BLACK-EYED SUSAN;

OR,

PIRATES ASHORE.

ILLUSTRATED.

LONDON:
TEMPLE PUBLISHING OFFICES, FLEET STREET, E.C.
1868.

BLACK EYED SUSAN.

OR, PIRATES ASHORE.

SUSAN'S SWEETHEART, WILL.

1

CHAPTER I.

ADMIRAL. What are you?

QUID. Boatswain, your honour.

ADMIRAL. What know you of the prisoner?

QUID. Know, your honour? The trimmest sailor as ever handled a rope. The first on his watch, the last to leave the deck. One as never belonged to the after-guard. He has the cleanest top and the whitest hammock. From reefing a maintopsail to stowing a netting, give me taut Will afore any able seaman in his Majesty's fleet.

Black-Eyed Susan. Act ii., scene ii.

———

OUR HERO.

WHEN Douglas Jerrold penned Quid's answer to the admiral, he gave the *beau ideal* of a true British sailor.

Although forty-nine years have elapsed since these words were first spoken by Mr. Lee on the boards of the Surrey Theatre, the 'national' drama is as warmly received by the sea-loving youths of England of the present generation as it was then by their fathers.

To those who have not had the good fortune to see the famous drama, a brief *résumé* of the plot may not be uninteresting. Those who have seen it we feel convinced will not begrudge the few moments spent in the reading.

Susan—the pretty black-eyed Susan, William's wife—is persecuted by her uncle, a mercenary, base-hearted scoundrel.

Being brought to the depths of poverty in consequence of her husband's long absence at sea, this Doggrass threatens to seize her furniture and turn her adrift upon the world unless she can pay the rent of the cottage which she inhabits with old Dame Hartley.

Tom Hatchett, the smuggler of Deal and captain of the Redbreast, conceives a passion for Susan, and, to ingratiate himself in her favour, he makes an arrangement with Doggrass, in which the latter is to make a distraint for rent.

Tom Hatchett then proposes to step in and pay the money, thus arousing Susan's gratitude.

He does so.

On the following day, with Bill Raker, the first mate of the Redbreast, he visits Susan, and tells her that his companion saw her husband die at sea by the swamping of a boat.

During the time he is telling the story, William, who has entered the cottage previous to the smugglers, creeps forward, and places himself between Tom Hatchett and the weeping girl.

William strikes the smuggler.

There is a struggle between them, and the gallant sailor wrests a cutlass from his foe.

An officer and two marines arrive at this moment, and capture the captain of the Redbreast and his first mate, and carry them off to serve the king.

William's happiness was not of long duration. For ere the day had closed, Quid, the boatswain, came to the public-house where the sailors were holding a carousal, and ordered them all on board.

Susan is struck with dismay at the cruel order, and William cheers her a little by telling her that he will ask the lieutenant, who is waiting on the beach for the liberty men, for leave until the next day.

He goes upon this errand, and before he returns, Captain Crosstree, who has taken a fancy to Susan, issues forth from the public-house in a state of intoxication.

He beholds Susan, and makes an overture which she resists.

Inflamed by wine, he attempts to drag her away.

William, hearing her screams for help, rushes in and cuts the captain down.

The rest is soon told.

He is tried by a court-martial, and sentenced to be hung at the yard-arm of the ship.

It is during the trial scene that Quid uses the words which precede this chapter, and in the same scene William makes the following splendid sailor-like and manly defence.

On being asked by the admiral if he had anything to say against judgment being passed upon him, he replies:—

'In a moment, your honours—damn it! my top-lights are rather misty. Your honours, I had been three years at sea. I had never looked upon or heard from my wife—as sweet a little craft as ever launched. I had come ashore, and was as lively as a petrel in a storm. I found Susan—that's my wife, your honours—all her gilt taken by the land sharks, but yet all taut, and with a face as red and rosy as the king's head on the side of a fire-bucket. Well, your honours, when we were as merry as a ship's crew on a pay-day, there comes an order for us to go aboard. I left Susan, and went with the rest of the liberty men to ax leave of the first lieutenant. I had not been gone the turning of an hour-glass, when I heard Susan giving signals of distress. I out with my cutlass, made all sail, and came up to my craft. I found her battling with a pirate. I never looked at his figure-head—never stopped. Could any of your honours—long live you and your wives, say I—could any of your honours have rowed alongside as if you'd been going aboard a Royal yacht? No, you wouldn't; for the gilt swabs on your shoulders can't alter the heart that swells beneath. You would have done as I did. And what did I? Why, I cut him down like a piece of old junk. Had he been the First Lord of the Admiralty, I had done it!'

His judges, though they felt as men for the prisoner's painful situation, could hold out no hope that his life would be spared.

So, when the fatal moment came, and the brave fellow mounted the platform, blessing those who were about to launch him into eternity, the captain he had wounded rushes in and stays the execution.

He had, in consequence of William having saved his life, written for and obtained the brave fellow's discharge.

This document had fallen into Doggrass's hands, and he retained it until, as he hoped, the execution would be over.

He was foiled in his villany.

When the admiral heard that William was not the king's sailor when he cut down Captain Crosstree, he ordered him to be set free.

Thus ends the play—a drama dear to our fathers, and loved by their sons, and owing to the splendid portraiture of William, rendered by the late T. P. Cooke, Black-eyed Susan became a household word through the length and breadth of our sea-girt isles.

Here begins our story.

Such is the hero whose life we would write; and in so doing, we will try to follow out the lamented Douglas Jerrold's wondrous conception of what a British sailor should be.

May the great changes which have taken place of late in our naval armaments—changes which have turned our splendid swan-like frigates into unseemly iron-ribbed structures of ugliness—leave our seamen as they were when they fought behind the nearly-departed wooden walls of Old England!

CHAPTER II.

A TRIO OF VILLAINS.

WHILE all the good folks of Deal were rejoicing at gallant Will's escape from an ignominious death, Doggrass was seated in his chamber—his brain busy recalling the events of the last few days.

The lines on that cold, mobile face seemed to have grown deeper, and the ferret-like eyes wore a malicious expression, since each well-devised scheme he had laid for Will's destruction had so signally miscarried.

'Curse him!' he muttered. 'He has beaten me at every turn. Through him I have lost my partner, Tom Hatchett; and when I fondly hoped that I had the discharge safely under lock and key, I hear that the fellow is free!'

The disappearance of that document from his desk was a matter which sorely puzzled even Doggrass's astute brain.

'Who could have taken it?' he went on, musingly. 'Suspicion points to that infernal Gnatbrain, that busy, meddling fool, whose tongue cuts like a two-edged sword. Yes, he must have taken it. I've no doubt by this time he is surrounded by a group of grinning sailors and their trolloping women, as he recounts the manner in which he saved that tobacco-chewing fellow from being choked. He would change his tune before long had not poor Tom Hatchett been taken. For as sure as the sky is above me, I would have had him taken aboard the schooner and rope's-ended until death by his own hand would have been preferable to living!'

Doggrass clenched his hand until his long nails penetrated his yellow skin.

The picture he drew of Gnatbrain rejoicing over the escape of honest Will from the yard-arm, was gall and wormwood.

But worse even than this was the thought of Will and pretty Susan's happiness.

'I have been foiled,' he resumed. 'Every well-laid plan has crumbled away at the very moment of success. Yet, were Tom Hatchett here to aid me, I should make another struggle to——ha!'

He turned his cadaverous face towards the closed window as this exclamation of astonishment came from his lips.

There was nothing unusual in the circumstance which caused the old framework to rattle; yet it made the man of many sins start and tremble.

'Bah!' he muttered, drawing his chair closer to the fire. 'I am growing childish when the wind suddenly rising pales my cheek.'

A lurid flash of lightning swept across the window, and from the dull, heavy roll of the surf upon the distant beach, he knew that one of those sudden tempests so frequent upon the sea-coast was gathering in awful yet majestic fury.

The heavens, which had hitherto been so placidly beautiful, were now darkened by heavy black clouds rising from the westward.

From amid these gigantic portentous omens of the elements' coming strife ever and anon blazed sheet after sheet of vivid lightning.

Silas Doggrass cowered before the flickering fire, and every blast of wind which shook the window-frame caused a shiver to pass over him.

The pattering of the rain-drops upon the glass, and the surge of the stormy waters as they broke in white, feathery, hissing foam upon the beach, brought to the stern, cruel man's remembrance a scene which had happened beneath that very roof.

And he crouched yet lower in his chair as the remembrance of that stormy night came upon him.

So great was his fear, that he dared not look beyond the pale of the firelight.

He fancied in the gloom there stood a figure—that of a man, his brother.

And Susan's father stood there—cold, and his clothes dripping with the salt spray.

And as memory opened the long vista of the sixteen years that had passed since he stood beside that dying form, a voice came upon his ears.

It was but his imagination that formed the words; yet, above the howling of the storm, he heard the tones of one who had long since mouldered into dust, ask—

'Brother, have you kept your trust with me?—kept the promise made, as hand locked in hand, and when my spirit fled from its earthly tenement, you swore to be a father to my orphan girl? Brother, have you done so?'

Cold drops of agony stood upon Silas's forehead as the female voice sank into a wailing bluster and was borne away upon the howling winds.

Had he kept that promise? Little wonder he hid his face in his hands, and sought to shut out the phantom, which he firmly believed stood in the sombre light, its pale face bearing a strange, mournful look, as though grieved more than angered by the wrong Silas Doggrass had caused his niece—the pretty Black-eyed Susan.

A heavy roll of thunder shook the house to its very base. It came like a requiem to the spirit's wailing voice; and Silas Doggrass sprang from his chair and gave utterance to a shriek of terror.

There was a response to his cry.

A response that caused his hair to bristle with fear, and his hands to grasp the back of a chair to support his trembling limbs.

Beneath his feet, beneath the floor of the chamber in which he stood, came a sound which caused his heart to stop its pulsations.

It was a low, groaning noise; as though a strong man, suddenly stricken by Death's cold hand, was battling with the pitiless destroyer.

This strange sound was succeeded by the shuffling of feet; and, at the moment when Doggrass's terror had reached its culminating point, the trap-door in the centre of the room was raised, and a pale, blood-stained face appeared above the floor.

Doggrass's fear passed away as he beheld this strange apparition; and, advancing to the open trap, he exclaimed, joyfully—

'Tom Hatchett!'

The smuggler of Deal drew himself painfully through the opening; then, staggering to a seat, said, in a faint tone—

'Some brandy, Doggrass; for I'm nearly spent.'

There seemed but little life left in the speaker, for he hung, limp and powerless, over the back of the chair.

Doggrass gave him a tumbler of brandy, and the fiery stimulant seemed to give him fresh life.

'Thanks,' he said, placing the glass upon the table. 'I feel better now.'

Doggrass saw the blood trickling from a wound

over Tom Hatchett's temple, and pointing towards it, said—

'You are bleeding. How did you get that wound?'

'I will tell you when we have brought Bill Raker round; that is, if there is any life left in him.'

'Raker! Is he'——

He is at the foot of the ladder. Get a light, Silas.'

Doggrass lit a candle, and Tom Hatchett, rising slowly from his seat, held it over the open trap-door while Doggrass descended.

He found the smuggler's first mate lying in a huddled heap, and, to all appearance, dead.

He looked up and told his companion so; but Tom Hatchett peered over the chasm, and said, fiercely—

'Bring him up. There may be a little life left in him yet.'

Doggrass was a strong man, despite his lean and attenuated form.

Lifting the powerless form from where it had fallen, he ascended the few steps which led to the chamber, and placed him upon the floor.

He was not dead. There was a faint pulsation of the heart; and, as Doggrass took his hand away from Raker's jacket, he uttered an exclamation of alarm.

The captain of the Redbreast looked up and asked—

'What is the matter?'

Doggrass held his hand before the light, and the smuggler saw that it was covered with blood.

'I thought so,' he muttered, 'that shot hit him in the breast.'

No words passed between them as they stripped the prone form to the waist; and when Tom Hatchett had sponged the blood stains away, he saw a small orifice near Raker's left shoulder.

'I can feel the bullet,' he said, touching the spot lightly with the tip of his finger. 'Here it is, against the bone.'

The blood still trickled from the wound, and the smuggler, knowing how soon his companion would bleed to death, took a clasp knife from his pocket, and, with no gentle hand, extracted the ball.

The pain endured by the wounded man must have been excruciating, for a shiver passed over his frame, and he attempted to rise.

'Keep still, Bill,' said Tom Raker; 'you will be better soon.'

The closed eyes partly opened, and the sufferer gave a deep groan, then lay as placid as though the angel of death had come upon him.

Doggrass bound up the wound; then, with Tom Hatchett's help, the prone form was carried to a couch, and a quantity of brandy forced between his set teeth.

Beyond this their surgical skill did not extend; so, leaving the first mate of the Redbreast to die or recover, the two men went to the fire.

Doggrass was the first to speak.

'So,' he said, 'you have escaped, Tom.'

'Ay,' was the answer; 'and, if I live, I will repay the fellow who caused me to be taken.'

Doggrass moved his chair closer to his companion, and his keen, grey eyes shone as he said—

'You owe this to William, do you not?'

'Ay, curse him! and you, too, for all I have suffered

'It was not my fault, Tom.'

'No, no; of course not. Did you not set me on to pay the money Susan owed?'

'Well?'

'Was it not your scheme that I was to pitch that yarn to your black-eyed niece about her precious husband having gone down during a storm?'

'It was. But I was not to know that he would return at the very moment of our success.'

'Perhaps not,' growled Tom Hatchett; 'but if I had not listened to you I should not have been taken.'

'You have yourself to blame for that, Tom Hatchett.'

The smuggler looked up, and demanded, fiercely—

'How myself to blame?'

'This way,' Doggrass said, smoothly; 'when you left the cottage where you saw her husband, you would have had plenty of time to have escaped the marines.'

'Perhaps so,' Tom Hatchett said, somewhat mollified; 'but I could not tamely endure a blow from that fellow.'

'Well, never mind that now,' Doggrass said. 'You had but little time to escape them; so let us see if there is not a way of having your revenge and Susan as well.'

The smuggler's eyes lighted up with passion, as he repeated—

'Have Susan?'

'Yes; but I will explain. Stay, first tell me the exact circumstances of your escape, that I may know how far you can aid my plan.'

'It's soon told,' said Tom Hatchett. 'You know, of course, that I was taken on board the guard-ship along with Bill Raker.'

'I am aware of that.'

'One question. What have you done with our schooner? I did not see her from the guard-ship.'

A cunning smile played over the cadaverous face, as Doggrass answered—

'Had her scuttled, and sunk'——

'The dev'——

'But in such a manner that she can float again in a few hours.'

'Good,' said Tom Hatchett. 'I would not have lost the little beauty for all India's wealth.'

Doggrass stroked his chin complacently, as he said—

'I thought it possible you would escape, so I kept the crew at hand. Say the word, and the Redbreast shall float before the sun rises.'

'I must hear your plan first respecting Susan; but first let me finish about my escape.'

Doggrass nodded an affirmative.

'From the moment we were taken aboard the guard-ship,' Tom Hatchett said, 'we did nothing but plan a means of escape; but owing to the bright moonlit nights no opportunity offered.

'This storm which is now raging was the chance. Bill and I dropped quietly through a gun-port into the sea. Our fellow prisoners must have given the alarm, for the waves were running too high for the sentries to hear the splash our bodies made. Anyhow, we hadn't gone more than half a cable's length, before the sentries began to fire, and, aided by the lightning, managed to hit us both.

'I don't know how we got to land, for my eyes were covered with the blood from this wound; but we did it; and, before we got a dozen yards more, Bill gave a groan and dropped flat upon the sand.

'There was no time to ask questions, for the battle lanterns had begun to move about the guardship, and spoke pretty plainly that they were having a lark; so I pitches Bill over my shoulder and ran as though the devil was at my heels.

'I didn't at first know where to steer for, until I thought of the vault under here; and knowing that we had so often stowed a cargo out of sight, even when the sharks were after us, I knew we should be pretty safe for a time. I can tell you, I was considerably done when I dropped poor Bill at the foot of the ladder. Didn't you hear him groan?'

'I did.'

'No wonder, poor devil! for his head hit against the lower step. That's all. Now, let's hear your —— Good God! They are here!'

As these words left Tom Hatchett's lips, the tramp of disciplined men was heard outside the door. Then came the words—

'Halt! Order arms! Stand at ease!'

Old Doggrass quietly inverted the candle, then drew a thick screen before the fire; these precautionary means taken, he turned to the smuggler, and said—

'Away with you down the trap.'

'But Bill Raker; they will '——

'Down with you, and leave him for me.'

While speaking, Doggrass lifted the wounded man from the couch and carried him to the trapdoor, and, before his burden had passed from his lean, sinewy arms, a stern voice outside called out—

'Open, in the king's name!'

Doggrass quietly closed the covering to the secret vault, and wheeled the table over it.

This done he went to the outer door.

CHAPTER III.

A SUBTLE PLOT.

THE dim light from a lanthorn revealed the cloaked forms of a naval officer and a party of marines standing in a half circle before the open door.

Doggrass met them with a smiling face; and shading his eyes with his hand, he said—

'Well, gentlemen, to what happy circumstance am I indebted for the honour of this visit?'

Silas was looked upon as a respectable member of society.

He was reputed wealthy; and, though a rigorous landlord, he gave away large sums to the public charity of the little town.

He was also one of the municipal body, and more than once he had headed the council when they presented a fulsome address to the admiral of a fleet just returned from the war.

Thus, bad as the man really was by nature, he managed to hold a pretty good position among his fellow townsmen, and was also well known to the officers of the fleet.

The young officer in charge of the party saluted the old rascal respectfully as he answered—

'The admiral's order, sir. We are to search every house within a mile from the sea.'

'Oh, indeed! You are quite at liberty to search mine from roof to cellar; but, may I inquire the object of your search?'

'Captain Hatchett and his first mate have escaped from the guard ship, sir; and as they are both wounded it is certain they have taken refuge near the beach.'

Doggrass smiled pleasantly as he said—

'It is scarcely possible the rascals have escaped! But surely you do not suspect they would seek refuge in my house—in the house of the chairman of the Town Council?'

'No, sir; but'——

The young officer hesitated, and Silas supplied the words—

'You must obey orders. Yes, yes; I understand. Pray enter. I know you must go through the form, in order to give in a truthful report.'

He stood aside to allow the officer to pass; and the latter, waving his men back as they were about to follow him, entered the passage.

So effectually had Silas cajoled the young fellow that he did no more than put his head inside the door, then withdrew, apologizing for the trouble he had given.

Doggrass affected to look upon it as a joke; and, to show how little he was offended, generously gave the lieutenant and the marines a glass of spirits each, and when they marched away, one said—

'Whatever people may say about old Doggrass he's the only one that has asked us if we had a mouth out of all the places we have been tonight.'

'He's a good sort,' said another; 'so good luck to him.'

Silas heard these comments, then closed and fastened the door.

He was not surprised when he entered the room to find Tom Hatchett and his companion seated at the table.

It took a great deal to surprise Mr. Silas Doggrass.

'I see you are better, Bill,' he said to the first mate of the Redbreast. 'But be careful of that bottle; too much of that is not good for you.'

Bill Raker set down the glass.

A sickly smile wreathed his lips as he replied—

'I expect it was the scent of them cursed marines as brought me round, for Tom says I opened my ports when they came to the door.'

Mr. Doggrass indulged in a quiet chuckle as he drew a chair near the table.

'You see,' he said, 'what it is to be respectable. That officer actually apologised for looking in at the door. He! he! he!'

'Curse, them!' Tom Hatchett said. 'They made my heart jump into my mouth. But never mind; they have gone; and as the scent will be pretty streng after us for some time, suppose we have your plan, for the sooner we are afloat the better.'

In this Doggrass assented.

Helping himself to a glass of brandy, he said—

'It's soon told. Now, in the first place, this fellow, whose neck so narrowly escaped the rope, has nothing to live upon for the present but his pay and the prize-money he has earned.'

'Exactly. And a pretty round sum that must be.'

'Yes, it is so. But suppose he had not the money, he would soon be compelled to go to sea again.'

'That's true,' Tom Hatchett said. 'But as he has got it, why, there's an end of the matter.'

'Not at all,' said Doggrass. 'He might *lose it !*'

He emphasised the last two words, and looked in such a peculiar manner at the captain of the Redbreast, that the latter at once understood his meaning.

'You've a long head, Master Doggrass,' Tom Hatchett said. 'But go on.'

'We'll suppose he has lost it, and, lastly, Susan upon his hands, he will find matters go hard ; and, as a matter of course, he will look out for a ship.'

'Exactly.'

'That's all,' said Silas. 'I give you the idea—can you finish it ? '

'Had the devil been at your elbow,' said the smuggler, 'you could not have hatched a better plan. Yes, I can fill up the places you have left open. Shall I speak openly ? '

'Do,' Doggrass said. 'We have no secrets from each other.'

'Very well. Here goes. In the first place, I am to find a man that will ease this William of his cash. I can do so : one that would cut a throat for a less reward than this.'

'Such a man in our present need would be a pearl beyond price.'

'Well, we can look upon that point as settled. Now, am I right when I say that I am to find the ship for him to take service in ? '

'Quite right, Tom Hatchett.'

'I can do that also ; and one word from my lips will prevent him from ever returning to England again.'

'Then, Tom Hatchett,' said Doggrass, rubbing his thin hands together, 'I advise you to say that word, for the sooner you have got rid of him the sooner will Susan be yours.'

'That prize in view,' said the smuggler, 'would make me sell my soul to the Evil One.'

'You can possess the prize without such a sacrifice, Tom.'

The smuggler's eyes shone with anticipated triumph as he listened to these words, and for some moments he gave his imagination play upon the bold and tempting reward old Doggrass held out for his share in the villany.

When he again spoke, his words somewhat unsettled even the steel nerves of his rascally old friend, partner, and patron.

'Look here, Doggrass,' he said, bluntly ; 'is not Susan your niece ? '

'She is.'

'And your only brother's child ? '

'Even so.'

Tom Hatchett bent forward upon the table, and looking old Doggrass straight in the face, said—

'You must think more of me than most men think of their fellows.'

Doggrass shifted about uneasily on his chair.

He felt this was but the prelude of a question he had half expected the captain of the Redbreast to ask.

'I do, Tom,' he said. 'Have I not every reason to value your friendship ? '

'To a certain extent, yes. But safely landing a cargo of contraband, and hoodwinking the king's men, would hardly make me stand before your own flesh and blood.'

'Mine is a strange nature, Tom,' said Doggrass. 'I care not for the ties of kindred. Why should I ? What has that girl done for me compared to your services ? '

'That's not the way I mean,' said the smuggler, his nature, though rugged, was hardly debased enough to believe that Doggrass was acting thus unless actuated by some powerful motive. 'Now, speak the truth, Doggrass. Does not Susan stand in your way ? '

Silas made a sickly attempt to laugh as he said—

'In my way—how ? '

'That,' Tom Hatchett said, 'is best known to yourself.'

There was a few minutes' silence, during which the captain of the Redbreast and his trading partner looked into each other's faces as though trying to solve the matter on the *tapis*.

They did not glean much from their examination.

Possibly both were too much in the habit of controlling their facial muscles.

'Look here,' Tom Hatchett said, breaking the silence ; 'let's start fair in this business. Tell me exactly the cause of your animosity to pretty Susan. I shall not be the less keen upon the work.'

'I should think not,' Silas said, 'considering the prize you have in view. Never mind my reasons for acting thus towards the girl ; they are weighty ones, you may be sure.'

'Will you not tell me them ? '

'Not now, Tom. *When Susan* is your *wife*—not before.'

Tom Hatchett saw the inutility of pressing the point.

But he made a mental resolution to discover the secret long before the time spoken of by Silas Doggrass.

'The storm is abating,' he said, rising. 'I must see about getting the schooner afloat before sunrise. Can it be done ? '

'Easily. The tide will be down in an hour or two, and by using the pumps you will clear the water out from the hold. But what is your hurry ? '

'I must go to Brest, and arrange about the vessel to take this William away.'

'True ; I had forgotten that. But about the fellow you spoke of—who will take care of William's cash ? '

'That,' Tom Hatchett said, 'will be in the rascal's pocket before the morning.'

Doggrass chuckled at the intelligence.

'You are invaluable, Tom Hatchett,' he said. 'I do not know what I should do without you.'

'There are plenty of rascals in the world,' was the blunt reply ; 'so you will soon get another to replace Tom Hatchett.'

'Perhaps so, Tom ; but not one I should like so well as yourself for a nephew.'

'I'm afraid,' the smuggler said, 'that I shall find a little difficulty in persuading pretty Sue to accept me, although her William will be gone for ever.'

'That will be your fault, Tom,' said the old villain. 'You have a fast vessel, and a crew of picked scamps. If you cannot take her for a month's cruise, even against her will, you are not the man I take you for.'

'What—carry her off ? '

'Ay. Don't look so astonished, man. Carry her off, and if she is not glad enough to become your wife when you return, it will be your fault.'

'But,' objected Tom, 'I should never be able to put my foot on this part of the coast after that.'

'Why?'

'The whole place would be up in arms, and ready to take up the affair.'

'Nonsense. If it should be necessary for you to take her aboard, I will take care that the whole town of Deal shall ring with Black-eyed Susan's elopement with Tom Hatchett, the smuggler, before your vessel is far from the beach.'

'A good thought, Silas. Well, I think everything is arranged. Take care of Bill Raker until I return. I suppose I shall find the men at the Devil's Gully?'

'You will; and glad they will be to see their old commander again.'

It was evident that Tom Hatchett was not unused to evading the king's officers; for, during the time he had been speaking, and signifying his intention to depart, he had taken a suit of black clothes from the cupboard, and now stood metamorphosed into a stout, demure-looking clergyman.

'I hope,' the reckless fellow said, 'that I shall meet the party of marines who are so anxious about my welfare.'

'Why?'

'Because I shall read them a severe homily about the sin of carrying carnal weapons for the purpose of taking the lives of their fellow-creatures.'

So saying, Tom Hatchett disappeared through the trap-door.

He left Silas with the wounded man, who slept heavily upon the couch, either from the effect of his wounds or the deep draughts of brandy he had imbibed.

The respectable Mr. Doggrass quietly closed the trap.

Seating himself by the fire, he muttered—

'Not that secret, Tom Hatchett; that is and will remain mine, and mine only.'

We shall see, Mr. Silas Doggrass — we shall see.

CHAPTER IV.

THE PLOT BEGINS TO WORK.

NEARLY three months have passed since the escape of Tom Hatchett and the first mate from the guardship.

So well had the smuggler played his cards, that all, save Silas Doggrass, believed the fugitives had perished in their desperate attempt to gain the shore.

With gallant Will and his pretty dark-eyed wife the time had glided imperceptibly away.

The young girl—happy in the thought that they were never more to part—passed her days in a state of celestial bliss.

Bliss that was unalloyed by any dark foreshadowings.

No power on earth could now part them.

Their hearts, at times saddened by the past, became the happier when contemplating the joys of the present.

It cost the handsome sailor many a pang to give up the live he so fondly loved.

Next to Susan, his thoughts were centred upon the mighty waste of waters, upon whose bosom he had passed so many happy years.

The old love of the ocean was strong upon him when he selected the little cottage in which they now dwelt.

It was a sweet spot this home of taut Will and Black-eyed Susan.

Before them lay the great ocean.

The music of the waves as they broke in feathery foam upon the base of the rock upon which their dwelling stood charmed the soul of the man with its weird, wild sound.

Towering high above them were the mighty cliffs—England's pride and defence.

Oft as Will sat at the open door beside his gentle child-like wife, and the red, dusky sun-glow was mirrored upon the water, his heart would fill, and the tear rise unbidden to his eye.

It was the great joy he felt which caused this feeling.

He had now all that he loved upon earth—his wife's soothing voice and caressive touch, and the ocean murmuring at his feet.

So the time passed on—not the smallest speck on the bright yet mystic future to mar their present joy.

When Will was so providentially saved from death, his first care had been to purchase the little cottage on the cliff.

His accumulated pay and prize-money made this an easy matter.

The remainder—about two-thirds of the whole amount—he put in a safe hiding-place.

With wondrous forethought for a sailor, he divided it into five portions, each portion he calculated would, with frugal living, last them twelve months.

Thus, without a care for the next few years, Will could have passed his days in idleness; but this to our hero would have been but a slow death.

Strong of frame, and blessed with an active mind, he soon began to feel depressed in spirits, solely for the want of occupation.

This state of things did not last long.

About fifty feet above Will's cottage was a cluster of fishermen's huts.

So, Will, to while away the hours that began to hang heavily upon his hands, made friends with those hardy toilers of the deep, and often accompanied them upon their perilous journeys.

One evening, when he had just returned from a successful cruise, Susan—who had been awaiting his arrival on the beach—suddenly exclaimed—

'Look, William! There's Gnatbrain and little Jacob ascending the cliff towards our home.'

Will shaded his eyes with one hand as he said—

'True, lass. There's honest Gnat and that grampus, Jacob, steering straight for our cabin. What the devil'——

Susan placed her hand over Will's mouth.

'You forget,' she said, archly, 'that you invited them to visit us this evening.'

'I?' Will began. 'Avast there, my girl! I will take my davy that I'——

'Said so,' Susan put in, 'on the night of the fleet sailing from the Downs.'

Will hitched up his trousers, and said—

'Perhaps I did, lass; for those fellows were so far in the wind through drinking our healths that I had to say all sorts of things to keep them quiet.'

There was a quiet smile upon Susan's face, as she said—

'No doubt you had some trouble with your old messmates.'

'Trouble, girl? Come, no tacking about; out with it. Damme! I drank them a safe journey—plenty of fighting, and lots of prize-money. What could I do less? They all drank to me, Sue, and I—I'——

'Had to be carried home,' Susan said, laughing. 'But come, Will, let us return.'

Then, with Susan's small hand passed over his arm, Will went towards their little dwelling.

They were met half way by Gnatbrain, who came towards Will, with extended hand.

'Great news, Will!' he said, 'great news! There will be stirring times soon.'

Will grasped the extended hand with his hard, sinewy fingers, until the pressure brought tears into Gnatbrain's eyes.

'News, you alligator!' he said, 'what's afloat? Has old Doggrass hung himself, because my neck escaped being lengthened? Or has young Jacob, here, found pluck enough to join the fleet, instead of chasing the crows from Farmer Stubbs' fields?'

'Neither, Will—neither; greater news than this. The'——

'Heave-to, lad. Now, come inside, and let's splice the mainbrace; then for your jaw. Come in, Jacob; don't stand there looking like—like—damme!—a fool!'

They entered the cottage, and Susan placed three tumblers and a bottle of rum upon the table; then brought a jug of spring water, and said to her husband—

'I will leave you for a short time, Will. I must go and see the old dame.'

'Right, my girl,' he said. 'She was kind to you when Will was away. Tell her, lass, that Will has not forget it, nor he ain't likely to. Here, give us one—that's it.'

She bowed her lovely head to receive her husband's kiss, then singing blithely, left the cot.

'There she goes,' Will said, gazing proudly after her matchless form. 'A frigate's a sign, Gnatbrain, to make a sailor's heart bump against his ribs; but my Sue, damme! she's more lovely than all the frigates in King George's fleet.'

'She is, indeed, lovely, Will,' assented Gnatbrain; 'and as good and true a wife as ever lived.'

'Hallo!' exclaimed Will, turning to Jacob, 'what's the worry, eh? What are the pumps at work for?'

Jacob drew the cuff of his jacket across his eyes, and blurted out—

'I was thinking, William, of the time when I served Susan's uncle—thinking how cruel I must have been to have began distraining her goods for the'——

'Avast, you lubber! Say no more about it. Damme! your heart wasn't in the work, Jacob, or you would not have been among the first to have welcomed poor Will, when he 'scaped from the yard-arm. Here, give us your flipper, man.'

They shook hands, and Gnatbrain said—

'I think Jacob's reformation was due to the lesson I taught him with the rolling-pin. Eh, Jacob?'

'Yes,' the little fellow said; 'you opened my eyes to my wickedness, when you knocked me down.'

'Drink, lads,' Will said; 'and you, Gnat, pay out the slack.'

'The slack, Will?'

'Ay, you 'long-shore lubber—the yarn — the great news you have brought. Damme! don't I speak plain English?'

'Plain enough, Will. Well, the news came this morning. I heard them reading it out of the paper when I was at the Dolphin. Great news, William, great news. England has declared war against France, and America has declared war against England.'

'No! What! and all this going on, and I to be ashore? I'——

'Remember Susan, Will—remember how she suffered before; and believe me, that if you were to go away, her precious uncle would be at his work again.'

'Damn him! He can't do anything now. No more sending her adrift without ballast, stores or compass. She has a ship of her own now. I'——

'You don't know him, Will. Even now he has thrust out poor old Peter Welsh. You know his son, Will? Young Joe Welsh, who sailed with you in the last trip you made.'

'Know him? Ay, and a better shipmate never handled rope or furled a sail. But what of the old man, Gnatbrain?'

'Well, you must know poor old Welsh lives in one of Doggrass's cottages—the next one to that where Susan lived.'

'Ay, I know. An old fellow, with long white hair, and almost bent double with the cargo of years he carries.'

'The same, Will. Well, of late, Peter has been ill—too ill to put his little fishing boat out to sea; and though he's lived in the cottage nigh sixty years, and always paid the rent as regular as the day came—yet, after all this,' Gnatbrain added, angrily, ' the old hunks won't give him a few days longer.'

Will brought his clenched hand down upon the table with a force that sent the glasses flying right and left, and caused little Jacob's heart to jump in his throat (not that this was possible, but the sensation felt more like it).

'Damme!' he said, indignantly. 'Bomb shells and skyrockets! The devil's limb! And would he serve an old man like this? One who has paid the shot as regular as a sailor's wife goes for her half allowance. Lord help him, Gnatbrain! Had I my will of the rascal, I'd—I'd—damme! I'd tie him to a grating every morning before breakfast, and rub him down with the cat.'

'So could I, Will. But the old rascal is far beyond the reach of such poor folks as we are.'

'Go on, lad. Tell me what he intends to do if the shot isn't paid to-morrow.'

'The old man, William, will have the very bed taken from under him, and ill and feeble as he is, he will be turned adrift—homeless and penniless.'

Will rapped out a great oath.

The honest fellow's heart was touched by Gnatbrain's story.

'Avast, lad!' he said. 'You've pitched a yarn strong enough to bring the salt water to a seaman's eyes. Poor old Peter! My shipmate's father to be turned out like a dog! Damme, Gnatbrain! it shall never be said that I saw him founder while I've a shot in the locker.'

'But, Will, you cannot pay the money. You've done nothing since you got your discharge, and'——

'Hark'ee, friend,' said Will. 'When I've been tossing on the billows, my Sue has been like a star, always guiding me to do right. When my shipmates spent their money at every port, I kept mine for Susan; and, thank God! I've enough to last me —to keep us in rations for the next four years. Old Peter shall have one year's supply—damme! he shall!'

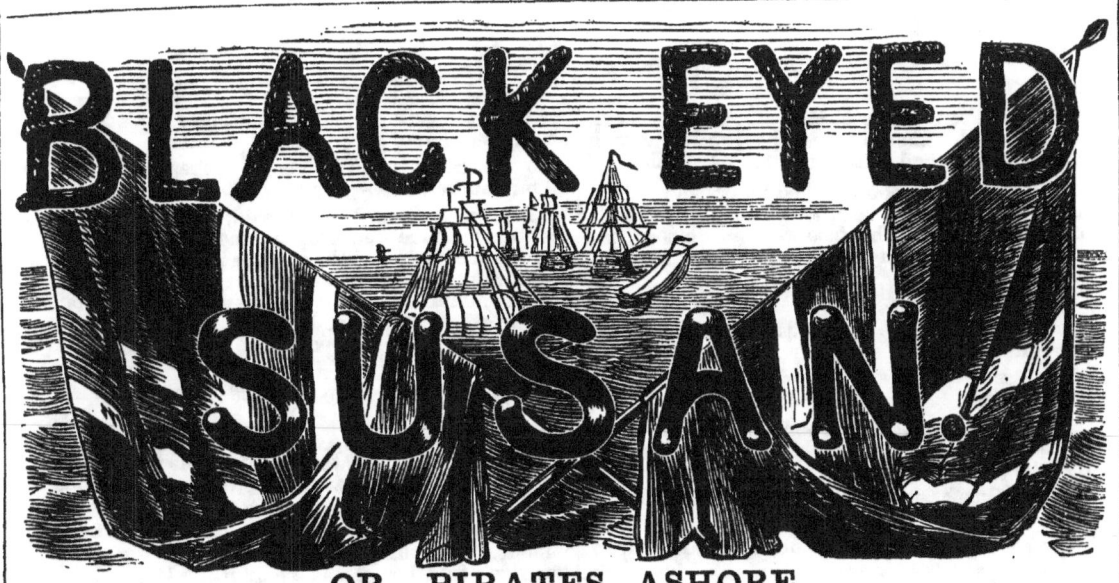

BLACK EYED SUSAN.

OR, PIRATES ASHORE.

THE REPRIEVE.

Will went to a sea-chest that stood in the room, and taking from thence a small box, opened it with a key, which he had fastened to his watch chain.

Gnatbrain and Jacob watched him open the box, and, to their surprise, he stood as though suddenly turned to stone, and his face went as white as one who had passed the mystic portals of eternity.

'What's the matter?' Gnatbrain began, and before he could utter another word, the box fell from Will's hands. Then, with a deep groan of agony, he sank upon a chair, and covered his face.

Jacob and Gnatbrain looked at each other in mute surprise.

Then their eyes turned upon Will, whose frame was quivering, as though he had been stricken with the palsy.

'Will,' Gnatbrain asked, 'what is the matter? You'——

The poor fellow raised his head, and, in a deep, mournful voice, said—

'It's gone! Every penny of my hard-earned money! Oh, God! Poor Sue!—poor Sue! She is a beggar!'

'Gone!' they repeated. 'What, the money?'

'All. Every shilling!'

And again he covered his face and rocked his body to and fro.

The blow had fallen heavily upon him.

At one fell swoop the bright visions of happiness he had so fondly dwelt upon were dashed away.

There was a silence of some minutes' duration, then Will arose from his chair.

Every outward sign of suffering had passed away.

He took the box from the floor, and looked at the lock.

An angry spot became visible on his cheeks, as he said—

'A pirate has fallen foul of this. See! here's the marks!'

And Gnatbrain and Jacob went towards him, and uttered an exclamation of astonishment when they saw the lock had been tampered with.

'How could this have occurred?' Gnatbrain asked. 'Has the box been out of the chest?'

'Never.'

'Have you no idea, Will, when the money was abstracted?'

'No more than you have,' Will said; 'for I've never opened it since the day Sue and I came to live here.'

Gnatbrain pondered for a few minutes over his answer, then asked—

'Do you remember anyone being here likely to know the contents of the box?'

'There has not been anyone here, Gnatbrain, but Will's friends, and his friends would not have done this.'

'I cannot understand it, Will, unless—unless'—

'Speak out, man, Don't hang back. Give me but one word that will put me on the pirate's track, and I will lay him by the heels before the sun sets this night.'

'I was about to suggest,' Gnatbrain said, 'that the box might have been opened before you came here.'

'No, lad, no; for I remember looking at——Ha! —damn it!—yes, that must have been the night.'

Uttering these strange words, Will strode across the room, his eyes flashing, and his hands clenched.

Gnatbrain and Jacob had not long to wait for an explanation of these strange words.

It soon came, and Will, as he spoke, looked like a lion baulked of its prey.

'Listen, shipmates,' he said, turning to his visitors. 'There was a night—the same night Sue and I came here, and the storm outside was so fast and furious, that we heard the very beating against the door and windows—— Hand me the grog, Jacob—when I think of it, it makes my body hot, and my throat as dry as a ship's deck under an African sun.'

He drank from the proffered glass, then resumed—

'Well, we were snug in our hammock, and Sue, as she listened to the tempest, told me how happy she felt now all my dangers were over, and I had not to go to sea any more.

'I told her, shipmates, that I had brought to an anchor, and nothing but death should take me from her side—told her of the ammunition I had stored away, and, damn it, shipmates! the very time I was paying out this, the pirate was overhauling my treasure chest.'

Gnatbrain uttered an exclamation of astonishment, and would have spoken, had not Will made a gesture to imply silence.

'I know what you would ask,' he said. 'You wonder I did not fall foul of him. I'll tell you; the wind rattled the windows and doors, and though I felt certain I heard some one in this room, Sue talked me over, and said it was but fancy. I found the door open when I came down in the morning, but again Sue was alongside me, and said it was the wind. That's when it took place, shipmates—and I deserve a round six dozen, for being a fool.'

Will quickened his angry strides while speaking, and those who looked upon his face, felt they would not have cared to have been the midnight robber, had the sailor's strong hand been upon his throat.

'Will,' Gnatbrain said, 'may I never see sweet Dolly again, if I don't point out the fellow that committed this robbery.'

'Eh—what?—you know him? Damme, Gnatbrain! tell me where he is, and by '——

'Hush, Will! Don't take His name in vain.'

'Right, shipmate, I will not; but tell me where this fellow is to be found, and I'd be foul of him before you could take in a reef.'

'I cannot swear that this is the man, Will; but at the time you say you were'——

'I say I were?—why man, isn't the box there to prove it? Say——but heave ahead, lad; only pay it out faster.'

'I'll try. You know Dick Harling?'

'Ay—a hang-dog looking lubber — half-fisher-man—half-smuggler; that lived no one knew how.'

'The same, Will. Well, at the time of which you speak, Dick became suddenly very flush of money, and for three weeks he was scarcely out of the Dolphin. Drunk at night, he slept on a bench in the tap-room, ready to begin drinking again the next morning.'

'Well?'

'So he went on, until one night he staggered out from the ale-house, and was taken by a press-gang.'

Will gave a howl of disappointment.

'He's afloat then,' he said; 'and out of the reach of my fingers. But never mind, I shall soon be on salt water again. If we meet, were I to be run up to the yard-arm the next minute, I will choke the—the—— D—n him! that I will! Ah!'

This exclamation of astonishment was uttered as Will looked out from the open window upon the ocean's glittering surface.

Gnatbrain and Jacob, obeying a natural impulse, turned round.

The sailor, and they also, became much interested with the object which caused Will's exclamation of astonishment.

'Beautiful! beautiful!' Will muttered audibly, as he leaned out of window. 'By heaven! she rides the water like a gull! Ah! she's bearing round. Away they go, up aloft; there goes her anchor. Look'ee, shipmates, I'd sooner command that little craft than be Lord High Admiral of the British fleet.'

CHAPTER V.

THE CAPTAIN OF THE GOLDEN ARROW.

THE object which had so strangely excited the sailor was a low-hulled, yet beautifully proportioned schooner.

There was something about her rig and the tapering masts which bespoke the graceful craft as designed more for war than peace; and, to Will's quick eye, the way in which the sails were handled, and the regular dip of the oars, as a boat left her side, told how those who handled them had received a man-o'-war's training.

Will and his companions watched the boat approaching, and the sailor, as though in answer to his envied thoughts, muttered—

'I know nearly every craft that carries the king's pennant, but there's none such a beauty as this. She shows no colours, yet she must be a man-o'-war, if not King George's, who the'——

He paused as a flag was run up, and the wind, catching the silken folds, floated it out proudly above the vessel's stern.

It was a strange device upon which the red sun now glittered, and the three who were so rapt in admiration of the little craft strained their eyes to read that which the fluttering silk for a time hid from them.

At last, the wind veering, displayed the banner as clearly as though it had been painted upon a board.

It was a golden arrow, upon a ground of spotless white, and Will, as he took his eyes from this strange symbol, said—

'Well, shipmates, I've seen many a flag in my time, but never none to compare with this.'

'It may be,' Gnatbrain said, suggestively, 'the property of some rich gentleman.'

'What, yer lubber—the flag?'

'Yes, and the vessel which carries it.'

'P'raps so,' said Will, doubtfully; 'but to my mind, that craft is well armed, and I don't think any 'long-shore gentleman, supposing he had a ship built like that, would arm her, and give the men a man-o'-war's training. No—— Oh, God! Look! It is Sue!'

With these words falling from his lips, Will sprang through the window, and ran swiftly towards a projecting point of the rocky cliff, and those who were startled by his strange words, and still stranger actions, rushed out of the cottage.

They were not more than a dozen yards, when both abruptly halted, and stood spell-bound with horror.

Their blood seemed to pause in its current, and their very feet to become rooted to the spot.

The sight that thus took such wondrous hold upon their faculties also caused those who were in the boat to ply their oars as though they were desirous of coming beneath the rocky projection already referred to.

Will, whose quick eyes had first noted the cause of these strange actions upon his friends and those in the boat, had suddenly paused, and now stood with one hand waving wildly towards the sea, the other clasping his brow, and from his white lips came, alternately, prayers and curses.

It was Susan, whose strange and perilous position had first caused her husband to spring through the open window, then to stand appalled at her danger—terrified—his courage rapidly leaving him, and a deathlike faintness stealing over his frame.

There was a cause for this.

He was powerless to save the life he loved from a terrible death.

A fate that would crush and mutilate her splendid form, and render those lovely features but a mockery of aught that was once human.

It was upon her return homeward, from her visit to the bed-ridden old dame, that Susan wandered out of the beaten track which led to her home upon the cliff.

She had done the same times before, in her search for the tiny wild flowers which grew among the crevices of the rocks.

Already one hand held a bright-hued group of her favourites, and, glancing towards her cottage, she was about to step over a fallen stone, and return homewards.

Before the step was taken, her eyes fell upon a cluster of white petalled flowers, which grew upon the very verge of the mighty cliff.

Susan saw not her danger, and, in a few seconds she knelt over the edge of the rock—one hand extended to grasp her prize.

The tips of her fingers touched the flower, but ere they closed around the stem, a wild cry of affright came from her lips.

The small projection upon which she knelt was swaying to and fro.

She knew the terrible meaning of this, and the attitude she had assumed for the purpose of plucking that tiny flower became one of supplication to her Maker.

She felt that her last hour had come.

Retreat was impossible.

One movement of her body would cause the stone to fall.

It was held in its loose setting only by the balance of her light form.

As her prayer went upward, her eyes were fixed upon the sunlit bosom of the waters, and in fancy she beheld her form lying mangled on that shore where she had so oft walked, leaning upon the arm of the man who was her all upon the earth.

It was hard to die thus, when she had but sipped of the cup of happiness which had been placed in her hands.

While her soul was thus filled with agony, she heard William's voice calling out wildly to her to remain still until he reached her side.

She held her heavy breathing, and held out her hands in mute supplication.

Slight as the movement was, it caused the stone to slip, and when she expected to feel herself whirling through the air, it stopped.

A wild hope sprang up within her.

She would be saved!

Oh, joy! and by him!

But, as the thought came to her mind, she looked around, and her prayerful words froze upon her lips.

The stone had been arrested in its descent by one of the sharp angles resting upon a small projection beneath.

This, she saw, by the sand and small rocky fragments which were dropping, would soon yield to the weight of the rock upon which she knelt.

It was at this moment that her agonized husband paused in his swift run.

He saw there was no hope—no means of reaching her.

Then, as his soul was harrowed by the sight, those mingled sacred and profane words came from his lips.

The pause was not long.

Again he bent forward.

If he could not save her, he could die with her locked in his arms.

In vain she implored him to keep away from the edge of the treacherous precipice. He heeded neither her wild gesticulations nor her words.

'Keep away, Will!' she said. 'One touch will send us both into eternity. Let me die. Back! back! as you love me!'

'No, Sue,' and his voice sank as he came yet closer, 'we will die together, or '——

From beneath the rocks came a sound that caused him to pause and look down upon the boat, which had just grounded.

He saw a young man leap ashore and make for the cliff, and as he began rapidly ascending the rugged side, he called out to Will—

'Back, man! if you wish to save her! Back! Don't you see the fall of a hand upon that loose stone will send it and its burthen upon the shingle. Back! I say!'

Will stood perfectly still.

He saw the speaker ascend the cliff with a celerity which astounded even the active sailor.

A tuft of grass, the smallest projecting stone served the stranger as a means of ascent, and as he rapidly neared the pale, motionless girl, Will's breathing became heavy, and the beatings of his heart became plainly audible.

He saw the gallant fellow's intention, and though he could not aid him, he followed every movement of the officer's lithe form with an interest that became fearful to endure.

The brave climber was soon near the terrified girl, but some distance from beneath the loosened rock, and when he became parallel with her, his voice could be heard calm—strangely calm, when all who stood near were trembling with excitement and dread—soothing and admiring Susan.

'Do not move,' he said, 'and you will be safe. The stone which supports you will hold out until I can grasp your hand. So—so. Keep calm, my girl.'

He worked his way sideways to her, then calling out for Will to creep to the edge of the rock, remained perfectly still, with his face pressed against the cliff.

'This way,' he said, 'the rock is sound here. It would take a broadside to dislodge a stone. That's it! Now, grasp my hand—so—tightly, for I fear when I have the weight of this poor girl added to my own, this tuft of grass will not hold us. Now, my girl, extend your hand towards me. Gently.'

Then, as she grasped his right hand, Will lay flat upon the rocky ground—one hand clutching the officer's left arm, the other the collar of his coat.

'Now,' he said, to Susan, 'place your other hand upon my wrist. Hold on for your life! There goes the '——

A rumbling noise, as the mass of rock fell—a shriek from Susan—then a cheer from the boat's crew, who stood beneath, watching the strange and terrible scene.

She was saved!

The officer, as the stone slipped from beneath her, grasped her small waist; and, for a few seconds, this human chain hung over the edge of the cliff.

Will holding the officer, the latter grasping Susan. They did not long remain thus.

Gnatbrain and Jacob had partly recovered their faculties, and came to Will's assistance.

Then the trio were drawn upon the level surface.

One soul-thrilling embrace took place between Susan and her husband, then the latter turned towards the brave man who had risked his life thus nobly.

'God bless your honour!' Will said, catching the officer's hand, and kissing it. 'You have saved one who is dearer to me than life itself. I can't reward you; but, in fine weather or foul, may the little cherub look down and bless you as I do.'

The officer gently disengaged his hand.

'I have done no more,' he said, 'than my duty; so, no thanks. I'm sure you would do the same for me.'

'Would I, your honour?' said Will. 'May the day come when you may want a stout heart and a strong hand! Then your honour will know how I will try and repay this. But come, here's my little cot. Come inside and rest, for coming aloft in that manner would take the breath out of the smartest foretopman afloat.'

The officer smiled, and offering Susan his arm, said—

'Permit me to '——

He paused when Susan drew back at the offer, and Will, who happened to turn his head that way, said—

'Come, Sue, my girl, let his honour convey you to our cabin. Think!—but for him, you would have been—been '——

The word stuck in his throat, and the officer, who saw how matters stood, came to his aid by saying—

'Never mind that little affair; try and forget it.'

'Forget, your honour? Never, until I go aloft, shall I forget how much I owe to—to—to '——

Will paused, not knowing how to address the preserver of his wife, and the officer, noting his embarrassment, smiled, and said—

'THE CAPTAIN OF THE GOLDEN ARROW!'

CHAPTER VI.

WILL TAKEN PRISONER.

THE sailor respectfully saluted when the gallant fellow proclaimed his rank.

Then, bidding Gnatbrain and Jacob good-bye, he followed the captain of the Golden Arrow and Susan to the cottage.

Will pondered over the name of the graceful vessel which lay so quietly upon the ocean's surface, and the result was a shake of the head, as he muttered—

'Never heard the name afore. But no matter; he is a brave man, and were a black flag flying from his vessel, I'd stand by him while I had a cutlass to wield, and five fingers to grasp the hilt!'

He was a splendid specimen of a naval officer, this captain of the vessel with the white silken banner flying over its taffrail.

Handsome as Adonis, and with a form so beautifully modelled that a sculptor would have vainly essayed to pourtray.

His speech was courtly, and his manners those of a gentleman—a polished, well-educated gentleman; and though so great a difference existed between him and his entertainers, his genial frankness and pleasant speech soon shook off the natural awkwardness they felt at having one so much above them as a guest in their humble cottage.

Seated by the open window, the young officer's eyes sparkled with pride when he saw his vessel riding at anchor below.

And Will, when Susan, after timidly thanking her gallant preserver, retired to the upper chamber, sat opposite the captain, and began to converse about the build and rig of the splendid ship.

The officer listened, with a pleased smile upon his face, to Will's words, and in answer to his question respecting the device upon the flag, said—

'That is the vessel's name. We have another flag when at sea.'

'The king's?' Will said, interrogatively. 'Though I didn't think there was such a clean-built craft in the service.'

'Not the king's,' was the answer. 'The flag, like that which you see now flying, is my own.'

A bitter smile wreathed the speaker's lips as he mentioned the king's name.

Then, suddenly changing the subject, he said—

'You are a sailor. Can you tell me where I am likely to pick up a few hands?'

Will's face became joyous in its expression.

He was bound by a tie of gratitude to the man before him.

Knowing that he should be compelled to go to sea again, he felt that to enter upon the Golden Arrow's books would be better than joining the fleet.

He was about to make the offer, when the captain interrupted him, by saying—

'I want good hands, William—such is your name, I believe?'

'It is, your honour.'

'Well, the men I require must be good sailors—quick of eye and bold at heart; for that ship, which now rides like a swan upon the waters, will soon be where none but brave men would care to find themselves.'

'Good sailors, your honour,' Will said, 'are hard to get now; for what with the press-gangs, and those who serve willingly, there's but few to be picked up.'

'So I had anticipated,' said the captain. 'But I can offer double pay to that which they will receive in the king's navy, and six times the prize-money. And more—if any of the men, such as I require, are married, I will give their wives two years' pay in advance.'

'You will, your honour?'

The sailor's eyes glistened as he asked the question.

'Ay, my man. And were they like yourself, I would not stop at giving four years' pay.'

'Damme!' said Will, 'if your honour likes, I will bear a hand—that is, if you will have me.'

'Have you! I should only be too glad. But you could not leave that pretty wife of yours, Will, and go on a long cruise in a ship which belongs to no country, and has no flag.'

'I have left her before, your honour; and as for the ship, I don't care what she may be. You are her captain — that's enough; and if we sail together, there may be a chance, your honour, of poor Will repaying a little what you have done for him to-day.'

'But your wife—does she know of your intention to go to sea again?'

'She does not, your honour. And I should not have gone, but for a—a—a pirate falling foul of my locker.'

The officer looked inquiringly at Will.

He answered the look by telling him of the robbery, and the narrow escape he had had from the yard-arm.

'You have but little to thank your country for,' he said. 'Still, I do not wish to take you with me without telling you the true character of my vessel.'

'I don't want to know anything, your honour —I only want to sail with you. I must go to sea, and I would sooner go with you than any captain, afloat and ashore.'

'Be it so. Here's my hand.'

'And mine, your honour.'

They shook hands.

In that grasp Will linked his destiny with that wild, chivalrous spirit which, during the great naval war, harassed the ships of King George tenfold more than the mighty fleets sent against them.

It was a silent compact, this linking of the fortunes and dangers of two brave men; and the gold-bedizened captain had good cause, before many weeks had passed away, to thank the good fortune which made him the preserver of William's wife.

'Here, William,' the officer said, placing a small roll of notes in the sailor's hand. 'Give this to your pretty wife, and tell her you shall be my care. And if this war which has begun lasts, she may hope to see you yet mount a gold epaulette upon your shoulders. No thanks. Be quick with your parting, for the Golden Arrow's anchor will be weighed at sunrise, and we have yet to pick up a few hands, if possible.'

'I will be with your honour in the snapping of a flintlock,' said Will. 'I know where we can find the very men you want. A few words to Sue —then we'll steer for the town.'

He went up stairs, with the roll of notes in his hand.

The captain, left to himself, gazed dreamily out upon the water, and mused.

'I would not have taken this man from his wife; but as he offered, and would, even had I refused him, have gone to sea, there can be no blame on my part. He seems a brave fellow; and, unless I am much out in my judgment, he will do me good ser'——

Will descended the stairs, and put an end to the officer's musings.

The sailor's handsome face was a shade paler than its wont, and as the captain rose to leave the cottage, Will said—

'I can stay here, your honour, until the Blue Peter's flying. It's my Sue who has asked the favour.'

'Certainly. Be on board before the anchor's weighed. But will you not accompany me to the place you spoke of?'

'Ay, your honour. It is after that I want to return.

The captain nodded assent, and, followed by Will, left the cottage,

Standing a little distance from the town was a public-house frequented by sailors.

To this place Will took his new officer.

The landlord, a one-eyed old sailor, readily conducted Will and his companion to a cellar beneath the house.

Here they found upwards of twenty stout-limbed fellows, who, having a dislike to the discipline of a man-of-war, were hiding from the press-gang.

A few words from Will, and ten of their number, selected by his companion, signified their willingness to enter the ship.

They asked no questions.

The captain was no niggard with his promises or his gold; and telling them, as an extra inducement, that the cat was not used on board the Golden Arrow, the men, after a parting glass with their companions, readily left their hiding-place, and in twos and threes repaired to the boat which was waiting for them.

The captain and Will saw them off, the former telling the coxswain of the boat to return for him in an hour.

Then they walked from the beach towards Will's cottage.

Here they parted—Will to take his farewell of Susan, the handsome, dark-eyed officer towards a palatial mansion, the residence of the Lord High Admiral of England.

The moon had by this time risen; and as the captain of the Golden Arrow threaded his way among a noble avenue of trees which led to the house, he wrapped his boat cloak around him, and seemed to be lost in a deep reverie.

He was.

But his profound thoughts did not make him the less careful of his mode of proceeding towards the house of Lord Harry Garthway.

At every rustle of a falling leaf, his hand went to the hilt of a heavy sword which hung at his hip, and, bowing his head, he peered into the sombre darkness, as though expecting to meet a foe behind every tree.

Coming opposite a blasted oak, he placed his hand inside a small orifice, and drew forth a folded paper.

A cry of joy came from his lips as he held the letter, and going to a small opening between the trees, where the moon's silvery rays fell with sufficient power to render the surrounding objects perfectly distinguishable, he read the contents of the strangely-acquired missive.

'Still true to you, Gerald (thus it ran); *but my heart is torn with fears for your safety. I saw your vessel arrive to-day, and my father, I fear, recognised its low hull and taper masts. Gregory Saunders was with him, and my heart filled with dread when my father told him to bring his gun brig round the headland and search your vessel. May you not meet. I know your proud spirit will not tamely submit to this man's insolence, and I tremble for your safety. Spread your vessel's white sails when you have read this, and escape while there is yet time. Fear not for me; I will never become the wife of Gregory Saunders.*

'MADELINE.'

'So,' he muttered, as he folded the paper, 'my foe is here. My rival, and placed upon my track by her father. Well, it is no more than I expected —no more than I desired. Let him come within reach of the Arrow's guns! then our long-standing debt may be settled. 'Escape while there is yet time!' No, sweet Madeline. Had I to cut my way through the tyrant's fleet, I would steal a few moments' bliss in your sweet presence.'

Muttering thus, and the fierce light deepening in his eyes, he reached the western side of the great house.

Could he be mistaken?

No.

Reclining on the window-frame, he beheld Lord Harry's lovely daughter.

Her eyes were turned towards the flashing lights of his distant home; and the small white hand which supported her head glistened in the soft light, as the rays of the night's glorious orb fell upon the rare jewels which were clustered upon the taper fingers.

Gerald stood entranced at the lovely spectacle, and his heart beat wildly as he noticed the sad, pensive look with which she regarded the distant ship.

She was thinking of him. The thought was bliss—celestial bliss. And, softly murmuring her name, he stood out from the shadow of the elms to where the silvery moonbeams fell upon his upturned face.

She heard his lowly-uttered word; and, changing her attitude, looked down until her light blue orbs met those which were upturned towards her.

Her start of surprise was followed by a deep blush and an exclamation, which partook of both pleasure and fear; then, as the white hands and the glittering jewels were extended towards him, she murmured—

'Oh, Gerald! why did you not heed my warning? Fly! There is yet time to escape from those who thirst for your blood.'

The proud lip curled somewhat scornfully as he answered—

'Gerald Stuart, Madeline, never turns his back upon a foe.'

She leaned further out of the window, and, in a low, supplicating voice, said—

'Hear me, Gerald. He is here, and I am a prisoner in my room '——

'Ha!'

'Hush. They thought you would come, and there is a party of armed men lying in ambush for you. Fly! as you love me. For pity's sake '——

'I were a coward to do so,' he said, and his hand gripped the hilt of his sword. 'A coward, and worthless of your love.'

'Gerald, they will kill '——

'Hear me out, Madeline. My ship rides below. Come, jump from your prison. There you shall be as a queen; there we will pass our days in such bliss that the '——

She drank in every word of his impassioned speech, and by the changing cheek and moistened eye, showed that a struggle was taking place between duty to her father and the love for that dark-eyed, handsome being.

The result is not difficult to guess; but, ere he could finish his passionate appeal, a rustling among the trees caused his weapon to leap from its sheath; and, turning in the direction of the sound, he stood face to face and blade to blade with Gregory Saunders, the captain of the Fire-Fly—his rival and his most inveterate foe.

Gerald sprang forward to meet him, his eyes blazing with fury; and, as their blades closed and the sharp, metallic sound went like a knife to Madeline's heart, Gregory Saunders hissed—

'Yield, traitor, or die!'

'Neither, at your hand—miscreant!' was the

reply, as the gallant fellow made a lunge at his enemy's heart. 'We have met, and foot to foot we'll fight out the quarrel until the green sward receives the blood of the conquered.'

The captain of the Fire-Fly retreated before the other's impetuous attack; and his ashy face and white quivering lips told of the recreant heart within.

A few moments would have seen him stretched lifeless upon the earth, for Gerald's stout, matchless skill made the other's tenfold his superior.

Gregory Saunders saw this, and his retreat became a cowardly flight; and, as the hot, impetuous youth followed, the coward called out—

'To the rescue! This way, my men This way!'

There was a rush of feet.

Then came the stalwart forms of a dozen of the Fire-Fly's crew upon the scene.

'Coward!' said Gerald. 'Is this your boasting? Is this the manner in which you tried to take me captive when we met.'

With the last words ringing out, he dashed at the king's officer, and, with one downward stroke of his keen sword, laid open the coward's cheek.

'There is a mark,' he exultingly said, 'that will cause you to remember our meeting. The next will be deeper still.'

Gregory Saunders dropped the blade he could not wield; and, blinded by the blood which poured from the gash in his face, reeled backwards and leaned against a tree for support.

The sailors, with that desire for fair play which is inherent in every English heart, stood leaning upon their weapons, hoping that their officer would face his foe.

From this attitude they were aroused by Saunders' frantic cries.

'Cut him down!' he yelled. 'Remember, a hundred pounds reward is offered for his head!'

The men made a simultaneous movement towards the gallant fellow, who stood with his sword levelled, ready to pierce the first who came near its point.

'Back!' he cried. 'Heed not the ravings of that coward. Back, I say! or there will be more blood shed to-night. Remember, I will never be taken alive!'

They paused.

The gallant seamen admired the brave man who stood thus unflinchingly before a dozen blades; and, had not the infuriated Lord Harry rushed to the spot, in all probability they would have suffered the captain of the Golden Arrow to have escaped.

One glance told the Lord High Admiral all that had passed; and, snatching a cutlass from one of the seamen, he advanced towards Gerald Stuart, exclaiming—

'At last we meet! Traitor—outlaw—pirate— die!'

'You seek your own destruction, old man,' said Gerald, as he caught the blow upon his weapon. 'Do not tempt me to slay you!'

Lord Harry foamed at the mouth with passion; and, in reply to Gerald's words, wielded his cutlass with a strength and skill that seemed wondrous for one so old.

Gerald still held the infuriated old noble at bay with as much ease as though he were a child; then, with a sudden movement of his supple wrist, twisted Lord Harry's weapon from his grasp.

'I could slay you,' he said, as the cutlass went whirling through the air; 'but, for the sake of her whom I love, I spare your life. Good night, my lord. When next we meet I will not be so merciful.'

He caught the cutlass as it descended and threw it at Lord Harry's feet, made a mocking bow, and turned from the spot.

Humiliated at his defeat, and fearful of losing his intended victim, Lord Harry snatched up the cutlass, and, calling upon the sailors to follow him, dashed in pursuit of the bold, fearless * * * *.

Gerald Stuart well knew his powers or the matchless skill with which he handled his weapon could not save him from a dozen blades; so, when he turned away from his foes, he retreated quickly towards his boat.

The chase was a close one, for the Fire-Fly's men were strong and fleet of limb, and urged forward by the heavy bribe offered by the savage old officer, they did their best to capture the fugitive.

So close were they upon him at times that, to save himself from their blades, he was compelled to turn and disable the foremost of his foes.

Four men had fallen to the ground by his weapon, and the remainder, rendered savage by their companions' fate, now pressed forward with an eagerness which showed the brute passion in their nature was aroused.

They rendered no appeal now to old Lord Harry's wish.

Blood had been shed; and it seemed that, tiger-like, it had awakened their thirst for more.

Gerald knew this; and, with lips compressed and his hand tightly gripping his crimson weapon, he put forth every energy to reach the boat.

There were but a few yards between the pursuers and the pursued, and the old noble, now seeing the latter's purpose, quickly ordered his men to separate into two parties.

The first were to keep up the chase and slay Gerald unless he yielded.

The second were to make a detour, and cut off his retreat to the boat.

The captain of the Golden Arrow knew not of this; and, in the imperfect light, mistook the men who suddenly shot across the bank for those of his boat's crew.

He discovered his error just in time; and while fiercely battling to cut a passage through them, Lord Harry and his party took him in the rear.

He was wounded, and nine weapons were seeking his life.

This unequal strife could never have but one termination.

That would have been the life of the noble-looking fellow who, although bleeding from several wounds, still fought—like a lion at bay.

His arm and eye began to fail him; and the proud spirit, mustering all the strength that was yet left, returned to make one desperate attempt to cut a path to the beech.

Hitherto the gallant fellow had only opposed his single blade against those wielded by his determined foes; but as he felt the cold faintness which follows the loss of blood creeping over him, he felt (and the thought gave his chivalrous heart a pang) that, unless he used the pistols which hung from his belt, his last moments were nigh.

So, while the right arm screened his body from the seamen's blades, the left hand grasped a pistol-butt.

There was a flash—a quick report—and one of his assailants dropped to the earth.

The bullet had passed through his brain.

'Close around the villain, men,' shouted Lord Harry. 'Quick—or he will use the other pistol!'

This sage advice was instantly followed.

Gerald Stuart's weapon was beaten down, and the hand which grasped the second pistol was disabled by a blow from the flat of a cutlass.

Setting his teeth hard, Gerald prepared to die.

He had already fallen upon one knee—his senses dazed by a blow upon the head.

Brave as he was, he could not help closing his eyes as he saw his assailants' weapons drawn back to deliver the fatal stroke.

Before a lunge could be delivered at his defenceless heart, a figure sprang into the very midst of his assailants—sweeping them back as though they were but blades of grass.

It was William, and in his hands was grasped a long oar, and twirling it around his head, it descended and struck the malevolent old admiral to the ground.

His voice rang out high above the groans of the wounded and the shrieks of the dying.

'Avast! you lubbers!' he cried. 'What! eight to one, and that one down and bleeding! Shiver me! Ah! it's the captain! the man who saved my Sue! Curse ye! you cowards!'

The strange and, in his sinewy hands, terrible weapon was not idle while he spoke, two more of the foe were stricken down, and the remainder, seized with a sudden panic, turned and fled.

They escaped but in time, for the armed boat's crew came running to their captain's assistance, eager to avenge his fall.

Will stooped over the handsome officer, who had swooned through the loss of blood he had sustained, and feeling a faint pulsation of the heart, the sailor said—

'Lift him gently, lads, for he is fouled by those lubbers. Curse them!'

Silent and sorrowful the crew lifted the bleeding form from the ground, and as they moved off towards the boat, Will said—

'I have four hours' liberty yet, shipmates. Tell him, when he comes to, that I shall be aboard before the anchor's weighed.' Then, as he walked towards his cottage, he added, 'I could go now, but for Sue.'

The old admiral overheard all this, and rising from the ground, leaped after his men, a wicked look in his cold, grey eyes, and a vengeful smile upon his lips as he muttered—

'So, Master William, you are one of this traitorous gang, are you? Very well—very well! You shall find yourself on a different ship before the four hours have expired.'

He hopped away upon one leg—the other had been fractured by the blow from Will's weapon.

Gallant Will slowly ascended the rugged pathway which led to his home.

He had slackened his pace to ponder over the late scene, and the part he had played therein.

'It's lucky,' he thought, 'that I heard the clashing of those cutlasses—luckier still, that I thought of taking that oar with me, or my new skipper would have been murdered, and—— D——n!'

Will turned fiercely as this forcible expression left his lips, and with one blow of his clenched hand struck a man to the ground whose hand had grasped the collar of his jacket.

The fall of his assailant was followed by the sudden rush of four armed men upon him, and before Will could shake them off he was thrown to the ground and firmly pinioned.

He was a prisoner, and in the power of the vindictive Lord Harry Garthway.

CHAPTER VII.

THE BUMBOAT WOMAN.

WITHIN an hour of the time that our hero fell into the hands of the malignant old admiral, the good people of Deal were aroused from their slumbers by the sound of a fierce cannonade.

And those who were not too much frightened by the roar of the guns went to the cliffs, and beheld a huge cloud of grey smoke hanging over the vessels thus engaged in close and terrible combat.

What nationality the ships claimed they were at a loss to conjecture; for, except the mass of rolling smoke and the repeated red flash of the guns, nothing was visible.

Some thought the French fleet had arrived.

Others imagined the close combat was between a revenue-cutter and a smuggler's lugger.

But the nautical element among them dispelled these ideas by saying that a cutter never carried such heavy ordnance as that which shook the windows of the houses near the sea, and shattered every pane of glass to small fragments.

So, huddled together, and fully expecting to behold a column of red-legged French infantry ascend the cliffs, they stood until the firing ceased, and that strange and awful calm which follows a naval fight took place.

Even then they were but little the wiser, for the dark hour, which preceded the coming day, prevented them from seeing the result of the fight.

So they pressed close together, and strained both eye and ear until the daylight came.

Then, to their surprise, they beheld the gun-brig, the Fire-Fly, rocking upon the water, a shot-torn wreck.

Her masts were out in two, and the upper portions, which yesterday's sunset gleamed upon in their lofty pride, were now dangling over the vessel's side.

Then, as the light grew stronger, they beheld the severe manner in which the brig had been handled.

Her bows were stove in; so was one side—and it needed no glass to show the gaping breaches that yawned from the bulwark nearly to the water-line.

'But where is the vessel that has worked this destruction?' was asked.

Many said, 'Sunk, of course. Could it be possible one of the king's ships had been so battered, and her antagonist yet afloat?'

No. The thought went against all reason.

So others, taking up the matter, said it must have been a French three-decker. No vessel of less dimensions could have so thoroughly battered the king's gun-brig out of all shape.

So they thought it was a glorious victory for the gun-brig to be afloat, although so severely handled.

A glorious victory, indeed! For was not the French line-of-battle ship at the bottom of the sea?

Those who laid this flattering unction to their souls were soon undeceived, and not pleasantly.

An old fisherman, armed with a powerful glass, after gazing at the wreck, turned the glass out to seaward, and, after a short examination of what seemed, with the naked eye, a mere speck in the distant horizon, closed the glass with a sudden snap, and exclaimed, with more force than politeness—

'I'm d——d if I didn't think so!'

NOTICE.—Another SPLENDID SHEET of the PLAY GIVEN AWAY with No. 3 of this Work.

BLACK EYED SUSAN.

OR, PIRATES ASHORE.

3   JACOB AT SEA.

'Think what, Joe?' a dozen voices asked.

'Why,' said Joe, tucking the glass under his arm, 'it's that there long, black-hulled craft as had a white flag flying at her peak as has been and smashed up the brig.'

'What! what! That little ship? Nonsense, Joe. The brig would have sunk her in no time! Tell that to the marines!'

'I tells it to you,' said Joe, angrily, to the sceptic. 'Here, look through the glass at that dark spot away to westward, and tell me what you see.'

So the sceptic glued his eye to the glass, and when he had obtained the proper focus, thus spoke—

'It's her, sure enough; and I can see them up aloft, repairing their foremast.'

So the idea of the French line-of-battle ship faded away; and the crowd, as they dispersed and went to their homes, shook their heads sagely, and whispered to one another that England's supremacy was gone, if a small vessel like that could batter one of the king's ships into a ragged wreck in such a short time as that.

And with this comfortable reflection they retired to their beds and the trembling spouses they had left therein.

During the course of the day the helpless brig was towed out of sight of the wondering crowds; and, despite every inquiry, they could glean no explanation respecting the strange occurrence, and an old sailor, who had lost a leg in his country's service and received sixpence per diem to make up for the absent limb, cynicly remarked (he must have been an ungrateful old rascal)—

'See here, mates; the captains and admirals is pretty fast a-palavering about the victories they gains, but they keep a victory of this kind precious dark.'

So saying, the old sailor with the wooden leg, and in receipt of sixpence per diem to compensate his loss, stumped away with a broad grin upon his face—whether caused by the words he had uttered, or a secret gratification at the battering the brig had received, we will leave to the charitable reader.

The affair gave much scope for the tap-room oratory of Deal; and, when the interest began to flag, the good folks were startled by another strange occurrence.

It was the report of a trial which had just concluded on board the Colossus, the guard-ship which lay about two miles off Deal.

None knew how the report originated, for the court-martial had been conducted with all the secrecy which the officers composing it could use; yet there leaked out sufficient to cause the sober inhabitants much gossip, and an equal amount of sympathy for the accused.

*   *   *   *

'Strange doings, Bill.'

'Very, Jack.'

These not uncommon words were exchanged by two men who had taken an officer on board the guard-ship.

They had just returned from the journey and dragged their not over clean-looking boat ashore; and this exchange of words took place as they stood with the moveable articles belonging to their skiff piled in a little heap at their feet.

There seemed to be a strange attraction in the big ship which lay in the offing to the watermen, for neither attempted to carry the cushions, rudder, or sculls away until they had indulged in a long stare at the old man-o'-war.

'So,' the first speaker said, breaking the long silence, 'it's poor Will that is to be hung to-morrow morning?'

'Yes, mate. Poor fellow! and they wouldn't let his wife go aboard to wish him good-bye.'

'No, the varmints. Poor thing—poor thing! Just as she thought he'd got clear of the service and the tyrants that think men are only fit to be tied up and whipped like so many dogs, he falls into this mess! I can't see how they'd any right to try him, when he didn't belong to the fleet.'

'From what that chap told me as was painting the side,' Bill said, 'they've made out that William belonged to that smart little craft which knocked the gun-brig into splinters, and then went through the channel squadron, firing her heavy guns right and left.'

'It don't say much for their smartness,' Jack said, 'if they let a little vessel like that punish them, and slip away.'

'They couldn't help themselves; she was in among 'em like a flash of lightning, and before one on 'em could get under weigh, she was hull down. Lor' bless you, Jack! there ain't a ship in the fleet as can walk the water like that one; and if I were a young chap, she's just the craft I should like to pitch my hammock in.'

'What is she, Bill? Not a Frencher?'

'Frencher!' Bill said, somewhat indignantly. 'Do you think a Johny Crapaud could do what she has done?'

'Don't know. He might, if he took 'em by surprise, as this one did.'

'No, Jack; it ain't in 'em, lad. They couldn't do it. But you was asking what this little spitfire is.'

'Ay.'

'Well, that's more than anyone knows, except them admirals and captains as has been and tried poor Will, and they keeps it dark enough.'

'So they did the trial,' Bill said; 'but it got out, somehow.'

'Yes, mate, the trial, but not the charge.'

'That, too, I heard,' said Bill, 'when you was carrying the officer's traps on deck.'

'You did? You've kept it pretty close, then, considering we've left the ship nigh an hour.'

'I've been thinking, mate—that's why I didn't tell you—thinking of that poor girl—pretty Black-eyed Susan as they calls her. Pick up the traps, Jack, and I'll tell you as we goes along.'

The speaker threw the sculls over his shoulder, and his companion, taking the unshipped rudder and the cushions under his arm, turned from the beach.

'This is what I heard,' Bill said, as they went towards the town, 'but mind you, Jack, I promised the chap as told me that I wouldn't get him into trouble by blabbing, so keep your tongue quiet, 'specially 'mong the women folk.'

'No fear of my jawing gear going to work.'

'That's right, mate. Well, the sailor said he'd heard it from one of the marines as stood guard over the prisoner that poor Will was charged with aiding and abetting the escape of an outlaw and a traitor, and a lot more names they called him. Besides this, the prisoner was charged with being in the service of a foe and a rebel, and for all this they sentenced him to be hung.'

'But,' Jack said, 'what did William say to it all?'

'He told 'em he was innocent, except breaking old Admiral Garthway's shins with an oar, and he said he wouldn't have done that, but he saw a young chap as had saved his Susan from falling over the rocks being tackled by six or seven men, and he didn't know but what they were robbers, seeing it was dark at the time.'

'Of course they didn't believe his defence?'

'Don't look like it, when he is to be run up to the yard-arm.'

Jack was about to deliver a sententious speech about the case, when Betsy, the bumboat woman, came running towards them.

She was a connexion of Jack's, and as she met that worthy, the good dame exhibited her broad, red palm, and somewhat astonished were the boatmen to perceive five gold pieces gleaming thereon.

'Why, Bet,' Jack began, 'what gold mine have you tumbled over?'

'The strangest thing in the world has happened, Jack. But come, let's go to the Dolphin and have a glass, then I'll tell you all about it.'

The watermen, like their brethren of the briny deep, never refused an opportunity to partake of the contents of a glass, or pewter, for that matter. So they closed at once upon Betsy's offer, and, I am sorry to chronicle, before they left the Dolphin, one of the gold pieces melted away, and this extraordinary fact had such an effect upon the trio, that they were compelled to cling to each other for support, when the landlord of the Dolphin discreetly turned them out of that hospitable house of entertainment, especially for salt-water gentlemen just home from a cruise.

*   *   *   *   *

The evening sun was setting in dusky splendour, and the brave fellow whose life was to terminate on the morrow sadly watched the few straggling rays that struggled into his gloomy prison.

The golden rays fell upon the marine's bayonet, as he paced to and fro upon the gangway, and caused the bright weapon to sparkle and glitter like a golden ball.

The officers were collected upon the poop, the midshipmen upon the quarter deck, and the crew, those that were not on watch, were grouped upon the forecastle.

There was a strangeness in the manner of these various groups that told of the morrow's dread scene; for the sailor, whether officer or seaman, liked not the thought of the coming execution. It cast a gloom over the whole ship, and none spoke above a whisper.

From this state of sombre quietude, those near the fore gangway were aroused by the marine going to the side, and calling out, in a loud tone—

'Hi! Keep off there! unless you want a cold shot dropped into your boat.'

It was something to break the gloom which had fallen upon the seamen, and they looked over the side at the person to whom the sea soldier was speaking.

It was a boat; and by the heterogeneous collection of things that were collected, seemingly in hopeless confusion, in her stern, they saw it was a bumboat, and those who were familiar with the sight of Betsy's portly form, beheld a dark-eyed, handsome woman in the good dame's place.

There was a good-humoured smile upon the comely damsel's face, as, disregarding the marines, she came close under the massive side of the line-of-battle ship, and to the surly admonitions, replied—

'Bother your cold shot, sentry. Would you destroy a poor woman's stock-in-trade, and upset her in that manner?'

'Keep off then, I tell you. There's no shore boats to come alongside until after nine to-morrow morning.'

The punishment was to take place at eight.

'Except mine, sentry. I'm to come. You ask Captain Crosstree if I'm not.'

'Captain Crosstree!' said the marine. 'Who told you he was aboard?'

'Listen to the man! as if I didn't see him, when he came in a shore boat. Go along with you, and tell the captain that Tom Frost's sister wants to speak to him, and you'll see how fast he'll come.'

The word was passed for Captain Crosstree, and, to the marine's surprise, that officer gave immediate orders for the bumboat woman to come on board.

The buxom girl ascended the sides in a manner that would not have disgraced the smartest sailor on board.

As she passed the marine she won that individual's goodwill, by slipping half-a-dozen cakes of tobacco in his hand.

He had only time to secrete the present in one of the pockets of his sparrow-tailed coat, when Captain Crosstree came towards the gangway.

He looked at the dark, handsome face, and said, interrogatively—

'You are sister to the man who spoke to me this morning?'

'I am, sir.'

'Well, has he sent me the promised intelligence?'

'He sent you this, sir.'

She gave him a folded paper, and the captain, hastily opening it, read—

'The vessel passed me this morning, when I was fishing, and, by good fortune, I got on board. They are repairing damages, and, from what I could glean, they intend to run her into the Thames and refit. She is well-armed, and full of men—but no doctor aboard; this I believe is the chief cause of visiting the Thames. They require a medical officer to attend upon the wounded. The vessel will be disguised when she comes within sight of land. Upon this point I cannot inform you, as I was ordered to leave before I could overhear their plan. The prisoner now under sentence of death will no doubt be able to furnish this intelligence, if properly managed. I should suggest that my sister, who is both pretty and wicked enough to tempt a saint, be sent to him, and if she does not get this necessary information, I'm afraid all the trouble we have been at will be lost. It can but be tried, and I see no other way.

'TOM FROST.

'On board the Mary-

'A smuggling lugger, you could have added muttered Captain Crosstree. Well, no matter what he is, he has done me a good service. This sister of his much resembles him in features.'

He raised his eyes, and caught the dark, expressive orbs of the smuggler's sister fixed upon his face.

'So, pretty one,' he said, 'you are, I presume, quite aware of the contents of this letter?'

'Quite, sir.'

'And willing to do as your brother wishes?'

'I would do anything to oblige you, captain.'

The look which accompanied these words went to the captain's heart, and a vague idea that he was secretly loved by the handsome girl was a source of no small amount of self-gratulation.

It was neither time nor place to indulge in a tender scene; so the captain, mentally resolving to soon become better acquainted with the dark-eyed beauty, gave her an expressive look, and said—

'I am going on board my ship in a few minutes. Will you follow me with the intelligence you glean from the prisoner?'

'It will be too dark,' she said, hesitatingly; 'and I may mistake your brother's vessel for yours.'

The officer's eyes sparkled at the prospective interview on board his vessel.'

'That is easily managed,' he said. 'I will hang two red lights over the stern, that you may distinguish the ship.'

'That will do,' she said, hanging her head. 'Now I will see the prisoner, and by telling him I have a message from his wife, he will be softened a little.'

The captain smiled assent, and making a sign to the sentry, the handsome girl passed from his admiring gaze.

'She's fit for a king,' he said, as he turned towards the poop. 'What splendid eyes and matchless form! It is a sin that she should follow such an avocation as bumboat woman. Pshaw! she has a soul above vending provisions to these coarse, vulgar sailors.'

The gallant officer did not think even this lowly calling was better than the position he would have given the handsome girl.

The memory of those dark eyes strong upon him, Captain Crosstree soon after left the guard-ship, and went to the frigate he commanded, and which lay a little to leeward of the stately vessels which composed the Channel fleet.

No sooner did his feet touch the deck, than he ordered two red lights to be displayed over the stern.

Then, his mind filled with vivid pictures of the anticipated interview, he paced to and fro the quarter-deck.

The time passed but slowly; and, to the amorous captain's surprise, the moon began to shed her pale light at intervals upon the waters, and still no signs of his visitor.

Peering over the frigate's side, he looked towards the guard-ship; and while fancying every dark speck was the coming boat, he was suddenly startled by seeing a flash of light stream from the liner's bows, and then the dull report of a gun came across the water.

CHAPTER VIII.

ON BOARD THE GOLDEN ARROW.

BOLD of heart, yet bitterly conscious of the doom he was about to undergo, gallant Will sat, with bowed head, brooding over the strange manner in which his new-formed happiness had been destroyed.

He thought of Susan; and the manacled hands were passed over his eyes, and from that stout heart, which had not quailed beneath the solemnly-uttered finding of his judges, now gave way to an outburst of grief, and salt tears of bitter agony welled up, and dropped through his half-closed fingers.

He had seen his wife once since he had been placed a helpless captive in the prison-cell on the middle deck.

He had seen her through the open port which gave light to his last home—the last before the tightly-sewn shotted canvas.

He had seen the boat in which she came to bid him an eternal farewell sternly ordered off by the red-coated sentries; and, in spite of her prayers and entreaties, Gnatbrain and Jacob, who were with her, were compelled to put the boat round, and row, slowly and sorrowfully, away.

Her last piteous cry yet rung upon his ears; and, in a voice anguished and hopeless, he moaned—

'I could have died better—could have worked the dead reckoning more like a sailor and a man, had I seen my poor young wife. It's hard to go aloft like this. But if my log is clear enough with the Great Captain above, I may yet see my Sue—may—may—yet'——

The strong man's voice sank into a low wail. The mental agony was too much for him; and, overcome with emotion, his head fell forward, and the powerful, muscular chest rose and fell with the workings within.

From this state he was aroused by the entrance of the handsome girl who had just left the impassioned Captain Crosstree.

Will raised his head; and, in the semi-darkness, seeing the outlines of a woman's form, a wild hope came to his heart, and rising as far as his manacles would permit, he said—

'Susan!'

The figure made no response until it came close beside the captive.

Then the sailor was startled by these words being whispered close to his ear—

'Not Sue, Will; but one who can do more for you than your wife.'

The tones of the girl's voice seemed familiar to him.

But ere he could make a reply to these strange words, a sailor entered, and suspended a battle lanthorn from the roof.

The man departed as silently as he came; and Will, when the light gleamed upon his visitor's face, said—

'Surely I'm not mistaken. It is'——

'Hush! Not so loud, Will. Yes, I am Gerald Stuart; and I have come to save you, or fall in the attempt.'

The sailor was for a moment dazed by this daring trick of his new friend; and before he could find words to express his disbelief in the ultimate success of Captain Gerald's plan, the latter drew from his pocket a small parcel.

He opened it, and the light fell upon a number of small saws, so fine in their structure that they seemed made of watch-springs.

'Hold out your hands, Will,' the gallant fellow said. 'That's it. Now, keep still, and your wrists shall soon be freed.'

For a few minutes nothing was heard save the deep breathing of the men who were playing such a dangerous stake for their lives.

Will was silent from sheer astonishment.

But when his wrists were released from the handcuffs, he seized the captain's hand, and murmured—

'God bless your honour! This is another debt I hope to repay.'

'Don't speak now, my good fellow. Here, take this saw, and work away at one leg while I operate upon the other.'

He did so, and in a few minutes stood upon the deck—his limbs free.

There was a greater difficulty yet to overcome, this was to sever the iron grating which covered the porthole.

Almost fearing to breathe, they set to work upon the iron bars; and, when one side had been sawn through, Will applied his herculean strength to them and wrenched the grating far enough aside to permit of the passage of their bodies.

'Get through, Will,' said his preserver, 'and drop quietly in the water. I'll join you when I've shifted this guise.'

While he whispered these words he rapidly unfastened the feminine apparel, and let it fall to the deck.

Will, who hung by his hands to the outside of the port, saw the light playing upon the hand, some uniform he had such good cause to remember.

Fortunately for the fugitives the tide was rapidly running out, thus they were able to rapidly drift out to sea without the slightest motion of their hands.

They well knew that the slightest splash would attract the notice of the watch on the guard-ship's deck, and scarcely daring to look upward at the dark forms which were partly visible in the gloom.

Silently they passed onward; and not until the huge hull of the liner had faded from their sight was a word exchanged.

Then the daring chief broke the silence—

'Safe, Will! Thank heaven and the bumboat woman who lent me her boat and her daughter's clothes!'

'Safe! Thanks to your honour's courage,' said the grateful sailor; 'but for that I should have been'——

A broad sheet of flame, followed by the boom of a distant gun, caused Will to stop abruptly.

'Your flight is discovered,' said the captain of the Golden Arrow. 'Quick, Will! for we shall soon have the whole pack of light vessels at our heels. Follow me.'

The young chief struck out quickly towards a bright light which hung over the bows of a low-hulled vessel some ten fathoms in front of them.

It was a race for life—and the two wasted not one of the precious moments in converse.

Cleaving the water with incredible swiftness, they soon reached the ship; and a dozen ready hands were waiting to haul them on board.

When Captain Stuart's feet touched the deck, he gave an order for the sails to be spread; then, as the canvas filled, and the gallant bark bounded forward, he turned to the officer on watch, and said—

'Cast loose a couple of guns, and answer their signal of alarm; then let them catch us if they can.'

The bright flashes of the guns were noticed by the distant cruisers, and by the moving lights, which gave the pursuing ships the appearance of gaunt spectres, the fearless chieftain knew that his foes were upon his track.

He had but little to fear from the ships that were to leeward.

His only danger lay in the possibility of coming across one of the outlying vessels.

For this he soon prepared.

The formidable guns which had battered the brig-of-war in such a short space of time were double shotted—the ports opened—the deck crowded with stalwart, armed men—and, fluttering over the vessel's stern, was the white silken banner with its strange golden symbol.

Thus did Gerald Stuart, the outlaw, rescue a prisoner from beneath the talons of a savage and bloodthirsty law; and with his strange banner flying and open port he defiantly waited for such of his foes as should cross his path.

Gallant Will's warlike soul was fired at the sight; and, throwing off his wet jacket, he seized a cutlass, and said—

'Let's come to close quarters, your honour. D—n them! I've fought for their flag, and twice they've tried to send me aloft! Let me now show how I can fight against them—and, damme! I'll'——

'You'll come below,' said the handsome young outlaw, smiling. 'We shall have plenty of fighting soon; but we cannot lay yard-arm to yard-arm with the whole of the fleet. We may catch one away from the flock; then, Will, you may have an opportunity of repaying a little of their kindness.'

'May I fall foul of those,' Will said, 'who kept my Susan away when the death signal was flying for her husband!'

'Never mind now, Will,' the chief said. 'Put that cutlass back, and when we've shifted these wet clothes we will come on deck, and perhaps—let us hope so—there may be another of the pack that would like to be served as we served the gun-brig.'

'The gun-brig, your honour?'

'Come below, and I'll tell you.'

Somewhat loth, Will followed his chief to the state room.

There was a fascination in those distant lights that held our hero to the deck.

He thought and hoped that those who had been so deaf to Susan's prayer would yet come alongside the Golden Arrow.

The vaunted British navy had not at that moment a fiercer or more implacable foe than taut Will—the man who had but a short time before been among the first to uphold the honour of king and country.

When the sailor entered the luxuriously furnished cabin he stood a few paces inside, and, fumbling with the rim of his hat, seemed afraid to advance further into the hitherto sacred precincts.

There was good cause for Will's bashfulness.

He had been reared in a humble home, and from his boyhood up to the time when he returned from his last cruise his dwelling-place had been the dingy forecastle of a man-of-war.

The rich carpet and richer furniture which he now beheld were too much for him.

As he caught sight of his sorry figure in one of the mirrors he felt how much he was beneath the splendour which surrounded him.

The captain of the Golden Arrow guessed the cause of the gallant fellow's timidity, and, with a few genial words, he soon brought Will to a chair which stood near the table.

'Now, Will,' he said, 'as we shall not have much time to talk over matters, the best thing for you to do will be to cast off those wet clothes, and jump into these.'

He pointed as he spoke to an officer's uniform which lay upon a locker.

The sailor, with a flushed face, stammered—

'What! ship those things, your honour?—gilt swabs * and all?'

'Yes, Will. I have lost my first officer during our fight with the brig, and from this time I appoint you first lieutenant of the Golden Arrow.

* Gold epaulettes.

That is more than the German king you have so long served would do for you.'

Gallant Will's heart swelled with pride, and he thought of the pleasure Susan would feel when she beheld him in that uniform which so well became his handsome form.

With fingers trembling with excitement, he changed his simple sailor's suit for the gold laced uniform.

The young chief, during the time this change took place, enlightened Will upon the cause of the heavy firing which had so disturbed the good people of Deal.

When he had, with sailor-like brevity, told how the Golden Arrow crippled her enemy, he added—

'That brig was commanded by my most pitiless foe. He has sworn to destroy me, not only because I am an enemy to the German who has usurped the throne, and who wastes the blood of his subjects and the revenues of England * to enrich a pack of needy Germans—not only would he hunt me down for the price that is set upon my head, but for another matter, of which you shall know more hereafter.'

Will was silent..

His chief's mode of expressing himself about the king was so different to that which he had been accustomed to hear that it caused the hitherto loyal sailor to feel as though he stood upon the brink of a great crime.

'This Gregory Saunders,' the young chieftain went on, 'tried to put his threat into execution the night you were captured. How he succeeded, that battered wreck can testify. Now, Will,' he added, his dark eyes sparkling, 'before we go further on our cruise I will tell you the errand of the Golden Arrow. It is simply to harass and destroy such of the British fleet as may come across her path, and, with heaven's help, I hope, before this vessel finds a resting-place in the ocean's bed, to strew the sea with the shattered wrecks of every light vessel which carries the usurper's flag.'

He paused; and while sipping a glass of wine, gazed at the silent sailor, as though to note the effect of his words.

'You will find,' he continued, 'that it is no idle boast when I say that we are a match for any vessel twice our size. The Golden Arrow's marvellous powers of sailing, and the heavy metal she carries—heavier, and twice that of the ordnance in any of the English frigates—enable her to cope with such unequal odds. More than this. When we are yard-arm with a foe, I could clear their deck in a few minutes with my small-arm men. You look incredulous. Listen. On board all the vessels which sail under the British flag you will find nothing but the old musket. Mark the difference. Every man on this ship has a long small-bore rifle, and well they know how to use them.'

Still no word from Will.

But for the play of his handsome features, there was nothing to tell that he had heard a syllable of his chieftain's explanatory speech.

He stood with his hands resting upon the heavy sword, which formed part of his new uniform, and, though he spoke not in reply, every word the commander of the Golden Arrow had spoken, had its weight with the brave sailor.

The wild, daring life Captain Stuart depicted, was congenial to the sailor's temperament. There

* It is a well-known fact that George the First made the strength and revenues of Great Britain subservient to the benefit and preservation of his Electoral dominions.

was something so fearless and free in thus traversing the pathless waters like a Nemesis, that suited the mind already so inveterate against those he had so well served, and been, in return, so foully treated.

This, and the vessel's singular speed, and still more singular armament—then, again, the rank which had been conferred upon him—helped to decide his wavering mind.

So, when the captain asked him if he would, after the explanation thus frankly given, accept the position, Will grasped the extended hand, and said—

'Will I sail with you? Yes. As long as a finger can pull a trigger, or a plank of the ship holds, I will be at your side.'

The captain returned the pressure of Will's hand, then pointing to the chair, said—

'Seat yourself, lieutenant, and let us drink success to the Golden Arrow and confusion to all Germans.'

Will drank the treasonable toast with as much sincerity as he had been wont to shout, ' God save the king! '

The clinking of their glasses frequently took place during the conversation which ensued after Will had thus outlawed himself from his native land.

Will soon became more accustomed to the change in his position, and to feel more at ease with his brave preserver. So, during a pause in their conversation, he asked how the captain had been so successful in effecting his deliverance.

Gerald Stuart laughed, as he answered—

'Very easily, Will. You must know I make it a rule to find out personally as much of the enemy's movements as possible, and, for this purpose, I am in the habit of assuming various disguises. After the battle with the gun-brig, I obtained the use of a small lugger, and, under the name of Tom Frost, went cruising about among the fleet, and by good fortune, I managed to run my ungainly vessel's jib-boom fast in the gear of a frigate's dolphin-striker. This vessel was commanded by Captain Crosstree'—

'Ah! My former officer!'

'Well, as I most particularly wished to glean some information about you, I scrambled up the bobstays when the vessels fouled, and soon stood in front of the captain. He, as a matter of course, rated me for my awkwardness in thus running against the king's ship, and, as a matter of course, I apologised, and, in my abject speech, made use of a few words which soon changed his anger into joy. I told him that I had been overhauled by a vessel, the description of which tallied with this bonnie craft.

'My gentleman was eager to hear about the Golden Arrow, which he was kind enough to call a pirate, and so far forgot himself as to tell me he had that very morning received orders to go in pursuit, and destroy the audacious craft which had so well punished the brig.

'This gave me a cue, and I told him I was going on board the pirate with some stores that evening. So I played my cards so well, that, under promise of a reward, I consented to bring him word of the exact condition and the hiding-place of the Golden Arrow. We then parted, and by mixing with the crew, I heard that you were to be hung up like a wet jib to-morrow morning.

'There was not much time to be lost. So, when I left the frigate, I obtained the loan of old Betsy's boat, and a suit of clothes, and in the evening went to the guard ship.

'I had written a letter under my name for the nonce, and in my female guise I brought it to Captain Crosstree. I was then the smuggler's sister, and in this letter I told him my sister would get the information he required from one of the Golden Arrow's crew, who was in irons in the guard ship. He swallowed the bait, and the result is '——

The officer of the watch came hurriedly into the state-room, and said—

'There's a large ship coming right across our bows, sir, and a frigate in our wake.'

'Are the men at quarters?'

'Yes, sir.'

'Very well. I shall'——

The roar of a gun above their heads caused the captain to spring to his feet, and Will, following the example, buckled on his sword, and the trio rushed up the gangway.

Before they reached the deck another gun was fired, then came a perfect salvo from the pursuing frigate, and scarcely had this died away when the advancing vessel discharged her bow guns at the Golden Arrow.

'That's my friend, Crosstree, in our wake,' the captain said; 'but as yet I'm not acquainted with the gentleman in front.'

Considering the little craft was between two huge foes, the fearless captain of the Golden Arrow betrayed but little anxiety; so thought his first officer, as he stepped into the midst of the grey smoke of the battle.

CHAPTER IX.

IN PURSUIT OF THE GOLDEN ARROW.

THE daring escape of our hero from under the very guns of the British fleet was more than Lord Harry Garthway could properly digest. He was furious when apprised of the occurrence, and when told that all attempts to recapture the prisoner had been a failure, he had scarcely enough self-control to resist the temptation of having the unfortunate messenger kicked out.

Smothered exclamations of disappointment and rage broke from his lips when the messenger had retired, and not even his battered shins could keep him from instantly setting out for the coast, and he boarded the frigate in a flaming passion.

'The captain!' he demanded, neither noticing nor returning the salutes of his subordinates. 'The captain!' was all he could utter, and strode the quarter-deck angrily.

The commander came instantly on deck, and saluted his superior.

'Well, sir,' demanded Lord Harry, turning upon him with eyes that blazed in their fury. 'Well, sir, and the prisoner has escaped?'

'Such is the unfortunate truth, my lord.'

There was a short pause, in which the high admiral had to strive hard to conquer his feelings sufficiently to speak with something like calmness.'

'And so, sir, you mean to say that a man was permitted to escape from one of his majesty's ships, surrounded by a fleet, and in this very port?'

'Such, unhappily, has been the case.'

'Case—case, sir! It's infamous!'

'It was no fault of mine, Lord Garthway,' answered the captain, somewhat coldly.

'No fault of yours, sir? I say it was. Had my instructions been carried out, it would not have happened.'

'Your pardon, my lord. Your instructions *were* carried out by me.'

'I will not be contradicted, sir. I say they were *not*. How comes it the traitor escaped, then? Could he do it alone? Who permitted anyone to see him? Was that my orders?'

'I believe not, admiral; but I was absent at the time. Captain Crosstree gave the permission for some bumboat woman to visit him.'

'Indeed! Who was the sentry on duty?'

'I do not know, but will discover.'

'Do, and put that man under arrest.'

'Pardon, my lord, he could not prevent the woman from entering when she had obtained the permission of Captain Crosstree.'

'It was neglect on his part to let them escape. Why did he not look after them? Do as I order you, put him under arrest.'

The captain saw how useless it was to attempt anything in the poor fellow's behalf, and he was called up to undergo the humiliating process of being handcuffed and thrust in prison.

Lord Harry did not seem inclined to stop at that. He made the most minute inquiries of who were on deck at the time, and if any addressed the bumboat woman; but on being told that nothing had been done without the orders of Captain Crosstree, he contented himself with imprisoning the marine, and sending for Captain Crosstree, who appeared shortly after the summons.

'So you have managed nicely to let the rebel prisoner escape, eh?' Such was the salute Captain Crosstree met with from the irritated old admiral.

'The news my lord, of the daring flight was as surprising to me as it must have been to you. I was on my ship at the time.'

'Indeed! Who gave the bumboat woman leave to see the prisoner?'

'I, admiral.'

'You, sir? And why?'

'To get some information from him as to the nature and equipments of the Golden Arrow.'

The admiral winced at the mention of that name.

He remembered his gun brig, and felt both ashamed and annoyed.

'I had already gleaned this information,' continued Crosstree, producing the written slip of paper given him by the supposed bumboat woman.

'Humph!' growled Lord Harry. 'You have managed to lose the prisoner—do the best you can to find him; and, if you take my advice, you *won't* return without having done so, and with the satisfactory intelligence that he and his schooner are at the bottom of the sea!'

Those words were spoken in a tone of warning or menace, that made Captain Crosstree's face flush. Still, concealing his feelings, he replied—

'I should be most happy, my lord, not only to undertake the commission but to fulfil it in a manner that will do honour to myself and justice to my country.'

'Do so. I expect you will have every preparation made, and be on his track by sunrise to-morrow.'

'It shall be done, my lord.'

'Sufficient.'

Then with a haughty wave of the hand, Lord Harry

turned away; but, now his excitement had cooled a little, he began to feel the effects of his damaged legs, on which he had been standing too long.

Lord Harry Garthway returned to his residence none the less good tempered than when he left it.

On entering his sitting-room he found Gregory Saunders seated at the table, with his head bound up and an ugly streak of black plaster across his temple and cheek.

'I hear, my lord,' he began, savagely, 'that the rascally traitor has escaped. It is to be hoped that the report is not true.'

The admiral threw himself into a seat with a savage growl of pain and rage.

'True? Yes, sir; it is true.'

Saunders made some comment, to which the old admiral did not reply. He was thinking, and his mind was absorbed in a deep reverie about Gerald Stuart and his gallant comrade, William; and the longer he brooded, the darker became his thoughts.

His breast filled with fierce hatred, and his heart beat wildly at the anticipation of having the two brave fellows in his power.

So lost he became, that his imagination conjured up the vision—a pleasing scene to him—of a yard-arm, with two dangling ropes tied into loops, one for each of his detested foes.

Then he came back to facts and realities.

The smashing of the gun-brig, and the escape of William, and the shame brought upon his house and name by the clandestine meetings of his daughter with a branded outlaw.

He worked himself into a state of frenzy, and only relieved himself by uttering some most dreadful imprecations upon the heads of his foes, and even his lovely child did not escape a bitter curse.

Saunders heard it, and the blood ran cold in his veins; for, bad as he was, he could not listen to it unmoved.

'Remember, Lord Harry,' he said, 'that she is your daughter. Would to God it were otherwise!'

'Otherwise, Captain Saunders! Otherwise! How can it be?'

'When that smooth-faced outlaw is out of the way.'

Admiral Garthway gave an exclamation in which was blended contempt and an amount of irony, not altogether free from a cutting sneer.

'Can we send a fleet in these times after him, and it appears that there is no one who cares about trying to capture him—at least, by the way his majesty's gun-brigs are allowed to be hammered to pieces.'

Saunders winced, and a flush rose to his cheek as he replied—

'The brig did its duty, my lord; and the men on board did theirs.'

'I did not say the contrary. But I tell you what it is, Gregory Saunders: you have lost your ship. I will get you another. It shall be the fastest sailer ever yet set afloat. It shall be well armed and manned by picked men. You want to marry my daughter. You shall. But I firstly wish to name the conditions. When you have hunted down, taken prisoner, or slain this outlaw and his accomplice, you shall have my daughter—with or without her consent.'

'This is a compact?'

'It is.'

'Then, sir, I will fulfil my part of it or die.'

He held out his hand as he said this, and the admiral took it, though a little indifferently.

Saunders had noticed the change in the old admiral, and thought it wise to put on as bold an appearance over the matter as possible.

Before he left, the old fellow was considerably mollified, and talked in his accustomed way.

'Everything will be prepared,' he said, as Saunders stood at the door to depart. 'And, when the vessel is equipped, you will lose no time in starting.'

'Fear not,' he replied, raising his hand; and all the feelings of his callous heart were stamped upon his evil face; 'unless you hear of my success over my hated foe, you will hear of my death. He or I conquers. It is war to the last.'

And he strode away in the most melodramatic manner.

Perhaps he thought it would leave some impression upon the admiral; but unfortunately Saunders was but a poor amateur actor, at the best, and its effect was entirely lost.

'That may be very well,' muttered the admiral, 'but I wish he would not talk so loud in the hall.'

Then he fell into one of his deep reveries.

He thought that his daughter's hand would be inducement enough for Gregory to dare anything.

Too well was Admiral Garthway aware of the inferior sailing of every vessel in the fleet, and did not put much faith in the success of Captain Crosstree.

The gallant captain—under whom William had once served—lost no time in having his vessel prepared; and by sunrise the anchor was weighed, and, true to his promise, he was on the track of the Golden Arrow.

Naturally, the first day brought nothing worthy of note, though Captain Crosstree overhauled every fishing lugger he came near, and questioned their captains or owners very sharply, but could gain no intelligence of the outlaw's fleeting vessel.

'No doubt,' said Crosstree to his lieutenant, 'the scamp makes good use of the sailing qualities of his vessel to get out of our way.'

'Does he know we are coming on his track?' asked the lieutenant, with a touch of irony in his voice that did not pass unnoticed, and the captain coloured.

He was of a generous nature, and on second thoughts saw his speech was boastful and vainglorious.

'He no doubt thinks someone is on his track.'

The reply was given pertly.

The smile on the officer's face was not pleasing to the captain.

'Still, Captain Crosstree, Gerald Stuart is more likely to stand a fight than a run.'

Those words were spoken without thought or any material meaning, but they were very true.

Could Captain Crosstree have seen a few leagues across the vast expanse of sunlit waters, he would have discovered the Golden Arrow gliding at a swan's pace through the sea.

Gerald Stuart had not escaped from a few gun scratches, and the loss of some particles of rigging in the brush with the Fire-Fly.

Small and trivial as the danger was, the handsome young rover would have them repaired, and the lovely vessel put in such trim as she appeared when anchored before the cliffs at Deal.

Captain Gerald Stuart, as he had said, had a purpose in thus venturing out with his fine craft, and gallant hearts of oak.

That purpose was not forgotten, and he waited patiently to see the canvas of some pursuing enemy's ship, as he said—

NOTICE.—Another Grand Scene of the Play ready. See next Number.

BLACK EYED SUSAN

OR, PIRATES ASHORE.

BOARDING THE FRIGATE.

'I came out to fight and destroy—not run away. My work is with those who are stronger than myself. I wage war with a power—with a nation—single-handed! I will defy it!—but I am not a pirate!'

William was at his side always, for the lion-hearted young sailor was as anxious as his captain for action.

He felt himself wronged—foully injured, and he felt he had risked his life for an ungrateful government, which he had served faithfully, and in return, got disgrace, and would have been brought to an ignominious death.

'And for why?' he mused, his heart swelling with feelings of strong passion and resentment for all he had suffered. 'For loving and dutifully serving my king and country, and defending the weak.' He smiled bitterly. 'I owe them a great deal. They have turned an honest true heart into a stone, that will bear whatever may be hurled upon it, without the slightest impression being left. Let them beware! If they fear what they make themselves, they shall have cause to fear me. My life—my gratitude—the life of one dearer to me than my own—poor, dear Sue!—is owing to the man I have sworn to serve, and I will do so while one drop of blood remains in me to give me power and life!'

Perhaps his thoughts had been helped into this dark and dangerous channel by the refined, but dangerous conversations of his gallant young chief.

Captain Gerald had calculated well when he had the Golden Arrow brought to under closed reefs, allowing the contrary winds to shift him here and there, in the hopes of falling in with an enemy.

*   *   *   *   *

The second morning subsequent to that on which Captain Crosstree left Deal, brought him in sight of a vessel which was as yet too far to clearly discern, but he had a presentiment that it was the Golden Arrow.

Captain Crosstree and his gallant crew were too used to hard service to display any great excitement, even though they had every reason to believe the ship in the offing was their anticipated prey.

The shrill whistle of Quid, the boatswain, brought every man to his post, and they awaited, in grim silence, the orders of their commander.

The gunners stood by their guns — a train of powder-monkeys formed a line from the upper deck to the magazine—the sail-trimmers stood with the ropes in their hands.

A flush of pride went over the features of Captain Crosstree as he gazed upon this grand scene.

To a sailor's heart nothing can be compared to the deck of a frigate before the action—when crowded with well-disciplined men, who await only the commands to begin preparations for the contest.

'Cast loose!' he cried to the gunners.

With one accord the men removed the wedges from the wheels, the ropes were cast loose, and the guns rolled heavily over the deck.

'Load, and prepare!'

One order followed upon the other.

They went from mouth to mouth, right down the vessel, from stem to stern—from the lower hold to the foretop.

The effect was wonderful.

A few words from that one man set everyone in motion, like supplying steam to a machine, every part of which was instantly set working.

Small arms were being loaded.

The clank of the ramrods down the long barrels of the marines' guns could be heard.

Cutlasses flashed, and reflected the sun's rays like so many will-o'-the-wisps over the scene.

The larger and more dreaded instruments were being loaded with their deadly discharge, and left with their dark, grinning muzzles against the ports, and the men prepared to run them out at a sign from their leader.

The vessel sped on towards the stranger, which could now be seen by the naked eye.

She was low in the water, rakish, and with such a clean cut about her as to make many of the old tars wish they were aboard.

She carried no flag as yet, and her sails were set as when she was first discovered—closely reefed, and the wind full in her teeth.

The scene on her deck seemed like a repetition of the one above described. It was similar in every way; only, if possible, looked more terrible.

The arms were fearful to look upon; the men a perfect legion.

But they were all well-picked, finely-built, stout of arm, bared specimens of which displayed such muscles as Samson would have been proud of.

They were all calm, rigid, with set mouths and bold eyes.

Their faces were faces of stone—so immoveable did they seem.

Their hearts were of steel, and their only thoughts their motto—'Victory, or death!'

The leader, too, as he now stood, would have graced a pedestal, and put to shame any statue on the face of the earth.

Young, with a classic face, set with the determination of a cold, relentless purpose, it was like one carved from marble; and from it went the rigid shade to that of his men.

The man-of-war came near—so near that each could see the other's men upon the deck.

The voice of Captain Crosstree hailed. There was no response; so, with a motion of his hand, he brought the sail-trimmers to their posts.

Then he hailed again—

'What ship?'

No reply.

'Answer, or I fire!'

Up went a white silken ball, that suddenly spread out in the breeze.

As it did so, the white cloud of sail fell like magic to the deck.

The swan-like vessel veered round.

Then it came abreast of the Britisher, broadside to broadside; and as the silken banner displayed its emblem—the golden arrow—a mighty roar rent the air, shook the ships, and disturbed the very waters of the deep.

The awful missiles of death went crashing against the frigate.

The work of destruction was begun, and it must go on.

'Traitor and rebel!' cried Crosstree, ''tis you, May heaven decide the battle! Fire!'

The vivid sheet of flame met a more vivid and terrible reflection.

There was crash upon crash, and the grey smoke rolling upwards soon hid the contending vessels in its troubled cloud.

————

CHAPTER X.

THE VULTURE AND THE DOVE.

UNSUCCESSFUL in his effort to obtain the assistance of the captain of the French lugger to carry off taut Will, Tom Hatchett, after a long stay at Brest, spread the Redbreast's wings, and turned her prow towards England.

It was while dodging the Channel Fleet that Bill Raker hailed a fishing-boat, and from its owner heard all that had occurred on board the guard-ship.

Tom Hatchett came on deck during the challenging between his first mate and the fisherman, and felt much elated at the news.

'You see, Bill,' he remarked, 'this husband of Sue's has saved me much trouble by taking himself off in this manner; and, considering the prospect in store for him, I don't think he will care to return.'

So, dodging the three frigates that had left the seaport, he saw that his road was clear to Deal; and, while ships were sent in search of the Golden Arrow, his smuggling craft was anchored in the bay.

The avaricious old scoundrel, Susan's uncle, was seated in his little room, pondering, as usual, upon the latest events.

He mused, as most wily-brained men do, audibly.

'How strangely everything has worked round to my interests,' he cogitated. 'That sea-roving fool out of the way—yes, out of the way, for a certainty. Now, if he comes back, it will be to get hanged, or—or' he thought, slowly. He would have smothered the accompanying idea, but it forced itself out, and he went on—'Or to carry Susan off with him. Humph!'

He fidgeted about in his chair, with his eyes staring vacantly at a smouldering fire, while his right hand wandered over the table in search of a glassful of brandy.

'I wish Tom Hatchett would come,' he went on, conveying the glass he had found, by striking his thumb against it, to his mouth.

After a pause, in which his thoughts wandered far back upon doings he thought forgotten, and their memories long since buried, he roused himself, and went on—

'I would not have that canting, tobacco-chewing foremastman come and run off with Susan for the world. She is safe in the hands of Hatchett—all will be well. If I could only communicate to —— Enter!' he added aloud, as a rap came upon the door.

It opened slowly, and Captain Hatchett entered the room.

It need not be wondered that his face wore such a beaming smile, as there was a large decanter of good brandy on the table, smelling strong enough to put a less keen scent on the track.

'Why, Tom, my boy!' exclaimed the old man, jumping up, and releasing his hold upon the glass he had been endeavouring to thrust upon the sideboard.

It had not gained a firm standing, and when he let go, it fell with a crash.

'I'm here again, Silas.'

'And just the man I wanted.'

'Indeed!'

'Yes. Have you heard the news?'

'News!'

'Ay, of that precious William.'

''Tis that which brought me here.'

'You are in the nick of time.'

'I am glad to hear it, Doggrass. Am I in time also for a glass of that water of life, as the French call it?'

'The term is somewhat out of place, then. But this is not *eau de vie*, but the finest Cognac. You ought to know. Try it.'

'Thanks; I will. It smells very much like the right stuff.'

'Now, sit down.'

The pair of unprincipled villains—the oldest was much the biggest scoundrel—sat opposite each other, each looking into his companion's face with a glare not hard to read or understand.

'Come, captain, you know me by this time.'

'I do,' and he laughed.

Doggrass was often inclined to think Hatchett was cynical, but not so rough as he seemed.

'Come, then, to business. You appear to think everything safe.'

'I do not, or I shouldn't have come here so quickly. The fellow lives, and, instead of being a prisoner, he has a friend in a position not to be despised.'

'Pooh! What care *we* for an outlaw, who by this time to-morrow might be strung up among his crew.'

'Well,' answered Captain Tom, coolly, 'so far as *we* go, perhaps not; but I would rather face a liner of the king's than that fellow's clean-cut schooner.'

'Does the panic seize you,' sneered Doggrass, 'as well as the champions in the village?'

'Panic! The devil himself couldn't frighten me! But, I'll give a man his due, and that fellow will smash the fleet before they get him!' replied Captain Hatchett, gravely.

'Then it only urges the necessity of immediate action.'

'Spin out your yarn, Doggrass,' Hatchett said, seeing his host waited for a reply.

'Need we go over the affair again?'

'No.'

'Well'——

'Well—I want to understand you. What am I to do?'

'As you said you would.' Get Susan in your power!'

'Hang it, man! Can I go and tear her away at a minute's notice?'

'I do not want you to do so.'

'By all the guns of a shore battery, did I ever come nigh such shuffling! Look here—pay it out, and none of your long-shore stoppages. Spin out until you've done, then haul-to.'

Doggrass shifted his little eyes about restlessly, and his right hand smoothed his chin, which was very rough for the want of shaving. Thus, meditatively, he began—

'You see, my dear captain, for *your* sake I would not have it thought that Susan went unwillingly. You must see Susan. You must be with her; and it must be known that you are at times in her society—it must be *seen*, for there is nothing like food for the ready eye of the village gossips to feed upon—and then you can work in safety.'

Captain Tom Hatchett began to meditate now, but he did not stroke his chin, for that was hidden by a long, shaggy, rough beard.

As we have said, Tom Hatchett began to reflect.

'You say wisely, Doggrass,' he answered, slowly. 'But how am I to see her?'

'That is easy enough.'

'You have a way of making everything appear so very easy, Master Doggrass; perhaps you'll spin out a little that I might see the right end of the halyard.'

'Here is a note. It is written in a handwriting the facsimile of William's. Seek her. Give her this, and say you have news from him. She, most likely, hasn't heard anything beyond the flying reports.'

Tom Hatchett's face brightened, and his eyes sparkled.

'But,' continued Doggrass, 'you must not go to her cottage on the cliff.'

Hatchett thrust his hands into his pockets, looked up at the ceiling, and emitted a low whistle.

'The deuce! How then?'

'Easily. I have done all for you. Since her tobacco-chewing husband met that pirate fellow, she has become wonderfully well off; and she goes out of a morning to commit little acts of charity, as she terms it.'

In spite of himself, a feeling of admiration rose in the breast, and a word of praise to the throat of Hatchett.

'There's no mistake, but that she's a craft built of the right stuff!' he exclaimed.

Doggrass scowled.

Captain Hatchett felt greatly inclined to hurl the decanter at the old scoundrel's head, but restrained the impulse, and his own feelings.

'Go on,' he said, swallowing a glassful of brandy as though it were water.

'You will meet her on her return home to-morrow morning. Try and be as near the market-place as possible, where plenty will see you.'

'Never fear.'

'You might do so three or four times. Who knows?—some sailor might insult her. You could be near, knock him down, *or appear* to do so; then offer her your arm, and walk off. Do you clearly understand?'

'Very clearly—that is to say, one of my men, for instance, who, with a guinea to heal the sore, would do it without a murmur.'

'Just so.'

'Continue.'

'A night or two after that, it might be reported that Susan had eloped with Tom Hatchett, of the Redbreast.'

'Enough. I can do the work now; I want no more. You want the girl out of your way. I'll make her my wife, fairly. Come now, does that do?'

'That is all I require, excepting her William might be troublesome, you know.'

'When he comes here I shall be far away, and he won't return again, I know; a price is set upon his head.'

Doggrass chuckled.

'Good, good. You will call upon me before the affair is finished—eh?'

'I suppose so.'

Another glass of brandy, and with the heavy sailor's cloak wrapped round the smuggler's form, his sou'-wester drawn over his eyes, he departed with—

'Good night, Doggrass. If I am wanted, let me know.'

'I will. Good night, Tom, my boy.'

'Confounded old rascal! What a hoary-headed villain!' muttered Hatchett, as he left the house of the respectable Mr. Silas Doggrass, and wended his way to the well-known resort of the sailors—the Crown and Anchor, kept by Peter Sharp, the one-eyed host, but who was more commonly known as Sharp Eye.

Captain Hatchett was a brave and a very careful man; and he knew that if compelled to stay in the seaport for a few days it was necessary he should go among his men a little, to keep them from getting drunk, and into street brawls, which invariably ended in some of them betraying himself and the ship's character.

While he did this his mind was occupied with the image of the pretty Black-eyed Susan, whom he hoped to meet on the following morn.

The lovely wife of gallant Will was anything but happy, although the means for a comfortable sustenance had been left her, and it was in her power to offer a comfortable home to Dame Hartley, and to help one or two of the starving families in the town.

It was only this that kept her from becoming perfectly wretched; and the thought that her beloved husband had such fearful disgrace clinging to his name—that the noose was dangling above his head, and he should then link his fate with an outlaw, to be branded as a felon, was indeed a trial to her young heart and pure mind.

The thought that both her life and that of her husband was indebted to the gallant Gerald Stuart made the pang of sorrow less bitter. But she could not drive the terrible reality from her mind that her husband was an outlaw, with a price fixed upon his head.

When these dreadful thoughts preyed upon her mind—and they usually did when her daily duties were finished, when, with her small gifts of charity, she had gone her rounds, and she found herself in the evening alone in her cot by the sea—then would she give way to these melancholy reflections.

Her heart well nigh bursting with grief—her brain on fire from the agony of her mind—then would she weep for him—weep long and bitterly—for his endangered life, his lost honour, his hourly peril, and his present road to sin.

Thus, with her hands clasped upon her breast, her head bowed, her gradually paling cheek wet with tears that flowed from a spring opened by the most poignant grief, she would remain for hours; and when worn out with fatigue, she would offer up a short prayer for his safety—a prayer that they might meet again—that she might get him from the dark road of destruction, and take him to some distant spot, where they might live happily together.

Alas! how these bright visions faded, and left her a full view of the dark, dreary future!

'If I could hear from him!' she murmured, on the night in question.

And the dreary feeling of desolation came fast upon her.

It would have been another night of heart-rending grief had not the good old Dame Hartley have coaxed her, with tears, to retire to rest.

'You know, my darling, you promised to go out and see that poor old woman in the hut.'

'I know, I know, good dame. But I cannot help it. Where is William — my William? I shall die. My heart will break!'

'Mine will, if you go on like this,' said the old dame, bursting into a flood of tears,

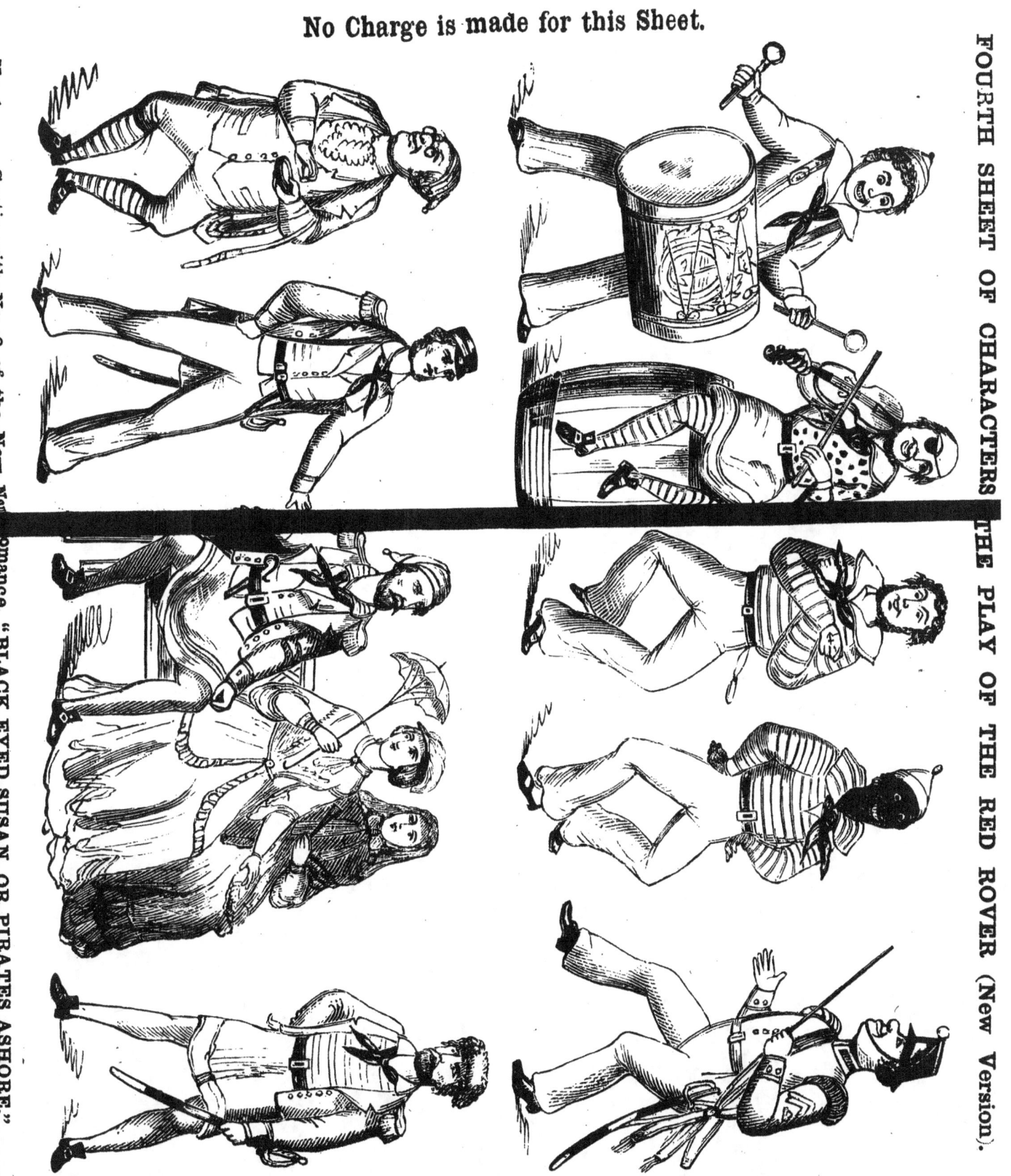

No. 4. Gratis with No. 8 of the New Nautical Romance, "BLACK EYED SUSAN OR PIRATES ASHORE."

Her sorrow touched the heart of Susan, who soothed the poor woman, and prepared to retire.

She did so, and Dame Hartley became a little tranquil.

Early next day, Susan was out with a basket on her arm, filled with some little delicacies for a poor, dying old woman, who would have perished long since had not Susan tended her.

It was well known that the beautiful Black-eyed Susan was not rich.

All she gave was out of the money left by her husband—a circumstance that made the people love her all the more.

But she knew plenty more would come, if her husband lived; so she thought if it was blood-money she could not do better than do good with it.

Thus our heroine spent her days during the first few weeks of her husband's absence; and when returning from the sick old woman, and in the centre of the town, she paused, as a man stood before her.

She drew back abruptly, as he said—

'Nay, don't be afraid. I've brought news from your husband. Here's a note. It's his handwriting. Do you recognise it?'

Susan looked up, and stretched out her hand, but let it stop midway.

She was eager to hear from William, but the man who held the note she doubted.

It was Tom Hatchett, captain of the Redbreast, who stood with the note a few inches from her hand, while her lovely eyes fascinated him to the spot.

CHAPTER XI.

NEVER CONQUERED.

GERALD STUART had taken his measures well to decide the unequal engagement in his favour, and from the deck of his matchless vessel he had watched carefully the enemy's proceedings.

He saw that parley would be out of place, and he determined to strike the first blow.

He did; and a successful one it was.

The first broadside was carefully aimed, and fired with a precision that did terrible execution.

The crew of the frigate, in their excitement, scarcely noticed the true nature of the damage done, but fought by their guns as only British seamen can fight.

Volley after volley of death-dealing missiles were hurled from the sides of either ship.

But owing to the swift and graceful movements of the Golden Arrow, and her low hull, the enemy could not get their fire to tell upon her with such destructive effect as theirs did upon the larger vessel.

Captain Crosstree displayed such cool courage and skill that, had not greater damage been done than he had suspected, the engagement might have ended differently to what it did.

As a fearful broadside was poured into him, a chain shot carried away the foremast, and it fell with a sullen plash over the side, its top impeding the frigate's movements.

'Cut away the ropes!' he cried, through his speaking trumpet. 'Ease the sails aft, and put the helm up. Come, work sharp, my lads! blaze away!'

He started from his post at the poop, and went amidships, as he gave this order.

Not half the starboard guns had sent forth their messengers of death. But ere he could inquire why, an officer from below approached him, and deported—

'The lower-deck guns are useless, captain.'

Crosstree bit his lips.

'And the vessel is settling down in the water. We have discovered a gap nine inches below the water line.'

Crosstree did not reply or change countenance.

He had noticed his ship lay lower in the water, but hoping it was nothing of any great consequence, he would not call the men from their guns, to dishearten them.

Gerald Stuart, from the mizzen chains, was enabled to see what was going on.

He perceived a little confusion among the men and also that the lower-deck guns were silent.

'Will,' he said.

Our hero was at his side.

'Could you manage to silence those upper guns?'

'I will try, sir,' William replied, not yet able to shake off his manner and tone of respect.

He was an expert gunner, and under his direction the broadside was prepared.

'Ready, mess——, my lads?' he cried, almost forgetting his former rank.

'Ay, ay, sir.'

'Steady, a minute! Look out for the sinking of the wave.'

He was watching the captain's hand, for the decisive movement.

'Now!' he shouted, 'fire!'

'Magnificent!' exclaimed Stuart, jumping from his post. 'Beautifully done, Will; if that does not silence them—why—— I thought so!'

The confusion on board the frigate was terrible.

Several guns were knocked over by this discharge, and the unfortunate men mangled.

The cries of the wounded and dying mingled strangely with the more hoarse and fierce exclamations of the living.

None cheered, or yelled their war-cry.

Commands were given hastily, and in loud, hoarse tones.

Sailors dashed about in every direction, and all the din and noise came plainly to the ears of those on board the Golden Arrow.

'Stop the firing,' said Gerald Stuart. 'Let us see what they will do.'

A word from Will, silenced every gun, and stopped the work of destruction for a time.

Again Gerald Stuart stood in the mizzen chains, with the speaking trumpet ready to challenge the foe, when he could get a favourable opportunity.

'Do you surrender?'

No answer.

'Do you surrender?'

A bullet from a musket whizzed past his cheek, and took a lock of William's hair off in its flight.

'That was near,' observed Stuart, carelessly, and he glanced up at the enemy's maintop.

As he did so, a marine was seen to fall head-first down from that elevated point, he had received a ball in his breast.

Gerald Stuart smiled.

'You see,' he said, turning to William, '*my* men never miss their mark. That was the man who fired at I or you—or both of us.'

This was true.

Men had been sent aloft with orders to shoot the commander or officers on the deck of the Golden Arrow.

Captain Gerald's sharp-shooters were picked men —men trained under his own especial eye, and their weapons, as he had said, were of a different and very superior kind to those used by the king's men.

The shot at the princely young chief was sufficient to set his 'sharp-shooters' at work, and the men in the maintop of the frigate fell one after the other, like so many monkeys caught in a tree, without the means of escape.

'Beautifully done, my lads!' said Gerald, encouragingly. 'Don't let them mount their perches. Now, I'll challenge for the last time.'

'Do you give in?'

'To an outlaw? Never!'

'I shall not pause to give you grace a second time.'

Crosstree gave a laugh of scorn, and a shot whizzed past the gallant young rover's head.

His face flushed, and he muttered—

'Well aimed, my friend; but the bullet is not cast that will take my life.'

He did not challenge again.

William walked forward.

'Hold!' he said, to a man before him, who was levelling his piece at Captain Crosstree. 'Pick off men and officers, if you like, but *do not* harm Captain Crosstree.'

The man paused irresolute, he dared not disobey; but the second attempt to shoot the chief he loved made the wish within him, to pick off the enemy's captain, almost irresistible.

William passed on without speaking again— when an honest sailor, he knew well how to obey; but now fortune had put power into his hands, he knew how to command without abusing that power.

The man took another wistful glance at the just distinct form of Captain Crosstree, and he mechanically raised his gun.

At the moment he would have fired—the injunctions of his officer having passed out of his head for the time, but he caught William's bold, flashing eye upon him, and the gun was lowered.

William knew the captain was safe then.

He went on giving instructions, and superintending the proceedings for the renewal of the fight.

Though he had displayed so much zeal in the cause of his friend, and a warm feeling of burning impatience for the contest, he did not forget that the vessel he was so powerfully aiding to destroy contained many friends of his by-gone days, messmates and companions of his youth, and the captain he had served under in many a glorious victory.

It was this thought that made him put his most sterling qualities into play. His only desire was to prevent the enemy from boarding. He pictured to himself his messmates—men he had eaten and drank with, slept, and fought by their sides— coming now in his presence to be cut down or maimed before him, and perhaps by his own hand, —while he imagined that by destroying their vessel, and placing the crew at their mercy, the fight would end.

But he was mistaken.

He had men of his nature to fight—men born under the same clime, bred in the same school, and taught to court death rather than live in dishonour.

He fancied now, amid this scene of death and destruction, he could hear the well-known words of his late brave captain ringing in his ears—

'Never give way, my lads; remember, it is better to die in glory, than succumb to an inferior foe, and live in shame.'

Many a time had William been one among the first to answer, with a loud cheer, those nobly spoken words, and as though to mark the workings of his brain, a hurrah that echoed far away came from the lusty throats of the king's men.

'Veer ship!' called Captain Gerald; and the sound of his fine manly voice awoke Will from his momentary fit of abstraction.

He went instantly to his commander.

'I am glad you are here, Will. I feel more safe with you at my side. We were out of place, apart, my friend.'

'I would not be away in the moments of danger for all the world could produce in wealth. My place is by your side. My body shall be a shield for yours, should such a thing be necessary.'

'Nay, my gallant Will,' replied the captain, with a smile. 'With you by my side I could face a hundred men; and, I think, protect my own elegant person (he smiled again); but you must try and call me Gerald. I like to hear the name from you. We are friends—friends brought together by a stronger tie than the usual string of friendship. We are captain and lieutenant'——

'We are, captain; and I'll stick to you like a barnacle to a ship's bottom, while there's life in us.'

Gerald shrugged his shoulders for a reply, and William understood it.

'Why do you veer the ship?' he asked.

'Do you not see that they intend to bring the larboard broadside to bear upon us?'

'Ay, true.'

'But I think we could prevent it, Will.'

'How?'

'You could at least.'

'By what means?'

'The two bow-chasers brought to bear upon the stern, below the water-line, would end the affair.'

William smiled gloomily, and passed his hand across his brow, while something like a sigh escaped his lips.

It seemed as though he was fated to be the destroyer of that which had been his home upon the sea.

Still he did so.

'It will be better—far better than having them struggling upon this deck.'

He did that portion of the work on which depended success—the ranging of the guns.

Patiently the guns waited for the word to fire, and William remained, thoughtfully, watching the frigate, which he now perceived was settling very low in the water.

A few random balls had been sent at the Golden Arrow, but without effect; and, after the short pause, Captain Crosstree expected that he would get a volley from a whole broadside.

He was not wrong.

He had been manœuvring his vessel, so as to get her larboard battery to bear upon the outlaw; but the damage he had sustained in his rigging and among his spars made the work dangerous slow, and tedious

At the moment his vessel's stern became a fair mark, William gave the word to fire.

A blinding flash lighted up the side of the Golden Arrow from the water's edge to the bulwarks.

A crash followed — and then more cries and groans.

The cannons pointed by our hero sent their missiles true to the mark.

They entered the stern below the water-line, knocked off the rudder, and did fearful havoc within.

Meantime, other shots flew among the crew; one — a chain shot — carried away the peak where the flag was defiantly waving in the smoke.

The next instant, the brave Captain Crosstree was seen nailing the standard to the stump of a mast.

A loud cheer broke from the crew, and even Gerald Stuart could not restrain an exclamation of surprise. William entirely forgot himself, and gave a shout that was heard all over the vessel.

'Stand to your guns, my lads—stand, to the last! If we can only get alongside, we will give the rebels something to howl for,' cried Captain Crosstree.

The men were now driven desperate; their ship was almost useless, their guns dismounted, and their men falling in heaps.

The dreadful strife had lasted more than two hours.

They loaded every gun that stood upon a carriage and fired, without waiting for orders or aught else; one discharge of grape and canister ripped up the planks of the quarter-deck at Captain Gerald's feet, and a splinter struck him over the eye, nearly stunning him.

At the same time, a ball cut the bulwarks away amidships, and rendered useless two of the upper-deck guns.

William gave a cry of pain.

A splinter, on which was still fixed a large bolt ripped open his left arm, almost from the elbow to the shoulder.

'My God! Are you hurt?' anxiously asked Captain Gerald, forgetting his own wound, and making to the side of William.

'No; it is nothing,' replied our hero, with a faint smile. 'I see you are hurt.'

'No—a mere scratch.'

'So is mine.'

Captain Gerald doubted the brave fellow. He saw the effusion of blood that poured from his friend's arm, and that the limb hung down as though useless.

'I beg that, as a favour, you will go to the doctor, and have it dressed,' Stuart said, earnestly.

'My place is on deck, Captain Stuart, while I have a leg to stand on, and I do not leave it.'

Captain Gerald knew William to be a man of his word, and therefore did not seek to persuade him.

Still, he called the surgeon, and ordered him to dress his lieutenant's arm.

Even that William would not allow, until his captain had let the doctor bandage his head.

To have held out against this would have only prolonged Will's agony, so the young chief permitted the doctor to attend him.

By the time William's wound was dressed a rapid change had taken place.

A contrary wind arose, and the frigate, not having any rudder, was dashed with the breeze full upon its beam towards the Golden Arrow, which slowly manœuvred out of its way.

Captain Crosstree gave a cry of rage; he had hoped they would have come to close quarters.

He saw, with regret, his ship could not float another twenty minutes. Still, the men worked at their guns, and with terrible effect; the shots were beginning to tell upon the Golden Arrow.

Captain Crosstree saw his brave fellows were getting tired and excited. They saw death staring them in the face.

The cry of—

'Let us board in the boats—anything is better than staying here, to be drowned like rats.'

'So you shall, my brave hearts,' Crosstree exclaimed, huskily. Aloud, he cried, 'Keep up a brisk fire, so that the smoke will conceal our movements. Have my boat lowered on the starboard side. Place the sick in the longboat with the ship's papers; let those who will follow me to that rebel take their places in the others.'

A faint cheer arose.

It was a daring, a bold, a dashing enterprise; it seemed like walking to death. But it was Crosstree's last effort—the last and only blow he could strike.

The firing was kept up until all hands but the gunners had gone into the boats.

Captain Crosstree then gave the order for all hands away. He was the last to leave. He went to the cabin, saw that the ship's papers were safely carried away, returned to the deck, to see that the flag was surely fastened, then he went into the boat.

At the moment the smoke cleared off, the frigate with a whirl and a mighty roar, sank to explore the ocean's depths, and a swarm of boats were seen to gradually approach the Golden Arrow.

The unexpected line caused a momentary stop of the cannonading.

It was impossible for Captain Gerald and William to suppress their admiration for the daring captain, and they found vent in very loudly-spoken words.

The boats were upon them before they had time to look round.

'Ready to repel boats!' he cried; 'but do not fire a shot until I tell you. Hit the boats with fourteen pounders, but do as little injury among the men as possible. Put them in the water, and they will be in our power.'

It was done.

As the boats came alongside, shots were dropped into them; but not before the men had got a hold upon the vessel.

Exasperated all the more, they boarded from all sides, and rushed, in spite of the terrible opposition, upon the deck.

'Fire upon them!' cried Captain Gerald, forgetting the feelings of compassion that had come upon him, as he strode forward with a gleaming scimitar in his hand.

William was by his side.

The fight was a short and fearful one.

Captain Crosstree sought out Captain Gerald. Their swords met.

There was a clash!

A loud ring of steel.

Then Crosstree stood defenceless.

'Spare him! He was my captain!' said William, coming forward in time to stay the other's angry blow, and he made a sign for two sailors to secure the prisoner, but the men surrounding him at that moment altered the case.

He stooped, picked up the sword he had knocked from his enemy's hand, and returned it with all the grace he was possessed of.

'Take it, Captain Crosstree. Such a brave man should never be dishonoured. Keep it.'

Crosstree did not reply.

He took it.

A fearful gleam was in his eye.

'I will,' he said, after a pause; 'but as man to man, foe to foe, foot to foot, and blade to blade, I challenge you to mortal combat. Come.'

———

CHAPTER XII.

IN THE LION'S POWER.

STRANGE rumours were afloat throughout the little town of Deal.

These rumours spread about wonderfully, and even the village gossips began to discuss and enlarge upon them.

Mrs. A would stand at the door of Mrs. B's house, and hold a confidential chat for an hour or two.

Of course Mrs. B was not to say anything about what she heard.

Oh, no! It is between ourselves. Decidedly. Of course, it may be untrue; but it is very much like a fact—very. Still, it is as well not to say too much as yet, for the poor girl's character may suffer. Truly—though we would be above harming a fellow-creature. To be sure we would. Still, if it is true—and I do not say it is not—why——

Mysterious looks are exchanged. A nervous twitch of the mouth indicates—such is my opinion. Then one gives a long-drawn sigh, and faintly murmurs a few more words of confidence, and then they part.

Undoubtedly, Mrs. B keeps what she has heard to herself. She is not in with Mrs. Chatterer when the 'troublesome children' are in bed. Oh, no! she wouldn't talk. Quite above it! She wouldn't defame a girl's character—the action would be beneath her. Still, one can't help saying a few words, and—lor' a mercy!—after all, everybody knows it.

You've heard, of course, Mrs. C? Heard! Oh, no! Lor'! Why, not that —— (voice sinks to a whisper)—has or is making up to that redoubtable Hatchett? No. Oh! bless me! Why, they are often together. Indeed! and married so shortly! Yes; but, you see, her husband's gone off in a pirate ship. Truly—how dreadful! But there, poor fellow! it was to escape from being hanged. To be sure it was; but still it is worse for her to be seen flirting with him! Flirting? Yes; they were actually seen walking arm in arm together through the town. Never! How dreadful (eyes are cast upwards with a look of unspeakable horror). Oh! well, Mrs. B, I always said she was a wicked jade, or I am sure her poor old ill-used uncle wouldn't have been so hard upon her. Yes, truly; and, if you remember, them was my very words. I do remember, now you speak (she was a great economist of the truth). Oh! well, it's not for the likes of us to run down a poor girl; for who knows but what we may be mistaken? Still, if—— Oh, yes! I assure you, Mrs. C, I am right. I saw her with these eyes of mine. Lor'! and what do you think? Can't say. Well, I've heard this, you know—only heard it. Well, well; what? Why she's actually going about as his wife, and me and Mrs. A is

quite sure she was never married again. Dreadful! I'm sure I don't know what girls are coming to, now-a-days! They wasn't so in mine. Nor in mine.

Two sighs—mutual feelings of consolation and suffering—arose.

The past arose also.

It is duly commented upon.

It affects their nerves.

A 'little drain' is resorted to, to quiet them.

Such is frail Mortality.

Frightful exaggerations had been made upon a piece of scandal that went about the town, though no one knew the author of it.

Though, had it been traced to its source, it would not have been far from the respectable Mr. Doggrass's door.

Poor Susan!

The pretty, black-eyed wife of our hero was new to the world's ways, in many respects.

She had hitherto escaped the biting, venomous tongue—the universal destroyer of character—one of the many fountains of misery—scandal.

No one could accuse her of impropriety or of unbecomingness.

But now the work of slander was going on, it would stop at nothing.

Poor girl!

She had innocently committed a fatal error in taking the forged letter from Tom Hatchett.

She committed a greater one in listening to the villanous untruths of the smuggler.

She was being drawn into the snare blindly, and would discover it when its meshes had got her safely within its folds.

Captain Tom Hatchett had very carefully carried out the schemes of old Doggrass.

Susan had the letter, read it, and believed it to be from her gallant young husband.

She thought Hatchett had become a friend, and trusted him, though sometimes a feeling of doubt would instinctively rise in her heart.

Still she was always civil and respectful towards him, stopped to speak when they met in the street, and did not object to his seeing her safely home at times.

She was molested one afternoon while on her way home, by a half-drunken sailor.

She screamed with fright, and would have run, only he held her by the wrist.

'Help!' she cried.

Help came.

The man was felled to the ground—at least, he lay there, though no one saw any evident signs of the blow, and she turned to behold Tom Hatchett.

Pretty Susan felt very grateful to Tom for that, who, after all, was extremely kind and respectful to her.

'It was lucky I was passing,' he said.

'Very. I am so grateful to you.'

'There's nothing to be grateful about. I'm only glad it was to-day instead of to-morrow.'

'What difference can that make?' smilingly replied Susan.

'Well, I'll tell you. May I have the pleasure of seeing you home?' Hatchet said, a cynical smile of triumph wreathing his lips.'

'Oh, certainly, Dame Hartley would like to thank you for your kindness.'

NOTICE.—With Next Week's Number of this Work will be Given Away the Grand Panorama Scene of the New Play of the "RED ROVER."

BLACK EYED SUSAN.

OR, PIRATES ASHORE.

5 TOM HATCHETT BRINGS THE FORGED LETTER TO SUSAN.

Gratis with this Number the Panorama Scene (first sheet) for the "RED ROVER."

Something like a flush of shame came over the sailor's face, and he turned his head away.

'But you did not tell me why you are so glad it occurred to-day instead, of to-morrow.'

'Because I set sail at sunrise. I shall, in all probability, meet your husband. Have you any letters for him?'

Susan's pretty black-eyes beamed with pleasure, and her face brightened up as, quickening her steps, she said—

'I am indeed much obliged to you. This is very kind.'

'Not at all; it's no trouble.'

'You are so generous, Captain Hatchett.'

'Am I?' he responded, with a faint sneer that Susan did not see.

'Would you?' she asked, 'bring an answer, if there is one?'

A sudden light of satisfaction started from Captain Hatchett's eyes, as he said,—

'Of course, I will; and even bring it myself to the cottage.'

Susan was now at the door of her cottage.

Tom Hatchett entered, and after Susan had told Dame Hartley all that had transpired, she left her and the captain, while she tripped away to write her beloved husband a note.

It was not long before she returned with a prettily written and folded *billet-doux*, addressed to William.

'I hope you will have a good voyage, Mr. Hatchett.'

'Thank you.'

As he walked very slowly towards the 'Crown and Anchor,' the note held between his fingers, with his eyes fixed upon the name inscribed outside, he became very thoughtful.

He was not naturally of a repentive nature, but he was deeply absorbed at the present moment, for while endeavouring to entrap the girl, for whom he had merely a passing fancy, he had become desperately in love.

'I would win her if possible,' he muttered. 'I will try all in my power to make her love me. I would like to get her consent to marry her. How sweet it would be!' and he actually found himself sighing.

'But if she should remain obdurate?'—he shrugged his shoulders—'why, then, by all the fiends that ever stopped a smuggler on his passage home, I will do as Doggrass has said.'

He had called upon Doggrass only once since the last interview we recorded, and he thought he would call, for a few minutes, to-night.

He found the old sinner at home.

'Ah! I thought you had cut me altogether, my boy.'

'I have been away.'

'So I supposed.'

'How does our little affair progress?'

Tom Hatchett related his success.

'Very good—capital!'

'I set sail at sunrise.'

'What!'

Captain Tom repeated the words.

'Without her?'

'Without her.'

'What a pity! Then you have abandoned the idea?—just as I had such a splendid scheme, too,' he walked the room hurriedly. 'All will fail; and I

thought you would have been the man to have aided me.'

'Spin out! Dash my toplights! I'll hear you.'

'Well, if you take her, I will find the means of communicating to her sea-sick William, and should he think of returning, I will say she went of her own free will; that would turn him against her, and you would have it all your own way.'

'P'r'aps so.'

'Don't you think it good?'—

'Very.'

The old man began to get uneasy.

'Listen,' continued Hatchett. 'I've got an idea.'

He then very quietly informed Doggrass of a plan of his own, which must have been a good one; for Susan's uncle did some steps that would have shamed half the dancing-masters in the nation.

Shortly after, Hatchett departed to his ship; which, at sunrise, was far away from the vicinity of Deal.

Our heroine had counted the hours since the departure of the smuggler. She waited for the moment he might return. How she longed for news from her husband!—never doubting Tom Hatchett.

She, above all persons, did not suspect that he would sooner have faced the British fleet than the vessel that contained her husband.

Nothing seemed so likely to her that William might have made use of him as a messenger, while out at sea, and not far off.

She understood perfectly that it would only be incuring death for her husband to come there, for a short time at least.

Day after day went by, still no news of her husband, or even Tom Hatchett.

A fortnight had passed, and the news of a serious engagement between the Golden Arrow and a frigate had taken place.

Susan heard those reports with beating heart.

Was her husband killed? Would he ever come to her again?

'I will go into the town to-morrow,' she thought, 'and glean all the intelligence I can of this dreadful strife.'

It was night now, as she sat by the fire; and already Dame Hatley began to doze in her chair.

Seeing this, Susan proposed that they should retire. Dame Hartley did so, delighted, and lost no time in getting into the land of dreams.

The room occupied by Susan overlooked the sea; she glanced out from behind a corner of the blind, but instantly retired with a shudder.

It was black as Hades without, and a low moaning wind, like the groaning of unhappy spirits, came with fitful gusts against the window.

She wondered at that moment where her husband was; and was perfectly lost in thought, when the boom of a cannon awoke her with a start.

Plainly the distant roar came upon her ears: it came nearer and nearer. She peeped out again from behind the curtain.

Nothing could be seen.

Suddenly, a flash, like a sheet of lightning, went past the window, and a report followed, that shook the house to its foundation.

She knew, then, a cannonading was going on below the reefs.

Suddenly, the sea became lighted up with ship's lanterns which could be seen like so many goblin light's floating about.

Then came another flash or two, and now a loud report, and all was quiet and dark as ever.

Still wondering what all this could mean, she stood with palpitating heart, and a strange mixture of hope and fear entered her breast.

Again she was aroused suddenly, this time by the sound of a footstep, and a face appeared at the window.

She stifled the cry that arose to her lips, thinking it was William; and opened the casement with trembling hands.

A figure sprang into the room—and she waited with every sign of fear and shame.

It was Captain Hatchett.

He looked excited; his clothes were bloodstained and he seemed tired, from long fatigue.

'Read this,' he said, throwing a note upon the table. 'If you would not wish to see me hung, you will lose no time in doing what the letter dictates. I have been chased by the armed dispatch-boat, the men saw me part company with the Golden Arrow; and it was only after a fight I got here. Make haste, for God's sake! We have not a minute! Fly—my vessel will be besieged in another ten minutes.'

Bewildered by his passionate appeal, and more and more by the letter, Susan scarcely knew how to act.

Still, she read that; and it was hard for her to realise her own feelings at that moment.

The message was from her husband, in which he said he was waiting some few miles out for her, and that Tom Hatchett would convey her in safety to his vessel.

'What shall I do?' she said.

'Come at once.'

'I will wake Dame H——'

'No, for God's sake, for my sake, for the sake of my ship and crew, come now! Do not pause! Do not hesitate, or I must return without you! Now, say, will you go to your husband?'

'Oh! yes, yes! William! my dear William! I *will* see him!'

'Then, come at once.'

'Wait. I will pencil these few lines to Dame Hartley.'

With hand so unsteady she could scarcely control her pencil, she scribbled a few words to the old lady, and hastily taking a few things she wanted, said—

'I am ready.'

'Come. We may even now be too late,' he said.

'Captain Hatchett,' she said, a vague chill of fear creeping upon her, 'you are not deceiving me?'

'If you think so, do not come.' And he stepped back.

'Oh, no! no! I must see my husband, at any hazards.'

'Come, then. We must run for it.' And clutching her in his arms, he sprang out of the window.

She insisted to be put on her feet outside; and they both hastened to the beach.

'Look!' she cried. 'What are those men?'

'Ha! My pursuers! Come on.'

They quickened their pace, and in a few minutes Susan found herself in the boat of the Redbreast, and in a few more she was in the vessel.

'Mine at last!' muttered Hatchett, as she sank, exhausted from fatigue, upon the sofa in the cabin.

The door was shut, and the lock turned upon her.

She leaped up, and tried the door handle.

'Am I betrayed? God of heaven! Can it be possible? And yet, no. No, it cannot be. He will take me to my husband!'

CHAPTER XIII.

QUID REMAINS TRUE TO HIS COLOURS.

CAPTAIN CROSSTREE'S daring act of bravery and defiance slightly staggered Gerald Stuart. How he could treat it he was for the moment at a loss to determine.

To fight the duel with a man who was only conquered by death was against the noble-minded young chieftain's nature altogether. He was not conceited about his own powers; but he knew the life of perpetual hardships and danger he had gone through had made him a perfect master of the sword.

He had fought with and vanquished professors of all nations, and felt assured his skill was superior to that of his gallant enemy.

To fight, then, would be death to one of them. How was he to act? How avoid this bloodshed? —the taking of a brave man's life, or losing his own?

'Captain Crosstree,' he said, perfectly composed, 'although I admire your bravery; but to accede to this unnecessary duel would be a folly best avoided. I have no doubt your skill is equal to your courage; but still, I cannot accept the challenge. I do not look upon you as my prisoner. You did not surrender—you were captured. Let that satisfy you; and be content with having your liberty as soon as I see any passing boat that can take you home.'

'Never—never! By heaven I will not give in! I will not surrender while my hand can grasp a weapon! I demand you as a man, and an officer, to fight. Remember, I bring myself to the equal of an outlaw and traitor, even to have my wish gratified.'

Captain Gerald bit his lips.

'Remember,' he said coldly. 'I spared your life once.'

'It were better had you taken it.'

'Still, I have not the inclination to do so, nor do I feel myself bound to accept your challenge. You may retain your sword; but go aft, and do not leave the quarter-deck.'

'I tell you I will never give in. You have sunk my ship; you have conquered my crew; but you will never vanquish me.'

'Pardon, captain,' said a young officer belonging to the frigate. 'But do you not think it unwise to thus hold out? You cannot strike another blow. Your men fought and died like Englishmen; the few remaining have surrendered their arms—you stand alone.'

'So be it, sir. You have surrendered with the rest. 'Tis well. I was responsible for the ship and crew. I shall be called to account. And it shall never be said that I surrendered, even when not a man was left to stand by me.'

William looked admiringly at his late captain, and a pang of sorrow shot through his heart to see him thus courting death.

Turning to Gerald, Crosstree said—

' Do you fight ? '

' No.'

Crosstree raised his sword, and made a spring forward. He would have cut Gerald to the deck had not two sailors leaped upon him, and pinioned his arms behind him.

Still he would not give in.

He fought and struggled like an enraged tiger, and held the sword hilt with such a firm grip that to wrench it away would have been to have broken his wrist or torn it from its socket.

William turned away with a sigh.

' Captain,' Gerald said, in a tone of firm decision, ' will you remain quiet, if liberty is given you? If not, I will have you ironed and confined.'

' Let me free, coward, and you shall see! You dastard! You fear to do the work yourself.'

It cost Captain Gerald a great struggle to keep his hand from the sword; but he conquered the rising passion, and said—

' Handcuff him.'

Crosstree made one sudden, unexpected wrench with both arms, and hurled aside his captors. Swiftly he dropped the hilt of his sword upon the deck—the point was held in a line with his heart ; and he threw himself forward.

William, with a cry of horror, made a leap to his side, and one swift pass of his sword sent the other's weapon whirling across the deck.

So near had been Crosstree's body, that the point cut his coat and scratched his breast; and he fell—unable to regain his balance—to the deck.

' Secure him ! ' cried William, angrily.

It was done, and without trouble. The excitement had been too much, and Crosstree had swooned.

They discovered, also, that he had been suffering from two severe wounds.

' Bring up the prisoners,' Gerald said. ' Let them form in a line along the deck. I would see them.'

The order was carried out, while Gerald Stuart slowly paced the quarter-deck conversing with William.

' Why do you have the men brought up in that manner ? ' asked the latter, throwing a rapid glance towards the prisoners.

' You are aware, my dear Will, that many of them are pressed men, and good sailors. We lost some hands, to-day ; we must replace them.'

' That is wise. To be short of men would be the first step to ruination.'

' There are many among them,' continued Stuart, not exactly heeding his friend's reply, ' with whom you are well acquainted, and, like yourself, good sailors and honest men. You might induce them to stay. You might still hold friendship's place in their hearts.'

' It is the meeting of the messmates I so long sailed with that makes me feel a little—little— that is——Damme! I feel like Plymouth Poll, when the Admiralty stopped her half-allowance.'

' I clearly apprehend you, Will; pardon me in reverting to the past, but I did not call them mess-mates—I said men, whose respect and admiration for you would make them stay.'

' And if you had my truest of friends what matters; I am not ashamed. I owe my present position to you; not to my own merit.'

' Pardon me,' replied Stuart. ' You merited all you have; I gave you nothing but that which

your own sterling intellects and abilities fitted you for. Remember you ought to hold such a position under the king's flag, had you been given your deserts ; and that would have been far more acceptable than the power given you by an outlaw.'

' You are more to me than twenty kings, and as many nations. What have they done for me ? ' he laughed bitterly. ' Death may follow this, but it may be a glorious one. Even should it come to the scaffold, it will be no more than my country would have done for me—the government I had served with all the ardour of my nature.'

' Forget it, Will. Do not fear the scaffold. My neck was never made for that — it's too well shaped,' he said, with a laugh; ' and so is yours. But we might die a glorious death. Remember our motto— I NEVER YIELD ! VICTORY, OR DEATH ! '

' They are two.'

' The first is my own; the other, the cry and motto of the crew.'

' Both are the right ones, and will never be forgotten by me.'

' The men await your orders, sir,' an officer said, coming to the young chief, who waved his hand in acknowledgment.

The lieutenant retired.

' Now,' Gerald said, and he walked slowly past the long line of prisoners.

A fine grim line they made, too; they were true types of the British sailor, broad of shoulder, grim, weather-beaten, powder and blood covered, black from the smoke, and most of them stripped to their waist.

' Any men but those of their own stamp would stand a poor chance indeed, against them.' muttered Gerald.

Among them were many of William's old messmates, and their glances were full of rugged dignity, and honest reproach.

He felt it too; he felt the colour start to his cheek's, and his own gaze shrank beneath theirs, and a fearful turmoil went on in his breast between the conflicting emotions.

He could stand contempt and rebuke, but he could not hold out against the look of pity, mingled with a still living feeling of friendship that still lived in the men for their own much loved favourite.

' All the hands that were pressed into the service stand out,' cried Captain Gerald.

A slight movement among the men, and twelve men stood out.

' Good,' muttered Gerald. Then he surveyed the remainder.

' I should like a few of them,' he said, turning to those who had not stood out. Then he summoned an officer to his side, and asked—

' Have you their names ? '

' Yes, sir.'

' Call them out.'

Taking a list from his pocket, the young fellow began to call out the names of the pressed men, loudly,

' Jack Adams.'

' Here, sir.'

A gruff old fellow stood out, cap in hand.

' What are you ? ' asked Gerald.

' Sailor, your honour.'

' What ship did you serve ? '

' None for these last for years, cap'n. I had my own fishing-boat—ay, and as fine a smack as yer

Issued from the Office of the "YOUNG ENGLISHMAN'S JOURNAL," 81, Fleet Street, London.

ever beheld. We were run down and collared. My boat was smashed by a few cold shots.'

'Very good, Jack Adams; you have not much to thank your country for. Are you willing to mend your fortune?'

'It depends.'

'Well, serve me. It's a free flag, but a good one; the pay is large, prize-money an equal share, no cat, unlimited food, and plenty of grog. It is a free ship; it is mine, and my cause you fight for; but I am neither pirate nor smuggler.'

'I'll join.'

The next man was called, and the next, and they followed the example of the first by joining.

The pressed men were more or less embittered against government, for being torn from their homes and occupations; and having smelt powder, and been in the din of battle, they felt a warm desire for excitement rising within them; and a free flag, good pay, no cat, and plenty of grog, was a good programme to depend upon.

The temptation became irresistible when Captain Gerald said he would give three months' pay or six in advance. This was a great inducement. Many men had wives or mothers who would be saved from slow starvation by this.

The ninth person was called.

'Pat Murphy.'

'Sure and it's me, your honour, as bears that honourable name!—and a stout, good-humoured, powerful Irishman, stood out.

One glance of Captain Gerald's experienced eye, told him the son of the Emerald Isle was not a sailor.

'What are you, or what have you been?' asked Gerald.

'Ah, bedad yer honour! and is it myself yer'd be after enquiring into; sure an' I've been a man all me life.'

'What has been your occupation?' asked Gerald, smiling.

'Bedad, yer honour! and it's hard to tell; for sure and I've had nothing to do, but whistle with me hands in my pockets while the taters growed, an'——

'Have you ever been a sailor?' interrupted Gerald, seeing that Mr. Murphy was too much an Irishman to speak explicitly.

'Bedad! no, yer honour. An' it is not the likes of meself as would want to be either. For shouldn't I have to learn all the tricks of a wild monkey afore I could hang on them there blessed ropes?'

'Are you willing to stay? You have heard my terms.'

'An' yer'd give me six months' pay?'

'Yes.'

'Shure it's myself as would die for you! Only say the word, and Pat Murphy 'll knock down the biggest man aboard.'

And the merry fellow skipped round with a good natured twinkle in his eye, as though he would, nevertheless, have given anyone his fist on their head had he been told to do so.

'I do not require any such illustrative proof of your good will; but you must fulfil some capacity. Can you cook?'

'Cook, yer honour! An' ain't I jist the boy, as could pail a murphy, or roast a fowl fit for the likes of yerself. Bedad, yer honour! an' there ain't a boy in ould Ireland as could turn out a dinner like meself.'

'Then henceforth you will be cook for the chief cabin and officers' mess.'

Pat did a wild flourish with his arms—several steps of a jig, — an original one too — at the same time he struck up in a loud voice—

'Sure I am a roving boy from Paddy's Land;
　I've a mind to be free and friskey,
With the girls I goes hand-in-hand;
　With the boys I can do me hot whiskey,
And I am good at a wake or a ball;
　We drink the health of the dead, sirs,
Me bludgeon is near at my call;
　And it's used to crack a thick head, sirs,
Fal the lal de dal, fal the la'——

'Come! come! This is no time for your concerts,' said Gerald, trying to speak angrily, for the capers the Irishman cut were droll enough to upset any man's gravity.

In spite of themselves, some of the men were in a roar of laughter.

The new cook went aft to finish his jig in the galley.

Captain Gerald now turned to the king's men.

William had addressed a short, eloquent speech to those who had been his messmates, in which he said,—

'You know me, shipmates, and knew that I couldn't hoist a false signal to you, and as plain sailing is better than tacking and double tacking, let those who don't want to enter this craft step for'ard; those who do, come abaft the mainmast. You know, shipmates, what I've got by serving the king, and you can see, if you use your top-lights, what I've got for serving the—damme—the skipper here. Lord love your hearts, there isn't a man among you but what would go abaft the mainmast if you knew what I know of this craft. Harkee, lads, there's not a cruiser in the King's fleet that can come up to this beauty; and as for grog aboard, why, bless you, she pumps it up like they do bilge water in the king's service. Then, again, prize-money! damme! at the end of the cruise you'd have enough to sink a jollyboat; so give the signal, lads, and those who don't want to stay, can go and be ——. No, no—not that ship-mates—I hopes they'll have six-water grog, and four banyan days every week of their lives.'

He also stated how he was to have suffered death for rescuing his gallant friend, and also the nature of the vessel and the necessity for him to have strong faithful hearts about him.

The stout honest hearts of his late companions were won, and the feelings of reproach and indignation vanished. They felt all he said was true, and that he had been made to suffer unjustly, and many volunteered to serve him, not for the money or privileges, but to prove that true hearts and strong arms could be found to serve him in the hour of need.

There were few that went forward after this appeal; and Will, to cement the bond, ordered the mainbrace to be spliced, and the fiddles set going.

Captain Gerald addressed Quid, the boatswain, who drew himself up, and answered, with manly dignity—

'Yer honour, I've no feelings of disrespect for you, but I do not take up with your cause. I was young when I followed the dangers of a sailor's life. I found a home on the sea, and bread for my wife and children, who—God bless them!—have been reared upon the king's money. I have served him faithfully for more nor thirty years. I've grown gray in his service, and I owe all that has been done for me to my Government; and may God desert me if I turn traitor in my old age—that's my answer, yer honour. And I can add, that the next man I would serve to the king, if in a better cause, would be Captain Gerald Stuart.'

He stepped back among his messmates, who gave a ringing cheer.

Captain Gerald felt all the admiration for him that it is capable for one to feel for an honest, noble-minded man.

'You have spoken well, Mr. Quid. I would not insult you by a second offer. Only, do not forget that should the king desert you in your old age you will find a friend in me. I require nothing in return but your good opinion, or the best you can form of a man whose life is a mystery to you and to all.

He strode to and fro for a minute, then turning to William, said,—

'Do not let any fishing-boats pass, as they must be made to convey our prisoners home.'

'Very well.'

'Ah! What is the meaning of that confusion?'

The confusion was the sound of a scuffle below deck, and the angry voices of some sailors.

'Come on, yer swab!' one was heard to say.

'Up yer come, yer skulking land-lubber, we'll ave you afore the skipper.'

A dismal groan followed this, and presently two old tars were seen dragging a form towards Gerald Stuart.

His first impulse was to laugh at the figure between the two sailors; it was most ludicrous.

It was that of a meagre, awkwardly-built individual who, in a state of terror, had brought his face to a look of pitiful supplication when he stood before Gerald Stuart.

'What means this? Who are you?'

'No one, sir,' he gasped.

'Where are you from?'

'The frigate as is gone down, yer honour. Oh, lor! you won't scragg me?'

'Very likely I shall.'

'Oh, lor! Oh, dear!' And he groaned most dismally.

'Who are you? What is your name?'

'Never 'ad any, cap'n. I've nothin'. Don't scragg me!'

'Nonsense; you must be called something?'

'Oh, yes!—oh, lor, captain!'

'What is it?'

'You won't scragg me?'

'Answer directly.'

'Yes—oh, lor! I is Dismal Jacob.'

'Truly. And the most appropriate appellation I ever heard in my life.'

CHAPTER XIV.

A DANGEROUS FLIGHT.

MADELINE, the beautiful, peerless daughter of Admiral Garthway, sat alone at the lattice window of her private apartment.

She was thinking of the gallant heart that was now far away meeting the dangers of the deep. She knew her father's hatred for the gallant fellow, and was aware that ships had been sent out to capture or destroy himself and gallant vessel.

She prayed long and fervently that he might not be injured. She shrank from the idea of rebelling directly against her sire's wishes, but she thought should he ever be slain, and he the cause, she should hate him even more.

An icy chill went to her heart. It was a dreadful idea this—to feel and know that she could hate her father just as inveterate as an enemy he had foully wronged.

'I would give my life,' she mused, 'to know he is safe. May God keep him from harm, and his—his—his——death from my father's door. I love both while he lives; but I should abhor my own flesh and blood were he dead.

She cast her beautiful liquid eyes up to heaven, and the silvery rays of the moon fell full upon her upturned face.

It was lovely beyond description in its complacent beauty. The depth of her soul was in that one glow of mute supplication for the Supreme Being to succour and preserve from misfortune the man who held her heart, her life. He was body and soul to her; without him the world would be a blank.

Her melancholy musings were stopped by Lord Harry sending for her.

'Why are you alone?' he angrily demanded.

'I do not feel well, dear father.'

'Stuff and nonsense. Some rubbish I'm sure. but I'll tell you what, Madeline—I will have no more of this—no more. Listen to me quietly; it is time you understood me.'

'I listen,' she replied, going cold as death, and rigid as a statue.

'I insist, as a parent, that this fretting is put an end to. Do not nourish any absurd ideas concerning that outlaw, whom I will hunt down to the end of the world, sooner than he should come back to disgrace my name and family. Listen to what I say, girl, and obey me. Make up your mind to marry Gregory Saunders, whom I have chosen for your future husband.'

'My lord,' answered the lovely girl, with a haughty calmness, quite new to her fathers, 'I hear what you say—I understand your intentions, but if you suppose that I will *ever* consent to marry that mean, despicable being, you mistake. Never! I say—never!' and she strode towards the door.

'Stay!' he cried. 'Harkee, girl. I swear you shall, or, by heaven! you shall be a penniless outcast; and, what is more, if it comes to my knowledge that you ever meet that pirate, or receive communications from him, I will have you hurled from my doors—I will, by all the stars in heaven! Now, remember that. God of mercy! to suppose that I should live to be disgraced by my only child!—to be despised, and to see that she would bring disgrace, shame, and misery upon me! Do you think that I would allow such an ignominious marriage? Bah! it is not the word for it—it would be an unlawful contract. And I have sworn, that should your clandestine meetings continue, I will not only have spies to watch you, and with orders to shoot him dead, but I will discard you for ever!'

'Do so, my lord,' replied the beautiful Madeline, more coldly than ever. 'You do well. Wait and see what your threats will bring forth; not the marriage with which you would tie me, so the word you used was out of place. Do you not think it would be better, in the second instance, in saying that becoming the wife of Saunders would be an ignominious marriage? No; you would perhaps say he is so brave, so noble. He is!' The cutting sneer and scornful curl of her beautiful lip cut the admiral to the quick.

Fearing his temper would get beyond his control, she hastened towards the door, as the quick tread of feet sounded in the hall; and ere she could leave the room, the door burst open, and Saunders rushed in, his face the picture of rage, disappointment, and ferocity.

'My lord!' he cried, 'Captain Crosstree has failed; his ship is sunk—his men cut to pieces.'

The admiral went a livid hue.

'How know you this?'

'The few remaining men have arrived in a fishing lugger. Captain Crosstree is on his way hither.'

The admiral turned in his blinding fit of passion, and beheld the smile of triumph that animated the beautiful face of Madeline.

'Leave the room!' he thundered. 'Get out of my sight, ungrateful, shameful girl.'

Madeline brushed by Saunders with a haughty stride, and gathered up her dress as though its touching him would contaminate it.

He coloured with rage and spite at this insult, but dared not say a word.

Long before the Admiral could cool himself down a little, Captain Crosstree entered.

He was pale, haggard, and fatigued; his care-worn appearance and look of deep sorrow did not fail even to strike Admiral Garthway, who checked his volley of passionate abuse and reproach, and demanded with all the dignity he could assume.

'What are your tidings?'

'Those of defeat, my lord.'

'Again! Oh curses! twice—two ships in succession. My God! what is to be done? What will be said if this goes on?'

He paced the room hurriedly, and his excited manner slightly frightened Saunders.

'Go on, Captain Crosstree—I would hear your account.'

The brave captain placed his written report upon the table, and in a voice that at times became faint from fatigue, he told how the engagement had taken place, and its termination.

In spite of his towering passion, the admiral could not repress an exclamation of admiration for the gallant manner Crosstree tried to board the enemy with the boats.

While concluding the narrative, Crosstree became so faint he could scarcely articulate.

'I did not surrender, my lord, even when my men had put down their arms. I challenged the leader to mortal combat. He refused to fight. I tried to cut him down, and would have done so but for his men. I did all mortal hands could do. The vessel sank with its flag nailed to the mast. Still I lost. Fate is in his favour, but I suppose I must suffer. Here, my lord, is my commission, if you consider it is forfeited, though God is my witness, and knows I speak truly, when I say I did my duty to the last.'

His commission dropped upon the table, and he staggered back with a faint, choking gasp to a seat, and the deathly paleness that overspread his face frightened the admiral.

Forgetting his disappointment, he rushed forward, and rang the bell furiously for assistance, and then went to Crosstree, whom he saw had swooned, and he soon discovered the noble fellow had received more than one wound.

His heart smote him for his hastiness, and a choking lump rose to his throat.

He had everything in his power done for the captain, and when he came to his senses ordered that he should be placed in the spare bed-room, and left there for the night.

Still feeling pity for the daring and loyal commander, and shame for his own conduct, he sat down and wrote something, which he afterwards sealed, and inscribed the name of Crosstree upon it.

Saunders shortly after departed. As he reached the lawn, he caught a glimpse of a white, lovely face, with Luna's pale light full upon it.

Drawing his cloak around him, he noiselessly drew back and darted behind a hedge.

It was not so much the desire to get from her presence as to prevent himself from being seen by a new-comer, who strode cautiously across the garden, to the spot above which stood the balcony of Madeline's chamber.

He took great care to keep in the shade; his features were well hidden, and a long cloak enveloped his form from head to foot.

Standing beneath the shade of a tall pear tree, he took a steady survey of the house. The moon throwing down a flood of its liquid light upon the casement above the lawn, the cloaked stranger saw the pale, sad, but strikingly handsome face of Madeline.

He started forward, though still with the same noiseless tread, and stood beneath the window.

The rustling of some leaves beneath his feet, and the shadow thrown by his cloaked figure over the gravel path, attracted the attention of Madeline.

She started. A slight cry escaped her, and, leaning forward, she said, faintly—

'Gerald.'

'Lady,' replied the stranger, in a tone of great reverence, but a voice that seemed more used to giving gruff commands, than making tender speeches. 'My lady, I am a messenger. Are you the admiral's daughter, Miss Madeline?'

'Yes,' she replied, excitedly. 'Alas! I wish I were not!' This was mused to herself.

'Then, lady, I come from Captain Gerald. I have a message—a very important one. Can you hear me plainly?'

Madeline came to the balcony, and leaned over.

'Yes,' she said, 'go on. Who are you?'

'Phillip Dafton, captain of the fishing lugger, and spy in the pay of Captain Stuart.'

'Ah! I remember you, my faithful friend, Where is Captain Gerald?'

'Lying a few miles out, lady.'

'Are you going to him?'

'Instantly.'

'I am glad. Tell him there is danger, great danger, he must not come near.'

'Lady, here is the letter he sent; he requires a reply. He also says his ship awaits you, in case it is not safe for him to come. My lugger has been fitted up to receive you. I have orders to carry you to his ship.'

He rolled the note round a stone, and threw it gently on to the balcony.

Madeline took it off, and eagerly read the contents.

Her face regained its wonted bloom, and her heart beat swiftly as she read the passionate contents.

Gerald implored her to faithfully trust his spy, and return with him, or he would run into the port, in spite of the fleet, and take her.

The letter was a true specimen of his ardent, impulsive nature; he spoke wildly of his intentions; his words were passionate, though full of love and pathos, and Madeline was in a wild delirium of joy.

But she wavered about taking that step which would part her for ever from her sire.

Then, again, she thought of his harsh words—his determination to make her fulfil the hateful alliance—and again her thoughts reverted to her handsome lover, and her eyes fell upon the note she still held in her tiny hand.

It was a hard struggle against temptation, and the lines which said that Gerald would come among the very fleet, where she went, haunted her.

'If he came,' she thought, 'it would be sudden death.' Yet he would, she felt assured. Then, again? what have I to keep me here.'

The stinging words of her angry parent still rang in her ears.

'To be discarded,—hurled forth like a dog, or marry that hateful being, Saunders! Never—never! Guide me O heaven! My brain is on fire! What shall I do?'

Conscience whispered that she would be doing wrong to thus disobey her father; but her heart's yearnings prompted her to give way to the impulse—that was, to go forth and meet her lover. She should be happy then; and if the worst came, she could but die on his breast.

Another perusal of his letter decided her.

'I will come,' she said, going to the balcony. 'In twenty minutes, I shall be ready.

Phillip Dafton again hid himself in the shade. He did not see another figure steal forth like a stealthy panther, and with just such a gleam in his eyes the wild beast of the forest would give. He did not go to the house, but hastened to the sea beach, and went on board a beautiful gun brig.

The moon began to wane, but her light was now and then obscured by a dark mass of drifting clouds.

Once, for an instant, it sent a flood of light upon the lawn at the back of Lord Garthway's residence, and in that instant displayed the figures of three persons.

Two females and one man, cloaked in sable wrappers.

The three darted among the trees, and were lost to view.

They travelled on rapidly towards the beach, and by their anxious lookings back, and the rate at which they travelled, it was easy to see they were flying from somewhere.

'Oh! Miss Madeline,' cried the second, a smaller female of the two, 'if our flight should be discovered!'

'Hush! for heaven's sake!'

'It will not, if we are cautious,' Philip said.

'Hasten, then, my good man. Where is your vessel?'

'Below the cliff.'

Hasten, then.'

Few words more were exchanged now, and another half-hour saw them at the rock's beach.

As though to aid them, the moon's bright rays were perfectly hidden, and the three forms were, like dim flitting shadows, cast upon the beach by the overhanging cliffs.

Low but distinct, a whistle rang out on the night air, and floated across the silent waters of the bay.

An answering signal came back upon the ears of the three fugitives. It was more like the echo of their own shrill whistle, wafted back by the breeze, than aught else.

A few minutes' silence.

A time of dreadful suspense, of agony of mind to one, and of fears and anxieties to the others.

Then came a sound like music to their ears.

It was the dull splash of oars which moved noiselessly in their rowlocks.

A minute later, and the boat's keel ground upon the beach. A few words were exchanged between Philip and the man in the stern of the boat.

The rowers got out, and stood respectfully on one side, while the lady was conducted in. Then followed the attendant by her side. Philip took the helm, and the crew reseated themselves.

Simultaneously the oars dipped into the water. A few rapid strokes, and the boat shot swiftly to the side of a little vessel anchored in the Downs.

With as much silence as was possible, the party embarked; its boat was hauled up; the ship's cable cut, and she drifted slowly out to sea.

Not a light was displayed. Not a man spoke. Orders were given in a whisper, and executed in silence. The beautiful Madeline stood on deck anxiously watching its progress, and every sail she saw looming in the distance she imagined on their track.

Her quick eye and ear told her that, by the silence and eagerness displayed among the men that danger was not yet past.

'Is there danger?' she asked, of Dafton.

'Lady, we are not safe until past the foreland.

Every sail was hoisted, and the vessel began to dash along. The crew stood grimly at their posts, and watched the vessel as it sped along. They did not feel safe yet. It was a time of anxiety for all on board.

The captain walked from one end of the lugger to the other, and at short intervals raised his night-glass.

His vessel was a quick sailer, and soon was in blue waters. Dafton breathed more freely, and the crew moved about with greater confidence.

'I think, lady, you might retire in safety now.'

Hardly had the words left his lips when a vivid flash lighted up the sea, and a king's ship was seen to run right across their bow.

Madeline had to lean on her attendant for support.

'Go below. For heaven's sake, go below!' cried the captain. 'Conceal yourself; I will swear you are not on board.'

Another shout. Still he sailed on, pretending not to see it or know its meaning.

Like the wind the gun-brig was upon him, and a voice, that froze the blood in Madeline's veins, cried—

'Lay-to, Philip Dafton, or I'll sink you with a broadside! Lay-to. I intend to overhaul you! No humbug. A word—another two yards, and I fire into you! and Gregory Saunders never breaks his word.'

'My God! we are lost!' cried the poor girl, sinking into the arms of her attendant, as the gun-brig swept upon them like some huge bird of prey, and Saunders, his demoniac face lighted up by the glare of the stern lantern, stood on the bulwark with a look of devilish triumph, and a taunting laugh broke from his lips.

'No—no, Mr. Philip Dafton! You do not fly away with your bird so easily.'

NOTICE.—With Next Week's Number of this Work will be Given Away another Large Sheet of Characters for the New Play of the "RED ROVER."

BLACK EYED SUSAN.

OR, PIRATES ASHORE.

6   WILL BOARDS THE FRENCH LINE-OF-BATTLE SHIP.

Gratis with this Number, a Sheet of Characters for the New Play of the "RED ROVER."

'Curse you!' muttered the spy. 'You have out-done me; but you may never live to boast of it! Beware!'

CHAPTER XV.

JACOB AT SEA.—(*See front page, No. 3.*)

THINGS had not gone smoothly with old Doggrass's late bailiff, Jacob Twig, or Dismal Jacob, as he had been named by the frigate's crew, for in an evil moment he had been tempted to enter the Dolphin and take a glass with two jolly tars, who charmed Jacob's ears by telling him they were about to join the graceful Golden Arrow, out of pure love for their old messmate, Gallant Will.

A couple of glasses made Jacob loquacious, and he told his new friends how he had helped to row the boat which held Susan, when she made that unsuccessful attempt to see her husband before his escape from the guard-ship.

'Tell him,' said Jacob, 'tell honest Will that Gnatbrain and I did all we could to help Sue to get aboard, but they would not let us come near.'

'All right, messmate, he shall hear on't. Have you anything else to say? But come, drink; don't be afraid of it.'

'I ain't. Yes, you may as well tell him that his old friend Gnat, is going to be married to Dolly Mayflower, and I'm to be best man.'

The jolly tars stood another round to drink the bride's health. After this Jacob's mind became a blank, until he found himself with a score or so of unfortunates on board the little tender, which lay off Deal.

The Dismal rolled his eyes as though doubting the reality of the scene which met them when they opened, after the hot grog had so effectively closed them.

There was a kind individual sitting near Jacob, who soon told the little man that the jolly tars he had met were a pair of rascally crimps; and after they had drugged him, he was bundled neck and heels into a boat, from thence conveyed to the tender.

Jacob heard all this in silence, but when the full force of his misery burst upon him, he turned his eyes upward, and gave vent to a succession of groans, which were only stopped by one of the company, who had no love for music, applying the toe of a hobnailed boot to the small of the Dismal's back.

Nothing more was heard of Jacob until the pressed men were called on deck; then, as he was dragged out by the heels from the darkest corner of the murky hold, he gave such evidence of a soundness of lungs that caused one of the seamen to cram a handful of tarred rope in his mouth, for the purpose, as the tar expressed it, 'of putting a stopper on his jaw.'

An hour after this, Jacob, with half a dozen of his companions, was sent on board the frigate commanded by Captain Crosstree.

Dismal Jacob is a character worthy of note. He was a man that could always be found if studiously sought for, though seldom seen, or, at least, noticed among the multitude of persons who come and go, rush to and fro, in the crowded streets of a city, or pass on in quest of their vocation, or perhaps pass away for ever.

Dismal Jacob—the only name by which he was now known—was a man of peculiar temperament and habits. He was a native of Deal; had never left the town in his life, until stolen by the press-gang; and his first voyage upon the perilous ocean did not prepossess it in his favour.

He was as ignorant of a sailor's life as he was of his pedigree. He did not like a sailor's life; the sea disagreed with him. Climbing the ropes was his constant terror, and the report of a gun would send him to the extremest corner of the ship.

The smell of powder had such an extraordinary effect upon his nerves, that he would be discovered, after the action was over, huddled all of a heap in some remote corner—his face the picture of abject misery, and his knees knocking together with a wondrous rapidity, and threatening the safety of his knee-caps to an alarming extent.

It is highly probable he derived his name from his disposition, which was a peculiar one—as peculiar as himself.

He was always groaning—fancied himself very ill-treated; never knew what 'good luck was'—that being an expression of his own—always got into other people's scrapes, and never got out of them without mischief. He was the butt of his companions; and, though he never shared in it, immense fun was often enjoyed at his expense.

Dismal Jacob, as related, was pressed, and sent on board Captain Crosstree's frigate; but no sooner had the engagement begun than he was missed.

No one could find 'the Dismal.' He had not been seen since the first shot was fired; though, strange to relate, the instant the vessel was known to be foundering, and the boats were launched, Dismal Jacob was seen, with his miserable face drawn to an extensive length, to emerge from a coal-hole, looking very much like an animated lump of the useful mineral among which he had burrowed.

He scrambled into the first boat he saw, and lay huddled up under the seat until quietly though forcibly dragged out by Quid to take an oar.

He did so, and, after three nervous pulls, missed his stroke, caught what is termed a 'crab,' and rolled off his seat backwards, lodging his head in the bow oarsman's lap.

'Haul up, you lubber! Can't you keep your beam ends?'

He whined out he would try, and shiveringly retook the oar. He might have gone on very well, only at that moment the Golden Arrow fired a shot that went so near his boat as to splash the water in his face.

The howl he gave made everyone suppose he was mortally wounded.

A second time he let go the oar, and rolled over; but the man behind him moved his knees, and Dismal Jacob rolled under the boat's seat, where he lay perfectly quiet, until he discovered that in sprawling out his hand his forefinger was thrust down the barrel of a pistol.

The bare idea that his finger was within six inches of a bullet was too much for him, and he uttered a groan that sounded like a last death cry.

'Get up, you lubber,' said the bow oarsman. 'Let's see where you're hurt.'

'Oh!' was groaned out.

'Are you hurt?'

'Yes. Oh! oh!'

'Much?'

'I'm dead—dead! Oh! oh! I shall never see the old town any more.'

'Turn over.'

'I can't.'

'Try.'

'I tells you that shot cooked my goose.'

'Prepare to board,' cried the officer.

Dismal Jacob gave another groan at this.

'They is going to board. I wish I was a-board, I does, nailed amongst the rest, on 'em, then I shouldn't a been here. Oh!'

The boat struck, and the sailors mounted the ship's side. Dismal Jacob sat up and saw an open port-hole. He found the use of his limbs then for he scrambled through it—discovered a half-empty shot-locker open, and dived into it, shut the lid with a bang, and remained nearly stifled until, dragged out by two of the ship's crew, and taken before Captain Gerald.

The princely commander of the Golden Arrow knew not what to do with his rum customer.

'Release him!' he said.

Jacob was released, much to his delight; and drawing the cuff of his sleeve across his nose, remarked, with a whining tone—

'I couldn't help it, captain it's me ways, it is. I ain't used to sich dreadful noises, I ain't.'

'You do not understand seamanship?'

'No, Captain, if you please, I don't.'

And he seemed glad of it.

'What can you do?'

'Clean knives and forks and boots, captain, and run on errands.'

Gerald Stuart burst out laughing, as did most who heard this.

'We have no commissions of that description on board this ship; still, if you could make yourself useful, you could stay—we want useful men, you know—if you prefer going back into the king's service, go.'

'No, thankee, captain; if it's all the same I'll stay here—I'll be useful, I will. I can brush yer clothes and trot about all day long, I can.''

Dismal Jacob had heard of the good rations, high pay, and prize-money.

He preferred it to the king's service.

'Very well, we will see,' said Gerald, waving him away.

Jacob turned round and gave a groan of pleasure and surprise; for, as he turned, he beheld Will, who had just come on deck from visiting the wounded.

'Bomb shells and capstan bars!' exclaimed Will, laughing; 'as I live, it's Jacob Twig! What cheer, young jibboom?—turned sailor, eh?'

'Yes, Will; but I'd sooner be scaring the crows in Farmer Stubble's field, that I would.'

'Lift up your figure-head, and take in a reef of that long jib of yours!' laughed the gallant tar. 'Damme, Jacob, we'll make a man of you!'

'Wish you'd send me ashore, Will, that I do. You don't know how all this fighting affects my nerves.'

'You'll get over that, Jacob,' said Will; 'and I shouldn't wonder if you don't turn out the best fighting man on board.'

'I should, though,' said Jacob. 'No, Will, it's the fault of my legs. My body's brave enough, but my legs take my body away. That's it——'

'Here, Jack!' Will called out to one of the men. 'Take care of this chap, and make a seaman of him!'

Jacob turned to see who was thus blessed with this onerous duty; and when a broad-chested, muscular seaman came towards him, he exclaimed—

'Wot! you don't mean to say it's you, Jack?'

'What cheer, yer land lubber! You here!'

Jack was one of Captain Gerald's favourite gunners—the smartest man he had on board at the long gun. Jack and Jacob had been acquaintances, and had not met for a long time. The meeting was a joyful one for the latter who required the protection of such a friend.

'Have you shipped among us, Jacob?'

'Yes.'

'Going to stay?'

'Yes, Jack; 'cos I can't do no other.'

'That's right. Be smart, and we'll make a sailor of you yet.'

'But I ain't got any more clothes. I ain't; so I can't be smart.'

'Clothes!' Jack eyed him askance, turned his quid, and continued—

'Look here, my hearty. Just learn to pay out your slack like a Christian. I don't mean anything about clothes when I say smart; I mean active.'

'I always is.'

There may be some truth in this remark, for a more active person in getting *out* of the way was rarely to be found.

Jack Happleton, or Happy Jack, as he was called, took his friend, and led him below.

'Bedad! and sure me honey, and is it the likes of yerself as is going to stay wid us, now?' cried Pat, dancing after Jacob Twig, with his sleeves turned up to the elbows, and his hands covered in dough.

'Those two will keep the crew alive, if I am not mistaken,' remarked Gerald to Will.

'That Irishman is a droll fellow, and that miserable Jacob will make a capital football.'

'Truly,' Gerald said, in reply, and linking his arm in that of Will's, they went off to converse upon matters of far more importance than the Patlanders antics, or the dismal one's misfortunes.

The Hibernian, from the moment he beheld Jacob, his brain was busy with an idea he had hastily formed for placing the unfortunate ex-bailiff in a predicament which, in the end, nearly proved fatal to his victim.

'Bedad!' mused Pat. 'It's an iligant idea, and by the tail of Ned Flanaghan's cotnamore (overcoat) I'll spake to the liftenant and ax him about it.'

He went aft and asked Will to appoint Jacob cook's mate, and having obtained the necessary permission, he took the dismal hero from Jack's keeping, and trotted him off to the main deck.

Here, outside one of the gun ports was an empty barrel, which had been on the frigate's deck when she sank into the ocean's mystic depths.

This barrel Pat had secured as it came towards the Golden Arrow, and safely fastened it by a strong cord to one of the iron rings near the port.

'Bedad,' he thought at the time, 'It's iligant fire's that same barrel will make.'

This idea had changed since Jacob became one the crew, and now, with his eyes sparkling with anticipated fun, he drew the luckless Dismal to the port, and, pointing to the empty barrel, said—

'Do you see that, you gossoon?'

'That tub?'

'Yes, avick!'

'Of course I do; but what is that to do with me?'

'A mighty dale,' said Pat. 'It's the cook's mate ye are. Now, bedad, if you don't look after the fire, it's but little the gintleman will have to ate.'

Jacob looked askance at the speaker. He could not see any affinity between the barrel which floated outside and Pat's remarks.

'Be me soul, ye spalpeen, there's but little rason to be got out of ye. Don't ye see, there's one shtring to that illigant tub?'

'Yes.'

'By the great Fin M'Caul, ye'll see more before ye have done, this night. Here, thin, ye spalpeen; take this rope and pass it round forninst the other; for one shtring won't do whin the ship goes, like the devil that she is, through the wather.'

'But,' objected Jacob, 'I shall have to get on the barrel.'

'In coorse ye will. So, out wid ye, avick! and when it's done it'll be done, as Moll M'Guinniss said, when she knocked out Biddy Rooney's eye.'

It was a long time before Jacob consented to emerge from the open port, and when he did so, and had seated himself across the barrel, the mischievous Hibernian cast loose the rope, and allowed poor Jacob to drift out from the ship.

To do Pat justice, he did not intend to quit his grasp upon the rope; but the vessel, careening over, twisted it from his hand, and poor Jacob was soon lost in the dark void beyond the glare of the ship's lights.

When the morning came, he was alone upon the waters, and close under his lee he beheld an immense shark, watching and waiting for the expectant meal.

CHAPTER XVI.

A DARING ADVENTURE.

THERE was just breeze enough to steady the sails of that incarnation of grace and beauty, Gerald Stuart's matchless ship.

The moon's bright disc appearing above the heaving bosom of the rippling sea, covered the heavens with a silvery gleam and streaming downward in one interminable line from the distant horizon, insensibly increased, until it played upon the white sails of the outlaw's ship.

What a glorious object she appeared, standing out white and ghostly from myriads of gem like stars, and the cloudless heavens behind formed so appropriate a background to the delicately moulded hull and the light pyramid of snowy canvas.

There was no sound on board the Golden Arrow to break the fascination of the scene, save the lazy creaking of the yards, and the rattle of the tiller ropes as the helmsman from time to time silently turned the wheel, as the needle told him the vessel was moving out of her course.

The watch were lying about between the guns, and line men whose hands were seldom away from their blades; they lay—grasping—cutlas or pike, ready in a moment to defend their floating home.

On the quarter-deck stood Gerald and Will. It was not the beauty of the night that wooed them while all else slept, for by the keen anxious glances they cast from time to time across the glittering water, it was evident they were waiting the arrival of a vessel, but whether friend or foe their faces did not form a sufficient index to judge.

Gerald Stuart was still dressed in his glittering uniform—but Will, who had found the closely fitting garments sorely inconvenienced the movements of his supple frame, had cast aside the garb indicative of his rank, and had assumed the loose, easy appearance he had so long worn under another pennant than that which entwined its whip-like folds around the topmast.

His dress, though fashioned thus, was of far more costly materials than worn by the seamen, and in place of white worsted trimming, his smart jacket was ornamented with silver lace.

Gerald, although he at first objected to the change, was fain afterwards to declare that his officer looked far better in this garb than that he had wished him to wear.

They had both been standing, since the moon had risen, with folded arms and thoughtful faces agains the taffrail, and so occupied were their minds with the object of this moonlight vigil that but few words passed between them.

'I cannot understand this,' Captain Gerald said, breaking a long pause, 'the fellow should have been here full four bells past.'

'Maybe,' suggested Will, 'he has been over-hauld, or—— Ah! damme! what's that?'

As he spoke, the dark outlines of a small vessel gradually rose above the line which seems to join the pathless sea with its arched canopy, and after the lapse of a few minutes, it needed no glass to tell the fashion of the stranger's rig.

She was very low in the water, and above her dark hull there was but a large square sail and a small jib. She carried no top-hamper; yet, with the wind coming over her taffrail, she cleaved the waters with the velocity of a sea-bird.

'It's the Curlew,' said Will. 'Ready, there, with a red light!'

As he spoke, a small red disc was run up to the Curlew's peak, and, after being stationary a few minutes, it was dipped three times.

Will took the red light from a seaman, and answered the Curlew's signal by waving it to and fro over the taffrail.

The reply was seen; for the distant light disappeared.

Then Gerald called out, in a voice which was heard all over the ship—

'Hands on watch, about ship!'

The men, without the least confusion, ran to their stations, and Will, whose quick eye followed their movements, no sooner saw they were in their proper places, than he said—

'Ready, O! ready!'

'Haul over the boom!' said Gerald. 'Ease it well over, men!'

This order was merely to keep the wind in the sail, and retain the power of bringing the stern from the breeze and the head towards it.

'Put the helm down,' said the young commander. 'Gently, you lubber, do you want us to heave stern-way!'

The beautiful fabric yielded to the pressure, and by the time the jib and fore-sheets were eased, she was gliding towards the little vessel, on board of which Gerald expected to find the proud and beautiful patrician maiden he so devotedly loved.

There was some obstruction in the running gear. When the men were raising the tacks and sheets taut, and Will, who loved his vessel next to

Sue, utterly forgetful of his laced jacket and super-fine cloth, rapped out a strong anathema upon the awkward man who, instead of loosing the weather brace, while the yards were being swung, held it tightly, and thus impeded the movement.

There was no lubberly work with such a seaman for an officer as Will, for he snatched the rope from the man's hand, and said—

'Look here, you lob-lolly boy, ease it—ease it! Do you want to disgrace the finest craft in the world with your ——.' He could get no further, so, raising his voice he shouted, ' Mr. Treblepipe—Mr. Treblepipe!'

'Ay, ay sir,' responded the boatswain, turning towards the disgusted officer.

'Show this fellow how to use a rope, and damme keep him on six-water grog and mouldy biscuit till he can do it.'

'Ay, ay, sir.'

The bosun made a note of the luckless wight's name—saluted Will, t'en left to see the decks swept and the ropes properly coiled.

The commander of the Golden Arrow smiled at this little scene, and muttered inaudibly—

'The King's service has given me a good officer at any rate.'

The lugger was by this time close alongside, and one of the Golden Arrow's men cast a grapnel among the small vessel's scanty cordage, and held her fast to the beautiful craft.

With a lover's eagerness, Gerald ran to the side, and was met by the burly form of Philip Dafton.

'The lady,' he asked, 'is she—— '

The fisherman doffed his cap as he interrupted the young officer's eager interrogation, by saying—

'She is not, your honour.'

'Then you have not delivered my letter.'

'I have, your honour; and the lady came aboard but before I could get out to sea, the Firefly gun-brig overhauled me.'

'Well, well—and—but proceed.'

'And I had to give the lady up.'

'Yet, you are here; did not Gregory Saunders seize your craft?'

He did, your honour, and took me in tow with a smart schooner he had taken before he fell foul of me, and as the Curlew was the hindmost of the three, I cut the hawser, and came to tell you.'

Gerald made no reply, and Will, who came to his side, was struck by the vengeful expression of his commander's usually placid features.

'Know you anything of Saunders's intentions respecting the lady?'

' From what I heard from the men he put aboard of me as a prize crew, I believe she is to be kept on board the gun-brig until she is spliced to that gentleman with the ugly scar you made across his sallow face.'

The fierce light in Gerald's eyes deepened as he heard this.

'Where are these men?' he asked. 'Bring them here. Surely, you must be mistaken. Harry Garthway would never force his child into this hateful union.'

'I'm not mistaken, your honour,' answered the sturdy owner of the fishing boat; 'for, had there been a priest on board, she would have been spliced to-morrow.'

'But the men? Bring them up. Let me hear their statement.'

'The men, your honour,' said Philip, coolly,

'can't come; for I took the liberty of pitching 'em overboard. Mine's a light craft, captain, and the weight of the king's men was too much for her.'

Gerald walked hastily to and fro the narrow limits of the quarter-deck, his brain busy with a rash project to rescue the maiden from Gregory's clutches.

As though resolved to carry out this plan, he paused, and facing Philip, said—

'After this, I suppose you will not be able to bring me information respecting the movements of my foes?'

'Mine is a swift boat, captain; but I don't care to trust her too close to a broadside of thirty-two's and well-trained gunners. But there are nooks enough in the cliff for to hide a larger hull than the Curlew.'

'Then you will still serve me?'

'Ay, Captain Stuart. Day or night, foul weather or fair, old Phil will do his best for the last of the——'

A meaning gesture from the young chief checked the completion of this sentence, and Gerald said—

'Thanks; but at present you can serve me best by coming aboard the Arrow. Go and collect your men. I want your lugger for a few hours.'

Philip betrayed no surprise at this request, and, touching his cap, was about to move away. Then, as though a half-forgotten circumstance had recurred to his mind, he asked—

'Is there a Will or William Howard aboard this craft?'

'Ay,' said Will, stepping forward; 'that's my shore name.'

Old Philip touched his cap at the sight of Will's gay trappings, and said—

'Well, your honour, there's a chap aboard my craft as wants to signal to you.'

'Tell him to steer this way.'

Old Philip went aboard the lugger, 'and soon re-appeared, leading a figure, which Will thought he had seen before.

It was that of a man a little beyond his prime, and the spare, sinewy figure was draped in that peculiar costume worn by the smugglers of the last century. A striped worsted shirt, black belt, with large square brass buckle, open jacket, baggy trowsers, and heavy deck boots, and upon the apex of this figure was a red worsted cap, the end of which, terminating in a heavy tassel, hung below his shoulder.

Will saw, as the man passed beneath the lights, which hung from the points of the lower yards, that his clothes were completely saturated, and hung about him in that cold, uncomfortable manner, suggestive of stiff joints and rheumatism at no distant period.

'So,' Will began, ' you—hallo! damme!—if it ain't Bill Raker, the mate of the Redbreast.'

'Yes,' cried Bill; ' but mate no longer; for our pretty bird is snapped up, unless Tom Hatchett follows the example of old Phil, and pitches the prize crew overboard, and cuts his tow line.

'Did you come here to tell me this?'

'No, Will, it's about Susan I came; for if ever a craft was in distress she'——

'Hand-grenades and tomahawks! What's the matter with my girl? Has that precious old ——. But go on. Bill Raker. No false signals, or up you go.'

Will pointed suggestively to the yard-arm, and the action was not lost upon Bill Raker.

'Phil Dafton can sign the log-book that I speak the truth,' said Bill, 'and'——

'Pay out, man—pay out! Do you want to keep a man with his blood tingling all over him like a feller's back tingles after the first dozen? Pay out, and with as little slack as you can.'

'Very well. It's this, then. During the first watch, Tom Hatchett brought your Sue aboard the Red——'

'The—the——. Go on. Damme! I'll keep quiet. Go on. But when I fall foul of that pirate, may my fingers be ——. Go on. D——n you! Do you wish to drive a man mad?'

'The Redbreast,' Bill Raker resumed. 'But before we got clear of the Downs, that infernal gun-brig of Gregory Saunders overhauled us to look for old Admiral Garthway's daughter.'

'Yes—yes!'

'Well, they sees Susan, and she hoists a signal, so I'm —— if they didn't take her aboard, put a prize crew on our craft, and took us in tow, while they looked after the Curlew, as had old Harry's girl aboard.'

'Well, where is she now?'

'She's with the tall girl they call Madeline; for, when Saunders overhauled the Curlew, and took the lady out, I heard her say to your Sue: 'You in the power of this villain? Cheer up, Susan, they will not desert us. You have a brave husband, and my devoted Gerald will not'——

'No, I'm d——d if he will! Here, captain, let's beat to quarters, and bear down upon'——

'Stay,' said Gerald; 'you forget the brig is by this time under the batteries of Lord Harry's three-decker,'

'Three-decker! Damme! if it was a twenty-decker I'd'——

'You'd follow my advice, Will. We must save them by stratagem, not by force.'

'I don't know much about straight Jems, but I suppose you know best, captain.'

'I do.'

'So,' said Bill Raker, resuming his narrative, 'they kissed each other; and, when I saw old Phil cutting his tow line, I dropped over the Redbreast's side and got aboard, for I wanted to tell you this.'

Will wrung the speaker's hand; then, obeying a gesture from Gerald, followed his commander to the state-room.

Here Gerald threw the contents of a clothes-locker into the centre of the cabin, but, not finding the articles he sought, said, in a tone of disappointment—

'We must go to Deal in the lugger and purchase a rig for this.'

'A rig, captain? What for the straight-eye-jem?'

'Yes, Will, just listen to my plan. They want a parson on board the Firefly to-morrow.'

'Yes, captain.'

'Therefore a boat will be sent early ashore to get one. That boat, Will, must take us on board the gun-brig, I as the parson, you as my clerk, and'——

'Damme,' shouted Will, in ecstacies at the daring scheme, 'we'll read 'em a lesson out of the ——'

'Steady, my enthusiastic friend, we are not there yet.'

'No,' answered Will, 'I'd give this left hand if we were.'

Gerald here again turned to the heap of wearing apparel, and to his satisfaction he found that he could muster a couple of suits of a clerical cut (for the young chief was in the habit of assuming many disguises) for himself and Will in the character of parson and clerk.

'Here, Will,' he said setting the example by doffing his uniform. 'Jump into this rig, and I'll talk meanwhile.'

The hardy pair were soon busy with their saintly garb, and many a round oath escaped them at the multiplicity of buttons which had to be fastened; but when the white chokers had to be tied, the oaths became both loud and deep, and Will in despair fastened his white cravat in a sailor's knot, and would have kept it so had not Gerald altered it.

When the pair were thus equipped, they could not, in spite of the weighty matter upon their minds, refrain from having a hearty laugh at the metamorphosis which had taken place.

Gerald struck a small gong which hung from the roof, and a Nubian boy appeared.

'Tell the master of the fishing lugger to send two of his men here.'

The boy salaamed, and went upon his errand, and when the fishermen came, Gerald told them to change their clothes, and select a couple of suits from his wardrobe.

They did so, and both being burly men, Will and his captain had no difficulty in hiding their clerical garb beneath the coarse fisherman's attire.

After the men had left, Gerald said—

'Those confounded buttons and loops stopped me from telling you my plan until now. It is this: we will fill the lugger between decks with our people, well armed, and you and I will navigate the craft. We must get ashore to-night, and look out for the Firefly's messenger, follow him to the parson's house, and when the good man leaves in obedience to the summons, we must make him a prisoner, then go on board in his place.'

'Bravo, captain!'

'Then we must rescue those we love; but how, must be left to chance and circumstances. One thing, we must have our boat close at hand, and when we go aboard the gun-brig, the lugger must creep close under her quarter, so that if the boat can't be reached, we must make a jump from the brig's taffrail, with the girls in our arms.

'It's as clear,' Will said, 'as the foreland light, and we shall do it.'

'I hope so.'

Each of them concealed a good Damascus blade under his fishing garb, then placed a pair of pistols in their breasts and went on deck.

Twenty of Gerald's tried hands were hidden in the lugger's hold, and as the two leaders were about to follow, Bill Raker placed a letter in Will's hand, saying—

'I found this in the Redbreast's cabin, and if it isn't old Doggrass's writing, I'm a Frenchman.'

It was, and Will saw the superscription was to Susan, and when the lugger's single sail was spread, he read the lying letter which had trepanned Susan on board the smuggler's craft.

So enraged was Will by the old rascal's treachery, that in spite of the danger he ran, when the lugger's little boat took him and Gerald ashore, that he went alone to Doggrass's house.

Gerald and the boat's crew stood to their arms awaiting the issue of this rash act, and Will, when he reached the house, was refused admission by an old crone, who was Doggrass's housekeeper.

The angry sailor stood upon no ceremony, for without a word he flung the old woman aside and strode into the hall, leaving the housekeeper in a horizontal position.

CHAPTER XVII.

A NIGHT TRAGEDY AT DEAL.

THE old party, who had been so unceremoniously hurled aside by the infuriated William, lay full length on her face behind the door, where she remained until her breath returned, and the voice of her master roused her shaken energies.

She felt convinced that the intruder was nothing more or less than a pirate who had come to rob her master, and perhaps murder him.

'Oh, dear!' she groaned, 'What shall I do?'

She did as most women do in such cases, which was to rush frantically into the street, and call as loud as her shaky voice would permit, for help.

The first ten steps she took placed her very unexpectedly in the arms of an individual who was hurrying along in great haste, and the sudden concussion brought a jerked 'Oh!' from him—a 'Yah!' from her—and she was thrown off her feet.

'Confounded old fool!' was the first impolite words that fell upon her ear as she scrambled to her feet.

'Oh, sir,' she cried, clutching him by the cloak, 'help. Master is being murdered—Mr. Doggrass.'

'Where?'

'Here, sir—here;' and she made a useless though powerful attempt to drag him to the door.

'Who is it?'

'Some sailor, sir. Oh, dear me! he rushed in with a drawn sword. Oh, dear!'

'Aha!' mused the stranger, 'indeed! Doggrass? Doggrass did you say?'

'Yes, sir.'

'It must be him—William, by my soul! My good woman, lock the doors, and bolt the windows, to keep the rascal from escaping. I will return in a few minutes with assistance; don't fear. I am Captain Saunders, of the Firefly.'

With that, he rushed off at a pace quite surprising.

'Nicely trapped,' he muttered; and dashing to the beach, he unmoored a boat, and rowed to the ship.

A messenger was dispatched to the Custom-house, another to the admiral, and he headed a file of marine

William knew nothing of this. It had all been done in silence, and he remained towering over his shivering enemy, his fine face distorted with uncontrollable passion.

Doggrass looked the miserable old dog he was, as he fawned at the feet of the man he had so foully wronged.

'William,' he moaned, 'think of my grey hairs. Spare my life, and I will tell you'——

'Pitch ahead, or by all the ropes of a seventy-four, I'll cut you down! No tacking, mister. Heave it out, shark, and go straight ahead, or I'll give no quarter, in spite of the white at your fore.'

'Yes, yes, Mr. William. I'll tell—I'll'——

'Heave ahead, you d——d old pirate—heave ahead! Where is my craft—my Susan—where is she? By the blue bed of Neptune, if she's stowed away by you, there'll be a hard account to settle!'

'No; I assure you I know nothing. It is reported that she eloped with Tom Hatchett. People'——

'Liar! Lay-to, curse ye! No more. Fire another shot like that, and by the blue bed of Neptune, I'll stop your jawing-tackle! Cursed old pirate! Look me in the face, and say you didn't write this—say you didn't—go so far as to hint it, and'——

He held up the note given by the smuggler to Susan before the old villain's eyes, and the gleam in his own brilliant orbs was like that of a tiger.

'I swear, I did not. I swear I had nothing to do with it. I'——

'Stop it! Heave-to, mate! heave-to! My sword has almost jumped out of my hand once or twice. No more! No false colours!'

'I swear, Mr. William,' whined Doggrass, 'I did not write it.'

'Who did?' he thundered.

'How should I know?'

'You hoary old rascal! Look to it! If harm befalls my Sue, I'll bear down upon you; and don't expect any quarter, for damme if you'll get it! You've been the cause of this, I know—you've always run down my smart little craft. Who stripped her of everything?—you! Who drove her into the enemy's waters?—you! Who put that pirate on to the track to fall foul of her?—you! Who—— Aha!'

He paused to listen.

The tramp of feet could be heard without.

Doggrass made an attempt to escape. Our hero caught him by the collar, and held him like a vice.

'Give signals of distress—just one—and, darn me! you'll suffer'——

'Let me go.'

'What! let you go? No! no! I'll keep you in tow, now; and if they want me, they'll have to fire at me through your old hull!'

Doggrass turned pale as a corpse, and he cast his eyes towards the door with an agonized stare.

The tramp of feet could be heard on the stairs; and, by the sound, William knew there must be a good number.

'Let them come,' he muttered. 'If they get alongside in a hurry, well, I'll surrender.'

How Doggrass's heart beat with joy and hope! He held his breath as the party paused outside the door.

'Help—in here!' he said, forgetting the warning he had received, in his excitement.

The door of the room was thrown violently open, and Gregory Saunders, at the head of eight marines, entered.

'Surrender, traitor!' cried Saunders.

Will laughed scornfully.

'I don't know what that is, captain. If you want me, take me. I never strike my colours, though you've a fleet against me.'

'Help me, sir?' whined Doggrass, trying to wriggle away.

'Unless you surrender in three minutes, I fire,' said Saunders. And he signed for the marines to level their pieces.

William put his sword between his teeth—took Doggrass in his arms, and held him as though he was a shield.

The three minutes had nearly passed.

'Ready—present'——

'Oh! no! no!—don't fire,' screamed Doggrass, who found his own breast held up in a line with the long deadly tubes of the marines' guns.

Gregory Saunders was in a dilemma.

The marines felt inclined to laugh at the sorry figure Doggrass cut in his night shirt, kicking and plunging about in terror.

William saw the bayonets were not fixed; and wishing to get out without bloodshed, he hurled Doggrass at Saunders, who fell back upon his men, and then to the ground.

The crashing of glass followed this, and Will with a leap went through the window into the street.

A crash that nearly shook the old roof off the house succeeded, and the bullets whistled over his head as he fell to the ground.

Fortunately he was not hit.

Saunders ran to the window and looked out, but the mist still hung thickly over the earth, and he could not clearly discern the figure of our gallant hero.

'After him,' Saunders cried, hoarse with rage; 'two run in here at the window and shoot him down, should you see him.'

The remaining six hurried off in pursuit of the fugitive. They saw his form looming in the mist, and fired again.

The vivid flash lighted up the street, and the report brought the people from their warm beds and houses into the street.

'He's hit!' cried Saunders, as he saw the figure stagger and fall; and he darted on at the head of his men, but paused ere he reached his anticipated prey, and waited behind his men with a cry of baffled rage.

'Reload,' he yelled, frantic at the sight of Gerald Stuart, with a boat's crew at his back. No time was given the marines to reload; before a ramrod could be drawn, the crew of the Golden Arrow were upon them with cutlasses, and they were driven back in confusion.

Gerald singled out his hated foe, but the craven cur slunk back amongst the crowd that had gathered round, and he kept out of the way.

A short conflict took place, the marines were outnumbered, and, after a very little resistance, they took flight.

Not a shot had been fired by any of Gerald Stuart's men. They had gone to work with the cutlass only, and driven the enemy off without any serious loss.

The bystanders still looked on in wonder and alarm. None knew what had been the cause of the fray, nor was the mystery likely to be solved.

Gerald Stuart called his men to convey the form of William to the boat. He had received a bullet, which glided across his skull, only going skin deep but doing enough injury to leave him insensible.

The crowd gave way for the sailors to pass, and the captain of the Golden Arrow commanded his men to make all possible speed. He saw lights flitting about in the distance, and he conjectured that the Custom-house men would be down upon them in a few minutes.

He was the last to leave the spot, following some yards behind his men, to see that none lurked in the rear; and when the forms of his boat's crew, with their inanimate burden, seemed to dissolve and become a portion of the gloomy mist, he strode on.

Some of the excited people of Deal followed; others stood in little groups and talked over the strange affair. It was from one of these little knots —or, I should have said, from one of the biggest parties of talking men and women—that a cloaked figure stepped from their midst, stretched forth his arm in a line with Gerald Stuart's handsome form —then came a crash and flash—one moment's terrible silence—and then a shriek.

It was a shriek of mortal agony, and was succeeded by the wail of a woman, the loud oaths of a man, and great excitement among the good folks of the town.

Gerald Stuart turned round. He knew the shot had been fired at him. It had whizzed past his head and sank in the brain of an unfortunate boy, who gave the awful shriek and died. Both parents were there. Mother and father saw their child fall, but they saw not the hand that did it.

The woman fell upon her son's form, and wept frantically.

She tore her hair, rolled about, called on his name, invoked blessings on his head, and a mother's bitterest curse upon the destroyer.

'Vengeance—vengeance!' cried the the half-mad father. 'Friends—neighbours—good people of Deal! Shall I not have *revenge?*'

A murmur answered him, which deepened into a loud shout, as he rushed frantically from group to group of excited people.

'The murderer! the murderer!' was the cry from every mouth, and everybody started with a rush to the spot where they had seen the flash.

'He's gone!' said a girl who was panting, and out of breath.

'Which way?'

'Where?'

'What's he like?'

Such were the numerous questions put to her by a score of men, and all expecting an answer at the same time.

'I don't know anything about him,' said the girl, striving to regain her breath. 'I saw him fire, and heard little Jemmy's screams. I knew his voice, poor little fellow, and I held the man who shot him by the cloak. Here it is. I pulled it off, though he did knock me down, and would have murdered me, had not my brother, John, caught him by the throat, and dashed the pistol from his hand. He cut my brother across the shoulder with a sword, and then dashed away. John's gone after him.'

'Which way?'

'Up High-street.'

'Let's hunt him down, my lads!' cried one excited individual.

'Who, you swab?' said a sailor, hoisting his slacks. 'The younker as battled with the pirate?'

'No, mate—the pirate!'

'Then I'm with you. Off we go!'

He was rushing from one place to another, calling on the slayer of his son, and brandishing a long, deadly knife, in a manner that greatly jeopardized the noses of all who got in his way.

'This way, Filham,' cried the hurrying mob.

'My son!—the hond!—curse him!—the murderer! the bloody wretch! My boy!—my boy!' and he tore his hair frantically.

There was a great hue and cry. All the men and boys dashed off, in a dozen different directions, to find the murderer of little Jemmy, as the boy was called. The party, who had started in the same direction as the heroic brother, John, fell in with the agonized father, who seemed to have lost his reason.

Gratis! Gratis! Another Splendid Scene with Next Week's Number.

BLACK EYED SUSAN.

OR, PIRATES ASHORE.

LEVI BEN MOSES RECEIVES THE REWARD OF HIS TREACHERY.

7

Presented Gratis with this Number, next Scene for the Play of
"RED ROVER."

'This way, messmate!' cried the sailor. 'We'll run the pirate down, or I'm a long shore lubber.''

Poor Filham, understanding that if he followed he would perhaps meet the man who killed his son, rushed on, and so swiftly, that few could keep up with him His face was ghastly pale, from excitement and fatigue—his eyes glared horribly—his teeth were locked—his lips parted—and ever and anon he would utter a cry of vengeance.

He suddenly came upon a little crowd of men. He leaped among them, and, brandishing his knife, cried—

'Where is he?'

The people shrank back. They thought a madman was amongst them.

'Its Filham,' said a faint voice, as the crowd closed with pitying glances round the distracted father.

They had all heard of the tragedy, and the name of the murdered boy, Like a pack of hungry wolves those who had followed the father came up breathless and perspiring to such a degree that they seemed like men who had just jumped out of a shower bath.

The sailor and individual who had started the chase elbowed their way through the crowd and came right to Filham, who was glaring distractedly about him, and asking for the man who shot his son.

'He's gone,' said a young man who was being supported by his friends—it was he who had spoken the father's name, and it was John, the brother of the brave girl who had endeavoured to stop the murderer.

"Gone!' said the father, in a tone of such deep melancholy that every heart was touched.

'Ay, father,' replied the young man. 'I caught him, we had a tussle and he wounded me. I can scarcely stand or breathe. A drop more brandy please.'

Brandy was given him, and he continued—

'He ran his sword into me, but I marked him. I cut him over the arm towards his neck, but I couldn't hold out, with this wound especially, as a lot of sailors came round, and he ran off with them to the beach.'

'He's a naval fellow then?' asked one.

'Yes, a captain. Poll's got his pistol and cloak. Poor lass! the coward hit her, too.'

'A ship's cap'n did you say?' asked the sailor, turning his quid.

'Yes.'

'May be, if I see his pistol I should know it, for they always haves 'em marked with two letters, and I knows all the capt'ns name werry right.'

It was agreed that the sailor should go back with them, and identify the pistol if possible.

Meantime, the father had stood perfectly quiet, like one turned into stone or paralysed; the knife dropped from his hand; he covered his face; his frame shook like an aspen; two or three deep groans that came from the inmost recesses of his heart broke from his lips; two large tears—tears of agony and sorrow—welled up, and trickled between his fingers to roll from them to the ground.

'My poor boy!' he muttered. 'My poor wife!'

Another groan, which shook the strong frame, and he fell huddled in a senseless mass at the foot of the sailor, who looked upon that face distorted in agony, and so white and immovable as to resemble death; and he swore to find the slayer of an innocent boy—the destroyer of a happy home, even should it be *his own captain.*'

'Shipmates!' he said, huskily, 'carry this poor fellow home. The dastard who did this ought to be hanged by one of his own crew.'

'Ought to be hanged by one of his crew!' seemed to echo back from the tops of the dark row of houses, as the mob moved silently and sorrowfully away.

CHAPTER XVIII.

THE POOR WANDERER.

KNOWING too well the rash impetuosity of his gallant friend and officer, Captain Gerald did not wait long with the boat's crew of the lugger, leaving orders with the men that they were to keep well on the alert, and be prepared at any moment he stepped ashore.

He wished to hear more news concerning the fate of his beloved, and he knew a man who was not at all unlikely to know something ; he was mine host at the Crown and Anchor.

'Good evening, my friend,' Gerald said, entering the inn.

'Ah, it's you, yer honour; hope you're well.'

'Quite, thanks ; any one here ? '

'Not many, yer honour—none in *our* room,' replied Sharp-eye, with a meaning grin.

'Our room' was a snug little private apartment behind the bar, kept by mine host for a very few of his most favoured customers, and Captain Gerald was one of those favourites.

'There has been some wild scenes in Deal, and I fear there'll more,' said Sharp-eye when they were alone.

'Indeed ! Why ? '

'Ain't the Redbreast laying out there under the guns of old Garthway's luger ; and ain't Miss Madeline and Susan prisoners ? '

'How do you know all this ? '

'Bill Raker's gone in the under room a short time ago, yer honour, and it strikes me, captain, this is dangerous ground for you. The escape of the Curlew has put all Deal on the scent, and the Downs is alive with vessels on the look out ; they suspects you'll be here.'

'They are not wrong, then. I am here, and for a good reason. My lieutenant, William, has gone to the house of Doggrass, and I fear his rash blood will put him in some scrape or other. I fear for him, and that is why I came ashore, though I entered the Downs with more dangerous schemes to carry out. What news have you heard ? '

'News, your honour, that the daughter of Lord Harry is to be spliced, by main force, to Cap'n Saunders in two days.'

'Two days?'—Gerald gave an inward laugh—'They may have some work to do.'

'That's likely, yer honour !' grinned Sharp-eye.

'And yer say as how Mr. William's gone alone ?'

'Yes.'

'Then pardon me, cap'n, for saying it's a pity. I say and know that Saunders's people is prowling about, and there'll be a row.'

'I will look after him. Why, I wonder was the marriage delayed for another day or two ?'

'That, your honour, I can't say ; but I knows it is so, and I knows that Lord Harry has a dozen or more armed men prowling about his premises in case you should walk that way.'

'Many thanks, my friend—that is as well to know.'

He took a little refreshment, and was left alone for a few minutes.

Now he began to form his plans. He had two days more than he had expected given him to make preparations.

Two days seemed a long time for him to wait in a state of anxiety for the terrible time to come—the time when he must either perish or gain his peerless bride.

A little cool reflection told him it would be as well to have a friend on whom he could rely on shore—that friend must be Sharp-eye.

He summoned mine host.

'My friend,' he said, 'I want your assistance if you could give it me.'

'For what, yer honour? You knows there's nothing but what I'd sacrifice for you.'

'I believe you, Sharp, and I trust you with them. Keep a good look out on every one that enters your house. Discover, if possible, who they are, their intention, and if one should ever turn up and prove to be a messenger from Lord Harry's ship he will be a messenger to the town minister. I want that man; he must not go until I have seen him.'

'It shall be done. Your honour can trust me you well know, and I have no doubt the fellow will be here.'

'Very good. I must now be away.' He said good night, and left the inn.

He wandered about without any purpose or definite idea of what he was going to do—he wandered in the direction of Lower Deal—the streets became darker and narrower, and all bore a more or less poverty stricken appearance.

The heavy mist lay—or seemed to lay—thicker in those poor localities than in the other and more respectable thoroughfares.

The rickety, irregular-built houses, shrank, as it were, as far back in the gloom, sinking to conceal their dilapidated appearance from the passers-by.

Gerald became reflective, and walked on, not taking any particular notice of the direction he was going.

He saw in some of those miserable structures poverty written in every brick—in the shattered windows, which were curtained with aprons, pieces of coloured rag, and others with an old bed-tick.

Each beggarly little window had its own secrets —its long, weary, and sad story—though each touching history was founded on the same basis— that of vice, poverty, sickness, and neglect.

He wondered how the inhabitants could sleep so peacefully, how such a place could become quiet, even at that hour.

The silence was unbroken by aught save the occasional squeal of some neglected infant, whose cries would ring out through the narrow, dirty streets, and every note of its weak voice denoted that hunger—the slow, fell destroyer, starvation— lurked within many of those dark, wretched dwellings.

It not only dwelt within, but the iron hand of poverty had one of its destroyed victims without. A figure, wretchedly clad in sable garments, staggered up the filthy street, and came towards Captain Gerald, who raised his eyes with a strange feeling of pity at his heart.

The form was that of a female—she was too far for him to see her face, which was covered by her hands—still he detected a feeble step, a slow, tottering walk—not the unsteady gait of intoxication—it was the slow dragging step of a care-worn form.

So noiseless did the woman come on, that he thought she must have had no boots on at all. When within a few yards of him the figure paused and leaned for support against one of the time-worn doors.

The face sunk lower into the hands, the head was bowed, and the form became bent and unsteady.

The round regular tread of Gerald seemed to rouse the apparently suffering creature, and she endeavoured to continue her walk.

It was useless.

With a groan that made Gerald's heart bleed, the poor creature sank upon a door-step and wept.

Gerald stepped up to her, and in a voice that was thrilling in its pity and feeling said—

'My poor creature, in the name of heaven I beseech you to tell me why you suffer?'

A long stifling sob, wrung from the woman's very heart's core, was the only answer, and such a sigh, or rather moan, of mental suffering came upon his ears that he laid his hand kindly on the bowed head before him, and continued—

'Do not fear to answer me. I mean well. In the name of humanity I ask you to tell me why you suffer thus. Could I not help you.'

'Could you give me the greatest gift on earth— that which is looked for—wished for—and yet feared—that which would end all my sufferings and ease this bleeding heart—that which would bring me eternal bliss and peace ever more—the' end of all things—death! then you would help me.

The tone of the voice struck Gerald with its sweetness of sound, the touching pathos with which the words were spoken, and the perfect though faint pronunciation of the words, told him the sufferer before him was not of the common kind.

The thin, white hands were removed and displayed a face beautiful even in its sorrow.'

The features were pinched and drawn in, the nostrils were pinched in, and the black rings round her sunken orbs, spoke too plainly of want—of hunger, and of no ordinary cares.

She was young, too—trouble had added many years upon her, and brought grey hairs to her head—but still she was scarcely beyond the days of youth.

'Come, you must not talk thus. Do not despair; you are too young to seek death. Life must be sweet to you——'

She smiled—a sad bitter smile; it spoke volumes —it spoke plainly of long and continued sufferings, and Gerald paused—a lump having risen to his throat that choked his utterance.

'Kind sir,' she went on, 'what interest can you have in a poor disconsolate outcast?'

'None, none, my poor young creature. I have the will and the feeling to do good; I merely follow the dictates of humanity, to help those in distress—to be a friend to the friendless, a protector to the weak, and a foe to the oppressors.'

There was no doubting the sterling honesty of his noble heart.

The poor sufferer saw it in his face, and she wep again.

'I have been so used to the world's frowns and bitter scoffs—so accustomed to look for degradation and insult, that your kindness overcomes me.'

Gerald Stuart saw she was getting fainter each moment.

'Tell me,' he said anxiously, 'where you wish to go—tell me what you want? Will money remedy all your'——

She stopped him again by another of those melancholy smiles, and large pearly drops stood quivering on the lid of either eye.

'Let me,' he persisted, 'at least conduct you to your destination.'

'Gracious sir, I could go alone if you would direct me.'

'To where?'

'The house of Lord Garthway.'

She attempted to rise, but would have failed had not Gerald assisted her.

She lifted her eyes to his, and thanked him with a sweet, melancholy smile.

Then he saw her go deathly pale; the smile die away, and her eyes become fixed on something behind him.

He turned quickly, and the form of a man drew back; the stranger had approached in perfect silence, and stood unknown to them there.

One glimpse at the face the suffering woman caught. She stared as though petrified into stone.

'Tis he,' she murmured.

Then her frame shook violently, a low murmur escaped her lips, and before Gerald knew what had occurred she lay huddled in a heap upon the dark, damp door step of the wretched house.

'My poor creature,' said Stuart, attempting to raise her from the ground.

He then saw she was senseless.

What could he do?

In an instant his mind was made up. He hammered at the door of the house, and called upon the inmates to open.

'Open the door!' he cried. 'Open, in the name of humanity.'

After an elapse of a few minutes, the ricketty door squeaked upon its rusty hinges, and a woman stood in the aperture, with a short piece of a wretched rushlight in her hand.

'My good woman,' said Gerald, 'for pity's sake take this poor woman in, and give her something to revive her—she is dying for want.'

The poor person, scarcely understanding what had happened, stooped to look at the form of the senseless girl.

The pale, deathlike appearance of the young creature touched her heart to the core, and she said—

'I will do all I can, sir; but there is not a crumb of anything in the house to offer her.'

'Never mind that; something shall soon be obtained.'

'Jack!' called the woman.

'Yes, mother,' answered a voice from an inner room.

Captain Gerald took the girl in his arms and carried her to the small parlour, and after looking vainly round for a sofa to lay her upon, he deposited the inanimate form into a chair, and began to chafe the cold wan hands.

The poor inmate of the house eyed him curiously; his cloak had fallen aside, and his handsome uniform was displayed by the flickering light of the candle.

'Could you bring me a little cold water?' Gerald asked.

'Yes sir, to be sure.'

The candle was placed in the neck of a bottle upon the low mantelpiece, and the woman turned to go, as a pale faced, but intelligent, lad entered the room.

He had nothing on but his trousers, a very ragged shirt, and a pair of old boots.

'Come here, my lad,' Gerald said, kindly.

'Do you want me, sir?'

'Yes. Could you run to some spirit stores, and procure some brandy?'

'I'll try, sir.'

Gerald gave the boy a crown.

'Is it for the poor lady,' the boy asked, his juvenile heart, touched by the sight of the deathly face.

'Yes, run along.'

'Then I'll make them open,' the little fellow said, bravely, and he scampered off without coat or cap, and was not satisfied with knocking up the tavern keeper and getting brandy, but he also summoned the doctor on his way back.

Jack fancied he saw a cloaked figure draw back as he emerged from the house, but his mind being so occupied by the strange circumstance that had occurred, he did not give it a second thought, and entered the house without looking to see whether the lurking figure was still there.

The door was securely closed upon him, when the same form silently approached from the opposite side and paused before the entrance to the hovel—for it was nothing better—and seemed to scan it with great interest. Once the person passed his finger across the door above the knocker.

It was evidently to ascertain whether there was any number to the house. There might have been, but he could not find it.

'I must know the house again,' the stranger muttered; and drawing a long naval sword he drew the point twice across the decaying wood, to the length of about three inches each way, making a cross.

Then he strode on, muttering darkly as he went—

"So, so! was it a dream, or could it have been her? By the furies, I must see to it! And Gerald Stuart here, too! Aha! that is good! We shall see, my fine fellow. If you are here, your friend William is not far off. Look to it! for it is easier to enter the Downs, than to leave them.'

Rapidly, now, he strode on, absorbed in thought; dark schemings, passion, hate, and deadly fear, were at work in his breast; a secret chord in his black heart had been touched that night; an evil mystery hung about that man, one, had the world known, that would have made Gregory Saunders a despicable felon, instead of a member of society.

It was while he walked on, thus meditating, he was accosted by the old housekeeper of Silas Doggrass, and heard that William was within. What followed is already known to the reader, in Chapter XVII. The poor wanderer met by Captain Gerald was like a phantom of the past to Saunders, and he lived in deadly fear while our gallant Gerald Stuart and William were free.

CHAPTER XIX.

INCREASING DANGER.

NIGHT dragged slowly on. The thick mist still hung over the Downs, and Deal was enveloped in the hazy shroud.

But the silence of a sleeping town no longer existed. On land and on the water the same excitement prevailed—lights glimmered duskily in the hazy atmosphere—the houses around seemed to send forth their inhabitants into the dark streets and stare down upon them with a sulky frown.

The Custom House was lighted up—officials and officious functionaries were everywhere and were everything—the local authorities ordered out their fat red-nosed hirelings, who paraded the streets full of importance and growing more bloated than ever.

The coastguards were roused from their sleep, and kept on the *qui vive*, and every man-of-war in the Downs had its men up and on the alert. The arsenal store-house was strongly guarded by the town force, in case of a siege from a desperate gang of pirates—a calamity that did not seem improbable, both to the official and officious members of the civil and government forces of his Most Excellent Majesty, King George I.

Every respectable and peaceful household of Deal was regarded with suspicion. The constables conversed mysteriously. Everyone and everything was all excitement, and yet there was scarcely one who could tell why the unexpected disturbance had taken place.

Many said pirates had landed, and were still lurking in the town; and those who *did* know a little, talked of dreadful doings, of the coast abounding with sea-robbers! that Doggrass had nearly been shot, and in his bed—a battle had taken place between a party of marines and a crew of smugglers or pirates—that a boy had been pitilessly murdered, and the felonious, red-handed, murderous, soulless, and so forth, brutes of creation had actually escaped to their ships.

Such was the cause of the excitement, and such was the state of Deal on the night of the 17th of ——, in the year of our Lord, Seventeen hundred and fifteen.

Lord Garthway had boarded his vessel, and had his men beat to quarters. The messenger from Saunders had reached him, though a little late, and he was prevented from making immediate investigations among the shipping by the reports from shore which continually came to him.

Many and various were the accounts of the tragedy, and they all more or less puzzled him. He frowned when he heard of the traitors escaping, and issued orders to the captain of the man-of-war to block up the entrance to the roads.

Owing to the intense darkness, they had to work very carefully, or a great deal of property would have been damaged among the shipping. To add to the admiral's annoyance, a heavy breeze began to arise, and the sea to run high.

Twice he had signalled for Gregory Saunders; each time no answer was given. Turning with rage and impatience, Garthway ordered a blank cartridge to be fired; and if the signal was not answered, a boat was to be put off, and the brig boarded.

But the signal was answered; and the report from Saunders' vessel was to the effect that he had arrived, and the rebels had escaped, and that he was severely wounded—a message that by no means improved the High Admiral's uncontrollable temper.

During this time of excitement and stirring events, the individuals who had so unmeaningly caused it all, were safe on board the Curlew, which was still under the cliffs.

William did not remain long in a state of insensibility or inactivity. With his returning consciousness returned his strength and eagerness. He

went on deck, and found Gerald gloomily striding the poop.

'Ah! Will, I am glad nothing serious ails you. What a night of events this has been, to be sure!' said Stuart, taking his friend's hand.

Will sighed heavily.

'It's like a dream to me. I feel like a lubberly youngster who's been kidnapped, and wakes up to find himself on a seventy-four.'

'Why did you come on deck yet?'

'I felt rather shaky aloft, and came up to see if it would clear the mist off a little. How did I come here?'

'I had you brought. Where is your wife?'

'Aha! I remember all now. Poor Sue! She's been run foul of by pirates and carried off.'

Will's voice became husky, and his frame trembled.

'Don't give way, Will; it will do you no good. Bear up. We are not beaten yet. She is a good girl, and would defy a legion of men. Tell me presently how you got into such a mess. At present it will require all our skill to take us out of here.'

Our hero shook off his lethargy a little, and glanced about him. The excitement that prevailed on shore as well as on the water convinced him that they were in an uncomfortable, if not dangerous, position.

'You see, we are in for it,' Gerald Stuart said.

'Ay, that's plain enough. But, what course do you intend to steer, your hon'——

A smile from Stuart cut short the word 'honour.' Will could not break off a habit that had grown upon him from his youth.

'The safest. You see, my dear Will, every ship is on the alert. Thanks to the darkness, they are afraid to do much; but morning will be here soon, and, when we are away, it will be a heavy conflict. I can see Lord Harry's liner getting under weigh; and the others will hover round him like a lot of bees. We cannot do better than run slowly out to sea. Keep on the disguise, and hoodwink them if possible. I can see that, ere this mist clears off, we shall have a storm, and that will keep them quiet.'

'We can't do better than get out into deep water; and, if they do run foul of us, why we can fight!'

Will felt desperate, and would have dared the whole fleet.

'True,' said Gerald, and he began issuing orders in almost whispers.

Everything was performed with as much silence as could be expected, and the Curlew lugger stood out for deep water.

No lights were displayed, and the gloom fell upon the vessel like a pall.

'With this breeze we could slip easily away—the thing is whether we shall be seen. Admiral Garthway seems pretty lively ahead there, and by the signals and boats that have been going about, a search is on the wing, and not a galley will even be overlooked.'

William did not reply. His heart was heavy, and he was in a sullen mood. He moved his eyes, if he did not his tongue, and could discern many lights darting about ahead, and he knew the men-of-war were laying across the mouth of the channel; behind them the vessels were being overhauled, and despatches had gone even so far as Woolwich to prevent any vessel from going without being overhauled.

'We are in a mess,' said Gerald, wishing to break the silence.

'Ay, like a salmon among a shoal of sharks.'

'Never mind, we must hope for the best. We can do no more than watch closely. I propose we keep watch and watch.'

'I couldn't sleep, cap'n. I am like a vessel in a storm, every timber in me shakes, and such a turmoil going on in my heart.'

'I could not rest either; so we will keep each other company.'

'Ugh! I shudder at the sight I saw to night, Will; short as my stay was on shore, I witnessed such a scene as I would not wish to see again. I pity you from my heart, yet I doubt whether you feared the worst; you shall hear.'

Gerald ordered the steward to bring up some punch, and drank to keep the mist from going to their lungs.

'I am a selfish lubber,' said Will, self-reproachfully, 'I've been groaning about myself, and never thought whether there wasn't anyone with greater trouble than myself. Forgive me, your honour, I'——

'Gerald, Will, Gerald'?.

The young captain took Will's hand, and said—

'Do not reproach yourself, we have both been unfortunate.'

'Spin out, Gerald, it does me good to hear of it, and teaches me to think of others.'

'I met with some one who has put invaluable knowledge in my power' continued Gerald. 'Providence works strange things. With all my hopes crushed and a heavy heart, I wandered about, not knowing or caring where I went. I traversed many of the streets of Lower Deal, and was arrested in my work by a distressed woman,—as I thought, at first, a beggar.

'She did not perceive me in the gloom, and, placing her hands over her face, she leaned against a door-post, and I heard her moan in anguish. I spoke to her, and at the sound of my voice she looked up. Imagine my surprise to find her, not only young, but a beautiful, delicate woman, with every lineament of her face and form speaking of better days and gentle breeding. My heart was touched. I begged her to tell me what I could do to aid her, and when she attempted to speak a third person came upon the scene. She tried to move away, but it was with great difficulty she could get up, and her eyes catching sight of the stranger, she staggered back. After a minute's speechless amazement, she spoke some words—I can say what it was—and I turned to see who the stranger was. He stepped back, and in consequence of the gloom I could scarcely see his face, but I could swear it was Gregory Saunders. I would have followed him, but the poor girl fell in a swoon, and I could but go to get assistance.'

'Who was she,' asked Will, becoming interested.

'You shall hear all,' he pursued. 'I had her taken into one of the beggarly little houses, and sent for assistance. I remained until she came to, and then put a few questions to her. She was afraid to say much, but told me she wished to see Lord Harry Garthway. I was struck by this peculiar wish, and asked why. "To prevent his daughter's ruin and dishonour." For heaven's sake, speak plain, I said. What mean you. "I mean that if she marries Gregory Saunders she will be *no wife*, and he will be a *bigamist*." I was horror stricken and bewildered at this unlooked for intelligence, and the narrow escape of Madeline. I questioned her further, but she would say no more, being tired. I left her plenty of money, thanked the poor woman of the house, gave her a piece of gold, with strict injunctions not to let anyone but myself see the lady, for such she is.

I left, and while striding leisurely back I saw an unusual excitement, and a file of marines going towards the house of your Susan's uncle. I guessed what was afloat, and called the boat's crew up to the rescue.'

'Ay, had it not been for that I should have been dead ere now. A second debt I owe you.'

'Nay nay, Will, only duty, you know, towards a friend. Let me continue.

He made William acquainted with the fatal tragedy that followed his victory.

'Poor little fellow!' he concluded, 'his dying shriek still rings in my ear. To think his young life should have been sacrificed for me, though, God knows, I would sooner the bullet had shattered my brains out than he should have suffered.'

'And the poor family?' asked Will.

'I stayed long enough to learn their name and address. I shall call upon them, and do all I can for them; the poor mother's anguish was heart-rending, and the father was like a lunatic.'

'Do you know who fired the shot?'

'Who would have done it but my most inveterate foe.'

'Ay. But are you sure?'

'From my heart yes, though I have no substantiated evidence yet.'

'It has been a night of events, and we are not the only sufferers.'

'Not by a long way, Will. Had you witnessed that scene, your heart would have bled. Aha! we must look out.'

During the time they had been conversing, the wind had risen to almost a gale, and the water was lashed into a foam by the close proximity to the reefs; the mist had thickened more; in fact it had now became so dense that a light placed at the forecastle could scarcely be seen on the quarterdeck.

'Make all taut above and below,' cried Gerald, 'it will blow pretty stiff soon, Will.'

'And she ought to be out of this port.'

'Yes, but we had better not. I do not intend to go far. I want the vessel to be off in the channel, and we could return to transact our *business*. I have sworn my *work* shall be done before I take a cruise, and it shall. Aha! silence fore and aft.'

Scarcely had the words left his lips than a king's ship run alongside, close enough to touch and would have run into her bow, but William sprang to the wheel and turned the lugger off two points, by which they lost the wind out of their sails, for a few seconds only though.

The crew were expert men, and they tacked instantly, and the Golden Arrow sped on as before.

'Hullo! What ship?'

'The Curlew, fishing lugger.'

'Lay-to!' shouted an officer from the gun brig.

'See you d—— first,' muttered Will.

'Pretend not to hear them,' laughed Gerald.

In vain did the officer call, he received no answer; and the rate at which the lugger scudded before the wind, was sufficient to confirm his suspicions, and he ordered a shot to be fired.

It was a rash act, taking into consideration the terrible darkness, and involved dangerous consequences. The shot was fired, whizzed past the Curlew, and struck a revenue-cutter amidships. The revenue-cutter was prepared for action, and this unexpected assault put her commander in a rage, he opened fire upon what he thought to be the enemy, and sent a rattling broadside into a war-sloop that was laying a little to leeward.

The sloop staggered under the shot, and an officer was struck by a splinter, and knocked off the poop. The captain had heard the challenge, and saw the suspicious vessel dissolve in the gloom; and when the flash came from that quarter, he thought he was only doing right to return the fire, which he did in earnest.

The revenue-cutter and sloop puffed away at each other, and brought all the ships in the Downs to that point. Immense excitement prevailed—the commander ascertained what sloop it was, and a frigate run down upon the supposed enemy: the cutter certainly stood in a favourable way for being smashed, had not the captain fortunately known that it was stationed in that one particular spot, and the mistake was discovered, though not until considerable damage had been done on either side.

This little friendly engagement had given our hero's vessel time to run clear of most the ships, and they were all but free, when the lights were hoisted and lowered from the mast head of a vessel, two blank cartridges were fired, then all was dark and silent as before.

It was the signal agreed upon to discover the rebels were running out. This Gerald did not know, and was staggered when a line-of-battle ship ranged itself right across his bows ready to swamp his.

'Lay-to!' thundered a voice he knew too well. It was the Lord High Admiral's.

'Every man below!' said Gerald, quickly. 'Jam down the helm, Will! My God! we are in for it!—ship ahoy!' he called, to gain time.

'Ahoy! why don't you lay-to?'

'We are afraid of running into you.'

'Haul up, or I fire.'

During this exchanging of words, the Golden Arrow had veered round, and was broadside to the liner.

'Now,' said Gerald, 'it's victory or death! Let her fly topsails—let go—that's it, my lads. Mr. Burkett, run below and tell them to fire the larboard battery below that fellow's water-line—now. Aha! Curses!'

Crash! a blinding flash, and deafening report. The Curlew shook from point to keel. Gerald was knocked off his feet, and William released the wheel with a cry of pain.

It whirled round, carried the man with it, dashed him into the scuppers; the vessel heeled over, the sails filled with a roar, and she tore on into the very teeth of the liner.

———

CHAPTER XX.

BOARDING THE FRIGATE.*

It was a terrible moment for all on board the lugger, the danger was imminent, and every man on board was paralysed by the sudden catastrophe.

The steersman who had helped William at the wheel lay in the scuppers, stunned and bleeding. Our hero had been struck by a splinter or some small shot, in spite of which he was the second on his feet—the voice of Captain Gerald aroused him, and he again leaped to the wheel.

Two stout fellows were at his side, and he brought the lugger round just in time to prevent a collision that would in all probability have proved fatal.

(* See front page, No 4.)

The lugger veered off her gunnel scraped the side of the three-decker, and she was hurled on by the wind.

Lord Henry Garthway was as much confused as any one by the sudden calamity, and owing to the darkness and the swiftness of the lugger, he was prevented from doing as he would have done—which was to pour a broadside into her deck, or order a company of men to board her—but the Curlew had shot ahead and swept past his stern, and when the guns were fired they hurled their missiles of death into the gloom only.

It had not taken one quarter of the time to occur that it has to describe, and the Admiral was left to either blaze away with his stern battery or veer his ship round and give chase.

He was choking with rage, and what he would have done no one knows, when his officer reported a brig was on the track of the lugger.

The Curlew made all sail out seaward, and having got a start kept it. Gerald never blessed the hazy darkness more in his life than he did on this occasion, and the wind, which was now blowing a perfect gale, aided him still further.

Lord Garthway would have followed too, but something very unexpected and unaccountable occurred, that made him stand on the poop of his vessel staring in speechless amazement through the thick black mist.

A terrible firing took place on the Downs. Signals were hoisted in every direction, and the sounds of a heavy engagement came upon his ears.

The cause was as yet a mystery to him. To ascertain the cause was his first impulse; but he was saved the trouble by a revenue cutter running alongside, and a young officer jumped on board the liner.

'There's a French privateer among us, Admiral, and some men-of-war we think, and Captain Hatchett is escaping with his craft.'

The roar of distant cannon, and crash after crash, confirmed the messenger's statement, and Garthway bore down upon them with all possible speed.

Morn had not yet appeared, and it was with great difficulty he could clearly discern his ships, and know one from the other.

The engagement attracted him, and told him the direction he should take, and he ran alongside the privateer, which had, under the cover of darkness, quietly captured two valuable prizes, and now was fighting to keep them.

The French schooner was well armed and full of men, but her captain saw his escape was almost impossible; indeed, to get away would be a miracle.

Still he did not intend giving up both prizes, so put a crew on board each, and while he engaged the king's ships, ordered them to make good their escape, and put themselves under the protection of a French frigate that lay a little way out.

They tried to do so, and the privateer waited the onslaught. Already two vessels were firing upon him, and the admiral's three-decker prepared to do the same.

The wind now blew a perfect hurricane; the waves rolled high, and the ships rocked about like corks upon the water, and to fire a broadside with any efficiency was simply impossible.

The sea ran too high for Lord Harry to board, and he called upon the enemy to surrender.

The privateer took no heed of the challenge, but attempted to run out, when a shot cut away her jibboom, with all its rigging and sails.

'Sacré!' muttered the commander. ' We shal be driven ashore. *Parbleu !*'

Such was the case. The heavy wash of the sea was gradually driving him ashore.

'Surrender !' cried the Admiral.

No reply.

' Do you surrender ?'

The tri-colour rolled to the deck, and the British sailors gave a shout.

While all this had been going on, our hero and Gerald Stuart were being chased by the gun brig.

It was Gerald's intention, though much against his inclination, to again board the Golden Arrow until he was safe from the clutches of the fleet. He knew his gallant craft was not far out, and should his spars hold good, he could outstrip the brig by two knots in every twelve.

It was a wild chase—every few minutes the lights on the gun brig could be clearly discovered, the next moment they would sink from view.

Not the slightest vestige of a light was displayed on the lugger, nor a gun fired to betray them, though the brig constantly sent a shot from one of their bow chasers.

'Look !' said Will, clutching Gerald by the arm, ' dash my buttons, there's a fifty-two coming down on our quarter with all the speed of a racer.

'You speak truly. Does she see us ?'

'See, captain! They must have sharp eyes It's the lights at their fore that betrays them.'

'At any rate, we must keep away—to hunt a frigate with this tub would be death. Silence fore and aft ! douse every light.'

'No fear, your honour, of their seeing us ; they're a good way off ; but they are sure to tumble in with the fellow on our track. Curse him, he follows pretty sharply ! Damme ! we shall have some work yet.'

The lugger bore off two points, and thus took her out of the line of the stranger.

William still stood at the wheel, and Captain Gerald took a rocket from a tin case. Lighting a match, he ignited the touch paper.

A loud hissing—a long line of sparks—a dull explosion—and a blue light wreathed for several yards through the murky air.

Then it faded away—darkness hid everything as before, and the lugger went on, everyone keeping a rigid silence.

A few minutes suspense, and Gerald gave an exclamation of pleasure.

Another blue light was seen a short distance from the weather bow.

'Safe !' said Gerald. 'We are seen.'

'It's the beautiful Golden Arrow,' said Will, warmly. 'Rouse up, you lubbers, fore and aft, and prepare to board the smartest craft in the world.'

Captain Gerald hailed the Golden Arrow, as the lugger was alongside, and our hero with the young chief and sailors jumped aboard.

'That was a Frenchman just passed you,' said an officer coming forward.

'Aha ! what build ?'

'A full-rigged frigate, sir. We would have stopped it or tried to, had not your orders been that we were not to enter into any engagement—so I kept out of the way.'

'You acted wisely, lieutenant. They are bold to come so far.'

'Dash my toplights !' cried Will. 'Mr. Froggy has tumbled across our pursuers. There they go !'

And there they did go—if he meant that they were firing into each other most furiously. Will saw the flash after flash, and heard the crashing of the destructive balls. His excitement was almost uncontrollable.

It was more than his blood could stand to see a fine engagement between a brig of his nation and a Frenchman and he not join in.

'Damme, if I can stand it !' he said, bringing his hand down on his thigh with a good sound slap. 'Captain, if you don't bear down upon those frog-eating swabs, I'll—I'll——'

'Such is my intention,' interrupted Gerald, coolly.

The Golden Arrow was put about, and the men called to quarters, and they eagerly waited to be upon the foe.

Rebels as they were, to have the enemy fighting under their nose was more than they could be expected to look calmly upon.

Each minute the engagement became more fierce. They were engaged at even quarters, and a deafening shout, coupled with cries, yells, and curses, told Will the Britishers had boarded the frigate.

'What carnage !' muttered Gerald, as he stood anxiously waiting for the Golden Arrow to run alongside.

He knew the gun-brig could not produce two men to the frigate's five, and the dauntless bravery of the English sea dogs thrilled him with admiration.

The cries of the combatants came plainly upon his ears, and by the dim light of the battle lanterns a fierce combat was going on.

Captain Logline was a young man, and ardent sailor, with an unstained character, a fine reputation among those at the Admiralty, and one who was now striving to gain that so oft wished for and rarely obtained—honour and glory !

He commanded the gun-brig in chase of the rebels, and when he fancied himself intercepted by the Frenchman, he engaged him without a word or thought to her size and power.

Now, he saw the folly.

Fearfully outnumbered, taken at a disadvantage and among the frigate's men, he saw his own gallant crew being cut up in every direction, and yet his courage did not fail him.

He cut his way like a tiger through the contending mass, and sought out the captain, who had just pitilessly cut a middy to the deck.

'*Diable*,' he muttered, facing round to meet Captain Logline's onslaught.

The young captain was a fine scholar, and heard the commander of the frigate give orders for grape and canister to be fired among the Englishmen, at a given signal, when his own men could draw off.

He did not think Captain Allan Logline understood him. Captain Logline did, and perfectly.

'Stay, lads !' he cried, at the highest pitch of his voice. ' Do not disperse. Keep up with the enemy, wherever they go, or you will be hacked to pieces by grape and canister.'

Vague as were his words, the brave fellows scented danger, and that all was not right, and they made a mental resolution to act up to their young captain's orders.

The gallant commander of the gun-brig was, with all the bold coolness of his nature, now goaded to desperation, and his foe found it hard work to keep his footing.

The wily Frenchman hacked his way forward to get among his men, and thus elude a sword he

BLACK EYED SUSAN

OR, PIRATES ASHORE.

GERALD STUART TO THE RESCUE.

could not conquer; but Captain Allen followed him up.

'Come to my assistance, someone,' said the French captain.

'Coward!' hissed Logline, between his teeth, and making a lunge at his shrinking foe that would have been fatal had not the pike of a sailor thrust off the blow.

The young Britisher's fury and prowess rose with his indignation. He felt now that two or three were upon him, he could defy the world.

One very rapid pass his sword made—his foe leaped aside to elude it. That was all Logline wanted. His weapon passed over and cleaved right through the neck of the man who had come to his captain's assistance.

'Now, dastard,' cried Allan, in French, 'do yourself what two of you could not.'

'*Mon Dieu!* thou are boastful.'

'We shall see.'

They were in the thickest of the fight now ; just at the foot of the mainmast, and men were falling in every direction.

The French commander tired now. Feeling his skill was getting less, his power leaving him, thought only of means to save himself.

Placing his back to the mast, he made a sign with his left hand. The signal was answered.

Logline, determined to put an end to the strife if possible, leaped round upon his foe, who staggered and fell as Logline gave a sharp cry of pain, and his sword dropped to the deck.

He had received the thrust as a shout behind told something had occurred.

It was a wild cheer. He heard a voice : he knew it was Will's cry.

'Come away, lads, here's one I'll make junk of.' That was the minute Captain Logline felt a blade enter his back, and he fell with a low cry as Will dashed past him with a reeking sword in his hand.

'My God!' murmured Logline, ' could you have been the one to have done this?'

He was not heard by Will, who had sprung upon the French commander. As he did so, a voice near him said :

'Coward! you have killed the captain.'

Not noting words he scarcely understood, Will simply caught his enemy by the throat and bore him down upon his knees.

'Dastard!' he cried, ' to shrink from fighting a man single handed!" and he put the point of his sword to the French captain's throat.

'*Mon dieu!* mercy!' gasped the coward.

It being all said in French, Will could not understand him, and seeing his presence was wanted elsewhere, he cut the captain down in his fury, and strode on.

He paused with a cry, as he saw young Logline laying in a pool of gore.

'Heavens! captain! who did it?' he cried, kneeling.

He was answered by a terrific shout, which told the Golden Arrow's crew had turned the battle—they had won.

'Who did it?' he unconsciously asked again.

This time the answer nearly petrified him to the spot.

'Messmates!' cried a voice,—' I mean the crew of the gun-brig—your captain didn't fall by the French foe, he fell by the first officer of the rebel ship—by that fellow in silver decorations — the rebel and traitor, William Howard.'

A groan came from the gun-brig's remaining crew, which deepened into a yell.

'Liar!' thundered Gerald Stuart. 'Recal those words, whoever he may be that utters them!'

He leaped forward with the intention of finding out the man, but was stopped by the lieutenant of the gun-brig, who stood at the head of his remaining crew.

William came forward, followed by the brave hearts of the Golden Arrow, and thus they stood, two deadly foes upon the enemy's deck, brought together by the one tie—one great tie of friendship—that of aiding their native brethren, and now they stood as deadly foes as ever.

CHAPTER XXI.

THE ARREST OF GREGORY SAUNDERS.

THE noisy, yelling mob, that had gone brawling through the streets of Deal like a pack of bloodthirsty wolves after their prey, returned without having overtaken the slayers of little Tommy Filham. They no longer yelled and hooted frantically. They made a silent melancholy group, and borne in their midst was Mr. Filham. The gloom that hovered over the town hung upon their hearts, and they retraced their steps in silence.

The sudden and very unexpected disturbances of the time cast a feeling of dread upon many. The wars, the press-gangs that prowled about, robbing many houses of their support, tearing fathers from sons and sons from fathers, with a ruthlessness unnatural. Then the scenes in their own quiet town, the death of little Filham and the late arrests, summed up, made a catalogue of incidents, bad enough to upset the tranquillity of any populace.

Poor Filham was borne on towards his no longer happy home—his trouble and grief for the time forgotten in the painless sleep of unconsciousness.

His wife bore up against her heavy affliction with that noble unselfishness, that strength of will so characteristic in woman—not that she felt the misfortune the less, for her heart was well nigh breaking, but she thought of her husband. Who was to tend and comfort him if she gave way? And her poor, darling boy—who could perform the last rites his cold clay claimed on this earth but her ?—none.

Then she looked up, and waited anxiously for the coming of her husband. He came at last, and was laid upon the dilapidated sofa in the little sitting-room ; and Mrs. Filham gave a cry, so much did his cold, stone-like face resemble death.

'He's only fainted,' said one—the sailor ; and those words recalled the wife.

None but the sailor and the brave John entered the house of sorrow, they walked stealthily about, rendered what service they could, and while the women was with the dead child, they remained to attend the father.

It was not long ere he recovered, though only feebly.

'What has happened?' he asked, as his wife entered the room. She stifled back the sobs that were choking her, and, kissing his aching lips, said—

'Sleep my husband; you will be better to-morrow. You are not strong enough to night to—to'——

Poor, heart-broken creature. She could not hold

out: a flood of bitter tears—tears of agony—welled up from the fountain of her grief-stricken soul, and streamed down her face on to the brow of her husband.

'Betsy, my wife,' he said, huskily, 'do not go on so. Oh, God! I remember—remember all now! Bear up my wife, we must not forget the dear lad is in Heaven. May God our Saviour receive his soul!'

Those in the room involuntarily bowed their heads and murmured, 'Amen.' Mrs. Filham rested her head on her husband's shoulder, and wept as though her heart would break.

'I do not forget, husband,' she sobbed, 'and I trust in Him; but it was very hard, poor darling boy.'

A moan was the only reply from the stricken father, and those in the room saw two large tears—liquid drops of a heart's agony—roll slowly down that strong man's face, and they turned away; perhaps the scene was too touching for them.

'Dash my toplights!' said the generous-hearted sailor, in a choking voice. 'It's no use my keeping up false colours, I've sprung a leak, and the pumps must go to wor'.'

So muttering, he put a large handkerchief representing the Union Jack up to his eyes, attempted to blow his nose, but failed; and he had to leave the room, as he afterwards said, or he would have been heard to 'blubber like a powder-monkey under the cat-o'-nine-tails.'

Jack, too, left the room, and sent his sister in to console them.

'Poll, my girl.'

'Yes, brother Jack,' replied Polly, who was still suffering from those inward spasmodic jerks and catching of breath, that is the usual sequel to a good cry.

"Suppose you fetch Mr. Milder, the clergyman?'

"Yes, Jack, I'll go.'

She went, and very soon brought back the reverend gentleman, who went kindly to Mr. and Mrs. Filham, who were alone when he entered. He spoke wisely, kindly, and in every way consistent with the present unhappy occurrence.

'Come, my children,' he said, 'will you read a prayer with me? You will find consolation only in that.'

'Willingly, sir,' replied Mr. Filham, who, like many other poor, honest, hard-working men, had a soul worthy, perhaps, a higher station, and he believed in a power higher and mightier than his own.

The reverend gentleman read them a brief, simple prayer, which was to the purpose, and understood; and the unhappy parents rose, strengthened in mind and body. Mr. Milder asked to be permitted to read a prayer over the dead, a wish readily granted by both parents.

'Wife,' said Filham, 'where is *she*?'

'In at Mrs. Morgan's.'

'She had better come, poor darling. She must know this some time or other, and she has heard, no doubt, a little. It would be a good opportunity while the Reverend Mr. Milder is here.'

'True, Thomas; I will send for her.'

Polly Morgan was dispatched to her house next door, to bring in the Filhams' little girl. She came in with an air of sadness, that told the child knew more than the mother thought.

'Come, Jenny darling,' said Filham, taking her arms and kissing the rosy lips with the passionate affection of a truly fond father.

'May I see dear Tommy?' said the child, beginning to weep.

'Yes, my love, if you promise not to cry, and listen to this gentleman, who will read the Word of God.'

The little one dried her eyes with an effort. The strength to do so was given her by the wish to see her brother.

Polly Morgan stayed with them; her brother Jack had gone outside with the sailor to find a remedy for watering eyes.

Sadly the little family went up-stairs and entered the room of the dead. It cost the husband a struggle to control himself: the wife could not. She broke out in another burst of grief; and poor little Jenny wept and sobbed until she nearly went into hysterics.

Polly cried again, and an unbidden tear rose to the eye of the worthy clergyman; and no wonder. The sight he beheld would have touched a harder heart than his.

The boy who, in life, was a bold, handsome lad, looked beautiful in the sleep of death. The bullet had entered the crown of his head and gone out near the top of the neck. The wound had been dressed by a surgeon. A light contraction of the nostrils and forehead was the only sign of his momentary pain, and a smile of sweet felicity dimpled the small, well-shaped mouth. The eyes were closed, as if in slumber, and the tiny hands lay outside the white coverlid of the little cot cold, though void the stiffness of death.

'My sister, my children,' said the clergyman, 'do not forget ye are but the creatures of God, and in this you see the work of his mighty hand—his will be done—and shall us poor mortals wail and fight against it? Let us rather bow to it, and pray that the soul of the departed may receive its just reward.'

Calmness among them was restored, and at each side of the bed knelt a parent; each held one of the little hands, on which was the chill of death. Jenny, her tiny fingers locked one in the other, knelt at the feet of her murdered brother—and thus they prayed long and fervently. When they left the room, they did so sadly, and with a tear of sorrow for the lost loved one; but it was silent grief, and came from hearts that had been comforted when they thought the world a-blank.

The door was locked, and the departed was left in silence and darkness. Mr. Milder left the house after a few words of kindness. The moon broke upon the dwelling where the aching hearts of that sad night slept peacefully, and wandered on in the world unknown, with the lost link of the love-chain that had bound a family together in happy contentment.

*　　*　　*　　*　　*　　*

So the dreary night passed. Morning came, and brought with it little change. The gloom within the house of that unfortunate family was as deep as that which pervaded without.

Very early John Morgan and his sister were sent for, and they came—the former looking pale and ill, the other sad and wretched.

'Good morning, Mr. Filham.'

''Morning, John,' replied the honest workman, without a smile of greeting for his young friend.

There was a short pause. John Morgan knew why he was fetched, but could not bring himself to begin a painful subject.

Filham saw it, and said sadly—

'It is useless for us to shun a subject that we must revert to. Poor boy! he is gone. God bless him! but to let his murderer go unpunished would only bring a curse upon me. 'Tis of this I would speak. Where are the things you wrested from the villain?'

'Here,' replied John. 'This is the pistol I took, and this is the cloak brave Polly tore off his shoulders.'

'Do you know either of them?'

'No: but Hawkins will be here shortly.'

'Hawkins?' repeated Filham, interrogatively.

'The sailor.'

'We can do nothing, then, until he comes; what letters are those on the pistol butt?'

'I cannot imagine what name they can stand for,' responded John, handing the pistol to Filham.

Scarcely had he examined them when Hawkins, the sailor, entered.

'Morning, messmates,' he said, extending his hand to both the friends. 'You are trying to get on the track of that red-handed pirate, I see. Tip us that pistol, and if there's any name why'——

He paused, and the colour left his cheek as he scrutinized the weapon.

Very slowly he turned the quid deposited in his cheek, as he examined the initials; the motion of his tongue ceased—his eyes expended, and he ejaculated—

'Thunder and lightning!' and by mistake swallowed at a guph the disgusting juice of the tobacco, and nearly bolted the quid.

Whether the juice and well masticated piece of tobacco was too much for his stomach, or that he was greatly surprised we cannot positively assert, but he turned deadly pale and let his arm drop to his side.

'You know the pistol?' asked Filham, excitedly. a small scarlet patch coming over each cheek.

'I think I know its owner.'

'The initials are'——

'G. S.'

'What names do they stand for?

'That, messmates, I can't swear to, anyhow; still they're mighty like Gregory Saunders, and'——

'And what?'

'Well, it's no use, out it must come; he is my captain.'

'Your captain!' cried Filham, jumping up with his hand to his brow. 'Good God! what had my poor boy done to him?'

'Avast! avast there, a minute, shipmate. I can't swear to it, you know; there might be more than one G. S., and pistols are very much alike; not only that, how do we know who used it.'

'We had better be cautious,' put in John Morgan, quietly, 'or serious trouble might fall upon us.'

'Ay, ay, that's true enough, messmate—true it is.'

'What am I to do?' groaned Filham; 'I cannot let my boy's murderer go unpunished.'

'Well, mate,' replied the sailor; 'I'm at your sarvice. I'll do all I can to discover the pirate. Look sharp after the cloak and pistol, so as no land pirate comes and bears off with 'em. I must go aboard to-day, but you'll hear of me if anything turns up. Don't run your head into danger, messmate. Let them there land sharks know of it, as I s'pose there'll be a c'roner's inquest; it's best to put it into the hands of them as understands sich matters; not that I knows anything about your long shore regulations, but it's the advice of an old sailor who sticks up for the rights of every man, and if Sam Hawkins can

help you he'll do it. Ay, damme! even though it's me own skipper I may have to run foul of.'

Filham saw the truth of the old sailor's advice, and followed it by giving immediate notice to the authorities that means might be taken without delay to discover those who did the deed. It was a matter that would require all the sagacity of the Deal authorities to sift, and measures were taken without delay to apprehend the individual who had so ruthlessly, though perhaps unintentionally, killed Tommy Filham.

Hawkins went on board his ship that day, some hours before he would have gone, that he might better his opportunity to discover how far he was right in his conjectures.

He was troubled by the curious circumstance, and felt more uneasy than he had ever been before. Never during his life had he been placed in such a position. Before he was rated captain's coxswain he had often cleaned his skipper's pistols, had loaded them while at Saunders's side, had, in fact, seen them more often than those he used himself, and therefore felt he could not be mistaken.

He was at a loss to know how to act. He, at times, thought it would be wrong to take any part in placing his commander in the hands of the law; then, on the other hand, he saw the desolate family and the murdered child. He remembered his oath, to unhesitatingly denounce whoever the person was who had committed the deed.

Thus perplexed beyond every degree of calmness, he wandered about the ship as though he was the only man aboard.

Captain Saunders had not yet embarked, and was not expected until seven in the evening.

Hawkins felt annoyed at this news; but on a little cool reflection thought it the most fortunate thing that could occur.

He and the captain's steward were warm friends. They had been companions on shore, and were almost as brothers. Hawkins instantly formed the idea that Fletcher would assist him, and he sought the steward.

'Did the skipper come aboard last night, Ned?' he asked, after having exchanged a few friendly words.

'Yes. Why?' replied the steward somewhat surprised at the suddenness of the question.

'Well, messmate, you'll know soon, only answer my question, without any tacking. What time last night?'

'Just before the fight in the Downs. He was looking frightened and exhausted, a cut across his face, and his clothes torn.'

Hawkins cut a quid and deposited it in his cheeks, and asked—

'Was he armed?'

'Yes, his sword; but only one pistol. Why all these questions?'

'One pistol!' excitedly asked the coxswain, not heeding the other's query.

'One pistol,' he repeated.

'Is it here?'

'No.'

'Can you get it?'

'I think so.'

'Do get it for me. Don't let the skipper know you want it—hide it for me till I return: and, without giving any further explanation, he ran up the companion ladder, went on deck, jumped into a boat and rowed ashore.

He first went to the house of Filham and saw the myrmidons of the law there, taking down

Filham's statement, and examining the pistol and cloak.

A long confidential conversation took place between the head functionary and the coxswain, and when the former left the house he took with him the articles for identification, and was accompanied by the sailor.

They went to the house of the chief magistrate, and from thence to the prison quarters, and a long debate was held between the head officers, and, when it ended, four men, the sergeant, bearing a warrant of arrest, and the sailor, issued forth, and an hour later they stood concealed by the darkness near the beach.

They had been there some time when the quick step of someone coming towards them roused the sleepy officers to a state of dignified activity.

The new comer was a naval officer. He approached very near, when a voice among the concealed group whispered—

'That's him!'

The executives made a rush — the serjeant, bloated out like a porpoise with importance, placed himself before the stranger, and said—

'Halt! in the name of the law! Are you Gregory Saunders?'

'I am.' And he drew his sword.

'Put that away, sir; its no use, there are six of us.'

'What want you?'

'You, sir. I have a warrant for your arrest.'

'On what charge?'

'That of killing a little boy named Thomas Filham, by shooting him through the head.'

Saunders reeled and turned a ghastly hue; the officers were upon him, he was held and hand cuffed, and led through the streets a fettered prisoner.

——————

CHAPTER XXII.

THE TRIAL OF GREGORY SAUNDERS.

A VAGUE, peculiar feeling of fear came over Gregory Saunders when he found himself a prisoner—and in the town prison. After the first shock was over, he had laughed the officers to scorn as they could not bring the indictment of murder against him.

For all that, he did not like his position; he did not feel so inclined to laugh it to scorn. By whom had he been charged? by whose authority, or upon what evidence, arrested?—questions he could not answer, and if any of his captors could, they would not; so he was left in an unpleasant state of misgiving.

Things connected with his past life came to his mind, and his cheek paled; the scene before the house in Lower Deal, with the strange wanderer and Gerald Stuart, still haunted him; although as yet nothing of real importance had come of it, it was a case of guilty conscience, and a dark secret hidden, as he thought, within the limits of his own black heart, haunted him, and he felt like a man about to be taken before a tribunal, and accused of forgotten, or perhaps unknown, crimes by phantoms, evil, mocking shadows that had come and flitted away in the past.

While deeply meditating, a last resource came to him—an only one. He was not prohibited writing to anyone yet. He therefore sent a messenger to Lord Harry Garthway, calling upon him to be his keeper and his judge, if he could not get him his liberty.

The admiral could not get him his liberty; but he sent a message demanding the prisoner, and had him conveyed to the flagship.

The Lord High Admiral went to speak to him.

'What means your arrest?' he asked, in a manner that puzzled Saunders.

'Have you not heard, my lord?'

'That is no reply to what I ask you.'

Admiral Garthway had heard, but wanted to hear what Saunders would say.

'I can scarcely tell you, Lord Garthway. Some absurd charge or other preferred against me by persons or person unknown to myself.'

'I will do all I can for you. Whatever you want ask for, and messengers are at your disposition, and we will settle the case to-morrow.'

Admiral Garthway left Saunders, then went ashore.

Gregory called the marine.

'Let paper, pen and ink be brought me.'

The man saluted, and retired The materials were brought, and Gregory Saunders sat down to write some dispatches or letters.

At the expiration of ten minutes, the sentry was summoned again.

'Send me a man who can go ashore for me.'

'Ay, sir.'

A sailor came—one of the liner's men. He entered the prison of Saunders, and when the door was closed, stood, cap in hand, waiting orders.

'You ill go on shore for me, and take this letter. If you see the man, bring him back with you. If he is not there, find out where he is. I know he is on shore, and don't forget my man that what you do for me I want you to keep to yourself. D'ye understand?'

'Ay, yer honour; yer wants me to haul up me jawing tackle. No fear, yer honour. If I'as to sail with secret orders, I'm not the lubber to break the seal afore the time.'

'Very good. Here's a guinea. You shall have four more when my business is done.'

The sailor pulled his forelock, made a scrape with his right foot, and took the letter, on which was inscribed the name of—

'R. ELFIN,

'Crown and Anchor.'

At one corner of the envelope was 'Private;' on another the word 'Important.'

The sailor went on shore and hastened to the tavern above named. The person wanted by the name of Elfin was not there, but mine host detained the messenger, and soon found the man required. He came swaggering in, and scowled upon the old tar—which was his interrogation of his business with the growl of—

'Hulloa!'

He took the letter, read it, and scowled more than before—from habit only—then he bent his dark fierce eyes upon the sailor.

' I'm to follow you?'

' Believe's so, messmate,' replied the tar, turning the quid in his mouth and eyeing Elfin mistrustfully.

Elfin was not prepossessing either in manner or looks. The sailor doubted him at first sight, and disliked him on acquaintance.

They returned to the ship, and Elfin was left alone with Gregory Saunders for some time, and when he left the liner he scowled perhaps a little more than was his wont; beyond that, there was no alteration in the man who as yet has been a stranger to the reader, but not so to many connected with this eventful history.

Gregory Saunders remained in a state of impatient anxiety for his trial; he felt a great deal of confidence in Lord Garthway, and he imagined an acquittal a certainty.

He did not pass such a miserable night on board the admiral's vessel as he would have done in the town gaol, and when the morning came he was fresh, and prepared to meet any charge—not only to meet it, but deny it; and the cynical expression of his face was strongly observable.

The captains and gentlemen arrived on board the admiral's three-decker, and the signal was given to commence the preparations for a trial by court-martial.

There was a great deal of bustle about it, especially as the liner was anchored in the Downs, and thus gave the men on many of the anchored vessels an opportunity to man the boats and loiter round the liner.

Any person that could possibly get access to the three-decker—either by creeping in at the hawseholes, or bribing the marines on deck—did so.

At nine o'clock the trial began. Gregory Saunders was brought in, and he evinced some surprise on seeing Captain Crosstree sitting there, no longer a captain but commander of the flagship, and rated to the rank of commodore. All this had been done by Lord Garthway, and when the brave sailor (Crosstree) recovered from his illness, he found himself a commodore.

The proceedings commenced; and, after the usual preliminary delays, the first witness against the prisoner was called. Polly Morgan was the one.

' What do you know of the prisoner?'

' Nothing, my lord.'

' Did you ever see him before that night?'

' No, my lord.'

' What do you know of the case?'

' That on the night of the seventeenth, my lord I was in the street before my mother's house—attracted there, as was most of the good folks by the noise of a fight and the firing of guns. I, like the rest, was eager to see what had occurred; but, when arrived at the spot, I saw—or, at least, could understand—nothing of the affair; marines were taking flight, and some sailors were carrying away a man who had been shot at; but the mist was so thick I could not see much.'

She paused to take breath, and regain her self-possession. The girl was modest and beautiful, and the position she found herself in was new to her.

' Proceed,' said Lord Garthway.

' I was standing with a crowd of neighbours inquiring what had occurred, as the leader or leaders of the party I heard called "rebels" strode away, when a man in a cloak stepped out from among a group of men. I saw him raise his arm, but the night was so dark I could not see that he held anything in his hand, though I saw him stretch it out'——

' Stretch what out?'

' His hand, my lord.' A bow indicated that she was to proceed, and she went on. ' I saw a blinding flash, heard a report, a scream, and then for a few seconds all was in terrible stillness—then everything was excitement and bustle. Poor little Tommy Filham had received the bullet in his head, and was killed.'

The girl became very much agitated at this point. The poor little lad had been a favourite of hers, and she had been loved in return with all the ardency of his nature.

Lord Garthway cross-examined her, and elicited a more perfect account of the child's death, which affected many of the gentlemen present. Those who were fathers themselves felt it keenly.

' Can you swear the prisoner is the man?' asked the High Admiral.

' I think so, my lord.'

' You cannot swear to him?'

' No, my lord.'

' What makes you think he is the man?'

' By his name, which corresponds with the initials on the pistol taken from him by my brother Jack.'

' When your brother Jack took the pistol, where were you?'

' Hanging on to the murderer of little Tommy, my lord. He struck me, but I would not let go his cloak. He would have killed me had not my brother Jack jumped upon him. The fastening on his cloak gave way, and I fell to the ground. By the time I got up, the struggle between Jack and him was over. Jack had got the pistol and a cut across the shoulder, but the ruffian escaped.'

' That is all you know?'

' All, my lord.'

' Very good; you can retire.'

Filham was called next, and he gave his evidence with the sound pathos of a suffering father and the truth of a man.

Jack came next, and was examined.

' You had a tussel with the man who shot the deceased?'

' I had, my lord; we fought when Poll had him by the cloak, and when he ran away, I ran after him, and we had another struggle; but I was wounded, and sailors came to his assistance, and he escaped.'

' Could you swear to the man if you saw him?'

' I could not positively swear to him, my lord.'

' Is the prisoner anything like the man?'

' Yes, my lord.'

' Can you swear he is?'

' I can't swear it, my lord. I would not wish to do so while the slightest doubt remains.'

' Then you have a doubt?'

' Men are very much alike Lord Garthway, and the night was dark.'

' Then upon what grounds had you Captain Gregory Saunders arrested?'

'I did not have him arrested, my lord.'

'Who did?'

'Another witness.'

'Let him appear.'

Hawkins entered; his hat he twirled in his hands almost nervously, and his eyes fell with an accusing stare upon Saunders, who went deathly pale at the sight of his coxswain.

Lord Harry Garthway saw the change come over Saunders, and he eyed him sternly.

'So you know the prisoner!' he said, abruptly.

'He is my captain, your most honourable lordship.'

'What are you?'

'Cox'n, my lord.'

'State what you know of the case.'

'I was ashore on the seventeenth, my lord, on leave, and spent the evening with some messmates at the Crown and Anchor; it was late afore I set sail from them to make my port. I knew the old party would be keeping watch for me, and made all sail I could until brought to by a gang of folks as barred my passage; while speaking with a stranger, I caught sight of Polly Morgan, as called by the good folks. I heard her giving signals of distress, and bore down upon her to see what was amiss. I had learned then, your honour, that a poor little fellow had been shot through the figure head by some lubberly pirate, and when the lass payed out her melancholy yarn, I was one of the first to go in chase of the pirate and her brother.

'Poor Filham was like anyone touched in the upperworks; he beat about like a Dutchman in a gale, and could not come up with the toe, nor could any of us—and when at last be hove-to, he could not keep his standing, he went down on his beamends and was conveyed home.

'Well, yer honours, I heard as how Jack and his sister—a brave little craft she is, too—had seized th' pistol and cloak of the pirate, and knowing so many of the gentlemen, I thought as how I could identify them; for yer see, yer honours, it was a cold-blooded deed, and my heart bled for the poor old people, who had lost their bright little lad in such a manner, and I felt as how I was a-doing justice, and I went back the next day, your honours, to Mrs. Filham's house, and saw the pistol and cloak. I knowed the fust, I thought, but couldn't recognise the cloak'——

'You knew the pistol?' interrupted Lord Garthway.

'I could swear to it, your honourable lordship.'

'Do you not think there might be two alike—I mean two pairs or more?'

'Yes, your honours, but not with the same initials.'

'Then you identified the weapon?'

'I—who, my lord?'

'Identified the pistol?'

'I ax pardon, your honour, but I only understands English—I—who?'

'Recognised the pistol—knew it?'

'Oh, oh! ay, ay! my lord, I did.'

'What initials did the weapon bear?'

'G. S., your honours.'

'Are the evidences here?'

'Yes, my lord.'

The pistol and cloak were produced, and examined, and darkened looks were bent on Saunders.

'Can you produce the other pistol?'

'No, your honours. Perhaps Cap'n Saunders will; as he only knows where it is.'

Lord Garthway turned to Gregory Saunders, and said—

'What have you to say to this charge?'

'A very little, my lords and gentlemen.'

'Do you plead guilty or not guilty?'

'NOT GUILTY.'

'Upon what grounds?'

'That of innocence, my lords. That pistol is not mine; I can prove it. That cloak never belonged to me, and I did not shoot the boy.'

'Have you any witnesses?' asked Garthway.

'I have, my lord.'

'Can you explain how those initials came upon the pistol?'

'Yes, my lord. The man who owns it is of a man that has the same initials as mine.'

'Who?'

'GERALD STUART, my lords—outlaw and traitor! Search the cloak, and see if it bears his name; and I have a witness who can produce the fellow pistol.'

'Let him appear.'

Some excitement prevailed now among the gentlemen sitting at the court. They scarcely knew what to think. All eyes were turned on the witness for the defence. None liked his appearance or his frown, and many doubted him before he spoke.

It was Elfin.

'Who are you?' asked the admiral.

'Rock Elfin, my lord—called mostly The Elf, or Elf.'

'What are you?'

'Once sailor—now fisherman. I was pressed on board the Golden Arrow, my lords, and served Captain Stuart. He was ashore on the 17th. I saw him and his crew. He passed me on the rocks, my lords, and dropped this.' He held up a pistol, the fac-simile to that which had been produced before. 'I do not know what made me pick it up, yer honour, but I did; and when passing through the town I heard as how there had been murder, and that a captain was taken up on suspicion. So I came aboard yesterday to see his honour, Captain Saunders. He told me to come to-day with the pistol, and I came.'

'You can swear to it?'

'Yes. It's Gerald Stuart's, and so is the cloak.'

'You know it?'

'Yes.'

He took the cloak, turned it inside out, and displayed a small elastic strap inside the collar, and on which was in full 'GERALD STUART.'

Dark as thunder grew the brow of the admiral. He examined the cloak. A short debate was held, and turning towards Saunders, the word—

'ACQUITTED!' rang through the ship.

———

CHAPTER XXIII.

THE PARSON AND CLERK.

SAUNDERS was free. The crime he had been charged with was now brought darkly upon Gerald Stuart—another sin added to his black catalogue. Rock Elfin was his accuser—the cloak and pistols were the evidence.

The Elf—as he was more commonly called—had turned traitor to his captain, though none could tell why. Perhaps for motives of his own; perhaps he aided Saunders for the same reason.

Nothing stood between Gregory Saunders now and his heart's wish—Madeline. The Lord High Admiral had given his permission for him to marry the lovely girl at once. He looked upon delay as dangerous to the interests of all parties.

Gregory Saunders watched Hawkins about like a panther. He meant no good to the man, and the coxswain felt it instinctively.

But Saunders worked out his evil in silence and in the dark.

Hawkins was coxswain still; his captain had never recalled the trial, or the scene at Deal in any way; but the old sailor knew it was not forgotten, and he was on the alert.

The Firefly lay off in the Downs—the Admiral's three-decker was some little distance off. The ship displayed no signs of anything like a celebration in any way; but the gun-brig did.

Among Saunders's many bad tastes was the one of show. He liked everything to be seen and known that bore any pomp or vain glory, and, in spite of the Admiral intimating otherwise, Gregory would make the marriage as public as he could.

It was to take place two hours hence, and many of Gregory's naval friends were to be present.

This was acting almost in direct opposition to the wishes, or rather the arrangement made by the High Admiral, but Gregory had a peculiar instinct, that of always quietly preparing against any unforeseen event that might jeopardise his life or his interests.

He knew too much of Gerald Stuart and his daring affair to imagine they would remain perfectly quiet while he was forcing the outlaw's idol into a hateful marriage.

He did not see by what possible means any interference could take place, but the many unknown sources from which the rebels obtained aid, gave him an unpleasant sensation about his heart.

There were boats of all shapes and sizes moving slowly about the gun-brig, or anchoring within a few cables' length of it. One little vessel, a lugger, attracted the attention of Gregory Saunders. It lay off on the weather quarter of the gun-brig quietly enough, but there was something in its position, the sails hanging loosely about, the ropes fastened in a manner that would require no trouble to undo them, they could haul up the canvas in a minute and be off, as it was moored by a rope-cable only.

One long cutter came direct for the brig and ran alongside.

The officer challenged—waited for a reply, and the new comers were ordered to board.

'For'ard, you lubbers!' called the officer; 'come for'ard, and help his reverance on deck.'

The sailors came forward with a broad grin on their faces. They saw a parson and his clerk making slow and laborious endeavours to get up the ship's side.

The men got safely on deck at last, and the sailors made way for them to pass.

The parson was, or seemed, an elderly man, with iron-grey hair, a pair of short whiskers, a little whiter than his hair; his eyebrows were shaggy, and of the same withered tint; he had been tall—was tall now, but for the stoop that brought his head forward and bent his back; he walked with the slow dignified grace of a servant of the great church, though his step was not so feeble as might have been expected, considering his age.

His companion was young, fresh-looking, broad shouldered, and had anything but a sanctified grace. In fact, the officer in the gun-brig mentally observed that he would make a better sailor than a parson's clerk. Perhaps he was right.

They went aft when Gregory met them. He did not exchange many words with the reverend father, as a great bustle on deck heralded the approach of the admiral's barge.

Had not that prevented his conversing with the churchman, he was too much excited by the coming great event to notice or talk with any one.

A salute was fired, the marines stood under arms, and the admiral came on board with his new friend, Commodore Crosstree.

The admiral was pale, and rigidly calm. Crosstree looked full of life and happiness, and he went to the poop to congratulate Captain Saunders on his good fortune, and so forth.

The admiral said but little; he glanced round upon the assembled naval men, and seemed slightly provoked.

'I did not wish this,' he said, when alone with Saunders. 'I did not wish it to be made a public show of. Why did you do it?'

'My lord, I was not aware it would give offence. I ask pardon. I thought, sir, Madeline would be less liable to hold out against our wishes when surrounded by so many strangers.'

'Lose no time, then; what is done cannot be altered,' replied the admiral, turning away.

Garthway did not look upon the matter in the same light as Saunders did. He was averse to strangers. The captains of his squadron witnessing forced marriage was not a thing likely to elevate a him in the eyes of his subordinates.

Strange it was, too, that the admiral had no real affection for his son-in-law. It is doubtful, too, whether he even liked Saunders as much as he did many of his young officers or commanders under him.

Gregory's friends could never perfectly understand the exact footing he held with the admiral. It was well known that Lord Harry stood his friend in many ways, and gave his daughter in marriage many said it was because Saunders, on the death of his aged father, who died covered in honours won in defence of his country, came to a large fortune, and, it was rumoured, Garthway married his daughter to the man who had the most money to keep her.

Those who were well acquainted with the admiral knew otherwise. Admiral Saunders had been Garthway's friend from boyhood's days. They had been mids together, had watched each other gradually rise, had fought for and helped each other, what one saw the other saw, what one supposed the other supposed, and so it went on until they grew aged men—were raised to the highest post of honour that England could give them, when Admiral Saunders died, leaving behind a son.

That son was Gregory. It was the dying sailor's wish that Garthway would look after the young man, who was the youngest boy and heir, the two elder having died. He wished him to continue the profession of his sire, and should he be worthy so much, asked Garthway to promise the hand of Madeline in marriage.

BLACK EYED SUSAN!

OR, PIRATES ASHORE.

'COWARD!' CRIED SUSAN, HER LIP CURLING SCORNFULLY.

9

Gratis with this Number the Fourth Sheet of Characters for the New
Play of the "RED ROVER."

This was all the dying father wanted.

He thought he had done all that could be done to make his son happy through life, little thinking the idol of his soul would turn out so unworthy of him.

'You will keep your promise, Garthway?'

'My old dear friend, I swear it!'

These were the last words that passed between the two old veterans.

Saunders died with his hand grasped in that of his loved friend; and tears ran from a fountain that one would have thought long since dried up, and fell upon the weather-beaten brow of the departed.

It does not seem such a mystery now why Gregory should be betrothed to Madeline, and there is no doubt that Garthway loved Gregory as a boy; but his affection had received the greatest shock it was possible to receive—that of disappointment: he was deceived in Saunders, and his hopes were blighted. Such a terrible disappointment altered Garthway altogether: *he* was the unhappy one, but he would not break his vow—the vow made over the dying bed of his true and tried friend, Admiral Saunders.

Admiral Garthway, stricken to the heart by the death of his friend, gave the required promise, and said he would look after Gregory as though he were a son of his own, and that Madeline should be his bride.

It is possible he would have delayed the marriage, and put Saunders to the test, to see whether he was worthy his daughter, had not the meeting between her and Captain Gerald made the alliance necessary to keep his name from dishonour, and his daughter from shame.

When every preparation was made, Madeline came upon deck with the pretty Black-eyed Susan.

Madeline was pale as death. Her lips were colourless, but her eyes shone with a light of fierce determination.

She cast her brilliant orbs round upon the assembled gentlemen, whose admiring glances she did not fail to detect.

'What mockery,' she thought, and her lip curled scornfully. 'They think it an honour that they witness a scene that should be the harbinger of happiness, little thinking the misery they would see brought upon me.'

When the parson came forward with his book, attired in his holy garb, her heart sank within her.

At first she had hope. She wondered whether he would go through the solemn ceremony against her wishes.

Then she thought whether he had any power to oppose her father. She felt he had not. She caught the eyes of the aged parson fixed upon her with a look of interest, and she returned his glance with one of silent supplication.

The longer she looked upon that kind, benevolent face, the more she seemed drawn towards the aged man, and presently a scarlet spot came vividly upon each cheek.

Susan seemed no less interested in the clerk, who did little less than devour Susan with his fine, expressive eyes.

Whether it was from the excitement of the trying moment, or the ardent gaze of the young churchman no one can tell, but Susan's beautiful bust rose and fell with great emotion.

The gentlemen were assembled. The quarter-deck had been fitted up for the occasion, and everything was prepared.

Lord Garthway dragged rather than led the beautiful Madeline to the small raised platform, where stood the parson.

As yet Madeline had not uttered a word, calm, cold, and passiive she was, and stood like a lovely statue.

Making the first preliminaries as short as possible, the minister said—

'Do either of you know any impediment why you may not be lawfully joined together in matrimony?'

There was a pause—a dead silence, and all eyes were fixed upon the pair. Saunders stammered some kind of a negative, when Madeline spoke in a voice, cold, but terribly clear and forcible—

'There is this impediment—our hearts are not and never will be linked together in the one and only lasting tie—love! It is a forced marriage, and one my heart, never—never will consent to'——

Surprise was manifest on every face but that of the admiral and Saunders. The naval gentlemen turned their eyes upon Garthway with a look that brought a flush of shame to his face, and he angrily said—

'*I* say there is no impediment; she is not over age, and it is *my* wish—who shall dare go against it? Proceed.'

The voice of the parson quivered slightly as he continued, and he could scarcely utter a complete sentence when he come to, 'Wilt thou have this woman for thy wedded wife?'

'I will,' replied Saunders, his eyes becoming fixed upon the old man with strange fascination.

The leaf of the Holy Book shook as though ruffled by the wind under the hand of the parson, as he went on, 'wilt thou have this man for thy wedded husband, to live'——

'Never!' came from Madeline's compressed lips.

'No! and damme, sir, if she shall. Avast! I can't hold out any longer! Make way, you swabs! Sky scrapers, and moonrakers, we'll see whether such a craft shall be taken in tow by that lubberly pirate! Haul off, d—— you!'

The effect of these words coming from the parson's clerk was astonishing.

Susan gave a shriek, and fell forward into his arms. Madeline echoed her cry, and started forward, as the supposed parson threw off his cloak, wig, and whiskers, and Gerald Stuart—the handsome, bold, young chief—stood defiantly before the shrinking Saunders, his long scimitar glaring before him, his arm round his beloved's waist and held to his breast, and his eyes flashing like burning coals, as he cried—

'No, nor shall she while I live! Make way. Ah! ah! you know me—Gerald Stuart, the rebel. Make way, or there will be blood enough shed to float this accursed brig in.'

'Ay, ay, haul off, you lubbers. Where's the man who'll stop Will and the smartest craft ever rigged—the pretty Black Eyed Susan?'

He, too, now stood out in his handsome uniform, and a long deadly cutlass grasped in a hand that knew well how to use it.

CHAPTER XXIV.

TREACHERY.

WHEN Captain Gerald and our gallant hero went ashore on the eventful night of the 17th, Bill Raker accompanied them for reasons of his own; and very good ones they were. Rough as he was, he had a kind of rugged fidelity to Captain Hatchett, and the knowledge of Captain Tom's peril while he was forced on shore, was enough to excite him on to hazard his own life to save that of his commander and companion.

He had given our hero to understand that he would not accompany their boat's crew, as he wished to have free liberty for a time at least, and he muttered—

'I shall rescue you, cap'n, or we'll swing together;' and he meant it.

A very little reflection convinced him that the Redbreast being towed under the stern of the admiral's three-decker, if it had entered the Downs at all, and to rescue the lugger and crew from the hands of Lord Harry was his first thought.

How to do it was as yet a mystery, and while he concocted a plan, he strolled on to the Crown and Anchor to consult some companions, and get their aid. It was work of very short time—he found men ready and willing to help him.

Having done this much, he appointed a time for them to meet, and went off to the house of Mr. Silas Doggrass, whom he found, as usual, at home, though not in the best of spirits.

Doggrass roused himself with a start when Bill Raker entered.

'All alone?'

'Yes,' surlily replied Silas; 'come in.'

Bill Raker did so, and made himself perfectly at home with Doggrass, and everything in the way of refreshment he saw on the table.

'Well, I s'pose you've heard?' queried Raker.

'What?'

'That your darling little craft, the Redbreast, is under Garthway's battery.'

'What?' almost shrieked Doggrass.

'It's true.'

'My vessel captured?'

'Yes—it's your fault, if you hadn't a-made Tom carry off your Sue, we shouldn't a-been in this plight.'

'Curses!' Doggrass walked the room excitedly. 'Lost—everything lost!'

'Not yet, Mr. Doggrass.'

'How mean you?'

'Well, such things have been as Robin Redbreast's flying away—even while under the cover of a sportman's gun.'

'Do you intend to try?'

'Well, Bill Raker's not the man to be spending his time among messmates ashore, while his captain's in the care of the enemy's jollys (marines). I intends getting at Captain Tom, if I can't do no more.'

'When?'

'To night. I came here to warn you of what had occurred, and to have the cellars below kept open, in case we want a hiding place.'

'Where is the girl?'

'Your niece?'

'Yes.'

'Well, the Admiral's taking care of her for you.'

Doggrass muttered a curse, and sat meditatively biting his thumb nail.

'Well, I must make sail now, Mister Doggrass; you'd better keep up, and on the look-out, though it's unlikely we shall want the underground den; still, it's probable we shall.'

'If you don't come back?'

'Well, you'll know our fate, anyhow.'

Doggrass left off biting his thumb nail now; and, after having swallowed a tumbler of wine, he paced rapidly to and fro, with his hands behind his coat tails.

There was not much fear of Doggrass sleeping while his lugger lay in the hands of the Government.

'Tom Hatchett,' he said, 'would never divulge our secret to secure his own safety.'

'Secret?' Bill Raker lifted his eyebrows interrogatively. He pretended not to perfectly understand his employer's meaning.

'Yes; he will not say who is *owner* of the lugger?'

Raker laughed scornfully.

'You fear for your neck, eh? You need not. Tom Hatchett is not the man to cry to get his liberty, even at the cheap price of your neck. Tom Hatchett told you, when he took the lugger, that in all cases he should act as though he was owner, captain, and everything else that was necessary.'

Bill Raker spoke rather more roughly than he would have done. Doggrass, doubting his commander, annoyed him.

Silas Doggrass, under the disguise of a respectable member of Deal—as one of the local functionaries—carried on his smuggling transactions to a very profitable extent.

He gave Captain Hatchett the Redbreast to do the illegal trading with, and had cellars large enough under his house to contain a city's wealth; thus he feared lest Tom Hatchett, seeing all means of escape impossible, would divulge the secret to obtain his liberty.

Tom Hatchett was a smuggler; but not such an unmitigated scoundrel as that.

'Good-night, Mister Doggrass. I shall make an attempt while the fog lies so low, and if I fail, why '——

'You'll hang,' put in Doggrass, turning sharply round.

'P'raps so.'

Bill Raker left the house not in the best of humours.

'D——d old shark!' he cogitated, 'to think he'd ever think that of gallant Tom.'

Retracing his steps to the snug underground apartments of the Crown and Anchor, he called his men together.

'Mates,' he said, as they gathered round him, 'it's hot work I wants you for. If we gain, why I'll make it a good night's work for you; if we lose we must take our chance. Take a moderate swig of drink, my lads, but don't have too much; I'll pay for it.'

A murmur, or rather a growl, of approval went round, and they drank success to the night's work, and health to Bill Raker.'

'Liquor up, my lads; time's running on.'

Ripe for anything now, the desperate fellows followed singly. Bill Raker and all of them met at the foot of the cliffs.

The mate of the Redbreast led them to a dark nook under the rocks, where a long boat lay moored. It was hauled up, the men got in, and a firm, steady boat's crew they made—nine in all.

'Now, my lads, give way.'

The oars fell with a simultaneous dip, and the boat shot ahead. Owing to the darkness, a man had to kneel in the bow of the boat to keep a look out.

Bill Raker knew exactly the spot where the

Redbreast lay, and steered his course without any trouble.

A small boat from shore was a too frequent occurrence to be noticed, especially as the pilot's galleys were up and down the roads every few hours.

Bill Raker noticed the unusual excitement that prevailed in the Downs, and guessed that Captain Gerald had been discovered. The lights displayed showed him that the admiral's liner had gone from its former moorings.

'Where is the Redbreast?' he thought. 'Confound the mist, I can't see a d—— thing.'

The boat still shot through the waters, and ere long, he sighted the dark hull of the Redbreast.

She was moored a little to seaward of an armed cutter, which was guarding three traders—two Indiamen, and one from Australia.

A little excitement prevailed among the men now, they were in sight of the lugger they intended to rescue.

It was a daring exploit, considering a half dozen men-of-war were within sight of them.

'Lay on,' said Bill Raker, in a low voice; 'muffle the oars, my lads, the jollys on the lugger's deck will hear us.'

The oars were muffled, and they continued to slowly approach the Redbreast. Bill Raker was vainly endeavouring to concoct a plan that would avert suspicion should they be heard, when a sudden firing broke out that echoed for miles around.

It was the engagement between the three king's ships, who mistook each other for the rebel.

This was an opportunity not to be lost.

'Give way—give way, my lads,' cried Raker; 'that infernal row would drown any noise made by us.'

A few rapid strokes, and the boat was alongside the lugger; the men kept from a collision, by placing their hands against the lugger's dark hull.

'Now, mates,' whispered the mate of the Redbreast. 'Look out, I'll sneak on board, and from a given signal from me, follow.'

With less difficulty than a monkey would climb a tree, Bill Raker mounted the lugger's side, rolled over the bulwark, and creeped along on his hands and knees to the hatchway.

He gave a grim smile of satisfaction; the engagement between the vessels off the Goodwin Sands, had caused the marines put on the lugger to guard the prisoners, to run aft, where they all stood leaning over the taffrail watching with great interest the fight, as they thought, with the rebels.

Bill Raker took from his pocket a large handkerchief, and let it hang over the bulwark, shook it for a few seconds and drew it up.

A head followed the handkerchief and the boat's crew began to ascend the lugger's side; every man on board then crouched behind coils of rope in the shade of the bulwarks, and under anything that would shelter them.

Bill Raker put himself in such a position that he could be heard when he spoke by all his men, and that by raising his head he could command a view of the sea.

'Mates,' he whispered, 'there are six marines to be overpowered, and it must be done in silence, and we are only nine to do——. Hist!'

They crouched lower still at his warning gesture, and he waited, straining his eyes to catch a glimpse of a vessel he saw coming slowly upon them, as he thought.

It was a long rakish barque he could see by the outline that loomed through the mist, and he wondered why it came down without displaying any lights.

He started, and gave an exclamation.

'Look out,' he whispered, 'here's a Frenchman coming down upon us. I expect she'll attack those Indiamen lying off on our stern. If so, we shall be able to have a scuffle.'

The men remained grasping their pistols and on the alert for any emergency. He stood up, hidden by the forecastle hatchway, and watched the stranger. Taking a night glass from the inner pocket of his coat, he watched every movement of the supposed Frenchman.

'They've hauled-to,' he said, just loud enough for his men to hear him.

'And they're up to mischief, I'll swear.' He went on slowly telling every movement made by the rakish-looking stranger. 'She's actually going to lower her boats'—a pause—'There they are—there they go. D—— if I saw such a thing; under the very nose of our men-of-war. Hush!'

The warning had scarcely left his lips when the men who had been looking over the stern of the lugger now began to move forward, when one spoke. Raker heard him say—

'I believe she is a privateer. Why, they are lowering boats.'

The marines rushed back, and tried to pierce the gloom with their eyes.

'We ought to fire an alarm.'

'Mates,' said Raker, 'Now's our time. There'll be a row, we had better be behind these gentlemen, and when the noise begins knock them overboard.'

With that charitable intention they sneaked aft, and crouched like cats over a mouse hole within a few yards of the unsuspecting marines.

The crisis was not far off. One of the marines, a little sharper than the others, caught sight of the pirate's boats creeping towards the traders, while the privateer sailed slowly down upon the armed cutter.

The 'jolly' fired his musket point blank at the nearest boat; the report roused the watch on the cutter, and the flash displayed to them the approaching enemy. The privateer fired into the cutter, and the boats boarded the merchantman.

The instant the firing took place the smuggler's crew came forward. One rush—a struggle—a few cries—then came half-a-dozen splashes, and the marines who had been put to guard Captain Tom and his crew were struggling for life in the water.

Swiftly had the daring fellows done their work, without bloodshed or loss of life—as yet.

'Take the wheel,' cried Raker, 'another cut the cable, and get under weigh.'

It was a moment of terrible excitement to them all. It was the time that would decide whether they escaped or would be captured.

Every man worked with a boldness and willingness that could not have been expected, even had the success of the daring exploit have interested them individually.

Bill Raker, with an expertness consistent only with the hazardous moment, cut the hawser, and the lugger drifted slowly along.

'Hoist her sheets,' he cried.

It was done; the canvass was set, a man kept

the wheel, and the Redbreast cleaved the water at a startling pace.

Bill Raker hugged the shore well, showed no lights, and thus escaped notice under the excitement that prevailed.

He saw Garthway's liner tearing down to the spot where the privateer was, and, laughing at his success and their blindness, he went below to see his captain.

Hatchett was down the aft hold, and Bill Raker had to take a lantern with him, and it was not without some difficulty he found his way and opened the hatch.

'Below!' he cried, when he had succeeded.

'Go to —— ! d—— you!' came up from the gloomy recess.

'Civil, anyhow,' laughed Raker to himself. 'That's what I call gratitude. Captain,' he called, aloud.

No reply.

'Captain Hatchett!'

'Shut the trap and leave me, curse you!'

'Ah! you are alive and kicking.' So saying, Bill Raker dropped quietly down into the hold, and holding the lantern in front of him, endeavoured to find his commander, by making 'darkness visible.'

'Cap'n—it's me!'

'Who?' replied a voice, the sound of which directed Bill Raker to the right corner, and the rays of the lamp fell upon Captain Tom Hatchett, looking pale and savage.

The light was too strong for him for the first few moments, and he had to cover his eyes with his hands.

'Come, captain—are you shackled?'

'Is it you, Bill?'

'Ay—ay.'

'Hold the light up to your face.'

Bill Raker did so, and Captain Tom Hatchett was able to see the welcome face of his faithful officer.

'Tip us yer fin, cap'n; I'm regular glad to see you again.'

Tom Hatchett did so, and, perhaps, had never felt a touch so agreeable in his life, as the genuine, friendly grasp of Bill Raker.

They had not secured Hatchett by chains, as many might expect, and Bill Raker soon set him free.

'How did yer do this, Bill? I thought the lugger was in motion.'

'I'll tell yer, cap'n, by-and-bye; we want all our time and words on deck; we ain't safe yet.'

'Have you freed the men?'

'What, afore you, cap'n? Not likely.'

'Then how did you get on?'

'Got a few hands from old Sharp-eye.'

'Ah! good. Come on, Bill, we'll give the king's men a warming now, if they try any d —— nonsense.'

The worthy pair hastened on deck, and saw the lugger still running before the wind at a very rapid rate.

'I thinks they miss us, cap'n,' said one of the men—'look.'

Tom Hatchett and Bill Raker did look, and saw a great confusion going on. Signals were being exchanged in every direction, and they saw a swift revenue cutter bearing down upon them.

'Get the lads up, Bill. Now my men hoist every inch of canvas the pretty bird will carry.'

Bill Raker soon had the crew of the Redbreast free, and no sooner did they appear on deck than they uttered a shout that rent the air.

'My lads,' cried Hatchett, 'that was indiscreet.'

The lugger scudded along; the men armed themselves, and in case they should be stopped Tom Hatchett had a red-hot shot prepared to hurl into the first vessel that should try to stop her.

'The breeze blows stiffly,' Bill Raker said; the night is dark, yet they seem to see us wonderfully well, and that revenue cutter follows, too, rather extraordinarily.'

'Yet we have no lights about,' observed Hatchett, mystified.

The cutter still followed pretty closely; and, what was more, several shots had been fired at the runaway lugger.

'We are seen by some means,' cried Hatchett, with an oath; 'discover the cause.'

One of the men accidentally caught sight of a glare of light on the waters; he looked over the taffrail and saw a lantern swinging about the aft cabin windows; he uttered an oath, pulled the light away, and took it to Tom Hatchett.

His brow grew black as thunder.

'We have a traitor amongst us—find the hound! By God he'll suffer, the skunk, he shall; muster up every man.'

Still shots were fired at them, and they saw by the cutter's lights she followed them.

Hatchett gave another oath.

'How is it? Who hung that light astern?' he shouted.

Before any could reply, Bill Raker gave a cry of rage.

Hearing the topmast creak more than usual, he glanced up and saw a blue light shining at the mast head.

With an oath he dashed up the rigging to haul it down when there came a report, a blinding flash, and he fell with a loud yell of agony to the deck, and the blue light still glared out in the night air, while Tom Hatchett and the crew stood transfixed with horror.

CHAPTER XXV.

THE YANKEE PRIVATEER.

IN the time of which we write, not only France carried on a maritime war with England, but America used to lay their clutches upon any vessel that happened to pass under their guns.

They had privateers, too, and they were somewhat more active than the French. The Yankee privateers were pretty bold: to wait outside a port and capture a wealthy trader as it passed was a matter of small consideration.

One was now cruising about in our waters with an indifference to our great navy powers, that spoke well of the commander's courage; or else it was conceit in his own powers that kept him there.

The one particular free sailer we now speak of was commissioned by the Congress to sail in our waters and make as many prizes as possible; not to engage an enemy of very superior force, as the Comet—the so-named privateer—was fitted simply for swift sailing and running fights.

Captain Nathaniel Ross was her commander

and a thorough fledged Yankee—a Yankee to the core, whose notions were based upon this li ne—'I guess and I'm a free born citizen,' a phrase he was constantly repeating, with a longer strain upon the disgusting nasal twang than even most of his race.

He was tall, with long, thin legs, big feet, lank, gaunt arms, with hands claw-like in the length, the nails were long, and from the wrist to the finger ends, scarcely any flesh could be seen; the skin was covered with hair.

His features were in keeping with his form, with hollow cheeks, sunken eyes, and a mouth that, when he laughed, his head seemed in danger of rolling down his throat.

The Comet was under a heavy press of canvass, and she skimmed over the waters like a graceful swan. To do them justice, few can build a smarter craft than a Yankee, and this was one of the smartest.

Captain Ross was on the deck with most of his officers, and the Comet was in its usual smart, fighting trim; everything prepared above and below decks.

'D'ye think we shall tumble in with a Britisher?' asked the first lieutenant of Ross.

'Guess I can't say,' replied Captain Ross, biting a piece of tobacco off a long roll he carried in his pocket.

'I should think we should run down upon one in these waters. It's the place I reckon,' continued Kimball, the first luff.

'Wal,' responded Ross, in his cool way, 'it's reg'lar sartin that if we don't get a tarnation good haul in the Atlantic, I'll cut off like a flash of greased lightning.'

'I guess a brush would do the boys good.'

'That's a fact.' This was another of Nathaniel Ross's stock expressions.

'This is a mighty smart craft, cap'n.'

'Smart!' echoed Ross, prolonging the word and his twang until none but those used to such language could have possibly understood it.

'Ay.'

'I reckon she'd go through the eye of a needle without touching.' Captain Ross ran his keen little eye over his fine craft with a glance of admiration. It is probable he thought it capable of performing the feat he had just spoken of.

'Deck ahoy!' came from aloft.

'Ahoy up there,' returned Kimball.

'There's something in the water, sir.'

'Where away?'

'On our lee sir.'

'Lee,' echoed Ross, scanning the dark blue waters. 'Younker, fetch my glass.'

A middy left the poop, and in a few minutes returned with his commander's telescope.

'Can you make it out?' called Kimball.

'I guess not, lieutenant; it's tarnation small.'

'Small?' muttered Captain Ross, raising his glass. It was a habit with him, as it was and is with many of Columbia's sons, to repeat the last words uttered by any person.

After a long scrutiny, Captain Nat lowered his glass.

'Now, my kiddies,' he bawled. 'Haul the beauty round and make for that infernal something. Be smart.'

Lieutenant Kimball, with some other officers, was vainly trying to make out the speck, which was only visible at every rise of the sea.

'Can you make it out, captain?' asked Kimball.

'Make it out?'

'Ay.'

'I guess it would puzzle Father Neptune himself.'

'Are you going to run down on it?'

'Looks mighty like it, don't it?'

'Certainly,' replied Kimball, in an apologetic tone.

'It's mighty fine to-day, luff; there's a reg'lar spanking breeze up. Let's try the Comet's speed.'

'Ay, ay.'

'She'll walk pretty smartly, Kim.'

'So I reckon.'

The snow-white canvas was hoisted, until the beautiful vessel seemed like a large white bird sailing gracefully, but swiftly, through the tinted waters.

The spray curled up the bows like crystal jets—at intervals dashing over the bulwarks and sprinkling the deck to the foremast.

Captain Ross was in every way delighted with the sailing qualities of his superb craft.

As yet, they could not clearly perceive what the floating speck was, though it was obvious to all that it was something that ought not to be allowed to pass unnoticed.

The glasses were at work again.

The Comet sped on, and the distant object became more discernible.

'It's mighty like a spar,' said Ross, glancing through his telescope.

'It's a funny shape, anyhow,' replied Kimball.

The second lieutenant—a young sailor of not more than twenty-two years' existence — was minutely surveying the mystery. He was possessed of very long sight, and he had a wonderfully powerful glass.

'Great Cæsar!' exclaimed he.

'What d'ye make out, Bunker?' asked Kimball.

'I make out, sir, something more than a spar there.'

'You do?'

'If it isn't the form of a man, I'm much out.'

'A man! You've mighty smart top-lights to see that!'

'I'll bet on it,' replied Bunker, with an air of assurance.

'I guess a bet is a fool's argument.'

'Great Cæsar,' retorted young Bunker, his face flushing angrily, 'you're tarnation polite.'

There is no other nation to be found where the people are so touchy as the Americans—a personal jest or unintended allusion is very often the cause of a serious quarrel among them.

'You're mighty quick, Bunker. I meant nothing.'

They were interrupted by the captain calling upon them.

'Lieutenant, I guess you'd better get the cutter's crew ready. I can make out the darned thing now; it's some poor cuss hanging on to a spar by his eyelashes.'

The Comet had gone through the water at such a rate that they were now almost upon the object of mystification.

By the aid of their powerful glass they could clearly make out a human form, but what it was floating upon they could not detect.

Captain Nathaniel Ross and his second officer displayed less excitement about the matter than any. He had the cutter's crew ready and the cutter prepared for launching, and then he coolly strode the poop, one hand resting on the hilt of his sword, the other playing with his long, red, pointed beard.

His little restless eyes wandered incessantly about, and he knew all that was going on around him, in spite of his apparent reverie.

'Now, younkers, up aloft, and furl the sails,' said Ross.

His orders were repeated by the lieutenant, and vociferated through the vessel by the juniors and midshipmen.

The Comet now lay gracefully upon Neptune's troubled bosom, and the cutter was let go from the davits. The men scrambled in, young Bunker took his seat in the stern sheets, Ross gave the word, and the men gave way.

They were within pistol shot of the ocean waif now, and all on board could detect a huddled-up form clinging like grim death to a floating barrel. Not many yards from the castaway there was a large and darker object, which Captain Ross made out to be a shark.

'Blazes!' he muttered. 'Lieutenant, veer the ship, and load the long gun. We must get in range, or its tarnation sartin Jack Shark will have a meal yet, by all the alligators of the Mississippi!'

Kimball bawled the necessary orders through his speaking trumpet, and the Comet moved slowly round until the long bow chaser was brought to bear upon the huge sea monster, which, innocent of the preparations being made to give it a pill of rather indigestible dimensions, moved sluggishly after the ocean waif.

'Got him covered, Kimball?'

'Ay—ay! cap'n.'

'Fire!'

A splash followed the report, and the water where the monster had been a minute before was dashed up to a great height. When it had subsided, and the smoke cleared away, all that was seen of the shark, was a long red streak that coiled round the floating castaway.

Young Bunker came alongside the poor wretch, whose pitiable condition touched their hearts. They saw a huddled up form clinging with the grasp of death to a floating barrel, fear, and the horrors of his position had distorted the sufferers face, and he looked horrible and ghastly, his eyes staring with a dull glare on the spot where the shark had been seen. His jaw dropped, and the colour on his sunken cheeks was that of a corpse.

'Great Cæsar!' ejaculated Bunker; 'if ever I saw such a dog-garned position for a man to be in! Look out, my lads; be careful how the boat strikes against the barrel.'

Five minutes more, and the wretched castaway was lying safely at the bottom of the cutter. The men pulled with a will back to the ship, and the castaway was hauled on board.

'Does he live?' asked Ross.

'I think so, sir.'

'Take him below, then; or it's pretty clear he won't live much longer.'

The inanimate form was conveyed below, just as the look-out reported a sail right on their bows.

'Stretch the canvass, my kiddies!' cried Captain Ross; 'let's see what the curs are made of.'

He hurled his well-masticated quid overboard, replaced it by a new one, and went below, leaving orders with Lieutenant Kimball to summon him when they had made out the stranger.

The deck was now left in charge of young Bunker, who kept the Comet at a fine running pace, and maintained a good look-out before the strange sail.

Ernest Bunker was very different to most of his companions on the privateer. He was a native of South America, and tolerably well-educated: had descended from a good, old, rich family—his grandfather having been a judge in Ireland; but in the last few years of his life, he had to emigrate for the new world, where he died, after bringing up a large and prosperous family. Ernest was the child of the old ex-judge's youngest son.

When he came of age, his father very quietly informed him his name was not Bunker, but O'Kelin, a revelation that considerably mystified the young lieutenant, and, like most secrets that could not exactly be understood, it was a source of great, though secret, trouble to him.

He was a well-proportioned young fellow, dark, with black moustache, and small pointed imperial, that greatly characterised his handsome face. He had, of course, the native twang; but it was moderated by his younger days being spent with a few well-bred and educated people.

It will be seen hereafter that this very brief and rough sketch of Bunker (so to be called) is not out of place.

He kept the vessel well on her course, and he had the satisfaction of seeing that they were nearing each other rapidly.

By the aid of his glass he could see the stranger was not a very swift sailer, or that she carried a cargo that impeded her progress.

She had no colours flying. The canvas was soiled, patched, and weather worn.

He was a young sailor, but an experienced one; he concluded directly the stranger had come a long voyage; everything bore an indication of it. She was an East Indiaman, he concluded.

'I wish I could see her colours,' he thought; 'never mind, I'll summon the skipper.'

Turning towards a middy, who was hanging half way over the bulwarks, and spitting in the water by way of calculating the vessel's speed, he said—

'Mr. Scraper, come here!'

'D'ye want me, sir?'

'Yes. Go below, and tell the skipper the stranger is approaching rapidly; it is in sight.'

The boy departed on his commission. He found Captain Ross sitting with his heels on the table, a glass of hot grog before him, and a huge cigar between his fingers.

'Wal?' was the greeting.

'The stranger's in sight,' said young Scraper, saluting.

'Made her out yet?'

'No, cap'n, she don't show her colours.'

'I guess it's likely she's got none to show. Wal, all right—skedaddle.'

Young Scraper took this graphic hint to depart, and scurried up on deck.

Lieutenant Kimball had joined Bunker, and they were making observations upon the distant sail, when Ross came forward with his slouching gait.

'She's a Britisher,' he said, at first glance, 'tarnation blazes. And unless I'm mightily bad off in my reckoning, she'll be a rich prize,' and he might have added, a tough one to get.

'Clear the decks, my kiddies, we'll give the cusses a peppering.'

The Comet was soon put in fighting trim, and a prime sight she presented to an observer—her low, dark hull, sharp prow, rakish masts, and clear decks; she carried twelve guns of very moderate calibre, and a bow-chaser—a complement of a hundred and thirty-six men, officers included, and sufficient arms for half as many more. She was about the most perfect model of warfare, speed, and grace, as ever was seen.

The stranger, seeing they were bearing down upon them, tried to get out of range. It was useless. The Comet was upon them, and within hailing distance.

'Ship a-hoy!' shouted Ross.

'Hulloa!'

'What ship?'

'The Lucy—Indiaman.'

'Lay-to, we want to come on board.'

'What ship, and who are you?'

'Look and see.'

Up went the Stars and Stripes, and a gun was fired.

The British sailors gave a cheer, hauled up the Union Jack, and fired a shot in return.

'Snakes and blazes!' said Ross, 'they'll show fight; there'll be a tarnation brush. Blaze away, my lads—blaze away, give it the cuss.'

His fire was returned bravely from the trader, and the crew cheered at every shot.

Captain Ross was getting in a rage, he did not expect this opposition.

'Prepare to board!' he shouted, 'look out fore and aft; look out my men—down, darn yer, down under cover, here comes a volley from the troopers on deck.'

The men crouched down under cover as a sweeping volley of musket balls raked the Comet fore and aft, and Captain Ross clapped his hand to his breast, with an oath, while the blood trickled slowly between his fingers.

CHAPTER XXVI.

BLACK-EYED-SUSAN DEFENDS HER HUSBAND.

DURING the time the mock ceremony of marriage was going on, the quiet looking lugger, spoken of before, let go her hawser, and drifted slowly towards the gun-brig, and when brave Will, unable to control his impetuous feelings, revealed himself, it had run almost alongside, scarcely noticed.

Captain Gerald found himself and officers in a more terrible position than he had expected. It had been, and was, a daring, desperate game to play, and none but the daring young chieftain could have done it.

It is doubtful whether even he would have attempted it had it not been that death was better —far better, to him than life, when his beloved was allied to a man she loathed.

He was driven to the most desperate fix now, but he did not despair; nor did the gallant Will. There was no retreating. They had dared much and must continue.

William had not gone so far as to look upon death as preferable.

His beloved captain and friend's bride was in danger, and his impulsive nature prompted him to dare anything. He would have gone through a burning frigate or den of lions, with as little thought as he had entered upon that daring scheme.

But now he could not be blind to the true peril of his position. After the first sudden shock had passed away, Admiral Garthway and the assembled gentlemen crowded upon them, and a body of marines rushed aft.

Every man on board was eager to prevent their escape, as, by doing such a service, they knew they would stand high in the Admiral's favour.

'Surrender!' cried Garthway, hoarse with passion.

'Never, my lord, while I have breath in my body,' replied Gerald. 'I have dared too much, to give in passively.'

'Surrender!' echoed Will, scornfully. 'I think you know me too well, to think I'd strike my colours to the biggest foe on earth.'

'Then cut them down!' thundered the admiral. 'Do not harm the women if you can help it; but stop them—cut them down at all hazards.'

'Look out men, fore and aft,' yelled Gregory, 'the rebels are upon us.'

Lord Henry jumped round, as a collision took place that threw some of the men off their feet. The Curlew lugger had dashed against the brig, and scarcely a shot could be fired ere the daring crew leaped on board, hacking right and left.

This brought every one into action, Captain Gerald tightened his grasp upon the lovely Madeline, and swinging round his terrific scimitar cut his foes down right and left. Will held Susan firmly to his breast, and followed his young leader's example.

It was very obvious they would have been shot down like dogs, had they not been shielded by the forms of the women.

Admiral Garthway and Gregory followed up Will and Gerald Stuart, but the few true and trusty friends closed round them, to aid their escape.

The stout, noble-hearted fellows would have stood there and allowed themselves to be cut down like blocks of wood under the wood-chopper's hatchet, if it would have secured the safety of their beloved leader and lieutenant.

'Fire into the lugger! Sink her!' Lord Garthway cried, furiously cutting away at the desperate body of devoted followers.

In spite of the fearful odds, they could not break the solid little square formed by the rebels, and while they were vainly endeavouring to do so, and the gunners were preparing to fire into the lugger, Gerald Stuart and gallant Will jumped on board.

Scarcely had their feet touched the lugger's deck, than a broadside was poured into her.

Madeline gave a shriek and sank to the deck. Will gave a cry of pain. They were both hurt.

The men hearing that their leader had boarded the Curlew, they did the same, followed closely by the enraged admiral, and his subordinates.

'No quarter!' he yelled. 'Cut them down!'

But when he caught sight of his daughter's lovely form stretched upon the deck, his cheek paled, and he uttered a cry.

Will, at the head of his few devoted followers, was striving to keep back the overpowering numbers, but he saw how vain it was. Not only had they the crew to contend with, but the gunners of the king's ship were battering in the lugger's side, below the water line.

'Will you surrender?' cried Garthway, 'I ask, for the last time.'

'Never!' replied Gerald, with terrible calm-

BLACK EYED SUSAN.

OR, PIRATES ASHORE.

THE INTENDING ASSASSIN.

ness. 'You have murdered my beloved, and I will die with her.'

He rose, picked up his blood-reeking scimitar, and standing over the motionless form of Madeline, fought like a Hercules.

Susan still clung to her gallant husband, who was foremost in the fight, and his reeking blade did fearful execution.

'Go below, my Sue,' he said, huskily.

'Never, dear Will, I shall be happy to die with you.'

Captain Gerald made his last stand. Now calling his few remaining men together, he placed them before his beloved, and at the head, with Will at his side, he fought over her, and seemed invincible, as did Will. Alas! their men were not. They were cut down like reeds. Six remained only, and that six stood up determined to fight to the last man.

The carnage was dreadful: the lugger streamed with blood. Still the merciless orders of Gregory Saunders continued.

'Cut them down!' he cried, when a shout made the blood rush from his cheeks.

'The lugger's sinking!' came from a dozen lusty throats.

'Stop firing, up there!' the admiral shouted through his speaking trumpet.

The order was too late—the mischief was done—they ceased working the guns; but the Curlew was already rapidly sinking.

Captain Gerald gave a grim smile.

'We can die together!' he muttered. 'Curse him, my hated foe! he keeps from my reach! Let me hold out until the lugger sinks, and they all shall go with us!'

But he began to tire; his brain swam, his eyes were covered with a film, a foam gathered about his mouth, and he felt he would sink exhausted to the deck in a few minutes.

'Do you surrender now?' cried the admiral, as the last of Gerald's men fell, pierced through the heart, with a pike.

'Never!'

'Nor I!' cried Will, springing forward, and driving his blood-streaming blade to the hilt in the carcase of the felw who slayed his last shipmate.

Ere he could withdraw his sword, a man leaped upon him, and, with one whirl of a marlinspike, felled him to the deck with a blow on the head.

Susan uttered a piercing shriek. She saw the enraged sailor, who stood like a fiend, draw his knife, and rush forward. She proved a brave girl, with a nerve of iron, in the time of need.

She did not swoon. With lightning rapidity she snatched up a loaded pistol, and, pointing it at the ruffian's head, cried—

'Touch him who dares!' Beautiful she looked, her hair all dishevelled and streaming down her neck, her eyes flashing wildly, her teeth set firmly, and her hand outstretched grasping the deadly instrument.

One of her tiny feet protected her husband's bleeding face, the other was resting upon the corpse of the last foe that fell by his hand.

The brutal sailor, in his fury, drew a pistol, too.

'Coward!' cried Susan, her lip curling scornfully, 'you've done what you'll never boast of.'

She fired—the man fell a collapsed heap at her feet, and ere another could take his place she held her position, with the reeking blade of her husband's grasped in the tiny plump hand.

It was like facing a tigress to face that infuriated girl. She looked like one of the forty furies—if we can imagine what they were like—ready to sell her life in saving her husband's.

'Hold, every man!' cried Lord Harry. 'Any one who touches that woman shall be flogged round the fleet.'

The carnage ceased now.

Not a man was left, save Gerald Stuart, and he stood wildly calling upon his foes to come on.

He still stood over the bleeding form of Madeline, and the blood poured from his scimitar in a crimson stream. His face was wild to look upon; his eyes were bloodshot, and rolled about in horrid glances; a thick foam was hanging about his mouth, and perspiration rolled down from his brow in large drops, and mingled with the blood upon his cheeks. His frame shook in his half-mad fury, and he called loudly to his foes to continue.

'My lord,' whispered Gregory, sneaking up, 'the lugger is going down.'

Gregory Saunders shuddered as he looked upon Gerald Stuart, and he kept out of the way, lest the young rebel should see him; and the very thought of having to face him in his present state made Gregory Saunders shiver.

'Let it sink,' answered Lord Garthway.

'But, my lord, you will go down with it.'

'Go to your duty, sir.'

Now the awful work of death was over, those who had been too willing to take part in it, turned away, sick at heart at the fearful scene—pitying the brave fellows who had fallen, their hearts touched to the core at the sight of Madeline and her lover, and their breasts thrilling with admiration for the beautiful Black-eyed Susan.

They could stand no more, and returned on board the brig, followed by Saunders, who had a vague sense of dread creep upon him while near the dreaded scimitar of Gerald Stuart.

'Rebel and traitor!' said Admiral Garthway, 'you stand alone! Not a man is left you! Look upon the bloody work brought about by you. I ask you again, will you surrender? If not, I will have you shot down.'

'Come, ye cowards!' was all Gerald would reply, in a hollow voice.

Garthway motioned for some of the marines to come forward.

'Stand in single file,' he cried.

They drew up in a compact line.

'Ready, present'——

A long row of deadly tubes were levelled at the gallant young chieftain's breast.

'Do you give in?' asked the admiral for the last time.

'Come on.'

'Cover him well, my men, with your muskets do not miss any of you. Now, Lieutenant Rice and Smaller, go and remove my daughter. Do not fear him. He shall be shot the instant you get her safely away. Make haste, sirs, move forward.'

Lord Garthway had some difficulty in speaking calmly. The sight of his lovely daughter touched him home. He thought how much she resembled her poor departed mother, as she lay there cold and motionless, and a choking sensation rose to his throat, and his eyes became dim.

He was by no means a cruel man, but duty was a stern law with him, and he would do his duty now to his king and himself.

'If,' he thought, 'my daughter is dead I will

shoot him where he stands; if she is not, and he won't give in—I will.'

The two lieutenants went towards Gerald, but slowly, they did not relish the business.

Rice, the more dauntless of the two, took a long boarding pike, and when close enough he struck Gerald's sword a blow that sent it whirling from his hand.

The tiger-like gleam in Gerald's eye deepened.

'You want *her*,' he cried, hoarsely. 'Ha, ha! come and take her.'

Swiftly he drew a long keen dagger from his girdle, and, stooping over the form of his beloved, he placed the point to her white breast, and said—

'You have conquered, but you'll never gain her. Another step, move hand or foot in any way that shall menace her, and you see her perish. We can die together; it is better than life, if we are parted.'

The murderous weapon was against her fair, beautiful flesh, and Lord Garthway saw he would keep his word.

He was nearly mad to know how to act, and to make his position worse, Crosstree said—

'Admiral, we are sinking; five minutes more, and we go down.'

'Oh, God! what am I to do?' gasped the admiral, 'he would not dare'——

'Would I not? Try, Lord Harry, try. Move a finger for your men to fire, and you see your daughter die.'

He was driven desperate. It was his last terrible resource, and he meant it.

Three minutes more, and everyone on board would be whirling to the ocean's depth with the ill-fated barque.

CHAPTER XXVII.

THE BLACK PLANK.

TOM HATCHETT uttered a fierce oath when Bill Raker fell from the rigging, and the crew gave a yell of rage. The mate of the Redbreast was picked up, and found to be bleeding from a wound in the shoulder.

'Are you hurt, Bill?' asked Hatchett.

'No, no, Tom; it's only a scratch. Don't let the fellow escape,' replied Raker, faintly.

One of the smugglers made a rush up the rigging; half way up he paused, for he caught sight of the shining barrel of a musket in a line with his head.

He thought of retreat; but others were coming up behind him, and he went up higher. His eyes were still fixed upon the cold, glittering tube when a blinding flash came before him—a deafening ringing in his ears, for half-a-second—a confusion of noise—a shrieking—a burning sensation came upon him — something hot entered his very heart; he gave a gasp, a groan, and fell quivering to the deck—dead.

There was no time given the assassin to fire again; men mounted the mizzentop from half-a-dozen different ways, and they caught the slayer of their companion, who was a marine—one of those who had been put to guard the lugger after it had been captured.

He was dragged down without mercy, and the green light was sent crashing from the masthead.

Captain Tom Hatchett waited for the shivering wretch; and the instant his foot touched the deck the captain of the Redbreast leaped upon him, gripping him by the throat; he would, in all probability, have killed the man there and then, had not one of the men called his attention.

'Devils of darkness! curse you! you'll suffer; hurl him into the black hole—put his limbs in chains,' he cried furiously; 'and let him wait until we are free.'

The shivering wretch was conveyed to the loathsome hole below the water line, his hands bound and his legs chained—there to await his fate whatever that might be.

He could not expect mercy, nor would he get any. His time was short to remain in this world, as he would soon discover.

Never had Tom Hatchett been in such a fearful rage as now. He could scarcely control his temper sufficiently to issue his orders. Bill Raker's wound was dressed, and he persisted in coming on deck.

'That d—— scoundrel! the sneaking hound! has nearly sunk us,' growled the exasperated Hatchett.

'He nearly cooked my goose,' replied Raker, 'curse him! I'd look over that, but to deliberately murder poor Jem, why'——

'He'll hang, by all the timbers of this craft!'

'He must have hoisted those lights.'

'Curse him! yes—to betray us.'

The Redbreast was making her way rapidly out to sea, with the wind full on her stern. She was a very swift sailer, and now that there were no lights to betray their position, the armed cutter was puzzled and could not follow up so smartly, and it was highly dangerous to fire at random, there being so many crafts about.

Poor Jem, as Raker had called the murdered man, was laid in his hammock, to remain until they could give his corse a sailor's grave with a little respect.

The revenue cutter followed on bravely, but the smuggler's lugger outstripped her.

'It's owing to that privateer, and the excitement caused by Gerald Stuart,' said Hatchett, 'that we got away like this.'

'Let this breeze keep up, and we'll soon have the bird clear of dangerous waters.'

As they ran into open sea they saw on their larboard, in the distance, signs of a conflict. The wind was blowing almost a gale, and Raker began to fear for the masts.

The lugger scudded along, heeling over, and going sometimes gunnel under water.

'Take my advice Hatchett, it's clear we shall lose a spar if you don't heave-to a little.'

'We must get clear o' that d——d cutter before we strike, or we shall be in for it.'

'Should the tops be torn away, we shall lose more by it than running a knot an hour less,' argued Bill Raker.

'It's so cursed dark,' muttered Hatchett. 'It's like sailing through a thunder cloud. If I could see what's on our track, it would ease my mind. Still—ready! lads, reef the tops, flying jib, fore jib, trim up the fore and aft square sail a little, —easy, easy at the helm, keep her well up in the wind.'

The men worked with alacrity, and the lugger went at an increased rate under her press of sail. She was a good barque, and hugged the wind closely.

'Does she make any lee way?' asked Captain Tom.

'No, she hugs the wind well. I think there ain't another vessel afloat as could tack like the

Redbreast, and that gives us another chance of beating our pursuers.'

'Ha! ha! Old Lord Harry will grind his teeth, when he sees we've cut our cable,' laughed Tom Hatchett.

'Ay! how nicely we cut off.'

'I thought I was going to see my last breakfast on board the flag ship,' said Captain Tom, recalling his captivity to mind.

'Not while you had a mate ashore,' was staunch Bill Raker's reply.

'Ay! I know, Bill; but how the devil did *you* get ashore?'

'I dropped into the Curlew lugger.'

'It's as well you did. Where did it take you?'

'That confounded Dafton run me alongside, and aboard the Golden Arrow.'

Captain Tom Hatchett faced his mate, and gave him a look of blank amazement.

'How the devil did you get on?'

'Well,' answered Raker, coolly,' I thought I was in a mess then. Fiery Will was there, and that good-looking young tiger, Stuart. He eyed the yardarm as a hint to me, and I took it. I felt skeered, cos, don't yer see, I hadn't found any good round lie to help me out o' the mess, but at last told him the liner had overhauled us. I pacified them by a lie that nearly choked me, to account for pretty Susan being on board, and when I said Lord Harry had them on the liner, their rage was taken from me to the Admiral, and so I got off.'

Tom Hatchett looked worried and enraged. The remembrance of Susan brought back many reflections of various nature.

At last he said, half aloud, 'It's as well I did not make an enemy of Will through it.'

'D'ye ever intend to try again?' queried Raker.

'I do.'

The mate of the Redbreast gave a whistle.

'Raker,'—Hatchett brought his hand down on his mate's shoulder—'I'——

'Ugh! Hatchett! Skyrockets! What a rap you gave my shoulder, cap'n! Whew!'

'D——n it! I didn't mean it, Bill. I'm a land-lubber to forget'——

'Haul up—haul up, Tom; it's all over now. Spin out the yarn my shout cut short.'

'Where did I stop? Oh! I intend to try again.'

'To get Sue?'

'To get Sue. Now, mate, we must stop our jawing tackle. Morn will appear soon, and, if I expect rightly, that d——d cutter ain't far off. We must look about us.'

The sound of strife had now died away. Nought could be seen save the heavy drifting mist, and the black rolling sea, which washed against the lugger's side, and billow after billow broke against the prow, and dashed over the deck

Lights were brought up now—the proper watch set, and the rest of the men went to their hammocks. Hatchett prevailed upon Bill Raker to go below.

The mate of the Redbreast went. His wound was still painful, and the loss of blood had weakened him considerably.

Captain Tom kept the deck now; he felt tolerably safe. With the instinct of a sailor, Hatchett took the lugger moorings, and made certain observations—only interesting to seamen. He used to get reflective sometimes—not that he had become sorrowful. Captain Tom Hatchett was neither a melodramatic hero, nor of that class of character always wanting to do right and being driven to do wrong. He was a matter-of-fact individual, but poorly educated, with good, seamen qualities, a very fair knowledge of navigation, a lover of money, and an inclination for excitement. As to his principles, they, perhaps, would bear less analysing than his past or present career. He had a notion of fairness in some things, and he was not the man who would take mean advantage of his superior strength over anyone. He looked upon smuggling as a profession, and if he took a fancy to anyone or anything he would not scruple at getting them or it. He believed in looking after 'number one,' and if any person wanted his service, and paid him for it, he would shut his eyes to all unpleasant sights, and close his conscience against right or wrong. He had a temper, too; and, when it was put out, Captain Hatchett was a dangerous man.

Now he was alone upon the lugger's deck, he was meditating upon the late events. He discovered he had a weak point—a very weak one. It was love for Black-eyed Susan; and he was concocting a plan to get her in his power again.

He never gave a thought to her husband, whom he hoped would get a spent bullet some day that would put him out of the way.

He was pondering this when the pale light of morn struggled through the thick, grey mist.

Scanning the horizon minutely, he was gratified to discover that nothing as yet could be seen in his wake.

The coming day brought with it unpleasant duties for Tom Hatchett to perform. His brow grew dark and his face surly, when he thought of the prisoner in the hold.

Captain Tom Hatchett was not brutal, but he would not overlook the cold-blooded murder of one of his companions. He looked upon all his crew as companions; discipline being very slight on board the smuggler craft.

'Call up the mate,' he said, to a man who was passing amidships.

'Ay—ay, cap'n.'

After having roused Bill Raker, the man passed forward, and bawled to his shipmates—

'Rouse up, ye lubbers, below there! Going to sleep all day? Tumble up, mates—tumble up!'

The men were out of their bunks and on deck in a few minutes. Bill Raker appeared, as the man at the wheel was changed.

'Wound any better, Bill?' asked Hatchett, wiping the damp from his face.

'Yes. I think it will be all right. Are we clear of the king's sharks?'

'It seems so. But the mist is still very heavy, and I can't see far. I expect we are. Haul up the lugger's course a bit. Poor Jem must be buried, and that —— hound shall feel what it is to play the spy and traitor!'

The Redbreast went at a very slow pace now through the waters; all hands were on deck and the murdered smuggler was brought up in his hammock which was to be sewn round him.

The men looked sullen and scowling as they beheld their dead mate, and a touch of pity could be traced in the hard lines of their weatherbeaten faces. Bill Raker appeared thoroughly savage, and Captain Hatchett's features plainly reflected the workings of his brain.

He was angered—calmly furious, and was determined to have revenge upon the slayer of his men.

'Bring the prisoner on deck,' he said, gruffly; 'Let the skunk see what he's done.'

The prisoner was dragged upon deck, and brought before Captain Hatchett, where he was held by the smugglers.

He wore the uniform of a marine, and Hatchett recognized him as one of those put on board the lugger.

'D'yer know why you are brought here?' asked Hatchett, firmly.

The prisoner's eyes wandered to the dead form laying stretched out near the mizzenmast; he paled, but did not reply.

'It strikes me you'd better make a clean breast of the matter, and spin your yarn without tacking. Did yer send those lights up?'

'Yes.'

'Both?'

'Both.'

'You're mighty cool for a man as will be food for the fishes.'

''Tis that which makes me so,' replied the marine, doggedly. 'I don't expect anything from you like mercy; I know you'll murder me—what can I expect from pirates!'

'Very well, you'll get what you expect, that's more than everyone can say. Curse you! why did you kill the man in that cold-blooded manner?'

'I wanted to keep my position.'

'To betray us.'

'To warn the ships you were escaping from?'

'You are making it pretty black against yourself—be careful.'

'Bah! What care I? I know my fate. It was a losing game from the first—life or death. When I was hurled overboard by some of yer, when I'd got free, I should, in all probability have perished, had I not climbed up a rope to the vessel's deck—had I been picked up by one of the man-o'-war's boats, there'd have been a court-martial and a flogging at the mast for letting you escape. So I did my duty and my best to betray you to them. When you discovered the first light I knew you'd soon discover me, and I was determined to fight for it.'

'Had you not killed the man, I should only have kept you prisoner until we were safe Now'——

Bill Raker interrupted the captain of the Redbreast by touching him on the shoulder, and drawing him aside, that they might exchange a few words unheard.

Captain Hatchett came forward now with an unreadable look upon his face.

'Do any of you know this marine?' he asked.

The men pressed forward and scrutinised the king's man from head to foot.

'I think I do, cap'n,' said one.

'Where d'ye remember seeing him?'

The smuggler considered for a minute or so, as though recalling some partly forgotten circumstance. The fog seemed to clear away from his memory, and he replied—

'The Crown and Anchor, sir.'

'Who with?'

'Myself, cap'n, and Jem, and a few others.'

Turning to the marine, Captain Hatchett fixed his fierce eyes upon him, and said—

'Did you recognise the man as he went up the rigging?'

'Yes—that is.' —— The marine paused, and hesitated.

'Did you shoot him from any particular motive?'

'What motive could I have?'

'How do I know? d—— you! I'm asking you.'

'No!'

'Did you know, Jem, at all?'

'Not that I know of.'

'Dash my toplights!' broke in the smuggler, who had been questioned by Tom Hatchett; 'hold fast, haul-to, cap'n. Damn me! I knows him now—the son of a sea-cook; let him say another lie as big as the other, and I'll choke him. He knows Jem, cap'n. I heard him swear to shoot Jem the other night, if ever he could get him. Don't deny it, you swab, or I'll choke you. Didn't he overhaul you when you'd been ill-treating as pretty a little craft as ever stood? Didn't he clap his grapnels on that windpipe of yours, and pour a good broadside into your darned figure-head, didn't he? Don't deny it, yer skunk; don't yer go to deny it!'

He did not deny it; perhaps he thought the smuggler would carry out his threat, and again, perhaps, the smuggler told the truth.

It looked very much like it; the man's look proved it, though, natural to the law of self-preservation, he would not condemn himself.

'That's enough!' furiously exclaimed Tom Hatchett, 'ye'll hang, d—— yer; it was a cool, cold-blooded murder; D'yer expect mercy?'

Captain Hatchett laughed a rough, dry laugh of mockery. 'Say yer prayers; ye'll walk the Black Plank as soon as it's rigged. Prepare the platform, my lads, for him, and two of you prepare the shroud for poor Jem; but he,' (meaning the marine,) 'shall go first. Let him see the work he did to the last minute.'

The marine looked round upon their rough, weather-beaten faces. If he had hoped for pity that hope vanished now. Nothing, save lowering brows and firmly set faces met his vision, and he saw in each determined countenance his death warrant. His cheeks paled, his head dropped upon his bosom, and he remained quiet—perhaps murmuring a prayer for his soul's forgiveness—perhaps silently cursing his slayers.

The smugglers did the work of rigging the Black Plank with great activity; they were anxious to get out of the waters they knew were dangerous to their safety—they were anxious also to avenge their messmate.

The ghasty-looking plank, with its sable coating, was rigged from the bulwark, and four of the smugglers stood by with loaded muskets.

A small platform had been raised on the deck for the culprit to walk up; at the foot of this platform they laid the corpse of smuggler Jem.

'Now,' said Captain Hatchett, 'bring the hound along.'

The marine was dragged to the platform, hoisted upon it, and then a piece of rope was produced to bind his hands.

'Blindfold him, he won't relish looking at the bullets as they come along,' smiled Hatchett.

'Mercy!' gasped the marine, unable to hold out any longer. 'Mercy! you dare not, you will not, you shall not, murder me.'

With all his strength concentrated into the one effort, he broke from his captors and leaped to the deck. He was like a madman: he fought and raved wildly; he snatched a hatchet up and howled in a voice that almost petrified the blood in the smugglers' veins—

'Come on! come on, ye cowards—murderers! I won't die—you shan't kill me—murder!—you shan't! Ha! ha! Come on.'

———

CHAPTER XXVIII.

STILL A PRISONER.

AT the very moment that Gerald Stuart placed the dagger to the motionless bosom of his beloved, and his foes stood looking on transfixed with horror, a strange, terrible reaction took place.

The form, so grand in its manly development, so powerful in its iron nerve, seemed suddenly bereft of all strength. The hand that held the dagger dropped listlessly to his thigh, his face turned ghastly pale, the eyes became dim, a foam gathered about the mouth, the handsome form shook with a few convulsive throbs, and Captain Gerald fell prostrate to the deck, motionless, powerless—swooning, or dead.

His dreadful convulsions—the short, terrible struggle—sent a chill of horror through the hearts of his foes; and how long they would have remained held by the lethargy, no one could tell, had not an appalling cry roused them to a full sense of their imminent peril.

'Off! come off! The lugger's settling down!' was the affrighted shout, and the slow sinking of the ill-fated barque gave an awful reality to the cry. None could doubt it then.

There was a wild rush to get on the brig—as jumping into the sea was highly dangerous, few could have kept up in the great whirl of waters caused by the foundering of the lugger.

Lord Harry Garthway leaped forward, clutching his daughter in his arms, and sped along the deck, and jumped from the poop to the bulwarks of the brig.

Susan would have gone down with her fallen husband, had not more than one brave fellow gone to their rescue. She had abandoned her position of defence, and, having thrown down her arms, she knelt by William's side and wept bitterly. She was but a woman after all; and now the excitement caused by the peril of her husband was over, she felt, and bitterly, the true horror of her position.

She would not move, or allow any one else to move her, until William was clutched by one of the officers who leaped to the lugger's side and on the brig, as the Curlew gave a terrific lurch that nearly threw the sailor who was carrying Susan off his feet.

He had just time to be dragged on board the gun brig, when there came a wild rush of waters—a roar, like that made by the pouring stream of a cataract—a cry from the lookers-on, and the Curlew sank beneath the ocean's depth, with a whirl that disturbed the sea for some distance round.

Great excitement was caused by the calamity. Small boats were hurried off with all possible speed to get out of the whirlpool; fishing smacks got out of the way; the gun brig was rocking like a cork upon the waves, and the sailors were rushing about on her decks in great disorder.

What number of wounded or maimed king's men had been saved from the Curlew were being hustled below to receive attendance, and their messmates were crowding round them to render what assistance they could.

The Lord High Admiral hurried to the chief cabin with his daughter, followed by the commander who carried Susan.

Captain Gregory ordered Will to be taken to the lower deck, where he remained, guarded by two marines, until he could be attended by the surgeon, who was pretty busily engaged.

His first attention was payed to Madeline, who had been struck by a flying splinter. Lord Garthway appeared very much excited. His face was pale, and his lips ashy—they quivered, too, as did his form, and his hand trembled as with the palsy.

The captains and officers, who had come to witness the wedding, seeing the serious turn things had taken, retired to their boats, and were rowed back to their ships. They left, out of delicacy, knowing their presence would only embarass, if not annoy, Lord Garthway.

Madeline came back to consciousness ere long, under the skilful hands of the surgeon, and her first inquiry was for her gallant lover.

'Hush! child!' said Garthway, excitedly; 'hush I will not have that name uttered in my presence.'

The old man spoke bitterly. His pride was touched—his family honour stained. It was a heavy blow to him. He would be a long time recovering from the shock.

'Have you killed him?' cried Madeline, weeping. 'Is he dead? Tell me! Oh, my father, tell me! Have you killed him?'

She sat up on the couch now. Her tiny white hands were clasped upon his arm, her two straining eyes turned up to his, and her pale lips quivered as she waited for the reply.

The admiral turned away, pained by the look of sweet supplication, and stricken home by what he termed his daughter's dishonour.

'He *is* dead,' murmured Madeline, in a tone of voice so chilling, so inward, that Garthway was startled.

'Come—come, my daughter,' he said, hastily 'I know nothing of—of—him you speak of. Return with me instantly. I cannot leave you here.'

He received no reply. There was no movement of the fragile creature at his side. She became a dead weight. The hands became a little tighter in their grasp. The eyes were fixed upon him with a stony, chilling, unconscious stare, and the lips were set like those of a marble statue.

'Madeline, my daughter.' Lord Henry spoke low and huskily. 'Madeline—God! how like her mother!'

The admiral's aged eyes became dim. His heart was touched. The one tender chord was struck, and he experienced emotions he thought himself incapable of.

Madeline had neither moved nor replied, and Garthway was aware that he spoke to an unconscious ear.

His daughter had swooned without any outward sign whatever.

Lord Garthway thought it wisest to have his daughter conveyed ashore at once, as he foresaw a scene should she come to her senses again.

The pretty Black-eyed Susan was with her.

She would have stayed with William, but Gregory would not allow her, in spite of her tears and heart-broken entreaties. The mean-spirited fellow only seemed to enjoy her misery until her persistance annoyed him and his spirit rose.

When he turned his back for a moment, Hawkins, the coxswain came forward and gently tapped Susan on the shoulder.

'Ax pardon, marm, but it's safest for yer to give

in; if yer would help yer husband, go ashore with the admiral's daughter. You'll find friends yet; I can swear to that.'

Susan saw the truth of his words. By going ashore, she might aid him; by staying, she might ruin him and herself, too.

It was a hard struggle for her to leave the ship without embracing her fond husband. She would not have done so—she could not; but Hawkins went below and heard from the surgeon that William was recovering rapidly.

She then tendered her services to Madeline; and the Admiral, in the excitement of the trying moment, never gave a thought to who she was. He felt too glad at having a female who could assist his daughter.

Black-eyed Susan did all that was necessary to prepare Madeline for a journey to her father's house.

She was conveyed ashore upon a litter—a post-chaise was found, and Madeline was driven quickly to her father's mansion, which was reached while she still remained in a state of insensibility.

Lord Garthway stayed behind to speak with Gregory.

'Have you the rebel Stuart, as well as that traitor William?'

'Gerald Stuart is not on board,' replied Gregory, with a malicious smile.

'What has become of the rebel?'

'I have made inquiries, my lord, and I can only learn that he was left on the lugger when she sank.

A look of great relief came over the admiral's face. The intelligence seemed to give him pleasure. He sighed deeply—a sigh as one would give when a great load is removed from a heavy heart.

'If I could believe it,' he thought. 'If it is so, what sorrow, trouble, and anxiety it would save me! She would forget him soon, and not have me to answer for his death.'

A doubt still existed. He could hardly credit that the man who had brought so much trouble to his house was thus suddenly removed from his path, and in a manner that exonerated him from any direct cause of his death.

'Are you sure?' he asked again of Gregory.

'He was, as you know my lord, senseless upon the lugger's deck when the panic seized the men, and they could scarcely get away with their lives. That fellow, William, and his wife were saved, I am certain. No one attempted to rescue the other rebel. The lugger sank swiftly.'

'And he went with it?'

'It is obvious that such must have been his fate, my lord.'

The admiral turned away, ordered his barge, and followed the litter containing his daughter to the house.

His last orders were, as he left the ship, that Willam should be strongly guarded and well secured.

Will was restored to something of his former strength, and then thrust into a loathsome hole, chained hand and foot.

'Caged again,' he muttered. 'Still a prisoner, and my captain, where's he?'

He tried vainly to recal the last part of the late fearful scene, but he could not. He remembered seeing Gerald Stuart fighting like a tiger to protect his beloved Madeline.

He was as yet ignorant of the lugger's fate.

William would have been at rest had he known what was the fate of his friend; but to be kept in a state of anxiety was torture to him.

He was guarded more now than he had been hitherto. His wretched pittance of biscuit and water was brought by a surly sentinel, who would thrust the repulsive food under the prisoner's nose, and retire without a word or look.

Two days had passed thus, and no idea was given him of when his trial would take place, or what they intended to do with him.

He wondered how much longer he should remain thus immured in the hold of the gun brig. Not one friendly face had appeared to cheer his dreary hours. He felt quite deserted—felt he was irretrievably lost.

The two days seemed a century to him, though the scene on board the lugger lived visibly in his memory.

He thought of his beautiful black-eyed wife, wondered whether she fell with him, or if she was a captive on his account.

He remembered the scene before he fell senseless to the deck; he recollected seeing but two or three of his brave followers left. His thoughts were torture to him. If he asked a question, he could elicit no answer.

While in this state of mental torture, one of his gaolers came with food. William watched him put it down, then scanned his face. This man had not visited him before.

'Messmate,' William said, in a low, hollow voice. 'If you've any feeling—any pity, answer me a question, mate, and with truth, as you wish for mercy from the Great Skipper some day.'

The marine paused, irresolute; he was not dead to all feeling of humanity yet, and the appeal made in a tone of voice so torturing, set his better nature at war with his callous sentiments.

'Mate,' continued Will, 'tell me—d'ye know ought of my wife—my Sue?'

'I don't know yer wife, 'xactly.'

'Where's the lugger?'

'Gone to Davy Jones's locker.'

'Where was my Sue, when the craft went down?' William asked, feeling his temples getting hot, and the blood rushing through him like molten lead—'where was she when I was shipped aboard this one?'

'Brought with you,' replied the marine. 'I remember now.'

'And—and—was—she—she'—

'Alive? Ay, mate, and kicking. Don't let your heart run into troubled waters about that—she's safe.'

The marine made his exit before William could interrogate him any further upon the matter.

He heard a long, heavily drawn sigh.

'Safe!' he murmured—'she's safe! Oh, God! perhaps it would have been better had she foundered with the lugger. I should have met her aloft with the Great Skipper; and now—she will live to see me *hanged!*'

Another sigh—a long, quivering gasp! It was from the inmost recess of his heart, and he buried his face in his hands. So he remained for a length of time—silent and motionless. He did not raise his head when a ray of light flitted across his dark, loathsome prison, when a heavy step sounded near, and the form of a powerfully-built sailor stood by him.

'Mate!' The word came from the intruder. It was spoken in a low voice, and a kind one. It sounded through the hold and echoed upon William's ear.

The voice of hope had found its way to the imprisoned sailor's heart, and he moved immediately.

'Mate!' repeated the new comer, 'it's a friend.'

Will raised his head now, and fixed his sunken eyes upon the sailor.

'I don't know you,' he murmured; 'why do you come?'

'I knows you, Mr. William. I may know yer more some day. I'm cox'n to Saunders; but I'm your friend. I'm here ashore while my cap'n's away, and I've news for yer.'

'You have, my friend! Good or bad?'

'Both, mate. I ax pardon, sir; lieutenant, I mean.'

'Nay, my'——

'Let me spin out. Your wife, sir—one o' the best of crafts, though I say it—is up at the house of Lord Garthway with his daughter.'

Will leaped forward and grasped Hawkins by the hand.

'This is true, mate—my Sue—my craft, safe?'

'Messmate,' replied Hawkins, solemnly; he seemed hurt by Will doubting him—'You're called rebel, assassin, pirate, and sich names, by my betters; you're an outcast with the law's brand on yer; yet I, Sam Hawkins, am your friend. What I 'says, is true—to doubt the word of an honest sailor is worse nor the cat.'

'Messmate,' Will said huskily, 'I ask pardon. Remember, mate, I didn't expect this. My Sue safe and well—well, say you?'

'Ay—ay! well, but you must let me spin out, or we shall be discovered by some d—— jolly, yer see. And I've got a paper with the news o' the fight in it, and it says, as how, when the lugger went down, Gerald Stuart was on its deck, immovable or dead, and he went down with it'——

'Hold! avast—avast! Oh, God! What my friend—my more than brother—my cap'n, dead—dead, gone down with that craft, and they let him go? Who says this—who dare'——

'I do, mate, and—and it's true.'

CHAPTER XXIX.

WHAT A WIFE CAN DO.

BLACK-EYED SUSAN did not leave Madeline even when they arrived at the admiral's house. Madeline had recovered a little. She recognised Susan; and, with some difficulty, articulated the one word—

'Stay!'

'I will not leave you, dear lady,' Susan replied. The answer was a tightening of Madeline's tiny fingers upon Susan's small, plump hand

Pretty Susan, like most persons brought up in a similar station of life, was a good nurse, had an excellent knowledge of ailments, and how they should be treated.

Seeing Madeline wished it, she stayed to nurse her companion, though her heart was nigh bursting at her husband's fate. It occurred to her she could render him more service by remaining with Madeline than she could otherwise.

A physician came to Madeline, and rendered what assistance he could. His opinion to Lord Harry was, that Madeline was in a state of nervous debility, that might prove fatal to her constitution.

'She must not, my lord, be worried, or made angry by anything. It is absolutely necessary that she should be kept very quiet. She should be strictly studied in every little wish.'

Such were the doctor's last words as he left the house and Lord Garthway to his own pleasant reflections.

Admiral Garthway was by no means a harsh or unfeeling man. He loved his daughter as a father should love an only child. His very affection for her made him so zealous in her welfare, and brought sorrow to his aged heart, as he thought disgrace and ruin would attend a continuance of her past misguided conduct with Gerald Stuart.

Many wondered why Gerald Stuart had become an outlaw. Few knew the real reason. Madeline was one of those few. She had known Gerald Stuart before he had become an outlaw—knew him as a fine, handsome boy, whom she loved as a playmate in her childhood, and their affection became stronger as they grew older. At length they were parted for a time—parted while she began to bud into the full prime of womanhood, and he fought his way up to honour and glory, in the service of his country.

She loved him more dearly during that trying epoch, waited and watched him ascend step by step the high, uncertain ladder—Fame. She saw him mount it boldly, fearlessly. He had nearly reached the top, then came a sudden, fearful change, the step beneath his feet gave way, and he was dashed to the bottom. He had toiled in vain; he could not remount, and he secluded himself from the world, broken in hopes, prospects, his future shattered to the winds, his name dishonoured, and himself ruined. Still Madeline clung to him—loved him all the more. Had it not been for that, his heart would have broken.

She knew he had been wronged; and though he was irretrievably lost to the world, she was satisfied to have him left her. Without him the world would be blank; with him she could live far away in some foreign clime, from the reach of the world's scorn.

The Lord High Admiral thought differently to this. He was an old, experienced man, and took things in a far different light.

He saw Gerald Stuart an outlaw—rebel—with a price set upon his head, and the gallows waiting for him—who would be driven away, hunted down, like a mad dog, and destroyed with as little mercy. He saw, too, this man ragging with him his only child—the last link left of his honoured family—taking her to ruin and dishonour, and placing a dark stain upon the escutcheon of his antecedents, and he would, if he lived to do so, prevent such shame falling upon the name of his revered family.

Whether Gerald Stuart had been driven into his present road of life, or whether he had gone into it from choice, the admiral did not trouble to discover. He saw him an outlaw—an outcast from society; and however noble his sentiments might be, he was a felon, and as such should be dealt with.

He felt himself bound in honour to give Madeline to Gregory Saunders—and they were to be married upon the first opportunity on shore.

He was anxious to see his daughter, and sent her maid up to know whether he could be admitted.

'She is asleep, my lord.'

'Let me be informed of her waking.'

'Yes, my lord.'

BLACK EYED SUSAN.

OR, PIRATES ASHORE.

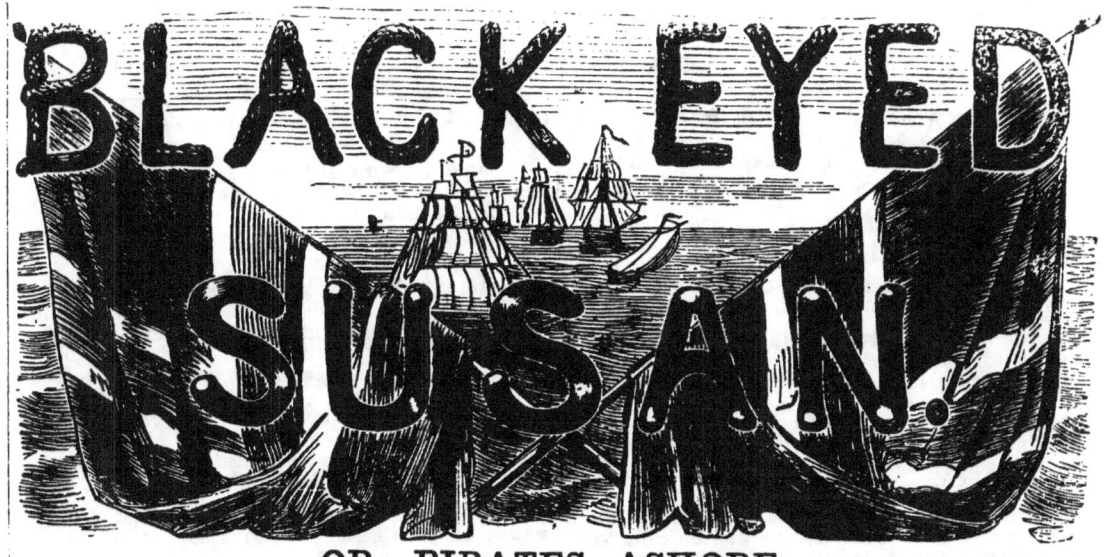

"LET ME GO TO MY HUSBAND."

11

Madeline was not asleep, but she feared to have any overture as yet. She was in a very weak state, and could utter only a few words at a time.

When she could speak, her first inquiries were of Gerald.

'Gerald!' she said, faintly, 'what has become of him?'

'Of whom do you speak, dear lady?'

'Of Gerald—your husband's friend and captain.'

Susan remembered then who she spoke of. In the excitement of her own troubles she had forgotten him. Now she recollected his gallant defence of Madeline. She had a vague remembrance of the last fearful scene when she was carried off the lugger with William. She had an idea of having seen Captain Gerald on the lugger's deck as she went down.

Her cheek paled as these recollections came upon her; for her heart sank with the misgiving that Gerald Stuart had not been saved from the wreck.

How could she break such tidings to the poor fragile creature by her side? But Madeline had watched the play of her companion's face, and she read there what sent the blood with a cold rush back to her heart.

'Tell me,' she implored, trying to sit up in bed, 'tell me what you know of his fate. Suspicion is only torture; let me know the worst.'

'Calm yourself, dear lady, and hope for the best. I know very little of Captain Gerald's fate. I can remember so little—everything was so horrible and dreadful; and the vessel sinking, too: and my poor husband, whom they tore from me. Nor was I allowed to see him.'

Madeline feebly took Susan's hand, saying—

'Tell me, dear friend, all you know and saw of the dreadful scene. Keep nothing from me.'

What had passed so lately was still vividly impressed upon Susan's memory; scenes she could not recal, without some emotion.

'You fell insensible while the dreadful work went on, and Captain Gerald fought nobly, like a lion, to protect you from the assailants. I should have gone to your assistance, but my husband fell, wounded, and would have been hacked to pieces had not I kept the infuriated sailors at bay. Oh, God! I shudder now at what I did. I dare not tell you, you would loathe me, and she covered her face with her hands.'

'Nay, do not fear to speak; I can imagine what you did. It was in the defence of him you love.'

'It was—it was! I fired the pistol I held, and, I fear, killed a fellow creature; but I knew not what I did. I saw his life in danger, the vessel sinking, and none but me left to help him. Every one of his faithful followers was cut up, and the lugger had then sunk level with the water. Lord Garthway had you removed to his brig, and would have had me carried there also, without my husband; but I would not stir until they had conveyed him on board—then I was torn away. Oh, God! the confusion and noise; the whirling of the waters; cries of the helpless, and shouts of the lookers on, as the vessel sank! Poor William was thrown into irons, and I kept near you, and thus came ashore.'

'Where was he—Gerald?' faintly gasped Madeline, turning upon her side, and fixing her eyes upon Susan.

'Pardon me, dear lady,' faltered William's pretty wife, 'if I say; I scarcely saw what occurred anywhere beyond the spot where my husband lay. Do not despair—someone conveyed Captain Stuart to the brig, where I daresay he is in captivity with my husband.'

'Would it were so! but I fear for him. I shudder to think what has been his fate, though it would be doing me a kindness to divulge it.'

'I know no more,' replied Susan, casting her eyes down.

Truly, she did not know what had become of Captain Gerald; but she remembered that when in that dreadful moment of excitement—when the rush came—when all on board tried to save themselves, she had seen Gerald Stuart upon the deck with no one near him. The same time then as he was conveyed on board the gun-brig and she caught sight—just one glimpse—of his pale stone face, as the water rushed with a mighty roar on the ill-fated Curlew's deck. The rest was a blank.

Madeline saw something of this in her countenance, and she sank back with a quivering sigh.

'My Gerald!' she moaned, 'my Gerald!' then she lay cold and motionless as death.

Susan bent over her and murmured her name.

'Speak,' she said; 'Oh, speak to me—look at me. Have my words killed you?' Her tears fell fast upon Madeline's fair, lovely face.

Then she knelt by her bedside, and still weeping, tried with such restoratives as were at hand to bring the sufferer to consciousness, and she kept imprinting burning kisses upon the pale lips of Madeline, and each time her efforts to restore her failed, she would weep afresh.

She heard not the room door slowly open, and a step pause upon the threshold. She was not aware the admiral stood there looking upon the touching scene, with an indescribable emotion in his breast.

He scarcely knew how to act. He wondered whether it would be right to thus abruptly break in upon such a scene; yet he saw his daughter lying there in a deathly stupor. Some change for the worse had come over her, and with a parent's anxiety, took a step forward as Madeline, with a deep sigh, re-opened her eyes and faintly murmured—

'Dearest, kindest friend, what should I do, left without such an one? Do not give way, I shall be better soon, and able to speak soon.'

Susan threw her arms round her neck, and kissed her pouting lips, now warm with the renewed circulation of the blood.

The admiral heaved a deep sigh of relief and paused irresolute; he recognised Susan, and a flush mounted to his cheek. The sigh attracted Susan, and she started up, turning her tear-dimmed eyes full upon the admiral.

'I ask your pardon, my lord, I did not know you were here,' and she attempted to dry her eyes, and she took a step towards the door, but Madeline said faintly—

'Stay.'

'Do not leave on my account,' said the admiral, with genial politeness so easy to a well-bred man.

He felt a little embarrassed, but not enough to show it. Approaching the bed side, he took his daughter's hand.

'My child,' he said, with dignified kindness, 'are you better?'

'So far as bodily health goes, my lord, yes,' she replied with an effort. 'It is the mind that requires a restorative, and a powerful one, or it may drag me down beyond all hope of recovery.' Clutching his wrist excitedly, she suddenly cried, 'Tell me—where is he—Gerald.'

A look of haughty anger came over Lord Garthway's face, but it passed instantly, and one of pain—acute mental agony—came upon it.

'Hush! my child!' he replied, with a slight tremour, 'utter not that name. Keep calm for my sake—for your sake—for that of your dead mother—your family honour, I beseech you! Ay, child! I implore you! I, your father, on my knees, beg you to forget that such a person ever existed.'

He sank upon his aged knees, his hands clasped upon that of his daughter, his silver locks falling back upon his shoulders, and his eyes looking imploringly into Madeline's.

She was mute for a time. How could she reply to such an appeal? Her brain was in a whirl, her senses confused. How was she to act, when her proud, aged sire, her only parent, was kneeling at her feet supplicating for what he had once endeavoured to obtain by force. It touched her to the heart, her eyes filled with tears, and they rolled in a silver stream down her cheek.

'Why, my lord, am I persecuted by a man I abhor? Is that honourable to the memory of my dear departed mother? Is my happiness nothing in the balance against *family* honour? Oh, my lord, my lord, rise.'

'Madeline, forget not I am your father. Why lord me? It is love for you that brings me here, Madeline, here on my knees. You are but an unsophisticated child yet; you know not the world's bitter scoffs and scorns you will bring upon yourself by such an alliance. You would live an outcast from society, and eventually he who dragged you to certain destruction will die upon the scaffold. Think, oh! my child! think of this, of your young life being blighted, crawling about on the earth's rugged surface, the wife of an executed traitor and felon.'

He broke down from emotion, his voice became husky, and his face excited. Susan had withdrawn from sight, out of delicacy.

'He is as the world or your disgraceful Government has made him. Nor can I exonerate you from a share in his downfall,' she replied, still weeping. Love for her father was not yet extinct in her heart. Certainly her affection would have been all he could have wished had not that hateful barrier stood between them. 'Tell me how you slayed him, how you' —— and her eyes blazed wildly, the tears for a moment were checked.

'I know nothing of him, child; repeat not his name.'

'I will. You must tell me what has become of him? Have you got him in prison?'

'No, child.'

'Then——then?'——she interrupted.

'He escaped from capture,' he went on. 'He escaped from me.'

'By death?'

'My child, I tell you he is *free*,' he involuntarily muttered—'ay, free from the persecutions of this world!' Aloud he went on—'My child, have I beseeched in vain? Mention not his name any more. I would be left in peace. Say no more. I will talk with you when you are better; at present remain quiet, forget the past scenes, and the past follies. Grant me this one wish, and you may not make one in vain. A father can do much for the sake of his child. Rest will comfort you.' He rose, kissed her pale cheek, and without giving her time to reply, strode towards the door. Ere he reached its threshold he started back with an exclamation. The form of a female was kneeling at his feet with clasped hands, and eyes upturned, with a look of earnest entreaty.

It was the pretty Black-eyed Susan, who thus knelt at his feet.

'What is it?' he asked, almost testily.

'My lord,' cried the supplicating wife, 'I ask you one favour, and hope, in the name of humanity, it will be granted. You have my husband in prison. If you cannot give him pardon, give him grace. Postpone his punishment, and mitigate the sentence. Grant this, my lord, for the sake of a young wife. Give me the power of seeing him. It will do much. I will exact a promise from him that if he be forgiven, pardoned by you, he shall discontinue his unlawful life.'

'You know not what you ask,' replied the admiral. 'He has the sentence of death passed upon him by a higher power than mine. I cannot recall it.'

'Father!' came from Madeline, who with a great effort sat up in her bed, 'be not hasty. 'Remember how much you owe her. She has been a sister—nay more than a sister—to me.'

'Hush! hush! my child, I do not forget, but I am not ruler of this world.'

'At least,' implored Susan, 'let me see him; let me go to my husband.'

The admiral reflected for a moment.

'Rise,' he said. 'I will give you an order to visit him—talk to him; see if he will petition his outraged Government. Let me know his ideas—conditions, if that is plainer—and I will do all I can. I will stop any further proceedings to the utmost extent of my power. I can do no more. The other portion rests with himself and my superiors.'

Susan leaped up, her hands clutched the flap of his naval coat, her eyes, streaming with tears, looked into his, and she sobbed—

'God bless you! God in heaven bless you! my lord.' Sobs choked her utterance, and Admiral Garthway put her gently aside, and left the room, his lips quivering with emotion.

When he had gone, Susan threw herself upon Madeline's breast, and then wept long and hysterically with joy.

Before she had composed herself a servant came up and presented her with a sealed letter. It was for Susan to see her husband, and to the commanding officer to keep William a prisoner on proper food and attendance until further orders were received.

Thus was William's life prolonged, and his hopes revived, for he felt that with time and health he would do the rest for himself. Susan kissed Madeline, and promising to return to the mansion after having visited William, she went off to the gun-brig to behold once more her heart's idol—her husband.

———

CHAPTER XXX.

THE TEMPEST.

DURING the time Lord Garthway had been with his daughter an incident had occurred in his house that, had he known it, he would in all probability have learned what a serpent he was nourishing to his breast in his adopted son-in-law.

Gregory Saunders, like all men of restless spirits—perhaps made so by an unquiet conscience—was ever prowling about, especially after such an event as had passed so recently.

He liked to know all that was going on, and for

that reason he strolled towards the mansion of Lord Garthway. He was, as usual, deeply buried in thought, and they run upon his ever-haunting subject—the poor wanderer whom he had seen befriended by Gerald Stuart.

That strange young creature seemed to strangely haunt him, and he thought so. At the entrance of Garthway's mansion he saw a lad looking about.

'What do you here?' asked Gregory, snappishly.

'If you please, sir, is this Lord Garthway's?'

'Yes. Why?'

'Then please, sir, I've a letter for him,' answered the boy, following Gregory to the door.

Saunders rang the bell, and a footman answered the summons immediately—the flood of light that streamed out upon the lad enabled Gregory to scrutinise him closely.

He started. He had a vivid recollection of having seen the boy before ; he could not remember where. Looking the lad hard in the face, he said—

'What is your name?'

'Jack, sir.'

'Jack, what?'

'Jack Murray, sir.'

'Where do you live?'

Jack, with a little hesitation, told him his address, with a description of where his house was situated.

Gregory Saunders started. This boy he now remembered well. It was the little fellow who had entered the house in Lower Deal, the one Gregory had marked with his sword point—the house containing the poor wanderer.

He was on the alert instantly.

'What can this boy want?' he thought ; 'what can he want with that letter? I must see to it.'

Turning to little Murray, he said—

'Come in. Go down to the servants. They will give you something to eat, while I get an answer from Lord Garthway for you.'

The boy went, and Gregory called a servant.

'Where is his lordship?'

'Up-stairs, sir.'

'Very good ; you can retire.'

Gregory Saunders entered the admiral's library with the freedom of one used to what liberty he chose to take in the house. Alone now, he broke the seal of the letter, which was well closed, and inscribed with the word 'Private' on the cover. Still he dared open it.

The first line brought a cry to his lips—not the nature of the words, but the handwriting. He sat, his face blanched with terror, as though he had seen a visitant from the other world.

His hands shook like an aspen ; his eyes started almost from their sockets, and his tongue clove almost to the roof of his mouth. It was some time ere he could summon courage to read the letter ; but fear of being discovered and questioned by the admiral, urged him on.

The letter ran thus :—

'Deal.

'To the Lord High Admiral,

'My lord,—For the sake of your honour, your daughter's happiness, and to prevent everlasting disgrace falling upon you, I send the following, to you no doubt an ambiguous, letter :—

'Beware of a fostered son you have about you—

he is as venomous as a snake—stealthy as a cat—dangerous as a wolf—and with the heart of an archangel ; take care, then, sir, keep your daughter from his clutches, or your name will ever live in ignominy. Marry your daughter to him, and she will be *no* wife, and he will have the crime of *bigamy* added to his number.

'Let this be sufficient. I am one who can only too well swear to what is here stated ; you will, see ere long the writer of this ; until then, I am

'A POOR WANDERER.'

'Eternal curses !' muttered Saunders ; 'It has come to this ! Ah, ah ! fortune seems to favour me My evil star has not yet fallen. Lucky star to direct me here just at this moment ! Had I not come,' he thought, his brow growing black, 'I should have been better under the waves.'

He shuddered to think what the consequences might have been.

'For him to know that I have a *wife* would be eternal ruin. She must be removed. I would not have such a barrier between me and my wishes not for ten lives. There is no time to be lost ; my measures must be taken surely and swiftly. I have enemies rising up in all directions. There is one gone. Ah, ah ! yes, Gerald Stuart no longer exists to oppose me—now for the other !'

He wrote on a slip of paper—

'Accept the blessings of a father and the gratitude of a gentleman. I have only one wish, and that is I might see my benefactress. The viper so long sheltered by me shall get his award.

'Yours, ever deeply grateful,

'GARTHWAY.'

This note was sealed up, and then Saunders rung for the boy—he came timidly to the door.

'Do you know who the writer of this note is?'

'I—I can find her, sir,' he replied with some hesitation.

'She wanted an answer?'

'Yes, sir ; I was to see Lord Garthway and get an answer—nobody was to see it but him, and he ought to have seen me.'

'Pooh ! pooh ! His lordship cannot be troubled with such little urchins as you. Here's a half sovereign for you ; run along, and say Lord Garthway'——

'Did not send it,' interrupted a cold, quiet voice. It was the admiral who had been near while Saunders interrogated the boy. Gregory stood as though stricken with the palsy ; his jaw dropped, and he felt that he would have given all he possessed for the ground upon which he stood to have opened and swallowed him up.

'What is this, Mr. Saunders? I would speak for myself.'

'My lord,' quivered Saunders, 'my lord—nothing.'

'A strange nothing, methinks. I will see it, Captain Saunders.'

*   *   *   *

Again on board the gun-brig Firefly.

To describe William's feelings when he heard the coxswain's account of Gerald's fate it would be almost impossible. All his excitement died away, he uttered no oaths or imprecations, nor cursed his enemies. The blow was a heavy one, and struck him home.

'My cap'n,' he mused, standing with his hands locked before him, his head bent, and eyes cast vacantly upon the ground, 'my friend, my skipper, my brother—and he gone. Oh, God ! I would have sacrificed myself ten times sooner. Give me the paper mate, I cannot keep my toplights clear from a mist, read the account out—read it, mate; I would hear all.'

Hawkins slowly read the following paragraph:

'After the bloody engagement was over Gerald Stuart, the rebel captain, swore he would murder the Lord High Admiral's daughter if they dared to touch him. Fortunately for the poor girl and his lordship, a strange fit of convulsions seized the would-be assassin, and he fell prostrate by the lady's side. At the same instant, those on board the lugger were warned of its foundering by the cry from the sailors and officers in the gun-brig, and directly a terrific rush was made by the conquerors to get on the man-of-war. They displayed great coolness, courage, and agility; not only did they save themselves, but William Howard, the rebel lieutenant, with his wife, was brought off. Lord Garthway nobly rescued his daughter. That was all that could be done in the time.' Ere a hand could be moved to save the wounded and dying, the lugger sank with Captain Gerald, the rebel leader, on its deck, and it is supposed he perished. Thus died one of England's greatest pests, and it is to be hope he finds that peace and mercy he failed to get in this world.'

Hawkins finished reading the badly-composed paragraph which had been, no doubt, scribbled down by a penny-a-liner who first heard the report.

'Then I have no hope,' said Will, sorrowfully. 'D'ye think it's correct?'

'Well, sir, as to its being correct, I knows he was on the deck when the lugger went down; but ye see there was plenty o' shore-boats sneaking around the crafts, and its my opinion he wasn't deserted in the scuffle.'

Any idea that conveyed hope to our hero's breast was better than the awful thought of his having perished.

'Mate,' said Will, looking Hawkins straight in the face, 'you say you'll stand by us?'

'Ay, ay, lieutenant, to the death!'

'Your hand, messmate. It's something to feel the flipper of an honest sailor in the hour of need.'

They exchanged a warm, hearty grip as Will asked—

'D'ye go ashore to-day?'

'I can get leave o' the luff.'

'Get it, mate, and make sail to the Crown and Anchor. You might discover something. If he lives and he can stand up he'll be there. Put this in your hat. He'll know you can be trusted then, and the brave lads will recognise you as a friend.'

William took from his jacket pocket a small golden arrow and gave it to the coxswain.

'I'll go, sir, and I'll do me dooty, whatsomever it may be. There may be a time when this arrow shall be my motter, and the sign above me figger-head. I must make sail now, or I shall be diskivered, and it would be six-water grog for a month—p'raps the cat.'

He went, leaving William alone, shut up in the narrow limits of his dark prison, to brood upon his future fate and that of his captain.

He was not left long to reflection. A marine came, preceding a visitor, who rushed forward with a loud cry—

'William!'

'What?' he cried, opening his arms. 'Sue—it's my Sue!'

He kissed her passionately, and she remained clinging to his breast, her utterance for a time choked by stifling sobs.'

'Oh, William!' she said, at length, 'I thought we should never meet again in this world.'

'No, lass, nor did I; but Providence hasn't deserted us yet, Sue. Tell me why they kept you away so long.'

Susan informed him of Gregory's harsh behaviour towards her, and he ground his teeth savagely. When she mentioned the admiral's kindness, his manly breast quivered with strong emotion.

'You are safe for a time, dear Will; and it rests with yourself whether you are free to live in honour, and win a name worthy you.'

'How, lass? How, my Sue? Let us have plain sailing. I'm not up in long-shore lingo yet.'

'Listen, then, dear Will! Listen without interrupting me, and I will tell you what I mean. The Lord High Admiral will give you a chance, and do all in his power to aid you, under the conditions that you will petition the Admiralty Board —that is, swear you will henceforth shun, or try to bring to justice, all malefactors; and that you will, if pardoned, live a loyal, honest life—that you will serve your country as you did once, my husband; that you swear to reform, and repent your past errors; that you would, were it necessary, as a duty to your Government, betray all those who uphold you in your outlawry. Then, my William, the pardon may be granted you, a new position given you, and a chance to wipe away the stain from your name and character.'

Susan paused, trembling with excitement, and she watched anxiously her husband's face.

He remained quiet, as though thunderstruck, for a few minutes, then stepping back, he said, slowly—

'Shiver my toplights, can I understand you rightly? D'ye mean to say I must go blubbering on my knees to those who drove me to what I am—that I must swear to betray him who gave me life? Oh, Sue, Sue! could you ask it—could you wish it? Sue, my good lass, my pretty little wife, do you forget who saved your life—who rescued you from a fearful death—who saved me from the yard-arm—who gave me and you, my Sue, means of support—who has been a brother to us? Would you hint at me turning traitor—hoisting pirate's colours, and go snivelling to those who set a sum on my life? Sue, you've pained me—you disgrace me. I answer, no! Never! Never shall it be said that honest William turned against his dearest friend, though death stared him in the face! No, Sue; you bring the red to my fore to think on't! I say again, never!—so help me heaven!'

Susan had expected this from her honest-hearted husband, but she was unprepared for quite so much determination. She tried again.

'Remember, Will, you lived long on the pay of your country. Do they deserve this from you? Ask your conscience, William—is it right to be fighting against your own flesh and blood?'

'Avast! avast!' cried Will, passing his hand across his brow. 'Avast, lass! those words go like a knife to my heart; but what can I do? God help me! I am doing wrong, Susan—wrong to my country; but they were the cause. But it shall never be said I wronged my dearest friend as well as my country. No, Sue; that would be double piracy. A traitor to both!—never! My life is not mine. My country would have taken it —Captain Stuart gave it me, and gave you yours. Mine is his, and in his defence will I lose it, sooner than turn double traitor. Avast! No more—no more, my Sue—a sailor never breaks his word to friend or foe.'

Susan sighed; but she was not dead to all sense of gratitude, nor was she so selfish as some might have been under existing circumstances.

Many would willingly have sacrificed the life of others to save their own, or one dear to them.

Like her husband, she remembered the debt they owed Gerald Stuart, and felt that she could only wait the issue of events, and trust in Providence.

Susan's stay with her husband was of limited time. That time had now expired, and she took a last farewell, arranging to come the next day for his final answer.

Night drew on now, and a rapid change was taking place in the weather. The wind blew high, the sea was being lashed into a foam, and the ships found it dangerous to move in some parts. Many lay to all taut, and with double anchors.

Commodore Crosstree was on board his vessel, and long experience had taught him how to prepare for what he saw was coming—an alarming tempest—and he issued an order for the vessels that were anchored below the Goodwin Sands to shift their anchors, and run out into the channel.

Gregory was not on board the Firefly, and after waiting some time in vain for his approach, the lieutenant sent a boat ashore for a pilot, and hoisted the lights and signals.

Scarcely had the boat touched the shore and the middy jumped on *terra firma*, than he saw a young man of remarkable appearance in the thick clothing of a pilot.

Coming forward, he said, with a haughty kind of respect—

'Is not that a signal for a pilot on yonder craft?'

'Yes sir, it is. I have come ashore for one. Are you of that calling.'

'Look,' said the stranger, showing his certificate.

'Very good, sir. Jump in, we have no time to lose.'

'You certainly have not,' replied the pilot, scanning the dark, threatening clouds that rolled in heavy masses above.

The pilot took his seat in the boat, and the middy was in the act of calling to the men to give way, when a sailor rushed to the spot, and shouted—

'Avast! hold on a minute, sir.'

'Who is it?'

'Cox'n Hawkins, sir.'

'Jump in.'

Hawkins jumped in, the men dipped their oars, and pulled briskly back to the ship, where they found the lieutenant anxiously striding the poop, impatiently waiting for the pilot.

He scrutinized the pilot closely; but there was no time to be wasted, and indifferent as to who the pilot was, so long as he was competent for the work and could undertake the responsibility.

'Are you ready, sir?' asked the pilot, going aft.

'Quite.'

Hawkins, who had been watching them unperceived in the gloom, now made his way below, and went to William, whom he found in a state of abject misery.

'Lieutenant,' said Hawkins, 'keep up, sir, friends are near. There's a storm coming on—a pilot's aboard to run the vessel away from the sands. *He* sent you this.'

William clutched eagerly at something held out to him by the coxswain. It was a small golden arrow, very much like the one William had given Hawkins, only it had one large diamond glittering like a tiny star near the barb.

'This!' he exclaimed, his eyes starting wildly, 'this was sent? Then I thank the Great Skipper for his mercy. *He lives.*'

The last two words were spoken in tones so low that Hawkins could scarcely hear them.

'I must go on deck, sir; a storm is brewing, and the hatches will be battened down. Do not be alarmed at anything you may hear. Summit, yer honour, might occur, as it has done afore, to open the tautest cage and let the bird loose.'

The coxswain, ere William could reply, left the hold and went on deck.

The vessel had already weighed anchor, and was going slowly out into a safe anchorage.

A heavy mist fell, darkling the air; the wind rose higher, the clouds sped along in huge threatening masses, and the sea was lashed into a foam.

Suddenly there came a crash, a distant rumble, a vivid flash, which seemed to quit the heavens like an electric streak of fire. Then came darkness, a moment's terrible pause; a second crash, which vibrated, re-echoed, and gradually died away. Now came the pattering of the rain, as it fell first in slow, large drops, then in a constant torrent.

The storm had broken in all its grand fury—the rain fell in torrents, rebounding from the vessel's decks and from the water to the height of two or three inches.

The loud roars of thunder came at shorter intervals now, and were followed by sheet after sheet of the electric fire.

Many were appalled by the awful fury of the tempest—the ships could hardly keep their moorings. Some were compelled to let go their anchor and beat about the Channel.

The Firefly, under the directions of the pilot, went slowly out towards the open sea. But as yet she had not passed the dreaded Goodwin Sands. This was the critical moment.

The hatches were battened down, all hands on deck, everything stowed away, and the sails furled.

The pilot stood on the poop with his trumpet, and the sailors rushed about here and there according to his orders. The lieutenant stood in a state of perpetual excitement watching, as well as the blinding rain and vivid flashes of lightning would allow him, the vessel.

As yet the pilot had not addressed a word to any one. He stood cool, as though going through a review; his face, which was singularly dark for an Englishman, wore a look of determination, and a set purpose was in his fine gleaming eyes.

'Look out, sir! look out, sir!' cried the lieutenant, excitedly; 'we shall run into some crafts ahead.'

A flash of light, of longer duration than any of the former ones, displayed some vessels being towed about right in their wake.

A deafening clap of thunder drowned the pilot's reply, if he made any, and something like a smile flitted over his face.

'Luff!—luff, sir!' almost screamed the lieutenant.

'Do so, if you can, with that amount of sail set,' said the pilot, ironically. Aloud, he called—'unfurl the skysail, and storm-sail. Let go her forejib a little more. Put the helm a-lee.'

His orders were instantly carried out; but the lieutenant became more terrified than before.

The vessel was rising swiftly to leeward—towards the Sands. He called to the pilot; but the howling blast drowned the sound of his voice. He moved forward, and a vivid streak of lightning, flashing right across his eyes, nearly blinded him. He staggered back, lost his footing, and fell.

The wind howled more furiously still, and the rain beat upon the sailors' faces. The helmsman was nearly blinded by the spray, and the electric fluid played round the vessel like a snake.

All was terror and confusion, and none was cool but the pilot. The tempest raged more furiously. The lieutenant regained his feet, and howled to the man at the wheel. Crash and flash—the vessel shook from the vibration of the air; the lightning blinded the men, it played round the capstan, coiled round the compass, and played upon the helm. Another flash—a long shriek of death agony, and then all was silent, save the heavy fall of rain.

What a cry of horror came from the crew! The man at the wheel had fallen a blackened, charred corpse, struck down by the lightning. The helm was deserted; the ship was tearing on in its unchecked course, journeying on to destruction, scudding furiously along, and direct for the fatal Sands.

Everyone was paralysed with terror. They rushed to the wheel; the pilot was the first among them.

'Back!' he cried, with a mocking laugh. 'Back, ye fools! What can save you now?"

One turn of the helm—the ship heeled over, the sails were blown away, her masts bent like reeds; she tore on, the water surging over her decks. There was a terrific shock, the men were knocked off their feet. The vessel was held fast, the roaring sea washed over the decks, and the wind howled like a thousand demons aroused.

The last the terrified crew had heard, as the ship struck, was a mocking laugh that echoed far above the roar of the storm, and a figure dashed from the helm.

The vessel was stuck in the dreaded Sands—going deeper each moment, and the men thought of those mocking words of the pilot—

'What will save you now?'

Ay, what will save them now?

CHAPTER XXXI.

THE ARAB.

THE British trader, was a harder prize than the Yankees imagined it would be. She was armed and full of men, and bringing some companies of invalid soldiers home.

The captain, a brave, cool Englishmen, and a thorough good sailor, was not one to give in without a struggle.

'A Jonathan, by jingo!' he said, when he saw the flag. 'My lads, shall we stand a brush? Remember the ladies and the wealth we have under our charge.'

'Fight, fight,' came from every honest old tar on board.

'So be it, my lads; we will fight.'

'Bring the guns up, my lads, load them to the muzzle, and let's see what a little British pluck will do.'

The four guns, all the ordnance the trader carried, were loaded to the muzzle, and brought aft to repel boarders. Every passenger took a part in the deadly strife, and all the soldiers who could stand up were called together, and put under the command of the officer—a young ensign who was compelled to return from India, on account of the climate.

'The poor fellows, in spite of their sickness, presented a good front; it was a long deadly line of tubes to face, and, as the captain remarked, if the enemy could be kept from boarding, they would give them enough fire to keep them down for a month.

He stationed the soldiers on the quarter-deck, that they might prevent the enemy from getting to the cabin where the ladies were.

A few of the youngest and most active men amongst the soldiers were brought amidships to help repel boarders there.

They managed to do so, too, most bravely. The Yankee thought to take them by storm. He was mistaken.

A seething volley was poured in upon his men from the passengers and crew amidships, which was followed up by the soldiers aft.

Still the grapnels were thrown, the two ships brought together, and the Comet's men made a second attempt. This time the four cannons were discharged, doing terrible execution.

They were followed up by a second volley from the soldiers, who worked bravely with their guns, and the young ensign stood like a hero at their head.

As the Yankees were beaten back, a bold, fearless fellow—one of the passengers—leapt forward, and unfastened the grapnels. The Yankee's vessel fell off a little, and the captain of the trader ordered the helm to be put head-a-port and the craft rounded off, leaving a gap of some thirty yards between the two vessels.

'Huzza! Capital!' cried the captain, in ecstacies. Beautifully done! Now, my lads, reload the guns, and we'll give the long-jawed thieves a warming.'

The sailors worked with a will, and the guns were reloaded. The young stranger, who had displayed such courage in unhitching the grapnels during the heavy fire, now strode to one of the cannons, a long brass gun.

With a quiet hauteur, he waved the sailor aside, and said, laconically—

'Fetch me the match.'

While the man went for the torch the stranger carefully elevated the gun, taking careful aim the whole time.

The match was brought. He took it from the man's hand, keeping his eyes still fixed upon the Comet, which was sailing round them, and, he saw, preparing a broadside.

He motioned for the man at the wheel to put the helm a-starboard a little; then he placed the match to the breech; a report, and the missile of death sped on its way.

A cheer from the sailors told its effect. The privateer's jibboom and figure-head was cut away, with all the rigging attached to it.

Captain Ross began to swear—

'Look here,' he said, 'I guess if yer don't give those darned Britishers a mighty strong pill, we shall get whipped to a certainty.'

A broadside that shook the trader from stem to stern was poured into her, and many of the brave fellows fell dead or maimed.

The passenger who had displayed such skill and courage quietly had the brass gun reloaded; and, turning to the captain, he said—

'Hoist what sail you can, and be ready to show a clean pair of heels.'

The sails were hoisted one upon the other until a good press of canvas was up. The privateer saw their intention, and Ross tried to run alongside again. He had sustained a heavy loss from the destructive fire of the Britisher, which was not yet out of the range of his guns.

The young passenger who had made himself so conspicuous, saw that more serious destruction would follow another such broadside as the last, and just as the trader began to move through the water, he fired.

It was aimed well; the shot took effect. It brought down the privateer's foretopmast—a little bit of mischief that brought her to with some little confusion.

Captain Ross swore an awful oath.

'Fire! fire! cuss ye!'

Much to his chagrin, the volley fell short, and the trader was scudding ahead at nearly eight knots an hour.'

'Bamboozled, by the furies!' cried Ross, looking after the trader with a half-comical air of amazement.

'Look here, my kiddies, rig a topmast and bowsprit—be smart—and we'll run her down yet.'

Captain Ross was not in a mood to give up his anticipated prize so easily, and he was determined to give chase, however great the distance might be between them.

Meantime the passengers and crew of the Indiaman were congregated on deck, their hearts elate with joy, and the lady passengers thanking their preservers with great fervour.

The captain mentioned how much they were all indebted to the personal exertions of the passenger, who still remained on the poop, his arms folded, and glaring with moody brow at the motionless privateer.

All eyes were turned upon him with some degree of interest, and many involuntarily uttered—

'The Arab!'

He was a man likely to excite interest in any one. Tall and beautifully built—such form as would have done justice to Apollo—with the strength of a Hercules. He was young, with a fine open countenance, large dreamy eyes, that burned with a soft, mellow light, but at times they were like the blazing orbs of a tiger. His complexion was not so dark as would be expected for an Arab, and many surmised he had European blood in his veins.

He had a kingly mien, and a proud, commanding air, that never failed to get civility and obedience. His English was almost perfect, his manners those of a thorough gentleman.

He received the fluttering compliments and gratitude of the ladies with dignified grace, but with an amount of coolness that told plainly it bored him.

The sailors gave him three hearty British cheers. He, of course, became now the centre of attraction; and even the late impending danger was forgotten in this new excitement, as he was privately termed by the ladies—

'The noble fellow! The *duck* of a hero! The beautiful Arab!'

The captain would have questioned him as to where he obtained his knowledge of seamanship, but seeing he looked anything but pleased at being so lionized, he refrained from doing so until some future period.

Captain Bingham gave a sumptuous dinner that day, with an excellent supply of wine, and the best things his stock would afford. The young Arab was asked to preside.

He declined with a graceful bow, at the same time thanking the captain for conferring the honour upon him.

'The fellow is a mystery,' thought the captain. Others thought so too.

While the passengers still sat over the table in the saloon, a man entered to announce that the Yankees had repaired their damages enough to give chase.

The captain, seeing the ladies looked frightened, rose, and addressed them calmly.

'Ladies, I assure you there is little or no danger to be apprehended from them now. We have had two hours good start of them, and you may rely the jury-mast they have rigged will not hold out long.'

This quieted the ladies' fears for a time, and they retired from the dinner-table. The young Arab went on deck.

The Comet was bearing down upon them at an unpleasant rate. The Arab fixed his piercing eye upon it for a few minutes, then turned away with a dissatisfied frown.

Captain Ross had lost no time in carrying out his intention of continuing the chase; and so soon as the mast and bowsprit could be rigged to bear sail, he put his matchless craft in motion, and, we must confess, it bore down upon the merchantman, hand over hand.

'Where's the man we picked up?' he asked, as the Comet scudded along.

'Below, cap'n.'

'Has he slipped his cable?'

'I guess not, sir,' replied the lieutenant.

'Can he come up?'

'I kalkelate so.'

'Let's see him.'

'Sneat!' bawled the lieutenant to a man who stood near the gangway.

'S—S—Sir!' replied the sailor, with some difficulty.

Sneat was an Englishman who had gone over to America some time before, and having nothing but misfortune, he wanted to get back to his native country, to do which he had to work his passage over. The poor fellow was afflicted with incurable stuttering—a misfortune that only made him the butt of his companions.

He was very good as an ordinary seaman—as the men used to call him "Jack of all trades."

Knowing the trouble he had to speak, he went down and told the doctor to send the castaway on deck.

He came—pale and feeble. He might have recovered more, had not the late firing been against him most dreadfully.

He looked a most deplorable figure, and Ross and the lieutenant laughed rudely at him.

'Great Cæsar!' muttered young Bunker; 'what an object!'

'Wal, my kiddy,' began Ross, 'and whe're yer from?'

'The sea, yer 'onour, I is.'

'What are you, and where bound?'

'I'm a cook's mate; me name's Jacob—I'm bound to serve on the Golden Arrow, I is.'

'Wal, and a nice-looking 'coon you are! Ha ha! I guess you'd make a halligator laugh. You're a mighty fine subject for a Britisher. What d'ye expect now you are here?'

'Nuffin—if you'll let me stay till I gets home.'

'Wal, I kalkelate you'll 'ave to be pretty slick

BLACK EYED SUSAN

OR, PIRATES ASHORE.

IN THE SHADOW OF DEATH.

and make yerself useful while yer stays. I guess you'd better mount the foretop and help the riggers aloft there. No idlers here, my man!—off you go!'

'Please, sir,' whined the Dismal, 'I never ain't been aloft, 'xcepting in Farmer Brown's loft, and '——

'Move off, cuss yer! and be slick, or, tarnation halligators! you'll get it hot!'

Fearing more violence at the hands of the privateer crew, Jacob went aloft, taking at least ten minutes to do so.

Night was drawing on now, and the privateer was near enough to see the trader's decks.

The wind blew in stormy gusts now, and some of the sails had to be taken in.

Captain Ross went below, leaving young Bunker and Kimball on deck.

Bunker was not in a very good mood. He had received a slight wound during the action, and that, and the loss of the prize, had put him quite out of temper.

He was startled by a shout from the man in the foretop, and Sneat came running aft, the picture of fright.

He paused before Bunker; his face undergoing the most painful contortions to behold in attempting to speak.

'Kuck—kuck—k——' he began, screwing and twisting his mouth about.

Bunker was usually the most patient with him; but, being out of patience to-night, he said, wrathfully—

'Sing, sing, d—— you, sing.'

Upon which Sneat bawled out—

'Jacob's gone overboard—overboard—overboard—Jacob's gone overboard — overboard—aha!' keeping time with his foot to the unmelodious strain.

In spite of himself Bunker could not help laughing outright. When he could control himself he said—

'Call all hands to the boats.'

Sneat forgot about singing out the orders, and began his usual contortions.

'Sing again. Great Cæsar! sing—that's the way to get it out.'

Sneat began to howl again with quite a serious face.

'All hands to the boats, my boys; all hands on deck; all hands to the boats, the boats; all hands on deck.'

He seemed quite to enjoy his own song, which set the ship's company in a roar of laughter.

'It's the only way to understand him,' said Bunker to Kimball. 'He can't speak under five minutes a word. He can sing; all stuttering people can sing perfectly.'

This is a well-known fact. It matters not how badly a person may stutter in talking, they can sing without missing a word.

'Put the ship back, and lower a boat to haul that lubber on board,' said Bunker.

The lubber—Jacob—would have long since been at the bottom of the sea had not one of the sailors thrown a plank over to him, which he clutched with the desperation of death.

The ship was put back, the cutter lowered, and Jacob again rescued from the deep. It was the cause of some delay, and Captain Ross did not forget to hurl a volley of epithets at the Dismal for his clumsiness.

'Crowd on all sail!' Ross called. 'Haul it up We shall lose her yet.'

Night's sombre shroud had now excluded the last blood-red rays of the sun, and only a faint glow of twilight struggled its way through dark clouds.

Captain Ross raised his glass to scan the Indiaman, which seemed to go ahead at increased speed.

Ross gave an exclamation.

'Tarnation devils! A darned pirate's running down upon her!'

The officers rushed to the vessel's side with their glasses, and by the last streak of twilight they could discern a huge, dark vessel running full upon the merchantman. The black flag of death was ominously conspicuous.

Captain Ross glanced up at his masts. They were already bending from the press of canvas, and the Comet went through the water like a racehorse.

'It's a mighty pity that daylight don't hold out,' Ross said, tapping his foot impatiently. 'Aha! Darned if I didn't think so! There they go!'

The loud report of distant cannonade came upon their ears, and echoed far across the dark, swelling sea.

Captain Ross spoke truly. A pirate had run down upon the unfortunate Indiaman when they thought themselves secure.

The Arab regarded the new foe for a few minutes in silence, and the captain of the trader was struck by the expression of his handsome face. He looked like a demon—his nostrils extended, his lips apart, teeth gleaming like fangs, and his eyes ablaze with a deadly glitter.

The sleeping devil was roused in him now.

'Blood will be shed,' he muttered. 'Let it. They shall not get this vessel without wading through gore to their ankles.'

Again the terrible instruments of death were prepared for use. He took them under his command, and waited patiently for the foe.

'Let me have a red-hot shot,' he said.

While one was being prepared, the pirate came thundering on. The black flag of death, with its ghastly emblem—its skull and cross-bones—was displayed visibly, flying at the peak.

A shot was fired for them to lay-to. Captain Bingham took no notice of it.

The pirate was almost within musket shot, and fired again.

This time the salute was returned.

'Put out every light. Do not let them see where we are,' cried Bingham.

The lights were put out, and nothing but the dusky canvas betrayed their whereabouts.

A murderous volley was sent from the pirate's hull; but, owing to the darkness, it did no material damage. As before, Captain Bingham had got everyone on deck ready to repel borders.

'Look out,' he called. 'They are upon us.'

Like a huge bird of prey the pirate swept alongside. The grapnels were thrown; but, ere they could touch, the young Arab fired the four guns from the poop and swept the pirate's deck.

Again the grapnels were thrown. They caught its bulwarks, and the vessels were swinging round to come broadside to broadside, when there came a crash and a roar that shook both the vessels.

Loud yells, cries, and curses came from the

pirate's deck, above which could be heard a voice, crying—

'Come on, my kiddies. I guess we'll give the curses a warming! They're caught both ways! Come on! Blaze away! Go it! Strike forward aft! Out with your bowies, you varmints! No quarter, my kiddies—no quarter! Give it the darned cutthroats!' and Captain Ross, at the head of his men, poured over in a living stream on to the pirate's deck. They were hemmed in on both sides. Escape was impossible. Death was terribly certain.

'Be quick! No mercy! No time! War to the death! War to the last man!'

CHAPTER XXXII.

A NEW FRIEND.

'MY lord,' said Saunders, every muscle in his body and on his face quivering with excitement and fear as the admiral stood holding out his hand for the letter, 'It is an absurd begging note; I will explain all when the boy departs.'

'Let it be so; and I hope you will do it satisfactorily.'

The admiral strode haughtily to his room, and Saunders breathed more freely.

'Go,' he said, 'to the boy—take back the letter, and keep your tongue tied.'

The lad went. He had a vague idea that something had gone wrong, and determined to keep nothing from his mother.

The admiral was not in his library, and Saunders' subtle brain went to work to devise some plan that would help him out of his dilemma.

He sat down at the table and hastily wrote a note, which he tore into shreds and scattered it upon the floor. This done, he had just time to rise from his chair and stand in a studied attitude before the fireplace when the admiral entered.

'Now, sir,' he said, 'an explanation would oblige me.'

'My lord,' replied Saunders, with a ready lie and assumed indifference, 'I took a note from that boy, and I confess it was addressed to you, but it being but imperfectly sealed, and judging by the bearer and the bad writing, I imagined it was but some begging letter; I read it and found it was from some destitute person in Lower Deal, whose husband had once served in your fleet. Knowing how much you were troubled at this particular moment, my lord, I enclosed a couple of sovereigns, as though from you, to the poor family. I did not wish to tell I had done this, my lord, as I wished them to think you had complied with their request. You already do a great deal, in fact, too much; I do a mere nothing for our starving brethren. I thought this an opportunity. There are the fragments of the note, my lord.'

He pointed to the shreds of paper on the floor. Those he had hurled there a minute before.

'This act does you credit, Gregory,' said the admiral kindly; his heart melted by the artful tale of the villain.

To better convince the admiral the cunning Saunders picked up some of the tiny pieces of torn paper, and placing them together, read a word here and there—such as :—

'Dying for want, your honourable lordship. He is starving—dying for want of nourishment,' and so on.

'Enough Gregory,' replied the old man; 'you had better stay here to-night, it is late.'

'I think, my lord, it is essential that I should go on board and see how things have been going on. About that fellow, William?'

'He must be treated leniently. His wife rendered my daughter a great service, and I was compelled to grant a short respite. I hope you will see that the orders she will produce are carried out.'

'I will, my lord.'

Gregory Saunders left Lord Garthway's mansion, but he did not go to the beach. A dark, subtle plot was at work in his brain. He felt he was walking on dangerous ground. He was not safe a minute.

He was wholly engrossed by the almost fatal occurrence of the night. He saw certain destruction staring him in the face, unless he found means to remove that terrible obstacle—the poor wanderer.

He went direct to the Crown and Anchor.

'I would be alone,' he said, returning Sharp-eye's greeting with a surly nod.

'Very well, sir,' replied mine host.

'Can you find Rock Elfin?'

'Yes, your honour.'

'Send him to me when he does come.'

Alone in a room, Gregory Saunders's evil brain went to work. Up to the last few months Gregory had had no cause to bring his evil nature out. What he really was, few knew. All his desires had been gratified; his prospects were very large and so forth, he could, therefore, let his dark nature lay dormant. Now they began to slowly peep out from behind the shallow surface that had so long concealed the wolf in his nature.

One can never tell what a man may be unless circumstances occur that bring both his good and bad points to the test.

When Saunders thought himself safe, and sure of the beautiful Madeline, and with the great fortune of the Lord High Admiral, he was content to live quietly, and assume a character best suited for the fulfiment of his desires. But now that he saw all his bright prospects about to be scattered to the winds, nature began to show itself.

He was now making a cool diabolical calculation in his own crafty mind.

'What chances have I,' he thought, 'if she should turn up now—all is lost—I am lost. Yet it will take a fortune to remove her. I must put mine in the scale with the prospective one. The chances are these,' he went on, holding up his fingers to better aid his calculation, 'unless I have that woman, with all other meddling persons, out of the way, Madeline is lost to me; the vast estates of his lordship and me are ruined, for I can see she is determined to bring about my downfall. On the other hand, should it cost me my fortune to get her out of the way, I could not only retain my character and my position, but there is another fortune, with her. It would pay me—that or ruin. I must choose. Bah! why should I think of the two? It shall be one, and only one. I will fight to the last, and let those who stand in my path, get out of it. I have repeatedly looked upon Madeline and his estates as mine, and the fiends themselves should not wrench them from me. It is the only course. It's a desperate game —at large stakes—it's worth the risk, even should I lose in the end; and it's worth the trouble to the gainer. No——'

A tap at the door.

'Come in.'

Mine host appeared with some wine, which he placed upon the table, and said—

'Elfin is here, your honour.'

'Let him come in.'

Elfin, the traitor, slunk in—the usual scowl upon his sullen face. He doffed his cap—if one can so term giving a cap a jerk nearly off the head backwards, and by the reverse movement, jerking it on again.

'I am glad you keep in the way when wanted, and that you can keep sober.'

Elfin favoured Saunders with a sulky stare, and growled out—

'Business is business.'

'That is undeniable; still, if you could manage to look a little livelier, and not let your voice get quite so affected by the fog, I should like it. The fog is very bad, I'll confess, and when you speak, your words are almost inaudible.'

'If my voice don't suit yer, Cap'n Saunders, don't have nothing to do with me.'

'Pish—quiet! I want you. I like you, and will pay for your services as they never have been payed for yet. That is very fair, considering I could hang you. Don't frown, you know what I allude to.'

'Yer can do as yer pleases,' replied the smuggler, with an indifference that surprised Saunders. 'I'm not the sort of cur to lick yer feet for my life; what I've done I'll do again; and when I'm nabbed, I can die game. Don't yer mistake me, Cap'n Saunders, I'll sell my services, and yer can trust me with any work; pay me for it, and yer need never trouble yerself about it after. It's a matter of business, and if I'm payed, I'm not likely to blow on myself, or anyone else. If I'm run down and captured, well, I am game to stand the weight o' my own affairs, which, if I do business, and am payed for it, it's no one else's.'

'I like your notions, Elfin. I can trust you, I daresay, providing I keep up to any agreement made by us.'

'Ay, ay!'

"Just so. Now, look here, Elf; you are not over flush with money; you havn't a boat that would carry a cask of brandy into port, and you havn't the means of getting one. I require your services—the work is desperate enough, and incurs great risk. Your neck is staked in the lottery, though I shall make every preparation I can to insure success. Should you succeed, you will possess a smart lugger and a crew; I shall give enough money to set you going. After my work is done, you can go to the devil, if you like."

The prospects of such good fortune actually brought a change in Elfin's face.

'Look here, cap'n, you'll find me a lugger?'

'Yes, a good one; and give you the means of getting men. The boat shall be well stocked with provisions, and armed with two guns, and small arms with ammunition for forty men—will that suit you?'

'Ay! I'll do the business, too. I don't care what it is—whether you pays for the *knife* or not. I'm game for anything that's business.'

'Here's money. Get a crew prepared for to-morrow. Be here to-morrow night at this time, or a little later. Meantime, I want you to put some fellow you can trust on the watch between here and —— street, Lower Deal.'

Saunders very carefully gave a description of the lad, Jack, who had brought the letter. He gave the man instructions to take from him any paper he might have about him, and prevent his going to the mansion of Garthway per force.

Elfin left soon after; Saunders remained at the Crown and Anchor until daybreak; then he left, followed by two rough-looking men and a girl of respectable appearance, pretty-looking, and tidily dressed.

They were not sufficiently near enough to Saunders for anyone to suppose they had any connection with him.

He walked briskly along, making his way through Lower Deal, until he came to the house, the door of which he had marked with a cross.

He walked close to the house, and paused so near the door, that a pocket handkerchief he dropped, fell upon the very step the poor wanderer had crouched upon the night Gerald Stuart saved her from dying for want.

Evidently he did not perceive he had lost his kerchief, for he strode on without looking right or left. He went straight on until he came to the door of a small beer-house almost opposite the spot where he dropped his handkerchief.

At the door of the beer-house he turned round, and fixed his eyes steadily upon one of the rough-looking men, who exchanged an almost imperceptible sign with him.

Then the ruffians began talking in a loud voice. One picked up the handkerchief. Shortly after a great dispute arose. The girl's voice was heard above all.

A serious quarrel seemed to take place between the three. The two ruffians began to bully the girl most shamefully. Words came to blows, though for what it is impossible to say.

The girl screamed 'Murder!' to the highest pitch of her voice. People began to thrust their heads out of the window. The ruffians continued to ill-treat the girl, who screamed for help much louder.

Little Jack—the boy whom Gerald had seen when he put the poor castaway in the care of the poor family—came running down-stairs, and opened the door, just as the girl was thrust against it, and, with a shriek, she fell into the passage.

'Cowards!' cried the brave little fellow, leaping forward and protecting the girl by placing himself between her and her brutal persecutors. 'Father! father! help! Here's some one being killed!'

The two ruffians did not wait for anyone else to come; they were satisfied with their work, and took to flight, as Jack's mother came rushing upon the scene of action, flourishing a huge rolling-pin in her hand.

'Where's the wretches?' she cried.

'They're gone, mother,' said Jack. 'But look at the poor girl; she's fainted, she has.'

'Poor creature; help me to lift her in, Jack.'

Jack rendered the required assistance, and the girl was taken into the little parlour, which had become wonderfully comfortable since the poor wanderer had remained with them.

Jack evinced some surprise when his mother began to restore the girl, to see she bore no signs of the late ill-treatment. Young as he was he thought it strange.

He fancied the girl came to her senses rather more quickly than was consistent with the strange treatment she had received.

Little Jack was a very shrewd boy for his age; he had, in the few years of his life, seen a greater insight into character, than many twice his age. He gave way to thinking, deeply too. He had a strange way of calculating upon passing events.

He would construct things that older people could see nothing constructive in whatever.

His juvenile brain was at work now.

'Why,' he wondered, 'did the girl faint. She was not hurt that I could see; and wasn't it funny she should have fainted in *our* door-way?'

His musings were cut short here by his mother calling him.

'Jack,' she said, 'go and fetch something for this poor girl, something that will give her strength.'

'Brandy, mother?'

'Yes, Jack.'

Jack went. The beershop nearly opposite Jack's house did not retail spirits, still he went in. The truth is he caught sight of a fur cap; it bore a resemblance to one he had seen when the girl fell back in the passage. Jack was curious to know more of the cap.

He rushed in, put a bottle on the counter, and called for a quartern of brandy.

'Don't sell it,' came from a stout personage behind the bar.

'Eh?'

'Don't sell it.'

'Oh! ah! yes, I had forgot.' The bottle was snatched up from the bar, the lad cast another look round towards the fur cap, and departed.

He had seen all he required. The fur cap did belong to a head he had seen—one of the men he had faced a short time since. What struck him as most peculiar with this man, and his companion was a naval officer. The boy recognised him as Gregory Saunders.

Jack made all haste home, and going mysteriously to his mother, said—

'I've seen something, mother?'

'Seen what, Jack?' The parent was in a back bedroom on the first floor of the house, attending to an invalid.

'Them two men, mother.'

'Which, Jack? What are you talking about?'

Jack was on the small landing, his nose against the crack of the bedroom door. He said—

'May I come in?'

'Yes.'

He entered, but kept a long way from the bed, on which lay a beautiful woman. Her complexion was so dark it was impossible to say whether she was foreign or not.

She spoke to Jack faintly but kindly, and he bashfully approached her couch.

'What,' she asked, smiling painfully, 'have you to tell? Sit there, and tell me.'

Jack's fond mother smiled with pleasure. She was proud of the notice the invalid took of her son.

'We've got another invalid down-stairs,' said Jack.

'Your mother has informed me,' replied the sick woman, who had signed the letter to Lord Garthway—'The Poor Wanderer.' 'But that is not what you were going to tell me.'

'No,' assented Jack, 'it was not. I went for a arrant'—he meant 'errand'—'and in the beershop over the way I saw two rough-looking men. They are them as beat the girl downstairs; and who d'ye think I saw with them?'—a pause—'that gentleman who gave me the letter last night, him as the great admiral called Saunders.'

The invalid started at the sound of this name.

'Are you sure?'

'Yes, mum, I am quite.'

'Did he see you?'

'I don't know, mum. He was talking to three other men—he was.'

The poor wanderer became thoughtful; Jack's mother turned pale.

'I don't like it, madam. Jack is very sharp; and after what occurred last night it ought to be seen to. I'll speak to my husband.'

The invalid became thoughtful—her lips were locked, and her brilliant black eyes flashed, while an olive tint came over each cheek.

'My good, kind friends,' she said, in pure English, 'I feel that danger menaces me. I know not how to act. How I wish *he*, my noble friend and protector, would come! Wait!' she said, with sudden energy. 'I will rise and occupy the arm-chair by the fire. I can then see your husband; he will give me his council. I must not waste any more time. No half measures must be taken, or I am lost. Oh, what would I give were I well enough to go out!'

Jack was sent downstairs, and the invalid got up, dressed herself in a loose-fitting dressing-gown, and, assisted by the kind, attentive woman, took her seat in a comfortable arm-chair by the fire.

'Is that girl still here?' she asked of Mrs. Murray.

'Yes, poor thing; they have hurt her foot, and she cannot walk. She asked if she could stay for a day or two. She would pay, she said, for her food and lodging. I——'

Both were surprised by a low, double knock at the door. Jack ran and opened it instantly. Mrs. Murray heard him exchange a few words with a stranger, then the lad came upstairs, and, peeping into the invalid's room, said—

'A gentleman to see the lady, mother.'

The beautiful sufferer's heart beat with joy. She thought it was Gerald Stuart.

'Let him come up,' she said.

A step, almost feeble, ascended the stairs. Her heart misgave her. It could not be that of Captain Gerald. She did not wait long in suspense. The stranger was ushered in by little Jack. The invalid looked up in mute surprise.

He was a man far beyond the middle age. Small in stature, with a hard impenetrable face, and quick, sharp eyes. Bowing courteously, he coughed, and said—

'Pardon, madam. I am from London. This letter will explain my business.'

He handed a small sealed letter to the beautiful girl. She broke the seal and read—

'DEAR MADAM,—*Events are about to occur that will, I fear, prevent me from being in your presence on the day I promised. I do not know what may happen, yet circumstances are taking a dangerous turn, and, perhaps, I may never be able to assist you hereafter. Still, I have taken the precaution to send you one in whom you can place implicit confidence. Trust him as you would me. He can be a very powerful friend in your cause. He is a man of intellect and experience—a lawyer by profession—Mr. J. Lorry by name. Do not hesitate to make him your confidant. State the steps you have already taken, and name those you wish followed up. An absent though watchful guardian,*

G. S.   C. A. G.

The beautiful reader of this strange epistle

turned it over and glanced at the seal, which was stamped with a small arrow. She knew there was no deception about it.

Looking up, she said—

'You are Mr. Lorry?'

'At your service, madam,' and he bowed with great courtesy.

'Pardon me not rising,' the fair speaker said, acknowledging his graceful salute with an inclination of the head. You, perhaps, can perceive I am an invalid '——

'Pray, madam, do not put yourself out of the way in the least. I regret to see you are suffering from severe indisposition, which I hope will not prevent you from at least transacting a little business to your own benefit?'

'Not at all. Be seated, sir. You know the writer of this letter?'

'I have that pleasure. We are old acquaintances. I am deeply grieved to say that since I received that letter with my own instructions, his fate has become a mystery.'

'What mean you? What do you suspect?'

'That he is dead—that he went down upon the lugger on which he had saved his bride from the hands of her persecutors—that he fell in her defence, and died an appalling death, while his rival triumphs with his bride '——

'No more! It is time I ceased to creep a nameless thing on the earth's surface. With your aid, I will proclaim who and what I am, and wrest the beloved of my departed benefactor from the grasp of a vulture!'

More beautiful than ever the outraged woman looked. She stood up—haughty, defiant, and determined. Mr. Lorry stood gazing on in silent admiration, not unmixed with awe.

———

CHAPTER XXXIII.
RESCUED FROM DEATH.

WILLIAM'S feelings were simply beyond description when the gun brig was hurled upon the Sands. He felt the fearful shock; heard the cries and curses of the crew above the howling of the storm and roar of the waters as they dashed over the vessel, and made their way through the smallest crevice.

The air became stifling and oppressive in his confined prison; he could scarcely breathe. Each minute he expected the vessel would be dashed to pieces, and sink beneath the boiling sea. What hope was there for him!

It was hard to perish like a rat in a trap. He made a desperate effort to get out. How useless were his endeavours! He was powerless to help himself.

The surging sea was now breaking through many parts of the Firefly, and came with a wild rush through the decks. the noise and confusion was bewildering, his brain began to whirl, his senses were confused, huge drops of perspiration broke out upon him. The air became more oppresive, he felt a dead, heavy weight pressing upon his chest.

Above the wild din and roar of the tempest he could hear the water surging through the ship, mingled with a strange noise. Crash after crash came upon his ears. The splintering of wood—heavy, furious blows, as though a demon was breaking the decks to pieces with some gigantic chopper. The crashing continued. It became plain—sounded nearer. The water poured through the vessel with terrible force; it penetrated to his dungeon, and his heart sank within him.

The ship was filling was the terrible conviction that forced itself upon his mind, and all hope died from his breast. He was powerless, helpless, compelled to remain inactive, and wait for death—wait, and watch its gradual approach, with no power to avert it.

He tried in vain to beat the hatch off and get out. He beat upon it wildly with his clenched hands, tore at it with his nails; all to no purpose.

The water was now above his knees, and was rising rapidly. Worked up to a pitch of mad desperation, he continued beating and tearing at the hatch in wild despair.

In his frenzy he called loudly for help. Who was to help him—who could get near him? Perhaps none lived to hear his cries.

His loud thuds upon the hatch met a responsive echo, it was the crashing he had heard now resumed, only much nearer to the hold. The sound incited him on, and he fought more madly than before. Presently he gave a cry, the crashing sound was upon the hatch that covered the entrance to his prison.

The water was now four feet deep, and William was nearly suffocated by the pressure of the confined air. His form shook like an aspen, his limbs lost their power; he felt himself sinking back exhausted, his senses rapidly leaving him.

Strange pains came upon him; he was like one in the infernal regions. The wild rush of the water wading on the vessel, the dull sluggish sound of it in the ship's hold, the howling wind, loud and repeated claps of thunder, combined with the repeated crash—crash, made the din an unearthly noise above all imagination.

He felt the cold, turbid water rising over his waist, he heard the crashing upon the hatchway, felt a cold rush of salt spray upon him; the confined air seemed to evaporate, then the hatch flew up; the bright edge of a hatchet gleamed upon him; a face, dark, terrible, and determined, appeared; the eyes flashed upon him. He saw the double row of gleaming teeth, and felt the hot breath of some demon-like intruder; he was clutched, too, by the neck. He felt himself being dragged through a surging mass of water, amid such wild unearthly noises as might be imagined to belong to the lower regions. Then came a fierce gust of wind. Something cold pelted down upon him. The murky mist enshrouded him like a pall; then he was hurled through the air, breathless, powerless, in a terrible lethargy. Down, down he went with a bewildering whirl, being dragged through the boiling sea. Every life motion of his body stopped, his breath being crushed within him, his heart nearly bursting; then everything passed like a shock; he was senseless to all feeling—darkness and oblivion.

*　　*　　*　　*　　*　　*

Two days since the fearful tempest—far out in the English Channel—a swan-like vessel skims across the waves, tinted by the blood-red rays of the setting sun. She carries no flag. On the deck the crew, all attired alike, lounge about the bulwarks, or play cards under the bulkhead.

On the poop stand the captain and first lieutenant; the latter looks pale and ill, as though only just recovering from a severe attack.

'God!' he said, continuing a conversation, 'I never shall forget the horror of my position that night. It seems, captain, like a horrible night-mare.'

'Never mind, Will; we are safe, thank Providence; and I think circumstances have turned out for the best.'

'Best!' echoed our hero, surprised, 'best, when you were nearly sent to Davy Jones' locker, and I was being slowly smothered in the hold of the sinking ship'——

'Ay, Will, even so. We are safe now. I escaped from what they thought certain death.'

'Ay, captain, you havn't spun out yer yarn about that yet.'

'It is simple enough, Will. I had merely fallen in a kind of stupor, lethargy, or swoon, and the immersion in the cold water roused me like an electric shock with the instinct of self-preservation. I struck out, and managed to keep myself afloat in spite of the whirlpool, which sucked me under more than once. But we have many friends about us, Will, and when I thought I should either perish or be discovered, a hand grasped my hair. I was dragged into a small skiff, and thus saved. I was not sorry it happened as it had. I knew no earthly power could save you, were I a prisoner too. I engaged a fishing boat, went on board the Golden Arrow, acquainted the crew with what had taken place, and took measures to insure your safety.

'The report that I was supposed to be dead soon reached me, and I am determined to keep up the delusion, as it will aid our plans. On the night of the tempest I went ashore. I had stained my face, put on a moustache, and the disguise of a pilot. Fortune favoured me. I got on board the gun-brig by the aid of Hawkins, with whom I had exchanged your token (the Golden Arrow) for mine, which you say he gave you. I was determined to steer the ships to the Sands, and I did so. You know the rest.'

'Cap'n, the debt I owe you will never be payed."

'Nonsense, Will, you owe me no debt; had I not saved you I would have blown Garthway's liner out of the water, and the Golden Arrow with it.'

'Poor Sue! Where's she now?' Will uttered, half aloud, his thoughts running more in that channel than paying attention to his captain's conversation.

'Do not fear, Will, she is safe, I have discovered, and when next we meet those we love, Will, it shall be to call them ours—for this time nothing shall prevent us from succeeding. Once safe on the matchless Golden Arrow we will run out into foreign water, and bid defiance to our enemies.'

Brave Will's chest expanded at the thought.

'I wish the time would come,' he said, wistfully 'I am heart sick of this—tired of being hunted like a mad dog from my native soil—from my own home—weary of the ceaseless turmoil—tired of even having to raise my hand in fury against my fellow countrymen—my superiors, nay, my messmates. It seems like flying in the face of the Great Skipper; it seems unlawful—it's *piracy!*'

'Will,' said Gerald, reproachfully, "not that—not that; call it rebellion and you are right. I do not raise my hand against the government. I do not acknowledge King George. He is not my king, therefore I am at liberty to declare war with those who war with my king.'

William looked the picture of surprise.

'Your king?' he echoed.

'Ay, Charles Stuart, the young pretender. He is unfortunate, Will; he needs strong arms and faithful hearts.' Gerald Stuart said this almost sadly.

'You may be right, cap'n, maybe you're not; my book larning has not been great, but I know him by report—maybe he is the right king, but Cap'n Gerald, I've eaten the bread of King George I've been brought up to serve my king and my country —to do my duty to all of his great ministers. I've fought under some of his great admirals, ay, and saved their lives, too, as I did Captain Crosstree's, God bless him! He has saved mine, too, though I was but a common sailor; and it seems disgraceful ingratitude to be raising my sword against those I was taught to honour and obey. I'm a traitor Captain Stuart. I feel it, here! here!' He struck his chest heavily with his broad hand.

Captain Gerald was too noble not to understand Will's honest feelings. He gazed at our hero with a look of mingled sorrow and admiration.

'Will,' he said, quietly, a tinge of huskiness in his voice, "you spoke only the sentiments of a warm, grateful heart. All men cannot have the same notions, perhaps we have not. I feel like one who has committed a crime, Will, in dragging you down the dark vortex of destruction with me. I can only make, or rather offer, a very slight redress, that of making you independent. You can then live on shore in peace. I know you would not forget your friend, and should God grant that I may live to surmount all difficulties and dangers, we might, in some future time, be happily united. I am willing to do that, and ask your pardon.' He ceased, his voice becoming more husky than he would have wished.

Will faced the speaker slowly. He felt, or thought he did, a reproach in Gerald's words, and his gallant, grateful heart smote him. An honest tear of sterling affection rose to his eyes, as he replied somewhat more huskily than Gerald had spoken—

'Cap'n, I ask your pardon. You've made me feel the ungrateful lubber I am. I wronged you— you, my most noble friend, a more than brother— it was base ingratitude. However, forgive me, Cap'n Stuart, I wish the words had choked me. To whom do I owe my life, my life's gratitude? Could I becomes yours, body and soul, Cap'n Gerald, it would but poorly repay the debt I owe you. Forget the words I spoke. Henceforth, your king is my king—your cause, as it was since we met, my cause; and to think of me doubting you, never, Cap'n Stuart! I can bear the stigma of being called traitor to my country and ungrateful to my king, but it shall never be said I played the ungrateful cur to my dearest friend on earth—pardon, your honour—barring Sue. Don't mention my going ashore again. When I do it'll be under a shroud, to return no more, or to rescue my wife.'

The two staunch friends locked their hands in a true grasp of lasting friendship.

'Grateful and true to the last,' said Gerald, giving Will a look of real affection.

The poor fellow could not reply. He loved Gerald Stuart dearly, and he felt he owed him his life; but he was sorely perplexed between the ideas of right and wrong. It was a relief to his mind to know he was fighting in the cause of a king, though a dethroned one. To desert his friend now he felt would be worse than deserting his country. The voice of Gerald broke his reverie.

'Do not, Will, let your gratitude for me prevent you from doing right.'

'Captain Stuart, I'm doing right in remaining true to you—true to my friend and benefactor.'

'It may be some consolation to know that your grateful government would only murder you, did you go back to them. I have been most foully wronged, Will; you shall know, some day. Enough of this conversation now. We must put our minds to other things. I have heard that the Admiral will marry his daughter to Gregory at the church; and his having gone so far as he has, I do not doubt but what he will do so. Not only that, Will, it is our duty to go ashore. Remember, my beloved Madeline and your wife are ignorant of our existence. God! the agony of mind they may be suffering on our account must almost drive them mad.'

'True, true, captain, we must go ashore. When?'

'At once; but listen, Will; if we wish our plans to succeed, we had better keep up the supposition that we are dead. I will contrive my disguise and appear as a Spaniard; you had better throw off your striking costume—a large black beard and a common sailor's dress will perfectly disguise you. We can then go ashore and learn what is going about; find means of communicating with your wife and my beloved Madeline, and then follow out circumstances to the completion of our schemes.'

'Ay, ay, captain; you've a noble piece of head-work, you have.'

'I think,' went on Gerald, not noticing the compliment, 'we had better not be seen together on shore, as the slightest thing will rouse suspicion.'

'True, captain.'

'Let us go below, the dinner bell rings.'

They descended to the chief cabin as the bell announced to the officers of the watch that that welcome meal was ready.

Pat Murphy made his appearance as our hero and Gerald sat at the table, where the doctor, with one or two other officers, waited their comrade's presence.

'Sure an' yer honours,' he began, looking nervously round upon the assembled officers, 'sure an' it's meself as would make a clain braist of it, yer honours. Och, one! and if it's yerself as will hang me for it sure an' I'd not murmur at it at all. Wurra! wurra! an' ain't it meself as desarves it.' He ceased his rapid talking to utter a groan.

The officers were both amused and surprised; the doctor coughed drily and put his handkerchief to his mouth to hide a smile; Gerald Stuart looked on in quiet wonderment not entirely devoid of a slight nervous contortion of the features.

'What am I to understand?' he said, pausing in the act of serving the doctor with some soup.

'Sure, yer honour, and its meself as understands too much. Wurra! And bedad, now it's meself as is committed murder!—och one!—och one!—an' it wasn't the likes of meself as would a' meant it. Wurra! wurra!' and he groaned in his agony of mind at some misfortune only known to himself.

Wondering what was coming after such a self-condemning prelude, Gerald thought it would be as well to put a serious face on the matter, and said—

'Your lengthened, ambiguous conversation is delaying our dinner. I should wish, cook, that you would be as brief as possible. Tell me plainly what it is you require.'

'Require, yer honour? Bedad! it's Jacob to be brought back to life I would be requiring; but seeing as how he can't be, I'll make a true confession to yer honour. Wurra! and if I'm hung, Jasus look down on me, for I shall go to him with murther on me soul.'

'Murder! Explain yourself.'

'Yer honour,' the cook went on, with a series of groans, 'sure an' I've murthered Jacob'——

'Really,' interrupted Gerald, with a wink at the

officers to look as terrible as they could, for all had heard of Jacob's disappearance—'steward, you had better call in two marines; they may be necessary. Now, sir, continue.'

'Sure, yer honour,'—another groan—'it's meself as didn't main it' (groan). 'Bedad, yer honours, an' I only maint to jist frighten the spalpeen. Virgin of Mercy! look down upon us. (Groans.) An' I hope yer honours won't be hard on a poor mortal as never injured a Christian in his life. (Groans.) Surean' I'm haunted night an' day by his ghost; och one an' the divil will have me soul now." (A prolonged groan.)

'You are not stating how the crime was committed?' Gerald looked very stern, the officers looked sterner. Pat Murphy began to think he really was a murderer, and with a series of most dismal groans, mingled with protestations, appeals for forgiveness, and even tears, he graphically explained how Jacob had been cast away upon the sea.

Captain Gerald must have been very much affected, for he put his handkerchief to his face, and his form seemed to shake with emotion, as his glistening eyes peered over the pink-bordered silk upon the officers, whose nerves were so unstrung by the dreadful account they could not control the muscles of their faces, and many turned away their heads. Pat thought to conceal their emotion (so it was), and his heart sank within him.

Gerald at length removed the handkerchief, and endeavouring to control a nervous twitching at the corners of his mouth thus replied, and every word sunk like a dagger's point to the culprit's heart—

'Mr. Murphy—by your own confession and free will, you accuse yourself of having most infamously taken the life of your fellow-servant and Christian brother—Jacob Twig. We, with all respect to your remorse and humanity, must confine you to the care of those marines while we debate upon the punishment. I can but anticipate that death will be the sentence found; if so, I will endeavour to mitigate it—if I fail, you will at least be consoled with the knowledge of my strongest authority being exercised in your behalf, and that though the gentlemen present may consider it their duty to pass such judgment upon you, they will still regret losing a good cook and, until this cruise, an honest, faithful subject."

A majestic wave of the hand consigned Pat to the marines, who received a wink from the captain that signified a great deal, and with sundry dreary groans of agony and sorrow, the cook was led away.

It would have relieved him could he have heard his judges five minutes after, as the cabin rang with unsuppressed laughter.

CHAPTER XXXIV.
FOUR TO ONE.

As some little interest may be felt in the fate of Pat Murphy, it may be as well to state here that after being kept in a state of 'dying suspense,' he was recalled by his terrible judges, whose faces sent a chill, a horror, to his heart, and he felt the flesh on his bones creep when Gerald Stuart rose and said—

'In the name of the jury, the gentlemen present, you, the prisoner, are condemned to die at the yard-arm'——

The prisoner interrupted by a long groan.

'Wurra! wurra! oh, sure, an' what did I leave my blessed mother for? Bedad! and it's hanged I'm to be. God bless yer honours! I can't go against your orders, for didn't I murder the poor chap, now, and, sure, though I didn't mane it. Jist'——

BLACK EYED SUSAN.

OR, PIRATES ASHORE.

THE TOILET.

13

Gratis with this Number a Sheet of Side Wings for the Play of the "RED ROVER."

'Do not interrupt, sir. You are condemned,' continued Gerald, prolonging each word to an unnecessary length, that its force should not be lost, or perhaps to witness the misery of the prisoner, ' to die at the yard-arm three months hence, should no tidings be heard of Jacob Twig. Until then you will continue in the berth of cook, but consider yourself a prisoner.'

Pat Murphy did not wait to hear any more. He gave a yell of joy that rang through the ship.

'Oh, an' God bless yer honour; it's meself as would die for ye. May the Virgin look down on ye.' The grateful Celt was on his knees before the young chieftain, and he kissed Gerald's hand with the affection of a dog.

'Enough,' said Gerald; 'go to your duty. It is all I could do for you.'

'Sure, an' bedad, yer honour, it's meself as'——

'Yes, yes, leave the cabin, please.'

'To be sure, yer honour; och one, and d'ye think Pat Murphy's the boy to shtay when he's had a jintle hint to go?'

He backed his way out of the cabin, and struck up a lively air.

> By the bright eyes of M'Karthy,
> I'm dead to ye all.
> For ranting O'Kelin
> I care not at all,
> An' Kitty me darlint,
> Bedad she's too small,
> For the jewel of a boy from Paddy's land."

In his delirium of joy he began to do a jig on the companion ladder.

'Sure an' it's meself as can welt the floor,' he cried, performing some steps that would make many of our modern dancers feel ashamed of their imperfectness.

What he meant by 'welting the floor' can only be imagined, as his foot slipped, and he came down the steps with such velocity that he performed a wild flourishing step before he knew he had lost his footing.

His singing changed to a groan. He had grazed his shins all the way up, and nearly dislocated his chin, which had come in contact with the top step.

Very much hurt, but much more mortified, the light-hearted Irishman went to his pantry, and drowned his misfortunes in a glass of good whiskey.

Captain Gerald and the officers enjoyed the amusement the affair afforded them with all the light heartedness of pleasure-seekers.

'I think he thought you really were going to hang him without a day's grace,' laughed the doctor.

'He is a great, honest-hearted, well-meant, simpleton,' replied Gerald, laughing. 'But enough. We have work—a heavy task, to perform, and pleasure is out of place.'

The officers rose from the table, bowed, and went on deck, followed by the doctor, and Gerald and our hero were alone.

'Now, Will, to business. I will not trust the Golden Arrow so far from our reach again. She goes where we do. We can run in under a disguise at night, you in a sailor's dress and beard, can go as a hanger on to the Crown and Anchor. I will leave Deal, and return in a few hours in a post-chaise, take up my rooms at the 'Three Admirals,' as a traveller from foreign parts. What do you think, Will?'

'I think, cap'n, one of those long-shore book learning sharks—lawyers—couldn't show the upper works you can.'

'Very likely not,' said Gerald; 'but now to put our scheme in practice.'

The Golden Arrow was put under its disguise. Every precaution was taken to avert suspicion. William assumed his garb of a middle-aged sailor, and that night the Golden Arrow anchored under cover of the darkness, in the roads, keeping as clear as possible from any other crafts.

Not a man was allowed an hour's liberty—nor did they want it. True to their leader—faithful to his cause—they wanted to serve him; and if serving him was to remain like prisoners in the narrow limits of the privateer's forcastle, they would bear it without a murmur.

To avoid any show, they were rowed ashore by two men in a light skiff.

That night, a post chaise, drawn by four spirity horses, dashed up to the well-known inn, the 'Three Admirals.'

The master of the inn came bustling out to see who the grand traveller could be. He went to the door of the vehicle and opened it, bowing low as a tall young traveller alighted.

He was dark, well-built, fashionably dressed, and handsome, with a dark moustache, and lustrous black eyes. He was closely followed by a handsome, delicate youth, dark as himself, as regards hair and complexion, but with an eye almost blue.

Mine host bowed to him too; he was distinguished looking, attired in a splendid dress, and certainly was not a servant.

The tavern keeper looked round for what he thought would follow, half a dozen servants. He was disappointed, only one came forward. He was short, thick, and clumsy looking.

The hotel master followed his guests in to the traveller's room.

'Your pleasure, honourable gentleman,' he said, respectfully.

A few words passed between the two travellers in Spanish or French, which the master of the house was not scholar enough to tell. Then the eldest of the two spoke.

'Have you an apartment fit for us to occupy for a week, or as long as it should be necessary for me to stay?'

'I have, most honourable sir.' Mine host scarcely knew how to reply. By the stranger's speech he was not English, so the innkeeper thought its foreign accent was very slight, and only perceivable at times. He thought the traveller must be a Spanish lord or duke. 'The first floor, sir, can be put at your disposal.'

'Let me have them at once."

The servants at the inn bustled about in every direction preparing the rooms for the grand travellers; and, to do them justice, they were not long in putting everything in a very comfortable state.

The apartments consisted of a sitting room, a drawing room, two bed rooms, and two ante-chambers—one adjoining the drawing room, the other the best sleeping chamber.

The travellers' luggage, which was very small indeed—much to the mental worry of the innkeeper—was conveyed to their apartments.

The travellers, escorted by mine host, went to the rooms, which were capacious, and comfortably furnished, though not elegant.

'I should like dinner in an hour," said the dark stranger, throwing himself into a comfortable arm chair. 'And Mr——.' He paused, and inquired the host's name by a look.

'Simmons, sir.'

'Simmons, I have travelled far. I am tired, and want to be at rest. Should anyone come inquiring about me, you will know nothing—do you understand?'

'Quite, honourable sir.'

'In fact, to speak in plain English, on what terms can you *mind your own business?*'

The worthy Simmons looked at the speaker in amazement, and felt a little indignant.

'The fact is this,' continued the traveller, 'name your terms for this apartment, with attendance, for my servant cannot do everything—in fact, anything I may require, or at any hour—it matters not. Name your terms, I will pay you in advance, then it will not matter to you whether these rooms are occupied or not, until the month expires. In fact, I wish you to act up to the old English adage, which you may know, 'Hear, see, and say nothing.' You have my card, use my name with discretion.'

Simmons glanced at the card handed him by his patron, and felt the dignity of his house rise greatly at such a guest. The card bore on its glossy surface—

'CONDE DE PALAMANA.'

'My lord, I perfectly understand you. I think you will find me all you wish. I never interest myself in any one's affairs, unless it is *for* such honourable gentlemen as yourself who may honour my house with their patronage.'

And he bowed lowly.

'Very good. Things are understood between us?'

'Quite, my lord.' He used the title at random, not knowing the exact meaning of *Conde*. 'I can well understand one of your lordship's rank not wishing to have any prying impostor know of your whereabouts; for the English adventurers are so very imposing on any foreign nobles.'

'Truly Dinner in three quarters of an hour. Should a messenger come for me, let him be announced.'

'Your orders shall be obeyed, my lord,' and he retired.

'Good!' said the supposed Spaniard, turning to his youthful companion. 'He readily takes me for a foreigner. How do I manage the Spanish accent, André?'

'Perfectly, Gerald.'

'Hush! Senor, or my Spanish name.'

'True; you did well to remind me. I shall not again commit that indiscretion.'

'That I am confident of. What is Wilk's doing?'

'He is below.'

'Ring.'

The handsome youth styled André rang the bell, A waiter answered the summons.

'Send his lordship's servant up.'

'Yes, sir.'

The man retired with a low bow, and returned in a few minutes—tapped at the door, and hearing a voice call 'Enter,' he strode into the room, and addressed himself to the Spanish count.

'Whatever message you have, my man, give to that gentleman, my secretary. He will inform me.'

The Spaniard spoke haughtily. He was reading, and did not like to be disturbed.

The waiter, stung with annoyance, and abashed, turned to the gentleman's secretary.

'Your master's servant is out,' he said, insolently.

'Fellow,' cried the Spaniard, hotly 'that gentleman, Don André, is my secretary. Address him like that again, and my servant shall kick you out.'

'I beg pardon, my lord.'

'Go.'

He went, cowed and humble.

'Andrew,' said the supposed Spanish Count, turning the name into English, 'we must, in the most trivial circumstances, keep up our assumed titles. Nothing but completley blinding both friends or foes will aid our schemes.'

'It would be a pity to let one false step destroy our desperate game,' replied Andrew, thoughtfully

If we have not introduced Gerald's companion before, it is because there has been no fitting opportunity. He and Gerald were like brothers; their affection for each other perhaps was stronger than that generally found existing between two of the same blood.

Gerald was all on earth to Andrew—father, brother, relation, and protector. The youth held no position on the Golden Arrow, as he was unfit for the service—unacquainted with the profession, and delicate as a girl.

While they were conversing together, Wilks came from the regions below stairs.

He was attired in a plain black dress of a gentleman's servant, in which he certainly did not feel comfortable, having been used to the careless easy attire he had so long assumed as steward on the Golden Arrow. He was a staunch friend to his young chief, and would sell his life to save him.

'You have been out, Wilks?'

'Yes, cap— senor.'

'Very good. Wilks, I can trust you I hope, without any fear?'

'Cap'n—my lord,' replied Wilks, seemingly hurt by the slightest shadow of a doubt being put upon his constancy. 'I went out to-night, but it was for you.'

'Faithful fellow, I did not doubt you. Wherefore did you go?'

'To get this.' He gave a printed bill and newspaper to the supposed Spanish count, who read the ormer with a gleam of satisfaction.

'The death of the rebel leader Gerald Stuart is well known.' He read aloud parts of the placard 'The traitor and deserter, WILLIAM HOWARD perished on the ——, by the sinking of the gun-brig Firefly, and thus escaped the punishment that would have been carried out upon him. . . . . His Most Gracious Majesty, however, will pardon such of the crew who had been led away by the outlaw, providing they will give themselves up within ten days of the above date, and will give such information as may be required concerning the rest of the rebellious band, and the resources of the aforesaid Gerald Stuart.' 'I daresay they will,' laughed De Palamana. 'Thanks, Wilks; you have rendered us a service. Now see about dinner.' He gave the proclamation, of which he had only read aloud a few lines, to his adopted brother, Andrew.

But the smile left his cheek, and his brows were knit in terrible anger as he glanced at a column in the daily local paper, headed 'Another Tragedy and Abduction.'

Then followed a lengthened and ambiguous account of the scene that took place in Lower Deal on the night of the tempest. The reporter founded his matter on the one incident of finding a girl in a pool of gore at the door-step, and on examination she was found to be still alive, though life was but hanging by a thread—a very slender thread indeed

WINGS SET 2

WINGS SET 2

'Mr. Lorry, we had better understand each other. I cannot, that is, I am not in a position yet to meet your demands, which'——

'Nay, madam, I cannot surely understand you. The instructions received from my friend and employer simply imply that I am to put myself at your service. The rest of the buisness is already settled, madam; you have nothing left now but to let us take measures. Firstly, let me know what has been done. I am acquainted with a little of this very serious affair, but only a very little.'

He received no reply for a few minutes; the invalid seemed lost in a deep reverie. She was inwardly blessing the forethought of her gallant preserver—and, without heeding her visitor's last remark, she asked,

'Did you say Captain Stuart went down with a vessel?'

'Such is the supposed death of him.'

'How was it?'

'Were you not aware, madam, that Gregory Saunders'—he pronounced that name very slowly— 'was being allied to the admiral's daughter, whom they attempted to force into the hateful union? It was through saving her he lost his own life—unless the report be untrue, or that they are mistaken. I hope, with all my heart, it is the latter.'

'Could my prayers insure his safety, or recall him to life, they should not be wanting; as it is, we must hope. If he has really perished, I swear to save his beloved from the clutches of a heartless scoundrel. Come nearer, Mr. Lorry, I cannot speak loud, it distresses me much.'

The excitement was too much for her, and she now found herself becoming weaker than ever. Mr. Lorry drew his chair towards her with a look of pity. He felt deeply for the young creature whose life had been blasted.

'I am not one to give way to presentiments, Mr. Lorry; but I cannot shake off the foreboding that I shall never live to accomplish my heart's desire.'

'Nay, madam, I'——

'Let me continue.' Her voice was getting fainter. 'I have been thinking seriously upon the matter. Should I never survive this illness, what would become of that poor girl? not that only, the villain would go unpunished. I propose, Mr. Lorry, that I place a copy, or the original proofs of my claim and identification in your hands, to be opened on my death by you, and measures taken according to circumstances.'

'Well,' replied Mr. Jasper Lorry, very slowly, 'though I hope your presentiment is merely a fancy, brought on by the anxiety of your position, still I commend you for wishing to take safe and certain measures. Have you done anything yet?'

'I sent a letter by the little lad here. By his account he was met at the door by a naval officer, who demanded his business, took the letter from him, sent the boy to the kitchen, read and answered my note. Fool he is to think I should not know his handwriting! Here is the reply.'

Mr. Lorry took the note and read it.

'From whom did this come?'

'Gregory Saunders, Mr. Lorry.'

'Humph! He must be a desperate villain, a dangerous man. Be careful of him. Shun everyone. Suspect everyone, friends or strangers, for you are not safe a minute from such a scoundrel. It is most fortunate I came to-day, for I see by report that next Sunday he will be married at the church to Madeline Garthway.'

He paused, seeing his hearer could scarcely move; a violent fit of trembling took her and she went paler still.

'It must not be,' she said, hoarsely.

'It shall not,' responded Mr. Lorry, calmly. 'I think were you to send another letter of warning to-night it would be as well. Fortunately I have a very old friend here at Deal, of my profession, he could help us.'

'But I do not wish too many to be in the secret of my affairs.'

'You misapprehend me; he will only assist me— follow my instructions without knowing the why or wherefore.'

'Proceed, sir.'

'That is all, I think. Open your case to me now, unless you are too fatigued, and I will take instant measures.'

'I will first give you my unfortunate story. I will then supply the proofs.'

Nerving herself to go through the unpleasant task, she began—

'I will not say anything of my pedigree, Mr. Lorry, as it is not wanted. Let it suffice when I say I am a half-caste. My father was English— my mother the daughter of a Queen—her own country. Of that I will speak some future time. Three years ago I was with my mother in Italy, where we had gone in consequence of my father's health, who derived no benefit from the change of climate, for three weeks after our arrival he died. My poor mother never seemed to recover the shock. She pined day and night, and I believe had not his love for me been a life tie to keep her on earth, she would have followed my father. I saw her declining health bringing the sure mark of the grim destroyer on her face, and I tried to make her happy. She cherished me all the more for being the only love link left her now. I had had a brother. I can just remember him when I was very young, and I loved him dearly, for he was a noble boy—handsome, bold, and yet gentle. Suddenly I missed him. I inquired for my brother of my mother. She would weep, and tell me to forget him; but, at length, after the death of my father, she told me my brother had been stolen, and, in all probability, murdered; for, though my father travelled nearly every part of the world, no tidings could be discovered of my lost brother, who was nearly ten years old when kidnapped. But of him, enough for the present.' She dashed a tear from her lovely eyes, and went on, 'While the death of my father was still fresh in the memory of my dear mother, a stranger came. He was Gregory Saunders—then a handsome, dashing youth—holding the position of captain. He had been sent out on some service, and in Italy we became acquainted. I certainly did not take a very great fancy to him at first sight—nay, I should never have thought of him had he not followed me everywhere I went, and when we became acquainted he was constantly with us. He told me he had received some damage in his ship, and that it would take two or three months to repair. Thus his stay was lengthened considerably. I need not follow minutely the cause of the serpent's progress. He managed at last to get my love and my consent, though my poor mother begged me not to marry him. Alas, how bitterly I regret not having done so! but love is selfish, and much as I adored my parent, I could not entirely control the promptings of my young heart. We were allied on his ship, and after the wedding breakfast he took me to my mother's. I then fell at her feet, and asked forgiveness for having married. Oh, God! I shall never forget the look of agony that came over her she when uttered the word 'Married!' My

God, forgive me for having gone against her will.'——

She buried her face in her hands, and her whole frame shook with emotion. It was some minutes ere she continued.

'I had, God help me! unwittingly sundered the last life-thread of her poor, careworn heart. She stood up, looking like one turned into a statue. She murmured : "I forgive you!" sighed—as she sank back into a seat, shed bitter tears of agony, and died.'

Again the unfortunate invalid broke down; this time she wept, so vivid was her dead mother's image before her.

Mr. Lorry could not trust himself to speak. Taking a handkerchief from his pocket, he placed it to his nose with one hand, and made a miserable attempt to use it, while with the left hand he put the corner of the large yellow silk to his eye.

Controlling, with some difficulty, her overpowering emotions, the outraged wife went on—

'Thus I lost my only parent and gained a husband. Despite of which I could not control my sorrow, and I would not leave the house of her I had loved alone. The burial took place a week afterwards, and I found myself in the possession of immense wealth. I now began to devote myself to my husband, whom I had almost shunned after the terrible calamity, and we lived happily until within a fortnight of his departure. I know not why, but I often felt a strange misgiving concerning him. I often had a suspicion—I know not why—that he did not love me; that I was deceived; that he had me married for my wealth.'

'He hinted at my staying in Italy while he returned home with his ship. I positively refused, being alone now, with no one but him to look up to for protection. I could not bear the idea of being left behind. I refused to comply with his demands. He had managed to get my affairs settled in his favour, and now would turn me off. He made it an excuse by saying that his father would disinherit him should he return with a wife. He promised to return as soon as a vessel could bring him, but I was doubtful of his sincerity, and I would not listen to him. I said if he went and would not take me on board his vessel I would follow in another. He did not reply, but turned away with a dark scowl. He left me shortly afterwards, and for two days he did not reappear. The second night I began to be alarmed, and thought of starting out to seek him, when a messenger came to say my husband was lying assassinated near the convent of ——. I knew not what I did. Snatching up a cloak and hood I left the house, and hurried rapidly to the spot indicated. I saw what I thought was my husband's form lying upon the ground, but as I darted forward, two cloaked figures glided from a dark recess upon me, and I was rudely clutched by them. I screamed—a cloak was thrown over my head—but not before I heard a voice say "Don't kill her with that, there are other means of getting her out of the way; let her be taken to the convent alive, but mind she never leaves it." My blood ran to water—I recognised the voice—it was my husband's—I screamed, and fainted. When I came to I was in a small dark cell of a convent, guarded by the sisterhood, watched night and day, left without hope, and scarcely life.'

'Two years passed in this living tomb, when I managed to escape by the aid of two monks. I have been ever since tracking the villain who thus robbed me, and would have had me murdered for better security, but Providence frustrated that. I had no money, therefore was compelled to sell what valuables I had, and did not get a very large amount for them. When I reached England I was destitute of a penny, and I reached Deal in a starving condition. I should have perished on the doorstep of this house had not Providence directed the steps of Captain Gerald Stuart this way. Such, sir, is my story, and tell me, shall I not have revenge?'

Mr. Lorry answered almost mechanically.

'You shall.'

The young wife lay back in her arm chair quite exhausted. Her eyes closed, and her cheeks so pale that Mr. Lorry thought she had fainted.

'I will summon assistance,' he said.

'Not yet,' she faintly gasped. 'I would not discontinue until my task is finished.'

Mr. Jasper Lorry felt a pang of sorrow and pity enter his heart. He did not like the symptoms. It boded no good for her to thus persevere in putting her affairs in his hands without any delay. He was not given to presentiments; but he felt there was one in this.

'While we peruse the documents,' he said, 'I should like to send the lad to my assistant—Mr. Longstreet.'

'Do so.'

Little Jack was summoned and despatched to the worthy old lawyer, Mr. Longtree, who accompanied Jack home.

By the time Mr. Lorry's assistant arrived, he had completed his business for the present. The papers and deeds which proved the young wife's alliance and her right, also her family connections, were carefully copied by Mr. Lorry, who placed the counterfeit documents in the invalid's possession.

'The originals shall be taken proper care of,' he said, 'until such time arrives as they will be wanted. Now, for the letter, and then I can leave you to rest for to-day.'

The letter to Admiral Garthway was written, and Mr. Longstreet called up to sign himself as a witness to the deeds copied by Mr. Lorry.

'I will conduct my business with you down stairs, Mr. Longstreet,' said the London lawyer, briefly.

Mr. Longstreet retired, rubbing the knuckles of his right hand in the palm of his left.

'Now, Madame Eurice, for such I am to address you.'

'It is only my Christian name, Mr. Lorry, but will do as well as any.'

'True, madam, I think now that you had better have medical attendance. I shall not leave Deal for a few days. During my stay I shall afford myself the pleasure of doing all I can on your behalf. Mr. Longstreet will bring an answer if there should be any. You will see me again in a day or two. It is imperative that no time should be lost in placing these documents in safe keeping. When we meet again I will pay a visit to Lord Garthway myself. I trust, madam, your health will have taken a more favourable turn. If so, I hope to see you lodged in more comfortable, at least more fitting, quarters, for one of your station of life than this.'

'Nay, I am comfortable here. I like the people. They are kind, homely, and honest. My requirements are small. This room is comfortable. Of the neighbourhood I care little. I am less likely to be interfered with.'

Mr. Lorry took a side glance at the small room. It was comfortably furnished, and, as he surmised, it had been done since the residence of the discarded wife.

He shook hands with the invalid, who gave a grateful glance, and he went below to his deputy after having dispatched Jack's mother to attend upon the invalid.

Mr. Lorry and his brother lawyer were shut up in a little back parlour alone, holding a low conversation. Jack had gone for an errand. His father had gone out, thinking, perhaps, that listeners were not wanted when secrets were going about.

They were not. Still there was one. Ellen Grevil (the girl who had been rescued from the street brawl) was standing against the back parlour door, her ear to the keyhole. She did not hear much—the lawyer spoke in a low voice, and all she could catch of any consequence was—

'These documents must be taken great care of. We do not know whom we have about us. It is dangerous even to trust oneself too far in this matter. Mr. Longstreet, you will convey this safely to Lord Garthway. You had better not go until after his dinner hour. This will explain all. You have the papers?'

A reply in the affirmative was all Ellen could catch, when she heard a step descend the stairs.

The girl skipped away, and went in the front parlour. No one entered; but she heard the lawyers come into the passage, and depart.

Now she breathed freely. A cunning light shone in her dark eyes as she took paper and pencil, and wrote a note.

Shortly after she might have been seen sitting at the parlour window, which was thrown open, her elbow rested upon the sill, her chin rested on the palm of her hand, while she played with a handkerchief with her right hand. She constantly cast an anxious glance across to the beer-house. Presently, a man—not prepossessing in appearance—came out, and approached her with a slouching gait.

No one was in the street at that moment—none but Ellen in the parlour.

She gave the man a quiet stare, as she would any casual passer-by, and seemed surprised to see him come directly towards her.

'Missus,' he said, gruffly, 'can you read that address, and tell me the way?'

The girl took the paper, and, in opening it, let it fall to the floor. Stooping, she quietly picked it up with her right hand, which contained a folded piece of paper.

She pointed out the way to some part of the town, and returned him the paper—*neatly folded*.

'Thank you, missus;' and the man went on, humming a low ditty. His voice sounded like the growl of a bull-dog.

Ellen seemed tired of sitting at the window. She closed it with a bang, and retired from the front parlour.

That day, at about four o'clock, Gregory Saunders received the following note:—

'*She is here—an invalid confined to her bed. Was visited this morning early by a lawyer from London. They were together some hours. Midday, the lawyer saw another of his profession. They arranged strange matters together. We're on the alert. The lawyer starts at six to-night to Lord Garthway's. He has with him papers from* HER, *and, using his own words,* '*They will disclose all.*' *Nothing more has passed yet. Doctor came, pronounces her worse. She has made dangerous disclosures to the lawyer who holds the papers and deeds.*
ELLEN.'

Saunder's lowering brow and deadly gleaming eye brought out the Satanic expression of his face as he destroyed the letter, and he gave a low, grating laugh.

'So, a meddling fool from London will seek the Admiral *to-night*, with papers that may *concern* me! Ha! ha! He may lose *his way*, and the papers too.'

Half-an-hour later, Elfin was closeted with Gregory Saunders.

'Mind you,' said the latter, with a warning frown, 'let that man reach the Admiral's house with those papers, and—you hang.'

'I never failed yet; I shan't now. How am I to know the fellow?'

'Instinct and circumstances must tell you when you follow the right one. Begone! You haven't much time to lose. He will be on the road at six; 'tis now five.'

Elfin left the house. His habitual scowl was more repulsive than ever.

'At six,' he muttered. 'Nice work. Never mind; I am well paid. Assistance might be necessary. I will get it.'

An hour later three dark figures were crouching from view on the road that led to the mansion of Lord Garthway. They kept well in any dark recess that afforded them shelter.

The night was quiet—the sky dark and cloudy. A distant church clock strikes six. The motionless shadows stir not. An hour drags slowly away; then another, and the clock strikes eight.

Slowly had the echoes died away, when a quick step is heard coming down the road, and the form of a man, evidently aged, appears. The step is feeble, though quick; and one of the terrible figures stands forth like an evil shadow in the path of the old man, who walks unsuspectingly on to the grim shadow—Death!

CHAPTER XXXVI.

THE REWARD OF CRIME.

BUSINESS had prevented Lawyer Longstreet from going to the Admiral's as early as he wished. Wondering what strange business his shrewd London employer could have on hand, he slowly and thoughtfully wended his way to Garthway's mansion.

He never suspected for an instant that anything was likely to happen to him—perhaps being ignorant of the nature of the business was the cause of his being so innocent of any evil design. Thus he went on—a very easy prey to the ruffian hirelings of Gregory Saunders.

The best part of the journey was accomplished, and he was in the most unpleasant part of the road. It was dark—the houses were few; still he did not feel any fear, but walked on quickly, his head bent, and his brain going meditatively to work.

He was within a few yards of the crouching shadows. They saw and waited for him. He did not see them. Unconscious of danger, he went on, his eyes cast upon the ground, his right hand grasping a good old-fashioned gingham umbrella, his left clutching the letter for the Lord High Admiral.

'Bless me!' he exclaimed, starting suddenly, as a dark shadowy form flitted across his path—'I thought—aha! Oh! God of mercy! help me—I am murdered.'

He reeled and staggered forward with a cry of intense agony, the blood pouring from a wound—a dagger thrust—in his ribs.'

He fell, as a hand grasped him by the throat.

'The letter!' he thought—his hand closed upon it. With that one effort his senses fled, and he was quiet and motionless.

The brutal hand was still on his throat, and a hoarse voice said—

'The papers! Where are they?'

Two forms kelt by the side of the poor old man who had so pitilessly fallen by the murderous knife—his pockets were rifled, his clothes cut up, to discover the papers.

With an awful oath, one of the ruffians spurned the body with his foot.

'Curses!' he cried, 'nothing but this letter.'

A low whistle—a danger signal—which came floating down the dark lane made the murderers start to their feet.

'The body! we shall be discovered. Quick!' The speaker and his accomplice dragged the lawyer's bleeding form along the road some thirty yards. A horse pond met their view.

'Now!'

The form was raised—a minute's awful silence—a dull splash—and the murderers stood glaring upon each other.

Another danger signal rang out on the night air. They turned and fled. The bloody knife was left in their flight on the spot where the deed was committed. A mask bespattered with the crimson life shower was left on the very edge of the pond. A solitary traveller passed; his foot went into the pool of clotted gore; he knew not what it was, and passed on.

Thus the deed was done. The murders had escaped; and nothing but the track of blood, the knife, and the mask was left to tell of the sanguinary work.

That night Gregory Saunders sat impatiently awaiting the arrival of some of his subordinates. His room was a private one at the Crown and Anchor. He wished to remain *incog.*; and mine host therefore had neither eyes nor ears when he was payed not to.

Ten o'clock struck. Gregory became fidgety.

'Can this be a failure, too!'

The idea seemed to strike him with horror. A perspiration broke out upon him, and his eyes became unnatural in their lustre.

Another hour passed. He now began to pace the room with angry strides.

'Curses! he comes not! Can he have failed in this? If so, I must——Bah! I get impatient. He comes!'

A stealthy step was heard upon the stairs. Presently some one paused outside the door.

'Enter!' he said.

Rock Elfin did so, with a more sullen air than ever. His scowl was threatening as he slouched in, and threw himself into a seat with a familiarity that brought a dusky tinge to Gregory's cheeks.

'Well?' was the impatient interrogation of Gregory.

'That's all I get for the trouble; not worth the business, I should think!'

He threw a folded piece of paper to his employer, who opened it eagerly, and read its contents. It was the letter written from the dictation of Mr. Lorry. It contained a more dangerous explanation than the former had.

The blood curdled in Gregory's veins as he pondered upon the probable results, if the letter had reached its destination.

'Good!' he said. 'This is enough! Where is the carrier of this?'

Elfin gave him a meaning, insolent stare, and felt inclined to break out in a hoarse laugh of mockery.

Not noticing the look he so well understood, Gregory said—

'I hope you did not go to extreme measures to obtain this paltry note.'

He used to make light of everything.

'Paltry note!' echoed Elfin, and his scowl became black as a thundercloud. 'Ah, well, it matters not, paltry or great, I'm payed the same. It's business! Look here, Mr. Saunders, you're work's done—you've got all you wanted—it's all the same, paltry or not, does it matter to you how I got it?'

'Certainly not. Only I should be sorry if you'——

He paused. The mocking smile of his ruffian hireling cut him short. He let the subject drop.

Pushing a decanter of wine towards his subordinate, he went on striding the room in deep meditation.

Elfin took a tumbler of wine, and began to drink it with a deliberate *nonchalance*, and taking as little notice of his employer as though he had not been in the room—as he would of a cat or dog.

Pausing suddenly in his promenade, the polished scoundrel fixed his glistening eyes upon his accessory, as though he would read him through, and said—

'Are you perfectly prepared to carry out my instructions?'

Lifting his heavy brow, and drinking off another tumbler of wine, Elfin smacked his lips, and replied—

'*Everything* is arranged. You've only to give the signal, and it's done.'

'So much the better. Did you go on board the lugger to-day?'

'Ay, and a smart craft she is,' replied the ruffian, with a look of satisfaction. 'The lads are ready, too.'

'Then you can do your work to-morrow night. Do not fail. There is nothing wanting on my part. I shall wait for you on board the lugger; and when you appear with *her* you shall receive the rest of the reward. You will not have much trouble if you are careful, as she is an invalid.'

'No fear. Ellen knows her game.'

'Very well. There is nothing left to arrange. Succeed, and you know your reward. Fail, and you will get a noose at the yard-arm. Mind you, Rock Elfin, if you should be discovered before you can get fairly away'——

'I'll blow the cursed blugger and all on boar out of the water. That's business. Ain't it?'

'That will do. Your know your work. Do it as soon as you like. Keep your eyes about you, and your companions from getting drunk.'

With that, Saunders left the room, and Rock Elfin to the wine and his own reflections.

'Good night, good night Mister Saunders,' muttered Elfin, clutching a goblet of wine. 'You have a nice chick; but its business—its business.'

*　　*　　*　　*　　*　　*　　*

The treacherous girl, Grevil, went on with her evil work with a cunning tact that could only be expected from one brought up in the heart of vice.

**Another Sheet of Side Wings for the "RED ROVER" to be given away.
See Notice Next Week.**

BLACK EYED SUSAN.

OR, PIRATES ASHORE.

THE APPEAL.

As she had said in her note to Saunders—which had been as a death warrant to the unfortunate Mr. Longstreet—Eurice was worse. She was very much so. The doctor came, shook his head when he saw her, and was silent.

He did not stay long. When he was about to depart, he said to her nurse—

'Do not leave her night or day,' and left the house.

The poor young creature, whose life had been so blighted, sank lower each hour. A lethargy stole over her brain and nerves, leaving her powerless and languid, wishing for death, were it not for the stern duty she had to perform.

The day after the visit of Mr. Lorry she revived a little. She sent for Mr. Lorry and the doctor; they came within a few minutes of each other.

'I did not expect to hear from you so soon,' said the lawyer, bowing to his client and the doctor. 'Ten minutes later and I should have been out. I cannot understand not having seen or heard anything of my deputy, Mr. Longstreet.'

''Tis that which made me send for you. I feel I shall not live long. I thought it as well to have a witness to prove I consign you to act solely in my name should anything happen; for that witness and friend I have chosen the doctor.'

'I am only too happy to render any little assistance I can in anything,' said that gentleman, with a kind smile.

'Have you,' continued Eurice to Mr. Lorry, 'a copy of the letter written last night?'

'I have, and signed by my deputy.'

'That is well.'

The deed was drawn up, in which she authorised Mr. Lorry to act in her name should an untimely death take her from this world.

The doctor, wondering at the mystery he saw in the scene going on around him, attested his name as a witness. Nothing more to be done, he and Mr. Lorry left the house together.

'Do you think there is any chance of her recovery?' asked the lawyer, as they walked along together.

'Well, her case is a strange one. Do you know, I really cannot say. The symptoms of death, she says, are coming upon her. Never during all my experience did I ever have such a strange case. Her malady is a mystery to me.'

'Strange; we must hope for the best. I will do myself the honour of calling upon you, sir, as perhaps you would like a little explanation of what took place to-day.'

'I should be most happy to see you, sir.' They arranged a time for meeting, and parted.

During the two days the girl Grevil had not been idle; she had won quite the affection of Jack's good-hearted mother.

The girl had a winning way of getting over people, and her remorse was so well assumed that it would have defied the closest observer to see any imposition about the girl. She volunteered to nurse the invalid while Mrs. Murray took a rest. Her offer was accepted; not so much for it relieving the anxious mother, who had learned to love the outcast wife as her own child, but because she thought the girl might be better company for the invalid.

A strange feeling of mistrust entered the heart of the outraged young wife as she looked at the girl Grevil. Her antipathy began to wear off on acquaintance; and ere the evening came she not only liked the girl, but felt less lonely when the girl was in the room.

Night of the second day drew on—it was the night of the tempest that had destroyed the gun brig.

Ellen was downstairs while supper was being prepared, and Mrs. Murray was complaining about little Jack being absent. The treacherous girl, with assumed generosity, offered to fetch the beer, and would hear of no denial, and had her way.

The meal was prepared shortly after. Ellen retired, and little Jack came in, his face flushed, his eyes beaming with wonder or intelligence.

His mother knew something had occurred.

'What has happened, Jack?'

'Oh, mother! horful—it's horful!'

'What, my son? what is awful?'

'There's been a murder!'

'Good gracious! what dreadful deeds are being perpetrated lately here.'

'Where, Jack?' asked his father.

'Not far from the great admiral's house, father.'

'Who is it?'

'Ah, nobody knows, they don't, 'cos they can't find the body. On'y there's a bloody track, a knife, and a mask been found; but that ain't the worst. They say as how Lawyer Longstreet is missing.'

This news had a strange effect upon Ellen. The blood seemed to stagnate in her viens, and she went deathly pale, and, fearing it would be noticed, she made an excuse to leave the table, and went upstairs to the invalid, and asked whether she could bring anything to her.

The reply was a negative. She expected it; but the excuse gave her time to control her feelings, and she returned to the supper-table. The conversation was kept up very late. The topic was the many strange doings in Deal of late. Jack, complaining of headache, retired to rest without taking anything beyond a cup of tea made by his mother.

Ellen watched it being prepared with a vicious gleam in her eyes, and she bit her lips till they nearly bled when the little fellow refused her.

It was now eleven o'clock when the girl, so old in the way of vice and crime, went upstairs to watch her patient. She said she would sit up on this occasion, not feeling tired. 'She could read,' she said, 'and that would enable Mrs. Murray to get a night's rest.'

Scarcely had she left the room when the good woman began to complain of a drowsiness.

'I feel very strange, John,' she said, to her husband, who was nodding in his chair. 'I cannot understand the feeling. I feel weak and giddy.'

'Eh, wife? What's that? You are over-tried, my gal, and want rest. Let us go to bed; a night's sleep will set you up.'

He drank the rest of the beer, and went with his wife to their sleeping apartment. Ere she could reach it a violent trembling seized her, and she was so weak she could scarcely stand.

Thinking it a momentary attack, brought on by over-fatigue, the husband assisted her into bed, and soon retired himself, and in a few minutes he fell into a kind of torpor. He was conscious, but powerless. He felt something was wrong, but he was unable to call assistance or rise. He lay in a deathly kind of trance.

Ellen found the invalid asleep when she entered the room. Treading softly, she crossed the room to where the sleeper lay, and, taking a small phial from her pocket, dropped a portion of its contents into a glass that contained a drink essential to the sufferer.

Either she was restless, or Ellen's presence disturbed her, for she awoke.

'What is the time?' she murmured. 'What is that noise?'

'It is the storm without, ma'am,' replied Ellen, answering the last question first. 'It's about half-past eleven.'

'I am very thirsty.'

'Will you take this?' asked the girl, eagerly clutching the drugged wine.

'Yes.'

Enrico drank the refreshing draught, and a few minutes after she was in a sound slumber.

The fearful storm raged without in all its awful fury. Above the noise of the elements there rang the shrill note of a whistle. The traitor girl, Grevil, started, and rose from her seat.

A violent trembling seized her, as the loud shrill note was repeated. She cast a glance of pity towards the invalid, then slowly approached the bed, and uncovered the sleeper.

'How beautiful and innocent she looks, and to think what a guilty wretch I am! Yet I dare not quail. I dare not refuse to do it. Again the signal! I must obey it.'

Trembling now in every limb, her cheeks pale, her eyes burning like living coals, with the flickering glare of the candle lighting up the dark shadows of the room, the girl began carefully to attire the sleeper in her daily attire. During the whole arduous process, Enrico did not awake. The girl had taken her measures too well; the powerful drug kept its victim in a deathly stupor. Having completed these arrangements, the treacherous girl descended the stairs shoeless, lest the noise of her footsteps might arouse little Jack.

Noiselessly she opened the front door. All was dark without. The rain fell in torrents, and the wind howled past her. She shrank back in horror, and would have retired, repenting the act she was about to commit.

'Is not the blood of one man already on my head?' she murmured, 'shall I be her murderess too, now'——

She was stopped by a dark form filling up the doorway.

'Ready?' asked a hoarse voice from behind a muffler.

'Oh, Elf, I have done it. They sleep like in death, and she is attired and insensible. Hist! the boy is not drugged.'

'Enough; out of my path, girl.'

Elfin, with two ruffian accomplices, entered noiselessly. They must have had no boots on. Ellen was unable to move. She stood transfixed with horror at her own devilish wickedness, and her hand was pressed upon her breast. Her head swam, and she felt as though she would faint.

The reappearance of Elfin with the inanimate form of the invalid roused her.

Putting herself in his path she said, imploringly,

'Rock, you will not hurt her. Take me with you to take care of her. Oh, do—do let me come.'

'Out of my way!' he exclaimed, hoarsely.

'Do not—promise me not to harm her. Ah! I see your intention in your eyes. I will come.'

'Curses! hold your tongue. Do you want to betray us?'

'No; but let me come—promise. Oh, Elf, for my sake—promise not to injure her. I do not want a reward. I only'——

'Mother—father, awake! Help! murder!' rang out from the dark end of the passage. It was little Jack's voice.

Elfin uttered a fearful oath.

'Silence that brat!' he cried; 'bring him with us.' Then turning with a withering look towards the girl, he said, 'You've done this, curse you. You shall accompany her—ah! ah—and have your reward.'

Loud and fearful was the piercing shriek that rang out upon the night air, echoing far above the noise of the tempest; and the girl, who had caused the destruction of others, felt her betrayer's knife buried in her bosom.

The cry was echoed by another. It came from Jack. Bravely the little fellow fought with a long iron poker, until a fatal blow sent him crushed almost to the bloodstained floor.

The scream had aroused the neighbours. The murderers whipped up their victims, dashed off with them to a carriage that stood not far off, leaving the unhappy girl, weltering in her gore, lying across the threshold of the street-door, the rain pattering down upon her cold, white face, and mingling with her life-stream that flowed from her motionless breast.

This was the reward for her services.

———

CHAPTER XXXVII.

HOW THE FRENCHMAN TOOK A PRIZE.

CAPTAIN TOM HATCHETT did not give the marine time to do much injury in his mad fury, half a dozen of the smugglers grappled with him, and he was disarmed in a minute.

His frenzied onslaught only helped to enrage Tom Hatchett, who now driven furious was dead to all feelings of mercy or remorse.

'Bind him!' he said.

One of the men tied the prisoner's hands with a large handkerchief, there being no rope handy; another blindfolded him, and a powerful smuggler lifted him on to the platform with as little trouble as any ordinary man would a child. The culprit struggled, but bound as he was he found it useless. His captor carried him to the end of the fatal plank, and stood him with his face towards the lugger.

Angered beyond control, Tom Hatchett cried—

'Don't tip him up my lads, a ducking would be too good. Curse him! he shall have the bullets.'

The four smugglers drew themselves up in a line; four long deadly tubes were brought to bear upon the poor wretch, who tried madly to release his hands.

'Ready,' said Tom Hatchett; 'fire!'

A simultaneous report, a blinding flash, and a loud scream of agony.

The smoke cleared away, and Bill Raker gave a cry.

The marine had burst the handkerchief asunder that bound his hands, and now clung with the grasp of death to the edge of the plank.

His cries of dying torture were dreadful.

'Tip the plank,' cried Hatchett.

It was done by one of the men who had fired. Then came a splash—a last despairing scream—and all was quiet. The murderer had gone to his last resting place with the stain of blood still on his hands.

Tom Hatchett soon shook off the momentary feeling of oppression that came over his men.

'Now, my lads, rouse up. Don't forget your messmate, poor Jem. Get him off, and the sooner we are out of these waters the better.'

The unfortunate smuggler who had been so pitilessly shot, was consigned to his watery grave; and the lugger was put in trim, her decks cleared, and the men at their quarters.

No signs of the pursuing enemy appeared yet, and Captain Tom had sundry various ideas of running into the coast, and getting a cargo that would make up for his late misfortunes.

'Should nothing occur to deter me,' Tom Hatchett said to Bill Raker, as the day drew on, 'we'll run into Brest, ship a cargo, and get back to Deal; and by Jupiter! nothing shall prevent me getting pretty Susan, should she not be with her confounded husband on board the Golden Arrow.'

'She's a dangerous craft to meddle with,' Raker replied, meaningly. 'She's a smart little spitfire, and with such a consort as William, she would defy a seventy-four.'

'Let her. I tell you, Bill, you won't dissuade me.'

'I don't want to, mate; I don't want to, but I want you to keep your neck out of danger—though I would try. Bill Raker can't always cut you loose, when in tow with the sharks.'

Tom Hatchett turned away moodily, his rough nature was roused, and he had a fierce tiger-like passion for Black Eyed Susan.

The day dragged slowly and wearily by, the men were tired; Raker was fatigued, and his wound pained him; Hatchett was sulky and troubled.

The mist began to clear off a little during the noon, but fell thick and heavy about dusk.

One of the men forward reported a vessel to be bearing down upon them.

Tom Hatchett scanned her through his glass.

'Confound the mist,' he said, 'she is almost upon us.'

'She's a smart sailor,' put in Bill Raker, coming forward; 'and by jingo, she's a French privateer, but she is not of French build.'

'Which is proved by her speed.'

'Ay, that's easy enough to see.'

'Do they sight us yet, think you ?'

'Look! would they come down upon us like that, if they didn't ?'

'Curse them! If we could show a clean pair of heels for an hour, darkness will aid us.'

'If,' repeated Raker, 'the Redbreast can fly; but she's got more than her match there.'

Tom Hatchett ground his teeth.

'Curse them! they shall not take us yet.'

'Not if I know it,' replied Raker. 'We'll try a ruse.'

The men were called up; the sails spread, and every effort made to show the unwelcome stranger a clean pair of heels.

Unfortunately for them, the stranger carried a nasty long gun at the bows, which hurled a shot right across the smuggler's quarters.

Tom Hatchett muttered an oath. Never had he so longed for darkness as on this occasion.

'Call up the lads,' he said; 'we will give them a warming at least before they do take us.'

The smugglers answered with a cheer, though they saw what rashness it would be to engage with the Frenchman.

The French commander seemed to suspect the nature of the Redbreast. He imagined there was a cargo on board worth overhauling, and was not disposed to lose the prize.

Tom Hatchett was not disposed to lose his vessel, and so kept out of the way. He was a fair judge of vessels, and he calculated the privateer to carry fourteen guns, about four times the number of men than he had, and was superior in every point of view.

'Twenty minutes more at this rate,' he chuckled, glaring admiringly at the Redbreast's prow, 'and we shall be out of sight, d——.'

A shot from the enemy cut away one of the lugger's spars.

The men began to get suddenly savage; they expected a bloody fight, and one that would not end in their failure.

'Bind another spar, my lads,' cried Hatchett, and his willing men did the best to obey.

'Can't we return a shot ?' suggested Raker.

'No; it would be losing time and distance. Let us keep on until compelled to haul to.'

Another shot from the Frenchman whizzed overhead.

'Ha, ha! you couldn't hit a haystack—ugh! the devil take you !'

This time a shot carried away the foretopmast, and threw the rigging into a tangled mass.

The Redbreast was losing speed.

Darkness came on, but not enough to hide the vessels from each other yet.

'Keep up, keep up, my lads; we'll——'

A well-aimed ball came with a crash across the lugger's stern, sending splinters flying in all directions, and so injuring the rudder as to make it almost useless.

Tom Hatchett uttered an awful oath.

The lugger only dragged through the water now.

Still he kept on with that dogged obstinacy so characteristic of him.

The enemy was so near now that a musket ball would have reached her.

She was less distinct than when first sighted, on account of the heavy blackness that enshrouded the vessels.

Tom Hatchett hoped this would help them to escape.

Each minute the privateer became less distinct, and in a quarter of an hour she was invisible.

But Bill Raker felt sure the foe was close upon their stern.

He was right. Hatchett was incredulous.

'Why don't they fire ?' he said.

''Cos they're charitable,' Bill Raker replied, with a grim smile, 'and don't want to spoil the pretty bird's feathers when they can get the bird without.'

Tom Hatchett gave a growl of savage rage.

'Take my advice, Tom; let the lads lie in wait under the bulwarks, in case he should come suddenly upon us.'

Hatchett growled assent.

The faithful little band, armed to the teeth, crouched beneath the bulwarks, and waited in terrible silence the coming moment.

'I thought so,' exclaimed Raker; 'look at that light! They are nearly upon us.'

The light of a ship's lantern flitted about for a few seconds only, then it disappeared, and all was dark as ever.

'Look here, Tom Hatchett, it's no use us trying to hold out against that crew.'

'D'ye s'pose I'm going to give in like a lamb ?'

'I didn't say so.'

'Spin out,' growled Hatchett.

'Well, get what you have of any value from below,

and come with the men and wait under the bulwarks aft.'

'What for?'

'To gain a victory.'

'How?'

'Well, I won't talk too loud, for the confounded crapo's ain't far off.

Tom Hatchett turned, and, placing his hand over his brow, pierced the gloom with his fierce little eyes, watching for the enemy, while Bill Raker communicated something to him that brought a gruff chuckle from the angered captain.

'It's all right,' he says. 'They are right upon us.'

'Silence fore and aft,' cried Raker, and he issued some orders in an under tone.

Dark as it was, they could see the enemy's prow almost upon them, and they were challenged.

The reply was given.

A shot was fired, and went crashing through the lugger's bows.

Tom Hatchett, in his rage, sent a shot crashing among the privateer's men, which slightly staggered them.

It was a terrible time for the smugglers, who crouched down, awaiting for the boarders.

The red glare of lanterns and torches showed plainly the privateer's movements. The crew waited at the side.

She looked wild and weird, coming swiftly as it were through the murky air, and the red glare of the torch playing upon their excited faces.

The smuggler lugger was as yet an undistinguishable sable mass, standing out in sombre relief from the dark background.

The coming foe gave a shout of triumph. They saw the lugger by the light of their lanterns and torches, but very indistinctly.

The sails had been lowered, but the flag was flying. Driven at bay, the smugglers were going to fight for their liberty and life.

Not a man could be discerned on the lugger's deck, and the black atmosphere hung like a pall over the smuggler's craft.

'Run right abreast of her,' said the Frenchman, eagerly. 'Grapple her, and then leap on board everyone of you. Rush right across the deck. Those English cunning dogs are crouching under cover.'

The captain deceived himself into the idea that he was too wide awake not to perfectly understand the enemy's movements.

In spite of his easy persuasives, his men did not feel as confident; there was something so ominous in running alongside and boarding that dark, silent ship, which kept on with only a jib flying.

Not a man could be seen, or a light. It was an awful uncertainty. No one knew what they were going to face.

The privateer's men were brave as most men are, but to board a vessel in a sombre gloom, that made it dark as Hades, without knowing what or whom they were going to meet, slightly chilled them.

'I believe mossoo's slightly skeered,' said Bill Raker, in a thick whisper to his captain.

They were both crouching with their men, waiting for the moment to arrive that would be death or liberty.

'Keep down, all of you. Here he is. Now, my lads, wait until the rush comes. Help them well over—don't forget to pour a volley from your pistols into them, then jump aboard from the clearest part of the vessel.'

'Ay, ay,' came in a faint whisper, along the lugger's deck.

The privateer was so close now, they could hear it skim through the water.

They waited breathlessly for the crisis.

It came.

A sudden collision. A crash—a shock. The grapnels were thrown, and the French privateer's men came over the side in a perpetual, howling stream of human forms.

It was a wild rush—a bewildering concord of cries, yells, and war whoops.

With the rash impetuosity of their nature they ran forward with a shout and a rush, and dashed on the lugger. Finding no foe to oppose them they rushed below. Every part of the vessel contained the intruders.

Then there came a report of firearms. The French rushed up from below, rushed from every point into each other's arm, and a wild uproar and confusion reigned over the vessel, and in the darkness, many of the friends and messmates cut each other down.

The captain, who was in the midst, sprang back towards his ship, attracted by the noise of strife. Never had he been so thoroughly taken in.

The smugglers who had remained like shadows during the boarding crouched lower still, and those men of the enemy who jumped down close to the bulwarks, were sure to fall on a knife or cutlass, and many died thus, not seen, and their low cry not heard in the din.

When Tom Hatchett thought nearly all the foes were over, he called—

'Now, my lads, up and board! Blaze away!'

The smugglers sprang up with a yell, discharging their firearms among the amazed Frenchmen, who were in the act of boarding, driving them in all directions.

The smuggler knew how much depended upon the issue of this fight, and cut away remorselessly. They cut down all in their path, and boarded the privateer from the forecastle as the French poured in upon the lugger from the poop.

'Out off the grapnels!' cried Hatchett.

Bill Raker jumped forward: they were cut off; and ere the enemy knew what had happened, the two ships were twenty feet apart. The privateer's crew, all but a few men, were on the lugger. The smugglers had taken possession of the schooner. Never had there been an exchange so neatly done before.

Panic-stricken by the furious onslaught of the smugglers, the poor sailors on the schooner rushed below stairs, crying—

'Hold, my men! batten them down, and hoist the canvas. Hurrah! splendid, Bill. This was a mighty stroke. What a notion of yours! D'ye hear them howl?'

'Ay, let them howl! He wanted a prize: he's got one—ah, ah!'

'Yes; exchange is no robbery!' laughed Hatchett.

The outwitted French captain was roused with fury at being thus juggled.

He found himself on the small smuggler lugger, with nothing in it worth carrying away, while the handful of smugglers had got his magnificent schooner.

He tore his hair, and howled out a lot of incoherent orders to his men, who rushed wildly about, ischarging their firearms at the runaway. A gun was brought to bear on the schooner; but darkness and distance made the attempt a folly.

The infuriated son of Gaul could not follow because he had, with his own guns, so damaged the lugger.

'Sacre! Diable! dirty English pigs!' he cried, as the schooner, with all its sails flying, bore rapidly away.

This is the way Monsieur Alexandre Treville took a prize; and what he gained by it cannot be very satisfactory to him. If so, he displayed his overwhelming joy very strangely, and at the great injury of his hair and moustache, which he abused most ruthlessly, tearing them out by the roots, and cursing his men for cowards, until passing the gangway, his foot missed the top step, slipped and he fell.

'Sacre! Diable!' he screamed, then lay quiet.

CHAPTER XXXVIII.
A THIRD MESSENGER.

UNDISTURBED by any interruption now, the foes of Gregory Saunders held a quiet, serious council.

In case any eavesdroppers should be prowling about, they kept up their assumed character with each other with a quiet gravity the serious nature of their business forced upon them.

Mr. Jasper Lorry sat quiet and thoughtful for a few minutes; he had not yet entered upon his business.

'Refresh yourself with a little wine. I'm sorry you came too late for dinner.'

'Nay, I've dined, my lord. Pardon me, in my zeal for your cause I had omitted to congratulate you on your safe arrival here. It was pleasant and unexpected to meet you thus.'

The supposed count bowed with a smile. He well understood the disguised meaning of his friend's words, and he replied—

'Yes; on some future occasion I will give you an account of my journey, which was well-nigh a fatal one.'

'Do. I should be most happy to hear all; but now'——

'To business.'

'Just so, my lord.'

'We cannot do better that hear what you have to communicate, Mr. Lorry.'

'Much, my lord, which is unpleasant.'

'I am prepared.'

'You have seen the reports?'

'I have.'

'They are ambiguous and botched-up compositions, and only bewilder you.'

'That I expected. Proceed.'

'I lost no time in coming here from London after the receipt of your letter. I saw the lady of whom you spoke.'

'Eurice?'

'Even so.'

'How did she greet you?'

'With all the welcome a prudent (pardon, I had forgotten you), devoted heart could give a welcome friend who had come to succour.'

Gerald's face became set as he listened to the lawyer.

'She seemed sinking fast, and her hourly pre-sentiment was that she would soon be called from this world. With the fear of that idea upon her, she went wisely to work. She made me executor, to act solely in her name, and the documents are in my pocket. I sent a letter by my deputy to the admiral. I have a copy of that letter, which never reached him.'

'How?'

'The soulless wretches murdered a poor old man on the way, and robbed him of the missive.'

'Cowards!' hissed our hero, from behind the beard.

'Bloodhounds!' muttered the count. 'Go on.'

'The body of the poor old man cannot be found. I intend to have a search throughout the country. That is not the worst; the same man who caused his death caused Eurice to be carried off—perhaps murdered, God only knows! Some girl who had been staying at the house a day or so was stabbed by the ruffians, and a little lad belonging to the house was carried, dead or alive, no one knows where.'

'Have you tracked the murderer?'

'No.'

'Nor where it was committed?'

'Yes.'

'Continue, Mr. Lorry.'

'I have taken immediate steps. I had the pond, not many yards from where the murder was committed, dragged. The lawyer's hat and silver snuff-box were found, but not his body. There hangs a mystery over the affair—one I must and will solve. Strange, the very night after the murder, that the outrage should have been committed in Lower Deal! but I have every reason to believe that I shall trace the doers of that, and very quickly.'

'How?' asked the Count.

'The girl who fell from a stab from one of the ruffians lies in a dying state—I will get a confession from her.'

'But she may know nothing.'

'SHE was an *accomplice!*' This was said with startling vehemence, and the lawyer's little eyes flashed terribly. 'I will proceed there now. If you could follow in a few minutes you will find me there, endeavouring to extort a confession from the treacherous girl.'

'Do so, Mr. Lorry; I will follow you. I have something to do, firstly, then to follow you.'

'Very good, my lord. Good night.'

Mr. Lorry withdrew, and our hero was left with his two friends.

'Now, Will, I want a messenger to go to the admiral's house.'

'You can trust me, cap'n.'

'Ay, I know that, Will; but you would be known. Here, we might escape notice; but get too near that Gregory Saunders, and, with his cunning, he would suspect and discover all.'

'No one knows me,' said Andrew; 'let me go—I wish it.'

Gerald Stuart became reflective for a few minutes. He was aware that Andrew was not known to any one; he was also aware of the danger any one ran in going on such a mission.

'You will grant my wish?' asked Andrew.

'But, my dear Andrew, do you know the danger you incur?'

'No, nor care,' was the bold reply.

'Go, then; and should harm befall you, let the

evil-doers look to it. You will take the semblance —the golden arrow. You will get beneath the window of Madeline's room, and cry like an owl until your signal is answered; then give her this sign, that will tell her I live.'

'It shall be done; fear not for me,' and Andrew departed.

'Now, Will,' said Gerald—they were alone—'I think I cannot do better than go to Mr. Lorry and discover who has abducted that poor girl. Should I do so, we will track him to the end of the earth.'

'Ay, we will.'

'I think, Will, it is safe for us to go out singly.'

'Ay, cap'n.'

'Then we will part for the present.'

Some arrangements were carried on in an undertone, and then Will left the tavern.

He had not gone many steps ere he came upon two men whose conversation attracted his notice.

They were Silas Doggrass and Gnatbrain. He was carrying on an animated conversation with Susan's villanous uncle.

'Maybe strange things will come to light soon, Mister Doggrass. There's been dark doings in Deal of late, but much will out sooner or later.'

Will distinctly heard these words from Gnatbrain, and feeling curiously interested, he strolled on in their wake.

'You're always prating,' retorted Doggrass, snappishly. 'Confound you and your croakings too! I wish you'd leave me to myself.'

'Ay, guilt and solitude go together,' rejoined Gnatbrain.

'Do they? Well, Gnatbrain and Doggrass don't; so I'll say good night!'

'Ah, say away, Mister Doggrass. I can afford to laugh now, for I know where your niece is. She's the companion of the High Admiral's daughter, who's going to be married on Sunday to as big a villain as ever trod the earth.'

With that he turned down a by-street, and Doggrass went on alone.

'Married on Sunday!' muttered Will, as he turned and retraced his steps. 'That's news for the captain.'

Meantime Captain Gerald had gone with Mr. Lorry to the house of Mrs. Murray to see the girl who had been struck by the knife of Elfin or his companions.

Captain Gerald was conducted to the room where the girl lay on a couch. Mrs. Murray had not yet recovered from the shock she had received by the loss of her son and the poor wronged wife whom she had learned to love.

Mr. Lorry requested that he might be alone with the girl, Ellen, and Captain Gerald.

The poor girl was suffering most acutely, and was sinking rapidly.

Her eyes lighted with a fierce light when she saw Mr. Lorry.

'I am glad you have come, sir. I thought I should die with no one to avenge me.'

'Fear not, poor misguided girl. Confess all frankly, that we may be put on the track of the villains who were at the head of the plot.'

'Captain Saunders.'

'Who abducted the lady and boy?'

'Rock Elfin.'

'What was he?'

'Once fisherman and smuggler, now Captain of the White Fox armed lugger.'

'You were a willing accomplice of theirs?'

'At the first I was, but I learned to love the lady in that short time, and it was in imploring mercy for her that I received this wound, which, I feel, is mortal.'

In spite of the part she had taken in the transaction, Captain Gerald pitied the girl from his heart.

'I think,' gently interposed Mr. Lorry, 'that it would be only just to have a written confession from this young person.'

'Truly.'

'I wish it, sir,' faintly gasped Ellen.

Mr. Lorry took pen, ink, and paper, and sat by the invalid's bed, waiting patiently for her confession.

It was tedious work, as the poor girl could not articulate a perfect sentence.

It was done, at length. A full and truthful confession—nothing was disguised from the lawyer, and he heard with pain that the unhappy girl had been the indirect cause of Lawyer Longstreet's death, though this could not be positively sworn to yet.

When the confession was finished, Gerald observed, with regret, that the poor girl was struggling madly to stifle back the cold hand of death, which was fastening its grasp upon her heart.

'You have nothing more to say. Is there anything that can be done for you?' asked Mr. Lorry.

'No, sir—nothing; but I should feel happier if that gentleman would forgive me for the share I took in the disgraceful business; but it was to save the man I loved, and to retrieve my fallen honour—for he promised to make me his wife—that I did it.'

'I forgive you with all my heart,' exclaimed Gerald, mournfully. 'Would to heaven, I could save you from death, that you might live to repent!'

'I do not want to live; but—but I should like the coward who betrayed me, and then thrust his knife to my heart, to be punished.'

'He shall.'

'That is all I wish to say. You forgive me. Beg the lady to do so when you see her. Say I died—I died—penitent'——

She could say no more. The doctor was sent for.

He came only in time. Five minutes after his arrival the resignated girl breathed her last.

'That was a cowardly thrust,' muttered Gerald. 'Poor misguided creature, I pity her.'

He then turned towards Mrs. Murray, who stood looking on and weeping.

'Be consoled, my poor woman, no harm shall befall your brave son. I have a swift ship, and these marauders shall be overtaken. God have mercy upon them, whoever they are—I will have none.'

He left a purse of gold with the weeping woman, saying she should not be forgotten, nor her son.

'God! what villany,' said Gerald to Mr. Lorry, as they returned towards the hotel.

'Yes; but you have them nicely in your power. Though the living witness is gone, we have proof enough to drag that villain Saunders to the scaffold.'

'And we will!' Gerald hissed the words between his teeth.

He entered the hotel alone, and ascended the stairs to his apartments.

'Has Andrew returned?' he asked of Wilks.

'No, your honour.'

'Great God! Can anything have happened to *him*! I must see to it.'

*   *   *   *   *   *   *

The brave youth Andrew never gave a thought to the late tragedy that had been committed in the lonely road he now traversed.

He only thought of fulfilling his mission—to do that he would have walked through a burning oasis.

It was a dark lonely road he had to traverse, but he kept well on the alert, and his right hand grasping a pistol by the butt.

It must be confessed he felt some relief when he saw the Lord High Admiral's mansion in view, and he quickened his pace.

By the instructions he had received from Gerald he knew what part of the house to find the window of Madeline's sitting-room.

Crossing the lawn he stood on the gravel path—in the shade of two gigantic vases—each containing a mass of choice flowers.

He threw his cloak aside, and waited silently to catch the slightest sound that would betray the approach of any one.

Taking from his breast the diamond barbed golden arrow, he imitated the cry of the night birds to perfection.

No notice was taken of it. He kept his eyes fixed upon the window, which remained dark as ever.

The night seemed to grow more gloomy. Sombre shadows seemed to flit around him. He heeded them not. He had his eyes only for that dark casement, ears only for a sound that might proceed from within.

Again his low, strange signal rang upon the night air.

Then all was silent.

He fancied he heard a stealthy step behind him. He turned; nothing could be seen.

Fixing his eyes upon the casement, he renewed his signal. This time he fancied he saw a light flitter about within.

'At last,' he murmured, 'she comes.'

Again he started.

A shadow was thrown across his path. He leaped round.

Too late!

Cold and gleaming, a long blade flashed before his eyes. He heard a surprised oath—then he gave a low cry of pain.

'Coward! dastard!' he said, reeled forward, staggered a few paces with his hand to his side, the blood gushing from a gaping wound to the ground beneath, and he fell full length and motionless, a dark form leaning over him, a fierce, cruel face looking into his unconscious eyes, and a blood-reeking blade, held above his chest, dripped its red drops upon his fair bosom.

CHAPTER XXXIX.

RETURNING TO LIFE.

WHEN Captain Gerald left the Three Admirals he met our hero. For fear of being seen together by any of their enemies, they adjourned to a secluded spot to carry on their conversation.

'I have heard sufficient, Will, to put us on the track of the villains who carried off that girl—that

you and me will follow and bring her back if alive, avenge her if dead.'

'Ay, but they've had a good start of us. When do you think of setting sail?'

'To-morrow.'

'Cap'n, you can't. I've heard some tidings, too. I followed that old shark Doggrass, who was in tow of Gnatbrain, and I heard a little of what passed.'

'It concerned us?'

'So much so that it informed me your Madeline was to be spliced on Sunday at the church.'

'Good heavens!' exclaimed Gerald, staggered by the information. 'Fate seems against us. I dare not go to leave her at the mercy of that villain. What can be done?'

'Well,' suggested Will, 'maybe I can offer an opinion. I say wait and save your beloved from that d——d pirate, and then set sail on the track of the dastardly cutthroats. The Golden Arrow is a quick sailer, and would soon overtake them.'

'That is our only resource, Will; we can do nothing else.'

'There be bad, bloody times coming,' said Will solemnly.

'I feel so too; but enough, I came out to seek Andrew; he has not returned yet.'

'Maybe he has come in while you were out.'

'Likely enough, Will; but I have a misgiving at my heart that all is not well. Come, we will return. Let us hope for the best.'

They went side by side to the 'Three Admirals.' At the door, Gerald paused, and a cold chill ran through him.

The people of the house were in a state of excitement. Lights were flashing about, and mine host looked the picture of terror.

'Oh, my lord!' he exclaimed, throwing his arms up, upon beholding Captain Stuart.' Oh, my lord! your secretary'——

Gerald waited to hear no more. He passed the innkeeper and his servants at a bound.

Will followed.

At the door of the apartments they were stopped by Wilks, whose face was convulsed with sorrow.

The poor fellow knew how deep was the love that existed between Andrew and Gerald, and he thought the shock would be too much for him.

'Cap'n,' he said, tremulously, 'don't go in yet. It will be too much for you'——

'Out of my path. I will know the worst!'

He thrust his faithful servant aside, and entered the chamber.

One step into the room, and he paused. All his passion vanished, his heart melted, and tears rose to his eyes.

Andrew lay in his bed—a deathly pallor over his handsome face, which was distorted at the mouth and nostrils with agony.

A medical man bent over him, and was tenderly dressing a gaping wound in his side.

Gerald stood looking on in mute horror—the agony of the sufferer could not surpass what he felt at the sight. Will was by his side, quiet and subdued.

'God! what coward hand did that?' Gerald exclaimed in an agonized tone of voice. 'Tell me, does he live? Is there hope?'

'Hush!' said the doctor, without removing his eyes from his patient; 'there is hope, but little hope.'

Another Sheet of Side Wings for the Play of " RED ROVER" will be given away with No. 16.

BLACK EYED SUSAN.

OR, PIRATES ASHORE.

THE FATE OF ANDREW.

' Is there *any* hope ? '

' Yes.'

' Thank God ! Save him ! restore him to me ; exert your skill to its utmost. Name your own price, I care not what it is, so long as you cure him.'

' I will do my best, sir ; the best for him that medical power can do. I cannot go beyond that. I have a request to make.'

' Name it.'

' That he will not be excited in any manner, nor e allowed to talk.'

' I will faithfully see to that. Tell me how came this ? '

' I know not, sir. That good person knows the sad details ; I do not.'

The doctor pointed with an instrument he held in his hand towards the end of the bed, to indicate the ' good person ' was there.

Gerald glared in that direction. He saw no one, and Will had vanished too.

But not far.

Turning round, he saw him near the door in conversation with an individual of peculiar appearance, who was carrying on an excited conversation in a low tone of voice.

Gerald would have gone forward to them, but Andrew opened his eyes, and murmured Gerald's name.

He waved his hand for Will and his companion to leave the room, as the talking might disturb the patient.

They withdrew, and closed the door.

' Andrew, my dear Andrew, how came this ? ' Gerald took the youth's hand as he spoke, and sat by the bedside.

' I should not question him now, at least yet, or medical aid will only be thrown away,' quietly observed the doctor.

Andrew smiled faintly. He tried to speak, but the effort was a painful one.

Captain Gerald swore a mental oath to avenge him ; to give back sigh for sigh, and pang for pang that the youth had suffered.

He was not the man likely to break his word either.

The doctor did all that could be done for his patient; then departed. Gerald watched by his loved friend's side for hours. No one but himself was allowed to wait on the wounded youth. He guarded him zealously.

William had been closeted in the sitting, or reception room with the stranger, who was honest-hearted Gnatbrain.

The first words Will addressed to him were—

' You here, messmate ? '

' Ay, Will, so I am.'

' More bloody work. How came it ? '

' I know not. I saw not the deed, but I heard the cry, and saved the sufferer.'

' Where, and how did you hear all this, mate ? '

' I am Lord Garthway's gardener now, and I hear and see much.'

' Maybe '——

At this juncture, Gerald waved his hand to them to leave the room. The conversation was resumed when they were alone.

' Well, Mister William, I don't know what made me go out in that part of the garden, I'm sure ; but I was there and heard the cry of pain. I rushed to the spot, and the murderer took flight, after havin robbed his victim.'

' Didn't you give signals of distress, and have the lubber captured ? '

' No.'

' No ! ' echoed Will, in surprise.

' It would be useless ; jackals only come when the prey has been found.'

William looked puzzled. He did not understand Gnatbrain clearly.

' May be,' he said, doubtfully.

' There is a bad game being played, William, but neither you nor yours will be the losers. Many strange things may come to light shortly, then let *him* look out.'

' Mate, I wish you'd try plain sailing. I can't make top nor tail of that.'

' P'raps not, p'raps not, but you'll understand all soon, Will. To end my story, I found the young fellow wounded, he murmured the name of this tavern, and I brought him here.'

' Mate,' said Will, as though struck with some sudden idea, ' you're gardener.'

' Ay.'

' Do you know Miss Madeline ? '

' I do.'

' And Susan ? '

' Well ; but I have not seen her since she's been at the mansion.'

' D'ye think you could ? '

' It's probable.'

' Gnatbrain,' would you do me a service ? '

' With all my heart, Mr. William, with all my heart.'

' Then find a means of seeing Sue. Give her this note ; if you cannot, manage to whisper in her ear that we—Gerald and I—are alive.'

' I will do it.'

Captain Gerald entered the room at that moment.

' He sleeps,' he said.

Will repeated what he had already heard from Gnatbrain.

' It is fortunate you are with his lordship. You could render us a service.'

' I would, willingly, sir.'

' Do you know anything of what is going to take place, there ? '

' Yes, sir, the marriage between Gregory and the Admiral's daughter.'

' 'Tis well I know this,' and Gerald's brow darkened. ' Could you, do you think, obtain a brief interview with Miss Madeline, or convey to her this note ? '

' I will do all I can, sir, towards it.'

' I shall be indebted to you, Mr. Gnatbrain, and your services shall not be forgotten. I should like to see you to-morrow.'

' I will put myself at your service, sir. Until then, good-bye.'

' Good night ; ' and Gerald wrung the honest fellow's hand warmly.

' An honest fellow that,' said Gerald, as Gnatbrain departed.

The worthy gardener was lost in meditation as he went back.

' Ah, ha ! ' he cogitated, ' maybe, Mr. Saunders, you'll sing a different tune soon. You don't expect to see the dead come to life, but they will the day your ruin is brought about, and it ain't very far off.

It's a good thing to be gardener. I see a great deal. I know as much as the jackals who went for their prey. I rescued it. He, poor youth, ain't the first I've saved. Ah! if they only knew who I'd got to bring agin them, Saunders would pray to be swallowed up in the bowels of the earth.'

Late as it was, he wended his way towards Garthway's mansion without the slightest trepidation.

Gnatbrain had a small, cosy cottage given him by the Admiral while he remained as gardener. It was on the grounds, to afford the opportunity of being near his work.

To this lowly little place he now wended his way, and though the road had been so dangerous to others he had no fears for himself. He was looked upon as a harmless nothing, and he chuckled when he thought of it.

'Ah, ha! harmless nothing. Yes, I am. Wait, my fine people, maybe you'll bite your fingers for not having crushed the harmless nothing. Maybe I'm not as harmless as you think,' and he chuckled gleefully.

He could now discern his little whitewashed cottage in the distance.

He approached it cautiously, and kept a sharp look out, as though afraid of being watched.

He gave two or three raps on the door ere he unlocked it to let himself in.

It was such a precaution as any one would take to warn a person within of their approach.

The rooms were all upon the floor; the door opened into the one usually occupied by Gnatbrain.

A small lamp threw its pale flickering glare upon the walls, making visible a lot of fantastic shadows that danced and flitted about like Will-o'-the-wisps.

Fastening the door very carefully, Gnatbrain took up the lamp and passed on to an inner apartment that was occupied by a sick person.

A man in the decline of life.

At a glance an observer would have seen by his face he had lately undergone great suffering, even now he ever and anon uttered a low, painful moan.

His eyes glittered with pleasure as Gnatbrain entered the room.

'Have you wanted for anything during my absence?'

'No,' feebly replied the invalid.

'Good. I have seen some friends. I shall most likely bring one to see you to-morrow,'

'Have you seen *him?*'

'Well—yes.'

'Did you tell him I live? It is sad to be here, and supposed dead.'

'Don't fear. The time's coming, it ain't far off, when you'll be brought to life. You'll be more than a phantom to one sinful wretch, at least.'

'But surely *he* might know it, Mr. L—'

'Hush! Walls have ears.'

The invalid gave a low groan.

'Are you not better?'

'Much—much.'

'Then have patience. You shall not be kept in this uncertainty after to-morrow, or Sunday; but it must be so till then. Others have to do the same. Men supposed dead are walking about in other forms. It's all for the best.'

'True, true, but, I care not how soon it ends!'

'It will do so, soon. Hist! What is that noise? Someone prowling about. Let them beware!'

Gnatbrain snatched a gun from the wall, and crept to the shutters, and placed his ear to the crack.

The voice he had heard came again.

A double click sounded ominously through the little room, as the gun-lock was pulled back, and Gnatbrain went on tip toe to the door.

CHAPTER XL.

A BEAUTIFUL TRIO.

THE long supposed death of Gerald Stuart, coupled with the many reports to corroborate the supposition was the cause of Madeline's lingering recovery from her severe attack of illness.

The peerless daughter of the Lord High Admiral recovered but slowly, not that she was confined to her bed, but she could not be about.

Pretty Black-eyed Susan was her constant companion. The two sad hearts found an echoing sympathy in each other's misfortunes.

About the same time as our hero, with Gerald Stuart and Andrew, were holding a council at the 'Three Admirals,' Madeline and Susan were seated together in the former's sitting-room, the window of which overlooked the lawn.

It was easy to see that both the young creatures were suffering from mental torture—grief.

Madeline was seated in a large arm-chair. Her head was resting on a large feather pillow, which brought out in bold relief the rich, dark curls that clustered in wavy masses over her snow-white shoulders, from which a scarlet cloak, edged with fur, had just fallen.

She looked beautiful in her negligent *dishabille.* One tiny foot and perfectly-modelled ankle peeped from beneath the hem of her morning robe.

Her lustrous eyes were closed, and her pouting, finely-cut lips were a little apart, displaying just a tiny streak of white pearl-like teeth.

She was pondering deeply—mourning for her absent lover—hoping against hope. An inward voice bade her not despair, and often she wondered if Gerald was really dead.

Late events had wrought a great change in pretty Susan. The peach-like tint had left her cheeks. The white, almost transparent, paleness that had substituted the former rosy flush rather added to than detracted from her beauty.

Her lovely eyes were shielded by the creamy-coloured drooping lids, her hands were clasped, and lying listlessly in her lap.

Both were awoke from their dreamy ponderings by the entrance of a tall, haughty-looking girl.

'I intrude, Miss Madeline?' she queried.

'No, Pauline; we need someone's presence to dispel this dreadful melancholy from our hearts.

Pauline seated herself between the two unhappy girls. With a smile of pity she took Madeline's hand affectionately between her own, and said, in a voice, peculiar in its clear, silvery distinctness—

'There is an end to all things.'

'I could, ay and do wish there was an end to my sufferings,' replied Madeline, mournfully.

Pauline pressed her hand. Pauline was a peculiar girl. She had been the attendant and companion to Madeline since the latter left school to become mistress of her father's mansion. They were more like sisters than lady and companion. Pauline loved her beautiful young friend (for she cannot be termed mistress in the relative position) with a passionate affection almost selfish. Pauline was not a year older than Madeline in years, but she was a haughty, determined woman, with a strong mind, powerful and decided will. To strangers and the opposite sex she was a cold, haughty, impassible girl. A look from her black, steady eye would awe a person. In fact, to some she was an inexplicable mystery.

With all her selfish love for Madeline, she did not look upon Susan as a rival. Upon first acquaintance she did not receive Susan very cordially. When the poor young wife's story was known, and the service she had rendered Madeline, Pauline liked her, pitied and would protect her.

Knowing Pauline's zealous affection, Madeline treated her as she ever did—with the same confidence and affection.

As the three girls—all young and beautiful—sat together, they made a lovely trio.

'I have had some news to-day,' Pauline observed.

'Concerning whom ?'

'The nation. I think the squadron your pa commissioned Captain Crosstree to be commodore of is ordered off in a few days to intercept the French, who intend helping the rebel Jacobites. Captain Saunders is in that squadron.'

Madeline's face flushed with joy.

'I hope he will go, then I shall be saved. God forgive me, but I almost wish he may—may'——

'Fall,' interrupted Pauline. 'Yes, I pray for it, for it would e'en be better to die in a contest, as honour would attend his death. Were he to live too long he might die in ignominy.'

Madeline looked interrogatively at her companion, who either would not or did not understand the look.

'I have just seen the gardener,' said Pauline.

'The gardener ? Ah, I remember. Well, dear ?' queried Madeline.

'He has been to the town, and he reports that a Spanish noble has just arrived at one of the inns there. That, of course, would be nothing to do with us; but he added, with great significance, "the Spanish noble has an English face," and that it was dangerous to allow his lordship's gamekeepers to be prowling about the grounds.'

'He is a strange man, Pauline.'

'He is, for even I cannot understand him.'

'But,' put in Susan, 'what suspicion has he ?'

'That I could not discover. You shall try if you like. I will conduct him here.'

'We will see him !' decided Madeline.

Pauline left the apartment, and was absent ten minutes or more, when she returned, preceding Gnatbrain, who entered the room bashfully.

'Are you going to the town to-night ?'

'I have been, Miss Madeline; but will go again if you wish it.'

'I may do so; but I wish you to answer a few questions. Have you any idea why his lordship has men lurking about the grounds ?'

'I don't know, miss, but I suspect Captain Saunders is with the admiral, and they are both in great excitement. It is the first time they have met since the Firefly went down with nearly all hands on board. Mr. Saunders has got some strange notions into his head, and he would have men stationed on the grounds with orders to shoot any lurking strangers.'

Madeline's cheeks went paler still.

'Are you one of those who keep watch ?'

'No, miss, I am not ordered to keep on the grounds, and I ain't ordered to keep off.'

Gnatbrain gave something like a knowing smile as he said this.

'Mr. Gnatbrain, can we trust you ?'

'Ask Miss Susan, miss.'

'He is a faithful friend of my poor husband's,' murmured the sad wife.

'Do you think it would be possible to discover if the lieutenant, Mr. William Howard, did really go down with the Firefly ?'

'I could discover that, I think, miss.'

'Do so, and I will reward you.'

'Yes, do, and I will bless you,' cried Susan, with an imploring look. 'You discover if my husband lives, and I will for ever bless you.'

'I will do all a man can do. But don't give way—wait and hope. You, too, Miss Madeline — your enemies have not got the game in their own hands entirely. No, Miss Madeline, let them have their own way up to the last minute; if nothing happens then to stop their game, why I will; for I can—yes, miss, I can.'

Without waiting for any more words, he turned round and withdrew, muttering as he went—

'If they only knew what I've got in my cottage—if they only knew !'

'I do know,' mentally observed Pauline, who, with the others, had overheard the remark.

'What can he mean ?' said Madeline, wondering.

'I know not,' replied Pauline ; 'but I'd advise the same measures. His lordship will seek you soon. Appear to accede to his wishes, and place your hope upon the last moment.'

A cry, low and subdued, yet of intense agony, startled the lovely trio.

It came from without.

From under the window.

Pauline was the first to break from the lethargy.

Approaching the window with a quick, gliding motion, she drew the curtains aside and began to unfasten the shutters. Ere she had the window-bolts drawn back another faint cry or groan came upon her ears.

'Oh, heavens ! what can it be ?' Madeline rose from her chair as the terrified words left her lips. Susan was by her side.

They stood clinging to each other in mute alarm, while Pauline—her nerves not shaken in the least by the mysterious cries—threw open the window and looked out.

'Hush !' she said, motioning the two affrighted girls to keep back.

All was dark without; the lawn was like a sable patch, thrown out in strong relief by the light gravel paths, across which flitted more than one dark shadow.

She knew not what the shadows were caused from. Something that caught her eye made a cold shiver pass through her frame.

A dark stain on the gravel path beneath the casement. Something seemed to whisper to Pauline what that dark stain was.

'Blood !' she muttered, inwardly ; and the other words followed involuntarily—' of whom ?'

'I see nothing, dear,' she said, in the usual manner she used to address Madeline.

A groan, faint though agonized, floated to the'r ears.

'There is something the matter. Oh ! Pauline, if it should be'—— She could say no more ; her look spoke the rest, as she clung wildly to her companion's arm.

'Something tells me there has been more dreadful work,' Susan gasped in an almost inaudible voice.

'Remain here; I will go myself. Do not stir, I beg of you, from this room until I return.' The cold, unreadable glitter was in Pauline's eyes as she spoke, her lips were set determinedly.

'What is all this?'

The voice was cold and haughty.

The beautiful trio turned and beheld the admiral, who had entered unheard.

Madeline threw herself forward on his breast, and fixing her beautiful eyes, tear-dimmed and beseeching, upon him, said—

'Father, something has happened—something, I know not what. Hark!'

Another groan, more distinct than the former ones, came upon their ears.

The admiral paled.

'What is this?' he asked.

'We know not. See—oh! do see.'

He strode across the room and rang the bell furiously. As he did so, Pauline went to Madeline.

'I will go e'en now. The admiral has sought you for some private motive. Do not hold out against his wishes. Hope on, and you won't hope in vain, though succour may not come until the last minute. Fear nothing—see him; accede to his wishes, in appearance only, and all will be well.'

Madeline pressed her companion's hand with silent gratitude. This would be a trying moment for Madeline, and she sank back in her chair. Pauline, with Susan, left the chamber, and Garthway ordered a servant to make a strict search over the grounds.

Then he turned, closed the door, and faced his daughter with an air of extreme uneasiness.

'Child,' he said, solemnly, 'you are better?'

'What should make me so?'

'Why those replies! Have you not returned to reason yet?'

'Alas! my reason, perhaps, has been too sound. I would it were not so now; I might, at least, find some relief in unconsciousness.'

The tone of voice, more than the words, made his lordship exclaim—

'Madeline — Madeline! would you break your father's heart?'

'God knows, not willingly, though my heart to others seems a matter of little consideration.'

'My child, listen—listen to me gravely. Do not forget, unhappy girl, that your father's life will now depend upon your future conduct. I have borne this long enough. I have suffered disgrace—such disgrace as will never be wiped out in my time. The accursed work of shame is cankering into my very heart. I cannot mix with my fellow men. I am here shut up, living away from society and my government, executing their commands and then retiring; but it shall end. I will lead an expedition against that rebel, Charles Edward; and my prayer is that I may fall in the honour of my country—that my blood may wipe out the stain that clings to me and mine, and through you—you, my only child!'

The old man broke down—his voice was thick and uncontrollable.

Madeline buried her face in her hands and wept; the idea of losing her only parent and protector was more than she could bear.

'Oh, no! no, you must not go!' she cried, starting up, and twining lovely her arms round his neck.

'Madeline, listen to me. I hope now that childish nonsense has left you, since the soulless wretch who so destroyed your happiness is no more.'

'Of whom do you speak'——

'Hush! girl. Listen to me. A squadron is going off to intercept the French. I must head it. Commodore Crosstree has the command of six ships, which are to cruise about to intercept the enterprise of the Spaniards. He, therefore, cannot substitute me. I may never return alive. Something whispers to me I shall not. But I could die happy, had you a protector. 'Tis my wish you shall have one. You know your husband, Madeline. I hope no foolish fancy will make him so distasteful. He is honourable—he loves you; what is more, it is a sacred compact that cannot be broken by any slight event. You are not well. I have therefore procured the necessary licence, and a priest will be here to-morrow, when you will become the bride of Gregory Saunders, who will protect you should I fall.'

'My lord, I may become an unwilling bride—a wife, but in name only. Do as you will, my lord, but force not too much upon me, or my bridal couch may be a *shroud*. Leave me now; you know my determination. As you will. I can only succumb in form. I *never* will yield myself to so despicable a cur!'

'Nonsense, child! when once you are his, and have got that romantic stuff out of your head, you will be happy enough. Remember! be prepared to-morrow at half-past eleven.'

Scarcely had he gone from the room, when the door of the outer chamber was burst open, and Susan, pale and terrified, ran in. Pauline followed. She was like a marble statue.

'What has happened?' cried Madeline, catching Susan's trembling form in her arms.

'Hush!' replied Pauline, in her cold, clear voice. 'There is blood beneath the window—a dark pool. I found this. I could not discover the cause of it. I followed a bloody track. Great heavens! this must end soon. It is *his* work. Let him look to it. Aha! Heaven of mercy! hark!'——

The two girls gave a scream and clung to their firm-minded companion as the echo of a report of a gun cracked past the open casement.

'Oh, God! oh God! when will this end?' murmured Madeline.

'When the dead arise from their graves to denounce the evildoer!'

CHAPTER XLI.

BRIEF AND TERRIBLE.

GNATBRAIN remained in a crouching attitude against the door of his hut, with his gun ready for instant use. The footsteps without died away, and when assured no one was prowling about, Gnatbrain went back to the sick chamber.

'What is it?' said the sick man.

'Nothing. All is safe now.'

'What do people want here?'

'Now, that's just what I'd like to know. Maybe I wouldn't give 'em a pill.'

'I wish I could get up.'

'No, no—not yet. To-morrow I shall want you. To-morrow Mr Lorry and the captain, with a *few friends* will be here, to memorize the wedding.'

Gnatbrain grinned at the hidden meaning of his words. The sick man only grunted, and looked peevish.

'Maybe,' continued Gnatbrain, 'maybe there won't be a row. He! he! he!'

'Hist! I can hear a noise again.'

'Can you, though. Well, now, it'll go hard this time if I don't collar 'em.'

The long, ugly-looking gun was again resorted to, and Gnatbrain crept from the sick chamber.

He did not go to the door this time.

At least, not to the front door, or entrance proper; he sneaked, tip-toe, to a tiny apartment—a lumber room—at the back of the cottage. The entrance from the field to this little domicile of gardening apparatus was a small one, and only known to the inexplicable Gnatbrain.

Unfortunately for spies and midnight prowlers, there was a chink at the side of a little grated window—this chink would contain the muzzle of the gun with great facility.

The muzzle was placed there on this occasion, and Gnatbrain crouched down below the window. His face wore a broad grin.

He meant mischief.

The stealthy fall of a foot could be heard without.

'He, he, he,' grinned Gnatbrain. 'Come a little nearer, my chicken. Did you ever have a sting from a gnat? He, he. You shall have a brain full now.'

He sniggered away at what he thought a capital joke, and played dangerously with the trigger of his gun.

The footsteps came nearer. He heard the latch of the door tried. The window shutter of the little sitting-room was being carefully examined, as far as Gnatbrain could tell, by some unwelcome stranger.

Then a shadow passed the grated opening above his head; then he listened; a footstep creaked. He held his breath. The gun projected a little further from the chink; then he waited again. Now his finger was on the trigger, and then—

He fired!

The rattling of the shots followed the loud crack.

Then came a howl. Such a howl—long, loud, and dismal.

'Murder! Help! Oh, lor', I'm shot! I'm dead! horror!

''Course you are,' muttered Gnatbrain, 'yer varmint.'

In spite of himself his hair rose on his head, as the dismal howls were repeated until they changed into a melancholy shriek.

Gnatbrain dropped the gun now, and crawled out to the scene of strife.

He took two steps, and his hair rose in horror. He could not move or speak; but in less than a minute he had conjured up in his mind's eye a grand trial of a prisoner for murder. He was the prisoner. He was convicted—sentenced—taken away—saw the gallows—and even had his head in the noose, all in that time. The next few seconds a cold, clammy sweat oozed out upon him, for another look at his own dreadful work finished the vision. *He saw himself hanging.*

*   *   *   *   *   *

The bridal morning of Madeline Garthway. Every person in the town was in a state of busy excitement. None was cheerful. A cold, chilly presentiment hung over their hearts. The admiral was the most depressed,

He could not shake the feeling off. Something was going to occur he felt sure. He was not the kind of man to give way to that kind of thing; still, he could not help it on this occasion.

He was constantly inquiring of the maid after his daughter.

The footman passed his library.

'Binns!'

'My lord!'

'Captain Saunders arrived yet?'

'No, my lord.'

'Damn him.'

'Yes, my lord.'

'Hold your tongue. Leave the room, sir. Tell me when he does come, and don't let me catch you grinning like that.'

'No, my lord.'

'Luff, go below, sir. Be smart.'

The flunkey retired, muttering as he went—

'Takes me for a dirty sailor! Haw—haw—how *horfully* wulgar. Go *below* and *luff.* Quite disgusting!' and his pampered nose sought a very intimate acquaintance with his eyebrows.

Lord Garthway was not in the best of humours this morning. He wished that the affairs were over.

'Confound that Gregory! He has been a lot of trouble to me,' and with his hands beneath his coat-tails he strode to and fro in his library.

He was suddenly startled by the sound of a heavy tread in the hall. He stood in quiet expectation to see a visitor.

He was not disappointed.

Gregory Saunders came. He was pale and excited.

'You look cheerful—d—d cheerful, sir, for a husband,' growled Garthway.

'I have reports from the Admiralty Board.'

'So much the better, sir.'

'That is not all, admiral.'

'Indeed! Won't they give you another vessel to get lost?'

Gregory winced.

'I care not about that. But I have suspicions that our foes are living yet.

Garthway opened his eyes with a blank stare.

'Yes, certainly. We have many foes still alive.'

'Ay, my lord. I speak of that cut-throat Stuart —the rebel.'

'How do you know this?'

'I do not. I surmise.'

'Pish! Wait till I've read this despatch, then I'll attend to you.'

Admiral Garthway read very composedly his orders from the Admiralty Board. They were brief and explicit—simply stating that, in eight days at the latest, he must be prepared to join his fleet and set sail for foreign waters.

He turned—his manner now calm and proud as was his wont—to Gregory Saunders.

'My boy, do not fear. Should the rebels still be in existence, they shall cause us no further trouble. In less than an hour Madeline will be consigned to your care. You cannot do better than make good the opportunity you have to spend a honeymoon by running over in your schooner to Naples or somewhere. Government cannot give you another ship yet; and they would not require you to go to war with that gilded nutshell. I must start for the fleet, and, once out on the main, the Golden

Arrow shall come to our aid. Should I survive the coming strife, we will return and live in peace.'

Gregory took his intended father-in-law's hand. He tried to smile, too, but failed. He could not. There was a cold, deathly hand grasping at his heart, crushing back every warm feeling of joy that his approaching triumph gave rise to.

In spite of himself, the visage of Eurice would rise up before him. The enormity of his crimes came with crushing force to his guilty conscience. Villain as he was, he dared not look the honourable old man, who had been his father's friend, and a sire to him, in the face.

Even his former crimes were but small in comparison to the one he was about to commit. Near as was the time, he did not feel that confidence a man on the brink of success should feel. The suspicion that our hero still lived unnerved him; if he did not fear being thwarted, he feared the judgment that would come some time or other.

The villain heaved a deep sigh of relief when the admiral left him to his own reflections for a few minutes.

A scene more animated, if not more cheerful, was going on above. Madeline was being prepared for the loathsome alliance.

Black-eyed Susan and Pauline were with her.

It would be hard to say which looked the most wretched.

There was a peculiar look of stern determination on Pauline's face; Madeline was pale and resigned; Susan was pale, timid, and sad.

'God, how will this, how *can* it, end?' murmured Madeline.

'Wait and hope,' replied Pauline.

'Wait! for what? Death, and hope for salvation?'

'Wait for the trial, dear; and hope for succour.'

'Succour! From whence?'

'From those who love and will protect you.'

Madeline sighed. She felt more like a person about to attend a funeral than a wedding.

'You know, dear Madeline,' put in Susan, trying to smile, 'people say if it rains in the morning it's sunshine in the afternoon.'

'Alas, yes, for some; but it rains in the morning with me, and becomes darker and more dreary at night.'

Madeline's maid entered.

She seemed to participate in the general share of gloom that was well distributed about the house.

'His lordship awaits with the *people* below for your presence, miss.'

'Say I come.'

'Bear up, dear; be calm, be firm; rely on me. You shall be saved at any hazard.'

Pauline kissed the pale brow of the unhappy bride; Susan gently kissed the ashy lips.

'Let us hope,' she said, tears chasing each other down her once dimpled cheeks.

Madeline trembled from head to foot. It was a terrible moment for her; and with one hand clasped in each of her friend's she was led from the room weeping.

The servants lined the hall to greet her. The sight of the menials gave the proud girl nerve to dash back her falling tears; and she assumed a calm, resigned air that was at that moment foreign to her nature.

Garthway met her at the drawing-room door, and led her by the hand to where Gregory Saunders stood with the minister.

Madeline entered the room, passive and obedient.

A slight shiver passed over her when she encountered Gregory's gloating eyes fixed upon her.

No word escaped her lips.

She now stood with her sire before the minister, who looked up in some surprise at the demeanour of the bride.

The solemn ceremony went on until the parson came to—

'Wilt thou have this man for thy wedded husband?'

A dead silence reigned throughout the rooms. Madeline spoke not, nor did she deign to look up.

Her lips were seen to tremble, and she grew paler still. Susan and Pauline drew nearer.

The parson repeated the question.

Still no answer.

'Cold, mute, and trembling, the suffering girl remained.

Gregory Saunders bit his lips.

Lord Garthway began to chafe dreadfully at such stubborn defiance.

The question was put for the third and last time.

'By my own free will—never.'

Those words broke the spell. Tears trickled down the unhappy bride's face, and she clung to Pauline for support.

Angered beyond control, Garthway strode forward and placed his hand upon his daughter's arm

'This is mockery, madam, this'——

He paused and listened.

Gregory Saunders stood dumbfounded, and a cold, creeping sensation at his heart.

'Keep up, they are here,' whispered Pauline in the bride's ear.

'My lord, is this farce to continue?' gasped Saunders, as the clatter of horses' hoofs sounded without, and a hum of voices at the hall door.

'Certainly not. Mr. Highpear you'——

'Three gentlemen want to be admitted,' cried the flunkey, entering the room and giving Garthway a card that bore the name of Jasper Lorry.

'I cannot see him now.'

'Pardon, my lord, you *must* see him now. The intrusion will be looked over, I hope, but delay would be dangerous.'

The voice was mild and calm that uttered those words, and an elderly gentleman strode firmly into the room.

Two men followed closely at his heels, two more entered in the rear.

'What means this?' cried Garthway.

'My lord, you can see,' and the quiet little gentleman bowed very low; then strode up to Saunders, and said—

'Mr. Gregory Saunders, R.N.?'

'Y—y—yes.'

'Just so. You are our prisoner.' As the words left his lips the two men, who had followed like poodles, stepped up, and adroitly slipped a pair of handcuffs upon the terror-stricken wretch.

'God!' cried Garthway, 'this outrage in my house! What does it mean?'

'That, my lord,' cried a voice full, rich, and manly, 'that he you were about to unite your daughter to is a *bigamist*, deceiver, traitor, and murderer; that he is steeped in the blackest crimes that can fit a soul for perdition. I denounce him as all I have said, as bigamist and murderer.'

'Who are you?'

The stranger threw aside his cloak and hat.

'GERALD STUART, from the sea.'

'William Howard, at your service; and that d—d lubber should have—Oh! Sue, my Sue!'

'Will!'

Like Gerald, Will had shed his disguise; and his manly form stood out in bold contrast to the shivering Gregory. Susan, with a cry, rushed into her husband's arms, and clung weeping to his breast.

Madeline no sooner heard the voice of her gallant lover than she fell with a shriek to the floor.

Gerald leaped forward.

Garthway stood in his path.

'Back, sir! What proof have you of this foul accusation? You touch not that girl. Back!'

'Proof, my lord—plenty! and another witness if you like!'

He strode to the door, and assisted a feeble form into the room.

It was an old man, supported by Gnatbrain on one side.

'Lawyer Longstreet,' said Gerald, coldly. 'The man that scoundrel paid to be assassinated, that the letter sent to warn you of his crimes might not arrive.'

Saunders stood petrified for a few minutes. When the spell did break, he uttered a shriek.

'Liars!—rebels!—accursed fiends!—it's a foul accusation, sir!—curse you!'

With a gurgling groan, he fell to the floor at the admiral's feet. He stood gazing on the scene in speechless incredulity and chilling horror.

'If it be so,' he murmured; 'if he would have ruined a father—and my daughter—may the God of heaven *curse him!*'

CHAPTER XLII.

THE LION BUCCANEER.

'LAND OH!'

'Where away?'

'On our starboard quarter, sir.'

The cry of 'Land oh!' now rang through the vessel; going from throat to throat; bawled from aloft to the deck; from the deck to the men; from the men to those below.

The cry had the same effect in all parts of the vessel. Men scrambled up from the lower decks, and lounged over the bulwarks to see what they could make of the land.

Unfortunately for their curiosity, it was night, and a very dark one, too.

The ship's lanterns threw a dusky glare on the deck, and displayed a scene novel as it was picturesque. The vessel was neither a king's ship nor a merchantman.

The craft was a three masted one, with a large black hull, clear cut and beautifully modelled at the bows. She was very high out of the water, with a large raised stern that rose ten or twelve feet higher than the deck amidships. She carried a raised poop and very elevated quarter-deck.

Her guns were many, and of very heavy calibre.

Her stern battery was very heavy, and the chief cabin contained six long guns, three aside.

Few vessels, half the size again, could not have boasted of such an armament.

The crew were a mixed set of men—Moors, Spanish, English; in fact, there was a sprinkling from all parts of the world. As a body, they formed a magnificent company of men. Each dressed according to his own caste or country, their costumes were most elaborate.

The most costly weapons were thrust carelessly into beautiful silken sashes, that adorned the waists of the men.

Some wore laced jackets over a blue or scarlet silk vest, others wore plain silk or velvet loose jackets, and a crimson or blue sash, with knee breeches, stockings, and shoes.

Each man was more or less armed, and a splendid set of dare-devil fellows they made.

Evidently the restrictions were not great on board the Fighting Lion. The crew, excepting those on watch, were employed in various games, such as cards or dice. Some playing musical instruments; others fencing with long thin swords, while some squatted languidly about, smoking fragrant cigars, and quaffing such wine as would have graced the table of a king.

Thus were the crew engaged, when the cry—

'Land, ho!' brought them like a swarm of bees to the vessel's side.

The commanding officer on deck took out his night glass and scanned the distant dark line that appeared as if it rose from the depths of the sea.

After a short scrutiny, he went to the compass and ascertained the ship's bearings.

'Ah,' he muttered, 'the Don wants a port near hear.'

'Crispina!'

'Senor.'

'Tell Don Cyril, land is sighted.'

The subordinate, a youth of about seventeen, hastened below to acquaint the commander of the proximity of land.

If the scene on deck was wild and picturesque, then that which presented itself when the boy demanded admittance to the chief cabin was novel and luxurious. It was the princely commander's private cabin, and the style it was fitted up must have far excelled the smoking room of an Eastern prince.

The floor of the cabin was richly carpeted; the sides were hung with thick rich silk tapestry, which met in a circle at the centre of the ceiling and hung down to the floor. At first sight, an observer would have thought the cabin was circular. From the centre of the ceiling where the hangings met, a large silver lamp swung gracefully with the motion of the vessel.

In the centre of the cabin was placed a large eastern lounge, luxurious velvet cushions were strewn round the cabin, beautiful costly arms of every nation were hung about the tapestry covered walls. Polished mirrors gleamed through the interstices of the silken hangings, and reflected the magnificence of the fairy-like bower in all directions.

The most curious feature of it all was a huge iron cage at the back of the cabin. The door was open, and the tenant of the cave, a monstrous lion—one of the finest specimens of the forest monarch. It lay crouched, its noble head resting upon its paws, at the foot of a velvet eastern lounge, on which reclined the owner of so much luxury. He was languidly smoking a costly hookah. To judge from its appearance one would suppose it had been the property of some eastern king. Don Cyril de Bragelio, the commander of the Fighting Lion, the prince of this wild, lawless

BLACK EYED SUSAN.

OR, PIRATES ASHORE.

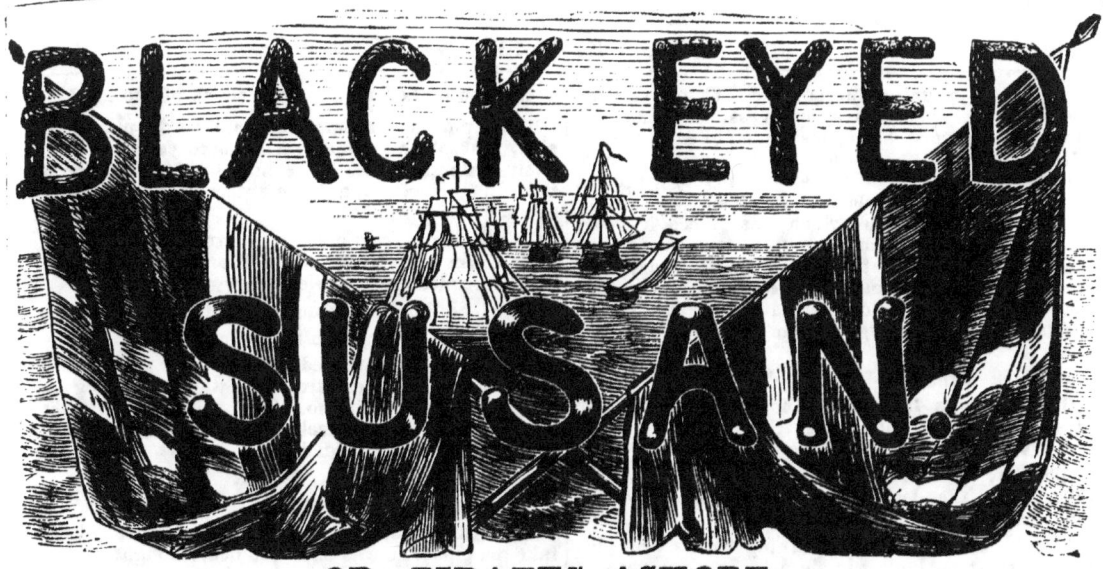

A WEDDING PARTY AND A FIGHT.

Gratis with this Number Set 2 of Side Wings for the Play of the "RED ROVER."

crew, was a young man, not more than five-and-twenty, dark, almost to swarthiness. A handsome moustache adorned his upper lip. He wore a laced silk vest, fitting like a skin, and showing his beautifully rounded chest off in all its manly grace, an ermine sash, with gold-fringed ends, was drawn round his waist, round which was placed a gold-laced belt, from which hung a curved sword; the blade was of Toledo steel, the hilt was ablaze with jewels. A jacket to match his vest fitted gracefully his well-made shoulders and small waist. A scarlet cap, with a large golden tassel, adorned his head.

A knock at the door startled him.

Turning to a little black boy whom he kept to attend upon him and supply the Turkish pipe, he addressed him in a foreign tongue.

The boy salaamed and went to the door. An officer from the deck stood there, and he gave the boy a message.

'Senor,' said the boy, returning to his princely-looking master, 'land is in sight.'

Cyril started from his couch and his eyes brightened. 'Land,' he muttered, 'now to see her I love.'

Throwing the long stem of his pipe to the little slave boy, he sprang up lightly from the couch, and would have started from the cabin had not a cry restrained him.

He turned in surprise and saw the cause instantly. In his anxiety to get on deck he forgot the lion was out of its cage, and the cry of terror came from the boy who feared the animal.

'Back, lion,' he said, patting the massive head of the brute, and pointing to the cage.

The monarch beast cowed his head, and rose from its crouching posture.

Cyril neither moved his hand nor eye, though he continued to speak kindly to the brute, which went passively into its cage, and the door was shut and bolted.

The form of the young chieftain was not one likely to instil awe into a beholder; it was more likely to command admiration. Yet he was known and feared. Foreign powers dreaded Cyril, the Spanish rover, or, as he was better known,

THE LION BUCCANEER.

Now on deck, he took a haughty survey of the sea around.

His presence commanded attention and respect, every lounger on the quarter deck saluted and withdrew, and silence reigned fore and aft.

'Calosso,' he said.

A tall swarthy man came forward. He was next in command, and a peculiar being too. Few knew his history, and it was generally supposed that he was Greek. Whether this was correct or not he never contradicted it.

He did not participate in the luxurious dress of his young chieftain. His was something of the Arab, or Algerian costume—white, with a large white turban. His legs were encased in high morocco boots, and a heavy scimitar, with a broad point, hung from his sash.

'This is the coast. How long has land been sighted?' asked Cyril.

'When you were apprised of it.'

'Good. Anchor off that dark point. You are steering out leeward. I will go ashore in a boat to-night.'

'To-night?'

'Even so.'

''Tis well, senor.'

'When you have anchored, let me know.'

Calosso replied by a gloomy shake of the head.

'You put me in mind of that sickly plant, the aloe, that blooms once in a hundred years, and my lively Calosso smiles once in a lifetime,' muttered the young chieftain, as he re-entered the magnificent cabin.

The lion rose from a sitting posture, and placed its nose against the iron bars of the cage, as a polite way of requesting to be let out.

'No! no lion, not to-night.'

He struck a gong with his knuckle.

The slave boy appeared. A stranger would have thought he had come from the wall, or sprang up from the floor. Not so. The cabin was in the centre of the quarter-deck. The officers' bunks and private berths surrounded it.

'My pistols and cloak, Anack.'

The boy retired to get them.

Cyril threw himself upon the lounge. He did not take his pipe : he was buried in deep thought.

'This is a desperate thing,' he cogitated. 'How will it end? Oh, Clarence, Clarence, my heart burns with a quenchless love for you. You warned me—but I must, I will see you again, beautiful dreamer, I '——

'Cyril!'

His name was pronounced in a voice low and plaintive.

He looked up, startled.

By his side stood an eastern beauty. She could not have been more than sixteen, and seemed more like the bright vision of a youthful dreamer of enchanted halls than a real being.

Her costume was well chosen, and set off her figure to its full beauty. She wore a long skirt of Oriental silk ; it was looped up to the knee, and displayed one magnificent limb in all its natural elastic loveliness. The boddice was cut sloping from each shoulder, and rose to a point at the extremity of her white and beautifully moulded breast, which was thus exposed to the ardent gaze of the young chieftain.

'Zona,' he said, gently, and took her tiny hand, 'why do you seek me?'

'You are going into danger, Cyril.'

'Nay, sweet Zona, if I go into as much danger as there is in your ravishing beauty, I indeed may fear.'

A gentle blush stole over the lovely creature's dimpled cheek, and her eyes glistened with ill concealed pleasure.

'Cyril, you must go?' she asked, wistfully.

He drew her gently to his breast, and a burning, passionate light was in his eye.

'Sweet Zona, your charms would tempt an angel to linger here, but I must away for a short time.'

'Away to danger.'

The princely fellow smiled confidently. The idea of danger he scorned.

'Should anything happen? Oh, Cyril!'

'Happen!' He laughed, and the lurking devil in his heart could be traced in the cutting sneer of his mouth.

'Fear not, Zona, you shall see me here again to-night.' He kissed her lovely neck, and led her like a trembling dove to her cage.

Cyril parted the silken hangings, behind which a polished mirror shone lustrously. Touching a spring, the mirror swung back, and discovered an aperture. It was the entrance to Zona's private cabin. It was like a miniature--though exquisitely furnished—divan.

'Come, pretty dove, retire to your cage.' He imprinted another burning kiss upon her white neck as she entered the 'cage,' as he had termed it.

She did not take her tearful gaze from him until he had retired to his cabin, and the well-carved door was closed.

He found Anack waiting with his cloak and pistols; Anack had been well trained, and he never intruded upon a love scene.

Cyril was equipped and ready to go ashore, when Anack announced the boat was ready for him.

He lost no time in being conveyed to the rock-barred shore. He evidently knew the ground by the way he avoided all dangerous points and effected a safe landing.

Dark as it was he found his way up the rocky path, and soon stood on safe ground.

On the brow of the cliff he halted; the moon burst from behind a mass of clouds and revealed to him a picturesque stretch of country and a sleeping village.

This quaint old place boasted of at least one mansion, and it was a grand old estate, not only the finest and most wealthy one in the old village of Sunblow, but for many miles round.

Situated upon a grand eminence, that commanded a view of the country round, stood the lordly house of the Earl Braymoor.

To this mansion Cyril, the young buccaneer, now directed his steps. He was well on the alert.

Keeping a watchful eye and ready hand, he entered the grounds, and did not pause until beneath the balcony of a pretty latticed window at the back of the mansion.

'Beautiful Clarence,' he murmured, gazing at the dark window, 'I know this is presumption—madness; but I cannot help it. I must see you; 'tis my fate.'

He removed a silken cord that had been coiled round his wrist.

'If I could only get up to the window to breathe thy name, dearest dream of my soul!'

Murmuring this, he took the cord, at the end of which was attached a leaden shot; this he held in his right hand, and took care to disentangle the cord; then, taking steady aim, he hurled the bullet over the balcony.

He gave a low cry of anger.

The leaden weight went with a crash against the window and shattered the glass.

'I shall be discovered,' he muttered, and coiling the rope he hurled it on to the balcony that it might not be seen, should anyone come out.

He crouched behind some plants, and waited breathlessly for the issue of the mishap.

All was silent, and he crept from his place of concealment. Fortunately the cord had not reached the balcony securely, and one end hung down within his reach.

He clutched it eagerly, and drew it until every fibre was tightened, to test its security.

''Sdeath! that was unwise. Ugh! I wonder how big the bump will be?'

The bump was caused by the bullet attached to the cord striking him on the head through his giving the rope an extra jerk—a proof that it was not secure.

'I never thought my head was so hard. Whew! I believe it's cracked. I'll lasso the balcony this time.'

He was expert in the use of that deadly instrument, the lasso—thanks to the tuition of Colosso.

The rope whirled through the air—whizzed round the stone parapet of the balcony, where it remained perfectly secure.

'At last.'

Hand over hand, with the agility of a monkey, he mounted it, and stood by the window of his beloved. The cord was drawn up after him.

An imaginary footfall beneath the balcony caused him to turn sharply.

Crash! His sword had smashed another pane of glass.

'God! I shall be discovered. Aha! her voice!'

A scream from within the chamber caused him to make instant efforts to remedy the misfortune.

'Clarence! beautiful, lovely Clarence! 'Tis I—I, Cyril. Do not alarm the house.'

This he cried—his lips against the shutter.

No reply came. Silence reigned within.

He waited, his heart beating against his side so furiously that he could hear the repeated thud.

'Lady Clarence, in the name of love, let me see you!'

A minute more the shutters opened, and the form of a female, young, proud, and beautiful stood there.

'Cyril—you here?' asked a low, tremulous voice.

'Ay, Lady Clarence; I am here.' He clutched the snow white hand in his own, and showered kisses upon it.

'Hush! Oh, Cyril! your rashness has brought ruin upon us. Hark! Servants are below. You will be discovered. Away!'

'Never, Clarence!'

Someone passed beneath the balcony. Lady Clarence trembled in every limb.

'Heavens! you must not be seen!'

She drew him into her chamber, in her terror for his safety, and shut the window. Then she turned with a low cry of terror. Cyril drew his sword.

A hand was laid upon the door-handle. Someone was about to enter her chamber. She went cold from head to foot. The look in Cyril's eyes terrified her.

'If it's a man,' he hissed, 'I'll kill him!'

CHAPTER XLIII.

WILLIAM BETRAYED.

GREGORY SAUNDERS soon recovered from his fit, and regained his feet. Pauline had Madeline conveyed to her room. Lord Garthway stood dumb with horror, his senses confounded, and his brain in a whirl.

'What!' he gasped, 'has it come to outlaws administering justice?'

'My lord,' replied Gerald Stuart; 'I come not as a foe. I come not to rob you of yours, but to save you from entailing shame—your daughter from misery.'

'My lord,' quietly observed Mr. Lorry. 'I am a man of the law. This case is mine. The evidence is in my hands. These gentlemen are my witnesses. I would not inflict unnecessary pain on you. Let those not concerned retire.'

'I will be responsible for the prisoner,' said his lordship, waving the men away, and with a stammering apology, he dismissed the clergyman.

None was there now but those connected with the case and Susan. Gregory Saunders was a prey to the most fierce conflicts which were going on in his breast. He shuddered to himself now he saw that a revelation was about to take place which would disclose all his dreadful guilt.

His soul shrank in horror as he reflected upon his frightful career of iniquity. The numerous crimes he had committed, and the agonies of mind he suffered as he thought his dark sins were about to be punished, was almost more than nature could bear.

More than once he felt he could scream in wild despair. Then a dogged calmness would come upon him, and with folded arms and knitted brow he waited, lose or gain, to brave it out, or be eternally ruined.

Lawyer Longstreet, whom everyone had supposed murdered, was led to a seat. Gnatbrain stood by his side.

Mr. Lorry went to the table, upon which he placed a pile of papers.

Resting his right hand upon them, he turned to the admiral and spoke, in the calm, unconcerned tone of a business man.

'My lord, much as I regretted this abrupt disturbance, it could not be avoided. You had upon two occasions been warned, but unfortunately the letters never reached you. The first that was sent, a boy, a little fellow conveyed it.'

'I saw no boy.'

'No, my lord. He was intercepted, the letter taken from him, and read.'

'By whom?'

'Captain Saunders.'

'You lie!' hissed the baffled villain, his eyes gleaming murderously upon the lawyer.

'I assure you, my lord, I do not.'

And Mr. Lorry related the incidents as told him by little Jack Murray.

The admiral's brow darkened, and he turned his eyes like an arrow upon the culprit. He remembered the circumstances of the letter, and now understood Gregory's unwillingness to let him see the answer.

'Go on,' he said.

'That letter, my lord, was sent on the 17th ult. On that day I received a letter at my office in London, requesting my presence in Deal. I came, and went to the house of Mrs. Murray, where I found a lady, evidently only half-bred English. She was young, beautiful, but unfortunately in a dying condition. She requested I would hear her history, and become her executor to act in her name. She had been foully wronged, my lord, robbed of her fortune, and then left to starve. Her wronger and husband was Gregory Saunders!'

'The unmitigated scoundrel! God of heaven, what villany! What ruin you would have brought on me! What have you to say!'

The admiral was livid with rage.

Gregory's pallid lips trembled; he did not reply.

'Read, my lord, for yourself.'

Mr. Lorry handed the documents given him by Eurice, and in which was the full particulars of her marriage history as she had related it to the lawyer.

The admiral read it, and his cheek blanched in horror.

'And this is the snake I was taking to my heart. God pardon him! for I will not!'

'My lord, the night I had those papers placed in my hands, and heard what had been done, I thought it prudent to send another letter to warn you in time. That missive was conveyed by Mr. Longstreet, who was waylaid and stabbed—the letter taken from him, and then the ruffians hurled him into a ditch. There he sits, my lord; it needs no proof to see he suffers.'

The admiral paused, his hand on his brow; the accumulating horrors appalled him.

Lawyer Longstreet with some difficulty stated what had happened to him.

'I do not remember being thrown into a pond, as I was insensible.'

He paused and glanced at Gnatbrain.

'My lord,' said the gardener, 'it was me who saved him. I saw the villains hurl him into the pond, and waited until they had fled from the spot. I then rescued him, and took him to my cottage, my lord, and restored him to strength. The wounds on the breast—'

'That is not all, my lord,' interrupted Lorry. 'You may remember that dreadful affair in Deal, in which a sick lady was abducted with little Jack Murray, and the accomplice of the ruffians fell a victim to their brutal passions. Either the poor girl was murdered to insure better safety, or to get her out of the way. Ere she died, my lord, I obtained her true confession; he whom she implicates as the chief instigator'——

'Enough,' cried Garthway, trembling from violent emotion—'this is sufficient. God! to think such a viper was reared in my house—would have been taken to my breast as a son! Why was I not warned of his consummate villany? Scoundrel! what have you to say for yourself?'

'That you can do your will, my lord, if you will believe these adventurers. Let them prove, by living witness, what they assert.'

'Base hound! would you dare deny the truth of these?' cried Gerald.

Garthway waved his hand for silence, then he turned towards the discovered villain.

'The proofs laid before me are sufficient to expose your guilt. I know not how you could so long elude justice overtaking you. God of heaven! what a round of sin hast thou gone through—crime upon crime—innocence and virtue, all a sacrifice to your base desires! Oh, God! I, your father's bosom friend—your protector and father in all but name—I, too, was to fall by your accursed villany; and my daughter you would have ruined—dishonoured for life. Oh, curse you! curse you! God! the words choke me when I think of your poor old father—the man of honour and nobility. Could he but come to ye from heaven, he would do as I do—curse you! —curse you under the light of day! Go, go, or I shall no longer keep these hands from thy cursed throat! Go, and may the curse of an outraged father—may heaven's bitterest curse be hurled upon you! Begone!'

Dreadfully agitated by the scenes of the morning, the admiral sank into a seat, and buried his face in his hands.

He was stricken—stricken in the tenderest part—his pride, his honour. When he thought that Gregory had been reared by him—had been treated as a son, had been made his heir—and then to turn upon him like a snake, not only to sting, but to crush and ruin him for ever—his brain nearly bursted with horror, and he groaned inwardly—groaned to think he had been so rewarded for his fatherly love to the villain, and when he remembered the noble old man, Admiral Saunders.

A clammy dew flowed out from every pore of Gregory's skin, and his limbs were bathed in a cold sweat. His legs almost sank from beneath him—his heart stilled its beating—his eyes rolled wildly, then suddenly gleamed with a set, deadly purpose. He was firm.

The men were coming in to take him.

With a cry, like a savage beast, he drew his sword, and leaped forward.

'Take me!' he cried hoarsely, 'take me, if you can.'

William put Susan aside, and drew his cutlass.

'Hold!' cried Gerald. 'Leave him to me.'

He drew his sword too.

It met the descending blade of the infuriated Gregory, as the officers entered the room.

He waved them back with his left hand, while with his right he used his sword.

The clash of steel roused the Admiral, and he sprang from the couch as a form dashed past him.

It was Madeline.

'Oh pray, pray, stop this strife!' she implored.

It was stopped.

Gerald dashed the sword from his opponent's hand. Much as he longed to take the law upon himself he abstained, and only struck the shrinking coward with the flat of his sword.

The officers no sooner saw the ruffian disarmed than they dashed forward and clutched him by the wrists.

Mad from pain and terror Saunders fought—fought in wild despair for his liberty.

The struggle was short but a fearful one. Gregory Saunders bit his captors, kicked and plunged like a madman, William, enraged beyond all control, stepped forward and secured him.

He held the prisoner while the handcuffs were thrust on, and he was dragged like a dog by the two officers of the law to a carriage that waited without.

'Go,' said Garthway. 'You shall have a trial; acquit yourself if you can.' Then he turned to his daughter and led her away.

Will still held Susan to his breast as though he feared losing her again.

'Sue, lass,' he whispered, 'we'll go back together. Will you come on the Golden Arrow?'

'Anywhere with you, Will.'

He pressed her closer to him.

'But' —— she continued; then hesitated.

'Spin out, lass; pay out the slack. Maybe you haul to without cause.'

'No, Will; but poor Miss Madeline, she will come too. Could I leave her in this moment of trouble?'

'Ay, true, my Sue, true. Love for you, lass, makes me an ungrateful lubber. No, Sue, sooner than you should be ungrateful to the Captain's lady—bless her pretty eyes!—I'll cruise about alone until she can run alongside with you. Maybe the captain will take her in tow. Maybe he'll get the old seventy-four (he meant Garthway) to surrender her. If he don't, why then, my lass, you must be as true to the lady as I am to her captain, and he'll come and carry off his prize when the lubbers are in their hammocks.'

He could not say more, as Lord Garthway turned to address Gerald.

'Captain Stuart,' he began, 'though political events make us enemies, and however selfish your motives may be, I cannot help expressing my gratitude for the service you have rendered me. I only regret your blind confidence and love for that wretched usurper, the pretender, should prevent you from becoming one of England's subjects.'

'Pardon for interrupting, my lord. Who drove me to this career? Was I not one of England's subjects? How have I been treated? Foully, most foully wronged have I been, and whatever my faults may be, I could not let you suffer from that villain's treachery. I will own, my lord, my senti-ments towards your daughter prompted it mostly. We knew each other when young; you were then, my lord, proud of me, and honoured me by your patronage; but, alas! prejudice steeled your heart as it did, and ever will do, many others. I may be a rebel—so-called, because I choose to fight for another king. Am I not as right in fighting and winning glory under one standard as another, so long as I acknowledge a sovereign. England has been my enemy, as yet I have been no foe to her.'

'Gerald ——, Captain Stuart,' said Garthway, correcting himself, 'this is no time to enter into a discussion. Like many other people in our time you were too quick, fancied yourself ill-used, and felt too proud to have a proper explanation with your Government. As you say, I knew you when I thought you were winning a road to honour; it may not be too late to retract even now—there is ever time to reform. Let it be so with you. Remove the stain of rebel and traitor from your name—regain your honour, and in some future time you reclaim the friendship of myself.

'But I have one stern request to make—I may feel for, and pity you, for a mad, head-strong passion like yours, for one beyond your reach, is to be pitied—I request that you will not seek to cast a blot of everlasting shame and dishonour upon my family name by continuing to force clandestine meetings upon one too young and unsophisticated to be aware of the disgrace attending it. I speak thus for your sake; for I would not be compelled to resort to severe measures, or become an unnecessary enemy towards you—tis my wish that blood should never stand between us—in spite of the great danger I incur in thus countenancing you under my roof. I allow you to depart in peace, and with your companion, whom, out of respect for you, I will let go unmolested. But be warned. Do not illuse this momentary triumph of yours with impunity. A price is set upon William Howard. The noose dangles above his head. Be warned!'

He strode from the room, after commanding Gnatbrain and the lawyer to follow.

Gerald turned to Will.

'I will meet you ere long at the hotel.'

'Ay, captain. Now, miss, there's a land craft without, let us make sail; we've done all we can do here, and the reward may be the noose at the yardarm, if I stay too long.'

He said this somewhat bitterly.

'My Will, dear!'

Susan uplifted her tearful gaze to his. She had felt strongly the admiral's words, and could scarcely reproach her gallant husband for his speech.

Twining his manly arm round Susan's supple waist, he led her away. Outside the mansion a carriage was waiting.

Will placed Susan inside, and seated himself; the door was shut, the coachman about to drive off, when the vehicle was surrounded by armed men.

Will leapt up.

'No good, Will Howard, we know you!' cried a rough voice. 'You're our prisoner!'

And a pistol was thrust almost against his cheek. Susan uttered a piercing shriek.

Her husband's danger was too terrible to be realized.

'Where is Gerald?' muttered Will, 'my captain, eh?'

Then he shielded Susan's form, and stood like a tiger crouching at bay.

CHAPTER XLIV.

' CAGED !'

GERALD STUART met Pauline in the hall; she drew him aside, and whispered, hurriedly—

'Go now. Be under the balcony at eleven to-night—Madeline will see you !'

'Nay, conduct me to her room.'

'I cannot.'

'Say rather you will not.'

'As you will.'

'Does she know '——

'Ay, all.'

'She is ill !'

Pauline did not reply for a minute.

Gerald clutched her by the arm.

'Girl !' he said, 'I must—I will see her ! Have you no feeling ?—are you dead to all human passions or heart's yearnings ?—are you stone ? Miss Clemence, you must conduct me to Miss Madeline ! Think you I can depart, and know she is here, near me. I must see her !'

He was wonderfully determined. Pauline's eyes gleamed just a little colder than usual, as she said—

' Is this gallantry to force yourself into the presence of a lady !'

When my presence becomes hateful, I will hear it from her own lips. Till then, bah ! Conduct me to her.'

'Come, then ; rashness brings danger. Be prepared.'

She glided away through a hidden door, and ascended a flight of dark stairs. At the door of her beloved friend she halted.

' Wait,' she said, and entered Madeline's chamber.

Two or three minutes of burning impatience passed. Gerald thought it an age. The door was re-opened, the curtains pushed aside, and a white arm was thrust forth. The white hand grasped Gerald by the sleeve, and he was drawn through the opening of the door into the room.

'Gerald ! '

'My love ! '

One step forward, and Madeline was clasped to his breast, and Pauline flitted like a phantom from the room.

The lovers were alone.

'Oh, Gerald ! this was rash. Why came you here ? '

'To see you, dear one.'

'Oh, Gerald, the fearful scenes of this morning ! To think that that villain would have pitilessly dragged me down to destruction.'

She shuddered, and clung to the breast of her lover.

'Your nerves are shaken, dear one.'

The voice so oft used in the work of tempest and battle—a voice, at the stern sounds of which a hundred men would fly, was low and sweet.

' The fearful doom I so narrowly escaped, was too horrible to be banished from my memory. Ah, Gerald ! I do not suffer alone. What must the heart of my proud father feel ? He was stern, Gerald, but is not dead to all affection for his only child.'

'I know it, Madeline ; I feel for him.'

' I shall never recover from the horror of this day. Oh, heavens ! what a fate mine would have been had you not saved me !'

Proud as she was, her feelings were beyond her control, and she wept long and bitterly.

' But, dear one,' Gerald whispered tenderly. He felt that to have spoken beyond a sigh, would have been profanation to her grief.

He was startled by the entrance of Pauline. She took Madeline Garthway by the arm gently.

' 'Tis time you sought rest,' she said. ' And you, sir, retire. Your presence is dangerous ; his lordship is coming.'

' Leave me now, Gerald, dear,' said Madeline, kindly. ' I will see you to-night at eleven.'

' At eleven. Oh, that it were'——

The report of fire-arms made him start.

Madeline uttered a scream.

'Go—go. Ah! what is that ?

' Will in danger !' he said, feeling instinctively it was so.

One passionate embrace. Pauline took Madeline gently away ; then led him from the room.

He went by a back entrance to the lawn, from thence he rushed, with drawn sword in his hand, to the front of the mansion, attracted hither by the loud altercation of voices.

He saw gallant Will bravely fighting against a company of armed men.

' Avast ! avast you lubbers ! D'ye think I'll be run down by a set o' land sharks ? Haul up, or damme you'll get a broadside.'

It was six to one—more than even Will's indomitable pluck and skill as a swordsman could stand against, without being overpowered sooner or later.

Gerald Stuart's unexpected presence altered the aspect of affairs.

Will's opponents paused. They saw one more gleaming sword, and a resolute hand to oppose them.

' Six to one ! Cowards, hold ! or there will be bloodshed.

Then Gerald leaped amongst them.

Help was not wanting now. The report of the pistol that had brought Gerald to the spot brought the Admiral's servants.

They did little after the first rush. They saw, as they supposed, their master's guests beset by ruffians. A second glance made them aware of a different fact ; the men's costumes denoted them to be men of the law.

Then the servants hesitated at interfering.

The leader of the officers spoke to Gerald, whom he did not know—

' Sir, this is an affair of the law in which it is dangerous to take any part.'

' My friends, to capture one you must capture both.'

The officers prepared for a second onslaught, when Lord Garthway appeared.

One stern glance he cast upon the scene, and his pale, haggard face flushed.

' What means this ?' he said, haughtily.

The sergeant explained.

' By whose authority do you proceed to arrest anyone on my grounds.'

' The magistrates', my lord.'

' Upon mine you retire. These gentlemen have my protection. Depart ! I give you thirty minutes to be away from my premises, and my game-keepers shall see that you do depart.'

Savage and crestfallen the men went slowly away.

They had been offered a price, for they looked upon Will as a bit of legitimate prey, and they mentally cursed the High Admiral for his interference.

'On his grounds,' mentally repeated the officer. 'On his grounds—men,' he said aloud. 'Off his grounds we can do our duty—MEN,' and he puffed out with importance. 'We represent the law.'

'Do yer, though? Well, all I can say is if the law's as good-looking as your lot, the sooner it's done away with the better. So off you go—a hop, skip, and a jump, or I'll fire.'

The chief officer turned to see from whence came the voice. He beheld one of Garthway's men who had heard the order for them to be turned off the grounds.

The fellow handled a long clumsy gun. It was loaded with duck shot of an unpleasant size.

'He! he! he!' grinned a country lad by his side. 'Fire! Mister Ben. Maybe ye'll make 'un run, an' won't I gi' un a prog with this old fork. It be mighty sharp, I tell 'ee.'

The urchin grinned mischievously, and the twinkle in his eyes showed he was ripe to put his threat into practice.

The imaginary sting of the shots, and the unpleasant as undignified idea of being helped by a pitchfork over the fence sent the valiant officer at a lively pace.

'Ha! ha! ha! they look worse nor our farmers stuck pigs a running from the whip. Father told I never to fear 'em, nor I doant.'

The servant followed the men off the grounds, and returned with the boy, who looked sullen and disappointed. He was vicious enough to regret not having the opportunity of using his pitchfork.

The officers, deeply galled at the treatment they had received, were only more bent upon making the capture.

'We'll have 'em both,' said the leader of the party, 'for it strikes me he is the well-known friend of that sailor. If not he's no bizness to interfere with the law. Let's wait in ambush; they must pass this way.'

And they remained in ambush. The promised reward and their own feelings for revenge kept them there without the noting the time they might have to stay.

Shortly after the departure, a carriage left Garthway's mansion, and neared the men directed to lay in wait. It came in sight.

Captain Gerald and William were within. Susan had been left with Madeline, as Gerald felt that danger was a long way from over.

'We have a task to do, Will,' said Gerald, as the carriage rattled along. 'Our bark to-morrow must see us on the ocean—our boundless home. Eurice, the outraged wife of that cursed villain, must be brought back. Then my fate shall be decided. Madeline is mine, or I shall be at the bottom of the sea.'

'Not that, cap'n,' said Will.

'I hope not, Will; to night I shall know my fate. I return to her. I will know all for certain. You will go, Will, and take command of the Golden Arrow until I come on board. Be prepared for instant departure, when I do so. Poor Andrew is better, he must be conveyed to the gallant craft. Our task on shore is done.'

At this moment, the carriage passed the spot where the officers were concealed.

They did not spring forward this time--the leading functionary did not know whether it would be safe.

'Snuffles,' he said.

'What now?'

Snuffles was a little dried up man, very snappish, and always miserable.

'Foller that carriage; it's my belief they're in there.'

Snuffles' eyes twinkled—he thought so too; and he thought of the reward, should he get the prisoner.

'All right; find yer here when I come back?'

'Yes.'

He darted off, and hung on behind the vehicle like a monkey.

The carriage drove into the town, and drew up before the 'Three Admirals.'

Snuffles slunk away, hid himself, and waited.

His expected prey was not seen during the day. Night drew on, and he still hung about. Andrew and Wilks went back to the Golden Arrow, as did Will, who took command, and waited for his gallant commander, who was hazarding his life to see his beloved.

The night was serenely calm, and Gerald found a melancholy feeling of despondency come upon him.

'If I were going to see her for the last time I could not be worse,' he thought, ' but I must shake the feeling off.'

Uninterrupted, he reached his destination beneath the window of the fair one he so madly, though vainly, loved. He paused.

To his low cry, a responsive signal came. A light for a minute shone in the window.

Then all was dark within. A low sound of bolts being withdrawn followed; then a rope dangled from the balcony.

Gerald gave a cry of joy.

Eagerly he clutched the rope, and ascended it, hand over hand. He paused at the casement, where stood a female form.

'Madeline, I am here.'

'Oh, Gerald, be cautious. I fear something will happen.'

'Nay, nay, love.' He kissed her hand tenderly.

'Oh, Gerald! I feel this is wrong, very wrong to my father. What should I be in the world's estimation, did they know I '——

'Madeline, why should me or you care for the world's opinions? Are you not sacred from all harm here? Though it be night, and your chamber, are you not safe from being sullied by a thought? Grant me ten minutes, only ten minutes' interview, my love, my adored one!'

'Gerald, I feel I dare not. Yet how can I refuse?'

'My dear, ere day dawns I shall be far upon the deep.'

'Would I were with you,' she muttered involuntarily.

'Madeline! my love! my life! come! You can trust yourself to me. Come, my bark lies out under the cliffs, my crew ready and willing, only too eager, to crown and adore you as their queen. Come, come, my beloved one; put yourself under my care, you shall be mine by holy wedlock in less than forty-eight hours.'

He was down on his knees now, his face full of burning love, his eyes shining with mute eloquence, looked into hers. She had trusted in him, and felt herself fascinated by his ardent gaze, his silent, passionate appeal. He trembled from the excitement of love.

It was hard for Madeline to look upon that pleading face and not yield to his wish—especially as she would only be yielding to the voice of love.

'Gerald, Gerald, do not. Leave' ——

Gerald listened. Each had heard something they thought.

'Madeline,' he urged.

'Hark!' ——.

This time he leaped to his feet.

The slight sound that had disturbed them had more danger in its stealthy silence than a greater disturbance.

In his eagerness Gerald had not thought of looking about to discover whether he was watched or not; and no sooner was he in the chamber of his idol than a little shrivelled form of a man appeared.

He crept forward to the rope.

Two little ferret eyes gleamed up. A low chuckle escaped the spy, and he drew his sword.

One stroke and he had severed the rope as high as he could reach.

He had stood upon tiptoe to commit the treacherous act, and the sudden relaxation of the rope caused him to lose his equilibrium, and he fell.

That was the noise Gerald had heard when he leaped up.

'Now,' muttered the spy, who was the crafty Snuffles, 'escape is cut off this way. Now to finish my work by rousing his lordship. He! he! a double reward.'

And he went on chuckling at the prospect of his 'double' reward.

He got it, but in a manner more terrible than he had ever dreamed of.

Gerald ran to the balcony.

'Betrayed, dearest!' he said, with frightful calmness. 'Betrayed, love; my rope is cut away. The hound who did it will rouse the house. Aha! I thought so. Hear that, Madeline? I will risk the jump. Your honour is at stake, and not even my life shall stand in its way.'

'Oh, no, no, Gerald! Let them come; rather that than you should court death.'

She held him back with all her gentle strength, as a voice, terrible in its significance, below warned them of their danger.

'Caged,' muttered Gerald; and a chuckle on the stairs told him he was, indeed, caged. He could jump from the casement; but men, armed to the teeth, were below.

CHAPTER XLV.

THE MURDER.

THE prison—all the horrors of a felon under the iron hand of the law—came in full force to Gregory Saunders. The hideous crimes he had committed came across his mind, and he pictured them in imagination a hundred times over in as many seconds.

Bad as he was, the blood that was upon his soul, of innocent people, haunted him. Conscience set its blighting torture to work. Remorse did not find a place in his heart; but, like all cowards, his present position, with his black crimes ever rising before him, cowed him—appalled him, and he shuddered.

He was a craven at heart. Death had unknown terrors to him; what came after death, or what might come after death, chilled his soul.

He would sooner live on in crime than repent and wipe out his sins by the sacrifice of his wretched life, that might at any moment be taken from him.

He paced the narrow limits of his cell like a caged tiger.

'I cast the die, and lost—lost!' So he muttered as he walked rapidly to and fro.

'Instead of this being my marriage day, I am a caged prisoner. But shall I give in? Not yet. I would sell my soul to perdition to obtain her—to make her suffer. It would be torture to that evil star of mine, her lover. I can try—I can fail again, or triumph' ——

And the thought brought a hyena-like grin from him.

'I must silence busy tongues; first to keep things silent—to keep my crew ignorant of my fate, then for escape—escape and triumph!'

He became calm now; his satanic temperament cooled down to devilish, cruel, calculative scheming.

Subtle plotting was his chief characteristic; to avoid the punishment of one crime he would go deeply into another.

He rang for the jailor.

The man came; he was ignorant of the charge against the well-known *protege* of Lord Garthway, and was civil to a degree.

'Bring me pen, ink, and paper.'

The man bowed and retired.

Ten minutes' impatient waiting, and then the fellow returned with the writing materials.

Gregory sat down before the paper and held the pen in his trembling hand.

He wanted to write to the man he had so foully wronged; the letter, a cringing, whining petition, was calculated to touch the old man's heart. Better for both had he refused all intercourse with the scoundrel.

Bribery could do much in those days—as much then as now; and Gregory Saunders, imposing upon his influence, his wealth, and late position, and upon the minds of the people, had the letter conveyed to his lordship.

The missive contained a canting kind of favour. Gregory spoke of being the victim of inveterate enemies—wanted to be tried before a court of justice, and such witnesses brought forth as could prove he was guilty of the crimes indicted against him. Until then, he begged his lordship would endeavour to have his humiliating condition kept a secret from the gossip of the town and his crew.

Lord Garthway respected his own name and honour, and wished the affair to be hushed up as long as possible.

The note he returned was to this effect :—

'*I have taken measures to prevent the matter becoming a general topic. You—or at least the crew you command—are ignorant of anything. Those who know of your arrest consider it an absurd mistake. I shall make private investigations in the matter, and should you think proper to confess fully to me how far your crimes have gone, and should they be less black than they appear, I will endeavour to get you free, providing you will swear to renounce all claims to anything in this land and go away. Hide yourself, conceal your name, and never let me see your face again, though the wrongs you have done me deserve a worse punishment than death. For my own sake I would get you away.*

'H. G.'

BLACK EYED SUSAN.

OR, PIRATES ASHORE.

THE LION BUCCANEER.

Gregory read it, and a settled purpose of sardonic import came upon his face.

'So, my lord,' the villain cogitated, 'you do not believe in my guilt. Ah! my game is up, I have lost. No—no, my lord, you shall not have it quite so much your own way as that. Luckily you have worked well in my favour. If I fail in the outset of my plan, I may then think of acceding to your proposal. Now for the first step.'

He sat down and wrote a second letter. By the same means as he had obtained a messenger for Garthway, he got one to take this to a man on whom he relied for assistance in his schemes.

The letter was addressed to—

'RODWIN BLAKE, ESQ.,
'Lieutenant of H.M.S. Sorcerer.'

Rodwin Blake was first lieutenant on the schooner commanded by Gregory, since the loss of his gun brig. Nearly all the officers were strangers to Gregory, and very few of his old crew were on board.

Blake received the letter with a positive feeling of annoyance. Blake and Saunders were old acquaintances. Blake felt uncomfortable from the day Gregory Saunders took command of the schooner Sorcerer.

Rodwin Blake pondered over the contents of the letter. Had it been a request, he would have hesitated in going to his captain; but it was a command that he dared not disobey.

His brow grew dark as thunder as he strode towards the prison. Gregory was a cruel, subtle wretch; he knew his man, and knew he would come.

'It was well I thought of him: I will make a ready tool of him. He might object at first, but dare not refuse when I tell him a little story.'

Saunders smiled fiendishly; it was a source of pleasure to him if he could drag anyone else with him down the dark gulf of sin.

His meditations were stopped by the appearance of the man he intended to make his dupe—or victim.

Rodwin Blake comes, looking sullen.

He evinced some surprise at seeing his commander in prison, affected a little indignation at what he termed an outrage.

He could say no less out of courtesy, and Gregory smiled cynically at his empty speech.

'I would be alone with my officer.'

The gaoler bowed and retired.

Assured of his being out of the way by the sound of his distant footsteps, Gregory was the first to break the awkward silence.

'Rodwin Blake, I am in difficulty.'

'That is obvious, captain.'

'I shall get out to-morrow—not without help—I have conferred the honour of my confidence upon you. I know your ambitious temperament, and should you succeed in rendering me this service, I may do something towards raising your sanguine hopes.

'You are Commander of the Sorcerer, Captain Saunders,' replied Blake, not a muscle of his pale face moving.

'Truly, but what I shall require done, must be accomplished silently. I wish you to carry out my intentions—only keep them to yourself.'

'The nature of the *duty* you wish me to perform I am ignorant of.'

He emphasised the word duty, pretending not to see that a private service was required of him.

Gregory Saunders gave him a cool stare, broke into a low laugh or scoff, then stepped forward and laid his right hand upon Blake's shoulder, his eyes fell upon the small grey orbs of his lieutenant.

The look was returned with a cold, impenetrable glance.

'Rodwin Blake,' Gregory began, slowly and with the confidence of a man who held a power—the power given him by another's secret, at his mercy. 'I shall want your services—not your duty, to-morrow night. Mutual confidence had better exist between us; we are men who never desert each other's cause. What think you?'

'What may the cause be?'

'Bah! Are you very particular as to the nature of your services?'

This was a biting sneer.

Blake saw it.

'Let me understand you. Do we stand here as captain and officer, or man to man.'

'Old associations will allow us to be here as friends, if you will—companions, or on equal footing—at least for the present.'

'Well, then, I rendered you a service once; it was unpleasant, and what the law would term a crime—still, I did it, but I swore not to follow up the road I had lately endeavoured to shun.'

'Pish!' Gregory laughed in his face; 'it was not the first crime you committed.'

'It was the *second*.'

'Then this service might make the third.'

'If I do it.'

'I think you will—I know your ambition to become commander of a vessel, and you think it would aid you were I out of your way. Ha! ha! you mistake. Desert me in the hour of need, and if I fall, you shall go with me.'

'You forget how much of your past life is known to me.'

'I do not. It is known to others, or I should not be here. You could do no more against me than others will. On the other hand you could help me. I did not desert you upon one very trying occasion. Come, let us swim together, or'——

'Go on.'

'You go down with me.'

'Is that a threat?'

'It is my intention.'

'I think you know me, Gregory Saunders, too well to think I would undertake ever to serve you from fear. What would you say against me?'

'More than you think.'

'Indeed!'

It was Blake's turn to sneer now.

'Ay! Would you, if you were asked, bare your breast?'

Blake's piercing grey eyes darted one rapid flash upon the speaker, then he was calm as ever.

'Do you not think it would prevent your liberty did the judges know that little device on your breast?'

Again his eyes darted that vivid flash upon Gregory—his hands worked nervously.

'Enough,' he said, coldly; 'I do not underrate a threat, but I will save you *this once*, then the debt I owe will be paid. Name what you require.'

'My ship and crew kept as safe, let them suppose I am still their commander, and keep them all ready for duty; sound a few, or get some men you can trust, and be here at twelve to-morrow night; be near enough to know all that may go on. I may require a dozen or more trusty hands.'

'For you to escape?'

' No.'

' How then ?'

' I will do all that myself. It is after I escape I shall want them.'

' Hem! there is a lady in the case?' And Blake gave one of his mocking smiles.

' There is.'

' I see all now. You want your liberty, your ship, a lady, and '——

' Freedom.'

' This must be done to-morrow.'

' Ay, the latest. What could I do without a vessel? That taken from me, and I am lost.'

Blake's brow grew cloudy.

' Are you aware of the danger attending such a step?'

' It will be less than I incur here.'

Blake gave his lip a doubtful curl.

' Should your crew imagine you are not lawfully their commander, you will find yourself among a legion of devils, who will tear the ship from your grasp, unless you can quell them and get them over to your standard.'

Blake was a few years older than Saunders, and twenty years more in the world's ways. He knew it would be far from an easy matter to turn the hearts of our honest British sea-dogs from their honourable course to the road of guilt.

Gregory knew this too.

' There are many among a large crew who would not hesitate to change their flag.'

' That is your intention?' Blake asked this abruptly.

Gregory regarded him in silence before he replied.

' No.'

' The vessel will be wrested from you. Will the crew show more clemency to you than any other person?'

' No.'

' How, then, do you mean to manage?'

' The schooner is a swift sailer. As yet my imprisonment is unknown, save to a few. The Lord High Admiral has the power of taking my commission; he will not do it yet.'

' You speak with strange confidence.'

' I speak what I have ascertained. His Lordship's honour is at stake—or his family glory, as he calls it—when I fall.'

' That is one point gained in your favour; you are thus safe for a day or two.'

' Ay—everything as it were. I might go aboard and take command of the schooner without causing any surprise. I shall fear nothing should my escape not be discovered for an hour or two. The men you bring had better be obtained from the crimps —fellows you can depend on. Even that, when we are at sea, would turn the balance of the scale in our favour. With a few resolute men to back us up, we could mould the minds of the crew to our own taste. Once out on the Pacific, I will defy Europe's power combined. There is plenty to do, and the men need not know they do not serve Government until it can no longer be concealed.'

' About the pay?'

' I can manage that when I meet them, providing you do a little business for me to-morrow.'

' Sufficient. Should everything go on well you shall hear from me. You must go now. Here I have written what I want down—what proceedings you must take. Let me know when you send.'

Rodwin Blake left the prison, and Gregory Saunders felt safe.

He knew the man he had to depend upon well; he was one not likely to break his word.

' He'll do it,' muttered Gregory. ' But he'll turn viper before long. I know you, Blake; but you won't get the schooner. Do my work, and I will crush you before you have time to sting. Now to settle everything. I must leave nothing undone. Ha! ha! this will be triumph, my proud beauty! When on board my craft we shall see who'll save you.'

The night had advanced far now. His subtle brain had done its plottings. He could go no further without liberty; that he intended to gain at the cost of life.

The time dragged slowly on his hands. He threw himself upon the pallet, and slept till late next day.

' Twelve hours more,' he thought, ' and I shall be free.'

He did not count upon failure.

The day seemed tediously long, as no one visited him, and he was left in ignorance of what was going on without. A messenger came, bringing a note from his accomplice—Rodwin Blake.

The epistle was brief; but its contents gave Saunders the most sanguine hopes.

' *Be prepared. I have succeeded.* (So it ran). *I shall be there at the time. Nothing yet is known. Your ship is ready, the men expecting their captain. Give the signal agreed upon, you will be heard.*
' *R. B.*'

The rest of the day soon slipped by. Gregory was absorbed in scheming his escape. The more he pondered upon the means the more difficult it became; and at last one fearful resolve was settled in his black heart.

He dared not let himself think too much upon the likely issue of his desperate plan.

Night came. The warder went his rounds to see the prisoners were in the wards.

Gregory was in his.

Then he waited until the gaoler's footsteps died away, and he rose again.

A taper he had bribed the man to let him burn he lighted; and he sat deeply absorbed in thought, and watching the flitting shadows which danced about his cell like so many dark phantoms.

The prison clock struck the hour of eleven—its solemn echoes rolled with unusual distinctness through the stone corridors.

' Nearly time,' he muttered.

The wind sighed and moaned without the prison walls. The night was dark—unusually so.

The cell in which Gregory Saunders was confined was near the street, and he heard the rising wind.

Taking from an inner pocket of his coat a long ivory instrument, he laid it very carefully on the table; by its side he placed a large silk handkerchief and a cotton one.

The ivory instrument was a long thin sharp knife. He opened the blade, then bound his wrist, and took the knife in his other hand.

' No,' he muttered, ' I won't do that, I'll try another game first.'

He unbound the knife, and took the huge stone ewer in both hands, held it above his head, and brought it down with a crash on the stone floor.

The noise echoed through the prison and roused the snoring gaoler.

He started up.

'What's that?' he muttered, and stared about him with a stupified air.

A noise proceeding from one of the cells made him curious.

He opened the door of Gregory Saunders' cell.

'What's the matter, sir? anything'——

'Yes. Look here; the ewer has fallen and broken. Could you bring me some fresh water and remove the pieces of broken earthenware? they might cut my feet.'

The man entered with a sullen air. If Gregory had not been very liberal with his guineas, he would not have gone at all.

Wondering how the accident could have occurred, the gaoler went forward, and stooped to pick up the broken fragments.

Could he have seen the devilish light in the prisoner's eyes, he would not have remained as he did.

Saunders strode noiselessly across the cell, and closed the door. Then he turned to the unsuspecting official, and slowly crept upon him.

With an instinct of danger the man rose to a standing position, and leaped back.'

'Aha!'

Gregory was upon him, his hand upon his throat.

'Silence, fool!' he exclaimed, and his blazing orbs gleamed before the gaoler's terrified gaze. He was fascinated by the glare, and saw his death written in their fierce light.

'What would you?'——

'Escape! One cry, and you die!'

He held the man by the throat with one hand, the other was placed upon his victim's mouth.

With the despair of death upon him the official struggled madly to get away.

Saunders set his teeth firmly, and the deadly glow of his eye became worse.

He got the man between the wall and himself.

They struggled madly, but the poor fellow could not move the fiend-like grip of the prisoner from his throat.

One faint cry escaped him as he was hurled to the floor, and Gregory planted his knee with brutal force upon the man's chest.

'Another cry like that, and you die!'

Keeping one hand upon the man's throat, he drew the knife with the other, and opened the blade with his teeth.

The sight of the murderous instrument lent supernatural strength to the gaoler. He partly threw the ruffian off, and disengaging one hand, caught him by the hair.

Gregory's face was diabolical in its expression of pain and fury.

He took the dagger in his hand.

The gaoler saw it coming, and caught the descending wrist.

'Help!' he cried.

'Curse you!'

Gregory tried to stifle his cries by pressing his cheek on the gaoler's lips. He removed his face with a smothered yell. The poor official in his terror, had bitten the ruffian's cheek nearly to the bone.

Maddened beyond all endurance, the murderous wretch placed his hand over the victim's mouth, then, with a brutal wrench of his right arm, he so twisted the gaoler's wrist, that he had to relinquish the knife.

The struggle was brief then. One smothered cry of mortal agony rang out through the prison, and Gregory Saunders sprang to his feet, his clothes blood-besmeared, his face streaming with gore, and a knife clotted to the hilt in his hand.

His teeth shone like fangs, and his blood-shot eyes were fixed with wolfish savageness upon the slowly and noiselessly opening door.

————

CHAPTER XLVI.

WILL SAVES THE LIVES OF THE CREW OF THE GOLDEN ARROW.

ONE of the boats from the Golden Arrow lay snugly under the cliffs. The crew sat within their narrow limits, like so many dusky, lifeless shadows.

A cloaked figure strode impatiently to and fro on the sea-shore. They were waiting for their chief.

Gallant Will, anxious about the safety of his beloved friend, commanded the boat's crew himself, and growing more impatient as the time wore on, he strode hastily up and down.

The danger Gerald incurred in thus desiring to see Madeline troubled Will, for the night was far advanced.

The distant crack of a pistol or gun-shot floated upon the night air, and echoed among the rocks.

Will heard it, and he started.

'Not far off,' he muttered; 'that meant something.'

Even the crew, who sat like shadows or grim phantoms in the boat started, and ventured to look up to ascertain the mistrustful sound.

They could find no clue in the darkness above. They remained as before, watchful and silent. Well on the alert, they strained their ears to catch the slightest sound.

Will had paused in his walk, lest the sound of his footfall on the sands should prevent his hearing.

The heavy clouds rolled on, darkling, in the air, the light of the twinkling stars alternately concealed by the sombre masses.

The wind seemed lulled a little into stillness, coming in playful gusts round the towering cliffs, and sporting along the narrow, rippling surface, in fitful gusts.

The very atmosphere seemed calmed into strange stillness; and Will stood, like a motionless spectre, waiting for sounds he felt certain would be connected with him. They came.

Another pistol-shot, so much like its former one—it must have come from the same spot—but so faint were its echoes that any but those listening for it would not have noticed it.

The air became darker, and its gloom sat upon the sailor's brow. More than ten minutes elapsed in anxious waiting, and no sound broke the stillness of the night.

'Half-an-hour more,' muttered Will, 'and if he comes not, I'll seek him with a crew at my back.'

The breeze freshened, and bore upon the air the echo of a cry—the murmur of voices.

It came almost like a sigh to those stationed beneath the rocks. Too well versed in these signs of danger to disregard even that slight sound, the crew rose as with one accord, and a low murmur broke from their lips—

'Our chief!'

'Ay, lads, your chief! He comes, and the sounds of strife tell us too plainly he brings foes at his back. Silence now, and all wait for my signal. Should you hear it, follow my footsteps with ready weapons—they will be wanted!'

'Ay, sir, and used.'

The friend of the young chief, so noble in his gifts of nature, strode away. He might lack what the world would term refinement, but he lacked neither courage nor honour.

He followed the directions of the sounds; he bore his naked sword upon his arm, and the well-trained hand grasped its hilt.

Not a great distance from the point of land where the boat lay, he halted.

He caught the sound of approaching footsteps. They came so near that he felt someone was not far off.

A figure came in view.

'The captain!' muttered Will; and it was so.

Bloodstained and exhausted, the young chieftain met his friend and officer.

'Will!'

'Gerald!'

'We have no time to lose, the bloodhounds have been on our track. It has been a fight for life, and blood has been shed.'

They reached the beach. The men saw their leader, and stood up in the boat with one accord, every hat was removed, and, as with one voice, the gallant, faithful fellows cried—

'Our chief—welcome.'

'Hush, brave hearts, the hounds of the law are after me, back to the ship, for my life.'

He was seated in the stern sheets, William was by his side, and the boat was pushed off. Then the sturdy rowers pulled with brave will and strength for their ship, and safety for their beloved leader.

Before the boat had got out of sight of shore a party of men were seen crowding to the water's edge.

A grim smile played about the lips of Captain Gerald as he watched them, and heard the loud clamour of their voices.

A vivid flash among them, followed by a crash, caused the boat's crew to pause.

'They want to betray us to the cutters,' muttered the man, which was just the case.

'Never mind. Give way, my brave fellows; once on board the Golden Arrow and I could defy ten such puny things as the revenue boats.'

'Are you wounded?' Will asked.

'I have received a scratch or two, it was heavy odds, Will, seven or eight to one—or more.'

There had been quite as many as that, and they took him at a disadvantage. It is probable his life would have been in greater danger had not Pauline aided his escape from the chamber of his beloved.

Madeline clung to him in supplicating terror. She could chance anything sooner than he should run into such danger as getting from the balcony, or leaping among armed men.

Not even her father would have dared to enter her room without her permission, and she hoped to delay time by carrying on a needless conversation.

At that moment Snuffles waited outside the door, and Lord Garthway demanded admittance to his daughter. Pauline appeared from an ante-chamber.

'Fly,' she said, 'danger hovers over you wherever you go.'

Taking Gerold by the arm she led him away, and said to Madeline—

'Admit his lordship.'

Recovering from the first effects of her embarrassment, Madeline admitted her father.

'Madeline, who has been here?'

The tearful girl was silent, she could not lie.

'Whom have you here, child?'

'No one, father.'

He looked at her very hard.

'Search the rooms, father, if you think so. Why am I thus disturbed and annoyed at this hour in the morning by any base-born hireling who chooses to make a noise here, under the name of the law. My lord, I wonder you have not more power than to allow me to be subjected to such insult. Is not my own chamber to be held sacred, even for a night?'

The admiral coloured.

'Go,' he said, turning to the valiant Snuffles, who waited outside the door, and was peeping through the chink with lustful eyes upon the maiden beauty. 'Go; you are on the wrong track, and cause me this annoyance again without cause and you will suffer.'

'But, my lord'——

'Leave the house, sir. Not a word.'

Cowed and crestfallen, Snuffles left the house and joined his companions outside.

Pauline Clemence took Gerald out by a side entrance. He thanked her kindly, and strode away in an opposite direction to where the officers stood in anxious expectation of their prey.

Unfortunately Snuffles joined them, and he was seen ahead and attacked.

He turned like a tiger at bay.

Angered by the number of assailants, and rendered savage by the humiliation of his beloved by his betrayal.

One of the officers fired a pistol, and the bullet struck him. The others rushed upon his heels.

He was rendered merciless, and the first man fell upon his sword.

'Back,' he cried, 'or you get no mercy!'

This remark made them braver.

Seven or eight to one was work they were not likely to fear. It was blood against weight, and in this case the former conquered.

Gerald put his back against a tree and fought bravely. Ten minutes, and his foes were put to the rout.

One man had stolen upon him unawares, and the barrel of the coward's pistol was within ten inches of the young rebel's head. Gerald drew a pistol too.'

'This is unfair,' he muttered. 'My life demands the deed,' and he fired.

The ruffian fell, a huddled heap.

So he went on. Fighting his way through his foes from the admiral's estates to the sea-shore.

Then he felt safe. On board his beautiful craft, the Golden Arrow, he would defy a fleet.

He was not long in getting to the haven of safety. The men pulled the boat through the water at a terrific rate, and only paused when it lay alongside the matchless vessel.

A loud murmur of pleasure from the crew greeted his ears, and the doctor and officers received him on the quarter-deck.

The medical man, with professional keenness, saw his weak state.

'You are wounded, captain.'

'Slightly.'

The reply, despite his efforts to appear perfectly right, came weak, and his step was feeble.

'Go below, captain,' said Will. 'You will lose nothing by a little rest and having your wounds dressed. You can trust the ship to me.'

Gerald wrung his hand.

'I know it, Will. It would be ingratitude not to comply with your wish. I leave all to you.'

He was conducted below, and William turned to the officers on deck.

'All hands on board?' he asked.

'Ay, lieutenant. We had some trouble; the men have been in sight of land a long time.'

'Ay, it's true. Now, get the boats out. All hands up!' cried Will.

'All hands up!' was vociferated from mouth to mouth, and the deck was crowded with a fine sturdy set of men.

Each one went to his post, and stood with a halyard in his hand, while others mounted the yards.

The hawser was cut, and Will cried—

'Let go for'ard—give her swing.'

'Let go for'ard,' was echoed, and the sails were lowered with beautiful precision.

The stiff breeze filled the sails, and the Golden Arrow stood gallantly out to sea.

'None too soon,' observed an officer to Will.

'You are right.'

He smiled as he watched the cause of the officer's remark. It was the flashing of lights in the roads, and William knew the revenue cutters were being put on their track.

'They will have to fly to catch the swiftest arrow that ever went without a bow,' laughed the subordinate.

'Let us get out into open sea, and we will engage ten of them,' remarked Will, and he meant it.

'There they go. Aha! I thought it.'

A gun was fired by the revenue men to warn the ships anchored within gun-shot, and Will could see a light that appeared to be floating along the top of the water following in their wake.

'A revenue on our track,' he said, laughing.

The Golden Arrow now made fine headway under the full press of canvas, and her course was steered to the coast of France, where Gerald hoped to gain some tidings of Elfin and his lugger.

'Pipe all hands below, and set the watch,' said Will. 'We need not keep the lads up for those toys.'

He alluded to the revenue cutters as toys.

Under the cover of darkness the vessel slipped past all the ships anchored in the waters, and now stood out under the full fresh wind that blew up the Channel.

William had not yet left the deck; though the men were below, and the watch was set.

Seeing nothing could be done now to accelerate the speed of the Golden Arrow, he turned to go below, when something of a peculiar nature caught his eye.

In two or three places he saw long wreaths of smoke curling slowly up. He stood transfixed with wonderment.

He clutched the officer on deck by the arm.

'D'ye see that?'

And he pointed to the vapour curling up the hatchway.

'Ay. Good heavens! What can it be?'

William walked forward.

'Don't rouse the lads,' he said, knowing the panic any disaster at sea caused among the men.

He stood over the fore hatch. The smoke seemed to wreath up from below, but from whence it came he could not tell.

He was about to descend the companion ladder, when he smelt something burning.

'God!' he exclaimed in horror, 'the ship is on fire!'

Scarcely had he uttered the words when there was a commotion below among the men.

'Fire! Rouse up, mates; fire!'

Then this was followed by the appearance of the men, who ran up on deck.

'Fire!' was taken up by those on the watch, and every man was out of his berth.

The first on deck at the cry was Gerald.

'Order, fore and aft; every man to his post,' cried Will.

He was heard. To be heard was to be obeyed.

'The smoke proceeds from the lower fore deck. Make an instantaneous search, and see whose lubber's things are on fire.'

Four of the crew went below. The deck was well searched; the men pulled the hammocks out, yet no signs of fire could be found.

The smoke was coming from some unseen quarter thicker than before.

The boatswain approached Will.

'It's somewhere below, sir.'

'Below!'

'Ay; down under the forehold.'

'The magazine!' cried Will. 'I will discover its source and its cause.'

'It is the work of a traitor,' muttered Gerald; 'muster the men on deck, let them stand ready with the fire buckets.'

'Ay, ay, sir.'

Gerald would have followed Will, but he foresaw that danger was nearer than the men supposed, and to leave them would have caused a general confusion.

Will, followed by some trusty hands, went to the lower deck. Rising from the cracks of the lower hold hatchway, were several little wreaths of smoke.

'Knock off the hatch,' cried Will.

The men did so, and Will jumped back with a cry.

The smoke came up in one dense cloud, and a few bright sparks shone like stars in the heavy vapour.

With an exclamation of horror, the men rushed back from the hold, and one, in his affection for our hero, clutched the gallant fellow by the arm.

'Come away, luff, for God's sake! It's under the magazine.'

'Avast! avast, ye lubbers! Would you have all hands on board to perish? Are ye cowards? or what are ye made of? Would running away save you? God! is there not one who will risk his life to save a hundred of his messmates? Avast! let go your grapnels, I'll go. Ay, alone, sooner than be followed by cowards!'

Will shook the man off indignantly, and drew his sword.

'It's the work of a traitor; and by the Great Skipper, he'll have no mercy.'

He said this as with reckless regard for his own life. He jumped below amongst the stifling smoke.

The daring bravery of Will made the men grow irresolute.

They could not turn and fly from the danger like cowards, when their daring lieutenant had gone fearlessly into the impending peril.

While they stood thus irresolute, Captain Gerald dashed down among them. He had seen the volumes of smoke; had heard the cry of the men, and came down to share the danger with Will.

'Lieutenant Howard?' he asked, excitedly.

'Below, sir,' stammered one of the men.

'And you stand shivering here like so many women? Cowards!' and he leaped down the hatchway. For an instant, he staggered, beaten back by the smoke.

Recovering himself, he endeavoured to glance round for Will.

The dense vapour was too thick; it had been confined so long that it was now like one huge unbroken cloud, and it nearly blinded, as well as suffocated him.

He could see nothing of the brave Will; but he heard a groan—low, deep, and stifling.

That was enough.

'Will!' he said; 'Will, where are you?' and he groped his way forward, as the men he had left above, stung with shame at their momentary fear, leaped down the dark chasm of vapour, with a cry of—

'Bring the buckets!'

'The buckets!'

A wild rush of feet followed; the crew darted forward, and formed a long line from the lower hatch to the bulwarks. The officers were among them, and directed the working of the crew with great velocity. Water was passed from one to the other, and a constant supply was given to those in the hold.

As yet, they could not use it. The source of the disaster was not discovered, and the captain and lieutenant were out of sight.

Will, with the daring impetuosity of his nature, dashed through the blinding smoke, past the magazine, to the farthest end of the hold.

Then he discovered the source of the conflagration.

A slow match had been laid from the starboard corner of the hold to the magazine. The work had been done carelessly and clumsily, and the match had set light to the planks and some bunks.

'Damme! the traitor shall suffer,' muttered Will, and he tore the slow match up, and trampled it out.

He was arrested in the act of calling to the men for water to be brought, and the hose set on, by a groan that proceeded from some one at his feet.

Half blinded as he was, and the inky darkness, prevented him from seeing who or what was there, when the smouldering timbers broke into a flame.

'Aha! Curses! Treacherous dog!' he thundered, hoarsely, and leaped at the crouching form near his feet.

It was a fellow in a smuggler's garb—not one of the crew—who lay crouched upon the floor, nearly choked with suffocation.

'Mercy!' he faintly gasped; 'mercy, and I'll tell all.'

'Mercy, you cursed pirate!—mercy? What mercy would you have given us? What mercy can you expect from me? None!'

His iron-like grip was upon the ruffian's throat.

The shivering wretch was dragged to his feet. He gasped, in piteous accents, to be spared; but Will's ear was closed to entreaty—his heart to mercy.

He held the cowering wretch by the throat, and his eyes shone through the mist like burning coals.

With his right hand, he raised his deadly scimitar.

'Breathe a prayer, traitor!' he cried; 'I'm going to strike.'

As he spoke, the floor beneath his feet broke into a mass of flames, with a terrible roar.

CHAPTER XLVII.

WARNINGS OF EVIL.

THE cause of Gregory's alarm was simple. The door of his prison cell had been left open, and swung back a little as doors often do when left unlatched.

Like a panther that has once tasted blood, Gregory Saunders thirsted for more.

It was a relief to him when he discovered the cause of the door opening.

At first he could not believe he had not been heard.

To him this cry of his victim had been like the shriek of a fiend.

Breathless and motionless, he waited for the coming of new foes.

None came;—the stillness was ominous. Not even a breath of wind penetrated the stone passage of the prison. Outside its partly open door a small oil lamp beamed.

Its flickering light only helped to make 'darkness visible,' and cast a lot of ghostly shadows upon the walls without.

The first paroxysm of fury over, the murderer shuddered at the pitiless deed he had done.

The prison clock tolled out the midnight hour. Solemnly it rang through the gloomy building, and came like a knell to the prisoner's ears.

A cold chill came upon him, a damp moisture broke out on his limbs, and he trembled in silent horror.

He was subdued now. The stillness of night awed him—the horror of the crime chilled him.

He dared not waste time. How could he best ensure success?

Filled with horror as he was, he could not perform the duty his safety would require without a shudder.

But fear made him bold—necessity made him less particular than he would have been on any other occasion. Choking down his feelings of repugnance, he lifted the body of the murdered man from the floor, and laid him upon the pallet in the cell.

He took the blood-stained coat from the dead gaoler's body, and with horrid calmness donned it with belt and keys.

Then he covered the corpse up, took the lantern and dagger, and left the cell, having locked and bolted the door.

He fully expected to meet with some one ere he had got far—even did no one appear in the passages he should meet the doorkeeper.

Should the fellow be asleep, how could he get out without the keys? To take them would be to wake the man—to wake him would be discovery—and discovery would be death.

He reasoned thus as he stole with stealthy steps through the dark stone passages, starting with a chill of awe at every gloomy shadow the flickering light of his lamp threw into the darkness around.

He was not of a very deep, calculative nature. He did not study the best means of surmounting the danger he expected to come, but went on, waiting the uncertain issue of his bold step, and acting as circumstances may direct.

The gaoler's coat he had put on with a vain hope that he might throw any of the officials off their guard.

He began to breathe more freely. He was in the passage leading to the door, and as yet no one had approached.

By the dim glare of a swing lamp, he could see the sleeping doorkeeper, and his heart beat quickly.

The danger of the present moment kept all his energies employed, and for the time the enormous crime he had committed vanished from his memory.

He trod lighter still, and blew the lamp out he carried.

The doorkeeper slept on, unsuspicious of the blood-stained wretch who crept with cat-like tread upon him.

Gregory Saunders scanned the door by the dim light.

One glance told him he must obtain the keys to get out. He turned slowly and surveyed the sleeper.

The man slumbered heavily. He was dreaming, and became restless for a few seconds. Unconscious as he was, Gregory's presence seemed to hover over him like an evil shadow.

The light went dimmer still; the silence was oppressive: the gloomy stone passage was like a vault of the dead.

There was a slight chink: the murderer's fingers had touched the keys that would open the door of liberty.

The sleeper started, partly awake. The lamp sent a blood red glow into his eyes. His hand went to the keys; the light became plainer; his eyes were open.

Only for a few seconds. The light seemed to vanish. He started—groaned; his hand went to his heart; his face wore a half-frightened, half-painful look; he sank back; and slept again—a sleep from which he would never wake. His soul dreamed on earth no longer. He was in the sleep of *death*—a dagger in his heart!

A shadow that had been thrown across his face passed off. The light flickered about from corner to corner of the corridor; the prison door opened with a loud clang, as hasty steps were heard coming down the stone passage, and the cry of frightened men echoed through the stone building.

Then the light went out, the door was opened to its extent, and the dark, phantom-like shadow passed out for a few minutes, returned, passed the door again, two dark, shapeless masses were hurled into the stone hall, then the evil doer passed out for good. The door closed with a loud clang, which sent the echoes through the sombre building, and caught up another sound more fierce and terrible.

It was like the noise of an earthquake. The prison shook to its base. The deafening report was followed by a fearful agitation: the prison roof was hurled in numberless pieces in the air. One sheet of flame shot up; then came a crash, and then dreadful cries of a multitude of human beings in fright or in agony.

*　　*　　*　　*　　*

The night after Madeline's secret interview with her gallant lover, she sat in her room with Susan.

'Do you know, Susan, dear, I really cannot shake off this feeling of coming evil. I am sure it is a presentiment.'

'What have you to fear, dear? he is in prison,' replied Will's pretty wife.

'I wish father was here, why did he go away to-day?'

'He will return to-morrow.'

'Ay! to-morrow, that is a long time.'

Madeline said this dreamily, she was thinking of something else at the time.

'I had a dream, dear Susan, but it was too fearfully vivid to be all a dream, I'——

She paused. Pauline entered.

'Is it not time you retired, dear?'

'I know not how to explain myself, Pauline, but—but—I fear to rest.'

'Your nerves are shaken, and you give way to foolish fancies. What can happen? the worst has passed.'

Madeline sighed.

She did not think so.

'Return to your bed, my dear Madeline, I am sure Mrs. Howard will stay with you.'

'That I will only too happily,' said Black-eyed Susan, tripping lightly towards Madeline, and kissing her pale cheek.

'I wish his lordship was here,' murmured Madeline.

''Tis as well he is away,' muttered Pauline. Then she spoke aloud—

'Fear nothing; I will sleep in the chamber below. The house shall be well secured, and men kept on the watch.'

She kissed the timid girl, took Susan's hand with courteous formality, and left the chamber.

'Strange,' she cogitated, as she went down the great staircase, 'strange that she should have a presentiment of coming evil. I, too, have had one—not a dream, a warning.'

She entered her sleeping apartment. A look of strange determination was upon her classic face.

'Should it be so,' she went on, giving vent to her thoughts, 'I shall be equal to the emergency.'

Taking a small oil lamp, she left the room, and went through the house, to ascertain whether the doors and windows were safe.

She had the nerve of a man; not one corner of the dreary building did she leave until satisfied of its security.

The wind moaned and sighed round the house dismally, and the branches of the gigantic trees without struck against the lattice windows, scratching and tapping with a ghastly sound.

Pauline heeded it not.

She was now at the foot of the staircase, and the echo of the church clock striking one was heard. The wind wafted the echoes through the house with great distinctness.

The sound died away.

She took only one step, then paused; her cheek went a little paler—not from fear.

Another sound was borne upon the moaning wind—it was the echo of a sudden report which reverberated through the air.

It seemed to cause a concussion so terrible, that the shock was felt even where Pauline stood.

The house shook as though loosened from the foundation, the windows rattled, and a mail figure on a pedestal in the hall fell with a crash.

BLACK EYED SUSAN.

OR, PIRATES ASHORE.

THE SHIP IN FLAMES.

' God !' murmured Pauline. ' Can it be an earth-quake ? See, it is *that*, I know ; I dreamed not in vain.'

Then a piercing shriek rang through the house.

Pauline knew the voice.

' Madeline !' she cried, and hastened up to her room.

She found Madeline sitting up in bed, and Susan trying to soothe her.

' Oh, what horror !' cried the terrified girl, and threw herself into the arms of Pauline, where she lay and sobbed like a child.

Susan was pale and trembling.

' Did you hear that dreadful report, Miss Clemence, and feel the house shake ?'

' I did. Was it that which startled Miss Garth-way ?'

' No ; she was asleep and dreaming.'

' Water—water, Susan,' gasped Madeline.

Swiftly Susan jumped from the bed and went to the water-bottle, and brought a glass of the crystal liquid.

Madeline drank it off at a draught.

' My dream frightened me,' she said, ' what awoke me like that. Ah, Pauline, it was dreadful—dreadful !'

' Hush, dear, the servants are roused.'

The terrified domestics came rushing up the stairs and crowded around the door-way.

The shriek that had awoke the house awoke them in terror.

Pauline faced them calmly.

' What is this ?' she asked, ' why are you all out of your beds ?'

' Oh, miss,' the terrified housekeeper said, ' did you feel the house shake ?'

' I did,' replied Pauline ; ' it was nothing—some explosion of gunpowder in the town, I daresay ; it will not hurt us, therefore I hope you will retire ; you disturb your mistress.'

' But I heard a scream, miss ?'

' The uncommon occurrence frightened your mis-tress ; she was asleep, and awoke in a fright. Are you satisfied ?'

The old housekeeper saw Pauline was getting angry, and she retired, followed by the rest of the female menials, who went, shaking, into their beds.

The plush-and-powder flunkey felt nervous, and slept with his lordship's valet.

The butler slept—we cannot say where, but he was observed to make towards the housemaid's room—of course there was nothing in that.

He went to see if she was frightened, only he did not come back to tell whether she was or not.

The house again resumed its quietude. Madeline was calmed, and, yielding to the persuasions of Pauline, slept again.

Pauline was not agitated from fear.

Still there was a nervous twitching at the corners of her mouth.

' What could it be ?' she thought, the inexplicable commotion of the scene returning to her mind.

The night had wore on, it was late now.

She entered her room with a slow, dreary tread.

She was sunk in a deep reverie, and everything she performed was done methodically.

The door fastened and secured, she laid the lamp down, and went to the window.

While looking out into the dark, night air, she shuddered.

' I am wrong to give way to these painful presenti-ments,' she murmured.

The wind groaned as it wafted past the casement—a gale seemed rising.

' Ought I sleep,' she went on. ' This is some silly fear.'

She was slowly disrobing—not with the intention of going to bed, but from force of habit.

She stood before the mirror, and began to undo the braidings of her hair.

She remained lost in thought, and her lips moved as though she was communing with herself.

Her wavy tresses hung down over her white shoul-ders, and sported over her beautiful bust, displayed by her unfastened *robe de chambre*.

In the act of brushing the silken wavy mass of hair, she paused and listened.

' That was something.'

She went to the door, which was fastened, opened it, and put her head out.

All was silent as the grave.

She remained thus for more than a minute, and became absent-minded as she stayed.

In this deep, meditative mood, she closed the door and returned to the dressing-table.

She renewed the occupation of hair-dressing the while.

' It was strange—I saw him last night in my wild fancy. Why should his form come before me, even in imagination ? Strange !'

She ceased.

Her hand became still ; her lips turned a livid hue ; her face went like marble white ; her eyes were fixe with awful fascination upon the looking-glass before her.

Wondrous nerves had that woman. She saw in that mirror the reflection of a form—the form of him she had just been murmuring so intelligibly about.

She was a stranger to woman's weak fears ; bold, decisive, and calm, she knew it was the face of no phantom.

Some one—a mortal, flesh and blood—had entered the room by the door with a stealthy step.

The intruder had a mask in his left hand ; his right was hidden by the folds of a cloak, which did not con-ceal the gleaming point of a knife.

She neither trembled nor screamed. The daring intruder, garbed in naval attire, could not see her face. She knew him, and slowly faced round.

' Aha ! not a cry, girl, or you die !'

The stranger started forward with uplifted knife.

' Victor !'

The would-be murderer halted, reeled, then stood as though transfixed with a motionless, speechless figure.

Pauline rested her left hand upon the table, her hair was thrown back from her shoulders, and her scantily-covered breast heaved and fell perhaps a little quicker than she would have wished.

Thus they confronted each other for a few minutes

Neither spoke.

The intruder she designated as ' Victor,' seemed struck dumb by her firmness.

He was a tall, slim man of about five-and-thirty He might have been more—he looked more.

He was well knit and well shaped, though we use the words slim. His features were perfect ; his eyes, cold grey, and twinkling ; his hands and feet were finely shaped and small; his lips short and thin, that only a thin streak of red could be discerned.

One glance would tell an observer he was a bold, iron-willed man. He has been introduced to our readers before, only as Rodwin Blake. Why Pauline styled him Victor, events will eventually show.

'Victor,' she said again, 'I expected this.'

He recovered himself now.

'You here?' he said.

'Ay, I might return the query. Why came you here? God of heaven, to think that you should meditate more crime. I know your purpose. I know your tempter; but, Victor, while I live you shall not carry out your evil intent.'

'Girl, where heard you this?'

'I was warned.'

'What of?'

'Your visit; it is to carry off Madeline. The crime-stained villain, Saunders, is here, but he shall not succeed. Victor, Victor. Oh, God! I never thought we should meet thus. Dare you think of attempting this crime. Would you raise your dagger again to me?'

He shuddered.

'I did not know you. Pauline, girl, there is no help. He is a fiend; he has me body and soul. He knows my secret, and I am sworn to serve him in this.'

'Hark! God of mercy! Victor, save her!'

A shriek, loud and piercing, came upon her ears; it was from Madeline. She drew a long dagger from its sheath, and dashed past Blake up the stairs to Madeline's chamber.

Then could be heard the steps of men. Doors were forced open; a terrible din; and screaming domestics rushed about in all directions.

Pauline rushed to Madeline's chamber. It was occupied by the men. The brave girl was struggling with two. Susan was in the clutches of a third.

'Release her,' cried Pauline, and she tore the mask from one of the ruffian's faces.

'Gregory Saunders!' she exclaimed.

Madeline shrieked. The ruffian turned upon Pauline with a murderous gleam in his eye, and as the noble girl tore Madeline, fainting, from the arms of a villain, Gregory raised his knife to strike the devoted girl, who turned at bay, with Madeline in her arms, a dagger in her hand, and fire in her eye.

'Touch her who dares!' she said, and even Gregory paused before the flashing eye.

But only for an instant.

CHAPTER XLVIII.

SEEKING THE EARL'S LIFE.

CYRIL, the lion buccaneer, stood in breathless anxiety, waiting to see who would break in upon them.

He held the fearless Lady Clarence to his breast, and his right hand grasped his sword.

Fortunately for them the door was locked, for someone paused without, and tried the lock.

'Clarence, my child!'

'Father!'

'You are safe?'

'Quite, father, dear. What made you ask so strange a question?'

'I heard a noise, my love, while passing from my library, and thought it proceeded from your chamber.'

'Were you not mistaken, father?'

'Perhaps so, child—perhaps so; but'——

'I will get up, my lord, would it make your mind any easier; then you could search my room.'

'No—no, child, sleep; I am satisfied. It must have been fancy.'

'That is well,' whispered Cyril, as the earl descended the stairs.

Lady Clarence remained quiet; she was listening to his retreating footsteps.

'Thank heaven!' murmured the beautiful Clarence, 'thank heaven he did not enter. I would not have him know you were here. Oh! Cyril, he, like many others, has heard of your mad career. Why did you become an outlaw?'

'Am I all to blame?' He asked this somewhat reproachfully.

'I do not say so,' Clarence replied, mournfully. 'But was it wise to take such a step?'

'Why not? I was in the way. I have been wronged, and those who did it attempted my disgrace. Can I go back to my father? No. Is there anyone to care for, or help me? No. And you—you, oh! beautiful Clarence, whom I loved to madness—you almost shunned me.'

'I, Cyril?' and her beautiful eyes were fixed with mute reproach upon him. 'You wrong me. I loved you as a friend—a brother.'

'I wanted more, Clarence.'

'I could not give it in honour, Cyril.'

'For why? Are you not your own mistress? Are you bound like a slave to become the wife of he whom they choose to allot you?'

'I was taught to look forward to the alliance from childhood, Cyril. Even if I could not love him, I had made up my mind to honour and obey as a wife should.'

'And this is what you call holy matrimony, when selfish interests are only considered and hearts wrecked?'

'Not wrecked, Cyril; I was not forced into it. I gave my promise before I knew you.'

'Not before you knew me, Clarence. Were we not companions when you came with your father to Spain? Was I not taught from my tutor to honour you, while at my father's mansion?'

'True, Cyril; but I knew of the reported alliance then, and I did not know you loved me.'

The words were spoken very softly, and Cyril thought the tiny hand nestled closer in his own bronzed palm.

He drew her quietly to his manly breast.

The moon's silvery light fell softly upon his handsome upturned face.

'Clarence! did you know the torture your coldness is to my heart you would at least pity me.'

'Cyril!'

'Clarence!'

'You are unjust.'

'I am in love.'

'Does that make you untruthful?'

'How, beauteous being?'

'You spoke of my coldness.'

'Are you not?'

'Cyril, I cannot forgive you. She gently disengaged herself from his embrace. 'I e'en know you have brought the scorn of society upon you. I alter not. You are the same to me. When did I ever reproach you for your folly—I can call it nought else.'

'Beautiful angel! Star of my soul!' Cyril exclaimed passionately, and took her hand between both his own.

'Cyril! I cannot listen to such talk.'

She tried to disengage her hand. He feared she was offended.

'Clarence! my beautiful Clarence! forgive me.'

He was on his knees now before her. His face was upturned to her own, his eyes flashed the soft light of love, his look of mute eloquence was irresistible.'

The peerless Lady Clarence remained silent. She turned her head away, but did not attempt to disengage her hand.

The beautiful face before her, so full of penitence, soon subdued her.

It was not the first time it had done so.

She knew her weakness, and feared it.

'Forgive me.'

These were the words of a contrite heart, and fell softly upon the ears of the lovely creature at whose feet he knelt for mercy.

'Rise, Cyril, rise!'

'I am forgiven.'

'Freely.'

'Clarence, my love!'

He was upon his feet, and he caught her in his passionate embrace.'

Clarence's heart fluttered wildly. The power the dashing Spaniard had on her made her afraid of herself.

'Cyril! you must go.'

'My love, not yet. I come to know my fate. My ship lies under the rocks. At dawn I set sail, I know not whither; I may go to death; then I shall trouble you no more.'

Clarence thought he spoke very sadly, and her heart was touched.

'Death! Cyril used to laugh at the grim phantom.'

'I almost court it now.'

'Is that right?'

'Can you ask it, Clarence? What have I to live for?'

'Much.'

'Much!' he echoed—'much! where?' and he sighed deeply.

'For yourself, your father, your name, and lost honour.'

'For the first I care little; my sire—what of him? I should be less trouble were I dead; and my honour—who took it from me.'

'You lost it by a rash act.'

'Do you deem me guilty of the deed?'

'No!' and she drew herself up with queenly grace.

'Bless you, dearest one!'

He stooped, and kissed her hand.

'I simply thought you rash, Cyril, and wrong to take to a lawless life.'

'I have not done so. I was tired of false friends and bitter enemies—tired of cringing life at court—tired of having to fight daily for my honour's sake—tired of living on with a hopeless love rankling in my breast—a love never returned. I longed for excitement, adventure—to be a monarch where I could rule with no one to gainsay me. I am a monarch, on the boundless ocean's wild domain. I alone rule there.'' (He stretched his hand towards the sea.) ''I have my slightest wish gratified. What is life without our desires are gratified?'——

'Still, Cyril,' she interrupted him, 'I hear you spoken of as an outlaw—as a nameless violater of the laws.'

'By whom?'

'Your enemies,' she replied, in a tone that conveyed a double meaning, and he understood it.

The dashing young Spaniard (known as the Lion Buccaneer) was an idol—a hero to dream of and worship—among the gentle sex of all nations.

Lady Clarence knew it, nor was she one of the last whose heart beat with dangerous admiration for the princely young chief.

'Would you give up this life?' she asked.

'Why should I?'

'For your own honour's sake.'

'I care for nothing—I have no one to care for—no one cares for me.'

'You are cared for, Cyril.'

'By whom?'

She did not reply. Her head sank upon his breast.

'Clarence,' he murmured, kissing the white brow, 'Clarence, dare I hope?'

'It were better not to, Cyril; we ought not to dream thus. It can never be. I do wrong to give you hope, Cyril. Think of me only as a sister. I will always love you as a brother.'

'She used the word love,' thought Cyril; and it gave him hope.

'We must part, Cyril. I cannot receive you thus. Is it honourable to my sire—my future husband?' She asked this, looking up into his expressive face.

'Love is always honourable,' he said; and tried to make himself believe it.

'But when it is where love should not be—how then, Cyril?'

He began to get more perplexed. He could not reply, so kissed her.

'You do not reply, Cyril.'

'Love is never where it should not exist,' he answered, desperately. 'It ought not to exist with your future husband, and it does not.'

'Why not, Cyril?'

'Because you were not made to become the slave of man.'

'I never shall be, Cyril.'

'Where matrimony is only a sense of duty, love is slavery.'

Lady Clarence did not see the point; so did not reply.

In her heart she loved the daring fellow before her. They had known each other when young, and this love strengthened as time flew on. But she was a haughty, honourable-minded girl, with generous instinct, and a true sense of right; and she tried very hard to stifle her love for him, that she might receive the man her father had chosen for her husband with unstained honour.

She tried to disengage herself from the fiery young aspirant's embrace, as she said—

'It is my fate, Cyril! I must bear it, so must you. I am satisfied to keep honour with my parents, and I could even live happy with you as a brother. Can you refuse me this?'

'Refuse you, Clarence!' he exclaimed, drawing her to him passionately. 'Ask me for my life, and I would give it freely.'

'Then you promise'——

'With a promise in return, dear one.'

'That'——

'Is—you will not enter into any hasty alliance: ask time of your sire.'

'For why?'

'I do not like the brother of the countess. I should like to know more of him, ere he takes my angel sister in bondage.'

Clarence hesitated.

'You have a motive for this, Cyril?'

'I have.'

'You will not tell me.'

'No, Clarence, dear, I will not. It is a vague suspicion of a selfish heart.'

'You, selfish, Cyril?'

'All love is selfish, beautiful dreamer, and I am so. I have a suspicion at heart: it is more a presentiment, and I want you to delay the decisive step until you hear from me.'

'I promise, Cyril.'

'Thanks, dear one,' he said; 'as a brother, I may kiss you.'

He held her fondly in his arms, and she nestled close to him. Perhaps she was glad of the privilege the fancied tie of brother and sister gave her.

She was less the proud woman now, and became more confiding.

'You will think of me only as a dear sister?' she asked; and he found her voice was not so firm as it might have been, with the hope of having her request granted.

'As a sister, if you wish it, Clarence; but I shall never love anyone else.'

He spoke earnestly and somewhat sadly. Clarence believed him, and he was all the dearer to her for it.

She thought of the man she was destined to be allied to. Her father's wife's half brother. And she involuntarily compared him as a cynical, selfish man of the world, with such a soul as a hollow society had left him, to the dashing impulsive being who stood before her in all the rich vigour of manly beauty and grace; and the conclusion of her mental comparison was not in the favour of the absent lover.

Lord Edmond Lichley was a handsome, coldblooded man of fashion, selfish to the core, with a sinister leer at the corner of his mouth, not prepossessing in his favour.

He became distantly related to the Earl of Greymoor by his sister, a woman of dazzling beauty, marrying the earl. She was his second wife.

It was to Lord Edmond that Clarence was affianced, and this was a dagger in Cyril's heart.

Lady Clarence had seen Lord Edward once, that was before she left school. She knew it was her father's wish that she should like him, and she tried to.

Between her and the countess there was a mutual secret antipathy. Clarence felt a chill in her presence, and mistrusted her. The Countess of Greymoor, for some secret reason, hated Lady Clarence from her heart.

There was a dark mystery attached to the earl's young wife, though no one suspected it but Cyril.

He had known the earl when his first wife was alive, and when Clarence was a confiding, innocent girl of seventeen, and a strange circumstance had made him mistrust the countess.

One thing Cyril had kept a secret from Clarence.

He had met with Lord Edmond in Madrid, and they became saloon acquaintances. Cyril could see that Lichley was not rich, and therefore concluded his sister was poorer.

This circumstance he accounted for her marrying the earl, a man much older than herself, and looked older than he was.

His reason for making Clarence promise she would not enter into an immediate alliance was a secret with himself.

He had met another stranger in Madrid—an Englishman of rank—poor, and of profligate habits. Cyril took a secret dislike to him, and was ever on the watch. He felt the man had a secret, and he wished to get a clue to it.

They drank together one night. The wine circulated freely, and the stranger imbibed too much. He became boisterous and unguarded. In drawing a handkerchief from his pocket, a case containing a miniature fell to the floor.

Cyril stooped and picked it up. The case opened, and he could not help seeing the portrait it contained.

'Aha!' he exclaimed, startled at what he saw, Edith, the Countess of Greymoor.'

He held the miniature in each hand, his eyes fixed upon it in mute surprise.

The words seemed to wake the stranger, his face went a livid hue.

'You know her,' he muttered. 'Dastard, how dare you open that case?'

He leaped forward with drawn sword.

Cyril started, and was on his guard, and his broad weapon flew out too, though scarcely in time. As he thrust out he felt a sharp prick in his shoulder. He might have died had not a young noble jumped between them, and he lost his life for the daring deed.

It was never known whose sword went through the young Spaniard. Cyril knew his did not, for his sword was not wet.

Both had been playing and gaming with the young noble, each was in his debt.

Cyril would have paid his, the English stranger could not.

Still the crime fell upon Cyril. People said he had always hated the young Spanish Duke, got in his debt, could not pay, and so took that opportunity of removing his creditor.

That was the cause of his disgrace, and he left his home for the sea.

The scene just described was passing through his brain, as he stood with Clarence held to his breast, and he became thoughtful.

'You are meditative, Cyril.'

'I? Hush, dear! What is that?'

Each listened. It was the sound of a stealthy footfall on the great staircase; doors were slowly opened and closed with stealthy silence.

Then a soft step ascended the stairs, a chamber door creaked back on its hinges, shut, and the lock shot with a click into the socket.

Then all was still.

'What is that?' asked Clarence, in alarm; and she clung with fear to Cyril.

'Nothing of any importance, dear one; perhaps a domestic who went below for some reason.'

'Nay, a strange feeling of fear comes upon me, Cyril. Methought I heard whispering when the sound of the first door being opened died away.'

Cyril had fancied so too; but thought it a fancy only

The words of Lady Clarence excited his suspicions, and made him think something *was* wrong, and he crept to the door and listened.

Lady Clarence was by his side.

' Footsteps, by heaven !' he cried. ' Stay, Clarence, where you are.' He opened the door, and crept out upon the landing. ' Do not stir, love. I hear voices. I will see the cause of this. Fear not for me ! '

' But my sire ?'

' Is safe while I am here.'

He kissed the pale cheek of the beautiful Clarence. drew his sword, and descended the stairs.

On the grand staircase he became more cautious.

He still heard footsteps ; they were heavy, and he knew them to be men's. Voices, too, came upon his ears—dark, sullen whispers, and he felt evil was going on.

' Aha !'

He paused, clutched the bannister with his left hand, his right tightened on his sword. He peered over into the hall, where he beheld three crouching figures.

' God of mercy ! What does this mean ? What dark work is beginning so soon ? They crouch by the door of the earl's library, and—they mean murder ! Fate brought me here to save you, my lord, and I would, were it nine to one, and it is but three. Ah ! they open the chamber door. I must follow !'

He crept down the stairs, keeping well in the shadow, and followed closely two dark forms entering the library.

The earl was there asleep in his chair. One of the cloaked ruffians approached the sleeper. A knife gleamed in his hand. It was raised—and fell—

Only to his side. A hand gripped him by the shoulder, and a sword's point was at his throat.

———

CHAPTER XLIX.

WILL'S BRAVERY.

THE fellow who had attempted to blow up the Golden Arrow was a paid hireling of Gregory Saunders.

He had gone on board under cover of night, and sneaked down into the hold and waited until the vessel went out to sea ; then he put his evil intent into execution.

Like most mean-souled wretches he was a coward, and he was not likely to endanger his own life could he help it.

To avoid such a calamity as death, he lit a very slow match, one that would give him three hours to escape.

When it was lighted, he started to leave the hold.

Now came his own punishment.

The hatch had been battened down, and his means of escape cut off.

He dared not, however, call at the hatchway for help. Doing so would be death. That he feared too much to court.

A clammy perspiration broke out upon him. His limbs shook with terror, and his teeth shut closely. He seemed lock-jawed with fright.

Finding his danger imminent, he thought of the only plan likely to save him.

To extinguish the match.

He staggered back to the corner of the hold with the intention of undoing his evil work.

He was too late.

The planks had caught fire ; the beams and some timber were smouldering, and would soon break out into a blaze, and a thick black smoke mingled with the close atmosphere of the hold, rendering it suffocating.

He groaned in abject terror.

To extinguish the rapidly rising fire was impossible.

He jumped upon the match he kindled, and not the smouldering planks ; he tore the burning pieces down with his hands until the skin peeled off.

All this was in vain.

It was out of his power to undo the work he had too well done.

He shrieked in mortal terror.

His eyes smarted from the blinding smoke, he was choking, and his tongue parched up in his mouth.

The hold was so full of the suffocating vapour he could not discern even the hatch. Sparks began to fly up, a little jet of flame shot out here and there, and the horror he felt was beyond all imagination.

The smoke began to make its way through the smallest crevice, and was seen on deck.

He heard the conversation above, and his limbs refused their support, and shaking in mortal terror he sank huddled up in one corner of the hold, where he was found by gallant Will.

It is probable William would have cut him down there and then for the dastardly act, had not the sudden bursting out of the fire compelled him to retire.

' Put the miserable cur in irons,' said Gerald Stuart, calmly. ' Come, Will, the danger of the moment requires all our energies.'

The men in their fury would willingly have torn the shivering wretch from the hands of Will, and wrenched him limb from limb.

When he gave him up to be put in irons, they would have done it, had not Gerald sternly bade them conduct the traitor to the bulkhead, and chain him up.

Knowing the penalty of disobedience, the men obeyed.

' I have removed the match,' said Will.

At the words, a cheer broke from the sailors. They felt their lives were owing to the noble fellow for his daring, indomitable pluck.

' Thank heaven for that, Will. Now, my lads, rig the pumps, and pass the buckets.''

' Ay, ay, sir.'

The men worked with a will. Truly they did, for Will was at their head directing the movements.

He never once flinched. He was in the thickest of the danger, doing the hardest part of the work, and even cheering the men on.

There was not an idle hand on board.

Even Pat Murphy worked like a Trojan. He was down in the hold by the side of William in a pair of sea boots and trousers, and a skull cap on ; his powerfully built body, and long brawny arms were naked. He handed two buckets of water to every one else's one, and skipped about with the rapidity of a monkey.

His noisy tongue was going all the time. He made light of everything.

Happy Jack, the gunner, was at his elbow, and a splendid pair of hard working fellows they were.

Happy Jack was not, nor had not been of late, on such good terms of friendship with Pat. He had the rough native instincts of a rugged honest heart,

and, like most generous natures, he would give his friendship and support to the weak.

With the rest of the crew, he could enjoy a little fun at the expense of Dismal Jacob, but he thought Pat's practical joke had gone too far.

The good meaning fellow had done nothing but picture to himself the torture Jacob might have suffered alone on the boundless sea.

But the present emergency made the worst of enemies friends, and Happy Jack would only have belied his name had he been sulky long.

'Och! bedad, me honey, it's a warming the varmint would been afther giving us.'

'The swab,' was all Jack could utter, ss he used the bucket with a will.

'Be smart, Sam, yer lubber,' he said. 'Damme! you are as slow as a loblolly boy with the water.'

Sam—or Yellow Sam, as he was called, on account of his straw-coloured whiskers—bent his long back, and worked until he was in a profuse perspiration.

'Och one, me darlint; bend your back, and make light o' the fun. Give a song, for its music hath charms. Oh, fal thra ral de ral.' He sent a bucket of water with terrific force. The handle gave way, and the bucket went with a terrible shock against the stomach of Yellow Sam.

'Ugh!' he cried, and went doubled up against the side of the ship's hold, he being breathless.

Happy Jack was in the act of sending a bucket of water too.

His arms were in full swing. He could not stop himself.

'Yeo—yeo—yeo!' he began to sing, and splash went the water, with a wild rush, into the ears and open mouth of the unfortunate Sam, who lay rolling about in the swamp, breathless and half stunned.

'Sure, an' it's the likes of yourself as needn't run away with my bucket.'

'Jump up, lad,' bawled Jack.

'Maybe he'd rather stay and take a rest, eh?

   ' " Me mother she's gone out to market,
      Me dad he's winking at home,
      The two snoring pigs ain't up to the rig
      Of snoring over a bone, a bone—
      Of snoring over a bone." '

Pat worked away, while Happy Jack picked his fallen companion up.

How long the cook's song would have lasted, it is hard to say, had not the boatswain's whistle called all hands to quarter.

The fire was put out, and all danger from that source over.

The men hailed the news with three hearty cheers.

The crew was summoned on deck, and an allowance of grog served out.

Thus refreshed, and with a short rest, the boatswain's whistle called them all to duty; and again all was noise and mirth; the officers vociferating one from the other to the men, who were putting the vessel in trim and stowing away the lumber.

Will, begrimed with smoke, and covered with wet and dirt, dived into a cabin with Captain Gerald.

'You had better change your rig, Will.'

He did so, and returned to the young commander quite refreshed.

'It was the work of Providence—that narrow escape from destruction, Will.'

'Ay, cap'n. I was well-nigh driving my sword through the pirate's carcase.'

'We may hear something from him.'

'Maybe we shall.'

The steward brought the wine on, and the two friends did it justice.

'Wilks.'

'Sir,' replied the steward.

'Send Lieutenant Burkett and the doctor below to me.'

The steward retired.

The officer and doctor entered the cabin.

'We had a narrow squeak,' observed the latter with a smile.

'We certainly had. Will you take wine with us?'

'Happily.'

Buskett said so, too.

'Steward.'

'Sir.'

'Fetch the captain of marines.'

Captain Longshot came.

'Captain, bring the prisoner here, under arms, will you?'

'Willingly.'

The valiant captain gave the necessary order to a subordinate, and the traitor was dragged before the young chieftain.

The shivering wretch was held between two marines.

Gerald's handsome face grew stern; it wore a cruel look as he eyed the terrified ruffian.

'Your name,' he said, coldly.

'Joe Bennet.'

'Did you attempt to blow up the vessel on your own accord?'

'No.'

'You were paid?'

'Yes.'

'By whom?'

'Captain Saunders.'

'How much were you paid to commit so dastardly an attack?'

'Twenty pounds.'

'Deplorable brute! And for such a sum you would, in cold blood, blow up a hundred of your fellow-creatures? Callous, brutal wretch! Take him away, Captain Longshot, and order him to receive two dozen with the cat.'

'Mercy!' gasped the man.

'That is the mercy I show you!'

'Mercy!'

He broke from his captors, and went down on his knees.

'Mercy, cap'n!' he implored.

'Give him another dozen,' said Gerald, coldly.

He could be pitiless at times; he was so now.

'Take him away.'

Shrieking for mercy, and trembling from fear, the man was dragged away, and given over to the hands of the boatswain and his mates.

Never had he received an order for the cruel punishment of flogging with so little repugnance.

'String him up, lads, and strip him, if he won't strip.'

The doctor stood by, and Gerald and Will were on the poop.

It was so dark that the battle lanterns had to be hung up by the side of the grating.

'Ready?' said the boatswain.

'Ready!' echoed the mate, who waited with the cat raised above his head for the signal from Gerald Stuart.

'Pro——' The word for the mate to commence was half way from his lips, when Will stopped him by clutching his wrist.

'Avast, captain! Look yonder.'

Gerald swerved round, and saw a light which seemed to be floating in the mist.

'That is in gunshot range, Will. What on earth can it be?'

He had his night glass brought.

'If that isn't the foretop light of a seventy-four,' said Will, 'why, dash my toplights, Mother Carey never had any chickens!'

'By heavens, you are right, Will. Pipe all hands to quarter; let the punishment be postponed.'

Joe Bennet was taken down, and his bloodshot eyes rolled about with an awful glare.

He had hopes of respite, and his rolling orbs lingered with a hopeful glance upon the distant light.

'Don't yer mistake, yer swab, you'll get it yet,' said the boatswain's mate, giving him a jerk.

He was thrust back into prison.

Silently as possible the men came to their posts. The guns, which were always kept in readiness, were run out, and the crew armed to the teeth.

'Friend or enemy,' said Gerald, 'she is a monster. Put out the lights, my men, 'tis that which betrays us.'

The light Will had sighted still shone darkly in the darkling air, and a strange vessel bore down upon them.

She was so close now, that with the naked eye she could be descried, looming out in the darkness like a giant shadow.

'We are taken at a terrible disadvantage,' said Gerald, 'should she prove a foe. I am certain it is nothing less than a seventy-four.'

'And a froggy,' put in Will.

'Do not reply, should they challenge us. We must fog them, and while they are considering in challenging the second time we will pour a broadside into her.'

The officers stood a silent, grim row of figures, waiting to convey Captain Gerald's slightest command to the men.

'Mr. Happleton,' said Gerald.

Happy Jack came forward, and pulled his forelock.

'Mr. Happleton, can you see the stranger's mast?'

'Ay, ay, yer honour, I've had an eye on that ever since the ship's been in sight.'

'Very good. Now, when I give the signal for the men to fire, endeavour to drop a shot into their foremast. I know you can do it if you like.'

'Ay, ay, sir,' replied Happy Jack, proud of the compliment.

Hitching up his trousers, and turning his quid, he returned to his long gun.

'We have thrown them off the scent a bit, Will,' laughed Gerald. 'We lay low in the water, and without a light to betray us we baffle them.'

'Maybe; but they're coming down on us smart enough,' remarked Will, watching the huge stranger.

'It's a line-of-battle ship, whatever country it may belong to.'

'And a nice mawling they may give us.'

'They'll challenge in a minute. Ah! I thought so.'

The challenge came.

'French, by Jupiter!' said Gerald.

'Starboard your helm,' cried Will.

They were challenged again.

Gerald Stuart did not reply to it.

'If you don't answer, monsieur, I'll fire into you.'

'Will you, though?' thought Gerald.

Aloud, he said—

'Give them their answer, my lads.'

The answer was given.

A broadside that shook the liner from stem to stern, and the concussion caused in the narrow space of air between the two vessels caused even the Golden Arrow to shake.

Happy Jack was not far behind.

He had been very impatiently waiting for the signal, and when it came his was the first shot to rattle over the enemy, and it struck the foremast.

So severely did it damage the mast that the weight of the sails, with the eddying gust stretching them out, brought the mast clean down with a crash.

'Mossoo's a swab,' muttered Happy Jack.

And then he swore an oath.

The French line-of-battle ship, while reeling from the shock, returned the fire in terrible earnest.

More than twenty guns belched forth their iron missiles of death; and, had it not been for the rashness in returning the fire so soon, it would have done dreadful havoc.

As it was, the Golden Arrow heeled over, and Jack the gunner was hurled into the scuppers, helped in his flight by Yellow Sam, whose long legs failed to support him at the moment he held the rammer down the muzzle of the gun; and when he lost his equilibrium, the butt-end of the ungainly instrument struck Happy Jack below the chest.

'It's no use hammering at that mountain of a hull,' cried Gerald; 'cripple her spars, my men.'

The enemy's men had left their posts in confusion and horror when the guns had been fired, and then saw the mast, with all its cordage, coming down among them.

Some moments of importance were lost through the men being seized with the panic.

The commodore bawled lustily to them to cut away the entangled rigging; and, after the first shock had passed, they did so.

By the time order was restored, and they prepared to re-engage the Golden Arrow, that beautiful little craft was sailing round the huge enemy.

Captain Gerald had the fire kept up, so as to cripple the enemy entirely.

The liner carried heavy metal, — heavier than Gerald had expected.

The enemy was not slow in returning the fire. One shot struck the Golden Arrow's rudder, and another went with fearful certainty through the rigging.

'Keep cool, my lads,' Gerald Stuart cried.

Will was among the men, cheering them on, and directing their work. He was confident of his courage and Captain Gerald's; but he knew there was enough in that huge liner to discourage any crew so inferior in numbers.

Few ordinary frigates would have engaged the line-of-battle ship as did the captain of the Golden Arrow.

The men were working the gun forward with a will, when a cry from the quarter-deck announced the destruction of the rudder, and the Golden Arrow was rendered helpless.

BLACK EYED SUSAN.

OR, PIRATES ASHORE.

SAVED FROM THE WRECK.

19

This only inspired the men.

'Give it mossoo, my lads,' cried Will, entering into the excitement with the true spirit of a British sailor. 'Give it him, he knocked our rudder off ; but, damme, we'll have his helm, ship, and all for it.'

A good humoured cheer followed this, and the men worked like Trojans. Naked to the waist, shoeless, and in most instances, capless, they fought, stopping only to have directions, and to follow them out.

With his own hands, Will continually fired the long gun.

'Hurrah!' cried Will, 'the mossoo's hauling down his sails.'

'He is helpless on the water, and can only fight,' remarked a junior.

'Aha! back, every one of you,' cried Will.

The men slunk back with a simultaneous cry of horror.

A shell came rolling along the deck, the match fizzing and burning as it came. Should it explode, death would be certain.

The men were paralysed.

The shell might explode in a second, or in a minute.

Gallant Will saw the danger.

'One life against a hundred,' he muttered, dashing forward.

'Great heavens,' exclaimed Gerald, 'what are you going to do, Will? Back, or it will blow you to pieces'

Will heeded not the words.

He wanted to save his companions, and, with reckless indifference he rushed upon the blazing shell, stooped so as to reach it with his hands, and rolled it into the sea through one of the open portholes.

There was a splash and a loud crash, the fearful missile exploded just as it touched the water.

Loud and deafening were the cheers that broke from the men, so enthusiastic were they that most of them left their guns to testify their admiration for the gallant fellow who stood, bewildered, before them.

'Captain Gerald took Will's hand.

'Noble friend,' he said, 'that was bravely done.'

'The lubberly thing was dangerously in the way,' replied Will. 'Ah! look out!'

As he spoke they turned.

The liner could not manoeuvre any longer, so it lay-to, and hoped by her superior mettle she could keep off the fire, and sink the vessel.

The Golden Arrow was just in uncomfortable range.

'Will, we must board them in the dark.'

'Ay, and now.'

'And now! Ready, fore and aft ; prepare to board in the boats.'

The men replied by a willing cheer.

The Golden Arrow had drifted off a little, and the enemy's fire was not so destructive. Not a speck of canvas was left up to betray them ; and the crew of the Golden Arrow, armed to the teeth, desperate and determined, embarked in the boats to cut off the huge foe.

A feat unexcelled for its daring.

The boats cleared off from the Golden Arrow.

'Silence, every one!' said Gerald; 'board the liner from all sides, and all at once.'

'That was near,' muttered Will.

A ball ploughed up the sea so near the boat as to dash the water into the faces of the crew.

The enemy kept up a fire at intervals.

'Look out! down, down! Wait for the signal.'

It was Captain Gerald who spoke.

CHAPTER L.

IN THE PATH TO LIBERTY.

HEMMED in on one side by the crew of the Comet, and confronted by the brave English tars of the Indiaman, the pirates stood little chance.

Captain Ross darted about like a meteor. His long thin cut-and-thrust did deadly execution.

His habitual coolness did not forsake him. He seemed to simply walk through the surging mass, cutting down all who stood in his way.

Knowing he was the most dangerous foe, the pirates tried to seize him.

Not a man remained on board the trader but its own crew.

The British tars looked round at their captain, waiting for the order to board.

Captain Bingham was debating whether he should make good his opportunity and escape, or help his former enemy.

The young Arab stood upon the bulwark ; his right arm was bared, and a scimitar of terrible weight was grasped in his hands.

'Follow,' he said.

And, obeying the instinct of courage, the crew of the Lucy leaped the barrier, and were among the combatants.

The pirates far outnumbered the Comet's crew, and they fought with bloodthirsty ardour.

Captain Ross saw his men could not hold their ground so well as he had wished.

The presence of the young Arab with the crew of the trader was a great acquisition.

Captain Bingham's brave heart caught up the fervour of excitement.

He was among his men, and in the thickest of the fight, while the invalid sailors watched any opportunity to pick off the pirates.

The wild cutthroat horde, hemmed in on all sides, fought more like raving fiends.

'Now, my kiddies,' cried Ross, 'give it 'em slick.'

And he strode on.

That gaunt, long figure was a dangerous foe, especially with a long thin cut-and-thrust to wield.

Ross now fought his way to one of the pirate leaders, and engaged him in his cool indifferent manner.

He noticed the pirate's eye glisten, and instinctively Ross thought there was a traitor at his back.

'Cuss yer,' he muttered.

Lunged out his long thin blade, which pierced through the body of his opponent like a flash of light.

He withdrew it, and jumped round, as a stinging sensation in his back made him wince.

When he jumped round he saw a pirate in the powerful grasp of Captain Bingham, and the Englishman's sword through his heart.

Ross's quick eye comprehended the affair in a minute.

'Guess I'm grateful, stranger; the cuss gave me a dig.'

'I was only in time,' said Captain Bingham, turning to engage another foe.

'Those Britishers are at home in war,' muttered Ross, and he engaged another foe too.

The vessel streamed with blood from end to end.

The pirates expected no mercy, and they got none.

They were a fearful horde, and held out with inhuman desperation.

They were being driven back inch by inch now, and the cries, groans, yells, and cheers were truly awful.

. Few prisoners were made. Cutlass, knife, pike, and tomahawk went to work.

Men were falling dead and wounded in every direction; it was cut and slash with all parties.

Even in some instances the Americans and English came together and fought, not knowing the nature or circumstances of the fight.

The light of a battle lantern displayed one of the Comet's men engaged hand to hand with one of the trader's crew.

Ross saw them.

'Tarnation seize you for blockheads! What are you fighting for? Darn you for stupid lubbers, it's the pirates we're fighting;' and he took his own man by the collar and hurled him among the pirate horde, where he had to fight his way out.

The young Arab had gone through the contending mass like any one invincible; his flaming eye was upon the pirate leader, and he seemed determined to have him.

Three times they met, and each time the pirate avoided him.

Still the young Arab watched him, and smote all who stood in his path.

He cut down a huge pirate who barred his passage, and was walking after the chief, when two men made a rush at each other in front of him.

They met furiously.

The Arab raised his sword to cut the one he considered the foe down, and a second glance told him they were allies.

'Fools! know you not your foes?'

And he hurled them aside.

The fellows looked at each other.

'Where from, mate?' asked one.

'The Lucy,' replied another, 'And you?'

'The Comet.'

'Then we are friends, for the time?'

'Ay, ay, mate.'

'Come on, down with the lubbers!'

Turned from foes to friends, they became staunch companions, and fought side by side; and their united strength made them equal to any three of the pirates who chose to oppose them.

The pirate horde now were driven up into a corner. The allies came together, and fought.

At the head of the two crews were Ross, the Arab, and Bingham. The pirate leader was in front of his remaining men.

'Charge them heavily—cut the hounds down—cover my retreat; and, sooner than they shall take us, I will blow the ship into the air.'

Caleb the Arab heard the words. He took one leap, and was in front of the pirate.

There was no getting away this time.

Captain Ross and Bingham kept the crew employed, and the Arab had the leader to his own mercy.

Caleb fought with a scimitar of prodigious size, and he seemed bent upon killing his foe.

The fight was brief but terrible—each fought with bloodthirsty ardour.

Caleb guarded a heavy blow aimed at his head, and struck in return at the pirate chief's chest.

His foot slipping at the moment, he lost his balance, and fell forward. Whether his scimitar slipped, and had struck the pirate with the flat of its blade, or whether the pirate wore armour, Caleb did not know.

But the cut-throat only staggered from the blow, but, ere he could recover his equanimity, the Arab struck him again, and he fell.

Leaping forward like a tiger, the Arab placed one foot upon the pirate's chest, raised his scimitar with both hands, hissed the one word—

'Die!' and slew him, by cutting the pirate's head off at a stroke.

The leader dead—the companion killed, the few remaining ruffians cried piteously for quarter.

It was not until Bingham interfered that they were listened to.

'Stop! d——n yer!' cried Ross, and his men ceased.

The scene of slaughter was dreadful, the pirate's vessel ran with blood from every corner, the dead and dying lay in heaps everywhere.

With a natural impulse, Captain Bingham and Ross turned and faced each other, and returned a look that said plainly—'Ought we be enemies after this?'

'Your flipper, stranger!' said Ross, extending his long, gorilla-like hand.

Bingham took it gladly.

'We shall part friends, at least,' he said.

'Guess so, stranger.'

'I am glad of it. I have a great responsibility in taking care of so many lady passengers. To take them safely home is all I wish.'

'Wal, I guess you can do it. Who's to stop you? But this here darned prize'——

'Is yours.'

'You're mighty quick in giving, stranger!'

Then, turning to his men, he bawled—'Do a rummage, younkers. Ransack the darned ship, and haul the booty on deck.'

The men were not long in doing this.

There was a great amount of wealth on board, and when displayed, the eyes of the crew were watering with a longing to get a share.

'I guess, stranger,' said Ross to Bingham, 'you can take anything that you like.'

Caleb took the pirate's sash and scimitar. Captain Bingham told Ross to give his men a little, saying—

'I do not require any of the booty. Had it not been for your assistance we should have been beneath the waves.'

Much to his wonderment, Ross ordered the men of the Lucy to convey boxes and bales on board the trader—curiosities of all nations, and some of no little value.

Captain Bingham valued the share given him at about one-sixth of the booty.

Young Bunker, who had discovered a box filled with lace and ladies' finery, brought it up on deck and sent it on board the Lucy, saying to Captain Bingham—

'Captain would you take this on board and distribute its contents among the lady passengers, as a remembrance of the officers of the Comet, and as a little recompense for the terror they must have been thrown into when our guns were opened upon you.'

'With pleasure, sir,' and Bingham grasped his hand; 'your name?'

'Bunker—second mate.'

Captain Ross gave a quiet grin.

'Tarnation moonshine!' he said, mentally. What he meant, he alone knew.

Preparations were made now for operating.

The soldiers and passengers of the Lucy were not a little delighted to see their commander and crew back again.

Soon after the battle the Lucy was speeding with a fair wind towards the cliffs of England.

Young Bunker was not forgotten. The things were distributed, and the ladies did not forget the name of the giver.

The pirate ship was looked upon as a very good prize, and Ross ordered the persons sick and wounded to be put on board.

'Ship enough hands to work her,' he said, 'and I guess you'd better put the useless skunks on board.'

The useless skunks were Jacob and Sneat. The Dismal had not been seen during the engagement. He took particular care to remain in a locker until nearly every man had gone on board the pirate hulk.

He only left the locker then to crawl to the bottom of the gangway, where he lay until the cook's mate, who happened to be there, saw him.

Hs stole back to his galley, and took a small piece of stale pudding which he made hot and cut round.

Then he went to the top of the gangway, held the piece of basted dough just above Jacob's head.

When the firing was most fierce, the fellow let fall the pudding.

'Oh! ugh! Who-o-o-o'—

Jacob clapped both hands to his cheeks, and rolled over and over the deck, howling most pitifully.

'There's a lubber,' laughed the mischievous cook's mate. 'He'll swear he was shot.'

Then he rushed down to the lower deck to play some practical joke upon the Dismal, who, however, was not to be found until the fighting was all over.

Sneat found him.

Sneat and Jacob had sworn eternal friendship.

'Send the crew up,' cried Ross.

They come.

'Now, younkers, go aboard the prize, and be smart.'

They went. Jacob was anything but smart.

Ross gave orders that the prize was to keep in sight until he had determined upon what course to pursue.

Then the Comet started away in full sail, the pirate ship following.

Sneat and Jacob went to their usual place on a coil of rope at the bows.

'Did you fight?' asked Jacob.

'Ye—ye—yes.'

'And get a wound?'

'W—w—why, yes, of kuck—kuck—k—course,' came out with an effort.

'Sneat, does you like staying here?'

'N—no, I d—d—do—'

'Do?'

'No, no, d—d—don't.'

'Nor more do I; I wants to get away, I does;' I don't like having to go aloft, they ain't nice lofts, they ain't.'

'How k—k—kuck—can we g—g—g—?'

'Gir who?'

'G—g—get away!' he got out with impatience.

Jacob, for want of better sense, always inter-

rupted the poor fellow, which made him ten time worse.

'I know how we can get away,' whispered the Dismal; 'by taking a boat.'

'A b—b—bo—'

'No, not a bow; a boat.'

'Y—y—you w—won't le—le—let me s—sp—sp—speak?'

'I would, if you could,' replied Jacob, with a grin at his own cleverness.

The jest was one too much for Sneat.

He felt hurt, and said so.

'Y—you might b—b—be like it yo—yo—yourself, some d—d—day.'

'I hopes not.'

'If I—I s—s—stutt—t—t—ter, I aint a kick—kick—coward,' replied Sneat.

'Is I?'

'The worst I e—ev—ev—ever knew.'

'I is?'

'Yes. Yo—yo—you'd run away from a k—k—cat.'

'Me! Why I could *shoot** the cat now, I could.

Sneat laughed. This was the first joke he had ever heard Jacob attempt, and he doubted its originality.

Perhaps he was right to do so.

They both laughed, became good tempered, and friends.

Jacob was really sincere about escaping; he was in constant trepidation since Ross made him mount the rigging.

They arranged it between them that the boat should be provided with provisions, guns, ammunition, and a sail.

Should they have to be on watch they could escape under cover of night.

'We is sure to get picked up, we is,' said Jacob.

'If n—not, it's b—better than being here.'

'Yes.'

They could not put their scheme into practice then.

Morn was nigh breaking, and the time would not be sufficient.

The two redoubtables kept together, building up castles in the air and planning schemes, and smuggling goods for the voyage.

The day seemed to drag slowly by. Towards night a very rough breeze arose.

Upon a little serious consideration they thought it better to wait the issue of a week or two; but the treatment of the fellow put in command of the prize was too brutally coarse, and Sneat could not bear it, and by morn gave Jacob a cuff.

'Now then, lisper,' cried the captain to Sneat, 'tell Miffenton to summon all hands on deck.'

Sneat went forward.

He became desperate—the noise was too much for him—and, remembering the injunctions of young Bunker, he began to sing.

'Mr. M—M—Mif—Mif—kuck—k—all hands on deck, me boys—all hands deck—all hands on deck, m' boys—all hands on deck.'

The men laughed loudly, and came on deck.

Thoroughly bent upon the purpose now, the two unfortunate friends kept a strict watch all day, and waited impatiently for night.

The time came, at length, for them to prepare.

---

* A nautical phrase for being sea-sick.

The crew slept.

The watch lay about the decks.

There was a man at the helm, and that was a source of great annoyance.

The wind was fair, a mist lay upon the water, and the sea was tolerably calm.

'I should li—li—like to kuck—kuck—k—knock that f—f—f—feller down.'

Sneat meant the steersman.

He had dragged the provisions, and what they wanted for the journey, on deck.

The boat hung up at the stern.

To touch it would attract the man's attention.

That would be discovery.

Discovery would be imprisonment to all parties.

Now, Sneat was not a coward. He was a man of determined character and great energy.

He saw the man who stood in his path to liberty, and intended to put him out of the way for a little time.

'He is the only block in the road to liberty,' remarked Sneat.

Taking a small spear in his right hand, he went up to the man.

Sneat did not want to hurt him, but should the fellow be obstinate he would get knocked down to a certainty.

The stranger looked up.

'What cheer, mate?' he said.

'W—w—what cheer?'

'Would you take the cursed helm for a few minutes, mate?' asked the sailor.

The fellow walked away, and left his post to Sneat. He laughed as he went below, thinking how nicely he had gulled the Englishman.

But Sneat knew his intention, which was to leave him at the post until next watch.

He did not mind this now.

If the man had not done as he did, Sneat would have knocked him down.

Now he lashed the helm in its position, and signalled to Jacob, who came out from under the bulwark.

He had laid shivering there expecting there would have been a tragedy.

'Is yer all right?' he shivered out.

'Y—y—yes.'

'What's we to do'

'Lo—lo—lower the b—b—boat.'

And they lowered the boat.

The provisions, arms, ammunition, and what few things they would require.

The boat was a large one, had a mast to be rigged at pleasure, and carried a large square sail.

Lowered into the water, she was dragged along after the vessel.

'G—g—get in.'

'How?'

'D—down th—th—the rope.'

The Dismal pulled a long face, and was some time ere he could summon up sufficient courage to go down the rope.

However, he did so, and was seated in the boat.

Sneat followed.

'All r—r—right,' he said.

'Yes, I is.'

'N—n—now then, k—cut loose the rope.'

The Dismal put his hands against the vessel to shove the boat off—a feat that was not necessary—as Sneat spoke.

'No, yer don't, darn yer!' a voice replied, from one of the cabin windows at the stern; and a hand grasped the shivering Jacob by the collar.

CHAPTER LI.

BOARDING THE LINE-OF-BATTLE SHIP.*

DARKNESS surrounded both the vessels and boats. There was no distinguishing the attacking party: so much the worse for the Frenchmen.

Gerald Stuart measured his chance very well. He waited until he thought each boat was by the hull of the enemy.

Then he gave the signal for attack; and the attack began in all its awful fury. One could not discern foe from friend, stranger from brother, or captain from shipmates.

Like a wilderness of monkeys the crew of the Golden Arrow climbed the liner's side, and was upon its deck fighting the foe before the French could completely understand what had occurred.

Will, followed by his boats' crew, scrambled up the French liner's side.

He had gone as far as the porthole. One hand was thrust in. He was drawing himself up when the grinning foes appeared at the opening.

The men from the Golden Arrow gave a cry of rage.

The arm of one of the grinning foes had thrust a pike out, and the point of it was within a few inches of Will's head.

Will did not shrink back, nor did a cry escape him. He hung on with one hand, while with the other he drew a pistol.

His position was a dangerous one. He swung back, not having anything to support him, and he could not take aim at the foe. The grinning enemy's pike was almost upon him when one of the crew fired.

The Frenchman fell back dead; his companion rushed from the spot.

'Come on!' cried Will, as he leaped in at the porthole, followed by his boat's crew.

They fought their way without much trouble on deck. A bloody engagement was going on there.

'All safe,' said Gerald, fighting his way forward to where Will was.

The crew of the Golden Arrow were completely outnumbered; but the surprise they gave the French was in their favour.

'Heavy work, Will.'

'Ay, captain. They are a few mossoos too many.'

The next stroke of his sword made one the less.

Gerald knocked an officer over, and then jumped forward to save one of his men from death.

'Will, this must not go on. Our men are scattered.'

'Call them together.'

'What I intend to do.'

'Maybe Mossoo won't have it all his own way. Take that, you lubber—two to one.'

(* See Illustration. No. 6.)

Will's sword smote the foremost as he spoke, then he turned and attacked the second, both of whom had been against one of his men.

The number of French was so overpowering that the crew of the Golden Arrow stood a certain chance of being cut up.

Gerald saw this, and called his men together. He had possession of the quarter-deck, and meant to keep it.

He called his second officer to his side.

'Burkett,' he said, fighting like a tiger while he spoke, 'we'—meaning Will and himself—'must make a stand here. The crew are closely pressed. Can you get round in the rear?'

'Yes.'

'With a company?'

'Yes, cap'n, and the reserved boat's crew are at hand.'

'Get them on the forecastle. When I give the signal, rush on to the foe.'

He cut a foe down, planted his foot on his chest, and holding up his red sword, cried—

'My lads, all but those of the pinnace rally round me.'

The pinnace was commanded by Burkett, and its crew followed him, while the remainder made one desperate and effective effort to get round their chief.

The vast crew of the French line were crowding upon the devoted band of staunch Englishmen who formed an invulnerable body of fine fighters.

There was no lagging, no pausing, with two such men as Will and Gerald at their head, they could only fight or die; many of them did both.

'Now, my brave lads, for a rush; use pistols and cutlass. Spare none till they cry for quarter. Follow!' cried Gerald.

'Ay, follow!' echoed Will.

Their reeking weapons were flourished on high for an instant, then they went forward. The crew followed.

The attack was as fierce as it was sudden, and the huge howling mass gave way before it.

The vast number of French made them strong, and the mounting force on the part of the English had given them nerve to press forward.

They thought victory certain.

Gerald made a rush at the captain, a little shrivelled-up being. Will rushed upon a huge French officer, whose moustache would have struck terror to any one with less nerve and more imagination.

The enemy's crew retired before the fresh onslaught. Gerald uttered a shout that was echoed by more than one of his officers.

That shout reached the ears of Burkett. He understood it.

'The signal,' he said. 'Now, my lads.'

From the pinnace the men mounted the chains, climbed the bows, and poured over the forecastle, and with such a war whoop as only their lusty throats could give, they were upon the French.

They gave a yell of fear, and in a panic they fled up the rigging; others fought and fled, and the English gained an advantage.

'Och one, yer spalpeens, an' it's the likes of meself as'll be afther you! Bedad, that's one for yer nob and the glory of ould Ireland,'

This was the inimitable Pat Murphy. Up went his huge cutlass, and down went a foe.

Those he could not reach on his left with his weapon, he shot out his fist, one blow of which was sufficient for any of the present members of the ancient Gauls.

'Hurrah for St. George!' shouted Will.

'Keep up the charge, my lads,' cried Gerald, 'and it will be victory.'

The double charge had made terrible havoc among the enemy.

Now they were driven back down the hatchways, or up the rigging, and many over the sides.

Wherever they went the brave British tars followed them.

Even over the side.

When Pat Murphy had knocked down a foe for the ' glory of ould Ireland,' he followed up another enemy. The Gaul, who seemed more like an acrobat than a sailor, saw him coming, and lost no time in getting out of his way.

The Celt was not to be done; he followed him up. The Frenchman fled to the bulwark.

'Bedad, now, stop a bit, will yer?' Pat uttered a most unearthly yell, and gave a wild flourish with his brawny arms.

His wild appearance and the frightful whoop so terrified his foe, he would not wait even to ask mercy.

In his terror he mounted the bulwark; he saw one of the Golden Arrow's boats below, and intended to have jumped into that, out of Pat's way.

Pat Murphy guessed his intent, and darted forward with a whoop.

'Bedad, ye murthering spalpeen! sure and I'll learn ye to strike a foe in the back!'

This, then, was the cause of the Celt's savage-like antipathy to his little enemy; he had killed one of the Golden Arrow's men from behind while engaged in fighting.

'Bedad and I'll slay ye,' muttered Pat; and he meant it. The dastardly act had raised up his most pitiless anger; and, like most Irishmen, he would have his revenge, as he said, mentally, ' if I die for it.'

The whoop and wild flourish mentioned above quite upset the flying Gaul's nerves and his equilibrium, so he toppled over the bulwark into the sea instead of the boat; and the enraged Irishman leaped the ship's side after him.

'Damme if that deed don't deserve the swabs!' * observed Happy Jack, in admiration and surprise.

He had just finished off one of his foes, and was looking round for his mate when he caught sight of Pat.

'Dash my toplights! I'll save the lubber, should he not beat the enemy.' And he went over the side too.

The captain of the liner no sooner saw the position his crew were in, and that Gerald was going to attack him, than he lucklessly got behind one of his men, and when that man had been cut down the commander had gone.

'Where the dev'—exclaimed Gerald—'Aha!'——

He caught sight of a form sneaking towards the chief cabin companion-way; he recognised the little commander.

' What does he intend doing?' Gerald thought, and followed him.

On the poop Captain Gerald was stopped by one of the liner's crew. A short scuffle took place; it did not last long. In less than two minutes Gerald Stuart strode over a prostrate form.

---

* Epaulettes.

'Fool! he would oppose me—at such a moment, too,' muttered Gerald. 'That little fiendish commander has gone down for some devilish purpose. A scream!—a woman in pain or danger.'

Gerald went down the companion ladder at a leap as a scream, loud and agonised, rang through the vessel.

Gerald ground his teeth, gripped his sword, and with blazing eyes jumped at the cabin door, from whence the cry proceeded.

It was locked, and resisted Gerald's strength.

A tomahawk lay on the floor near him; this time he went against the door with the weapon in his hand.

There was a crash—the door went in, shattered to pieces, and Gerald leaped over the splintering fragments as another prolonged shriek greeted him.

But the cry was as much of hope as fear, and it was followed with—

'Oh, save me, monsieur!'

Gerald could speak French like a native, and he understood the words spoken by—as he could see at a glance—a girl unusually lovely for a French lady.

She was struggling madly in the arms of the commander of the line-of-battle ship.

'Let monsieur approach,' he said, with a savage grin, and his bloodshot eyes rolled horridly, 'and I will slay you!'

He threw his struggling victim at his feet, and placed the point of his blood-stained sword to her neck.

In her terror, the instinct of self-preservation did not desert her.

Freeing one hand, she pushed the point of the blade away.

Gerald Stuart saw the act, and he hurled a pistol at the old ruffian at the same time. The blow staggered him; and, ere he could recover himself, Gerald took such a spring as a tiger would take. Fearful lest the wretch should recover, and injure the girl, Gerald made a sweep of lightning rapidity with his sword.

It met a check, but not enough to stop it—the French commander's neck being the check. The scimitar swept through, and not even a cry from the foe ere his head fell, with a sickening crash, at the feet of the terrified girl.

'Oh! monsieur!' she screamed, and fainted.

'Death to ill-treaters of women!' said Gerald, and he turned to remove the unfortunate girl. 'Ah! that's the shout of victory! My brave lads never cry anything else—if they were conquered, they would die.'

It was victory.

Gallant Will saw his captain go, but was engaged with the huge officer with the fierce moustaches, and could not follow.

He knew the fate of the commander was sealed, and felt safe.

Ever calling to his brave crew to keep up, he fought on until he had backed the fierce-moustached individual near the mast. Then, with one swoop, he shattered his blade, leaped at his throat, and cried—

'Surrender!'

The officer did not understand the word, but he did Will's blazing eyes and determined look, besides which Will's sword-point was at his throat, and that could leave no doubt as to the nature of the word.

'Oui, oui, monsieur!' cried the desperate officer.

William did know oui meant 'yes,' so he released him, and, with a shout, hauled down the enemy's flag.

Treacherous and cowardly, his foe—the man he had just given life to—arose, and sneaked a few paces off on his hands and knees.

A sword lying at a little distance attracted him. He clutched it in his hand, then stood upright, and crept, tip-toe, towards the unsuspecting Will, who had hauled the colours down.

The intending assassin was almost upon his victim, when a cry made Will jump round.

It was a shriek of warning from one of his crew.

'Coward!' he thundered, comprehending his danger at a glance, 'cowardly swab! was this what I saved your life for?'

The words were wasted, but his action was not. He cut the traitor to the deck, and gave the one cry—

'Victory!'

'Victory!' shouted the crew with a wild hurrah, as the last of the remaining Frenchmen put down their arms, and cried for quarter.

Their looks and actions told the brave fellows from the Golden Arrow they had surrendered, and there was not a man on board the gallant rebel's craft that would have struck down an unarmed man.

If one dared, and was discovered, he would suffer the penalty—that was death!

The line-of-battle ship was won, and William felt proud of the victory.

He looked round for Gerald.

'Call all hands aft,' he said to Burkett.

This was a custom with them, to know who were dead or wounded.

The men came aft in a body, and those Will could not remember by sight, he called out their names.

'Murphy,' he said, 'I don't see the lubber. Murphy and Happleton are missing.' Then turning his eyes upon the many lifeless forms upon that bloody deck, he sighed and cogitated, 'Poor fellows! half-an-hour ago most of them were well and happy.'

The names of the favourite, Happy Jack, and the no less favourite Pat Murphy, caused a general stir.

Not one had seen them fall.

'I saw them go overboard,' said Yellow Sam, coming forward, and stanching the blood that flowed from his leg.

'Get the wounded ready, lads, to carry on board the Golden Arrow,' said Will. 'Maybe it's best for the enemy's wounded to remain on this craft. There's a bloodsucker on board, and he can understand them—old Mixins won't. Get the boats ready for embarkation. Have you battened down the hatchway on the prisoners?'

'Ay, ay, sir.'

'Be smart, then.'

Will turned away, and went below to see Gerald.

He found him leaning over a lovely little girl, beautiful as a goddess.

'I need not ask how the battle went on,' smiled Gerald.

'No, captain; the liner's ours.'

'Have we sustained much loss?'

'Five or seven dead—thirty-one wounded.'

Gerald sighed.

'It might have been worse.'

'Ay, captain, much. That is your work.'

He pointed to the decapitated body.

'He would have murdered this poor little creature.'

'Then he deserved more than that,' sighed Will. 'The pirate ought to have been hanged.'

'He had better be removed, ere that poor girl recovers.'

'True.'

Two men were called down, and they removed the ghastly sight.

'The skipper's sword's awfully sharp, mate,' remarked one of the sailors.

'Ay, ay, and he's got a d——d nasty knack of cutting heads off.'

'Ay, he knows how to do a clean shave.'

'And ye don't want the second one either.'

They both laughed—laughed gaily and heartily, and not ten minutes before they were staring death in the face, and neither knew whether he should ever cross the Golden Arrow's deck again.

They were at the vessel's side. The cold body of the Frenchman was hauled over into the sea—the head followed.

Neither went far. The huge prowling monsters of the deep were under the ship's side waiting for their food.

They were getting it.

'The men are preparing to go on board the Golden Arrow,' asked Gerald.

'Ay, with the wounded.'

'Not the enemy's.'

'No.'

'I will send the doctor into the cockpit to them; they will understand their own medical man better than ours.'

The French physician was at that moment attending to the senseless girl. When he had finished, Gerald told him to go to the cockpit, and attend to the wounded.

'Do you know anything of this young lady?' Gerald asked.

'No, monsieur.'

The doctor was a polite, mild-tempered little man, and evidently good-natured and obliging.

'Is she related to the late commander?'

'I know not, monsieur. The captain brought her on board one night, but never let her leave the cabin.'

'I see. You had better go to the cockpit, the crew are there.'

'Good, monsieur; I will go.'

He went, and Will watched him go with a grimace.

'What lingo,' he said.

Gerald smiled.

'Hist! she awakes.'

The sufferer opened her large beautiful eyes, and glared with a vacant stare, then with a beaming smile upon Gerald Stuart.

'What an angel!' thought Will, meaning the captive.

'You are better?' asked Gerald.

'I am well, monsieur, I thank you.'

'You were not hurt?'

'No, monsieur. I should have been, perhaps, killed—perhaps more than killed, had not your good ship come in sight, and caused Monsieur Thoret to go on deck.'

Monsieur Thoret was the late commander, who had gone in much shorter way to his grave than he had to the fight.

The poor girl's eyes filled with tears, and her tiny hand trembled in Gerald's soft palm.

Not understanding the language, and not liking to see a woman cry, Will went from the cabin.

He had got to the companion ladder, when there came a loud shout and the rush of feet.

'What the devil's the matter?' muttered our hero dashing up the steps and along the quarter-deck.

He saw the men rushing about in all directions; some were staring aghast at what had caused the cry.

'A ghost! a ghost!' some shouted; and Will started forward—his cheek even paled.

Pat Murphy, as he had been in the fight—naked to the waist, blood and smoke-begrimed, appeared—at least, his head and body to the waist did—just above the bulwarks at the bows.

He looked ghastly and horrible in the dark mist. There was no mistaking his face, pale and shadowy now; but the crew knew him.

'Wurra!' came in a sepulchral tone along the deck; and the men stood chilled with horror, for they felt there could not be any mistake now.

And there was not.

————

CHAPTER LII.

THE WOLF OF THE WAVES.

GREGORY SAUNDERS would have thrust his dagger to the heart of Pauline, had not Rodwin Blake stepped between them.

'Touch her,' he said, 'and I'll tear your heart out.'

The look that accompanied these words made the villain pause.

Pauline would have fled with Madeline. She started forward, got as far as the door, then she recoiled, with a scream.

'Fire! Great God!' she cried, 'they have fired the house.' And she staggered back.

Her strength was leaving her now. She heard a struggle going on behind her—Black-eyed Susan fighting to get to her aid.

All attempts were useless. Pauline was clutched roughly, Madeline torn from her arms, and Rodwin stood before her.

'God!' she said, 'and it's you.' A low moan broke from her lips, and she fell a huddled heap at his feet.

The marauders had fired the house. The rooms were full of smoke; the back-stair even was in a blaze; and the flames were shooting up in more than one direction.

Madeline was now an unresisting prize, for she had swooned.

Susan was the only one left with full possession of her faculties.

She struggled with supernatural strength.

It was useless with the ruffians she had to deal with.

Then she screamed loudly for aid.

'Help! Oh, help!' she cried.

'Bring her along,' cried Saunders. 'Curse her She will be safe among the crew.'

A very brief struggle went on between the two brutal captors and Susan. The words of the ruffian, Gregory, struck terror to her heart, and under the rough, brutal handling of the wretches who held her, she fainted, and was carried off.

The last to leave the burning house was Rodwin Blake.

He had stood contemplating, with a mournful look, the inanimate form of the beautiful Pauline.

BLACK EYED SUSAN.

OR, PIRATES ASHORE.

THE MISSING DEED.

'It is safer for us all that she should come; but not a finger shall touch even a hair of her head.'

Most tenderly he took her in his arms, and bore her from the ill-fated house.

Horses waited without for himself and captain.

He took the one left for him, mounted with the burden in his arms, and rode swiftly away.

The hired ruffians were told to disperse, and get back to the ship without being seen.

There were many among them that would not have gone back only for the reward that awaited them.

Susan's brutal captor's were the last of the party.

Though Gregory had started before Rodwin he soon overtook him.

'Come on,' he said; 'every minute may be fatal. Where are you going? We dare not ride down an open path like that, we should be seen. Your escape is known everywhere by this time.'

Gregory did not reply, but followed his accomplice.

Madeline lay across his saddle before him, and his face wore a look of fiendish triumph as he rode on.

Imminent as was his peril, he even dared to press his burning lips to hers.

'Come on,' said Rodwin.

'You need not stay,' said Gregory, with a frown.

He did not like the tone in which his late officer spoke.

Blake smiled scornfully.

The sea beach was soon reached.

Now they could hear tell-tale sounds. The alarm bells of the prison were ringing, guns were being fired, and the place was in a state of great excitement.

'None too soon,' said Blake, dismounting.

'The boat?' queried Gregory, following the other's example.

'Is here.'

Saunders conveyed his victim to the boat, placed her in the stern sheets, seated himself, and waited impatiently for Blake.

He followed, and took his seat beside him, with Pauline in his arms.

'Give way!' cried Gregory.

Wondering much at the ladies' insensible condition, and suspecting more, the sailors pulled back to the ship.

Madeline was conveyed to the cabin, and Blake conveyed Pauline to a private berth, locked the door, and put the key into his pocket.

Then he returned on deck, and ordered a boat to shore.

'Wait,' he said, to the coxswain, 'for the men.'

Then he went down to the senseless girl again.

The boat went to the shore—only six or seven of the men were there.

Having orders to bring the men back, the coxswain had nothing else to do than to remain till they came.

He lighted his pipe, and did so with characteristic indifference.

Those of the party on the beach, who knew more of their late doings than he, felt anything but comfortable.

The loud, and not far distant, report of firearms came upon their ears, and from where they stood they could hear that Deal was once more in an uproar.

The prison had been partly blown down, the mansion of the Lord High Admiral set on fire, and the prisoner Saunders gone.

The frightful turmoil that raged everywhere was better seen and known by Susan's abductors than any of the other hirelings, as they were behind.

Having had to go by a different route to the sea-shore, they came to the dark, frowning cliffs, about the time Blake had sent the boat for them.

'Look out,' said one.

'Hullo! who's ahead there?' said another.

A number of dark forms could be seen, moving about under the cliffs.

Susan revived again, and looked wildly about her.

The hot breath of her captor fanning her cheek told her all.

With all the strength of her lungs she cried for help.

Shriek after shriek broke from her lips.

'Curse you! I'll strike you, if you ain't quiet,' hissed the wretch in her ear.

She did not heed him, but screamed again.

'Hullo! whom have we here?' cried a voice, the owner of which made a rush towards the flying party.

'Susan! by all the shots in a locker! Pretty Susan! Rally round, lads! By —— we'll give the devils something! Come on, Bill.'

'Ay, ay, Tom.'

Susan's abductors found Tom Hatchett and Bill Raker, with half-a-dozen men at their back, stopped the way.

'Surrender the lass to me, or '——

'See you d——d first.'

Captain Tom did not speak again.

'Come on,' he said. 'Cut them down; no quarter.'

His cutlass flew out, and he darted at the man who held Susan.

Bill Raker followed him.

Several pistol shots were fired, and some wounded on either side.

'Oh! save me!—save me!' cried Susan, feeling even a sense of security under the protection of the smugglers.

The voice of the woman Tom Hatchett so selfishly loved calling upon him for aid, went to his heart's core, and his blood boiled within him.

He rushed at the man who had placed Susan on the ground, and holding her with one hand, he drew a pistol with the other.

He pointed it at Hatchett's head, pulled the trigger, and fired.

'Curse you!' said Tom Hatchett, lifting up his sword. 'You haven't the bullet that could kill Tom Hatchett.'

Susan had madly clutched the ruffian's arm, and, at the risk of her life, had knocked the pistol up.

The bullet went in the air.

Tom Hatchett was saved.

He repaid the brave act by cutting the ruffian down with his sword, and taking the terrified girl in his arms.

More than one man had fell.

Bill Raker, who usually followed the precepts of his faithful ally, no sooner saw him fall by Hatchett's sword, than he brought one down dead.

The rest, panic-stricken, fled.

Raker did not follow—they had not time. A detachment of officers were coming along under arms.

'Back! back! to the boat!' cried Captain

Tom, or, by heavens! we shall be arrested on suspicion!'

Side by side with Bill Raker, and followed by the men, Captain Hatchett lost no time in regaining his boat.

That sped swiftly to the ship. His ship was safety, and he cared not for all the authorities of Deal put together.

Tom Hatchett had no longer got the Redbreast. He commanded the beautifully equipped French ship he had captured by the ruse.

He conveyed Susan to the chief cabin, which was spacious and handsomely fitted up.

He placed Susan on a couch, and retired on deck to watch what was going on.

He could see Gregory Saunders's ship.

'Those curs belonged to him,' he remarked to Raker, meaning Saunders.

'Ay, there's no mistake about that.'

'They're aboard.'

'Sure to be now.'

Raker was right.

The ruffians hired by Saunders were on board the schooner.

The first question Gregory asked was—

'Where's that girl?'

The boldest of the men stood forward and told him.

'Ah! that cursed Tom Hatchett! Let him beware!'

He mentally resolved to keep a sharp look-out for the smuggler, thinking of course that he only had the Redbreast to tackle.

'Put out to sea,' he said to an officer. 'Be smart; the last man upon the yards will have two dozen.'

Awed, and not a little alarmed at the threat, the men executed the orders as soon as they were uttered.

Gregory strode the deck, his head bent, his brow knit.

He was reckless now, fearless while in power. Success made him presumptuous. He had now thrown off the yoke of a government, and would sail the seas his own master, king of all around him, with no one to issue an order but him.

Neither heart nor conscience smote him now with the enormity of his sins.

Crime had no terrors for him. He was going swiftly down the dark vortex—destruction. His wealth, lawless position, his power and success made him not only a villain but a tyrant.

If the power remained in his hands another week he would make that vessel a floating hell, and the crew a legion of fiends.

Rodwin Blake was below. He had returned to the little cabin where Pauline lay.

He felt the slow motion of the vessel as he watched the unconscious girl, and knew they were going out to sea.

His usually rigid features wore a strangely-gentle look.

Once he stooped forward, as though he would have kissed the pale sleeper's brow.

But he recoiled with a shiver of horror, as though he thought the contact would sully her innocence.

In an instant the expression of his face passed, and gave way to one thoughtful and gentle.

Suddenly Pauline opened her eyes.

Vacantly she scrutinised the cabin; then her eye fell upon Blake; a cold shiver passed through her frame.

She passed her hand across her brow, and turned her head away.

'Pauline.'

The name, spoke in a voice singularly low and musical, made her start, then she turned slowly to the extraordinary being by her side.

'Where am I?' she asked.

'Going out to sea.'

'Victor, for what am I saved! Oh, God! do you intend to add to my sufferings again?'

'Peace, girl, peace! The look that made his face handsome died away; he was cold, rigid, as ever, and his voice took that peculiarly low, keen, sound, cold and thrilling.

Pauline recovered her habitual self-possession, and she sat up on the couch, and looked Rodwin full in the face.

'I thought,' she began mournfully, 'I should be left alone with my sorrow that I might forget it if I could. I thought you—you—dead, or far away, and you are here—here with him—here to do me wrong, and to help in one of the foulest deeds ever meditated.'

'Pauline, I have been your foe, you think. I helped in the affair to-night, because I was obliged.'

'Obliged?'

'Ay, compelled! My life depended on it. I was in his power.'

'His power!' echoed Pauline, her finely-curved lip curling in withering scorn. 'Were you in his power before?' 'And that prompted you to kill him?'

Blake shuddered.

'Pauline.' His voice was husky now, 'listen to me. I was in this viper's power then.'

'Did that make you slay your own brother?'

Pauline spoke coldly and bitterly.

'Listen to me; do not interrupt me; hear all, and if you do not forgive me that one crime, why——we shall nev—can you forget, Pauline? Is it so long ago since I loved you?'

'Alas, no! would I could forget it.'

'I loved you madly. I loved you to distraction. I told you so.'

'And I——'

'You did not spurn me; you hesitated, bade me wait; you loved my brother.'

'I did.'

'I did not know it. I was jealous. My pride was hurt at your polite refusal. Stung to the core I left your presence, and sought solace at the gaming-table. I won—then lost—loss after loss. My money went. I got in debt. I became mad with wine and excitement. I staked my brothers and my own estates. I had nearly lost, when that cruel fiend, that devil in my path, Saunders, came to me. 'The dice your foe is using are loaded,' he said.

Rodwin went on with his sad story in a cold, passionless strain. Not once did he raise the pitch of his voice.

He made no gesticulations.

Swore no oaths.

Nothing but the deepening gleam in his eyes and the compression of his lips betrayed the incarnate fiend that was stirred up in his soul.

'In my mad passion, I struck the cheat across his face. He jumped up, and hurled a decanter at me; and I'——

He paused, while the light in his eye grew cruel.

'And you what?'

'Slew him.'

'Did that compel you to exile yourself?'

'It did, as you shall hear. I took up my money, and held up the dice to the company present. The cheat had many friends there. In the excitement, the dice were taken from me, and suddenly I heard a clamour. Two dice were brought, smashed to pieces. Half-a-dozen of the company present swore they were the dice I had said were loaded; but they were not.'

'Were they the same dice?'

'I say no; the company said yes. I was called a murderer, and beset by the whole company; and had to fight my way out. I did so, with the help of that infernal evil star, Gregory. I told him I must flee, and he gave me a chance of escape.'

'With him?'

'On his vessel. Thus I left you.'

'And I, wondering what had become of you, thought you had committed suicide, and pined myself away until on a sick bed. I would have consented to your suit sooner than that, but when months passed, and you came not, I yielded to the protestations of your brother. He, too, pined for you; and when I told him of your love, he spoke nobly—manly—and as only such a soul as his could speak. He said he would sacrifice me, could it make you happy. His was no selfish love, for he would have given you comfort at the cost of his heart's happiness—his life.'

For the first time for some years, a visible change came over Rodwin.

His frame shook with emotion, and his lips quivered.

'No more—no more!' he said, striking his chest with his clenched hand, 'lest I slay myself at your feet.'

'That would not repay for the past. I will finish. Finding you never came back, he urged his love, and I accepted him; for you know, Victor, I always loved him the most, though I liked you both. I could then have loved you as a brother, and he as an idol to'——

'Enough, let me finish; my time down here is short. I went with Gregory. He was on a three years' cruise. He stayed in Italy some time, and married there; robbed and wronged the girl, and left her. I was in his confidence; his secrets were in my keeping. He knew it, and feared me. Once it came to my ears that he had induced me, with his artful lies, to slay that man in the gaming-house, because he was in his way. I told him of it, and I threatened to denounce him.

'He did not reply, but I saw that he meant mischief. One day he took a prize. It was a bloody contest, for he had a horde of pirates to contend with. He slew the leader, then addressed the men, and when the fight was over, and I came on deck, I was told to go on board. We dined—had a banquet. I drank too much wine, and slept.

'When I awoke—oh! God! I remember an aching pain at my chest. I slid from the cot to the floor, and stood before a mirror; and when I looked upon myself, I thought I should have torn myself limb from limb. The hound—the inveterate fiend—had had me *branded*.'

'Branded!' cried Pauline, starting up.

'Ay, girl.' He trembled violently now, and his ace became distorted with passion. 'Look, look,' he cried, tearing open the breast of his coat, and displaying a ghastly device branded on his chest.

'Great God! that emblem'——

'Is the WOLF OF THE WAVES.'

On his chest, printed in with red and black ink, was a wolf's head; two flags crossed behind it, each bearing the ghastly emblems of death—the skull and cross-bones; and under these were the letters—

'V. S. C.'

'Yes,' he went on, hoarsely, as Pauline covered her face with her hands, and shrank back, filled with horror; 'yes, the "Wolf of the Waves"—that was the appellation given to the ravaging monster who had commanded the horde. I knew I had been drugged, and that done while I slept, I felt I was lost. The hound had me in his power. I staggered on deck. I forgot to say I found a note. It was from Saunders, and to the effect that if I went home I should find *you* in the arms of Munroe, my hated foe. This helped to set my brain on fire; and when I went on deck the crew hailed me as their king and captain.

'I felt fate was against me—the noose was round my neck, and Gregory was ready to hang me. A thousand pounds were offered for the Wolf of the Waves; and his name, as you may remember, was Sorman Camet. The two initials of my surname corresponding with his, left me powerless, and I accepted my fate.

'The crew—a wild horde—were ruled only by a hand of iron. I was put amongst them—amongst this horde—and, by God, I ruled. My first thought was to get home to slay the man I hated—that Harvey Munroe; and I came. I saw you in the garden, in the shubbery, with, as I thought, him. My heart grew black; the scenes I had gone through of late hardened it. I rushed forward, and with my sword'——

'Hush, hush, for God's sake! Can you talk of it? Can you, Victor? My heart will burst.'

'I will continue. I knew not who your lover was. I rushed forward, cut him down, and saw in the bleeding form'——

'Your brother!'—she burst into tears. 'Your brother!' she continued; 'and you his slayer.'

'That was not all. I'——

'Not now—not now. Oh, God! Poor, poor Julian! I'——

'Hear me.'

'Not now. Hush, hush!' Her voice sank to a whisper; her eyes became fixed in a glassy stare, and she fell a dead weight in his arms.

CHAPTER LIII.
TERRIBLE TIDINGS.

THE day subsequent to that on which Gregory Saunders was denounced by Gerald Stuart and Mr. Jasper Lorry, Lord Harry Garthway, with the last-named gentleman, started for London.

The admiral was determined to sift the villany of his dastardly *protege* to its base, ere he took any final steps.

The distance is something over seventy miles. The admiral had not three days to spare, and they travelled by the quickest possible means.

Neither money nor trouble was spared.

'I think we shall arrive by daybreak to-morrow,' observed the lawyer, as they were whirled along in a post-chaise and four.

'To-night would be none to soon,' replied the admiral.

He looked troubled and unhappy. In appearance he was five years older than he had been the day before.

'Were it not for your anxiety, my lord, I could perform the journey alone. The sad event that took the suffering lady from us was so unexpected, or I would have kept the documents here.'

'It was a wise precaution, Mr. Lorry.'

'I hope it may prove so,' and the lawyer sighed involuntarily.

Strange to say he felt troubled about the documents.

'Has the affair become published?' asked the admiral.

'No, my lord; none but myself and the witnesses knew of it until I came to you. Even the officers I brought to the house are unaware of the motive of the charge against the man.'

'I am glad it is so.'

They had covered more than twenty miles of ground now. An inn was in sight.

Mr. Lorry proposed a change of horses.

'Act as you wish, Mr. Lorry; do not try to study me. I place myself in your hands.'

The stay was not a long one. Fresh horses were put in, the travellers partook of a little refreshment, and continued their journey.

Ere night had placed its sable pall over the earth, more than half the journey was done.

They gave up the chaise, which returned to Deal, hired a fresh one, and then started on again.

The horses were good, the post-boys fresh, and they went at a spanking pace.

The moon was in all its silvery splendour, and threw its subdued light upon landscape and habitation.

Here and there, where the ground was most open, and the trees less thick, the liquid-like rays of the night queen penetrated the vehicle for an instant.

Then it would pass rapidly away, and leave the carriage filled with gloomy fantastic shadows.

The travellers were silent.

Mr. Lorry mentally enjoyed the splendour of the scene—he liked it, and though his active brain was at work, he could fully appreciate the grandeur of the night.

Lord Garthway did not sleep, though he sat back in the carriage silent, as though he were.

He was given to retrospection. It was one of his weaknesses. He was fond of calling up the realities of the past in the shadows of the present. He did so now.

He seemed unconscious of Mr. Lorry's presence, and of the moon's bright rays that threw a flood of light across the landscape.

Deeply absorbed in his meditation, he was alive to nothing around. He was dreaming—dreaming of the past—his younger days—of an old and loved friend, and a fine, noble stripling of a boy.

In the dim goblin shadows that flitted about the inside of the old vehicle, the admiral traced, as it were, the form of his old friend, Admiral Saunders and Gregory, as a young and gallant officer.

The face of his old friend wore a look of intense mental anguish and pity.

Garthway's heart whispered to him he had been a father to Gregory, and the shadow seemed to call back—

'You have.'

Again and again did the admiral hear the words still ringing in his ears, as they were spoken by his dying friend—

'You will look after my son. You will be a father. You will give him your daughter, should he deserve her; but should he turn a scapegrace, discard him.'

'Ay, discard him!' involuntarily sighed the unhappy admiral. Would that heal this wasted heart, bring back my daughter's happiness, my honour?'

He paused; but his heart answered him—

'No.'

Then he gave a start.

The carriage had given a jerk; the post-boys lashed their whips. Mr. Lorry put his head out of window, pulled it in again, and sat down.

Everything relapsed into its former silence. Mr. Lorry closed his eyes, and crouched up in a corner, the clustering trees obscured the best part of the moon's light, and the shadows in the interior of the vehicle became more gloomy.

The admiral dreamt again; his imaginative mind conjured up the future in the shadows of the present, and he relapsed into a state of semi-unconsciousness.

He suffered all the torture of a stricken heart, and the dread uncertainty of the future. He could not in honour save the villain, and the enormity of his crimes demanded even retribution at his own hands.

So the admiral's mind worked and worked; the post-chaise rattled on; the night became more silent; the darkling shadows of evening died away, and left an unvarying gloom, out of which seemed to rise a thick roll of mist, and that mist bore the form of the admiral's old friend, and in his uneasy sleep, Garthway spoke—

'My old friend.'

The eyes of the phantom of his dreams regarded him with love, and gentle pity.

'I am come, old friend, to console you. I parted from the world of sin and sad cares, and left with you my son. I thought he would have been the pride of your home and an honour to his father's memory. Pine not, my friend—grieve not. You have been a kind father to him, he has been a basely ungrateful son. Like a viper he lay dormant, until powerful enough to help himself, then he stung the nest he was reared in. My old friend, how sad is it we should have to meet thus. Do your duty to yourself and your God, and to my memory. He has erred, he has sinned, and darkly. Let him be punished by his outraged fellow-men, and He above will rejudge him. Wipe the blot from your name that he cast upon it, and forget the thing—the earthworm of ingratitude. I would he were dead. I could sorrow over him departed, living, I shun the very air his presence pollutes.'

'Then I am forgiven. I'——

'My old friend, I sorrow for you for the trouble I have brought upon you; but the world is little else than cares. A better time will come.'

The old friends shook hands. The eyes of the dream-phantom still were fixed upon Garthway's; his lips moved, and he seemed about to speak.

'Last stage, sir. Refreshment, sir? Last change to London.'

'Eh? Oh, yes.'

The post-boys dismounted. The vehicle had been brought up with a jerk, and an ostler had shouted in at the sleepers with all the force he could command in his lungs.

'We do not stay,' said Mr. Lorry.

'Not stay, sir?'

'No—right on.'

Only a few minutes' delay, and they went right on The post-chaise rattled on. Both travellers now kept awake.

London—the grim old city, with its toppling houses and smoky-looking structures, lighted up by the cold grey light of morn.

They breakfasted now; and when at length it was time to repair to Mr. Lorry's office, they went out, and reached it a few minutes after the confidential clerk got there.

'Mr. Tomkins!' said Mr. Lorry, calling his confidant into the inner office.

The grim face of Tomkins startled Mr. Lorry.

'Have you any bad news?'

'Yes, sir,' replied Tomkins, with a glance at the admiral.

He was too much of a lawyer to speak before a second party.

'You can speak,' said Mr. Lorry. 'But, firstly, has Baggs entrusted anything to your care?'

''Tis of that I would speak, sir.'

'Indeed! Go on.'

'Poor Baggs came home, sir, brought back in a cart, his head cut open; he looked nearly dead. Unfortunately he had been nearly murdered, and robbed.'

'Robbed!' exclaimed Lorry, displaying so much excitement that the confidential was surprised.

'Yes, sir, of the papers entrusted to his care.'

A look of blank despair came upon Mr. Lorry's face. Lord Garthway looked vexed.

'Would you accompany me to my residence, my lord? I shall get a clue ere night.'

The admiral rose and followed Mr. Lorry.

The confidential made a mystic sign to the under clerk to make him hush his humming.

Humming in the house of Lorry while a lord was going out was too much for the slight nerves of Mr. Tomkins, who bowed Garthway out.

At the door Mr. Lorry turned to his confidential.

'You will come to me to-night.'

'Yes, sir.'

'Letters, and so forth.'

'Perfectly so, sir.'

These few words exchanged settled the business of the day with Mr. Lorry.

The lawyer paid a visit to the humble lodgings of the faithful Baggs, the assistant messenger to the more ancient firm of Mr. Jasper Lorry and Co.

Poor old Baggs almost wept when he saw his master.

'I could not help it, sir—I couldn't.'

'Nay—I know it.'

'But you will trust me again, sir?'

'Yes, Mr. Baggs, when you are well enough.'

He could not glean much from poor old Baggs. The poor old fellow had been waylaid and nearly murdered—left for dead—and robbed.

The story was wearisome, but full of cold-blooded work.

Lorry knew the doer.

Gregory Saunders.

That day was spent in looking over copies of papers and deeds, and adopting means to discover the robber.

Early the following morning the methodical Tomkins was disturbed out of his cool, clock-work kind o' temperament, by the entry of a stranger.

A youth, bold, handsome, and good-humoured, and attired in the uniform of a middy.

''Morning, long tails.'

'Sir!' This came very indignantly from the confidential of Mr. Jasper Lorry. To be called 'Long-tails' was too humiliating.

'Why, you look as lively as a parson in a storm. Come, spin out, ship-shape. Is this Mr. Lorry's, or Dorrys, or some Orry or the other?'

'These, sir, are the offices of Mr. Jasper Lorry.'

'All right, mate. Where's the skipper?'

'Skipper!'

Mr. Tomkins was puzzled.

'Ay, you lubber; haven't you a skipper?'

'Sir, I should understand were you to speak English.'

'Why, you swab—Oh! if I had you on board for a week.'

Mr. Tomkins turned white at the bare imagination of being on board for a week.

'Look here, you land shark. Where's the skipper, Lorry?'

'You want Mr. Lorry.'

'Why, of course I do, you lubber. I have been asking for him this ten minutes.'

'I am sorry to say he is not here yet.'

'Oh, you are sorry to say Mr. Lorry's out, eh? Ha, ha! There's eloquence for you, by jingo! So am I. Where's he bound for? Where does he cast anchor?'

'You labour under some misapprehension, sir, Mr. Lorry has no anchor.'

The mischievous mid opened his eyes in affected surprise.

'Tell you what, old fellow,' he said, 'if you spin out such cable as that, you'll spoil your jawing tackle. Now, look here. On my soul, it's too bad. I started at eleven bells last night, and have travelled ever since, and to find the skipper out, it's really too bad, especially under the fearful circumstances. Is the Lord High Admiral with Mr. Lorry?'

'Yes, sir. That is, you mean Lord Garthway?'

'Who else should I, you lubber? D'ye know where he is?'

Mr. Tomkins had tact enough to see that this young gentleman was a favoured midshipman of the great admiral's, and for the sake of one, he was civil to the other.

'He is at Stanhope's.'

'Stanhope's?'

'Yes—hotel.'

'What port is that?'

Mr. Tomkins guessed what the mid meant, and turning to the under clerk said—

'Conduct this gentleman to Stanhope's.'

The under clerk obeyed, and they left the office. Mr. Tomkins was not sorry for it. He felt as he said—

'Upset for the day,' and he could not get the words out of his head.

'Eleven bells—skipper—swabs, and lubbers,' were constantly buzzing in his ears, and he made a mistake in his items for once.

'That horrid sailor,' he would mutter. 'Eleven bells—be smart—lubber—ugh!'

It took Mr. Tomkins nearly a week to recover his usual gravity.

The under clerk looked upon the middy as a young lion to be humoured in every way.

Thus no time was lost, and the mid soon found himself at Stanhope's, and before the admiral.

Garthway was seated at the breakfast table languidly taking the morning meal.

When a servant ushered in a visitor, he looked up, expecting to see Mr. Lorry.

'Good morning, my lord,' the middy said, saluting.

'You here, Richards?'

'I started last night, admiral, at eleven bells, and, after riding the whole night, arrived here half an hour ago. Beg pardon, my lord, for not appearing more ship-shape, but the nature of the business would not allow of any delay.'

'What brought you here?' asked the admiral, a vague feeling of alarm coming upon him.

The middy's face wore a look of melancholy, and his travel-stained and fatigued appearance suggested all manner of things to the admiral's mind.

'This letter, my lord, written by Captain Stanton. It will explain my appearance, my lord.'

Garthway noticed an uneasy look come over the youngster's face, and marvelled more still.

He broke the seal of the packet and began to read the letter.

The middy watched his face, which went pale, then red, and then almost convulsed. Young Richards turned away. He knew the nature of the intelligence, and the effect it was likely to cause.

'My God!' gasped Garthway, and he let the paper fall from his hands. 'Boy, do you know the nature of this?'

'Yes, my lord.'

'But—but——God help me, if this is true!'

'Alas, my lord! I am too sorry to say I am the bearer of such news; but I saw'——

'You saw—saw it?'

'Yes, my lord; I saw your mansion a ruin, and half the prison blown down.'

'And'——

'The prisoner put there by you escaped.'

'And my daughter?'

'It is said, my lord, that your daughter, with her companion and Miss or Mrs. Howard, has been abducted. I will retire, my lord, until you wish to see me.'

And the mid backed his way to the door.

Admiral Garthway motioned for him to stay.

He could not speak yet.

The blow was too crushing. His house burned down, his daughter gone—abducted—perhaps dishonoured.

'Horrible!' he gasped, and buried his face in his hands.

The middy turned away with dim eyes. With all his rackety mischief, he had a good heart, and was a good sterling nature. Moreover, he loved the admiral—would die for him, and the ruin and trouble that had come upon him, went to the middy's heart, as much as a personal grief would.

The terrible silence was broken by the entrance of Mr. Jasper Lorry.

He paused in the door way.

He saw something had occurred.

'I intrude,' he said.

'No, no, I want you.'

'He went forward; then the admiral rose, and placed the sad tidings into the lawyer's hands.

Young Richards was looking out into the street through the glass of the windows.

Agitated as was the admiral, he noticed his favourite middy's emotion.

'Raymond,' he said, and even in the midst of his overwhelming trouble the admiral spoke kindly.

'My lord.'

And the middy turned his pale face towards him.

'Take a seat at the table and breakfast; you must be tired.'

'Nay, my lord, I could not'——

'Nonsense; be seated. I must leave you here for a few minutes. When I return, be ready to accompany me back.'

Raymond saluted, and took a seat before the sumptuous meal.

He would not have done so, but he looked upon it more as a command than an invitation from one so much his superior.

Mr. Lorry, if quieter or showed it less, was as much concerned, equally surprised and horror-struck at the news as the admiral was.

'My lord,' he said, 'what are we to do?'

'I shall return immediately. Let me have an hour with you.'

Lord Garthway left the hotel pale and trembling with the lawyer.

The middy sat down with a sigh.

He undoubtedly felt very grieved at the misfortune of the admiral; but he was only a midshipman after all. He had travelled all night and was really very hungry; so it must not be thought he was unkind in sitting down and doing ample justice to a meal as good as it was inviting.

'Poor old admiral!' he thought, while making an attack upon a fowl. 'I am deuced sorry. I daresay he'll chase the skunk of a pirate who did it; if he should, why, I'll spit him—the pirate, not the admiral.'

At the expiration of three quarters of an hour he began to push the plates from him and stretch out his legs.

'What a wise fellow he was,' cogitated the mid, 'who said, if it were not for our bellies, our backs could wear gold—I think that was it. If so, he might have used some word more delicate in sound than *belly*. It's quite true, though. Here's a lot to pay, and for my breakfast! Thank goodness, I haven't got to pay for it, though.'

The admiral returned. Raymond was very quiet now; he was quick-sighted, and could see the mental anguish Garthway was suffering.

Not an hour was lost ere they set out for Deal. If they travelled from thence quickly, they returned much quicker.

It seemed a long, tedious journey; a melancholy silence was kept up on every side.

Captain Stanton and the admiral's head-servant met him in Deal.

'Drive me to my house,' the admiral said.

They did so, and the captain spoke on the journey.

'My lord,' he said, lowly, 'we may not be too late even now to save the lady. The most curious incident that occurred, my lord, was the disappearance of the Sorcerer.'

Admiral Garthway gave an inward groan; he knew whose doing it was.'

The carriage stopped before his own mansion. He alighted from the carriage and stood upon the lawn, where Gnatbrain and several others were waiting for him. The admiral did not speak; a look of the most silent agony came over his face.

'Ruin!' he murmured. 'My child gone, my home destroyed, my honour blighted, my life and happiness wrecked; and he the cause of it all! May God pardon him, for I will not.'

Then his head drooped upon his breast; he clasped his hands, and stood in mute anguish, looking vacantly upon the dreary, charred ruins of what, two days before, was a noble mansion.

If his grief was silent, and to a degree hidden, those who saw him withdrew from his presence.

They knew the proud man's feelings of lost honour and ruin, and they felt it sacrilege to trespass upon him.

———

CHAPTER LIV.

MARIE DE SURBETTE.

THE unexpected appearance of Pat Murphy on the bulwark was enough to scare the men.

'Och one, me honeys, and it's meself as is here. Sure, an' bedad, an' is it the ould jintleman you'd be afther taking me for?'

This broke the spell of horror, and caused a laugh.

Some of the men rushed forward, and took the honest fellow by the hand.

'Bedad, an' I've been nearly kilt. Sure, thin, I'm glad to see you, och one.'

He climbed the bulwark, and leaped upon the deck, followed by Happy Jack.

Gallant Will went forward, and took Pat's hand.

'I thought you had gone to Davy Jones's,' he said.

'Not yet, yer honour; and it won't be a lubberly Frenchman that'll take me there.'

Will laughed, and thought it very likely.

Pat Murphy would have been called upon to give an account of himself had not Will ordered the men to attend to the wounded and bury the dead.

The sea rolled high, and the night was terrifically dark, so that any idea of embarking on the Golden Arrow until daylight was banished.

The rebel schooner had drifted nearer the liner; but a jury-rudder having been mounted, the men on board were able to keep her off.

The prize lay like a log upon the water.

Will went below to see how Gerald was progressing.

Gerald Stuart was getting on very well, indeed.

So Will thought.

Captain Stuart was seated by the side of the French girl, her head reclined upon his shoulder, her tiny hand rested in his own.

The scene was too interesting to be intruded upon, so Will retired, wondering if his captain was really the angel he thought he was.

Captain Gerald was not a saint, but he was as good, and better than most men.

If he held the weeping girl to his breast, it was only from sympathy.

He would have had a hard heart indeed had he treated the young creature—a girl in years—with less kindness.

'Have you no friends?' he asked, continuing the conversation, which for a moment had dropped.

'Alas, monsieur, I have none.'

'No parents?'

'No. My father died many years ago; my mother, he told me, had left him when I was ten years old, and she has not been heard of since.'

'Poor child; and so you were left without a friend.'

'Monsieur, the captain was my uncle.'

'You mean the old sinner I killed?'

'Yes; he had my fortune, and was my guardian. He wanted me to marry him. I would not; and he brought me here on board the vessel. I know not what my fate would have been had you not saved me.'

'Poor little one! He had the vicious intent of making you marry him?'

'Yes, to get my fortune.'

'And now he is dead, it is yours, of course.'

'Yes, monsieur; but, alas! what can I do? I cannot live alone, and the law would take it from me until I am of age.'

'Will they?'

'If I go back.'

'Then you shan't go back.'

The girl smiled sadly.

'Would you like to stay in England until I can go to France and help you get your rights?'

'I should like to stay in England, and'——

She paused and blushed.

'And what, little one?'

'With you?'

'My little one, you do not know who I am.'

'You are an Englishman.'

'That's true.'

'And a good, honourable one.'

'People say not.'

'People are wicked, and say bad things of any-one.'

'But even my Government discard me.'

The girl smiled doubtfully.

'Here's a go,' thought Gerald. 'She won't believe a word I say. She wants to fall in love with me, and then, I suppose, will want to marry me—and I know that will never do. She's an innocent little thing. I must take care of her, and see if there is any chance for Andrew.'

'But,' he said, aloud, 'if you stay in England, I will come and see you often, but I cannot remain with you.'

'I should be happy would you come and see me.'

'I will promise you my protection; in fact, I will put you somewhere safely, in a house or apartments. Should I be able to reach France safely, I will see your wrongers, and have your fortune transferred to England—how would you like that?'

'Yes, very much. Ah! you Englishmen are so kind and so generous.'

'Are not Frenchmen? In fact, I have always heard they were perfection, especially as regards their conduct to women.'

The girl became silent, and sighed sadly.

'So I was taught to think,' she replied, 'but, alas! an early, sad experience of the world soon opened my eyes to the hypocrisy of mankind.'

Gerald was surprised to hear her speak thus. He imagined her to be a simple, innocent child, but he found an early contact with the world had made her a woman in some things.

'Yet,' he said, wishing to hear more of her sentiments, 'yet we English are generally thought rough, brusque, wanting in delicacy and refinement.'

'Yes,' assented the girl, with a touch of irony, 'and by a nation where the vilest immorality goes on beneath the mask of refinement. The French are a wretchedly sensual race. They would stand with their hat off for half-an-hour in the street while talking to a girl they, perhaps, have foully outraged. A man of my nation would not enter the presence of his wife even in anger with his hat on, but he would leave her to drag on a wretched, lonely life, while his nights were spent in the arms of his mistress, and his days in the cafés, and that is what they would call refinement and honour. Give me the honest, independent mode of an Englishman. They are gifted with the refinement of nature, and if they lack

BLACK EYED SUSAN.

OR, PIRATES ASHORE.

'THE WOLF OF THE WAVES!' SHE EXCLAIMED.

that obsequity our countrymen are so full of, they do not lack morality.'

'In many cases, no.'

'It is your national character, monsieur,' said the girl, firmly.

'You have received a severe lesson for one so young.'

'I have. I have been left to the mercy of society; I have trusted in those whom I looked upon as friends, and by them been betrayed. There is no constancy in my countrymen. I blush to say it, but there is not.'

'Yet you trust me.'

'You are English.'

Gerald smiled.

'Are there no treacherous Englishmen?'

'Yes; but I should know them. You are proud and noble, generous too. I do not know why I think so, but I do. You would not betray a trust!'

'I would sooner suffer death.'

'You did not slay that man who sought my life from any selfish motive?'

'Certainly not.'

'You promised to be my guardian, to protect me while I was thus helpless in the world?'

'True.'

'And for what?'

'To make you happy.'

'And in return, you will expect'——

'Your gratitude and esteem. I will be frank with you. What is your name?'

'Marie.'

'I will be frank with you, Marie. I am in love—have loved since my boyhood, and when that love dies out, I shall no longer exist. I will love and cherish you as a brother, a guardian. Will that make you happy?'

'Very,' replied the loving little creature, her eyes becoming dim. 'Then does that not make it true, what I say? You cannot love me because you love another; you tell me so before my affections are turned to you. You promise to become a brother, and protect me, and all from an unselfish motive of goodness—greatness. Ah, mon Dieu!* I wish I had been English.'

'But I am only one of a nation, and perhaps should not be so kind were I not in love.'

'You would always be honourable and generous.'

'I hope so,' replied Gerald, finding that to try to make himself appear no better than anyone else was a signal failure. 'But you would find one of your own countrymen who would do as much.'

Mademoiselle Marie shook her pretty little head.

'I don't think so,' she said. 'If one offered to marry me, it would be for my money; if he were in your place, he would ask, and perhaps by some cruel subterfuge compel me to become his.'

'They must be an unprincipled set.'

'They think they are not; it is the fault of their blind conceit.'

'How?'

'That of imagining they are perfection, while their sordid animal appetites make them brutes.'

'Glad I'm not a Frenchman,' thought Gerald; 'this vicious little puss is their most bitter enemy.'

'You must have had some previous insight of English character.'

'Yes; my mamma was half English—that is, my grandma was all English.'

'I see.'

'We used to have English friends come. I liked them all—I did.'

'But you don't give the ladies of sunny France such a bad character, I hope.'

'They are, in most cases, bad enough; but should be pitied, not abused.'

'Why so?'

'Because French young ladies are little better than slaves. We have no will of our own, and no privileges—our own mistress only when within the precincts of our own chambers.'

'That is bad.'

'It is cruel, monsieur. We are scarcely in our teens when all such things as playthings are moved from our sight, and matrimony is the next thing we learn to think of and look after; we have no choice.'

'How?'

'Our husbands are chosen by the parents; and, whether we like him or not, we have to enter the state of bondage—frequently slavery; for we are sold more like slaves than won like women and wives.'

''Tis bad indeed.'

'Why, we are denied the privileges of our domestics. They put on their white, frilled caps, which are their safeguard, and they go out unmolested by anyone.'

'And you.'

'We, monsieur; ah! mon Dieu, we cannot cross the street without being accompanied by an old servant of either sex; so that we are never alone. Virtually, we do not belong to ourselves. Watched almost night and day more like captive slaves than the daughters of a Christian land.'

'That, in itself, does not speak well of your countrymen, when a young girl is not allowed to walk through the streets in safety.'

'True, monsieur; and the consequences of this servile kind of life, are, in all cases, more or less grave.'

'I suppose so.'

'What can you expect? Young, passionate girls kept like that until they are the age to marry, and when they do they are like slaves set free—mad—nothing but mad with the joys of having the reins of freedom in their own hands; and they know not when or where to stop. They go to as much the extreme one way as they were kept in extremes the other.'

'Well, give me England after that, though she is but the Isle of the Sea.'

'I would ask for nothing greater than that.'

'What?'

'To be English.'

'And yet the climate is usually sneered at. It is said that we never see the sun.'

'Bigots say anything. I am but a child in the world's ways, and perhaps have no right to argue; but let nations say what they like of England. Where will you find stronger—more hearty men, than your countrymen? Where will you find such bravery. individually or collectively?'

The remark rather staggered Gerald.

He had never thought of this point of argument.

'If the strongest—the hardiest men are bred and born under the climate of England, can it be so unhealthy—so unbearable as our countrymen would make out?'

'Truly no.'

---

* An expression often used by the ladies of France.

Gerald was struck with the wisdom the girl displayed.

'You are a great judge of character.'

'It is my strongest point, or my greatest weakness.'

'The former. Ah! here is morn, the beginning of a new day.'

'I like the morn, yet I am not anxious for the day to pass quickly.'

'Many people have the same taste.'

'Ah! but each day that comes, is one nearer to our end.'

'You would not like to die?'

'Not yet. I should like to be good—very good. I do not fear death; but I have a love for the world. I know what to expect, and expect what I find in frail humanity; but no one knows what may come after death.'

'Perhaps life begins there. Our wretched existence upon earth being, as it were, to perform as much as our desires will let us, the will of Him above, and to secure eternal bliss hereafter.'

Gerald rose as he spoke, and sighed.

The dark beauty by his side remained wrapped in deep meditation.

Captain Gerald was disturbed by the entrance of Will.

'Well, Will?'——

'The morning light has discovered a spanking—I should imagine by her size, British—line-of-battle.'

'Aha!'

'Far away?'

'Yes; I can only just see the dark line of her hull as yet.'

'Good! I will come on deck. Will, you have the whip ready for this young lady.'

'I'll see to it,' replied Will, retiring.

'What did you say?' inquired the French young lady.

'I ordered the whip to be got ready for you,' said Gerald, translating it into the phrase with the same meaning.

'Ah! mon Dieu! what have I done to deserve the whip?'

Gerald laughed heartily, and explained that it was a chair which was hoisted up by a rope fastened to the topsail yard.

The whip being an especial accommodation for ladies.

This set the mind of Mademoiselle Marie de Surbétte at ease.

'I must leave you for a few minutes,' said Gerald.

'Very good, monsieur.'

Gerald Stuart went upon deck.

He found, to his surprise, that the wounded men of his crew had been conveyed on board the Golden Arrow.

Such of the provisions and ammunition as Will thought necessary were conveyed to the rebel craft.

The brave sailors had not been idle during the night, for all traces of the late dreadful carnage were gone, and the vessel put in 'ship-shape.'

Captain Gerald turned to look at the approaching stranger.

To the naked eye she was but a huge white speck.

He scanned her through his glass.

'A Britisher,' he muttered, seeing that much at a glance.

The boat came alongside, and Will stepped on deck.

Gerald could see that the preparations for the embarkation of the lady were completed.

The staunch friends went down to the cabin together.

'Should the stranger prove a foe, Will, we shall look odd.'

'We can fight.'

''Tis a large vessel, or I mistake much.'

'So was this.'

'Truly. Ah! Will, we must trust to circumstances. Now, let us see what there is worth conveying on board the Arrow. Firstly, there are the things belonging to this young lady.'

'Maybe there's something worth having in the chief cabin,' suggested Will.

'Have you looked?'

'Not yet, Gerald; I left that to you.'

'Will you point out your personal property, and that of your uncle's,' said Gerald to Maria de Surbette.

'I will, captain.'

'Have you any in this cabin?'

'My own boxes.'

Everything belonging to the young lady was put carefully under lock and key, and then conveyed to the boats.

Gerald also asked her to see that everything belonging to the late captain was secured, and she was to retain the keys.

This she refused.

'All his effects are yours,' she said; 'yours by the right of victory.'

'But I suppose he had in his possession deeds concerning your fortune?'

'Which are safest in your hands.'

Seeing it was useless to argue, Captain Gerald made a sign to Will, who called four men to his assistance, and the effects of the chief cabin of the liner were transmitted to the Golden Arrow.

The stranger was so near now that it could be plainly seen by the naked eye.

The schooner was not in a fit state to engage a powerful enemy.

Neither Captain Gerald nor Will were likely to surrender without a struggle; therefore, the men set to making such preparations for holding out as long as they could.

Tired as the men were, on account of having had no rest the night through, they would not shirk another fight; they were ripe for it, in fact.

By the request of Will, the cross of St. George was hoisted.

The stranger acknowledged it by hoisting another, and the admiral's flag.

'I know the vessel,' said Gerald.

'Ay! and I've seen it before.'

After the exchange of signals, a boat was put off from the British liner, and was pulled vigorously towards the Golden Arrow.

'Deck ahoy!' cried a voice from the pinnace.

'Ahoy!' replied an officer.

'In distress?'

'No,' answered Gerald; 'will you come on board?'

It was Raymond Richards—Admiral Garthway's favourite middy.

'Admiral sent me, sir,' he said, saluting Captain Gerald, 'to see what has happened.'

'Which Admiral ?'

' Garthway.'

Gerald penciled a few lines on a piece of paper.

' Give his lordship this. Tell him I captured the liner with a hard struggle,'

' When, sir ?'

' Last night ; and she damaged my rigging most dreadfully.'

' Talk about the Gnat and the Lion,' said the impertinent young mid, with a quaint look at the line-of-battle ship, and then at the Golden Arrow.

Gerald smiled. The idea of the Gnat and the Lion tickled his fancy.

' But you see, sir,' he said, ' I did not drive my big antagonist mad, but captured him by sheer hard fighting. Come, take my message to the admiral.'

He went.

The paper bore only two or three lines.

Admiral Garthway read them, and ordered his gig to be manned.

His face flushed and his eyes sparkled, when the middy told him of the engagement.

' God ! ' muttered the admiral, as he descended the ship's side, ' what bravery ! and to think his Majesty should lose such a commander—stupid, mad youth ! '

The gig shoved off, and Captain Gerald Stuart waited anxiously for the presence of the admiral.

CHAPTER LV.

JACK MURRAY AND HIS CAPTORS.

ROCK ELFIN carried the wronged wife of the villain Saunders on board the lugger. Little Jack Murray was conveyed on board too.

The brave little fellow was wounded and bleeding.

Elfin was in a brutal humour, afraid of discovery, mentally calculating the loss it would be, and the rage of his employer made him desperate.

Eurice was conveyed on board without any difficulty.

She had not recovered from the effects of the drug. Jack was senseless from the ill-treatment of the ruffians.

The smugglers lost no time in getting as far out to sea as possible.

The whole of the first night went, and every means was resorted to to get the lad Murray back to a state of sensibility.

Elfin had endeavoured to bring his captive back to consciousness, but she lay like one dead.

Nothing could be got between her teeth, she did not seem to breathe.

Brute as he was, a pang of pity shot through his breast, but only pity—remorse he was a stranger to.

The callous ruffian made it his boast that he looked upon everything as a matter of business.

He thought the poor young wife was dead. Remembering the delicate state of her health when the brutes took her from her home, this did not seem unlikely.

So the long dreary hours of darkness passed, and when morning came she was just the same.

Rigidly cold and motionless.

Elfin always went himself, he could not trust his men, he could himself.

' She is dead,' the ruffian thought. ' Well, it's all the better. I almost hate to do anything unpleasant there. It's a pity such beauty will get in people's way. But there, it's business, and I'm payed for it.'

With that he left the cabin.

He had left some wine and biscuits within reach of the sufferer should she come to.

When he got on deck one of his ruffian associates, with a coarse laugh, said—

' Going to leave the cub down below altogether ?'

The cub was poor little Jack Murray. Down below was the loathsome hold of the lugger.

Elfin had simply forgotten him as yet, and recalling the brave little fellow to mind brought a scowl to his brow.

' Yet the whelp might be of some use,' he thought, after a little meditation.

The day had nearly passed, and dusk began to throw its sable shadows over the sea.

' Bring the whelp up.'

Jack was brought before the ruffian. He looked haggard, exhausted, and bloodstained.

Rock Elfin eyed the boy as a man would an injured dog.

' How d'ye like your lodging ?'

The ruffian said this with a savage grin.

Little Jack gave the brute a look of quiet scorn, but did not reply.

' Oh, you've lost your tongue, eh ! '

' I might have lost my life for all you care, you brutal coward ; let me get free, untie my hands, and see whether I can't take revenge for the way you wounded me. Your cowardice is as great as yourself, for you even fear to let me, a boy of fourteen, have my liberty.'

Elfin laughed.

' You know too much, youngster. Deal would be too hot for me if you were to go back.'

' What do you intend to do, cowards ? Murder me ? Why did you not do it ? Why did you keep me here to torture me ? Oh ! if my hands were free ! '

' Well, it all depends on yourself whether you live or not. If you remain quiet, you'll live ; if you try any tricks you'll suffer.'

' Why was I stolen from my home ?—did I harm you ? '

' You were in the way, youngster, and you'll be one of us.'

' Never ! I'd sooner die first. If you think to make me stay you are mistaken. Give me my liberty and I will go the first chance I have. Let me get arms into my hands, then look out. Coward ! you are dead to all feeling. You know not what it is to have children, and God would not allow you the guardianship of young '——

' Hold ! curse you ! ' cried Elfin, rushing forward, and gripping the boy by the arm.

Unconsciously the boy had touched upon some secret spring in the ruffian's heart, for his face was almost convulsed, and the passion became so terrible, that even the men slunk back.

' Cursed brat ! ' he cried, ' you know not what you have said. Speak again, and I'll strangle you ! What is more, you shall stay. You shall have your liberty, but be careful how you use it, or by —— I'll crush the life from your heart ! You shall see whether I fear such a brat. Attempt to escape, and you shall be shot. We will see who shall be master here ! '

Then turning to his ruffian men, he cried, hoarsely—

' Let him go free—let him walk the deck, and, mark you, let him alone. If any dare to touch him, why you'll suffer.'

He released his grip upon the boy's arm. Jack nearly fell to the deck from pain and weakness. When his hands were untied, and he was left standing upon the deck, he reeled back. The blood rushed through his veins. A peculiar stinging sensation came over him. The blood rushed to his head, his brain was in a whirl, and he fell to the deck insensible.

His young frame had suffered to much. Elfin stepped forward with a low cry, more like a savage growl than aught else.

'Is he dead?' involuntarily exclaimed Elfin, going forward.

'Looks like it,' replied one of the lawless wretches, with an unfeeling grin.

Elfin snatched the boy away from their hands, and carried him to the cabin where Eurice lay.

He placed Jack upon the floor, took some brandy, and attempted to pour it between the lad's clenched teeth.

The attempt was a failure.

'He shall not die,' muttered Elfin. 'God, are those words true?—that the power of having or rearing, or obtaining the love of a child is denied me now? I will see.'

He chafed the lad's cold hands.

'How like,' he muttered—'how like'——

Then his eye caught sight of the pale, motionless form of Eurice.

She lay still, calm as ever.

Beautiful she looked too, in her marble-like paleness.

The stone-like heart of Elfin was for a moment touched.

But his only thought of remorse was—

'What a pity she should have been in his way.'

He continued his operations with little Jack, whose teeth at length unlocked, and a low moan escaped his lips.

'Aha! he lives!' And Elfin's eyes glared with a savage kind of glee.

He poured some brandy down the boy's throat.

Then he left him.

Elfin was not safe yet, and he rarely left the deck; at any moment he might be run down by a king's ship.

Shortly after his departure on deck, little Jack recovered his senses and a little of his strength.

Two or three minutes elapsed ere he could recover his recollection.

When he remembered what had occurred, he felt some surprise at finding himself in a comfortable little cabin.

He turned on his side, raised himself up on his elbow, and glared round him.

'The lady!' he exclaimed, starting.

He had a great deal of nerve for one so young; but the sudden and unexpected sight of Eurice lying apparently dead gave him a shock.

Leaping to his feet, he went to her side.

'Poor lady!' he said, taking her hand with peculiar tenderness, and bursting into tears.

The poor little fellow was but a child; the sight touched him home. Like most boys of his age, he could not look upon so much beauty and goodness without a certain amount of love and reverence entering his juvenile soul.

'They've killed her,' he sobbed. 'If I was only a man I would kill the cowards.'

While he stood weeping over her, he fancied he felt a slight twitching in her arm.

'Perhaps she's only asleep,' he thought.

He dried his tear-dimmed eyes, and watched her face closely.

He remembered his mother had felt her heart to see if it beat, and thus discern if any signs of life remained.

Poor little fellow! In his childish innocence he thought it nothing less than a sin to uncover the lovely bosom and ascertain if there was any pulsation of the heart.

He feared to attempt it.

'Lady,' he said, 'do wake.'

Her lips twitched nervously.

His heart beat with a joyous hope.

Brandy, water, and biscuits were upon the cabin table.

He took some of the fiery spirits and gently poured some between the parted lips of the unconscious beauty.

Then he watched its effect.

It was almost magical.

The powerful drug had done its work; its force had passed. The system, no longer held dormant by its influence, resumed its sway; the blood circulated, the muscles of the body relaxed, life returned; with life came consciousness, and the sleeper awoke.

'Oh, lady, I thought you were dead.'

The childish, familiar voice struck upon the confused senses of Eurice with a welcome sound; she clasped the juvenile's hand in hers.

'Where am I?' she murmured. 'Was it a dream?'

'Oh, no—no, lady, it was real—all real.'

Eurice gave a groan, and fixed her eyes upon Jack.

She remembered him. She noticed his haggard appearance and blood-stained face; she saw the tears coursing each other down his sunken cheeks, and drew him to her breast.

'Poor little fellow; what has happened? I am not at your house.'

'No, lady, you are on the sea.'

'The sea!'

'Yes, lady.' And he told, in a few words, how she had been abducted; how he had fought for her, and been struck down, and conveyed on board the lugger.'

'Great heaven! then I was drugged,' she exclaimed, in horror. 'And you have suffered through me. But who did it—who drugged me?'

Her face blanched in horror at the thought.

'Not—not'——

'Not mother, nor father,' said the little fellow, artlessly. 'It was Ellen Grinel—that girl.'

'Treacherous creature! God will punish her for it. Oh, God! then I am in the hands of those who will show no mercy.'

'They are cowards and wretches, lady; but they shan't hurt you while I live.'

'Are you not a prisoner?'

'No.' And he informed her of what had passed between him and Elfin.

'Poor child! it is little better than death,' she replied.

'Hush! we might be heard.' He went forward, and fastened the door, looked round the cabin, saw they were alone and secure, then he returned to Eurice.

'I think they suppose you are dead. I wonder

why I was brought down here, and why the leader of these men should show me mercy? He has left food and everything that is wanted. I will go and see what they are doing. If anyone comes, don't let them see you are awake, until I come back.'

He stole out of the cabin on tiptoe, and went on deck, keeping well in the shade.

He saw Rock Elfin in conversation with his first accomplice—a fellow who acted as a sort of lieutenant.

There were a crew of thirty-five men on the White Cat, and Elfin rather liked the idea of officers.

'Strikes me,' Jack heard the smuggler say, 'she's dead; if she ain't, she seems like it, and if she don't wake up, we'll shove her in a canvas bag, and sink her. It'll only be paying duty to the dead—eh, Jem?'

Jem laughed, as though he liked the idea.

'But if she wakes up, couldn't you make better use of her than that?'

The look that accompanied the ruffian's words left no doubt as to their meaning.

'Look here, Jem, that's out of the business. It's my work to take her away, and not let her go back, but I ain't paid for anything else; and if I did it, and the captain should find it out, why—well—summut. It ain't nothing to do with my business, so don't you think it, mate.'

'Well, if you is so partickler, turn her over to some one else—to me. I'll'——

'Look here, Jem, get out—go for'ad. Whose master here? Another word, and I'll show you.'

Jem slunk away.

Elfin watched him, and saw the sullen look of vindictiveness the ruffian gave him.

'Wait,' muttered Jem, 'wait. Yer won't get it all yer own way. I could command this craft quite as well. Maybe I'll do it; and then who'll stop me from having her—her, her. Ain't she a beauty. Now I'll go and have a look at her.'

He went, closely followed by little Jack, and locked the door just as Jack threw himself against it.

Unable for the moment to know how to act, the little fellow kicked at the door with all his juvenile strength.

It was to no purpose.

He heard a struggle going on inside. The ruffian, Jem, had gone direct to the terrified girl.

His look, his flaming eye, was sufficient to warn her of him.

She jumped up from the couch, and made for the door.

The smuggler stood before her, his back was to the door, his hand turned the key.

'Mercy'! gasped the terrified girl, going on her knees.

'I ain't going to hurt you,' the brutal wretch replied, with a leer. 'If yer are careful yer may live, and get yer liberty.'

'Liberty! Oh, how?'

Poor girl! she grasped at the faintest shadow of hope.

'Well, yer see, it's likely I shall be captain here, and if yer behave yerself, and don't squall out when I come near you, maybe I'll give yer yer freedom, only you'll have to *love* me first.'

'You! repulsive wretch! Base thing! dare to approach me, and'——

'Ah! ah! ah! that's a good un. Why you can't help yourself.

The brute took her by the waist, and drew her to him.

She screamed loudly for help, and, weak as she was, fought bravely.

But her strength was nothing in comparison to the smuggler's.

He stifled her cries with one grimy hand, with the other he forced her back upon the couch and held her there.'

One last frantic effort Eurice made.

She dashed his hand from her mouth.

'Help!' she screamed.

'Who's to help you?'

'I am.'

The cabin window was dashed open, and little Jack, his clothes pouring with water, jumped in.

The ruffian was staggered, and released his hold upon the girl.

Little Jack leaped at the ruffian's throat, and said—

'Unlock the door, lady—unlock the door.'

'Cursed whelp!' the cowardly smuggler cried, and drawing back his fist, he struck the noble boy a blow on the temple, that felled him to the floor; the blood trickled slowly from the boy's pale face.

Eurice had the presence of mind to act upon the lad's advice.

She rushed forward and unlocked the door, as her persecutor caught her by the shoulder.

'Curse you!'

It was Elfin who spoke, and who entered the cabin.

He caught his subordinate by the throat, dragged him from the cabin, and up the companion-ladder to the deck; then held him at arms' length, drew back his right hand, and then shot out his fist.

The blow fell with crushing force upon the ruffian's temple.

He groaned, and fell a huddled heap under the bulwark.

Then Elfin retraced his steps to the cabin, and looked, with a savage glare, upon the scene before him.

Eurice was again insensible.

'Ah, she's dead now,' he muttered; and did not trouble to see whether she was or not.

But he went to Jack. He dashed water on the boy's pale and bleeding face, and swore an awful oath against his accomplice, Jem.

It was not long ere Jack came to; he guessed Elfin had saved him, and felt grateful.

He had no time to thank the smuggler, as he rose and left the cabin the instant Jack opened his eyes, saying—

'You'd better help each other.' And strode on deck.

'Where's Jem?' he asked, savagely.

'Down below, cap'n. You've nearly cooked his goose. He ain't opened his toplights yet.'

It was well for him he had not. Elfin was in the humour to strangle him should he come on deck.

Little Jack, with the nobility of a true, generous nature, did not think of his own hurts, but jumped up, and went to the assistance of Eurice.

He could not lift her upon the couch, so administered what restoratives he could find to bring her to her senses.

When she came to, she clasped him in her arms.

'Brave little fellow!' she said. ''Tis to you I owe my life.'

Then she kissed his haggard cheeks and pale lips.

The good little fellow felt repaid, and ready to fight for her ten times more.

'They won't touch you, any more,' he said. 'I will go and see if I can get something for you to eat. Don't be afraid, lady, I'll lock the door, and put the key in my pocket.'

He did so, and went on deck.

The night had grown darker—the sea rolled high—the lugger rocked about like a cork upon the water.

The night watch was out, the rest of the crew slept. Elfin kept up an uneasy look-out himself.

Jack Murray drew back when on the deck. He saw a figure creeping towards Elfin, who stood near the bulwarks.

The figure crept closer and closer, and at length stood just behind the unsuspecting smuggler.

The lugger gave a lurch—the dusky shadow stepped forward.

There was a savage oath, a cry, and Elfin was hurled overboard by his ruffian subordinate, Jem.

The cry roused the sleeping watch.

Jem Crambury sneaked away.

Little Jack looked on in horror.

He was thinking whether he should say nothing about it, and let the ruffian sink who had brought so much misery upon his family.

But his better feeling prevailed. He remembered that Elfin had been merciful to him.

'Your captain's overboard!' he cried, and took one leap into the sea.

Those who saw the deed could not repress a cry of admiration.

Jack had clutched a rope with one hand as he leaped over the side.

The crew rushed forward and put back the lugger as quickly as they could.

Meantime Elfin was splashing about; he was a good swimmer, but the sea ran high.

He was encumbered with big boots and a heavy coat, and stood a poor chance of keeping up long.

Nothing but his immense strength kept him up at all.

But when he saw the lugger receding from view, his heart sank within him. It was as much as he could do to keep his head above water.

He sank deeper and deeper still, and now he felt he could no longer hold up.

With a bitter curse against the traitor who did it, he made one last desperate effort to keep up.

Useless—he went down; his head went under, and his effort to rise upon the water was useless, when he felt a hand clutch him by the collar.

It was a tiny hand—a juvenile one, and he instinctively felt it was Jack's; he saw the lad's pale face as his head appeared above the water.

'Lad,' he gasped, hoarsely, 'save me.'

'As long as I can keep up. I can't last very long.'

He was but a child—his strength but feeble, and the weight he had to bear enough for a man. How could he keep up?

CHAPTER LVI.

THE CHASE BEGINS.

GERALD STUART had Admiral Garthway received with all the honours due to his station.

Lord Harry greeted him with well-bred politeness.

'My lord, would you step down into my cabin for a few minutes?'

The admiral bowed assent.

'Do I err in thinking you will not attempt any hostilities towards me, my lord?'

'You do not.'

Gerald Stuart bowed.

'It is an unexpected pleasure, meeting you so soon. I'——

Gerald paused. The pale, haggard face of the admiral worked convulsively.

'Great heavens! My lord, you are ill.'

'No, no; it is nothing—nothing.'

'I have no right to doubt, my lord; but if I dare judge by appearances '——

'Chut, chut! You sent for me?'

'I did, my lord. The line-of-battle ship you see is a prize I took last night. Here are the papers and credentials, which I will place in your hands with the prize. She would be of use to the government.'

Admiral Garthway looked as he felt—surprised.

'But I could not say I took it.'

'Why not, my lord? You could if you chose.'

'How, sir?'

'By engaging and conquering me. I think the government would not exactly let that pass without awarding honours to the man who did it.'

'This is useless talk, Captain Stuart.'

'It is truth, my lord.'

'Very likely.'

'Unless you accept the prize, my lord, I shall sink it. I cannot afford the men to man her; she is full of prisoners.'

'I will send here '——

'Thank you, my lord. Pardon me—but is there any fresh news that causes you to be afloat without a squadron?'

Lord Garthway paced up and down the cabin with a moody brow.

'Captain Stuart,' he said, stopping suddenly.

'My lord?'

'I have fresh news—strange news—terrible news. God help me!'

He put his hand to his brow, and again paced the cabin.

'My lord, for the sake of bygone days—as a friend of my boyhood—I implore you to trust me. Can I help you? May I know the nature of this news?'

'Yes, boy, you shall. Listen. A day after your departure I started for London. I was fetched the following day—taken home with all possible speed, and found my house in ruins; my daughter gone, with her attendant and friend; the prison of the town half blown down; and the vessel commanded by Saunders gone—he with it. He, sir, did it all. He has my daughter; and it is to hunt him down that I am out without a convoy.'

'Madeline! Pardon. Your daughter gone, and in the power of that wretch! Oh, God!'

Gerald staggered back and sank into a seat.

He pressed his hands to his burning temples.

'Curse him—the villain, the pirate, the traitor robber! My lord, even without your permission, I will hunt him down—I will track him over the seas, over the face of the earth, but I will find him, and, when once found, let him look out.'

Gerald Stuart rose—his face was flushed and convulsed—his eyes glared wildly, his hands worked nervously.

' I have a swift-sailing vessel—it would outstrip any afloat. Trust me, my lord, should he elude the Golden Arrow he will be more than mortal—that is, should he not fall into your hands.'

' 'Tis well, Captain Stuart. You have spies and agents that might help you. You have a swift vessel and a daring crew. Hunt him down, show him no mercy, bring him or his head to me, return my daughter, and you shall have such protection as I can give you.'

Gerald Stuart drew his sword and raised it on high.

The point was poised to heaven, the back of the blade touched his lips.

' Hear me, O Heaven!' he murmured. ' Help me, guide me on the track of the villain, and I swear to hunt him down ; not to rest night or day, nor to go on shore, unless compelled from necessity, until the wretch who could rob a father of his honour and his child lay dead—dead at my feet, or in the bottom of the sea.'

The admiral turned away—a chill crept upon him.

He knew the man too well to doubt that such an oath would be uttered in vain or in the heat of the moment.

He felt that should Gregory escape his clutches, he would, sooner or later, fall a prey to the fierce young chief of the Golden Arrow.

' My lord, enough ! Your daughter shall be restored, if alive—terribly avenged, if dead.'

Lord Henry grasped the excited young chieftain's hand.

' Gerald !'

The captain of the Golden Arrow looked up, and his heart softened.

His name pronounced in a kind voice, and by the admiral, brought to his mind, with the rapidity of lightning, his past days.

' Gerald !' said the old man, ' my heart is not dead to gratitude or old love. I loved you once, and I may again. Do this for me, aid me, drop the rebel flag, and the reward shall be a father's gift—a father's blessing.'

' Lord Henry,' replied Gerald with emotion. ' Death alone shall prevent me from fulfilling my oath. As you can see by the work of last night, England's foes are my foes. I cannot abandon the rebel flag yet, but I promise never to use my energies against a ship of his Majesty's.'

' Enough—we must part. I will keep a southern course entirely.'

' Good, my lord. I will follow up the one I have taken. We shall run him down ere long.'

' Let us hope we shall do it in time.'

' With the help of Heaven, we shall.'

Gerald Stuart conducted the admiral on deck. He was saluted again with great honour, and returned to his liner.

' I will take charge of the prize,' the admiral had said, and kept his word.

Gallant Will noticed Gerald's excited face.

' What has happened ?'

' Happened, Will ? You shall hear in a minute ; order the master up.'

The old fellow came aft.

' Oakham.'

' Yer honour.'

' How long will it be ere the Golden Arrow is in trim ?'

' She can sail in half an hour.'

' The rudder ?'

' Is fixed, your honour. All is taut aloft ; we can do the rest while she is in motion.'

' Hoist every stitch of canvas she will carry, and sail in an N.N.E. direction.'

' Ay, ay, sir.'

' Mr. Burkett.'

' Captain.'

' Give a parting salute to the admiral, dip the colours three times, and then put the Golden Arrow to the uttermost of her speed. Risk spars and masts on the vessel for aught I care, but while she holds her planks together she must sail as she never sailed yet.'

Mr. Burkett, the second officer of the Golden Arrow, understood the chief, and he knew something had occurred.

He did not wait to question, but carried out the orders to a letter.

Gerald took Will below.

' Will,' said Stuart, as they entered the cabin, ' the news from the admiral is terrible.'

' What, in the name of Neptune, is it, Gerald ? '

' Listen. Gregory Saunders has escaped.'

' What !'——

' Wait ! He had the prison blown up, the house of Lord Harry Garthway blown down, and he has fled with your wife and Madeline.'

' With Sue ?'

' With all who were with, and attempted to save Madeline.'

' Sue ! The cursed pirate got my Sue ?'

Will groaned aloud.

' Poor lass ! When will thy troubles end ? Oh, Father of Mercy !—and what might be her fate ? Oh, curse him, cursed pirate. Captain, are we on his track ?'

' I hope so.'

Will rocked himself to and fro with his face buried in his hands.

' We are on his track.'

' I have sworn an oath not to rest day or night until the hound is hunted down, Will.'

' And when that time comes '——

Will grit his teeth.

' I've heard talk of hell's tortures ; he shall suffer them, and he shall suffer worse for Sue.'

' Don't give way to despair, Will. We must bear up. Be vigilant, on the look-out, and on his track, and we shall find him. The Golden Arrow sails swiftly, and he who can elude her must be something immortal.'

' Ay, true. I will bear up. Poor Sue ! Should harm befall her, I will tear the villain's heart from his body, and hold it in his face while he gasps for mercy.'

He clutched a goblet from the table, and drank deeply of wine.

Gerald did the same.

The steward, Wilks, announced breakfast at that moment.

Neither Will nor Gerald could do much justice to the meal ; still, the young chief did not forget to give special instructions to the steward concerning the food of Mademoiselle Marie.

Will was too excited to seek rest. He walked hastily about the quarter-deck, watching the vessel's progress, casting many glances at the masts and

BLACK EYED SUSAN.

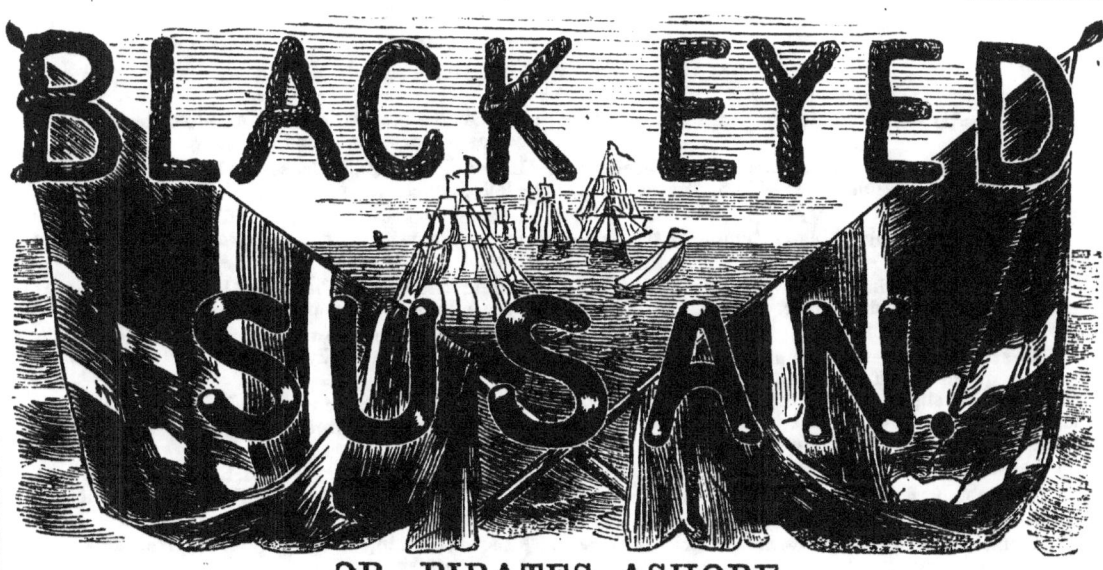

OR, PIRATES ASHORE.

'HE FORCED HIM BACK, WITH HIS HAND STILL UPON HIS THROAT.'

spars, and ever and anon trying the log to discover the speed.

Gerald Stuart sought his adopted brother, Andrew, and told him the terrible news, winding up the heroic catalogue of horrors by saying—

'And now I have something pertaining to the beautiful to show you.'

He left the wondering Andrew in the saloon-cabin, and presently returned, leading the blushing French girl by the hand.

'Here, Andrew, here is someone for you to take care of; teach her English, and read to her. She must not be slighted while compelled to stay on board; and my troubles will not allow me to pay much attention yet to the young lady.'

Andrew's beautiful blue eyes sparkled brightly.

'This is indeed happiness!' he said, taking the girl's hand gently in his own.

'Would mademoiselle allow me the honour of becoming her teacher?'

Mademoiselle said she would, with a pretty smile; and Andrew led her to a seat and a charming conversation went on.

Captain Gerald had gone on deck.

In this new trouble, Will and Gerald found solace only in each other's company. So Andrew was left with what he very facetiously termed—

The dark fairy of the Golden Arrow.

He heard from her lips how she had come in the care of Gerald, and what had passed between them.

'And you have no friends?' he asked.

'None, now, but the noble captain and yourself; and I could be happy with that.'

'And on this bark?'

'If I might stay.'

'But what would the world say?'

'Much, I have no doubt; but it has done so before. The world has an evil tongue, and is ever ready to use it. I no longer study or fear it while I'm doing right in the sight of my Maker, and following the dictates of my heart.'

'But this wild life would be very cheerless without a female companion for you.'

'Female friends do not always bring happiness.'

And she gave one of her bitter sighs.

Andrew looked at her in mute admiration, and because he could find no suitable answer,

'Would you like to speak English?' he asked.

'It is the great wish of my life.'

'Then you shall, if you will have so unworthy a master.'

Marie gave him a look of gentle rebuke.

'I have such books as will help us,' he went on, 'and you shall take the first lesson when you like.'

'I am ready now.'

Gerald Stuart had given up his own private cabin, which performed the duties of library and private sanctuary to his young charge. Adjoining this was a berth that comprised a sleeping apartment—it was safe and sacred from all intruders.

So the little French protegee was safe.

To the library Andrew led her, and began the pleasing occupation of teaching her English, and so wiled many hours away.

On board the vessel was a cabin boy of about fourteen years old—a boy that loved Captain Gerald with all the ardency of his young heart.

Knowing this, and thinking it would help him in the task of teaching his pupil English, Andrew put the lad at the disposition of Mademoiselle Marie, as her constant attendant and safeguard.

Knowing it would please his beloved benefactor, the lad, Lionel, accepted his post with delight.

The boy was a fondling, picked up in a dying condition by Captain Gerald, and taken to the Golden Arrow.

Gerald Stuart had been repaid for his trouble by the boy's love and recent gratitude.

The day dragged slowly by with Gerald and Will, who remained on deck, watching for the slightest sign of a sail.

With Andrew the day passed better, and when evening came, he relinquished his task of master with a very bad grace.

Neither Will nor Gerald Stuart had taken any rest on the previous night. Gerald saw and felt the necessity for it now.

'I shall turn in, Will,' he said. 'We shall want rest. What say you?'

'Ay, soon.'

Gerald left him on the poop, and went below to seek a little rest.

Will's mind was too much abstracted to seek sleep.

Long after night threw its sable tint on the deck, he strode to and fro on the poop.

The watch was set, the men silent and in their hammocks.

The breeze shifted, and the Golden Arrow sped on its course. The sails would flap now and then, a rope creek, or a gull strike against the fleeting vessel, but there were no noises of any consequence to break the solemn quietude of night.

At length, worn out and weary, Will wrapped a huge cloak closely round him, and, with his arm placed at the back of his head and resting on a gun-carriage, he slept.

It was not long ere his distracted imagination carried him far away in the land of dreams.

At first they were a confused jumble of nothings, running one upon the other, leaving nothing tangible or to be remembered; but the mist seemed to clear away, as he saw clearly in his visions some faces and forms he knew—saw his wife, and his heart beat.

The scenes of his past life were recalled. He went through his courtship again, his marriage, and his happy home on the cliff.

The form of Doggrass would arise, and stand like a grim phantom of evil between him and his wife, and Susan would disappear.

The scene would change rapidly, and he travelled from place to place, country to country in search of his young wife, and after going through a multitude of trials and disappointments, he found her.

Again the scene changes—he was upon the deck of the admiral's liner, his neck was in a noose, his wife was pleading for his life.

He felt the rope tighten—he saw his wife dragged away—heard the order for the men to haul him up, heard the scuffle of feet, felt himself suspended in the air.

Then all became a blank—his senses confused—he went on in a world of darkness, then the scene opened, far away.

He was on the track of the villain Gregory. He was following him up and down upon the sea.

He saw his hated foe—saw his wife in his hands —fancied he could hear the cry of his wife in his vessel for help.

He struggled wildly to get at the tormentor.

The veins in his forehead and neck rose like cords;

his face became scarlet, and he ground his teeth with fury.

His clenched hands struck the deck as he thought in his weird vision—invisible hands held him back—held him from his foe—the abductor of his wife.

He turned round, and at length reached Saunders. He caught him by the throat, hurled the ruffian down upon the vessel's deck, was about to clutch his Sue, when something seemed to rise between them.

Some huge sea monster, and he started back.

Started in horror, while the ship sailed away, and Gregory Saunders stood at the stern with Susan in his arms—a malignant grin upon his face, and a demoniac gleam in his eyes.

Will strove madly to get at the monster before him, which gradually took the shape of Doggrass.

In his frenzy he screamed aloud, and rolled about as though in convulsions. The phantom of his dream still stood gibing and mocking him. Gliding forward, and with outstretched hand, he grasped the agonized husband by the shoulder, mocking him the while.

'Where—where is my—my wife—my Sue? What is '——

'Sail, oh! lieutenant! There is a stranger on our beam.'

Will leaped to his feet—a cold dampness was upon his limbs, his brain was on fire, his tongue hot and parched, his eyes ached, and glared wildly about.

Morn had broke while he slept.

The watch had been changed. The first ray of morning soon broke slowly through the grey mist of the new day.

Far away he could see a speck.

It was a vessel in full sail, and going directly from them.

'The cursed pirate!' he muttered. 'My glass—hoist every stitch of canvas. Ah! ah! I know the bark—it's him, and my Sue is on board!'

The masts of the Golden Arrow groaned under the load of canvas, and bent like reeds.

The crew were called up and stationed at their quarters, and Captain Gerald came upon deck, watching the terrible chase with eager interest.

CHAPTER LVII.

THE BEAUTIFUL DEMON.

CYRIL'S was a nature the world would call generous. He was gentle and forgiving, too, in some things; but to see these ruffians creeping, in the shadow of night, to murder an aged noble in his chair, and while asleep, roused his fierce blood.

'No mercy,' he said, and drove his sword through the villain's neck he held in his grasp.

The would-be murderer fell dead at his feet; his cry of agony roused the household.

The second intruder would have escaped, but Cyril said, very calmly, but in a voice not to be doubted—

'Move a step, and I'll kill you.'

The earl had sprung to his feet.

'What is this?' he cried, and, with the instinct of danger, pulled furiously at the bell-rope.

'My lord, I was in time to save your life.'

The domestics, in a terrified group, came round the door.

'Take this scoundrel,' said Cyril, hurling the second ruffian towards the butler; 'take him, and keep him in safe custody.'

He was dragged away, and put in safe custody.

The earl, recovering from his bewilderment, turned towards Cyril with extended hands.

'Cyril!—from Spain?' he said.

''Tis I, my lord.'

'How came you here?'

'You shall hear anon; at present——the countess comes. I will see you alone.'

The countess came.

The Earl of Greymoor turned to greet her; he did so with a strange look in his eyes.

'What has happened?' said the countess, rushing forward and throwing herself upon the earl's breast.

'Nothing, thank God, my love, though much might have occurred. Retire to your chamber; this is no sight for you—nor for you, my love.'

The last words were addressed to Lady Clarence, who entered—her beautiful face the picture of fright.

The countess turned when the earl's daughter entered, and her eyes fell upon Cyril.

She started.

'My preserver,' said the earl.

The countess held out her hand frankly.

Cyril took it, and fixed his black, piercing eyes upon the beautiful woman with a look that made the colour leave her cheek.

'Whatever the world may say of you,' she said, with a very good attempt at a bland smile, 'we at least owe you a debt of gratitude.'

'I doubt whether we really do,' thought Cyril; 'for, if my suspicions are correct, you had more to do in this than you would care to own.'

But he did not say so.

He bowed with courtly grace, and lightly touched the delicate fingers with his lips.

'Come,' said the earl. 'I am safe, and the scene here is not fit for you. Let me conduct you to your room.'

'Nay, I will go with Clarence. Come, my dear. We, of course, shall see your old friend in the morning?'

The earl bowed assent, and the countess left the room with her daughter-in-law.

When she was alone in her own chamber the smile left her ruddy lips, and the soft glow went from her cheeks.

Her face was paler, her mouth shut closely, her eyes glittered dangerously, and she looked pitilessly cruel as she stood with her face turned towards the door, and her tiny hand clenched until the nails cut into her delicate flesh.

'Her lover,' she muttered. 'Ha! And 'twas through him. Cyril, beware, and you, too, my lady. Ha! this is a secret I will hear more of.'

Now she paused, and fell into thinking.

The Countess of Greymoor was a dangerous woman—a beautiful demon, and at the present moment she looked it.

'Cyril,' the earl said when they were alone, 'Cyril, how came you here? It is an unexpected visit, and has become a pleasure. I shall ever be indebted to you.'

'Nay my lord, the debt is paid by your friendship, if I can retain that love. The world, my lord, is turned against me.'

'I have heard strange rumours, Cyril.'

'Of me?'

'The name and description is that of you.'

'I will not deny it, my lord, e'en should I lose your friendship. It is I. I am Cyril the Lion Buccaneer; but what the world would say of me is like most of the world's sayings—full of injustice and falsehood.'

'I believe you, my young friend. I believe you, because I would not so insult the memory of my old friend, your father, as to believe what the world says is true.'

'Yet my father believed it.'

'He knows this?'

'He must. He threatened to disinherit me, unless I left Spain.'

'And you left?'

'What else could I do?'

'True.'

'You have heard how I came to be an outcast?'

'That unfortunate duel in Spain?'

'Ay; but believe me, my lord—believe, on the beauty and purity of your daughter—I swear the deed was not committed by me.'

The buccaneer raised his right hand, and cast his eyes to heaven as he spoke.

The earl was a man of peculiar lasting love, and gentle instincts.

He believed the handsome young outcast, who had been a friend of his daughter's in their earlier days, and he believed Cyril had been wronged.

Maliciously—foully wronged.

He held out his hand. The Lion Buccaneer took it gratefully.

'And my old friend, Cyril, your sire?'

'He lives, and, I hope, is happy.'

For the first time, perhaps, in his life, Cyril sighed sadly.

The earl noticed it.

'I think, Cyril, you could get forgiveness.'

'I shall not sue for it, my lord. I am a Don Bragelio. I asserted my innocence. I called heaven to witness it. I was doubted. My father's love was poisoned against me. I shall not sue again. I do not wish it. I am happy as I am.'

'Happy, Cyril? Happy as an outcast?'

'That is what the world calls me, my lord,' replied the buccaneer with a strange smile; but I am out of the reach of justice. I have not broken the laws of my country or humanity yet, therefore I am safe. I am not a pirate nor freebooter. I am called a buccaneer. My flag is my own, and I sail my own master—the sea my kingdom; and because the world does not know what to call me. I like the life, my lord. I always was a wild, reckless fellow, and the roving existence, when I am away from an ungrateful society, suits me.'

'But your honour—your family pride?'

'Is still with me. Let those who attempt to take it beware.'

His brilliant eye flashed again.

'You speak strangely, Cyril—in riddles; and pardon me if I say I cannot understand.'

Cyril laughed.

'To you, my lord, I would willingly make everything clear. All I wish is a promise that my secret will be respected; and I know a promise from the Earl of Greymoor is as sacredly kept as an oath.'

'You have my promise. But, hark! Who comes?'

'A servant, by all appearances,' thought Cyril, as the earl's confidential entered.'

'The chief constable, my lord, has just arrived, and wishes a few minutes audience.'

'Show him in.'

The head functionary of Greymoor entered with becoming dignity and deportment.

'My lord,' he said, bowing low, 'I hope my very early visit has not disturbed you.'

'The strange and serious events of the night have kept me up, Mr. Crawley.'

'No doubt, my lord—no doubt. It is really dreadful—dreadful—if what I have heard is true.'

'I should have been pitilessly murdered, squire, had not Providence sent a friend to my aid. He killed one of the ruffians on my behalf; the other is in safe keeping in the cellars.'

'I will have the ruffian removed. Have you any of their motive?'

'That is the only thing that troubles me. I cannot imagine why they did it.'

'We will examine the living ruffian, my lord. We will see into it as soon as possible.'

'To-morrow.'

'As you wish, my lord. To-morrow.'

'You will take a little wine, Mr. Crawley?'

'Not this morning, my lord. 'Tis only just daylight; too early. Shall I wait upon your lordship to-morrow morning?'

'Ay, it would give me pleasure.'

'I will,' said the worthy magistrate, bowing himself out.

He had come with a sufficient number of men to remove the ruffian and the dead vagabond, and they were removed from the earl's mansion.

The attempt upon the earl's life struck horror to the hearts of the domestics. He was a man universally loved, and the danger he had escaped was less easily forgotten by his servants than by him.

'I think,' he said, returning to Cyril, whom he had left in an ante-room, 'a little coffee would do us good.'

Cyril thought so too, and said as much.

'I suppose the countess will not make her appearance until late. No doubt the occurrence upset her,' remarked the earl.

'She was deeply affected I think, my lord. But, Clarence, she bears too strong a love for her father to be away from him after such a danger.'

'She is a dear girl,' involuntarily muttered the earl.

'My lord, have you no idea why your life was sought?'

'None,' and struck by the tone in which the question was asked, added, 'Have you?'

'I have suspicions; but, like all uncertain surmises, they are best kept to myself.'

'Yet, if you have any grounds for your suspicions'——

'They are too vague to build upon, my lord; but still, as you love your daughter, pay attention to what I say. For heaven's sake, keep on your guard. Trust no one, for you will find the serpent—and ready to sting—where you would expect to find a dove. Beware, my lord, of the person you love best—the love is dangerous.'

'Good God! what can you mean?'

'I only mean——trust in me, my lord. I have mentally sworn to watch and wait for the unravelling of a mystery, and I will do it. I discover much in my travels, and learn a great deal.'

'But would you accuse'——

'I accuse no one, my lord.'

'It is a mystery.'

'Let it remain so, my lord.'

'How could the men get admittance to the house?'

'There lies the mystery.'

'How came you here, Cyril?'

The buccaneer blushed deeply.

'Cyril'—the earl laid his hand upon the young chief's shoulder, and spoke very gravely—'Cyril, own the truth. Tell me—for I would not doubt you; I would not deem you guilty of so dishonourable an act as to worm your way into a girl's affections when '——

'Hold, my lord; you wrong me. I will own a tendency that way. Hear me; you shall know my secrets, and what has occurred since we parted in Spain.'

He paused for a minute, and leaning gracefully upon the corner of the mantel-piece, he rested his head upon his hand, and began.

'When the misfortune came upon me in Spain, I felt hopeless indeed. You wonder why I took to the life of a rover. I was alone; my own parent discarded me. I had enemies where I thought to find friends; and the lovely girl who had been my playmate—whom I had watched gradually blossom into the beauty of womanhood and the grace of an angel —you tore away her love—or, at least, her hand was given to another.

'Was not mine a hopeless life, then? I found solace in excitement, pleasure in danger; and I wandered away—became the restless wanderer of the seas, because its wild freedom suits me.

'I went in disguise to Madrid not long since, and there learned something that concerned us, my lord; and when I set sail I mentally resolved to dare all to see the playmate of my younger days—the idol of my soul, Lady Clarence; and heard from her own lips that you had given her to an English nobleman.'

'Not I, Cyril; it was the countess's wish. Nor did I know of your love.'

'The countess did, my lord. It was my intention to have come and seen you, had not that occurred that so cursed my life. But you know how I was prevented? Your ideas wrong me, my lord. Could I do less than hope to see, for the last time, the idol of my soul? I had promised never to urge my suit—to come between her and your wife; but I ask one boon, my lord?'

'What is it, Cyril?'

'As you love your daughter, as you forgive me for my visit here, do not enter into a hasty alliance with Lord Lockley.'

'That I will promise.'

Cyril paused—he was striding about the room— and took the hand of his aged friend.

'Thank you, my lord. You will not regret either your promise or your friendship. People call me outcast, freebooter, and many other unpleasant names; but to you, my lord, I will reveal myself. Look!'—

He held a small silver case towards the earl, who took and drew from it a small sheet of parchment, from which hung two heavy seals.

They were royal seals.

The earl's countenance lighted up with joy.

'This is indeed joy, my boy. You no longer need fear losing my friendship or love, nor shall you further live on so blindly '——

'Nay, my lord. I would have it kept a secret as yet.'

'As you will.'

'You believe me now?'

'Ay, and let those who would defame your name look to it, for they will have to answer me for it. But Cyril, on your honour, as you respect me, you will not take advantage of my daughter's love if she has any for you. I dare not give you hope, though I love you, Cyril; for the countess has made the intended alliance public. I grieve for you; I pity my daughter, and am sorry for myself; but what is done cannot be undone.'

'As yet, no; but we will wait.'

'We will wait; any power shall not set aside that, for '——

A messenger from Lady Clarence interrupted the conversation.

It was to know whether she could breakfast with the earl. His reply was to the effect that her presence would give him pleasure.

Cyril's heart bounded with joy, his face flushed, and his eyes sparkled.

The earl saw it, and gave a sigh.

His unusually early breakfast was served, and Cyril accompanied his host to the breakfast room.

Lady Clarence was there.

She ran forward and threw her arms round her sire's neck.

'Ah, papa, how dreadful! how shocking it was! I could not rest until I had seen you.'

The earl patted her little head tenderly.

'I am safe, darling.'

'Yes, but it was dreadful.'

'Well, then, there, forget it, my child,' and h1 led her to a seat. 'You have Cyril to thank for your father's life.'

She lifted her beautiful eyes, and gave the buccaneer a look that repaid him for what he had done.

During the morning meal Cyril kept up an animated conversation, so as to dispel the sad incidents of the night from the mind of Lady Clarence.

'How would you like to see a buccaneer's vessel, Lady Clarence? Do you expect to see something very dreadful?'

'Oh, no! I should like to see one so much,' and she clapped her little hands. 'Will you take me?'

'If you would permit me, my lord, or if you would come too.'

'Certainly! Why not? Would you like to see the young rogue's vessel, Clarry?'

'Very much, dear papa.'

'Then you shall.'

The earl was glad of anything that would remove the impression of his late danger from his daughter's mind.

He had also a peculiar lingering love for Cyril, whom he had known and loved as a boy, and since the young chieftain had given him the silver case with the parchment document and seals to preserve, his slight restraint wore away.

'I should like to see the rogue's vessel,' smiled Greymoor, his benevolent face a-glow with pleasure. 'I suppose it is like a fairy bark?'

Cyril smiled.

'I have heard of a beautiful lion you have, and from which your name arose.'

'Truly, Lady Clarence, you shall see it, and hear its history.'

Delighted with the idea of visiting the corsair's ship, and seeing the wonderful lion, hearing its history, and seeing the daring crew of corsairs, Lady Clarence tripped away to perform her toilet.

In her romantic mind there was something very

beautiful in going to see a wild horde of daring rovers.

Earl Greymoor sent a message to the countess.

A reply came—brief, and to the point.

She was indisposed at the present moment, did not feel inclined to leave her chamber, or see anyone yet.

The message was brought before Cyril, and the earl turned away with a nervous twitching of his nether lip.

'Dare I suspect?' he inaudibly muttered, ' no—no, I dare not.'

Lady Clarence appeared. She looked beautiful, radiant with pleasure, a-glow with the freshness of morn upon her cheeks, and her eyes sparkling with joy.

Greymoor was debating how he should perform the journey.

'We will take the break,' he said, 'drive as far as the rocks, and then walk.'

'Could you spare a messenger, a confidential person?' asked Cyril.

'Yes.'

The earl summoned the groom of his chamber.

'Cyril turned towards the earl's confidant.

'Would you ride down to the cliffs, and when in sight of a boat you will see near the shore, wave this?' He gave the man a small roll of silk. 'Should a stranger in naval attire ask you from whom you come, give him that ring, and if he returns one similar, give him this note.'

The confidential servant retired, pleased with the confidence reposed in him.

Shortly after, the party set out for the rocky-bound shore.

Scarcely had the earl, with Cyril and Clarence, left the grounds, than the countess was up and rang for her maid.

'They are gone, Pastora?'

'Yes, my lady,' replied the maid, an Italian, nearly as beautiful as herself, and younger, though she did not look it.

Pastora was extremely confidential. Her mistress could trust her with any secret. The countess knew it, and kept her for her value on that account.

In private they stood on a more familiar footing than lady and lady's maid.

Throwing herself gracefully into an easy chair, the countess fell into a deep reverie, while Pastora quietly prepared the toilet,* she sat with one hand clasped in the other, her lovely orbs cast down, and her flowing tresses hung about her shoulders in enchanting disorder.

Pastora stood behind her chair, and began the operation of dressing the luxurious hair; and while the countess sat in this quiet, dreamy state, and her face had the complacent look of an angel, her brain was filled with terrible thoughts.

'Cyril was in the house,' so ran her ideas, forming themselves into unspoken words. 'He must have been with her. Tremble, my haughty Lady Clarence, for I will bring you down yet. That for him—the old dotard! I'——

'What is that noise on the back staircase, Pastora?' she asked, aloud.

The beautiful Italian went to ascertain.

'A rough-looking man, who evidently knows the secret entrance, wants to see you, my lady.'

---

* See front page No. 13.

'Hasten, then, with my toilet. I will see the knave.'

A dangerous light burned in the lovely woman's flashing eye as she spoke.

Had the unwelcome visitor seen it, he would have retired, and thought himself fortunate.

Pastora completed the toilet.

The countess put on a long morning robe, and waited for the visitor.

He came—a rough, surly-looking, brutal man—such a one as, if met in a long lane on a dusky night, would be shunned with the utmost caution.

'Your business!—and how dared you trespass through that passage?'

So spake the countess, and the man stood momentarily awed.

'I hid there all night. I know you. I knowed you when you come and hired me; so I thought I'd see you this morning.'

'For what?'

'Eh?'——

'Speak, insolent dog!'

'Insolent dog, am I? Well, I don't know; he ain't dead yet, is he?'

'He'——

'Yes, the earl; and they can't hang me for what I didn't do, can they? But they could the woman as paid us to do it.'

The countess went pale as marble, and quite as cold.

She clenched her hands and lips—then waited for the ruffian to proceed.

'I wants the reward, I does. It's worth it, for keeping quiet. And I wants you to get my mate out of the jug.

'Jug?'

'Yes, prison.'

'And if you have the money, and your companion is released?'

'Oh! then, I'll do whatever you wish.'

A terrible look came in the eyes of the beautiful demon.

'Very well, I will do it; but you must go abroad.'

'Whenever yer likes.'

'And your companion shall be released.'

'If he ain't, he'll split.'

The countess coloured. The language was too coarse and vulgar for her delicate ears, and she shuddered.

'He'll blow—tell all about it.'

Now she understood it.

'You speak faintly,' she said.

'So would you, ma'am, if you'd been in that passage all night.'

'Since I still want you to do something ere you go, I will pay you well for it.'

'What is it?'

The countess fell into a deep reverie.

'You require the full reward?' she said.

'Yes.'

'But I promised you a thousand pounds among the three of you.'

'Well, if one chooses to get killed, it ain't my fault, is it?'

'But you did not succeed.'

'No, but it's all as well 'cos we ain't; if we'd done

it, we couldn't a told, but now we only attempted it, we can tell who told us to do it.'

' But if you are paid?'

' Ah! that makes a difference, it does.'

' The money will be between you and your companions.'

' Yes,' growled the ruffian, discontentedly.

' Then I'll pay you when he is out of prison, or you will not share it.'

' He is a blab, and no good.'

' How much is he worth?'

' Worth?'

' Yes; I think, as you say, he is not to be trusted; he is a coward and a sneak.'

' If he was to split,' growled the ruffian, ' I'd slit his wizzen.'

The beautiful temptress stepped forward, and, though she loathed the act, she put her hand on his shoulder, and said, with a smile—

' I am in danger; you could help me out of it. *He* is in the way, and a dangerous companion for you. Would you go and see him, and take him some *wine*, it would remove him from danger, and the reward should be doubled, and all yours.'

The beauty of the speaker intoxicated the ruffian. The hand upon his shoulder thrilled him through. He looked up; the smile he saw went to his heart's core, and he gasped—

' I will do it!'

CHAPTER LVIII.

THE MEETING.

' HAVE I killed her?' broke from Rodwin Blake's lips, as Pauline fell forward into his arms, cold and senseless.

He held back her head, and looked into the rigid face.

' Pauline! speak—speak to me!'

She answered not.

He chafed her cold hand—stroked back the hair from her marble brow.

' Pauline!'

His voice again took an almost silvery tone of tenderness.

' Pauline! Speak to me in, the name of—of *Julian*!'

The pronunciation of that name acted like magic upon Pauline.

' Julian,' she murmured, ' can you mention the name of the brother you *murdered*?'

' Pauline, hush!'

' Oh, Victor! what am I brought here for?'

' Safety; and you are safe.'

' Victor, I implore you to let me be with Madeline! You will give me my liberty?'

' Yes.'

' But Madeline—where is she?'

' Safe yet; but listen, Pauline; let me finish my story. When I committed the fearful deed that has ever haunted me, I returned to the place where my ship lay, and found it gone. I came to England, changed my name, and took the lieutenancy on board the Sorcerer. I have watched Gregory Saunders wherever he went, and I swore to have revenge whenever I should find an opportunity. You hear me, Pauline, and he shall suffer tenfold what I have. You would scarcely think I could live so long by the side of a man I so bitterly hate

without driving my sword through him? But I do. I would not have revenge that way. I hate him. I watch him like a cat watches a mouse, and the revenge I will have shall repay me for the time I have waited.'

Pauline shuddered. She knew the nature of the speaker.

He was no idle boaster.

' I will leave you, Pauline, for an instant, and see to him. If the girl is alone, you shall go to her.'

Blake discovered Gregory on deck. Then he went and conducted Pauline to the cabin where Madeline was kept a prisoner.

There was a secret antipathy between Saunders and Rodwin Blake.

Gregory feared him, and Rodwin knew it.

Rodwin would work out his purpose with a cold, unflinching nerve.

He knew Gregory would sell his soul to get him out of the way, and he kept a strict watch.

Rodwin worked in the dark.

Secretly he had the game in his own hands, and he had only one regret—that was, Gregory Saunders was not a worthy antagonist.

The Sorcerer was speeding out to sea, and Gregory kept up his assumed character as lawful captain of the vessel.

He feared the outburst that would follow his treachery being discovered. He could not trust his crew—or very few of them.

One man he watched with the eye of a hawk— Tom Hawkins, the coxswain.

Gregory had an idea the old fellow knew all about the late affair.

The old fellow did, and had mentally sworn to keep a watch upon his captain, and save the love of Gerald Stuart at the cost of his life.

Gregory Saunders was slowly pacing the quarter-deck now.

Rodwin Blake approached unheard.

Gregory was muttering darkly, when the pirate's cold hand fell upon his shoulder.

Gregory shuddered.

' We have sailed well.'

The words were spoken in a cold, meaningless tone. It had neither triumph nor joy in it.

Gregory turned and faced him.

I have succeeded. Now comes the triumph.'

' I should not be in too much of a hurry.'

' You would not. I never wait while the power is in my hands.'

' You should be careful how you use it.'

Gregory laughed scornfully.

' Base dogs! They would not dare question my right.'

' Indeed!'

' No; they are too used to a servile life to dare to gainsay my wishes.'

' Do not be too sure. There is one there who would inform the men the nature of your crime.'

Blake pointed to Hawkins.

Gregory ground his teeth.

' I have my eyes upon him,' he said.

' Take my advice. Wait until you are a little further out to sea, and sound your men.'

' Wait—wait. Shall I wait any longer?'

' Wait at least a day or two. Leave the men to me. I will see to them.'

' What would you do?'

'Secretly discover who would alter their course. Get their names down ; and, if they are the greatest number, you can do as you like with the rest.'

'I will leave it to you.'

Gregory said this because he could not help himself.

It was one of those things in which he was lost. He could not act himself, and, much as he mistrusted and feared Blake, he was willing to let him do it.

'I can remove him then,' he thought, 'should he dare thwart me.'

Like most men who have gone deeply into crime, Gregory Saunders gave way to the next degrading vice—

Drink.

He dared not remain quiet, or entirely sober ; his conscience would not let him.

He was too much the coward to stare fate in the face, and he sought oblivion the better.

Rodwin Blake smiled when he saw this. He knew how much a man's mind is worth when stupified with drink, and he went on working silently, though dangerously, in the dark.

The second day passed, the third night came. Gregory had been seen on deck very little. Rodwin Blake seemed to take absolute command of the ship.

Gregory was half-mad with drink when he sent for the officers of the ship and Blake.

Rodwin had foreseen this, and had prepared the men he had hired on the night of Gregory's escape, with several others of the crew, who were ready to do anything for the daring adventurer, and when he heard the orders for the officers to see Gregory in his cabin, he stationed the men he could trust near the door.

They were armed to the teeth.

The last two days most of the officers and the crew had had a dogged reservedness about them.

The ship's duties were done, but few words were said. The harmony of the ship's company was broken up, and the men worked away with a gloomy air, and talked in little groups to each other.

The officers came, and bowed coldly to the captain, who sat at the head of the table, endeavouring to disguise his half-drunken condition.

Blake sat by his side.

Wine was brought in by the dozen, large silver goblets were placed upon the table, and Gregory told his subordinates to drink.

The men did so, but almost in silence, and the officers continually exchanged meaning glances with the second lieutenant.

Gregory Saunders saw the dull indifference in which they all partook of his hospitality.

'You are not merry, gentlemen.'

'We are not, captain.'

The reply started Gregory, and he looked up with a drunken stare.

'How ? What ails you ?'

'On behalf of myself and brother officers, Captain Saunders, I shall act as spokesman.'

'Well ?'

'It is usual for the government orders to be made known ere this, I believe.'

'Do you ?'

The lieutenant did not reply.

'Whose master here ?'

'You are ; but we have heard something which would put your right aside.'

'From whom ?'

'One of the crew.'

'Enough. Go on deck. I am master here, and you have to obey me. Go to your duty ; and, remember, insubordination will be death !'

The officer turned to his companions.

'Not a word !' thundered Gregory, staggering to his feet, 'not a word. I am commander, and will be obeyed.'

The officers went on deck : Gregory followed them.

'Officer of marines,' he called, 'arrest that man !'

His finger pointed to Hawkins, and the poor old fellow was arrested—none knew what for.

'Why am I arrested ?' said the old boatswain, indignantly.

'Silence, sir !' String him up. Give him two dozen.'

The men murmured. The second lieutenant of the Sorcerer turned quietly to the excited captain, and asked, gently—

'What crime is the boatswain, Hawkins, accused of ?'

'That is my affair, sir ; do as I order.'

'I] believe,' persisted the lieutenant, Mr. White, 'I believe it is usual for the offence or crime, as it may be, to be brought before the officers ere such extreme measures as flogging are resorted to.'

'String that hound up, I say !' almost shrieked Saunders, 'string him up !'

Not a man stirred. The murmur grew louder. Threatening looks went from one to the other. The purport was dangerous to the lawless wretch who commanded them.

'My lads—messmates,' cried Hawkins, 'you can rebel without fear of punishment. He is a traitor to his king and country. He was thrown into prison for murder and bigamy, that's having a lot of wives, that is,' said the old fellow, wishing to leave no doubt upon the minds of the men. 'He was thrown into prison for his villany, and escaped by murdering the poor fellows who guarded him, and why he wants me flogged, is because I appeared against him at his trial ; more than that, he's got the Lord High Admiral's daughter on board, the cursed pirate ! and he'll hang yet !'

The men groaned in disgust at the man who had been their leader.'

'Messmates !' cried Hawkins, in a louder key, 'will you see me flogged like a dog for nothing ?'

'No ! no !'

The crew, roused to a pitch of desperation, gathered aft. Lieutenant White saw how matters stood, and addressed Gregory.

'Mr. Saunders,' he said, 'your proceedings are unlawful. This dare not proceed.'

'Dare not !' echoed the baffled villain, with a drunken stagger ; 'dare not ! Who dares dispute my right ?'

'I do, in the name of justice ; and will dare more. Unless this ship's course is put back, boatswain Hawkins released, and we are allowed to return into port by our own free will, I shall arrest you as a traitor.'

Saunders foamed at the mouth with fury.

'Mutiny, by God !' he yelled, drawing a pistol from his belt ; and with a pitiless laugh he shot poor Lieutenant White through the head.

Then the tempest broke. The men gave a simultaneous cry of horror and revenge, and rushing forward, would have torn Gregory from the quarter-deck but for the appearance of Rodwin Blake.

BLACK EYED SUSAN;

OR, PIRATES ASHORE.

'MATE,' SAID THE SMUGGLER, 'D'YE KNOW YOU'RE IN DANGER?'

'Hold. fools!' he said—his peculiar, cold, keen voice ringing in the ears of the excited men.

Even the appearance of this iron-willed man would not have restrained the crew, but he had forty men, armed to the teeth, at his back; each held a long-barrelled gun in his hand, and covered a man with the deadly tube.

Boatswain Hawkins had already been cut down and given his liberty.

Saunders, sobered by his recent danger, and his heart quailing with fear, fell back among the men with Blake.

'This is very much like mutiny,' said Blake, glaring round upon the men. 'What does it mean?'

The sailors were silent.

'How many of you wish to grace the yard-arm?' continued Rodwin Blake.

'Now,' said Saunders, coming forward—he saw the strange power his confederate had over the men, and he wanted the power entirely in his own hands; so he came forward, and under the pretence of being lenient, he thought to gain his men's favour—'I have for some time been the commander of most of you on board; you have been led to battle and glory by me. Is it not so?'

'Ay, ay!' came rather sullenly from some of the crew.

'You served me and your country well. I never neglected the interest of my government by word or deed; but I am now, through the work of my enemies, under the hand of the law. Were I to return to port, there would be a prison for me. That is the gratitude I should receive. Would you all desert me in the hour of need?'

The sailors were silent.

'If I desert my country, I shall not turn my guns against it. I shall fight under another flag until I can repay you, my lads, for your devotion, and when this cruise is out, you, one and all, shall be made independent, and do as I shall—live abroad.'

The low murmur that came from the men sounded very much like approval.

'We, or I, shall be termed by my country a traitor, but you will now have the appellation of smuggler or pirate. The hazard is small. I simply wish you to stand by me during this cruise; you shall have sufficient money after that to live in comfort. Is that not fair?'

'Ay, ay, sir.'

'Let those who will not join me stand out. They shall be put ashore on the first opportunity.'

More than one-third of the original crew of the Sorcerer stood out.

'Very well,' said Saunders. 'I shall give you all until to-morrow to decide, and they who choose to alter their minds between this and then may do so. Now, to your duty, my men.'

There was a faint cheer, and the crew went one by one to their duty.

Rodwin Blake had been a quiet spectator of the scene. His lips curled in quiet contempt; for, much as Saunders thought he had the cards in his own hands, Rodwin held the ace, and would play it ere long.

Gregory gave him a look that spoke plainer than words—

'I am master!'

Then the traitor went below.

A small cabin had been fitted up for Madeline, but Blake, knowing she was not safe a moment, had the berth made into two small cabins that Pauline could

be near the admiral's daughter to render assistance should it ever be necessary.

Gregory stole to his cabin, and again sat over the wine, while Rodwin Blake kept upon deck.

Gregory Saunders kept himself quiet for a few nights. He thought he ruled supreme there; and his sinister brain was working to know how he could get Blake out of his way.

He had taken to drink, and this alone damped his energies, and left Rodwin his master in every way.

Saunders drank to drown remorse; drank to sustain his brutal courage and instinct when it was waning; and, while he was doing this and dreaming of his triumph to come—triumph over Blake, over Madeline, whom he thought his, and that he had only to seek her to find her in his power—while, I say, he spent his time thus, strange things were going on among the men.

Blake was often among them. Hawkins was with them. The men skulked about in little knots, talking and whispering together, and Saunders knew it not.

Four nights passed after the mutiny.

Saunders had been drinking more than ever, and his head was filled with a lot of maudlin notions of his power, and so forth.

He upbraided himself for being a fool, and putting off his desire so long. He would seek Madeline now.

The night was late—quietness reigned through the ship.

Gregory staggered up from his seat, and stole towards the door.

Drunk as he was, he had cunning enough left to know that a noise would betray him.

He slipped off his boots.

Then he stole towards the cabin in which Madeline slept.

He found the door locked, and a fiendish grin overspread his face.

He was not baffled.

He possessed a duplicate key, and opened the door noiselessly.

A tiny night lamp burned in the cabin, and displayed to his burning gaze the lovely sleeper, as she lay—her lily shoulders uncovered, one beautifully-moulded arm lying outside the bed-covering.

His blood grew almost to fever heat. He trembled from the intensity of his unconquerable passion. His breath came short and thick.

The sight of the sleeping beauty almost sobered him.

In his wild excitement he forgot he had left the cabin door open, and a gush of wind coming down the hatchway shut it with a loud click.

Madeline started, turned, and opened her eyes. Saunders drew aside, and concealed himself behind a curtain.

With instinctive modesty, Madeline, in her dreamy stupor, covered her bared shoulders, and again fell off to sleep.

Then Gregory stole from his hiding place. He clutched a small phial in his hand, and he crept on tiptoe towards the slumbering girl.

He was by her bedside—leant over her; his presence seemed to trouble her even in her sleep.

She turned and shifted about, and at the moment he thought she was going to awake, he drew the cork from the neck of the phial, placed the tiny bottle to her nose, and put his lewd grasp upon her shoulder.

A short fierce struggle went on with the poor defenceless girl. She seemed choking and fighting to keep off a terrible lethargy that stole upon her.

But it was useless; the powerful drug was too strong, and she lay inanimate and in a state of semi-consciousness.

A low, exultant chuckle broke from the villain's lips as he contemplated his devilish work; but it died away, as a tall majestic form stood before him.

It was Pauline.

She had entered noiselessly from her cabin by the communicating door. The expression of her face was beyond description.

Her eyes glared with all the suppressed fury of a tigress; her hand clutched a long, keen dagger. She was in her night robe, and her hair hung down her back and over her shoulders.

The first feeling of fear passing off, Gregory stood spell-bound with her beauty.

'Ha! ha!' he said, 'I did not know there was so much beauty within my grasp, or'——

He paused. Pauline took one step near him: the dagger was uplifted, and she said—

'Begone!'

He read by her look that she would not speak again, and he shuddered as he contemplated himself weltering on the floor—her dagger in his heart.

———

CHAPTER LIX.

CAST UPON THE SEA.

WHEN Tom Hatchett got Black-eyed Susan in his power by defeating the ruffian hirelings of Gregory Saunders, he went without delay to the house of the respectable Silas Doggrass, to acquaint him with the fortunate occurrence.

'Aha, Captain Tom, my boy!'

'Well, old stick, how d'ye bear up in this foul weather?'

'Pretty well, Tom—pretty well. Have you heard of my last misfortune?'

'No, mate.'

'Why, not that Susan has been stolen from the house of his lordship?'

'Has she, though?'

Doggrass looked up.

'You don't seem concerned about it much.'

'No, Mr. Doggrass; nor do you—at least about the loss. It's *her money* you are thinking of—eh?'

He poked Silas in the ribs with his thumb, and laughed loudly.

'Pish!—a paltry nothing.'

'Is it, now? Well, why the devil did you take her away from her husband? Would you have paid me handsomely for doing it, if the cash was a paltry nothing—eh? Ah, well, old stick, don't get into a funk about nothing. You're all right, and your money's safe.'

'How? What do you mean, Tom?'

'Mean? Why, the pretty lass is on board my craft—safe, old man, in my cabin, and there by fair means.'

'Fair means!' said the old sinner.

'Ay, old choker—by fair means. I rescued her from the —— pirates, who stole her from the house of the admiral.'

'Gad, Tom, that was a good stroke!'

Doggrass brightened up wonderfully—rubbed his hands, grinned all over his face, and patted Tom Hatchett on the back.

'Come, now, Tom—can I trust you this time?'

'How?'

'You won't bring her back?'

'Don't fear, Doggrass; *I* shall not bring her back. I've a spanking ship now, and can go anywhere. You are all safe now, Mister Doggrass. Get the lass's money' (he strode towards the door and stood in the passage), 'and enjoy it.'

Then he shut the door with a bang, and left the house.

'And enjoy it!' muttered Doggrass. 'Humph!'

* * * * * *

When Black-eyed Susan awoke from her unconsciousness, she found herself in the cabin of a vessel, and by the violent rocking, she guessed the craft was ploughing through a heavy sea.

A deep sigh escaped her; her senses were as yet confused; she was ignorant of what ship she was on, or whose hands she had fallen into, when the door slowly opened, and a little black girl entered.

She glanced timidly round, and approached the bed on tip-toe. When she found Susan's beautiful eyes fixed upon her, she started.

'Oh, missy, you so frighten Zebra!'

'Come here, child.'

The child—who was, in truth, nearly sixteen years old—went to Susan's side.

'Where am I?'

'On massa's ship. Massa good and kind to lady; he good and kind to Zebra, too.'

'Who is your master?'

'Cap'n Hatchett. He no hurt you. He lub you, Missey Susan; no be afraid; de cap'n no hurt you.'

'I am not afraid, child; but I knew not for the moment where I was. I remember all now.'

'Will missey take somet'ink to eat and drink? Zebra, pour some ob dat down missey's t'roat; dat bring you to. Me go now, and fetch the chocolate for missey.' And the kind-hearted little black girl ran off without giving Susan time to refuse.

Zebra was not a full-bred mulatto; she was half-caste; and, if not exactly beautiful, there was a pretty expression on her face at times.

She was not long ere she returned with a large hardware cup of steaming chocolate, a cold fowl, and some bread. She placed them before Black-eyed Susan; and, in spite of her depressed spirits, she felt tempted to partake of it.

On another tray, lying upon the swing-table, were wine and biscuits; and gallant Will's pretty wife could not help inwardly noticing the attention paid her.

'You no like that; you want wine.'

'No, thank you, Zebra; I do not feel inclined to take anything.'

'But, missey, take dis. Oh, do, or you make poor Zebra cry.'

Susan saw the faithful little nurse was really hurt to think she would not touch any of the refreshment, and, therefore, partook of the chocolate.

'Where do you sleep?' she asked of the black girl.

'On de floor, near missey's bed, if she let me.'

'Nay, my good child, it would be unkind of me

to let you,' replied Susan, touched by the girl's sudden attachment.

'Den Zebra sleep on de mat outside de door.'

So Susan saw there was nothing to be gained by not allowing her faithful attendant to remain, and, upon seconds thoughts, she altered her mind.

The child would be a safeguard to her, and Zebra stayed.

It was nearly morning now; and, in spite of the violent agitation of her mind, Susan now slept, and after a few hours' troubled slumber, she awoke to find her dark-skinned attendant stealing softly about the cabin, putting every little thing in its place, and preparing the cabin for the day.

Susan felt very wretched, as she thought of the fate of Madeline and Pauline.

After she had breakfasted, little Zebra informed her that Tom Hatchett wanted to see her.

'I will see him soon,' she replied; and Zebra carried the message to Tom Hatchett.

'All right, my little ebony. Say I won't trouble her till afternoon.'

Susan's attendant only laughed at being called 'little ebony,' and ran off to her mistress.

Susan was glad of this respite.

She knew she had him to thank for her safety; but she also knew that he would do as much as that purely from self-interest. Still she felt assured she would have to see him, and she was safer in the power of Tom Hatchett than Gregory Saunders.

Late in the day Tom Hatchett entered her cabin. He had dressed himself for the occasion, and, certain it is, that he had not been seen so smart for many a long month.

'Hope you are better, Miss Susan'——

'Mrs. Howard, Captain Hatchett.'

'Excuse me, Mrs. Howard, but knowing you so long under the name of Pretty Black-eyed Susan, I could not bring myself to remember you had been married.'

Tom Hatchett's seemed to lose his roughness while in the company of the woman he was mad enough to love.

'I have you to thank, Captain Hatchett, for my deliverance from those monsters. But why did you bring me out to sea?'

'Because I couldn't help it,' said the gallant captain, after a pause.

'Could not help it?'

'No. Where was I to take you?'

'To my cottage on the cliff. Dame Hartley would have taken care of me.'

'Would she?' thought Tom Hatchett. 'So would Doggrass.' Aloud he said, 'I will tell you, Susan, for I can't call you anything else. You have unknown enemies. Had I left you on shore you would have seen a worse fate than this. Your life was in danger while near that accursed Deal. More than that, I could not stay in the roads. My time is short to journey to Brest, and I therefore brought you with me. I had another reason besides.'

'Another reason?' asked Susan, wonderingly.

'Ay. There was no one to take care of you—no one.'

'William would soon come home.'

Tom Hatchett laughed.

'You are mistaken there. He come home? Bah! He's got a dozen wives before this, if he is alive at all.'

Susan went deadly pale, and her hand went to her breast to still its wild throbbings.

'False!—'tis false, Captain Hatchett!' she gasped.

'Is it? Why did he go away?'

He paused as though for a reply, but did not get one.

'Was there not room enough on the Golden Arrow for you? Was he *compelled* to leave Deal? Could he not have taken a house for you away from that infernal town, and placed you in security?'

Susan was staggered. This way of looking at things was new to her. She did not doubt the motives of her husband for a minute; yet a vague idea that he *need not* have left her so, stole upon her.

'What,' Hatchett continued, 'would have become of you, had you depended upon *him* for aid? and yet, while he is prowling the seas, those you despise are watching over you.'

Susan hung her head in abject misery.

She understood him.

'Perhaps the king's ship drove him away,' she pleaded.

'Did the king's ship drive me away. No, Susan, you were in danger, and to have saved you I would have dared all England's fleet. Yet you do not thank me for it. You want to know why I did not leave you on shore. I will reveal all to you anon—all that now should have been kept from you.'

He went almost to her side, and continued, in a low voice—

'Know you, Susan, that had I left you in Deal, there would have been an old vampire close upon you, and for gold that old villain would sell his right hand —his heart's blood, did it not kill him, and for gold he would have *spilt your blood*.'

Susan shuddered and covered her face with her hands.

'Oh, horror! who can this monster be? I have no gold.'

'No, but he has, belonging to you. It was left, Susan, by your father, and he, your uncle Doggrass, has that money, and while you live he cannot use it. Thus it was to save you, Susan, that I brought you away—to save you, and because I love you.'

Tom Hatchett clutched her hand in both his own, and went down upon his knees. It was the first time in his life he had ever done so to a woman.

'Susan'—he said—' Susan, don't despise rough and uncultivated Tom Hatchett. I could be gentle to you—give you wealth and happiness in plenty. Do—do not spurn me.'

Susan was horrified at this passionate appeal. At first her eyes flashed in terrible anger, but she remembered her defenceless condition, and feared to make her captor a foe. She thought her misery would never end, and, thoroughly overcome, she burst into a bitter flood of tears.

'Captain Hatchett, I pray you—I implore you to get up—to leave me. Is this your boasted friendship and kindness? Oh, God! I wish I had died on the cliffs from which I was rescued, and then my troubles would be at an end. False friends surround me on every side, and they are the worst enemies.'

She dashed the tears away, and boldly confronted Captain Hatchett. He had long since risen to his feet: he looked troubled and concerned at her grief.

'No, Captain Hatchett, I cannot—will not, listen to your proposal. I am in your power. You may kill me, keep me in captivity, do ought you list, but you will never make me faithless to my beloved husband. Leave the cabin, if you are a man—much less a friend.'

Captain Hatchett was deadly pale, a fearful struggle seemed going on within him. His fingers worked nervously, and his ashy lips quivered as though he had been seized with the cold.

''Tis well, Mrs. Howard; you have said enough. My crime has been in loving you—my deeds that of kindness. You may think better some day. When I return from Brest you shall be put ashore in Deal, and then you will see who was or is your enemy; and, should you ever think better of Tom Hatchett, remember you were the first woman he ever loved, and, so help me heaven! you shall be the last.'

And he kept his word.

While Susan was bewildered, scarcely knowing what to understand, he left the cabin.

Little Zebra entered instantly, and ran to her weeping mistress, and wept too.

Susan was not annoyed with Captain Hatchett's company during the rest of the voyage. If she went on deck he always gave her the weather side, after passing the ordinary compliments of the day.

While the vessel lay in at Brest lots of nice little delicacies were sent from shore to Susan without a word from any one, and in her heart she thanked Tom Hatchett for his manly, disinterested kindness.

He had soon completed his arrangements in the port, and was ready to sail in less than a week after his arrival.

But he was very prudent, and waited for night that he might steal out, under cover of darkness, with his contraband cargo.

The night turned out very favourably for his purpose. The atmosphere was thick, or what is usually known as 'muggy,' not a star shed forth its twinkling light, and the sea was running sluggishly.

A stiff breeze blew off shore, and this was an addition to the facilities Tom Hatchett had to run out.

Everything was conducted on board with necessary silence, and the gallant schooner soon left the still waters of the harbour.

'Safe!' said Tom Hatchett, the moment the vessel was in the open sea; but he had never so gravely erred in his life.

It so happened that some interested person or persons had very wantonly pried into the affairs of other people, and also the rakish schooner, commanded by Tom Hatchett, and the day previous to his leaving the port, the governor had been warned, and his suspicions aroused concerning this craft that came and went like a phantom in the darkness, and the consequences were very grave.

A fully-manned brig stood outside the harbour in wait for Tom Hatchett's craft. This the gallant smuggler did not even suspect, or he might have been a little better prepared to meet his foe.

Not many minutes after he had flattered, or deceived himself, that he was safe, Bill Raker uttered an oath.

'D——, Tom, look there.'

'Hallo—a ship by St. Peter!'

'She doesn't show any lights.'

'No, and where the devil's she coming to '——

'Bah!' exclaimed Raker, clutching Tom Hatchett by the arm, 'it's a trap.'

Tom Hatchett seemed to fully understand what his mate meant, for he uttered a fierce oath.

'We're too late to fight.'

'And if we did, the noise of the guns would bring half a-dozen lubberly Frenchmen down upon us.'

'What's to be done?' asked Tom Hatchett, in despair.

'Wait, and let's see what she intends doing.'

The purpose of the brig was very obvious—without a light, her sails half furled, her men on deck, and the guns protruding from the port-holes—in this war-like style she came full upon the beam of the smuggler's craft.

'The game's gone too far, Tom, for us to do any good by being d—d obstinate.'

'Shouldn't think of it,' replied Hatchett. 'But there's Mrs. Howard—she mustn't fall into the hands of these French lubbers. There's only one choice. Get the jollyboat ready and launched on the lee side. I'll palarver with the fellow while you do that.'

'What good is it?'

'You'll see.' Then he turned to his men,—'My lads, it's no use us being obstinate; we had better give in quietly. Some of you hide in the coal-boxes or anywhere. There may be a dream of retaking the craft. Conceal some small arms about you.'

The French brig was so close now that her bowsprit almost scraped the schooner, and her commander hailed—

Hatchett answered with—

'Ahoy''

The French captain shouted for two or three minutes, but Tom Hatchett understood very little of what he said, and therefore remained quiet.

Monsieur began to get angry at receiving no reply, and at length a voice shouted in broken English—

'Ahoy!'

'Ahoy!' shouted Hatchett.

'Am I speaking to de captain of de schooner?'

'Ay—ay.'

'Den you must lay to, or monsieur le captain will fire into you.'

Opposition was useless, and while the brig bore round to put the men on board, Tom Hatchett went below to Susan.

'Mrs. Howard, I am very sorry to intrude, but we are in the hands of the French; and, unless you come on board at once, we are lost.'

Susan in strange wonderment allowed him to lead her on deck.

'Boat ready?' asked Tom, in a thick whisper.

'Ay. Everything there.'

'Come on, then.'

'No, you go with Mrs. Howard, Tom. I'll stop and see if I can't outwit these gentlemen yet. Take my advice, Tom. Don't endanger her life. Run into port. The boat and the men are ready.'

Then Tom Hatchett and Susan were lowered into the jollyboat, and they crept slowly from under the lee of the vessel. The sea was rougher and the wind stronger than Tom Hatchett had expected. The boat rocked fearfully, and was dashed about like a tiny cork.

The men looked at each other. Susan clung to Captain Tom in wild terror, and he was bewildered. In a few minutes both vessels had faded from view in the darkness. No shore light could be seen, and he was ignorant of the course the boat was taking.

The men plied their oars and pulled unceasingly for hours. Still no sign of land, and a terrible idea forced itself upon Tom Hatchett, and he shuddered, for he saw now it was too late to avert their fate—that they were drifting hopelessly out to sea.

So the wretched night passed, and when morning came the smuggler captain saw the prospect of death by wreck or starvation before them.

The men in the boat stared blankly at each other;

then their glances, full of pity, fell upon Black-eyed Susan. She sat in the stern sheets of the boat. Her face was overcast with a shadow of despairing gloom.

To many it would seem as though we overrated the horrors of their position, considering they had a good boat and had only been cast upon the sea the previous night. But in the excitement of the trying moment when the vessel was boarded by the Frenchmen and Tom Hatchett had to make his escape, the necessity of provisions was forgotten.

Thus Tom Hatchett's forebodings were not without just cause. They had drifted far out to sea during the night. There was no sign of a ship or land. There was every indication of a calm setting in, the horror of which, without water or food, few could possibly survive.

A calm did set in. The sun poured down a flood of scorching light, burning and blistering the human beings confined to that fragile boat.

The first part of the day passed without any apparent signs of the men's sufferings, but towards evening they felt their insides were being gnawed with hunger, their throats parched with thirst, their lips blackening and cracking like parchment.

Tom Hatchett was silent, and hung his head down in abject misery. His selfish love for the beautiful Susan Howard made him inwardly curse himself as the cause of her misfortunes.

Night came, and brought with it a little respite from the burning heat of the day. But, alas, it soon passed: another day followed. The still polished surface of the treacherous ocean appeared as though it had been burnished. Not a breath of air was stirring, and the sun glared down from the centre of the spotless azure canopy above like a monster ball of fire, and the horror of their position began now to steal upon the boat-load of human beings.

The oars were deserted, the sail hoisted as an awning to keep the blistering rays of the sun off, and the men crouched beneath it while the boat lay almost motionless on the water.

None had tasted either food or drink since they embarked in the tiny vessel, and now the men were becoming mad under the tortures of their trying situation. The men's faces were distorted and ghastly; their eyes unnatural in their glare—wolfish, in fact, and their jaws dropped, until their features were pitifully horrible.

Two days and two nights they had been cast upon the sea, and now the poor fellows were nothing better than skeletons. Black-eyed Susan bore up bravely; but the mental suffering she went through could be seen by the convulsive workings of her face.

The third day came: still the wind kept off. The pitiless sun sent its blistering flood of light down upon the poor castaways. The remorseless ocean looked glaring and transparent as before. Hunger increased—thirst became maddening. Greedy, longing eyes were cast upon the sportive wavelets, and famished, blistering tongues lolled out, in eager anticipation of the treacherous liquid.

All of this Tom Hatchett saw, but did not notice, because he felt it. But he fancied he detected something more to be feared. Long, lingering glances had been cast upon Black-eyed Susan; and then the starving wretches had looked meaningly into each other's wolfish eyes, but exchanged no word to betray the terrible purport in their hearts.

Many groaned and raved in mad delirium. One, a huge burly smuggler, dragged himself to the gunnel of the boat, and dipped a baler into the sea.

Susan saw the act, and, turning to Tom Hatchett, she said, in a low, hoarse whisper—

' Save him.'

' Stop him!' cried Hatchett; ' take it away, or he will go mad.'

The drinking vessel was snatched from the man, and he was hurled to the bottom of the boat, where he lay, cursing and raving so terribly that Susan shuddered, and buried her face in her hands.

Then the men drew into a little knot at the bow of the boat, and held a conference. Tom Hatchett shivered from head to foot; he saw long-bladed knives being drawn, and clutched in long bony hands, with murderous intent. The points of the weapons seemed to menace Susan, and bloodshot wolfish eyes were cast pitilessly upon her, and the crew turned their faces towards Tom Hatchett.

The crew crawled forward. They exchanged, or simultaneously uttered, a few stupefied words—' One to save all '—and they crawled on.

Black-eyed Susan looked at them with a fixed stare, in which could be read patient resignation.

' I shall die,' she said to Tom Hatchett. ' I have looked forward to this. May God forgive the deed, and rescue the poor creatures from their suffering.'

' No, no,' Hatchett said, with difficulty; ' they shall never kill you until they've finished me. I am armed. Let me get before you; let me '——

' Too late! Let me die.' A bony hand clutched her dress.

' Never! Back, curse ye! or '——

But the men paused not; they crowded upon each other, all looking at their anticipated prize, like so many demons or vultures.

———

CHAPTER LX.

WILL AMONG THE FRENCH.

WILLIAM HOWARD was totally lost to the movements of the men and officers around him; he did not even notice that Captain Gerald stood by his side.

If slowly, the Golden Arrow gained surely upon the strange sail; and that gave him hope. His excited brain already pictured the poor helpless girls at the mercy of the scoundrel who had dared so much. His heart beat wildly.

' Do you think her English?' inquired Gerald Stuart, breaking the heavy spell that held Will in a trance-like torpor.

He turned with a deep-drawn sigh, and while closing the glass he had held so long in his hand, replied—

' The Great Skipper alone knows, captain; but I hope it may be that infernal pirate. Maybe it is. If so, by all the bright stars that lead the mariner on his course, I will strangle the life from his black heart And may God forgive the deed.'

' We shall come up with them yet, Will. But that craft yonder seems too small to be a cruiser.'

Will raised his eyes wearily.

' Maybe,' he said, again scanning the strange sail. ' Why, it's a cutter!'

The Golden Arrow had run down so swiftly that the exact size of the distant vessel could be discerned.

Will gave an inward groan while Captain Gerald watched the cutter with growing interest, and shortly after left the deck.

From a huge box in his cabin he took several large

rolls of silk. He selected one and unfurled it, displaying the banner of the Pretender.

This he took upon deck, and ordered it to be hoisted at the mizzen peak; and the white flag, with the golden arrow worked upon it, to be hoisted to the mast-head.

A stiff breeze was blowing, and the rebel flag was spread out, and was seen by those on board the cutter.

The effect was a strange one. The sails the cutter had kept flying came with a run to the deck, and, veering round, she stood towards the Golden Arrow, much to Will's astonishment.

The cutter answered the signals hoisted by Gerald, and run up the rebel flag. The vessels were so near to each other now that Will could already define every outline of the beautiful little craft.

'The Freux,' he said; 'maybe that's something I never heard of.'

'It's a French name,' smiled Gerald. 'If I mistake not, meaning Rook.'

'Then she's a Frencher.'

'Not exactly, Will. She is on the same mission as ourselves, and an agent of the Young Pretender.'

Several signals were exchanged before the cutter became too confiding. It was satisfied at last, and stood off the weather quarter within hailing distance.

Gerald challenged the captain of the cutter, and was answered respectfully.

'Any dispatches?' shouted Gerald.

'Many, Captain Gerald. Things have begun in arnest. Lay-to, a boat shall come alongside.'

'I will prepare. Any one coming on board?'

'Yes.'

Both vessels became stationary upon the sun-lit sea, and a small boat, propelled by four rowers, put off from the cutter, and ran under the stern of the Golden Arrow.

The tiny craft contained two personages besides the rowers. One was the commander of the cutter, the other was evidently a personage of rank. He ascended to the deck of the Golden Arrow, and was quickly followed by the captain of the Freux.

The crew of the Golden Arrow were drawn up in regular state order; every one was dressed as he would have been at a review. The officers, Will included, stood by Captain Gerald in full uniform, and met the personage from the cutter with as much pomp as they would an admiral.

'Ah! my lord, I did not expect to see you here,' said Gerald.

'I did not think I should have been here so soon, but the crisis is at hand.'

'You will come below, my lord?'

'Yes. I have much of information to give you.'

'Secretly?'

'No. Those you can trust may be present.'

'Captain Smith, you will accompany us below?'

The captain of the cutter said he would, and followed the person Gerald had addressed as my lord to the chief cabin.

The persons seated round the table were Captain Gerald, Will, the second lieutenant, Andrew, Captain Smith, and the nobleman.

Gerald Stuart summoned Wilks, and ordered some of the best wine to be brought in; and when this was done, the cabin door closed, and the men left to themselves, they commenced business.

Lord George Clare broke the silence.

'We had feared your vessel had been destroyed or captured, Captain Stuart, from not having heard of you for so long. I was not so much surprised when I was in England; but, not hearing of you in France, was more than I could clearly understand.'

Gerald Stuart blushed.

'I hope you do not entertain any suspicion of my fidelity to the cause. But events, private occurrences (he thought of Madeline and blushed again), have kept me upon the sea, and so actively employed that'——

'Nay,' smiled his lordship. 'I have heard something of it by report. A lady was in the case—enough to know you are still faithful to the cause is all we want.'

Young Lord Clare—he was not more than twenty-five—drank a goblet of wine, which he seemed to approve of greatly.

'That is prime old vintage,' he said, pushing his glass towards Gerald. 'But I must continue. I suppose you have heard the Tory party in England have been persuading the Chevalier de St. George (viz., the Pretender) to come over. He expects to be met and joined by the Tories on his arrival in Great Britain.'

'On his own resources?' asked Gerald.

'No. He, like the rest of his family, has ever found a staunch ally in the King of France. Of course Louis has the matter hushed up as much as possible, but he aids the Chevalier in every possible manner.'

'He has great faith in Charles Stuart.'

'He believes that the throne of England will yet be the seat of the Chevalier.'

Gerald Stuart hoped it would be so, but he had doubts upon the subject.

'The Duke of Ormond and Lord Bolingbroke are in France. I saw them the night previous to my departure, and from them I heard how things are going on.'

'Can they do any good to the cause over there?'

'Well, yes. They keep up a continual correspondence with the Tories in Great Britain and are now at the service of the prince. The most important points are, a fleet is already being equipped in Havre for Charles Edward. There is no doubt that Louis XIV. will assist him in every possible manner.'

'The long-looked-for time is coming.'

'It is very near; and, unless you forsake your allegiance, your presence will be required at Havre. Take these letters, you will find instructions in them. But take care, spies are everywhere, and we may fail yet.'

'There is not a day to spare.'

'Not an hour. Put about at once. Sail direct for Havre, and let your energies be employed to their utmost in aiding the schemes of our prince. Get there safely, and others of our brotherhood will help you on.'

'You are not going back to France yet?'

'I cannot. The cutter has a cargo which I must look after.'

'Ah!' sighed Gerald. 'I can understand.'

'Have you anything on board the Golden Arrow?'

'Much that is necessary for the followers of the prince.'

'Then if we can find room for them on board, the better. You can disembark all you have, and sail with a clear ship.'

'True,' said Gerald, half dreamingly. He was thinking of Madeline, and Will was thinking of Susan.

He had appeared to join in the animated conversation between Burket and Captain Smith, but his ears were listening to catch every word that passed between Lord George Clare and Gerald.

The blood left his veins, and he felt sick at heart at the mere idea of having to follow the fortunes of the Pretender, while his wife was in the power of a lawless man like Saunders.

Lord George Clare rose from the table while talking to Captain Gerald.

'I am very sorry. I feel for you, knowing what you must suffer by having to give up the search after—perhaps—all you hold dear to you; but, Captain Stuart, remember your oath, duty to your sovereign before to yourself. He needs every strong arm and willing faithful heart about him that can be had, and in appealing to Captain Gerald Stuart I do not appeal in vain.'

Young Lord Clare was a man of strong and determined energies. He would have sacrificed his heart's blood, much less its love, for the young Prince he had sworn to follow.

'My lord,' responded Gerald, with equal promptitude, 'duty to my prince never was neglected, and shall not be now.'

''Tis well. Gentlemen,' turning towards the officers, 'adieu. Now, Captain Stuart, let what you have to be removed to the Freux be done at once. Time is precious. I must return on board.'

He went on deck. With him went the rest of the party, Captain Smith and Gerald bringing up the rear.

'There will be no danger in us running alongside each other? I have a few boxes to transmit to your ship, Captain Smith.'

'No danger, whatever. The sea is beautifully calm.'

Gerald turned to Will.

'Run the Golden Arrow a-beam of that craft, Will, and fix the grapnels.'

The Golden Arrow was soon run abreast of the Freux, and they were locked to each other; then the crew went to work, and in less than an hour numerous boxes and barrels were hoisted up from the hold of the Golden Arrow and deposited in the depths of the cutter's hull.

The casks and chests contained arms and ammunition for the rebels.

The arrangements being completed, the captain of the cutter retired from the Golden Arrow, followed by the young Jacobite leader, Lord Clare.

He paused with his foot upon the bulwark to address Gerald.

'Captain Stuart,' he said, turning his bronzed face towards the young chief, 'Remember—your king, and your oath.'

The grapnels were cast loose. The ships parted company, and sailed in opposite directions.

Captain Gerald turned gloomily towards Will.

'Fate,' he said, is against us; we can only trust to chance and providence to recover those dear to us, duty to my prince demands the sacrifice.'

'It's a great sacrifice,' Will said, with a heavy sigh.

'Yet I need not drag you into this, you never gave your oath to Prince Charles.'

'No,' bravely responded the gallant sailor, 'but I have given my oath to you, Captain Gerald, and I follow you, whatever the cause may be you risk your life in.'

'Then, Will, we must hope to discover some clue to the fate of those we love, and do our duty at the same time.'

Sail after sail was spread out upon the Golden Arrow, until, like a feathered arrow shot from a bow, she sped gaily through the deep blue sea.

No stoppage or interruption took place on the voyage, and at dusk one evening they found themselves in sight of Havre.

Even from the distance they were from the bustling seaport, lights could be seen dotting out in the darkness. The harbour was crowded with ships of nearly every description.

Darkness and a thick fog soon fell upon the sea, and the Golden Arrow was compelled to crawl in at little more than a snail's pace.

She ran right under the bowsprit of a French liner, and had not Will been at hand with his ever ready skill and courage, the gallant rebel craft would have suffered.

Havre was not then as it is now or even as it was sixty years ago. It was dull, badly lighted, the houses had a more cheerless aspect, and the harbour was, at night, as dreary as it was possible for any seaport like Havre to be.

At length, and after a great deal of labour, and difficulty, the Golden Arrow was anchored amidst a crowd of vessels, with the French pennant flying at her peak.

The vessel now being safe, there was an opportunity of exchanging a few words.

'Now, Will, I can lose no time; I must go ashore at once, and probably shall have to stay some time to further our plans. I shall perhaps take apartments. The Golden Arrow will be under your command, Will, and Andrew will be the medium of communication between us two.'

'Supposing the lubbers of Frenchmen should run alongside?'

'Never mind that, Will; show these papers, and remember whatever may occur, act as your conscience may dictate. You are commander here.'

'Shall we be in this port long?'

'I expect not, Will.'

William had not forgotten Susan. He had no wish to remain.

A boat was prepared for Captain Gerald and Andrew, who was to accompany him.

Gerald and Will parted warmly, and as the boat parted from view, a strange unaccountable feeling came over Will—a kind of presentiment stole upon him, that he should not see his gallant friend again, and Gerald's last words were still ringing in his ears.

'You are captain now, Will.'

This he had said as he went on the ship's side into the boat.

The tiny vessel was now out of sight. Will had a challenge given from one of the ships, and an answer given by Gerald. Then all was quiet as before. Nothing but the dull wash of the sea against the vessels' sides could be heard, or the moaning of the wind through the bare rigging.

The cutter containing Captain Gerald and Andrew was pulled swiftly through the water, rounding the ship, and touched the landing ship before the occupants could exchange many words.

'Shall the boat wait, sir?' asked the coxswain, raising his glazed hat.

'No,' said Gerald, briefly. 'Return to the ship as yet, and keep a good look out for the shore boats. Good night.'

'Good night, yer honour, but—but'——

BLACK EYED SUSAN.

OR, PIRATES ASHORE.

KEEPING OFF THE FOE.

'Well, speak out, Brace,' said Gerald, pausing good-humouredly.

'Well, cap'n, if so be as I'm not bold in 'dressing yer honour jist now, I should like to say that which is the thoughts of my messmates as well as myself.'

'Well, well.'

'Pardon, cap'n, but yer a-going ashore among them there furriners, and maybe they're not mighty pertickler; and if yer thinks there's any danger, yer honour—well, yer would be granting a favour to poor Bob Brace and his messmates to let 'em foller yer.'

This address—so full of rough, uncultivated eloquence—touched the young commander of the Golden Arrow.

The proof of their fidelity was so simple and yet so strong.

'Mr. Brace, I thank you and the other brave hearts, but I do not fear danger—there is none to fear. If there was, my journey should be performed with you, my brave lads, at my back.'

'Yet, cap'n,' persisted Bob Brace, mournfully, 'I feels summit here,' and he struck his chest with his huge hand—'summit that says danger hangs over the skipper. Maybe, cap'n, if you won't let us come, you'll allow your faithful old Bob to touch your hand.'

Old Brace and the cutter's crew were chosen and favoured men of Gerald's. He had known them when on board an English frigate as a junior officer. His appeal of rugged affection brought a large lump to Gerald's throat.

Andrew turned away.

'Certainly,' gasped Gerald, trying to appear as though it did not concern him a bit, 'certainly. Silly fellows, what good can that do you?'

But, however, he gave his hand to the old coxswain, and exchanged a fervent grasp.

Then he caught sight of the anxious, upturned faces of the men.

He could not resist the impulse, and shook hands with each one, but old Bob would have the last shake.

Then Gerald turned away.

'Now, yer lubbers, what d'ye mean by staring and blinking there?' said old Bob, huskily. 'Any one would think as how you was a-taking leave of your mammies. Can't the skipper go ashore without all this fuss?'

Then he blew his nose very loudly, and the handkerchief covered the whole of his face—eyes and all.

'Well, Bob,' said one quite as old and weather-beaten as him, 'we ain't a-making no fuss—we ain't,' and he drew the cuff of his coat across his eyes.

'O' course not,' echoed the other.

Whether or not, no one attempted to touch an oar until the form of their chief was out of sight.

'I say, Tom.'

'Hullo! Bob.'

'Did you see them two figures pop out from that corner?'

'No, Bob.'

'Well, I did; and, shiver my timbers! they're follering the skipper.'

And he jumped up in the boat with the intent of leaping ashore.

CHAPTER LXI.

BOB BRACE IN THE HANDS OF THE SPIES.

'Stop here, lads! Damme, I'll run the lubbers down if they're on the track of the skipper.'

There was no preventing him. Bob Brace sprang from the boat to the landing-steps, and the next instant was out of sight.

Quick as he was, Captain Gerald and Andrew were nowhere to be seen. Nevertheless, the old salt was not going to be so easily baffled; he therefore dashed round the corner at which he had seen Gerald disappear.

All to no purpose; he saw no one but a few Frenchmen lounging about, or strolling through the dirty thoroughfares. They favoured the hurrying sailor with a stare of surprise as he passed on; but that old Bob did not care a wit about.

He went up one street and down another; still no trace of his captain could be found, and he was in blank despair.

'I'll give it up,' he thought, and began to rapidly retrace his steps.

All this time his companions were waiting anxiously in the boat for his return. Long they sat smoking or chewing in silence.

An hour flew by, and old Bob came not.

The men began to get tired—tired of staring at the dark, cheerless pier; tired of the sombre hulls of the ships, standing out like huge monsters of life; tired of glaring at each other and listening to the dull washing of the sea; and tired of waiting.

'I say, Tom,' said one of the men, removing his pipe from between his lips.

'Ay, mate.'

Tom did not remove his pipe; he was thinking.

'Maybe the lubber's lost himself, Tom.'

'Very likely, mate.'

'Werry likely! It's more nor that—it's sartin. Come, mates, it's no use us squatting here like so many monkeys in a canoe on the lakes of the Calliste.'

'Who's he, mate?' inquired a third member of the cutter, eyeing his companion askance.

'Don't yer know?'

'Sartin I don't, Jarvis.'

'Well, yer see, it's yer ignorance. When you've travelled as much as I have, Peter, maybe you'll know more about them there places.'

'And the lakes?' grinned Tom.

'Never mind about 'em, Tom. All I knows is, it was on that blessed island—leastways, I think so—that I ever seed the fust mermaid.'

'Whereabouts does that island lay—what's the latitude?' inquired Peter, provokingly.

'Look alive, mates,' said Tom, seeing Jarvis was perplexed. 'Let the yarn stand over until we get on board; at present we must think o' old Bob.'

'Ay, ay,' growled Jarvis, with a sigh of relief.

'Well, spin out, mate. What was yer going to say 'bout Bob?'

Jarvis took the pipe from his mouth and faced Tom.

'I say, Tom, mate—damme, we can run a clear course now.'

'How, mate?'

'Why, you can parley vous France a little—leastways, I heerd yer say so.'

'Course I can parley vous France,' echoed Tom, with a hearty burst of laughter that nearly stifled him.

Jarvis felt instinctively that something he said was the cause of the merriment, and he turned away in deep disgust, which he showed by pulling vigorously at his short pipe.

The other men laughed because Tom did to such an immoderate extent.

'Go on, mate,' he said, vainly endeavouring to stifle his merriment.

Peter gave a grunt.

'Should like to know _hoo_ could go on, with you going on like a ape—all jabber.'

No offence, mate,' replied Tom. 'Spin out your yarn. I think you left off by asking, 'You can parley _vous_ France,' and he laughed again.

'It's no use talking,' Peter said, appealingly, to his mates. 'He's mad—quite mad.'

However, Tom left off laughing, and, Peter cooling his indignation, condescended to finish his observations.

'Well, I was going to say mates that, being able to understand the land lubbers, he and another on us ought to go ashore and look for Bob. Maybe he's lost himself.'

This idea was readily believed by the cutter's crew. Old Brace must either have lost himself, or got into some danger.

Tom Tiller with Peter went ashore, leaving the boat in charge of two sailors, and when they got ashore they knew no more where to look for the missing coxswain than they did to find the captain.

All this time Bob Brace had been on a wild goose chase, and ultimately got himself into a scrape. We left him threading his way back to the harbour. He would have reached there safe enough, but unfortunately he became aware of the lamentable fact that he had lost himself in the labyrinth of dirty narrow streets, all of which looked very dark, very unwholesome, and very beggarly. Each turning had a double row of tall houses, which was so much alike that Bob could not distinguish one street from another—at least by the shops or buildings.

Wherever he turned, he saw mean-looking wineshops, slovenly Frenchmen, bakers and butchers. With true British pluck he did not despair of finding his way, and very probably would, had he not suddenly caught sight of two cloaked figures turning the corner of the street some distance ahead of him.

Now there was actually nothing in the appearance of the men in cloaks to excite any one; but old Brace was positive in his own mind that the personages were those he had seen follow Captain Gerald.

Without any idea of what he could do should he overtake them, he started off in 'full chase,' mentally resolving to bring the individuals on their 'beam ends,' unless they at once told him where his skipper was.

He forgot at the time that they would probably address him in French.

All of this he did not give a thought. Away he went, flying up the street like a madman, and dashed round the corner. He had seen the two figures disappear. Then he was brought to a stand still by a frightful collision.

'Hold up, yer lubbers!' he gasped, staggering back against the wall.

For a person to hold themselves up after being run against by a man of the old coxswain's stamina was a matter of failure only. The unlucky individual uttered a fearful oath, and then lay gasping on his back, and staring blankly at the oil lamp that swung from a cord run across the road from the opposite windows.

'Ax pardon, yer honour,' said Bob, helping the Frenchman to his feet.

'Pardonne!' echoed the injured one, understanding that word by its great similitude, 'pardonne, monsieur! Parbleu! Aha, Anglais?'

None of which Bob Brace understood; but taking it for granted his apology was accepted, he strode on.

'_Ma foi!_ Non, monsieur.' The Frenchman stopped him. He would not have done so had he not seen two of his own countryman coming towards him.

'How now, mate?' asked the old sailor, shaking off his foe's grasp. 'Maybe you want that jibsheet o' yours flattened out. Make way, you lubber; don't stand shouting there.'

Then he gave monsieur a punch that sent him spinning out of the way. Now monsieur had—when shouting—told the two new-comers that he thought the old tar an escaped prisoner, or something of that kind; and, therefore, when old Bob began his wild goose-chase again, he was confronted by two more monsieurs, each with shaggy moustachios, dirty faces, and rough hands.

The old coxswain was not likely to let two Frenchmen stop him without giving them, what he termed, a broadside.

He came to a standstill rolled up his sleeves, and squared up to them with all the grace of an expert pugilist.

The monsieurs stared at each other, jabbered a little, then glanced at Bob's two sunburnt fists, and they became undecided how to act.

Old Brace soon decided the question.

'Yes, you lubbers, come on.'

The man he had knocked down came up to the men. He was an officer—old Brace could see by his uniform.

'Messieurs,' he said, turning to his countrymen, 'I should not let this man escape. The injury he did me is nothing; but he may be a prisoner, and he ought to be given into custody.'

This was all very fine. To talk of a man being in custody, and giving him into custody, was a very different affair.

'But, monsieur,' said one, 'he is English, and will fight.'

'_Parbleu!_ and can't you fight?'

The men did not like to say they could not, and tried to look brave over the matter.

Old Brace, who was tired of all this delay, said—

'Luff, yer lubbers, luff, or, damme, I'll spoil yer figger heads.' And he set about doing it with a will. He went into them right and left, never thinking that three to one was very heavy odds.

We are sorry to say the old sailor had that mistaken notion in his head of one Englishman being equal to any number of Frenchmen; but he was soon taught that, though the sons of ancient Gaul were deficient in the art of self-defence, and in most cases made bad sailors, they had courage, and plenty of it.

We will admit that one of the messieurs was placed _hors de combat_ in a very short space of time, and the second was on that way, when the officer took Brace by the necktie, and hurled him off his feet.

'Damme, you lubbers!' he exclaimed, half in rage, half in astonishment. He could scarcely realise the fact of being hurled down by a '_monseer_.' He struggled madly to get up; but the three were one too many.

'Sheer off, yer swabs!'

The 'swabs' would not, and poor old Bob found

himself being gradually overpowered, when two new comers appeared on the scene.

Bob looked up, and stared at them in mute surprise.

They were two individuals cloaked from head to foot, and the old sailor could have sworn positively that they were the phantoms who had led him such a wild goose chase.

One of them turned and addressed the officer in pure French. The other looked fixedly at old Brace, and suddenly electrified the old sailor by asking—

'Who are you ?'

The poor old coxswain, with his hands tied behind him, only stared at the speaker.

'Who are you, my man ?'

'Bob Brace, at yer service.'

'Are you ? ' smiled the stranger. 'It appears to me you are unwillingly at the service of those gentlemen.'

'Gentlemen ! ' echoed Bob ; 'them mounseers gentlemen ! Only untie my grapnels, and see whether an old salt can't polish off six of 'em.'

'Very likely, but firstly, how came you in this plight ? '

Old Brace soon explained, and then the two cloaked individuals held a conversation in an undertone, and in a foreign tongue, which ended at last, and the gentleman who had electrified the sailor by addressing him in English, spoke to him again—

'I see you are English, and I suppose belong to one of those ships *for* England, lying in the harbour.'

He fixed his eyes upon the old sailor to note the effect of his words.

They had no effect upon him, because he did not understand their exact meaning, therefore replied simply—

'Ay, sir. I belong to an English ship lying in the harbour there, but not one of King George's.'

'Ah ! '

The exclamation broke involuntarily from the stranger, and he exchanged glances with his friend.

'Well, I suppose you are right in your statement, and therefore the men have no right to keep you a prisoner. I will release you, after which I want you to answer me a few questions.'

'Ay, ay, yer honour, and right glad am I to do so.'

He was released. His late antagonist departed, and he accompanied his two newly-made friends. Both of them spoke English with such perfection, that old Bob knew they were of that nation.

They conversed freely and in a friendly, humoursome strain with old Bob, until he took an immense fancy to them. They passed up a street which seemed narrower and dirtier than the others. A little more than half way up this turning was a wine shop. It had a quiet appearance, and was signalized by the word 'café' written upon the wall in large letters. Few persons were inside, and its very quietness gave it a suspicious appearance.

The trio entered this very silent café ; a nod was exchanged with the host. The strangers raised their hats, and passed through into a private room. Old Bob wondered why they should want a private room, and had a slight misgiving come upon him when one of his companions asked him what refreshment he would take.

His mind was soon made up, and refreshment, cigars, and tobacco were brought in. Each took what he fancied, and a conversation began.

The coxswain was questioned upon many subjects

rather closely, which he did not like, and became anything but gushing.

'How long have you been in this port ? ' asked the darkest of the two strangers.

'Not many hours, yer honour.'

'Did you come from England ? '

'Well, s'pose so.'

'Did you see anything of a cutter while crossing ? '

'Cutter ? Saw lots on 'em.'

The strangers began to look vexed. They could elicit no information from old Bob whatever.

'Come, you don't drink,' said one, rather impatiently.

'Well, yer see, sirs, I've been drinking, and maybe ye'll excuse me ; but I never takes *too* much when on dooty.'

'You are not on duty.'

'Gentlemen, I'm on dooty, and must return to my craft.'

'Not yet.' The dark stranger rose and strode across the room and locked the door.

Bob Brace sprang up.

'Hullo ! pirates, eh ? Now, sheer off.'

The two men laughed. The poor old sailor was in the hands of the English spies, whose work it was to frustrate the attempts of Louis XIV. to aid the Young Pretender.

'Look here, my man, we are not going to hurt you ; but I should advise a little discretion with your valour. I want a few questions answered concerning your ship and captain. Don't make a noise, or be obstinate, or '——

He finished his sentence by drawing a pistol and pointing it at the old fellow's head.

Bob Brace drew himself up proudly, uncovered his gray, flowing locks, and said—

'Maybe, sir, you are an Englishman, but, damme, you haven't the spirit of a dog. Shoot—shoot if you wish. I don't fear death ; though the man who would point a pistol with a threat at an old and unarmed man, is too much the coward to fire.'

The spy coloured, and lowered his weapon.

'I did not intend to harm you, but we must know what you can tell us. Come, now, what is the name of your ship and your captain.'

'Look here, sir, once for all. Yer may roast me alive, and then yer won't get one word out of me that will betray my captain.'

'Fool ! How can we betray your captain. The French are not your enemies. It's the English and King George.'

'Oh ! yer knows that much. Then, if I may ask, whose enemy are you ? Very much like ours.'

'Will you answer my few questions ? '

'No.'

'Very well. Listen. We know you and your captain. You are of the Jacobite party. Your ship is in the pay of that rebel, Prince Charles ; and, unless you divulge what you know of your mission and intention and your commander's name, you shall be given over to the secret committee as one of the rebels, and a confession extorted from you by means of such hellish torture that your very flesh shall creep, your blood turn to water, your heart freeze with horror, and your brain burst with agony. Will you consent ? '

'No ! '

"DRAWN TO MADE UP BY DE-BREY UPON STEAM: OR PIRATES ASHORE."

Issued from the "YOUNG ENGLISHMAN'S JOURNAL" Office.

CHAPTER LXII.

THE BAL MASQUE.

CAPTAIN GERALD STUART left Andrew when they had reached a certain part of Havre. His mission was a secret one, and like many others of that dangerous period, those concerned in them dared not let their own brother know the nature of their undertakings.

So careful was the Captain of the Golden Arrow to avoid the slightest possible chance of being watched, he lingered for some time in the dark narrow streets, to see that no one was near him, then he suddenly disappeared into a tall, gloomy building.

He stayed there some hours, and when again he came forth, some adjacent church clock struck the hour of eleven.

' 'Tis late,' he muttered. ' I must get back; danger lurks everywhere. So we have a lot of King George's spies about here; 'tis well I am warned. There will be a disturbance soon, I'm thinking. Let us only succeed in hoodwinking the spies, and if a force is not landed over the water, with the Chevalier at their head, to the astonishment of the forces of Great Britain, it will be strange to me. Ha! a carriage! Who comes?'

Gerald drew his cloak tightly around him, felt that his pistols were safe, and strode on. The rattle of carriage wheels came closer, and a rather stylish vehicle came round the corner of a narrow street. It was going along at a rapid pace, and presently whirled past Captain Gerald. He could not see the occupant, but his quick eyes caught sight of female attire.

' A fair one returning from a ball or soirée,' he thought. ' Aha! careless ass!'

By the last two words of his soliloquy he meant the coachman, who, turning the corner of the Rue de —— something—we regret having quite forgot the name—however, the wheel of the carriage caught against a post. The post being much firmer and a great deal stronger than the carriage, the latter toppled over with a loud crash, and the wheel was splintered off at the axle-tree.

A loud scream from the inside announced the terror of the occupant, and another from a heap of mud in the centre of the road told the unfortunate fate of the driver.

The horse, in its sudden fright, would probably have run away, but fortunately for the persons concerned, the trace got under its leg and tripped it up.

All this occurred in a very short space of time, in fact, before Gerald could reach the scene of distress.

His first act, naturally, was to run and extricate the lady from the interior of the overturned vehicle.

She trembled slightly, Captain Gerald could feel, and as he led her to the footpath she thanked him in a voice so musically thrilling that Gerald turned in surprise to look at the speaker.

By the aid of a dingy oil lamp swinging just above their heads he could see a pale but beautiful face, almost heavenly it looked under the dusky, flickering glare.

The eyes that looked into his were large and dreamy, and the whole expression of the lady's countenance was ravishingly lovely.

' What an angel!' thought Gerald.

He did not know how dreadfully he was out in his calculations.

' Mademoiselle,' he said, ' you are not hurt?'

She looked up into his handsome face, and—a smile lighting up her whole features, she replied, in pure English—

' I am unhurt, I thank you, sir. The shock frightened me.'

' Have I the honour of addressing one of my countrywomen?' asked Gerald.

' I presume you mean by that, English. Yes, I am.'

Gerald raised his hat and bowed very low.

By this time, the coachman had got up. His appearance was highly suggestive of a short pile of animated mud.

' The vehicle is useless,' said Captain Stuart.

' True, sir; and we can procure none to-night. What shall I do?'

' Under the circumstances, there could be no objection to me accompanying you to your residence,' said Gerald, hoping she would not refuse him.

' None whatever, kind sir; but the trouble it will be to you.'

' Nay '—Gerald spoke reproachfully—' do you forget I am English?'

' No, and therefore I must consent.'

Gerald escorted her home. The distance was not far—he wished it had been. Never in his life had he been so thoroughly charmed as by the lady he was thus strangely thrown into the company of.

She seemed as gifted and highly-bred as she was lovely.

She had a winning, childlike frankness about her, too, that made Gerald feel almost a reverence for her.

He went to the door of her *maison*, where he left her in the care of an old lady who appeared to be her guardian, or housekeeper, or perhaps some relative.

Gerald had to tell his name, to satisfy the curiosity of the fair creature, after which he was cordially, though formally, invited to visit them the next day, that the lady might return her thanks for the service he had rendered her.

The apartments occupied by the lady whom Gerald had designated in his own mind as the ' Beautiful Mystery,' was elegant in the extreme. She seemed to be well off, too, judging by the style in which everything was done.

She seemed entirely her own mistress. The old lady Gerald had seen was a faithful housekeeper.

The Beautiful Mystery, when she had entered her apartment, was confronted by some one she evidently did not expect.

A gentleman — handsome, tall, well-built, and English.

' You here, my lord!' exclaimed the lovely girl, starting back.

' I have been waiting for you, Catherine. What made you so late?'

' An accident. It might have been more serious had not I found a friend.'

' Indeed!'—there was something like a sneer in the way this was uttered—' may I inquire the nature of the danger and the friend?'

' The stupid coachman dashed the wheel of the carriage against a post, and the vehicle was overturned.'

The individual she had styled lord started.

' Who saved you?'

' An Englishman—Captain Gerald Stuart.'

' Aha! English, Catherine?'

' He was, my lord.'

But why lord me, Lady Catherine? Any one would think we were strangers. But tell me now of this gallant countryman of ours. Was he a naval captain?'

'I think so.'

Then I wager 'tis he.'

Who?'

'Some one we are looking out for, a friend of Charles Edward, the Pretender, and a man who would pause at no daring plan that would get a fleet away from here to aid the usurper. This fellow must be stopped. Shall you see him again?'

'Perhaps.'

'You must. You will be at the bal masque?'

'I shall, I think.'

'Then we must go, and—he must go. Remember, Catherine, the effectual removal of this Englishman would upset the plans of the Pretender's allies, that the great schemes would fail, even those with the King of France. What would be our reward, think you? Pardon from our king, and we could return to our native land. You know this is the bond. If we fail we shall live in exile; if we succeed, we return to wealth, honour, and freedom.'

The beautiful Lady Catherine sat down on a sofa, and laid her head dreamingly back—her eyes were half-closed.

'Remember,' her visitor continued, 'your brother's life is in danger should we fail. See him—the stranger—again, if you can, and make him divulge enough of his personal history to put you on your guard. He must come to the bal masque.'

'Very well, my dear cousin,' said Lady Catherine, with a more friendly smile than she had hitherto greeted her visitor. 'But it is now very late, and I wish to retire. I will seek this dangerous Englishman, and the rest will be left to you.'

The cousin did not seem to relish his cool reception. However, he took Lady Catherine's hand, and, kissing the tapering fingers, left the house.

'By heaven!' he muttered, as he strode hastily along, 'she is beautiful enough to tempt one to marriage, but I will see if I cannot win her without that, as I cannot think of losing the charming little French countess. Her fortune would render me a god among my fellows.'

During the time these little incidents had been taking place Captain Gerald Stuart returned to the hotel, where he had left Andrew.

The next day Gerald sought Will on the Golden Arrow, which was lying out some little distance from the pier, and in perfect readiness to run out to sea any minute.

'Aha! captain,' said William, coming foward with a flush of pleasure on his wan face.

'Why, Will, you look as though you had been cruising among the crafts of the other world. What on earth ails you?'

'Maybe I was a little concerned about you, captain. What else could make me look bad?'

The gallant fellow averted his head as he spoke. He did not, in his unselfishness, say that the unknown fate of his wife was rankling into his very heart.

'Nay, Will,' answered Gerald, 'I know what brings you down to this; but bear up. We shall not stay here more than a week; and, remember, we have others on the track of the villanous Saunders. Keep a sharp look-out, Will. The ships yonder are fitting out for the service of our king and cause. We shall leave port with them. Be prepared to receive everything on board that may come with the private signal.'

'Ay, ay.'

'Should I not return in a few days, and your ships should start, even one at a time, and you should receive the secret orders to set sail, do not wait for me—command the ship. I may no longer be in existence. The place is full of hazards, spies, and every attempt that has lately been made to aid an unfortunate prince, has been discovered and frustrated.'

'Captain,' said Will, 'then, now, I can account for our missing men.'

'Missing men?'

'Ay; Bob Brace fancied he saw two strangers follow you when you first went ashore, and the brave old heart followed, in case they meant foul play. The crew in the cutter waited for him some time; but he never returned, and his two messmates went ashore to find him. None of them has been back since.'

Gerald felt alarmed for their safety.

'Keep the men on board, Will; I will see after those foolish fellows.'

'Will you stay on board to-day?'

'I cannot, Will; I have an appointment.'

He had—a dangerous one.

*   *   *   *   *   *

Three nights later the Grand Hotel of Havre was lighted up until the place seemed perfectly illuminated. It was the night of a grand bal masqué. All the swell people were there—friends and foes, and, alike, unknown to each other.

Captain Gerald Stuart, the morning before, had received a note that somewhat puzzled him. It ran:—

'Be at the bal masqué to-night. Be on the watch for a silver domino. On approaching the wearer draw your handkerchief across the back of your hand. Do it carelessly, to avoid notice.'

'Umph!' thought Gerald; 'who the deuce can it be here? Surely no one but she whom I saw yesterday—the Beautiful Mystery. Well, 'tis strange; one thing is favourable. I should have gone without this. I must be there.'

He went. It was late when he arrived. The saloons were crowded with the gaudily-arrayed revellers, and bristling and gleaming with the countless number of lights.

It was a scene of dazzling, seductive splendour; and Captain Gerald passed over the threshold of the thronged salons to watch the company, and take a momentary glance around in search of the silver domino.

Music and dancing were at their height; masked partners were going round in the giddy whirl; bursts of laughter ever and anon filled the rooms and rang through the darkling thoroughfares.

Gerald waited, screened from view, for the dance to end. It was not long ere the music ceased. The giddy revellers led their unknown partners to a seat, or retired with them to get a little cool air on the balconies.

Captain Gerald took one calm survey of the whole company; he could see no silver domino. Then pulling his own mask over his face, he strode in with the kingly mien that caused him to be so much the admiration of his crew.

He was attired and armed as a fine corsair chief, and by his side hung a huge, curved scimitar. Every dark, thrilling eye—gleaming like stars through the holes in the masks—was turned upon him, and a low buzz of admiration went round.

He was met midway by a tall, dashingly-dressed

cavalier in a plain black domino. They exchanged a few words in a low voice. This was the personage to whom Gerald paid secret visits; but his curiosity being aroused by the letter he had received, Gerald did not pay much attention to his companion, but kept his eyes employed for the silver domino.

'Look,' said the stalwart cavalier to Gerald—'look well at these two men coming towards us; note the one in the costume of a captain of the guard.'

'And the statesman?' queried Gerald—meaning the captain's companion, who was in the state robes.

'I do not know him—I think not, at least. He is a mystery, and a dangerous one. The man you have to fear in France is the captain of the guard. Hist! they will hear us.'

They drew aside as the statesman and captain passed. Gerald heard the former say, in English—

'I will see you to-night, after I have seen her; then I will divulge something'——

The remainder of the sentence was lost, as they passed out of ear-shot.

'You hear?' said Gerald's companion. 'English, too!'

'Yes. Aha! Pardon me; I will rejoin you in a few minutes.'

Gerald spoke hurriedly. A sudden hush had come upon the company as the form of a lady, elegantly attired, entered the room. She wore a silver domino.

She strode in with regal grace; and Gerald, his heart all in a flutter, strode towards her, and drew his handkerchief across the back of his hand.

She gave a sudden start, then made an almost imperceptible gesture for him to follow her.

He strode leisurely across the saloon, and passed so close that he heard her whisper—

'Follow me. I am in danger. Be cautious.'

He started at the words. Who could she be? What danger could menace her? He was mystified; but he followed.

It was well he did so.

———

CHAPTER LXIII.

A SLENDER CHANCE OF LIFE.

BLACK-EYED SUSAN saw the danger she was exposed to, in all its terrible reality. Not only was she in immediate danger, but faithful Tom Hatchett would in all probability lose his life in a useless attempt to save hers.

The poor unfortunate sailors were no longer men, they were brutes—demons thirsting for blood, hungering for human flesh. Poor fellows, even then they were to be pitied, not condemned. All human instincts had left them. Their minds were left only in an animal state.

They were mad—mad with hunger and thirst.

Susan looked upon the meagre, wan-faced, wolfish-eyed creatures, and she went sick at heart, though she pitied them. She felt her time was come, and prayed for future salvation; prayed to God to forgive the poor maddened wretches for the deed she felt sure they would commit.

Tom Hatchett did not know—or, at least, had forgotten—prayer; but he remembered the name of the Deity and breathed, called upon his Maker, though only by name, for succour.

Like a pack of vampires they approached the captain of the smugglers, who stood, in the last hope of despair, waiting for them.

His quiet, determined resistance caused a momentary check.

'Lads,' he said, in a voice so low and hoarse that it was scarcely audible. 'Men, think, for God's sake, think of what you are about. Pause—pause ere you take such a step.'

The word 'think' sounded like mockery to the starving brutes. Think! Alas! they no longer had any senses beyond the one lingering craving for blood and human flesh.

'Cap'n,' said the leader of the men—his voice was as weak and hoarse as Tom Hatchett's had been. 'Cap'n, we must do it—we must. We don't want to sacrifice you. But the lady, God! she must expect it.'

The other poor wretches seemed deprived of all power of speech.

They only looked on.

That look told all. Long, bony, eager hands grasped long knives, and then they took one staggering step forward.

The cold, gleaming blades of the assailants gleamed before Tom Hatchett's gaze. He saw their blood-shot wolfish eyes glaring into his. He knew they were creeping forward—creeping towards the woman he loved, to suck, like vampires, the very blood from her veins.

He shuddered—his senses swam. He felt as though he would sink to the bottom of the boat powerless. How his heart sickened!

'Susan,' he gasped, as a film came over his eyes. 'Susan, 'tis for you,' and he fired a pistol point blank at the nearest assailant.

A sharp cry of agony—a groan—then came a dead, a terrible silence—a stillness under the scorching sun, out upon the ocean, unbroken even by the vast world of waters dashing against the boat.

Susan gave a shivering groan and buried her face in her hands, for there was something so horribly suggestive of what would follow in that stillness that she feared to look up.

Tom Hatchett seemed to recover. The report of the pistol brought back his senses, and though he shuddered in pitying regret for the dead, he uttered a deep sigh of relief for the momentary safety of Susan. But what followed made him sink to the bottom of the boat and hide his eyes in horror.

The suffering, inhuman wretches had only wanted food, they cared not from whence it came.

They had got it.

Wolfish eyes looked into wolfish eyes, hungering jaws gaped at hungering jaws, but no word was spoken, though the sentiments of each one was understood by the other.

The bleeding form of the sailor Tom Hatchett had shot was dragged away to the prow of the boat. More than one greedy mouth was glued to a gap in the neck or breast of the dead man, and his fellow creatures—his late messmates—drank, with a wild delirium of joy, his heart's blood.

The cannibalistic meal over, the castaways revived and became stronger, excepting Tom Hatchett and Susan. They were drooping more each minute.

A deadly lethargy came over Susan now; her head sank back on the gunnel of the boat, her eyes shut, and her senses partly fled, but her agony did not entirely leave her.

In her trance-like sleep she was suffering the tortures that would more than punish those doomed to perdition.

Captain Hatchett watched her, spoke to her.

His words were not heeded.

She heard him not.

He then glanced towards his men. They were lying huddled all of a heap at the end of the boat, thirsting after their horrid repast.

Darkness at length came on. The breeze stiffened and the surface of the ocean became ruffled to almost cause a rocking motion of the boat, the moon appeared in a watery maze, and at short intervals was hidden by the passing clouds.

Some of the occupants of the boat began to rave, groan, and curse in their disturbed and agonised slumber. Tom Hatchett sat wide awake listening to them, sat not only chewing, but eating, and swallowing with gusto, the last remains of his tobacco.

'It's no use,' he muttered at last, 'I must do it.'

On his hands and knees he stole forward amongst his groaning men, and there he crouched down still—crouched and groped at the bottom of the boat. Whatever he searched for he found.

He pulled his sleeping companions aside to get further under the bow of the boat, and when there he remained for many minutes. When at length he rose his head his eyes were wild and unearthly in their glare, his mouth was blood stained, and altogether he looked as much a brute as his companions.

He rose to a kneeling position, and as he did so a pair of burning eyes glared into his, and a low, fierce chuckle saluted his ear.

Then he looked up.

The sight he saw made him shudder.

It was one of his men. The most powerful of the party was watching him. It required no second glance to see he was mad. He grasped a long, clasp knife in his hand. There was no mistaking his intention.

'Adams,' said Tom Hatchett.

'Ah, ah!' replied Adams. 'More blood—blood—yours,—y—yours!'

All his remaining sense was concentrated into the one brutal thought—blood.

The smuggler captain could see that was the extent of his companion's words, and he saw that his life was not safe for one minute from the madman's hands, and with the instinct of self-preservation, he drew his knife.

Then he spoke again.

'Adams,' he said, 'put down that knife.'

Adams only muttered the one word, 'Blood,' and stretched forth his hand, as though to clutch his captain by the collar.

The maniac's laugh rang in Tom Hatchett's ears, as he felt his hand upon him.

No more words were wasted. There was a sudden scuffle, a feeble struggle and cry. The boat gave a lurch, heeled over, the rising waves dashed the spray into the faces of the sleepers and over the forms of the combatants, and a long cry of fear and agony finished the momentary incident, and a form rolled out of the boat into the sea.

That was not all.

An awful sound followed. It was like the collapse of some huge monster's jaws. The outcasts felt instinctively a shark had got his meal.

They rose in bewilderment; the night had come over dark, and they saw dimly an erect form before them, and a superstitious dread came over their hearts, which increased when the form crept aft without speaking a word, and took the post by Susan, where Hatchett had lately been.

It was Tom Hatchett, but the sufferers were not aware of it.

Black-eyed Susan still lay insensible. The night grew darker, the waves rose higher. There seemed every indication of a storm.

The poor maddened wretches, suffocating with thirst, prayed for one, their cannibalistic meal had increased their tortures.

One poor fellow lay at the bottom of the boat in a wild delirium—a raving madman. It was he who had been so eager to drink the blood as it flowed hot from the heart of his scarcely dead companion.

The three men who still retained their senses huddled themselves up at the bow of the boat, groaning in agonised despair.

The heavy masses of clouds seemed to descend until they floated on the water.

Tom Hatchett sat trying to steady the boat, and prevent Susan from being hurled out.

'Bail the boat out or she will fill,' cried Tom Hatchett at the highest pitch of his voice, which was not very high.

Only two of the tortured sailors were able to obey. These did so with some lingering sense of self-preservation. The very moment they knelt down with their heads bent to perform the duty, something large and cold fell upon their necks. Each paused and turned his face upwards.

A gasping cry of delirious joy broke from their lips. A few large drops of rain had fallen; others were following thicker and faster.

The danger of the water in the boat was forgotten. The famished sailors threw themselves upon their backs, and with their mouths wide open, eyes shut, and hands and feet stretched out, they awaited the coming of the glorious blessing.

Tom Hatchett poured forth the gratitude of his heart in two fervently spoken words—

'Thank God.'

Then, baring head and breast that the soothing liquid might fall upon his burning skin and cool the heated blood in his veins, he rested Susan's head upon his jacket with her face towards the sky.

The falling of the rain might revive her; and, while he awaited for this, he spread out the small canvas sail to catch the crystal drops; also his cap and boots were placed in such a manner as to catch the rain as it fell.

Who can portray the joy in his heart as he stood under the increasing shower!

While he stood thus, he fancied he heard the flapping of wings. He turned sharply, and glared out into the darkness. He could see nothing of the nature of a bird; but he was suddenly struck heavily by something alive, and the next instant a frightened water fowl fluttered at his feet.

It had evidently sought refuge from the storm on the tiny mast of the boat; but, perhaps, through injuring its leg or wing, it could not retain its position, and fell violently to the bottom of the little bark.

Hatchett did not stay to think of the probable cause of its presence. He saw food that, under the circumstances, would be welcome to the woman he had so insanely loved.

The bird was clutched, killed, and concealed from the wolfish eyes of his companions. Then he continued catching the rain water.

A low moan from Susan announced the return of her senses. Tom Hatchett went to her side. From out of a tin bale in the boat he poured water down her throat.

'Lay still,' he said. 'Remain quiet a minute.'

While she lay quiet, returning a fervent prayer for the succour they had received in the moments of

BLACK EYED SUSAN.

OR, PIRATES ASHORE.

A RANDOM SHOT.

dire agony, Tom Hatchett tore the bird's feathers off, wrenched the legs from the body, and offered one to her.

'Eat,' he said. 'Eat; it is all I can give—all.'

Susan hesitated. She remembered the pistol being fired, the death of the man, and shuddered.

'Eat,' continued Hatchett. 'It's good. It's a bird sent by the Great Skipper to keep you from dying. Take it Susan—for God's sake, do.'

The simple, unaffected appeal, had its effect upon Susan, and she ate of the fowl, and what many of our readers would scarcely believe in—she enjoyed it too, and did not stop until the second leg had been demolished.

Then she thought of her faithful protector, the starving men, and she pushed his hand away.

'Oh, selfish, ungrateful creature that I am,' she said, 'to forget there are others besides myself! You, Captain Hatchett, want as much as I do.'

'No, no; go on with it.'

'No more. The men—think of them.'

'They have had *food in plenty; so have I.*'

'Food? From whence came it? Oh, God! Can *you*—you have—surely no '——

'Hush! Don't seek to know. Have this; 'tis for you; it was sent from heaven—ours came from hell.'

The latter part of his speech was uttered in a voice low, but so intensely impressive that Susan shuddered. Still she ate no more, and Tom Hatchett put the remains of the bird away for her, should they live until the next day.

He was hungry—he could have eaten the whole; but rough as he was, he could be unselfish.

Susan thought the worst of this danger was over. Water had been sent them—the men were no longer dying of thirst. But she did not observe how fearfully the storm was increasing, and the wind rising almost to a pitch of fury.

Tom Hatchett did.

He called upon the men to bale out the water. While they were doing so, the wind rose to a hurricane; the waves rolled mountains high, and the boat was tossed upon the billows like a cork.

Each person inside had to hang on like grim death.

Tom Hatchett saw the frail bark could not hold out much longer, and his heart sickened for the safety of Susan. How could he possibly give her a chance of life?

He soon thought of one. He collected four of the boat's oars, lashed them well together with a piece of cord, and dragged them aft.

'Susan,' he said, 'it's the only chance of life I can give you: let me lash you to these spars.'

Susan lay in a helpless lethargy, and although she faintly expostulated, she had no power to prevent Hatchett, who did what he wished with a little gentle force.

It was the last he could do; then, like the rest, he hung on to the boat's side as it was whirled higher than ever in the air. The waves washed over the boat; then it descended, almost submerged; again it rose, this time higher still, borne on the very crest of the waves, and again fell. The waters came with a mighty rush upon it.

A series of wild, unearthly shrieks resounded on the air. The mighty waters whirled on in their fury, carrying the boat keel upwards along with it.

Where was its living freight? Were they added to the mysteries of the deep?

CHAPTER LXIV.

THE SILVER DAGGER.

THE bal masqué continued in its brilliant sea of animation. Music rang out through the saloons; merry laughter and animated discourse all mingled with it.

It was indeed a joyous time. Every one seemed happy and lively, and had any one suggested the probability of a tragedy taking place amidst that scene of pleasure, they would have been laughed at.

But no one suggested it, and the revel went on, the revellers keeping up the fun of the night, in happy ignorance of anything unpleasant occurring.

The revellers were preparing for another dance, and many longing eyes gleamed through the ghostly masks at the form of the dashing corsair, and Gerald was not quite dead to the slight sensation his appearance caused.

But all his attention was given to the lady with the silver domino. He saw the individual in state robes approach her, and she started at his appearance.

Gerald could see the person of the supposed statesman was distasteful to the unknown beauty. He noticed, too, a fearful gleam in her eyes as the gentleman in robes addressed her.

He wondered at the cause and drew near her.

At first Gerald thought he was merely asking for the name of the silver domino in the next dance.

He was wrong.

The robed stranger went close enough to the unknown beauty to say in a hissing whisper—

'Lady Catherine, follow me.'

She started, and a chill seemed to run through her frame. The music struck up at that moment, and the dance began.

'Your presence will not be missed. Come now,' continued the speaker, 'or will you refuse me?'

The deep, livid glare of the eyes that followed this was a menace—a terrible one. Lady Catherine saw it.

'Who are you who dares thus address me?'

'Ha! ha! You do not know me? Stuff. Drop this farce. Will you follow?'

And he walked on.

Lady Catherine walked mechanically forward, and they entered one of the *bosquets.* Drawing in the shade of the shrubbery, the statesman spoke again.

'I have tracked you,' he said, 'even here. Your flight was useless. I know its cause—to join your exiled cousin, and lure him on to destruction, by your cursed beauty—to lure him on until, should he be reinstated, you will grasp at his wealth—his title, and spurn him, but you shall not. I have found you. I give you four-and-twenty hours to leave Havre with me. Refuse, and by heaven I will drag you down from the pinnacle on which you stand, humble, and denounce you!'

'Beware how far you brave me.'

'Ha! ha! Stuff! Your tragedy-queen humbug won't do with me. Do you consent, or '——

'Hush! who comes?'

The statesman drew aside.

A stranger approached with a careless air. He was a dashing little don of a Frenchman, and with the gallantry of his race he went up to Lady Catherine, and begged her to enter the devious, whirling dance that was going on.

She started, and a glance of joy shot from her eyes. Here was a chance of getting away from her tormentor. He saw it, and read its purport. At a stride he was by her side, and fiercely ejaculated the one word—

'Engaged.'

The courteous little monsieur nearly leaped up.

'Pardonne, monsieur,' he said, 'I was not aware of it.'

'I am not,' said Lady Catherine, haughtily. 'Allow me to choose my partner.'

'Be careful,' said her tormentor in English, 'leave me, at your peril!'

'Parbleu!' said the Frenchman, biting his moustache. Monsieur, that lady denies your right, she had accepted me.'

'Out of the way, fool. This lady is a friend of mine; dare you interfere?'

'Mon Dieu! Oui. You are a strange friend, monsieur. You force your company upon a lady; certainly, only an Englishman could do it. Mademoiselle,' he continued, turning to the lady, 'grant me the favour of being the champion of one so lovely.'

He proffered his arm, which was taken by the lady, and with a galling smile, he turned to go.

His rival stood before him, but addressed the lady in English.

'Catherine—another step, and I will put my threat into execution. You, monsieur,' he cried, turning fiercely, 'release that lady's arm.'

'Never!' came very emphatically.

With that, he gave the discourteous Englishman a push, and strode on with the lady in the silver domino.

But not far. The Englishman was wound up to a paroxysm of rage, and he made a bound forward. He did not touch his rival, but grasped the lady so fiercely by the arm that she gave a low cry of pain.

This was a direct appeal to monsieur's chivalry; he felt it was. His fiery temper was aroused, and releasing the arm of his fair prize, he was about to jump at the insulter, when the dashing form of the corsair came up.

He was beforehand with the Frenchman, and clutched the daring insulter by the collar, hurling him forward some two or three yards.

'Base cur!' he said, fiercely, 'had you a weapon, I would cut you down.'

'Monsieur,' said the Frenchman, 'I am the one he has insulted. Leave him to me, and take the lady from the room.'

Voices sounded near—two or three couples talking merrily; among them was the tall captain of the guard, who had been the companion of the insolent statesman.

He gave Gerald a long, curious glance as he hurried Lady Catherine away, and Gerald saw by the look that the man was a foe, and had seen his rough usage of the man who had dared to insult an unprotected lady.

Captain Gerald led her back into the saloon from observation, and she thanked him for his timely aid in removing her from so embarrassing a position.

The parties, who for a minute had sought the cool air of the bosquet, passed into the grand saloon again to rejoin the dance.

'Diable!' he said, his eyes blazing furiously. 'A miserable pig! By the God above us, I would make carrion of your corse had I a sword by my side.'

It was fortunate for the insulter the Frenchman's costume was not adorned with a weapon.

'Now, monsieur,' continued he, 'unless you apologise for the many insults I will strangle you.'

And his fingers worked as though he would much rather it should be so than the other mode of settling the quarrel.

The Englishman laughed mockingly.

'Miserable fool, go and join the insipid girls—their company is all you are fit for.'

'Is it?'

The fiery Frenchman was roused up, his vanity had been touched by the preference displayed by the English beauty. His heart had literally jumped at the anticipated joy, and the man before him had robbed him of all, besides insulting the loveliest woman in the saloon.

He did not waste any more words, but, with the impetuosity of his race, leaped upon his foe.

So unexpectedly did he make the attack, his enemy was completely taken off his guard, and thus got the worst of it.

A brief struggle took place, and the Frenchman forced his foe back until he got him against a low balcony—his hand was still upon the insulter's throat—his neck upon the stone work, until his face was purple.

The Frenchman had let his temper master him so much that he would have strangled his foe but for the sounds of approaching footsteps.

Then he released his grasp upon the other's throat, and left him almost lifeless, huddled beneath the shrubs.

They concealed his form from view, and the strolling revellers passed the spot without noticing the inanimate form.

During this little episode Gerald Stuart had conducted the lady through the dances, and treated her with all the winning courtesy he was gifted with.

When he turned to suddenly look at her, he found she was regarding him fixedly, and with a passionate fire in her glare he could not fail to read.

When the dancing was for a time over, and she leaning upon his arm, strolling about the building, she spoke to him strangely.

'Watch well,' she said; 'you have enemies where you least expect to find them. I will point them out to you—men that you would fear if you knew them.'

Gerald laughed lightly.

'I fear!' he said. 'I never feared a mortal yet.'

'Not an open foe.'

'Nor one that works in the dark.'

'You speak boldly.'

'I have cause to do so. I have defied England's power before now, and shall do so again.'

Lady Catherine glanced at him admiringly.

'But,' he went on, 'point out these men I am to fear; let me know them, and I will guard against all danger.'

'Be on the alert, then.'

Gerald had led her to a recess in the window, and

they were looking up to the star-lit sky, when he addressed her in a voice singularly sweet.

'Tell me,' he asked, 'lady, by what name—by what token I may know you again.'

While he spoke, the image of Madeline seemed to rise before him—rise from the grave, in death's spotless shroud, and accuse him of his falsity.

He shuddered slightly, and a feeling of repugnance for the beauty by his side came upon him; but he caught sight of her beaming eyes, and her coral-like lips, wreathed in smiles, and the feeling passed away.

This strange woman held a mystic power over him; he did not feel himself while with her.

'Why,' she said, 'do you wish to know my name?'

'Surely this is not to be our only meeting?'

'Alas!' sighed the beauty, 'it were better it should be so. I am surrounded with trouble and misery; I know not life's joys or pleasures. The world does not seem the same to me as it does to others, and there are times when I wish I was dead.'

The sadness of her voice touched Gerald, and he took her hand.

'Talk not so,' he said. 'You'——

He paused; the look on her face startled him. He followed the direction of her eyes, and saw her late insulter was coming towards her.

'Do not fear him,' he said.

'Nay, stay one minute; the music has begun for a dance. I will return; wait for me here.'

As she passed away, Gerald fancied her sleeve caught in something in his belt, and gave it a twitch.

He thought nothing of this, and she passed away.

She met her tormentor.

'Follow me,' she said.

And he followed.

When alone, out on the balcony, she turned and spoke again.

'Now, mean-souled insulter of women, tell me your wishes.'

'Aha! you have come round at last.'

'I! Bah! Speak, or I will no longer bear these taunts.'

'Then listen. Outside is a closed carriage waiting for us. Come with me at once, while the noise of the revel is at its height.'

'Man, I cannot—will not. Cease to annoy me here. You perhaps know my house. Come there, and let me see you.'

'Do you intend to come with me now?'

'No.'

'Enough. You have wronged and ruined me. You have turned a fond heart to the bitterest gall. You have cursed my existence, you beautiful demon. But, unless you comply with my wish now, I will have revenge. Let me inform you that, among the revellers, are two officers of the law brought here by me, and I have only to give a sign; then your proud beauty will be humbled to the dust.'

He had worked himself up into a fit of passion; he had clutched firmly at her arm, until she shrank back from the agony. He put his head close to hers, and said something in low, hissing whispers.

He raised his hand as though to tear the mask from Catherine's face. She shrank back with a low cry. He laughed mockingly, and persisted in his work.

'Bah!' she said, her whole form quivering with emotion, her eyes blazing fearfully. 'You have dared too much. Your life is a curse. Let i end.'

The music at that moment in the saloon struck up louder than ever. One or two of the lights near the balcony flickered out. The stars seemed to retire one by one from the blue canopy; and when Lady Catherine suddenly left the balcony to join her corsair partner, that one large bright star was twinkling down upon a pale, stone-like face.

The face was unmasked. It belonged to the statesman—the man who had threatened Lady Catherine. The eyes were open, the mouth a little apart, the features looked as though they had been passion-distorted, then surprised, and then turned to stone.

Motionless, colourless.

From the breast was trickling a long, dark stream of blood, and protruding from the left side was the silver hilt of a dagger.

There he lay; half an hour ago full of oaths of vengeance, and terrible threats—life and animation. Now his might have been a face carved upon the stone of the balcony for all the difference that could be seen at the first sight.

Inside the saloon the lady with the silver domino was dancing with the dashing corsair.

The revel was at its height. Everyone was going round in a delicious whirl when suddenly the band stopped.

The dancers paused.

A cry rang through the saloon.

Every eye was turned in wonderment towards the large door-like windows leading out upon the balcony. There stood one of the revellers—his mask thrown off; his face pale and haggard; and his finger pointed to something behind him.

Every one made a rush to the spot, and there beheld—the one star still twinkling down upon it—the lifeless form—the bloodstained form of the unfortunate and mysterious Englishman.

Some of the ladies swooned and fainted, while the men blocked the doorways.

Two individuals approached, unmasked.

They were officers of the law.

'Who did it?' was the cry. 'Every one unmask.'

Everyone did so. Captain Gerald, who was within a few inches of the corpse, felt his fair companion shudder, as she removed her silver domine.

The sergeants scanned every face. Then one stooped and plucked the silver dagger from the murdered man's breast.

'Whose is this?'

Gerald started back with a cry, and ere he could speak, the tall captain of the guard before mentioned snatched it out of the officer's hand, and pointing to Gerald, said—

'It's his!—the corsair's. 'Twas in his belt last night.'

'Yes, yes!' cried several of the company. 'The corsair's, the corsair's!'

Gerald staggered back with his hand to his brow, his bosom bursting in horror. He *had* worn the dagger. How was it he had not missed it before?

'It's a lie!' he gasped. 'I am innocent.'

Lady Catherine seemed suddenly turned into stone, struck dumb with horror, and as the officers, with drawn swords, approached Gerald Stuart, she gave a low, gasping cry.

But the sight of his foes' arms and handcuffs roused all the blood of his fiery nature. Out flew the mighty corsair's blade; one terrible whirl he made to clear a circle round him; then he said—

'Stand back all! Fools! I am innocent; and by heavens, the man who dares approach me, dies!'

There was a general hush.

CHAPTER LXV.

A TERRIBLE WRECK.

THE fate of Rock Elfin seemed awfully certain. The men, wondering at the deed, and who could have done it, were for the moment paralyzed. Rough and brutal as Elfin was among his men, he was respected and liked. They could not get on without him.

Many a fierce oath was uttered against the traitor's hand, which was as yet unknown.

Blue Peter, an old, trusty hand of Elfin, gave a cry of admiration as little Jack Murray leaped into the sea. He saw something must be speedily done, and took the command on himself.

'Put down the helm. Put the lugger back. Now lower a boat,' he yelled.

The men worked with a will.

Every floating article was thrown overboard, and a boat prepared to sail at a minute's notice.

Meantime brave little Jack would have perished long since had he not been an excellent swimmer.

From the moment he jumped overboard he did not lose his presence of mind.

Bravely he kept himself above water.

He saw the ship put back, saw the boats lowered, but could not call loud enough for them to hear him.

His heart leaped with joy when Elfin, by a motion of the hand, kept himself afloat. He fancied he was safe.

But when five minutes elapsed, and he saw no signs of a boat coming, his heart sank within him.

Poor little fellow!

He had striven manfully to save his powerful enemy, but during the time the preparations were being made for his rescue, he had become almost exhausted.

He could not hold out five minutes longer.

It was already a trouble to keep his head above water.

Then followed a slight struggle—one great effort—a few bold strokes, and the exhausted swimmer rises to the surface of the ocean.

In one arm is the inanimate form of Jack Murray.

A cry from the lusty throats of a boat's crew near at hand—words of succour.

A loud cheer from the lugger came to Rock Elfin's ears, and he struck out manfully for the approaching boat.

He was nearly exhausted, and the weight of the boy greatly impeded his progress.

He saw the boat coming slowly on, but its crew had lost sight of him.

'Help—this way!' he shouted, faintly. 'To your left—to your left!'

A huge wave dashing over him drew him under and stopped his further cries.

He soon came to the surface again.

'I cannot hold out much longer,' he murmured. 'Why don't they come? Help! help!'

'Bear up, bear up, cap'n. We are at hand,' said a cheery voice.

Elfin gave a gladdened cry. His senses then fled, and he would have sank with the motionless form of Jack Murray had not a powerful hand grasped him by the arm, and he was dragged into the boat.

'Now, my lads, pull and be d—d to you,' said Blue Peter, who had come out with the party.

The boat fairly leaped through the water, and, in a very short space of time, was by the lugger's side.

They were then hauled on board, and lifted upon the quarter-deck.

Rock Elfin's iron will was not conquered yet. Poor little Jack Murray was taken below; and Elfin, being supported by two of his crew, stood endeavouring to heave the water up that had gone in his inside.

'Brandy!' he gasped. 'Brandy!'

It was given him, and he drank deeply.

The men could see by the vivid light in his eyes that his fierce passions were aroused, and they shrank back from him.

Elfin's weight helped to drag him down.

'Keep up, my lad,' he gasped; 'do not tire yourself by motion. Keep steady.'

The smuggler was nearly exhausted—almost beyond all hope.

Little Jack would either rescue him, or they would die together.

He fancied he heard the sound of voices.

With renewed hope and energy, he battles desperately for life.

He caught a glimpse of a boat.

A faint cry escapes his lips.

Another effort, and he rises to the summit of the waves.

But he was hurled back by a huge mountain of water that came upon him with a mighty roar.

Down, down he went, the water howling and hissing like a death knell in his ears. Elfin went with him.

Would they never rise again?

His nose and head were ready to burst.

His brain was in a whirl.

At one moment he seemed to be going down a huge chasm, the next he seemed to be ascending amid a mighty rush of the liquid monster.

Then he seemed to be hurled about like a cork upon a river, still he would not release his hold upon Rock Elfin.

Death stared them in the face—death around them.

Unconsciously he made an effort to save himself—Elfin had released him.

The motion of his body brought him upwards.

The cool sea breeze fanned his brow.

Oh, for five minutes only of that delicious air!

But it was not granted him.

Blood poured from his mouth and nose.

His arms were raised above his head.

His face became rigid and distorted, and he gave a gasp, and lay dead or senseless.

Then he sank again, perhaps never to rise more.

But there was a cry of anguish from a human being near the spot.

A huge form dived down in the water.

Down it went like an arrow cleaving through the air.

It was Rock Elfin, who had partly recovered his strength by having removed his heavy boots and jacket, when Jack Murray had helped to keep him up. It is a common thing for a good swimmer to undress in the water.

He dived low, and caught the boy by the collar.

His very passion prevented his immediate recovery. When, at the expiration of twenty minutes, he could speak, he said, with a fierce oath—

'Where's Jem?'

'Below, cap'n.'

'Rout him up. Tarnation devils, he'll suffer!'

Jem came on deck with a hang-dog sullen air.

Elfin's face was fearful to behold.

'Curse you for a mutineer! Do ye dare look me in the face, d—— you! Why did you do it, eh?'

The ruffian made no answer.

'I'll tell you. To get me out of the way, but you didn't; and now you'll get what you deserve. Now, strip. String him up, lads, or by the fiends I'll make you all suffer alike!'

The craven's heart quaked as he heard this order.

The villain shook like an aspen.

But he did not move.

'Strip!' the smuggler thundered.

Blanched with fear, and filled with malice and hatred, Jem made a move.

'Give him seventy. If he don't strip in less than two minutes, let him have a hundred.'

The quailing wretch's tongue clove to the roof of his mouth.

His things were torn off—his back exposed.

He was lashed to the grating.

The acting boatswain stood by.

A signal from Rock Elfin, and the lash fell.

Jem gave a loud cry.

But at the second and third lash, he writhed and yelled dreadfully.

When a dozen had been given him, he shrank as far as the bonds would let him.

His shrieks were fearful.

The terrible punishment was continued.

His cries began to cease.

His head fell upon his breast.

A thick white foam gathered round his mouth.

His body was completely lacerated, and was covered with gore. At last, he hung a collapsed heap in his bonds.

The sentence was completed.

His bindings were cut, and he fell a huddled, awful mass to the deck.

All turned away, sick at heart.

Each man returned to his duty, and the cut and bleeding form was carried below, and placed in a hammock.

Now Rock Elfin had vented his fearful passion, he sought the brave boy who had risked his life to save him. With a peculiar tenderness in every action, he attended to the boy, and at length brought him to consciousness.

Two days the little fellow lay in a dangerous state, and no one to wait upon him but Elfin. The third night had come on. Jack lay chafing at his helpless condition, thinking of Eurice — wondering if she were better, if she had been menaced by danger, or if she was dead.

While these distressing thoughts were passing through his brain, the door of the little private berth was softly opened, and Eurice, pale and trembling, entered.

On catching sight of little Jack's wan face, she ran forward and put one hand on each side of his head, and holding his lips towards hers, kissed him fondly.

'Brave boy,' she said, the tears running down her cheeks, 'you risked your life for the man who would have murdered you.'

'No, no,' said little Jack, crying too—he did not know whether it was with joy at seeing her safe, or because she cried. 'Since I was taken from the dungeon in this ship, he has treated me kindly.'

''Tis strange; he's ever coarse and brutal towards me.'

'Because,' said Jack, knowingly, 'he fears to let any weakness enter his heart about you; because he has been paid to take you away. He is a bad man; but some men, who would seem better, and remorseful, are much worse. This Elfin never follows the dictates of his heart.'

'How, simple child? He would kill me.'

'No, he wouldn't,' answered Jack, stoutly.

'Would not?'

'No, miss; b'cos he'd have done it before. He was paid by the wicked brute of a captain to carry you off, and put you somewhere.'

'Perhaps in a convent?'

'What places are those?' asked Jack, innocently.

Eurice explained.

'But I will beg for you,' Jack went on. 'He is kind to me, and p'rhaps would help you if I were to ask him. But hush!—he comes.'

Rock Elfin came to see after the boy he so strangely liked.

He scowled when he saw Eurice.

'You here!' he growled. 'Who the devil told you to take such a liberty?'

'Nay,' pleaded the frightened girl, 'the boy was kind to me; I came to assist him—to return my gratitude for his kindness to me.'

'Daresay. S'pose I can look after the cub? Any better, younker?'

'Yes, thank you.'

'Want anything?'

'No, thank you.'

Elfin slammed the door, and left.

Eurice parted with Jack soon after.

The next day he was better, and able to get up.

Strange to say, when he was alone, Elfin made his voice almost gentle; and Jack, thinking of the poor, suffering girl, whose fate was such a terrible uncertainty, sought Elfin in his cabin.

Rock Elfin looked up in surprise.

'Well,' he asked, 'what d'ye want, brandy, eh?'

'No,' replied Jack, 'I am well now. I want nothing but a favour.'

Elfin elevated his eyebrows.

'Favour?'

'Yes. For God's sake, do not harm the young lady! Let her go back—let her leave the vessel with me.'

Elfin jumped up.

'What!' he said, 'd'ye know what ye're asking for, younker? Get on deck, and thank yer lucky stars for the good fortune you've had in being treated so well. Look here, youngster, don't come here trying yer yarns. Go on deck. You've got your life and your freedom—now go.'

' My life,' said Jack, bursting into tears; ' my life you gave me. I risked it to save yours—I could do no more. I tried to save the man who injured me. My freedom you may take—place me in that awful dungeon—let me be eaten by the rats—kill me—only have mercy to the poor lady.'

Jack knelt and clutched Elfin round the knees.

The tears ran down his cheeks, and he sobbed pitifully.

' Boy, you know not what you ask. I dare not.'

' Dare not? You are as strong as him who made you do it. You have a vessel and crew. Do you fear a man half your age and size?'

' Fear—ha! ha!—no; but it's business. But listen, boy: he made me swear to take the young lady away. I will do so; but she won't get hurt by me, or while under my care. I will put her away—if she can get home, she may. That's all I can do. Mind you, don't you tell her that much, or p'rhaps I'll alter my mind. Now go, and keep her company.'

He felt a great deal of relief when Jack was gone.

' D—n the gal!' he muttered, ' I'll put her on shore; and if the cap'n sees her again, sarve him right—I can't help it. D—n it, I ain't afeard of him. Maybe, he'll never see me again.'

With that he went on deck.

He did not think that reparation had come too late. An evil hour was coming. It was not far off.

Night came.

The sky was hidden by the dense black clouds; not a star shone forth to throw its twinkling light upon the heavy, black, rolling sea.

It was a dreary, dismal scene to those who were upon the deck of the smuggling vessel.

So dark was the scene around that the White Cat seemed as though enshrouded in the folds of a huge black pall.

The solitary individual at the helm could not discern the mast from where he stood.

The clouds seemed to roll swiftly but ominously past, and float about upon the water; and rain began to fall in huge drops, with a loud patter, on the lugger's deck.

Then began a fearful tempestuous night; the sea ran mountains high, and beat against the vessel's side with a roar like thunder; huge masses of thick, murky cloud—behind which lurked the most furious part of the storm—rolled across the sky; rain poured down in torrents.

The wind howled and shrieked through the rigging, and caused the lugger to shake and tremble, and threatening every minute to rend the masts from their sockets. A lurid flash of lightning lit up the scene for miles around.

The next instant all was darkness as before.

The waves seemed to soar higher, each moment lashing the waters into a perfect sea of foam.

Though the elemental war raged so furiously, the lightning darted about like forked tongues of flame, and the thunder that roared and reverberated through the arches of heaven, shaking the earth like some terrible earthquake,—a fair, pale, and tearful face might have been seen at the lower port window of the vessel.

It was poor Eurice. Little Jack Murray was with her when the cry of ' All hands on deck!' reached his ears.

' Let me go,' said the boy. ' It is safer. Wrap yourself up—I will take care of you.'

And they went on deck. The hatches were battened down, and every one had to cling to something for support.

Everything that could be done was performed—every stitch of canvas taken in, all lumber thrown overboard, but useless. The storm had come upon them suddenly—too suddenly to be guarded against.

The men clung on to every article that afforded support, and groaned in terrible fear.

The timbers, creaking with the terrible strain, were bilging apart; the masts and spars were carried away with a fearful crash, and the bulwark stove in.

The dismasted ship, with her groaning load, was drifting helplessly on, and the waters breaking over her bulwarks, mingled with the fast rising waters in the hold.

At that instant a loud, wailing shriek came from the nearly submerged decks of the unfortunate lugger.

It came from Eurice.

The men were being dashed about at the mercy of the waves.

The ship was sinking fast.

What a fearful panic reigned among them all!

Those who had now nearly recovered from their horror lowered a boat.

They leaped into her anyhow.

All huddled in a heap.

The boat passed from the ship's side, and rose high on the crest of a huge wave.

It was but for a moment; even as they looked the mighty waters hurled it back against the vessel.

A cry broke from the men; the boat was crushed to atoms, and the crew left to contend against the fury of the raging element.

No power could have saved them; and the rocking ship, ploughing on its retarded course, left them in the midst of the foaming sea.

One by one the poor fellows seemed to sink from view, and seek eternal oblivion.

' Fools!' said Elfin, ' no boat could live in this storm.'

' Then we shall all perish together,' said Eurice.

The men prayed, moaned, or wept, and some in their anger cursed the very elements.

Little Jack Murray clung tightly to Eurice, and when he could speak his words were—

' We will die together.'

Heavily water-logged, the vessel's progress became slower, and she sank down deeper in the fretful sea, till her black hull was near the water's edge.

And the surging billows sweeping her decks, hurled the ill-fated men into the sea.

Pale but determined—like the hardened but courageous criminal that, standing beneath the fatal beam, looks calmly round, resolute to meet his fate if the end has come, yet unwilling to take leave of dearly-loved life while the slightest chance remains—stood Rock Elfin by the wave-washed bulwarks, looking into the leaping sea.

His last hour seemed come, and he shrank not from it; yet while prepared to meet his death, he eagerly scanned the prospects of life.

And now came the final crisis.

The lugger reeled for a moment with the violence of the waves; then the groaning timbers rove apart, the foaming waters broke over her, every living soul was washed from her deck.

Spars, beams, cargo, and human beings were all whirled round in the frothy cauldron, and those who were in the midst of those angry waters saw with dismay that the fearful danger cut short their slender chance of existence.

Little Jack Murray, when he saw the last moment had come, clasped Eurice in his juvenile arms.

' Cling to me,' he cried; and she did so.

Scarcely had he spoke, when the lugger sank. He saw Elfin's last effort was to get to him. Then he saw no more. Borne on the very summit of the waves in the terrible darkness with his burden, stunned and bleeding by the fury of the ocean, he closed his eyes, clasped Eurice to his heart, and only waited for death to relieve him from his agony,

----

CHAPTER LXVI.

A FIGHT IN THE BALL ROOM—GERALD'S FOES INCREASE—WILL TO THE RESCUE—HOT CONTEST—CAPTURE.

GERALD STUART was looked upon with horror by the company when the dreadful deed of mystery had become known to them all.

None could imagine why he did it, or even when it was done.

Officers were called in, the festivity quite broken up, and the grand revel had turned to a shuddering tragedy.

Gerald dashed aside his mask, and stood in haughty defiance before them. His brave heart swelled with indignation at the base charge against him, and his eyes were fixed with a gleam of suppressed fury on his accuser.

The minute or two he had stood looking on in bewilderment an incident that occurred in the early part of the evening flashed to his mind.

He remembered that when the beautiful mystery, Lady Catherine, left him upon one occasion, that he felt a sudden twitch at his sash, in which was fastened the silver dagger.

' God,' he thought, and a pang shot through him, ' Could it be that she would ——. Ah! no, by heavens, it were sacrilege to harbour such a thought against one so innocent and beautiful. Aha! they come.'

His enemies did.

They were increased in number.

The guests made way for them to come forward, and Gerald, casting aside his mask, spoke in loud, clear accents.

' Gentlemen,' he said, ' I am an Englishman. Among you all—one of you—that man accuses me of basely murdering some unknown gentleman. Listen. I swear to heaven I am innocent of the deed. I own the dagger was mine, but it must have been taken from my sash, or else it fell from it during the dance.'

There was a hush.

The horror the ladies had evinced for Gerald now slightly gave way. With the quick and impartial perception of their sex they could see that the few words he had uttered were truth.

He began to grow interesting.

Lady Catherine stood by his side, cold, haughty, and silent. She had regained her self-command.

The leader of the officers stepped forward, and addressed Gerald with a grandeur that would at any other time have been laughable.

' Monsieur,' he said, with a sneer, ' we, of course, do not doubt your assertion, but the evidence is against you, and you must answer to our judges for the crime, and if you can clear yourself of it you will have every opportunity. But I hope, as a gentleman, you will surrender.'

' Certainly,' said Gerald, with a provoking smile, ' I cannot say anything against your hoping that I will surrender.'

' You mock me, monsieur.'

' That would be bad taste.'

' Bah! Will you give in?'

' No.'

The officer turned to the company present.

' Ladies, would you one and all kindly withdraw? the scene may terminate badly, and it would prevent a great deal of embarrassment to my men if you would leave the room.'

Most of the ladies turned dreadfully pale, cast a pitying look at Gerald, and allowed themselves to be led away by their friends or partners.

Lady Catherine was the only female that stopped, and she faced the officer with queenly grace. Her mask was removed, and she looked almost like a being of another world, so marble-like was her features.

She spoke in a bold, steady voice, and her eyes seemed to search into the officer's very soul.

' Take care,' she said; ' you have a man of another country before you, charged with murder upon the slightest link of evidence—bah! say rather—faint suspicion. He has no positive accuser, and his life you dare not menace. Be discreet with your zeal, for though he may oppose you, you dare not kill him; if you do, I will charge you with murder, as I warn you not to. He,' pointing to Gerald, ' is innocent.'

Then she strode away.

Gerald was dumbfounded—the officers bewildered.

Several of the gentlemen returned to the saloon, and mingled with the officers to aid in the capture of Gerald Stuart.

He was asked to surrender for the last time.

' Take me if you can,' was the reply.

Then the fight commenced.

The officers rushed forward; but the flashing blade before their eyes, as Gerald drew his scimitar, kept them back.

' Diavolo!' he exclaimed; and his eyes flashed bright as the steel he held above his head; ' back! The first who takes another step forward, falls.'

The officers were awed by his calm ferocity. He stood firm as a statue; every muscle and sinew was in play; his chest expanded, and his eyes gleamed dangerously.

There was a silence of some moments; the officers stood irresolute, fearing almost to attack the stranger charged with the foul murder.

Gerald did not move an inch; he stood firm, and determined to fight for liberty.

' Surrender,' said the officer, with official dignity.

Gerald laughed mockingly.

BLACK EYED SUSAN.

OR, PIRATES ASHORE.

READY FOR ACTION.

'Surrender for the crime of another? Never!' he said.

'It will be better for you to give in at discretion; if you are innocent you can prove it. This resistance will go against you.'

'Where is the chance of proving my innocence?' said Gerald, keeping his eyes on the leading officer; 'if I am taken, I shall have to suffer for the crime, and the real criminal will go at large. Where is the chance to vindicate myself of the foul charge? I am accused of the murder; I should have to suffer for it, if the assassin is not found.'

The officer was growing impatient; and the gentlemen, who quite believed Gerald to have committed the murder, urged the men on to take him.

'Will you give in quietly?' demanded the leader, angrily.

'I am innocent, and on that principle I shall fight for my liberty. Take me if you can.'

'Forward!' said the leader to his men; and, setting the example to lead them on, he drew his hanger, and rushed upon the masquerader.

Gerald brought his weapon down from his left shoulder with a terrible sweep, and struck his assailant a fearful blow across the brow with the flat of the blade.

The blow stunned him; he reeled, the sword dropped from his hand, and he fell back into the advancing ranks of his men.

Incensed by the fall of their leader, the officers rushed upon the captain in blind fury, and the gallants helped to capture him.

Gerald Stuart did not wish to kill the men; he did not want to be taken, and he could not keep them back by threats.

He retreated as they advanced, using the flat of his scimitar, knocking down the foremost of them.

The men pressed upon him more boldly, seeing his fear to kill.

Then his anger rose.

'Back, bloodhounds!' he thundered. 'I have avoided bloodshed till now.' And he struck down an officer with a fearful gash across his head. 'Back! or he will not be the last.'

'Down with him!' shouted the gallants.

The officers made a sudden rush at him; Gerald was thrown to the ground, and the officers swarmed around him.

Two secured his arms behind him, others held his legs, and one burly ruffian drew from his pocket a pair of handcuffs.

'Let's have the darbies on, mates,' he said, unlocking the iron circlets.

Gerald struggled fiercely to free his hands. He knew if he once got them on, his case would be hopeless.

By a sudden effort, and with wonderful strength, he drew up his legs and freed them from the grasp of his captors, at the same time twisting over on his back he shot up his feet over his head and struck two of the officers violently on the mouth.

The two officers reeled back. Before any of the others could secure him, he sprang up on his feet, but in an instant he was surrounded, and his arms pinioned behind him.

'It is no good to resist, you had better go quietly,' said one of the gentlemen.

'I am innocent, and I won't be taken,' answered Gerald, and he tried to break from his captors.

'Now, my blade, we'll just 'ave these ere bracelets on,' said the ruffianly speaker, and he brought the handcuffs again. 'Give us yer fist.'

Stuart grinned savagely, and displayed a double row of very white and well-shaped teeth.

It was impossible for him to attempt to oppose these men. He was held from head to foot by the rough hands of his uncouth captors, and it galled him bitterly to find himself overpowered.

'One,' said the officer, slipping one of the iron rings over the wrist of Gerald's white wrist.

'Two,' exclaimed the captive. By a sudden jerk he freed his hand, and struck the officer senseless at his feet by a blow on the head with the heavy irons swinging at his wrist.

'Three,' said another of the officers, administering Gerald a blow under the left ear that felled him to the floor.

Then the others fell upon him, but before they had time to execute their design, the casement at the end of the saloon was dashed open, and a clear voice sang out—

'Avast there, yer lubbers! Clear out, or damme I'll scuttle a few of yer.'

Every one started up, and turned their eyes towards the window. The gallant sailor Will sprang into the saloon with naked cutlass, and heedless of the officers' menacing looks dashed through them to the rescue of his captain.

'I heard you was in danger, captain, so I came,' he said, assisting Gerald to his feet, and keeping the officers back by making a circular sweep with his weapon from side to side.

'Thanks, my gallant Will,' said Gerald, gratefully, and he grasped the sailor's hand. 'You have arrived only just in time, the bloodhounds would have dragged me to prison for murder.'

'Murder!' repeated Will, in a hoarse whisper, and he looked at his captain in horror.

'But—bu—t—'

'No, Will, I did not do it. I am as innocent of the crime as you are,' said Stuart.

'I know you are, captain. Who said you did do it?'

'My stiletto was found thrust to the heart of the murdered man.'

Will looked bewildered.

'It is a mystery,' said Gerald. 'I missed the weapon from my belt. I must have some enemy at work, who plucked it from my sash while dancing, and has committed this foul deed to bring it home to me. The stiletto bears my initials.'

Will listened in grim silence, and his anger rose in fury to think of the treacherous scheme that had been laid for the destruction of Captain Gerald, whom he loved as a brother.

During this time he had kept the officers at bay by the motion of his sword; he lowered it now, and turning fiercely upon the men, demanded what they wanted.

They did not comprehend what he said, and Will was as ignorant of what they were saying.

'What are the jabbering apes talking about?' he asked.

'They tell me to surrender; and you, they say, had better not interfere.'

'Shiver my timbers, captain!' exclaimed Will, wrathfully. 'Is that what the swabs say? Well, if we don't give 'em a lacing, we ain't Britishers. Keep a clear course there, yer lubbers!' he added, flourishing his cutlass. 'By my love for pretty Sue, I'll be amongst you like a red-hot shot. Now then, lay-to if you want a peppering.'

He made a rush amongst the officers. They were taken aback by the daring, furious assault, and before they could recover their wonted equanimity, he had beaten his way to the door, followed by Gerald Stuart.

They had not descended more than half-way down the stairs, when the hurried rush of feet, and the frantic shouting of the officers in the saloon, assured them that the fellows had come to their senses, and did not mean them to escape.

'Come, Gerald,' said Will, 'or the lubbers will let daylight in our backs.'

They hurried down the long passage, followed closely by the enraged officers.

Will pulled open the door, and was in the act of leaping out into the street, when a body of soldiers, with lowered bayonets, drew up in front of the door.

Will drew back, with a fierce exclamation.

'It's no use, Will,' said Gerald, laying his hand on the other's arm, to prevent him using his weapon. 'I must go.'

'Then I go, too,' said Will. 'But let us have a try to get back. We can get out of the window.'

Gerald looked round. The officers stood in a square block, completely obstructing their way to the stairs.

There was no hope now; before and behind they were hard pressed by the foe.

The officer in command of the guards called upon them to surrender.

'I am wrongly accused of a murder of which I am innocent,' said Gerald.

'That is nothing to do with me,' said the young *parvenu*. 'You are my prisoners now. Do not put me to extremities by resistance; it will go against you.'

Gerald laughed satirically. It galled him to be spoken to in such a manner by a bare-faced boy. He saw how utterly impossible it would be to think of escaping; and to save the humiliation of being asked to surrender his sword, he threw it scornfully at the feet of the young officer.

Will looked on in some astonishment. He had listened to the foregoing conversation, but did not understand a word that was spoken, and it puzzled him to know how Gerald could talk with them.

'Give up your sword, Will,' said Gerald.

'I am not going to give up my sword.'

'You will have to, or they will take it from you.'

'Well, then,' said the gallant sailor — and he snapped the blade across his knee—'they can have it now.' And he threw it across the road.

The soldiers closed around them, and they were led away to prison.

CHAPTER LXVII.

GREGORY SAUNDERS KEEPS THE RATS COMPANY —A STRANGE SAIL—ITS ASSOCIATION WITH RODWIN BLAKE—HIS OLD SHIP AND CREW— HIS APPEARANCE AMONG THEM.

FOR a time we must turn the attention of our readers to the Sorcerer and her commander—the ruffian Saunders.

He was kept standing in Madeline's cabin, confronted by the beautiful and iron-nerved girl, Pauline, whose hand clutched a dagger with deadly intent.

The ruffian quailed with fear; for if she should give an alarm, her cries would bring Rodwin Blake, and he feared the man he had so foully wronged.

But a deadly glare came in his eyes as he regarded the lovely, palpitating form of Pauline. The phial he held in his hand contained a deadly drug—so dreadful and spontaneous in its effects, that if placed to the nostrils of anyone, it would deprive them of their senses.

He leered wolfishly at the beautiful girl, and a coarse grin overspread his face. He uttered no word or sound, but quick as lightning, he hurled the contents of the bottle into Pauline's face.

One long scream she gave.

'Victor!' she cried, then reeled, and would have fallen to the floor, but Gregory caught her in his arms, and the diabolical grin on his face deepened.

'Ah, beauty!' he thought, 'you shall pay for your interference.'

He was about to put his hot lips to hers, when a cold, iron-like hand gripped him by the throat, and curdled the very blood in his veins.

'At last,' came in a whisper of deadly menace. 'That is all I wanted, to get my clutch upon you. By hell, you shall shriek in your wild agony of torture for this! You shall have those infernal foul lips dried up—that infernal lewd grasp rendered powerless. You shall suffer all that I can devise for you.'

The ruffian's hold relaxed. Pauline fell to the floor, and he looked up.

Rodwin Blake was his captor.

'Let go; dare'——

Rodwin's laugh cut short his speech.

'Ha! ha! Fool! D'ye think you are master here? No, you are no longer captain. I have waited my time, now you suffer.'

Saunders went sick with fear. Blake did not say much, but it was his look—the tone of voice, the cold, pitiless—almost devilish cast of features that covered the brute in man's form.

Without another word or any great exertion, Rodwin Blake dragged Gregory upon deck—dragged him to his own quarter-deck, and hurled him, like a dog, into the arms of half a dozen men.

Then the spell broke.

'Hounds!' cried Saunders, trying to break away. 'Beware, I am your captain.'

The men laughed loudly.

'Is you now?' said one.

'Dogs! Have you dared mutiny?'

'Oh, no, it's you as mutinied; and we look on it as our duty to put you in irons. Lieutenant Blake's commander now; so be civil.'

This was a crushing blow for the villain.

The truth instantly flashed to his brain.

Blake had done his work fearfully in the dark. He had won over the crew, and the man he most feared on earth was now in his power—his captor, judge, and avenger.

A clammy sweat broke out upon him.

He dared not hope for mercy.

Blake, who had stood watching his fear and horror as the crew came up and every face showed its satisfaction, now came forward.

'Saunders,' he said, 'your blind conceit led you astray. You had the man you most feared always near you. You were a fool; for *he* worked in the dark. You will have plenty of time to think of what passed between us some time ago, and it may do you some good to know that I intend to have back a cry for cry, a pang for every pang that I have suffered. You shall revel in blood, as I did, and have to rule a pack of demons. Now, my lads!'

He turned to his men as he spoke.

'Put him away in the hold among the rats, where he will have plenty of company and time for reflection.'

'Oh, God! No, no! not there! not there!' supplicated the outwitted villain.

Blake laughed in savage mockery.

Then he spoke again—

'Curse you!' he said. 'Think yourself lucky you have even this mercy shown you; for my first impulse, when I saw you in the cabin, was to tear your heart out—ha! ha!—but I've *saved you for something worse!*'

And he laughed again.

'Now, men, take him away—load him with irons. No words, no cry, or you shall be forgotten altogether when you are there.'

Then the shrinking wretch was dragged away, irons placed upon his limbs, and then he was thrust in the loathsome hold of the vessel, and left to fight for life or become the food of rats.

His wild, unearthly cries died away as the hatch was closed over him, and the men, without a feeling of remorse, left him, and returned to their duty.

Rodwin Blake reigned supreme.

He had waited long—he had suffered much—but his time had come. He triumphed now—revenge would follow.

Aye, terrible revenge; and he was not the man to swerve an inch in his purpose, terrible as it was.

He had the vessel put in order, the men in their places, appointed his officers, and then went below to look after Pauline.

With what joy did she receive the news of their enemy's fall, and that they were no longer in his power.

'But the men,' asked Madeline, 'will they be constant?'

Blake smiled grimly.

'I reign supreme,' he said. 'I am liked and feared—mistrusted, yet depended upon—but I am safe.'

He was true in what he said.

Truly the men did not love him, but he had mastered a brutal tyrant—he had not asked them to turn traitors to their king—everything went on in man-of-war fashion; and, though many advocated a return, they feared the man whose terrible passions and power was so under his own control that he would subdue himself ere he conquered others, but when roused—a demon.

Three or four days passed.

A biscuit and water were given to the captain at intervals, but not a word was exchanged with him, and he was more than once on the verge of madness.

At dusk of the fourth day, a sail was reported.

Blake came on deck with his glass, and saw, to his surprise, that the strange vessel was closely followed by a smaller one, which he instantly conjectured must be a prize.

He was right.

The larger of the two came on at a sweeping pace, and Rodwin Blake never once moved his glass from the time he began to scrutinize the coming ship.

The men who were watching him saw his face change until it looked like one carved from marble.

The glitter in his eye was terrible, and when he turned his gaze upon those around him they literally recoiled.

'All hands up!' he said.

His cold, cutting voice sounded through the vessel, and roused the men from their very hammocks.

'Prepare for action!' was the next order.

The men looked astonished, and not a few moved.

He turned upon his officers, his aspect unchanged, excepting the look in his fine eyes, which, as he said—

'See my orders obeyed!'—

Warned the subordinates to do so without so much as a look of remonstrance or interruption.

The first few minutes of excitement over, everything was conducted in an orderly well-disciplined manner. Every man on the deck was well armed and the guns prepared for use.

Now they could afford a little time to speculate on the stranger, and suddenly a cry of mingled horror and joy rang through the ship.

At the masthead of the coming vessel they saw spread out in the dusky air of eventide, the ghastly device of piracy.

The black flag, with the skull and cross bones.

The stranger was a pirate.

How every heart beat with excitement and with nervous desire to begin the fray—with what gusto the men began to sharpen their cutlasses, reload their pistols, and put a point on the boarding-pike that made them dangerous to touch with the finger.

No sooner was any order issued than executed, and a smile of satisfaction wreathed the lips of their iron-willed leader.

It was observed that not once did he take his gaze from the direction of the pirate barque, and when at length it was within gun-shot, one short, savage, and blood-chilling chuckle left his lips.

'Prepare to fire! Steady! Let every shot tell, or there will be none of you left to tell of this day's work. Yon vessel is the "Wolf of the Waves."'

Then he added to himself—

'And I was its commander. Ha! ha! The traitors will not expect to see me.'

How his hand tightened on his sword, and he laughed in silent joy—or, rather devilish exultation.

At the mention of that dreaded name, a low, fierce murmur broke from our English tars, and they literally thirsted for the fray to begin.

No doubt existed now in the minds of the men but that the vessel in company with the Wolf of the Waves was some unfortunate prize.

No sooner did the pirates see the actual size of the English vessel than they set up a yell, hoisted another black flag, and run the guns out.

Then they fired a shot for the schooner to lay-to.

'Top man away—furl sails!' cried Blake, and in a few minutes the schooner lay almost motionless on the water.

Another yell from the pirates denoted their pleasure at what they thought submission, but how soon that yell changed into a whoop of bloodthirsty rage when a broadside from the English schooner was hurled amongst them with a terrible effect!

Cries, groans, and curses blended with the roar of cannon and sharp fire of musketry.

The pirate leader was furious at this unexpected attack, and he gave the pitiless order for them to run alongside and board, and to give no quarter nor mercy.

In spite of the terrible firing, the vessel was run alongside the Sorcerer, but Blake saw it coming, and his orders were then—

'Prepare to board. Wait until we touch their ship. Give them no time to mount our rigging. Board with a rush, and under the cover of the fire from the marines.'

Then the vessels came together with an awful concussion.

One wild whoop the pirates gave and dashed on the bulwarks, but not over.

A tremendous volley poured in by the British marines drove them back, and ere they could renew the attack, the boarding party was among them.

'Cut them down! cut them down!' yelled the pirate leader. But he stopped in his orders, his jaw fell, his face grew livid, and his arm dropped to his side powerless, as his eyes were fixed in awful fascination upon the leader of the British crew, who had been the first to leap aboard.

He was in the midst of the wild disorder, and facing the chief. The bloody strife had begun, when, in a voice of thunder, he yelled—

'Stop, one and all! D'ye know me? Will you strike the Wolf of the Waves?'

He tore aside his vest, and displayed the device. The contending parties paused—his own men from wonderment, the pirates from horror, for they beheld their late leader—a man not one on board would have menaced with death, even in his sleep.

They feared his very presence.

Wonderful was the effect of his presence. The mighty roar of battle ceased as though by magic. Every arm was stayed, and all eyes turned towards the being whose simple presence could do so much.

He stood quiet and rigid as a statue. He was on the poop, looking down like a grim avenger upon his men.

His teeth just gleamed between his lips, his eyes were immovably fixed upon the wounded leader, and without one sign of actual passion, he addressed them all—

'So we've met again. Was I expected? No, nor wanted. Look ye here—are you all traitors? whose work was it? Point him out. No lie, no word of deception, or, by the fiends eternal! I will exterminate the whole horde of you! Who is the traitor?'

A terrible silence seconded his words. A few heads were turned, and eyes looked occasionally at each other, but no one spoke.

The Wolf of the Waves had fixed his glittering orbs upon the chief of the pirates, and that man stood as though paralyzed with fear.

'You won't tell!' thundered Blake, leaping down, and, with a tiger-like spring, he was upon his treacherous lieutenant, and caught him by the throat.

'Miserable cur!' he cried. 'You dared to mutiny when I was far away. Curse you! you know your fate.'

He hurled him off his feet with mighty power, and putting his foot upon his chest, raised his blood-stained sword.

'One word,' he cried, 'from any man among ye that shall be in defence of this viper, and I'll smite his head off at a blow. WAS HE THE TRAITOR?'

One minute's awful stillness.

Then came a simultaneous answer—

'Ay, ay.'

'He made you mutiny?'

'Yes, yes.'

'You swear?'

'We do.'

'By what means?'

'He said you were dead, my chief,' said one, a tall, fine pirate, evidently first in command.

Blake laughed, and removed his grasp from the cowering wretch's neck.

'Take him,' he cried, 'put him in irons, and place him below. Let me see how quickly that is done, as a proof of your allegiance to me.'

Nearly the whole crew of desperadoes made a movement towards the unlucky traitor, and he would have been torn to pieces had not Blake called—

'Put him in irons, d'ye hear? The man who uses a knife or weapon of any kind, shall share his fate.'

That saved him being torn to pieces, and he was taken below, and confined in the hold.

'Now,' Blake went on, 'each crew back to his ship. Haul the prize alongside. Everything and every man in his place, and I give you twenty minutes to do it in. Then you shall see a sight. You shall have one among you that you shall turn into a demon ere you let him go.'

Then he went below to the state cabin. He saw, in a state of affrighted dishabille, a lovely woman.

She seemed dying of horror and fear. When he entered, with his breast still bare, a loud cry escaped her lips, and, starting back, with her hand upon the table, and her hair flowing over her lovely shoulders in rich disorder, she seemed to be almost stifling with some great emotion.

Then her eyes fell upon the ghastly device on his breast.

'Oh, God! 'Tis you, the Wolf of the Waves!' she exclaimed, ' and here!'

'Where should I be?' he said, his passionless voice unaltered, 'but here, *and with you.*'

CHAPTER LXVIII.

SAUNDERS AMONG THE RATS—PHANTOM SHADOWS—A TIME OF HORROR—HIS TERRIBLE FATE ANNOUNCED BY RODWIN BLAKE—BRANDED AS A PIRATE—OUT UPON THE DEEP.

WHAT a terribly bitter time it was to Gregory Saunders, after his imaginary power, at the moment he thought his triumph complete, to be thus humiliated by his foe.

He had need to fear him, too. He remembered the evil he had worked to Rodwin Blake, and he was aware that the whole fearful purpose of Blake's life was revenge.

And this was the way he began it.

Death, at the time, would have been mercy; that mercy was denied him. He was to suffer tortures untold.

And then the fate in store for him made his flesh creep.

What an age the first day of his captivity seemed!

How dreadful was the darkness ! how agonizing the stillness !

The nauseous air was stifling, and his heart sank with dread.

The first hour passed in fierce, vengeful thoughts. Evil passions were at war in his heart, and he harboured wild thoughts of revenge.

The second hour brought a change.

He was somewhat cowed. He thought more of himself—of his position ; how long he was likely to remain there ; if it would always be as silent and as dark, and the air as close—odious.

Then a strange feeling came over him, that he was not alone in the hole.

It was a strange, varied fancy, but it grew upon him stronger each minute, and at last he could not shake it off.

He stopped his own breathing, and listened.

No sound, save the sullen splash of the waters against the copping of the vessel. He tried to pierce the darkness ; but after straining his eyes until they nearly bled, he gave it up.

He could see nothing save darkness.

Still the feeling crept stronger and stronger upon him that he was not alone.

Aha! What was that?

The almost noiseless passage of some living thing past his feet. There was a faint scratching which reached him each minute. Truly he was not alone.

There were rats in plenty.

Yet he could not shake off the feeling, and going down upon his hands and knees he crept round the narrow limits of the hold.

Every few minutes he would recoil with a deadly chill all over him. His hand would come in contact with some slimy little reptile. Once his hand came full upon a large live rat, who did not approve of so extraordinary and never before experienced a liberty, and to testify its disapproval it caught the tip of Gregory's finger in its little mouth, gave it a nip, uttered a squeak that sounded like a modified scream of joy at the cry of pain it elicited from the daring intruder, and glided off in triumph.

Though common sense told Saunders that the only occupants of that tomb were rats beside himself, he could not shake off the superstitious awe, and he sat himself down in one corner with his back to the beams of the vessel, so that nothing at least could get behind him.

Wise precaution—only wait.

Now he sat, all thoughts of his crime gone from his mind, which was now full of horror, and the third hour came.

The horrors of that were well nigh too much for him.

He gave way to retrospection—at least he could not help going on—letting his thoughts run upon times gone by ; and in the dark and terrible hold, amid the unbroken silence and the blankness of a tomb, he had conjured up in his mind's eye bygone friends or enemies, kindred, and companions. Then the scene changed, one by one his past victims rose up before him, and filled his soul with horror.

He shut his eyes, tried to sleep, covered his face in his hands—all to no purpose.

The phantom shadows would rise up. They would make themselves visible to his disturbed imagination, and they would not be turned out of their legitimate spot of darkness and solitude.

So he sat and stared at the blank air—stared at imaginary shadows which took the form of those he had, perhaps, hurried from this world, by his own hand.

Stared until his eyes smarted, his head seemed ready to burst, his blood dry up, and his mind wrought horror upon horror—fancy followed fancy, until he uttered an irrepressible shriek.

A scamper of tiny feet followed the cry, and he was aware that it had scared away a troop of his foe.

The reptiles that had so unceremoniously bitten his finger some time before this, had gone to communicate to its fellows the intelligence, and no doubt painted the monstrous biped animal—or, in other words, Gregory Saunders—as a wonderful being that put himself in such ungainly shapes, emitted unearthly noises, but still upon being bitten, the benefit derived thereof by the biter was very great, and in every way satisfactory.

So the rats congregated, and, with the large one as their leader, they came out to look at the gigantic wonder, and, we dare say, all were more or less astonished, and felt that the present time was a great epoch in their short career.

But while they, perhaps, were discussing whether to trust themselves too near, he uttered an unearthly (to them) shriek, and they halted.

His cry seemed to break the spell. He crouched up in the dismal corner, and for the time his tortured brain was relieved from the view of the phantastic shadows.

But the rats came again.

He heard a persistent nibble, nibble, nibble—scratch, scratch—nibble ; then a silence.

Perspiration oozed out of every pore of his skin. He knew, from the experience of others, that the rats, on getting used to his presence, would attack him with impunity.

Actually, while he was devising some means by which he could at least keep them off, he felt a sudden nip on the blade-bone of the back—a burning sensation followed, and he jumped up with a sharp cry of agony.

One of the treacherous little wretches had got behind him, and drove him out of his corner ; and being thus disturbed, he kept going round and round his dark prison, thinking motion would keep off his foes.

It did for a time ; but fancying at last he did not intend to give them a chance, a whole pack of the vermin attacked him openly, and he had to fight for it.

We will not dwell upon so horrible a scene. Let it suffice that his time passed in this manner; either in a delirious kind of raving and talking to imaginary persons around him, or in moaning, or fighting with the rats, hour after hour passed ; each one was worse than the other ; the hours rose into days, and he was little better than a madman.

He had, in times of despair, blasphemed and laughed in scorn at anything earthly or unearthly ; at others he had raved and wept ; and at length he tried to pray.

Mockery.

The words would not form themselves ; if they did they seemed to stick in his throat.

His cheeks were sunken and hollow ; his hands and legs torn by the rats ; his eyes sunken back ; and his mind almost unseated.

On the fourth day, when he sat huddled up in the corner, waiting for death—trying to pray for death—he heard the loud roar of cannonading.

That revived him.

But it did not last long, and again the silence of death reigned around him. He wondered at the cause, and while he was wondering, he had heard a noise above his head; the hatchway was removed, and two forms dropped into his loathsome prison.

One of the new-comers carried a lantern, and the light so dazzled the eyes of the prisoner that he was compelled to cover his face with his hands.

Shrinking back into one corner of the hold, he gasped, hoarsely—

'Away!—go away!'

'Avast, skipper—yer is wanted on deck; and a good thing it ain't the devil as wants yer; so be easy. But he'll have yer soon.'

'Ay, come on deck, mate; we've no time to lose, and orders not to lose any.'

Gregory Saunders was clutched by the sailors, and dragged forward.

'Let's have a look at yer,' said the holder of the light. And he let the glare fall full upon his face.

Even the rough hearts of those men were touched as they looked upon that face, so full of abject misery.

The sunken and torn cheeks, the drooping jaw, sunken orbs, tattered clothes, and torn limbs—lacerated by the rats—caused his appearance to be wearied and horrible.

'Come on, skipper,' said the lamp-bearer, less roughly.

The sight touched him, but he had no great pity for the man who could wrong his best friend, and attempt the ruin of his daughter.

They took the suffering wretch upon deck, and the shades of night darkening the air, he was able to bear the faint twilight shadows.

The scene that met his gaze startled him.

There were three ships, side by side. On the poop of the centre one stood his cold-blooded foe, Rodwin Blake.

The deck of the large pirate barque was crowded with men.

'Knock off his irons,' cried Blake.

It was done.

Gregory Saunders stood before the man he detested, free—every limb at liberty; yet he dared not move.

Standing in a group on the deck of the vessel Saunders lately commanded, were fourteen or fifteen men he had employed on the night of his escape from prison—men, whose very souls were steeped in blood, and they were hired on that account.

They were ordered to go on board the Wolf of the Waves, and range themselves on the starboard side with a lot more men picked out for some purpose.

'Bring Despardo on deck,' said Rodwin Blake.

The traitor, who had been taken away in irons, was brought on deck again, and guarded by two men; he stood by the side of Saunders, awaiting the ordeal.

He did not wait long.

The vessel that had been in company with the pirate ship was a well armed corvette.

Blake pointed to this, and addressed Saunders—

'That ship,' he said, 'is going to be yours, and that crew.'

He pointed to the men on the starboard side.

'That crew will man her. You wanted to revel in blood—to glory in power. You shall. You wanted to rule demons—you've got 'em now, curse you!

Look up. D'ye remember a time gone by when I was in your power, when I fell under the effects of a drug, you had me branded, and I was put among the men to rule as leader, or lose my life? So shall you be; but I tell you what I am going to do. D'ye remember, I swore to have revenge? Ha! ha! I shall keep my word; but see how.'

He pointed to a long narrow platform that had lately been erected, and Saunders shuddered.

'Look yonder; that's your flag, your device, and you will have that branded on you as this,' he cried, striking his breast on the device thereon, 'as this was on me. Do your work, men.'

Half-a-dozen of the bloodthirsty brutes rushed forward, and clutched Gregory Saunders in their rough grasp.

That long, narrow platform had been erected for him.

For what?

Let us not dwell too much upon the incarnate work that followed.

He was strapped down, implements were brought, a man stood over him, tore the clothes from his breast, and when it was done, he began to work upon it with something that made the poor wretch scream in awful agony.

One half-hour passed thus, one half-hour of horror—bitter, dreadful horror, and when at length he was put upon his feet, his form was distorted, a foam hung thickly upon his lips—upon his breast was something worn.

A vulture, in blood-red colour, was branded on his chest, in its claws was a dying dove.

Saunders was in a kind of lethargy; he had his senses, knew the awful scenes that were going on around him, but seemed without the power to move.

Rodwin Blake, pointing to the mast head of the corvette, caused Gregory to look that way. He saw a black flag with a blood-red device on it, or a fac-simile of that upon his breast.

Blake spoke—

'You know your doom, and your flag, this is your crew, and there's no shrinking from the work. Hear me. The vultures have sworn to me to keep you as their leader, to see that you don't shirk your work; night and day you shall ravage the seas, you shall revel in blood until your heart is sick; you must lead them on, or they'll find a way of making you suffer. Go; remember your duty until we meet again.'

He waved his hand. The men gave a terrific cheer, and went on board the corvette.

Blake took up a bottle of wine.

'Now go,' he said. 'And you, Despardo, go with him. Here are your instructions; don't break the seal until daybreak. Maybe you'll like your fate when you read it. Ha! ha!—I've kept my oath! Go, and hie to the Red Vulture. Long live the service!'

He dashed a bottle of wine against the ship's bows as the Wolf of the Waves veered off a little, and Gregory stood on his ship's deck, among his legion of fiend-like men.

He turned his face to his foe.

'We shall meet again,' he cried, the spell broken. 'Then, beware.'

'You know your fate—fulfil it, and take with you my curse, my bitterest curse—the curse of an old man you wronged, and that of his daughter—the curse of your dead wife! And when scenes of blood have driven you mad, come back to me, and suffer the last ordeal, for we shall meet again.'

———

CHAPTER LXIX.

THE BEAUTIFUL MYSTERY IN THE CELL OF THE
CONDEMNED—THE ESCAPE—WILL'S PERIL AND
RE CAPTURE.

TIME wore but slowly with Gerald Stuart and his companion, Will, in their dungeon home. They saw no change, knew not day from night, and every hour seemed an age.

The jailer came and went, but never spoke. He would leave their pitcher of cold water and loaf of dry bread morning and night, and they saw no more of him until he came his nightly rounds to see that all was secure.

The silence was torturing, the sombre gloom oppressive, their senses became dull and heavy, their limbs cramped, and they grew tired of each other's presence.

At first they had tried to kill the lingering hours by conversation, but of that they grew tired, and relaxed into a mood of melancholy despondency.

Gerald Stuart had cherished a hope of being released. He had friends in Paris, and he wondered why he had not heard from them. Had they, too, condemned him of the dark murder of which there was such damning evidence of the deed brought against him by the silver dagger?

Then, on second thoughts, he found relief. His identity remained unknown up to the time of his capture, and he had been apprehended for the murder as the corsair with the silver, the blood-stained weapon, the evidence of his guilt.

'I shall be spared at least the calumny of my friends,' he meditated, 'but should they hear of my capture for the murder, what can they think? I shall be branded as an assassin, be accused of a murder of which I swear to the immaculate God I am innocent of! But who will believe it on such infernal proof? My dagger was found in the dead man's breast, and I must die for another's crime.'

The creaking of the cell-door made him start. He looked up. He had got used to the regulated hours of the prison. This was not the time for his jailer to come, and he wondered at the unusual visit.

A veiled lady entered the cell. The jailer placed a lantern on the stool, and with a haughty wave of the hand she demanded him to leave her.

The lady uncovered her face, when the man had gone, and revealed her lovely features.

Gerald gazed upon her in raptured wonder and admiration. He recognised the beautiful creature, Lady Catherine, and marvelled much to see her there.

Her large eyes were full of tender pity, and two tears hung on her long lashes like diamond dewdrops; then she started, and her countenance changed as her gaze fell upon a hudled heap in one corner.

'You are not alone, Captain Gerald?' she said, in a sweet, tremulous voice, and her magnificent bust heaved with concentrated emotion.

Gerald did not answer. He remained with his eyes fixed upon the lovely creature before him, his every sense was enthralled by her dazzling beauty.

The lady seemed vexed by his silence, then she dissembled, and her looks were all tender pity.

She went towards the prisoner, and laid her little hand on his shoulder.

'Captain Stuart,' she cried.

The music of her voice fell upon his ear like a charm; he started to his feet, and impressively took her hand.

She did not resist. He pressed a fervent kiss upon her fingers, and looked steadily into her brilliant orbs, as though he would have reached her very soul to know the secret of her visit.

The lady returned the gaze with a steady look, that sent a thrill of rapture through his every nerve. She felt his hand close around her arm with a nervous pressure, and a pleasing flush mounted his pale sunken cheeks.

The lady smiled secretly, but there was meaning behind that smile—a look of triumph.

'To what am I indebted for the honour of this visit, madam?' asked Gerald.

'You rendered me a service when my carriage was overturned,' she answered. 'I have come to see if I can be of any assistance to you.'

Gerald thought not of it, he wondered what interest she could have to get admittance to the prison where the regulations were so strict.

'Who is that person?' She pointed to the corner of the cell.

'My first lieutenant,' replied Captain Stuart.

Lady Catherine gave the gallant fellow a friendly glance. Will dropped his gaze and blushed. He had drawn himself up to a sitting posture, and was scanning their mysterious visitor intensely when he met her brilliant glance.

The miseries of the prison confinement had wrought a pitiful change on the hearty, robust fellow.

His cheeks were sunken and haggard, his eyes wild-looking, and his frame shrunken and drawn up as though with cramp.

'This is a fearful place,' said the lady, and she shuddered.

'I don't care how soon I get out of it,' Gerald remarked; 'but when I am removed, I suppose it will be only from here to the headsman.'

His deep-toned, melancholy voice sent a cold thrill through her.

'Not so,' she said, 'I have come to release you.'

'You!' exclaimed Gerald, and Will started up.

'That is, I have done my best to secure your liberty,' she said. 'Here are the means of escape.'

She drew from under her cloak a curl of strangely platted cord and a paper parcel.

'In what way will these aid us?' Gerald sighed despondently, as he took the cord. 'Immured within these four walls, I see not the use of this.'

The lady coloured indignantly.

'You are ungrateful,' she said; 'but come, don't despair; I must forgive you for your want of courtesy. The means of escape do appear very small at present, but then I have not told you all.'

Gerald bowed low.

'Pardon me, lady,' he said. 'I have grown uncouth in captivity.'

The lady acknowledged the apology by a sweet smile.

'In that parcel,' she said 'you will find the implements used for cutting through iron. It will take about an hour to cut through the bolts and lock of your cell door, begin you work when the jailer has gone his last round.'

'But,' put in Gerald, 'the scraping will bring the fellow in, who keeps guard outside all night.'

Lady Catherine smiled incredulously.

'There is a small bottle of liquid with the tools,' she cried, 'which will prevent all the grating

BLACK EYED SUSAN.

OR, PIRATES ASHORE.

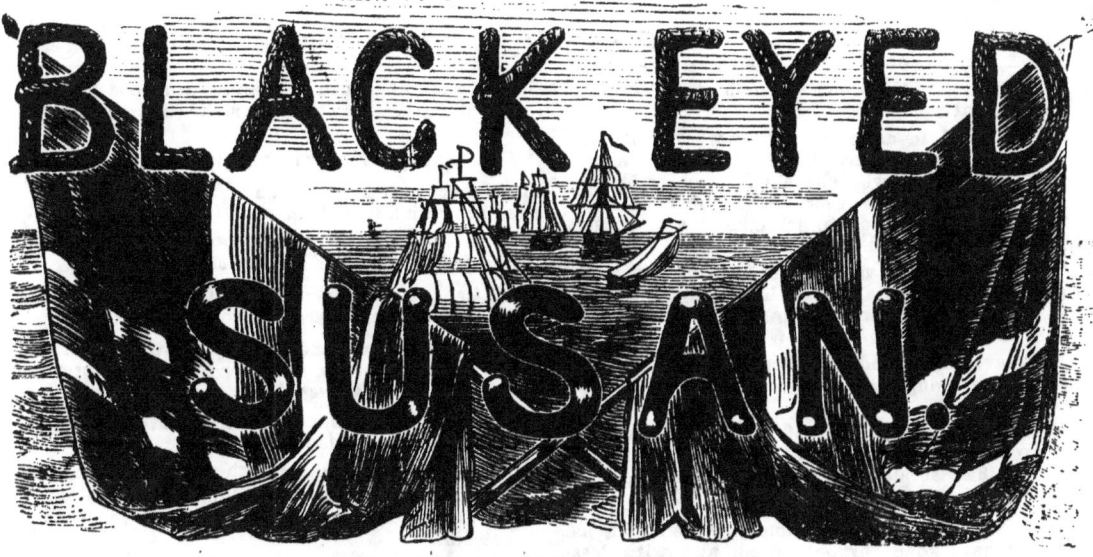

SUSAN'S PERIL.

sound, and soften the iron, so you have nothing to fear from that.'

' What am I to assign for this mark of interest you have taken in my behalf madam ? ' asked Gerald, wondering why she should trouble herself about him. ' I shall ever be indebted to you. Name anything I can do to serve you in return for this generous act, and I am your slave.'

' Come to me when you are free,' she replied, ' and I will then tell you the cause I had for your liberation. Come the instant you are free. I must now go.'

She waved her hand and departed, leaving the captives wondering what motive she could have for their liberation.

No sooner had the sounds of the jailer's footsteps died away along the stone yard, after his last round at night, than Gerald set to work with file and saw.

He and his lieutenant worked alternately.

The saw went through the iron with the liquid, as it would have gone through wood, and with less noise.

The last bar to liberty was sawn through—the ponderous door quietly and cautiously opened.

A man—a malignant-looking ruffian—stood at the entrance, with a pair of long-barrelled pistols, waiting for the prisoners.

Will, quick as thought, pounced upon the fellow, snatched the weapons from him, and dragged him into the cell.

The man was taken too much by surprise to utter a cry, and, before he could recover from the shock, he was gagged and bound hand and foot.

All this was done in a few seconds and in profound silence.

Will placed the pistols in his belt, and reconnoitred the place, to see that all was clear for them to proceed, while Gerald Stuart made a noose in one end of the rope with a slip knot, to throw over the spikes of the high wall.

' It is all clear, captain,' said Will, returning. ' There ain't any pirates about.'

Gerald closed the cell door after him, and cast the line, with the loop in it, over the wall—a very high wall, thickly studded with long iron spikes.

The rope hitched, Gerald gave it a twitch to ascertain its strength, and began to mount hand over hand.

Will followed him when he had got half way up ; so, by the time Gerald was at the top Will, was half way up.

It would have been much better for him had he been at the top too.

He felt a sudden tug at the rope, that nearly precipitated him over.

Looking down, he saw the jailer they had left in the cell coming up the rope after him, with a very formidable weapon held in his teeth.

Will was so astonished at the appearance of the fellow that he remained stationary, looking down in blank dismay.

The voice of Gerald from above awoke him to the danger of his position.

' Avast there, you lubber ! ' said Will.

The jailer held on grimly just beneath him with one hand, and inserted his sword in that part of the sailor's person where his ' slacks ' fitted most tightly.

Will gave a spasmodic shout of pain, and fairly sprang up the rope.

Will heard the fellow giggling. The insult of being laughed at, added gall and wormwood to his injured dignity. He took a pistol and spitefully said—

' Take that, you lubber ! ' and fired.

The lubber got it in the shoulder, and he fell on the stones with a dull thud.

The pistol report and the agonised yell of the maimed jailer roused his brother officers.

Will had gained the summit of the wall when a troop of armed men swarmed into the prison yard.

A shout from one, and the rapid advancement of the others, as they drew up under the wall, informed Will that he was discovered.

He hauled up the rope and threw it over the other side as a clutch was made at it.

Gerald slid down it like a flash of lightning.

Will was not slow to follow him. His head was on a level with the top of the wall when a volley was fired at him.

The bullets whistled over him ; one carried off his cap, and slightly grazed his head.

For the moment he thought he was shot. Forgetting his position in his terror, he clapped both hands over the injured part, lost his equilibrium, and fell back.

Instinctively he twined his legs, while falling, round the rope ; and there he hung, with the desperation of a wild cat.

The rope, not being very thick, and being extremely finely plaited, it did not give much purchase, and presently he felt himself gradually slipping down.

His position was a critical one. He was now more than fifty feet from the ground, and the idea of descending that distance on his head was a torturing contemplation to a man with his faculties.

Will broke out into a cold sweat. He was going down faster ; he felt that his feet would unlock ; and then—horror !

He experienced, in an instant, as the thought flew through his brain, all that must follow such a collapse—the fall through the air, with its stunning sensations ; the shock as he reached the stones ; the torturing pains that shot through his limbs, drawing up every muscle, as if each one was being torn from his body ; then came over him the sickening feeling of death.

In frantic despair he shrieked aloud, and by a desperate effort threw his body up over his feet, and clutched the rope, and with wonderful velocity slid down.

Gerald caught him in his arms, and was startled by the wild expression of his looks.

' Will ! Will ! What ails you, man ? ' he inquired, in great alarm.

' All right, captain,' replied Will, shaking himself ; and he laughed at his own fears. ' I thought I should have taken a dive from aloft into the other world.'

' Are you hurt ? '

' Well, it may be I am, but I don't feel it. The lubbers let fly at me, and a shot carried away my forelock with it.'

' Go, then, Will—return to the ship. We shall have the sharks upon us in a minute.'

' Ay, ay, captain. But it strikes me that pretty craft that came to see us to-day didn't show her true colours ; and it may be you will want a helping hand. I didn't like the look of her top-lights ; they were too much like treacherous beacons luring one on to destruction. So, if you do not mind, I will cas anchor near the port you'll run into, so that I shall be at hand on the first signal of distress.'

'Have no fear on my account, Will; I can manage a woman,' replied Gerald.

'But there may be others laying about ready to overhaul you.'

'She cannot mean me harm, or she would not have effected our escape. Come, Will, you return to the ship; one of us are wanted there. Let the lads know that I am not in danger, and get everything ready for going under weigh to-morrow.'

Will parted with the captain very gloomily; he felt that he was going into danger. He walked slowly away, suddenly stopped, and looked back.

Gerald's graceful form was fading in the distant gloom.

Will stood, irresolute, and watched him till he was out of sight.

'I don't like to disobey orders,' he mused; 'but, damme! I can't let him go alone.'

And he started after Gerald at a run.

He had not got far when he was confronted by a body of men, whom he knew to be the prison officials in search of him.

He was in a fix.

They were six, well armed.

He was alone, and without any weapon of defence.

For all that, he did not intend to be taken.

The men were jabbering at him in French, which he did not understand.

'Sheer off, yer swabs!' he shouted, and, like a tiger breaking through a jungle, he leaped amongst the men, scattered them right and left, and made off with all speed.

His flight did not last long.

One of the Frenchmen—a meagre little fellow, fleet of foot as an antelope—darted after him and when within arm's-length he aimed a blow at Will's head with the butt of a gun, that brought him senseless to the earth.

The others were soon surrounding him, eager as a pack of wolves.

And the gallant sailor, unconscious of his danger, was again in the hands of his foes, being borne away to prison.

CHAPTER LXX.

TOM TILLER AND PETER IN SEARCH OF BOB BRACE.

TOM TILLER and his companion, Peter, whom we left on their fruitless search for the old coxswain, lost themselves amongst the narrow, dirty little streets of Havre as the night drew on.

'It strikes me, Peter, the old cuss has lost himself,' observed Tom Tiller, alluding to Bob Brace.

'D——d old fool!' growled Peter. 'Should like to know what business he had to go arter the skipper. He's allas doing summat clever. If he hadn't gone we shouldn't ha' got into strange water.'

'Ne'er mind, Peter,' said Tom, consolingly, 'I daresay we shall be able to steer out of here into clear water.'

Peter grunted. He was in a bad humour, and being out of tobacco did not console his feelings. He would not ask his companion for any—he could not condescend to do that in his present mood—so, in desperation, he thrust his hands into the depths of his pockets, and looked all the disgust he felt at his forlorn position.

Tom Tiller regarded him askance.

'Peter,' he said, 'don't be out of temper.'

'Out of temper, be b——d! who's out of temper?'

'Well, mate, it's all right.'

'Is it?' grumbled Peter. 'I should like to know where we are.'

'Oh! somewhere about France. Why don't yer have a smoke, Peter?'

'Can't smoke a empty pipe, can I?'

'Ain't yer got no bacca?'

'If I had I should smoke it.'

'Oh! well, here yer are, mate,' and Tom pulled out a dirty piece of twist from a corner of his pocket.

Peter took it and thanked him with a grunt. Cutting some of it into small shreds, he crammed the bowl of a short black clay, and commenced to puff away vigorously.

'Don't be down, mate,' said Tom.

'Who's down?' asked the other, indignant at being accused of such a thing now he had a pipe of tobacco, 'I'd like to know when we're going to get back to the ship?'

'When we find our way there.'

Peter pulled away fiercely at his pipe, and watched the white clouds he puffed forth ascend and melt into the air.

'Perhaps you'll ask yer way?' he said, turning suddenly upon his companion, 'I would, if I knew the lingo.'

'All right, mate, we shall get along all right, when we get out o' this cussed place. S'pose yer won't say no to a glass of grog?'

'S'pose I won't,' Peter grunted, more quietly. 'I am as dry as a red herring.'

They turned into a little café, a dingy, dilapidated-looking place from the exterior, but the interior presented quite a different appearance.

The place was spacious, brilliantly lighted up, and thronged with a gay company.

The old tars entered shyly, and Tom, with what little French he knew, made the landlord understand his wants.

He was astonished to hear two rather pretty and very showily dressed young women conversing close to him in broken English.

Old Tom gave them a furtive glance. He looked remarkably wicked, and the girls were not in the least bashful.

'Ah, monsieur,' said one, with an arch smile, and she laid her hand on his arm, 'we are Anglish.'

'Ah me!' answered Tiller, with an air of impertenence.

'None of that, Tom,' said Peter.

Tom gave him a look of disdain.

Peter moved to the other end in deep disgust.

'D—d old fool, s'pose he's going along of 'em.'

And to smother his indignation at such depravity, he drained off his grog at a gulp.

For an old salt, Tom Tiller made capital progress with his fair companion. They seemed quite to understand each other.

The girl whispered something in his ear that brought a ruddy glow to his weather-beaten face.

He gave her a ravishing look, and then cast his eyes inquiringly towards his companion.

Peter looked awfully miserable. Leaning over the counter, with his head supported in his hand, he cast a longing glance towards the girl disengaged, despite his disgust at the proceedings of his messmate.

'Go and trice up my mate,' said Tom to his companion's friend.

The girl seemed delighted, and advancing towards the discontented sailor, glided her arm through his, and looked persuasively into his face.

'Hallo, here!' said Peter.

'Well, monsieur, we are very cross.'

'Cross be d—d, I don't want none of your overhauling, so clear out, or damme—'

The girl patted his cheek.

Peter's look of astonishment was great. His features relaxed into a smile.

'Ah!' said the girl, smiling and touching him again on the cheek, 'me taught we wasn't angry.'

Peter felt his resolution giving way. At the time he was grumbling he was half disposed to hug the girl to his heart.

'Sheer off,' he grumbled, trying to shake her off his arm. 'I don't want no petticoats hanging round my neck if my mate is such a fool.'

'Oh, monsieur, dat am very wrong. You do not love de ladies,' and the girl gave a look of disappointment.

Peter could not hold out any longer, the despairing look conquered him. He sidled up to his companion.

'Well, mate?' said Tom.

'Well, mate!' grumbled the other. 'You've done a d—d nice thing, ain't yer?'

'What's the matter?'

'The matter! who the blazes told yer to send the ass to me?'

'Well, mate, I likes to act square, an' it warn't right for me to 'ave two while you had none.'

Peter began to sober down.

'What are yer going to do, Tom?'

Tom gave him a comical glance, and looked towards his fair companion.

'Well, mate, I reckon I shall take a cruise along of her,' he said.

'And what am I to do?'

'Take a cruise along of the other.'

'Got any silver?' whispered Peter, in the other's ear.

Tom nodded, gave his companion part of what money he had in his pocket, and with the girls hanging on their arms they sallied out.

Peter became quite sociable, and chatted on gaily. He told Tom he thought he should soon be able to speak French if he had his companion for a governess.

The girl told him he could visit her whenever he chose, and Peter fell quite in love with her.

'Never clapped my toplights on such a figurehead afore,' he said, confidentially, to his messmate.

His opinion was greatly altered though with what occurred.

They were taken to a house in one of the back streets, and shown into a neat little room, where they were requested to wait while the female parties went out to get refreshments, having previously extorted from the simple, generous hearted fellows what money they had about them.

Peter and his companion waited in anxious anticipation for their return.

Half an hour passed. They did not come.

Tom Tiller became uneasy, a suspicion of the truth struck him.

They had been fleeced.

His face lengthened lamentably. He dived his hand into his moneyless pockets, and swore mentally.

'I know it,' exclaimed Peter, suddenly.

'Knew what?'

'It's all through you.'

'How is it?'

'I didn't want to come.'

'I didn't ask you to.'

'It was through you, and pretty fools we look here, fleeced by two girls. D—d if I am going to be done though.'

'Nor me either. I'll either have my money back or —'

He kicked over the table by way of finishing his sentence.

The noise brought some one up stairs.

Tom Tiller took up the poker, and sprang up as the door opened.

Two burly bullies entered.

'Now, my kiddies,' said Tom, brandishing the formidable weapon menacingly, 'tell us where them cussed shemale pirates are gone.'

The two Frenchmen were roused by the fury of the sailors.

'What are you making a noise about?' asked one of them.

'Look, here,' Tom answered them in French, 'we ain't agoin' to be done. Where are the gals?'

'Out, and you had better go, too, or we shall pitch you out.'

The old fellow burned with rage; a threat of being pitched out by two Frenchmen was more than he could stand. He swung the poker round his head and sprang towards them.

The Frenchmen retreated.

'What did they say, mate?' asked Peter, who did not understand a word that was spoken.

'They said they would pitch us out,' answered Tom Tiller, wrathfully. 'Them pitch us out, us two Englishmen, why—why—why, bust me, I'll eat 'em alive.'

'Pitch us out, did they say?' Peter rose quiet and terrible.

The Frenchmen were as ignorant of what had been said as Peter was when they spoke, and they advanced courageously to carry out their threat.

Peter pounced upon one like a tiger, and sent him to the ground before he knew where he was.

'Pitch us out, curse yer, will yer?' He clutched the fellow by the ears, and bumped his head on the hard oaken floor.

Tom Tiller leaped on the other, and knocked him down with the poker.

He was up again, though, in another moment, and planting his foot in Peter's side, sent him rolling over.

Then Peter's antagonist got up, and served Peter as Peter had served him. But he did not keep at that game long, Peter hit him a blow under the nose that sent him over like a ball.

Then Peter got up, rolled up his sleeves, and met the Frenchman like a prize fighter.

The Frenchman did not understand pugilistic science, so, instead, he used his feet.

One blow in the stomach doubled Peter up, it was followed up by the other foot, that struck him under the nose as he bent forward, and put him erect, rattled his teeth, and made him see at least fifty Frenchmen dancing around him.

Peter was confused beyond action by the attack and kicks rained upon him in rapid succession.

'That's yer game, is it?' Peter waited his opportunity, clutched the Frenchman's leg, and, by a sudden jerk, hurled him over the banisters.

The Frenchman fell heavily at the bottom of the stairs.

Having disposed of his antagonist, Peter went to assist Tom Tiller, but at that moment Tom prostrated his foe with the poker.

The fellow lay quietly, but when his companion came limping up stairs, armed with two huge sticks, he sprang to his feet and took one of them.

A terrific encounter then ensued.

Tom Tiller and his opponent fought hand to hand, but where Tom got one blow the other got several unmerciful stripes with the poker, his body felt like a bag of jelly, but he would not give in—the worse for him.

Peter got some awkward cracks from his opponent before he got the stick from him, then the game changed and the Frenchmen cried for quarter.

Peter, thinking he was being sworn at, belaboured the fellow the more.

In the midst of the uproar the two girls appeared upon the scene of action.

The fight stopped.

The two Frenchmen sneaked off like the beaten curs they were, swearing vengeance on the Anglais.

The girls smiled at their defeat.

Tom and his companion, forgetting their antipathy towards the girls at the sight of their smiling faces, embraced them and were happy.

The girls had merely come up to stop the row, and get rid of the Englishmen, but the Englishmen were not to be got rid of, so they had to submit to the compact they had formerly agreed to, and each, with her chosen companion, retired to a separate room.

In the night Tom Tiller was awoke by a noise in his room. He started up in bed. He was alone.

He swore again he had been outwitted.

His chamber door was open. He saw a dark form entering, crawling along on all fours.

Tom clutched the water-bottle, and threw it at the object of his surprise.

The bottle hit the object, and smashed on his head. There was a howl, and the object rolled on his back.

Tom sprang out of bed, and pounced on the intruder in a storming rage, increased by the disappointment at finding himself alone.

The intruder was his late opponent, the Frenchman. He came in for revenge, and Tom gave it to him.

While Tom was rolling about on the floor fighting with the Frenchman, a disturbance occurred in the next chamber.

The vindictive Frenchmen had thought to attack the sailors while asleep, and reek their vengeance in full.

They were a little out in their calculations; sailors do not sleep too sound, as they discovered on entering.

Peter, like his companion, was disappointed to wake up and find himself alone.

But he awoke in time to see a white form making a rapid exit from his room with a bundle under its arm.

Peter jumped out of bed and ran after it. At the door he caught in his arms a man who was entering.

It was the other Frenchman, and Peter threw him to the ground.

This was the noise that Tom had heard.

Tom had laid his foe *hors de combat*, when Peter entered, dragging with him the other Frenchman by the hair.

'Damme! I thought so!' he said, throwing the Frenchman down, with a jerk that made his head ring as it came in contact with the bedsted leg. 'I've lost my kit, Tom.'

A frightful suspicion struck Tom, and he looked round for his clothes.

'Clean gone,' he said, with a look of blank despair, 'socks, boots and all.'

'The long shore lubbers—the pirates!' Peter exclaimed, 'this is a nice state of things. We can't go back to the ship like this!'

And he looked down at his long hairy legs, bare from above his knee.

'That's sartin,' replied Tom.

His eyes fell upon a pistol lying on a side-board, but it was empty.

Seizing one of the Frenchmen by the throat, he thrust the cold barrel in his ear.

The Frenchman shivered, and turned up his eyes in terror.

'Now, yer lubber,' said Tom, in a tone that made his captive's blood freeze in his veins, 'bring back our clothes, b—— yer, or cuss me, I'll blow yer brains out!'

The Frenchman consented if Tom would only remove the pistol.

'Not a bit of it!' replied the sailor, priming; and he pulled the trigger on full cock. 'Now then, lead the way, or'——

The Frenchman broke from him, and darted forward.

Peter tripped him up with his foot as he reached the door.

Tom pulled him to his feet, and thrust the deadly tube deeper in the other ear.

'Try that on again,' he said, 'and you are a dead man.'

The Frenchman looked timidly into his face.

'I mean it,' said Tom.

His looks confirmed his words—they were remorseless.

The Frenchman did not make a second attempt to escape. Dutiful as a child—an obstinate one, compelled into compliance by force—he conducted his captors to a room below the stairs.

Peter jumped past them as they entered, and threw himself against a door on the opposite side, to prevent the exit of the female dupes.

'No, yer don't,' he said. 'I want to see that all my things are right afore yer go.'

Tom Tiller placed his captive against the door by which they had entered.

'If you make a move to go, I shall let fly,' he said, warningly.

Then he commenced to examine the things, while Peter guarded the other door.

'Two watches, one bacca-pipe, and a box gone,' said Tom. 'Where are they?'

He looked towards the girls.

They looked uneasily at each other.

' Give 'em up,' said Tom, severely, ' or, cuss me! —I don't care for yer sex—I'll let fly.'

He levelled the pistol at them. One of the girls gave a frightened shriek, and clung to Peter for protection.

Peter glided his arm round her supple waist. She was in *deshabille*, just as she had escaped from him; he could feel her warm form palpitating, and it sent an intoxicating thrill through him.

' Come, that'll do, mate,' he said, giving way beneath the influence of his interesting position. ' What d'ye want to frighten the lass for? Cuss the watch! She's welcome to it for what I care.'

And he kissed the lips of the pleading, upturned face.

' Ah, well! I ain't a-goin' to lose mine,' said Tom, firmly. ' They don't get over me. I ain't a fool; so give up the watch, whichever of yer's got it; I means to 'ave it.'

' Dare dey are,' said his late partner, pointing to a table on which a small work-box stood.

Inside this box he found the missing articles. Tom then began to dress.

Peter did not seem in any hurry to follow his example.

' Hallo!' shouted Tom, ' my prisoner's gone.'

Which was a fact. But it did not much matter now, and Tom did not trouble himself about it.

' Well, yer swab, how long are yer going to stand there?' said Tom, turning to Peter, in deep disgust.

Peter only pressed the daughter of Eve closer to his side, and gave her a look full of meaning. No, he did not wish to stand there!

' Well, I shall go without yer.'

' You can go,' said Peter, quite content to remain behind.

' Ugh, yer lubber!' And Tom turned on his heel to leave; but he was met at the door by the two Frenchmen, armed with ugly-looking blunderbusses.

They brought these from their shoulders in a line with his breast.

Tom scampered back.

Peter gathered up his clothes and rushed to his fair companion for protection.

The tables were turned now.

The girl was not ungrateful. She took him by the arm, and they passed through the other door.

Tom was left deserted. The other girl followed them. Tom thought that was the best thing he could do, and with a bound he leaped through the aperture, and closed the door after him.

The Frenchmen swore like troopers, and rushed after them, bent on their destruction.

Things had taken a very serious turn.

Peter stumbled several times while being led along, in trying to get his legs into his trousers.

They entered another room. They must escape by the window—they had no alternative. The Frenchmen could be heard coming after them.

Peter drew his fair girl to his side, and gave a sigh as he kissed her.

The enemy were in the room.

Peter turned. He saw his messmate scrambling out of the window, and hastened to follow him.

There was a shout from the Frenchmen. A loud, double report as Peter mounted the window-cell, and he fell, giving vent to a wild shriek.

He had got a bullet somewhere.

Tom Tiller raised him to his feet, and he limped away, making all manner of curious faces, as if he was hurt, of which there was little doubt, for he could not sit down.

The morning had not dawned when they made their unceremonious exit, and night came on before they sought another place of rest and refreshment, and they were as far away from their ship as they were the night previous, lost in the labyrinth of dirty little streets of Havre.

They had put up at an inn, but they had got no money.

They were in an uncomfortable dilemma, and how to get out of it they knew not.

The host was not a man of prepossessing appearance, or they would have stated their lamentable condition to him, and trusted to his feeling of humanity for the rest.

As it was, they would have to face it out. They had had what they wanted, and would give mine host what he did not want if he was not civil.

They were puzzling their brains how to get out of this mess, for it was late and time they set out again to find their ship, when the clamour of angry voices smote their ears.

Tom Tiller started to his feet.

' By God!' he exclaimed, ' that is Bob Brace's voice I hear.'

They listened.

The voices grew louder.

' Do you still refuse to say what you know?' exclaimed a voice.

' I do,' was the determined answer, and the speaker was Bob Brace.

' Fool! you court your death by refusal.'

' I fear not death, so that I save my captain,' replied the old sailor.

' Then take it, grey-haired hound.'

This was followed by a cry and heavy fall.

Tom and Peter in wild terror rushed towards the direction of the room whence the voice came.

The landlord tried to obstruct their way.

Tom Tiller, with a demoniac glance, clutched him by the throat, and hurled him furiously aside. Then passed, and burst open the door, and were transfixed with horror at the sight that meet their view.

On the floor lay the old coxswain, his face ashy pale, his grey hair matted with blood, and over him stood a masked and cloaked figure, dagger in hand.

CHAPTER LXXI.

GREGORY SAUNDERS BEGINS HIS CAREER AS RED VULTURE, THE PIRATE—A BLOODY DEED —BLACK-EYED SUSAN IN HIS POWER.

WHEN Saunders sailed from the vessel commanded by Rodwin Blake, he stood on the bulwark, his eyes fixed upon his foe and his hand raised on high, he invoked all the curses of Satan on his enemy; and when, at last, nothing met his view save the dark, turbid waters, he turned towards his vile horde of ruffians.

He was a demon in soul now.

His purpose—power, triumph, and REVENGE.

Far into the night he was striding his quarter-deck, like an unchained demon.

Who can tell what was going on in that man's breast?

Released from a loathsome prison, placed in the pure air, and on the deck of a swift-sailing and well-armed vessel; with a bold, bloodthirsty crew, ready for rapine and murder; his feelings would have done honour to Satan himself.

At first, many a bitter qualm passed over him.

He could not bear the thought of coming face to face with any of his late brother officers, or gracing the yardarm of Admiral Garthway's ship.

'Curses! my curses on him!' he muttered, and meaning Rodwin Blake, not Garthway. 'Curse him! he has kept his word—worked like a snake in the grass! Fool that I was, not to have slain him when I had him in my power!'

He did not like the idea of being *compelled* to lead on the legion of demons to bloodshed and pillage.

He had opened the sealed packet Blake had given him, and read its contents.

A portion of it ran thus :—

'The crew have sworn by a terrible oath to explicitly execute my wish in every way. They are sworn to serve you, to stand by you in victory, or to the death. They will uphold you in all things as their leader; but YOU have a part to perform in the compact.

'That you let no ship pass, of any nation, that will afford plunder for your men; that one-third of the booty shall go to your crew, the rest to yourself and officers; that they shall have everything they require; that you keep no WOMAN CAPTIVE on board your ship more than SIX DAYS, or she will then become PUBLIC PROPERTY. Go against one of these rules, and you will be torn from your seat, taken amongst the crew, and tortured to death as they might think fit.'

'God!' he thought, 'what power the fiend has over the minds of his men.''

He was interrupted in his wanderings by the ghostly face of Despardo appearing before him.

'Captain,' he said, 'I suppose that devil meant me to stand as first officer.'

Gregory turned his haggard face towards the speaker.

One long, hard look he gave him, and then turned away, without utttering a word.

Hastily he strode the deck; Despardo stood watching him with a malignant gleam in his eye.

After a few minutes he approached the pirate again.

'Captain,' he said, 'remember your duty. Is this doing it? Look at the ship—where is she going?—Where are we going?'

'To hell!' interrupted Gregory fiercely.

'We know that; but look at the men getting drunk and doing nothing. Some here must have a voice.'

'Send them aft, every vagabond one on board.'

'All hands to muster; now, boys, come aft.'

The pirates, who had been waiting impatiently for this, came aft in a body, and turned their dark, evil faces towards their new leader.

He faced them with the stern look still upon his face, and his haggard, wolfish eyes, glanced from one to the other.

At length he spoke.

'D'ye know what I'm here for?'

'Ay, ay!'

'So be it. I am your leader.'

'Ay, ay!' louder than before.

'Very well. Now listen: I'll keep to the compact; by the devils that aid us you shall have enough of me. It was your own seeking, and you shall have blood and rapine in plenty. I shall be your leader, and you'll mind me, too—ay, in all things. Let me hear a murmur of discontent, and the man who utters it, dies. Let me see one of you going against my orders, and I'll shoot him without a warning. Let a traitor be found among you, and he dies a sudden and awful death. There is no cat—no restrictions beyond what I have said. You have wines or aught else in the ship's store in plenty; but understand me, I'll take the ship wherever I like, and whenever I please, and you'll follow me in all things. Here is your first officer, in obeying him you obey me—but the others as you choose. Now, put the Vulture in trim, and shape her course for the Pacific. Have the arms ready—guns shotted, and let me see how you can do it—away.'

Then he left the vessel under the care of Despardo and went to his cabin.

What a change to his imprisonment in the hold of the Sorcerer!

It was not until late the next day that he was seen, and then a sail was reported to have hove in sight.

That took him on deck.

A vessel was discerned at windward. The Red Vulture was brought round and put in chase, and she bore down upon the merchant ship—for such they saw it was—and ere the sun had set, they were within gun-shot.

The deck was crowded with people; the British flag was flying at her peak.

Everyone seemed to be watching the suspicious conduct of the pirate craft. Gregory could see they had their glances upon him.

'Hoist our colours, and give them a shot.'

Up went the black flag, with its ghastly device on it. Its effect was magical; for the merchantman seemed in dreadful confusion, and every stitch of canvas was hoisted in hope of getting away.

Vain hope.

The Red Vulture bore down upon them, and hurled a deadly broadside into her—sent the seething death-dealing missiles among women and children—old men with grey hair and palzied limbs were cut down, and lay weltering in their blood upon the snow-white deck of the good ship Lucy.

But the tragedy was to come.

*　　*　　*　　*　　*　　*

Nearly a week before the Lucy fell in with the Red Vulture, she was sailing gaily through the blue waves of the sun-lit ocean, when one of the men who had gone aloft to execute some duty, descried a speck on the bosom of the blue sea.

Not knowing what to make of it, he reported the circumstance to the mate, who instantly took his glass up to the mizzen top, and surveyed the object for several minutes without uttering a word.

Evidently the distant speck puzzled him.

'It's something,' he muttered, at length, and by something he meant it was a matter that ought to be looked into.

Ordering the man to keep a sharp look out upon it, he descended to the deck, and had the vessel's course altered just enough to put him in the track of the object that was now creating some interest among the crew and some of the early-rising passengers.

'It gets larger as we approach it, Mr. Hudson,' said the captain.

'As it naturally would, sir,' smiled the mate, 'but

the important feature is, does it take any special form ?'

'There is the puzzle.'

Many of the passengers came round the captain and mate, and the inquiries of the lady portion of the "community" were asked at, what Captain Brown afterwards remarked — 'Nineteen to the dozen.'

Being naturally a good-natured, easy-tempered man, he replied to as many as he could in the space of time given him to reply.

On his right was an old lady—very fidgetty, very quaint, very talkative, and very fond of having all the conversation to herself—on his right was a young lady, fair, gentle, and beautiful, and her questions were put in such a sweet, childlike way that he really took a pleasure in answering them.

'Bless me !' cried the old lady. 'Dear me ! but what do you see, Mr. Captain ? I see nothing, that I really don't; but then, my eyes are not so strong now; but they were matchless once, sir—yes, matchless as— do you see better now, captain ?'

'No, marm.'

'Captain,' said the young lady, artlessly, 'may I look through that glass of yours ? It is a very large one. Do you think I could hold it ?'

'Why, yes, miss; or I could, and you can look just the same.'

Her beautiful head was against his shoulder as he held the telescope for her to scan the object.

'Why, captain, it is a spar, I think you call it.'

'I saw that, miss. You have a pair of sharp, as well as pretty eyes,' the old sailor said, with an amount of enthusiasm quite astonishing.

The young lady blushed, and continued—

'But I see something else, now. There is some one clinging to the spar.'

'What !' fairly shouted the old sailor, snatching the glass away, and putting it up to his own eye.

'Damme ! that is—pardon, young lady, but such is the case.'

Now there really was cause for excitement, and plenty of excitement too.

The vessel neared the spar, and now it could be seen with the naked eye.

Captain Brown ordered a boat to be got ready, and when within fifty yards of the castaway, the Lucy hove to.

Scarcely had she done so, when a cry broke from every throat on board.

'It's a woman.'

'Great heavens ! Poor creature ! Come, my lads, be smart,' cried the captain, his generous heart well nigh overcome at a sight so touching.

Never before did the sailors display such true British alacrity and willingness as on this occasion.

The boat was lowered, manned, and shoved off before the orders had left the captain's mouth.

The mate was in the boat, and his eyes became dim, and his voice husky, as he said—

'Steady, lads. Mind, for God's sake, or we may strike the poor creature with the boat.'

He saw, too, with some surprise, that it was not a spar she was clinging to, but four boat oars locked together.

Carefully, very carefully was the castaway lifted into the boat, and gently placed on the men's jackets at the stern.

Then they pulled swiftly but silently back to the ship, for the sight touched them deeply.

How gladly did Captain Brown receive the sufferer on board his vessel, and how interested the passengers became when they saw it was a young and lovely woman.

But she seemed to be beyond all hope of recovery.

The young lady who had been the first to discover her, proffered her services as nurse should she recover, and her offer was gladly accepted by the captain under these much-wished-for circumstances.

The poor suffering girl was carried below, it was thought beyond all recovery; but after long and patient attendance a faint spark of life yet lingered in the young heart, and every effort was made to kindle it into a flame.

More than one heart grew sad as they saw all their perseverance failing to restore her.

But humanity urged them on; it was a good cause, and a thrill ran through every one on board when later that evening the lady was pronounced to be—

'Alive, and progressing favourably.'

But four or five days passed, and she had to keep her couch—a wild fit of delirium set in, and she raved incessantly.

Raved of a boat filled with starving men, of a storm, and the wreck of the boat's crew. She raved of husband, and of terrible deeds done, and implored to be saved from her enemies, until the young lady sitting by her couch grew alarmed at the terrible things she heard.

But at length this passed off, and she made rapid strides towards recovery. She recovered full possession of her senses, and was surprised to find herself with friends, and a young and beautiful girl nursing her.

When able to speak, she told her terrible history, and when finished gave her name,—

Mrs. Howard—or known more as Black Eyed Susan.

How the captain rejoiced and skipped about the deck at her recovery. How the passengers rejoiced, and laughed and chatted in little groups about the deck.

The gloom that had hung over them all passed away, and all was happiness upon the good ship.

Captain Brown came up on deck, and with a countenance radiant with joy informed the passengers that he should have a little merriment on deck, under an awning, as the lady—Mrs. Howard—was going to be brought up on the poop.

With a feeling of interest in their hearts the passengers waited to see the castaway, whose beauty had got whispered about long ere this, and many of the men passengers were wishing her husband had never been born.

When she came, her presence caused a slight commotion.

Pale, but beautiful as ever, Black Eyed Susan faced her many friends, and thanked them with a gentle smile, when a lounge of cushions was prepared for her, and she was gently conducted to it.

The young lady who had been a sister to her since she had been on board, was as merry as she was good and pretty, proposed a round of amusements. But even while a merry laugh rose upon the air, there came a voice from aloft like a knell or evil omen. It was not an unusual cry or voice, but the words on this occasion seemed to come strangely solemn.

'Sail, oh !'

An unbroken stillness reigned throughout the ship, while Captain Brown and his mate were trying to make out the stranger.

BLACK EYED SUSAN.

OR, PIRATES ASHORE.

THE WRECKERS AT WORK.

She was a corvette, and bearing down straight upon them. Ay, and at a rate that proved to the sunburnt skipper that to run from her if they had any cause to do so, would be vain indeed.

She displayed no flag, and it was hard to guess at her nationality.

Some alarm was evinced when it came upon them, as it seemed, with the evident intention of coming along-side or running them down.

At length when within gunshot, Captain Brown was about to signal, when a cry of heart-rending horror came from the whole ship's company.

A black flag, with a huge crimson patch on it was drawn up, and upon inspection, the red spot took the form of a vulture worked upon the ghastly ensign.

' God of heaven, help us ! ' cried the captain, as a long, wailing shriek from the women curdled the blood in his veins.

' Ladies,' he cried, ' go below if you please. Gentlemen, you will remain on deck to help us to keep off the bloodthirsty villains. Now, my lads, up with the canvas, and trust to our speed and Providence.'

But just as he spoke, a broadside was fired into them, mowing down the unfortunate beings upon the deck.

Even while the long, wailing shrieks of the maimed and wounded rang upon the air, the pirate barque dashed alongside, grappled with the Lucy, and, with a yell that would have awakened the dead from their graves, the bloodthirsty wretches poured over the side, hacking remorselessly at women or old men.

The Red Vulture was at their head. He leaped on to the poop. Susan was clinging to her young friend, struck powerless with terror when the pirate came. With a bitter laugh he took her by the hair, drew her head back, and raised his blood-stained scimitar. Poor Susan murmured one short fervent prayer, and closed her eyes, that she might at least shut out the sight of the coming blade.

CHAPTER LXXII.

LADY CATHERINE'S LOVE FOR GERALD — HIS INDIFFERENCE TURNS HER AFFECTION TO HATE, AND HE FINDS A BITTER ENEMY IN HER.

IT was past the midnight hour when Gerald Stuart reached the residence of Lady Catherine.

It was a strange time to see a lady, and he hesitated about knocking; but it was by her request, and he had given his word to keep the appointment.

His word was his honour—he could not break one without staining the other ; still he hesitated.

All was very quiet around. He glanced up at the windows; a steady light burning in the room of the first-floor decided his resolution.

He knocked gently, and was almost immediately admitted, announced, and shown into a magnificent apartment.

Lady Catherine advanced towards him in her regal beauty, and received him, blushing and confused.

Gerald wondered at her embarrassment.

' Has she fallen in love with me ?' he thought.

Then he smiled at his own conceit. The idea he thought absurd, that the noble, superb creature—who must have dukes and noblemen of the highest rank at her feet pleading passionately their love—should deign to look upon him with the slightest favour.

The lady watched him closely ; she seemed to read his thoughts, and a cold smile distorted the beauty of her face.

Gerald looked round the apartment in admiration. He had never seen anything to equal it. It outrivalled in splendour the chamber of a prince.

The walls were hung with costly drapery, of an eastern make, trimmed and decorated with masses of flowers, worked in coloured silks and gold-lace, and festooned round a massive chandelier of crystal glass pending from the ceiling.

The floor was covered with a rich carpet, soft as down, into which the foot sank imbedded. The furniture was elegant in every way.

The lights burned with a low, subdued gleam ; the air was filled with an oppressive odour that thrilled one's senses, and seemed to carry him away in a dreamy daze.

Gerald was aroused from his reverie by the trembling hand of Lady Catherine being laid on his arm.

He started, looked up into her face, and was surprised to see her standing by his side, blushing and confused.

A smile lighted up her face, and she assumed her wonted grandeur.

' You must wonder at my strange request to see you to-night,'' she said ; and her soft little hand tightened on his.

Gerald did wonder ; there was no denying the fact.

' It was my only opportunity,' she continued, ' to say that which I almost dread to speak.'

Gerald wondered more and more ; he discerned her agitation, and ascribed it to quite a different cause to that from which it arose.

' Speak, lady,' he said. ' I owe my liberty—my life to you ; and if there is anything in my power that I can do to make you happy, do not hesitate to name it.'

' Gerald Stuart,' she said, slowly, and in a tremulous voice, ' your life is in my hands. It rests with yourself whether you are given up to your 'foes or not.'

' What mean you ?' cried he, starting to his feet, startled by the lady's strange words.

' Fear nothing from me,' said the lady, with one of her winning smiles ; ' I have dared much for your sake—risked even honour and life for you.'

She cast herself, in a careless, graceful attitude, on an ottoman at his feet.

' For my sake ?' said Gerald, subdued by her bewitching grace. ' I do not understand you.'

' Come,' she said, ' we shall understand each other better presently.'

She rose on one elbow, and took his hand.

Gerald, in a sort of stupor, sank down by her side.

Lady Catherine watched him as a cat would a mouse, and there was a look of lurking triumph in her large luxurious eyes.

Gerald struggled to resist the intoxicating influence of his beautiful temptress.

Other men, of a less passionate temperament but a weaker mind, would have given way now.

It was a tempting situation—the place, the silent hour, were all in accordance with the thoughts that tempt men to risk their honour for half the favour Gerald had put in his way; but he resisted, fought against the overpowering influence, and almost scorned the beauty by his side.

She was attired in an azure robe, hanging loosely around her gracefully-developed form, low in the neck, displaying a bust of surpassing magnificence.

Her beautifully-moulded limbs were perceptible through the thin gauze wherever it clung to her.

Her tiny feet were encased in blue satin slippers, and between the foot and the bottom of her robe was displayed an ankle that would have set an anchorite dreaming.

Yet all this Gerald resisted.

She threw herself helplessly into his arms, her glowing cheeks rested on his shoulder, and her waving tresses fell about him like a cluster of golden thread.

He felt her heaving breast and palpitating heart keeping time with his own, and her hot breath on his cheeks.

Gerald felt his resolution melting. He did not wish to take advantage of the lady's trusting confidence, but he could not withstand much longer if he sat there.

Disengaging her arms from around his neck, he put her gently from him.

'Lady,' he said, and his voice was thick, 'lest you should regret the generous act of liberating me from prison, I will leave you now, and to-morrow I can wait upon you at your own pleasure.'

Lady Catherine looked at him reproachfully.

A shade of disappointment came over her glowing cheeks, and an angry flash marred the beauty of her liquid orbs.

'Ah! you do not find my company agreeable,' she said, playfully; but there was a tinge of bitterness in her tones.

'On the contrary, madam,' answered the astonished Gerald, 'your company is so delightful, I dare not stay too long. Man is such a weak mortal, he is not master of his own passions; so, lest I should regret by protracting my stay, you will excuse me leaving.'

'You are in love,' said Lady Catherine.

Gerald coloured.

A shiver passed through the lady.

Her cheeks turned ashy pale, and she almost glared at him.

'You are unwell,' he said, anxiously.

'A little faint,' she answered, with a sickly smile.

Gerald got some water. The lady thanked him, and drank.

She recovered her former self; but with her queenly dignity, there was a repulsive coldness in her manner that brought back to Gerald a deep, almost reverend respect for her he had felt on their first meeting.

She was still pale and agitated.

Gerald got in a stew, he thought the lady unwell, and he believed himself to be the cause of it, and now he wanted to make amends for his unkindness.

He wanted to fetch a physician, he wanted to call her maid, but she objected.

Gerald was undone.

It was a most awkward situation for him, but not a disagreeable one.

He began now to see what he could do to atone for the past.

He cast himself at her feet, and taking her hands in his own, began to tell her a few anecdotes of his adventures. He was naturally very eloquent, his voice was thrilling, and he assumed a gaiety he did not feel, to cheer up the lady he accused himself of crushing.

His lively manner and amusing stories soon brought the wonted glow to her cheeks, and her eyes assumed an expression of tenderness as she looked into his handsome face.

'Then, really,' he said, gaily, 'I did not think I possessed such power.'

Lady Catherine sighed.

'Ah!' she said, 'you possessed more power than you are aware of.'

'Really now, dear lady, you do me honour; but, come, you must tell me a story now. You said my life was in your hands.'

'That is '—— and the lady hesitated.

'Is what?'

'That you owe me your life.'

'Ah! true; but as my life is no good to you, you will but '——

'Stay, sir, 'tis your life I want.'

'The deuce you do. Really, now, I shall begin to think I have hitherto undervalued myself, since I have so many bidders for my life; but, of course, I must give you the preference. You, I am sure, will be a gentle, indulgent mistress.'

'That depends upon yourself,' smiled the beauty.

'I will be a most obedient servant, if you will promise to keep me from my enemies.'

'Ah! that is what I desire,' she said, artfully coiling the treacherous cord around him. 'It was for that purpose that I risked the danger of effecting your escape from the prison.'

'And I owe you my life's gratitude.'

'Ah! we shall see your gratitude. Did your friend escape, too?'

'Thanks to you, kind angel of deliverance, he got safely away. But I hope you do not want him in your service too.'

'Ah! you are jealous.'

'I am selfish. I should not like another to share thy favours with me.'

'Good,' thought the lady.

'Well,' she said, if you promise to be loving and obedient I will not take another, and you shall find in me a very kind mistress.'

'I fear you would spoil me with over indulgence if I may class my future expectations with those of to-night.'

The lady blushed.

'If you are intrusive you may find me severe.'

'Then I will promise not to do anything to deserve your displeasure.'

'We shall agree then,' and Lady Catherine took his hand.

'Now,' said Gerald, 'what position shall I hold in your service?'

'A favoured one.'

Gerald bowed.

'I could wish for nothing better,' he said.

'Now,' she said, 'I must tell you what you will have to do.'

'There will be nothing you can name but what I shall do with pleasure.'

The lady bowed in her turn.

'I hope so,' she said. 'Firstly, then, my life is made miserable by the persecutions of my cousin, Lord Wylie.'

I will undertake to rid you of him,' Gerald said, smiling; 'no man shall persecute you while I remain in your service.'

'Then,' she replied, 'I shall want you to remain with me always.'

'Then until you get tired of me I shall always find too much pleasure in serving you. The next thing, my lady, when I have disposed of your cousin.'

'I shall place myself entirely under your protection.'

'You shall never have cause from me to regret your confidence.'

'Then that is all. I wish for you to protect me from my enemies, and take me back to my native clime.'

'Command me, lady, and I will obey; but when we return to England, will you discharge me?' he asked, regretfully.

'No,' she answered with beaming eyes, 'I shall want you to be with me always, and do you think you can leave your mistress?'

'For a servant, dear lady, I must serve with a love that may make me forget my station.'

'You are getting bold, Gerald,' she said, and a happy smile illumined her face.

'That is not my fault, dear lady. As I said, man is such a weak mortal, that he has no control over his passions at times, but I promised to be very good, and you shall have no cause to regret the indulgence you may show me.'

'Then in case you should be tempted to forget your station, be something more to me than a servant,' she said.

She shook like a timid child as she spoke these endearing words, and a moisture gathered in her eyes.

Gerald was silent for some moments. He did not wish to take the import of her words. He felt for her, and would have saved her the pain she would feel when he confessed the truth to her.

'A brother, then,' he said; 'let me love you as a brother.'

An expression of pain passed over her lovely features. Gerald saw with regret the fearful struggle she was having with her feelings. Her breast rose and fell, and tears of agony rose to her downcast eyes.

'Can't you be anything more to me?' she asked, pleadingly.

'What more would you desire? What more dared I think of becoming to you?'

'Gerald Stuart,' she said, sternly, and her voice was faint. She trembled like a fluttering bird, and the sorrow on her face sent a pang of remorse to his heart.

It was a fearful moment of suspense to both. Gerald, who wished to disguise his knowledge of her pleading affection, could not give her a thought without menacing the memory of the saintly maiden to whom he was betrothed, and Lady Catherine, trembling to confess her strange love, but fearing, lest he should avow the truth that he was given to another.

'Gerald Stuart,' it was by a desperate effort that she nerved herself to speak, 'must I confess to you?'

'What am I to hear?' he asked, assuming a look of surprise.

'Oh,' she said, 'there are none so blind as those that won't see. Gerald Stuart, I love you!'

Gerald was touched by her plaintive voice.

'Lady,' he said, regretfully, 'I am deeply grieved that you should have cast your affections on one so worthless. I cannot return your love. My vows are plighted to another.'

The truth struck the lady heavily. She sank back helplessly, and covered her face.

Gerald was moved by her emotion. He tried to offer her consolation in the love of a brother, but she repulsed him.

'You mock me,' she cried, starting up.

Her face was cold and rigid; her eyes were fixed upon him with a staring glance, and as she stood before him in her angry beauty, he thought he had never seen a more perfect woman in his life.

'You have trifled with me,' she went on vehemently; 'scoffed at my weakness—insulted me—spurned my love and honour! but take care how you continue your iniquity.'

'Lady, the fault was not mine,' Gerald said. 'I will do all I can to defend you from your enemies. Had my affections not been given to another, I should have loved you. But, alas! dear lady, we cannot tear the heart from the ideal of our affections. Let me share your love as a brother—let me be your guardian—your defender—all that I can, but that I can never be.'

'Then I must hate the only man I ever loved,' said the beauty, remorsefully. 'I cannot bear the thought that you should love another. I have done much to serve you—offered all, and been rejected—had my beauty and honour spurned by the only man that I would yet yield to. Think not that I am a wanton. I have had princes and the noblest peers of the land lay their wealth and coronets at my feet, for half that which I offer you. Kings have been on their knees at my feet, pleading, and yet I have rejected all. I offer to you that which others would have died to obtain, and thought it bliss.'

'I bitterly regret having been the innocent cause of offending,' said Gerald, 'and if there is aught in my power that I can do to atone for the wrong, there is nothing that shall impede me from executing your command; but love I cannot return.

The lady's face grew demoniac. In that moment her strong love for the gallant captain turned into the bitterest hate.

'I would have saved you,' she said. 'Man, you shall return to the dungeon, and die on the block for the murder at the *Salon*.'

'But I am innocent of the crime.'

'I know it. Ah! ah! ah!' she laughed, demoniacally. I am the criminal, but you will be the sufferer. 'Twas a deed I did to get you in my power. Gerald Stuart. You have sealed your death warrant by your refusal.'

CORP. STIFF

PIRATE

HOMESPUN

PIRATE.

GUINEA WOUNDED

GUINEA DEAD

PIRATE.

DICK FID

PIRATE

CHARACTERS in the Play of "Red Rover."—Gratis with No. 28 of "Black-Eyed Susan."

Gerald sprang to his feet.

'Devil!' he said, 'in angel's form! If I die, the vengeance of heaven will follow you.'

The lady gave a wild cry, and left the room.

CHAPTER LXXIII.

ROCK ELFIN AND JACK MURRAY PICKED UP BY THE MAN-OF-WAR—ELFIN'S DANGER AND TERRIBLE REVENGE—FIRING THE SHIP—ALONE ON THE TEMPEST-TOSSED WAVES.

THE terrible wreck of the White Cat left Elfin and his crew fighting desperately with the furious waters of the deep. The crime-stained ruffian clutched a grating, and made a leap after little Jack Murray, whose juvenile arm was supporting the delicate form of Eurice.

With death staring him in the face, the poor little lad clutched madly at a floating spar, and clung to it with a grip that death alone would ever cause him to relax.

The storm began to abate. He tried to look about him.

Not a sign of face or form of any of the sailors of the ill-fated lugger could be seen.

His limbs were getting weaker, and his power was rapidly going.

The sea was calming down, and the first streak of morn was breaking, when a peculiar commotion in the water attracted his attention. With an instinct of danger he clutched the form of Eurice nearer to him. What he saw made him shudder, and the blood froze in his veins.

A shark was surely but swiftly approaching.

Tears of bitter agony coursed down his cheeks.

'What have I done,' he cried, 'that I suffer thus? Oh, God! Lady, lady, we must—indeed we must—die now.'

One low, quivering sob escaped him, and nature gave way; he was senseless and motionless, at the mercy of the sea and the shark.

* * * * *

He had not seen a boat approaching, in quite a contrary direction; nor did he hear the rattle of musketry as several shots were fired at the voracious monster of the deep.

But it was so, and he was saved, and taken on board an armed ship.

'There has been a wreck somewhere here,' said the captain. 'Three castaways this morning! Well, doctor, do your best, and save the poor lad, and that poor girl, too.'

The doctor did do his best, and he saved them. When Jack came to his senses again, he was in a sailor's berth, on a man-of-war brig.

He learned, too, that a man had been picked up besides himself and Eurice. By the description, he knew it was Rock Elfin. He started, and turned paler than death.

'Do you know him? Perhaps he was lost from the same wreck?' added the doctor.

'He was, sir.' And Jack told how he came there; how Eurice came there; and who sent them both.

The captain was called, and he heard, with great patience the statement made by Jack. When the lad had finished, his face grew dark as a thunder-cloud.

'Am I harbouring such a villain on my ship?' he cried, going on deck.

'Boatswain,' he said, 'send that man, Tom Smith, aft to me.'

Tom Smith, *alias* Rock Elfin, came aft, with a tumult of conflicting passions in his breast.

'My man,' said the captain, sternly, 'I wish for your statement again. What was the name of your ship?'

'Crocodile—gunboat brig.'

'Your name?'

'Tom Smith.'

'You lie, you infamous scoundrel! The vessel was a lugger—the White Cat. Your name is Rock Elfin, and you are a pirate and smuggler.'

'Who's your proof?' cried Elfin, livid with rage.

Captain Stanley stamped his foot upon the deck, and the doctor came up, leading Jack Murray, who looked more like a corpse than aught else.

'There, sir, is my proof?'

Elfin gave a cry, and staggered back, white and trembling. The commander of the brig required no further proof, but ordered him to be kept under the hatch in safety.

It was done, and he was a shut-up prisoner—and not the only one, for the brig had lately captured a schooner of redoubtable character, and the best portion of her crew was on board.

But Elfin found a friend on board; and that night, when all had retired to rest, he came, like a phantom of evil, upon the deck, and prowled about, to execute a base purpose in his heart.

He crept on his hands and knees.

He had determined to escape.

How did he do it? Most diabolically.

Creeping along in the darkness of the lower deck, he sought the hold amidships. It was long and tedious work, but he succeeded in removing the hatch. Unseen and unheard, he dropped down into the black, murky hole, and groping his way about, he reached the opposite corner.

Then he deposits on the floor a bundle of something very much like tow rope, and oily rags; then he carefully lighted a torch, and when it was well ignited he held it to the ignitable mass.

Slowly and deliberately he kindles the ends of it into a small flame, which presently bursts into a lurid glare, which lighted up his swarthy features.

With the flaming brand in his hand, he approached a heap of what appeared to be rubbish, but in reality were pieces of tar rope, a lot of tar, with several pieces of oily rags.

For a moment he gazed round the hold.

He then placed his torch to the greasy, tarry ropes.

A thin column of smoke rose up towards the hatchway. Then came a slight flame—a lurid glare, and, though the heat was suffocating, he did not move from the spot.

Nor did he move until he saw the whole heap begin to blaze.

In several parts of the ship did this fire-fiend go, and presently disappeared.

A dense smoke began to fill the vessel.

A suffocating heat swept through the barque. Several jets of flame began to make their way through the cracks of the hatchway.

Suddenly, with a tremendous roar, a mass of fire came hissing and rushing through the hold, in which the destroyer had first began his deadly work.

The officer on the poop saw it, and heard the raging fire below.

For a moment he seemed rooted to the spot.

Recovering his presence of mind, he leapt from the poop, and gave utterance to that ominous word—

' Fire !'

' Fire !' he shouted again.

This time a terrible commotion is heard below.

At this same moment the door of the captain's cabin was burst open, and the heartless destroyer of that noble vessel, with the still flaming torch in his hand, blazing, and sending a terrible glare over the cabin, in the face of Rock Elfin.

In a voice of thunder, he cried—

' Awake, captain !' the ship is in flames, and in twenty minutes she will be blown in the air.'

Captain Studley sprang out of bed, and reeling back at the fearful intelligence, and terrified at the awful appearance of the gipsey, who still held the torch above his head.

Without another word, Elfin dashed up the companion way, and was lost in the gloom.

Captain Stanley was so bewildered and confounded, that he stood rooted to the spot.

But the cries of—

' Fire !' in all directions, recalled him to his senses.

As he hastened up the companion way, he heard the loud cries of his first mate, giving orders to the men.

When he reached the deck, all was terrible consternation and confusion.

The sailors were panic-stricken.

Not even the angry tones of the mate's orders could call them to their duty.

The brave commander's cheek paled, when he saw the fearful havoc the fire was making.

But keeping his presence of mind and coolness that was so necessary in such a case, he cried in a loud, commanding voice—

' Now, lads, rig the pumps, and get the buckets; come, work with a will, and this shall soon be put out.'

Excitement was at its highest pitch.

The captain expected the ship to blow up every minute.

He had a quantity of powder in the aft hold, and yet his bravery, coolness, and skill never deserted him for one moment.

He seemed to be all over the ship at once.

Aiding or encouraging his men in their duty.

His greatest trouble was in keeping the prisoners in order.

They had, with one accord, battered away at the hatchways. Desperation lent them strength, and when order was most needed they were howling and shrieking on deck.

Then they began to fight with each other, to battle for their lives and the boats, and in being too anxious over getting the latter, they lost the former.

Things were coming to a dreadful crisis.

' Save yourselves, my men ; waste no more time in trying to aid those blinded fools, who, in their evil passions, will destroy each other.'

The captain had hardly finished speaking, when the mainmast fell with a crash close to his heels, burying one of the men, who was cursing most awfully his fellow prisoner for not letting him get in the boat.

The captain remained on the hot and scorching deck until every one of the sailors had gone in the boats.

He then lowered himself over the vessel's side, at the same time making a sign to the second mate, who was trying to get the prisoners embarked.

Getting in a rage, and fearing he should lose his life if they did not hasten, he drew one of the pistols from his belt, and said in a fierce voice—

' The first man that attempts to get in the boat out of his turn I will shoot down like a dog, I will, by —— '

This threat partially awed the men.

But not for long. They were mad with fear and excitement, and mad at being free, though through the awful circumstances.

They would not follow Captain Stanley or obey the mate.

They, with the most horrible execrations, hurled charred pieces of wood into the boat.

One threw a piece of flaming rope at the captain.

At that critical moment he beheld a flame curling up by one of the lower deck cabin windows.

' Pull, pull for your life !' he shouted to his mate. ' We have no time to lose—the powder will catch ! '

Seeing their terrible danger, they pulled from the ship.

At the same instant, the prisoners made a rush to where they beheld a boat hanging to the davits.

With a cry of agony, the foremost dashed back.

A huge mountain of flame shot up in front of him.

They ran howling and shrieking to the other side of the vessel. Their only hope of escape was gone.

Their tongues were parched with burning thirst.

Their faces began to whiten.

With agonized glances, those men gazed into each other's faces to find help that they knew not where to find.

The ship was burnt almost to the water's edge.

It was a miracle the powder had not caught.

The agony of those poor wretches became awful to bear.

They called frantically to the captain.

He did not hear their cries.

If he did, it was impossible to help them.

With a last, despairing shriek, many threw themselves overboard.

While many others had gone raving mad through the suffering, from which they were soon released.

Crying, yelling, cursing, and frantically calling

upon some imaginary deliverer for help, they dashed about utterly regardless of the flames.

Presently, there came one wild, despairing shriek from the tortured wretches, followed by a terrible roar.

The next instant, the remains of that ill-fated ship with those human beings, were blown into the air.

And their mortal suffering was ended.

Nearly a score of poor wretches were sent before their Maker with a curse upon their lips.

Blown into the air.

Their limbs torn asunder and hurled in different directions.

The captain and his boat's crew had been horror-stricken spectators of the appalling scene.

They were not far, and could detect at the distance they were, the human forms among the spars, rigging, beams, sparks, that amid a dense cloud of smoke filled the air.

Then all was over.

Nothing but a few pieces of charred wood were left of what was a few hours before a noble ship.

Darkness spread its veil over the last traces of the fatal scene.

Where was Rock Elfin all this time. He had taken the cutter, and alone committed himself to the mercy of the sea, and the tempest. He had escaped, and he gave not one thought to those who had suffered—not even to poor little Jack Murray, or Eurice. Both of them had been conveyed by the captain's order to the jolly boat, that they might be under his especial care.

Meantime Elfin was leaving the terrible spot as quickly as he could.

Every minute brought with it fresh torture of the mind and conscience, and fear for his safety.

By morning, his form began to look haggard, and his eyes began to get a wild, restless appearance.

It had been a terrible oversight of his, not to bring water—an article that in such a case is invaluable—a blessing existence could not continue without.

It was a thoughtless oversight, but all the groaning imaginable would not bring the crystal fluid.

He still kept upon the watch.

'Unless assistance overtakes me shortly, and this heat should continue, I am lost—lost!' he muttered, in a hoarse whisper.

He beheld his situation in the true light—hopeless, horrible—and he was helpless.

He sat, mute and apparently stupified, and reduced to such a state of weakness, that even when the sun went down, he would be too far gone to propel the boat.

When the glorious sun went down, throwing a blood-red glow upon the sea, a gentle breeze sprang up.

Elfin gave a sigh of relief as he felt it wafting past his heated brows.

Suddenly he started up, and gave a smothered cry.

Only a faint streak of the setting sun could be seen, and a change had taken place in the hitherto cloudless sky.

A huge black speck, far away in the distance, began to roll slowly towards him. It seemed to bring with it a dark mist. Then the heavens looked black and threatening.

A storm was brewing.

A distant rumble came upon his ears; then it deepened into a loud roar, and then died away.

In the dusky light of the darkling heavens, he saw the outline of a vessel. But so very far away. He gave a low cry of joy; his eyes dilated, his chest expanded, and his whole frame shook with mental excitement.

But dared he hope? His own vile heart had placed him where he was. The tempest was coming on in redoubled fury, and the probability of the vessel seeing him, or its coming near, was very small.

The fury of the raging element in the short space of time alarmed him.

The sea ran mountains high, with a roar like thunder; huge masses of thick, murky cloud—behind which lurked the most furious part of the storm—rolled across the sky; rain poured down in torrents.

The wind howled and shrieked past his ears, and a lurid flash of lightning lit up the scene for miles around.

The next instant all was darkness as before.

The waves seemed to soar higher, each moment lashing the waters into a perfect sea of foam.

Though the elemental war raged so furiously, the lightning darted about like forked tongues of flame, and the thunder that roared and reverberated through the arches of heaven was enough to strike terror to the heart of any human being.

Rock Elfin clung like grim death to the boat, and he looked about him for the vessel he had seen.

He had with him a pistol, which he fired in hopes of being heard. Vain idea!

A deafening thunder clap drowned the sharp report, and it was borne away by the shrieking wind.

Death was horribly certain now; every ray of hope left his villanous heart. He thought of Jack Murray. Where could he be in such fearful weather? The unfortunate one that he had sent to perdition.

Now the boat was crushed amidst the mighty roll of waters, and he had nothing now to cling to.

He thought of the past. His many errors came flocking to his mind, and he screamed aloud in the agony of his soul. But it did not last long. He was carried high up into the air—then he descended—he felt as though he had received a sudden blow that seemed to shatter his limbs.

Then he lay amidst a burning whirlpool, and with a groan that was forced from out of that quivering heart by the agony he endured, his senses fled, and, for the time, Rock Elfin was dead to the world.

CHAPTER LXXIV.

THE ASSASSINATION.

THE night was dark, and the rain fell in heavy showers, whilst the wind that had been gradually increasing with the setting of the sun, blew a fearful hurricane.

It was dark, we said, but during the momentary flashes of lightning that accompanied at regular intervals the heavy claps of thunder, the forms of two men might be seen crouching in a hollow of the lofty cliffs that guard the coast of Dover.

They were seafaring men to all appearance, and it was evident by their attire, and the pistols stuck in their belts, that their profession was anything but a peaceful one.

In fact, we may confidentially state they were smugglers. Their names and the object of their mission we must keep a secret until the progress of our tale discloses it.

'It's a rough night, mate,' said one, glancing at the bronzed visage of his companion, as the flash for a moment illumined his cheek, 'and I fear,' he added, 'it will prove less fortunate to us than we expected.'

'Well, we can't grumble if it does,' replied the other, carelessly, 'we can't always have luck.'

'True, mate. But it isn't pleasant to be crossed at every point. That affair with the coastguards sticks in my gullet, and all the brandy I pour down my scuttle hatch— which you know is noways trifling —won't wash it down.'

'No, nor help to cure that wound on your arm,' rejoined the other. 'That gullet of yours will be the ruin of you, if not all of us, some day.'

'Avast heaving, mate! Don't begin preaching; it is not a very pleasant night to listen to a sermon, and our position is not the most enviable.'

'Right, mate, right,' replied the other; 'and if the skipper does not venture to land to-night, we shall have all our work for nothing.'

His companion shrugged his shoulders.

It was evident he was not much pleased with the prospect.

'Well, mate, I'll tell you my opinion of the matter,' he said. 'It's not likely he'll run down on a lee-shore, so I propose that we pay a visit to old Dan.'

Old Dan was the proprietor of a snug little domicile known as the Anchor Apeak, and though strongly suspected of acting in concert with the smugglers, and assisting them to dispose of their contrabands, he was too 'cute for the coastguardsmen.

To this house, after carefully concealing their pistols, they accordingly repaired.

The hour was late, but they found both a hearty welcome and a willing guest in old Dan.

The smugglers, on entering the cheerful parlour, drew back and cast a wistful glance on the host, for there was a stranger in the room, whose appearance they did not at first approve of.

A smile from Dan silenced their suspicions, and seating themselves by the warm fire, they soon made themselves comfortable.

The stranger, whosoever he might be, made himself very agreeable, and chatted pretty freely so that the trio were soon on intimate terms.

The warm grog might have assisted in doing this, but be it as it may, the smugglers, throwing aside their rough nature, made themselves quite at home.

There was a melancholy expression on the stranger's face, however, that they did not fail to notice; and after they had sat awhile, one of the smugglers ventured to ask what it was that made him look so sad.

'I will tell you,' said the stranger, yielding at once to the smuggler's earnest entreaty. 'It was love.'

Then, in a softer tone he went on—

'You must know I once loved a fair and beauteous damsel. Loved her, aye dearer than my life, and we were happy, until a foul fiend, who styled himself a friend, crossed our path.'

'Her father was averse to our union, and this friend, in whom I confided too much persuaded me to elope with her.'

'There is not much harm in that,' remarked one of the smugglers.

'No, but you have not yet heard all, we were to murder her father to render our success complete.'

'And did you?'

'You shall hear.'

'I listened to his proposal, and assented. Enough,' said he, 'we understand each other. Go and speak to her, and let us make haste.'

'I pressed his hand as a friend, and as he did not let it go, but kept looking at me with a singular expression, I added: 'I'll tell you what it is. If I had any advice to give you, it would be to say nothing to her about that matter. We will arrange the thing without her expecting it, nor you either; make yourself easy—that's my affair.'

'Ah!' said I, 'I did not know that. That will certainly be better. Besides, those farewells!— those farewells!—they weaken one.'

'Yes, yes,' said he, 'don't make a child of yourself, that's much the best way. Don't kiss her, if you can help it; if you do, you are lost.'

'I gave him another good grasp of the hand, and left him.

'He seemed to me to keep the secret well.'

'Night came on suddenly. It was the moment I had resolved to seize. But that moment has lasted me till the present time, and I shall drag it along all my life, like a cannon-ball.'

'That moment, I assure you, I can't understand it yet. I felt the deepest rage seize upon my whole heart, and at the same time something or other, I don't know what, was forcing me to obey, and pushing me forward. I summoned my men, for I was then captain of a ship, and said to them—

'Come, a boat in the water; put the girl into it, and keep rowing off until you hear the report of firing; you will then return.'

'There must have been something in the air which forced me on. I caught a glimpse of the old man— oh! it was horrible to see!—walking by the side of her I loved! I shouted like a madman, 'Separate them!—we are all a set of wretches — separate them!'

BLACK EYED SUSAN.

OR, PIRATES ASHORE.

LITTLE JACK SAVES THE LIFE OF SUSAN.

The smugglers, who by this time had become interested in the old man's yarn, were suddenly disturbed by the report of a gun that caused the old casements of the Anchor Apeak to rattle so tremendously as to threaten destruction to the glass.

'More work with those audacious smugglers,' remarked Old Dan, tipping his customers a sly wink. 'There will be an end to it some day, I suppose, and then we peaceful inhabitants will cease to be alarmed and frightened out of our wits.'

The smugglers returned the glance.

'I suppose there will be an end to it some day,' suggested one, giving his muffler an extra twist, and feeling his neck as though to make certain it was not a rope he had round it. 'They give us trouble enough ; a fellow cannot enjoy a comfortable glass without being disturbed.'

With this the worthy pair arose, and, bidding their companion a good night, strolled out into the darkness, which was rendered the more intense by the heavy showers of sleet that faced them, and caused them to shiver in spite of the warm clothing that encased their burly and muscular forms.

With caution they approached the edge of the cliff, and, shielding their eyes as possible from the blinding sleet, gazed long and wistful over the storm-lashed sea.

Far out beyond the broad belt of foam that marked the spot where the dark rocks lay hidden they made out the dim outlines of a vessel laying to under a close-reefed mainsail and storm stay sail.

It was too dark to make out accurately her rig or build, but a small blue light that shone for a moment from the masthead satisfied the smuggler that it was the vessel they were on the look out for.

'The captain's mad,' remarked one, 'to run in such a night as this !'

The companion did not appear to heed what he said.

Crouching down behind a small hillock that afforded some shelter from the blast, he busied himself in lighting a small lantern.

It showed a red light, and as soon as he had trimmed it he held it before him in such a manner that none but those to seaward could observe it.

It was soon answered.

A bright red light shone for a second from the ship, and then all was darkness.

This elicited a growl of approbation from the smugglers, who, having placed their pistols in readiness and concealed the lantern, moved slowly away.

'The landsharks are on the alert,' said one, as a blue rocket shot up from the coastguard station. 'Black Peter is on the move I daresay, but I question whether he will be foolhardy enough to attempt to launch a boat amongst the breakers.'

'No,' replied his companion, 'I don't think old Doggrass will care to leave his warm nest on such a night as this.'

'It matters not, we can do better without him, we can—ah !'——

The cause of this exclamation was another rocket shooting through the air and the whizzing of a shot in the direction where the vessel's light had been seen.

'Blaze away, my hearties !' growled the first speaker ; 'the more powder you waste the less you will have for an emergency.'

Taking a bye-path, the smugglers journeyed on in silence, keeping a sharp look-out on either hand, for, in spite of the weather, the sound of the alarm gun had brought many from their beds.

Their way lay near the coast-guard look-out, and, diverging a little from their track, they took up a position where they could watch, unseen, the movements of the dim figures that glided spectre-like about in the darkness.

One of the party they could see was vainly trying to light a watch-fire, which, owing to the boisterous wind and dampness of the materials, seemed an utter impossibility.

At length his efforts were crowned with success.

A bundle of tarry rope was ignited, and a flame shot up, throwing a ruddy glare on all around.

'To the boats, men !' they could hear the bluff old lieutenant say. 'We can launch them under shelter of the peak.'

'Madness, madness !' replied one of the men ; 'we shall sure to be swamped.'

The lieutenant took no heed of his words.

Hitching up his sea-boots, and tightening his sword belt, he led the way down a steep path that led to the foot of the cliff, followed by a score of his men.

The glare of the watch-fire aided them greatly in their perilous descent, so that they were not long in reaching the beach.

'Quick, lads ! bear a hand,' was the cry of the lieutenant, as he shielded his eyes from the spray, and gazed around upon the horizon.

His men were on the alert in an instant.

The dim outlines of a vessel, shooting with the swiftness of an arrow round a projecting headland, could be seen by those most experienced.

A heavy yawl was soon brought from its concealment, and a score of stalwart fellows ran it down to the edge of the serf and strove to launch it.

Their first efforts were unavailing.

The boat reared up on ends, staggered for a moment, and was then thrown back violently on the brave fellows, who were submerged to the waist, almost crushing them, and breaking the arm of the coxswain.

Vexed not subdued, the brave fellows made another attempt with the like success, but without injury to themselves, and a third attempt proved more successful.

The boat, with her staunch crew, stood out amidst the breakers—a dozen pair of sturdy arms plying the long ash oars, and the bluff old luff seated with the tiller in his hand.

All was silent, save the heavy breathing of the men, or the rush and roar of the angry waters as the boat glided over the mountainous billows.

The old lieutenant sat silent and moody.

His whole attention was bent on the steering of the boat.

It required all his skill to steer through the broken water, so that he could not even bestow a glance towards the headland where the smuggling craft had disappeared.

A muttered curse came from the old luff, as one billow, more lofty than the rest, reared its crested head a few fathoms in advance of them, and, with an angry roar, dashed over the bow of the boat, half filling her with water, and jerking the rowers from their seats.

The tiller was jerked from the hand of the luff, and the boat, left to her own guidance, fell off broadside to the sea, a toy to the angry waves that dashed pitilessly over her, and disappeared.

The scene that ensued was harrowing in the extreme.

The gallant fellows strove, but vainly, to keep themselves afloat.

One by one they disappeared beneath the boiling surf, until at last only two remained.

These were both good swimmers; but despite their skill and resolute courage, they would have shared the fate of their unfortunate companions, had not the oars of the yawl befriended them.

To these they clung with the tenacity of men who knew it was their only chance for life, and they were rewarded by being dashed upon the beach, exhausted and almost lifeless.

Their comrades—who had watched their heroic struggles with feelings most acute; for what can be more harrowing than to see a fellow man sinking down into the dark vortex of water within a few yards of assistance, and yet to be unable to render that little help which might save him?—soon carried them to a place of shelter, and, by the aid of stimulants, restored them to a state of consciousness.

By this time the party had been reinforced by a file of marines and a body of troopers—who took good care, however, to have no hand in anything that pertained to nautical affairs.

They were there only to intercept the smugglers, should they attempt to escape shorewards; or in the event of a capture, to convey them to prison.

Sergeant Gill, who had charge of the marines, was the most gallant amongst them; in fact, he had only been raised to his present position a few days, therefore his zeal for the service was great.

'Come on, Plumper,' he cried to his corporal. 'Lead the boys up; a little salt water won't hurt them. Come on, my hearties! We'll show these lubberly coastguard fellows that a royal marine can conduct the business better than they can.'

He turned fiercely to his men, and flourished his sword in a manner that was supposed to be expressive of his feelings.

'Come on, you rascals!' he shouted to the marines, who had taken advantage of the shelter of an old boat reared on end, in the form of a hut, to shield them from the biting blast.

He had scarcely given utterance to the words, when an unforeseen accident occurred.

The sharp report of a pistol was heard at no great distance, and the horse that bore the corpulent form of the captain of the troops dashed towards the sergeant at terrific speed.

Sergeant Gill had not time to get out of the way, but flourished his sword in a most menacing manner, to which the maddened steed only replied by an angry snort, and dashing full against him, sent him rolling down the steep hill at a velocity that not only deprived him of breath, but threatened to break every bone in his skin.

In the meantime the troopers had wheeled round and faced about in the direction whence the sound had proceeded.

All had heard the report, but none had seen the flash.

With fierce, flashing eyes and determined visages they prepared to charge, and dashed headlong through the darkness, in the vain hope of bringing down the foe.

For more than half a mile they pursued their reckless course, heaping curses on the smugglers, who had been the cause of disturbing their rest, and turning them out of their comfortable quarters on such a dreary night.

The voice of a man brought them to a sudden halt.

'Hullo!' thundered the foremost trooper, bringing his horse up with a jerk that threw it on its haunches.

'Are you looking for smugglers?' queried the man, approaching.

'Smugglers be hanged!' burst out the enraged trooper. 'We are looking for a scoundrel that has shot our sergeant's horse. He took him in the rear, the coward; and, if we do come across him, woe be to him.'

'Was there only one?' asked the man, affecting simplicity.

'We can't tell. We saw no one. But, whoever it may be, they have pretty sharp heels.'

'That accounts for it then. I just saw two fellows, well mounted, tear down the road ahead of you. One called to his fellow to make for the 'Three Admirals,' but the other shouted that it was dangerous, so they took the road to Sandgate.'

'Oh! did they?' said the enraged trooper, and without more ado he turned to his companions, who wheeled round and darted down a cross-road that soon hid them from sight.

'One enemy the less,' muttered the man; then, giving a low whistle, he was soon joined by another.

They were the two smugglers we have before noticed.

'A bad shot that, mate,' said one. 'You hit too low.'

'Well, perhaps it's as well I did so,' replied the other, carelessly. 'It's no use taking life when it can be avoided. Those fellows won't be back for two hours at the least. The coastguardsmen can't launch a boat in double that time; and, as for the marines, they ain't worth a pin in the dark.'

So saying, the worthy pair reprimed their pistols, which they carefully placed beneath their jackets; and, taking a path through a dense corpse were soon out of sight.

In the meantime Sergeant Gill had scrambled to his feet; and, on looking round, he inwardly cursed his men, pouring a bitter incentive on the head of the unfortunate captain whose horse, smarting with pain, was galloping hither and thither, then walked to the edge of a cliff so as to get a view of what was passing on the beach.

The ruddy glow of the watch fire lit up the scene with awful splendour, and disclosed to his astonished visage the shattered boat washed upon the beach and the coastguardsmen dragging the mangled corpses of their unfortunate companions clear of the boiling surf.

Forgetting his misfortune for the moment, Sergeant Gill stood watching the terrible scene until a bright light far out at sea attracted his attention.

It was immediately answered from the shore.

Then a blinding flash appeared for a few seconds on the deck of the distant ship, revealing the hull and towering masts of a frigate. Then all was darkness as before.

CHAPTER LXXV.

WILL HOWARD'S ESCAPE FROM THE FRENCH PRISON.

CONSIDERING the rough handling Will had received, he was not so much hurt as might be expected.

Six burly soldiers carried him to the guard-room, from which, after certain preliminaries had been gone through he was handcuffed, and cast into a dismal cell.

It was here he found himself when he returned t

consciousness, and his first thoughts on discovering his position, were of Gerald Stuart.

'Caged again,' he muttered, savagely. 'This seems to be my lot; the hand of fortune turns against me of late, but I'll bear up against it all, and if I once get the wind in my favour, I'll teach these frog-eating rascals a lesson.

Thus thought Will as he ruminated in his dark and dreary dungeon, the offensive odour of which was worse than poison to him, who had been accustomed all his life to the fresh sea air.

Then he thought of his Sue, his lovely Black-eyed Susan, for whose life he would freely have laid down his own, and a deep-drawn sigh unconsciously escaped him.

For some time he sat, his brow gloomy and overcast, thinking of the strange events that had befallen him of late, the damp atmosphere of the place causing the perspiration to hang on his brow in heavy dews.

Presently he raised his hand to wipe the clammy sweat from his brow.

This act reminded him that his hands were manacled, and a bitter groan of agony escaped him.

'Will! Will!' he muttered to himself, you must not give way like this! you have a duty to perform, every hour of your imprisonment increases the danger of your friends,' and, with a desperate effort, he tried to break the heavy manacles.

He failed, and a sickening sensation passed through his frame at his defeat, but to his joy, he discovered they were very much larger than his wrists.

Suddenly recovering himself, he slipped the manacles from his wrists, and groped around the wet walls of his prison.

While he was thus engaged, he heard a deep, hollow moan, that appeared to come from the further end of his cell.

A groan that seemed to strike terror to his heart, and cause the very blood to curdle in his veins.

For a moment he stood powerless, and he felt as though he should fall to the floor.

'What can it be?' he thought. 'Surely it must be fancy—some horrid imagination of my brain.'

But he had not long to conjecture, for another groan, hollow and sepulchral, sounded in his ear, and he clutched at the slimy walls for support.

'God! what can this mean?' he muttered, half aloud; 'am I a victim of fancy or am I visited by the inhabitants of the tomb?'

Another groan echoed through the vault, and this time he was certain he was not deceived.

Summoning up his courage, he said—

'Be you man or demon, speak, I conjure you.'

Another groan was the only answer.

'What can this be?' he thought; 'is the place haunted? or are they playing me some trick? Be which it may be, I will solve the mystery.'

Nerving himself to the utmost, he continued to grope round the cell, and to his horror another groan fell on his ear, causing him to start; and, as he did so, his hand came in contact with a cold clammy substance like the face of a corpse.

A thrill of horror ran through his frame, and with a shudder he withdrew his hand.

'God! this is awful,' he muttered.

He knew he had touched something, he was certain it was not the damp walls—no, it was flesh of some kind, but of what kind he could not imagine.

He tried to move from the spot but could not, he was rooted to the spot, and his very hair seemed to rise up on his head.

The qualm of fear passed away, and was succeeded by a feeling of curiosity. Stretching out his hand he discovered that another prisoner shared his gloomy cell.

'Speak, friend, who are you?' cried Will, compassionately.

A faint murmur was the only reply.

'Can you not speak, my friend? Can you not tell me who or what you are?'

A faint murmur emanated from the lips of the wretched man, and Will stooped down to hear, if possible, what he said, for he felt anxious to know for what crime the poor emaciated wretch had been cast into that fearful dungeon.

Will could not hear all the man said, he was so feeble, and appeared to be on the brink of the grave.

By what few words he could catch, he learnt the man had been imprisoned for some imaginary crime, and was waiting for his trial.

But as they had nothing to substantiate the charges, they were putting it off until he should want no judging in this world.

As he had lain in that damp dungeon three months, and he saw no chance of being released but by the grim monster death, he prayed hourly for him to come and end his wretched existence.

'Can it be so,' cried Will, 'can it be possible such fiends are allowed to dwell on the earth? No; 'tis too horrible to think of, my brain reels at the very idea.'

Turning away from the groaning man, he muttered to himself—

'Surely they mean to serve me as they have served this poor mortal. No, it must not be; it would drive me raving mad.'

Seating himself upon the stone bench, he relapsed into a state of dreamy thought, and conjectured in his own mind the most horrible scenes.

He was aroused from his reverie by the sound of approaching footsteps in the passage leading to his cell, and the bolts were once more withdrawn, and two jailers entered the dungeon.

The jailers were two stalwart men. One of them carried a lamp and the other came to bring the food for the prisoners, and a piece of black bread and a jug of water. The brave seaman could not but observe the fiendish smile that played on the lips of the jailers, and his lip quivered with rage.

'Here's your supper,' said the foremost of the jailers, 'if you have not had it already; I dare say the fresh air makes your appetite pretty keen.'

Will eyed the speaker narrowly, and although he was burning with indignation, he did not answer him, but kept his eye fixed firmly upon his features, upon which was branded the deepest villany.

'Do you hear me?' growled the fellow. 'Come, lay hold of your grub, if you want it; if you don't want it say so.

'How am I to hold it,' cried Will, holding his hands so as they could not observe they were unfettered, 'when my hands are fast.'

'You'll get used to that, old fellar,' interposed the other with a sneer; 'you are not used to such fine lodgings; you want to come to France to learn high life.'

'Oh, he'll learn in time, Janot. I lay he won't be so independent when he gets used to our ways.'

'No, he'll learn how to respect us when he knows who we are.'

'You are right, old boy,' replied the other.

'Now then, my pippin, lay hold of your grub,'

'I cannot,' answered the sailor.

'Oh, you can't, eh? Well I can't stand here and hold it all night.'

'Then lay it down,' cried Will.

'I will, I can assure you, for my arms are tired of holding it.'

'Thank you,' said Will, in an assumed tone.

The jailor was about to place it on the floor, but before doing so he looked up in the sailor's face, saying—

'You must be careful, mind you, and not grease the carpet.'

'I'll grease you, directly,' thought Will.

'It's as fine a drop of wine, and as rich a piece of cake, as you have tasted,' said the jailor, placing the prisoner's food on the floor.

'Indeed!' replied Will, dealing the stooping jailor a crashing blow on the back of the neck, causing him to fall insensible on his face; and then springing at the other one, he grasped him by the throat.

The lamp fell from the man's hand, but luckily was not extinguished, and the two struggled fiercely to gain the mastery.

Will clutched his foe tightly by the neck, and flung him to the floor, still retaining his hold. Over and over they rolled.

At length Will got the upper hand, and placing his knee on the chest of the jailor, held him down, and clutching his throat tighter, caused him to writhe with agony; then dealing him a terrific blow under the ear, knocked him senseless.

Hastily seizing the lamp, Will hurriedly examined his fellow prisoner, and a feeling of pity was excited in his breast.

'I wish I could take you with me,' cried Will, in a tone of sympathy. 'I would willingly; but I have yet to escape myself.'

'Do not trouble yourself about me, friend,' murmured the man, feebly. 'My time has come; my life hangs upon a thread, and that will soon be broken. Farewell! Fly while you have time.'

'Good-bye,' cried Will, as a tear stole down his cheek; then, taking the emaciated hand of the miserable man in his own, added mournfully—

'May God help you; good night.'

The gallant sailor could scarcely utter these last words, he was so affected by the miserable appearance of the prisoner; and, hurrying from the cell, he took the precaution to close the door after him and shoot the bolts.

Shading the lamp with his hand, he hurried along the corridor; and, as he passed the various cells, a melancholy gloom came over him and he quickened his footsteps.

On arriving at the end of the corridor he perceived a flight of stone steps, and on ascending them he was surprised to see the jailer's room. Here a strong door barred his progress. It was locked!

What was to be done? He had no key?

'Very likely,' he thought, 'it is in this room.'

On a long bench or settle lay the wife of one of the jailers; she was asleep, and over her head hung a huge key.

'That key,' thought Will, 'must be the one I stand in need of. I must have it.'

Noiselessly he crept into the room, and reached over the sleeping woman, and was about to seize the key when a heavy hand was placed on his shoulder.

Glancing over his shoulder he caught sight of another jailer, and, quick as lightning grasping the key, dealt the man a terrible blow between the eyes.

So sudden had been the blow that the man had not time to utter a word, and he fell on the floor without a groan.

The woman moved slightly on the bench, but did not wake, and it was well for her she did not, for Will was rendered desperate, and much as it was against his inclination, he would have been compelled to serve her the same.

His next movement was to unlock the door, through which he passed, and traversed a long passage. He was rather perplexed on reaching the end, for two passages branched off in opposite directions.

Which one to take he did not know, but there was no time to consider hit or miss.

He took the one to the right which led to another flight of steps, which the sailor quickly ascended.

A gush of air extinguished his light, and his heart bounded at the smell of freedom as the fresh air fanned his heated cheek.

He proceeded as cautiously as possible, for he could hear the measured tread of the sentinel, and as he advanced he discovered that he had taken the wrong passage. He had ascended to the ramparts.

He was about to turn back, but the moon that had hitherto been obscured by a passing cloud shone full upon him, at the some moment the sentinel turned to retrace his steps.

'Who goes there?' he demanded, pointing his musket towards our hero.

'A friend,' answered Will, as coolly as possible.

But this would not satisfy the sentinel, and advancing towards our hero, he said—

'The password?'

The seaman was completely puzzled. Here was a greater difficulty than any he had met with as yet, for he was unarmed, while the sentinel held a loaded musket with fixed bayonet.

The soldier, seeing his embarrassment, and wishing to show his authority, rushed towards him, gesticulating fiercely, and made a feint at him, as though he were going to run him through.

Will, who noticed he was rather forward, and knew he must shortly decide one way or the other, cried, in a commanding tone—

'Hold!'

'Give the password, or I'll skewer you,' roared the sentinel.

'I will in one moment,' replied Will, fixing his glance on the soldier.

The soldier, putting on one of his fiercest looks, held the bayonet close to the sailor's breast.

Will saw his only chance of escape would be by fighting, and, as he was unarmed, he could not well do that, so he quickly formed his plans.

Looking the soldier boldly in the face, and making a movement as though he were about to speak, he stepped forward and seized the bayonet.

The soldier was thrown quite off his guard; but as soon as he became aware of the sailor's intentions, he tried to snatch it from his grasp.

But his efforts were useless; and the sailor, taking advantage of his movement, seized hold of the stock with one hand, and with the other dealt the soldier a desperate blow on the nose.

The soldier uttered a growl of rage, and Will wrenched the musket from his grasp, and stood over him the next moment in a threatening attitude.

'Mercy! mercy!' cried the soldier, cowering beneath the stern glance of the sailor.

'I'll grant you the same mercy as you would have granted me, you rascal!' vociferated Will, angrily, holding the bayonet to the soldier's breast, who shrank in dismay from the glittering blade. 'Take off that coat, you coxcomb!' he cried, 'and be sharp about it, or I'll assist you.'

'Mercy! mercy!' cried the soldier, sinking on his knees.

Will could not suppress a smile as he gazed upon the trembling wretch, who but a minute or so before had been so full of boast, and giving him a severe kick, he cried—

'Now, then, pull off that coat, you have worn it long enough.'

'Spare me! spare me!' cried the soldier, imploringly.

'I'll spare you to some tune directly, if you don't do as I order you,' cried Will, seizing him by the collar and giving him a severe shake.

This was quite enough for the soldier; he did not wish him to repeat the dose, and reluctantly pulled off his coat.

Scarcely had he done so when Will was upon him, and bound and gagged him, and then dragged him in the shadow of one of the guns.

Having attired himself in the soldier's clothes, he took a cartridge from the soldier's pouch and smeared his face with some of the powder, wetted, in imitation of a moustache, then shouldering the musket, he rushed to the guard room, shouting as hard as he was able—

'Prisoner escaped!'

'Prisoner escaped!'

The officer on guard rushed from the fire where he had been sitting half asleep, and confusedly cried out—

'What's the matter? What's wrong?'

'The prisoner's escaped!' cried Will, in alarm.

'D—n the fellow,' cried the officer, rubbing his eyes, for he could scarcely see, coming so suddenly into the dark, 'where has he gone to?'

'He went that way,' cried Will, pointing in the opposite direction he intended going.

'How did he escape?' cried the officer.

'I saw him scale the wall,' answered Will, in well feigned accent.

'Come on, your lazy dogs,' cried the officer, then dashing down the street indicated by Will, he ordered his men to follow him up closely.

No sooner had they left than Will dashed down the opposite street as fast as his legs would allow him.

'You cursed French dogs,' he muttered, 'I'll learn you to be more watchful.'

CHAPTER LXXVI.

WILL HOWARD TURNS SMUGGLER—A DESPERATE STRUGGLE FOR LIFE.

ON gaining his liberty Will's first thought was to look after his friend Gerald Stuart, but as he had not the slightest recollection of the streets he left him in, nor what part of the town he was then in himself, he was at a loss how to act.

In wandering about he found himself at last upon the quay, a circumstance of which he became too fully aware in being surrounded by a body of soldiers.

A phalanx of bayonets were immediately pointed at his breast, and as he was totally unharmed, to resist being captured seemed nothing short of madness.

'Surrender! You are my prisoner,' cried the officer in French, a language to which Will was not totally a stranger, but as liberty at the present moment was as dear to him as life, he did not mean to give in quietly.

The soldiers could see this in his looks.

His teeth were firmly set, his hands clenched, and a fire of determination gleamed in his flashing eye.

'Avast heaving, you lubbers,' he shouted, half mad at the thought of being taken,—'avast there, I say, or by the powers of Neptune I'll swamp you all.'

The soldiers did not understand a word he said; but his gesture implied what he meant, and for a moment they drew back.

In that moment Will saw his chance.

Seizing the musket held by one of them, he wrenched it from the soldier's grasp, and bringing the butt down heavily on the officer's head, he laid him prostrate.

All was now confusion.

The soldiers swore most furiously.

'Cut him down!—pink him!' was the general cry.

Again they rallied, and surrounded the gallant tar, who by this time had brought his weapon in a position of defence.

'Stand off!' yelled Will, describing a circle with his weapon, within which circle the soldiers, though willing, dared not put a foot.

But he might as well have roared at the wind.

His single arm would have been like a reed among so many.

He would have fallen, pierced by the bayonets of his merciless foes, had not an unforeseen accident occurred.

A party of smugglers were repairing to their boat, after paying a visit to the fat old landlady of the 'Pig and Dolphin,' and in passing that way they were surprised to hear the voice of a fellow countryman in distress.

The captain, who like his men was about three sheets in the wind, no sooner heard it and caught sight of the Frenchmen, than, cutlass in hand, he rushed to the spot.

'Hurrah, lads! To the rescue!' he shouted to his men, who, excited by the spirits they had imbibed, and naturally indignant at the idea of an Englishman falling a victim to the frog-eating crew, needed no other incentive.

A desperate conflict ensued.

The smugglers' cutlasses told well upon the unwieldy arms of the soldiers.

For some minutes the conflict raged with unabated fury, until many of the soldiers were stretched upon the ground, and Will and the smuggler captain were laid for dead.

A sharp scuffle then ensued.

The Frenchmen were put to the rout.

Then, raising the bleeding men, the smugglers beat a retreat to their boat, and were soon on board a tight little brig.

For a moment her white sails fluttered in the wind; the sharp click click of the windlass sounded on the night air, and the gallant barque, yielding to the breeze, sped gallantly out to sea.

When Will recovered from the wound he had received, or rather gained sufficient strength to speak, he looked around, and asked—

'Yeo, ho, there, my hearties! What ship is this I am aboard?'

'The saucy Kitty,' was the bluff reply.

'How did I get here?'

'Drove hard on a lee shore, and I picked you up.'

'Damme, that's generous. What name, mess-mate?'

'Got none.'

'That be hanged.'

'It's a fact. May I never swab a deck or keel-haul a Jew, if it arn't.'

'Well, damme, you know what I mean. What name do you sail under? What flag do you up-hold?'

'The flag of freedom,' replied the man, enthusias-tically. 'We are smugglers; and, if I am not mis-taken, your name is Will Howard. I am a native of Deal, so cannot be deceived.'

'Wrong — wrong, man,' exclaimed Will, not knowing the character of the man who had thus recognised him.

'Well, shiver my mizzen!' said the man, rubbing his eyes, 'if that arn't good. Do you think you can bamboozle old Sam?'

'What, Sam Fowler?' queried Will.

'Yes, old Sam. Why, damme, Will, you soon forget an old top-mate.'

''Tis the way of the world,' muttered Will; 'but,' he asked, glancing curiously round, 'what craft do I find myself on board, eh?'

'The Fleetwing,' replied the smuggler; 'and as taut a little craft as ever kissed blue water; but our captain, poor fellow—poor Tom Swinford—you know him—he's'——

'What, what?—speak!' ejaculated Will, as a slight recollection of the conflict flashed to his mind. 'Is he hurt?'

'Hurt? Worse, Will—he is dead!'

The feeling-hearted tar sank back on the coil of rope that had served him for a pillow, and a ghastly pallor overspread his features.

'And I am the cause of it,' he said.

'No, no; 'twas fate, Will; but as we have lost our best friend. and the night is likely to be a rough one, the men have asked me to—to'——

'Well, go on.'

The smuggler hesitated.

Will saw his dilemma, and kindly assisted him.

'You want me to pilot you?' he said.

'Aye, that's it—we want you to be captain.'

Will agreed. After hearing the account of the *melee* with the French soldiers, he made up his mind to steer boldly into the coast, and, if possible, effect a landing that night in the teeth of the custom-house officers and the many cruisers that swarm in the Channel.

It was a desperate resolve, but those who knew aught of the character of the man who stood cap-tain of that gallant little brig knew it was no idle boast.

Sure enough, as old Sam had prophesied (he was the mate), the night was a rough one.

The wind that blew directly for the coast increased to a violent hurricane.

The sea rose like a mountain and dashed the little bark about as though it were but a cork.

Will used the utmost caution.

He had now two enemies to contend against—the elements and man.

All sail that was not necessary to the steering of the ship he had securely furled, the storm sails bent, and an extra hand at the wheel.

And so he steered in, his eyes fixed on the tower-ing cliffs until, at length impatient, he displayed the light we have before noticed as proceeding from the deck of a distant vessel.

'All right,' he muttered, as it was answered from the shore by a red light. 'Aha! they are on the alert, then.'

By this time the wind had abated a little, thus enabling them to show more canvas, and hauling the ship to about four points, Will steered along the coast.

He had scarcely rounded the headland, where he had hoped to land his cargo under shelter of the cliff, when a schooner shot out from a little bay, and laid across his bow.

Will's quick eye detected her in an instant, and, by a dexterous movement of the helm he brought his ship to the wind, just escaping the raking fire that passed by like a shower of hail, and bringing his broadside guns to bear upon the schooner's hull.

This was the signal for a fight.

A battle that none but the stoutest heart would have courted.

Broadside for broadside was exchanged like light-ning.

Grape and chain-shot flew about in heavy showers.

The crashing of splintered wood, mingled with the shouts of the men, made the din almost deafening.

At length both vessels touched.

The captain of the schooner was on the quarter-deck, when the glare of a match revealed to him Will's features.

'Will Howard, the pirate,' he shouted to his lieutenant. 'A reward is out for his capture. Heave round, my lads; he must not escape. By all the furies, we must capture him!'

The lieutenant dashed forward among his men, and urged them to their utmost exertions.

'Boarders away,' he shouted. 'Cut the rascals down, but spare the captain.'

This they found was a task much easier said than done.

Old Sam had crept over the side and cut the grap-lins, whilst a couple of hands hauling in the main try-sail sheet caused the brig to fall off.

An execration of rage burst from the captain of the man-of-war schooner on finding himself thus baffled, for his bowsprit being cut through with a chain shot and all his sails riddled with grape, rendered his vessel unmanageable.

A loud shout of defiance came from the deck of the smuggler as she skipped away before the wind; but a bitter oath was extorted from old Sam when he descried a frigate with open ports and the crew at their guns bearing down full upon them.

Will cast an anxious glance towards her.

He could see that the commodore's flag floated from her main.

'Confound it,' he muttered, 'they have scented me out. See, the schooner is signalling to him.'

Will was well versed in the man-of-war regula-tions. His long stay in the service had learnt him that which was now very useful to him.

'W. H., pirate,' he replied to an interrogatory of old Sam's; 'so I must away. My life is not so pre-cious as to command the lives of the whole crew.'

Sam stared at him, thunderstruck.

'What, topmate! do you mean to strike?'

'Yes—and hard, too, if I get yard-arm and yard-arm with this confounded new-comer. But I am wasting time. I must make one desperate attempt for life; and if unsuccessful—well, damme! I'll '——

'Avast, captain,' cried Sam, as Will sprang to the boat, and commenced lowering it. 'What do you intend doing?'

'I mean to save you, if possible.'

'How?—impossible!'

'Then I'll try it. So farewell, Sam, if we do not meet again.'

There was a fire in his eye that marked his predominant will; and as the boat touched the water, he leapt in, taking in his hand a smouldering torch.

Seizing the oars, he pulled for a low point of land, and, as he had anticipated, the frigate was hove-to, and her boats lowered and manned.

This gave the brig an opportunity to slip away.

'Hurrah! Hunt the rascals down!' yelled the commodore. And the fatal words lent vigour to the gallant Will, as he beat to his task; and his boat sped on swift as an arrow.

It was a hazardous run for life, and there did not seem much hope for the pursued.

The commodore watched the smuggler round a rocky point, and, as he believed, draw into the shore. He was afraid his own boats would not come across him in time, and so he pointed another gun at him, this time with perfect aim, so true, indeed, that the ball struck the flaming torch from the smuggler's boat, and left him in total darkness.

The commodore foamed in fury at his own folly.

He had given the smuggler his only chance of safety.

Running up lanterns from the yards of his vessel, he endeavoured by continual discharges of unshotted guns to throw a light on the receding boat, but the smuggler captain, by skilful rowing, baffled his attempts.

Straining hard at the oars he pulled vigorously out to sea; scarcely a splash betrayed which way he went. He was calmer now, and knew what a terrible risk he had to run the gauntlet.

He was far from the shore when he heard the regular dripping of water, and knew that one of the pursuing boats was near.

It was too dark to see, but he drew steadily away, and then rested on his oars to allow the boat to come by.

The men were rowing cautiously, and he heard them conversing about the certainty of his capture.

'He's a devil to fight,' he heard one say, 'and we'd better settle him with a bullet, as soon as we catch sight of him.'

The smuggler was so close to the speaker that he might have pulled him from his perch.

Another man spoke.

'We shall have a reward for catching him—sure to get something, I suppose.'

He did get something.

The smuggler had sat still as a statue. As the boat glided by, carefully balancing himself, he leaned over and caught the blade of the oar the man was in the act of dipping into the sea.

Giving it a sudden wrench he twisted it out of the man's hand so violently, that the fellow went sprawling on his back, while the boat lurched half over.

'The devil! I've caught a crab,' spluttered the man.

He caught something else.

The smuggler captain gave him a drive in the ribs with the oar that sent him back again as he was try-ing to rise, and nearly knocked all the breath out of his body.

While he was lying prone, he caught sight of a pair of eyes flashing upon him from the darkness.

With a sudden yell of affright he clutched at the oar, crying—

'Here he is—the smuggler—catch the devil—he's here.'

The sudden warning caused the boat's crew to start up quickly, and the smuggler captain, by an adroit movement, capsized them all into the sea.

This accomplished, he thought it time to pull into shore. With long steady strokes he made for land, while the crew struggled to regain their capsized boat.

He had chosen a place some distance from where the frigate lay, it was where a little creek ran into shore. There were no other lights here, and he had a better chance of escape.

If he did not run foul of the officers of the customs or the coast-guard, who were always on the look-out at such points as these.

Peering through the darkness, he saw a favourable landing-place, and as his boat grated on the sand stepped to the beach.

At this moment a vivid light went up from the frigate—a light so bright that it revealed the scene for miles around, and betrayed the spot where he had landed.

With a loud hurrah, the men in the other boats, who had been lying in close, made for the shore, and the smuggler knew that unless he could speedily elude their vigilance the most gallant defence would not avail to save his life.

A few rude habitations were scattered here and there about the rugged coast, but a little way inward were some mansions of large dimensions. Many of these were familiar to our hero, and it was his object to keep as far away from them as possible.

He took care, too, to be as much in shelter as he could.

Blue lights and rockets still went up from the frigate, which was signalling to those on shore to intercept the smuggler, and the smuggler had now to be close as he went in order not to be seen by the revenue officers who were turned out to capture him.

The commotion behind him assured him that his pursuers had landed, but he did not so much regard those who were in his rear. He feared more the foes who were in his front.

All of a sudden, as he was creeping by the rocks, a light flashed upon him, and he found himself confronted by a party of custom officers.

A cry from them, uttering his name, a rush, a swift report, followed by another, a gleam of steel, and he had forced through their midst—how he knew not. Scathed but untaken. He heard their shouts of rage and pain as he went like a meteor through them, and then he bounded fleetly away.

A short run brought him to the edge of a little stream, widening inland from the creek, here and there was a heavy boat, in which a roughish-looking man was seated leisurely listening to the sounds of pursuit and strife.

When he saw the smuggler he divined how matters stood, and standing up in the boat, stretched out his long gaunt hands to take the daring fellow.

'You've just dropped in the right spot,' he said, with a grin; 'make up your mind to stay till they comes. I'm the boy to take care of you till then.'

He laid his hands on the smuggler's shoulder.

The smuggler shook him quickly off.

BLACK EYED SUSAN.

OR, PIRATES ASHORE.

WILL IN THE HANDS OF THE BLACK PIRATES.

'Fool!' he said, 'a word and I send a bullet through your brain!'

He thrust a pistol against the fellow's temple.

The man looked at him in open-mouthed dismay. He had not seen that he was armed, and so made sure of an easy capture.

He was careful of what brains he had, and hesitated what he should do.

The gallant smuggler, ever prompt in action, very speedily took him by the throat, and having forced him to the boat, leapt in and knelt upon his chest, while he gagged and bound him.

Then, with giant strength, he hurled him on to the river's edge, and taking his seat in the boat, rowed away as his pursuers came upon the scene.

He was out of their reach long before they could get another boat ready and follow him.

We will leave him now for a short time, and proceed to the residence of Sir Henry Warberton, a proud and haughty gentleman who dwelt with his family in a magnificent mansion facing the sea-coast, and situate a few miles from the place where the action had taken place between the frigate and the schooner.

Accustomed to continual actions between the smugglers and the revenue vessels he would have taken little notice of the affair if the contending vessels had bombarded each other under his very walls.

He knew that such affairs were very speedily over, and generally ended without much damage being done.

But the tumult of this night's battle had prepared him for some more serious conflict, and when the explosion took place he was standing at his window, and so beheld much of the animated scene that followed.

After the escape of Will came the cessation of firing, and, supposing that the engagement had terminated with the destruction or capture of the smugglers, he troubled himself no more about it.

He had guests that night, and the costly dinner was followed by a gay masquerade, which was to be kept up until a late hour.

Sir Henry's grown-up children—a son and two daughters—were present.

The sisters were twins, and were each strikingly beautiful.

The brother was young. He was named after his father, and, though inheriting the family pride, was noble and brave to a high degree.

The two sisters had been dancing with the partners whom they had chosen for their father's guests. They were each in costume, and looked entrancingly lovely as they retired from the dance.

Ellen, the taller of the two, remained in the dancing hall; but Beatrice, her younger-looking sister, strolled through the spacious gardens to enjoy the cool night air.

She had heard the distant sounds of strife, and was wondering how the engagement had terminated, when she heard a sudden tumult of voices, followed by the clash of steel.

An instant after a youthful figure sprang lightly up the rocks, above which her father's dwelling stood. He held a pistol in one hand, and a sword gleamed in the other. Beatrice shuddered, for she saw that it was red, but she had no time to dwell upon that. The young smuggler, for such he seemed to be, had only got a little way up the rocks when two of his pursuers advanced upon him.

Beatrice saw how his graceful figure was drawn erect, and how his kindling eyes flashed as his keen sword circled above his head.

She saw his assailants lunge at him with their weapons, and she suppressed a shriek as it seemed that he was run through his head, but while she looked, he whirled the cutlass from the grasp of one, and hurled the other headlong to the earth.

A loud shout now rose on the air, and as the young smuggler sprang higher up the rocks, a party of custom-house officers, armed with cutlass and pistols, covered him with their weapons.

Her heart seemed stilled as she heard them summon him to surrender.

His undaunted reply answered them.

Then there was a blinding flash, and she saw him stagger and fall.

He rose again instantly, but seemed faint and overcome. He was bleeding and half-stunned, but as if nerved to exertion by the approach of his foes he drew himself erect, and seizing the first who came, thrust him down upon the remainder.

A moment more, and he had vanished from her sight.

The guests were pouring from the house with her father. The tumult had brought them forth, and Beatrice, horror-stricken by what she had witnessed, withdrew from observation.

She knew not why, but the youthful smuggler had interested her in his fate, and she was sadly hoping that he might not be killed, when, with a single leap, he came from behind the rocks that formed a wall round the house, and stood suddenly before her.

Too startled to speak, she gazed upon him with her large eyes dilating, and her fair bosom heaving in pity as well as alarm.

The brave Will stopped in surprise at seeing her, and then stepped towards her and said—

'Lady, I am hunted to the death. Will you betray me to my foes?'

'Alas! what have you done?'

'Enough to make my life valueless. They come —and I must defend myself to the last drop of blood.'

Beatrice looked at the noble figure before her, wounded and bloodstained, faint and almost overcome.

He yet seemed so noble and gentle that she could not bear the idea of his being slain.

'Alas!' she cried, wringing her hands, 'they will kill you—can you not escape?'

'That is impossible, lady. I thank you for taking an interest in my fate, but I am doomed, and can only sell my life dearly.'

His hand clenched on his reeking cutlass.

She stepped towards him timidly.

'Oh! no—no,' she cried. 'Don't sacrifice your life. Escape.'

'Lady, there is no way. Shiver my timbers, they have hove me short at last.'

'There is. Hide in this house—in there—it is my chamber—enter by the balcony—quick—they are coming—oh, heavens! you are lost.'

He had stayed to fall on one knee and take her hand in grateful respect.

Now he saw his pursuers advancing, and with one light bound he leapt to the balcony. The folding windows were open, and he noiselessly stepped on to the carpeted floor.

He was hardly out of sight when the officers came up the rocks; at the same time her father, accompanied by his guests, came rushing to the spot.

'Seek your chamber, my child,' he cried, as they

went past; 'a noted smuggler and pirate is concealed about the place; his hands are red with blood, and he would murder you should you fall in his way.'

They went past her, little dreaming that her trembling, fragile form almost secured from their sight the young smuggler whom they were seeking. They went, and left her standing there, mute with fear and horror at what she had done.

CHAPTER LXXVII.

DOINGS OF THE RED VULTURE.—SUSAN AGAIN IN THE TYRANT'S POWER.

NOT many days elapsed before Will was again afloat on board the brig, making a course down channel, with a favourable wind.

He would have returned to Havre, only that it was too hot for him; and as he doubted not that Captain Stuart would leave the port as soon as possible, he thought it useless to run into unnecessary danger.

'Susan—my own darling Sue!' he ruminated, as he paced the brig's quarter-deck. 'What would I not give, had I the tyrant here that holds you in his power!'

The voice of his mate put an end to his solitary musings.

'Shiver me, captain, if I didn't hear the boom of a gun!' said the bluff old smuggler.

'Nonsense!'

'So you may say; but if that warn't a gun, why, old Sam never heerd one.'

At that moment a distant boom was heard rolling over the waters; and on looking to leeward, where a dense cloud of mist had been hovering since day-light, but was now drifting gradually away, they beheld two vessels apparently engaged yard-arm to yard-arm.

'A pirate—confound him!' yelled Will. 'Clap on every stitch she will carry, my lads! Hurrah! Down with the pirate's flag!'

What would have been the feelings of our hero had he been able to glance upon the deck of one of the vessels, from whose scuppers the blood was pouring in a purple stream?

It would have frozen him with horror.

Just at this moment it was that Red Vulture, the pirate, had seized upon his lovely victim, and was holding the gleaming scimetar to her snowy throat.

A startled cry from one of his crew arrested the deadly blow.

Gregory Saunders cast his bleared eyes around.

A vessel, bearing down upon them under a cloud of sail, met his gaze.

It required but a glance to see that her guns were run out, and ready for action.

With a bitter oath, Gregory hurled the woman from him, and leapt into the midst of his men.

Despardo was by his side.

'You will not leave the work unfinished?' he said, huskily.

'No—by all the furies, I will not!' was the brutal reply.

'Then give your commands. Our time is but short. We shall have hotter work when this fellow heaves alongside.'

Gregory waited to hear no more.

He shouted his orders to his devilish crew.

Then arose the din of musketry, and the clash of steel, mingled with the shrieks of women and the groans and prayers of men.

The crew of the Lucy, taken by surprise, had made what defence they could, but the pirates dealt death with unsparing ferocity, and the deck of the ill-fated ship was heaped with the slain.

Foremost in the conflict was Gregory, his tall form towering above his men. Armed with his scimetar, he slew all that came before him.

His was no arm unused to strike.

The blade fenced off every blow that threatened him, and dealt death indiscriminately around.

In the midst of this deadly strife, he found himself confronted by one of the passengers.

He was an elderly, distinguished-looking man, and stopped suddenly on beholding Saunders.

'Good heavens!' he exclaimed, 'you here in this sanguinary business. For God's sake stop this dreadful massacre!'

'I will,' cried Gregory, savagely, and with a sweep he sent the old man's head rolling at his feet.

For a moment he gazed in satisfaction at the work of his guilty hands, and then pressed on to fresh slaughter.

Who can describe the frightful scene that ensued.

The deck presented a frightful spectacle.

The bodies of the slain lay under the feet of the combatants; the shrieking women stood apart, their loud screams deadening the reports of the fire-arms, as they beheld husband, brother, or friend fall before them.

Quarter was asked, but none was given.

It was not until the last of their antagonists sank beneath his numerous wounds that the carnage was stayed.

Then the pirates rushed *en masse* down the gangways, and into the cabins, and, having ransacked the vessel for its valuables, soon appeared on deck laden with rich spoils, for the Lucy was freighted with silks and specie, and had amongst her passengers many who had brought much wealth on board; she had besides a number of casks of wine, and these were hauled upon deck.

Others of the crew dragged from their hiding places the hapless females, who had sought refuge in concealment, and whom they now looked upon as their lawful prey, and two ruffians brought forth from below an aged, white-haired man.

They brandished their red weapons before him, and when he clasped his thin, white hands together, and prayed to heaven for that mercy he knew he would not receive from his brutal captors, they drove their cutlasses into his breast, and hurled him overboard.

Despardo proceeded to superintend the carrying away and secreting of the booty thus lawlessly gained.

'What do you intend doing with these?' asked Gregory, pointing with his blood-stained blade to the unhappy women whom the pirate crew held prisoners.

'Prizes,' was the laconic reply.

'A pretty arrangement, truly; but see, they are shipping the wine on board. You will not burden yourself with that at the outset, will you? we have plenty of rum.'

'The lads will look for a drinking carousal,' Despardo replied.

'Then while I'm captain, they do not have it. What! at the very commencement of our cruise, ere we can have the vessel trimmed to avoid suspicion, you take on board two such dangerous articles as wine and women—the very ingredients of discord. The ship will be in a mutiny in a week, and remember, British men-of-war are always fishing in these waters; this fellow (pointing to the approaching ship) may be one for aught we know.'

Despardo wrinkled up his features with a puzzled air.

Gregory's words surprised him.

'What are you driving at?' he said. 'We should have a mutiny if we were to deprive them of their prizes.'

'Leave them to me!' thundered Gregory. 'Have you done with the prize?'

'Well, I reckon yes.'

'Then if you will return I will manage the crew.'

Despardo went back to his vessel, and Gregory walked aft to the men.

'Now, then, get ready to ship off. Leave those barrels—we have wine enough on board. Fire the ship, and leave her.'

The ruffians murmured at being deprived of their intended carousal; but Saunders was not a man to be questioned, and smoke issued in various directions from the ship.

'Now, men, get on board your own vessel at once. On board with you. Leave those ladies here. Away with you,' he continued, as the crew began to remonstrate.

They sullenly obeyed.

'Ladies,' said Gregory, 'I have rescued you from a fate which, as Englishwomen, you would, I know, have thought worse than death. You may thank me for that. I must leave you, as the flames are rising round us. Farewell! you will without doubt meet your fate with becoming firmness.'

He spoke in a tone of quiet irony, and, waving his hand to them, followed his men on board his vessel.

Suddenly he paused.

The features of one of the women, whom he before had not minutely surveyed, arrested his attention.

'Susan, by all that is holy!' he muttered, 'the wife of one of my *friends*. This at least will be a little towards revenge.'

He raised her in his arms, gave the order to sheer off, then went below.

Then the grappling irons were unfixed, and the two vessels parted company; the pirate ship bearing away on her course, and leaving the ill-fated Lucy to her doom.

And now from the deck of the Lucy rose a succession of wailing shrieks as the wretched women, conscious of the fearful fate to which they were left, clustered to the bows of the vessel, and beseeched for mercy.

But they appealed to hearts that exulted in destruction; the pirate crew laughed at their entreaties, and scoffed at their terror.

And the smoke of the burning vessel became more dense, and the forked tongues of flame shot up around them; and their screams of agony and despair died in the distance as the pirate ship bore away from her stricken prey.

*   *   *   *   *

A fire at sea!

How terribly thrilling when even the first dread rumour spreads from tongue to tongue, and while there is yet a chance that the exertions of the crew will subdue the flames.

But, oh God! how frightful to those poor doomed creatures who had seen their defenders, their kindred, slaughtered before their eyes—who had knelt by the gashed, disfigured body of some loved one, and tried to kiss him back to life.

How they huddled together and flew from the maddening tongues of fire, and shrieked for mercy till it seemed strangely hard that Heaven could see their distress, and turn a deaf ear to their plea for succour.

The devils in human guise had too well fired the ship, and circling flames narrowed the scanty spot upon which these despairing women clustered, until the frenzy of their agony made them leap into the bosom of the sea, seeking their release from the torments of that floating hell.

And farther and farther away sailed the destroying vessel—fading at last in the distant gloom, passing out of view like a spectre of ill; but not losing sight of the burning wreck, whose place was revealed by the red glare, diminishing as the wind bore them away, but growing more vivid even as it became less to view.

———

CHAPTER LXXVIII.

THE MEETING WITH THE PIRATES.

OWING to the thick, sulphurous smoke, the smuggler brig was not perceived by the shrieking wretches, whose fate now seemed doubly sealed, until she had approached within hail.

Will's first thought had been to give chase to the dastardly pirate, but on discovering that some of the unfortunate passengers were still living, he made up his mind to save them if possible.

A boat was instantly lowered, and Will, followed by half-a-dozen of his sturdiest followers, leapt in.

Their efforts at first seemed useless, but owing to the daring spirit of the gallant Will, two of the women were rescued from the burning ship.

Having seen the last one left fall a victim to the flames, Will returned to the brig, and used his utmost to restore to consciousness those he had rescued.

From the narrative of one of the ladies he concluded his wife was one of the unfortunate passengers, and when he learnt that the pirate had taken her with him, his heart swelled with indignation.

'Cheer up,' said Sam, on observing his captain's low spiritedness, 'we may yet run on board him.'

*   *   *   *   *   *

A week had nearly passed, and the smugglers, whose destination had previously been the port of Lisbon, found themselves beating about the West Indies.

The crew were lying listless about the deck, when they were suddenly aroused to action.

'Sail-ho!' sang out the look-out man from the masthead.

It was the evening of the succeeding day.

Captain Will sprang to the binnacle.

'Where away?' he asked.

'Off our starboard quarter, sir.'

Will adjusted his telescope, and took a survey of the horizon.

Far, very far away, was the faint indication of a vessel.

She was coming in their track, a minute's examination proved; and our hero, with a satisfied smile, handed the glass to his mate, while the crew, with curious interest on their faces, gathered about the quarter-deck.

'Sail-ho!' again sang out the look-out.

'Where away?'

'Off the stranger's lee.'

He gave our hero the glass.

The two vessels were coming plainly in sight.

They seemed close together, but the one they had last seen was the bigger of the two, and by the manner in which she gained upon the other, evidently was the swifter sailer.

As Will gazed across the sea, an excited look crossed his features.

'I could have sworn,' he observed to old Sam, 'that I saw smoke about the stranger's bows.'

'Not at all unlikely,' was Sam's reply. 'There's plenty of warm work in these seas; and the looks of that big craft don't please me at all.'

A few moments of anxious suspense ensued.

All was silence on board.

Presently everyone started.

Boom came the sound of a gun across the sea.

Another—then a quicker succession of shots.

There could be no uncertainty now—the two vessels were engaged.

William cast an anxious look around at the lowering sky.

'Have all sail spread,' he shouted; 'we may come up with her before darkness sets in. Clear the decks and run out the guns; and boarders, look to your pikes and cutlasses.'

'Besides,' he added, 'who knows but this may be the fellow we want.'

A score of willing hands sped about the ship—sheet after sheet was unfurled, till the masts bent like reeds beneath the pressure of the gale.

The wind was blowing stiff, and the brig leapt swiftly across the intervening space.

In a little while could be seen an occasional sheet of light leaving the sides of the two vessels, over whose hulls the smoke hung in dense clouds.

The booming of the guns was more startling but less frequent. The weaker vessel was yielding to the superior force of the enemy.'

'The little one is beaten,' said Will to Sam.

'Yes; they have taken her. I hope we may be in time to do the same for them.'

'See,' he cried, 'they have fired the ship!'

As if it had been flooded by instantaneous liquid fire, the smaller vessel, all in a moment, was ablaze from stem to stern; but her big opponent did not even then cease firing into her, and half a dozen shots brought her so low in the water, that her speedy destruction by fire and leakage was certain.

Whether her crew and passengers had been removed, or were left to their terrible fate, it was impossible to conjecture; but a determined look settled on the faces of the smugglers as their ship began to forereach upon the victorious cruiser.

Having accomplished her swift, ruthless work, the strange vessel, deigning her pursuer no notice, now spread her sails, and shaped her course in another direction; but she went at an easy speed, as if glutted with the plunder of her prey, and at every leap of the ship the distance between them was lessened.

Now that they got closer, the appearance and build of the enemy they were so soon to encounter were the subjects of curious observations.

She was a rather ungainly craft, heavily laden, and carrying an enormous weight of sail; her hull was low, and so oddly shapen, that had her masts been cut down she would have looked like a huge tortoise upon the waters; her prow was sharp and like a beak in shape, and her figure-head was a monstrous vulture painted red, and with its talons extended on deck as if to seize its prey; her decks were crowded with men, and the long lines of dark muzzles protruding from the portholes revealed how deadly was her armament.

The unfortunate vessel she had captured, and which was now blazing to the water's edge, had no more chance in an encounter with so formidable a foe than a dove had in contending with a vulture.

'Give her a gun,' cried Captain Will, 'she shows no colours, but that will bring her to.'

The gun was fired.

Scarcely had the sullen roar died away than, as if by magic, the stranger's yards were stripped, and she lay to under bare poles, her motion as abruptly arrested as if a giant hand held her in her course.

'The pirate means to fight,' Sam remarked. 'I should like to send her a shot that would sink her. Hullo! that's in reply to ours, I suppose. Not badly aimed either; by jove I thought my head was carried away in splinters.'

'A puff of smoke had come from the stranger's sullen hull, and, as Sam spoke, a big cannon ball came tearing up the beams of the quarter-deck, and knocked its way out at the other side.

Before Will could reply, a gaunt, thin, cadaverous-faced vampire, who acted as doctor or sort of bloodletter, crawled aft.

He had a case of instruments in his hand, and quietly squatting down on the splintered deck, he said drily—

'Ha! you've got a tough devil there, my young bloods. I shall have all my work cut out to stop all the veins they open before you are two minutes older. Here, boy, bring me a basket for the legs and arms, we shall have plenty knocking about here presently.'

The boy—an ungainly, blubber-faced lout, with a hideous grin about his face—sidled up to his master, and began unrolling bandages as he sat beside him and looking to the points of murderous-looking implements.

'Come,' Will said, 'we can't have you on deck; you must do your work below.'

'Ay—ay, my fine captain; they'll do work enough for me first up here,' said the smuggler, as he sidled away followed by his assistant.

The stranger vessel had as yet shown no colours, and in silence her gun had been fired.

The men who had swarmed upon her decks were nowhere visible; but now a little ball was run up her halyards, and her flag unrolled.

A black banner, with the device of a monstrous red vulture in the centre.

Will's own banner had already been run up.

No sooner was the flag of the stranger seen than one of the females, who stood beside our hero, uttered a startled cry, and exclaimed—

'The Red Vulture! 'tis he. Keep your vessels apart or we are all lost.'

As if in reply, a deep hoarse laugh came from the stranger's deck, and a voice cried—

'Now, devils, give them their salute.'

A swift, sudden, and deadly broadside answered this command, and the weight of metal pounded against the hull of the brig. It was well that her sides were protracted by a coat of sheathing, or that well-directed volley would have sent her foundering to the bottom of the sea.

As it was, it did some damage, and our hero's deck was strewn with the wounded bbfere he well understood the sudden attack.

'Salute them in return,' Will cried. 'Lady, your place is below. Sam, be ready with your boarders. Fire or no fire, we will not shirk the guns.'

The lady descended, with a warning look on her beautiful face, and then began the swift and deadly cannonading, for which the smugglers were so famous. While their light vessel, under a heavy press of canvas, flew like a bird, as she obeyed the manœuvres of her skilful commander.

Their telling fire, and the skill with which she evaded his deadliest volley, evidently baffled the leader of the stranger pirates, whose deck was almost untenable.

In the hottest of the fight his deep voice resounded amid the din, as he gave some order to his crew.

A moment after, a blinding flash shot like lightning from his bows, and the brig was visited with a perfect hail of what seemed living fire.

For the moment, the seething balls of fire ran from stem to stern, and made a mimic hell of their deck.

The smugglers fled stricken from their guns, as they strove to escape from the ravaging flames, but the angry tones of their dauntless leader recalled them to their duty.

'Back to your guns!' he cried, leaping amidst the fiercest raging fire. 'See, I am nnharmed! Fear not this harmless flame. Keep up your fire—deluge their deck with iron hail! Boarders, prepare; I, alone, will stay here while you take their ship!'

The flaming missiles blazing furiously at our hero's feet, cast a lurid glow on his excited features. He seemed more than mortal as he stood unscathed amidst the terrible element, and his followers, with a ready cheer, served their guns with deadly effect.

The pirate captain was paralysed at receiving this storm of shot and grape from the vessel he had encircled with fire.

His fierce voice again rang out its commands, and with sudden swiftness his canvas fell, and his vessel drew away.

Captain Will, standing dauntless in his perilous position, looked through the smoke and saw a burly-formed, stalwart man, with a massive head set on immense shoulders, looking at him from his shattered decks.

He was dressed in a rover's costume, a black, bushy beard encircled his chin, and his belt was crammed with huge pistols and short cutlasses.

'Ahoy there!' he cried; 'are you the smuggler, and Will Howard?'

'We are,' our hero replied, 'and defy you.'

'Then I fight you no longer. I'm sorry I've encountered you. Look to your holds, or the fire we've given you will blow your ship to pieces. I can give you no help—I've too much powder on board. We shan't fight if we meet again. You'll know me—I'm Gregory Saunders, the Captain of the Red Vulture!'

'And my wife?' asked Will, in a voice of thunder.

'Is safe. Fear not for her.'

'Where is she?'

'No matter ; be satisfied. You will u ever see her more.'

Will's indignation knew no bounds.

'Scoundrel pirate !' he shouted, half mad; 'she is in your power. Release her, or I'll——'

The pirate silenced him with a wave of his hand.

'I have spared your life,' he said, 'be satisfied. We part to meet no more.'

He waved his hand, and stepped down from the carronade on which he had been standing, and as his vessel answered her helm, and sheered off from the scene of action, the smugglers saw with consternation that the liquid fire, running like mercury about their decks, had set the holds in a blaze.

The position of our hero and his crew was critical in the extreme.

The burning ingredient, whatever it was, seemed harmless so far as its flame was concerned, for Will had thrust his hand into it without being even scorched ; but it dropped a glowing mass like red hot mercury, and this ate its way through every beam and plank, and was lodged in all the crevices of the ship.

Prompt and collected in the deadliest peril, Will sprang from his dangerous position, and issued his swift orders, himself aiding in the efforts to put out the fire.

In this they could succeed so far as the material of the ship was effected ; but the blazing liquid proved to be inextinguishable, and burned as vividly under water as on the deck.

Our hero's crew and our hero himself looked blankly in each other's faces.

The fire was travelling to the powder magazine. One spark there, and the noble vessel with its daring crew would blow in pieces.

Now that the last echoes of the cannonade had died away, a strange silence reigned.

Noiselessly the smugglers kept at their dangerous task of putting down the fire, while our hero, with a select party, saw to the powder magazine.

Their only chance of safety lay in keeping the blazing element from this place, and a direct approach of the flames was prevented by a barricade of iron plates, with which they shut off the place where the powder was stored.

The worst danger, however, lay in the fact that the insidious ingredient, working its way through the beams, might at any instant fall from over their heads, and instantly compass their destruction.

With this peril before them, our hero and his chosen band set to work.

Their resolve was a desperate one.

Every barrel of the explosive material was hauled from the storing place, and thrown singly into the sea.

The powder in bulk was well saturated by means of a hose kept playing upon it, and after an hour's imminent peril—any moment of which might have hurled every living soul into eternity—the last barrel of powder was, amidst a cheer that proclaimed the salvation of the ship, hoisted out at the lower porthole.

The task of quelling the fire was comparatively trifling when this was accomplished, and the smugglers worked less quietly now that the fearful imminence of their danger was past.

It took them a long time to extinguish every trace of the fire, and when this was effected, the crew gathered round their leader to thank him for preserving their lives.

He was paler than he had ever been before.

He had fully realised their jeopardy, and though danger was his proper element, and defiance of death his kindred nature, the threatened destruction of his ship and crew had quelled the usual fervour of his dauntless breast.

Every inch as brave and staunch a sailor as ever, he looked sadly upon the havoc around him, and his beautiful vessel, charred, riddled, and splintered in all directions, seemed a perfect wreck.

And now, even though they had saved themselves from their threatened fate, their position was still harrowing.

Will gazed with bloodshot eyes after the pirate's fast receding ship.

'God of heaven!' he gasped, almost choking, 'this is too much to bear; my wife, my all, in the power of that fiend.'

For a moment his feelings seemed to overpower him, and he would have fallen to the deck had not old Sam come to his aid.

––––

CHAPTER LXXIX.

ROCK ELFIN MAKES HIS APPEARANCE IN ANOTHER CHARACTER.

IT was one of those unenviable mornings, calculated to damp even the most cheerful of spirits, that a snug little schooner lazily made her way through the dank mists that hung over the ocean, and caused the snowy sails to hang motionless against the masts.

She was a light little craft, and had it not been for the profusion of sanguinary visages that here and there showed above the bulwarks, a beholder might have taken her for a king's ship.

Her calling was far otherwise, however.

She was a pirate ship.

The dealer of death and destruction—her captain and crew a set of the most bloodthirsty wretches that ever sailed the sea.

The men were in no enviable mood—the weather, and a run of ill luck rendered them morose, and they leant upon the gun carriages, casting ominous glances over the sea, or watching the fishing tribe disporting in the blue depths of the ocean.

The captain paced the deck like a caged lion, while his officers amused themselves by playing cards on the after hatch.

The cry of 'Sail, oh!' brought them to their feet.

Every eye was now fixed in the direction of the ship's head.

'I hope it arn't another Johnny haul taut,' ejaculated one of the pirates.

'No fear o' that, Bill; her spars arn't lofty enough.'

'I lay it's some Yankee liner.'

'That won't be much of a haul, then,' growled the others.

'It won't pay us for our dunnage,' he said, holding up the breast of his shirt, and displaying two large holes made by a musket ball.

The shades of evening now spread a mantle over the wide expanse of waters, and the approaching vessel could not be clearly made out by the naked eye.

Ever and anon the men would cast an anxious eye towards the poop, where the captain was intently peering through his glass.

Every ear was on the alert to catch the least sound.

They now listened intently for some order.

'What do you make her out to be?' inquired the mate, who had been trying to pierce the gloom.

'Look for yourself,' was the rejoinder, as the captain handed him the glass.

'I should think she's an Indiaman.'

'I am sure she is, or I never saw one, and if I have not seen her before it's strange to me.'

'When do you suppose you've seen her?'

'Don't ask so many questions. Go forward, and do what I told you. If this is the vessel I take her to be, she is well manned and armed, and also freighted with a valuable cargo.'

On came the doomed ship.

The crew and passengers had all come on deck at the cry of 'Sail oh!'

They were anxiously peering at the vessel they supposed was an outward-bound merchantman.

Darkness now reigned around, as the two vessels rapidly neared each other, for the moon had not yet risen, so that the unsuspecting crew could not see the deadly instruments of war that projected from the bulwarks of the brig.

They had now neared to within hailing distance.

'What ship is yours?' cried the pirate captain, in a clear voice.

'The Water Lily.'

The captain smiled inwardly.

'Where are you from?'

'Calcutta.'

'Whither are you bound?'

'London.'

'You'll never get there, then,' muttered the pirate.

'What ship is yours?'

'The Vivid.'

'Where are you bound to?'

'Madras.'

'Are you from London?'

'No.'

'Where then?'

'Cardiff.'

'Oh, indeed.'

'You have had rough weather?'

'No, pretty fair. We lost our mainmast in a fog —a vessel ran into us.'

'Just so. Ah, some careless fellow, I presume?'

'I have a letter I should like to send by you if you have no objection, and if you have any spare rope, as you are so near home, I should be much obliged if you could let me have it.'

'With pleasure.'

'I'll send a boat.'

Both vessels by this time had hove to, and they were laying almost motionless.

In the twinkling of an eye a boat was dropped from the quarter davits of the brig, and half-a-dozen resolute fellows having been secreted in the bottom, she shot rapidly under the quarter of the brig, pulled by six of the crew, who had doffed their terror-inspiring garb, and now assumed the appearance of merchant seamen.

A few rapid strokes brought them alongside the Water Lily, which was a fine East Indiaman of fifteen hundred tons, and was loaded with costly merchandise.

The pirate captain seized the rope ladder that had been placed for his accommodation.

With a spring he gained the deck.

The captain stood ready to welcome him.

'Step down into the cabin, if you please,' said the captain.

He quickly accepted the invitation.

When they arrived in the cabin, an exclamation burst from the lips of the captain.

'What, Elfin, is it really you?'

'It is, Mr. Jones,' was the cool reply.

'Glad to hear it, Elfin; you are an old friend of mine.'

'Ay, one of the oldest, I should think.'

'Drink,' said the captain, handing him a tumbler of pale brandy.

'Here's towards your good health, Captain Jones.'

'And here's towards your success. I suppose it's the first voyage you have been, captain, since last we met?'

'It is,' answered Elfin.

'I suppose you have not a very valuable cargo for the first voyage?' inquired the captain.

'No, not so valuable as yours, if I conjecture rightly.'

'Well, you see, Elfin, we are frieghted well this voyage, and under the lazarete,' he whispered, 'are diamonds and precious stones to the value of half a million.'

A smile passed over the features of the pirate, unobserved by the captain.

'Yes, valued at half a million,' he repeated emphatically, 'but I am obliged to keep it a secret from the crew, or I fear they would murder me to get possession of it.'

Another smile passed over the features of the pirate.

'Have you anything else valuable on board?' inquired Elfin indifferently.

'Yes, down the after hold are elephants tusks, valued at two thousand, and under my bed,' he said, in a tone of confidence, 'there is specie to the value of five thousand pounds.'

'They have great confidence in you, captain, to place you in charge of so valuable a cargo.'

'And have you no supercargo on board?'

'None.'

'You have ladies on board. If I am not mistaken I saw two as I came down the companion.'

'Yes, an elderly lady and her daughter. They are on their return to England, after having amassed a large fortune in India.'

'Indeed.'

'Yes, Elfin,' he said, familiarly, 'if you or I had only one half the riches this ship contains, we might lay up in dock for the remainder of our lives, instead of washing about the stormy seas.'

A fearful scowl rested on the features of the pirate as the captain entered one of the state-rooms, and his hand clutched a dagger concealed beneath his clothes.

He was about to enter the state-room, when the captain returned, bearing a heavy box in his hand.

This is their treasure,' he said, 'and if the crew only knew what the cabin contained, my life would not be worth a straw.'

Elfin moved uneasily on his seat.

His hand clutched firmer the hilt of the dagger.

At length, resuming his former coolness, he inquired—

'I suppose you carry arms for fear of a surprise?'

'Yes, we have eight carronades on deck, and in yonder locker there is a plentiful supply of small arms.

'What, do you mean to say you don't keep them handier than that?' exclaimed the pirate, surprised.

'I have them there in case of those pirates that infest this part should attack us, but I dare not trust them to the men under any other circumstances.'

He had placed his mouth close to the ear of Elfin to utter the last words.

Elfin chuckled inwardly.

His eye flashed fiercely.

And he felt within himself that he could not contain himself any longer.

The captain now returned to the state room to replace the box.

The eyes of the pirate flashed fire.

He rose cautiously from his seat.

A dagger gleamed in his right hand.

With a spring he bounded forward.

In his impetuosity he had capsized the decanter, and the captain turned his head on hearing the sound.

The face of the captain assumed a look of hatred as he saw the bright weapon in the hand of Elfin.

'Perfidious wretch!' cried the captain, as, with a dexterous movement he caught hold of the weapon, and dashed it from the hand of Rock Elfin.

A bitter oath rolled from the pirate's lips.

'Curse you!' he said, 'you have been deceiving me the——'

His speech was cut short by the sound of approaching footsteps on the deck, and, springing like lightning up the ladder, he dropped into the boat.

In another moment he was on board his own vessel.

*　　　*　　　*　　　*　　　*

The pirates on leaving the merchant ship were elated with their glorious prize.

A goodly store of treasure had they, and enough grog to swim in for a month.

But they did not put it to that use.

They poured the fiery liquid down their insatiable throats until they began to quarrel among themselves.

Rock Elfin had to use violent means at length to bring them to order; and next morning, when the fumes had worked off, he gave his first and second mate, who had shown the men no good example, a severe reprimanding.

'Sail-ho!'

The voice of the look-out stopped any further conversation, and as the mate seized his glass, Rock Elfin, pale with ill-suppressed rage, left the quarter-deck.

'Sail-ho!' came from the masthead again, and the cry was taken up by the man on the forecastle.

'Where away?' asked the pirate.

'On the weather quarter, sir.'

'Can you make her out, Stevens?'

This was the mate.

'Not distinctly, sir. There's a mist over the sea which partially hides her hull and lower rigging'

By the aid of his powerful glass, the pirate saw the strange sail beating up to windward.

It was not the Golden Arrow he knew by the difference in size, and, glad of anything to break the

BLACK EYED SUSAN.

OR, PIRATES ASHORE.

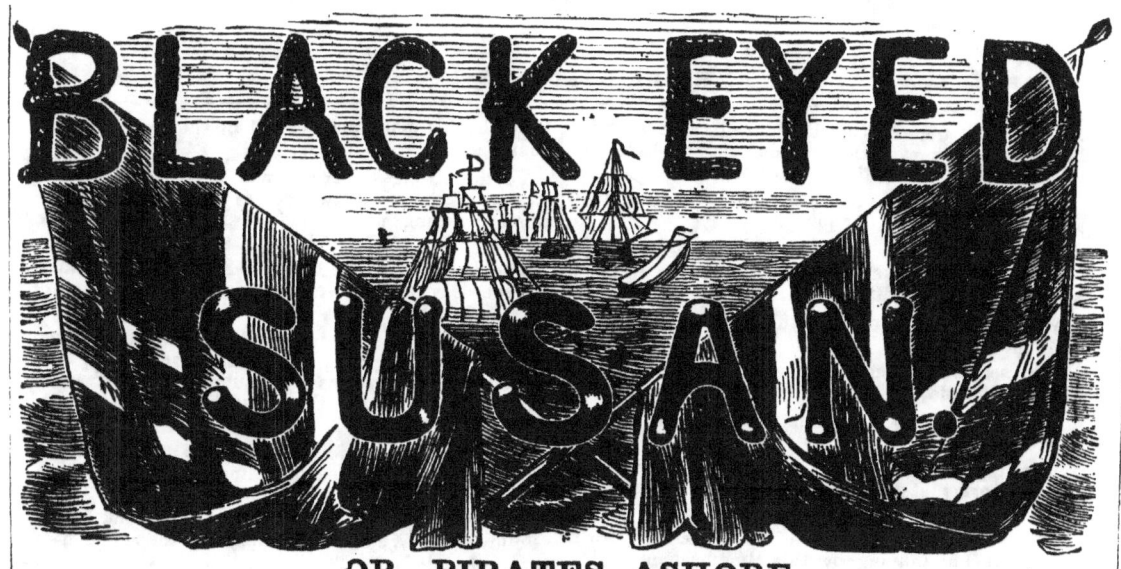

'TELL ME,' SAID THE ADMIRAL, 'IS YOUR NAME NOT SUSAN?'

heavy weight upon his spirits, he had the crew beat to quarters and everything made ready to give the stranger a warm reception, if necessary.

There was something in the appearance of the stranger that puzzled the pirate.

One moment she would seem as though about to bear down upon him, and the next she would start off upon a directly opposite course.

Watching the ship closely, the Captain said to his first mate—

'She seems as though she were drifting before the wind. What do you think?'

'I have thought so for some time, sir, but did not like to make the remark.'

'Strange,' mused the pirate leader; 'there have been no storms lately. Surely the vessel cannot have been abandoned.'

He placed his glass to bear upon the stranger's decks, her hull having by this time become distinguishable to the naked eye.

What he saw sent a red spot to his cheek, and turning to Stevens, he said—

'Pipe all hands below. This is an empty vessel.'

The crew, relieved from their stations, crowded to the side, to gaze upon and wonder at the strange behaviour of the coming vessel.

It was near evening when they ranged alongside.

Captain Elfin's words were verified—the brig was deserted, and at the mercy of wind and waves.

The schooner was brought round to the wind. The sails for a moment flapped against the masts.

The young chief, though watching the coming vessel, turned his eagle glance upon the men, and asked, sternly—

'Do you wish that vessel to run into us?'

The men were silent, and hung down their heads.

In their eagerness to execute the order that would bring them alongside the stranger, they had allowed the wind to be forced out of their sails.

Elfin turned to the helmsman, and said—

'This is partly your fault!'

'I put the helm down, sir,' was the reply, 'as ordered by the officer of the watch.'

Elfin walked quickly to the wheel, and seizing the spokes, said—

'Yes, you did! a landsman could have done it as well. Look here, sir!'

The man's face coloured at his leader's rebuke.

'Bear in mind,' he continued, suiting the action to the word, 'put the helm down spoke by spoke; not suddenly, by doing so the ship loses her way. Do it slowly, and she keeps her velocity in coming to the wind.'

He resigned the wheel as he spoke, and the helmsman, looking after his light form, muttered—

'I'd sooner have three dozen any time than one of his quiet looks!'

The pirate chief went back to his station on the quarter-deck, and in a voice that could be heard all over the ship, said—

'Mr. Martin!'

'Ay—ay, sir!'

'Hand in the main sheet, ease off the jib, and lay her alongside.'

These orders weare carried out, and the vessel was soon brought alongside the stranger.

It was not the work of a minute to throw the grappling-irons; the next, the pirate chief, followed by his mate and several of the crew, went on board.

To the strongest-nerved man there is always a strange feeling of awe comes over their minds when boarding a deserted vessel upon the wide ocean.

The quietude of the decks, the sails set, perhaps, for the very reverse weather in which the desolate bark is found.

The mystery that attaches to her being in this lone state tends to augment this strange sensation, and make the flesh creep, as the thought of some fearful fate having come upon the crew will force itself upon the mind.

The pirates paused for some minutes upon the deck, and gazed with saddened feelings upon a crimson stain near the step of the mainmast.

'There has been foul work here,' said Rock Elfin. 'Follow me. We shall, perhaps, find the solution of that red trail.'

He went quickly down the after-hatch, followed by his men.

They were soon clustered at the open door of the state room—clustered in a silent, horrified group at the terrible sight within.

Some of the bodies yet warm, and the blood slowly oozing from deep and ghastly wounds. A group of slain men and womed—some of the latter scarcely in the first bloom of womanhood—lay upon the ensanguined carpet.

To fill the horrible picture, two infants were pinned by long knives to the panels of the cabin.

Not a word was spoken by the pirates until their young leader, plucking one of the weapons that had drunk the innocent babe's life from the little corse, took it to the light, and said in a hushed voice—

'It is a Moorish weapon—here is the clue to the foul deed.'

A whisper began among the men until it rose, and was taken from lip to lip, and the words swelling into a chorus, proclaimed the miscreant who had suffered this deed to be committed.

'The Red Vulture!'

'You are right, my lads, it is his fell work, and he cannot be far away from us.'

Elfin lowered his knee, and raising his right arm on high, said vehemently—

'Hear, and aid me, lads, in my vow to sweep this demon from the sea! Yes,' he added, with vehemence, we must cut short his desperate career, for he forereaches us, robs us of our lawful rights, and leaves us as you see, nothing but the bones to pick.'

He pointed to the emblems of a ghastly black flag, that had been left by accident on the deck of the doomed vessel.

CHAPTER LXXX.

A BOLD DASH FOR LIFE.

To explain how our hero returned on board the smuggling brig we must take our readers back a few chapters.

It was mostly to the sudden lull of the storm that Will owed his escape from the brig, but he was still in danger. From his concealment he could hear the voices of his persecutors as they rushed about in the darkness, making their cutlasses ring again as they thrust the bright blades in every hole where it was likely for the smuggler to be concealed.

His fair protector stood trembling at the casement, peering through the opening of the curtains, breathless and in terror.

She could see torches glaring hither and thither, lights flickering about, and occasionally a bitter oath reached her ears as the sailors were met with disappointment.

Will's thoughts now reverted to the brig.

Had his scheme proved successful, or had she been intercepted, he wondered.

Then his thoughts turned to the fair girl who had so nobly sheltered him.

She who had braved her father's anger—she, who at the risk of tarnishing her honour, had admitted him to her chamber.

Presently a voice beneath the terrace startled her.

'Come on, lads, he is here! I saw him go this way,' growled a bluff old tar, 'and damme, lads,' he added, 'we will run him down.'

The words fell like a thunder-bolt upon her ears, and trembling in every limb, she stood as though transfixed with terror.

Her tongue clove to the roof of her mouth, and the scream that arose ta her lips died away unuttered.

It was well for the smuggler it did so, for that cry of alarm would have brought his pursuers, who, like a pack of wolves, were panting for his blood, to the place of his concealment.

In his exhausted state he would no doubt have fallen a prey to their vengeance, had not fate ordained it otherwise.

Although he would have sold his life as dearly as possible, yet eventually he must have succumbed to the overwhelming number of his enemies.

As Will gazed upon the pale features of his fair protector, he tried to subdue the pang of remorse that shot across his soul.

He was about to speak, but his lips were sealed.

Alarmed at the thought of having sheltered so black a villain, and who, if her father spake true, had added murder to his crimes—and she had seen the blood-stained sword in the hand of the smuggler —feeling alarmed for her own safety—for she was alone and unprotected, and wholly in the smuggler's power—she was overcome with fear, swooned away, and would have fallen to the floor.

Will, seeing her stagger, flew to her assistance, and caught her in his arms.

Having laid her gently upon her bed—for it was the lady's own chamber in which they now were—he procured some water, of which there was plenty in the apartment, and gently bathed her pallid brow, and moistened the compressed and colourless lips of the apparently lifeless young lady.

The approaching voices of his pursuers awoke him to a sense of his danger and the awkward predicament in which he was placed.

They had searched every spot in the vicinity of the mansion where it was likely a man could conceal himself.

The voices of the men sounded just under the balcony by which he had entered.

From his position he could hear their conversation.

'It's no use of us searching in that direction,' said a gruff voice. 'I believe he is in the house, for the last time I saw him he stood somewhere about this spot.'

'Then search the house, by all means,' said Sir Henry, who had assisted in the search from roof to cellar, 'for I shall not be easy till I know he is not in the neighbourhood.'

A strong guard being posted round the mansion, to prevent the escape of the smuggler, they commenced a rigid search of the interior.

Beatrice was now slowly returning to consciousness, and when at length her eyes opened, their pale blue orbs rested upon the pale but handsome features of the smuggler.

A thrill of horror ran through her frame.

A faint cry of alarm arose to her lips.

Then again she swooned.

Although only a few minutes had elapsed since the smuggler had entered the apartment, it appeared to him as though it were an age.

Oh! what—what would he have given if the fair being before him would only return to consciousness, that he might assure her of her safety, and that he might also convince her of the delusion under which she laboured when she believed him to be the murdering, blood-stained villain which the words of her father had incited in her breast.

The sound of approaching footsteps in the corridor leading to the chamber, aroused him from the dreamy stupor into which he had been thrown.

He had scarcely time to conceal himself beneath the bed when the door opened, and a dozen men-of-war's-men, armed with sword and pistol, headed by the lieutenant and Sir Henry, entered the room.

Sir Henry, on seeing the position of his daughter, as she lay on the bed, her small and delicate hands clasped as though in great agony, placed his hand upon his heated brow.

As he glanced towards the half-open window, his face assumed an ashy paleness, and his corpulent frame was seized with a violent trembling.

He was about to speak, but his lips refused their duty.

A parching thirst seemed to dry up the words as they mounted to his tongue, and it was evident by the expression of his face that he was fiercely contending with the emotions that were working in his breast.

There lay his daughter, in the flower of her youth, immovable and inanimate as a statue, the long tresses of her dishevelled hair hung down the side of the bed.

Her bosom of snowy whiteness lay bare and exposed to the rude gaze of those assembled.

At length he found speech—

'Great heavens!' he cried, vehemently, 'has the villain dared to pollute the chamber of my daughter with his unholy presence? And, oh!' he exclaimed, in a voice hoarse with emotion, 'has he dared to violate the person of my daughter, if so I'll hunt him like a beast of the forest, even were he to assume the form of a worm, that burrows in the earth, I would find him.'

'It's evident someone has been here, Sir Henry,' said the lieutenant; 'for see, here is a basin of water. It is probable he may have escaped by the window.'

So saying, he rushed to the balcony.

'Below there!' he shouted.

'Ay, ay, sir.'

'Have you seen anyone pass out of this window?"

'No! no! no!' answered several voices.

'Keep a good look-out, then, for the pirate is not far off.'

Sir Henry had been so deeply engrossed in the thought of his daughter's violation, that he was not aware of the presence of so many of the sailors.

And now, seeing them gazing on the inanimate but lovely form of his daughter, whose disarranged clothes were drawn up above her knees, he turned angrily towards them, and ordered them to leave the room.

'A lady's chamber,' he said, 'is no fit place for a host of armed men.'

Having closed the door and window, Sir Henry, by the aid of stimulants, proceeded to restore the lovely Beatrice to consciousness.

Having procured a small bottle from one of the drawers in the apartment, he placed it to the nostrils of his dearly beloved daughter, and a burning tear coursed down the old man's face, as he imprinted a kiss upon her marble brow.

In a few seconds she opened her eyes, and in as many more was able to speak.

The first question he asked her was, whether or no the smuggler had entered her apartment.

Being answered in the affirmative, a groan of agony burst from his lips, for he feared his worst doubts were confirmed.

Springing to the middle of the chamber, he swore, with a bitter oath, to find the smuggler that night, be he hid where he might.

The daring Will, who during this time had been concealed under the bed, had listened with intense interest to their conversation, and a flush of indignation mantled his brow as he listened to the vile imputations of Sir Henry, who had charged him with the violation of his daughter.

As he lay he formed a daring project.

He was determined to deny the false accusation.

Creeping noiselessly from his place of concealment, he stepped sharply to the centre of the room.

With a look of defiance he faced his two inveterate enemies.

Had his Satanic majesty appeared before them they could not have been more astounded.

Before they could recover from their surprise, the barrel of a pistol was presented at the head of each.

'If you raise any alarm,' he said, in a tone of firmness, 'it will be the signal for the death of both of you.'

Beatrice, on seeing the supposed pirate threatening her father with death, uttered a piercing scream.

Will spoke.

'Hear me,' he cried, vehemently, 'hear me, Sir Henry. I have heard you pronounce me a murderer and pirate. I deny the accusation; what I have done has been done in self-defence.'

'And, again,' he continued, 'I have heard you accuse me of violating your daughter. Of this charge, too, I swear I am innocent, and declare it in the presence of your daughter.'

At this instant a crash sounded in the casement behind him.

A bullet whizzed past the smuggler, grazing his boot and entering the leg of Sir Henry, who fell to the floor with a groan.

'Treachery,' roared the lieutenant, springing to the window.

Beatrice flew to the assistance of her father, and, raising his head, supported it on her snowy arm.

The smuggler, tearing a costly scarf from his neck, bound it round the leg of the wounded man.

In the confusion caused by the shot Will saw his only chance of escape.

Bending on one knee, and imprinting a kiss upon the delicate hand of Beatrice, he said—

'Medical attendance is required. I will go fetch a doctor.'

The lieutenant was engaged in loud altercation in the balcony.

The smuggler, well knowing there was no time to be lost, hastily left the room.

Will threaded the various corridors without meeting a single person, for the guests who had been waiting in great anxiety, and eager to ascertain the result of their search, were now growing uneasy at their long absence, and on hearing the report of fire-arms, had rushed to the garden to ascertain the cause.

Having arrived in the hall without interruption, he speedily attired himself in the great coat and hat of one of the guests.

Thus disguised, he emerged into the garden.

He had not proceeded far, when his progress was arrested by the stalwart form of one of the man-of-war's men, who threw himself in his path.

Where are you steering to?' said the sailor, placing his brawny hand upon the shoulder of the young smuggler.

Will grasped the butt of a pistol he had concealed in the breast of his coat, and affecting surprise at the conduct of the sailor, thus threw him off his guard.

'What, have you not heard that Sir Henry has been badly wounded, in attempting to capture the smuggler?'

'What,' said the sailor in amazement, 'the genelman that lives in this big house?'

'Certainly, he was shot, when standing face to face with the smuggler.'

'Well, shiver my timbers!' said the sailor, taking an extra nip at his huge quid, that caused his cheek to protrude as though he were suffering greatly from the toothache, 'only to think of him shooting the genelman, after us chasing him about all night.'

'And was the smuggler in the house?' he inquired.

'Yes, he was in yonder room a few minutes since.'

'Are you quite sure it was him?' said the sailor, who could scarcely believe it to be true.

'I am positive, I was in the room at the time.'

'And where are you going now?' inquired the sailor, eyeing him narrowly. 'Our orders are to arrest anyone that offers to leave the mansion.'

'Oh, indeed,' rejoined the smuggler, affecting to be surprised, 'but you will not dare to detain me, I am going to seek medical aid, for the gentleman, I fear, is dangerously wounded.'

'Oh, then you are under sailing orders. I am sorry I detained you so long, but duty is duty, and we must attend to it.'

'You are quite right, my good man,' said Will, 'and though this delay may prove dangerous to the wounded gentleman, the fault will not lay at your door.'

'But before you go,' said the sailor, 'tell me which room you see this covey in, for I would not mind giving a month's grog, much as I like it, to have a fair look at his figure head.'

'Have you not seen him, then?' said Will, affecting surprise, which would certainly have allayed any suspicion that might have been lurking in his breast.

'No; but I will to-night if there is the least chance, for he must be a devil in human form to have escaped us as he has done. I have to thank him for this,' he said, raising his tarpaulin hat, and discovering a ghastly wound in his forehead, from which the blood was oozing.

The daring smuggler gazed at the wound, which assumed an ugly appearance, and he now resolved to make him the only recompense then in his power.

That was to obtain him an interview with the smuggler, so that he might form his own opinion whether he were flesh and blood.

'Well my friend,' said the smuggler, 'you want to see this pirate, as you call him?'

'I do.'

'Then you shall see him; but mind, only on one condition, that is, you must promise me that when you see him you will keep silent.

'Rather queer conditions, old fellow,' said the sailor, turning his quid, but nevertheless, I comply with them.'

'Come this way, then,' said the smuggler, taking a path that led towards the back of the mansion.

Then stopping abruptly he said,

'You see yonder casement?'

'I do.'

It was plainly to be seen, for, from the window indicated by the smuggler shone forth a bright light.

Beneath the window might be seen the figures of many men moving rapidly to and fro.

'That is the room in which I saw the smuggler.'

The sailor's eyes were now turned in the direction of the window.

Will, in the meantime having divested himself of his disguise, added—

'And here is the smuggler!'

The sailor turned, and beheld with astonishment the smuggler, his arms folded.

His first impulse was to rush upon Will and beat him down.

But a pistol grasped in either hand of the smuggler restrained him.

Seeing himself baffled, the sailor was about to raise an alarm, when Will silenced him with—

'Is that how you keep your promise? One word, mind, and I fire. I am desperate, so be careful what you do.'

The sailor muttered something Will could not hear.

As Will was planning some means to rid himself of his unpleasant companion, a rustling amongst the bushes startled him.

Will half turned his head to ascertain the cause, but before he could do so he found himself surrounded by a dozen stalwart men-of-war's men.

'Surrender, Will Howard! You see, I know you,' cried a gruff voice. 'Yield quietly, or we will use force.'

Will glared for a moment with a look of deadly hate at the speaker.

Whipping his cutlass from its sheath, he closed with his would-be captor.

CHAPTER LXXXI.

WILL HOWARD HAS A MIRACULOUS ESCAPE.

As many of the guests of Sir Henry witnessed the strange scenes of that eventful night, on hearing the fugitive was Will Howard, the pirate who had so miraculously escaped from his just punishment at the yard-arm, their excitement was at its highest pitch.

Sir Henry, believing him to be a villain of the blackest dye, his hands red with the blood of his victims, afforded his pursuers every facility in his power to capture the gallant smuggler.

Who can imagine the dismay of Sir Henry on hearing the smuggler had escaped, but a great weight was removed from his bewildered brain when he heard from his daughter's lips that she had not been molested?

But when she informed him that it was she who concealed the brave smuggler in her apartment, and that it was at her own instigation, she believing him to be the injured party, he had entered by the window.

The appalled look that came over his face at these words was indescribable.

He sank back into the chair, glaring like a maniac at his dismayed daughter.

Beatrice trembled like a leaf.

Her eye dropped beneath her father's savage glare.

At length she spoke.

'What have I done, dear father, thus to incur your anger?'

'What have you done?' he shouted, in a frenzy of rage, grasping her arm. 'You have sheltered a black, polluted villain from the hands of justice. If it had not been for your folly, ere this he would have been safely lodged in jail.'

'Do not chide me, father,' she cried, clasping her hands in despair. 'When I saw the man hunted to the death as he clambered up the rocks, and the light from my window poured its mellow light on the pale but noble countenance of the pursued, he appeared too mild and too gentle to be thus ruthlessly slain.'

'Ah!' he said, lightening his grasp upon the maiden's arm, 'it was love that prompted you to shield the villain, and you, having invited him to your chamber, have played the harlot beneath your father's roof.'

He paused in a gasping sort of way as she shook off his grasp.

Beatrice suddenly stepped back a pace, her sweet face glowing with spirit, and her glorious eyes flashing as she said—

'Father, if I may still call you by that name, dare you accuse me of playing the harlot? Do you doubt my chastity? What proofs have you to warrant such an accusation?'

'What further proofs are required,' thundered Sir Henry, 'but your own words; your own instigation prompted him to enter your bedchamber; you concealed him from our view with your person; and when, having searched the house, we enter your chamber and find you prostrate, your hair dishevelled, your clothes disordered, and your breast and limbs uncovered, and the villain concealed beneath the bed?'

The countenance of Beatrice assumed an ashy paleness, and her fortitude gave way.

'Father, father,' she cried imploringly, dropping on her knees and clasping her hands supplicatingly, 'spare my feelings I implore you.'

He was about to spurn her from him, but she clasped his knees and clung frantically to him.

Then, with an inarticulate murmur on her lips, she fell to the floor in a swoon.

Sir Henry, forgetting his wound in the excitement of the moment, sprang to his feet and fell heavily to the floor.

With great difficulty he dragged himself to the further end of the room to procure the basin of water with which the smuggler so recently bathed her marble brow, and slowly and painfully he dragged himself to where his daughter lay insensible.

It was some minutes ere the lovely maiden showed any signs of returning consciousness.

And as her father gazed upon her death-like features, and wiped the cold dews from her brow, a pang of remorse shot through his soul.

In that lovely countenance he could see the striking likeness of her mother, who had long since finished her weary pilgrimage on earth.

As he bent over her, lost in deep contemplation, a silent tear rolled down his aged cheek.

'Can she be guilty?' he murmured, half aloud; 'no, I cannot believe it. My over-heated brain has conjured up imaginations too horrible to dwell upon.'

'Oh that I could be assured of her innocence !' he thought; 'but everything appears so suspicious, and her own words only confirm those suspicions.'

He was aroused from his lethargy by a loud knock at the door.

One of the domestics entered, followed by the surgeon, who had been sent for to dress the wound in Sir Henry's leg.

On entering they found Sir Henry bending over the prostrate form of his daughter.

Beatrice, having been placed upon her bed, and her maids summoned, the usual restoratives were applied.

Meantime Sir Henry had been conveyed to his chamber, where he received the necessary attention he required.

The surgeon, who was a skilful practitioner having examined the wound, which by this time had assumed a dangerous character, extricated the bullet with great dexterity, and bound up the wound.

He was placed in bed by his attendants, where we will leave him a prey to his own imagination.

While this scene was being enacted between Beatrice and her father, a scene of a different nature was being enacted in the grounds surrounding the mansion.

Will Howard, having cleared a road through the host that had so suddenly surrounded him, made his way to the shrubbery, and was lost in the darkness.

The old admiral foamed with rage, and soundly rated the lieutenant for letting him escape, while the lieutenant in turn swore fearfully at the men.

Lights flashed in all directions, and the lieutenant, boiling with indignation, followed by a body of men, rushed wildly about the grounds.

In vain they searched every rock, and every spot for a mile round, where it was at all likely a man might be concealed.

At length one of the men caught sight of a dark figure as it stood in bold relief on the summit of a neighbouring rock.

He drew the attention of the lieutenant towards it.

With a yell of triumph he bounded forward, closely followed by his men.

Nothing impeded their progress. Onward they dashed like a pack of wolves.

Through bushes and brambles their way lay; but, nothing daunted, they dashed through them, tearing their clothes and flesh in the excitement of the chase.

They now ascended the steep and rugged side of the rocks.

Above them they could see the object of their search.

Only a few yards more had they to ascend ere he would be within their grasp.

Another moment, and the dark object had disappeared.

With an angry gesture the lieutenant scrambled to the summit of the rock.

Through the darkness he could see the dim outlines or the same dark figure on another projection not far distant.

'Onward !' he cried. 'He cannot hold out much longer; he is almost winded.'

Onward they went again, reckless of danger.

Every moment brought them nearer to the dark form.

They had now neared it to within a few yards, when the lieutenant, who was foremost of the pursuing host, stumbled and fell, whilst the others following closely upon him, ere they could check their headlong speed, followed suit.

And it was well for them it was so, for a few yards in advance of them a dark chasm stood ready to receive them with extended jaws.

With a fearful malediction the lieutenant sprang to his feet.

On the other side of the gulf stood the object of their pursuit.

'Do either of you know how we can cross this gap?' he interrogated, fiercely.

'I do, your honour,' answered one of the seamen, drawing a plug of the favourite weed from his mouth about the size of an ordinary hen's egg.

'Lead the way, then,' he cried, imperatively.

'All right, your honour; but you must keep your lamps trimmed, for it's rather an awkward gangway.'

'Hold on a bit, old cock,' he said, shaking his fist at the motionless figure as it stood like a statue on the other edge of the chasm, 'we'll soon heave our graplins aboard of yer.'

He led the way along the edge of the chasm, and dropping down on all fours like a cat, bade them follow him.

They did reluctantly.

He now proceeded along a narrow bridge formed by the trunk of a tree, thrown across the gulph; they followed him cautiously, for the night was pitchy dark, and below them yawned the chasm.

One false step and they must be dashed to pieces.

The seaman, who had undertaken to guide them, had by this time crossed to the other side.

When he turned in the direction where the figure had last been seen it had disappeared.

By this time they had all gained the opposite side.

'Curse this fellow !' roared the lieutenant. 'They ought to have made him Will-o'-the-wisp, for he beats all I ever came nigh. I think it would puzzle the devil himself to catch him.'

'You're right, your honour,' said the seaman; 'they say a starn chase is a long 'un, and I think he has led us a good chase to-night, and we arn't had a toothful of grog over it either.'

'You're right, Bill,' said another of the seamen, replenishing his quid, and giving it an extra nip, as he thrust it into his cheek. 'I think it's time to splice the main brace. I know if I wore braces they would have had to be spliced long before this, for see here, mates, I'm flying signals of distress: they hang about me like Irish pennants, as old Pipes call 'em.'

As he spoke he held up his arm, and displayed a number of ribbons—for they were nothing else; his jacket and trowsers were one mass of tattered rags, torn by the rocks and bushes.

Meanwhile the lieutenant had been trying to pierce the gloomy darkness that reigned around. At length his eye rested on an object, on a prominent rock, as though it were in a recumbent position.

He pointed it out to his men, and they darted off like a pack of hounds in full cry.

The ground over which they were now almost flying, was of so rugged a nature, that they had great difficulty in keeping their feet.

Still onward they flew, feeling certain of obtaining some reward if they could only capture the daring smuggler, who had up to this moment eluded all pursuit, and escaped from the many snares that had been laid for him.

Buoyed with this hope, they overcome all the difficulties that lay in their path.

The rocky nature of the ground compelled them at length to slacken their speed and to proceed more cautiously.

'He's off again, yer honour,' said one of the sailors.

True enough, the dark form now stood erect.

It was rapidly moving away.

The lieutenant, who was almost exhausted, as were his men also, and burning with vexation, levelled his pistol, the report followed, and a blinding flash, and the retreating form dropped to the earth.

With an exultant cheer they now dashed forward, each eager to be the first to capture the daring young smuggler.

A few moments brought them to the spot.

The lieutenant, believing his foe to be harmless, having previously shot him, and claiming the preference of being the first to capture him, ordered his men to stand back.

This order they dared not disobey.

Brandishing his cutlass above his head, the lieutenant stepped boldly up to his crouching victim.

He was about to order him to surrender and lay down his arms.

His bullying propensities far exceeded his bravery.

When his wounded victim had allowed him to approach to within a few feet, he charged him in the stomach with his head.

A hearty roar of laughter now burst from the stentorian lungs of the sailors as they saw the lieutenant panting on the ground, for the figure they had been chasing for the last two hours turned out to be an old goat.

The shot had entered his flank.

As he lay in agony on the ground, on seeing the lieutenant brandishing his cutlass in rather unpleasant proximity to his face, with a final effort he butted his victorious captor in the stomach, and had almost knocked the breath out of his body.

It was his last effort, poor beast, he now lay writhing in agony.

One of the seamen, in order to put an end to his misery, drew a pistol from his belt and shot him through the head.

The report of the pistol caused the lieutenant to spring to his feet.

'Blood and thunder!' he roared. 'What is the meaning of all this?'

Another deafening laugh was the only response.

Burning with indignation, and stamping his feet with rage, he looked round at the men with bitter irony.

'I'll learn you to laugh the other side of your mouth, my beauties,' he cried, fiercely. 'Black list and six-water grog shall be your portion when I get you on board the frigate,' and he added, turning to one of the petty officers, who gloried in the rate of captain of the afterguard, 'I'll be the means of taking the stripes from your arm and placing them on your back.'

The laugh had now subsided, but a kind of tittering seemed to have taken hold of the group, and, the more they tried to look serious, the louder it grew.

Mortified at being thus defeated, and indignant at the behaviour of his men, he led the way back to the mansion.

CHAPTER LXXXII.

THE MEETING ON THE CLIFF.

WILL had scarcely made good his escape from the man-of-war's men, when another danger, of which he little dreamed, awaited him.

He was making his way towards the beach, and when on the summit of a lofty cliff a sound startled him.

It was the voice of a female in distress.

'Silence, my pretty one,' he could hear a gruff voice say, 'you might as well howl at the wind, as to sing out here. Come quietly, and you will come to no harm.

'Never! I will never yield to your proposals,' replied a female voice.

Will started from his listless apathy.

'The voice,' he gasped, 'it is the same. I could swear to it. No other lips but those of my tight little Sue can utter such music.'

Will leant over the cliff, for the sound was beneath him, and ascending the rugged path he saw a woman being led by two men; in the rear two others followed, and they appeared to be well armed.

Will's blood fairly boiled with rage and indignation when it flashed to his mind that his Susan was in the power of Gregory Saunders, and that the villain was now almost within his reach.

He would have rushed to the spot where they stood, but a deep crevice intervened.

'Unhand me, villain!' he heard the woman say, and she struggled to free herself.

'No, by my soul, I will not,' was Gregory's reply; 'were the evil one to step between us I would make you obey me.'

'Liar!' shrieked the woman—and this time Will was certain it was the voice of his Sue—'Liar! coward! I defy you.'

'Be it so,' growled Saunders. 'Well, 'tis no matter; you are in my power, and you shall know it.'

Will could stay to hear no more.

With one bound he cleared the gap, and, darting down the steep path, he came face to face with his foe.

Susan screamed.

She recognised her husband on the instant.

'William, dear Will!' she ejaculated.

'Aye, 'tis I, dear Sue,' he replied.

Then, turning fiercely on Saunders, he hissed—

'Coward! scoundrel! we have met at last.'

Saunders started.

Had a spectre arisen before him he could not be more astonished.

'Ah, is it you?' he gasped.

'It is; you are not deceived,' replied Will. 'There

is a long account between us. It must be settled, and at once.'

'Be it so, then,' said Gregory, savagely.

As he spoke he stept before Will, thrusting Susan behind him with one hand, and with the other drawing a pistol from beneath his coat.

Will's quick eye detected his movement, and, dashing his pistol aside, he closed desperately with his adversary and forced him back against the cliff.

'Help—help,!' gasped Red Vulture. 'Help, lads—quick!'

This cry would no have reached the ears it was intended for had it not been for Susan.

She gave a startled cry, for the villain in his fierce passion had nearly hurled her off the narrow path.

It was with difficulty she regained her footing, for, as she gazed down the vast steep, it made her brain reel and her heart to fail her.

It was only for a moment that she felt thus, and then her former courage returned.

'Villain!' she hissed, seizing the pistol from Gregory's hand. 'You shall pay the penalty of your crimes. Long enough I have borne your insults, now I '' ——

She could say no more.

A firm hand grasped her by the arm, and her throat was firmly gripped by a ruffian, who sprang up the crag behind her.

'Not so hasty, my pretty one,' a gruff voice hissed in her ear. 'Not so hasty. You forget you are among friends.'

It was Gregory's lieutenant.

He did not recognise Will, but, when the smuggler captain relaxed his hold of Stuart and dealt him a terrific blow, he drew his sword.

Will's fate now seemed sealed.

Two desperate villains to contend with, and he almost unarmed; whilst, to add to his danger, his wife's life was depending upon his success.

A third ruffian now made his appearance, and seeing Gerald leaning back against the wall, his life nearly squeezed out of him, he was rather startled.

By this time Will had seized his Sue and placed her in safety, and armed only with his knife, he stood ready to defend her to the last.

'Aha!' laughed the third comer; 'so you have turned meddler. 'Ay, well, you shall be well paid for your interference. A bullet through your brain, and then the lady will be glad of our company again.'

'Coward!' cried Will, 'did it take three of you to bring her here? Surely, one would have been sufficient; but rascals, like locusts, go in swarms.'

'Quite right,' answered the man, nettled at the words; 'and as you are not one of us, we can dispense with your company.

Will's eye flashed as the fellow raised his pistol, and had it not been for Susan, who clung tenaciously to him, he would have sprung upon him.

Fortunately for Will, the weapon missed fire, and before he could draw another from his belt, a low whistle was heard on the beach below.

The lieutenant's notice had been already attracted by something, and he was lying flat down, trying to peer through the darkness.

But the distance was too great for him to discern anything clearly.

He could just make out the dim forms of several men moving about on the sands, and the dim outlines of a boat laying on the beach.

A white light at that moment shot up from a neighbouring cliff.

'The sharks, d——n them!, vociferated Gregory, who, by this time, had recovered a little from the violent usage he had received from the smuggler.

'The sharks!' echoed the luff, starting to his feet. 'Then those fellows I saw flitting about were smugglers.'

'Ay, the coastguards; the land sharks are in their wake. They'll be down upon 'em in a crack,' chimed in the third comer, a bluff, burly-looking fellow.

'Then we must settle our business quick,' said Gregory, huskily. 'This fellow has been the cause of delaying us. What say you if we drop him over the cliff?'

'Agreed,' was the response.

And, before Will could utter a word, he was seized by two of them, Gregory himself undertaking the charge of Susan.

But Susan nobly defended herself. She knew that it was not so much her life he sought, or he would not have spared her so long.

The villain had a base design at his heart.

An old mansion that had been left him by his father, and was now in ruins through his neglect and profligacy, stood in the neighbourhood, and to it he intended taking her, until he could mould her to his views.

The chance that now offered itself of ridding himself of Will Howard seemed most opportune; and though Susan shrieked and struggled with him, he kept urging on his accomplices to settle the gallant tar.

But he was too strong for them.

The thought of his Susan being left in the hands of such villains, inspired him with fresh vigour, and he hurled one of his opponents from him, causing him to roll over the crag.

Seeing the fate of his companion made the lieutenant shudder, and in a moment Will saw his chance of freeing himself of another disagreeable, if not dangerous, customer.

Concentrating his power into one mighty effort, he seized the lieutenant by the throat, and forced him to his knees; then, dexterously extricating a pistol from the lieutenant's belt, he dealt him a severe blow over the head with the butt of it.

The fellow fell stunned by the blow, and bleeding from a nasty lacerated wound on his forehead.

Like lightning Will sprang towards Gregory Saunders, who was struggling with Susan to get possession of the pistol.

''Vast heaving, you cowardly swab,' roared Will, rendered desperate; 'sheer off, or by the 'ternal God I'll brain you.'

The fierce tone caused Gregory to pause in his exertions.

'Confounded idiot!' he hissed, 'do you not know I hold your life in my hands. One word would bring the coastguards about you; they would make a good haul in capturing Will Howard, the pirate.

'Perhaps so, but where is the man that will take him?' said Will, his eye flashing fiercely; 'it will not be you, I fancy.'

Gregory made a feeble attempt to laugh.

It was but a ghastly smile, rendered more ghastly by the grey sickly light.

Torches glared here and there, pistol shots whizzed about, and the clash of steel made the rocks ring again.

Will knew well the cause of this.

The coastguard had surprised a band of smugglers; they might be his own crew for what he knew.

BLACK EYED SUSAN!

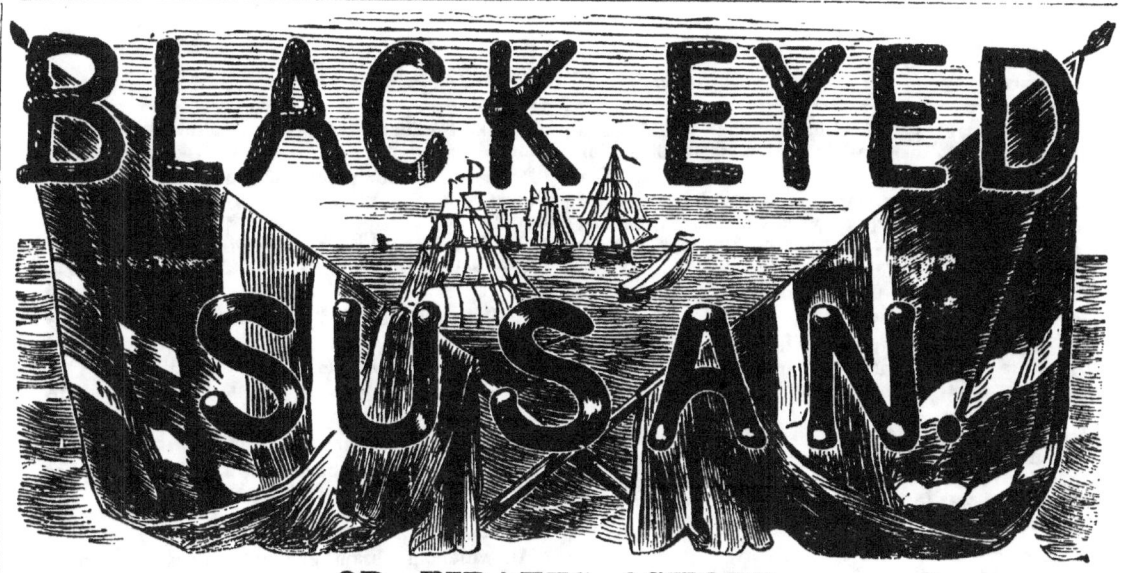

OR, PIRATES ASHORE.

SUSAN DEFENDS HERSELF AGAINST TOM HATCHETT.

The thought galled him, and he would have rushed down to their assistance had it not been for Susan.

While he was ruminating, a noise above startled them, and to their surprise a score of sailors, headed by a lieutenant, were seen descending the narrow path.

Gregory, with the fleetness of a deer, took to his heels, and made for the beach.

Will would have followed, but Susan, faint and overcome with the sufferings she had endured, was unable to walk.

'Come, come, dearest,' he said, 'try and keep up. It will grieve me if these men tear me from you, though it would not be without a struggle; yet I do not wish to use violence against those who, like myself when I was in the king's service, only obey their orders.'

Susan heard him not.

She had fainted.

Will was now driven to desperation.

What to do he scarce knew.

He could have made good his own escape.

But to fly, and leave her whom he held dearer than life, would have been worse than facing the mouth of a cannon.

'Well,' he muttered, 'let them take me. I must trust to Providence.'

As the words left his lips, a body of armed men rounded a projecting crag that had concealed him from their view.

'Hullo! Heave ahead!' cried the lieutenant, on beholding Will; 'here is one of them, and, by Jove, he has got a cargo!'

'Yes, you have one, Lieutenant Fordham,' said Will, bitterly. 'I will give myself up to you, for I know you will treat her kindly.'

He pointed to Susan as he spoke.

The lieutenant started.

He evidently felt hurt.

'What, Will!' he said, 'is it possible I find you here?'

'It is, and it is also fortunate that you are known to me,' replied our hero, 'or ere this you would have received the contents of this pistol.'

'You are in jest.'

'I am not, I am desperate.'

'Mad, as they say.'

'Yes, mad; and who has driven me to this madness?'

The lieutenant turned away, his men were crowded round and listening.

Many of them knew Will, more than one had been shipmates with him.

'Seize him, lads,' cried Lieutenant Fordham, 'he has broken the laws of his country, rebelled against his king, and must suffer.'

Will reluctantly gave up his arms, and suffered himself to be led away, two of the seamen assisting Susan to follow, she having partially recovered.

They had not proceeded far when they were met by another party headed by the very lieutenant that had been so severely reprimanded by the commodore.

A feather would almost have knocked him down when he saw Will Howard a prisoner in the hands of a junior lieutenant, for he turned ghastly pale and staggered like one shot.

Few words passed between them; the good fortune of the one had incurred the displeasure of the other,

for unlike Fordham, the first lieutenant was of a malicious disposition.

Being the senior officer, the first luff, or "Old Bilboes," as he was termed by the sailors, took charge of the prisoners, ordered his men to fall in, and having scanned Susan narrowly, remarked—

'We will take her with us, a female pirate is a novelty.'

Fordham bit his lips with suppressed indignation.

He regretted having fallen in with Will.

He almost wished he had let him escape, even in the presence of his men.

Bilboes, on the other hand, was in ecstacies.

Only one thing troubled him, and that was, what story could he frame to make it appear as though he had captured the smuggler, and thus retrieve his fallen character?

His villanous brain was not long in forming a scheme.

'Take the woman to the boat-house, Lieutenant Fordham,' he said, raising his voice to a tone of hauteur; 'I will see after this fellow. Fear not; he will be safe with me.'

Fordham, though inclined to do so, dared make no reply.

The laws of the service made him a slave to his superiors.

So he obeyed.

The boat-house alluded to was a rough but strongly constructed shed.

It was used by the coastguards as a temporary prison as well as a boat-house.

When Bilboes gave the order for Susan to be led away, it seemed like taking a load off the heart of the gallant Will.

He felt he could trust her with his late officer, and he glanced gratefully towards him.

It took some time to lead Susan, in her present weak state, to her temporary prison.

It was but a cheerless place when they did arrive there.

'Well, sir,' asked a bluff old salt, 'how shall we find a bed for this blessed gal?'

'We must make a shake-down with the boats' sails, I suppose,' answered Fordham, rather puzzled.

'Well, sir, it's rather a rough billet for a woman,' said the old man-of-war's man; 'for, let the woman be ever so bad, she's the wife of an old messmate; and though the 'great guns' that formed the court-martial said he was only fit to dangle like a jewel-block from the yard-arm, he was as taut a sailor as ever trod a plank.'

Fordham turned his head to conceal the struggle that was working in his breast.

A struggle between duty and his better feelings of humanity.

He knew that Bilboes would return as soon as he had lodged Will in safety, and made out a good report to the commodore; therefore, if he intended saving Susan, he must set about it speedily.

To rid himself of the two sailors was his first thought.

'Go to the village,' he said, 'knock them up at the inn, and ask them if they have any spare bedding. Go, both of you, and bring plenty, for this cold night air will kill the poor creature if she is not properly tended.'

The good-hearted tars waited to hear no more.

'Come on, Bill,' he said, addressing his companion.

And the two soon disappeared.

When they were gone Fordham said to Susan—

'Come, lass, we must not stay here. Your safety depends only in flight. If the first lieutenant returns before we are gone, you may give up all hopes of escape.'

'But I have done nothing to deserve this treatment,' answered Sue, her eyes dimmed with tears ; ' why am I——'

'Hush, I hear footsteps,' said the luff, interrupting her. 'The rocks seem alive with armed men. A smuggling craft has been detected in landing her cargo, and a pirate vessel, supposed to belong to your husband, has been seen in the offing. Come on. Trust to me, and I will try to save you.'

Susan could not reply : her heart was too full.

Fordham led her gently from the shed.

Glancing carefully around, he descried several men prowling about the rocks, evidently in search of some one.

'He went this way, I tell you !' shouted a voice, which was easily recognised as Bilboes. ' Cuss you all, for a set of swabs. How the devil did he manage to escape ?'

'Can't say, sir,' answered another voice. ' We ought to have pinioned him ; for he is as slippery as an eel. Hang me, if ever I saw anything done so quick in my life.'

'And well you shall remember it,' answered the luff, in a tone of bitter irony, ' I will teach you your duty when you go on board.'

A sullen growl came from the sailor, he knew too well the meaning of those words.

Fordham waited to hear no more.

'Your husband has escaped,' he said, ' let us fly at once.'

'Which way, oh which way can we go ?'

'I scarcely know, we appear to be surrounded.'

'Yes, they are coming this way.'

Fordham gave an agonised look.

'Too true,' he muttered, ' but they must not see you here, or the old villain will doubly avenge himself on you, especially as Will has escaped. Our only way,' he added, ' is by the cliff.'

A few steps brought them to the edge of the cliff, but the descent seemed impossible.

Fordham glanced towards the gorge down which the boats were taken to the beach, but he feared being seen by the sailors.

'Fear not, lass,' he said, taking Susan by the waist and running swiftly with her to a part of the cliff which was more rugged and broken, and where a stream of water was pouring down into the sea like a cataract. ' Cling to me, and we will descend at all hazards.'

The descent was indeed perilous, and had not Fordham been a man of no ordinary strength, it would have been fatal.

Cautiously but rapidly he made his way from crag to crag until he touched the beach, and a prayer of thanksgiving escaped his lips as he did so.

He had scarcely descended, however, when two men sprang upon him and seized him by the arms, whilst a third took hold of Susan.

'Gregory Saunders !' burst from Susan's lips.

'The same,' muttered the villain, coolly, ' I have watched your descent with the anxiety of a friend, ay, more so, a lover.'

'Wretch !' gasped Fordham, struggling to free himself.

It was no use.

He was held too firmly.

'Now, lads,' cried Gregory, ' to the boats with them, we have waited long enough. Now, boys, bear a hand,' he added, as shouts were heard upon the cliff. Hurrah, shove off.'

When the last of the sentence was completed, Fordham found himself in a boat, and six sturdy fellows rowed it from the beach.

Meanwhile the gallant smugglers were engaged in a deadly conflict with the coastguards.

Scarcely had the boat touched the beach, when a host of the land sharks poured down upon the sands, waving their cutlasses in the air with one hand, and grasping a pistol in the other.

Then commenced a fearful and bloody onslaught.

The smugglers fighting for their gallant leader.

The coastguardsmen for duty, honour, and prize-money.

So furious did the smugglers contend for their rights and privileges, that the coastguardsmen could not withstand their furious assault.

At length they turned about and fled, closely pursued by the smugglers who carved their names in their backs, and signed their death warrants in their own blood.

At length, having gained the bloody and dearly bought victory, the smugglers having first attended to the wounded, proceeded to land the valuable cargoes.

The daring smugglers fought bravely.

Their assailants dashed on to them like hungry wolves, and threatened to crush them beneath their overwhelming force.

Now did the brave smugglers miss their gallant captain.

Oftimes did they fancy they heard his manly voice urging them on above the din of strife.

Desperately they battled against their implacable foes, who fought savagely to wrest the boats from them in the hope of sharing a glorious prize, for they were loaded with merchandise of the costliest description.

The battle was at its height, and the human mass heaved to and fro, struggling and wrestling like the surging billows of a storm-lashed sea.

Bravely did the little crew struggle to keep possession of their boats, and beat down the intruders as they tried to board them.

Upon the beach and in the boats the clash of arms and report of the pistols, mingled with the cries and groans of the fallen, told how well they fought for their liberty.

It was evident the bold smugglers must soon give way to their more formidable opponents.

Although there were already more of the coastguardsmen laying amongst the slain, yet still their numbers greatly exceeded that of the boats' crews.

Again the smugglers rally, and with a shout of victory or death they boldly dash on their foes.

Their bright blades glitter in the feeble rays of the moon as they cut right and left, dealing death and destruction around.

Now they are surrounded by the coastguards, who are cutting them down with their blood-stained weapons, as though they were trimming a hedge.

Then again the little band appears to gather fresh strength, and they carve their way elbow-deep in blood through their enemies, who surround them on all sides like a wall.

Again the coastguardsmen beat them back, and drive them from their boats, and now they are fast losing ground.

Still unconquered and unsubdued they fight gallantly, shoulder to shoulder.

But it is evident they cannot hold out much longer, for there is scarcely one of that brave and daring little band but what are bleeding from their wounds.

Still their bold and resolute spirit will not allow them to yield.

They would sooner fall, hacked into a thousand pieces, rather to be taken.

Weaker and weaker their little force is growing, whilst the coastguardsmen almost number three to one.

And just as they are about to fall beneath the remorseless fury of their opponents, a shout is heard.

And old Sam, headed by a body of smugglers, came to their rescue.

Madly they rush upon the coastguardmen, and cut and hack them down like sheep beneath their deadly stroke.

'Cut them down, my brave men,' cried the lieutenants, 'we must not let these lawless robbers escape from their well-merited punishment.'

'Lay on, my gallant sea dogs,' roared Sam, 'lay on for the love of your gallant captain.'

'Follow them up,' he cried, as the coastguardsmen began to retreat.

'Show them no mercy, give them no quarter, let them have cause to remember this night's work.'

It was plainly to be seen that the coastguardsmen were fast giving way, whilst the smugglers followed closely upon them.

'Well done, my gallant comrades,' thundered Sam, 'give them blood for blood.'

Than this, the smugglers needed no other incentive.

Foot by foot they pressed the coastguardsmen to give way until they forced them into a narrow gorge, when, turning suddenly, they beat a safe retreat to the boats, and made for their brig.

When about half way between the ships and the shore they were startled by the sound of a voice that seemed familiar in its tone, but proceeding, as it appeared from the depths of the sea.

'The captain,' cried Sam instinctively. 'Back, all of you, he is swimming in our wake.'

The men did so, and the captain, bleeding and almost exhausted, was hauled into the boat.

CHAPTER LXXXIII.

THE STRANGE SAIL—THE MEETING BETWEEN CAPTAIN STUART AND ROCK ELFIN.

THE sun was just breaking through the azure sky, when the captain of the Golden Arrow stepped upon deck.

'Well, Johnson,' he said, addressing the officer that had been temporarily appointed in the place of Will, 'what luck, think you, we shall have to-day?'

Bill Johnson was a bluff, old tar, he had weathered many a gale as the saying is, and was cradled on the deep. His age, to his own knowledge, which was certainly imperfect, was verging on to the allotted space of man, three score years and ten, yet he was as nimble as any one on board, and as for eyesight, there was none dare question his vision.

'There's a speck yonder, captain,' he said, not heeding the captain's question, 'that I cannot make out. It is not a cloud I feel certain, for I have taken its bearings, and find it moves to the southward without rising.'

'Is it a ship, think you?'

'Well, it's summit. I can't say as to its being a ship, if it is, why, damme, I never see one like it afore.'

Captain Stuart took his glass.

Carefully he surveyed the distant mystery.

'Confound it!' he said, 'I can see nothing but a mist, but as you say, it moves, and in a different manner to what one might expect.'

'Ay, that's the queerest part of it,' said old Bill, chewing most tremendously at the huge quid of tobacco in his cheek, 'I should like to find out what it really is.'

'You shall, if there is any possibility of doing so,' said Gerald, himself as anxious as any one on board to know what it could be. 'Quick! brace up the yards.'

'Luff, luff! There, steady her at that,' he said, turning to the man at the wheel, and the Golden Arrow shifted her course about four points, bringing the strange object in a line with her jibboom.

Four long and tedious hours the Golden Arrow kept on her course.

Old Bill all the time kept his glass at work, his jaws keeping on the move with the working of his mind.

They found that they gained rapidly on the object of their chase, which had proved such a mystery to all on board, and to their utter surprise, about eight bells in the forenoon watch the mist gradually dispersed, and revealed to them a low, black hull of a ship of war.

'A pirate!' burst involuntarily from every lip.

Gregory Stuart looked astounded.

Recovering himself on the instant, he said—

'A pirate in truth, and a strange one. To your guns, men! We will give them a broadside.'

He had scarcely given the order, and the men had not yet got to their respective stations, when the strange vessel opened her ports, and discharged her port broadside.

The effect was magical.

The Golden Arrow's crew, mad with rage, flew to their guns, and ere the report of the treacherous broadside had died away, they returned it in right good style.

The guns of the Golden Arrow were pointed one degree below the water line, and the iron shower buried itself in the stranger's hull with such force, as to cause her to heel over considerably.

The long, deadly tubes of the Golden Arrow still poured its iron hail, and as the concussion stilled the air, the vessels drew gradually towards each other.

Captain Stuart stood on the quarter deck.

As the smoke rolled away, he was able to make out the captain of the strange ship.

'Rock Elfin!' he ejaculated, and his hand closed on his pistol-butt. 'Rock Elfin, the villain! By heavens, he must die!'

Scarce knowing what he did, he raised his hand mechanically, and drew the trigger.

A laugh of scorn and defiance succeeded the report.

Rock Elfin had caught sight of him.

He anticipated his intentions and evaded the shot by stepping nimbly aside.

A cry of baffled rage came from Captain Stuart.

SCENE.—Interior of the "Foul Anchor," for the Play of the "Red Rover."—Gratis with No. 32 of "Black-Eyed Susan."

'Villain!' he cried, 'you have foiled me. But I will be revenged! I will blow your ship to atoms, and your crew, the rascals, shall suffer with you!'

'Hurrah, my lads!' he shouted, as he leaped among his men. 'Double shot your guns, and fire point blank!'

'Ay, ay!' was the cheerful response, and then the work began in earnest.

The crew of the Golden Arrow, stimulated by the voice of their daring leader, worked their guns with such admirable dexterity, that it seemed the enemy must soon give in.

It was not so, however.

Rock Elfin had a chosen crew of desperadoes, whose souls were wrapped up in the work of desolation and plunder—men who knew that their lives depended on their success.

Rock Elfin, himself, though callous and indifferent of life, could not think of yielding.

'Come on, lads!' he shouted to the hideous-looking wretches that surrounded him, we will dash alongside and board her.'

A yell of approbation greeted his words, and the crew prepared to leap over the side.

'Stay,' said Elfin, in a voice only audible to his own men; 'be not too rash. Give them a broadside first.'

The sudden silencing of the Golden Arrow's guns enabled Elfin to talk to his men. He did not know, however, what was the cause of the firing so suddenly ceasing.

Had he have done so, his heart would have leapt with joy.

The Golden Arrow had taken fire between decks, and all hands were employed in keeping the flames from the magazine.

Captain Stuart was in an agony of mind, but he did not betray it. All his nerve was required to give the men orders, and exert himself to the utmost.

It was while he was thus engaged, that Elfin gave the order to fire.

The Golden Arrow staggered under the shock, but f the two, Elfin suffered the most.

His mainmast had been partially cut through, and the wheel-spokes had been torn away, carrying away with them the man at the wheel.

This rendered the ship useless.

She fell off before the wind, and Gerald Stuart, on seeing this, hauled his own ship to three or four points, and thus left to himself, renewed his exertions to quench the fire.

It was midnight before this was accomplished, and then fearing that a storm might overtake them, Captain Stuart ran for the nearest land.

The watch was set, but owing to the damaged state of the vessel's hull and rigging, the men were not allowed to turn in, so to wile away the time, it was proposed that each should spin a yarn.

Many and various were the stories, and called forth many a hearty laugh, but at length they began to tire.

Then old Tom Starboard, who had sat quietly chewing his quid, and listening to the various stories of weird sights and adventures, pulled up his trousers, and giving a slight jet of tobacco juice for the benefit of a boy who stood grinning by him, said—

'Now, messmates, yer yarns is pretty good, but I've one as will beat 'em all into fits.'

'All right; go ahead.'

And Tom did go ahead in the following style:—

'In a lonely part of the bleak and rocky coast of Scotland, there dwelt a being, who was designated by the few who knew and feared him, the Warlock Pirate.

'He was, in truth, a singular and a fearful old man.

'For years he had followed his dangerous occupation alone; adventuring forth in' weather which appalled the stoutest of the stout hearts that occasionally exchanged a word with him, in passing to and fro in their mutual employment.

'Of his name, birth, or descent, nothing was known; but the fecundity of conjecture had supplied an unfailing stock of material upon these points.

'Some said he was the devil incarnate; others said he was a Dutchman, or some other ' far-away foreigner,' who had fled to these comparative solitudes for shelter, from the retribution due to some grievous crime; and all agreed that he was neither a Scot nor a true man.

'In outward form, however, he was still ' a model of a man,' tall and well-made; though in years his natural strength was far from being abated.

'His matted black hair, hanging in elf-locks about his ears and shoulders, together with the perpetual sullenness, which seemed native in the expression of features neither regular nor pleasing, gave him an appearance unendurably disgusting.

'He lived alone, in a hovel of his own construction, partially scooped out of a rock—was never known to have suffered a visitor within its walls—to have spoken a kind word, or done a kind action.

'Once, indeed, he performed an act which, in a less ominous being, would have been landed as the extreme of heroism.

In a dreadful stormy morning, a fishing-boat was seen in great distress, making for the shore—there were a father and two sons in it.

'The danger became imminent, as they neared the rocky promontory of the pirate—and the boat upset. Women and boys were screaming and gesticulating from the beach, in all the wild and useless energy of despair, but assistance was nowhere to be seen.

'The father and one of the lads disappeared for ever; but the younger boy clung, with extraordinary resolution, to the inverted vessel. By accident, the Warlock Pirate came to the door of his hovel, saw the drowning lad, and plunged instantaneously into the sea.

'For some minutes he was invisible amid the angry turmoil; but he swam like an inhabitant of that fearful element, and bore the boy in safety to the beach.

'From fatigue or fear, or the effects of both united, the poor lad died shortly afterwards; and his grateful relatives industriously insisted, that he had been blighted in the grasp of his unhallowed rescuer.

'Towards the end of autumn the weather frequently becomes so broken and stormy in those parts as to render the sustenance derived from fishing extremely precarious.

'Against this, however, the Warlock Pirate was provided; for, caring little for weather, and apparently less for life, he went out in all seasons, and was known to be absent for days during the most violent storms, when every hope of seeing him again was lost. Still, nothing harmed him: he came drifting back again, the same wayward, unfearing, unhallowed animal.

'To account for this, it was understood that he was in connexion with smugglers; that his days of absence were spent in their service—in reconnoitering for their safety, and assisting their predations.

'Whatever of truth there might be in this, it was

well known that the Warlock Pirate never wanted ardent spirits.

'So free was he in their use and of tobacco, that he has been heard, on a long and dreary winter's evening, carolling songs in a strange tongue, with all the fervour of an inspired bacchanal.

'It has been said, too, at such time he held strange talk with some one who never answered, deprecated sights which no one else could see, and exhibited the fury of an outrageous maniac.

'It was towards the close of an autumn day that a tall young man was seen surveying the barren rocks, and apparently deserted shores, near the dwelling of the pirate.

'He wore the inquiring aspect of a stranger, and yet his step indicated a previous acquaintance with the scene.

'The sun was flinging his boldest radiance on the rolling ocean, as the youth ascended the rugged path which led to the Warlock Pirate's hut.

'He surveyed the door for a moment, as if to be certain of the spot.

'Then, with one stroke of his foot, he dashed the door inwards.

'It was damp and tenantless.

'The stranger set down his bundle, kindled a fire, and remained in quiet possession.

'In a few hours the pirate returned. He started involuntarily at the sight of the intruder, who sprang to his feet, ready for any alternative.

'What seek you in my hut?' said the pirate.

'A shelter for the night—the hawks are out.'

'Who directed you to me?'

'Old acquaintance!'

'Never saw you with my eyes—shiver me! But never mind, you look like the breed—a ready hand and a light heel, ha! All's right—tap your keg!'

'No sooner said than done.

'The keg was broached, and a good brown basin of double hollands was brimming at the lips of the Warlock Pirate.

'The stranger did himself a similar service, and they grew friendly.

'The pirate could not avoid placing his hand before his eyes once or twice, as if wishful to avoid the keen gaze of the stranger, who still plied the fire with fuel and his host with hollands.

Reserve was at length annihilated, and the pirate pecularly said—

'Well, and so we're old acquaintances, ha?'

'Aye, said the young man, with another searching glance. 'I was in doubt at first, but now I am certain.'

'And what's to be done?' said the pirate.

'An hour after midnight you must put me on board ——'s boat. She'll be abroad. They'll run a light to the masthead, for which you'll steer. You're a good hand at the helm in a dark night and a rough sea,' was the reply.

'How if I will not?'

'Then—your life or mine.'

They sprang to their feet simultaneously, and immediate encounter seemed inevitable.

'Psha!' said the pirate, sinking on his seat, 'what madness this is! I was a thought warm with the liquor, and the recollection of past times were rising on my memory. Think nothing of it. I heard those words once before,' and he ground his teeth in rage—

'Yes, once—but in a shriller voice than yours! Sometimes, too, the urchin rises to my view; and

then I smite him so——bah! give us another basin-full!'

He stuck short at vacancy, snatched the beverage from the stranger, and drank it off.

'An hour after midnight, said ye?'

'Ay—you'll see no urchins then.'

'Worse—may be—worse,' muttered the pirate, sinking into abstraction, and glaring wildly on the flickering embers before him.

'Why, how's this?' said the stranger. 'Are your senses playing bo-peep with the ghost of some pigeon-livered coast-captain, eh? Come, take another pull at the keg to clear your head-lights, and tell us a bit of your ditty.'

The pirate took another draught, and then proceeded—

'About five-and-twenty years ago a stranger came to this hut—may the curse of heaven annihilate him'——

'Amen to that,' said the young man.

'He brought with him a boy and a girl, a purse of gold, and———the arch fiend's tongue to tempt me. Well, it was to take these children out to sea—upset the boat—and lose them.'

'And you did so?' interrupted the stranger.

'I tried—but listen. On a fine evening I took them out. The sun sunk rapidly, and I knew by the freshening of the breeze there would be a storm.

'I was not mistaken. It came on even faster than I wished.

'The children were alarmed—the boy, in particular, grew suspicious.

'He insisted that I had an object in going out so far at sunset.

'This irritated me, and I rose to smite him, when the fair girl interposed her fragile form between us.

'She screamed for mercy, and clung to my arm with the desperation of despair.

'I could not shake her off.

'The boy had the spirit of a man.

'He seized a piece of spar, and struck me on the temples.

'Now, you villain!' said he, 'your life or mine!'

'At that moment the boat upset, and we were all adrift.

'The boy I never saw again—a tremendous sea broke between us—but the wretched girl clung to me like hate.

'Perdition!—her dying scream is ringing in my ears like madness!

'I struck her on the forehead, and she sank—all but her hand, one little white hand would not sink!

'I threw myself on my back, and struck at it with both my feet, and then I thought it sunk for ever.

'I made the shore with difficulty, for I was stunned and senseless, and the ocean heaved as if it would have washed away the mortal world—and the lightnings blazed as if fiends had come to light the scene of warfare!

'I have never since been on the sea at midnight but that hand has followed or preceded me. I have never——'

'Here he sank down from his seat, and rolled himself in agony upon the floor.

'Poor wretch!' muttered the stranger, 'what hinders now my long sought vengeance? Even with my foot—but thou shalt share my murdered sister's grave!'

'A shot is fired—look out for the light!' said the young man.

'The pirate went to the door, but suddenly started back, clasping his hands before his face.

'Fire and brimstone! there he is again,' he cried.

'What?' said his companion, looking coolly round him.

'That infernal hand! Lightning blast it! But that's impossible,' he added, in a fearful under-tone, which sounded as if some of the eternal rocks around him were adding a response to his imprecations.

'That's impossible! It is a part of them, it has been so for years; darkness could not shroud it, distance could not separate it from my burning eye-balls. Awake, it was there; asleep it flickered and blazed before me. It has been my rock ahead through life, and it will herald my death!'

'So saying, he pressed his sinewy hands upon his face, and buried his head between his knees, till the rock beneath him seemed to shake with his uncontrollable agony.

'Again he beckons me,' said he starting up. Ten thousand fires are blazing in my heart—in my brain! Where, where can I be worse? Fiend, I defy thee!'

'I see nothing,' said his companion with unalterable composure.

'You see nothing!' thundered the pirate, with mingled sarcasm and fury. 'Look there!' He snatched his hand, and pointing steadily into the gloom, again murmured, 'Look there! look there!'

At that moment the lightning blazed around with appalling brilliancy, and the stranger saw a small white hand pointing tremulously upwards.

'I saw it there,' said he, 'but it is not her's! Infatuated abandoned villain!' he continued, with irrepressible energy, 'it is not my sister's hand—no! it is the incarnate fiend's who tempted you, and who now waves you to perdition—begone together!'

'He aimed a dreadful blow at the astonished pirate, who instinctively avoided the stroke.

'Mutually wound up to the highest pitch of anger, they grappled each other's throat, set their feet, and strained for the throw, which was inevitably to bury both in the wild waves beneath.

'A faint shriek was heard, and a gibbering, as of many voices, came fluttering around them.

''Chatter on,' said the pirate, 'he joins you now!'

''Together—it will be together!' said the stranger, as with a last desperate effort he bent his adversary backwards from the beetling cliff.

'The voice of the pirate sounded hoarsely in execration as they dashed into the sea together; but what he said was drowned in the hoarser murmur of the uplashing surge!

'The body of the stranger was found on the next morning, flung far up on the rocky shore—but that of the murderer was gone for ever!

'The superstitious peasantry of the neighbourhood still consider the spot as haunted; and at midnight, when the waves dash fitfully against the perilous crags, and the bleak winds sweep with long and angry moans around them, they still hear the gibbering voices of the fiends, and the mortal execrations of the Warlock Pirate!—but after that fearful night, no man ever saw the PHANTOM HAND.

CHAPTER LXXXIV.

THE CASTAWAYS.—TIMELY ARRIVAL OF THE GOLDEN ARROW.

'PORT!' shouted the captain to the helmsman, who was endeavouring to steer the good ship Talavaria through a narrow channel between the reefs of jagged coral by which the captain found his ship suddenly surrounded.

The captain had been hastily awakened from his sleep by one of the passengers—a young man named Albert Langham, who had, during the passage from Madras, fallen in love with the captain's daughter, Martha Gould.

The mate—a Spaniard—had long cast an anxious eye on her beautiful figure, and now he looked upon the landsman as a rival.

A fierce, deadly fire of jealousy was aroused in his breast—a desire for revenge, which he was determined to satisfy, with what direful effect we shall see.

Presently a crash was heard, and Albert Langham rushed to the hold.

'We have struck the rocks—have pierced her side!' said Albert, in dismay; 'and 'tis through your neglect.'

'Aye! aye!' gasped the Spaniard, turning pale; 'the craft is stoven in. Santa Maria, help me!'

Thinking at that instant only of himself, he was about to make a rush for the deck, when a sudden fiendish thought darkened his brow, and sent the fires of fierce exultation to his eyes.

He peered through the hatchway once more. He heard the surging rushing noise of the water as it poured like a torrent into the hold, and saw his hated rival clambering actively up the rope by which he had descended.

A mocking laugh broke from the lips of the Spaniard.

'Wretch! dog!' he shrieked, 'the hold of this ship shall be your tomb.'

And he seized the hatch, intending to fasten it over the opening.

But at that instant he was dashed aside by the strong arm of Albert's old chum, Tom, who had flown to the rescue of his beloved shipmate.

The Spaniard seemed resolved not to lose the satisfaction of destroying his rival, and he now sprang upon the old tar with a sharp clasp-knife in his hand.

Tom, by a well-directed blow, knocked the weapon from his grasp, and seized his antagonist by the throat.

Then a struggle took place, but did not last long; for the foot of the Spaniard soon slipped, and he fell headlong through the open hatchway.

In his descent his form struck against that of Albert, dislodging the latter from the rope; the next instant both men found themselves in the water of the hold, which had now become very deep, and was becoming deeper each moment.

As they were good swimmers, they were not long in gaining the rope; but the hand of Langham had scarcely come into contact with it, when he felt the fingers of the Spaniard squeezing his throat. In vain did he strive to release himself from this vice-like grasp, and presently he began to experience the horrors of suffocation. The pain in his head and throat was terrible; his brain seemed to whirl, and he knew that he was becoming unconscious.

In the meantime the water in the hold had been rising higher and higher each moment, and the two men were now much nearer to the opening in the hatchway than they were a few minutes previously.

Peering through the opening, Old Tom Treever could no longer be deceived in regard to the situation of his chum; and quickly lowering himself by the rope he dealt the Spaniard a kick upon the head, which caused him to fall back senseless into the water. Then seizing Johnson by the cuff of his jacket, the old tar assisted the half unconscious youth in his efforts to climb the rope, and finally pulled him through the hatchway into the steerage.

'Quick, quick, my lad?' he shouted, seizing Albert by the arm, and drawing him towards the companion-way. 'They are lowering the boats!'

'No, no!' cried Johnson, 'we must try to save the second mate. Villain as he is, we must try to save him, and——'

He was interrupted by a succession of piercing cries from the deck above, and quickly recognising that beloved voice, he dashed up the companion-way, under the impression that Martha Gould had been washed overboard.

When he gained the deck, he perceived the young girl standing by the quarter-rail, partly surrounded by the protecting forms of a group of seamen, among whom was her father. Upon seeing him she threw herself upon his bosom, and he then learned that it was her fears, excited by his non-appearance, that had caused her to utter the cries he had heard.

Albert wished to go back to the steerage to use his efforts to save the mate.

But the captain and several others opposed him, and he was pulled by main force into one of the three boats that had been lowered.

A few minutes afterwards the ill-fated vessel went down.

Old Tom Trevor significantly nudged the elbow of Albert, near whom he was seated.

'There, lad,' said he, 'there she goes, and you would have gone with her had we allowed you to go back to the steerage after that rascally Spaniard.'

'Heaven be praised, dear Albert, you are now safe!' murmured Martha, on the other side of her lover.

'Safe at present—that's true enough,' muttered the old tar to himself; 'but where he and all the rest of us will be afore morning remains to be seen. Ho! ho!' he added, with a quiet laugh, as the sound of a hearty 'smack' fell upon his ears, 'the lad is at his old tricks. Blow me, if I believe he could help kissing her if we was in the midst of the Maelstrom!'

As though there was a charm that would preserve her from harm in the form of her lover, Martha clung closely to him the whole of that long, weary night.

The gentle girl felt safe with him she so fondly loved.

In her innocence of the deadly peril that surrounded them, she talked hopefully of their safe return to the island of her birth—old England.

Albert listened to her girlish voice.

He had not the heart to undeceive her, to tell her of the thousand dangers that awaited them, situated as they were upon the dangerous, trackless ocean, without food, without shelter, without even a compass to guide them.

Wearily that night passed; but she, the gentle girl, slept with her head upon his shoulder, the young seaman's boat cloak wrapped around her fragile form to keep it from the chilling blast that swept and moaned over the troubled waters.

Morning came, and the castaways found themselves upon the open sea.

Not a speck was visible on the mighty waste of waters, and faint and exhausted, the rowers rested upon their oars and gazed hopelessly around.

The heavy sea had borne them far away from the dreaded reefs.

But a new danger threatened them—a horrible, fearful death, thirst.

Fiercely gleamed the sun upon their defenceless hands, drying up their tongues, until they were swollen and blackened for the want of a drop of water to allay their torture.

So passed the first day.

And the suffering crew, now no longer able to raise their oars, allowed the boats to drift at the mercy of the white-tipped waves, which seemed to dance around them as though mocking their sufferings.

The second morning came, and hunger and thirst filled up the measure of their woe.

In the stern sheets sat the captain, supporting his lovely child's head.

For she had succumbed to her misery, and now lay with her head nestled upon her father's breast, one arm thrown around his neck, the other hand grasped by her lover.

With a hopeless look of resignation, she gazed first at her father, then at the pale but uncomplaining young seaman who held her hand so fondly in his heated grasp.

'Father,' she murmured, looking piteously in his face, 'fater, must we all die? Is there no hope? Not one drop of water to save us from going mad?'

A sob of agony broke from the captain's lips, and pressing her head yet closer to him, he murmured,

'There is no hope, darling; none. Oh, God!'

And the strong man's head fell upon his breast in utter desolation.

A fearful cry from the bow of the boat caused them all to start.

'Twas the cry of a madman, a poor, frenzied wretch, who had partaken of the salt water during the night.

It had maddened him.

And now, with fierce, bloodshot eyes, he was trying to hurl himself into the rippling wavelets that danced so invitingly before him.

The poor fellow was held by two of his messmates, but the madman's strength dashed them aside, and with a piercing cry he sprang from the gunwale into the water.

One splash told the sad tale.

A terrible cry followed.

Oh, horrible—horrible!

Another, and another scream from the doomed wretch.

In speechless horror the sufferers turned their bloodshot eyes towards the spot where the seaman had disappeared, and beheld the water streaked with blood.

No need to ask the cause of these fearful screams, for a crushing, cracking, soul-sickening noise now could be heard.

Then the white belly of a shark could be seen, as it rolled over, crunching the bones of the ill-fated seaman in its fangs.

'Poor fellow! he's gone,' said the captain, huskily. 'Now, for God's sake, abstain from drinking the salt water.'

No reply came from the men.

BLACK EYED SUSAN

OR, PIRATES ASHORE.

'HIS HEART SANK AS THE HUGE MONSTER APPEARED.'

They sat silent and hopeless.

Many were evidently thinking it would be better to end their sufferings as their messmate had done than linger in such fearful agony.

Captain Gould evidently read the thoughts that were passing in their minds, for he resumed—

'Do not give way yet; there is hope for us. We are now upon the seas frequented by our men-of-war.'

'Ay, ay, captain,' said young Albert, 'we have escaped thus far. Let's trust a little longer to that sweet little cherub that sits up aloft.'

'Well spoken, boy. Come, my lads, let's try and bear up against the wind, which, if I mistake not, is drifting us back again.'

Although the captain's heart was filled with agony as he gazed at the now senseless form of his child, he strove to cheer his suffering crew, and keep them from ending their wretchedness by abstaining from the sparkling water which leapt around the bows and sides of the boat, as though luring them to partake of the fearful draught.

The pale-faced crew made no effort to use their oars.

They were now sullen and fierce; and, to Albert and the captain's horror, they now brought their heads closely together, and from the low, fearful whisperings, and the wolfish glances they cast towards the fair girl—who now lay senseless, huddled upon a couple of boat cloaks in the stern—it was evident they had come to some determination whereby they would be able to slake their parching thirst.

Captain Gould and Albert exchanged one glance full of terrible meaning.

Although no words passed between them, they read in each other's pallid face and sunken eyes the fearful meaning of the low consultation held by the crew.

It needed no explaining.

'They were about to murder the young girl, and drink her blood.'

A wild look of agonised despair gleamed from the wretched father's eyes as this appalling knowledge came to his mind.

Albert, too, trembled like an aspen, but quietly picking up a tomahawk from the bottom of the boat, he placed it behind him, with a determination to defend the lovely girl to his last drop of blood.

Captain Gould saw the young seaman's act, though his heart told him the attempt to resist above a score of desperate, half-crazed men would but end in death.

He followed the young seaman's example, and, in breathless silence, awaited the coming of the conspirators.

One look of agonised reproach Albert directed towards his old messmate Tom, but it was disregarded.

The old seaman had lost his senses by the terrible sufferings endured since the ship foundered, and now, like the remainder, greedily awaited the moment when, vampire-like, he should be able to drink the fresh, warm blood from the young girl's veins, instead of suffering such horrible pangs as he now endured from his parched and cracking throat.

Albert saw there was no hope for assistance from his messmate, and, with a groan of terrible anguish, he gazed upon the lovely form of Martha.

Unconscious of the terrible fate that stood over her, she still lay at rest. A dreamy trance had come over her, and she was soothed by the most delightful vision.

Babbling little streamlets, clear murmuring rills, seemed spread before her.

So strong was this delusion upon her mind, that she could feel the liquid stream laving her hands, which she used as a drinking cup.

Several times she sought to raise the coveted draught to her lips; but the water seemed to run in mockery through her fingers, and, falling into the stream, went rushing away.

From this tantalising vision she was awakened by a terrible cry.

Opening her eyes, she beheld a strange and fearful scene.

There, within a few feet of where she lay, was the form of a sailor, the blood welling out from a wound in his shoulder.

From the fallen man she glanced towards her lover, who, with flashing eyes and head erect, brandished a tomahawk, and kept the angry boat's crew at bay.

Martha shuddered. One glance at the blood-besmeared blade of Albert's weapon showed the cause of the sailor's wound.

In affright she rose to a sitting posture, and gazed around for her father.

What could it mean? He, too, stood before her, grasping a large hatchet.

The frenzied crew, awed by the determined front of these resolute men, stood for a moment, with their wild, bloodshot eyes fixed upon their victim.

The sudden fall of one of their number had checked their advance.

A moment they stood irresolute; then, with a wolfish cry, they sprang towards the fallen man.

Horrible, dreadful to relate, they dragged him to the bow of the vessel, and to the wound in his shoulder, made by Albert's tomahawk, several of them glued their parched lips, and, vampire-like, greedily sucked his blood.

In vain the poor wounded wretch sought to escape from them.

Vain were his faint moans and struggles. He was thrown down, and the famished sailors bit and fought with each other to obtain a draught of their fellow-creature's blood.

This for a moment appeased them; and, worn out by their struggles with each other, they for a time lay motionless in the boat.

The seaman who had served for this horrible repast had ended his sufferings in this world.

He lay across one of the thwarts, a stiffening, ghastly corpse.

Another night passed, the succeeding morning bringing with it fresh horrors.

A horrible desire for the possession of the hapless Martha had seized upon the wretched seamen.

Again the scene of the preceding day was enacted, but this time with better success by the wolfish crew.

Throwing the dead body of their late messmate overboard, they rushed upon Albert and Captain Gould, both of whom, from having kept awake the whole of the preceding night, were so exhausted and worn out that they could not muster sufficient strength to stand upon their feet.

Howling like so many wild beasts, the seamen bore down upon Martha's protectors.

A few blows from a stretcher rendered them senseless, and the poor girl was dragged to the bow of the boat.

No time was lost by them.

Her white neck was uncovered, her head thrown

back, and one of the maddened, inhuman monsters opened his clasp-knife to open a vein in her neck.

They did not wish to kill her outright, but to draw her blood from her drop by drop, until she died from exhaustion.

By this means their lives would be prolonged longer than by slaying her outright.

Poor girl! she gazed piteously at her inhuman butchers, and sought feebly to push aside the rough hands that encircled her neck.

With frenzied impatience they gathered round her, every eye directed to her fair neck, every tongue wishing for the moment when they should begin the terrible repast.

Her clustering curls were rudely pulled aside.

Already had the sharp point of the knife touched her fair skin, and a minute drop of blood began to show itself.

At this moment a feeble cry came from the stern sheets, and Albert, pointing with his thin, emaciated fingers towards the the west, cried out—

'Hold, hold, for God's sake! There is a sail in sight.

'A sail!'

'A sail!'

Came from the dry, cracked throats of the wretched men as they dropped Martha's head, and turned to look in the direction pointed out by Albert.

Yes, there was a sail—a small speck yet, but every moment becoming larger.

A faint cry of joy came from their lips, and many laughed and cried by turns, others sank upon their knees in silent prayer at their unexpected deliverance.

Larger and larger the vessel became, and the longing eyes of the hapless wretches were filled with delight.

Louder and louder became their joyful cries, for the vessel was bearing right down upon them, and every heart swelled with a delicious feeling of joy as they discerned the massive bow and bends of a noble frigate.

Dashing the waves aside, she came nearer and nearer; but suddenly, and while every heart beat with joy, the Golden Arrow, for such it was, hauled up her course, and shot upon another tack.

Then from the poor wretches there came one long cry of agony, and many of them sank to the bottom of the boat senseless.

The reaction had been too much for their weak state, and when they saw the vessel alter her course, they fell as though suddenly stricken by death's icy fingers.

Half stunned and bewildered, Albert now crept from the stern-sheet, and, tearing off his white shirt, fastened it to the blade of an oar.

For some time it fluttered, then a gust of wind suddenly catching it, tore the sleeve away and bore it eddying towards the frigate.

'We are seen! we are seen!' he gasped in a faint voice. 'See, one is tacking towards us. Thank God! thank God!'

Yes, they were seen.

Captain Stuart at the very moment Albert's signal of distress was blown away had given an order for a boat to be lowered.

Gerald sprang to the quarter davits, and shouted—

'Cutter's crew this way.'

The men sprang towards the captain, who was already busy casting off the gripe.

'Be sharp there,' said the captain. 'I can see a woman's form huddled up in that boat.'

The cutter was soon ready, the rope gears cast off, and a cheery 'Give way' from Gerald Stuart was followed by the dip of oars, and the gallant frigate's boat sped on her errand of mercy.

The news soon spread that a couple of boats were drifting about on the open sea, and many anxious eyes watched the cutter as she flew through the water.

CHAPTER LXXXV.

THE SAILORS AGAIN.

THE castaways were kindly received by Captain Stuart and his crew, Gerald devoting his own cabin to the lady's use, her father gratefully thanking him for so doing.

One of the sufferers—a stout, athletic seaman, who had received a desperate wound from one of his maddened shipmates—created much interest.

The ghastly wound on his shoulder necessitated the removal of his shirt, and, to the surprise of all, his body was completely covered with drawings of birds, fish, and animals of various kinds and variegated colours.

A murmur of surprise emanated from the crew; for, though used to seeing persons tattooed, they had never seen one so much so as the wounded man.

'The wound is dangerous, I fear,' said Gerald, who undertook the task of dressing and bandaging the wound. 'I fear it will turn out serious. Carry him below, and let him rest quiet. We shall enter some harbour, I hope, before night,'

The order was obeyed; but, scarcely had the seaman been placed in his hammock, than he seemed better.

'I hope the captain will not land upon any of these islands,' he said, feebly; 'if he does, we shall be all murdered.'

'Why?'

'These islands are infested by pirates of the most bloodthirsty and cannibalistic principles of any islanders I have ever seen. I have'——

'What? Go on.'

He had paused as some thought entered his mind, and a quivering sensation for a moment shook his frame.

Some horrible thought had occurred to his mind.

'Well, what was it?' again asked the interrogator.

'Oh! nothing. Do not pain me unnecessarily.'

'But do you know aught of these islands?'

'I do; but no matter.'

'If it concerns us, it must matter. Let us hear it, it may perhaps turn to our advantage.'

'It is nothing of importance. I was taken by the natives, that is all.'

'And they tattooed you?'

'Do not ask me.'

'Then let us hear your story.'

'I will tell you,' he replied, in answer to their earnest solicitations, 'though the story may not be very interesting to you, and though my blood curdles in my veins at the very thought of it.

'I was a cabin boy on board the Nancy, and being a favourite with the captain, was permitted to accompany the officers on shore.

'We had landed several times, and obtained water and fruit; and the scientific gentlemen had even been upon the hills, and as yet the people had showed no disposition to molest us.

'But at length the sailors began to defraud the natives, and abuse their women, entering the huts and helping themselves to whatever they fancied.

'The sailors were thus the aggressors, as white men have always been whenever there has been trouble with the natives of the group.

'They are a simple, kind-hearted people enough, but are easily excited, and irascible, and resent an insult more readily, perhaps, than civilised people would.

'When we landed the last time the party was attacked by a large number of natives, who had secreted themselves in the woods.

'The good captain was the first man to fall, and then the doctor, who had come on shore to gather plants and flowers; but myself and two other boys, who happened that morning to accompany us, were saved by hiding ourselves among the rocks till the fight was over.

'We remained secreted till we were forced by hunger to leave our hiding-place and go in quest of food and water.

'When we ventured out, we found to our horror that the ship had sailed.

'The officers, no doubt, supposing we had also been murdered, made no efforts to return to the shore, and we were left to an uncertain fate.

'We had not been long wandering through the woods in search of fruits to allay our hunger, when we were discovered, and surrounded by a party of natives.

'We now gave ourselves up for lost, and expected momentarily to be brained with their heavy war clubs.

'But with much shouting and jabbering, they led us off in triumph to the old King Toriquo. The chief received us with great joy, and for three days a great feast was held, in which the dance of victory was performed with great rejoicings.

'We were permitted to join in the universal carnival, and feasted high on fish and fowl and other delicacies.

'After the feast was concluded, the king took us to his own house, and continued to feed us on the most nourishing food, till in a few weeks we had become as plump as young pigs. In fact, I began to suspect that the old cannibal was getting us in prime order for another feast, in which a more delicate dish was intended to tickle the palate of the savage chief.

'All this time we had been treated with marked kindness; our tarry clothes had been taken from us, and we had been furnished with gaudy suits of fine matting, trimmed with gay-coloured feathers, similar to those worn by the king and his attendants.

'We were not, however, permitted to leave the hut except for a little while in the morning, when we were taken to the shore, and made to bathe in a lagoon within the coral reef.

'One day one of our comrades, the youngest of our number, was taken from us—for a walk, as the chief gave us to understand.

'We never saw him again, and we had no doubt he had been eaten by the cannibals. Whether the poor lad was devoured there, or sent to another island, we could not ascertain. Since, I have been told he was carried to the other side of the island and roasted. On that occasion, I remember, Toriquo was absent several days.

'We knew what fate we were reserved for. No death could be so revolting as that which we were satisfied was in reserve for us, and we determined to starve ourselves, or barely eat enough to keep life in us.

'In a few days we had the pleasure of finding that we lost our flesh as rapidly as we had gained it. But the savages did not long permit this, and they began to stuff the food down our throats, as I remember to have seen done by turkeys and geese in my native country.

'We, however, determined that we would die by our own hands, or force the cannibals to kill us in a fight, sooner than be led out to the sacrifice for which they had reserved us.

'Not far from the king's hut stood an isolated rock, that had fallen from the top of a high cliff. This rock was approachable only on the sea-side, and that by a narrow and irregular crevice.

'Our attention had been called to it on landing for the first time by the officers, who observed it might be valuable as a place of defence, in case of a sudden attack upon our watering party; for it was below this rock that a fine, fresh water stream emptied itself into the harbour.

'It occurred to me that if we could get possession of the fire-arms of our murdered shipmates, we might gain this rock, and by courting another mode of death, escape that we had so great a horror of.

'I knew the muskets, together with the cartouche boxes containing the ammunition, had been deposited in the chief's house, and were suspended from the walls.

'The building was never guarded, though it contained all the trophies the people had ever taken in all their wars; and we would have no difficulty in entering it unseen, while the indolent natives were enjoying their mid-day slumber.

'The use of the muskets, which they termed in their language "thunder sticks," they were altogether unacquainted with, and regarded them as supernatural instruments, which only "devil's men" could handle with impunity.

'They appeared to hold them in great fear, and no one person ever ventured to handle them.

'I observed, when the guns were used in the victory dance, no less than four men were employed in bringing each one to the ground, where they were laid, while the savages danced around them in a wide circle.

'They expressed a great concern, lest the thunder sticks would die for the want of food, as they termed the powder and ball, and desired us to instruct them in the manner of loading them.

When thus appealed to, we expressed as much ignorance as themselves, asserting that as we were not yet men, we had never been initiated into the secret.

'I conferred with my comrade, Jack Douglass, and we determined to put our plan into operation that very day. Accordingly, when the savages were asleep, we stole cautiously from our hut, and, entering the chief's hut, selected such of the weapons as we knew were in best order, and loading our shoulders with a couple of powder horns each, and as many cartouche boxes nearly filled with cartridges, started for the rock; first taking the precaution to convey to our fortress a large calabash of fresh water.

'As soon as they missed us the savages raised a great noise, and spread the alarm, by sounding conch shells, and beating their hideous drums.

'The woods and hills were searched in every direction where it was possible for a man to penetrate; and it was not till the next day that they bethought them to examine our rock o. . . .ge.

'At last one enterprising young savage approached the rock, but had scarcely entered the passage to it than I fired, and tumbled his carcase upon the beach below.

'The report of the gun aroused the country for a great distance around; and it was but a few moments before the rock was surrounded by hundreds of the excited natives, armed with javelins, clubs, and bows and arrows.

'We were beyond their reach, and so easily defended was our little fortress that we had no fears so long as our ammunition held out. We only acted on the defensive, shooting down only such as had the temerity to attempt the passage of the crevice.

'We so managed that but one musket should be empty at a time. Jack loaded while I fired.

'In this way I had despatched four of our assailants, when old Toriquo approached to the base of the rock, and made signals for a 'palaver.'

'We had been prisoners long enough to pick up considerable of their language, for boys easily acquire a strange tongue.

'The old chief promised, if we would come down, and be good boys, and learn them the use of the muskets, they would not only treat us kindly, but he would adopt us as his sons.

'We knew enough of these islanders to mistrust their most sacred promises, and refused to surrender.

'But the old king, to prove his sincerity, dispersed the natives, and for several days supplied us, with his own hands, with abundance of food and water; and at length won so far our confidence that we consented to return with him to his hut. In short, he was true to his promise, and we were adopted into his family with much ceremony, and received our warrants of nobility, as you may perceive by the tatooing which has so attracted your attention.

'In the course of a few years, after I had married the daughter of one of the under chiefs, and could speak their language perfectly, I was promoted to a rank equivalent in Europe to that of a duke or prime minister, or chief adviser to the king; and on the death of my old protector, I was honoured with the supreme government of the island.

'But things were not permitted to remain long in this blissful state.

'The day of the great sacrifice was close at hand, and the natives sought, by every means in their power, to quarrel with us.

'As king, my life was partly insured; but my friend, Jack Douglass, whom I had promoted to as high an office as I could without incurring the savages' displeasure, was looked upon as a victim.

'I could constantly hear the mutterings of the tribe and the hints thrown out; but I mastered the dreadful sufferings of my mind, and determined to hold my superiority to the last.'

'Ah, cuss 'em!'' ejaculated Tom, who had been listening in breathless suspense, 'they deserve hanging.'

'Worse than that, you will say, when you hear all.'

'Well, go on.'

'A week almost of unutterable torture I passed, during which the preparations for the human sacrifice were being made.

'Many of their own tribe were doomed to suffer, but they wanted a white man to complete their dainty meal.

'I could see there was no chance of Jack escaping unless we used force, and accordingly I formed a plan.

'Only one of the tribe—and he I could not well do without—I let into my secret.

'He was a tall, muscular fellow, and hitherto I had found him faithful; but, alas! he proved himself a traitor.

'Our plan was that we should work at night, get one of the largest canoes down on the beach, provision her, and fit her out with sails, secret her in one of the narrow creeks, and when an opportunity offered make good our escape.

'We worked hard that night, the Indian assisting with a will, completed our task, and returned to our huts, resolved the next night to take our muskets and ammunition with us, and bid farewell to our island home.

'Nothing transpired the next day to arouse our suspicions that the savage had betrayed us, so we waited until night set in, each hour seeming to us like a day.

'Darkness at length set in, and with it we crept out and proceeded cautiously towards the beach, our black assistant leading the way.

'Presently we heard a noise.

'It was the savages' war-whoop.

'The bushes cracked and were thrust aside, and we were instantly surrounded.

'Surrender, white-faced traitors!' yelled the savages, pointing their long spears towards us. 'You have offended the Great Spirit in trying to escape.'

'Remonstrance, in the shape of words, we knew were useless, so we had resource to our arms.

'The two foremost fell by our muskets, and we should probable have done some slaughter, had not our treacherous friend crept stealthily behind Jack, and felled him with his heavy club.

'This sudden and treacherous act caused me to turn, and I felt myself pierced through the arm.

'Rendered powerless, I was seized, and we were borne to the village in triumph.

'Insults were now heaped upon us in every form.

'On me the more so, as I had been the king; and thus we lingered till the day of the grand festival arrived.

'Jack Douglass—poor fellow—was the first to suffer, and I had to witness the horrid spectacle.

'They first drew out his nails, then skinned him by degrees, making the skin peel off by means of a lighted brand of pinewood.

'The brave fellow bore the horrible torture as long as he could without a moan; and, at length, overcome with pain, he swooned.

'This was a happy relief; but the savage wretches soon restored him to consciousness, and danced around him as his shrieks and cries filled the air.

'At length, nature could stand no more. He fell at the foot of the stake, a corpse.

'My turn came next; and when the fierce miscreants turned towards me my blood fairly boiled with madness.

'In the moment I seemed endowed with supernatural power; and, snapping the cords that bound me, I seized the knife from the hand of my tormentor, and plunged it in his breast.

———

CHAPTER LXXXVI.

THE RED VULTURE BEARS AWAY HIS PREY—
SUDDEN APPEARANCE OF RODWIN BLAKE.

THE boat bearing Susan from the shore had scarcely touched the vessel's side when Gregory leaped to the deck, and, in an impetuous tone, gave the order to make sail and trip the anchor.

The order was readily obeyed.

And now the white sails fluttered to the breeze for a few moments, and then expanded like a cloud.

As the pirate gazed upon the advancing boat with eyes dilating, a horrible smile illuminated his ghastly features.

And in a thick voice he muttered half aloud—

' Ah ! Will Howard, I have foiled you this time. The Red Vulture is once more afloat, and many will soon have cause to remember it. Fire, blood, and plunder shall be our watchword ; rapine and horrors shall mark our track, and through a sea of blood will steer the Red Vulture.'

Oh, what a tale of terror sounded in that wild laugh that rang o'er the sombre waters of the bay !

With a quick but noiseless motion every order of the stern captain was obeyed, even when he ordered the men to give three cheers.

With alacrity they flew to the bulwarks of the vessel, three exultant cheers vociferated from their throats.

For they had been led to believe that the land-sharks, having captured Will, were now on their track thirsting for their blood, and the dark forms they saw gathered on the beach were the coast-guards.

They were unable to discern the features of the dark figures in the boat, the dim outlines of which they could see by the doubtful morning light was full of men, and were engaged in hot pursuit.

Full well did Gregory know this, and he increased their excitement by the vehemence with which he gave each fresh order, not allowing them one single moment for reflection.

' Now, my lads,' he almost roared ; ' cat and fish the anchor, run out your studding-sail booms, secure the boats and make all ready for sea. Come, move sharp, unless you want to swing at the yard-arm, or dance a hornpipe from the cross-beam of a scaffold. Do you not see the bloodhounds of the law already close upon us ? '

At these words the crew flew about the decks headed by Despardo, who, heaping curses on the pursuers, inspired them with fresh vigour.

The stunsail booms were quickly rigged out and tacks and halyards hove.

In a very short time the little brig flew through the water with lightning speed.

Her long black hull appeared almost buried beneath the towering clouds of canvas now spread to the wind.

A blood red flag, embellished with the ghastly emblems of the profession in which they were about to be engaged was run up.

The skull and cross-bones now fluttered in the breeze, and on sped the little craft on her errand of destruction.

The Red Vulture could not have been better adapted to the wishes of Gregory Saunders, for she was built for speed, and provided with six brass guns of rather heavy calibre for vessels in those days.

With her crew of thirty well-armed and resolute fellows, she proved a formidable opponent to any vessel who might dare to cross her path.

The pirate captain, Despardo, and his chief officer were standing on the poop, holding a short conference as to the best mode of proceeding.

As the pirate captain stood beside his companion, and the pale grey dawn of morning irradiated his swarthy features, clearly defined, there was an unmistakable character of malignant treachery in the deep-set glaring eyes, of unmitigated, cruel, tigerish ferocity, in the thin scornful lips and large white glittering teeth, that remaind, while heavy masses of damp black hair fell in clustering elf locks on his ample shoulders.

' Forward, there ! Pass the word for the second officer ; let him come aft for orders," cried Gregory, in a clear but subdued voice, at the close of their short but evidently decisive consultation.

' Dick Stedfast,' he resumed, as that individual made his appearance on the poop, ' let all the men be mustered aft.'

' Ay, ay,' he replied, as he hurried forward to obey the order.

In another moment the deck was crowded with a group of stalwart, fiend-like forms, whilst the resolute expression of their weather-beaten, and sun-tanned features added to their terror-inspiring garb, shirt and skull-caps of crimson serge giving them a formidable appearance.

' Now, lads,' he said, in a commanding tone, ' we attack, plunder, and destroy. You all know the meaning which these words convey, therefore you require no further explanation ; but hark ye,' he cried, fiercely, ' the first man among you who betrays the least signs of treachery I'll send a bullet crashing through his brain.'

This fearful threat, uttered in such an impressive manner, seemed to have the desired effect, and a smile of satisfaction played on the lips of the Red Vulture as he gazed silently on their awe-stricken visages.

' Sail oh !' now sounded from the mast-head.

With an impulsive movement, Gregory sprang to the side, and scanned the horizon with his glass.

' In stun-sails !' he thundered, ' and clear away. ' She appears to be an Indiaman,' he said, turning to Despardo, who stood at his elbow.

The day had set in with thick and foggy weather, and a vessel could be only indistinctly seen at the distance of a mile.

Looming like a gigantic mass through the haze might be seen a vessel of no small dimensions, braced sharp up on the wind, as though she were steering for the English Channel.

It was apparent to all that she would cross the bows of the Vulture, and that shortly.

Speculation was rife as to the probable extent and costliness of her coffers, and the rapacious hearts of the pirates beat high in the anticipation of an easy capture and a glorious prize.

Saunders, who had been anxiously watching, now hailed her in the usual way.

He received no answer.

The vessel crossed the bows of the brig, and appeared to be indifferent to her movements, as she hauled her wind and proceeded in the direction of the stranger.

The brig soon overhauled her, for she appeared to be a sluggish sailer, and in a very few minutes ranged alongside.

' Ship ahoy !' thundered Saunders, for the second time.

He waited impatiently for an answer.

No answer came.

'Ship ahoy!' he almost shrieked, in a frenzy of rage.

At that moment a blue ensign was run up to the peak, and two rows of ports, each presenting the black muzzle of a gun, appeared to his astonished gaze.

What a change came over the features of the pirate as he saw the guns, with their dark, yawning chasms, ready to deal forth death and destruction.

For a moment he stood as though rooted to the spot, but hastily recovering himself he flew to the wheel, and by a dexterous movement of the helm, he bore down on the breeze at the same moment the men squared the yards.

'It's a British man-of-war,' he thundered. 'By heavens, she will knock us to pieces, Despardo! We are no match for a frigate of forty guns.'

'Loose the royals; run up the stunsails,' he roared.

At that moment a deafening roar rent the air, and a shower of shot flew harmlessly by the brig.

Whilst the vessels having changed places, the pursuer being now the pursued, flew rapidly before the wind.

The Red Vulture was evidently increasing the distance between her and the pursuing frigate.

A shot from the bow of the frigate carried away the port topmast stunsail boom.

The sails were now dragging the water, thus causing an impediment to their progress.

'Cut away the hamper!' roared Gregory, 'and drag two of the guns aft.'

The order was quickly obeyed.

The frigate had gained considerably on the brig, and it was apparent to all on board both vessels that the frigate would soon be alongside of her, whilst the sailors were already in the nettings, waiting to board her as soon as she should draw sufficiently close for them to do so.

'Try your hand at that gun, Dick,' cried the pirate captain; 'and mind, dread the consequences if you miss your mark.'

'Drop down,' cried Dick, 'or them turkeys won't miss their mark.'

They had scarcely time to fall to the deck, when a shower of bullets from the muskets of a body of marines mustered in the bow of the frigate shot over their heads, lodging in the spars and different articles on the deck.

'They say a starn chase is a long 'un,' said Dick, as his eye glanced along the barrel of the gun; 'but, d—n me, I would sooner have a short 'un, for it's growing rather hot.'

A bright flash at that moment, followed by a loud, crashing sound, told how truly Dick Stedfast had directed his aim.

Now the foretopmast of the frigate came tumbling down, causing those assembled on the forecastle to rush aft.

Many of the boarders in the forerigging and chains were knocked overboard by the falling mass of spars, sails, and rigging.

A smile of satisfaction lighted up the swarthy visage of the pirate as he patted Dick familiarly on the shoulder, and bade him try his hand upon the other gun, which in the meantime had been loaded by Despardo and several of the crew, and now stood ready for him.

'Ay, ay,' was the rejoinder, as Dick sprang lightly to the other gun, and leaned forward in a stooping attitude to ensure his aim.

'Try the maintopmast, Dick,' ejaculated Despardo.

But Dick only threw himself down flat on the deck at the rear of the gun.

As he looked through the port he saw the barrel of a musket pointing in a direct line for his head, and scarcely had he fallen down when a bullet whizzed through the port and ploughed up the deck a few feet in his rear.

Like lightning he sprang to his feet again, and took his station at the gun.

A loud report followed.

The maintopmast swayed to and fro, and in another moment fell down before the mainsail, bringing its mass of sails and cordage down with it.

A yell of defiance now rose from the brig as she dashed away from the frigate.

At the same instant the frigate made a yaw to one side, and delivered a broadside from her main-deck guns.

Another yell arose from the brig.

The iron shower flew past the brig, tearing up her decks, and killing and wounding many of the crew, and cutting the mainmast to its centre.

With a rending noise the shattered spar, with all its entanglement of sails and cordage heeled over, hissing like red hot embers, into the foaming sea.

Just then a startling cry of mortal agony, unearthly and appalling, aroused the pirates from the trance-like stupor into which they had momentarily been thrown, and turning their eyes in the direction whence the sound had proceeded, they were horrified at beholding the mutilated body of Dick Stedfast, whose legs had been shot off at the knees, and now he was clinging to the capstan for support, as he tried to walk upon the stumps.

A ghastly expression on his countenance, and a death-like pallor on his brow, he gazed with a wild, fixed stare of vacant horror at the huge black mass, almost obscured by the fog.

'Shipmates,' he said, in a tone of agony, 'I must have one shot at that cursed frigate. Load her with grape.'

The spectators listened in wonder to the words of the wounded man, and appeared like men who had awakened from a fearful scene.

'Do you hear me?' he gasped, as he fixed his unearthly glare upon their awe-stricken features. 'Will you load that gun, that I may be revenged for the loss of these spars?'

A thrill of horror ran through the crew as he pointed to the now severed limbs as they lay near the stump of the fallen mainmast.

Scarcely knowing what they were doing, several of the crew moved aft and loaded the gun.

Dick's eyes lit with a lurid glow as he impatiently watched their every movement.

And while they were yet running out the gun, with an herculean and final effort of his fast-ebbing strength, he hobbled along the deck.

The crew started in horror, as the clump, clump, caused by the bones striking on the deck, fell upon their ears.

At length, faint and exhausted, he reached the breech of the gun, but ere he could fire, he fell exhausted.

It was only a miracle as it were that the pirates escaped a just retribution.

Not only the crew, but the captain, stood appalled at the shocking mutilation of Dick Stedfast.

The commander of the frigate, who was no other

than Captain Crosstree, burning with indignation at the audacity of the pirates, rounded his ship to, with the intention of giving them a raking broadside.

In doing his bowsprit, that had been sadly shattered by a stray shot, snapped off near the gammon, and the frigate became unmanageable.

*   *   *   *   *   *

Next day the pirates, enraged at their defeat and thirsting for fresh plunder, glared eagerly about the vast extent of sea line.

But no ship was in view, so, with morose and savage looks, they went below.

'Sail oh!' at length brought the captain from his cabin.

Gregory looked pale.

'Where away?' he asked, hoarsely.

'Ah, a glorious prize,' he muttered, as he glanced in the direction indicated, and then added—

'Now, Despardo, I hope we shall have some luck.'

Despardo gave a grunt of assent, and Gregory Saunders walked forward to the quarter-deck.

'Boatswain!' he roared.

The second officer, Dick Stedfast, lay below, under the care of the surgeon.

'You know our motto,' he resumed, as that personage made his appearance on the quarter-deck. 'We attack, plunder, and destroy. Clear for action, and bear down.'

What an electrical and appalling effect did that shrill cry of 'Sail ho!' produce upon the Red Vulture's lawless crew!

In an instant all signs of idle lassitude and of careless abandonment had vanished.

There was a heavy tramp of eager feet as they rushed upon deck, and a moment or two had sufficed to swell their number greatly.

Crowding the lee bulwarks with savagely glittering eyeballs and hungry, wolfish countenances, they glared upon the distant outlines of their anticipated prey; for with the Red Vulture's robber crew, to sight a merchant vessel was almost tantamount to her capture and destruction.

The brig's head now turned in the direction of their prey, which appeared to be a ship of large dimensions, though only a sluggish sailer.

Every inch of canvas that could be spread was set on board the Red Vulture, and right gallantly did she bear down before the breeze.

The heavy and cumbersome merchantman appeared to labour heavily in her endeavours to breast the surging waves.

It would have been an easy task for the little brig to have overhauled her had she not have been in so disabled a condition; for as yet time had not permitted them to refit topgallant and royal masts, and repair other damages she had received in the fight.

All that day did the pirate captain and his bloodthirsty colleague pace the deck, watching the progress of the vessels; and towards evening they had neared to within a mile of each other, when, to their astonishment, they observed the strange vessel shorten sail.

It was evident they would soon be able to overhaul her.

A smile of satisfaction irradiated the swarthy visage of the Red Vulture, and there was a look of treachery in the deep gleaming eyes, and his scornfully curling lips proclaimed an unmitigated and tigerish ferocity.

Despardo, with his right hand grasping one of the shrouds of the main rigging, eyed the doomed vessel, whom he already believed to be within their grasp, with remorseless cunning.

The sun had now sank below the horizon, and evening began to throw her shades around, when the unwieldy and apparently indifferent merchantman hauled to the wind and appeared to the astonished pirates, whose gloating eyes had never for one moment lost sight of her since morning, as though about to cross their bows.

Intently did they watch her movements, and various were their conjectures as to her probable intentions.

The starboard side of the strange vessel up till now had been the only one visible to those on board the pirate ship, and now the stranger stood boldly across their bows.

Now they were on the starboard side of the brig, and suddenly, even whilst the pirate was considering the best mode of attack, she squared away again, thus exposing her port side to the view of the astonished crew, as the vessels ranged alongside each other, their heads both pointing in the same direction.

Picture their dismay as the strange vessel exposed to their view her port side, from which bristled a tier of guns, their black muzzles pointing directly towards the Red Vulture.

Before they could recover from their astonishment, a terror-inspiring vision met their gaze.

It was a black flag with skull and cross-bones, showing them to belong to the same class of bloodthirsty ocean ravagers as themselves.

For a moment Gregory Saunders stood astounded at this sudden change in the aspect of affairs, as the apparently inoffensive merchant vessel was changed into a death-dealing Nemesis.

It was evident all their combined energies would be required to beat off the attack of their superior antagonist, for a tier of eight bristling guns protruded from her dark sides.

Her hitherto apparently deserted decks presented a scene of life, as the hideous and bloodthirsty crew, who had hitherto been concealed from view, thrust their heads above the bulwarks and presented a stern front, so bold and formidable that for an instant the Red Vulture and his companion, paused, panic-stricken and irresolute, knowing not which course to pursue.

Bitterly did they curse the fate that had allowed them thus to be drawn into the trap of their formidable enemy.

Concealment was now no longer necessary, and the crew of the Red Vulture, who had hitherto lain crouched at their quarters, taking cursory glances at the strange vessel through the open ports, were now glaring at her with eyes dilated and knitted brows.

'Prepare for action,' roared Gregory.

But the crew paused a moment to take one more look at the strange sail to calculate what chance they were likely to have against so great odds.

Their decision was but momentary.

They knew full well that in such savage, lawless warfare as each waged against their fellow-men, no mercy, no quarter, would be shown or granted by their implacable foes.

Through the resistless force of sheer necessity their battle cry must be, 'Victory or death!'

And, goaded thus, the outwitted ruffians rushed like raving demons to the fray.

Despardo, assisted by a party of the pirates, was busily engaged in bringing round the three brass guns from the port side.

BLACK EYED SUSAN.

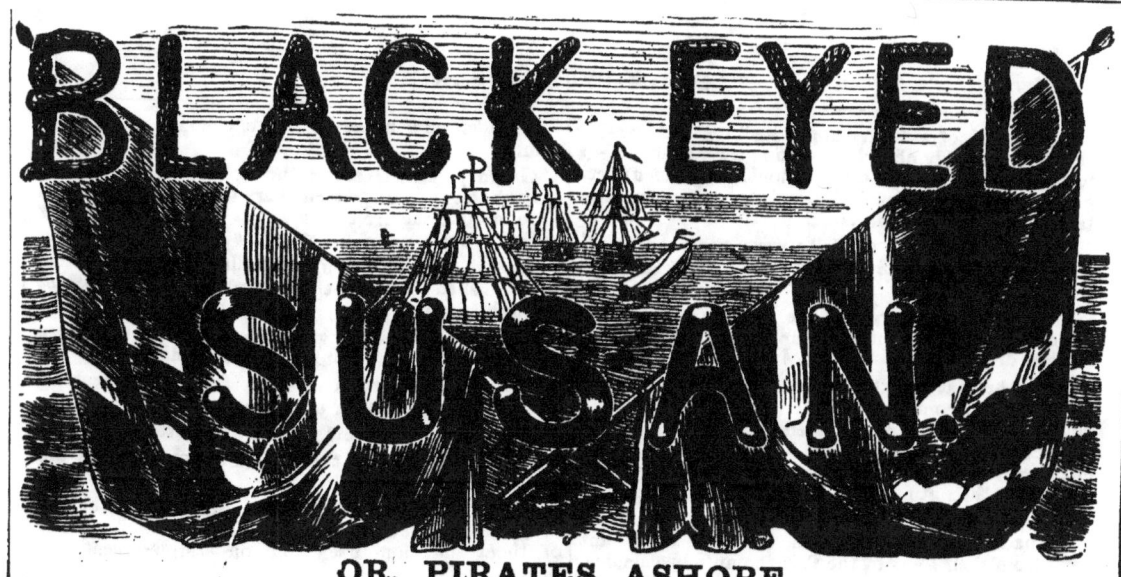

OR, PIRATES ASHORE.

'STAY, MY BROTHER, DO NOT SLAY THE WHITE MAN'

By the aid of skilfully-applied slings and levers, they were quickly placed in position, and their bright muzzles thrust through the ingeniously-contrived portholes, which until now had remained unobserved by their astonished assailants.

So ingeniously and skilfully were they contrived, that it appeared as though they were thrust through the solid bulwarks.

Their blood-red flag, with the ghastly emblems of their profession, was now run up to the masthead, as a token of defiance.

It was he that had thus lured them on by his crafty and ingenious contrivances, for which he was so renowned, had been hotly engaged in the morning with two French gun-brigs, who had fallen upon him unawares, and had but just escaped from the withering fire of their guns when he was sighted from the deck of the Red Vulture.

He had lost many of his men, who had been shot away from their guns by the Frenchman's broadsides.

His vessel had sustained serious damage to her hull and rigging.

Seeing the Red Vulture suddenly make sail and turn her head in the direction of the rover, as though about to give chase, and not knowing exactly what kind of vessel it was, or what force he was likely to be opposed to, he thus lured them on, hoping that under cover of the night they might fall upon the pursuing vessel, and thus, by stratagem, achieve an easy victory.

All day the carpenters and crew had been employed in repairing the shattered hull and rigging of the Rover.

Having patched up some of the worst wounds, she was now able to attack any merchant vessel that might happen to cross her path.

The shattered condition of her crew rendered her unfit to contend with any well-armed vessel.

He had well surveyed the little brig.

By the disabled condition of her spars, he conjectured she might be only one of the many vessels which abounded in those waters, carrying on their nefarious practices of conveying slaves from the coast of Guinea to New Orleans and other parts of America.

The brass guns he saw protruding from her sides only strengthened his suspicions.

Not doubting but what she had wherewith on board to purchase her freight of living souls, he bore down in the gloom of evening to reconnoitre her, little doubting but that she would soon be wholly in his power.

This being the case, conjecture his surprise on beholding a vessel well manned and armed, bearing the ghastly emblem of the Red Vulture.

For a few seconds the rover and his crew of mercenary wretches stood stupefied.

This allowed the crew of the Red Vulture time to recover from the trance-like stupor that had fallen upon them also.

The loud boom of cannon sounded over the waters, and a blinding flash, followed by a fearful crash, aroused the Rover crew from the listless attitude they had been thrown into by their sudden surprise.

A wild yell of defiance arose from the Rover's deck.

A responding volley crashed through the Red Vulture's planks, disabling several of her crew, and doing other damage.

Still, on flew the iron showers, tearing huge splinters from the stout oaken sides of both vessels, and tearing away the rigging or anything that impeded its headlong course.

Broadside for broadside was exchanged with deadly aim.

Gregory dashed along the deck, heedless of the iron shower and shattered spars that fell in profusion around him, cheering on his men and inspiring them with fresh vigour by his presence.

'Stand to your guns, my gallant tars!' he cried, as he dashed amongst them, brandishing his cutlass above his head.

Right well did his gallant crew obey the stern mandate of their still sterner commander.

The sweat poured in streams from their reeking brows, as broadside for broadside was exchanged.

Now the vessels drew near to each other.

The violent blast of the cannon seemed to still the air around.

Many had fallen on both sides under the withering fire, and the crews of both vessels—at least, parties of them that had been told off—stood ready to board.

Like a swarm of rats the crew of the Rover dashed aboard the Red Vulture.

Though they were met with a stout resistance, yet eventually they gained the deck.

And now came the climax of the deadly conflict.

With the agility of maddened tigers, a score of the pirates, led on by their chieftain, gallantly opposed their intruding and sturdy foes.

Fast and furious waxed the fight.

Its fast-contending human waves, rolling, wrestling hither and thither, like the surging billows of a storm-lashed sea.

Already nine of the pirates lay writhing in agonies upon the slippery, blood-stained deck.

Still, the survivors fought with a stubborn and unyielding ferocity which only the dread, inevitable alternative of a bloody and fearful death could have inspired.

Those who were not actually engaged in the hand-to-hand conflict, emulated their comrades by continuing the service of their guns with the same obstinate persistence.

Exhausted at length by their superhuman struggles, the crew of the discomfited Rover saw that their only chance of safety lay in retreat.

With a sudden, simultaneous, and irresistible rush, they succeeded in cutting their way to the gangway.

With a desperate leap, they precipitated themselves on to the deck of the shattered Rover.

'Stand to your guns, men,' cried Gregory, 'they shall not forget the Red Vulture. 'Give them a double-shotted broadside.'

A loud cheer was the response.

Then came a mighty, sense-oppressing roar, that shook each vessel from stem to stern, and caused them to vibrate with the shock.

It was a broadside fired simultaneously from both vessels, and now they lay enveloped in a wreath of smoke and sulphurous vapour.

Gregory Saunders and Despardo had fought side by side during the whole of that sanguinary fray, spreading dismay and carnage wherever their deadly weapons flashed among their foes.

The crew of the Rover had all fled precipitately to their own vessel, leaving their chief, Rodwin, still battling fiercely on the deck of the Red Vulture as he wielded his deadly weapon in his bullet-shattered hand.

CHAPTER LXXXVII.

SUSAN ON BOARD THE RED VULTURE — THE
CAPTIVES IN THE HOLD.

DURING the fight Susan was below in the cabin, trembling with fear; but when the firing ceased, and the oaths of the combatants had silenced a little, she breathed a sigh of relief.

She shuddered though as Rodwin Blake was brought into the cabin, bleeding and exhausted.

There was a fiendish smile on Gregory's face as he gazed upon his inveterate foe.

Turning fiercely to his men, he said—

'Bind him securely, heavily iron him, and let him be thrust into the lower hold. I have not forgotten the time I passed with the rats. They may deal more lenient with him; if not, he will learn a lesson not easily forgotten.'

A cruel smile wreathed his lips as he spoke, and when he had finished, he burst into a low, mocking laugh.

Despardo did not seem to relish the speech.

He seemed like a man standing between two tottering rocks, one of which must sooner or later fall upon his devoted head.

The stern mandate of his chief he knew must be obeyed: but in doing so, he incurred the wrath of Rodwin Blake, who, he knew, would not fail to have revenge if he once more got into power.

Rodwin Blake was pale as death.

Weak and wounded as he was, yet he still had sufficient strength to control his features.

He knew it would please his enemy to see him suffer and hear him beg for mercy.

No. He would rather die than humble himself thus far; and, though his broad chest rose and fell with the violent emotions that convulsed his breast and racked his very brain, he would rather suffer than complain.

'Gregory Saunders,' he said, in a voice of firmness, breaking the silence that succeeded Red Vulture's speech, 'do with me as you think fit. I can bear it; but, remember, I may yet have another day of victory.'

'Ha, ha!' laughed Gregory, 'that will never be. The Red Vulture will float for ever, and, while she does, you may depend upon it, you will accompany her as a prisoner.'

'That may be your opinion,' replied Rodwin, scornfully, 'but it is not mine. You have neglected to read the orders I gave you. If that woman is on board another day you know your fate, and you know she has a husband that will be revenged.'

Gregory laughed again, this time more hollow and sepulchral.

He felt the truth of Blake's words, and an ominous presentiment crept over him.

'Take him away, men,' he said, hoarsely; 'I will bear his taunts no longer. Let him be doubly ironed, mind, and dread the consequence if you do not do your business well.'

About a score of the rovers who had failed in gaining their ships were already incarcerated in the loathsome den.

Amongst them was the young lieutenant who had so nobly taken Susan's part.

He had been thrust below at the first onset of the fight for fear he might do mischief.

'Well, Despardo,' said Rodwin Blake, when they were below, 'see that you attend well to your duty; but see that you do not make those irons fit too tight, for my wrist is sadly shattered.

Despardo trembled slightly. He did not much relish his task.

He quailed beneath the dark piercing eye revealed to him by the lantern's sickly glare.

'There, will that do?' he asked, as he bound the wound up with a portion of his scarf, and fitted the largest manacle he could find.

'Admirably,' replied Rodwin, calmly; then added, meaningly—

'I may do as much for you some day.'

'I fear not,' muttered Despardo, and having seen to the security of the rest of the prisoners, he returned on deck.

Rodwin had made good use of his eyes during the time of manacling, and now he was in darkness he knew exactly the position of his companions.

He had not failed to recognise the uniform of the lieutenant, and a thought flashed to his mind.

It was of escape.

Drawing closer to the luff, so that he could whisper to him, he said—

'How long have you been here, comrade?'

The lieutenant shrank away from him.

'I am no comrade of yours,' he said, 'though chance has thrown us together.'

'Tush, man; this is no time for preaching. You are a prisoner like myself; would you not escape if a chance offered?'

'Certainly; but there is not much chance.'

'There is.'

'Name it.'

'Not till I know your true sentiments.'

'Well, I'm a prisoner.'

'That's not what I mean. How far would you go to free yourself?'

'The length of my chain.'

'Well, if you are so dull,' said Rodwin, nettled, 'what measures would you have recourse to?'

'Any.'

'That will do.'

'What mean you?'

'That you shall be free if you prove true.'

'But that would avail me nothing, unless''——

'Unless, what?'

'It matters not.'

'It does. Speak.'

'Unless I could take with me one who I believe to be on board.'

'A female?'

'Yes. Have you seen her?'

'I have. But do you know she is'——

'What—what?' asked the luff, eagerly, a presentiment of evil crossing his mind.

'Married?'

'I do; and 'twas for respect of her husband, who was once a shipmate of mine, that I fell into this cursed trap.'

'That will do. I want to hear no more. I know you will join me in the plan I have arranged for our escape.'

'I will gladly if I can but save her.'

'You can do that, never fear,' said Rodwin, huskily, pressing the lieutenant's hand as he spoke.

The lieutenant heard the grating voice, which was anything but prepossessing, and, had it been light, he would have seen the cunning light in his companion's eye that, as a beacon warns the mariner of the proximity of rocks, told of a fierce, deceitful disposition.

————

CHAPTER LXXXVIII.

ADMIRAL GARTHWAY FALLS INTO A TRAP.

WILL'S return to the smuggling brig was hailed with joy.

He was greatly fatigued with his long swim, but soon recovered.

His first thought, after venting his spleen in no pleasant terms on the heads of his captors, was of his Sue.

This was of little use he knew, so he set about preparing his ship once more for sea.

A shot hole was discovered near the water line, which necessitated the ship undergoing repairs, so he steered her into one of the little bays, and awaited the light of day to accomplish his purpose.

Scarcely had the anchor been dropped, and the sails snugly furled, when a man-of-war was seen rounding the headland, much to the chargrin of the smugglers, who were preparing for a night's repose.

The man-of-war dared not venture far into the bay on account of the shoals, so she hove-to outside, and lowered a boat.

Two officers seated themselves in the stern, and four men pulled to the brig, evidently to overhaul her, for they had not the slightest idea that it was Will Howard's ship.

Will, in the meantime, was not idle.

He attired himself in a different rig, and giving a few hasty orders to his men, waited anxiously the boat's approach.

'What ship is that?' bawled one of the officers.

'The Curlew,' was Will's ready reply.

'Where from?'

'Oh, ah! we will come on board then.'

'Just as you like.'

Will assumed as careless a tone as possible, though in his heart he felt good to drop them a cold shot.

The officers sprang on board nimbly.

A cunning gleam was in their eyes.

They felt sure by the rig and cut of the vessel she was something more than a coaster.

They were not deceived.

No sooner did the first one reach the deck than he disappeared.

So did his companion.

Two burly smugglers had seized them, and conveyed them to Will's cabin.

'Well,' said Will, 'you have paid me a visit, have you?'

'We have,' answered the first comer, 'and dearly shall you repent this insolence. Do you know that we are '——

'Quite sufficient. We know enough of you to assure us that you are not gentlemen. How dare you come on board unasked?'

'Do you know that we are'—began the officer again, swelling with indignation.

'I told you we know all about it,' replied Will, with the utmost nonchalance, 'so hold your tongue. Sit down and have a glass of brandy if you like. Then lend me your clothes.'

He pointed to the tallest of the two, whose clothes seemed to fit Will admirably.

The fellow screwed up his visage in a style that seemed to say, 'not yet, my boy.' Then, suddenly assuming a fierce gesture, he said—

'Impudent scoundrel! what mean you?'

'What I say. I am not joking.'

A fierce light shone in the eyes of the officer at these words, and his hand closed on the butt of a pistol.

Before he could use it, however, old Sam grasped his wrist and wrenched the weapon from him.

At a signal from Will the officers found themselves surrounded by several of the smugglers, who, without saying a word, denuded the officer aforesaid of his uniform, which was instantly donned by Will.

The officers were then gagged, securely bound, and placed in Will's state-room.

The smuggler captain then went on deck, and approaching the bulwarks just near enough for the sailors alongside to see his uniform, shielded his face, and in an assumed voice said—

'Go on board at once. Tell Admiral Garthway the captain of this vessel, which is a smuggler, has surrendered his ship. Ask him to come on board to make arrangements.'

The men, thinking it was the senior officer of the two—who was the first lieutenant—who spoke, obeyed at once.

'Thus far we have been successful,' said the captain to Sam. 'If the old admiral does come on board, he will have cause to remember it.'

'Ay, that will he! Nothing could have happened better.'

Old Sam was in ecstacies; and when he saw the boat push off from the man-of-war, with the old admiral in it, the water welled from his eyes with laughter.

Will stood aft, with his back to the gangway, as though busily perusing a document, when the old admiral mounted the side with a pompous air.

'The captain's in the cabin, sir,' said Sam, touching his forelock deferentially. 'Will you go down to him?'

The old admiral did not deign an answer; he was too full of wrath at being received thus coldly by his officers; but he walked slowly down the companion-way.

Will followed him, and carefully drawing the slide over, so as no sound should reach the deck, stepped into the cabin behind the astonished admiral, and closed the door.

The admiral stood for a moment astounded at finding the cabin empty.

The thought instantly flashed to his mind that he was trapped.

Before he could turn to raise an alarm or draw his sword, he was seized from behind, a couple of stalwart smugglers forced him into a seat, and Will dexterously took possession of his weapon.

This was done so quietly, and so momentarily, that the sailors alongside, who had been handed a bottle of rum by old Sam, had not the least inkling of what was going forward.

'Ah! you recognise me?' said Will, fixing his glance upon the admiral's keen, grey eye. 'We have met before, you know.'

'We have, scoundrel?' said the admiral, sarcastically. 'I thought you were safe in jail.'

'You were mistaken; but we have no time to lose. Here is pen, ink, and paper. Write, and I will dictate.'

'Never, base villain!' vociferated the admiral, trying to rise.

The smugglers held him fast, and one of them, placing the cold muzzle of a pistol to his ear, made him start.

'Now go on,' said Will, authoritatively; 'no nonsense, mind. I am resolute; if you do not write as I dictate, you may look out.'

There was something in the tone of Will's voice that assured the admiral that the smuggler captain was in earnest, so he reluctantly consented.

Taking the pen in his trembling hand, he wrote slowly the words Will commanded him.

They ran thus—

'The vessel has surrendered. Make all sail to the Downs. I shall travel over land and join you soon.

'ADMIRAL GARTHWAY.'

This letter was given to the boat's crew, who were ordered to pull swiftly on board and return as soon as possible.

It seemed an age to the chafing admiral during the absence of the boat, and he heaped his incentives on the head of his captors pretty freely.

*   *   *   *   *

If it had not been for the respect the smugglers had for Madeline's feelings, the old admiral, her father, would have been made the subject of their free frolics.

As it was, he got off comparatively unmolested, but with a farewell salute that in no way tended to lessen his chagrin or his discomfiture.

The boat in which he was returning to the shore had not time to leave the ship's side before several of the crew hurried to the bulwarks, bearing in their midst some immense sacks.

They challenged the admiral.

'Boat ahoy!'

'To the devil with you!' grunted the old admiral.

'Here's a present for you!' old Sam sang out.

Amidst the giggling of the ship's crew, a well-filled sack was dropped over the side.

'Here's another!' Sam cried; 'take it ashore, you lubbers!'

A second sack dropped over.

This almost smothered several of the crew, and narrowly escaped the commodore's head.

As the second sack went over, the boat left the vessel's side.

The party in the boat, suspecting the truth, hastily undid the fastenings of the sacks, and enabled the cadaverous, woe-begone visages of the two officers who had gone on board to capture Will to peer ruefully forth.

How they had been maltreated since that fatal hour when they had been made helpless captives, will be discovered hereafter.

Suffice it, after enduring untold tortures, to which the smugglers had subjected them, they were crammed, more dead than alive, into the sacks, and thrust over the vessel's side.

The jolly fellows lined the bulwarks as the second load tumbled into the boat.

'Good-bye, admiral,' they cried to Garthway, who sat in the stern, looking like a living corpse; 'you'll hear of us at sea.'

They waved their caps and cheered lustily, until the boat was out of hail.

The big war ship was now speeding swiftly away.

There had been a minute's conversation going on at the quarter-deck, and Will thought they were going to risk all by not obeying the admiral's order.

But they evidently thought better of the idea, and bore away.

The admiral expected, however, that the smugglers would make good their escape.

Such was not our hero's intention.

With the audacity peculiar to his headstrong nature, he resolved to remain in harbour a little longer.

A resolve that was near being fatal to them.

The admiral reached the shore in a state bordering on madness.

If he had been able, he would have given orders forthwith to have Will's ship blown into the air.

This, in his present condition, he was unable to do.

But he closed with the first opportunity of having the smugglers attacked, and their leader slain.

The first luff, as soon as he got safe out of reach of those at whose hands he had received such frightful treatment, recalled to Admiral Garthway the purpose that had taken him on board.

The irate veteran pricked up his ears at the mention of the smugglers.

'We cannot help it now,' he said, bitterly; 'it is most unfortunate that we should have allowed ourselves to be so tricked.'

The precious pair of pirate catchers looked as if they thought the result had been deucedly unfortunate for themselves, seeing that they had not only lost their chance of reward, but had been mercilessly ill-used in the bargain.

'Now, if any man,' hissed the admiral, 'could be induced to attack their ship, we would grant him an indemnity.'

'That is to say,' observed the first luff, 'if he can beat them at sea, he may marque.'

'Ay,' the little admiral cried, 'and such a reward as you never dreamed of shall be his if this pirate is taken, with his lawless crew.'

'Hum,' growled the luff, 'those beggars can fight. If this pirate captain has not a good stomach for fighting, he had better leave them alone.'

'I know a man that will just suit,' said the second lieutenant.

'What sort of a man is he?' inquired the admiral.

The officer gave a description of the man.

He was one of the most merciless pirates who ever infested the seas.

Every clime he had visited, he left a track of blood, and the ocean dotted with burning wrecks.

No one knew his name, and such was his prowess in combat, that few cared to dare him to a personal encounter.

Added to this, he was a most consummate hand at eluding pursuit and avoiding suspicion, by assuming new devices wherever he went.

The vindictive admiral listened with pleasure to these details.

'Where is your man to be found?' he asked.

'At the Crown and Anchor.'

'Humph! A den of thieves.'

'Silence!' Admiral Garthway exclaimed. 'Remember this pirate has, with impunity, cast defiance in our teeth, and we must not be particular, so long as we take him in the end.'

'Humph!' growled the disappointed officer; 'I don't think he'll be taken yet.'

' We shall see,' was the old admiral's dry response. At all events, I'll see this fellow to-night at the Crown and Anchor.'

One of the rowers, at that moment, seemed so absorbed in listening to the arrangements, that he missed his stroke.

Any one might have supposed that he was more interested in listening to what was going forward than in rowing the admiral ashore.

Such was the fact.

He was one of Will's numerous friends, and his purpose there was to hear what was likely to go forward, and report accordingly to his old chum.

Perhaps it was owing to this interesting individual being amongst the rowers, that early the same evening, a tall, well-formed young fellow might have been seen sauntering leisurely towards the rendezvous, known as the Crown and Anchor.

His bearing was unmistakably nautical.

His dress was a sort of half naval undress, over which he wore a long blue cloak, beneath the folds of which hung a very serviceable sword.

Any one peering beneath that same cloak could have got a glimpse of a pair of finely-mounted pistols and a short dirk.

He evidently knew the nature of the men he was about to meet that night.

The Crown and Anchor was a big shantling building, in a densely-populated part of the town, the Alsatia of the place, for in it were congregated some of the worst type of humanity—men who had fled thither red-handed from their crimes—men who defied the law's control, and banded together in a desperate league within the sanctuary of this ill-omened quarter.

The narrow streets and alleys along which the stranger took his way were thronged with disreputable characters.

Lots of ill-looking ruffians, their brutal visages stamped with the haggard traces of crime, got in our adventurer's way, but he invariably walked straight to their midst, putting them aside without the least discomposure.

A look of his unquailing glance sufficed to convince the cowed rascals he would be dangerous to meddle with further.

Arrived at the Crown and Anchor, the door of which swung wide open, he sauntered in.

The landlord, with bare, brawny arms, took a swift survey of his person as he entered, and glanced after him with a sinister leer as he strode past the groups at the bar.

As our readers may imagine, the Crown and Anchor did not bear a very good repute.

There were rumours of deeds done within its reeking walls that made the heart shudder.

If there was a place where the worst characters were to be found in plenty—fellows ready to do any bloody deed—this establishment was the one.

Indeed, such was the ferocious instincts of the brutes who took shelter there, that the bravest officers of justice shrank from crossing its fatal threshold.

It was the nightly rendezvous of smugglers, pirates, and even at times coastguards.

True, their visits were not always purely to study what they saw there.

If there was an enemy to be stabbed in the dark, or a fair woman to be carried off, it was at this haunt they found the ready instruments of their will.

The room into which our adventurer now strode was of huge dimensions, and more than one hundred lamps lighted its dim corners.

Tables innumerable were placed before rudely constructed seats, and at those tables were sitting or standing groups of the most curiously mixed characters it would be possible to describe.

Rough seafaring men — fellows of undoubted piratical habits; slim youths, sickly with dissipation; men, who by their bearing, if not by their disguised costumes, could be seen at a moment's glance to belong to the higher walks of life.

Leaving the stranger in this loathsome haunt, we will now return to our hero, Will Howard.

CHAPTER LXXXIX.

In grim silence, and enveloped by a mystic cloud of invisibility, the death avengers rushed upon their foes.

Like an avalanche the gallant lads swept the broad decks of the pirate ship—thrusting their bright steel in the pirates' bodies, and driving the fear-stricken crew like a herd of sheep towards the fore part of their huge vessel.

Foremost in the death struggle could be seen the splendid form of the gallant Will, and close beside him was Sam, his dark eyes watching for every blade that was levelled at the fearless boy's heart.

Mighty were the efforts made by Will and Sam to reach the steel-clad form of the pirate.

Efforts that were for a time unavailing.

The grim leader of the pirate horde rallied his band, and led them onward to repel the attack of the smuggler's gallant crew.

Wielding his scimiter high in the air, he shouted—

' Follow me, pirates—hurl back those rascals into the sea. Were they demons we could outnumber them. Follow! follow!'

Animated by the tone and example of their mystic leader, the corsairs bore down in overwhelming numbers upon the small band of smugglers.

There was a short but sickening scene of strife.

The smugglers fought and fell without yielding one inch of vantage ground.

Now amid the dreadful strife did Sam and his leader perform such prodigies of valour that the fierce-headed foemen who fell beneath their mighty arms formed a rampart of quivering flesh before the gallant pair.

Will Howard, though so fiercely engaged with the terrible odds before him, watched with eagle eye every movement of the pirate gang.

He saw, with mingled feelings of bitterness and pain, that the enemy's best marksmen, who filled the tops, were pouring down a shower of bullets from their long matchlocks upon his brave, unyielding men.

Others he saw were crowding the open hatches, and with their long-barrelled weapons were taking sure and deliberate aim at his crew.

' Go,' he said to Sam, ' and lead a party to the quarter-deck. Tell them to pick off their enemies in the top.'

The old smuggler hastened to obey the order, a proud smile on his lips at the honour thus bestowed upon him.

He had not taken more than three paces from his leader when a ball from one of the very men he was sent to dislodge entered his arm.

He fell at our hero's feet, the proud smile still upon his lips.

A smothered cry of rage came from Will's lips at the sight, and his face became convulsed with passion.

Sam, though wounded, soon gained his feet.

Will assisted him.

'That ball,' he said to Sam, ' was intended for me; keep them in check here. I'll go myself and dislodge those fiends.'

He cut his way through the savage horde, and leaving a trail of blood in his path, reached the quarter-deck.

'Quick,' he said to those that followed him, 'hand me a rifle. Now to make them clear the tops.'

With a deadly, unerring aim he began the work.

At every flash of his rifle a turbaned pirate came whirling through the air, stricken to death by the angry boy.

As long as there remained a foe along the rigging did the gallant smuggler captain and his companions keep up a stream of fire.

The next moment Will beheld Sam's kingly form stretched prone upon the deck, and heard the pirate's mocking laugh of triumph.

Then Will, with eyes ablaze with passion, strode forward and faced the hideous monster, who, raising his scimitar, rushed forward and shrieked—

' Thus will I avenge his fall !'

He pulled the trigger.

Horror ! the treacherous pistol flashed in the pan.

Then the pirate, with a yell of joy, sprang towards his antagonist to cut him to the deck.

But as his flashing blade descended it was caught by the blade wielded by Will Howard.

The hideous pirate foamed at the mouth with rage.

Every feint, every cut, every slash he made was met by the splendid swordsmanship of the graceful captain.

Had the pirate not been defended by a breast-plate Will's sword would have passed through and through his body.

At that moment Will fancied he heard a female voice ascend from the hatchway.

The pirate chief stood between him and it.

His only thought was to cut him down—for it might be the voice of Madeline.

Dashing boldly at the fierce pirate, he beat him on one side, and bounded down the steep ladder.

All was darkness; but the gallant captain groped about in the vain hope of finding her he sought.

A noise through the chinks in the bulk-head warned him of his error in descending the wrong hatch.

'Fool that I am !' he ejaculated, huskily; and sprang to the ladder to reach the deck.

Here he found himself surrounded.

A score of the dusky crew, attracted by their leader, had surrounded the hatchway.

They were armed with every kind of weapon, and one of the officers bore in his hand a lantern, by which he had intended to descend in search of the gallant Will.

For a moment our young hero's case seemed hopeless.

His crew were forwarned of the vessel.

He shouted, but they could not hear his voice above the din.

Will hesitated but a moment.

He had lost his cutlass in descending, but seizing a short scimitar from the hand of the nearest pirate to him, he cut right and left.

In an instant he gained the deck, and soon found himself surrounded by his followers.

They were but few, and opposed to the overpowering numbers of the pirates were compelled to give way.

Will's eye caught a glimpse of the pirate chief.

He flew madly towards him.

His men, believing he had beaten a retreat, rushed to the side and gained the brig.

The graplings were removed, the breeze filled her sheets, and she sped swiftly away.

Will Howard was left alone on the Pirate's deck.

It was some moments ere he discovered this.

Still he did not repine.

Grasping his weapon firmly, he did fearful execution among his inveterate foes, who tried fiercely to take away his life.

Many a sharp weapon's point rang against his blade as he hurled himself against the bristling line of steel.

Many a death cry followed the swift downward stroke of his scimitar, as a Moslem foe fell headlong down the steps, his skull cloven in.

While he fought, like an enraged tiger, with the crowd who stood before him, another party came in rear, and would have decimated the gallant Will had not aid suddenly come.

Help so sudden and powerful that Will, for the first few moments, could scarcely believe the truth.

He felt a towering, muscular man place his back against his shoulders—heard the cries of rage and astonishment that fell from the lips of those who sought to creep upon him.

He knew, too, that a massive weapon was wielded by his unknown friend, and at every stroke the crowd counted one less.

Still the odds were fearful.

Although the gallant fellow who had come to Will's aid was a Colossus in stature, and Will's bravery and skill was worth a dozen ordinary men, both must soon have fallen, for the Moors gained strength every moment.

While the fight was at its highest, the voice of the unknown whispered to Will—

' Be of good heart; boats are coming to the rescue.'

' They will never reach us.'

As they spoke, both were naturally plying the work of death.

Neither could turn their heads, eyes and hands were wanted to repel the forest of weapons that were opposed to their single arms.

' They will not,' was the answer. ' Keep close to me; we must swim for it.'

' Never,' said Will, firmly. ' I will die; but leave this vessel without revenge—never !'

An exclamation of disappointment came from the unknown, and, as he plied his massive weapon, he said—

' It is certain death for us to stay. I will force my way through this crowd of devils. Keep close and follow.'

' Death, first !'

' Be it so,' was the answer. ' I care not; yet were I in your place I would live to be avenged for the miscreant's treachery.'

Will remained silent for a few seconds.

He felt that his adviser was right; yet the stubborn

bull-dog nature would not let him yield until the last moment.

'What is your plan?' he asked.

The reply did not come immediately.

Will's colossal friend was fiercely engaged with three of his late companions — three who seemed more than all who opposed him to seek his death.

When the glittering axe had settled the trio, he answered—

'Swim for the boats—regain your ship; there is no other plan.'

'Be it so,' said the exasperated Will, jamming the point of his sword between the teeth of a powerful pirate. 'I will follow you.'

The herculean fellow swung his axe round with both hands with such terrible swiftness, that the foremost rank of his adversaries were mowed down as though the swift lightning's flash had stricken them.

He followed the momentary pause that ensued by stepping forward.

Will stepped back at the same time.

Thus back to back they fought — a lane to the bulwarks.

Another moment, and the deadly axe would have crushed the last who stood between them and liberty.

Before the mighty arm could accomplish this last stroke, the pirate, foaming at the mouth with passion, came upon deck.

Until now he had been kept below by the surging crowd that barred Will's descent into the cabin.

But as the gallant pair clove their way to the vessel's side, the pirates gradually left the blood-stained hatchway, and enabled their savage leader to ascend.

He saw at a glance what had taken place, and his eyes blazed like living coals.

He beheld the giant frame towering high above his men, wielding that terrible axe.

Sancho, so was the giant termed.

He had received the soubriquet from his companions.

If he had another name, none on board the pirate vessel knew it.

His nationality was as little known as his name.

Though his skin was dark enough to have proclaimed him of African descent, his massive features possessed that frank, handsome outline only to be seen among the Saxons.

His language was pure English; though it was well known he was familiar with several tongues.

Some among the pirate horde thought he had sprung from an English father and African mother. Others, judging by his tanned skin, inclined to the belief that he was an Indian.

Many of the keenest among the Moorish gang had noticed that Sancho's hands and face at times seemed of a darker hue than usual.

Those who beheld this came to the conclusion that his skin was stained by the sable die, which concealed his nationality, and required renewing from time to time.

Whatever opinions were entertained by his fellows none dared to openly question him.

His marvellous strength and fiery nature and his reticence, stopped prying curiosity, for he rarely exchanged a word with those with whom fate had placed him.

He seemed like a lion in the company of wolves, and, like the gallant forest monarch, he was more dreaded than liked.

Had the pirate horde been less engaged when the panic so suddenly fell upon them, they would have noticed that the tremendous weapon wielded by Sancho was the only one that was idle during the fray.

Both the axe and its gigantic owner were absent from the fight.

And had they sought the giant they would have found him leaning leisurely against the foremast, his large, dark, expressive eye following the graceful form of Will with more of love in them than hate.

They would have seen, too, that when danger of more than an ordinary kind menaced the gallant fellow, as he, like the God of battle, moved among the combatants, the massive axe clutched by its owner, and his attitude changed from calm repose to that of the jaguar about to spring.

Then, as Will extricated himself from peril, a proud look swept over his features, and he became a passive spectator of the fight.

A cynical look, that settled upon his face when the Moors were driven back by the smugglers, showed that his sympathy was not with his companions.

Such was the mystic being who had come to Will's rescue when the fiery boy was pressed hard by the Moslem pirates.

So great was the terror in which his mighty arm was held, that unless a score of Moors crowded upon him, by the mere force of numbers, none would have faced him.

The pirate would have sooner beheld two-thirds of his crew pass over and aid the smuggler than the redoubtable Sancho, the man whose single weapon was a host in itself.

'So,' hissed the pirate, when he came within a few paces of the chief and Sancho, 'thus you beard me? Die, recreant dog!'

He levelled a pistol point blank at the head of his late follower.

Sancho felt the ball tear a furrow across his cheek as it sped forward, and, with a deep cry of rage surging up from his broad chest, he bore down his Moslem foes and sprang towards the pirate.

The latter knew the fearful weight of the uplifted axe.

He knew that, despite his steel breastplate and chain mail, he would be but as a fly beneath the terrible weapon.

He dared not stay for the onset of the angered giant, but with a curse of baffled rage ran among his Moors, and yelled—

'Where are your pistols and matchlocks? Shoot the renegade—shoot him!'

A matchlock ball whizzed past Sancho's head; and knowing that his giant strength would not save him from a bullet, he strode towards the spot where the gallant young smuggler stood, with his back against the bulwarks, battling fiercely with his foes, and cried, as he swung his axe round—

'Now, leap for it; away! I will prevent you treacherous scoundrel from having your life.'

Will thanked him with a look, and cutting a Moslem's pikestaff in two, he sprang upon a gun, from thence to the bulwarks.

He stood and turned to see whether his gallant friend, the Hercules, could force his way through the crowd, and beheld, to his joy, Sancho spring upon the same gun from which his foot had just alighted.

The Colossus paused for a moment, and with a swing of his steel axe, awed back those who would have stayed his leap into the sea.

BLACK EYED SUSAN!

OR, PIRATES ASHORE.

BLACK-EYED SUSAN ON BOARD THE PRIVATEER.

One withering look of hate he bestowed upon the pirate, then with unerring aim, he sent his ponderous weapon flying through the air.

'This,' he said, 'until we meet again; that is the first mark from Sancho, the Avenger.'

The spiked missile struck the miscreant pirate upon his steel corselet, hurling him to the deck, and crushing through the glittering metal as though it had been a sheet of glass.

He waited until he saw the pirate's mouth and nostrils streaming with blood, then turned to Will, and curtly remarked—

'Some of his ribs are broken, I expect. Now, jump; they are loading a dozen weapons for our benefit. Away! he will be safe from mischief until we meet him again.'

Will plunged into his element, the noble ocean, followed by his mysterious friend.

As their bodies cleft the waves, the sharp ring of a dozen matchlocks told what their fate would have been had they stayed another second.

When they came to the surface, the pirate vessel had passed on far ahead, and from her stern the guns were pouring forth death upon the gallant smuggler's boats.

'It will be some time before we are picked up,' remarked Sancho to his companion. 'Should those devils see us, they will come in vain.'

An answer trembled upon Will's lips; but ere he could speak, Sancho called out, suddenly—

'Sink—sink! we are seen.'

Twenty long barrels blazed out from the pirate's side, and the water where the gallant pair had been floating was dotted with minute sprays of foam by the well-aimed bullets.

CHAPTER XC.

THE CONSPIRACY AGAINST WILL'S LIFE—HOW WILL GOT ON BOARD THE BLACK PIRATE SHIP.

THE arrival of the strange visitor at the Crown and Anchor created no excitement in the guests assembled; they were accustomed to all kinds of comers, and each was too intent on business of his own to note what passed between others.

The stranger, for such he seemed to be, as no one recognised him, probably from his disguise, sat some time sipping the hot brandy with which he had been served, his eyes fixed on the door, as though in expectation of some one entering.

At length a tall figure, dressed in a thick reefing jacket, big sea-boots, and a big hairy cap, that half concealed his face, strode carelessly in.

He cast a meaning glance at the stranger, and seated himself close by his side.

'Good evening, friend,' he said, in a half-whisper.

'Good evening,' was the reply. 'You are late.'

'Business detained me.'

'Indeed!'

'Yes; and as I have but little time to spare, we will to business at once. Your name is '——

He whispered in the stranger's ear, so that none might hear that name mentioned.

'That is my name,' said the stranger, fixing his dark eye on his companion. 'Have you come from the admiral?'

'Yes; he has a little job for you.'

'Good! Name it.'

'You know Will Howard?'

'The smug'——

'The same,' said his companion, interrupting him. 'A heavy reward is on his head. You can earn it if you like.'

'Name the conditions.'

'You have a fast ship, a powerful crew, and more, your men will not stand at trifles.'

'What mean you?'

'Simply this, that they will not ask too many questions when gold is to be earned.'

'Certainly not. So you mean, if we cannot do it by fair means, treachery must be employed.'

'Anything, so long as you effect his capture,' answered his companion, a cynical smile wreathing his lips. 'If you can destroy his ship, and take him captive, the reward will be doubled.'

'It shall be done. But you know how I am circumstanced; I am almost penniless. That last affair has almost ruined me.'

'What do you want?'

'I need scarcely say money.'

'Oh! ah! I forgot. The admiral has sent you one hundred pounds. This, mind you, is out of his own private purse.'

'Then I can draw a little on the reward?'

'No, no—that will never do.'

'Why not?'

'It is not known that he has employed you. What has passed between us must never be known.'

'Ah! I see. A little work in the dark, eh? Well, who will give me my reward when I have captured this fell villain?'

'The admiral, of course.'

'And he is to have the praise for doing my work?'

'Exactly.'

'Well, it matters not, so long as I get the money. Give me the hundred pounds, and as much more as you can shell out.'

'That will not be much.'

'How so?'

'I am poor; therefore can give but little on my own account.'

The stranger eyed him closely.

'Come—say fifty,' he said, in an ironical tone.

After shuffling for some time, he handed a packet of notes to the stranger, who seemed satisfied, and they left soon after as they came, separately.

One hour later, a small boat, with a single occupant, might be seen leaving the beach, and heading in the direction of a vessel that lay at anchor in the bay.

'Ahoy, who's there!' cried Will, who stood on the poop as the boat drew near.

The boatman gave a peculiar whistle.

'All right,' said Will; 'pull on the port side.'

The man obeyed; made his boat fast to the ladder, sprang up on deck, and followed Will into the cabin.

For nearly an hour they remained in close conversation; then the man returned to his boat, and pulled ashore in silence.

'Get under weigh immediately,' said Will to his chief mate; 'it is not safe to ride here till morning besides, if it were, it would add to our danger in slipping through the Channel.'

'Ay, very thoughtful, skipper,' said old Sam, elated at the thought of once more getting to sea.

* * * * * *

What Will's intentions were on the purport of the missive the mysterious boatman had brought no one, not even old Sam, knew.

He kept his own thoughts, and allowed the smugglers to surmise what they liked.

A week had passed in this manner, when Captain Will, like his men, began to grow uneasy; they had scarcely seen a vessel during all this time, but now a ship was descried on the starboard bow.

Thick, hazy mists hung on the water, so Will went aloft, glass in hand, to reconnoitre.

It was a large vessel, heavily armed—of what country Will could not determine, but resolved to run down upon her and overhaul her.

While the brig crept unseen towards the strange vessel, Will from the masthead beheld a sight that sent the hot blood from his cheeks and caused every fibre in his frame to thrill with excitement.

Old Sam, who stood with folded arms at the foot of the mainmast, watched the varying hues of his young leader's face.

'Something,' he thought, 'of more than ordinary import is going forward upon that vessel.'

Suddenly a cry of rage fell from the captain's lips; and, dashing the glass to the deck, he glided down a rope and stood beside Old Sam.

'You are strangely altered,' said Sam. 'What has happened?'

'Enough, Sam, to pierce a stronger brain than mine.'

'Its nature, captain?'

'The vessel,' said Will, 'that we are gliding invisibly towards is that of the Black Pirate's.'

Sam uttered a short cry, and his dark eyes shone with fury.

'The fiend!' he hissed through his clenched teeth. 'I shall rend that covering from his face, and'——

Will had never beheld Sam's features so passive as they were in this instance.

'Sam,' he said, interrupting his companion, 'you know this fellow?'

'I do. Did you know how much of that ruffian's early career has blended with your path? But—I'—

Go on, Sam.'

'Some other time. I have said too much already.'

'You have not; you spoke of my father. Tell me—do you know him?'

There was a strange quivering motion perceptible upon Sam's lips as he answered hastily—

'I did.'

Will's heart beat strangely as he gazed into the speaker's dark eyes.

'Sam, he said, 'you are not what you seemed when you were brought upon the flag-ship by the press-gang.'

'Another time,' said Sam, hastily, 'you shall know all. Do not ask me any more questions now, but tell me what you beheld on the deck of that vessel.'

'Ha! what is that? A woman's voice in distress!'

'It is Madeline's.'

'Madeline's?' said Sam, in astonishment; 'and on board that vessel?'

'I fancy so.'

'What fearful mystery is this?' said Sam. 'Should that fiend harm her, the measure of his sins will be filled to overflowing.'

'You speak strangely, Sam.'

'Perhaps so to you. The strangeness may pass away when I tell you that between Madeline and the pirate, as he is called, there exists a close tie of blood.'

'Does he know it?'

'No. Neither must you know more until the fitting hour comes. Now, tell me what you beheld upon the deck.'

'A strange and horrible scene,' said Will. 'A man was bound with cords and a woman was clinging to his neck.'

'Ha! Proceed.'

'That black devil was standing near them, and, from what I could make out, he seemed to be torturing the unhappy girl.'

'—— and furies, drive the ship on faster; we may be too late to save them.'

'We are moving as quickly as the strong wind that is full against us will permit. Behold, we are within musket-shot.'

Peering through the white cloud of vapour, Sam beheld the huge hull of the pirate ship close upon them.

At the moment his eyes discerned the deck of the pirate ship the inhuman wretch was calmly standing by and watching his myrmidons torturing a fair girl.

Sam gnashed his teeth with rage, and his dark face became convulsed with the terrible conflict of harrowing feelings in his heart.

'Fierce monster!' he shouted, as his hand sought the hilt of a heavy blade that hung by his side, 'all the devils in Satan's gang shall not save you from my hand when we meet.'

A hand was placed upon the angry seaman's shoulder; he turned, and beheld Captain Will.

The gallant smuggler, though appalled at the horrible brutality taking place on the pirate's deck, was singularly calm.

'When I have crossed blades with the devil in human form,' he said, with great quietude, 'it will be time for you, Sam, to take your weapon in hand.'

Sam's brow became as black as night, and in his sudden anger he uttered words that he would have given worlds to have recalled.

'My quarrel,' he said angrily, 'dates from a time before you came into the world; therefore I have a prior right in this matter.'

An angry flush came to Will's handsome face.

'I am master here,' he said proudly, 'and all who serve under my flag must obey. I tell you that my hand and no other shall punish this miscreant.'

Sam stamped his foot upon the deck, as he said passionately—

'You do not know to whom you speak!'

'I do,' was the quiet reply; 'I speak to my officer—a man in whom, it appears, I have placed too much trust—one, of all others, who should be the last to use mutinous language.'

The angry chief turned away from Sam, and placed himself in front of a number of gallant lads, who, with drawn weapons, were awaiting the moment to throw themselves upon the pirate's deck.

How they succeeded has been already shown in Chapter 89.

CHAPTER XCI.

THE RED VULTURE IS FOILED IN HIS VILLANY.

WHILST Rodwin Blake was engaged in conversation with the lieutenant in the vessel's dreary hold, the Red Vulture and his companion in crime stood upon the deck of the fated vessel, their faces seemed to be rather paler than usual, and presented a haggard appearance.

As they watched with anxious eyes, the dark clouds rising from the distant horizon, they could not help feeling that some dreadful calamity awaited them.

The wind, which now blew in anything but a favourable direction, seemed to increase, and blew in fitful gusts as it howled mournfully through the cordage which clattered against the masts, and died away in low monotonous sounds.

Each were wrapped in deep thought as they gazed in the direction of the gathering storm, which ere long they felt certain would burst upon them in its fury.

With an impetuous motion Gregory seized the speaking trumpet.

'Boatswain, call all hands,' he cried, fiercely.

The heavy tramp of eager feet rushing up the forward hatchway, told how promptly the pirate captain's injunction had been obeyed.

In the space of a very few minutes the gallant ship lay beating to the wind under double reefed topsails.

Each moment increased the fury of the gale, whilst the rain, in large heavy drops, came down like a deluge, and seemed as though, in its fury, it was striving to beat them to the deck.

The pirate crew looked at each other in superstitious dread, and an awful presentiment of some approaching evil had taken possession of them.

'Close reef the topsails,' thundered Gregory. 'Go you, Despardo, see they haul up the earrings well on to the yard, for I fear we are going to have another fearful night of it.'

Despardo hastened to obey the injunction, leaving the Red Vulture buried in gloom and abject thought.

'Curses on that fellow!' he muttered, half aloud. 'He seems to haunt me night and day, and now even I can feel his withering grasp upon my leg. He says I shall not be freed from his infernal machinations until I land the cussed girl and her mother in England. That I cannot do.'

'It would be madness to venture into the English Channel. No, no—those waters swarm with danger too much now, like a sugar cask with wasps and hornets; and what with king's cruisers on our weather bow, and land-sharks under our lee, I might soon find myself dangling under the brace-block at the fore yard-arm of a line-of-battle ship.'

His soliloquy was abruptly broken by the appearance of Despardo.

'They are snugly reefed,' he said, wiping the rain from his grimy face. 'The earrings are well hauled out, and the lugs well up on the yard, and I have examined every point, and find them securely tied. I think we can stand against a good blow now.'

'I am not afraid of the storm, Despardo; but you know that ill-luck hangs on to us like grim death to a nigger, and so he will as long as we have that woman aboard. I was in hopes the wind would have held favourable a few hours longer, and then we should have been able to run through the gut; but now the wind blows right dead in our teeth.'

'Are you going to run through the Straights of Gibraltar, then?' inquired Despardo, in surprise.

'I am.'

'Then the sooner this wind changes the better, for I don't much like beating about this part. What do you intend doing when we get through the Straits?'

'I thought of running along the coast of Barbary, and leaving her in charge of one of the many friends I am acquainted with there.'

'Oh! indeed,' said Despardo. 'Then you don't mean to ask my permission whether you may thus dispose of her?'

'Why should I?' inquired Gregory, coolly.

The eye of Despardo lit with a lurid glow, and he eyed the captain sternly as he listened to these words, and gazed with a look of mingled rage and deadly hate upon the strangely repulsive features of the captain.

'Oh! I see it all now,' he said, fiercely. 'You want to have all the game to yourself. Ah—ah!' he laughed, savagely; 'but you'll not do with me as you please; you shall find Despardo a match for the Red Vulture.'

'What?' cried the pirate, in a frenzy of rage, 'do you think I will submit to this?'

'I don't clearly understand you,' was the cool rejoinder.

'You very soon will, then,' said Despardo, hoarsely.

'Oh, indeed, we shall see. But this is no time to bandy words; we have sworn to stick to each other through thick and thin, fire and water, calm or storm, and now I think we had better make it up over a glass, for I feel as though I want something to warm me. I am drenched to the skin.'

'I am not much better,' said Despardo, eyeing his dripping clothes.

'Boatswain!' cried Saunders.'

And as that individual promptly appeared, he cried—

'Just keep an eye to the vessel for a few minutes, and see that she is kept cleverly full and by, and if she should break off, if only one point, or there is the least change in the weather, let me know directly.'

'Ay, ay, sir,' replied that worthy functionary, as he dashed the rain from his sou'-wester, 'I s'pose if I see any signs of a strange craft or anything of that sort I am to give you a hail, your honour?'

'Certainly,' said Gregory, as he disappeared down the companion ladder.

The storm still raged with unabated fury, and the vessel made but slow progress through the water, as she lay under double-reefed topsails, labouring heavily as she breasted the billows defiantly, whilst the sea assumed the form of one vast plain thickly intersected with high and lofty snow-capped peaks.

When Despardo got to the bottom of the ladder the cold sweat stood in thick beads on his haggard lineaments, and he was compelled to clutch the steps of the ladder for support.

A feeling that he could not overcome crept over him, and he almost feared to enter the cabin.

At length, mustering courage, he stepped into the cabin.

And now he started back as he beheld the scene that was presented to his gaze on entering the cabin.

There stood Gregory, near the after lockers, his left arm encircling the small waist of the lovely Susan, whilst with his right hand he was endeavouring to wrench the dagger from her grasp, which she held in her delicate little hand.

Without waiting for a moment's reflection he sprang upon him, and having seized him by the collar, he bore him to the deck, and held a pistol closely to his head menacingly.

'Would you murder me?' cried Gregory, in terror.

'I will if you offer to touch that girl again,' growled Despardo fiercely, whilst his eyes glowed with the fierceness of a hungry wolf. 'If you dare touch her again I'll blow out your senseless brains.'

'Let me rise,' said Gregory, seeing him lag in his purpose.

'Not till you have sworn ——'.

A scream from Susan as she fell fainting to the floor caused Despardo to turn his head.

In that moment Gregory saw his chance; with a violent jerk he disengaged himself from the knee of his adversary, and mustering all his strength, with one final effort he grappled with Despardo, threw him to the floor, and placed his knee upon his chest.

'What have you got to say for yourself now?' inquired Gregory, in an exulting tone; 'suppose I send a bullet through you brainless skull, eh? Do you think it will be more than just?'

Despardo could only reply with a scowl.

Gregory could have easily settled his score with him, but he knew full well it would not be to his advantage to do so, for one without the other they would be powerless; besides, the crew on hearing the report might rush to the cabin, and the sight of their murdered officer might creat a mutiny, especially after the strange incidents they had witnessed.

The voice of the boatswain caused him to start.

The vessel lurched heavily.

'It's coming on to blow great guns, captain,' cried the boatswain down the companion; 'we must take more canvas off her, or else the sticks will soon go over the side.'

Gregory sprang to his feet and rushed upon deck, and Despardo followed as quickly as he was able, for he had been so fixed under the table, that it took him some few moments to extricate himself.

At first they could not see anything, for a pitchy darkness reigned around, and they had to wait a few seconds until their eyes became a little used to the darkness.

On either side of the tempest-tossed vessel the angry billows rose majestically, and threatened to crush the gallant craft with the fury with which they dashed against her sides.

All around presented a black mass of roaring billows, their tops crested with snow-white seething foam as each angry wave rose, and then rolled away with a hissing sound.

Whilst the threatening aspect of the sky added to the dismal scene, for the dark black masses of sable clouds overspread the canopy of the heavens.

Every sail was now furled save the main-topsail, and that was taken in to the close reef.

And the little vessel lay to in the furious gale, whilst many anxious eyes watched eagerly for the least sign indicating the assuagement of the storm.

The crew were, most of them, crouching under the lee of the long boat, or in other parts of the vessel, where the least shelter might be obtained from the heavy showers of spray that blew furiously over her bows and weather bulwarks.

Whilst matters were going on thus on deck, a scene of a different nature was being enacted in the hold below, which we must leave for another chapter.

CHAPTER XCII.

RODWIN BLAKE AND HIS MYRMIDONS HAVE RECOURSE TO DESPERATE MEANS.

It was a terrible time for Rodwin and the gallant luff in the damp, fœtid dungeon of the ship.

The storm still raged furiously.

The heat became oppressive.

The stench of the bilge-water amounted almost to suffocation.

Damp vapours floated about in the murky air, and the oaths and fearful execrations of the pirates added greatly to the misery of the lieutenant.

In the meantime Rodwin Blake made good use of his ears. He had crept close to the hatchway, where above the howling of the wind, he could hear Gregory giving orders to his crew.

He could hear the 'pat, pat' of feet as the men hurried to and fro on deck to execute their various duties.

'Confound it!' he hissed savagely, as he groped his way down the ladder and crawled to the place allotted him; 'they have hove her to under the close-reefed main-topsail. The hands will not have to go aloft again until the storm lulls.'

'That makes things no worse,' remarked the luff. 'How do you propose taking the ship?'

'I was in hopes the hands would have gone aloft. We could have forced the hatch, made for the cabin, secured the captain, armed ourselves, and kept the men aloft until they chose to join us.'

'And if they would not mutiny?'

'We could shoot them; it would be their own choice.'

The lieutenant said no more; he longed to be free, but he did not care to resort to such murderous means.

Besides, he felt in his heart that the wretch with whom he was forced to associate would not scruple in insulting Susan, even though he had professed to be her friend.

'Can we not take the ship by any other means asked the luff, after a moment's pause.

'Well, we might; but I cannot see clearly how, yet.'

'If the hatches yield easily, we might secure the watch on deck and batten the watch below in the forecastle.'

'That might be done if we were sure the men had turned in; if not, the least sound will bring them on deck, and what could we do amongst so many?'

'We have not tried.'

'Neither do I mean to,' answered Rodwin, sullenly. 'I have a better plan in view.'

So saying, he crept towards the bulk-head and tried each plank, through the chinks of which he could here and there force his finger.

One of them he found yielded a little.

He took one of his manacles and gave it a prize.

It opened more.

The wood was very old and eaten with the rusty nails.

Presently it gave way; and Rodwin, who, spite of his wounded wrist, was very powerful, soon removed another.

Thrusting his huge body through the opening made, he found himself in another part of the hold.

The ropes, blocks, and cordage told him he was in the fore peak, and an examination by groping round the vessel's side to ascertain its form assured him such was the case.

He was in that part of the hold immediately beneath the forecastle, where the sailors slept.

A fiendish thought seized him on making this discovery.

By climbing on to a transverse beam he found he was enabled to reach the deck above, which formed the forecastle floor.

A few minutes served to find the hatch, and a slight pressure told him that it was easily moved.

Groping his way back to the dungeon, he whispered huskily to his men—

'Now, lads, I have found a road to liberty; the pirates are asleep, a sleep from which they must never more awaken.'

The rovers needed no further explanation.

They fully comprehended the meaning of their leader's words.

Noiselessly shaking off the irons that Rodwin had previously loosened, they followed him through the opening in the bulkhead.

Blake soon mounted the beam, and, assisted by a stalwart ruffian, raised the hatch and slid it noiselessly aside.

Pausing for a moment to listen if the pirates breathed, and having satisfied himself that they were not suspected, he thrust his head up the hatchway until his eyes were clear of the floor.

A lamp slung from the beam above shed a dull light around, the motion of the ship causing it to flicker greatly, but giving sufficient light for Rodwin to see the faces of the pirates turned towards him.

They were asleep.

Such a sleep as only the watchworn sailor knows, into which they fall so soon as they turn in their hammock, and from which they awaken at the first sound of the boatswain's voice.

Rodwin drew himself cautiously up.

His keen eye had discovered a large bowie knife stuck in the belt of one of the sleepers.

In an instant his hand was upon it, and before the ruffian that followed him had risen to his feet, the sleeper's head was almost severed from his body.

Then the murderous work commenced.

The pirates' long knives were brought into active use.

Two minutes sufficed to change the sleeping hammocks into winding-sheets.

Rodwin Blake gave a demoniacal smile as he looked around at the work of himself and his trusty confederates.

'One task is accomplished,' he muttered, hoarsely. 'Now, lads, to the deck.'

The sound of a pair of heavy sea boots overhead warned them that some one was approaching.

'It is Despardo,' he whispered to his men. 'Keep close. Let us hear what he wants.'

They had scarcely drawn back when Despardo thrust his head over the scuttle hatch, and shouted—

'All hands wear ship.'

'Ay, ay!' growled Blake in an assumed tone. Then added, glancing at his men, 'we will wear her for you.'

Despardo could only distinguish the 'Ay, ay!' for the wind howled fearfully, and the sea lashed over the bows, as the vessel rode over the foam-capped billows.

The Red Vulture had been hove to, and Gregory, who, since the quarrel with Despardo, had been keeping a good look out, found that a strong current was driving them on to a reef of rocks.

By wearing the ship and running her away a few points, Gregory hoped to clear them, though, bringing the ship round before the wind in such a sea was dangerous in the extreme.

'Now, lads,' whispered Rodwin, 'we must be careful, or our plans are all spoiled. Attend well to me, and all will go right.'

'Now then, tumble up!' thundered the voice of Despardo, impatient at the delay.

'Ay, you will see us in time,' growled Rodwin, a malicious gleam darting from his eye.

CHAPTER XCIII.

TOM HATCHETT BETRAYED IN THE HANDS OF CAPTAIN CROSSTREE.

BOOM! boom! It was the signal gun; a man-of-war was making for the Sound.

Something of importance was going on, if we may judge from the numerous groups that gathered near the water-side, and the hurrying to and fro of messengers from the port admiral's quarters to the fort.

*   *   *   *   *

Captain Crosstree, after the engagement with the pirate, put into Gibraltar to repair damages and refit masts and rigging, and while there he by chance scented out that Tom Hatchett the smuggler was in the vicinity.

He would have escaped, however, had not a treacherous friend betrayed him.

One night, as he was returning to his boat, a party in ambush seized him and conveyed him to the frigate.

'Well,' said Captain Crosstree, 'we have found you; ay, caught you at last. You will swing for it this time for a certainty.'

'How so? On what charge do you arrest me?'

'You are proclaimed as a smuggler and pirate. You have fired upon a king's ship,' was the reply.

Captain Tom turned deathly pale at these words.

His ship and crew were out of danger, but now he had no chance of escape.

The captain narrowly watched his changing countenance.

He was a shrewd man, and strongly suspicious.

As a natural consequence, he had already concluded that the first word Hatchett would utter would be a lie, and he was prepared to answer him.

Tom Hatchett quailed beneath his searching glance.

He felt the hopelessness of his position, and trembled for the consequences should he not escape.

'Well,' he said, trying to look straight in the captain's face, 'you will, of course, let me have liberty till I am found guilty.'

This boldness seemed to astound the captain.

'You speak well,' he said, sternly; 'but you forget you have not yet satisfied me who your allies are.'

Tom's brow darkened.

'Who told you I had any? And, if so, who made you my judge?'

'I am no judge, and well for you it is so.'

'How is that?'

'Because I should hang you at once.'

'Ah, for why?' interrogated Tom, fiercely, forgetting for the moment where he was.

'Because that hang-dog look of yours proclaims you guilty.'

'Curse your insults!' hissed Hatchett, savagely, his brow corrugating, and his large white teeth grating horribly. 'I should like to twist your ugly neck!'

The captain gave a low mocking laugh.

It stung Hatchett to the very soul.

His blood began to course wildly through his veins, and his fierce eye glistened serpent-like.

The captain did not think for a moment that he meditated mischief. He did not know the smuggler's fiery nature.

Before he could either think or conceive any idea of his intentions, Hatchett was upon him, and clutched him by the throat.

The captain's sword was by his side, but Hatchett took care that he should not use it.

He held him like a vice, and caused him to double up with pain.

'Curse you! You would like to choke me with a rope, would you? But I'll drive the vile breath out of your carrion carcase!' hissed the smuggler.

Snatching a tompion mallet from its bracket, he wielded it in fiendish triumph over the head of the almost lifeless Captain Crosstree.

Then raising his arm to its full extent, so as to give more force to the blow, he prepared to bring it down with crashing violence on to the bare head of the captain.

Luckily for Captain Crosstree, the sentry at the cabin door had heard their loud talking, and listened.

From listening he got to peeping, and he had fortunately contrived to open the door sufficiently, and in time to see the captain's danger.

To lose a moment would be endangering the captain's life.

He gazed in silent horror at the deadly weapon, poised high in the air, ready to deal the fatal blow.

Without a word he pushed open the door.

With a bound, like that of a hunted deer, he sprang forward, and with one blow of his fist, felled Hatchett to the deck.

So sudden and unexpected had the blow been dealt, that Captain Tom, half-stunned, could not imagine from whence it came.

As he rolled his eyes round, and rested them on the marine, a volley of oaths burst from his lips.

'Curse you!' he hissed: 'you shall pay for this.'

The marine, having raised the captain's head, so that he should not choke, then sprang upon Hatchett, and held him down, whilst he called lustily for help.

His cry was soon answered.

A host of blue jackets and marines, and a dozen or so of the officers, soon made their appearance, and scrambled over each other in their endeavours to be first.

The smuggler was at once heavily ironed, and placed under arrest.

Captain Crosstree was conveyed to his state-room, and placed in a swinging cot.

The first lieutenant and sailing master, after holding a short conference, came to the decision that they had better return home, and report the circumstances.

Tom Hatchett wondered what could be their intentions, when the heaving motion of the vessel told him that they were at sea.

His last thoughts were that they would return to England.

When one of the sailors informed him of this, he turned pale, and trembled.

'Death, death,' he muttered 'will be my fate, and I cannot escape it. Ten thousand curses light on the chance that brought me here. The fiend of darkness seems to be working a spell against me. But I will not die without a struggle—I will not yield to the grim monster tamely—I will not die alone. These hands must once more wear the crimson gloves.'

He shuddered at his own fiendish thoughts, and threw himself down on the coil of hard rope that constituted his bed.

*   *   *   *   *   *   *

The same boom that had aroused the peaceful inhabitants of the town gave Hatchett to understand they were in port.

The smuggler, who had been confined in a close hold, was not sorry when informed that he would be allowed to walk on the main deck a few hours, to stretch his cramped limbs and breathe a little fresh air.

But when he heard from the captain's own lips who had betrayed him, he shook like a reed stricken by the wind.

'B—t him!' he muttered, his teeth grinding together like millstones. 'By the powers of darkness, if I live I will be revenged!'

He hurriedly paced to and fro the narrow limits assigned him, and glanced occasionally at the open ports.

'What would I give to be free!' he thought. 'Oh, liberty, how dear thou art, especially to those who do not possess thee! Would to heaven I could free my hands from these shackles, and could have but one short hour of liberty.'

It was growing late, and dusky shadows began to fall upon the waters.

Hatchett looked wistfully towards the dim outlines of the shore.

Boats were passing to and fro.

All around seemed to be so happy.

The sailors over his head were hurrying about with busy tread, humming snatches of songs or whistling some favourite tune.

The smuggler alone seemed sad.

His heart was heavy as lead.

His brain was almost turned to madness.

Suddenly a smile irradiated his dusky visage.

Some thought has beamed its cheerful rays into the dark recesses of his heart.

And yet it would appear he had no cause to rejoice, for in one short half-hour he had to return to his dreary dungeon.

It so happened that the marine who kept guard over him was the very same who rescued the captain.

With musket loaded and bayonet fixed he paced to and fro.

His watchful eye was alert to the least movement of his prisoner.

Something at length attracted his attention, and he stood for a moment with his back to the smuggler.

In that moment Tom saw his chance.

His dark eyes lit with a fiery glow.

His teeth grated horribly, and a demoniac smile played upon his features.

Clenching his hands firmly, and gathering all his strength, he, with a desperate effort, snapped the chain that held his wrists, and with a savage growl sprang upon the sentry.

Seizing him by the throat, he bore him down on his knees, and, though the marine tried to free himself, he clutched him so tightly that he could neither move nor speak.

The veins of his face became black and swollen.

His tongue protruded from his mouth, and his eyes almost started from their sockets.

Then a convulsive quiver shook his frame.

The death rattle sounded in his throat, and all was over.

He was dead.

Hatchett gave a ghastly smile when he had completed his fiendish work.

'So perish all who thwart me,' he hissed; 'now to save my own life.'

Unfastening the bayonet from the dead marine's musket, he placed it in his belt, climbed through one of the open ports, and dropped noiselessly into the water.

Cautious as was this movement, the quick ear of the sentry on deck heard the rippling of the water, and looked over the side.

It was too dark for him to distinguish more than that a man was overboard.

He could not see his face.

Hatchett was a good swimmer, and he struck out boldly for the shore.

He was the more invigorated by a sudden bustle on board the frigate, and the flashing of lights as they were carried past the ports.

That they had discovered the dead body of their comrade he did not doubt, and that they were searching for himself at once flashed to his mind.

Desperately he renewed his efforts, but the shore was some distance, and he made towards a group of boats that lay at anchor midway between him and the beach.

He was rapidly nearing them, and buoyed himself up with the hope that if he could get into one of them he might lie concealed until all was quiet, then pull ashore and pass through the town in the night.

But this hope died away, as the splash of oars fell on his ear, and on turning he beheld, to his horror, a boat fully manned pulling swiftly towards him.

An officer stood in the bow of the boat directing the men in their movements, and as they drew near, he could hear him give each order plainly.

Hatchett's case was now desperate in the extreme.

He began to feel a weakness creeping upon him at the very moment all his strength was required.

With a bitter curse, he bent himself to his task again.

A few yards more, and he would gain one of the boats.

But his pursuers were gaining fast upon him.

His strength was fast failing him.

His clothes were weighing him down.

His heart sank within him.

That he could not hold out much longer he became too painfully aware.

A hazy mist began to float before his heavy eyes.

Nature had become thoroughly exhausted, and he was relapsing into a dreamy state of unconsciousness when a strong arm grasped him by the collar.

A gruff voice sounded in his ear, and he found himself a prisoner.

But the stubborn unyielding nature of the smuggler captain would not allow him to submit to his captors without a struggle.

Another pair of sturdy hands had seized upon him, and was assisting in dragging him into the boat.

Another moment and he would be totally in their power.

Then a circumstance that he had forgotten occurred to him.

He remembered that he had placed the bayonet in his belt.

Quick as thought he grasped it and plunged it into the breast of one of the men, and drawing it quickly, thrust it into the shoulder of the other.

With a cry of agony they both relaxed their hold, and before their comrades could recover from their alarm, Hatchett dived under the boat's keel, came up the other side, and swam towards his place of rescue.

Although panting from exhaustion, Hatchett did not lose his presence of mind.

Naturally crafty, he soon thought of a plan for deceiving the sailors.

As might be supposed, they were looking for him on the side where he had disappeared.

Taking advantage of this, he exerted all his remaining strength, and soon reached the nearest of the boats anchored.

Luckily a piece of rope hung over the stern, and grasping this, he drew himself close under her quarter, leaving only sufficient of his head out of water to allow him to breathe.

The sailors cursed and swore horribly at losing the murderer of their shipmates.

They pulled diligently round, and passed once or twice so near to him that he could have reached out his hand and touched them.

At length, after pulling round several times, and having searched most of the boats, they returned gloomily to the frigate.

Hatchett watched them gleefully.

He drew breath freely.

When they had proceeded far enough to render him secure, he scrambled into the boat, took off his clothes, and wrung them.

The boat he had so fortunately selected was half-decked over, had a mast, stepped sails bent, and was moored with a rope cable.

This he soon cut, and let the boat drift out to sea with the ebb tide.

Thus far clear, he set the sails, and as the breeze was freshening, he edged along under lee of the land.

As he sat at the helm, guiding his solitary bark, thoughts of the past floated through his mind.

He pondered over the strange incidents that had placed him there, and he began to think of the future.

'Curse them all for a set of fiends!' he muttered, savagely. 'I have lost both ship and men through their officiousness, but I am not unavenged. Three of them have atoned for it with their blood.'

'Yes,' he continued, thoughtfully, 'I am now alone, penniless, friendless, and at sea, as it were in a shell. To whom shall I fly for help—of whom shall I ask for succour?

'Ah, I have it,' he cried, his eye brightening. 'Old Doggrass is in my debt. He shall act honourably and dup up, or feel how deeply I can sting.'

He glanced at the bayonet as he spoke, and a cruel smile wreathed his lips.

When he made this resolve, he was far out of reach of his pursuers, and now his fear had subsided, the cravings of hunger took possession of him.

He had eaten little of the hard biscuit and cold water that had formed his prison diet.

BLACK EYED SUSAN

OR, PIRATES ASHORE.

WILL HOWARD FANCIES HE SEES A SAIL.

His mind was too worried to eat.

Now that he was free, he felt as hungry as a wolf.

Fastening the helm, he crawled into the narrow place that formed the cabin, and afforded only sufficient room for two people to sleep.

As he crawled in on his hands and knees—for it was not high enough to sit upright in, let alone walk —he was startled by what appeared to be the growl of a dog.

This banished his hope of finding anything to eat, and caused him no little alarm.

It was no enviable position to be cooped up in that narrow place with an animal of doubtful size and amiability.

But Hatchett did not dwell long on this.

He still had the bayonet in his possession, and he commenced poking about with it, having first wrapped a thick woollen scarf round his wrist, in case the monster might seize him.

As yet he had met nothing but wood; but on making a side-thrust, the point of the bayonet came in contact with something soft.

The next moment a growl, not of a savage, as he had imagined, but of an angry man unpleasantly disturbed from a sound sleep, made him draw back.

'H—l and furies!' growled the man, 'what are you up to?'

With the assurance that he had a man to deal with, Hatchett gathered fresh courage.

'Sorry to disturb you, my hearty,' he replied.

'D—n you, and your sorrow too!' growled the man.

Hatchett judged from this that he had a rough customer to deal with.

'Well, you're not over polite,' he said.

'So you'll find, if you don't sheer off,' was the reply.

Captain Hatchett was no coward, but the fierce tone of the speaker caused him to tremble a little, and to consult in his own mind the best means of defence.

CHAPTER XCIV.

THE STRUGGLE ON BOARD THE RED VULTURE.— GALLANT HEROISM OF SUSAN.—THE MONSTER OF THE DEEP.

'Now, lads, prepare for a struggle if it is necessary,' said Rodwin, huskily, as he concealed the blade of his long knife beneath his dress, keeping the haft ready to his hand—an example followed by his men. 'We may meet with some resistance,' he added. 'If so, you know how to act.'

'Never fear,' growled the wretches whom he addressed as lads; 'we will end as we began.'

A heavy sea striking the vessel in the fore channels caused her to lurch heavily, and Rodwin, looking up the hatchway, saw that the night was pitchy dark.

Everything seemed in favour of the rovers.

Could they but once get aft without being observed they felt sure of an easy victory.

Such, however, was not to be the case.

Rodwin had scarcely left the scuttle hatch, and taken two paces along the deck, when a figure sprang up from behind the riding bitts, and aimed a terrific blow at his head.

Had the blow taken effect, Rodwin's career would have been ended; as it was, he fell to the deck, and scrambled to his feet again, half drowned.

'Confound you, you skulking hounds! I'll learn you to move sharp,' cried a voice that he immediately recognised as Despardo's; 'man the braces, you lubbers; we are drifting on the rocks.'

'Curse you!' exclaimed Rodwin, forgetting in the anger of the moment the caution he should have preserved.

Despardo might not have recognised the voice; the shrieking of the blast, the roar of the bursting surge, and creaking of the spars, as the vessel laboured heavily, drowned the sound; but a circumstance occurred that revealed all.

A vivid flash of lightning, that for an instant rent the sable clouds, shone full on Rodwin's face, then again all was dark.

Both stood for a moment as though spell-bound.

At first both seemed rooted to the spot.

Rodwin was the first to recover.

In an instant his left hand closed on the knife, and he made a deadly thrust at Despardo.

'Die, villain!' he hissed, his white teeth gleaming in the darkness.

But Despardo stepped back, and, aided by a lurch of the vessel that sent him sprawling in the lee scuppers, thus escaped the deadly aim.

Gregory was pacing the deck with nervous strides, swearing within himself at the sluggishness of his crew, little dreaming what was passing forward.

The voice of his chief officer aroused him to a sense of danger.

'Help! mutiny!' shouted Despardo, believing the crew forward had assisted in Rodwin's release. 'Quick, or we are lost!'

Gregory Saunders stood for a moment stagnated.

The word mutiny had filled his soul with dread.

The strict discipline of his ship had kept his men hitherto staunch to his flag.

A twofold danger had now fallen upon him—a mutinous crew and a reef of rocks almost aboard them.

Saunders's temper was not the one to allow him to stand by ruminating.

With the bound of a panther he leapt forward, and springing his sword, which he was scarcely was without sleeping or waking, prepared to use on the refractory pirates.

As he passed the long-boat's bow, a stinging laugh brought him to a stand.

His name was uttered in a well-known voice, and he found himself face to face with Rodwin Blake.

'Ah! the prisoners escaped,' was his hasty ejaculation.

'Ay, prisoners no longer, but free men!' yelled Rodwin, brandishing his knife. 'This ship is ours; I am captain now.'

'Never!' gasped Gregory, almost choked with passion. 'When I am dead you may command.'

'Then die!' hissed Rodwin, fiercely, a savage glitter darting from his eye. 'We cannot both live and hold command.'

Gregory parried the deadly thrust with his sword, and shouted to the remainder of his men, who were listening to the angry altercation, to seize upon the prisoners.

'Let them!' yelled one of the rovers, the same stalwart fellow that had assisted to raise the hatch. 'If they can do it, why, then'——

A pistol-bullet fired by one of the Red Vulture's men passed close to the speaker's ears, breaking off his speech abruptly, and within an inch of silencing him for ever.

Mystified as to the fate of their companion, the pirates fell to in real earnest.

Rodwin Blake rallied his men, and a fight, bloody and cruel, commenced.

Fearful oaths came from the combatants on both sides.

Groans and shrieks of agony, mingled with the fierce blast.

Then, the thunder pealed forth, the lightning in flashes rent the sky, and the ship, totally at the mercy of the waves, her helm having been lashed hard down fell off in the trough of the sea, and pitched and rolled in such a manner, as to threaten instant destruction to all on board.

Rodwin cheered on his men, unmindful of the storm, his object being to gain possession of the after part of the vessel, where the arms were stowed.

The pirate crew still outnumbered his little band, but what few there were were desperate to the extreme.

In the meantime the cabin had been taken possession of by another.

It was Lieutenant Fordham.

He had taken no part in the fray.

His sole object was to preserve Susan from the hands of her ruthless captors, or to perish with her in the attempt.

Fordham had marked well all that passed.

He had surveyed the white, seething breakers that were now close to the ship.

He had taken the bearings by the compass, and he saw that nothing but fatal ruin could befal the ship.

In the midst of this confusion, and while the struggle for mastery was at its height, the main topsail split with a noise like a discharged cannon.

The mainmast began to creak and groan with the rolling of the ship.

Two of the weather backstays were carried away, and the main topmast sprung above the cap.

Deprived of the only bit of canvas that could be shown in the teeth of such a gale, the Red Vulture turned broadside to the sea.

A heavy wave broke on board her, and swept her deck; and as the gallant ship quivered with the violence of the shock, the mainmast went by the board.

Lieutenant Fordham was on the poop.

He clung, with suspended breath, to a stanchion, and when the mass of water had rolled away, he saw that the deck had been swept of nearly all its occupants.

A shout at that moment made him aware that he was recognised; and Gregory, who had been washed as far aft as the chestree, and was clinging to the main tack cleats, rushed towards him.

'Away, fiend!' thundered Fordham, seizing a handspike from its becket—"away! or, by heavens, I'll brain you!'

Gregory gave a fiendish laugh.

'Ah! you can bark well,' he said, with a sneer.

'And bite, you will find,' interposed Fordham, a deadly fire lighting in his eye, as, tightening his grasp on the handspike, he met the blow of Gregory's sword, and, with a blow, sent him reeling to the bulwarks.

Scarce rid of one enemy, the young luff found himself opposed to another.

It was Despardo.

He bore Gregory no love, but seeing the captain used thus roughly made his blood boil.

'Scoundrel! what mean you by this?'

'Need you ask?'

'I demand.'

'Then take my answer.'

So saying, Fordham levelled a blow at Despardo's head, but, ere it struck, the handspike was wrenched from his grasp.

The lieutenant was surprised at seeing who had done this.

'Rodwin Blake,' he said, huskily, 'what mean you?'

'Enough blood has been spilt already,' was Rodwin's reply. 'There is but three of us left. If we have any regard for our lives, we had better be friends.'

'Friends!' iterated Despardo, 'how can we?'

'Well, friends to ourselves, then. You see the hopeless condition of the ship; these rocks will soon be our graves—combined, we may yet run her clear.'

Fordham listened in silence. He would have dared anything for Susan, but he feared for her safety in the power of two such men.

'Well, what say you, youngster?' asked Rodwin, observing Fordham's silence.

'There are three of you without me,' said the luff. 'It ill becomes the officers of a king's ship to become a pirate.'

Gregory was just recovering from the blow, and Fordham had included him in the trio.

'Cut the whelp down!' growled Gregory.

He had scarcely uttered the words, when Fordham leapt down into the steerage, and entered the cabin, closing the door after him.

Susan was sitting by the table, wringing her hands in despair—her dark eyes filled with tears—her tresses hanging dishevelled over her shoulders.

'Oh, tell me—are those wretches coming down?' she cried, piteously.

'They are.'

And before he could say more, a thundering knocking was heard at the cabin door.

'Where can we go? Can we not fly?' she asked, in despair.

'Alas! no. There is no escape but by the cabin window.'

'Then I will choose that way. It will be more preferable to trust to the mercy of the waves than to such wretches. Farewell, kind protector—farewell!'

So saying, and before Fordham could stay her, she leapt on the transom lockers, dashed open one of the windows, and leapt headlong into the sea.

Fordham stood for a moment, petrified.

'Lost! lost!' he cried, tearing his hair—'lost for ever!'

He glanced out of the port, and saw her rise to the surface, her tiny hands clasping a portion of shattered spar.

'Brave girl!' muttered Fordham, 'with thee I will peril all.'

And ere the words had left his lips he was by her side—one arm entwining her slender waist, the other clasping the spar.

Swiftly the current swept them onward, and it was a great relief to the luff when he found they had cleared the reef.

On board the Red Vulture the fore topsail had

been loosed, and they were evidently trying to save the ship during a partial lull.

'Thank heaven, we shall yet be safe,' said Fordham, as his keen eye caught sight of land.

But a motion of the water near him caused him to look that way.

Horror! The blood froze in his veins.

A shark was rapidly approaching.

The hope that had buoyed him now died away, and his heart sank within him as the huge monster appeared.

CHAPTER XCV.

THE STORM—CAST ON THE ROCKS—AN EPOCH IN THE LIFE OF LITTLE JACK.

THE night was black, and the awful thunder rolled, while the forked lightning's vivid flashes flitted round the ill-fated brig Antelope.

She drove before the wind; her sails were torn to ribbons; her mainmast rocking in the gale, snapped and went by the board; her rudder was unshipped, and she was left to the mercy of the raging waves.

At length she drove upon the rocks, and went to pieces.

Day broke on the wreck, but the hazy atmosphere and the drizzling rain added to the dreary aspect of the surrounding cliffs.

Little Jack was one of the few survivors; he had lashed himself to the trail-yard, which snapped asunder as it went overboard.

The furious billows dashed him to and fro; one wave would wash him on shore, while the succeeding one would take him out to sea again; but, fortunately, the tide was ebbing, and, at length, a friendly wave cast him so far on shore that the next failed to reach him.

Here he lay some time insensible; at length returning reason showed him his forlorn situation. He disengaged himself from the fragment of the mast to which he was attached, and, crawling into a crevice of the rock, sought a temporary shelter from the pouring rain.

Here he pondered on his hopeless condition. Without food, without shelter, and scantily clad, even hope seemed to desert him; and, reclining his drooping head on his trembling hand, he gave way to despair.

The boisterous weather gradually moderated; the clouds divided, and a gleam of sunshine lighted up the rocky eminence.

More dead than alive he crawled from the crevice; the sunny ray cheered his heart; he knelt in prayer, and returned thanks for his deliverance from death.

He gazed upon the wreck, which lay within a quarter of a mile of the main land, but not a living soul was to be seen.

He thought he heard a sound beside that of the murmuring waves—he listened—he was not deceived. The distant chiming of church bells struck upon his ears—he sprang on his feet—hope and joy at once took possession of his breast; he was near the habitation of man. He ascended the cliff in order to ascertain his situation, and, to his great joy, discovered he was within a mile of a village; thither he bent his way, weak and fainting from fatigue and hunger.

He arrived at the door of a fisher's hut: he paused, and feared to knock, lest he should meet a refusal. At length he mustered sufficient resolution, and tapped gently at the door.

'Who's there?' inquired Jane, the cottager's only daughter, as she opened the latticed window.

'A poor shipwrecked sailor boy,' replied Jack, 'who craves both food and shelter.'

'Wait awhile, and I'll tell my father,' said the gentle girl, as she disappeared from the window.

A few moments elapsed, the door flew open, and little Jane, followed by her father, appeared.

'What did he say? food and shelter?' ejaculated the old fisherman, as he approached; 'he shall have both, poor boy.' As he concluded, he bent an eye of compassion on Jack. 'But, tell me, boy,' continued he, 'where does the wreck lie?'

Jack pointed in the direction, and added it was within a mile of the village.

'Here, lass,' cried the fisherman, 'take this poor lad, and give him some dry clothes and something to eat, while I go down to the seashore and see if anything can be saved from the wreck, before our land-sharks hear of it and go down to plunder.'

'I'll take in the poor boy, and get him some breakfast,' said the girl. 'Come, poor sailor boy,' continued she; 'lean on my shoulder, and I'll lead you in.' He did so, and the affectionate girl conveyed him into the cottage.

Old Keeler, the fisherman, took his oars, called up his boy, and bent his way to the sea-shore.

Here he beheld the hulk of the vessel jammed between the rocks; she was now lying high and dry.

He approached her, but not a living soul was visible.

He went on board, and descended into the cabin.

Heavens! what a sight was there!—the lifeless bodies of the many who had been unable to escape from the wreck.

He found two chests uninjured; with difficulty he got these on deck.

The tide was now rapidly rising, and his boat being brought alongside he lowered them into it, and made the best of his way homeward.

On his way he was observed by Black Bill and some other wreckers, who immediately guessed what had happened, and without delay spread the news through the village.

The wreckers were soon on the alert, and hastening down to the strand, commenced the work of plunder.

When Keeler reached the cottage, he found the boy much recovered.

He opened the broken chest, and supplied him with clothing.

Jack was anxious to go to the wreck, in case there should be any living person on board.

Keeler knew it was useless; but not wishing to check the good feelings of the youth, he agreed to accompany him.

They went by a bye-path, not wishing to meet any of the plunderers.

The boat was therefore sent afloat from a small creek which ran alongside of the cliff.

They could observe the wreckers busily engaged in plundering the vessel.

They turned from the scene with disgust, and ascending part of the cliff, intended to watch their departure.

Jack made a sudden pause. Keeler looked at him with surprise, and inquired the cause.

'I am not quite sure,' said Jack, 'but I could

SCENE.—The Rover's State Room, for the Play of the "Red Rover."—Gratis with No. 36 of "Black-Eyed Susan."

almost swear I saw a hand raised above yon low crag.'

They looked towards the spot. Jack was not mistaken; a hand was seen raised for a moment.

'I am right! I am right!' exclaimed Jack; and, hastening toward the spot, he descended quickly, followed by Keeler.

'Gracious heaven! it is my captain!' exclaimed Jack. 'Thanks to Providence, he lives! he lives!'

He threw himself by his side and raised him. Keeler applied the brandy-bottle to his lips; then lifting him in their arms, they carried him to the boat, and shortly after brought him safely to the cottage.

By strict attention and the supply of every needful comfort, he soon partially recovered from the many bruises with which his body had been wounded, and was sufficiently restored to be able to travel.

One of the chests which Keeler had rescued from the wreck belonged to the captain, and contained money and valuables to a large amount.

A chaise was procured from a neighbouring town, and the captain, after thanking and rewarding the old fisherman, took his departure, accompanied by Jack, who declared himself resolved never to leave him as long as he would accept his services.

They travelled swiftly, and soon reached London.

The family of the captain were mourning his loss, because the news that had reached them was that every soul had perished with the wreck.

When he entered the room, a burst of joy broke from the anxious family, which was increased to admiration on the captain taking Jack by the hand and saying—

'Now let me introduce my preserver.'

Jack felt abashed, and returned their compliments with such modest and retiring manners as strongly prepossessed them all in his favour; and his continued good behaviour so charmed the captain, that he failed not to use his interest in his behalf.

One morning he called Jack into his private room.

'Jack,' said he, 'you will be obliged to quit us soon.'

'Sir!' exclaimed Jack, 'do I hear aright? Leave you, sir? In what have I offended?'

'In nothing,' replied the captain. 'It is in consequence of your exemplary conduct that I have made interest at the Admiralty, and have procured for you a midshipman's berth on board the Defiance, as trim a ship as ever floated on the ocean's bosom; and her commander as bold a sailor as ever stepped on shipboard.'

Jack felt the obligation, and testified his gratitude for the captain's solicitude, but candidly confessed he would rather have remained under his present master's command, though even in a more subordinate situation.

The captain assured him that he would most willingly retain him; but he was not then in commission, and he told Jack it might be six or eight months before he was appointed to a ship; but he promised whenever opportunity offered, that he would certainly take him on board.

They parted. Jack waited on the captain of the Defiance, and, in consequence of his excellent character, was most cordially received on board.

Yet his ardent mind was not satisfied with his only being employed as an officer of the navy; he sought to understand the full management of a ship, and the method of steering by the compass.

He availed himself of every opportunity of getting into the company of the ship's master and his mate, and, by degrees, acquired so much knowledge, that, in the course of two years, he was considered one of the best steersman in the service.

The first opportunity which offered itself to display his seamanship was during an action off Lisbon, when the master and his first and second mates were successively marked out and killed, while at the wheel, by the enemy's marines.

Jack soon returned to England, and visited the captain who had behaved so generously towards him.

He complimented him on his great success, and offered him a home during his leave on shore.

Jack gladly accepted the offer, though he would not have done so—he would rather have returned to the poor cottager—had it not been that a face at one of the windows had attracted his attention.

The window belonged to a house just opposite the captain's, and the pair of black eyes that anxiously wandered from house to house, as though in search of some one, sent a thrill through his veins.

Jack took no heed of this, further than mentally resolving to find out who this might be, for the more he gazed at the window the more fascinated he became.

———

CHAPTER XCVI.

TOM HATCHETT MAKES NEW FRIENDS—THE PLOTTERS.

TOM HATCHETT was not long in making friends with his strange companion; he did it more for policy than friendship sake.

'Well, old trump,' he said, familiarising his voice, 'how comes it that you are all alone in this tub? Where are your mates? have you any?'

'Of course I have,' growled the man.

'Oh, I hope they are better tempered than you.'

'Why?'

'Because they might answer me civilly.'

'Well, it's a way I've got; but if my mates had been here the civility they would have shown you would have been to chuck you overboard again.'

'Indeed.'

'Yes, but I'm not that way inclined; so take a pull at the grog bottle, for I see you are all of a shake.'

He was right; the cool air after Tom's immersion was anything but invigorating.

Hatchett pulled strongly at the bottle, and seemed greatly benefited by it. He became talkative, and his companion opened into conversation more freely.

From the conversation Tom soon gleaned that his companion belonged to a band of no good repute—a set of fellows half-bandit, half-smugglers.

It mattered not to Hatchett who or what they were. He was an outcast from all society but such as he had fallen into. The only one he could resort to was old Doggrass, and he felt assured he would not speculate on another venture.

The boatman edged his craft along under shelter of the cliffs until they were some distance from the harbour; then, shooting his boat in under an overhanging rock, leapt on the beach.

'Here,' he said to Tom, 'it won't do for me to take you aboard without axing the captain's leave; you can stay here till I return.'

'What, alone?'

'There's baccy and grog to keep you company.'

'But how shall I know that you will return?'

'Don't consarn yourself about that.'

'Is that you, Bill?' cried a voice.

It made Tom start at first; he could not imagine whence it came.

'Silence!' whispered his companion. 'Keep yourself out of sight.'

Tom drew back into the little cave, and took a good survey of the pirate, for his dress betokened him as such—thick woolly trousers, a coarse red shirt fastened at the waist by a belt, and a pair of brass-mounted pistols stuck therein.

John Hatchett smiled.

He felt he had fallen in with a desperate set of fellows, and it made him rejoice.

Having provided our adventurer with the rough comforts the boat contained, Bill, for so we must call him, stepped into his little craft, set the sail, and sped away to the northward.

Tom followed him with his eye, until a point hid him from view; then lighting his pipe and seating himself on a huge stone, he began to ruminate.

For more than an hour he sat thus, and having imbibed pretty freely, and worn out by his late exertions he fell asleep.

He was awakened at length by a gruff voice saying—

'Well, lads, it's a 'tarnal shame, and I wouldn't stand it no ways.'

Tom sprang to his feet, and stared about in astonishment.

He was alone in the cave, and yet the voices sounded near.

A faint glimmer through a crevice in the rock arrested his vision.

He placed his eye to it in the hope of gaining some clue to the mystery.

He could see but little. It was a large cave, dimly lighted, but by the sound of voices, he concluded that a dozen or more persons were assembled within.

The conversation up to this time had been carried on in a lower key, but as the controversy grew hotter, the voices of the speakers grew louder.

Bill's voice was easily to be recognised from the rest.

He was trying to impress something on the mind of one of his listeners, who appeared very difficult to teach.

Tom could hear the man say—

'Most likely; but let us come to the main point.

'That is the main point,' replied Bill, with great emphasis. 'You don't want to work for nothin', do yer?'

'Certainly not; but let's hear what you want us to do.'

'Well, look here, mates,' said the pirate, in a confidential tone, 'I know you dosen't like this fellow more'n I do, and I know there's many aboard as don't, cos they told me so when they came to fetch me ashore. Now, if I can make it all right with them, we can soon manage the rest.'

'Not so easy as you imagine,' said the robber, thoughtfully. 'The skipper fights like a devil; and as for his men, I have seen sufficient proof of their courage to assure you they are no cowards.'

'That may be; but you don't suppose I'm such a cuckoo as to tell 'em what I'm arter, do you? We must do it quietly, on'y we mustn't hurt that blessed gal.'

'What will you do with her?'

'Oh, never mind about her, she'll be right enuf.'

'Most likely,' answered the robber with a sneer, then added—

'If you think you can manage it, we will assist you.'

'Right you are, my pippins,' replied Bill in ecstacy, 'give us your fin. I warrant I'll make reg'lar sea dogs of you afore long. You can just stow your blessed carcases among the rocks till I come ashore for you; but whatever you do keep your lamps trimmed on the schooner.'

'Stay!' cried the men, as Bill turned to depart, 'we have not got any lamps.'

'Lord bless your hinnercent souls,' said Bill, 'don't you know what I mean? Ain't you got a pair of eyes in your blessed heads?'

'Is that what you mean?' asked the fellows, in surprise.

'In course it is, and when you sees a red light come down on the beach, and I'll let you know how I'm gettin' on.'

So saying, the pirate again descended the cliff, leaving the robbers, for such they evidently were, to talk over the affair between themselves.

On arriving on board, Bill set to work sounding the crew.

And having found that many of them were averse to the change, and prejudiced against the captain, he found it no difficult task to excite them to mutiny.

Before he had been on board an hour he had gained the hearts of the pirate crew.

Having succeeded so far, he set to work arranging his plans; but it was a task of no little difficulty that he had undertaken, and it required both time and caution to accomplish it successfully.

This he well knew, and he paced the deck all that night forming plans, and then as quickly abandoning them.

At break of day the captain brought a lady on board, and placed her in the berth prepared for her; and then proceeded on deck to view the vessel.

Then the captain descended to the cabin, where his chief officer was seated examining a chart.

'Well, captain,' he said, 'what do you think of her (meaning the schooner)? Do you think her equal to the task I have 'lotted out for her?'

'I cannot answer you, unless you first inform me what that is,' answered the captain.

'Sit down,' said Tomkins; then continued, 'I have learnt that there are two vessels richly laden shortly to leave Oporto for England, and I thought of running down and easing them of their cargo.'

'That is no difficult task,' said the captain, thoughtfully. 'But most likely they will be guarded.'

'A small war sloop is waiting for them. She will accompany them to the channel.'

The pirate captain bent over the chart, and marked out the course the vessels would most likely take; then said, addressing the lieutenant—

'We must be speedy. See well to our fighting gear. This chance must not slip through our fingers. Have you plenty of ammunition on board?'

'Ay, captain. And those six brass guns, though small, are perfect beauties; so that if we once get them within range, they will even astonish the Britishers.'

'How does she sail?'

'Like a witch.'

'And is she quick in stays?'

'She is; and on a wind there is nothing can touch her.'

'That is well,' replied the pirate, proudly. 'Let everything be ready for sailing by daybreak tomorrow morning.'

'All right, captain,' said Tomkins. 'I will see to it at once.'

So saying, he ascended to the deck, and the captain joined the lady in the state-room that had been fitted up for her reception.

The remainder of that day was employed in watering the ship and provisioning her for the cruise.

Meanwhile Bill was not idle. He bound the men by oath to secrecy, and heightened their excitement by telling them of the rich booty to be obtained if they were only true to each other.

To this they readily yielded, and it was agreed that at midnight they should arise and slaughter those of the crew who had not joined the mutiny.

That night, when all on board save the sentry that paced the deck was supposed to be slumbering, the traitor placed a red light over that quarter of the schooner nearest the shore, then left the vessel in a small boat.

On reaching the beach he was joined by the bandits, and they proceeded to a part of the beach where they might converse without being observed, for the moon was shining brightly.

He then laid down his plans, which were that after killing those on board who would join them, and securing Tomkins (for it was considered advisable not to sacrifice him until they had gained all the information that they needed), they were to take possession of the ship, and murder the captain.

The bandits listened until he had finished, then he who had been spokesman at their former meeting, asked—

'Is Jones in the cave?'

'He is, and he must die,' replied Bill, fiercely, 'and every man who leans to his side.'

'That will be difficult, will it not?'

'Not in the least. You will join us when we come on shore, and we can take them by surprise. Are you afraid?'

'I am not,' replied the bandit, sullenly. 'But can we not do with less bloodshed?'

'We cannot. Dead men tell no tales,' answered the pirate, with a meaning look. 'Not one must escape who knows the secret.'

'I agree with you in that; yet I do not like the idea of murdering my comrades in cold blood.'

'Your comrades!' said Bill, scornfully. 'They are not your comrades now. Was you not forbidden to see them again on pain of death?'

'True. Yet still they gave us a chance of our lives. It is not them, but the captain that should be punished.'

'That cannot be. One and all must die. Not even one of my own comrades will I spare that offers the least resistance.'

'Of course, you know best. But how can we assist you?'

'You must go to the secret trap, raise it carefully, and descend the steps as softly as possible. You can lay there concealed until you hear us make the attack from the beach. Then you must fall upon them in the rear; and if you are as courageous as you look powerful, your help will be better than ten in the front.'

'We lack neither power nor courage to use it,' answered the bandit, fiercely. 'My hatred to the captain will nerve my arm. He has brought us on a wild-goose chase, separated us from the band where we were happy and doing well, and then wanted us

to join the pirates, or return to the stronghold without money, and alone.'

'For this, of course, you wish to be revenged,' said the crafty pirate. 'It is now in your power. One bold stroke, and we shall not only be victorious, but,' he added, with great emphasis, 'we'll be rich.'

'We will,' replied the bandits, as with one voice. 'We will be revenged on the skipper for casting us off.'

'Farewell, then, for the present,' said the pirate, as he turned to the boat; 'but mind, keep your weather eye lifting. One false step and we are lost.'

'Fear not. We will go at once,' said the bandits preparing to ascend the cliff.

Tom stood for some moments after the conversation had ceased, as one thunderstruck.

What could be the injustice the captain had used towards them he could not imagine.

However, he was content to leave it as it was for the present, and it was not long before he found out the secret.

CHAPTER XCVI.

WILL HOWARD GOES ON A FRESH TACK—THE HURRICANE—CAST ON THE SHORE.

EXASPERATED at being defeated in his purpose, Will returned to his ship, vowing vengeance on the Black Pirate crew.

Sambo followed him up the side, his dark eye flashing fiercely.

'Curse him, Will!—curse him!' he exclaimed. 'He will meet with his punishment some day.'

'And mine be the task to do it,' resumed Will Howard. 'Madeline, I fear, is in his power. I must rescue her if any possibility exists.'

'There is none, I fear,' said the giant.

'That remains to be seen.'

'But surely you would not do '——

'I would do anything—venture anything to save her from the fiends.'

'It is impossible to do it now.'

'How so?'

'Night is drawing on, and the sound of the guns would soon bring a man-of-war down alongside of us.'

'And what of that?'

'Well, it would not be pleasant.'

'To him it would not.'

'Nor to us, I fear.'

'Well, what do you advise?'

'Put it off for a day or two. I know the rendezvous of these pirates well.'

'You ought to, if you do not. But I hardly like to leave that poor girl in their hands.'

'It must be so. I see no other choice.'

Will at length yielded.

It was with great reluctance, though.

His eyes were riveted on the pirate ship as long as she remained in sight.

At that moment old Sam stepped to Will's side.

'Beg pardon, your honour,' he said, touching his forelock, 'but we have just discovered that the foretopmast is sprung. That breeze last night has done it.'

Will bit his lip.

'There is a place within a few leagues of this,' said Sancho, 'where we might lay safe.'

'That is deuced awkward,' he said. 'We must fish it for the present, and run in some out-of-the-way place to refit another.'

'Is there any chance of getting another spar?'

'Plenty. The wood grows there in abundance.'

'Then we will go there.'

Will then went aft to consult the man at the wheel; and after the wants of the wounded smugglers who had been able to get back to their ship had been attended to, the watch was set.

*   *   *   *   *

Darkness set in rapidly as the gallant brig sped on her way.

Will did not leave the deck, and Sancho kept his place by his side.

Grouped upon her deck were many officers and men, who, as soon as the sails were spread and the ropes coiled down, seated themselves upon the guns to enjoy the evening breeze.

'A yarn! a yarn!' clamoured a noisy personage in one of the groups.

'Ay, ay, my hearty!' was the cheerful response of a bluff old salt; 'and a tough 'un you shall have, too.'

He thrust a huge plug of tobacco in his cheek, gave his pants a South Sea hitch, and then began—

'Well, mates, it's no use spinning the old yarns over again, so I've stowed them down in the orlop-deck, and now I'll begin a fresh one.

'It's some time since I heard my brother spin the yarn, but I think I can remember it, so here goes.

'Our regiment was laying in the West Indies, and deuced hot it was (I mean the weather), I can assure you.

'So hot, indeed, that what with it and the mosquitoes we could get but little, if any, sleep.

'There was a light air stirring, and, leaving the window open, I resumed my place in the hammock, and, while viewing the prospect before me, and inhaling the fragrance of my cigar, sweet and pleasing ideas of country and of home rose gradually within my mind.

'The landscape slowly faded from my view; the thoughts of kindred, of friends, and of the green banks of the Shannon, continued to mingle undefinedly with lofty palm trees, smoking mountains, cigars, swfzzle, sentries, grand rounds, rum, and p isoners of war; in a word, I was fast asleep; and so might have continued till the morning, had I not been awakened by an unusual commotion in the men's guard room, separated from mine by a thin wooden partition only.

'The confusion of tongues at Babel was order and regularity compared with the uproar I now heard; but at intervals I thought I could distinguish the low moanings of one in pain.

'To snatch my sabre from the table, and run into the adjoining room, was the thought and work but of a minute; and if the confusion of noises only was astounding, the scene that met my eyes on crossing the threshold was perfectly alarming.

'A huge wood fire—that incongruous but invariable appurtenance of a West Indian guard-room—threw its fitful beams on the rough and marked features of the whole assembled guard, who were congregated round a black soldier of my regiment—nay, of my own company—who lay on the hearth, agitated almost convulsively.

'His face, as the fire-light gleamed on it, was deadly pale. Yes, my friend, a black man can look pale; and nothing can be more horrible than the colour which at such a time the negro assumes. The blood forsakes the countenance; the lips become a dull, yellow white; a circle of bluish tinge surrounds the eyes, the red veins in which, being swollen and filled with blood, seem of the hue of fire; while the ivory whiteness of the teeth imparts to the whole face a character almost demoniacal.

'I elbowed my way with difficulty through the circle, for authority seemed lost.

'I shouted, stamped, swore, and at last was heard.

''That black spalpeen has run away from his post, and never stopped to look behind him,' says the sergeant.

''Where was he stationed?'

''In the archway by the prisoners' quarters.'

''Turn out the relief, then, and post another sentinel.'

'I, at length, by dint of shaking, kicking, roaring, and thumping, drew an answer from Blackie himself, who gasped out, as his mouth opened and shut like a dying dog-fish—

''Oh, Massa Coptin! oh, Massa Coptin! me savee—sartin me safe—sure me go da *kicke raboo* —me die—me go da Guinea—me see da Jumbee!'

'I was but a new comer in the colonies, and did not understand him. I demanded an explanation from the sergeant.

''Sure, and plase your honour, he says he saw the *White Gentleman*, that is the devil, yer honour.'

''The superstitious scoundrel! The prisoners have been endeavouring to terrify him,' exclaimed I; 'turn out the relief this instant; take off his accoutrements; make a prisoner of him, and follow me to his post.'

'This was soon arranged. The sergeant and three men were selected; the word was given—' With ball-cartridge prime and load!' and off we went towards the massive archway dividing the lower from the upper compartment of the fortress, where the sentry had been posted, and where the French prisoners were locked up during the night-time.'

'We reached the spot. I advanced alone up the archway, but saw nothing; and at last slowly and pensively returned to the soldiers I had left beyond the arch. All there continued still, and remained so for upwards of half an hour; at the end of which time, weary of inactivity, I placed one of the men on the duty which his fellow had abandoned, and proposed returning to the guard-house with the others.

'Scarcely had I turned my back for this purpose, when shrieks of terror burst from the newly-placed sentinel, who, after about a second, presenting his musket down the archway, flung it violently from him, and fled precipitately, as also did the sergeant and his comrades.

'My eyes followed the direction of the levelled musket; and I do not fear being accused of cowardice when I say I followed the example set, and also ran away; for never did a more fear-inspiring object meet the human vision than that on which my terror-stricken gaze was now riveted.

'The moon, as it shone brightly into the avenue, showed me, near the summit of the arch, and almost on a level with my head, floating towards me, a human form, self-sustained in air, the arms of which were stretched out, as if to enfold me within their grasp.

'It was clad in a short tunic of transparent white, which showed more pure in contrast with the pitchy darkness behind it.

'The head was not quite severed from the body,

BLACK EYED SUSAN.

OR, PIRATES ASHORE.

LITTLE JACK AND SUSAN IN THE CLOISTERS.

37

but hung upon the breast, attached to the breast by a slight portion of the skin on one side.

'The legs were tossed to and fro in such a manner as clearly showed that the bones had been broken in many places ; and from the severed neck a stream of crimson blood gushed over the white raiment even to its feet.

'Covering my eyes with my hand, I fled towards the guard-room, and had nearly reached it, when the sound of distant laughter from the vessels moored below the fort struck on my ear, as if a ray of sunlight had pierced through the thickest darkness.

'The consequence of my conduct flashed at once upon my mind. I halted—my breast heaved—my knees trembled, and a profuse perspiration rushed from every pore.'

'Mustering every energy that fear had left me, I slowly retraced my steps. The feelings of the condemned criminal, as he paces between his cell and the fatal gibbet, would be a state of bliss compared with what I suffered, as I endeavoured to muster in my mind every motive that could stimulate me to exertion.

'At last I stood trembling and breathless on the spot I quitted. Slowly I raised my eyes, and shuddering, closed them in terror, though nothing met my view within the dreary void before me.

'The heavy-toned bell of the fort tolled the hour of one. Reassured, I gazed more earnestly towards the summit of the arch, and beheld, while the deep note of the bell yet sounded in my ear, the same frightful object emerging, as it were, from the solid masonry of the roof.

'It now hovered over my head in a horizontal position, which, as it floated nearer and lower, was changed for an upright one ; the breast dilated and swelled, as when one draws a heavy respiration ; no sound accompanied the motion.

'Despair gave me courage. At my feet lay the loaded musket of the sentinel. I seized and cocked it, viewing the object of my dread more earnestly. The respirations were continued, and I now saw that the head was but one unshapen, battered mass of red raw flesh.

'Assuming as military a tone as terror would permit, I shouted—

' ' Who goes there ? '

'No answer.

'Again and again I shouted the soldier's challenge, though each time fainter and fainter. I now fancied I could almost touch it. Bringing the gun to my shoulder, I took aim—I fired.

'The loud echo was repeated a hundred-fold, reverberating hollowly from the arch before me, and more sharply from the graveyard beyond.

'Thick smoke filled and obscured the passage.

'I could not have missed—my courage was the nerve of despair.

'Slowly the breeze dissipated the dense smoke ; and there, fluttering wildly, like an eagle over its prey, and certainly now not more than two feet from my head was this " thing of fear and dread."

'I sprang upwards, and clasped it in my arms. I felt a slight resistance. Something snapped loudly ; and a cloth, cold, dark, and damp, as the covering of the dead, enveloped my head and shoulders.

' 'Twas no " unreal shade." I felt 'twas substance.

'Terror vanished, and I became on the sudden strangely valiant. Sounds of human life were around and about me ; the prisoners were alarmed, and talked loudly in their quarters. Lights moved towards me from the guard-house, with the sound of measured footsteps. It was the sergeant and the entire guard.

'They moved in line, steadily, and with ported arms, ready for the charge ; and low at my feet lay the object of this warlike preparation.

'And what was it ?

'*A shirt of white linen!* which had been pinned by the sleeves to a drying-line, reaching from a window of the casement to the opposite one ; to the collar were pinned *a red nightcap* and a pair of *red garters* (the seeming stream of blood), and to the bottom was attached a pair of stockings (the joint legs of my ghost!)

'The line being rather slack, it had been wafted backwards and forwards in the breeze that blew down the passage, causing it to advance and recede ; and, as it bellied with the wind, it seemed to dilate and diminish in form, causing the before so evident respiration, and giving it the appearance of supernatural animation.'

When the old salt had finished his yarn he was cheered lustily, and, after taking a pull at the lee braces and a swig at the grog-can, Ben Bobstay, another old salt, was called upon to spin them one of his old twisters.

Before the yarn commenced, a termination was put to their merriment by the hoarse shout of the boatswain.

'Hands about ship.'

The men flew at once to their respective stations wondering at the cause, as the wind when they set the watch was blowing favourable and it had not yet shifted.

One glance from an experienced eye was sufficient to account for this.

The dark outlines of two rocky projections that formed the arms of a bay were just visible, and within the bay the mast-head light of a frigate riding at anchor was plainly to be seen.

To tack ship and run down the coast was Will Howard's intention ; but before eight bells at midnight the wind rapidly increased, so that he was glad to give that rocky and irregular coast a wide berth.

Then a calm that gives warning of a pending gale gave the smugglers some uneasiness.

They were prepared for it, but could not tell from what quarter to expect it.

For two hours they were kept in this suspense, when the wind suddenly chopped off the land, and the gallant little craft, owing to the damage to her fore-top mast, was compelled to scud before the gradually-increasing tempest.

This was a source of great annoyance to Will.

He did not wish to leave the vicinity of the coast, hoping to fall in with the black pirates again.

Every hope of this was now banished, the hardened aspect of the sky told them they need not expect a change as yet.

For several days this state of weather continued, when one morning they found themselves in the midst of several islands.

The weather had been misty and thick, so that they were unable to take the sun, and, in the manner the ship had been running, it was impossible to place any reliance on the log, therefore they lost their reckoning.

Will was at a loss to conjecture what islands they had run down among. Sancho, and even old Sam, whose experience in nautical matters was great, could not imagine where they were.

The vessel was running under close-reefed main-top-sail, double-reefed fore-course, and the fore top-mast stay-sail, to dispense with either of which would be to heave her to at once.

Will stood for some seconds, his eye fixed on the

low land ahead, in a state bordering on bewilderment.

'Can these be the Windward Islands?' he asked of old Sam.

'I should say not, captain,' said old Sam, after a moment's pause. 'If they are, the old tub must have flown across the Atlantic. No, no; they cannot be.'

'There are trees on this island,' said Will, pointing to an island on the port beam. 'If we can bring up under its lee, we may get another spar.'

'I am afraid the sea runs too heavy,' said Sam.

CHAPTER XCVII.

THE STRANGE VESSEL.—THE TWO VILLAINS.

LIEUTENANT FORDHAM was in evident peril.

The sea-monster had certainly decided upon one of them for a meal.

Susan was happily in a state of unconsciousness, and the brave fellow, who was determined to save her if possible, was heartily glad she was so.

Although terribly exhausted with his late efforts, the thought of the terrible fate that menaced one or both nerved him with fresh vigour.

Besides the huge monster, which was now only a fathom distant, the fins of several other sharks could be seen gliding rapidly towards them.

Fordham had not many seconds to consider how to act.

Events had passed in less time than we have been able to record them; but he was a man of strong nerve and astonishing quick perception.

Clasping his left arm firmly round the waist of Susan, he threw himself away from the spar, so as to cause the shark to deviate a little from his intended course; and when the sea-monster had measured its mark, and felt certain of its intended prey, and was about to turn over and seize its victim, Fordham and his senseless burthen disappeared beneath the waves.

The shark was the first to appear again on the surface, and when it did so the water was tinged with crimson streaks.

It lashed its tail furiously, sprang some feet out of the water, and then suddenly dived beneath.

By this time Fordham was clinging to the spar again.

A long bowie-knife was between his firmly-compressed teeth.

It was the only weapon he had possessed himself of in the Red Vulture's cabin.

One hasty glance the gallant fellow cast along the foam-capped waves, to catch a view of the rest of the monsters which he knew must be near him.

The fins had disappeared, and this troubled him much, as he knew not from which quarter to expect he next attack.

He prepared himself, however, for another desperate struggle, sweeping the sea with his ever-watchful eye, as he rose with the waves.

Suddenly the water became agitated at some distance from him, which led him at first to suppose it was caused by a ripple, or the current running over a sunken reef, but which turned out to be a shoal of sharks in chase of their wounded companion, whose track was marked by a trail of blood.

A terrible conflict ensued, as each fought for a share of the carcase, and Fordham breathed a sigh of relief when they disappeared again.

His attention was now drawn to the land whither the spar appeared to be drifting, but it was some miles distant, and he feared in his exhausted state that he would be unable to hold on with the additional weight of Susan until they should be swept ashore.

Feeling that his strength was gradually giving way, and that the cold was beginning to pinch his limbs, he took the scarf from his neck, and, pressing it round Susan's body, lashed her to the spar in such a manner so that part of her body was out of water.

With a small piece of rope he found adhering to the broken mast he then secured himself, and, yielding to the dictates of nature, soon all was lost in oblivion.

*　　*　　*　　*　　*　　*

'Ho, ho! my chicken; a pretty good landfall we have met with!' were the words Fordham dimly heard uttered. 'A naval officer, eh? and in company with as pretty a little craft as ever sailed.'

'Well, shiver me! it is strange,' muttered another voice.

'Strange! Damme, man! strange, do you call it? Why, it's as plain as that scar on your cheek where that fellow caught you with his boarding pike. By my soul! I could swear—and you know I am not much addicted to that—that this fellow has fallen in love with some captain's daughter, and slipped his cable.'

'Well, captain, that may be your opinion, but it ain't mine.'

'Ain't your'n? What do you mean?'

'Why, I don't believe a fellar would slip his cable from a good ship, and put to sea with such a precious freight as she seems to be, with no better craft than the head of a splintered mainmast. No, no; I can't enter that in my log.'

'Well, how do you reckon they got athwart our bows?'

'I should say they've been wrecked.'

'Wrecked, be hanged!' And the captain accompanied his words with an oath. 'Do you think that spar ever belonged to a king's ship? No, no; but this fellow, by his rig, evidently belongs to the king's navy.'

'That may be; and p'raps he has had charge of a prize. There's lots to be picked up in these waters; it's only a wonder we have escaped so long; but as time's on the wing, as the landsmen say, and as we have had but little luck of late, I propose we run down towards the reefs.'

'And what good will come of that?'

'Why, this fellow will come round by that time, and he may tell us where to find the bones; there may yet be a good picking amongst them.'

The captain remained for a moment silent.

He had evidently some other project in view.

Presently he said—

'There's some sense in your proposal; but as the wind's falling light, and I don't wish to get becalmed in such an unpleasant spot, especially in the presence of a frigate, we will wait and see how things turn out.'

At this moment a draught of brandy that had been rather unceremoniously poured down Fordham's throat by one of the rude attendants, caused him to cough.

'Ah! he's coming to, Ned,' said the captain. 'Rub him well; I thought he'd soon righten.'

'There was little danger of that from the first,' interposed the man who had proposed running down to the reef, and who served in the capacity of mate;

'there's no such thing as killing those fellows by water, they get too much of it in their grog. If you make a hole through his bread locker with a cold shot'——

'There, belay at that,' said the captain, testily; 'your yarns, like the Dutchman's cruise, have no end. Heave-to a little, and let your jawing-tackle rest.'

By this time Fordham began to show signs of returning life, and the captain, who was anxious to learn how he came lashed to the spar in company with so beautiful a female, gave the men instructions how to act.

Susan was not so far gone when picked up as the lieutenant—the position in which she was lashed kept her freer from the water, and she had had a good sleep.

As soon as she was released and found herself in a ship's cabin she fainted; and the captain, having placed her in his berth and wrapped her up warm, left her to herself, more to keep her beauty from the amorous eyes of his mate than from any motive of delicacy.

'Well, sir,' said the captain, his voice assuming anything but a pleasant tone, as soon as Fordham was sufficiently recovered to sit up, 'what ship is it you have escaped from ?'

Fordham glanced around in unfeigned astonishment, and cast his eye distrustfully from one face to the other.

The captain grew impatient at the delay.

'Speak out at once,' he said, angrily. 'We know your true colours. Let us hear how you came to desert your ship.'

Fordham saw at once how matters stood.

He had heard part of their previous conversation, and he framed his answer accordingly.

'I have deserted no ship,' he said. 'My vessel— a small schooner—has foundered.'

The captain's brow darkened.

'Liar !' he ejaculated. 'How do you account for this uniform ?'

'Easily. My vessel was freighted to carry despatches to the captain of the man-of-war on this station—that is, if we are not far from where you picked me up.'

'We found you among the islands,' interposed the captain.

'Well, I was sent to him with despatches, which, I believe, was to apprize him that Red Vulture, the well-known pirate, and one Rodwin Blake were cruising in these waters, and'——

'He was to capture them ?'

'If possible.'

'Well, go on.'

'A heavy gale, that you have no doubt felt, deprived us of our foremast; in the morning a squall took the mainmast by the board, and our vessel, having sprung a leak, went down.'

'With all hands but you ?'

'I suppose so, unless you found a lady—my wife —in company with me on the spar.'

Fordham kept a keen eye on the captain as he spoke these words.

The captain was a man well schooled in villany; his hardened features did not relax a muscle as he replied—

'There was a female with you—your wife, perhaps' (he laid great stress on the word); 'but she was dead.'

'Dead !' gasped Fordham, clasping both hands to his head. 'Were you sure ? Is her body on board ?'

'No,' was the reply; 'do you think I make my ship a floating coffin ?'

Fordham heaved a deep sigh.

The tone in which the captain spoke was sufficient to let him know the character of the men he had fallen amongst.

Too cut up at the thought of Susan's loss, the gallant luff did not notice the glances exchanged between the captain and mate, as they left him to himself to hold their own private consultation.

'Well, captain,' said the mate, as they entered the private cabin, and seated themselves at the table, 'if you ain't as fine a pilot on a dark coast as I know. What put it into your head to tell the feller that the gal was under hatches ?'

'What, indeed. Need you ask ?'

'It seems queer.'

'Everything seems queer to you, when it's as plain as a chart to anyone else. Didn't he ask about her ?'

'Nat'ral enough. He said she was his wife.'

'How do I know that ? I suppose you would have me give them my state-room to themselves ?'

'Why, as to that, it amounts to the same thing. You have given it up to her, and there's room enough for two.'

'I know that, but I have not given it up yet.'

The mate put the silver goblet he was drinking from on the table, and stared full in the captain's face.

'Do you claim her as a prize ?' he asked.

'Anything you like,' replied the captain, sullenly. 'My wife, if it suits you better.'

The mate rose from his seat with an oath.

'Your wife !' he hissed, fiercely. 'Do you forget the ship's articles ?'

'I do not,' was the sullen reply; 'but you seem to forget I am your captain.'

'Captain be d——. You know we are all a right to share alike.'

'But not in this case.'

'In everything—we share the danger, and we share the spoil.'

'So you shall. But this woman must be an exception. I will take her on shore. She shall be mine; I swear in defiance of every one.'

The mate said no more.

The captain had baffled him by saying he would take her on shore.

There was a gloomy aspect in his countenance that told he was not satisfied; though, seeming to submit, there was a dark purpose hidden under the grim smile he gave as he resumed his seat.

'Well,' he said, 'putting that down as settled, how do you mean to act with her hu—— I mean with the man ?'

'That must depend on circumstances. I am not going to run my neck into a halter to spare him, I can assure you.'

'Not likely. I know I should feel uncomfortable dangling from a yardarm ; but if we stay here we are most likely to have a good chance of it.'

'That's certain, if Red Vulture and Rodwin Blake have made this their cruising ground. A man-of-war, too, is the last thing we should care about meeting. We must clap all sail now on the other tack.'

'What ! to capture the smuggler ?'

'Yes ; we must have Will Howard if possible. He's a dangerous fellow ; but we must lay our plans well.'

'We can do that if our shore chaps prove true ; if

they keep a good look-out for his landing, we can hunt him about at sea.'

'Much easier said than done,' growled the skipper; 'but we must get rid of this officer fellow as soon as possible. In the meantime, I will draw from him all he knows, and as he thinks his wife dead, he'll be very glad to get away with a whole skin.'

'But should he betray'——

'Bah! How can he? What does he know of us? and at a pinch I'll swear he will not refuse to take an oath of secrecy in payment for his passage. I wish, though, he had delivered his papers first, for the capture of those two ships would have left us a clear sea to work in.'

'And a glorious time we might have had of it. With our swift little craft, that would float in less water than I mix with my grog, we could have been kings.'

Eight bells was now struck, and ere its sound had done reverberating through the ship, the boatswain's voice was heard turning up the watch.

The mate strode gloomily to the deck.

'How have you got the wind now?' he asked.

'Well abeam,' replied the boatswain, holding up his brawny palm. 'There is not enough to fill an old woman's apron; but it's fair, and that's what we don't get every day.'

The mate muttered something that was only heard by the ears it was meant for, and he and the boatswain walked to a secluded part of the vessel, and a low and earnest conversation then ensued.

So soon as the mate's footsteps on the cabin ladder died away, the captain rose, and entered his state cabin.

Susan was sitting on the cushions of a sofa, her brain all of a whirl, and at the greatest loss imaginable to conjecture where she could be.

She started at his touch, for she did not see him enter, and the scream that rose involuntarily to her lips was suppressed by his terrible frown.

'Well, well,' he said, vainly endeavouring to soften his harsh voice, ' you seem comfortable, if not happy. I should think by your manner this is not the first time by a great many you have been on shipboard.'

'Perhaps not; but that concerns you little. How is it that you intrude?'

'Intrude, aha!' and the captain laughed. 'Intrude, my dear lady; sure it is no intrusion for a captain to enter his own cabin.'

'Are you the captain?'

'I am.'

'Then perhaps you can answer my question?'

'Name it.'

'Was there another besides myself saved?'

The captain stood mute.

He was working up his dead reckoning. He had answered that question to the officer, but he was rather at a loss how to answer the wife.

'Was it your husband?' at length, he asked.

Susan was now as much perplexed, but, a thought suddenly crossing her mind, she answered, ' Yes, it was.'

'Well, he certainly was there, but——'

'But what? Is he dead?'

'Aye, and buried some hunhred miles from here.'

Susan clasped her hands in despair.

'Merciful heavens!' she gasped, ' can it be true?'

'True enough, but not so bad as you seem to take t,' said the hardened skipper. 'You have lost but ne, there are hundreds more to be obtained.'

Susan made him no reply, and, as she stood silent

before him, her dark eyes shaded by their long silken lashes as she bent her gaze on the floor, he became desperately enamoured of her.

'I even,' he cried, in the moment of excitement, 'I, the captain of this ship, would not hesitate to sacrifice myself at the shrine of such an idol. I would worship you, and make you the happiest of all women.'

Susan stood for some moments like one thunderstruck at this sudden outburst of the captain's.

'Sir, do you know to whom you speak?' she asked, sternly.

The captain stood for a moment in silence.

The contraction of his features and the working of his broad chest told how hard he contended with his rising indignation.

'Ah!' he vociferated, 'this comes of making women offers, leaving them to their own choice. Had I said you should be mine you had not dared to say nay, but as it is you shall be mine. I will substitute the dead.'

Susan gave a stifled cry.

The word 'dead' rung in her ears like a knell.

Not wishing to make a scene between himself and the mate, the captain closed the state-room door, and left Susan to compose herself.

———

CHAPTER XCVIII.

THE DEVIL'S HOOF—CAPTAIN WILL AND SANCHO GO ON A VOYAGE—THE DISCOVERY BY THE INDIANS.

WILL and his officers kept a good look-out, the result of which was to assure them that their vessel was running into a bight of rocks which was completely embaying them, and would evidently bring upon them certain destruction.

Dark looks were on the hardened features of the smugglers, and ominous predictions dropped from the lips of some of the oldest.

Captain Will was the calmest of them all.

In spite of the darkness he had been able to discover that the rocks ahead, and on either side of them, formed a kind of horseshoe in shape.

'Think you we have got amongst the Carribbees?' asked Sam, venturing to break upon the captain's silence. 'If so, and we get cast away, the savages will make short work of us.'

'Savages!' reiterated Will, 'there is plenty of time to think of them. We have something else to contend with before we reach land. I am afraid we have hit upon a group called the Devil's Hoof.'

'The devil we have!' burst from Sam, suddenly. 'Then, there is no chance of beaching the ship; but I think, if I remember right, there is a channel to be found through it, though it is not known to many, and used only on a pinch by pirates in eluding a a chase.'

'You are quite right, Sam; but who is to find a channel so obscure on such a night as this? Besides, we may have to haul on either tack, and the ship yaws like a mad bull, driving dead before it.'

'Well, it's a venture, you know, captain.'

'Too well I do. What sail do you think we dare show in the teeth of this gale?'

'The peak of the main try-sail just above the rail, and the fore top-mast stay-sail might steady her a bit. The hands can manage the top-sail braces.'

'True, we will set to work at once. What has to be done must be done quickly. You must take the wheel. I will keep a look-out on the bowsprit, and Sancho can pass the orders to the men.'

It was dangerous work, for no sooner was the canvas loosed from its fastenings, than it threatened to lash itself into ribbons, and threatened destruction to the brave fellows who strove manfully to control it.

Their efforts were at length successful.

The stay-sail was hoisted, and the main try-sail was so arranged as to show but a small portion of its head above the bulwarks.

This fresh impulse to the vessel, small as was the increase of sail, made the vessel feel her helm, and Will took his station between the knight-heads.

Vainly he strained his eye along the white belt of foam that marked where the deadly rocks lay for the least opening, until they were close upon the reef, and then the cry of ' Port !' burst from the captain's lips.

' Port it is !' Sam shouted ; and the vessel bore off under guidance of her helm ; and at another shout from Will to ' Starboard hard !' she luffed up, and shot between two black-looking objects that reared their heads about a fathom clear of the foam.

' We're in the channel !' burst from several lips ; but ere they could utter another sentence the vessel struck with a force that brought down both masts, and a towering sea, that leapt like a mountain over the stern, swept the deck of every living soul.

When the wave had passed, Will found himself jammed with the fallen rigging on the bowsprit, and he had only time to cast his eye along the deserted deck when another sea rolled aboard, broke, and swept him, rigging, and bowsprit all away.

It was now Will's courage was put to the test.

Clearing himself of the entangled mass, he buffeted hard with the waves, and contrived to keep himself from being dashed into fragments against the rugged projections until he found himself at last left by a receding wave upon the beach.

With just sufficient strength remaining, he drew himself clear of the surf, and after a short time he rose to his feet, and went in search of any of his crew that might chance to be thrown-ashore.

His search was for some time fruitless, and he began to suspect that he was the only survivor, and he prayed for daylight that he might get a better knowledge of his situation.

Daylight did not, however, come until its prescribed time, and with it brought fully to his mind the horrors of his situation.

The land presented the appearance of one unbroken mass of rock, barren as the palm of his own hand, and with not so much as a tree in sight.

Laying on the beach were the bodies of two of his late crew, so dreadfully disfigured by dashing against the rocks, as to be totally unrecognisable.

With a solemn feeling of awe and thankfulness for his own preservation, he drew them clear of the surf, and placed them under shelter of a crag until he should feel better able to bury them.

He then continued his journey, and discovered he was upon an island, a small stream of water, not deep enough to float a sloop, cutting him off from the rest of the rocks.

Weary with his exertions, and faint for the want of food, Will now began to think of some mode of sustaining life until he should be relieved from his present deplorable condition.

There had been plenty of provisions on board the ship, but he could see no signs of any being washed ashore, and not the slightest vestige remained of the ship, nor the least sign to indicate where she had struck.

Will did not yet despair ; he had nothing but the one object, that of search, to occupy his mind, so he waded through the water from one rock to another, for about a quarter of a mile in the direction he supposed the remains of the brig to lay.

Here his search was rewarded by discovering a piece of spar, and on nearer approach he found it jammed between two rocks, and on trying to extricate it, for it was covered with cordage, and he thought it might be useful, his ears were startled by a groan.

For a moment he seemed paralyzed.

Recovering himself suddenly at the thought of a human being lying there, he set about at once to discover whom it might be.

The groan came from beneath a mass of rope that had been coiled down by the sea and left in a small hollow in the rocks.

Owing to his weakness Will found his task difficult, but he was rewarded for his pains, and a cry of joy burst from his lips.

' Sancho, my friend, is it you ? ' he exclaimed. ' You are sadly hurt, I fear ? '

' But little, I hope,' said the herculean fellow, assisting Will in his endeavours to release him.

' Well, shiver me,' cried Will, as his tall friend drew his lank form erect, ' if I ever saw anything to equal this. It would not at all surprise me now to hear of a seventy-four stowing her launch into a water-cask to preserve it from the sun.'

' Nor I,' answered Sancho, glancing at the small hole he had just left, and into which it would have taken him all his life to get again, that is, if he were ever successful ; ' but never mind, that's over, so let it pass.'

' But this spar and rope we must not lose,' said Will, and he commenced making active preparations to get it to land.

' Hold on,' said Sancho, who from his extraordinary elevation could get a good view around. I see something like the bows of the old ship.'

Without wasting time in further parley, the two set off in the direction indicated by Sancho, and they soon had the satisfaction of beholding not only the bows of the old ship, but a great quantity of the stores.

' If we land there in safety they will last us some time,' said Will ; and as he spoke he selected several things from the disordered pile, and then he and Sancho made for the main rock or island.

The vessel had evidently gone to pieces on a receding tide, and the things had been thus providentially left in the hollows of the rocks, for Will had discovered a small keg of rum and some biscuits, part of which had not been spoiled.

* * * * . *

' Well, we have passed just a week on this blessed spot,' said Will, one morning as he crawled to the opening of the little tent they had erected ; ' and now I grow tired of this solitude and long for a change.'

' I feel the same, but what good is it ? We can only ramble about from rock to rock.'

' I don't know so much about that, Sancho. We have enough to make a raft. What say if we try, and start on a bold venture to reach the land where we have noticed the trees ? '

' I leave it all to you. Where you dare go I dare accompany you.'

' Well, I'm for the venture.'

' Good. We will just have a mouthful, for we have but little more left of our stock, and then we will set about it; for my part I can't bear the thought of being starved on this rock.'

The meal was soon completed—a few crumbs of mouldy biscuit and an oyster shell of grog, and then the pair set to work.

The spars were laying on the beach just clear of the waves, and Sancho rolled them down to the water, whilst Will lashed them firmly together.

It took them some time, for the work was laborious; but, when completed, the raft was so constructed as to float anywhere, and capable of being managed anyhow, but close hauled.

Will had fixed up a pole, and rigged it so as to set a fore and aft sail, and taking with them what they deemed necessary, they set out on their hazardous voyage.

The breeze was just blowing lightly, and having calculated how long it would take them to reach the distant shore, they set a kind of watch, sleeping alternately, and calling each other when necessity required.

Forty-eight hours they had estimated the run, and it was the evening of the second day of their departure from the rock that the raft began to draw in shore.

The country appeared hilly, and well-wooded trees intermixed with plants growing close to the beach, but no sign of habitation could they see, nor the vestige of any human being moving about.

It was nearly dark when they had settled on a spot suitable to land.

A small inland creek that formed a kind of cave they chose, and, running the raft amongst a cluster of trees that grew some distance in the water, they moored her securely, and stepped to land.

The spot was well chosen, and served for two purposes; the trees shaded it from the heat of the sun and from the prying eye of any of the natives, if there were any, that might chance to prowl that way.

A cursory survey of the place was at once taken.

Fruit appeared in abundance; birds, too, seemed to be very plentiful.

Leaving our hero to gather some of the fruit, Sancho stepped on board the raft, and soon possessed himself of several good-sized fish that had attracted his attention while landing.

These were soon cooked, and discussed with much gusto by our adventurers; for they had scarcely tasted any food since they left the reef.

Having finished their meal and made up their minds to explore further inland in the morning, the weary adventurers formed a tent of their sails, and were soon sound asleep.

At the first break of day, Will was astir, and, leaving Sancho to cook a good supply of fish (for they did not wish to betray their concealment by the smoke in the daytime, when any of the inhabitants might be about), went to reconnoitre.

Every step he took bore fresh evidence of the provision of a boundless providence; bread-fruit seemed to grow in abundance, and cocoa-nuts lay scattered around.

Charmed by the sight, and forgetting, in the rapture of the moment, the direction he was taking, he soon found himself in a delightful grove, and he strolled through it in a deep meditative mood.

A dense wood now barred his way, but as he had noticed a rising ground beyond, he pushed on through it, intending to get a good view around, when, suddenly, a loud cry was heard, and the foliage was greatly agitated.

At a loss to conjecture the cause, he stood for a moment rooted to the spot.

With eager eyes he stood looking in the direction of the sound, scarce knowing what to expect, but prepared, as well as any unarmed man could expect to be for any emergency.

He had not long to wait.

The growl of a fierce Indian sounded on his ear.

Before he could look around for any place likely to conceal him or even attempt to fly, the brushwood parted, and a body of painted savages surrounded him.

A collection of war clubs, tomahawks, and spears, held in a menacing manner, told him it was useless to offer any resistance.

Obeying the order that was imparted to him by gestures and horrible contortions of the leader's face, he followed the chief through the brushwood, surrounded closely by a dozen warriors of the tribe.

This was something new to Will.

Never before had he been so near to an Indian warrior, and it was a novel position he was in, for he knew not whether they regarded him as a friend or a prisoner.

Emerging from the thicket, they came on to a large open plain, and being joined by some fifty more, all armed in a semi-barbarous manner, it set Will's brain on the conjecture.

The bodyguard that had formed round him at first still held their council. Whether to protect him from violence on the part of the tribe or for fear he should escape he had yet to learn.

Amongst the Indians he noticed were several squaws, and one woman, who by her dress was somewhat related to the chief.

When Will heard the latter's voice it recalled to him the voice he had heard in the wood. It must have been her that betrayed him to the tribe.

When she approached to view the stranger, there was a kindliness in her smile and such a glance of admiration in her eye that revived the confidence in Will's breast, and made him hope that all would yet turn out well.

Gradually the throng began to swell.

The tribe had evidently disposed themselves for a morning hunt, and as the grim warriors began to pour into the open space, Will had good opportunity to examine their exteriors.

Four besides the one who appeared to be the chief carried rifles, and the rest were armed with all manner of clubs, spears, and javelins.

One party—for they seemed to be in regular divisions—carried long bows, and were provided with a bundle of arrows.

Suddenly our hero's thoughts were turned into another channel.

A party of chiefs were holding a consultation, and by the glances frequently cast towards him he could see he was the object of their conversation.

While he was watching with anxious eyes something touched him lightly on his shoulder, and a voice, that seemed musical when compared to what he had expected, whispered in his ear—

' Fear not, my brother. Be firm; I will aid you!'

Soon after the chief signed to the guard, and Will was rudely seized, his arms pinioned behind him, and he was led into the midst of a circle formed by the chiefs.

' My son,' said the chief, ' you have trespassed on our domains—the land the best warriors of our tribe have watered with their life-blood. The pale-faces have no right to tread upon its soil. Whence come you, and for what purpose?'

Will for a moment was at a loss for an answer, but recovering himself instantly, he replied—

'I am a wanderer. My canoe' (pointing to the sea as he spoke) 'was swamped by the Great Spirit. I came here to seek the means of returning to the home of the paleface.'

'Does my brother speak true?' said the chief, after a moment's pause. 'Does he not come with canoes at his back, and the spear-sticks' (meaning the bayonets) 'at his command, to drive us from our land, and bury his hatchet in our hearts?'

'He does not, I assure you,' replied Will.

The chief eyed him distrustfully.

Will had attired himself in the suit of one of the unfortunate officer's that had met with such a disagreeable reception on board his ship, his own having been torn in shreds, and these being the only ones that chanced to wash on shore from the wreck.

Will noticed this, but with a sailor's careless indifference he was thinking of Sancho and the mess of fish, for the morning air began to sharpen his appetite.

'If my brother speaks true,' said the chief at length, 'it will be well; but if he speaks false, he shall feel our wrath.'

The chief then left with the chief followers of his tribe, and Will was left to the care of four armed warriors, who soon raised a tent, for the sun was growing warm, and provided him with food.

Will was hungry, and ate ravenously, for, though the food, with the exception of a fresh-killed bird, was of the coarsest description (to use his own words), 'it was not to be sneezed at even by a ship's captain.'

He was left to himself while eating, the Indians having sense enough to retire, and he was not sorry for it.

Presently the back of his tent was gently raised, and to his great surprise the Indian girl crept in.

He was about to utter an exclamation, but a motion of the Indian girl warned him to silence.

'I have come, my brother,' she said, 'to warn you of the danger that is at hand. The chiefs do not believe you; they say you have a strong force of warriors at hand; say, is it so, that Oona may know whether it is right for her to speak to the brother of the pale faces?'

'Oona is wrong,' said Will, his dream of release and his meal terminating at the moment the girl uttered these words. 'Can you not see the pale face is alone?'

He pointed to his hands, to his belt, and then to the lance she held in her hand.

The girl's eye suddenly brightened.

She understood at once his meaning.

'You have not come on the war trail?' she said.

'No, you see I am at peace.'

'How came you here?'

'Why ask that?'

'The homes of the pale faces are so far away.'

'My canoe,' and he pointed towards the sea to make her understand.

'And is it there still?'

'No, the spirit of the great waters dashed it on the rocks.'

'And your brothers?'

'All gone.'

'All?'

'Yes.'

There was something so romantic in the story, and the face of the sailor looked so depressed when he mentioned the loss of his crew, that Oona felt at once what he said was true.

Will saw his chance.

He found his story, together with his attire, had worked the same magic on the girl as it might had she been of a different colour, and he did all he could to encourage it.

'But you said your warriors would kill me,' said Will, craftily, reverting to the subject. 'Are they not braves that they would kill a pale face unarmed?'

'They are braves, my brother,' she replied, seemingly hurt at this allusion; 'but until my brother the chief is certain you are not on the war trail he must hold you as a foe.'

'But can you not tell him?'

'The voice of a woman is no use.'

'Ah! I see. The voice of a woman is not heard in council.'

'Not so loud. Remain quiet, and I will save you yet.'

She imprinted a kiss on his hand, and disappeared before Will was aware of her intentions.

A sudden commotion in the camp caused Will to look from his tent, and then he beheld Sancho in the midst of six fierce fellows, who had evidently determined he should not escape.

Sancho's eye glanced round the encampment, and it was a relief to him when it fell on Will's sunburnt face.

He was led at once before the chief, who became distrustful.

He had had visitors of mixed colours, and he began to grow wary.

Sancho was put to a strict examination, and as his story agreed with Will's, and as he (not like our hero) had told them he and Will Howard were companions, and that the raft lay moored where they could satisfy themselves of the fact, a strong party proceeded there accordingly.

When the chief returned he was angry.

He had been sore disappointed, for though he did not expect to find more whites, yet he had hoped to get hold of a prize worth having.

In this he was disappointed; and in the anger of the moment he seized his rifle and hurried towards Will's tent.

Oona saw him.

She had seen the thunder in his countenance and the fierce glare of hatred in his lightning glance too often to be deceived in their meaning.

Following closely on her brother's heels, she caught him before he could enter the plain, and clutching him by the arm, she said, with an air of deep earnestness—

'Stay, my brother. Do not slay the white man.'

The chief spoke not.

The cloud on his brow grew darker.

'He must die,' he replied, sarcastically.

And before Oona could urge another word, he tore himself from her grasp, and hurried towards Will's tent.

———

BLACK EYED SUSAN.

OR, PIRATES ASHORE.

THE PERILOUS DESCENT.

CHAPTER XCIX.

THE TRIAL—OONA SAVES WILL'S LIFE—THE
TRAIL OF BLOOD.

FAR away from the sounds of the rushing sea were the prisoners carried, Captain Will scarcely being able to exchange a word with his companion.

The warriors of the tribe had agreed to put them to death, in spite of the pleadings of Oona.

Takoka, her brother, was a great chief, but even he dared not go contrary to the decree of the council, nor would he have done so had he been able.

The wigwam allotted to them was large and airy, insomuch as it admitted both light and air at the roof, and Will began to feel rather anxious for his position, which was right under it, for fear the rainy season might set in.

Two days had passed since the arrival at the village, and the prisoners had received no other visitors but the Indians who brought them their food, and acted as guard over them.

The third day, however, they were welcomed with a cheerful sound; it was the voice of Oona conversing with the Indian on guard.

'How is this,' she asked, her voice assuming a tone of hauteur, 'that I am not allowed to enter? Do you refuse to let me pass?'

'Waugh, I do,' growled the savage.

'Beware! Remember Oona's revenge is sharp.'

'And Tokoko's,' suggested the savage, 'is sure.'

'My brother speaks well,' said the girl, suddenly recovering; 'but Oona is free to all the wigwams. You know you would not dare stop me before Tokoko?'

The Indian gave another savage growl, and Will could see he placed himself in front of the entrance of the tent to block the way.

A short controversy then ensued, and Oona walked away, leaving the prisoners in none of the best of moods.

Next morning Will was taken before the chief, and put through a close examination, it having been reported by a scout that palefaces had been seen hovering about.

Will denied all knowledge of this, but it was useless. He was accused of leading the enemy to their camp. and was condemned to suffer death.

Sancho was also condemned, but the colour of his skin lightened his sentence.

He was to be the chief slave for the remainder of his life.

This was not altogether a pleasant prospect, but it was so far satisfactory: the liberty of one might be the liberty of two.

This was Sancho's opinion, and he soon put it to account.

He was armed with a rifle and dressed in skin and feathers, one tuft adorning the upper part of his head.

The captain saw him as he passed his wigwam, but he took no apparent heed, for the guards were keeping vigilant watch that no communication passed between them.

Sancho was provided with fresh quarters, and the guard, as usual, was kept inside, and out of Will's wigwam.

Tokoko had informed our hero that two suns would set before his execution, and the gallant sailor hoped that in that time something might occur to effect his deliverance.

Oona, not being able to visit him, was a source of great discomfiture to him.

He also regretted the absence of Sancho, for, though they had not been able to discourse freely, they were enabled to exchange meaning glances with each other before.

Towards night, however, now that the Indians on watch had been relieved of half their duty by the absence of Sancho, they began to grow less attentive, and seated themselves and began to doze.

Will watched them with his keen eyes, and heartily wished his arms were free.

He would have had a sharp struggle for liberty had they been, but, as it was, he was obliged to be content with watching them.

More than once he wished he was like them, and could have gone to sleep to drown his thoughts, for his watchfulness began to be a burden to him.

Towards night, when the moon was peeping through the straggling clouds, he fancied he could see a form through the opening of his prison flitting about in the gloom.

He laid and watched in an agony of mind, and his eyes ached with his anxious gazing.

At length it came closer, and he now became certain it was a human form.

Presently he could discern a female dress, and as the moon peeped out he discovered the face of Oona.

Gliding noiselessly by the drowsy sentinel, she crept into the opening, and, seeing by the light through the roof that the Indian inside was reclining with his head on his knees, she approached our hero.

'Oona, is it you, my sister?' he asked, in a suppressed voice.

'It is,' she replied, mournfully.

The tone made our hero start. It seemed to bode no good.

'Why have you risked so much to come here?' he asked.

There was a pained look on his features as he spoke.

He feared the Indian would awake and see her; that an alarm would be raised; and he trembled for the consequences.

'Why,' she replied, 'need my brother ask?'

'But your life is in danger, is it not?'

'Waugh,' she said, and fixed her dark, lustrous eyes full upon him. 'Does the son of the palefaces want so much to understand?'

Will was now more perplexed than ever.

A slight misgiving seemed to have taken possession of him.

Oona saw this, and to relieve him she said—

'Has my brother forgot that Oona has a heart? Can he wonder if she loves you?'

Of all things this was what Will had least expected to hear.

The girl had openly confessed her sentiments, and they were what he most wished not to hear.

It reminded him of Sue, of his cot on the cliff, and it sent a pang to his heart.

Seeing how matters stood, and that the girl, if not able to liberate him, might do much to assist him, he said—

'But my sister cannot love a paleface?'

Oona drew herself haughtily erect.

A flush suffused the deep olive of her cheek.

Pointing through the opening above her, she said—

'Can I love the moon?'

'You can, for there is no one to hinder you.'

'And who is to hinder me loving my pale brother? The heart of Oona is free as the buffalo to roam where it likes, until smitten by one whose dart is keen enough to pierce it.'

'My sister speaks true,' muttered Will; 'but who would try the venture of throwing away a kind heart on a condemned prisoner?'

'Condemned! Ah, but the sentence is not yet fulfilled. The paleface must not die while Oona lives.'

'Impossible!' cried Will, his excitement overcoming his prudence.

And before he could say the word, the savage awoke and sprang to his feet.

He glared savagely at Oona, and made a thrust at her with his knife; but she stooped to evade the blow, and at the same moment picked up the hatchet that lay on the ground.

It had slipped unconsciously from the savage's hand in his sleep; and he drew back from her threatening attitude as she rose and brandished it above her head.

'Back, false warrior!' she hissed, her aspect suddenly changing to that of a demon. 'Is this how you obey the commands of the chief? The whiteface might have been hid behind the hills had it not been for me.'

The wretch cowered; he saw how helplessly his negligence had thrown him into her hands.

'Oona,' he said, 'give me the hatchet; let it be buried between us for ever.'

'Is it for a warrior to make conditions with a woman?' said Oona, her dark eye flashing fiercely, and her curling lip denoting the scorn she felt towards him. 'Topaski, you have raised your knife against me, and it is but right the hatchet should drink your blood.'

A slight spasm went through the savage's burly frame.

His fierce eyes peered beneath his shaggy brows.

He was meditating something, and well Oona knew it.

As he sprang towards her to get possession of the gleaming axe, she brought it down with a dull crash, and before the Indian could close with her he fell a corpse.

As the body fell with a dull thud upon the earth Oona seemed suddenly to recover her senses.

The deed was done, and now she repented her rashness.

The Indian outside too was now beginning to stir.

One glance she cast towards him, and then her mind seemed fixed upon a plan.

Drawing the dead Indian with a strength that seemed not to belong to her to one side of the wigwam, she bounded lightly to the entrance.

The hatchet was firmly clasped in her hand, and it was evident she would not fail to use it if occasion required.

The Indian did not thoroughly awaken, luckily for him, or probably he would have fallen into a sounder sleep than when his head fell again on his knees.

'My brother must now be quick,' she said, turning to Will Howard. 'The thongs once broken you must fly.'

'And you?'

'Will follow like the deer of the forest. Come quick, or we may not get the chance.'

For some moments after she had cut the bonds Will's arms were too cramped for use, and as the blood began to circulate, it occasioned him much pain.

It was joy to Will to find himself thus free and his

arms unfettered, and his thoughts were now of Sancho.

'Come, come,' said Cora, seeing he made no attempt to leave.

'Where is my brother?'

'He must remain.'

'Here with these'——

'Yes.'

'Never, I cannot go without him.'

'Is not Oona going to bear you company?'

'True, but without Sancho, my friend—no, never!'

A look of displeasure settled on the Indian girl's face.

'Does the sight of Oona offend you?' she asked.

'No, far from it; but Sancho, I cannot leave behind.'

'He is far from here.'

'Where—where?'

'On the other side of the camp.'

'I will go to him at once.'

'It will be death. Let us escape at once.'

Will cast an anxious glance through the opening of the hut.

'May I ground on a lee shore and serve a meal for a shark, if I go and leave him!' he said, clenching his hands which were yet scarcely free from cramp.

The girl, in defiance of the colour of her skin, seemed to understand well what he said.

'You must not stay for him,' she said, 'if you value your life and mine, which will be sacrificed if we are discovered.'

Will was struck by her tone and the altered manner of her voice, and it occurred to him she was not what she seemed to be.

She appeared to notice this, and as though to divert him from the subject, she placed in his hand the hatchet, and led the way to the opening.

The sentry was still sleeping, though evidently by his restless manner he was not in deep slumber.

Oona stepped cautiously forth. She held the long knife she had taken from the Indian beneath her dress.

'All is clear,' she said in a subdued tone; 'my brother must make his way alone towards that opening in the trees; I will join him soon.'

Glad to get his freedom at any price, though he was not now afraid of meeting with a savage as he had the hatchet, our hero stepped lightly over the sward, and made his way to the spot indicated.

A few minutes would have brought him safe, but, as he was turning the angle of a hut that lay in his way, he fell across a prostrate body that was crouching in the shade.

He expected to hear the usual growl, but not a sound was uttered by either party, and before Will could gain his feet he felt himself clutched by a pair of brawny arms that held him powerless, and the cold blade of a knife was instantly at his throat.

'Wretch!' he gasped almost unconsciously, and it was well for him he did so.

The knife vanished like magic, and he was lifted bodily to his feet; then a voice whispered in his ear—

''Tis I, captain; 'tis Sancho.'

It took Will a moment to recover breath.

The perspiration was rolling off him in beads.

'Thank God, Sancho!' he said, 'it is you.'

'And, thank God, you spoke! for if you had not you your glass would have been run out.'

'Ah! you meant it.'

'I did. It would have added another to the list.'

'What, have you killed any one.?'

'I have, four; there lays one.'

Will looked in the direction indicated, and saw a body stretched on the grass, the head having rolled some distance away.

Will shuddered, and was about to make some remark, when Sancho warned him by a look, and dropped on his knees.

Placing his ear carefully to the ground, he listened.

'A footstep comes this way!' he said, springing to his feet, at the same moment dragging Will after him into the shade.

Quick as the movement was, they had only time to conceal themselves when a figure, muffled in a tiger skin, shot past them.

The figure passed so close to them—for it was evident whoever it was did not wish to be seen—that it touched their dress, and they waited with bated breath until it had gone out of sight.

Presently they heard a loud thud, as though something had fallen.

Then a horrible yell was raised.

Will divined the cause immediately.

The figure had fallen over one of the dead bodies, and this was the death wail.

Not daring to move, the pair stood speechless.

They could see the dark forms of the Indians flying about among the huts.

They could hear the incessant howls, as a tiger bereft of its young, and they set about to devise some means of safety to themselves.

The wigwam under which they were sheltered had long since been evacuated, and its occupants mingled amongst the group that was yelling not many yards away.

'We must climb a tree,' whispered Will, 'it is the safest.'

'Where can we find one?'

'We must crawl to that group.'

'That will not shield us.'

'It must for a time, captain.'

Will saw that every moment delayed was dangerous.

He agreed to try and reach the tree; but as he was about to make a start, he saw it suddenly surrounded.

It chanced to be a tree almost idolized by the savages.

They climbed up its trunk and brought down handfuls of its leaves.

This Will afterwards learnt was to cover over the dead, for according to their custom it was believed that if the moon shone on the wound before the sun it was a sure sign of the escape of the murderer.

Will was thankful he had not gone there now.

Time was short, however, and they had not much to spare.

Crawling into the deserted wigwams they found a large pile of skins, and, rolling themselves into them, they were completely out of sight.

'So far so good,' said Will; 'but how are we to get away from here when we feel inclined to?'

'We must trust to Providence,' was Sancho's reply. 'We are here, and we must do as best we can.'

'That's evident,' muttered Sancho; 'but how are we to escape, providing we are not caught here?'

'Take a bold dash for it.'

'Hush! they approach.'

Hurried footsteps were heard.

The glare of a pine torch was seen through the crevices, and then a long, low wail, dismal and horrible, echoed on the still night air.

'They have discovered the other body,' whispered Will.

'And they will find many more,' was the careless reply.

By this time the wail had been taken up till it echoed from a hundred throats; and Will fancied, above it all, he could hear Oona's voice giving directions where to pursue the murderer.

The shouts now became louder than ever.

The fury of the Indians increased at every step; for Sancho had left a trail of blood behind him that showed how determined he had been on releasing his captain at all hazards.

The search for the murderers—for now they had discovered that Will had left his wigwam—became general, and the wood was searched in such a manner that would have surely put an end to the escape of the fugitives had they sought its shelter.

CHAPTER C.

LITTLE JACK SEES THE STRANGE FACE AGAIN —THE FATAL MISSIVE—MYSTERIOUS DISAPPEARANCE OF LITTLE JACK.

CAPTAIN LISTON, the gentlemen who had proved such a kind benefactor to Jack, did not appear a man possessed of great worldly riches; at least, if he was, he made but little display of them.

The house he occupied was but small, and the neighbourhood not of the wealthiest.

But Little Jack was treated kindly, and we may say he was happy, with the exception of an ardent longing to find out who inhabited the strange old house opposite.

The old-fashioned windows with their heavy damask curtains were a source of great annoyance to him.

He often wished that glass had not been invented, and that the gorgeous drapery had been put to some other use.

The old captain's motto was, "Early to bed and early to rise," and this afforded Jack many hours of silent meditation before he could close his eyes in sleep.

Hour after hour he would watch from his little window that overlooked the street the strange house, and note with particular earnestness those who entered or came out of it.

One of the constant visitors was a tall, middle-aged man, of military appearance, and the person who usually accompanied him was a man, gray with age, of a strangely sinister aspect, and stooping in gait.

It was strange, Jack thought, that they only came at dusk, and invariably left as the old church clock proclaimed the hour of twelve.

This was sufficient to rouse the romantic ideas of Little Jack, that is, if he had any; at least, it gave him food for many hours' conjecture, and he resolved in his mind that before his leave was up, to solve the mystery of the strange house and its mysterious occupants.

The captain's retired habits did away with all hopes of learning anything in that quarter, and as he was encouraged to go abroad but little, his whole thoughts were supposed to be devoted to study.

This enabled Jack to retire unobserved whenever an itching to watch seized him, and thus it was that the learnt that only one person, and that an old woman, visited the house in the daytime.

It was one afternoon as he was watching the departure of the elderly dame, that his attention was attracted by a face appearing at the window directly opposite his own.

The first sight caused him to start involuntarily, and he muttered to himself—

'Yes! 'tis the same face that haunts me in my dreams—that has caused me so much uneasiness since I have come to reside here.'

It was some moments ere he could recover himself sufficiently to take another view. The sight seemed to have thoroughly unnerved him.

At length he ventured to approach the window; but to his disappointment the face was gone.

For nearly an hour he sat musing, absorbed in thought, when, unconsciously turning his head, his eyes met those of the strange, pale face.

This time he had courage to look, and he saw features, though strangely altered, that he had seen before somewhere, but where, for the life of him, he could not call to mind.

As he sat thus entranced, she observed him, and then he saw for the first time that she held a small slip of paper between her tiny, wasted fingers.

The truth flashed instantly to his mind that that slip of paper contained some information that the lady was a prisoner against her will, and that this was the only chance she had of communicating it to the outer world.

Jack, young as he was, had had some experience in these matters, as we have already seen.

When the lady opened the window slightly, and slipped the missive out, he watched narrowly where it fell, and, as it was in a retired spot, he resolved to get possession of it that night at all hazards.

Like most boys, Jack had taken full dimensions of the captain's house, and, though he had never had the opportunity of slipping from the window of his dormitory as many schoolboys do, and scaling the orchard wall to possess himself of the fruit, he had often climbed to the roof of Mother Rickett's house to dislodge his neighbour's pigeons. Therefore, he was well skilled in the art of spout climbing, and he was resolved when night set in to put his skill in practice.

How long the hours seemed to him!

He fancied the sun had forgot to set at its usual time.

He watched the little missive as a miser watches his hoarded treasure, and at times when his eyes had been fixed on it longer than usual, he fancied it had been borne away by the winds.

In this manner twilight crept on him faster than he was aware, and it was not till he saw the strange visitor we have before described that he discovered that he discovered it was getting dark.

His cap was in the hall, but, not wishing to disturb the family or let them into the secret of his adventure, he resolved to go without.

It was not without a slight tremor he trusted himself to his frail support, which was easily reached from a landing window, for he was some twenty feet

from the ground, and, moreover, a greenhouse was directly beneath him.

If he did slip he well knew the result.

If his life was not the forfeit, he would be maimed for life, and at once call upon himself the anger of his generous patron.

However, Jack had no time to meditate.

The spout appeared a good one of its kind, though his weight certainly tended greatly to the injury of its fastenings.

It loosened from the wall, and this gave Jack the better handhold, so that he was soon on the frame of the greenhouse, and his sailor propensities soon took him clear of the garden-wall that skirted a bye-lane.

Here Jack paused for a moment to gain breath, and to think of which should be his next proceeding.

'The missive—the missive!' thought Jack. 'I must get that and learn the first secret.'

Cautiously creeping from the lane, he took a good survey of the street, and, darting across the road, he beheld the object of his anxious watch.

It had fallen close to the wall on a board or kind of cellar-flap, on which anyone seldom, if ever, walked, it was so far from the regular path.

A cry of joy burst unconsciously from the boy's lips, and his eye dilated as he rushed forward to seize the tiny scrap of paper; but scarcely had he grasped it when an icy chill went through his veins, and a horrible whirling seized his brain. The flap gave way, and he disappeared down the dark opening it concealed.

———

CHAPTER CI.

TOM HATCHETT IN HIS NEW HOME—HE LEARNS A STRANGE HISTORY—THE CONSPIRATORS— THE TRAITOR—THE FAILURE WHICH PROVED A DOWNFALL OF LUCK TO THE SMUGGLER.

THE ex-smuggler, Captain Tom Hatchett, met with a good reception from the rough beings who were to be his future companions that night, and good justice did he do to the grog that seemed to flow plentifully.

'Hurrah, my lads! Strike it down the main hatch,' he shouted, 'and here's a jolly good health to you, Mister Skyscraper, for introducing me to such company, and a successful voyage to us all.'

'Ay, ay! hurrah!' was the general response to this, and the grog flowed freer and disappeared much faster.

But Tom was no fool.

It would have taken a longer head than Bill's, cunning as he was, to have bottomed the thoughts of the crafty smuggler.

He drank freely, it was true, and never missed a turn, but it would have taken as much rum to have knocked him over as would have bred a mutiny in a whole fleet.

Bill had not long joined them. He had pulled ashore by himself in a small dingy; but careful as he was of evading his turn to drink he was already becoming half dazed.

Tom noticed this, and seizing an opportunity to draw him aside he said—

'Now, my hearty, we have sailed thus far together, what say you if we get our tacks aboard, and see what course we're going to steer.'

'What course? Leave that to me, my boy,' replied Bill, evasively.

'To you? No, no.'

'What! are you tired of it already?'

'Not just yet.'

'Well, make yourself happy like the rest.'

'Who's unhappy?' said Tom, craftily.

'Well, that's right, my boy. Make yourself jolly, like these topers. See how they pour it down, just as though they were striking molasses into a ship's hold.

'That's very good logic, but we're going to sea.'

'And you'll have just the same time of it. Why, we're loaded with rum and ballasted with shot. Hang me for a parson, if I know what more you want.'

'How about the craft?'

'Well, she's as tight a little fiddle as ever was handled. Sharp as an axe, taut as a fire-bucket, and as for a long chase, why George's own yacht couldn't touch her.'

'So far all speaks well,' said Hatchett, affecting ess earnestness than he really felt, 'but how about his skipper that's to have his life lines eased?'

'Well, as to him, he's nobody.'

Bill spoke this in a manner that convinced Tom he did not care about him knowing too much; and Hatchett, on the other hand, was determined to know all.

'And how about the gal he has aboard?'

'What gal?'

'Why, I heard 'em say there was a gal in mess.'

'Well, p'raps so; but she's nobody.'

'Well, that's good,' said Tom, affecting a laugh; 'two nobody's in a ship, eh? And I suppose they occupy the space between the mainmast and the pump, what they call no men's land? Ha, ha, ha!'

This terminated the conversation for a time, for two of the half-drunken fellows were having a fight, and it required not only the voice of Bill, but the display of a brace of pistols, to quiet them.

This over, Tom resumed his task; he was not likely to relinquish it after he had so well begun.

'I say, old fellar,' he commenced again, 'I tell you what it is: if we are to be shipmates, we must have no playing in the dark, you understand; for if I find you hoisting false colours to me, I shall let daylight into your carcase with one of those very same fellows you have been playing with just now.'

This bold speech made Bill stare.

He was totally unprepared for it.

One glance was sufficient to tell him the nature of his man, and he had long before taken the dimensions of his burly frame, and calculated upon his strength.

This, however, only served to favour Tom in his eyes.

He was just the sort of fellow he wanted, but he did not care about making him a confidential.

Tom, however, insisted upon knowing more, and Bill was compelled, though reluctantly, to satisfy him.

This he did in the following manner.

'Well, old oss, and damme, you seem a hard-mouthed 'un, I just tell you a little of the yarn; but mind, I don't want you to blow it amongst all hands; those skunks, cuss 'em, must be kept in the dark.'

'I understand.'

'Well, you must know, our skipper that was took the offer of a good round sum to capture Will Howard; I daresay you've heard of him?'

'I've heard his name broached; but what of him?'

Tom had to struggle to keep his countenance at mention of Will's name.

'Well, he's turned pirate, they say; and this old admiral, I forget his name, offered to add to the government reward if we could catch him. Our old skipper sniffed at the bait; at first it seemed too good, 'specially as his craft—Will's, I mean—was larger than ours.'

'Yes, yes. Well?'

Tom began to grow impatient.

'The bargain was struck, and we were all promised a handsome reward equal to the danger of the service, but you see we never found him.'

'But how came these men here?' asked Tom, seeing the story was only partly told.

'They were to assist us on land for fear he took to burrowing. You understand?'

'I do, but I can't make out how he came to give up so easily.'

Bill would have fain kept this part of the story to himself, but seeing no way of escape he resumed—

'We cruised about in the latitude laid down so long without so much as smelling him, that our lads got tired of it, for it was tack and tack, bear and haul, watch after watch. At last we fell in for a regular sneezer that made us all cough again, and in fact we never thought the craft, good sea-boat as she is, would ever fetch where she started from.'

'And that frightened you?'

'No, but our skipper had a 'culiar turn o' mind. He's as queer a fish as ever I sailed with. We sights a piece of wreck, picks two half-drowned casts off on it, and he bears away for home at once.'

'What were they, then?'

'Why, a man and woman.'

'Ah! Dead?'

'No.'

'What were they like?'

'Well, I didn't see much on 'em. I heard that the fellow was a luff from some frigate, and the gal '——

He paused.

'What of her?'

'Oh! never mind now.'

Tom's curiosity was too much excited to be put off in this way.

'Go on. Let's have it, you old blubberfin. You've just got to the best of the yarn.'

Bill still hesitated, but Tom managed to wake him up, and he said—

'Will Howard's wife.'

'His wife!' ejaculated Tom, for a moment thrown off his guard.

'His wife, yes; is there anything strange in that? Why, everybody knows, at least the chaps in our line, that he married Black-Eyed Susan.'

'They do; but it's not everybody that's seen her and chaps in our line, you know, take delight in seeing a pretty lass; and I, for one, would'nt mind springing half the rhino of a twelvemonth's cruise to see this pretty girl.'

'Well, as for beauty, I don't think she's much handsomer than any other gal. As for my Poll, of Portsmouth, why, I wouldn't give half the salt water she squeezed out when I left her, for all the Black-Eyed Susan's that ever spread bunting.'

'Avast! there, mate. You know we have all different fancies. Maybe I might think the same if I'd seen her, but as I have'nt, I should very much like to.'

'She might suit your taste.'

'So I think, for one of my mates once said he see her on Deal beach, and she spread as neat a clew and showed as clean a forefoot as any ship in the fleet that there lay moored in the Downs.'

'That may be, but she's only a woman after all.'

'So I suppose; but I expect I shall get a look at her when we go on board the Nooker.'

'That you won't.'

'How's that?'

'She's not there.'

'Lying again, old thunderbolt, eh?' said Tom, slyly.

'No, by my soul; the old hag on board is not her.'

'Old hag,' reiterated Tom. 'Well, where is the young 'un.'

'Gone.'

'Gone?' echoed Tom.

The news seemed to surprise him; in fact he was almost thunderstruck. He had hoped to see Susan, and get her in his power.

'Well, damme, if ever I saw a fellar so struck over a woman,' said Bill, noticing Tom's sudden change. 'Now, I bet if you'd seen her you'd a thrown your grapplins and boarded her, spite of her being married.'

Tom gave the speaker an angry look, and Bill, to soothe him, said—

'Well, she's gone ashore, and our skipper's gone to take care of her. Before they went a long-shore lubber dressed in parson's togs came off to the ship several times.'

'And what became of the man?'

'I put him ashore, poor devil; and that's how I fell in for you, or you fell in for me.'

Tom Hatchett dropped his cheek on his hand, and began ruminating while this part of the story was being told, but Bill, having got so far, was not going to give in till he had quite finished his yarn.

'When he went away—the skipper, you know—this new 'un takes his place, and, says I, this game won't do, old oss; we must have a throw for it; the ship's as much mine as yours.'

'You were going to mutiny?'

'Mutiny be d—d. How can it be mutiny for a fellar to take his own?'

'P'raps not.'

'All would have been right. The chaps are all on my side; and we should have been at sea now, only Jones turned shark and we had to give it up.'

'Is that Jones that's ironed in the cave?'

'That's him, the cuss. He won't spoil us this time. We shall board her in the boats—one forward and the other abaft—and take 'em before they could turn a handspike.'

'The signal's hoisted,' said one of the men, interrupting the discourse.

'What is it?'

'A blue light over a red.'

'That's right; all goes well.'

Bill returned the signal, and then returned to the cave to muster his men.

The word was now passed, but the half-drunken wretches had some difficulty in recovering their feet, and when they did the cry was raised that Jones had escaped.

The men who had been keeping guard were found doubled up on the floor, and the others, as soon as they found Jones was gone, cried loudly for vengeance.

The sentries were pulled roughly to their feet.

A dozen hands were outstretched to reek what they

thought just punishment on them, when Bill ordered every man back.

'I am your leader,' he said, with a tone of desperate meaning in his voice. 'I am your leader. Let my hand be the first to strike.'

But his boast was uncalled for.

A hand had already done the horrid work.

A deep gash in the breast of each of the men showed where the treacherous knife had robbed the men of life.

Bill recovered himself a little on seeing this.

With a bitter malediction on the head of Jones, he shouted—

'See to the boats!—see to the boats!'

They were found to be safe, and it was concluded at once that Jones had fled inland, or was hiding among the rocks.

Whichever it might be, it was not thought expedient to look for him, as torches would be required for that purpose; and as the time for boarding and taking the schooner had arrived, they took to the boats at once.

None of the robbers knew Tom Hatchett; and as the leader placed implicit faith in him, he gave him charge of the boat that was to board on the bow, and took the command of the other himself.

With muffled oars and steady stroke, the boats shot rapidly on.

All seemed silent on the deck of the schooner.

One solitary figure alone was seen on the poop.

This Bill took for the dark outline of the man who had given the signal, and whose watch it was then supposed to be.

Swiftly and silently the boats sped on, all in them confident of success—their weapons ready to their grasp—their minds filled with the thought of blood.

Bill's boat was the first to touch the side, and as she drew under the quarter, he seized the rope placed for him, and leapt on to the deck.

Instantly he was seized and pinioned.

The rest of the boat's crew were as quickly served the same.

Then Bill gave vent to a fearful oath.

Jones, the traitor, stood before him.

Tom Hatchett approached more cautiously.

He approached the bow with a wide sweep.

This was so that he might reconnoitre, and he fancied he saw the glow of a slow-match through one of the ports.

Making a feint to dash on board, he gave his boat another sudden sweep, and, as he expected, the mouth of the gun opened.

Had Tom not steered the boat, it must have been instant destruction, for a dose of grape tore up the water still marked by the boat's course, and a volley of the most horrible abuse followed the roar of the gun.

'Let those stand to be peppered that like, say I,' said the smuggler. 'I'm for sheering. What say you, mates?'

'Sheer, sheer! we have had enough!' cried several voices, simultaneously.

Tom took this for granted; and, chuckling inwardly at the thought of having so easily gained a boat and a full crew, he headed the boat for the shore.

Too crafty to lay there to be trapped, the resolute smuggler gathered all that was useful, and placed them in the boat, and as they pulled away and were about to round a sharp point, they saw a boat coming from the schooner to intercept them.

CHAPTER CII.

JACK'S NARROW ESCAPE IN THE VAULTS.

LITTLE JACK was more shaken than hurt by the fall.

His unceremonious descent seemed to have quite unstrung his nerves.

When he rose to his feet he felt dazed and bewildered, and a large bump on his head marked the spot that he had suffered most on.

It was a bump of no mean size; but Jack saw now that he should wind up his adventure.

Once only he looked up the hatchway, as he termed the hole he had fallen through so suddenly, and thought of returning home; but he found the hole was too high up for him to reach it.

This was a sad beginning, indeed, and so Jack thought; but he was not a faint-hearted boy. He felt certain there were some other means of egress; so he set about finding it.

All was pitch dark.

But he groped about until he found a wall, and following it up with his hands, he was in hopes he might find an outlet.

He did at length.

It seemed a passage, for he could easily stretch to each wall, and he walked along, cautious, but yet more in confidence.

This terminated in what appeared to be a large vault.

He groped along the wall to his left a great way, and yet found no opening or impediment.

Jack now began to grow faint-hearted, and he tried to find his way back.

But a shoal of rats chasing each other caused him to turn round and face the sound, for he feared they would attack him.

When the sound ceased sufficiently to assure him they were gone, he found he had stepped incautiously from the wall, and though he stretched out his hand he could feel nothing.

For a moment he stood bewildered, for in the excitement of the moment he feared he had not turned exactly as he was before, and his conjecture proved true, as he took step after step, and yet came no nearer the wall.

His case was now hopeless in the extreme, but, determined to find one wall and grope his way back, he kept steadily on.

It was some time ere he reached anything, his progress was so slow.

But at length he felt a cold, slimy wall, and he followed it up in the direction as nigh as he could guess of the way he had come.

At length, he found the passage, as he supposed, by which he had entered, and he moved along it at a quick pace.

But to his horror, instead of finding it end, as he expected, the walls diverged on either side, and he lost one altogether.

This was a complete disparagement of his expedition.

He wished the note had been far away before he had seen it.

However he travelled on through the inky darkness, hoping that his troubles would soon end.

But alas! he did not know the nature of the place he was in.

Had he done so, he would not have ventured near the place for worlds.

As he journeyed onward through the intricate mazes (for in truth it seemed such, for the walls began to grow uneven, and in some places formed a regular, or irregular, zig-zag), he found the air begin to grow offensive.

A horrid damp, fetid smell seemed to rise up from the earth each time he set his foot upon it.

More and more oppressive the stench became, until the brave boy felt ready to faint.

Then the horrors of his situation flashed fully to his mind.

'Can it be possible,' he thought, 'that I am to die here in this horrid vault, without a single friend near, and without a single soul knowing my fate? No, no—it is horrible!' he burst out suddenly. 'It cannot be. I must bear up against this horrid stench, and try for liberty.'

Then as he journeyed on, and still met with more defeats than success, his blood went like ice, and then coursed through his veins like red-hot iron. His brain seemed to be on fire, and his imagination was too horrible for description.

More than once he felt in his bosom for the fatal missive.

It was there, safe—much safer than he who bore it through that horrible den.

At length he found himself in what appeared to be a small, vaulted chamber.

He groped around it.

He found there was another opening opposite the one he had entered.

He would not venture to pass through there yet, and he still continued his search, his hands having to serve him as eyes, when suddenly he came across a small niche.

Much faster than he had put his hand in it was it withdrawn. A cold icy subject had caught his fingers, and at the same moment a horrible rattling sound was heard that seemed to follow him as he recoiled, then fell at his feet with a dull crash.

This was the crowner of all.

Of all that little Jack had passed through nothing equalled this.

For a moment he stood like one paralyzed, and then he fell down in a swoon.

When he recovered he found himself laying on the damp floor, surrounded by a heap of bones, human, he little doubted.

Scrambling to his feet, his first thought was to escape from the horrible place, and in his hurry he got into the passage he wished so much to avoid.

Here he found his way difficult.

It was literally in the chamber of death, bones strewed the ground on all sides, let him turn his foot which way he might.

It was anything but a comfortable position for one so young to be placed in, the bones rattling and rolling beneath his feet, impeding his otherwise not very fleet progress, and the thought that almost within a stone's throw his own comfortable little bed lay waiting ready for its occupant.

At length the dungeon of death was passed, another passage traversed, and to his joy a flight of steps were gained leading upwards.

This was indeed joy, and our adventurer set to work to reach the top with renewed vigour.

Here he was doomed to disappointment again.

A large studded door stopped his progress.

He tried it; it would not yield to his youthful pressure.

This was really disheartening, sickening; and he had a hard matter to keep from swooning again.

He did master the feeling, however, and to his

BLACK EYED SUSAN.

OR, PIRATES ASHORE.

SAVED!

surprise, if not joy, he saw a faint gleam of light streak through the keyhole.

That some one was in the room beyond he had now not the least doubt; but he feared to raise an alarm, as he did not know the nature of the person whom it might bring to his aid.

Presently he looked through the keyhole, and saw a form flittering about. Then his quick ear caught the sound of a footstep coming stealthily towards him.

'Who can it be coming thus to my aid, and at such an opportune moment?' he thought. 'How did they become aware of my presence, I wonder?'

He would not have wondered long, had the owner of those stealthy footsteps seen him crouching like a rat in one corner of the threshold.

Presently a key was thrust into the rusty lock, and turned, but much against his inclination the door was not opened, and what surprised him most was, the steps were plainly heard retreating.

That some deep mystery was in the case he had now but little doubt, and that he was about to be the hero of some wild adventure, if he was not already one, seemed to be most clear.

He waited till the footsteps were no longer audible, and then, finding the key was still in the door, he tried it, and found it yield.

A moment sufficed to place him on the other side and close the massive door; then, threading the oaken passage as noiselessly as possible, he came to another door less thickly studded but as cumbersome as the first.

He found this yield, but not so readily as the first; and, on passing through, he found himself in a large wainscoted chamber, dimly lighted by a lamp pendant from the ceiling.

The oaken floor was here and there discoloured by large patches of what appeared to have been blood; and it made his young heart shudder as the thought occurred to him that more than one dark deed had been done in that room, and the more he thought of it the more his memory reverted to the dungeon of bones, and associated the dark blood stains with the many fleshless skeletons he had travelled over.

If his thoughts were horrible before, they were now tenfold, the dim glimmer of the lamp aiding his heated imagination to all kinds of horrid-looking spectres rising up from behind the antique chairs and quaint old furniture.

With a weight of horror hanging at his heart, he fled precipitately towards a pair of stairs; but, ere he reached them, something on one of the tables attracted his attention.

It was a pair of pistols, and had evidently been recently placed there, at least, so he judged by the dust around, as they were quite clean and both loaded.

Thrusting them beneath his jacket he took one more glance around, and he fancied the whole place had become suddenly animated with spirits.

Each chair seemed to have its occupant; others were gliding about, and still they kept pouring up from every hole and crevice in the floor.

As Jack stood and viewed this real or imaginary sight, his hair fairly rose on his head.

His limbs shook with a fearful trembling, and in a state of frenzy he rushed from the spot.

On, on he went, heedless whither his oscillating limbs took him, until he was suddenly aroused to a state of consciousness by the sound of a human voice.

Human voice—how sweet it sounds! especially to one who has been immured in a tomb, as it were, like little Jack had been.

It acted like a magic spell to the ears of the gallant boy.

The sounds were of distress—supplication, and emanated from a female.

This was enough for Jack. All his former fears fled. He thought of the missive, the pale face at the window, and the purpose that brought him from his home on that eventful night.

Boy as he was, he had sufficient knowledge of the world not to rush pell-mell into the room from which the sounds emanated, and the door of which he could see was ajar.

Proceeding cautiously, he ventured just near enough to peer in, and then he saw a sight that made his blood curdle.

Down on her knees was a lovely female, in the act of supplication.

Over her stood a man—a very demon in appearance—and he was evidently trying to force her to sign her name to a document that lay on a table.

'Spare me! spare me!' Jack heard her say. 'If I sign the deed, it will benefit you but little, and prove my ruin.'

'Bah!' the unrelenting wretch exclaimed. 'Has not your uncle sanctioned it?'

'My uncle! God protect me from such a wretch! My bane—my persecutor, you should have said.'

'Call him what you like, he is nevertheless your benefactor, your guardian. His better judgment must guide your acts. Sign at once, or I may be tempted to use violence.'

'You dare not, and yet I have had proof sufficient during my stay here to convince me you would not stand at trifles.'

'I stand at nothing,' was the brutal reply, 'especially when my acts are legalized. Your uncle, Mr. Doggrass, has given free power to act in this.'

'As I said before, my uncle has no control over me. My husband is the one to be consulted.'

There was a calmness in the tone, and a stolid expression in her eye as she uttered these words, that made the villain start.

'If you are bent upon a refusal, and still remain obstinate,' he said, in a half-hissing tone, 'I will resort to other means.'

'Wretch! monster! Were William here, you would pay dearly for this brutality; even my uncle would feel his just resentment.'

'William! Ha! ha! The pirate, the outlaw who dare not show his face, whilst a yard of hemp is in the country. He would resent your wrongs as you term them! Ha! ha! You have judged wrongly when you think I am to be frightened by such a bubble as he.'

Susan, for doubtless our readers have already recognised her, sprang to her feet, and made a move towards the door.

The villain prevented her reaching it.

He clutched her by the long, streaming hair, and drew her back.

A desperate struggle, in which he gained the mastery, then ensued.

He forced her back upon her knee, and clutching her throat with one hand, with the other brandished a glittering dagger above her heaving breast.

'Now!' he hissed, 'will you submit?'

Susan could not reply: she was almost choking.

This enraged the fiend. There was still a bold look of defiance in her jet black eye; and, though it would have been against his interest to have slain her, yet he could scarcely restrain his hand from striking the fatal blow.

'Sign the document, demon in woman's form!' he hissed, his whole frame quivering with the intensity of his passion. 'Remember, no human ear will ever learn your fate if once I strike. The secrets of this house will remain as long as it stands. You may be missed, but none shall find you.'

'Mercy! mercy!—wretch!' was all Susan could articulate.

'Wretch,' repeated the man, savagely; ''tis a nice word, and the last you shall utter. It is as well that none but our own ears have heard it, and none but our own ears shall hear your dying groans.'

He raised the gleaming poignard, and was about to bring it down with one fell swoop, when a voice arrested him.

'Hold, monster! I have seen and heard sufficient to assure me that you, not her, most deserve a violent death. Release your hold, or a bullet may serve to relax your grasp.'

The wretch quivered.

The blood flew to his cheek at being threatened by a boy, and especially when that boy held his pistols and his life, as it were, in his hands.

CHAPTER CIII.

OLD DOGGRASS HAS AN UNPLEASANT VISITOR — THE ATTACK ON THE SMUGGLERS.

THE old tower clock had long proclaimed the hour of midnight as old Doggrass made his way to his wretched abode.

If the abode was wretched, how much more so was its occupant?

As the candle shed its flickering ray on his pale, sunken visage and unkempt hair, it proclaimed him what he was—an outcast from all society.

Seating himself at the table, he sat for some moments absorbed in thought, his features working in a manner that would have puzzled any one to determine the object of his thoughts.

Presently he rose, and, unlocking a small drawer, spread its contents on the table before him.

Several papers he threw from him, and some he piled in a heap, his eye brightening or becoming gloomy as he ran over the different superscriptions.

At length one caught his eye.

It was well thumbed, and the writing outside seemed almost obliterated, yet the word Meriton was still visible.

'Aha!' chuckled the old villain to himself; 'this is the last will and testament of her father. I promised to see his wish fulfilled, which was that, if she came of age before being married, she was to have five hundred pounds, the balance of his assets.

'But she has been a bad girl to me, a most ungrateful niece. She would never marry as I wanted her, or she might have been well off; but, of course, if people will be headstrong, and don't know how to value the advice and good services of a true friend, why they must go to the dogs.'

Doggrass sat for some few moments lost in contemplation.

Presently he broke out in his musings again.

'Five hundred pounds! What a paltry sum for old Meriton, who was once the greatest man hereabouts, to leave his only brat, his daughter. Not but what it was as much and more than I would have done, for it is more than she deserves, the baggage, it is.'

Having thus soliloquized, Silas once more collected the papers, and having hastily deposited them in their former place, mixed himself a stiff glass of grog.

Once more taking his seat he then began ruminating aloud.

'Yes, she will be twenty-one to-morrow, and I hope that she will then become to have sense. Who would have thought that five years had elapsed since the day she showed me open defiance by marrying that beggarly sailor! But there, I hope she will become more tractable, and that Lord Travers will be able to make her give up all pretensions to the smuggler and pirate, who will certainly involve her in ruin.'

At this juncture a tap at the shutter startled him.

Vacantly he stared around, as though scarcely believing what he had heard.

He was not accustomed to visitors of late, and he willingly believed that a false alarm had startled him.

A second knock soon undeceived him, and wondering who it could be, and mindful of his own personal safety, he took a pistol from a shelf and cautiously approached the door.

'Come, bear a hand,' cried a voice as he began fumbling at the fastenings; 'you seem to move as snug as though you expected a squall.'

'I little expected seeing you,' was Doggrass's reply. 'What wind has blown you on the coast again?'

'The same as ever, though I daresay it's freshened a bit.'

Old Doggrass stared at his visitor, who, without any ceremony, seated himself and finished what grog remained in the tumbler.

'Tom Hatchett,' he said, as soon as he could recover sufficient breath, 'how comes it you are here? I heard you were in bilboes—that you had been betrayed into the hands of the Philistines—and '——

'You find it all a lie.'

'I can't answer for that.'

'Can't you see I'm free?'

'I can; but under what conditions and by what means you became so, I cannot understand.'

'Then ask no unpleasant questions. The act alone of calling upon you is quite sufficient proof of the great esteem and friendship I hold towards you, who have been one of my oldest and staunchest friends.'

'Well, well,' answered Doggrass, glancing furtively at the clock if you have any business to transact, do it at once.'

Tom Hatchett watched his agitated mien.

'I have business,' he said; 'but there is no occasion to hurry that, I see. Come, pour out some grog. My sharp walk along the cliffs has left me rather dry.'

Doggrass obeyed reluctantly. It was evident the presence of his friend caused him no little uneasiness.

'Well, now,' said Tom, helping himself, 'after being so long away, it will be fresh news to hear what has been going on in these parts. I suppose it's grown too hot for smuggling, and you have taken up with something more respectable?'

'Respectable!' echoed Doggrass. 'Well, you may say that—that is, if taking poverty by the hand is respectability. There was a chance once of gaining an honest living; but now the sharks have all the pickings, leaving honesty nothing but the bones.'

'But you don't mean to say this is your case?'

'I do. I am ruined.'

'Well, there is nothing like making a clean breast of it, as the beak said to old Ned when he failed in running a cargo in the teeth of the coastguards; bu there are many *ifs* and *ands* to be added and deducted before the statement can be logged.'

' Then you disbelieve me ?' said old Doggrass, with a well-meant scowl; ' and, I suppose, my word will be set down as nothing when I tell you that you run a risk in being here.'

' Well, as to that, I feel little concerned. You would not betray me I know; and, as I have run some risk in coming here, and am likely to incur the same by leaving, I think it safest to remain where I am.'

' And should your presence be suspected——'

' There will be no harm in that, so long as I am not found.'

' You may have been watched, and seen to enter here.'

' In that case we must depend on circumstances.'

' And I must bear the brunt ?'

' I have done the same for you.'

' I know; but those days have passed. I am growing old now, and wish to live the remainder of my days in peace.'

' A glorious notion, indeed; and for this peace, as you term it, you wish to turn off your old friends. Well, I am sorry for that, and, indeed, I feel greatly disappointed, as I have incurred all this danger—though I look upon it as a pleasure—for nothing, and find my only true friend has deserted me.'

' Well, as to that, we have parted now some months, and neither of us seem much the worse for our separation. I have been easier in mind, certainly, and that's about all.'

' That may be all very well, but have you forgot our former friendship ?'

' All—everything, excepting that you are here, and the sooner you are hence the better I shall like it.'

' Plain sailing, by my stars !' ejaculated Hatchett, opening his eyes. ' This is opening a broadside in your teeth. Come, come, Doggrass, where have you learnt all this ?'

' Experience has been my teacher.'

' Ha ! ha ! experience ! and well you have profited by it. Had I chosen to have acted the rogue as you have done, how many cargoes might I not have run unknown to you ? Doggrass, you are a villain.'

' Those are indeed hard words,' said Doggrass, soothingly.

' Still they are true. You have proved a false friend to me.'

' In what way ?'

' By pretending poverty, when I come to ask a favour.'

' I have not heard it asked yet.'

' Well, then, I want you to assist me.'

' Yes.'

' I was caged, you know, and my vessel and all in her I expect has been taken; but as I have escaped, and have mustered a boat and a dozen hands, I only want you to give me a lift.'

' In what way ?'

' Why, assist me to get a small lugger.'

' What use would that be when you can't hold a craft five minutes ? If you had one to-day, to-morrow I should expect to hear you were towed under the fort.'

' Too bad—too bad ! You ought to know Tom Hatchett better.'

' Well, I know that.'

Hatchett's cheek flushed.

' Doggrass,' he said, ' beware how you tamper with a desperate man. I follow a desperate game, and, as you know, I shrink from nothing.'

' Then you would threaten me ?'

' No; 'twas but a caution. Say whether you will assist me, or whether I am to seek elsewhere that you owe me ?'

' Owe you, scoundrel !' exclaimed Doggrass, starting to his feet. ' Owe you ? By heavens ! things have come to a pass. Owe you ! What man in Deal can say I owe him a penny ?'

' I can; as for others, I know nothing. You never paid me for the affair of your niece.'

' I gave her to you, but you was fool enough not to stick to her.'

' Well, that may be true, but she's on shore again.'

' How know you that ?'

' I know the ship she came in.'

' And where she stays ?'

' Perhaps.'

As Doggrass began to grow more anxious in his inquiries, the smuggler grew more sullen in his answers.

' When did you see her last ?'

' Not many hours since.'

' You did ?'

' Of course. You seem to think it strange !'

' I do. It is strange if you have seen Susan.'

' Why, have you shut her up in some castle ?'

' We-e-ll, not exactly, you see; but I don't care about her being exposed to every prying eye. Her husband, that rascally sailor, will never dare show face here again; he is branded as a pirate, and a swing from the yard-arm will welcome his return.'

' Not so bad as all that, I hope, Master Doggrass ?'

' Yes, sir; and you'll find it true.'

' Well, that's a point I won't argufy. I know if I am caught what they'll do to me; but, then, I've never sustained the injuries he has. Poor lad ! it was a cruel thing of you to have him pressed on the very day of his wedding.'

Doggrass shuffled in his chair.

' Had you been me,' he answered, at length, ' you would have done the same.'

' Never, Doggrass—never. I loved the girl, and who the devil could resist such a pair of black eyes ? But to force a brave lad like Will to fight for the king would have been the last of my thoughts.'

' Well, let it rest at that. More than once I offered you her hand, and you were fool enough to let the chance slip, and '——

' Now I am poor I suppose I may cast off all hopes.'

' Certainly. I would not give her to a beggar, and you are but little else.'

Captain Hatchett's brow grew dark as night.

A spasm passed through his frame as he strove to check his rising temper.

' Look you here, Doggrass,' he said; ' do not add taunts to insult, or I may forget the friendship that has existed between us.'

' What, would you murder me in my own house ?' exclaimed Doggrass, with ill-concealed terror, as his eye caught sight of a pistol the smuggler held beneath his coat.

' I would silence your prattling tongue. But, hark ! what is that ?'

'Footsteps, I could swear.'

'Then I must hide.'

'Not here. Fly by the back way.'

'It is dangerous to break cover,' said the smuggler, sullenly. 'Let them burrow me out. It will take more than one to take me, and these dogs I have found never fail to bite hard.'

'Fly! Escape quickly!' gasped Doggrass, in abject terror. 'If there is a skirmish in my house I am ruined for ever.'

'Well, you say you are in poverty, so it can take but little to ruin you,' replied the smuggler, with provoking coolness.

Doggrass looked around in abject terror.

The footsteps were gradually sounding nearer.

'There are three or four of them,' he said.

'And there are two of us. We have the advantage of a good battery, and that makes our numbers equal.'

Presently a halt was made at the door, and a loud knocking followed.

'Open, in the king's name!' thundered a voice.

'Who is it disturbs us at this hour of the night?' cried Doggrass, with a slight tone of indignation in his voice.

At the same time he was trying to remove a large table that seemed to resist all his efforts.

The knocking was repeated with greater violence, and threats were uttered of breaking down the door.

'Quick! quick!—lend a hand here,' cried Doggrass, in accents of terror. 'Ah, 'tis no go. You must secret yourself where you can.'

Hatchett was a man of burly frame, and it was with some difficulty he contrived to squeeze his burly carcase beneath the table they had vainly been trying to move.'

The smuggler was anything but pleased with his new position.

He would sooner have met his foes face to face.

However, he placed his pistols to his hand, and muttering a deep curse, awaited the issue in no pleasant state of mind.

Old Doggrass then approached the door, throwing his clothes into disorder as though he had hastily dressed.

But his services were not needed.

The door came in with a crash, and a dozen well-armed men instantly filled the place.

'Ah! Mr. Doggrass! we have you now,' said the lieutenant in command of the party. 'There is no chance of escape. Turn up the smuggler you have sheltered beneath your roof.'

'Smuggler!' gasped Doggrass, in well-feigned surprise. 'I have none here!'

''Tis a lie! He was seen to come this way.'

'Well, Lieutenant Pike, if you are so well-informed, you will perhaps tell me how he gained admittance. It must have been by the chimney, as my door has not been opened since dark.'

'Liar!' again shouted the lieutenant, 'and that to your teeth. Harry Rowlock, the waterman, swears he saw that infamous Tom Hatchett edging along the cliff, and he says he made straight for here.'

'Harry Rowlock is mistaken; the old fool is losing his sight, or he would not have rowed athwart hawse the admiral's barge as he did yesterday.'

'That has nothing to do with this case,' said the lieutenant. 'His eyes are perhaps better than you think; 'twas he first reported Bill Raker being seen on the beach, and now I have positive proof he was right.'

'Bill Raker!' gasped Doggrass, in surprise.

'Ay; you know him well—the mate of the Redbreast.'

Silas stood for a moment astounded.

'We're wasting time here, sir,' said one of the party, addressing Lieutenant Pike. 'Those fellows are slippery as eels, and every minute we give them ——ah! what's that?'

'The click of a pistol, by Jove! Now, lads, prepare. Search the house, and if we don't have them this time, my name's not Pike.'

In an instant all was in an uproar.

Doggrass was thrown down by a party mounting the stairs, and in his fall one of Hatchett's pistols went off, lodging a ball in the leg of one of the sailors.

One of the sailors, judging by the direction of the shot that it was fired by Doggrass, dragged him to his feet with very little ceremony; and Hatchett, feeling himself no longer safe, crawled out behind, and began to seek for some means of escape.

This was no easy task.

A party of the sailors were overheard tumbling over everything that might or might not reasonably hold a man; whilst the remainder were ransacking every hole and cupboard.

Hatchett glanced his eye at the door, but a half-dozen sturdy fellows were guarding it; then his attention was called to a window near at hand.

This seemed his only chance; so having re-primed his pistols, and secured a little note that had slipped from Doggrass's pocket in his fall, he crept towards the aforesaid window.

It was deep in the shadow.

He reached it unperceived, and would have doubtless escaped, but some clumsiness in undoing the fastening betrayed him.

'Aha! the smuggler!' burst from one of the sailors; but ere he could dash forward and capture him, Hatchett cleared away both frame and shutters with his heavy sea boot, and standing on the naked sill kept his enemies at bay.

'Back, all of you!' cried Hatchett, his voice husky with mingled desperation and rage. 'Back, I say, or by —— your life shall be the forfeit.'

For a moment he stood thus, his dark, restless eye seeming to take in every movement at a glance, and as the footsteps of the men descending from their fruitless search met his ear, his case seemed rendered one of the greatest desperation.

One wild look he cast around, and then his mind seemed resolved.

With a cry of defiance, he raised his hands aloft; then, taking aim, fired point-blank into the faces of the men who were anxiously watching a chance to pounce upon him.

This staggered them for a moment; and when they recovered from the shock Hatchett had disappeared.

A dozen men, headed by Pike, were at the window in an instant, and they could just make out a dark figure gliding swiftly away in the gloom.

The shots from half-a-dozen pistols whistled through the night air, and above the din the voice of Lieutenant Pike was heard shouting—

'To the beach, lads—to the beach! Rescue this rascally scamp, and then for the smuggler.'

Hatchett had had a good lead, but in spite of this his pursuers followed swiftly on the trail.

'There, there he goes!' shouted one of the sailors, as a dark figure emerged from an opening and darted swiftly towards the cliffs.

It was evident Hatchett's heavy deck boots and

thick woollen coat were telling on him fast, for his pursuers, much lighter dressed, were hauling upon him hand over hand.

Once he stumbled, and then a shout came from his pursuers, but he soon regained his feet, and sped on as before.

He was fast making for an angle of the rock where he would be hidden from his pursuers, and Pike, seeing this, levelled a pistol and fired.

The smuggler fell, and a shout of joy burst from the sailors, who had now began to slacken their speed ; but to their mortification, the smuggler they had thought had been dropped by a bullet, sprang to his feet and darted away.

' A clever ruse, d——n him !' hissed Pike, foaming with rage. ' Curse the fellow ! he will run us all out yet.'

' Ah ! he's a bird not easily caught !' growled one of the men, ' or he would never have run so long. It 'll be a queer rope, I fancy, that will hang him yet.'

' You are right, mate,' interposed another, whose breath told that he was close upon done. ' I'll lay it 'll be the rope cable of a Chinese junk.'

This conversation was put an end to by the smuggler gaining the summit of the cliff, and, as a dozen pistols were levelled at the form of the smuggler, as it stood out in the bold relief, a shout was heard, and a party of smugglers made their appearance.

CHAPTER CIV.
THE GOLDEN ARROW FALLS IN WITH A PRIZE — THE TREASURE CHESTS — THE PIRATE'S DOOM.

LIKE three caged beasts were those left on board the Red Vulture.

Rodwin Blake dared not close his eyes in sleep.

Everywhere he went he fancied the gaze of his companions was fixed upon him.

Gregory Saunders and Despardo had taken up their abode in the cabin ; but Blake had domiciled himself forward, where the dreadful tragedy had been enacted.

The bodies had been removed, but the floor of the forecastle was here and there stained with patches of blood.

It was an unpleasant position for one callous and hard-hearted as he was even ; but as circumstances were he was compelled to make the best of it.

As it required all the energies of the whole of them to keep the ship within any bounds at all, the life of each was invaluable to the others ; thus it was that they had a kind of security in each other.

Had it not been so, Rodwin Blake would have stood but little chance between his two foes. Nevertheless, he was ever on the watch against treachery, and fear never let him close his eyes in sleep.

For three days this torture was kept up, and care and the want of rest was beginning to tell plainly upon Blake, when they were blessed with the joyful sight of a sail.

Saunders eyed her steadily with his glass, but it was some time ere he could determine whether she was a cruiser or a vessel trading on the coast.

Despardo took his turn at the glass with like success, and Blake, who still stuck to his dominions forward, ascended to the cross-trees.

Presently he descended, and venturing as far aft as the mainmast, said—

' Well, Saunders, what do you make of her ?'

' I can't say positively,' growled Saunders.

' Can't you form an opinion ?'

' Perhaps I can ; but it is best kept to myself.'

Rodwin Blake bit his lip.

He never held any conversation with his companions, only on such occasions as when it took the whole of them to manage a sail or trim the yards. Saunders and Despardo undertook the steering of the ship between them.

' Will you lend me the glass ?' said Rodwin, after a pause.

' Go forward, and keep your place,' replied Gregory, in a tone that deeply humbled Rodwin. ' When you are required aft, we will call you.'

A deep oath came from Rodwin's lips.

A fierce fire lighted in his eye.

' Curse you !' he muttered ; ' if it were not two to one against me, I would make you recall those words.'

A light, mocking laugh rang in his ears as Gregory joined Despardo at the helm, and this seemed to fire his brain with madness.

By this time the strange vessel was bearing down on them fast.

Blake had walked forward ; and, leaning upon the bulwark, was surveying the stranger with keen and anxious eye.

Nothing escaped his earnest gaze, from the set of her royals to the rake of her lower masts.

Presently he started.

' The Golden Arrow, by heavens !' he ejaculated.

' Yes, yes, it must be ; I cannot be deceived,' he again broke forth. ' No vessel but her could glide so smoothly through the water, no prow but hers could cleave the water with so gentle a ripple.'

While he was ruminating, the strange sail swept alongside with the grace of a seabird, and a voice from the quarter-deck hailed the Red Vulture.

Gregory Saunders scarce knew what reply to make, but a word from Despardo soon overcame this difficulty.

' The Lake, from Havanna to London,' he answered, boldly.

' You seem shattered up aloft. Have you had bad weather ?'

' We encountered a heavy gale, and lost most of our crew.'

' You are in distress, then ?'

' Yes. A little help to put us to rights and the loan of a few men would be very acceptable.'

' I will oblige you as well as I can,' was the reply, and the vessel, that had already been rounded to, made active preparations to lower a boat.

Gregory's perception had not been so keen as Rodwin Blake's.

He had failed to recognize the Golden Arrow, owing to her different disguises, but Rodwin viewed her with the eye of an experienced seaman.

Gerald Stuart boarded her in person, and commenced at once taking mental notes of what was required up aloft. Then he directed his attention aft, where Gregory was standing dumbfoundered.

' Well, well,' exclaimed Gerald, an angry flush suffusing his cheek, ' who would ever have dreamed of the Lake turning out to be the Red Vulture ? What means this ?' he asked angrily. ' Why have you practised on me this deception ?'

Gregory quailed beneath the searching glance.

He knew not what to reply.

The Golden Arrow was the last of all ships he would have wished to meet.

'Come, what have you to say?' asked Captain Stuart, angrily. 'What villainy have you and Despardo been up to that I find you thus circumstanced?'

'Nothing particular,' replied Gregory, mustering courage. 'I told you we met with a fearful storm and lost all hands.'

'And you two are the only survivors?'

'Nay, there is one more forward.'

'Let him be brought aft,' said Gerald, motioning to his men.

He was instantly obeyed, and Rodwin Blake, haggard and careworn, was led on the quarter-deck.

Captain Stuart started on seeing him.

'What, Rodwin Blake here? 'Tis a strange wind that has blown three such rogues together. How came you here, Rodwin? You have, no doubt, already invented a tale.'

Rodwin Blake, having nothing to conceal, told his tale as plain as possible; and when Captain Gerald had listened to it with all patience, he made a gesture to his men and descended to his cabin.

Without ceremony, Gregory, Despardo, and Rodwin Blake were seized upon by the Arrow's crew and taken on board that ship.

Meanwhile, Captain Stuart possessed himself of all papers of any value; and then, giving the ship over to his men to avail themselves of any treasures they might find, ordered them to set fire to her.

'Now then, my hearties,' said Ned Marline, the captain of the main-top, and whose especial duty it was to see the captain's order carried out. 'Now then, my hearties, bear a hand, or you will have to tumble aboard before you've overhauled half his lockers.'

'Avast heaving, topmate!' said old Bob Brace, turning a huge quid in his cheek, and giving his pants a fresh hitch. 'It's no good being in a hurry when you get hold of a good job. It's a 'tarnal shame of the skipper to make matchwood of such a craft as this, when half-a-dozen of us could run her in port, and make a pretty good cruise of it.'

'Well, as to that,' growled Marline, 'the skipper knows best. Duty is duty, and if he gives us the run of the cargo, I think we ought to be satisfied.'

'Cargo! well, damme, I've run across nothing yet worth having. The hold seems empty, and all I can see worth the least trouble of moving is these two heavy chests.'

'And what's in 'em?'

'Shot, I lay a wager!' interrupted Tom Tiller; 'shot, my hearties, you may wager your grog. It's what they trim ship with.'

'What do you suppose they want to trim ship so nicely for?' inquired Ben.

'Why, these kind of ships always does it if they want to ease her forefoot on a wind; why it's much easier than transporting the bow gun aft. Besides, it might be wanted.'

'Then what do you take her to be?'

'Well, Bob, I'll tell you. I've taken the dimensions of the truck and kelson, and I conclude that she's a slaver.'

'Nonsense.'

'So you may say, but I knew it. She's a black birdcatcher, and so you'll think if you look at her hold.'

'Well, you've sailed long enough on the coast to know, Tom,' said Marline, scratching the small tuft of hair that stuck on his head like a bunch of half

teased oakum; 'and of course I won't argufy the point; but this I must say, if you mean to overhaul these chests it's time we began, for we shall soon tire the skipper's patience.'

Bob Brace, Tom Tiller, and Marline then set to work to discover the contents of the chest, which, after five minutes' careful survey, were found to be so strongly made and so heavily bound with iron, as to puzzle them how to proceed.

Bob stood some time cogitating and punishing the huge quid that distended his cheek in a most horrible manner.

'Three locks, by jove!' he muttered; 'they were not put there for nothing. If we could once open them, I know they would reward us.'

'Och, sure and bedad! and what's all the row about?' broke in Pat, who suddenly made his appearance, cutting a ludicrous figure.

His face was as black as a sweep, and the perspiration was rolling down his lank cheeks in large beads.

'What, Pat! where on earth have you been to?' asked Bob, endeavouring to look serious.

'Where an airth? by jabers, and it's meself that thinks I've been somewhere else; if I may judge by the heat, I've been nearly roasted.'

'And how's that?'

'Why, do you see, I heard the ship was to be desthroyed, and, thinking there might be something useful in the way of cookery, I comes aboard.'

'Well?'

'First thing I claps eyes on was as fine a set of coppers as ever graced a galley, and, sez I to myself, "Pat, we must have 'em."'

'So you've been fool enough to try and get them aboard?'

'By my sowl I have; and, had the lazy spalpeens give me just one lift, I should have done it; but, bad luck to me, they ran away, and while I was inside tugging for bare life, they set fire to the galley.'

'The devil they did; and is the ship on fire.'

'By the powers it would have been, had I not stuck to it; not that I cared a pin for the ship, but I couldn't stand and see the coppers roasted—indeed, indeed.'

'Bravo, Pat,' said Bob Brace, tapping him on th shoulder. 'Now, we've got a tarnation job here, and if you like to give us a pull through with it, why, shiver me, you shall have the coppers, galley and all; at least, what's left of it.'

Pat began to roll his eyes most wondrously at sight of the huge chests.

'Well, what's in 'em?' he asked.

'That's just what we want to know,' said Tom.

'Indeed—and sure then give us a lift.'

The sailors commenced a laugh. They thought Pat was beginning his jokes.

Pat, however, was in no humour to be laughed at.

Placing his broad shoulder against one corner of the chest, and setting his feet against the bulk head, he swung the chest round with evident ease.

'Bravo, Pat!—bravo, Pat!' came from several of the group; but Bob's face was fearfully elongated.

If it could be moved so easily, he thought, there could be but little gold in it.

Pat, however, now he'd begun, was not so easily disheartened.

Having examined the locks, and found they were too strong to force, he had recourse to another expedient.

With assistance he soon turned it bottom upwards, and, as he had expected, found that it was not so securely bound on the underneath side; so with a formidable axe he commenced a desperate assault on it.

It was not long yielding beneath the Irishman's prowess, and a hole was formed large enough to examine its contents.

At first their labour seemed of no use, but by degrees sundry sparkling little stones were brought to light, and the little party found themselves as rich as Jews.

The second chest was now the subject of discussion; but this, they found, resisted strongly.

Pat, however, mastered it at last, and to their joy they found it contained gold and silver, which they quickly transferred in sacks to their own ships.

Faithful to promise, Pat's coppers were hoisted into the boat, and then the Red Vulture was committed to the flames.

While this was being enacted on board the Red Vulture, a scene of a different nature was going on on board the Golden Arrow.

The three prisoners were arranged before the captain, and severely cross-questioned, but as nothing but what tended to their guilt could be drawn from them, Captain Gerald retired to consider what punishment they deserved.

Gregory Saunders he would have run up to the yard-arm without a moment's hesitation; but as this punishment seemed too severe for all of them, and as he wished to serve them as near alike as possible, he hit upon another plan.

Two of the Vulture's boats had been used in conveying the treasure on board, and into each of these he ordered two days' bread and water to be placed.

A pair of oars, but no sail nor anything that was likely to serve as one.

Into one of these Gregory was placed, with instructions not to touch anything until without the range of the Arrow's guns, under pain of being fired into.

Next, Despardo was placed in the other boat, and when it was deemed an impossibility for them to reach each other, the second boat was cut adrift.

Now came the turn of Rodwin Blake. He looked ghastly and careworn, and his eye wandered restlessly about the deck.

'Now, Rodwin,' said Captain Gerald, 'it is time we part. Remember, when next we meet, if we do ever, the long reckoning between us will be settled. I give you the chance of your life, and if you escape the punishment you so well merit, death, I hope you will turn the remainder of your days to a better account.'

So saying, he gave a signal to his men, and Rodwin, more dead than alive, was led into the boat.

It was now getting dark, and a damp, heavy mist was beginning to fall on the ocean, when the order was given to cast off.

A deep, wailing groan came from the boat as it disappeared in the gloom, and Captain Stuart, seeming satisfied with the manner in which he had disposed of the trio, descended to his cabin.

CHAPTER CV.

DEATH OF THE SCOUT—WILL'S DESPERATE ENCOUNTER WITH THE SAVAGES.

WILL and Sancho saw no chance of escaping from the wigwam in which they had sought shelter. From the cursory glances they could obtain, they concluded the whole place was alive with savages.

As Sancho had been formally rigged as one of the savages, and wore one of their skins, he sadly wanted to go out and reconnoitre; but Will would not hear of this.

'It will be exposing yourself to unnecessary danger,' he said. 'We will stick together, and share whatever comes between us.'

Sancho did not much approve of this.

He expostulated, and urged the necessity, but all to no purpose.

'Do you not see,' said Will, in a voice now grown husky, 'that the torches are glaring all around. Every tree, every bush will be searched, for they suspect we are in the vicinity. See you not,' he added, pointing to a dark figure that was clinging to what appeared a chief—'see you not that Oona is trying to put them off the trail?'

The rest of that night was well calculated to try the nerves of the gallant pair.

Hunger and thirst were telling upon them fast; but when it was considered that their life was at stake, this was borne with cheerfulness.

The gray streaks of morning at length began to appear, and a cold, chill air rendered the situation of our adventurers the more miserable.

'We must be moving out of this,' said Will, 'if we have any regard for our lives. If we remain here, we must surely be discovered.'

'But how are we to get away?'

'I know not; but certain it is we must. I have been thinking of something this last half-hour that has totally made up my mind.'

'And what might that be?'

'Well, I have thought that Oona might prove treacherous. These Indian girls can hate as deeply as they love. If she fancies I have slighted her passion, she will be one of our deadliest foes.'

'But I do not think she is an Indian born,' said Sancho, musing.

'Ah! What reasons have you for your suspicions?'

A sudden thought had reverted to Will's mind, and he asked the question with more earnestness than he would have wished to betray.

'From what little I gleaned, while in the wigwam, I believe her to be the daughter of some settler that has been slain in their savage warfare, and that the chief has adopted her from childhood.'

'That,' replied Will, 'may account for the strange fancy she took for me; but, however, we will not trust to her. We must place all dependence in ourselves.'

Sancho agreed to this; and, as it was getting light, he ventured to peep through a hole he had made in the side of the wigwam.

All was now hushed. Whatever the Indians were doing was done in silence.

'See here,' whispered Sancho, drawing Will to the hole; 'there is a scout within a few yards of us. He is leaning against a tree as though drowsy with his night's watching.'

'True,' said Will; and there was a hollowness in his voice. 'He is armed with a rifle, and has a well-filled pouch.'

BLACK EYED SUSAN.

OR, PIRATES ASHORE.

GERALD STUART ENGAGES THE MAN OF WAR.

For a moment Will seemed lost in thought.

His fingers played nervously with the handle of a long scalping knife.

'One blow,' he muttered, 'would do it; but yet I cannot bear the thought of being assassin.'

'But we must do away with idle reasoning,' said Sancho, who had heard sufficient of the words to make out their import; 'it is life for life.'

'True, but it is cowardly to strike a sleeping foe. The hand of Will Howard is as yet clean of such a dastardly deed.'

'Then let mine be the task,' said Sancho, his dark eye flashing with a sinister gleam. 'They stand between us and liberty, and that liberty is life to us.'

It was some time ere Will would yield the point, and when he did, it was with a mighty effort to master his feelings.'

'No, Sancho, never shall it be said that Will Howard was afraid to do his own dirty work; you are a faithful follower, and already have you blood enough on your hands.'

Without further hesitation Will dropped flat on the earth, and drawing himself to the opening, took a good view of the figure of the scout.

He could see many more about, but too distant to observe his movements.

Wreaths of curling smoke here and there indicated that some of the squaws were astir, and Will, yielding to the pressing exigencies of the moment, crawled through the grass almost with a serpentine movement.

Cautiously he approached the savage, for it was evident he was not asleep, though in a kind of dreamy daze, and when he had approached near enough, he sprang to his feet and buried the gleaming knife to the hilt in his broad shoulders.

One fearful gasp the Indian gave, and tried to turn and face his murderer.

But the blow was too surely death, and he sank upon the sward without so much as a groan.

Will was not long in divesting him of his rude accoutrements, and, giving a signal for Sancho to follow him, he dashed into the forest.

But swift and silent as the deed had been done, it did not escape the watchful eye of one on the opposite side of the plain.

It was Oona, who was returning to her tent after a fruitless search for the object on whom she had so strangely fixed her love.

Unconsciously a cry burst from her lips, and ere its echo had died away, the savages poured from their huts like so many bees, and, taking a cue from the direction in which her eyes were still riveted, dashed into the forest like so many howling fiends.

It was difficult travelling for Will and his companion. The thick growth of the underwood impeded their progress greatly, whilst the howling of the savages told plainly that they were gaining upon them fast.

Denser and denser the forest seemed to grow, and Will's legs suffered much from the brambles; still, on he went, Sancho following in his wake.

At length the forest grew more clear, the brushwood became less entangled, but the howling of the savages grew nearer.

The border of the forest was at length gained, and before him rose a steep acclivity.

Before ascending he paused.

To his horror, Sancho was nowhere to be seen, and the shouts of the Indians on either side told him that they had forereached him.

Will's first fear was that Sancho had fallen into the savages' hands, and he was about to return to aid him if possible, when he found it an utter impossibility to retrace his way even for a few yards.

He was now alone, and deeply did he feel the helplessness of his situation.

But our hero did not forget himself.

Gliding steadily forward, scanning every tree, bush, and covert, he gradually ascended the mountain that rose before him, till at last he stood upon the verge of a rocky gorge, and beheld, compressed by its narrow channel, a mountain stream roaring and foaming fifty feet below him.

There was something congenial to his nature in the wildness and grandeur of the surrounding scene, and for a minute or two he paused here in a contemplative mood, leaning on his rifle and letting his eyes rest upon the foaming waters below.

Rocky peaks stretched up around him, with bushes fringing their dark, jagged sides, and here and there a tall pine standing sentinel and overshadowing them.

Far below, the eye fell upon an undulating forest that stretched away into the blue distance.

The gorge where Will stood was about twenty feet in width, and the sides were perpendicular.

On the opposite bluff of the stream, about one-third of the way down to the water, there was a narrow shelf, running zig-zag with the different strata, and being mostly concealed by bushes which shot out from here and there a crevice and overhung the boiling torrent.

At the point exactly below him, upon which his eye fell as it went down to the water, there was an angular projection of the rock, with a deep fissure just behind it, barely wide enough to admit the body of a man, but extending back some distance, and gradually enlarging into a small cavern.

Little did our hero think, as his eye chanced upon this spot, how much his life would depend upon this peculiar formation of nature.

While he thus stood, with his gaze bent below him, he was suddenly startled by the whoops of savages, and glancing quickly round, he saw them bounding down the rock behind him, and spreading out to the right and left, so as to cut off his escape in either direction.

A moment was sufficient to acquaint him with the startling fact that, if he would avoid either captivity or death, there was no alternative but the fearful leap before him, and as he had escaped almost by a miracle, he was not a second in making his choice.

The leap could only be death, and he feared that less than again falling into the clutches of his barbarous enemies.

There was not a moment to be lost.

They were almost upon him; he could not even venture back three paces to gain headway for the spring.

So crouching down a little, he bounded from the rock on which he stood, with the full effort of his will and nerve.

But owing to a slip of one of his feet, he fell slightly short of the opposite verge, and came down upon the shelf we have mentioned, where, catching hold of the vines as he struck, he saved himself from a backward plunge into the seething torrent below.

Will paused for a moment to gain breath.

Even here he was not safe.

He had sufficient presence of mind to know it, and act accordingly.

Swinging himself round the angular projection of the rock, at the peril of being precipitated into the roaring rapids, he had just time to glide into the fissure leading to the cavern, when some three or four shots were fired by the yelling Indians above, two of the balls flattening against the rock by his side, and one grazing the skin of his shoulder.

'It is my turn now,' muttered Will, as he faced about, brought his rifle to his shoulder, and took a quick aim at the most prominent figure of the disappointed and yelling group.

Then came a flash—a crack—and, bounding outward from the rock, the savage fell headlong into the roaring waters, which whirled his body out of sight in an instant.

The wild yells of surprise and rage which followed this death-shot of the bold sailor would have sent a cold chill of terror to the heart of anyone less courageous than Will; but he, with a quiet gleam of satisfaction lighting up his bronzed features, replied with a loud, taunting laugh, that rendered his enemies almost mad with fury.

They took care, however, to draw back and keep themselves out of sight; and muttering to himself, our hero drew back also, and hastily reloaded his rifle.

'Well,' thought the intrepid Will, as he glanced curiously around his rocky abode, which was scarcely ten feet in diameter, 'this looks like getting into new quarters. If I had but Sancho here now, with another rifle, we might polish off the whole lot. It's a pity there are no provisions; if there were any, we might hold out a whole siege.'

Having reloaded his rifle, and adjusted his long knife ready to his grasp, Will ventured as far out towards the light as he thought prudent, and there took up his watch, hoping to get a sight of another of his foes, that he might send him after the first.

For half-an-hour he watched in vain, and was beginning to think they had all retreated, when he fancied he saw a very slight motion, as it might be the movement of a small stone on a larger. He was not deceived, however, and carefully poising his rifle, he waited till he could just catch a glimpse of two black, basilisk eyes rising slowly above the rock to peer down at his place of refuge. Then his finger pressed the trigger, and a ball passed into the painted forehead, just above those gleaming orbs, and crashed through the brain of the savage.

Loud yells from others quickly resounded, and half-a-dozen dusky, almost naked figures suddenly appeared along the edge of the chasm, and poured a volley of balls at the spot from which a wreath of blue smoke was rolling outward.

Will Howard sprung back the instant he fired, and thus allowed the balls of his enemies to harmlessly flatten against the rocks within a foot of his head.

Then, with another taunting laugh, he quietly proceeded to reload his piece, and once more set himself on the watch.

Hour after hour went tediously by, and still Will saw nothing of his foes.

Had they gone and left him?

It was not probable, but rather that they were on the watch, waiting with cat-like patience to shoot him whenever he should attempt to escape.

He felt himself completely caught in a trap, and thought it not unlikely that the Indians would keep a guard over him until he should venture forth alive or starve to death where he was.

This was not a very pleasant reflection; but our hero had been through so many perils already, and had in his time so many hair-breadth escapes, that he did not attach the weight to it he otherwise might.

Something, he fancied, would yet happen for his rescue.

But the day proved a long and tedious one; and, when the shadows had filled the valleys and the descending sun was gilding the highest peaks, he began to experience a keen sense of hunger and thirst.

Tired, too, of watching in one position, and anxious to see what chance there might be of his getting to the world above during the coming darkness, he ventured rather boldly through the fissure, got upon the shelf outside, and took a quick survey of the rocks above and below him.

He was there only a few seconds, but in that time a lurking savage fired from the opposite heights, and, staggering back, Will fell into the fissure, believing himself mortally wounded, and hearing the triumphant yells of his foes at the result.

On examination, however, he discovered, to his great joy, that the ball had struck an iron tobacco-box in a side pocket, and glanced off, leaving him only slightly bruised.

Knowing that the savages now believed him killed or badly wounded, he instantly resolved not to undeceive them, thinking they would either depart or remain and seek to get his scalp.

'If they do come,' he muttered, 'they will find me worth several dead men yet.'

The result proved that he had correctly surmised, for about two hours after sunset he heard a slight noise at the mouth of the fissure, and soon saw it darkened by a human figure.

He suppressed his breathing, and allowed the figure to advance a few steps, and then struck it to the heart with his long knife.

The savage fell without a groan; and, securing his weapons, he dragged the body back, and prepared himself for the next.

Creeping stealthily to the shelf he found a rope made of twisted deer-skin dangling from above.

By this the savage had descended, and by this, doubtless, another would follow.

Fixing himself where he could easily look upwards, he remained for an hour on the watch, and then beheld in the dim light another human body carefully descending.

Waiting with secret exultation till the second savage was near his level, Will suddenly reached up and cut the cord above his head, and, with a wild yell, the Indian went swiftly down into the foaming rapids.

From this time for several hours Will heard nothing more of his enemies, and resolved at last to dare all, and conquer or die, he reached up, seized hold of the still dangling rope, and, with great exertion, drew himself to the level above.

Scarcely had he reached the surface, however, and was preparing to look around, when he found himself seized by a pair of powerful arms in such a manner that all resistance would be useless, and, yielding to his fate, he found himself once more a prisoner.

CHAPTER CVI.

THE TRAITOR—THE SMUGGLERS SURPRISED.

STARTLED by the sudden appearance of the smugglers, Lieutenant Pike had some difficulty in arranging his men.

'Now, lads,' he shouted, 'we had these sea-robbers before. There is nothing to do but mow them down, and show them that the laws are not to be trifled with with impunity.'

A general shout came from Pike's party, which was answered by a derisive cheer from the smugglers.

'Surrender, miscreants!' cried the lieutenant, boiling with rage. 'Lay down your arms, and we will give you quarter.'

'Quarter be d—d!' cried Hatchett. 'Show your liberality when it is needed. We will never give in while a man remains standing.'

'Then take the reward of your obstinacy,' said the lieutenant. 'On to them, lads; let them taste your steel.'

The sailors made a rush; but a pistol volley point-blank checked them; and, before the smoke had cleared thoroughly away, the smugglers had disappeared as suddenly as they had come.

A cry of rage burst from the lieutenant's lips when he found himself thus baffled.

'Follow them—let them not escape,' he shouted.

His men made a rush; but it was fruitless. The only man they saw was a wounded smuggler, who had been shot through the calf.

'Aha! seize him!' cried Pike; 'he will make one rascal the less.'

Two of the sailors led him up the cliff; and, as he seemed in great pain, he was taken to the jail at once, and his wound attended to.

Lieutenant Pike accompanied him, and it was not until he had wrung from him a promise, by the aid of threats and promises, to betray the entrance to the smugglers' stronghold, that Pike left him.

There was a smirkish smile on his lip when he left the prison, and he hastily took his way to head-quarters, to prepare for a grand attack.

*   *   *   *   *   *

The moon had scarcely risen, and by its fitful light might be seen the dark forms of several men flitting along, like so many spectres, beneath the towering cliffs.

The wind blew in fitful gusts, and the roaring of the waves as they rolled on the beach was the only sound that broke upon the ear.

'Hold!' cried the foremost of the men, who was no other than the lieutenant.

Then turning to two of his companions, who were midshipmen, he said—

'Take your men with you, and conceal yourselves about these rocks; for, if my eyes do not deceive me, yonder is our vessel, and it appears to me to be steering for this point.'

'It is,' replied one of the middies, peering through his night-glass; 'and though she has been slightly altered, I could swear to her build.'

'Go, then, and be ready at my call. I will climb the cliff and watch her. The coast-guardsmen, I have no doubt, are on their way to the cavern by this time.'

So saying, he commenced to climb the rugged cliff, and the midshipmen, followed by the blue jackets, disappeared among the rocks.

A few minutes previous to this a body of officers and coastguardsmen might be seen wending their way through a thickly-wooded dell.

''Tis strange,' said one, 'that we have not seen the lieutenant; he has no doubt taken the sea-shore as it is low tide; if so, it will enable us the better to proceed unobserved.'

'You don't expect to see him, do you? because I don't. He has, no doubt, turned faint-hearted.'

'Perhaps so. I have not had a very good opinion of him since the affair with the schooner; 'twas rather strange, you know.'

'It was. But we must observe great caution now. Where is the guide?'

'Here I am,' answered Tom Truck, the smuggler that had been wounded; 'we must pass through the defile; not a word must be spoken, for these very rocks have ears.'

Tom now led the way, and the others followed in single file, for the passage was so narrow that it would not allow two to walk abreast.

After having crossed a deep gully, Tom pointed to a small hole, and whispered to one of the officers.

'This leads to the secret cave, we must proceed with caution.'

The officers crawled through, and were followed by the men, but the treacherous smuggler waited till the last had disappeared, and trembling with fear, entered the gloomy passage.

The officer was the first to enter, and, crawling on his hands and knees, cautiously groped his way, for the inky darkness of the passage rendered it difficult; and it was not until he had received several bruises that he arrived at a sharp curve, and he saw with pleasure, a few yards in advance, the faint glimmer of a light.

Drawing his sword noiselessly from its sheath he listened, and he could hear the murmur of voices.

In the cave the smugglers, little dreaming of danger, especially in that quarter, were carousing, when Bill Raker, who was engaged in conversation with Ned Rocket, fancied he heard the rattle of a blade on the hard floor.

Turning his eyes in that direction, his suspicion was confirmed by the glitter of a sword at the entrance to the cave.

Whispering a few words to Ned, he rose to his feet, and, seizing a cutlass, waited in silence the appearance of whoever it might be.

The smugglers, turning their eyes in that direction, soon understood the meaning of this act, and seizing their arms were about to rush headlong on the intruder, but Ned Rocket, rising from the chest on which he had been seated, motioned them to be silent, and with lowering brows they grasped their pistols and stood ready to fire.

Bill Raker, with the cutlass held above his head, kept his keen eye fixed on the sword as it gradually advanced, and his brow darkened as he beheld the arm of the officer.

At length a head was cautiously thrust through the aperture, and with crashing violence the blade descended.

A cry of horror came from the cavernous passage, and the next moment the enraged smugglers, rushed to the entrance and discharged their fire-arms amongst the terrified officers.

The shrieks and cries of the baffled men told how deadly had been their fire, and the smugglers, seizing their cutlasses, pursued their retreating foes.

Scrambling over the writhing bodies, the smugglers soon overtook them, and the coastguardsmen, who had little dreamt of meeting with such a reception,

THE FOUL ANCHOR.

SIDE WINGS for "Foul Anchor" Scene, for the Play of the "Red Rover."—Gratis with No. 40 of "Black-Eyed Susan."

could make but little resistance, whilst the smugglers, foremost among whom was Bill Raker, taking advantage of their panic, brought down a man at each thrust of their deadly weapons.

The traitor, on hearing the first alarm, made a precipitate retreat, but the coastguardsmen, owing to the intense darkness and their ignorance of the place, were less fortunate, and as they scrambled over each other to gain the small outlet, they completely blocked up the narrow passage, and thus afforded the smugglers every facility of killing or capturing them.

The shrieks and groans of the wounded echoed fearfully through the cavern, and when torches had been procured, their fierce glare disclosed a horrid spectacle.

Leaving several of the smugglers to guard the prisoners and bind up the wounds of those who were not dead, Bill Raker, assisted by the others, searched among the rocks, but not one living soul could they see.

They were about to give up the search and return to the cavern, when the report of a pistol caused them to start.

'See to your pistols,' cried Raker, setting the example; 'we have an enemy in another quarter. That shot was fired from the crow's nest.'

Scarcely had he uttered these words, when three more shots, rapidly following each other, sounded on their ears.

'To the beach,' cried Raker. 'Bear a hand, my lads; some of our comrades are in danger.'

The smugglers with lowering brows followed Bill Raker down the crag, brandishing their bright cutlasses, and each grasping a pistol in his hand.

The sounds that had startled Raker were occasioned by Hatchett being surprised by Lieutenant Pike and his party while landing from the lugger.

No sooner did the boat touch the beach, than Pike darted forward, and, levelling a pistol, demanded him to surrender.

'Do you think I will tamely submit to you?' was Hatchett's reply. 'If so, go back and tell those who sent you, they have mistaken their man.'

'I come not here to parley or bandy idle words. Surrender in the king's name, or I must use force.'

'Force! Aha! I defy you!'

'Yes, force. You will find I have sufficient,' replied the lieutenant, boiling with rage.

'Where? I can see but yourself; and were I not backed by a stout boat's crew, you could not take me single-handed. Where—where is the force you boast?'

'Here,' cried the lieutenant, holding the bow of the boat with his left hand, and placing a small whistle to his lips, then shouted, 'Bear a hand, my lads. He cannot escape us this time.'

Scarcely had the sound of the whistle died away, when a dozen men sprang up from behind a rock, and a score more made their appearance from other places where they had lain concealed.

Hatchett cast a scrutinizing glance around; then, turning to the lieutenant, he said, sternly—

'Take your hand off the boat. This is my property.'

The lieutenant bit his lip, and shouted to his men, when Blue Peter, springing into the bow of the boat, drew a pistol, and pointed it at the lieutenant's head.

Hatchett, seeing this, rushed forward to stay his hand; but ere he could so, he drew the trigger, and the ball went crashing through his brain.

The brave lieutenant threw up his arms, pressed his hands to his forehead, and fell on the sands—dead.

The middies, seeing their officer fall, rushed to the boat, and, uttering cries of revenge, surrounded the boat's crew.

But the smugglers, no way daunted, rallied round their chief, determined to fight for their liberty; one of the middies and two of the blue jackets lay bleeding on the beach, when the sailors, seizing the boat's painter, ran the boat up high and dry, and tried to dislodge the smugglers from their temporary ambuscade.

The clash of weapons rang on the night air, and the groans of the wounded, mingled with the shouts of the combatants, echoed among the rocks.

Captain Hatchett cheered up his little band, and formed a crescent with his trusty blade, whilst Blue Peter, who fought gallantly by his side, kept his opponents at bay.

Already two of the smugglers lay bleeding in the boat, and the remaining few were nearly exhausted with their almost superhuman efforts, when the remaining middy, with an exultant shout, tried to beat down the captain: but Tom Hatchett, whose keen eye was ever on the watch, parried the blow, and ran his sword through his throat.

At that moment a loud shout was heard, and Bill Raker, followed by the smugglers, came to the rescue.

The sailors, who were true hearts of oak, although the odds were now against them, would not give way, and a pistol volley from the smugglers brought down several of them, amongst whom was one of the smuggler's crew.

The sailors fell one by one, preferring to be hewn down rather than to yield, and the smugglers eventually became masters of the spot, although they had suffered so severely.

The dead and wounded were quickly cleared away, and then the daring smuggler once more entered the cave.

But he was now an altered man. The smile had disappeared from his brow, the bright fire of his dark eye had lost its lustre; and his followers could not but notice the changed and haggard appearance of his features.

On entering he glanced around, and when he saw the signs of the late conflict, his cheek blanched.

But shaking off his momentary weakness, he called Bill Raker, and from him learnt that they had been also attacked by the coastguard.

The captain listened in silence to this recital, and when Bill Raker had concluded, he said, in a tone of bitterness—

'When will this work end? Not only does it grieve me to take the lives of those brave men, but it saddens my heart when I see my brave comrades bleeding around me. What have you there?'

'It's a piece of paper, captain, I found while searching about the rocks. I have not yet read it. It may be of importance.'

'It is, truly,' said Hatchett, with evident embarrassment. ''Tis well it was not lost.'

CHAPTER CVII.

THE GOLDEN ARROW PURSUES HER WAY—THE MARTINET—AN UNWELCOME CUSTOMER.

THE morning after Captain Gerald had so summarily disposed of the three pirates turned out to be hazy, and Captain Stuart, who had given orders to be called at the first dawn of light, hastily ascended to the deck.

The wind was at south, and the Golden Arrow was close hauled on a bowline, heading about south with west, her larboard tacks aboard, and her royals gently lifting.

'Keep her well full, let her move through it,' said Gerald, as his keen eye glanced aloft. 'There is but a capful of wind.'

Ben Brace was at the wheel, and the captain's voice rather startled him, for as the wind was steady, the vessel required but little steering, and like most sailors in the first morning watch, he felt a little drowsy.

Captain Stuart joined the mate.

'There's a treacherous bank rising to windward,' he said, 'that I don't much like the look of. Have you seen anything during your watch?'

'Nothing. In fact we have scarcely been able to see the flying jib until now, the fog has been so heavy.'

'That's rather provoking,' Gerald half muttered. 'I wish this haze would drfft away. To-day is the fourteenth, and a vessel that I wish to speak ought to be somewhere in these waters.'

'Is it the Martinet?'

'The same. The wind has been fair for her.'

'Shall I place an extra hand on the look-out? I have a man between the night heads, and one on each bow.'

'It will be as well. Send a hand on the fore-topsail yard; let him keep his eye well to windward.'

'Send my coxswain, Tom Tiller,' he added. 'He has an eye like a needle, and is every bit as sharp.'

'Ay, a shrewd fellow is Tom, and as steady a hand as any aboard,' muttered the mate, as he went forward to rouse Tiller out of his snug berth.

The mate knew where to find him.

When it was not his look-out or wheel, and the decks were dry, he was always coiled snugly alongside the gun of which he was captain, and made himself a comfortable though not over soft pillow of one of the quoins.

A slight touch brought him to his feet.

'Hullo, what's up?' he said, looking askance at the mate. 'It is not four bells yet. You are not going to wash decks.'

'Four bells, you sleeping lubber! Why, it has scarce struck two. I really believe the ship and all hands might go down without your knowing it. You are like a booby; no sooner do you settle than your head's under your wing, and you are as immoveable as a stanchion.'

'Well, as to that, there's nothing to do. We may as well sleep as to mope about. It gives more room to those who wish to stretch their limbs to walk about; and, as to my thinking, a sailor can never shorten his life lines by the amount of sleep he gets.'

'Well, well, let that drop. The captain's woke up with the devil on his back. He expects to meet a ship in these latitudes, and he wants a good look-out kept.'

'Ah! that alters the case. When eyes are wanted you'll always find Tom's lamps trimmed. What kind of a craft does he expect?'

'Can't say. But tumble up on the topsail-yard, and think of a short allowance of grog if you are caught napping.'

'Don't fear for that, though hang me for a mummy if a fellow won't have all his work to unbatten his eyes against this fog.'

An impatient gesture from the mate cut short the discourse, and Tom, having filled his cheek with an antidote against the fog in the form of a small coil of tobacco, sprang aloft as nimble as a cat.

Captain Stuart paced the deck with an impatient stride.

His watchful eye glanced occasionally at the thick black vapour that rose higher on the weather bow.

Then he would fix his gaze aloft at the sails, which flickered against the mast, and told that the light air was gradually leaving them.

'Calm—calm,' he muttered; 'it is no more than I expected.'

'Have you placed the man aloft?' he asked, as the mate walked aft.

'I have, sir; but he cannot see a cable's length to windward. To leeward it seems brightening up, and he fancies he can see a sail down on our lee quarter.'

'To leeward?' and the captain slipped his head beneath the spanker-boom. 'My glass; let me see if I can make her out.'

Gerald Stuart took a long and searching look, and occasionally wiped his glass in the vain hope of rendering his vision more clear.

'There is something, but I cannot make it out,' he said to the mate; then, handing him the glass, he added—

'See whether your eyes are clearer than mine.'

'There is something,' said the mate; 'but whether a ship or only a cloud I cannot determine. In another hour the sun will show itself, and perhaps eat up all this fog.'

'Another hour!' echoed Gerald. 'In that time we may be laid by the heels by a regular souther.'

Gerald once more took his glass.

'It is a vessel,' he said; 'this time I am not mistaken. She is hauling up under our lee. She carries a better wind than us.'

'Mast-head there!'

'Ay, ay, sir.'

'Can you make out the vessel on our lee quarter?'

'It's a heavy ship, bearing up under all plain sail.'

'Does she carry stay-sails between her masts?'

'No. When she fell off a bit just now I saw she had nothing but her trysails.'

'Do you think she's a man-of-war?'

'I can't say; her hull is too low to make her out.'

'All right. Keep your eyes well about.'

'Trust to old Tom for that. Curse the fog! it's enough to choke a hoss, let alone an old sea-dog like me.'

This cost Tom another coil of the favourite weed, and then he once more resumed his watch.

Presently he shouted at the top of his lungs—

'Sail on the— hard up, hard up!'

Ben had the vessel perfectly under command, and a slight turn of the wheel caused her to fall off.

All hands on deck were instantly on the stir. Two men ran to ease off the spanker-sheet, and the forecastle-men flattened-in the head-sheets.

For a moment all hands stood with bated breath.

A huge mass of canvas appeared out of the heavy haze, looming in the fog like a ship of double dimensions.

In an instant Captain Gerald was at the weather-rail.

'Where are you going, you bats?' he shouted. 'Has your sight taken leave of you, or are you all asleep?'

It was evident both vessels had sighted each other at the same moment. for the stranger had hauled-to a couple of points, and thus a collision that might have been fatal was averted.

'We are not blind,' was the answer of the agitated captain; 'but the look-out has fallen asleep. Mr. Martin, put another man on the look-out, and place that fellow in irons.'

'What ship is that?' asked Gerald, eyeing the vessel narrowly.

'The Swallow,' was the quick reply.

'That will do,' said Captain Stuart. 'Your name is Henson, is it not?'

'You grow inquisitive,' answered the other.

Then giving his men orders to trim the sails again, he was about to keep on his course.

'Martinet ahoy!' shouted Gerald, seeing the captain's intentions. 'Heave-to; I would speak with you.'

By this time the Golden Arrow had been brought to the wind again, and preparations were being made for her going about.

The captain of the Martinet had noticed this; and, as the Arrow was a ship almost double his size, and as he did not like the stranger's movements (for he failed to recognise the Golden Arrow—she assumed so many disguises), he thought it best to give her wide berth.

As soon, however, as Gerald hailed her as the Martinet, the captain began to feel more confidence.

Still he was mistrustful.

He had despatches of great importance, and a heavy responsibility was on his head.

Something he whispered to his chief officer, who immediately went forward, and Captain Stuart soon after saw that the men were crouching at their guns.

'Well, Captain Henson,' said Gerald, after his ship had gone about, and his vessel ranged at a respectful distance alongside the Martinet, 'when this nonsense is ended we will to business.'

'Indeed,' was Henson's cutting reply. 'Perhaps you have mistaken your customer.'

Captain Gerald bit his lip.

'Is not your vessel the Martinet?' he asked.

'The Swallow, I believe. I answered your hail.'

'Well, be it so. Your name is Henson, is it not?'

'I am not quite certain.'

'Confound the fellow,' muttered Gerald. 'He is as obstinate as a mule. I dare not give him the countersign before these men.

Captain Henson stood on his poop, longing for the wind to freshen.

He well knew that several British cruisers were on the look-out to intercept him, and he felt great uneasiness at the officiousness of the stranger.

Presently a thought struck him.

In his embarrassment he had never thought to ask the name of the strange ship; in fact, if he had done so, he never expected to get a true answer.

At length he said, leaning over the quarter netting—

'May I make bold to ask what ship yours is?'

'The Dart,' answered Gerald, determined to be even with him on this point.

'And your name?—if I make not too free.'

'Gerald Stuart.'

The mention of the name caused a general change in the captain.

'I am at your service,' he said. 'Your ship is the Golden Arrow, I presume, though paint has altered her much since last we rode together?'

'Ah, you remember me at Havre?'

'I do—and the gale that nearly sent us both on shore.'

'Well, now you are satisfied with my identity, perhaps you will not mind stepping on board?'

'With pleasure.'

In a few minutes more both captains were in close conference in the cabin of the Golden Arrow.

What passed between them was known only to themselves; but when they returned on deck, they seemed the best of friends, and were wonderfully chatty.

Seven bells had been struck by this, and the sailors were anxiously awaiting the boatswain's pipe to breakfast. The haze had cleared away to make room for the sun, and old Tom Tiller had been called from his station aloft.

'How bears that fellow now?' asked the captain of the mate, as he cast his eye towards the northern horizon.

'He still bears up, and we have raised his hull,' answered the mate.

'Can you make her out?'

'Well, at first I took her to be a whaler, but now I confess I am puzzled.'

'Think you she is a man of war?'

'She's painted deuced queer if she is; she seems to have no ports.'

'She certainly does not,' said Captain Gerald, after surveying her with the glass. 'Let us have your opinion, Mr. Henson.'

'For my part, she has a roguish look,' said Henson. 'She is no whaler; she has the build of a frigate, but her ports are well concealed.'

'I will try her, and see what country she belongs to,' said Gerald. 'Here, Mr. Happleton, hoist the stars and stripes.'

No sooner did the flag unfurl itself from the gaff than the British flag was hoisted from the stranger's peak, and Captain Henson, with a hurried good-bye, went on board his own ship.

CHAPTER CVIII.

THE ABDUCTION—LITTLE JACK SETS HIS WITS TO WORK FOR SOME PURPOSE—THE SMUGGLERS OUTWITTED.

WHEN the first surprise occasioned by the appearance of little Jack had subsided, the villain burst into a loud hoarse laugh.

'Lay down those babbling toys, boy,' he said. 'See you those pistols are not primed, and when you have done that, devil's imp as you are, perhaps you will answer me how you came on these premises.'

Jack was not a moment in ascertaining the fact of the pistol not being primed.

'Confound my luck,' he muttered, but with astonishing presence of mind he only threw one down, and retained the other, grasping it by the barrel.

Lord Travers, for such was the villain's name, laughed a bitter sarcastic laugh.

'Ah! young madcap,' he said, 'it would have been better for you had you not made yourself so officious. You have pryed into the secrets of this house, and dearly shall you pay for your temerity.'

Susan, in the meantime, had fainted.

She now lay helpless on the carpeted floor.

Lord Travers's face was ghastly white, and as he turned from the helpless girl and directed his attention to the boy, there was a look almost amounting to fiendishness on his distorted visage.

Seizing Jack by the arm, a feat that made him the recipient of a heavy blow from the pistol-butt, he swung him round and hurried him from the room.

Jack struggled manfully, but his efforts were, of course, useless against one of such superior strength, and that strength doubled as it were by a fit of madness.

'Villain! would you murder me?' cried Jack, as he felt his throat tightly clutched.

'Were I to do so the world would be none the wiser,' was the brutal reply; 'but as I do not intend doing so, I hope this will prove a lesson to you for the future.'

Before Jack could reply or frame his lips to speak, he heard the creaking of hinges, and the next moment he went flying into the street.

With reeling brain and mind perfectly bewildered, Jack staggered across the street, and without so much as bestowing a look on the house he had just left, he leapt the garden wall and soon gained the quietude of his own room.

It was then that the startling scenes flashed vividly to his mind, and now he had time to reflect, he felt more anxious than ever to penetrate the mystery still further.

Sleep that night seemed totally to have deserted him, so, seating himself at the window, he was soon lost in a deep reverie.

From this, however, he was soon startled by the rumble of wheels, and on looking out, to his surprise he saw a coach and pair standing within a few paces of the mysterious house.

Two men had already alighted, and were prowling about, evidently in search of some easy entrance.

A faint light was glimmering at one of the windows, and to this their attention seemed diverted.

It was some distance from the ground, but this difficulty was soon overcome; a third party came and assisted one to mount on the other's shoulders.

Jack saw the window raised and one of the men disappear, but he was not many minutes before he returned and handed his companions what appeared to be a large bundle encased in a blanket.

Jack saw them place it in the coach, and then the thought flashed to his mind that it must be the female either dead or alive.

Quick almost as thought Jack was in the street, and, concealing himself in the shade, he watched the movements of the trio.

Jack could see that they were dressed different to ordinary landsmen; in fact, he took them for fishermen, and, as two of them domiciled themselves inside with their burthen and the other seated himself on the box, Jack took the liberty of perching himself behind.

At first the coach sped slowly, evidently not to make too much noise; but, as soon as they cleared the streets, it rattled off at a pretty brisk rate.

As yet he had no assigned reason for pursuing his venturesome journey.

Curiosity alone seemed to urge him on.

At length he fancied he heard a female voice.

He felt certain of it, for it gradually grew louder.

Jack climbed up and placed his ear to the little hole at the back of the coach, where he could hear what was passing within.

'Consummate villain,' he heard a female say; 'is it thus you take advantage of one who is already persecuted almost to death?'

'Nonsense—nonsense. You mistake kindness for some other harsh word. I heard they wanted to force you to marry Lord Travers, and I thought it would be a charity to give you a chance to marry a sailor if you wanted to marry.'

'This is indeed cruel. You know I am married already, that my heart can never love another, and that while Will Howard lives I am his wife.'

'Aha! those silly notions seem planted in your head as firm as ever mainmast was stepped aboard the Redbreast. But you'll alter, for the wind cannot always blow from one point.'

'Indeed you are mistaken; and so you will find.'

A signal from the man on the outside of the coach brought the conversation and the whole of the conveyance to a dead stand.

'We'd better freshen up here, hadn't we, captain?' said a gruff voice. 'It's the last chance we shall have.'

'Yes—yes,' growled Hatchett, thrusting his head out.

Two of the men then entered the inn, leaving one to keep guard; and Jack, watching an opportunity, managed to creep round the other side of the coach and hold a few minutes' conversation with the occupant.

Short as the space was, something was arranged between them, and when the smugglers (for such they were) returned, Jack took his former place.

Jack could see by the change of scenery that they were rapidly nearing the coast, and he could learn by different bits of the discourse he could pick up that that they were drawing close to their destination.

This was the time for Jack to set his wits in motion.

The vehicle was ascending a steep incline, and the horses were just using their own pace, when Jack, stepping up to the off hind wheels, did something, and then darted into the hedge.

Presently the wheel began to waddle, and the coach with a crash suddenly came to the ground.

Jack was on the spot in an instant, and liberated those inside, for the man who was driving found himself jerked into a ditch.

Susan, of course, who appeared to be badly hurt, was lifted out, and while the smugglers were lifting the body of the carriage, she, under the guidance of little Jack, made away with all speed.

A fearful oath burst from Hatchett when he discovered this.

'This is the work of that young villain, I swear,' he cried, hoarsely. 'Bring them back, lads—bring them both back.'

But the fugitives had a good start, and were close upon what appeared the brow of the hill, and Hatchett, fearing they might escape, cried, with a fearful oath—

'I will bring one down at least.'

But his rage knew no bounds when he discovered that both pistols were gone from his belt, and he redoubled his exertions to overtake them.

Fear lent Susan wings, and she seemed almost to fly; and she distanced her pursuers greatly.

But alas! her exertions were of little avail.

A large chasm stopped their further progress.

Jack was almost mad.

He could see the brutal smugglers exerting all their efforts to overhaul them.

'Good heaven!' he said, 'help us out of this dilemma, for those brutal ruffians will kill us!'

BLACK EYED SUSAN

OR, PIRATES ASHORE.

IN PERIL.

A ghastly smile wreathed Hatchett's features when he found them brought to a stand.

'Clap on sail, lads!' he shouted to his accomplices. 'We shall soon overhaul the runaways, and then may I never more float on salt water, if they slip my grapplins.'

Jack could hear this humane speech, and his blood fairly boiled.

They shall not have us,' he said, 'if it costs me my life.'

He had caught sight of an old tree that projected nearly across the gulf, and, at the risk of his life, he seized it, and formed a bridge with his body for Susan to cross.

Susan nerved herself for the desperate passage. One false step she knew would consign her to a fearful death.

Scarce daring to look down into the giddy depths, the brave girl stepped on the outstretched form of her gallant companion.

But ere she could take another step the smugglers were upon them.

Hatchett rapped out an oath, and was about to drag her back, when, drawing the pistols from their concealment, she levelled them at his head and cried—

'Back, villains!—back, every one of you! The first that moves a step forward dies!'

CHAPTER CIX.

SILAS DOGGRASS FINDS HIMSELF IN JAIL.

WHEN Lieutenant Pike and his party hastened from the house in pursuit of Captain Hatchett, old Doggrass was struggling desperately under the weight of an old-fashioned eight-day clock.

It had been knocked down in the *melee*, and fallen across Silas's chest, almost depriving him of breath.

'This comes of having so much lumber,' said one of the sailors, who had as much as he could do to lift the cumbersome piece of furniture.

'Ay,' replied the other; 'and if you had not been in such a hurry, it might have saved the hangman a job.

Silas heard this remark, but did not seem to understand its significance, for he said—

'Sorry for intruding at such unreasonable hours, Mr. Doggrass,' said the sailor, who had assisted Silas to rise, winking at his companion; 'but our orders are not to leave till you are sufficiently recovered to accompany us.'

Doggrass started.

He looked at the sailors thoroughly amazed.

'Me go with you scoundrels? What do you mean?'

'That you must go with us to pay a visit to old Locket the jailer.'

Doggrass's eyes opened to their fullest extent.

His face, too, greatly elongated.

'You are joking surely,' he said.

'Not a bit of it; so pull your old hull together after the shaking you've had, and then we'll make sail.'

'Had we not better pipe to grog first?' asked Doggrass, the thought occurring to him that he might win over the sailors.

'We shan't object to that,' said one; 'but mind, we can't trust you alone in the spirit room.'

'Why not? Do you distrust me?'

'No, no; but it might not be safe.'

'I don't understand you.'

'Well, you might miss your road in coming back.'

'No fear, no fear,' said old Doggrass, trying to laugh. 'You are a thoughtful set of fellows. I am afraid you take too much interest in my welfare.'

'Not at all; our orders were to look after you well, and I am sure, after the squeezing you've had, you will require a little care.'

Doggrass muttered an inward curse, but concealed his disappointment as much as possible.

He found his *ruse* could not succeed, and he wished he had not proposed the grog.

As it was he could not well withdraw, and he began fumbling at one of the cupboards.

He did not wish the sailor to visit the cellar with him for two reasons, firstly, because he hoped to be able to bar the door after him, and make good his escape by a secret passage; and secondly, because he did not wish the fellow to see what it contained.

His motto was to keep every one in oblivion, an thus it was he had run clear in his villainy so long.

He was some time fumbling at the cupboard, but at length he drew forth an old, mouldy bottle and filled three glasses, desiring the sailors to drink.

The sight of the spirits was a temptation not to be easily resisted by the sailors.

One of them (Tom Steerwell), however, had had great experience in capturing smugglers; and, as Doggrass had been so long fishing it out, he fancied the contents of the bottle had been drugged.

'Drink—drink, my lads,' said Silas. 'You do not seem to have much appetite for it.'

'I should like to see our host drink first,' said Tom. 'I am sure you stand most in need of a comfort.'

Doggrass gave the fellow another inward curse.

'I am afraid you study my welfare too closely,' he said. 'This is the second time I have had to thank you for your kindness.'

'I need but little thanks,' retorted Tom. 'What I do is done freely.'

'Too freely—curse you!' muttered Doggrass to himself as he sullenly raised the glass and drank off its contents.

The sailors did not hesitate to follow his example, Tom Steerwell rather maliciously hinting that if Doggrass should go aloft he might make a pleasant journey.

When the grog had been discussed, Silas began to show signs of uneasiness, which his companions did not fail to notice.

They were suspicious that the place had some secret ins and outs unknown only to Silas himself, so they kept a sharp eye on him.

One precaution they took was to keep the candle out of his reach; and as some officious person had previously taken possession of Doggrass's pistol, they felt no uneasiness on that score.

'Well, are you ready to accompany us?' asked Tom, after waiting as long as his patience would allow him.

Doggrass scowled, and muttered something unintelligible.

'I think as how that it's time, Tom, that this backing and filling was put an end to,' said the other sailor, anxious to get away and see what was going on outside. 'We shall lay on our oars here until daylight breaks in upon us.'

Tom was evidently of the same opinion.

Taking a small roll of sinnet from his pocket, he rather unceremoniously laid hold of Doggrass, who, in spite of his struggles, soon found his arms firmly pinioned.

Silas was completely astounded at the sudden turn things had taken; even the manner of his captors seemed suddenly changed.

Having completed the pinioning, Tom coolly drew a pistol from his belt, and holding it in a suggestive manner, said in none of the pleasantest of tones—

'Now, my hearty, come along, and don't let us have any nonsense, for if you do you will find us a brace of tough 'uns.'

Doggrass made no reply, but with a scowl that spoke plainer than words, he walked on between the two sailors.

Lockit, the head jailor, was in no pleasant humour at being disturbed in his sleep; but when he learnt that Doggrass had been brought in a prisoner, his astonishment banished all other thoughts.

'Doggrass! Doggrass!' he muttered, leading the way up a dark stone passage, 'who ever would have thought it?'

A shudder passed through the prisoner's frame as he gazed round at the cheerless walls of his cell; and the sullen reserve of the jailors made him feel more acutely his position.

'Take care of him, Lockit,' he heard Tom say as the door was closed; and then a cold, bitter laugh fell on his ears.

Presently all was silent, and he was left to his own reflections, when he burst into a fit of passion, heaping curses on the head of Tom Hatchett.

CHAPTER CX.

SUSAN AND LITTLE JACK IN THE CLOISTERS.

STARTLED by the daring act of Susan, the smugglers drew back in alarm, whilst Hatchett, uttering not the most pleasant epithets, bit his lips with rage.

It was well that the smugglers were not provided with fire-arms.

They had only brought the one brace of pistols with them, thinking they would not be needed, and of these Susan had ingeniously taken possession.

In this desperate strait Susan's courage never once forsook her.

Taking advantage of the smugglers' confusion, she reached the tree, and with a desperate leap, gained the opposite ridge.

Here she kept the smugglers at bay from attacking Little Jack, whose position was critical in the extreme.

The bough on which he leaned was old and decayed, and he could hear it crack, and feel it gradually yield beneath his weight.

With a desperate effort he slid his feet from the rock and clung to the tree, which threatened each moment to precipitate him into the gulf beneath.

It was a trying moment for the daring boy, but perseverance and indomitable courage brought him through it in safety.

Clasping his legs firmly round the cracking bough he reached up to where it was more solid, then drawing himself up by the mere strength of his arms, soon stood by the side of Susan.

To attempt to follow him the smugglers at once saw would be madness, for could they reach the tree, one of the bullets would certainly find its way into the body of the adventurer.

Thus baffled, they could do nothing but return to the coach, which was still staying in the road.

This they did, promising to return with a good force to hunt the fugitives down at any risk.

Jack heard their threats, but little did he dream that they would put them into force.

He did not know what an awkward position he was placed in.

When the smugglers had gone, Jack and Susan pursued their way leisurely, for they were certain the smugglers could not return soon, and all communication was quite cut off by Jack more effectually breaking the tree.

That they were near the sea Jack felt certain. He could smell the salt breeze, but when he was brought to a standstill by a view of the ocean, and found himself on the verge of a towering cliff, it made him start.

'Prisoners, by heaven!' he said to Susan, as he glanced around and found that the chasm completely cut them off from the main land, and left them on an isolated rock.

Susan for a moment turned pale.

'Prisoners! What mean you?'

'That we are caged. Nothing without wings can leave this place.'

'Can we not return by the road we came?'

'How can we? Have we not caged ourselves?

'We have, certainly,' said Susan, with much perturbation; 'but we must find some way of escape. Our enemies will return, and we shall be lost.'

'If we are not already,' said Jack, whose heart now for the first time began to fail him.

It was Susan's turn now to use her energy.

She saw that the boy had outdone his strength.

Securing the pistols, she commenced a closer survey of their situation by walking round the rock and examining its sides.

The only discovery, however, that she made was that the sides were perpendicular as a wall, and that without some artificial means there was no way of leaving the surface.

Deeply impressed with these thoughts, she was returning to where she left little Jack gazing meditatively on the sea, when she fancied a stone on which she chanced to tread gave back a hollow sound.

She tried it again by stamping her foot, and this time she felt certain a hollow cavity was beneath.

She now called on Jack, and they both began to consider the best mode of raising the stone.

They had nothing but their fingers, and these were but poor implements; but Jack, on scratching away the sand, discovered an iron ring.

Even now they were at a loss to know how to raise it, for their strength was not of great magnitude; but Jack after a while conceived a plan.

Placing the barrel of one of the pistols through the ring, one clasped the barrel, the other the butt; then with a sudden jerk they wrenched it from its place.

A pair of stone stairs then presented themselves to their astonished gaze, down which Jack at once descended.

This led to a long subterraneous passage, which Jack traversed until he came to another steep flight of steps.

Jack hesitated a moment before going further; but a faint glimmer of light at the bottom dispelled the apprehensions he at first felt, and he descended boldly.

Here was another long passage, which terminated in a series of vaulted chambers, some built and others hewn-out of the solid rock.

Jack cast his eye around, and from the relics that remained he judged that a monastery had once stood there, and that he was now in the cloisters.

There he was joined by Susan, who had followed unperceived close upon him.

'Well, Jack, who would have thought of the existence of such a place ?' she exclaimed. 'I, for one, I am sure, would not.'

Jack was too absorbed in his meditations to answer.

There was a strange look about the place which he could not make out.

Having pointed out the peculiarities of the place to Susan, and devoured all with his gaze that his eye could reach, he set about a stricter search.

From one cloister to another Jack went until he had counted twelve, each similarly shaped, and lighted by a small loop-hole punctured through the side of the rock.

Jack viewed the place in surprise.

At the farthest end he discovered another trap leading downwards, but which was entirely blocked up with stone and earth, the results of an explosion.

'This has been a refuge for smugglers,' he said, 'at one time, and they have doubtless been betrayed.'

'And blown up this place to make good their retreat,' suggested Susan.

'It looks like it. Ah! what's that ?'

This exclamation was caused by something hanging in a gloomy recess.

Jack approached it with caution to get a nearer view.

''Tis the body of a man hanged !' he exclaimed, half in terror.

Susan trembled slightly and clung to his arm.

'Are you not deceived ?' she asked.

'No ; I feel certain it is a man.'

'Perhaps it is the traitor.'

'Most likely they hung him on the spot.'

A closer examination proved that Jack was right.

It was the body, or rather skeleton, of a man dressed in a guernsey and coarse flannel trousers ; a kind of petticoat, that was crumbling into dust, reached from the waist to the knees.

Susan trembled and withdrew to the other end of the cavern.

'We must leave this place. I cannot stay here,' she said, in a voice almost inarticulate, to Jack who had followed her.

'Neither can I,' replied Jack. 'And here is our first step to freedom.'

As he spoke he sprang forward and drew out a coil of rope that was half concealed by accumulated dust, and began to measure it in in sailor fashion by stretching out his arms.

'Forty fathoms,' he said, when he had done ; 'that is more than we shall want to reach from the cliff to the beach. We may find some retreat by that way.'

'I trust in heaven we may,' replied Susan, who now began to look upon the place as loathsome.

Shouldering as much of the rope as he could carry, Jack hastily ascended the steps, Susan picking up the remainder of the coil and following him.

Jack's surmise was correct.

The rope was some fathoms longer than they needed it.

Fastening one end securely to the rock, Jack began to descend with the agility of a cat.

Susan watched him and trembled slightly.

It seemed a perilous descent for one so young.

It was a relief to her when the rope ceased to be agitated and the signal was given that he was on the sands.

Once on the beach, Jack soon took a survey of his position.

It was a hopeless one.

His heart seemed to sink like lead.

A heavy stream of water, coming from some sub-terranean resource, rushed down the chasm that formed a gully on either side and cut off all communication from any other part of the beach.

Jack's eye took this in at a glance.

Still he was determined not to be beaten.

For some moments he stood in deep meditation gazing at the waves that purled at his feet, then suddenly he turned towards the rock.

It was jagged and uneven, so that he could not view it all at once, so he leisurely walked on, hoping to fall in with some cave or fissure.

In this he was successful.

He discovered a large cave, and what had been a flight of steps until the motion of the water had destroyed them.

Jack concluded at once that this had been used by the smugglers ; and as there was no way of his ascending, had he felt so inclined, he continued his search along the beach.

A cry of joy burst from his lips as he rounded a narrow crag, which, with another, formed a kind of bay.

High and dry upon the beach lay a raft that had either been deserted or the unfortunate occupants washed off.

It was heavy, and too much for the boy to launch ; but as it had floated there, he doubted not that the tide would float it again ; and as the water was gradually hemming him in, he found there was no time to be lost.

To ascend the rope was but the work of a few moments, and then he communicated to Susan the result of his discovery.

'But do you think it advisable to trust ourselves at sea ?' asked Susan, anxiously.

'I can see no other way of leaving this place.'

'Can we not try to cross the gulf ?'

'We can try ; but it would be useless.'

'Then we had better remain here. Providence may assist us.'

'The smugglers may assist us,' said Jack, meaningly. 'Depend upon it, they will pay us a visit before long.'

'They said so ; but do you think they will come ?'

'I feel certain of it. They know we are trapped. If we do not embrace the opportunity of escape, we shall fall into their hands.'

'But we have no provisions—no water.'

'That is true ; but, as you say, we must trust to Providence. We may fetch in-shore a little further along the coast.'

Susan was about to argue further, when Jack sprang to his feet.

'Here they are !' he exclaimed. 'By heavens, they are close upon us !'

Susan turned her head.

Her cheek went ashy pale.

The smugglers had approached to the other side of the chasm.

So noiseless had been their proceedings, that they had not before attracted notice.

They were each well armed with a cutlass and a brace of pistols, which showed they were bent on success.

One of the fellows carried a coil of rope, at one end of which a grapnel was attached.

This he coolly threw into the boughs of the tree, and being satisfied that it had fairly hooked itself, he drew the rope tight; several of the party held it firm, thus forming a temporary bridge.

Tom Hatchett placed his cutlass between his teeth, and motioning several of his men to follow, grasped the rope with both hands, and then proceeded along it, hand over hand, with the alacrity of one who had been well trained to such work on shipboard.

At this juncture Susan, who had stood as one petrified, gave a loud shriek, and fell into the arms of little Jack.

CHAPTER CXI.

WILL HOWARD AND SANCHO GET LOST IN THE BACKWOODS.

WHEN Will Howard found himself seized by the herculean arms and raised to the edge of the abyss, he thought he was once more in the hands of the savages, and gave himself up as lost.

He was relieved, however, when he found himself face to face with Sancho.

'Thank God! captain,' said the giant, 'that you are here. I feared those devils would have picked you off.'

'''Tis a wonder how I have escaped,' said Will; 'but how in heaven's name came you here? I took you for an enemy when first I felt your grasp.'

'Seeing you were nearly winded,' replied Sancho, 'I stopped to throw them off the scent, not dreaming that they would scatter as they did.'

'Did they see you?' asked Will, excitedly.

'Two of the foremost sighted me through the trees, but I drew them off by turning sharply to the right. They let fly a shower of arrows at me, which I escaped by darting behind a tree; they then lost sight of me in a dense thicket, and concealing myself in some high grass I saw them all rush by.'

'But how came you to know I was here?'

'The firing of rifles soon told me that the chief and his party had come upon you.'

'Creeping from my hiding-place I concealed myself in a bush where I could see all that passed, and more than once I fancied you were hit.'

'As I could do but little I lay quiet until they were tired out, and when they had gone, I came here just in time to see you ascending the rope.'

'Which way did the rascals take?' asked Will.

'They disappeared in yonder thicket; they no doubt are in search of me.'

'They may return.'

'Most likely, when they think you are quiet.'

'Our escape, then, must be made at once. Which way do you propose going?'

'To the left, round yonder cluster of trees. It will be impossible to find our way back to the raft.'

'To the left, then, let us go. We may fall in with a stream of water. As for food, I fear we shall run precious short.'

'Food!' exclaimed Lawks, his lips seeming to smack at the very idea. 'I feel as hungry as a wolf, and about as particular as to what might fall in my way as a shark.'

'We may meet with something as soon as it is prudent to use the gun,' said Will. 'At present I feel almost contented with nibbling the stock.'

During this latter conversation our adventurers were walking on as rapidly as possible, and they were not long in gaining the shelter of the trees.

Not daring to stop, and wishing to place as much distance between them and the Indians as possible, they pushed their way onwards until they came to a small stream, where they slaked their thirst, and refreshed themselves with a good wash.

Here several birds were flying about; but much as they wished, they dared not fire a shot; so they contented themselves with a little rest, and then started onwards.

On reaching a clearing, they were enabled to look about them, and they found that they were travelling on the brow of a rising piece of ground, from which they could command a distant view.

Down in the hollow, at the distance of about a mile, a thick brake extended from left to right, and in the distance beyond they could discern the bend of a broad river that was lost to view in a densely-wooded forest.

Will was now getting thoroughly exhausted, and he did not hesitate to tell his companion that rest, if not food, must he had before they could venture to proceed farther.'

Sancho, whose strength seemed exhaustible, heard this with sadness.

'Can we not manage to gain the bank of yon stream you can see winding through yon grove,' he asked.

'I will try, though it will be a task,' replied Will, whose feet and hands were fearfully cut by scrambling about the rocks.

It was nearly half a mile to the place Sancho had pointed, and as they neared it they were suddenly startled by seeing a wreath of smoke curling up between the trees.

Sancho started back and clutched Will.

'Stay here under shadow of this tree,' he said. 'I will go forward and reconnoitre. It may be a party of Indians encamped.'

Will stood under cover of the tree, his rifle ready for any emergency.

Sancho went forward, wrapping his skin round him so as to be able to use his right arm, the hand of which firmly grasped his spear.

Will stood watching his gliding figure until it was lost to view in an agony of suspense.

Presently he heard the well-known signal that all was right, and then he saw Sancho enter the clearing and waive his spear.

Will was greatly delighted to find that the fire belonged to a trapper who was cooking a huge buffalo steak, using his ramrod as a spit.

'Welcome, strangers,' said the trapper in the regular yankee nasal twang; 'glad to see you. A stranger about this part, I guess?'

Sancho's thoughts were too deeply absorbed in the steak which was sending forth a delightful odour to notice the conversation.

The sharp nip of hunger began to pinch him frightfully.

Will sat, or rather dropped down on the stump of an old tree, and replied to the trapper's hurried remarks—

'We are strangers. We have lost our way, and want to find a track to the nearest sea-port.

'Well, I guess you'll have a tarnation job. There's not one within a hundred miles from this, I calculate.'

'We might find it did we know the direction.'

'We'll talk of that by-and-by. Just see to the cooking of that steak, and then let's hear how you managed to lose yourselves.'

Sambo officiated as cook, and Will recounted their adventures, and when he had done the trapper rose to his feet, and approaching Will, said—

'Wall, you've got through a good deal. Did you ever try your hand at bone setting?'

Will did not notice till now that his left arm was slung in his pouch-strap, and it flashed to his mind immediately that the man's arm was broken.

'I cannot boast much of my ability,' Will replied; 'but it will not be the first broken limb I have set if I get yours into place. So I will try my best.'

'And I guess I'll be thankful,' said the trapper; 'for it pains me some, I assure you.'

Will soon had doctored the wounded limb, and bound it up with splinters which Sancho cut from a piece of log, and the trapper appeared much easier.

The meal being ready, consisting of buffalo, biscuit, and cold water from the stream, they all set-to vigorously, Will intimating in the meantime a desire to know how the trapper met with his accident.

'Well, I'll tell you, friend,' said the trapper, anxious to satisfy his curiosity.

'You must know that I arrived here yesterday about this time, and thinking it was a fine place to camp for the night, I tethered my old 'oss and kindled a fire.

'The wood being green did not burn up so fast as I liked, and thinks I, I'll take a stroll, and see if anything's moving.

'Well, I looked down the slope, and sees the brake yonder, and I fancies I saw a drove of what I took to be wild hogs.

'This seemed a glorious chance, as I hadn't drew trigger for three days; so I takes old kill-deer with me and hurries down to the swamp, but when I got there, there wasn't signs of a living critter.

'Well, I was a sort of vexed, and I thought I'd go on and get a drink outen a might nice spring that run inter the river, and jist as I had reached the bank, I heered a kind ov a scrapin' noise over my head; and as I looked up to see what made it, by the Holy Moses! rite up thar, on a big limb that stuck strait out from a sweet-gum, I seed two great fiery eyes starin' rite at me.

'I'm darned, stranger, if they didn't seem to burn rite into mine, they war so hot; and then behind them eyes was one of the hugest panthers I ever seed—and, I tell yer, I've seed some. She wor a rale seven-footer, from snout to root.

'I know'd by the shake of the varmint's tail she warn't going to set thar long.

'She war fixin' to give me a call. So I jist fetched old kill-deer up, and held her betwixt them red, fiery eyes of the critter, and let drive.

'Well, will you believe it! the infarnal varmint didn't budge an inch.

'I sorter reckoned I'd killer her, and sorter reckoned not. She lay close to that 'ar limb, but that long, furry tail of hern hung loose like a bit of moss, and kind o' swayed in the wind.

'"Well," said I to myself, "I'll prospect the darned thing." So I drew out my gunstick, and inter the sweet-gum in no time.

'I got outen on the limb whar the critter lay, with her toe-nails a stickin' into the bark like grim death.

'Thinks I, "Old mother painter, I'll fetch yer," and at that I give her a dig in the ribs with all my might. Mercy on me, but warn't the fat in the fire then!

'She warn't hurt a bit—only my ball had tickled her skull a little, jist under the scalp, and she'd sorter got asleep like.

'But that thar dig in the ribs woke the critter up. She riz rite up, and wheeled upon me.

'The way I got down outen that sweet-gum I can't tell—'twas somehow dreadful quick, I reckon; but one thing I do know for sartain, that 'ar varmint war down as soon as I war, and she lit onter me like a coon onto a corn-hill; and the way, stranger, that thar critter tore me was awful.

'See here,' and the trapper stripped open his shirt-bosom, and exposed to view his hairy breast, covered with the gashes made by the talons of the panther. But that don't begin with my back and hips. Well, we rolled and tussled—for I fit as well as I could with nothing but my teeth and fists—till we both fell down the bank.

'Down thar the water war tolerably deep, and I reckoned if I only had the varmint inter the water, I mought drown her.

'I managed to slip a little lower down on to the drift wood below, and as the critter made a lunge arter me, she slipped off a smooth root down betwixt some logs.

'"Now," says I, "Dan, is your time;" and as she souzed inter the drink, I reckon it war my turn to jump, and so I catched the critter's tail, and quicker than I could tell it I whipped it under one log, and betwixt two others that lay close together, and getting a good brace for both feet, held on like grim death to a dead nigger.

'The painter war awful mad, I tell yer; but 'twarn't no manner of use. I had her good, and held her down under the drink for more'n ten minutes. She pulled at one end of the tail, and I at the other; but then, stranger, we war both on us pulling for life, and as I valid mine mor than hern, I pulled a little the strongest, for you see I had the advantage.

'Well, it turned out at last as I got the best of it, and I was jist thinking what a glorious skin I should peel off him when I slips on a wet log and breaks my arm.'

'That was unfortunate, indeed!' said Will; 'but if the animal is there still, we can skin it for you.'

'Not to-night, friend; we'll have a pipe, and then we'll freshen the fire, and I'll share my blankets with you, for I see you stand in need of rest.'

The trapper was right, and in less than one half-hour from the time he spoke they were all three sleeping soundly.

———

CHAPTER CXII.

GREGORY SAUNDERS ENGAGES THE PRIVATEER.

CAPTAIN HENSON had scarcely got on board his ship when the vessel that was coming up on the wind fired a gun from her bow, as a signal to heave-to.

The Martinet had on board despatches of importance, and Gregory had been sent to meet her, to convoy her in safety up the English Channel, which place was alive with English cruisers.

Gregory eyed the stranger for a moment; then giving a signal to Captain Henson to keep out of harm's way, he deliberately waited the approach of the stranger.

The movements of the Martinet did not appear to please the captain of the new-comer.

He fired two of his heaviest midship guns, which, however, were badly elevated, the shots dropping in the water, and after bounding from wave to wave, disappeared a few fathoms short of the Martinet.

Gregory's brow grew dark, as the smoke, intermixed with flame, shot from the vessel's hull; but he smiled when he saw the result.

He gave a few hasty orders to the mate.

That officer walked forward immediately, and communicated some instructions to the boatswain, whose shrill pipe was soon heard in every part of the ship.

The courses were hauled up, and the men in silence hastened to their guns, which were cast loose, and preparations made for an engagement.

Both vessels were heading towards each other, and closing rapidly.

Captain Stuart was now able to form some idea of the size of the vessel he was evidently bound to give battle to.

She was a heavy ship, and carried four guns more than the Golden Arrow; but there was something about her trim and rig that gave Gerald reason to expect she was not a regular man-of-war.

Tom Tiller was at the wheel, and he had an excellent opportunity of viewing the heavy, lumbersome ship, with her towering mass of canvas, as she stood across the Golden Arrow's bows.

'Have you made her out yet, sir?' he ventured to ask of Captain Stuart as he approached him to glance at the compass.

'Not distinctly; yet there is something about her that makes me think I have seen her before.'

'You have, sir; and so have I. She anchored a few cables' lengths from us when we lay in the downs.'

'What, is that the Lotus—the privateer?'

'The same, captain; I could swear to it.'

'And I think you are right. I can now recal to my mind many points about her.'

He turned away, and walked towards the mainmast.

Addressing the mate, who was standing there, he said—

'Keep the hands steady at their guns. See that shot and shell are well supplied, and boarding-pikes ready to hand. Send the riggers into the tops, and let the sail-trimmers stand by to execute my orders quickly.'

'You intend fighting her, then, sir?'

'Certainly; and if I gain the day, I shall be well repaid. She is but a privateer, and surely we can beat her.'

As he spoke the vessel ranged abreast about twenty fathoms to windward of the Golden Arrow.

'Ahoy! What ship?' was bellowed in a hoarse, discordant voice from the poop.

'The Golden Arrow,' was Gregory's cool reply.

'Heave to, then.'

'I have hauled up my courses; is that not sufficient?'

'No. Back your main-yard.'

'You had better send some one on board to do it.'

'Insolence! Do you refuse to obey me?'

'Until you prove your ability of taking command of this vessel.'

'That shall not be long first. You have insulted me by not heaving to at my first order, and shown contempt by not hoisting your colours. Now, it is my duty to chastise you.'

'Ready about there!' he shouted, at the pitch of his voice. 'Hard a-lee!' he thundered to the helmsman, making him fairly start.

Then, as the vessel came up to the wind and paid off on the other tack, he gave the necessary orders, until the vessel's head stood in the direction of the Golden Arrow.

Meanwhile, Gregory was not idle.

The Lotus was a little on his weather quarter, and as he had his ship in full play, he gave the wheel a slight touch, bringing his ship broadside to the approaching vessel.

Then he gave the order to fire.

The effect was magical.

The guns had been well layed, and the iron shower struck the Lotus, raking her fore and aft.

Her decks were torn up, several of her guns dismounted, and the shouts and groans that came from her deck told of the havoc it had made among her crew.

The privateer captain, hoarse with rage, flew about the decks trying to rally his men from the sudden shock they had received.

'To your guns, you lubbers!' he shouted to the sailors, who were standing mute, gazing at the destruction the Golden Arrow's terrible broadside had inflicted; 'to your guns—the last man at his station dies!'

The men, as though suddenly aroused to life, took up their places, and a party of idlers carried away the wounded.

Captain Bullyton was true to his word.

One poor fellow, who had received a blow from a handspike as it was hurled up from the deck, stood half stunned, and the privateer captain, observing him, deliberately took a pistol from his belt and blew out his brains.

This served as a warning to the rest, and Bullyton gazed in evident satisfaction at the effect it had upon them.

Both vessels were now abreast, and broadside after broadside were discharged from them with terrible effect.

The Lotus being high out of the water, was a good target for the gunners of the Golden Arrow, who planted their shot with steady aim in the former's sturdy side.

Bullied and confused, the gunners of the Lotus fired but indifferently, more than half their shots passing over the Golden Arrow's low hull, occasionally cutting away a stay, or severing some rope, which was instantly stoppered by the active riggers.

Captain Stuart stood coolly upon the quarter-deck, watching the progress of the fight, and availing himself of every advantage that offered.

His silken banner, with its golden device, fluttered defiantly in the gentle breeze, whilst the English ensign that hung from the peak of the Lotus drooped as though too lazy or too dispirited to unfold itself.

Captain Bullyton, on the other hand, was rushing about half frantic.

His hoarse voice mingling with the roar of battle, and his features gesticulating horribly.

'Serve those guns a little quicker,' he shouted to his officers, who had charge of the different divisions, 'by heavens, that bumboat will batter us to tinder before we make a hole in her.'

The officers, like the men, were confused.

They shared in the excitement of the captain.

More than half the crew had been killed or disabled, and the men found it difficult to clear the dead and wounded from the recoil of the guns.

Every now and then the dull splash could be heard in the cessation of the firing as a body was committed without ceremony to the deep.

As the battle continued, Bullyton's manner grew wilder.

He could see that the fight was fast turning against him.

'Grimton,' he shouted to his chief officer, 'come aft.'

That personage, who was superintending the foremost division, walked aft.

His uniform was scarcely distinguishable for blood and the black grime of powder; his men had been well kept at their work, and, in fact, were the only ones on board that fought with any firmness and energy.

'Grimton,' said the captain, as the officer approached, 'it is no use battering at that fiend any longer; we may keep on firing until we have not a plank to stand on.'

'What do you intend doing?'

'Board her; my patience will not allow me to stand here and be battered like a stone fort; we must board her, and trust to our swords.'

Grimton dashed forward and passed the word for the boarders to make ready, leaving a few men to work the most effective guns.

Captain Stuart, on the other hand, was in the utmost of good humour, in which his men seemed to share, for they plied their guns, carried away the wounded, or cleared the deck of the dead, as though they were only going through their ordinary drill.

Bob Brace was at his favourite gun, which, from its extraordinary length, he had christened the Telescope, and Pat was serving as handspikeman in lieu of one of the hands that had lost his head.

Happy Jack was serving as loader, and many were the jokes passed between him and Pat.

'Hurrah, my honey, shove in the praties!' cried Pat, as Jack thrust the ball down the muzzle. 'By my faith, they'll not find them over maely, and if they get one in their sthomach they'll not need any more, by my sowl.'

Bob was as happy as the rest.

He glanced his keen eye along the narrow tube of his favourite piece, and more, he could see as well through the blinding smoke as if it had been clear.

Truth was, he had well laid his gun at the onset, and chalked both bed and quoin, so that he only had to replace it when the gun was run out, which enabled him to plant each shot well into the enemy's side.

When, by chance, the smoke did clear, he would then mark the position of the vessel, and if there was a chance of dropping a pratie, as Pat termed it, through a port, he did so.

Thus matters stood when the impetuous Bullyton dashed his vessel alongside and prepared to board.

His men were mostly stalwart fellows, and well armed, and he doubted not that they would sweep all before them.

He was mistaken, however.

As they prepared to leap over the side, a party of the Golden Arrow's crew, led by Gregory himself, sprang up from the bulwarks, and hewed them down as they leapt into the wire nettings.

'Fiends! curse them!' yelled Bullyton, who had hoped to pour his men on the deck of the Golden Arrow unperceived. 'Hack them down! Our victory is certain!'

As the ships came together, Marline secured both bows to together by heaving a grapling on the rigging of the bowsprit, and as the vessels held together crunching and grinding, the gunners on both sides double shotted their guns, and peppered into each other at close quarters.

Bob's gun chanced to come abreast one of the ports which had been lowered, and the gun secured; and Bob, on discovering this, sent Pat into the galley to heat him one or two shots.

The Irishman soon appeared with a large iron pot, in which he had placed the red-hot metal, and having hinted to happy Jack that it was nicely "roasted," and would not require "paaling," he hastened back for another.

Having battered away the port, Bob directed his fire towards the magazine hatch, which he soon had the satisfaction of seeing smoking, and a second shot being buried in the mainmast between decks, soon burst out in a blaze.

As soon as the gunners discovered the fire, they were thrown into confusion, and rushed upon deck to procure assistance and water; but every one seemed crowding to the bulwarks, trying to gain a foothold upon the enemy's deck.

Above the clash of steel and the cracking of pistol shots, the voice of Bullyton could be heard shouting and cursing at his men.

More than once he tried to force his way to where Captain Stuart was standing encouraging his little band, and driving back the long pikes of their infuriated boarders.

He had spied Captain Stuart through the smoke which was wreathing up from the rapidly discharged guns, and had tried two pistol-shots at him, but without success.

Lieutenant Grimton had fallen at the first onset at the head of his party; and now that they had lost the only officer on whom they could rely or place any confidence, these men, like the rest, were thrown into disorder.

Presently the grappling parted, and the ship swung aft, and Captain Gregory, who was about to make a sally on to the Lotus's deck, was thus prevented.

Turning angrily to discover the cause, he saw Pat coolly leaving the bowsprit with an axe in his hand.

'Arrest him!' he shouted to Marline; 'let him be brought before me.'

He pointed to Pat as he spoke, and Marline, aided by two seamen, marched Pat unresistingly on to the quarter-deck, whither Captain Stuart had already gone.

'Scoundrel! what mean you by this conduct?' asked the captain, scarcely able to control his passion.

'Sure and bedad, it was to save your honour from being blown up,' replied the Irishman, with perfect sang froid.

'Blown up! Confound you; and we have lost a glorious victory through you.'

'Sure, and it's meself you have to thank for not losing yourself altogether.'

'What mean you, scoundrel?'

Pat pointed to the Lotus.

Captain Stuart needed no further explanation.

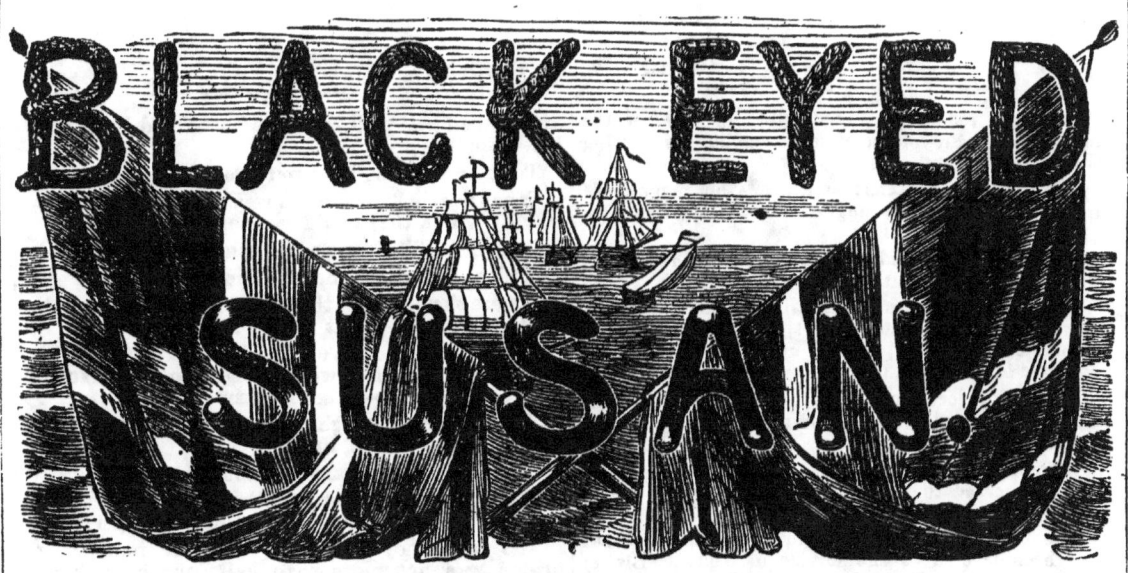

BLACK EYED SUSAN!

OR, PIRATES ASHORE.

DEFENDING THE PASS.

A bright red flame was making its way up the mainmast, and a volume of dense smoke was pouring up the fore-hatch.

'On fire, by heavens! and near the magazine,' exclaimed Gerald, his anger suddenly changing to surprise.

Bob Brace was still hammering away at the Lotus's hull, ignorant of what was passing on deck.

'Stop that useless firing; it is only waste of powder,' said Captain Stuart, on observing this. 'Confound the fellow, he will never leave off unless you give him an actual order.'

This was indeed truth; as long as a plank of the Lotus floated and he had a shot to fire, Bob would not have left off.

Attention was now directed to the burning ship, which appeared to be deserted, and Captain Stuart determined to board her in the boats.

The two cutters and captain's gig (the jolly-boat had been devoted to the service of Rodwia Blake) were lowered and manned and soon pulled alongside.

On ascending to the deck it was found extremely hot, and Captain Stuart found that his worst fears were realized.

The ship was deserted, and Captain Bullyton was gone.

Not that Gerald had any wish to make prisoners of the captain or his few surviving men, far from it; he did not care about his vessel being lumbered up with a parcel of useless lumber as he termed it.

Away on the quarter, pulling for bare life, they could see the remains of what had once been the crew of the Lotus.

Captain Stuart for the first time during the engagement forgot himself so far as to give utterance to an oath.

Then, descending the cabin to see if there were any papers or anything of value left—which he little expected—he gave orders for all the arms laying about the deck to be placed in the boats.

Gregory cast his eye round the cabin with a feeling of bitter mortification as he saw the drawers turned out and the floor strewed with papers.

He was about to ascend to the deck again, for Tom Tiller had stepped down to warn him it would be dangerous to trust themselves on board much longer, when a neatly-folded packet caught his eye.

Hastily he seized it, and ran his eye over the writing outside.

'Thank God, now I am happy,' he cried. 'We have surely gained a brilliant victory.'

The paper he picked up was the letter of marque which Bullyton in his hurry to escape had dropped.

As the fire was taking fast hold, Gregory went on board his own ship; and, seeing the Martinet laying-to, he bore down on her at once.

CHAPTER CXII.

ESCAPE FROM THE SMUGGLERS — A NIGHT ON THE RAFT.

TOM HATCHETT, confident of success, and deeming it impossible for the fugitives to escape as soon as he had crossed the gully, gave a loud huzza.

'Come on, lads,' he shouted, 'remember your reward if we capture this cursed pair of imps that has given us so much trouble.'

Urged on by this fresh stimulant, Bill Raker and several of the crew soon joined their captain, and rushed pell-mell to where Susan and Jack had last been seen.

To their surprise they were gone.

What puzzled them more was they could see no way by which they could escape.

Presently Bill Raker spied the rope.

He leant down on the cliff and looked over.

'There they go, d— them!' he muttered between his teeth; 'but I'll cut their journey short.'

Without a moment's consideration of what he was doing, and filled with thoughts of vengeance, he drew his knife and severed the rope.

Hatchett caught sight of the gleam of the knife, and rushing forward, cried—

'Hold, fool! what are you about?'

He was too late, however, the mischief was done and they had no means of pursuing the fugitives.

The rope they had used for their temporary bridge was not more than half long enough to reach the beach.

Hatchett stamped and swore like one mad at finding himself thus foiled, and he did not fail to heap a volley of abuse on his mate Bill Raker.

The mate's temper was not such as to allow him to brook this treatment, and he in turn cursed and swore at the captain.

This commenced a serious quarrel.

From words they got to blows.

In the heat of his passion, Hatchett drew his cutlass, and threatened to run Raker through.

Bill could not stand this, so he also drew his cutlass, and the pair fell to in good earnest.

The smugglers looked on in a state of mingled surprise and alarm, for the combatants fought desperately, and evidently intended killing each other.

One of the crew endeavoured to part them, but he got a nasty wound for his pains; so he let them fight on.

Both Hatchett and Raker were good swordsmen, and it was some time ere either could gain advantage of the other, though Raker once nearly forced Hatchett over the cliff.

How long they would have fought in this manner there is no knowing, had not Raker slipped, and the sword of Hatchett passed through his shoulder.

Raker never recovered his equilibrium, but fell to the earth uttering a deep moan.

Seeing his mate wounded, Hatchett turned quite a different man.

'It is no use staying here longer,' he said; 'let us leave this place; it seems that nothing but bad luck attends us.'

The men raised Raker to a sitting posture, and bound up his wound; then two of the smugglers bore him away on their shoulders.

When Susan screamed and fell into little Jack's arms, the poor boy was for a moment stupified.

The shouts of the smugglers, however, brought him to a sense of his position; and, securing Susan firmly to his waist with his scarf, he slid gently over the cliff, and lowered himself on to the raft.

He had scarcely touched his foot upon it, when, on looking up, he saw Bill Raker glaring at him, and he had only time to step aside and pull Susan after him, when the rope fell with fearful violence.

Swiftly the raft glided away with the tide, and the wind setting off the land drifted it seaward.

Susan watched the receding shore with aching eyes.

Her heart was filled with grief, and she sat herself down, and relapsed into a kind of dreamy reverie.

Incident after incident flashed vividly to her mind, and the form of William seemed to rise in visions before her.

Night at length came, dark and cheerless; and in the wind seemed to come a kind of driving sleet.

Little Jack, worn out with fatigue, had fallen asleep, leaving Susan to enjoy her thoughts alone.

Poor girl! hers indeed was a cup of bitterness; and there she sat on that dreary night, anxiously peering through the gloom, fancying each moment that she saw a sail bearing towards them, until at length, like little Jack, she fell into the arms of Morpheus.

CHAPTER CXIII.

LORD TRAVERS VISITS DOGGRASS IN JAIL.

Two restless days and sleepless nights Doggrass passed in his dreary prison, without seeing a soul except the stolid and almost brutal jailer who brought him his food, and visited him occasionally to assure himself he had not escaped.

On the third day he was startled by the key grating in the lock at an hour unusual for him to be visited.

He was surprised to see a man, cloaked and muffled, let in by Lockit.

The jailer looked at the new comer, who had previously slipped a gold piece in his hand, and said in a meaning tone—

'Remember, ten minutes is all I can allow; even that is greatly exceeding my duty.'

He then looked the door, and Silas and his visitor were alone.

For some moments Doggrass stood gazing at his strange visitor as though he would pierce him through.

The other met his gaze steadily.

Throwing off his disguise he said—

'You know me now, Doggrass? and as our time is but short, let us not waste it.'

'Lord Travers!' exclaimed Doggrass, a beam of hope lighting up his wan visage. 'I feared I was quite deserted.'

'You were deceived, but that is not what brought me here. I have strange news to tell you.'

'Have you succeeded?'

This was asked as though the querist was scarcely able to draw breath.

'I have not,' was the reply; 'far from it.'

'How is that?'

'Patience, and I will tell you.'

'But'——

'Wait patiently.'

'How can I? Remember, we have but a few minutes.'

'Well, to be brief, she has foiled me.'

'What!—escaped?'

'Just so.'

'Confound the wench! Hang her, she is a regular vixen.'

'She is indeed, and I have found her so to my cost.'

Doggrass scowled horribly.

His ghastly features turned a kind of ashy gray.

His voice was thick and husky as he asked—

'How did she escape?'

'I cannot say, it is a mystery.'

'Were you absent at the time?'

'Yes, but I left everything secured as usual.'

'And you have no clue, no suspicion of any one?'

Doggrass was growing uneasy.

He began to suspect Travers was playing him false.

The noble lord was to have come out handsomely had he succeeded in getting Susan to sign the document, which was to denounce her husband as a pirate, and express her determination of never more submitting to him as his wife.

A mock marriage was to follow, and this accomplished, was to take her to some retired spot as his mistress.

All this the old villain had planned without the slightest remorse, but he now began to doubt Lord Travers's honesty, and fancied he had taken her away, and finding him helpless and in difficulties had invented the tale of her escape.

Lord Travers did not for a moment suspect such were his thoughts, and he answered quite earnestly—

'Clue! not the slightest; and the only one I can suspect is a boy, of whom I know nothing.'

'A boy,' echoed Doggrass, thoughtfully.

'Yes, a vagabond. He entered the house I know not how and when. By kindness and soothing, I was about to prevail on the girl to sign her name. His presence altered her mind.'

'And she refused?'

'She did, d— her, most obstinately.'

'And what of the boy?'

'He managed to possess himself of my pistols, which, fortunately, were unloaded, and after a brief struggle I threw him into the street.'

'Did you notice him sufficiently to know him again?'

'To his identity I could almost swear.'

At this juncture they were interrupted by the jailer, who announced that they had already exceeded the time allowed.

Lord Travers stepped up to him, and slipping another gold coin in his hand said—

'We need but a few minutes more to settle our affairs.'

Lockit growled something unintelligible, and then disappeared, not forgetting his usual caution to close and lock the door after him.

Having completed this arangement, Lord Travers again seated himself, and with a face that betrayed evident concern asked—

'Well, what do you advise?'

'I can advise but little, and do less,' replied Doggrass, 'seeing the helpless state I am in. I a prisoner here, and God knows how it will end.'

'Have they anything strong against you?'

'Nothing.'

'That is strange. How came they to confine you?'

'A smuggler who I once befriended gained access to my home in my absence, and secreted himself and'——

'You did not know it?' interrupted Travers.

'I was as innocent as a babe,' said Doggrass, craftily, 'till a party of men-of-war's men burst open my door, entered my house, and the ruffian was discovered.'

'What do you suppose brought him to your house?'

'I know not, except it was plunder—perhaps murder.'

Doggrass saw with satisfaction that his tale was taking the desired effect on his visitor, whose influence he knew was at that time very great with the chief magistrate.

'This must be seen to,' said Travers, after sitting a moment in deep thought; 'it will not do to let the innocent suffer unjustly; besides, at this critical moment I find I need your advice and judgment.'

'And now,' he continued, taking a small note-book from his pocket, 'tell me the name of this audacious scoundrel that has caused you to be thus persecuted.'

Doggrass paused for a moment hesitatingly.

At length, deeming it the best course, he replied—

'Tom Hatchett, the smuggler!'

Lord Travers started, but recovered himself instantly.

'I know him well,' he muttered to himself. 'He did a job for me, but then I paid him well, and that clears me off all obligations.'

Having made a note in his book, the jailer once more appeared, and Lord Travers, deeming it imprudent to bribe the jailer further, whispered a few hasty words in Doggrass's ear and then left the cell.

CHAPTER CXIV.

CAPTAIN BULLYTON REACHES LAND — WILL HOWARD PLAYS A TRICK ON THE PRIVATEER CAPTAIN.

WITH the first streak of morning Will was astir, and having roused Sancho to replenish the fire that had smouldered all night, he took his rifle and sallied down to the cave brake.

It was a wild spot, and being in a hollow was a kind of swamp.

Through its centre ran a clear and refreshing stream, and Will did not fail to recognise in his wanderings the spot where the trapper had had his desperate fight.

Upon the bank he saw what he supposed to be the remains of the panther.

Some ravenous beast had devoured it all but portions of the skin.

Whilst our hero was gazing silently and in deep thought at the remains, a rustling in the brake startled him.

Clutching his rifle, he turned to see what it was.

He was surprised to see a huge bear with its head thrust through the canes, and the want of food recurring to Will's mind, he determined to have a shot at him.

Unfortunately, he had not brought his shot-pouch with him, but still he was determined to try his hand at a single shot.

The huge monster was still glaring at him immovable, as though uncertain whether to attack him or retreat.

Will raised his rifle, took steady aim, and fired.

The ball hit the boar in the shoulder, and staggered him a bit.

Then suddenly he reared on his hind legs, and with a terrific grunt made a desperate spring at Will.

This was so sudden that Will had not time to club his rifle and prepare for the attack of the infuriated beast.

It failed in fixing its large fangs in his throat as it had intended, but came with such force as to cause Will to stagger, and had it not been for a tree behind him he must have fallen.

Quickly recovering himself he dealt the ferocious brute a desperate blow with his rifle that seemed to stun him.

But only for an instant.

He quickly returned to the attack, and Will, grasping his rifle in both hands, as he came on with open jaws, caught him in the mouth, and forced him back; then, whipping his knife from its sheath, inflicted a deep gash in its chest.

As the boar reeled with pain, Will followed up the attack, and he soon had the gratification of seeing it roll over in its death agonies.

On returning to the camp he found that breakfast was awaiting him, and after they had refreshed themselves they parted from the trapper and proceeded in the direction pointed out by him.

A week's travelling, which was not unattended with great hardships and vicissitudes, brought them in sight of the coast, and the wanderers were thankful when they saw the blue sea stretching before them.

Having discovered a cave in which they might sleep, and an abundance of turtles' eggs, they resolved to take up their abode there until some chance vessel should rescue them from their perilous position.

The abundance of eggs they found next morning, led them to hope that they might fall in with a turtle, though they had no appliances for cooking it or making it savoury.

Having walked about till they were tired, they seated themselves down to rest, and each became absorbed in his own meditations.

Suddenly Will started to his feet with an exclamation—

'A sail! a sail!' he cried.

There was a white speck on the ocean, and Sancho, having shaded his eyes from the sun, and looked in the direction, pronounced it a delusion.

'It is strange if I am deceived,' muttered Will. 'I feel certain it is a sail.'

'I feel assured you are wrong,' said Sancho, 'it lays too low. If it is a sail, it must belong to a boat, and what boat would ever cruise about in this wild spot?'

'We might ask the same questions of ourselves,' answered Will; 'who ever would have thought of us being here?'

Sancho said no more, he leant on his spear in silence, and Will continued his survey.

A half-hour more brought the object so near, that Will felt certain he was not deceived.

He fancied he could make out a black speck like a boat.

Patiently he waited, and anxiously he watched, as it drew nearer and nearer, and then he could make out that it was a boat with some dozen or more occupants.

The light breeze propelled the boat rapidly shorewards, and the sun disclosed to Will's anxious gaze the bright uniform of an officer in the stern sheets.

'The crew of a shipwrecked vessel,' remarked Will to Sancho.

'Most likely,' replied the giant, recovering from his reverie, 'they have a good boat.'

The strangers were no little surprised to see Will and Sancho awaiting them, and they indulged in a hope that they had lit upon a settlement.

Their disappointment was great on hearing the truth, and they were for running down the coast.

On hearing that turtle eggs were in abundance, and the men expressing a wish to stretch their cramped limbs, the captain changed his purpose, and resolved to stay for the night.

This was good news to our hero.

He led them to the cave where some of the provisions were temporarily stored, to admit of the boat being cleaned out.

A flag was then displayed on a staff at the top of the cliff, and Will had the satisfaction of seeing another boat, propelled by oars, making for the spot.

Will then made himself as agreeable as possible to the captain, and told him a story of his shipwreck which was partly a fabrication.

He did this purposely, and then learnt the captain's story.

It turned out to be Captain Bullyton and part of his surviving crew, two of the boats having parted company with them during a breeze one dark night.

Will no sooner learnt that the Lotus had been engaged with the Golden Arrow, and that his new-made acquaintance was a man to be shunned instead of courted, than he fixed upon a plan.

This he communicated to Sancho, who seemed to share in his ideas, and the pair waited patiently till night should enable them to put their plan into exercise.

Captain Bullyton was much pleased with the place; he ordered the water breakers to be filled, and a great quantity of the eggs to be gathered.

The men cheerfully set to work; it was a change to them after being confined in the narrow limits of the boat.

The second boat now drew near to shore, and the occupants, six in number, leapt to land with as much delight as their fellows.

Will saw that the last arrived boat, a cutter, was well supplied with provisions, two or three bags of bread, and a barrel of salt pork, besides two good sized water breakers.

She was provided with a long sail, but the mast had been broken, and Will looked upon her with envious eyes.

The cutter was hauled into a little creek where the pinnace was undergoing a thorough scrub, and subjected to the same treatment.

A shout from a party of the sailors startled all hands, and in looking to ascertain the cause, they saw two of the tars labouring along under the weight of a huge turtle they had slung to the middle of a pole.

Sancho and one of the crew, who chanced to be the cook, soon dissected the prisoner, and having cut it up in pieces, placed it in a large iron pot, in which they were about to boil some of the pork.

This was a welcome feast to all.

The privateer's men had been subsisting on raw salt pork and dry biscuits since they had lost their ship.

Whilst the crew were thus engaged, Captain Bullyton and Will Howard were preparing for their departure.

The conquered captain seemed to have lost a great deal of his former blustering.

In fact he was rather humiliating to our hero.

He showed him his compass, and opened his case of nautical instruments, so that he might express an opinion of their qualities.

He also showed him his writing desk, and a secret drawer in which he had concealed his money and valuables from the crew.

Of all these things Will made a mental note, and marked well the spot where they were stowed, and when it was announced that the turtle was fit for eating, they sat down and had a jovial repast.

The captain and his officers dined with Will.

The others had to get theirs how they could, or wait till some one had done, for their tin plates were but scanty, and a spoon was a luxury very few could boast of.

Large shells in some cases served as soup plates, and smaller ones as spoons, whilst cocoa-nut shells, or anything that was found hollow, were brought into requisition.

Captain Bullyton, short as had been his preparations, had not forgotten his wine, nor a well-filled beaker of rum that was always kept in his cabin.

This was a luxury to Will.

A luxury of which, till now, he had not dared to dream.

He took a mental note of these, and chatted pretty freely as the wine went round.

Night at length came, with its deepening shadows, and the men who had been told off went upon watch.

One man was to look after the boats.

Another was to guard the entrance to the cave, and a third was to keep sentry on the heights for fear of an attack from the Indians.

These men were to keep watch for two hours each, which time was reckoned by an hour-glass.

No sooner had the men been disposed of, than Will set his thoughts to work.

His inventive mind soon performed the duty assigned to it.

He listened, and found that all but himself and Sancho were asleep.

Sancho, at a given signal, crept noiselessly from the cave, saluting the sentry as he passed him, and went towards a small green spot on the bank.

Here he collected the leaves of a certain plant; they were dry, and he crumbled them in his hand.

Having breathed upon them, he held them tightly until the moisture of his hand softened them, and then he retraced his steps.

'The air is rather sharp,' he said, to the sentry, 'and your captain seems rather sparing of his grog.'

'He is, curse his long carcase,' growled the man, his imagination conjuring up the comfort he might derive from a glass of rum.

Sancho had touched the right chord, and he meant to follow it up.

'I have a nip in the bottle, mate, if you like to accept of it,' he said, placing his mouth to the privateer's ear as though fearing to breathe too loud about the precious liquor.

'Accept of it,' said the man, ejecting a mouthful

of tobacco juice, 'I should like to find the tar that would ever refuse it. Why, you might just as well try to run a vessel in the wind's eye, as turn a sailor against his grog.'

Sancho did not wait to hear the finish of his remark, but walked into the cave.

Will was waiting for him.

Sancho gave him a portion of the leaves, and the two distributed them in small quantities under the nostrils of each of the sleeping men. Sancho then returned to the sailor with the promised bottle, which held about a pint.

He allowanced the sailor out to about half, which he drank with great gusto; then, with the remainder, he cheered the heart of the man who kept guard over the boats.

Whatever that bottle contained besides the rum, it had a magical effect.

The sailor in charge of the boats was soon sprawled his full-length, and when Sancho passed the other man, he was crouched down against the rock snoring like a stentor.

Deep sonorous sounds emanated from all the occupants of the cave except Will, who was busy carrying various articles to the entrance.

From there Sancho conveyed them to the creek, and deposited them in the cutter.

Amongst the articles was a bag of the best biscuits, several bottles of wine, a small keg of spirits, the captain's compass and instruments, and also the desk containing the coin.

To these were added several pieces of pork, a quantity of the turtles' eggs, and a breaker of fresh water.

The foremast of the pinnace served in place of the broken spar, and also gave them less to apprehend in case of a pursuit.

When all was ready, Will and Sancho stepped in, and, as the wind was contrary, they had to use the oars.

This they did freely, but, as they were leaving the mouth of the creek, a musket-ball passed close to Will's cheek.

'Close work; one would think the fellow had been a barber,' said Will, as he glanced up to where a white wreath of smoke was dispersing.

The sentry on the cliff had been aroused by the splash of oars.

Seeing the boat moving away, and believing that some of the crew were trying to desert, he fired his musket with the double intention of hitting the men and raising an alarm.

But he might as well have tried to wake the rocks as to wake his comrades—they were too well drugged.

Although there was not much fear of the privateers being able to pursue them, Will did not care about trusting too much to Providence.

Putting all his strength on the oar, he urged Sancho to do the same, impressing on his mind the disadvantages they would have to work under in case of a pursuit.

In the first place, the boat was heavily laden, and was notched for eight oars; whilst in the second place, the pinnace would be fully manned, and twelve oars would prove too much for their two, however strong they might be, or with whatever will they might work.

Again the crack of the musket was heard from the cliff, and again the bullet whizzed over the boat, this time striking Sancho, and causing him to fall from his thwart.

A cry of anger escaped Will's lips, and he poured an invective on the head of the sentry, as he threw in his oar, and assisted Sancho to rise.

CHAPTER CXV.

GERALD STUART AND THE BRAVE LIEUTENANT —THE FIGHT WITH THE MAN-OF-WAR.

WHEN the Golden Arrow ran down alongside the Martinet, Captain Henson complimented Gerald on the manner in which he had silenced such a formidable enemy.

'That I count as nothing,' answered Captain Stuart; 'it is only the commencement of the dangers we shall have to conquer.'

'I hope you are mistaken.'

'I fear not; in fact, I have assurance of what I say.'

'Indeed—a token?'

'A token if you will, and a pretty plain one.'

'What might it be then?'

'A paper I discovered on board the privateer.'

'Relating to us?'

'Yes, stating the strength of our armament, the number of men, names of officers, and a full description of both vessels.'

'Then we have been betrayed?'

'Most undoubtedly so, and the traitor was well informed.'

'This is awkward, and makes our venture dangerous.'

'Yes, we may say doubly dangerous,' answered Gerald, 'for I have no doubt these papers have been distributed freely among the fleet and cruisers.'

'Well I leave it entirely to your judgment how we shall act,' said Henson thoughtfully; 'we must run the gauntlet at all hazards.'

'And we will too, and in safety I hope.'

Gerald spoke in the tone of one who was well assured; he did not speak hastily; he weighed well each word before he uttered it.

Captain Henson was not a man easily frightened, but when Gregory mentioned the paper his cheek slightly paled.

The manner and tone of Gerald, however, partly dispelled his fear, yet he could not dispel the presentiment that all would not be so well as Gerald had anticipated.

Towards evening a schooner passed them, and Gerald hailed her.

She was from Falmouth, and her captain reported the channel alive with cruisers; he had passed a squadron formed of light frigates and corvettes in the Bay of Biscay, and that morning he had sighted a gun-brig that caused him to heave-to.

This was not pleasant news for the captains, and Henson was so far impressed with the idea of being captured, that he said as much to Gerald.

Captain Stuart only laughed at him.

'I can settle the largest man-of-war we may meet in the channel without firing a shot.'

This seemed too incredulous for Henson to believe and imagining that Gerald was getting as far as boasting, he walked away to pace his quarter-deck.

Gerald knew the meaning of this.

In fact it needed but the eye of a casual observer to read his thoughts in his looks.

It was no wonder, then, that a man like Gerald Stuart, who had devoted most of his life to the study of human nature, should see through the transparency.

He could see that he was disbelieved, and felt rather hurt, but considering the great thing he had promised to a stranger of only a few hours' acquaintance—a man who knew nothing of him, only by hearsay, he was not surprised.

'No matter,' he muttered to himself, 'he shall see that I make no rash promises if the opportunity offers; but however it may be, I will give him sufficient proofs of what I say, not being boastful, as shall induce him to place reliance in me for the future.'

Darkness was now drawing on a pace, and as it was necessary for their general safety that both vessels should keep at a respectful distance during the night, and yet not part company, Gerald gave Henson a few necessary orders.

It was before arranged that, should an enemy appear, the Lotus was to be edged away out of danger, and the Golden Arrow was to be left to do the fighting, and that in case of two appearing, and Henson failing to get away, he was to select the lightest.

As Gerald had anticipated, the night was pitchy dark, though the weather was moderate; and to prevent the ships losing each other, a horn lantern was displayed at intervals in the fore-rigging of the Golden Arrow, and answered by a red light from the Martinet.

Nothing of any consequence occurred that night, but in the morning a vessel was discovered within a mile of them.

As the twilight brightened, Gerald could see she was a man-of-war, and he had not the least doubt it was the gun-brig that had spoken the schooner.

To run from such a small vessel was the last thing Gerald would have thought of, though, when he signalled to Henson, and told him he was about to engage her, a scornful smile played on that officer's lips.

'Now,' he muttered, 'why don't he put his boasted power to the test? If he can—as he boasts—defeat a liner without firing a shot, he ought to settle this fellow by shooting peas though his speaking-trumpet.'

Thus reasons Henson.

But he did not know the power his colleague possessed.

Gerald Stuart never did anything rashly.

He laid out his plans with the tactics of a general, and though on this occasion he was going to fight the brig, he did so out of policy to prevent a failure that might have proved their utter ruin.

The brig was stationed there, and no doubt was acting in concert with the Lotus; therefore the captain or lieutenant in charge of the brig must know something of the privateer.

At least, this was Gregory's review of the position of affairs, and whatever his purpose was, he determined to fight the brig.

For this purpose he threw his vessel saucily across the brig's bows, and waited a quarrel which he knew must eventually ensue.

Lieutenant Fairfop, in command of the brig, which was named the Fawn, was astounded at the audacity of Gerald, and, hoisting his colours, he fired a gun as an intimation of the indignity he felt at the daring and wilful insult.

Gerald Stuart stood coolly watching his antics, which was to take two or three paces along the deck, stamp his feet upon the hard planks, and then stroke his whiskers as though he was trying to stretch them.

In this manner he amused himself for some minutes; then, when the Golden Arrow was clear of his bows, he approached the side, and yelled—

'You scoundrel—you! What do you mean by such conduct? I have a mind to teach you respect to your superiors.'

Gerald replied with the most provoking coolness.

'When an officer in the king's service can forget himself as you have done, I fear there is little hope of his teaching others.'

'What!' yelled the infuriated Fairfop; 'is your presumptuous insolence such as to allow you to lecture me—I, a lieutenant in the king's navy?'

'Were you an admiral, you would not frighten me with your bullying.'

'Insolent rascal!' cried the lieutenant, now boiling with rage. 'Recall that word and apologize.'

'My apology is here,' replied Gerald, in a tone of bitter irony. 'Come on board and take it, if you dare!'

He tapped the hilt of his sword as he spoke.

Fairfop was now in the height of his passion.

He stamped his foot, tore his whiskers, and went through so many pantomimic tricks as to make him look perfectly ludicrous.

'Pirate! fiend! whichever you are,' he yelled, at length, 'come on board and let me examine your papers. Such words could never emanate from the loyal subject of a king.'

'Poor, deluded wretch!' cried Gerald, his lips wreathing in bitter scorn, 'you little know to whom you speak. But, when you have proved yourself my master by deeds, not words, then will I obey you.'

'You defy me?'

'I hurl defiance in your teeth.'

'And refuse to obey my commands?'

'I have answered you already.'

'Then dread a just punishment. I bear no insult with impunity. You have not only insulted me, but the king's flag.'

'I would trample upon it were it here!' replied Gerald, tauntingly.

Fairfop fancied he heard a mocking laugh ring over the waves.

He turned towards the Golden Arrow.

He viewed her from the truck to the waterline.

All on board was silent.

With the exception of two men in the tops, who appeared to be at work, there was no one to be seen but Will and the helmsman.

'Well!' he ejaculated, 'there is nothing formidable in her appearance—nothing that I can see to make him so infernal saucy; but I will humble him, he wants teaching manners; and Lieutenant Fairfop of his Royal Majesty's Navy shall be his tutor.'

As Fairfop had said, there was nothing pretending in the appearance of the Golden Arrow.

Everything was as quiet as it was possible to be made.

Only two guns showed their dark muzzles, and besides these there was not the least sign of a port, much less a gun, along the whole side.

Fairfop could not help smiling, though it was faint, at the little game he was about to enjoy.

Already he was picturing to himself a battered hull, riddled sails, mangled bodies—the captain vanquished and at his feet begging for the life he was only going to spare to torture.

At this moment the drummer caught his eye, and he shouted to the second lieutenant—

'Mr. Sternall, beat to quarters.'

Mr. Sternall, or Allstern as he was termed by the sailors when in conversation amongst themselves, owing to a rather unusual prominence on a certain part of his person, passed the word without hesitation, and the men flew with alacrity to their guns.

Again Fairfop fancied he heard that ringing laugh mocking him, and he grew red, then ashy pale, as his fierce gleaming eyes turned to the Golden Arrow.

'Man the starboard guns!' he shouted, at the pitch of his voice.

The starboard guns were manned, and the quartermaster was ordered to bring the ship round, so that the broadside might tell full upon the Golden Arrow.

Again the mocking laugh sounded in Fairfop's ears.

'Give the order to fire as soon as the guns bear,' he gasped to Sternall.

He could not speak.

Rage choked his utterance.

It seemed as though a great ball was sticking in his throat.

Presently the word 'Oh!' burst from him, as if it had been jerked up, and he staggered back to the companion-way.

The cause of this exclamation was, just as the second lieutenant was about to give the word 'fire!' the whole side of the Golden Arrow opened, as it were, and her hull bristled with guns.

A blinding flash, a loud report, and then a crash.

The deck of the Fawn was suddenly turned into a slaughter-house.

Dead and dying strewed the deck, blood poured from the scuppers, and the scene was one of terrible carnage.

In the midst of this the voice of Captain Stuart would be plainly heard directing the movements of his crew.

'Double shot your guns, and keep your match in hand,' he cried.

Fairfop was astounded.

He had not yet had sufficient time to recover his self-possession, and give the order himself to fire, as Sternall had received a blow from a piece of splintered timber in that very part of his person that held him up to ridicule, and was now panting on the deck.

'A pirate, by heaven!' gasped Fairfop, as soon as he could give utterance. 'Lay your guns well, lads, and fire steady.'

The seamen of the Fawn were a fine body of men — they were volunteers from various ships; the prospect of prize-money had been an inducement for them to enter upon the cruise, which was expected to be attended with some danger.

Crash went the Fawn's broadside, and as quickly

was it responded to by the Golden Arrow; when Fairfop, seeing they would have no chance with the big guns, he having been staggered by the first fire, dashed his vessel alongside, and attempted to board.

The ships came together with a concussion that made both ships reel; and Gerald Stuart, taking time by the forelock, leapt on to the brig's deck.

Then commenced a fearful struggle.

The men, as we have before said, were tough and tried, and were fairly lost for the want of a good officer to lead them.

Bob Brace, Marline, and Tom Tiller, having forsaken the guns, followed close upon their captain, forming a kind of body-guard.

The man-of-war's men, who were trying to board on the quarter, rushed forward to prevent this unceremonious intrusion, the boatswain leading the way, waving his cutlass.

Amongst the foremost was Forecastle Joe, a brave but lumbersome fellow, who, with musket at the charge and fixed bayonet, stood ready to receive Captain Gerald on its point.

He was mistaken in his man.

Captain Stuart dashed aside the gleaming steel, and with a well-directed blow laid the fellow almost open to the waist.

By this time all hands were called into play.

Fairfop had recovered his equanimity.

Sternall had also recovered from his shock.

One insertion of a sail-maker's needle (in the wounded part), which the mischievous cabin-boy had some how become possessed of, was sufficient to bring him to his feet.

As the two bodies of men came together it seemed like the conflux of two mighty rivers.

They were brought up by a sudden check, that threw each party backwards.

Fairfop, instead of in front, was now behind, cheering on his men; and Sternall, deeming it best to follow his commander's example, was some distance behind him.

This gave Stuart many advantages he otherwise would not have had.

He was able to lead his men here and there through the surging throng, and, as his powerful arm descended and added another to the ghastly pile, his men strove their utmost to imitate him.

Foot by foot, inch by inch, they gained their way aft.

Desperate was the struggle upon that slippery deck.

Fierce was the contest when they saw their comrades fall.

Still on—on slowly but surely, Gerald cut his way.

Sometimes the men fell back terrified at his presence, then the gap was filled by better and braver men, who only rushed to court death, and fell by Stuart's gleaming weapon.

At length the mainmast was gained, and Gerald tried to cut a way to where Fairfop stood, himself doing nothing but shouting to his men in the wildest manner.

At last Fairfop and Gerald met face to face.

The coward quailed.

He could not withstand Gerald's steadfast eye.

'Now,' said Gerald, 'I come to offer you my apology; take it, if you are able; if not, give up yours to me.'

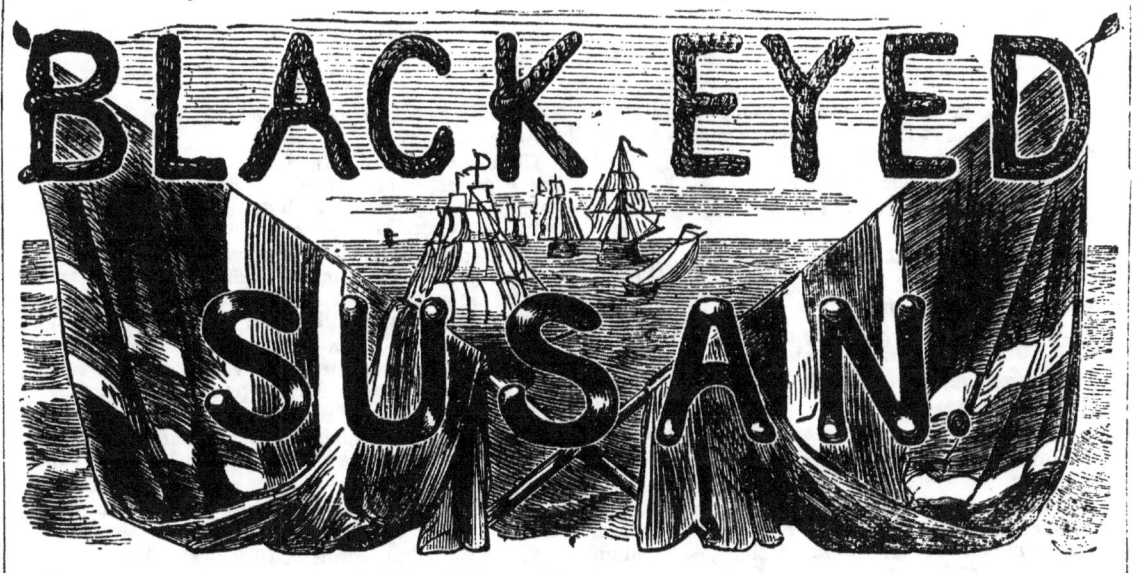

BLACK EYED SUSAN.

OR, PIRATES ASHORE.

THE MEETING.

He waved his sword over the lieutenant's head, who was obliged to put up his sword to defend himself.

Gerald did not wish to kill him.

His aim was to humble him.

This he did.

With a skilful turn of the wrist, he wrenched Fairfop's sword out of his hand, and caught it in his own brawny palm.

'Now!' shouted Gerald, pointing a pistol at his head, 'whose turn is it to apologize?'

'Mercy!' gasped Fairfop, as the cold barrel touched his heated brow.

'Surrender, then, and end this bloody slaughter.'

'Never!' cried Fairfop, struggling between fear and duty.

'Then you will fall a victim to your obstinacy!' thundered Gerald. 'Repent before it is too late. See, your men are falling on all sides, and cannot hold out much longer.'

'Pirate, I have given you your answer,' cried Fairfop. 'I will fall with my men, if it must be so.'

Stuart saw that all argument was thrown away upon the lieutenant.

Pride rendered him headstrong.

Captain Gerald did not wish for his life, so he caught him by the collar, and drew him from the midst of his men, who were vainly trying to protect him, Captain Gerald's body-guard keeping them at hot work.

Bob Brace and Marline stuck together, and Tom Tiller, with a party of foretopmen, followed in their rear.

Lieutenant Sternall, with a few marines, one or two middies, and a party of blue-jackets were struggling desperately on the quarter-deck, whither they had been driven.

'Give the miscreants no quarter! Charge them, Corporal Buff! Let them see that we have a little pluck left.'

Sternall had scarcely given utterance to these words when Pat, who had joined Tom Tiller's party, rammed the staff of his boarding-pike between his teeth, and sent him rolling behind the binnacle.

Seeing the lieutenant fall, and believing him dead or mortally wounded, Colonel Buff grew faint-hearted.

His men were thrown into confusion; and as Tom Tiller and Pat incited their comrades to action, the marines threw down their arms and begged for quarter.

The quarter-deck—in fact, nearly the whole of the brig, was in possession of the boarders, and Tom Tiller cut the peak halliards, and let the colours come down by the run.

Fairfop's few adherents were the only ones now in arms, and these, though desperate and resolute men, were soon overpowered by unequal numbers.

The lieutenant gave a groan of bitter agony when he saw his ship in the hands of the boarders.

Captain Gerald mustered the prisoners.

By the ship's books he found that nearly two-thirds of the crew were missing.

The slaughter had been terrific.

Having placed the officers aft, and the rest of the prisoners in the waist, Captain Stuart placed a strong guard over them, and then descended to the cabin.

Strict orders were previously given that nothing was to be removed from the brig without his sanction; and this was acted upon to the very letter.

Gerald, on entering the cabin, began ransacking the drawers, in one of which he found an exact copy of the document he had found on board the privateer, describing his ship and the Martinet.

He also found a book of private signals, which was as precious to him as a mine of wealth; and having concluded his search without finding anything more of value to him, he went upon deck.

The prisoners were looking, with woe-begone visages, at their captors, who they expected each moment would have orders to put them to death.

Their faces elongated greatly when Captain Stuart ordered Marline, Ben Brace, and Tom Tiller to provide themselves with hatchets from the carpenter's chest.

Everyone looked at the captain in silent wonderment.

What were his intentions? was the thought of all who heard that order.

The appearance of the three sailors, each armed with a formidable axe, soon put their minds at rest.

'Lay aloft there, and disable everything above the cross-trees,' he said, sternly. 'Let the top-gallant and royal yards and masts be cut through.

Turning to a group of men, amongst whom was Pat, who were doing nothing, he said to them—

'Get your knives to work, cut adrift the lanyards of the lower rigging, let every shroud be cast loose.'

Addressing himself to Fairfop, who was gazing dismayed at the mutilation of his splendid little ship, he said—

'I will not deprive you of your vessel, but I will take care to clip her wings so that we may have a good start before you can come up with any of your confederates, for I see by your list that they swarm about here like bees. It is fortunate I fell in with you as it gives me a chance of '——

'Eluding the yard-arm,' cried Fairfop, in a fit of desperation. 'Pirate, beware! for though you disable my ship, we may yet meet again.'

'I trust so, and under the same circumstances,' replied Gerald, tauntingly.

By this time the work was completed aloft, and the armourer having spiked the guns with their own priming wires, which Gerald had ordered to be filed into certain lengths, they prepared to return on board the Golden Arrow.

Before doing so Captain Stuart once more addressed the commander.

'Lieutenant Fairfop,' he said, 'I am sorry that necessity has compelled me to use such stringent measures, and so far degrade his majesty's officers; but had you proved successful, you would have dealt less leniently with me. I now bid you farewell, and leave you to repair the damage, and give you full permission of acquainting the admiral of the station, the fact of your having been honoured with a visit, not from a pirate, but the captain of the *Golden Arrow, Gerald Stuart!*'

'Gerald Stuart!' gasped the lieutenant; the name fell on his ears like a thunder clap.

Clasping his hand to his brow, he stood like one petrified, and for some minutes after Gerald and his men had regained their ship, and cast off the grapplins, he stood speechless and immovable.

Gerald then bore down on the Martinet, which ship, as before, had sailed out of reach of the cannon, and had laid to watching the progress of the fight.

This second victory of the gallant captain raised

him high in the estimation of Captain Henson; but still the words of Gerald Stuart hung on his memory.

'If he could have gained his end without bloodshed,' he soliloquized, 'why did he not do so? It was his boast,' he added, half-aloud, 'and though I cannot but admire him for his courage, yet I abhor him for his self-conceit.'

Gerald could read in his features that a certain amount of confidence was wanted between him and the man who was bound to him by a mutual tie.

At first he attributed it to jealousy in not allowing Henson to share in the conflict; but a remark from Henson brought the whole truth rushing to his mind.

'Aha! you have not yet learnt to know the man you accuse so unjustly,' he muttered to himself; 'but ere we reach our destination, I may have an opportunity of—but there, it is no use surmising.'

Little did he know how soon his power would be put to the test.

Gerald turned to give some order in the trimming of the sails, for as the Golden Arrow sailed much swifter than the Martinet, it was necessary to take in the light canvas.

As he did so, his eye caught sight of a speck on the horizon in a line with the jib-boom.

Gradually it rose higher and higher as the vessels rapidly approached, and disclosed a cloud of canvas, that left no doubt on the mind of Gerald of the nature and size of the vessel that bore it.

He was not deceived. Laying down his glass, he said to the mate, 'A line-of-battle ship, by all that's holy; we shall be but a bumboat alongside of her.'

CHAPTER CXVI.

AN UNEXPECTED CHANGE.

SILAS DOGGRASS sat brooding in his cell, counting the hours as they dragged slowly by, and thinking himself totally deserted.

A week had passed, during which time he had heard nothing of what was passing in the outer world.

Even his friend Lord Travers had not visited him.

This gave him great anxiety.

His suspicions now seemed fully confirmed. Lord Travers had proved himself a traitor.

'Curse him!' Doggrass burst out, suddenly rising from his seat, and glancing at the grated window, through which the light feebly struggled; 'could I but once gain my liberty, he should find that Silas Doggrass is not so tame as he thinks.'

There was something demonical in his expression as he clenched his long hands, and went through the ceremony of strangling some imaginary foe.

A noise at the door disturbed him, and as it opened he glanced sheepishly towards it, as though he was fearful of anyone detecting him in the act.

A smile irradiated his visage as Lord Travers, cloaked and muffled as before, entered.

'Well,' he half grunted—for his suspicions were not yet allayed—'you have come at last?'

Lord Travers was rather startled at this reception.

He gazed some moments at the prisoner before he made an answer,

'Yes, I have come at last,' he said, 'but my visit seems to give you some uneasiness.'

'Uneasiness!' growled Doggrass; 'were you chained up here from day to day, as I am, you would feel uneasy. I thought you had forgotten me entirely.'

'Quite the reverse.'

'Then where have you been?'

'In London.'

'Ah!'

This was said with a sigh and a look of incredulity. Silas believed he had been in London, and that he had Susan hidden there somewhere.

'Do you believe me?' asked Travers.

'Not in the least; but you will please explain what business took you to London.'

'Friendship for you.'

'Indeed, how was that?'

'I have been trying to obtain your release. I failed in persuading the magistrate here that you were innocent, and I tried what I could do for you in London.'

'And you failed?'

'I certainly did not succeed.'

'Then I am lost!'

'Not quite—there is yet a way of escape.'

'How?'

Travers pointed to the window.

Doggrass shuddered.

He was a coward in heart.

'No other way?' he asked.

'None!'

'Then I must trust to fate.'

'What!' exclaimed Travers, 'are you faint-hearted? You must dispense with these girlish scruples; the way to liberty is open; it needs but a little energy on your part to leave these hated walls.'

'To talk is one thing, to act is another,' said Silas, impressively. 'When you walk in and out the doors are open; should I try to escape, I might either fall and break a limb, or get a bullet in my carcase.'

'Then I have risked my liberty for nothing,' said Travers, wrathfully. 'See, I have brought you rope and other necessaries.'

'You are kind, very kind,' said Doggrass, emphasizing his words. 'I am sorry it is not in my power to reward you.'

Travers did not notice the smile of bitter irony that played on his lips as he spoke, or doubtless he would have left him to his fate; as it was, he pitied him, and sat some moments in thought.

'My mission has been useless,' he said, at length; 'but I will not desert you, Doggrass. I will yet try my influence, and see what can be done.'

At this moment the door grated on its hinges, and the bull-dog head of Lockit was thrust through the opening.

The look on the jailer's face spoke as plain as words what he wanted; and Travers, waving an adieu to the prisoner, followed the turnkey out.

* * * * * *

All Deal was thrown into the utmost consternation when it was reported that Doggrass had been tried and acquitted.

In the various taverns it was discussed, and especially at the Crown and Anchor.

Even the old fishwives, when they went in to get

their dram, discussed the subject; and various were the comments as to how his release had been effected.

It was believed by the inhabitants that old Doggrass was a miser—that he had heaped up riches in some secret place; and it was hinted by more than one party that this had something to do with the verdict.

They put it down that bribery had blinded the eyes of justice.

In this they were utterly at fault.

Lord Travers had some wealthy and influential friends in the great town of London; and though they had not given him any reason to hope for the prisoner's release when he stated the case to them, yet what he said had great weight in Doggrass's favour.

They thought it over, and hoodwinked many things that under other circumstances would have been taken as evidence; though one great thing in the prisoner's favour was that on his house being searched, nothing to lead them to believe he was a dealer in contraband was to be found.

What spirits they did find were considered necessary, as Doggrass at times opened his house as a tavern, though it was often closed, as he had too much work on his hands to attend to that business.

His house had for many years been known as the Dolphin, but of late the owner, through some whim or other, changed its name to the Three Luggers.

Many people whose business was not sufficient to employ their minds, without troubling their heads with other people's, expressed their surprise at this, and puzzled their brains to find out what could have induced him to do so.

Doggrass must have been deaf as well as blind to remain ignorant of what was passing in the minds of his customers, some of whom were even bold enough to ask questions on the subject.

But Doggrass always had an answer for them, and quietly hinted that if his liquors—which were certainly of the best—did not suit them, they might go elsewhere.

Once free from the jail, Doggrass had his house put a little in repair, and the sign, which had become almost obliterated, revived.

He then opened his house to the public for the sale of liquors, more as a blind than for anything else, as the rents of his houses brought him in a pretty tidy income.

Dame Howard had now become destitute in the extreme. The poor, scanty pittance the parish allowed her scarcely kept life and soul together.

Her neighbours, poor as herself, could not help her; and Doggrass saw a chance of retrieving his lost character by doing at least one act of charity in his life.

He took her to his home, and made her his housekeeper; and as she was almost entirely deaf, he felt a security in her he would not have done had she possessed all her faculties.

Charity, they say, covereth a multitude of sins; and so it did in this case.

Doggrass was looked upon as a most humane man; and the misery he had brought upon the dame in former years, by robbing her of her only child, seemed to have been forgotten.

It was now Doggrass's policy to make himself as affable as possible towards his customers—a task which was to him extremely hard.

It required a great effort on his part to bring a smile on his hardened visage; and as most of his customers came only to see and hear what they could, it required the utmost caution on his part.

It was some relief to the mind of Doggrass to know that the smugglers had not been seen about the coast since the terrible conflict between them and Lieutenant Pike's party.

That officer prided himself that he had driven them from that part of the coast; and, as a strict watch had been kept on the entrance of the cave, and no one had been seen to leave or enter, his words seemed verified.

The landlord of the Three Luggers, to maintain his respectability, closed his house as a rule at an early hour, and sent the old dame to her bed.

Could anyone have seen the old villain then, it would have done their eyesight good.

Hour after hour he would sit brooding over his real or imaginary wrongs.

He would think of Lord Travers, and wonder how it was he had not seen him since their last interview in the jail, and then he would think of Susan, who, he little doubted, was concealed from him by the lord's treachery.

After venting his spleen on those he considered his enemies, Doggrass would sip up his grog, and then proceed to ogle his treasures.

His first precaution would be to ascertain if Dame Howard was asleep, and then he would bolt the door leading to the stairs, to make sure of not being interrupted in that quarter.

He would then proceed to one corner of the room where one of the beards, worked by a secret spring, would fly up, and disclose a square hole built of bricks.

Here his treasure was concealed, and Doggrass often boasted to himself that none but himself knew of it, and that the men who built it, and constructed the secret cellars under his house, had long since crumbled in their graves.

It was thus he had been employed on dark, cheerless nights, the wind howling fitfully round the old gabled building, and the rain driving in showers against the shutters, creating anything but a comfortable sensation in the mind of the listener, when he was suddenly disturbed.

A heavy peal of thunder, that seemed to rend the heavens, shook the old house from roof to base, and made the landlord tremble for the safety of the Three Luggers.

Awe-stricken with the violence of the crash, Doggrass closed the hole, and, taking the candlestick in his trembling hand, he tried to direct his steps towards the stairs, but they seemed powerless.

Another peal made the old house tremble as though trying to outvie its master, who was shaking like a reed.

'God protect those at sea on such a night,' he muttered, unconsciously, as his eye glanced at the shaking doors, and the wind swept into the crevices with a fearful wail.

So involuntary had the words been uttered, that he actually wondered whether or not he had heard the sound of his own voice.

Conscience-smitten and filled with superstitious fear, he stood clutching the balustrades unable to ascend the stairs, though he made several desperate efforts to do so.

The image of Will Howard flashed vividly to his heated imagination, and then his thoughts reverted to Susan.

'Great God of heaven!' he muttered, 'where can she be? I dreamt of her last night—a fearful dream. I trust no harm has come to her, for, though she is of an obstinate, aggravating temper, she possesses a noble spirit. She has caused me worlds of trouble through her headstrong will; yet I cannot forget she is of kindred blood. A tie exists between us; she was my sister's only child.'

How long he would have gone on in this manner there is no knowing; the floodgates of his hardened heart seemed, for the first time in many years, to have been suddenly opened, had he not been disturbed and startled by a loud knock at the door.

Thoughts flashed to his memory of Hatchett's visit, and he paused in breathless suspense until it was repeated.

Presently a voice, totally strange to him, was heard in the lull of the tempest, shouting—

'Open the door. Be quick, for God's sake! Life is almost gone.'

CHAPTER CXVII.

CAPTAIN BULLYTON GETS BIT—THE PURSUIT OF THE FUGITIVES—ON BOARD THE SLAVER.

THE sentry on the cliff having fired twice, and received no answer, rushed down to the beach; and seeing a darkie laying rolled up in his rug in a hollow in the cliff, he gave him a kick with his foot to rouse him.

This fellow had escaped Will's notice, but he slept so soundly that a cannon-ball would not have roused him had it struck him anywhere but the spot the sailor had assailed with his boot—viz., on the shins.

However, the sailor was successful, and Sambo sprang to his feet with a howl—one hand being pressed upon the aching shin, and the other scratching violently at his woolly head.

'What you do dat for, massa fast, eh?' yelled the negro in a squeaking voice. 'By gor a'mighty! you do dat agen, you feel dis darky's knife.'

'Rouse up, fool, and let's have none of this nonsense,' cried the sailor impetuously. 'Do you not see that boat? Some of our men are deserting us. Quick! rouse up all hands; they seem as dead as logs.'

'Aha!' ejaculated the darky, turning up the whites of his eyes as though he had made some important discovery. 'See here, massa Jack, dey been drugged. Yah, yah! He, he, he!'

'You fool! drop this nonsense, or damme if I don't hammer your thick head till it's as big as a pumpkin! Turn up the hands; lend me a hand to wake them.'

'Yah, yah! He, he, he!' grinned the darky in spite of the sailor's threat. 'Dem fellows know what dey about. By gor! you shake all night, you no wake de men.'

'I'll shake you, cuss your black hide! if you keep giggling there,' thundered the sailor, shaking his fist threateningly at the negro. 'What do you mean by this foolery?'

'No foolery; Sambo sabby all he say. Look here on massa captain's face.'

The sailor looked, and seeing nothing but a few powdered leaves, took no heed of it further than believing the darky was making a fool of him.

'Sink me for a swab if I can stand this!' cried the exasperated sailor, glancing through the opening of the cave at the dark outlines of the receding boat. 'D—n it! this is as bad as being jammed between two winds, or laid in irons. By Jove!

there is one of our boats leaving us; and all hands, sentries and all, fast as a church, and about as easy to move as the chain cable of a three-decker.'

While the sailor was thus easing his mind, and venting his spleen on a huge quid of tobacco which he was chewing vigorously, and shifting from one cheek to the other, Sambo had lit a pipe, and was puffing the tobacco-smoke up the nostrils of the sleepers.

By this time the sailor's intellect began to grow clearer, and a true knowledge of what was actually the matter with the sleepers gradually dawned upon his mind.

'Bravo, Sambo, my hearty! Pull away!' he said, in a much more pleasant tone than he had hitherto addressed his companion with. 'Unbatten their eyelids, or the fellows will be too far for us to overhaul.'

Sambo puffed away vigorously, until, as the saying is, he was black in the face; and the captain being the first to recover himself, started up almost choked.

'Curse you for an infernal black scoundrel!' were the first words that left his lips. 'You deserve keel-hauling. What are you at, you imp of darkness? You will choke all hands.'

The black looked up in wonderment, and stammered out—

'By gor, massa, I do no harm; I only '——

'Silence, you devil's imp! It was a bad day when I shipped you. If I had towed you astern until you had bleached as white as the rind of a pork-piece, we should not have been laying here upon these hard stones; hang them! they have dented into my flesh, and made my bones ache as though they were dislocated; and you, you son of Hades, are trying to choke us with tobacco. What were you about—smoking the mosquitoes?'

'Beg your honour's pardon,' said the look out man, who slipped out during the skipper's speech, and only ventured in when his storm of passion had subsided a little—'beg your honour's pardon for waking you, but some of the hands are deserting. I have fired a shot or two at them, but it was no good; and on coming down here, I found you all snoring like great guns, and about as much life in you as a main-sheet block.'

'What do you say, deserters? What boat have they taken? where is the sentry in charge of them?' yelled the captain as soon as the trance-like spell in which he had listened to the sailor was broken.

'They have taken the cutter,' replied the sailor 'and both sentries are as fast asleep as boobies on a yard-arm, and are playing the bag-pipes to'——

'Cut your yarn short,' thundered the captain. 'Which way did those fellows take?'

'To the nor'ard your honour. See,' he added pointing, 'you can just make out the boat.'

'Go, then, at once, man the pinnace, and pull like blazes after them. Here, boatswain, muster the hands and see who is missing.'

When thirteen men had manned the pinnace, it did not take long to muster the rest, and it was soon announced that their own men were all present, but that the strangers were missing.

At this intelligence, the brow of the privateer captain grew black as a thunder-cloud, and the volley of oaths that poured from his lips was enough to bear down all before it.

The sentry on the entrance of the cave, and the man who had been set to watch the boats, were at once placed under arrest with a promise of having a warm coating under their shirts in the morning.

In the meantime, Will Howard and Sancho bent to the oars with a will. Of course they were ignorant of what was passing on shore, but as they felt certain of being pursued, they wished to place as much distance between them and the shore in as short a time as possible.

'Give way, Sancho,' cried Will, down whose reeking brow the perspiration rolled in streams; 'it's pull devil pull baker with us now. Confound it, how the boat seems to hang water.'

'And no wonder. Look at the weight in her; we have stores to provision a ship for a long voyage.'

'Well, we are well stored if we are fortunate enough to escape; but we are a long way from the shore now, and as I see no boat yet make its appearance, we may as well freshen with a nip of the captain's brandy.'

'Agreed, it is capital stuff. I sampled one of the bottles, and it seemed to give me new life.'

The pair ceased rowing, and Will half-filled a panakin from one of the bottles, then adding a little water, gave it to Sancho.

Sancho swallowed the spirit with a smack of the lips which implied he was not often used to indulge in such a luxury.

Will then helped himself to the same, and the pair thus refreshed renewed their work with fresh vigour.

At this time the moon, contrary to the wishes of the fugitives, peeped through the dark mass of clouds, and Will fancied he could make out a dark speck in their wake.

'If that is not a boat,' said Will, after a careful scrutiny, 'may I be drilled for a lubber. Heave round, Sancho, my hearty, we'll do them yet.'

'I wish they had given us another half-hour's start,' said Sancho, peering at the boat, for such they had little doubt it was. 'We ought to have settled the fellow on the cliff.'

'It matters little now; we have entirely to depend upon our own exertions. If we flag, we know the consequences.'

In spite of Will's cheering words he could not be blind to the fact that the boat was rapidly gaining upon them.

Whenever the moon struggled through the murky clouds, they could see the boat plainer.

The chase now became a hot one.

Will fancied more than once he could hear the oars as they jerked in the rowlocks.

'Heaven help us,' he thought, though he did not communicate his fears to Sancho, 'for we are now past all power of our own.'

Swiftly the cutter sped through the water, but still the boat grew larger as it crept steadily up astern.

At length he could keep his thoughts to himself no longer.

'They are walking down on us hand over hand,' he said to Sancho; 'we may have a tussle for it, and as pulling like this is only wasting our strength in vain, I propose we set the sail.'

'Just what I was thinking, captain. This light air will keep her going, and we can pull at leisure if it is needed.'

The sail was set, and the wind, which was not very strong, kept the boat going at about the same pace as the oars.

A shout from the privateers told how conscious they were of their advantage.

Will replied with a taunting laugh.

If they were going to overhaul them, he considered it best to urge them on, and let the collision take place, and trust to Providence for their further safety.

'See to your arms, Sancho,' cried Will. 'Look well to the priming; remember, we cannot spare a shot.'

'There is no fear,' replied Sancho, 'but what every one will bark if it has not the chance to bite.'

They had not neglected to arm themselves well, and provide plenty of ammunition.

Sancho had about a dozen pistols, which he had borrowed from the sleeping privateers, and these were ranged in a row ready to his hand.

Will had four in his belt, beside a cutlass.

As his duty was to steer, Sambo had to watch the movements of the privateers.

Crouching down, with his eye just clear of the gunwale, he could see the men pulling, and the coxswain standing up in the stern sheets.

'Pull, my hearties—give way a few strokes,' he could hear the coxswain say. 'Hurrah! we shall soon drop on 'em like a cold shot from a forecastle chaser.'

A flash, and a sharp report followed this speech, and a dull splash was heard in the sea as the coxswain fell over the stern, stricken by a shot fired by Sancho.

'One the less,' said the giant, coolly, reloading the discharged barrel.

This caused a sudden commotion in the boat, and as the tiller was deserted, the boat yawed, allowing Sancho to count the number of foes they had to contend against.

As the body of the coxswain did not rise to the surface, another supplied his place, and gave the order to pour in a volley.

As only four of the men, besides the coxswain who had been shot, were armed, the volley was nothing compared to what it would have been, and now our adventurers had discovered this fact, they felt greater confidence in themselves.

The volley did no material damage, besides cutting a hole in the sail, and, as Will and Sancho laid flat down when the order was given, there was little fear of their being hit.

Sancho was on his knees the instant the bullets whizzed past, and another well-directed shot wounded the new coxswain.

His place was quickly supplied by one who inherited a fiery temper from his captain.

'Fire into them, my bullies!' he thundered. 'Cut them up as small as junk. D—— 'em! they ought to be strung up.'

The disorder in the pinnace had impeded her progress, and allowed the cutter to forge ahead, evidence of which was given by the pistol-shots dropping into the bottom of the boat.

Sancho had one pistol which he had reserved for a long range, and as the privateers, swearing and calling them anything but gentlemen, sat down at their oars, and began to get good way on the pinnace, he fired a pistol in a line with the men on the starboard side of the thwarts.

A good shot was Sancho, and perhaps never before in his life did he have such an excellent opportunity of displaying his skill. Two men dropped their oars at this shot, and those who were armed, sprang up and returned the fire.

One of the shots almost proved fatal to our hero.

It took off the crown of his hat as though it had been cut with a knife. Another cut a button from the breast of his coat.

'Sharp work, as they say, when the enemy rakes you fore and aft. What say you, Sancho?' said Will, holding up his crownless hat.

But Sancho either did not, or pretended not, to hear him.

He was taking another deadly aim.

A sudden lurch of the boat probably saved the man's life for whom the ball was intended, for the bullet went through the planking of the boat just between wind and water.

'By G—— we are sinking!' they could hear one of the men exclaim, and then the order to bail out was sufficient to tell them what damage was done.

From this time the pinnace began to flag in her movements, and it was evident the privateers were growing disheartened and weary of the chase.

This was welcomed as a good omen by the fugitives, as if the privateers had come up with them, they would have had but a poor chance against such unequal numbers.

The breeze, too, was freshening, and the cutter began to feel her weather helm.

This decided the conflict.

The privateers, well-knowing the cutter's sailing qualities, and having lost one of their masts, which Will had transferred to the cutter, they gave up the chase as hopeless, and having fired their pistols as a farewell salute, turned stern about, and headed for the shore.

'That is a wise trick on their part, and a fortunate circumstance for us,' said Sancho, 'for if they had persevered in the chase, I should have given them a few more pills, while on the other hand, a stray shot might have found its way into one of our carcases.'

'They have managed to knock a hole in the boat,' said Will, looking down at his feet, which was over the ankles in water. 'Bale her out, Sancho, and let us see the extent of the damage.'

Sancho set to work, but the water did not seem to diminish, and they became anxious to learn where the hole might be, so as to thrust a plug in.

A pint panakin was the only baler they could find, and it was some time before Sancho began to gain on the new enemy that threatened them if not with death, with a good deal of extra labour.

If the appearance of the water caused them uneasiness, they were more surprised to see it suddenly abate.

Sancho bailed the boat out dry, and they were pleased to behold that no more took its place.

This was a blessing, and as they were both fatigued and the pinnace was leaving them fast, they proposed taking a little refreshment.

Sancho gladly acquiesced in this.

He was sweating at ever pore.

A quantity of brandy was poured into the panakin, and Sancho went to the cask to procure some water, but to his horror, it was empty.

A feather might almost have knocked him down on making this discovery, and he seemed fearful to break the news to his companion.

The thought flashed to his mind that the labour he had bestowed in bailing out the boat, had been devoted to the throwing overboard the precious liquid.

It was some consolation to think that they were not totally deprived of the means of moistening their palates, and Will, from whom the direful news could no longer be kept, cheered his companion by reminding him that they still had some bottles of wine.

But as is mostly the case, both seemed to be seized with an insatiable thirst, and as they had eaten freely of the salt meat that had been served out to them for their suppers, they felt their loss most keenly.

The brandy revived them greatly, but did not quench their thirst. Consoling themselves as well as circumstances would permit, for they had started on an uncertain voyage, one sat watching and steering, while the other tried to close his eyes in sleep.

The wind was very unsteady during the night, so that the boat had made several courses, and in the morning land of no sort could be seen.

With nothing to direct their course but the rising of the sun, the two adventurers pursued their way, trusting to Providence to guide them to some port.

Exposed to the burning sun by day, and the chilling air at night, the horrors of their situation began fully to develop itself.

The wine was soon consumed, and the brandy would not quench their burning thirst.

The salt pork and dry biscuits they were unable to masticate, and thus the fourth day passed without the least indication of rain in the heavens.

It was the morning of the fifth day, and when their spirits began to give way, that a sail was sighted.

Sancho, who was laying on one of the thwarts trying to banish his uncomfortable thoughts by sleep, and inwardly cursing the bullet that had pierced the water-cask, sprang to his feet at the joyful sound.

The boat's course was immediately changed, and then opinions were passed as to what the strange vessel might be.

It was a small vessel, battern-rigged, and appeared to be carrying little sail, which led them to suppose it was a fishing vessel.

As they neared, this supposition grew stronger. Only two men were to be seen, one steering, the other standing in the bows, as though surprised at seeing a small boat so far from land.

Will and Sancho were both gasping for a drink, and, reckless of all consequences, they were about to run alongside the stranger.

But the man who was clothed in the garb of a common seaman waved them back and shouted—

'Where are you coming to, you lubber? and where do you hail from?'

Will was not prepared for this question, but had sufficient presence of mind to answer.

'Our vessel struck upon a sunken reef, went to pieces, and we are all that escaped from being drowned. We are short of water if you can give us some.'

'Just so; but you don't suppose we carry water to supply every one we meet; you have nothing to give us in return.'

Stung to the quick by this inhuman reply, Will felt half inclined to put a bullet through the fellow, and try to obtain by force what it appeared they could not get by fair means.

Not wishing to use violence unless compelled Will tried once more to soften the fellow's iron heart.

'We could spare you a little salt pork and

biscuit,' he said; 'and a brace of pistols, if you stand in need of them.'

The man pricked up his ears at the mention of the pistols.

His face suddenly relaxed its hardened expression.

'We have enough provisions for us two,' he said, 'but the pistols may be useful. If they are loaded discharge them, and then come alongside.'

All the pistols but a brace Will carried in his belt had been stowed under the stern sheets, and as Will was glad to procure water at any price, he gladly accepted the terms.

The pistols were discharged, and the cutter laid alongside, but scarcely had they touched, when a dozen bloodthirsty-looking wretches sprang up from a covering of canvas that Will had taken for the deck, and he and Sancho were bound hand and foot before they could recover from their surprise.

One glance was sufficient to satisfy Will that they had fallen into a nest of pirates—a set of hideous-looking wretches, from whom they might expect no mercy.

While Will and Sancho were being seen to by their rough attendants, another party jumped into the cutter, and stripped her of every movable article, and the prisoners had the mortification of seeing the pistols ranged before the man who appeared the captain.

A consultation was then held, but as the conversation was carried on in Spanish—a language of which Will was in total ignorance—he was unable to tell what it was about.

From their gestures and the fierce looks occasionally cast towards them, Will concluded that they were discussing their fate.

One fellow, a dark, swarthy ruffian, with high, prominent cheek-bones, and long, straggling hair, was evidently thirsting for their blood.

His long, bony fingers twined serpent-like round the haft of his long, gleaming knife, and his dark, restless eye seemed to wander from the face of one to the other.

There were about fourteen in all of the ruthless villains, but the party seemed devided in their opinion, and, as the excitement of either party increased, their voices grew louder.

One of the parties appeared to be an Englishman, and he burst out in that language.

'What's the use of making them prisoners? they will eat more than they are worth. Set them adrift say I, or else give them a taste of Long Tommy.'

The snake-like fingers were again twisted round the haft of the formidable knife, as Long Tommy was mentioned, and the restless eyes wandered to the captives.

The captain replied to the Englishman in Spanish, and he seemed to deliver his speech pretty warmly, for his face was flushed, and his eyes seemed starting from his head.

At length the captain's party seemed to have conquered, for he walked up to the prisoners and said—

'The men crave for your life, as it is a rule with us to preserve none but women; but as you have offered no resistance, and I can make more of you by exchanging you to one of the Barbary cruisers than by taking your life, I shall not let the opportunity escape me.'

'Thanks; you are very considerate,' thought Will. 'But I hope before that we shall have some opportunity to escape.'

As Will made no reply, the pirate remarked—

'You don't appear gratified for the service I have done you.'

'We are very,' replied Will; 'but our throats are too parched to speak.'

The captain supplied them with a tin of water, which he held to their lips while they drank.

'A thousand thanks for your kindness,' said Will, with well-affected gratitude. 'I shall ever remember the kind interest you have taken in our behalf.'

There was no deception in this latter part of Will Howard's speech.

The thoughts of the pirate's treachery were too deeply graven on his memory.

He felt as though he would have given a fortune, had he possessed it, to have had the chance of throttling the hardened wretch.

Hopeless as seemed their case, Will did not despair.

Something seemed to buoy him up, and bid him have courage, and bear with patience the insults and cruelties that might be heaped upon him.

The "demon," as Will had christened the fellow with the long knife, seemed to take a delight in passing to and fro the place where they lay helpless, and each time he passed he indulged in a grin that showed his yellow, fang-like teeth.

To describe the miseries they endured would be impossible.

Cramped and sore with laying on the hard ropes that formed their bed, and their flesh swollen with the ropes that bound their limbs, they were compelled to bear the rays of the scorching sun that blistered their faces and hands, and made the skin to crack.

One of the brutal wretches, when any duty required him to move from one end of the ship to the other, took a delight in jumping on their bodies, and, as he was not particular on what part of their person he alighted, he not only caused them much annoyance, but a great deal of pain.

Thus a week passed, during which time a small sloop had been boarded, her crew slain, and, as the cargo consisted chiefly of sugar, she was scuttled and sunk.

On the seventh day a sail was sighted in the western hoard, and as she proved to be a brigantine, and had the appearance of a trader, the pirates gave a shout of glee.

All sail was crowded, and the vessels had hauled up to meet her, and the dusky wretches, whose aid would not be required till they commenced the work of slaughter, laid down in the bottom of the boat, and the deceitful canvas was drawn over them.

The feelings of Will and his companion were anything but pleasant, when they found themselves laying cheek by jowl with the inhuman crew.

They could fancy their hot breath filled the place and rendered it almost stifling.

As the saying is, "What can't be cured must be endured," so were the prisoners obliged to put up with it, and they longed for the vessel to come alongside, so that the cover might be removed, and they once more breath the pure air.

The brigantine was a swift sailer, and the pirate vessel would have had some difficulty in overhauling her the way the wind was; but the pirate hoisted an old shirt as a signal of distress.

The captain shortened sail at this, and allowed the pirate to overhaul them.

BLACK EYED SUSAN

OR, PIRATES ASHORE.

THE SPY.

'What are you short of?' cried the captain, as soon as they were within hail.

He was a short man, with large, bushy whiskers, and his voice was as strong as a lion.

'Everything,' replied the pirate. 'We have been driven off the land, and as we have no quadrant aboard, we are not likely to find it again in a hurry.'

'Have you no compass?'

'A shaky one; there is no dependence to be placed in it. The iron work round the binnacle attracts it.'

'Have you never discovered this before?'

'It is my first trip in her.'

'Well, if you take my advice, it will be the best. Drop under our quarter, and come on board; I will give you the longitude and latitude if you require them, and see what I can spare from our *stores*.'

He placed great emphasis on the last word, and then gave the mate, who was standing aft, orders to throw over a rope.

'He shall have all he requires,' he muttered, as he walked forward.

The captain of the pirate vessel did as he was directed, and grasping the rope, he skimmed up with the agility of a cat.

The men crept stealthily from beneath the canvas, and followed him with no less agility, keeping close under the counter so as not to be seen.

When the pirate captain disappeared over the bulwarks, the rest, deeming concealment no longer necessary, sprang up, and tried to climb up the ship's side by the eye-bolts, or anything they could get hold of.

But they failed in this, and many of them fell back into the boat. A coating of grease would not allow them to hold on.

One of the fellows fell on the canvas under which Will was lying, and it was only by a miracle he escaped being smashed.

Like monkeys swarming up a pole the pirates still continued to climb, and those who had failed in pursuing the other route picking themselves up, and having uttered sundry oaths, followed their companions.

Will and Sancho lay in an agony of suspense, expecting each moment to hear the sounds of strife, or the groans and shrieks of the victims, but all was quiet, as though nothing was going on.

Had they been able to have seen upon the brigantine's deck, this would have been explained.

As each of the pirates appeared above the bulwarks he was seized, a pitch-plaster dabbed over his mouth, and two men taking them out of the hands of the receivers, dragged them across the deck, where they were concealed by the brigantine's mainsail, which was lowered down to the deck.

'Aha! nicely trapped, eh?' said the captain of the brigantine, as the last of the pirates, who had not the honour of having the pitch-plaster, as it was too late to raise an alarm, found himself disarmed, and in the clutches of the receivers, two black-bearded, athletic seamen.

'Caught like a set of thieving foxes as you are, eh?' continued the captain. 'How would you like four dozen under your shirts to keep you warm these cold chilly nights? I can oblige you, you must know, for our boatswain is fond of his favourite tabby.'

A volley of curses was the only response, and

had the pirates not been securely bound, they would have made a desperate resistance, unarmed though they were.'

'Well, you are a nice set of fellows, I am sure,' said the captain, tauntingly glancing along the line of rage-distorted faces, 'and your leader is a bold man to lead you into such a trap. You are now on board a slaver, traffickers, as they term us, in human flesh; but we are not sea robbers, nor dealers in human blood. I could read the character of your craft, you see, although you tried to blink me with false colours; but you found me too old a sea hoss for you.'

'You are a clever fellow,' replied the pirate captain, strongly excited, 'but mind you are not trapped yourselves like our own. It's a desperate game you play.'

'Cool, certainly,' said the slaver, who appeared to hold his profession in high estimation, 'to class us on the same footing as yourselves. But there, as we have plenty of room on board, and a short trip will do you no harm, you can lay in the hold, until I consider what punishment you deserve. Here, bosun,' he added, 'hand these fellows down below.'

'I guess I will, and that tarnation sharp,' said the boatswain, motioning several men forward.

The sailors were not long in placing them between decks.

Without removing the lashings they passed a strap under the arms of the pirates, and hooking on a tackle from the main-stay, hoisted them off their feet, and dropped them on to the slave deck.

Here they were received by two stout fellows, who seemed well practised in the work.

They placed them on the deck about a yard apart, and secured them to a stout iron bar that ran fore and aft the deck.

Cursing their fate, and heaping bitter invectives on the ship and all belonging to her, the pirates were left to their fate and their own reflections.

In the meantime the mate and a party of his men had boarded the pirate vessel, and they were elated at finding the pistols and a bag of Spanish doubloons the pirates had taken from some unfortunate vessel.

Will and Sancho were still buried under the canvass, and not knowing what kind of a reception they might meet with from the new comers, resolved to lay quiet, and trust to chance.

A circumstance, however, prevented them from doing this.

One of the men, on going forward to haul in the bow rope, stepped on Will's stomach so heavily as to force the wind out of him, and make him grunt.

The man, on hearing the noise, started as though the devil had hold of him, but on recovering himself, tore up the canvass with an oath, and discovered the two unfortunates.

'What the devil have you got there?' growled the mate, whose ghastly visage Will fancied he had seen before. 'Live stock, eh? D—n it, we shall get a cargo without going to the coast.'

This speech was sufficient to convince Will that the brigantine was a slaver they had given chase to and captured in the frigate he was in, as they returned from the Cape of Good Hope.

'Shall we sling 'em aboard?' said the man addressed, 'or let 'em lay here to navigate her to the bottom?'

The mate was about to make some jeering remark, when Captain Sheerpole looked over the quarter, and in a tone of surprise, said—

'Hallo! hand them up, lads'; let's see what stuff they are made of. Perhaps they won't object to a voyage to the coast.'

'We shall, greatly,' thought Will; but glad to get released from his horrible position, he said nothing.

Owing to their cramped condition, they were obliged to be assisted up the side, and the captain ordered them to be placed on a hen-coop.

The mate eyed them maliciously.

In his heart he wished that the hen-coop had been turned adrift with them on it.

Prudence forbade him expressing what he thought, so he kept silent.

'Well, my hearties, what misdeed brought you to this forlorn state?' asked the captain, eyeing Will's uniform, which, it will be remembered, belonged to one of the officers in his Majesty's navy, though it was now sadly torn and disfigured by dust and grime.

Will told him the same story as he had told the pirate.

'Ah!' ejaculated the captain, and his eyes twinkled beneath his shaggy brows; 'a fine tale, no doubt, for the marines, but us old sea-dogs can't hoist it in. "Honesty is the best policy," young man; so throw overboard all deception, and pay out your yarn in a straightforward manner.'

'It is the truth,' said Will. 'Why should we throw out false colours when there is nothing to gain by it?'

'That is just what I want to hammer into your timber head,' said the captain. 'Dishonesty and ingratitude are the two worst things a man can be guilty of.'

'We are guilty of neither,' replied Will, meeting the captain's glance steadily. 'In the first place, we could not rob you in this condition; and in the second place, you have done nothing for us deserving of our gratitude.'

'Oh! then you don't consider we have released you from those piratical swabs, that would doubt-less have made junk of you before another sun had set?'

'It was not at all probable.'

The captain bit his lip.

He found he had a wary customer to deal with.

'Now, to be candid,' he said: 'are you not deserters from a ship of war?'

'Oh, if that's what you are driving at,' said Will, carelessly, 'I can only say you were never more right than you are wrong in the present instance.'

'Then how came you by this uniform?'

'There are many things in a man's private life that he does not wish everyone to know,' replied Howard, glancing significantly at the captain; 'for instance, I might ask you where you got this ship, where you are bound, and what cargo you intend freighting her with.'

The captain remained for some time silent.

It was a secret he could not divulge to every-one.

Will's answer, however, had established him in his confidence; and well knowing that two men in their position could do him no harm, he said—

'To such a question, to a man on whom I could rely, I should reply—the West coast of Africa, to ship a cargo of niggers, that I hope will pay me handsomely. We are rather short-handed, and if you and your companion like to join me, I will put your names on the ship's books.'

Our hero had as much aversion to becoming a slaver as a pirate, for he looked upon one equally as bad as the other; but as circumstances would not permit him to choose the life he would lead, he consented, determined to escape the first op-portunity that offered.

Sancho, who had no particular choice so long as he was with his friend, also gave his consent, and the captain ordered them to be released and supplied with food, of which they stood in need.

The appearance of a sail directly in their wake aroused the captain to action.

'Sink the pirate's craft!' he cried to the second mate. 'We must not hang about here any longer. By heavens! we shall have one of the cruisers down on us in a crack, and find ourselves in irons or strung up at the yard-arm in the turning of a handspike.'

'Aye—aye!' cried the mate; 'follow me, lads.' And slipping over the side with a heavy crowbar, he soon dashed a hole through the bottom of the boat.

The sailors cut away the masts, so that the vessel following them might not see her sink; and having cast off the rope, she rapidly filled and went down.

The captain took his glass and ascended to the crosstrees, where he seated himself, and surveyed the stranger with an uneasy glance.

His quick eye soon detected her to be a frigate that had given them chase the night before, and he gave orders to clap on all sail.

CHAPTER CXVIII.

SMUGGLERS AND THEIR WRONGS—UNWELCOME NEWS.

TOM HATCHETT, enraged at his second defeat, and angry with himself for having wounded his mate, returned to his vessel in no easy mood.

'Curse the fellow!' he muttered. 'What made him be so hasty? But there, perhaps it was my fault, though he has to suffer the pain.'

With this consolation he walked forward, and gave the order for the anchor to be hove up.

There was a want of energy in the manner the men worked, and Hatchett did not fail to notice this, and well knew what was the cause.

He would have given anything to have recalled the quarrel, and regained the confidence of his men; for he judged by their actions that he had lessened, if not totally lost it.

Bill Raker was a favourite with the men; for when Tom Hatchett was taken by the frigate's crew, the mate worked the ship out from under the very muzzles of the guns of the fort, and eluded the vigilance of a gun-brig that was cruising off the mouth of the bay.

Besides this, the object of Tom's visit to Gibraltar was a mystery to them, and one that incurred great risk without the smallest profit.

Tom had not been so many years in the lawless profession without knowing that excitement and good runs was all the smugglers required; and as they had had but little of either lately, he knew they were discontented.

If his mind was uneasy at seeing the men crawl-ing about, it would have been much more so had he heard their conversation.

'Well, Ned,' said one, as he took hold of a hand-spike, as though he did not care whether he lifted it or not; 'what do you think of this game, eh ?'

'Rather queer work, I think, Jem.'

'So I say; and if old Tigersides would cut down Bill Raker with so little remorse, how much less would he think of serving us the same ?'

'You are right there, mate; but let him begin with any of us for'ard, and he'll see a sight he won't much care for. Why, hang it ! I'd put a hole through him as soon as look at him.'

'And I too. As it is, I don't like the idea of him getting off scot free.'

'Well, Jem,' said Ned, eyeing his mate closely, 'if the lads were of my mind, they'd parbuckle him at once, and let him know that, smugglers as we are, and have a leader, we own no master.'

'Well, the argument's good, but the work is dangerous. We'd better wait and sound the crew before we do anything rash; for some of them fellows in the cave think that without Tom we couldn't live; and we owe our successes to his influence with old Doggrass.'

'True again, mate; but as we have done without the aid of that old land-shark so long, we can sartinly do without him again. Besides, as he's got into trouble through Hatchett, he won't like tackling it again.'

'Don't you run away with that idea. He will come out stronger than ever if he gets off, as I heard he would; for though he's as timid as a lubber on his first cruise, when he sees broken water on his lee he keeps the lead going, and knows just how to act.'

'Ah, with his friends, he has much influence in Deal, I know; but if he gets fairly on the rocks, the devil himself wouldn't get him off.'

Their conversation was cut short by the sudden appearance of Tom Hatchett amongst them.

He had walked the quarter-deck, listening for the click of the windlass, until his temper was worked to that pitch that he could bear the delay no longer.

'Now then,' he shouted, 'what is it to be ? Am I captain, or are my orders to be obeyed no longer ? If you want to break up the band, do so. I will seek another crew; you can find another leader.'

Ned stepped boldly forward.

'Tom Hatchett,' he said, 'your conduct to-day has been anything but satisfactory. Since you have raised your hand against Bill Raker, what security have we for our lives ?'

'The same as ever. Was it not his own folly ? Think you I am mad—a fool, to make war among ourselves ? Return to your duty like brave men, as you are, and let not this paltry quarrel part us, who have shared danger and toil together for so many years.'

This speech had the desired effect; and Tom, seeing the tide of opinion had once more turned in his favour, followed it up.

'Now, lads,' he continued, 'I mean to give up this girl-hunting. I see it brings us no profit, and puts us to considerable risk. Old Doggrass has been pressed into the stone frigate, and if he finds no port-hole to escape, why, we must shift for ourselves. We will make a trip to Holland, and if he gets loose, and hears that we have got a good freight, and money is to be gained, he is not the man to throw a good chance overboard. He will assist us; and if not, we must take a smggsler's chance—a full purse, or a dangle from the yard-arm.'

A loud shout greeted this speech, and Captain Hatchett rejoiced at having averted what might have proved a sad disaster, returned to his place on the quarter-deck.

A bumper of brandy restored good fellowship amongst them, and the smugglers returned cheer-fully to their duty, and hove the anchor up with a will.

When the sails had been set, and the anchor hoisted on to the gunwale, the Laughing Bird, as the vessel was named, once more sped through the water like a thing of life.

The smugglers had nothing to do now but lounge about the decks and talk over the past events, which was anything but what Hatchett desired, as it was his wish that they would be forgotten.

Idleness breeds discontent, and in no place more than on shipboard; so that it was no wonder the smugglers began to growl again.

An incident, not altogether pleasant, turned their thoughts, however, in a different channel. A man who was working aloft reported a cutter bearing down on them.

'Let her come,' growled Hatchett, glad of any chance of diverting the men's attention; 'it is not the first one that has honoured us with a visit.'

Hatchett, though apparently so indifferent, did not appreciate the cutter's visit; on the contrary, he wished she might blow up or sink before she could get much closer.

But in this he was not to have his wish, for in spite of the curses he heaped upon her, the cutter came steadily on.

She had rounded a bluff, and came suddenly in sight of the Laughing Bird, and her commander, who chanced to be Lieutenant Pike, 'sweated up' his peak and throat halyards, tightened his jib and foresail, and hoisted a gaff topsail and square sail.

'He means mischief,' cried Hatchett, with an oath. 'If we had not lost time in that useless wrangling, we might have been half-a-mile further out in the offing.

'And if we had not been bound on a foolish errand, we should not have been here,' returned Ned, who was trimming the main-sheet.

Hatchett did not reply, but he darted a glance at Ned, which implied all he would have said to him had he dared.

In the present excited state of the crew, Hatchett was aware that he must be careful of his words and doings, or risk losing his command; so that his silence was not altogether voluntary.

Ned was aware of this, and, like most people who gain an advantage, he was determined to make good use of it while it lasted.

Captain Hatchett now had a double anxiety on his mind.

The Laughing Bird had her heavy sails bent, and the light air, which sent the cutter spinning through the water, scarcely moved the smuggling craft.

'Trim sails !' cried Hatchett, rendered desperate. 'Move sharp, or, by my soul, I'll move you ! The first man who flags in his duty, or disobeys my orders, shall have the contents of this.'

He clutched a pistol as he spoke, and placed the hammer at half-cock.

Hatchett glanced around to see what effect this threat had on the men.

It was favourable, he had once more got command of them; they could see by his dark flashing eyes and darkened brow that he uttered no trifling threat.

'See you there,' he continued, drawing his form erect, and throwing power into his voice; 'see you there; that vessel is coming down on us hand over hand. You know her character, and the fate that awaits us if she is allowed to board us. For myself, I mean to escape if possible; if not, I am prepared to fight to the death. They shall never take Tom Hatchett alive; and if you are cowards, and desert me, a spark in the magazine will settle the difference between us.'

'We are no cowards,' cried several of the men; 'and we will prove it. Give your orders—we will obey; and let all disputes be forgotten. We fight for the same cause, and whilst a plank of the old ship floats, we will stick to her like barnacles.'

'Well said, comrades,' cried Hatchett, glancing aloft. 'The wind freshens; clap on every rag we can stretch to woo it. Sweat every rope taut, trim the sheets, and clear the guns for action.'

Throwing off their heavy deck boots, the smugglers obeyed with alacrity, and after the ropes had been hauled taut and belayed, they cleared away the guns, and then stood grim and silent as the deadly tubes on which their hands rested.

Lieutenant Pike, who had considered the smuggler as good as captured, swore bitterly when he saw there was a chance of her escaping.

'Give them a shot,' he cried, to the gunner; 'let them have it home.'

The shot flew on its destructive mission, but Lieutenant Pike had the mortification to see it drop a few fathoms astern of the Laughing Bird.

'Try again,' he cried. 'Elevate another degree; try for her mainmast—we must cripple her; they must not escape us, the rascals! Do your best, men our honour is at stake. If we succeed our reward will be great.'

Thus urged, the gunner stripped to the waist, and his eye once more glanced along the deadly tube.

CHAPTER CXIX.

SILAS DOGGRASS AND HIS MIDNIGHT VISITORS.—
VILLANY UNMASKED.

THE clamoring at the door increased, and had not the men threatened to burst open the door, it was likely they might have knocked till they were tired.

Doggrass, with the recollection of Hatchett's visit full in his mind, would have gone to bed in spite of the words he had heard uttered, which he considered only a ruse.

Before opening the door, however, he was determined to see who it was.

Creeping upstairs, he possessed himself of his pistols, and pointing one—a formidable horse pistol —at the group around the door, he shouted—

'Now then! what do you want here, this hour of the night?'

'Open the door, you surly old bear,' was the gruff reply. 'Do you mean to keep us here all night? We are almost perished, and this poor girl has scarcely any life in her.'

'What girl?' demanded Doggrass brutally. 'Don't bring a parcel of people here to die. It is not likely a poor man like me can keep open house to everyone that chances to be storm-ridden.'

'What shall we do, then?'

'Go to Farmer Thrivewell's; he keeps a barn especially for the use of persons in your situation. Go away, my man, and do not disturb me again.'

Something like an oath came from the man's lips.

'Cold blooded tyrant! do you know who we have here?'

'No one that I wish to see.'

'It is your niece, Black-eyed Susan.'

A vivid flash of lightning revealed the forms of three men dressed as seamen, and one of them bore in his arms the form of a female.

Had the lightning stricken Doggrass, he could not have been more appalled.

How he descended the stairs and opened the door, he knew not.

He only saw the forms of the men as they hurried in, and then all seemed oblivion.

When he recovered, he found the three men around a table, on which they had lain their senseless burthen.

By their side stood a bottle of his best cognac brandy, to which they had helped themselves pretty freely, and a little of which, diluted, they were trying to pour down the throat of the senseless girl.

Doggrass's first act was to call Dame Howard, and having carried Susan upstairs by the assistance of one of the men, she was left in the old dame's charge.

The next thing for Doggrass to consider was how to rid himself of his company, the men appearing pretty well satisfied with their new quarters, having helped themselves to more brandy, and seated themselves very comfortably.

'Here's to your good health, Master Doggrass,' said one who appeared to be the leader of the gang. 'I am sorry we had to disturb you; but, as you see, the girl, poor thing! could not have held on much longer. I thought she would have parted her cable while you were palavering out of that port.'

'It would not, perhaps, have mattered much if she had,' said Doggrass, assuming an indifference he did not feel. 'She has been nothing but trouble to me. But where did you pick her up?'

'Where indeed! Where you little expect.'

'Well, well! where was that?'

'At sea.'

'At sea!' repeated Doggrass, scratching his head.

'Aye—on a raft.'

'At sea, and on a raft! How, in the name all that's holy, did she get there?'

'That is just what I want to know; but certain it was, that's where and how we found her. She was almost starved, and, in fact, was on the very point of slipping her wind, when we ran athwart her.'

'This is strange; but I have no reason to doubt your word, though really I cannot believe it without something to confirm it. How long is it since you found her?'

'A fortnight to-day.'

'Ah! that is about the time!' muttered Doggrass. 'Was there no one with her?' he asked.

'Indeed there was a sprat of a boy; but of him we can say but little.'

'How so?' asked Doggrass, growing nervous with excitement.

'He was dead.'

'Dead ?'

'Ay! If not, he was next to it.'

'Did you not rescue him ?'

'What use would it have been lumbering our vessel, which is but a small sloop, with dead hands ?'

'But you surely did not leave him ?'

'We surely did ; but we left him above hatches, though my mate here wanted to bury him.'

'What, throw him overboard ?'

'Certainly. You do not think we could dig him a grave, do you ? Besides, we were heavy laden, and it was night.'

'Where were you bound ?'

'To Jersey, and we took your niece with us. She wanted to give us the slip, but we did not see it, especially as we thought she was rather loose in her upper works, and expected you would well reward us for our trouble.'

'Reward you ?' echoed Doggrass, changing suddenly. 'What reward could you expect ?'

'We trust to Providence for all we get,' said the skipper (for such the speaker was). 'If we make a good haul, we say we are lucky ; and if not, we curse the unlucky fate that attended us.'

'If I were to follow your example, I should often curse my fate,' said Doggrass. 'Your visit here to-night, instead of profiting me, has done me much harm, and now you talk of reward.'

'Well, if you are too poor,' said the skipper, laying great stress on his words, 'to give money, you can spare us a little grog for the boys of a cold night ; and that ham hanging there would be very acceptable.'

'Indeed ! and what next will you want ?—my house, I suppose—the very roof from over my head.'

'I do not know, Master Doggrass, what you think of it, but I consider it poor pay enough when you consider we have had to turn out of the cabin to let her occupy it ; and then there was a fortnight's rations.'

'Ah, well, so there was, though I doubt whether much of your salt beef or hard biscuits passed her lips. Here is a sovereign amongst you, and you can have the ham.'

'And the brandy ?'

Doggrass handed them a bottle each, which appeared to satisfy them, and they left.

By this time the storm had lulled considerably, and the sailors made their way rapidly towards the bay, where the sloop lay at anchor.

As they neared the cliffs, one of them, named Bob Braddon, turned to the skipper, and, in a voice that well suited the occasion, said—

'Confound it ! I must go back ; I've left my knife, and I would not part with it on any account.'

'Knife be d——d ! You don't mean to say you are going back for that ?'

'I must, I tell you. I would not lose that knife for any money. I'll go and give the old devil another turn, and if he's in bed, why, he'll have to turn out.'

The skipper argued the point, but it was no use ; Bob Braddon was not to be turned from his purpose.

He was not long in reaching the Three Luggers and he knocked loudly at the door, much to the annoyance of old Doggrass.

'Who the devil's there ?' he asked, thrusting out his night-capped head, for he had already commenced to undress.

'It's me.'

'What the deuce do you want ?'

'I've got a message from the skipper.'

'Devil take the skipper, you and all !' growled Doggrass. 'Can't you come in the morning ?' he asked.

'I shan't have time ; we are going to trip anchor at daylight.'

Doggrass gave a growl of dissatisfaction, and, hastily slipping on his clothes, opened the door.

He would not have done so, however, had he had a previous intimation of the character of his visitor.

'Now for the message,' said Doggrass, trying to look calm.

'Be seated first. It may take some time to spin the whole yarn,' said the sailor, perching himself on a corner of one of the tables.

'Be quick about it,' said Doggrass, impatiently. 'Remember you have disturbed me twice this night.'

'I am sorry for it ; but as we must all yield to circumstances, as the stout spar yields to the blast, so you must bear with it.'

Doggrass looked with amazement at the speaker ; around his lips he detected a faint smile, and, in an impetuous tone, he said—

'What mean you, scoundrel ?—how dare you take this liberty with me ? Leave my house at once, before I am compelled to use force.'

Doggrass was a stout-built man, and in his younger days had been possessed of prodigious strength ; but the sailor was more than his match now, for his form was lithe and supple, and he had youth also in his favour.

Having eyed his companion for a moment, the sailor replied—

'Sit down, man. It will require patience and a cool head to listen to what I have to say. Can you remember so far back as ten years ?'

Doggrass grew pale, and a trembling took possession of him, which he tried to conceal.

'Ten years !' he said ; 'so many things have occurred in that time that it would be vain to try to recollect so far back.'

'Indeed ! Overhaul your log, man. You must recollect. You cannot have forgotten a *circumstance* that transpired at that time.'

'Whatever it was, it is past,' said Doggrass, wishing in his heart the floor would sink in with the man. 'I do not keep a clerk in my memory to record all events.'

'Well, it's not over pleasant at times ; but if you will listen I will freshen the nip of your memory. Ten years ago, in this very town, there was a man whose business was of that nature that it needed to be kept secret from the eyes of the world, and the more especially a certain set of land crabs that pryed into every hole and corner where the smell of a certain narcotic assailed their nasal organ.'

'A philosopher, by heaven !' exclaimed Doggrass, trying to look calm.

The sailor took no heed of his remark, but went on.

'To effect this, deep cellars were secretly built beneath a certain house, and three men, well skilled in mechanism, were engaged to do the work. A large sum was paid to them at the completion, and they were bound by oaths to secresy.'

Doggrass clenched his hands convulsively, and his eyes were riveted on the speaker's lips, as though he could see each word as it was uttered.

'Well,' continued the man, 'it was thought impossible for three men to keep such a secret long, as large rewards were offered for the capture of certain parties who traded in a certain commodity, for the stowage of which these cellars were evidently designed. It was thought one man was sufficient to know of the existence of such a place, and that the owner of the house under which the cellars were built.'

The sailor paused, then, fixing his eyes on those of Doggrass, he continued.

'The inventive brain of the villanous employer was at work, long before the job was completed, to devise a means of sealing the lips of the workmen, and it occurred to him that there was great truth in the saying, "dead men tell no tales." He thought it over, and, as it suited his present case well, he set to work again to devise a means of putting his terrible project into action. He was not long in doing this. The sudden death of a wealthy merchant left his only son involved in difficulties; a bill for one hundred pounds became due, and the hard-hearted discounter threatened the unfortunate son with imprisonment if it was not immediately paid.'

Doggrass started from his seat.

'Enough of this,' he said; 'I can listen to you no longer.'

'But you must. Sit down, and hear me out; you may then find out the names of these parties, if they have slipped your memory.'

'I will not hear another word,' gasped Doggrass, hoarsely.

'You must. I will not leave until my mission is fulfilled. This man—this fiend in human shape, taking advantage of the power he held over the son, invited him to his house, plied him with liquors, and made him take an oath to serve him for one night only. The reward was to be the liquidation of the debt and twenty pounds. From that moment the fiend never lost sight of his victim, but constantly probed him with the recollection of his poverty, and hints of the power he held over him. On the other hand, he reminded him of the inducement held out, and promised him a bright future, if he well fulfilled the work he had in store for him.

'Up to this the youth—for he was but little else, and unskilled in the ways of the world—had not the least idea of the service required of him, and in fact he cared but little, for his brain was kept muddled with drink, so that he had no guidance of his thoughts or actions.

'At length the day arrived for the workmen to return to town, and then the subtle plotter broached the subject to his victim.

'He induced him to drink several glasses of brandy before doing so, under the pretext of strengthening his nerves.

'The young man listened to the wily tempter in a state bordering on abstraction, whilst the wretch informed him that the three men were not to reach London alive; if they did, he might judge what would be the consequences.

'He then laid down the instructions, which were that he was to conceal himself on a lonely part of the road, which they would travel at night, and armed with a brace of doubled-barrelled pistols, shoot each one, and not leave until he was certain they were all dead.'

Doggrass sat rigid as a statue during this part of the narration; his cheeks and lips went of an aspen hue, and his hands were clenched so tightly, that the blood was ready to flow.

The eye of the sailor was fixed on him, and seemed to burn into his very soul as he went on—

'The bloody deed was not so hard to accomplish as might have been supposed. The men were half drunk, perhaps drugged, and their fire-arms were loaded with damp powder.

'The deed was done, and the carriage over-turned, and the *murderer*, on searching for the money, which, as a further inducement to the committal of the crime he had been led to believe they had about them, found it to be a parcel of base and useless coin.

'I—for no doubt you recognise me—stood for a moment paralysed with horror at the crime I had committed. I was sober then, and the horrors of my position flashed to my brain like seething lightning. Fearing to show my face in Deal, I fled to London, and shipped in a vessel for a voyage round the world. Since then I have kept to the profession of a sailor, and after shipwreck and pirates, you see me here.'

'And what, in h—— name, brought you here?' exclaimed Doggrass, as his blood coursed again through his veins. 'Murderer, I will denounce you!'

'Murderer!' hissed the seaman through his clenched teeth. 'Utter that word again, and it shall be your last. Murderer! Who made me so? Richard Silas Doggrass, the smuggler, robber, and land pirate.'

The eyes of the speaker flashed fiercely, and his hand grasped a knife, the blade of which was near six inches long.

'Murderer!' he hissed again. 'And will Silas Doggrass denounce me?'

'I will, unless you leave this house, and promise no more to molest me.'

'On condition that you show proofs of the deed.'

This staggered Doggrass; he had not thought of this.

The only proof he had was the work of the murdered men.

The sailor saw his dilemma, and seemed almost to read his thoughts.

'Now it is my turn,' he said, 'to talk about turning informer. My proof,' he added, pointing to the floor, 'is substantial; there is little fear of its being wrecked, like yours, at the sight of the first breaker.'

There was so much truth in his words, that Doggrass could not deny them; in fact, he did not attempt to, but expressed a wish of coming to terms.

'There is some sense in that,' said the sailor; 'it reminds me of a skipper, who finding it impossible to beat off a lee shore, picks the softest place to rest his ship's keel on.'

Doggrass gave a ghastly grin.

He found himself hemmed in like a fox, but still hoped by a struggle to save his brush.

'I should think you receive but poor remuneration,' he said, craftily, 'for toiling on the coast? I wonder you do not take long voyages. An expedition is now fitting out for the Polar Seas. I will procure you a berth, and supply you with an outfit.'

'It will be time to talk of that when the business which brought me here has been settled,' was the curt reply. 'There is a little debt between us that has been standing over this ten years.'

Doggrass turned alternately red and white.

His eyes were riveted on a paper the sailor drew from his pocket.

He handed it to him, and he grasped it in his thin, claw-like fingers with the tenacity of a bird of prey, then his eye glanced eagerly over its contents.

'Do not destroy it; it is but a copy of the original,' said the seaman, as Doggrass was in the act of rending it to pieces; 'the other is safe, and will remain so, till the debt is paid.'

The paper alluded to was a promissory note for the amount of ten pounds; it was the balance of the twenty pounds Doggrass had promised him for murdering the workmen.

This sum, trifling as it was to Silas, was a large amount to the seaman, who had to labour hard for a trifling pittance; but, seeing that Doggrass was in his power, and having learnt from Rowlock, who had boarded the sloop to see whether his services as boatswain would be required, that Doggrass had had a narrow escape from the law, he was determined to make a good job of it.

'And should I refuse to acknowledge this,' suggested Doggrass, 'what could you do?'

'Open the eyes of those you have so often gulled. Remember, I hold a secret that would prove your ruin.'

The look Doggrass gave him was more expressive than a thousand words.

'There,' he grunted, savagely, throwing down ten sovereigns on the table, 'take it, and give me the'——

'That will not *square* the debt,' said the sailor, interrupting him; 'it must be squared.'

'Curse you! What do you mean?' ejaculated Doggrass. 'Ten pounds is the sum.'

'There is ten years' interest. Ten times ten will be just one hundred.'

'One hundred pounds!' cried Doggrass, perfectly astounded at the man's audacity. 'You claim good interest. It is more than I possess.'

'You can borrow it.'

'Of whom?'

'Your banker. It is no use beating about the bush, Master Doggrass. You are sailing in a dangerous channel when you play with me.'

'But'——

'No excuse, you old miser, so overhaul your shot-locker.'

Doggrass was silent.

The machinery of his villanous mind was in motion.

'One hundred pounds!' he thought. 'I have often risked life and liberty for less than this. Why should I part with my hard earnings without a struggle? He possesses a secret, too, known only to himself, Tom Hatchett, and Bill Raker. They would be puzzled even to find the entrance from the beach, as I have removed the marks. What is to prevent me taking his life, and settling two jobs at once? It will rid me at least of a customer that bids fair to be a troublesome one.'

The sailor sat watching him, little dreaming of what was passing in his mind.

'Well, have you made up your mind? What is it to be?' he asked, at length.

'With such odds against me, it would be madness to argue further,' said Doggrass, with a tone and expression he knew well how to assume. 'I will give you the sum, though I must own it is exorbitant.'

'You forget the risk I run in earning it.'

'And the risk you run in obtaining it, you might have added,' thought Doggrass, as he ascended the stairs to obtain, as the sailor thought, the money.

Presently he returned with a long bag, which, by the faint light of the candle, appeared to be well filled.

'Now the debt shall be *squared*,' he said, with great emphasis, a smile of triumph wreathing his pale, thin lips.

The sailor was in ecstacies at the success of his scheme, and his eyes shone with glee as Doggrass thrust his hand into the bag.

But his look was changed to one of horror, when, instead of the glittering gold, as he had expected, Doggrass drew forth a pistol loaded and primed, and held it pointed at his head.

'Now the debt shall be squared,' he repeated, sarcastically. 'It shall not be said that Silas Doggrass—or, if you like it better, Richard Silas Doggrass—has not rewarded you for the trouble of your visit.'

The sudden revulsion of feeling caused by the appearance of the pistol held the sailor for a moment in a state of helplessness.

Doggrass eyed him with a sort of malicious glee.

He wanted to take his life, yet he longed to gloat over his sufferings.

His finger was on the trigger, and it wanted but a slight pressure, and the ball would crash into the sailor's brain.

It wanted but a moment for the sailor to regain his self-possession, and then with a lightning movement he grasped the pistol, and tried to wrest it from Doggrass's hand.

In this he failed, and a desperate struggle ensued.

'Treacherous scoundrel!' cried the sailor, 'is this how you fulfil your promise?'

'Aye, and 'tis no more than you deserve!' gasped Doggrass, almost choked with rage at letting the opportunity of putting a bullet through his foe slip by.

'Then I can only say, you are a villain of the blackest dye.'

'Aha! talk on,' laughed Doggrass, hysterically, and forcing his adversary back over one of the tables, he strove desperately to regain the pistol. 'Talk on—I feel you are still in my power.'

'Be not too sure.' replied the sailor, hoarsely, bringing himself forward with a violent jerk, that made Doggrass fall back a step, and gave the sailor a bit of advantage; but the struggle was ended by the pistol going off, and wounding the sailor in the shoulder.

A stream of blood began to pour from the wound, and the sailor, staggering, fell back upon the floor.

"As Doggrass gazed at the apparent lifeless form, a tremour, occasioned by fear, crept over him; but his fierce passion returned with the thought of his victory, and he at once set about removing the evidence of his guilt.

Removing the heavy table that had so firmly resisted his efforts on the night of Tom Hatchett's

BLACK EYED SUSAN.

OR, PIRATES ASHORE.

BLACK-EYED SUSAN'S VISIT TO THE ADMIRAL.

visit, he placed the light on the top step of the stone staircase, and then raising the form of the sailor in his brawny arms, descended into the gloom of what appeared to be a vault.

He was not many minutes gone, but when he reached the room he looked cautiously round.

Everything was as he left it.

Hastily closing the trap, he replaced the table, on which he stood the flickering light, and then wiped up the blood, leaving a large damp spot as the trace of the dark tragedy so recently enacted.

Having finished, a violent trembling seized him, so that it was with difficulty he reached a chair, and sank back into it.

A bottle of brandy stood within his reach, and in the absence of a tumbler, he gulped down the fiery liquid from the bottle.

Cold beads of sweat burst out upon his brow.

The trembling increased as though he had been suddenly seized with ague.

His bloodshot eyes rolled in fear around the gloomy chamber, and as he wiped the sweat from his brow he gasped out—

'That face—it still is fresh in my memory. Good God! Is it possible I have been watched. I could swear it was human; but the eyes, they seemed to pierce me through, and seethe my brain like red hot embers.'

Again he wiped his brow, and his bleared eyes wandered round the room.

He tried to rise, but could not.

Then again he burst out—

'Fool that I am to let this weakness overcome me! It was but fancy. Who could have watched me? I am growing childish. No one knows the secret of the cellar; so what need have I to fear discovery?'

One more effort he made to rise, but his limbs were weak as an infant's; and, as he sat alternately cursing and praying, he fancied he saw the same pale face, and the same dark gleaming eyes, glaring at him through the open door that led to the stairs.

'Curse it! it is no delusion,' he said, in a voice scarcely articulate; 'it is the same face, the same glaring eyes I saw gazing at me through the trap; be it spirit or human, I will follow and solve the mystery.'

Starting from his chair, on the impulse of the moment he tried to walk towards the door, but the effort was too much for him; he dropped into the chair again, where we must leave him, a prey to the most horrible thoughts.

CHAPTER CXX.

GERALD STUART OUTWITS THE ADMIRAL—THE TABLES TURNED.

TRUE enough, as Captain Gerald had anticipated, the vessel that had shown itself was a liner; three white streaks traversed her sides, and they were dotted at regular intervals with the muzzle of an engine of death.

Captain Henson wished his vessel far away.

This time he could not depend on Gerald's protection, and he glanced towards his consort as much as to say so.

Gerald saw his look, but he had other things to think of at the time, so he gave him instructions to act as before, and keep out of the range of the guns, for, said he—

'They cannot sail two ways at once, though their vessel is large enough for six; so keep a good offing; I will play them a game; and if I get beaten, you will be out of the way, so good-bye.'

Henson, though far from being a coward, needed no second invitation to place as much water as possible between his ship and the man-of-war.

The line-of-battle ship looked like a giant bearing down on its pigmy foes.

The snowy sails expanded like a cloud, the water surging from her massive bows, and the admiral's flag flying proudly in the breeze.

Captain Henson could count more than forty guns on her one side, which led him to conjecture she was a ninety-four; and this alone was sufficient inducement for a small vessel—an enemy in particular—to give her a wide berth,

Contrary to expectations, however, he saw the Golden Arrow sail boldly up to her, and heave-to in answer to the gun that communicated that order in its stentorian boom.

He could not see what was going on on board the Golden Arrow, it is true, only that she hoisted an English flag, and lowered a boat.

Gerald had long since made his preparations.

His suit had been changed, his hair assumed a different colour, his eyebrows, moustache, and whiskers had altered, and, in fact, he had a different aspect altogether.

The crew stared at him in wonder when he came on deck and ordered the gig to be lowered.

His coxswain, Tom Tiller, and Marline, who were superintending the lowering of the boat, exchanged curious glances with each other, and Bob Brace ventured to predict, in a tone of the greatest solemnity, that 'it was all up with them.'

Happy Jack even shared in this belief, and his face assumed an aspect quite foreign to his nature.'

'Yes, it's all up with us,' he said, echoing Bob's words. 'We shall swing this time sure enough. We shall have the yellow jack over us, and go up in the smoke of the bow chaser.'

'Now, my hearties,' said the mate, 'cut these confounded yarns. Why, hang me! you look like a purser's ghost.'

'You'll hang soon enough,' remarked Happy Jack. 'The fore-topmast stun-sail tack, and a tail-block at the yard-arm, will send you aloft quicker than ever I saw you mount a shroud.'

The boat touched the water, was hauled up to the gangway, and Gerald stepped boldly in.

It was a daring act, but one from which the daring spirit of Gerald Stuart did not flinch.

The officers waited to receive him at the gangway, and on the quarter-deck he could distinguish Admiral Garthway. He had a spy-glass under his arm, and was evidently surveying the Golden Arrow with the care of one who tries to call his memory to something he has seen before, but since forgotten.

Gerald Stewart noticed this, but, confident in himself and certain of success, he seized the man ropes when the boat touched alongside, and ascended to the deck.

'Well, sir,' said the admiral, fixing his eye on him as though he would pierce him through, 'what ship is that?'

'The Lotus,' was Gerald's firm reply.

'And by whose permission do you carry those guns?'

'The admiralty's.'

'Indeed! then you have some authority for it?'

'A letter of marque.'

'Produce it, if you please, and let me examine it.'

Gerald drew a packet from his breast, and handed t to the admiral.

Admiral Garthway examined it minutely.

There was a suspicion lurking in his mind.

'Is your name Bullyton?' he asked.

'I am proud to say it is.'

'Humph! And you are'——

Gerald handed him the despatches.

Admiral Garthway read them, and found they corresponded with his own.

Glancing his eye at the Martinet, which was edging away under all sail, he asked—

'What ship is that? She was in company with you when you were first sighted.'

This was close work for Captain Stuart; but he was not long lost for an answer.

'She is a homeward-bound West Indiaman,' he replied; 'and, being suspicious, I boarded her.'

'And overhauled her papers?'

'Yes; but she was not the vessel I took her to be.'

'You mistook her for the Martinet, I suppose? She is about her build and rig. Her paint certainly differs from the description; but that is easily changed.'

The admiral was still suspicious.

The more he gazed at the supposed Indiaman, his suspicions grew stronger.

Turning to Captain Stuart, he said—

'Were it not for the letter of marque and the despatches which have evidently come from the Admiralty and correspond exactly with my own, I should have thought you were deceiving me, and I should consider it my duty to overhaul your vessel.'

Gerald Stuart knew the character of the man he had to deal with too well to doubt his word.

Once, when his keen, penetrating eye was fixed on him, he fancied he had seen through his disguise.

It required an effort to control the feeling that crept over him.

Nine hundred men were ready at a word to obey the stern mandate of their still sterner commander.

Willing hands would have seized him and his crew, and run them up to the yard-arm.

One false word, one false look, he knew, would have betrayed him, and then nothing could save him.

But Gerald was not one of those who meet troubles half way. He felt confident in himself, and this made him sure of success.

Seeing that the admiral bestowed more than ordinary interest on the Martinet, he drew his attention from her, by saying—

'I gained some useful information from his Majesty's gun-brig, Fawn. Lieutenant Fairfop boarded her a few days since.'

'What might that information be?' asked the admiral.

'He fell in with the Golden Arrow, the rebel ship we have been so long in search of. She was in company with a French man-of-war, but he gave them chase.'

'Ah, a brave fellow, Fairfop. Did he engage them?'

'The French ship took to her heels; and the Golden Arrow, after receiving a few shots from the Fawn's bow-chaser, escaped in the darkness.'

The old admiral, who at first showed symptoms of glee in anticipation of hearing of a glorious sea-fight, now fairly foamed with rage.

'Curse him!' he vociferated, stamping his foot on the deck, 'I wish I had him under my lee, I'd let him feel the weight of our metal; but there,' he added, consolingly, 'we shall have him before long. If he ventures near the channel and escapes the traps laid for him, I will eat my head.'

A smile passed over Gerald's features as the admiral went on describing the number and size of the various ships that formed the channel fleet, describing how it was divided into squadrons, the ground they were to cruise on, and the names of the various officers in command.

This was valuable information to Captain Stuart, and he listened in wrapt attention to every word.

When the admiral had finished, he appeared quite excited.

'What do you think of that, Mr. Bullyton?' he said, clapping Gerald familiarly on the shoulder; 'do you think the cunning rascal, 'cute as he is, can escape now?'

Gerald was some seconds ere he replied.

He had scarcely heard the admiral's last words

He was wondering whether any of the man-of-war's men had been holding a confab with his boat's crew through the lower deck ports, and he was rather fearful that a word might be incautiously dropped, and being caught and carried aft by one of the men, he might find himself a prisoner.

It did not diminish his fears when he saw one of the officers walking leisurely for and aft the lee-side of the quarter-deck, as though waiting for a chance to speak to the admiral without offending him.

Suddenly recovering himself, Gerald replied—

'It certainly seems an impossibility, admiral, for them to escape these well-laid plans; but this audacious rebel has so many schemes, and is so daring and cunning, that there is yet a chance of his escaping.'

'Think you so?' asked the admiral, evidently displeased.

'I do; and from what I have seen and heard of him, I should not wonder if he were to escape from under the very muzzles of your guns.'

'What!' ejaculated the admiral, starting, and eyeing the captain with a glance that was anything but pleasant. 'Dare you insult me on my own ship?'

'I certainly do not, and if I have unconsciously offended or hurt your feelings, I am truly sorry for it, and crave your pardon.'

'Well, well, I was too hasty,' said the admiral, cooling down; 'but the breeze begins to freshen, and before another watch, I expect we shall have to reef, so step down in my cabin. I have some excellent Madeira.'

Gerald would rather have returned to his ship, but as a refusal would offend, and perhaps excite suspicion, he followed the admiral below.

As he was about to step on the companion ladder, Gerald cast his eye in the direction of the Martinet, and saw that she was nearly hull down, for Captain Henson made good use of his time, and clapped on all sail.

Admiral Garthway poured out the wine and motioned Gerald to be seated.

'Make free,' he said, 'with true seaman generosity. And then laying a chart on the table, he pointed out the course he intended taking, and also that of the channel fleet, after which he gave him a small book of private signals, used only by flag-ships when the commanders wanted to hold private intercourse, apart from the rest of the officers.

'Gerald now considered it time to be leaving, as the dash of the sea under the counter and quarter-galleries gave evidence of the wind's rising, and he was about to acquaint the admiral with that fact, when he beckoned him to keep his seat.

'Now, Mr. Bullyton,' he said, 'I wish to know what course you intend steering, as your letter of marque only gives you permission to act below the Eddystone, and not further into the channel.'

As the daring captain had succeeded so far, and had ingratiated himself into the admiral's favour, he hit upon a bold plan.

'I have had a sharp contest with a French privateer,' he said, 'and that has run out my ammunition. I have plenty of shot, but as for powder, my magazine stands much in need of replenishment, so that I shall have to run in the first port I can make.'

'That will waste time, which is too precious to throw away, especially at the present moment. I will spare you a few kegs, if you like.'

'This was just what Gerald did like; in fact, it was the very thing he aimed at.

'I will accept them gratefully,' he said, 'and give you a bill upon the owners.'

'I do not need it,' said the admiral, completely thrown off his guard; and summoning the officer of the watch, he ordered ten kegs of powder to be placed in the boat.

Captain Stuart having explained the course he intended to pursue, and his reasons (fabulous of course) for doing so, thanked the admiral for his kindness and condescension, and then shaking him warmly by the hand, wished him success, and then returned to the Golden Arrow.

It was a great relief to the crew when Gerald mounted the side, and they obeyed the order to brace round the yards, and put the vessel once more on her course, with an alacrity almost beyond belief.

'I don't care,' said Marline, 'how soon we lose sight of her, for damme, every timber in my hull has been on the shiver ever since we hove-to. As for the skipper, why, hang me! he must be sheathed and doubled bolted, to trust himself a-board her!'

'You are right, bosun, he's a tough old plank; he's sheathed and clamped like an ice ship. Why, bless your heart, nothing pauls him, and his nerve is as firmly weather-bitted as ever was a cable.'

The speaker, Tom Tiller, was trimming the spanker sheet as he described the qualities of the captain, and as he dipped his head under the boom to get a last fond look, as he termed it, of the floating castle, he burst out—

'Damme! Marline, they smell a rat. See, they're about, and heading this way!'

'They have discovered the trick played upon them,' said Captain Gerald, as he returned from the cabin, where he had relieved himself of his false colours, and heard the sailors remark—'She is rigging out stun-sail booms, and intends giving us a smart chase, but if this wind holds we need not fear them. We will hoist every rag, and show them our heels.'

'Sail loosers aloft. Rig out studding sail booms,' roared the boatswain; 'rest of the watch round in the weather braces. All ha—a—nds make sail,' he shouted down the hatchway.

The men swarmed up the hatchways, and flew to their respective stations.

The booms were rigged out, and the stunsails bent.

Long white streaks shot up from the deck and expanded like a cloud, and the Golden Arrow, under the snowy cloud, sped gallantly through the water.

The Martinet was now more than hull down and had hove-to, but the sudden filling of her sails showed that they had kept a good look out from aloft; for now the line-of-battle ship gave chase, she followed their example by clapping on all sail.

Skysails and royals were now brought into requisition, although the aspect of the sky warned the mariner of his danger in carrying such lofty sail.

The masts creaked and groaned, the yards bent, ropes cracked, and the ship strained under the additional weight.

'All hands!' again shouted the boatswain.

'Get up preventive backstays, reeve preventive braces, haul taut the boom guys, see sheets and halyards clear for running well, secure your tacks, and have all ready to let fly.'

The masts began to bend, the vessel rolled, and, as she ran before the gradually increasing gale, heavy seas rolled up on her quarter and washed the decks.

The man-of-war came bowling along at the rate of nine knots as sailors term it, her immense sheet of canvas bellied out to the breeze, her hands in the tops ready to shorten sail at a moment's notice.

Boom, at intervals was borne down on the breeze, as the bow chaser was fired, and the white smoke rose and mingled with the head sails.

'He is feeling his way,' cried the mate, 'but I don't think he gains on us much; that last shot dropped a good quarter of a mile in our wake.'

'No—and every shot he fires wastes his powder and checks his way. He loses a quarter of a knot every time he fires.'

'Do you think so, sir?'

'I do not fear what I saw by the last two shots, each time they have given greater elevation, and by the report, if I am not mistaken, they increase the charge. See there how she yaws.'

As he spoke another shot was fired; and, before the report had been swept past by the breeze, the admiral's fore-topmast stunsail boom went down with a crash, and the sail was useless.

'Bravo!' cried Marline, who had noticed this; but scarce had the words left his lips, than the sudden gust that had caused this mischief, carried away their own main-top gallant stunsail boom, and hands were sent aloft to secure the sail before it did further damage.

'Rig another one,' cried Gerald. 'There is only a capfull of wind; by heaven! if we fail to nurse it, we shall find ourselves in the claws of the British lion.'

'Ay, ay,' cried Marline, and the boatswain's voice, was heard shouting—

'Away aloft! Bob Brace, take two hands with you, and send that lubber of a Pat down here. What the devil is he doing up there? He may be a smart hand at reefing the cook's coppers, or taking the soundings of a soup kid, but as to bending a tack, splicing a grommel, or lashing the heel of a boom, why damme! the captain's grog monkey would do it better.'

'Now then, old dumpling dust,' cried Bob, as he scrambled up the topmast rigging, and grasping the top-gallant stunsail halyards, swung himself out on the end of the topsail yard. 'Lay down out o' this, the bosun wants yer.'

'Faith, sure! and what can he be afther wanting of me?'

'He'll soon tell you. I expect he wants you to shake a reef out of the pudding bag, for you've hauled us so d—— close lately, that I've had to reef my bread locker. My bread bag hangs like the slab reef of a seventy-four, my pants hang like a purser's shirt on a handspike, and, if you don't slack out your sheets and steer a little freer with the beef kids, I shall soon pass my examination for being hauled starn first through the eye of a ring bolt.'

The boatswain's voice put an end to their edifying discourse.

'Now, then, look out for the boom—look smart, lads. Why, damme, you move as nimble as if you had the shot locker or a cable trunk lashed to your starn. 'Sway away! belay there! Make fast every inch.'

With plenty of hands it was only the work of a few minutes to set the sails, though, to those who were not actually engaged in the task, it seemed much longer.

The man-of-war had not gained on them during this performance, but hands were aloft repairing her damage; and the bow gun was silenced for a time.

'She steers wild, I fancy,' said Gerald, eyeing her narrowly; 'what do you think?' he asked of the mate, 'she yaws most horribly.'

'Something wrong with her tiller ropes, I should say; and if she keeps on at that rate, she'll soon carry her sticks over the side. Well, I hope she may, that's all I know; for I don't like the idea of having an elephant like that hanging on our heels.'

'Nor I; but as they say "what can't be cured, must be endured," so we must throw overboard all our dislikes and trust to Providence and Dame Fortune for the rest.'

At this moment Bob Brace, who had ascended to the crosstrees to see if all was secure aloft, hailed the deck.

'Hallo!' roared the boatswain, 'I wish you'd belay your throat halyards, and come below.'

'There's a sail on the port bow,' cried Bob.

Captain Stuart looked up.

'It's our consort, is it not?' he asked.

'No; she is on the starboard bow.'

'What does she look like?'

'I can only see her topsails.'

The captain took his glass and went aloft.

'It's a stranger, by Jove!' he said to Bob, as he sat astride the crosstree, and wound his left arm round the top gallant rigging to steady his glass.

'A man-of-war, I'll be bound,' he added. 'She is giving chase to the Martinet. I wish Henson had given me the despatches, as I advised him to; but there, they would not have been much safer; to-morrow may see us in the hands of those d—n

sharks in our wake. I only hope he will not turn fainthearted, and destroy the papers that have given us so much trouble to preserve so far.'

It was some minutes before he returned to the deck; before he did so, he was thoroughly convinced that a ship-of-war was in chase of the Martinet.

'Ill luck! ill luck!' he muttered, as he hastily paced the deck. 'Confound it! I wish we could shake this fellow off; he hangs on to us like a bloodhound.'

'And his fangs will prove as sharp,' said the mate, who chanced to overhear the last of his speech.

'I know it; and that knowledge is none the more consoling for being true,' said the captain, testily. 'But we are leaving her, and that is a consolation.'

The line-of-battle ship still continued to be unsteady, and the stunsails were lowered, and she was hove up in the wind.

'The wheel ropes have fouled or carried away,' said the mate; 'I thought so at first. Good luck, that gives another knot.'

'And much we need it; for we don't know how soon we may have some of our own tackle carried away. Everything holds on taut at present; but the wind freshens.'

'If they hold on till dark, we may dodge him. There is no moon, and'——

'But the Martinet!' cried Stuart, stamping his foot; 'it is for her safety I feel most concerned.'

He took his glass, and once more went aloft to get a glance before the dusk hid them from them.

Both vessels were running before the wind, and wreaths of smoke issuing from the sides of each told him that they were engaged.

'A running fight, by heavens!' muttered the captain. 'After all, Henson has more pluck than I gave him credit for.'

Darkness, aided by the smoke, soon hid both ships from his view, and he descended to the deck to watch the progress of his own vessel.

CHAPTER CXXI.

A DARING DEED—THE SCENE IN THE VAULTS— HORROR.

SILAS DOGGRASS could not rest until he had satisfied himself that Dame Howard and Susan had retired to bed.

He glanced curiously at the door, peeped through the key-hole, and as all was darkness, he sought his own chamber.

Had he seen the dark flashing eyes fixed on him, the pale face, or the trembling figure, crouched in the shade, it would have caused him much uneasiness.

It would have explained all.

It would have accounted for the pale face that haunted him.

But he did not see this, and like a thief he stole to his room, and tried to sleep.

As soon as the door was closed, and all was silent, the figure crept from the place of its concealment, groped about, and entered one of the rooms.

Having procured a light, her dark eyes wandered to the bed on which Dame Howard soundly slept.

'God of heaven!' she murmured, 'give me but strength to bear the horrors of this night, aid me in the mission which it is my duty to fulfil.'

Wrapping a cloak around her, she took the light and left the room.

Along the dark passage she glided like a spectre, descended the stairs, but found to her mortification that the door was locked.

She recollected now that she had seen him place something in his pocket.

'It must have been the key,' she thought. 'I must have it, let the risk be ever so great.'

A moment's hesitation, and then she retraced her steps. But a sound startled her as she traversed the gloomy passage.

The storm had burst out afresh.

It had only partly lulled, as the strong man pauses in his labour to get breath and redouble his exertions.

It was the rain beating on the roof that startled her with its sound, and after listening to the wind as it whistled and roared until a cold chill crept over her, she proceeded.

There were several doors, but she had noted well the one in which Silas had entered.

She listened.

In fancy he could hear him snoring.

Placing the candle in a nook, where its light was screened, she carefully tried the door.

It yielded.

In his excitement, the old villain had forgotten to turn the key, and so she entered.

Noiseless, trembling at every sound, scarce daring to breathe, she strained her eyes to pierce the gloom.

Near the window she could see the faint shadow of a bedstead, and reclining upon it, she could just barely discern his form.

He moved.

He was not asleep.

What she had mistaken for his snoring were a succession of moans.

The guilty wretch could not sleep.

Conscience haunted him.

He thought of his illgotten wealth.

Thoughts of the horrible deed flashed vividly to his mind.

He rose up and glared timidly around.

In fancy he herd a sound.

'It could not be,' he muttered; and then, as though terrified at hearing his own voice, he fell back and buried himself in the clothes.

Horrible indeed was the position of the intruder.

Cold dank sweats poured from her brow.

A trembling like ague shook her frame.

Fear crept over her, and she thought of retiring.

Thoughts of the danger she had risked, and how near her aim was accomplished, gave her fresh strength.

She groped about until she found the clothes, the pocket—the key.

Having got what she sought, she was about to leave, but by accident she stumbled against a chair.

Doggrass started up.

'What can it be?' he muttered in accents of terror.

'I will knew,' he added; 'be it ghost or human, I will not be afraid.'

Susan crept under the bed.

The perspiration poured from her in streams.

She repented her rashness; for she had seen enough of her uncle to know that he would not stand particular how he silenced her, should she be discovered.

'He would murder me,' she thought; 'his hands are already wet with blood; he would murder me with the same feeling that he murdered the sailor.'

In silent dread the villain groped about, dreading he knew not what. At length, satisfied with his search, he went to the door, turned the key, and withdrew it from the lock.

Susan's predicament was now awful.

How could she leave the room?

She was certain of being discovered.

She was puzzled, too, as to where he could have put the key.

'Find it I must,' she thought. 'At least it is better to be discovered in trying to escape, than to lay here and be found at last.'

Creeping from her concealment, she searched his clothes again.

Doggrass was now in a kind of dose.

The storm was howling fearfully.

The thunder shook the old house, and the lightning illumined the room.

She was about to rise, when the thunder startled her. and the momentary flash was sufficient to enable her to see the door.

In an instant she was there.

The key turned noiselessly in the lock.

She stood outside.

Trembling in every limb, she paused and listened.

He had not followed her; but it occurred to her that he might wake up and go downstairs, so she locked the door after her and left the key in it.

This done she took the candle, and made her way to the trap, which she partly raised.

'He lives, thank heaven!' she murmured, as a groan sounded from below.

With caution, then, she descended.

In a nook between two barrels she found the object she sought, for he was laying apparently dead.

Hastily ascending the steps again she took a bottle, half-filled with brandy, and, raising the wounded man's head, she poured a little down his throat.

This revived him.

She next examined his wound.

It was a nasty place she found on wiping away the clotted blood, but not dangerous, and she soon bound it up.

Susan had explored the place before when living under her uncle's roof; for she was not free from that weakness to which women are so prone—curiosity.

It was that that had led her into the adventure of that night.

She knew the place well, and recollected that there was a little room fitted up with a mattrass and chairs—a place Doggrass had prepared for fear he might, like many other people, have to hide his face from the light of day.

To this place, as soon as the sailor had sufficiently recovered, she led him, and, having ministered to his wants, she left, promising to return as soon as circumstances would permit.

With this assurance the wounded man, having drank a good tumbler of spirits to numb his pain, laid down, and tried to seek that repose of which he stood so much in need.

Susan had a most dangerous part to act.

She had to trace her way back to her own room, and to visit the room of her uncle to replace the key.

He might awake, perhaps he had already, and was anxiously awaiting her return.

Dame Howard, too, might have missed her, and, in her excitement, aroused Doggrass; if so, she was lost.

All was silent, save the howling of the storm, and, as she retraced her way, confidence returned.

With a firm step she approached her uncle's bed room, and noiselessly turned the key; but, as the door opened, a flash of lightning lit up the room, and she saw a sight that froze her very blood.

CHAPTER CXXII.

THE TREACHEROUS MATE—THE RISING OF THE PIRATES.

THE Slaver Captain was right in his surmise; the sail that had appeared so suddenly astern was a Yankee cruiser, that had been dogging them from port to port.

She was reported a swift sailer, but as the slave ship was only in ballast, it did not cause them much apprehension concerning their capture.

A heavy press of sail and a stiff breeze soon bore them on their way, and before eight bells sounded the first night-watch, the Yankee was out of sight.

Will soon recovered from his cramped state, and as soon as he was able to walk about, he made himself well acquainted with the armament of the vessel; then leaning over the vessel, his seaman's eye glanced fore and aft her dark side, and took in at a glance the symmetrical beauty of the hull.

'A regular clipper,' he muttered to himself; ' 'tis a pity so smart a vessel should be put to such unholy purposes; would I were her skipper, I would put her to some better use.'

His meditation was suddenly interrupted by the sound of a footstep, and on turning his eyes towards the deck, he saw, moving stealthily along under shadow of the boats, a figure which he took to be the mate's.

Remembering the look he had given him on his first coming on board, he fancied he intended mischief to himself, and prepared accordingly to meet him.

He was deceived, however.

The mate had not observed him.

His whole thoughts were taken up in concealing his own person from the observation of the watch, who lay sleepily about the decks.

Knowing that it was not the mate's watch on deck, Will observed him narrowly, and with more than idle curiosity.

'This fellow is up to no good,' he thought, ' or why should he sneak about in this manner? The look-out is at his post, and the 'All's well' was given to the second mate when the half-hour was struck.

Thus thought Will, and laying his hand on the rail, so that if he were discovered it might be supposed he was asleep, he kept strict watch on the gliding figure.

As is customary, the captain's watch was kept by the second mate, so that the captain might be on deck at any exigency. As all appeared secure, he, the second mate, was leaning over the taffrail, thinking of a fair young girl, who had smitten his heart with her beauty on his last sojourn ashore.

Thus it was that he did not notice the mate creep from the companion way, and skulk on all fours to the lee side of the boats, and pass along as far as the fore-hatch, which was open, and disappear.

No sooner was his head below the combings of the hatch, than Will slipped off his shoes, and, creeping as noiselessly as a mouse, put his ear to the hatchway, so as to catch the least sound.

Will knew that the captain of the pirates was confined just beneath him, and he had no difficulty in recognising his voice.

'Fool!' he heard him say, ' what do you want disturbing us at this hour? We have had enough of your hard tack and bilge water, for a time at least. Let us have a little sleep, if there is such a thing to be had aboard a slaver.'

'Sleep! Ha! ha!' retorted the mate, and he gave a slight laugh; ' it is well you can sleep, moored as you are fore and aft, with these chains— 'tis well you talk of sleep.'

'I talk of nothing but what is practicable,' growled the pirate, with a savageness in his tone.

'Then you are fortunate. Did you feel your imprisonment as keenly as I should, sleep would not visit your eyelids.'

It was too dark for the mate to see the scornfu smile that played on the pirate's lips as he replied—

'Experience has taught me this.'

'Experience!' echoed the mate.

'Ay, had you been chained to the oar of a galley as many years as I, it would teach you to sleep so sound, that the roar of a cannon would not wake you.'

A smile played on the mate's livid features.

'There you were worked both body and brain,' he said, placing great emphasis on his words. 'Here the brain alone is employed. There you had change of scene; but here all his one dull monotony.'

There was a peculiar tone in his speech which the slave took for irony, and, in a fierce voice, he replied—

'Away! taunt me not. It is not enough that you have illegally imprisoned us. Away, fiend! It is well my hands are fettered, or I would chastise you as you deserve.'

It was far from the mate's intention to incense the pirate. Will could see his drift at once, and his object became more apparent, when the mate, moderating his tone, said—

'You mistake my visit; I came here with good intent, to '——

'Taunt me, as you have proved. Away, false fiend!'

The mate bit his lip with passion.

He scowled horribly, and felt half inclined to dea l the pirate a blow with the butt of his pistol.

It was well it was dark for both parties; it precluded them seeing each other's visage, and confined them to the hearing only of words.

It was some moments ere the mate could sufficiently master his temper to speak.

'I have mistaken my man as you have mistaken my motives,' he said, at length. 'You told me you had served at the galleys; if so, you must among other amiabilities you were taught, have learnt to control your passion, or you would not have escaped, as I doubt whether they gave you a free pardon.'

'They did not; I took it.'

'And quite right to. I consider that freedom is best under any circumstances.'

'When it can be obtained.'

'True; but you escaped the galleys.'

'That's evident; but I see no chance here as yet.'

'You have been here no time.'

'Quite long enough to be pleasant.'

'Then you would not remain had you a chance of escape.'

'Fool! Try me. Away, scoffer! How could I escape without aid—without a friend? I have neither here; so leave me. You need not trouble about our safety; you will find us here in the morning.'

The mate bit his lip the more violently. With with all his cunning he could not make the pirate understand his meaning without speaking much plainer than he cared to do.

'Speak not so hasty,' said the mate, in a voice greatly modified; 'supposing you had such a friend of which you speak?'

'Well?' growled the pirate.

'Would you refuse his services?'

'Does a drowning man refuse the aid of a plank?'

'He does not if it is within reach.'

'Then why ask me such a question?'

'Because I can assist you.'

'Can! But will you?'

'There is little doubt of it. Listen.'

'I am all attention.'

'In the first place I am mate of this craft; and, as the captain has insulted me, I wish to be revenged.'

'Quite natural.'

'Well, I shall have to keep the middle watch; I will take the ship, and you must help me.'

'Must!' ejaculated the pirate, in well-feigned surprise. 'What, with these irons on?'

'They shall be removed.'

'And my men; what of them?'

'They will share the same. We shall want their assistance.'

'Good. When do we begin?'

'Soon after you hear eight bells struck. In the meantime I will procure the keys of your shackles, provide muskets and cutlasses, and all that is required.'

'How many of the crew will aid us?' asked the pirate.

'None; and none we want. I would not trust a man of them; they must all die, every man, even to the cabin boy.'

''Tis well I am with you. But what are we to do with the ship?'

'Run into some bye port, ship a few more hands, change the vessel's name, and trade on our own account.'

'Good; a capital idea, master mate. If you do as you propose, we may depend on success.'

'Of that I have no fear. So farewell till after midnight.'

The mate turned to the ladder, and Will resumed his old place.

Crouching as he had done before, the mate slunk to his berth, but he did not turn in.

The remainder of his watch below was spent in forming his plans, and planning how he should gain possession of the key of the arm-chest.

It was in the captain's state-room, and he was afraid of waking him.

He more than once thought of settling him, and went so far as to draw a huge knife from its sheath, and examine its edge.

Then his heart seemed to fail him.

Fear or some other cause made him return it to its place.

Perhaps he thought that it might be necessary to call the captain, and then his plot would be discovered before its time.

Will Howard watched him until he saw him enter his berth, and then he joined the second mate.

That officer stared at our hero in surprise.

Walking aft was an infringement of the laws of the ship, as no foremast man was allowed on the quarter-deck unless he was to perform some duty, such as trimming sail, steering, or assisting in heaving the log.

He was about to make some remark when Will stopped him by saying—

'I have something of importance to tell you.'

'Pay out the slack and be sharp,' was the gruff rejoinder.

'Will felt rather piqued, but as it concerned himself and Sancho as much as the rest, he restrained his indignation, and acquainted the second mate with all he had heard.

'As I suspected,' muttered the officer, thoughtfully. 'From the first of his setting foot a-board, I did not like the fellow. I told the captain so, but the fool would not listen to me.'

'Has he been long with you?' asked Will.

'Too long for me. He has been here a month.'

'And his name?'

'He keeps that to himself. But we know him as Walter Gregory.'

'Ah! as I suspected. His face appeared familiar to me. Where did he ship?'

'Havanna.'

'Did you hear how he came there?'

'He was picked up in a boat at sea. He was as mute as a maggot when he shipped with us, and as lean as a hop-pole. But since he has blown out, he gets big both in body and words.'

'Ah! a bully, as he always was. I have a mind to go down and tackle him in his berth. His name is Gregory Saunders, a black-hearted scoundrel, and one that I owe much to in the way of grudgery.'

'Take my advice, and do no such thing,' said the second mate, grasping Will by the collar, and drawing him back as he was about to hurry towards the cabin-ladder.

As Will turned, the light of the binnacle fell on his face, and the officer could see that his brow was knitted, and his lips compressed.

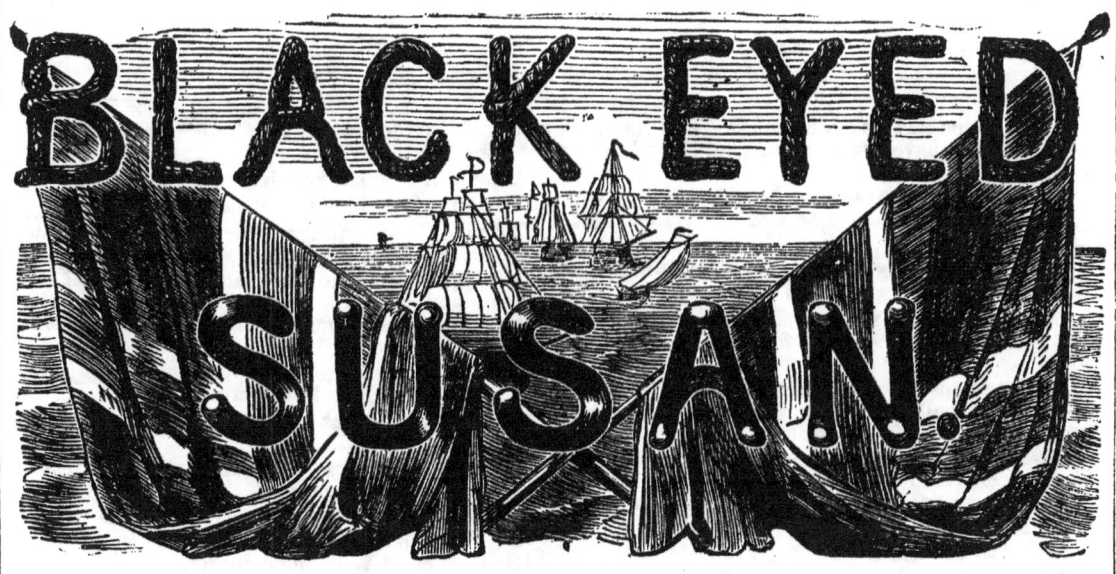

BLACK EYED SUSAN.

OR, PIRATES ASHORE.

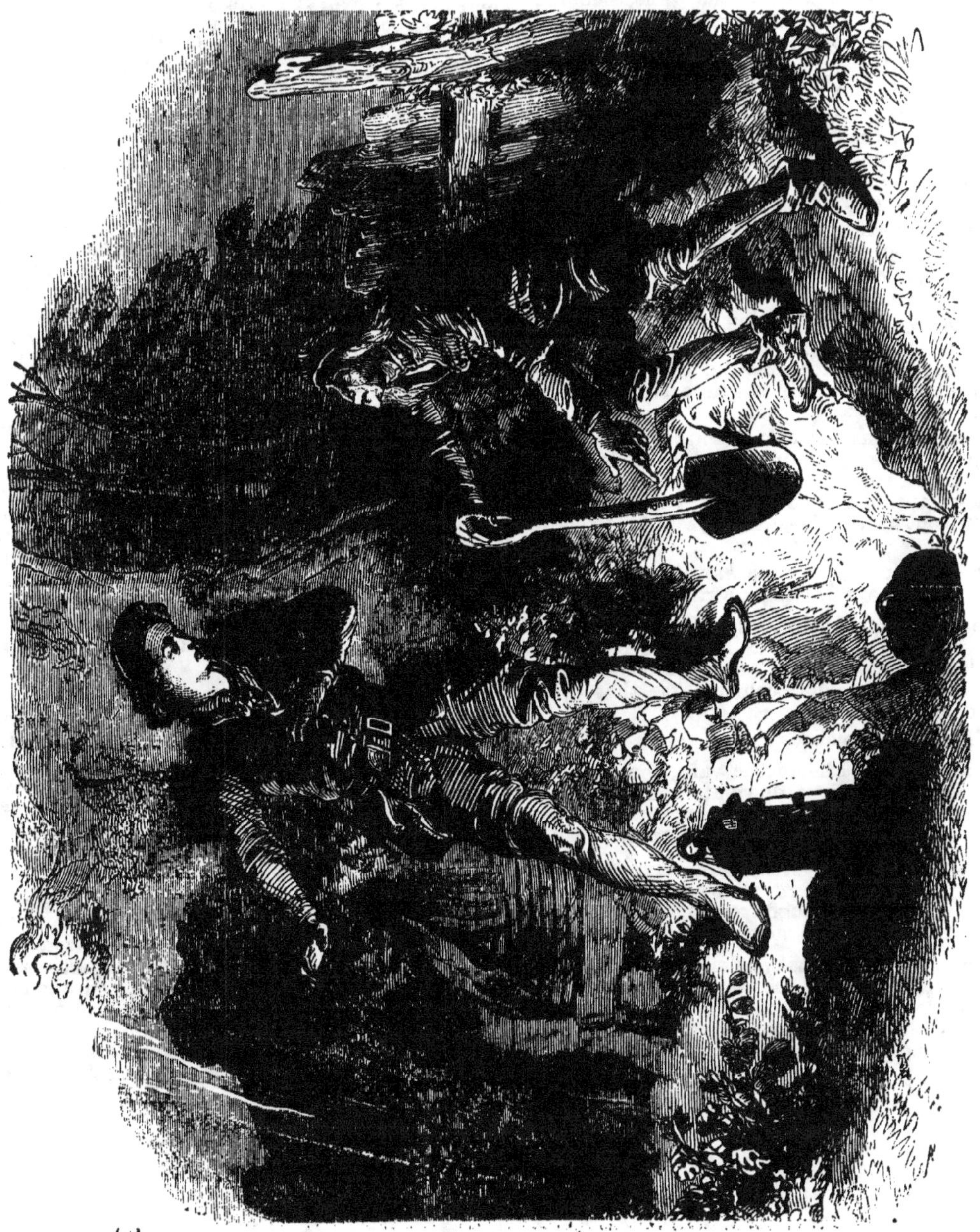

THE MIDNIGHT SEARCH.

'Why do you stay me?' demanded Will, hoarsely' 'What motive have you in preserving the villain's life?'

'A great motive, inasmuch if you were to set foot in the cabin, your life would be forfeited. Besides, you'——

'What, for ridding the ship of a black-hearted wretch like'——

Hush! you have not proved him such. Leave him to me. I will answer for all the harm he does.'

'And perhaps get a few inches of steel in your carcase, or a bullet lodged in your skull, to make up for your deficiency of brains.'

'Heed well your words, young man, before you speak to me,' said the second mate, galled by the sharp retort; 'you make pretty bold on so short an acquaintance!'

Will walked away.

He had done all that was necessary in that quarter, and he sought Sancho, so as to put him on his guard.

They had retired to a spot where they thought no one would hear them, but they had not noticed a form coiled under one of the guns, and they started when, in the midst of their narrative, the stranger jumped to his feet, and seated himself beside them.

'Well, what want you?' asked Will angrily.

'Well, mates, don't speak so cross; why you talk as sharp as the cox'n of a jolly boat, or a new fledged middy when first put on duty in a king's cutter.'

'For the matter of that,' said Will, vexed at having been overheard, 'its no seaman's action to turn eavesdropper.'

The man, a jovial devil-may-care sort of fellow, set up a laugh at this.

'Curse you, for a swab!' cried Will, almost losing his temper. 'If you grin at me, I'll stop your baccy chewing for a month, by unshipping a few of those tusks you use as a substitute for teeth.'

'Avast, shipmate, don't be angry,' said the sailor; 'we both row in the same boat, what consarns you consarns me; and, as I've slung my hammock aboard this hooker, its a dead sartinty I don't want anyone 'cepting myself to swing in it.'

'Do you think either of us want to swing in it?' asked Will, his eye flashing angrily.

'No; shiver my mizzen, why you're all aback if you think so; but you see as how I've been carefully balling off the yarn you've been spinning, and I've heerd enough to convince me that somebody does.'

'Who is this somebody?'

'Well, as far as I heerd the yarn, I should say its them dam scorpions down atween decks; but, damme, if they swings in my berth, the murdering swabs, cuss 'em; hang all pirates, say I.'

'Pirates!' iterated Will, derisively. 'I have, certainly, fallen amongst a most refined set of devils; you talk as though you were on board a king's ship instead of a slaver.'

'It was not choice that put me aboard this 'ere craft, shipmate,' said the sailor, returning the scornful look with which Will regarded him. 'When a fellar's out of depth and can't swim, he must collar anything that'll float him.'

Ay, if its only a grindstone,' replied Will, tartly. 'But how came you here? Let us have the yarn.'

'That will I, in the turning of a handspike.'

'Belay that, and let's have the yarn.'

The sailor having plugged his cheek with about a fathom of pig-tail began—

'Well, you must know my mother was a washer-woman, and the first wessel I ever seed was a earthen one called a butter boat, and this I used to swim in'——

'Curse you, for a lubber; bowze taut your jawing tackle, and tell us how you got here.'

Six bells were that moment struck, and Will said, impatiently—

'Now for the yarn; it wants but an hour to midnight, so waste no time.'

'Well, here goes; but don't heave me to again to get soundings '——

'Go on!' cried Will, impatiently.

'As I was going to say, I was cap'n o' the main-top in the Saucy—but there, never mind the name, as I've reasons for keeping it under hatches. Well, it was my turn, being as I belonged to the port watch to have first turn ashore. We had twenty-four hours' leave, and pretty short commons, too, seeing as how we had been at sea six months; but no matter, we were glad enough to snatch at that, as old Jack Shark would have said, for we'd had plenty o' drill and but little luck.'

'Cut it short, mate, cut it short.'

'Damme, shipmate,' said the sailor, 'I've lost my reckoning agen.' Then, giving his quid two or three vicious twists, he went on. 'I forgot to tell you we were in New Orleans, and a mighty fine place it are, if you only manage to dodge Yaller Jack, and as fine a place as I knows on to get rid o' the yaller boys. Well, as I was saying, our time was but short, and, as we were bent on a spree, why, in course, we meant to make the most on it.'

He paused for a moment to masticate his quid, and as Will had had sufficient experience that to urge him on was only to prolong the story, kept quiet.

'Well, as I was saying, we went ashore, and my chum Jack, who, by-the-bye, was cap'n o' the fore-top, says to me—says he, "Bill, old ship, we sticks together mind, like barnacles." "Ay," says I, "old top, and woe be to the fellow as tries to part us, that's all." Well, off we goes to old Mother Harper's—as nice a dame as ever you met—on a cruise, and she had two of as plump darters as ever you clapt eyes on, and as they were out o' commission, Jack and I makes up our minds to moor there till our leave was up.'

'Well, how did it end?'

'Why, Jack and I told 'em we were going to have a week's holiday, and that we'd lots o' prize money coming to us; but the starbowlines was to have twenty-four hours' run first; for, do you see, as we wern't werry well fledged, we wanted to get tick, which we meant to pay with the fore-tops'l. This was jolly enuf for us, do you see, for we'd planned it all, knowing we was going to unmoor directly the starbowlines came aboard'——

'Seven bells!' muttered Will; 'only one half-hour. Pay out the slack, you lubber.'

'Well, to cut the yarn short, we were jolly enough, swayed away on all top ropes, set the chain-pumps going on the rum cask, and when our time was up, we were so top hampered that we could'nt budge tack nor sheet; consequence was Starbowlines comes ashore, capsized all the yarns we'd spun so finely, and we were left in the hands of three reg'lar gudgeons that would give no quarter, and show no mercy.

'Into us they battered their double-shotted broadsides till they started every plank in our blessed hulls, crippled our timbers, and tumbled us down into the orlop deck, where we righted, and scrambling on our pins begun groping about in the dark.

'We was all on a gasp, for our throats were parched, but the devil a drop of anything could we find, only bumped our sore and bruised lower masts against empty casks, which made Jack swear most tremendously, and I followed suit.'

'So you broke your leave?'

'How could we do any other? the she-tigress kept us battened down until the liberty men, all but our two unlucky selves, got aboard, the frigate tripped anchor, and was far away.'

'So you joined this craft?'

'Wait a bit. Jack and I, as soon as we got into daylight, thought of returning the broadsides we'd received, but thinks we if we do, we shan't get any grog, and we were as dry as a bread locker, so we kept quiet cos our rhino had all melted, and we were treated reglar hansum by the old dame and her darters; they let us swill away at the grog tub as much as we liked; and some how we lost our reckoning, and when I came to, I find myself swinging in a hammock on board this hooker.'

'Ah, they sold you. But hush!' Will spoke in a whisper, and kept his eye fixed aft; 'it's just on eight bells; stick to me, and keep a handspike within reach.'

'Ay, ay! That's what I heard you palavering about. Well, you'll find Bill Clewline can hit d—d hard if its wanted.'

'All right; keep snug till the watch is mustered.

Eight bells were struck, the watch relieved, and the second mate went below.

The mate glanced aloft, and ordered a pull on the lee braces, having gone through several, if not necessary preliminaries, customary ones, for most mates have a habit of altering the trim of sails to lead the captain to believe that he is paying more heed to the sailing of the vessel than the officer that has just left the deck, though, as it often happens, the sails have to be trimmed as they were at first to make the vessel steer her course.

It was so in the present case, but the second mate took no heed of it.

He went to the captain's berth, and woke him.

Will Howard, Sancho, and Bill Clewline did not go below with the rest.

They concealed themselves about the deck, for they were afraid to breathe a word to the crew, not knowing how many might be in the mate's confidence.

The first half-hour was passed in silence.

One by one the watch relinquished their walk, and picked out the softest plank they could find for a snooze.

Hard enough was the softest, but nevertheless the sailors were soon asleep, as the sky was unclouded, and the wind, as well being fair, was steady, so that there was little fear of their being disturbed.

Not long had Will to watch from his ambush the coming of the mate.

He walked forward with a stealthy tread, and descended the hatchway.

As he did so, Will noticed he carried a bundle of what he took to be cutlasses, wrapped up in an old piece of tarpaulin.

He was below some few minutes, and Will's quick ear detected a slight rattling of chains.

'At their work, Sancho,' he whispered.

'Ay, Captain Will, and we'll be at ours soon.'

'Hist!'

The mate's head appeared above the hatch.

He walked aft silently as he came.

He returned soon with another bundle, but as it was too heavy, or for some other reason best known to himself, he did not carry the whole of it down at once.

After taking a cautious survey around, and assuring himself that all the watch but those on duty slept, that the look-out man was looking ahead, and that the man at the wheel could not observe him, he opened the bundle, and, selecting half, descended the fore-hatch ladder.

Will's time for action had arrived.

'Now follow me,' he whispered to his companions.

In an instant they had possessed themselves of the remaining weapons; and, as the captain and second mate appeared aft, bearing a loaded pistol in each hand, the mate's head popped up the hatchway.

A lump of oakum well-tarred, that Will had previously prepared, was thrust into his mouth, and Sancho, fixing his giant grasp on his shoulders, lifted him to the deck without the least trouble.

Scarcely was he disposed of when the pirates in a body rushed up, and Will was so taken aback by this unexpected rally that he had only time to cut one down before he was surrounded.

Sancho and Bill were similarly situated; and, though they cut about most lustily, they were well nigh overpowered.

Sancho had his foot planted heavily on the mate's chest; but the villain dug his nails into the calf of his legs until the pain caused him to move.

'H—— and furies!' yelled the mate, 'we are betrayed. Lay on, my bold fellows. Rip them up with your knives.'

This was easier said than done.

The three brave fellows they found themselves opposed to knew how to use their trenchant weapons.

The captain and second mate flew to their assistance; but neither of them dare fire for fear of shooting their own friends.

The mate somehow gained his feet, and giving vent to an oath as well as he possibly could in his condition, for the tar glued his lips and burnt his tongue, he drew his knife, and viciously plunged it to the hilt in the breast of one of the sleeping men.

The fatal blade had effectually done its work.

Not a groan came from the wounded man; he merely rolled over, and expired.

Again the red blade sought its victim, but this time with less success.

By some means the sleeper moved, and the keen blade was imbedded several inches in the deck.

He made a vigorous effort to withdraw it, but it was too firmly embedded, and as by a sudden wrench the blade snapped, the mate himself was firmly grasped by the back of the neck.

With a desperate effort he tried to free himself, but he was in a vice as it were, and a horrid oath burst from him.

'It's no good,' said Sancho, whose iron grasp it was that held him. 'You are a prisoner now, and must put up with your deserts.'

'Never!' yelled the mate. 'Unhand me.'

'I'd sooner split your windpipe,' said Sancho.

'Ay, give him to me,' cried the captain, grasping the mate's collar, and placing a pistol to his ear.

The guilty wretch shuddered.

The cold barrel seemed to deprive him of all power.

To the quarter-deck the captain led him, and placed him against the companion-way, where he stood unresistingly—his cowardly spirit cowed, his sanguinary nature for a time subdued.

The fight forward was desperate though but short. The clash of arms aroused the sleepers, and hearing that the pirates had been released and had mutined, they soon armed with anything they could get hold of.

A gun-rammer dashed out the brains of one of the pirates, and the ramrod of a musket was thrust through the body of another.

CHAPTER CXXIII.

THE FIGHT WITH THE CUTTER—THE SMUGGLERS GAIN A GLORIOUS VICTORY.

TOM HATCHETT prided himself on the sailing of his craft the Laughing Bird, but when he saw the revenue cutter overhauling him with the slow but steady movement of a snake, it gave him some uneasiness.

The past events of the day had served to ruffle his temper severely, but when he saw his vessel about to fall into the hands of his inveterate enemies, it sent a pang through his burly frame that seemed to gnaw his very vitals.

The smugglers, now the danger had drawn near, began to feel their position acutely.

They worked with a will, strained their muscles at the sweeps, but the Laughing Bird seemed to move no faster. It was as though a drag was holding her from cutting through the water.

So it seemed at least to those on board her, though to the cutter's men it seemed as if she was flying.

Both crews were equally interested in her welfare, though from different motives.

Lieutenant Pike was not idle in the meantime.

He used every endeavour to facilitate the speed of the cutter.

At one time he would be giving orders for some alterations of the sails, at another he would be giving directions to the man at the bow gun.

'Try her again, my lad,' he said to the gunner; 'we are slipping through the water; now, aim at her spars, she cannot baffle us this time.'

The gunner did his work well.

A shot went through one of the sails of the Laughing Bird.

This brought a cheer from the man-of-war's men, and a volley of oaths from the smugglers.

Hatchett stood calmly watching the shot until it had passed and dropped ahead of the Laughing Bird, then he sprang into the rigging and went aloft.

'All right as yet, lads,' he shouted; 'it has only grazed the spar. I feared it had cut it through.'

With these words he descended to the deck. There was a look of bold defiance in his eye.

His brow was knitted, and his lips compressed.

'Lay aft here!' he shouted to a party of his men, who were watching the cutter with anxious gaze.

'We are losing ground fast,' he added, as the men gathered round him. 'Quick, lads! Give them an answer to that insolent shot. They have spoilt a cloth in one of our best sails, and nearly carried away one of our sticks. We will learn them that we are desperate men, and set some value on our lives.'

A long brass gun, mounted on a carriage of the same metal, was wheeled aft, and the gunner stood, match in hand, ready for the word to fire.

But Lieutenant Pike had watched their movements narrowly.

A cloud of white smoke rose from the cutter's bows, a shot whizzed through the air, and the smuggler, who held the match, fell headless to the deck.

Such an oath, as we dare not repeat, fell from the lips of the smugglers as they picked up the mangled remains of their comrade, and consigned it to the deep.

Captain Hatchett seized the match.

Stepping to the rear of the gun, he shouted, sternly—

'Muzzle to the right; well—elevate—down—ready?'

As the last word left his lips he applied the match, and a ringing cheer burst from the smugglers as the cutter's topmast fell.

'Bravo, captain! nobly done!' cried one of the crew. ''Twas a—— H—l and furies! look there!'

This last ejaculation was caused by a fearful crashing sound.

The mainmast swayed to and fro.

'Stand clear!' yelled Hatchett, mad with rage.

The warning was only given in time to be obeyed.

The mainmast had been cut through with a shot, and the smugglers had scarcely cleared out of its way, when it came crashing down on to the topsail, smashing the wheel, and sending the spokes flying in all directions.

Hatchett and his lawles screw were now fairly mad with rage.

Escape seemed hopeless.

Two alternatives only were left them—to fight or yield, for run they could not.

'What say you, lads?' cried Hatchett, pointing to the advancing cutter, which was now only a few fathoms astern. 'What say you, shall we '——

'Fight to the death!' shouted the smugglers, simultaneously. 'Fight to the death—we will never yield to our foes!'

'Nobly said, and if you act as bravely, we may yet have a chance of escaping these bloodhounds of the law.'

'Clear the deck, and get the guns to work again.'

The smugglers set to with a stern determination.

Hatchets, knives, and cutlasses were brought into requisition, but the mass of cordage had embraced the whole of the quarter-deck and its contents in its entanglement, and the smugglers, though they hacked and cut at the tough hard ropes, got on but slowly with their work.

The cutter's men, confident of a prize, and elated

with success, sent cheer after cheer from their sturdy lungs, until the voice of Lieutenant Pike ordered them to desist.

'Silence!' he shouted. 'Until the victory is gained, let not another voice be heard. Obey my orders, and a glorious prize shall be our reward.'

Not another word was heard but Pike's stern orders.

'Load the bow gun with grape,' he said to the gunner, 'but reserve your fire. We must take these lawless wretches alive, if possible. A dance from the yardarm or a swing from the gallows is the only death they merit. Hard a port, there! Steady! lay her alongside.'

As he spoke, the cutter shot swiftly up by the smuggler's quarter, but before she could be laid alongside, the guns of the Laughing Bird discharged their whole broadside into the cutter.

This daring act seemed to paralyze the movements of the cutter's crew.

The smugglers had concealed their intentions till the last moment.

Shrieks, groans, and oaths mingled in the air.

The voices of the two commanders were heard above the din, and the rattle of blocks and flapping of sails, as the ships now unmanageably hung in the wind, added to the horror of the scene.

'Surrender!' cried Lieutenant Pike, eyeing Hatchett viciously through the smoke that had not yet cleared away. 'Surrender, and I grant you quarter, and a fair trial before your necks are stretched.'

'And if I refuse?' asked Hatchett, with a sneer.

'I will sweep you and your sacrilegious crew from the face of the deep. I will mow you down with grape and canister, and rid the coast of one of its greatest scourges.'

'Then fire away, and be d——d to you! I fear not your threats any more than I respect your laws. Now away; let fate decide the victory.'

Lieutenant Pike, galled at the daring effrontery of the smuggler, lost the cool determination he was so well known to possess.

'Boarders! Man the guns!' he shouted in a breath.

This confused the men, and they ran hither and thither, knocking each other over, and cursing each other vociferously.

Hatchett, seeing their disorder, took advantage of it immediately.

On a given signal, another deadly volley was poured into the cutter, and many of the brave seamen, who were preparing to board the smuggler, were blown away from the very muzzle of the guns.

It was the smuggler's turn now to cheer, but they soon found themselves hand to hand with the gallant tars.

Springing over the bulwarks in every direction, the man-of-war's men, cutlass in hand, swore vengeance on the slayers of their comrades.

Their excitement was heightened by the shouts of Lieutenant Pike.

'Hurrah, lads! Down with the murdering rascals!' he thundered, at the pitch of his voice. 'Cut them down!—give them no quarter!'

The smugglers met them with more firmness than might have been expected from such lawless men.

Hatchett, armed with a good stout sword, distinguished himself by his prowess, and having discharged both pistols, he threw them away, and fought a road to the head of his men.

'Back with the fiends, the tyrants! Drive them off our decks!' shouted Tom Hatchett to the smugglers. 'Back with them! Drive them overboard if they do not yield.'

'Yield! What, to an outlaw?' cried Pike, almost choked with rage. 'Yield! British seamen yield to a nest of infamous wretches such as own you as leader? Never!'

'Then die!' hissed Hatchett savagely, as the lieutenant stepped before him; but the blow he aimed at him was well warded, and then their blades again crossed.

This was the first time the two leaders had had an opportunity to engage each other closely, and the opportunity was not thrown away by either.

Each sought eagerly for the other's life.

Both equally panted for each other's blood.

Point, parry, and thrust were given in turn, and more than once the victory was almost decided in favour of Lieutenant Pike.

Meanwhile the battle raged furiously.

Dead, dying, and wounded lay around in heaps.

Blood poured in streams from the scuppers, and it was difficult to keep a foothold on the slippery deck.

This almost proved fatal to Tom Hatchett.

He was hardly pressed by Pike, and in springing back to ward a blow, he fell.

'Yield thee now!' yelled the lieutenant, exultingly.

'And thou too!' cried a voice; at the same moment Lieutenant Pike fell forward with a deep gash in his side, from which the blood copiously flowed.

'Ah, Bill! how came you here?' asked Hatchett, as soon as he could recover from his surprise, 'thanks, comrade. I'——

'Not a word of it. Bill Raker has not forgotten his duty. But see, we have no time for idle talk.'

Bill Raker was right.

A dark mass of clouds was rising in the weather horizon, and the aspect of the sky as the sun sank behind a bank of heavy gray was as angry as could be.

The men-of-war's men who, from the moment their leader committed the fatal error in delivering his order, had not fought with the energy as was their wont, on losing sight of the lieutenant and missing his voice, fought for a moment with stubborn determination.

But it was only for a moment.

A stalwart fellow dressed in blue serge and begrimed with powder, strode in amongst them, shouting—

'Make good your retreat, lads. See, the storm will be down on us in a crack.'

As though by mutual consent the combatants on both sides paused in their deadly work, and cast their eyes towards the spot were the lurking danger threatened.

Then, taking advantage of the moment, the man-of-war's men sprang on to the bulwarks, and leapt on to the cutter's deck.

A few sharp strokes of an axe served to sever the ropes that bound both vessels together; and as the breeze, the forerunner of the gale, sprang up, the Laughing Bird swung off, and turned her head in the direction she had formerly been pursuing.

It was then, and not till then, that the cutter's

crew became aware of the ruse played on them by the smugglers.

The man who had ordered their retreat, instead of the boatswain as they had supposed, was one of the daring smugglers, who, having disguised himself in the suit of one of the dead sailors, had by this device cleared the deck of the Laughing Bird of all foes that were in a condition to fight.

Lieutenant Pike, who with the rest had gained the cutter, and, in fact, had been assisted in doing so by the strong arms of the disguised smuggler, expressed his opinion of the smuggler's conduct, in spite of the pain of his wound, in no gentlemanly terms.

'Curse them! hang them! Oh! they have robbed us of a fine prize, and heaped upon us more —oh!—disgrace than we shall wipe off in a month.'

'Hang 'em, ah! I should like to, yer honour,' said the man who was binding up the wound with the gentleness of a bear. 'But I shouldn't a cared so much if the rascals hadn't a knocked this confounded hole in yer honour's upper works.'

'Make haste, man, and get done. Oh! Gently, hang you! You—oh!—handle one like a lump of old junk. Confound you—do you think you are parcelling the main-stay, or seizing the lanyard of a bowsprit shroud?'

'Beg your honour's pardon, if I '——

'Oh!'

'Boo!'

The first exclamation was wrung from the lieutenant, by the sailor holding his shoulder in his iron grasp, and hauling on the bandage just as though he was passing a strip of tarry canvas round a rope that had been chafed (which process is termed parcelling). The second mournful note was forced from the sailor; through the lieutenant unconsciously planting his foot on his stomach, and giving him a jerk that, independent of sending him flying against the main mast, nearly deprived him of breath.

'Now, then, you clumsy fool, see if you can use more care,' said the lieutenant, angry beyond bounds, and wincing with pain.

'Beg your honour's pardon,' said the tar, deferentially; 'I didn't mean to hurt you. I'm as gentle as '——

'A bear. Curse you! And if you are not quick, and learn a little more manners than the aforesaid animal, I'll see what a good round dozen will do towards loosening your hide.'

The sailor made no reply; but the frown on his visage was enough to indicate his thoughts. Before finishing off with the lieutenant he gave him a parting nip, taking care, however, to keep well in his rear.

Lieutenant Pike gave a hideous groan, and turned, as well as his wound would allow him; but the revengeful tar had disappeared, and no doubt enjoyed a quiet grin to himself.

The cutter was sadly disabled, and, as the gale gave token of approach, the remnant of the crew, after carrying the wounded below and clearing the deck of the dead, set about repairing the rigging and making all snug, for fear it might overtake them before they could get into port.

The smugglers in the meantime had refreshed their spirits with a cheery glass of grog, and laughed most merrily at the trick played on the cutter.

One party being told off to look after the wounded, among whom were many of the cutter's best men, the rest set to work clearing away the deck and repairing such damage as was necessary.

Bill Raker, weak as he was, did good service.

Under his guidance the quarter-deck had been cleared of its encumbrance, the spokes of the shattered wheel lashed so as to enable them to steer, providing the weather was not too bad, and a stunsail boom lashed across the stern, where the taffrail had been smashed away.

*   *   *   *   *   *

As had been predicted, the night set in gloomy and tempestuous.

Dark heavy masses swept across the sky; the wind howled in fitful gusts, and the rain descended in a regular deluge.

The smugglers, taking a near cut through a channel beset by myriads of rocks, the passages of which would have proved certain destruction to any other but Tom Hatchett and his mate, who alone knew its secret windings and intricate mazes, gained anchorage in a bay where they could lay secure from any danger of the elements except lightning, which now began to play about in the dark canopy of the heavens.

Before the storm had reached its present fury, Hatchett had contrived to land all the wounded and see them all comfortably housed in a cave close by, and well bedded on heaps of dried sea-weed and ferns.

This was a secret cave which the smugglers used as a reserve, and to which they only resorted in time of need, such as the present, or when it was thought prudent to keep out of the way for a short time, in consequence of the country being too hot for them to carry on their desperate calling.

Hatchett and his crew were well matched.

Nothing seemed to touch them, and nothing seemed impossible for them to do.

But of this anon.

We left the Laughing Bird riding snugly at anchor, Tom Hatchett and Bill Raker, wrapped in their pea jackets and heavy deck boots, standing by the wheel in deep and earnest conversation, heedless of the blinding showers that beat pitilessly upon them.

'I tell you, it will be useless depending on old Doggrass; the old rascal is as close as a jambing hitch. You might as well ask a parson to part with his gown as ask him for money, unless you can give him double in return.'

'Well, don't be angry, Tom; if you've asked him as you say, it's evident you must know; but still there is no harm in trying again. I am one who never despairs, and gives nothing up for a bad job until I'm certain it's a failure.'

'Ah! you are plucky, Bill, I know; and you have about the greatest amount of cheek of any of my acquaintance, except old Silas himself. What say you if you pay him a visit?'

'I am agreeable,' replied Raker, not observing the cynical smile on his companion's lips; 'I am agreeable, my boy. How much do you think we need?'

'Two hundred, beside our own resources. Look you, if you can, for this confounded rain that comes down, as though the world had turned bottom up and the sea had exchanged places with the sky.'

'Ha—ha!' laughed Bill Raker, heartily. 'You are never at a loss for a simile; but, hang me, if that don't beat all! Ha—ha—ha! Well, what say you if we get below, for that hit you gave me makes me feel develish stiff; and, though my outside skin begins to moisten, my innerworks are as dry as a cinder oven.'

'Ah! 'tis well for you that fate cast your lot among smugglers; for, if you had had to pay duty for all the spirits you have poured down your insatiable throat, it would have cost you a pretty fortune.'

'Ha—ha! you are about right my boy,' and the smuggler laughed heartily. 'It is a privilege that but few enjoy, to drink the king's health at his highness's own expense.'

'True but let us talk of something more important; When do you start on your journey to Deal?'

'At once, if you like. I will repair to the cave, and I can visit the old boy first thing in the morning.'

'It will not do. You will be recognised, and we shall be lost.'

'Fear not for that. I will disguise myself so effectually that my own mother would fail to recognise her own hopeful progeny.'

'Well, let us go below. Stay, what's that? A light on the beacon, by heavens! What can it mean?'

Hatchett said no more, but rushed down in the cabin.

He soon returned with a lantern and a rocket.

'Have you seen it again?' he asked of Bill.

'Yes. 'Tis red with a bright flash.'

'A vessel in sight. What can he mean? No one will venture to seek us here, surely?'

The light appeared again from a high point on the cliff, and Hatchett held up his lantern, which was provided with different coloured glass, each covered with a tin slide.

By means of the different lights—red, blue, green, and white—Hatchett held a conversation with the smuggler on the cliff, the purport of which was this—

'Cutter in the offing—dismasted—fast driving on the rocks—tar barrel burning.'

Hatchett held up the light again, and the signal was answered immediately.

'The cutter is driving on the gull's wing,' he said, turning to Rocket. 'What think you?—is it prudent to attempt their rescue?'

'There is only one danger, if we escape a wet coffin,' answered Bill.

'And that is'——

'The discovery of our whereabouts.'

'Yes, we have baffled them pretty well, and it would be a folly to shove our heads in the shark's jaws.'

'It would, as you say; but it would be against our laws to see a lot of brave fellows drown, while there's a chance of us saving them.'

'Well, just as you like, Captain Tom. Shall I turn up the lads, and man the yawl?'

'Yes; it would be no more than we should expect from others, though I have not the least hesitation in saying I believe they would string us up the next minute had they the chance.'

'Ahoy there! turn up lads! man the yawl!'

About a dozen smugglers answered the summons. They poured up the hatchway incredibly quick for their lumbersome attire, and as the rain poured down their backs, they swore tremendously.

'Well, what's up?' growled one, as he seized hold of the painter to haul up the boat, which was towing astern.

'A ship in distress, you grumbling swab! Now bear a hand!' cried Rocket.

Heedless of his wound, Bill seized the rope and slid down into the yawl, followed by the rest.

'All right there?' he shouted.

'Ay, ay,' was the much cheerfuller response, for the smugglers, though indifferent to the laws made by their rulers, were obedient to the laws of nature, and those of their own making.

'Let go, captain!' shouted Rocket, who was seated in the stern sheets. 'Now, lads, give way cheery.'

The men bent vigorously to their oars, and Hatchett strained his eyes after them until they were lost in the darkness of the night.

———

CHAPTER CXXIV.

GERALD STUART AND THE TIGER FRIGATE.

'Martinet, ahoy!' shouted Gerald Stuart, through his speaking trumpet, as he hove his ship to alongside the dismantled vessel.

'Ahoy!' replied Captain Henson. 'What cheer? Where have you left the liner I saw chasing you at sunset?'

'She is all right. I left her with her foremast hanging over her bows.'

'Did you settle her according to promise, without firing a shot?' asked Henson, doubtfully.

'That did I. But what have you done with the frigate?'

'She is not far off.'

'Out of sight, seemingly?'

'But not out of mind. He gave it me pretty hot.'

'So it seems. Did you beat him off?'

'We hit a warm one somewhere, but it was so dark we knew nothing for a fact. He hauled off, and we lost him before daybreak.'

'You have reason to believe he is about here, then?'

'Not far away. Hang him! he has cut away my topsail sheets, unrove half my running gear, carried away two of my spars, and left me almost a hulk as you see.'

'Quite bad enough, but not what I expected to see.'

'How—what do you mean?'

'I expected to see your ship all in pieces, and you floating on a hen-coop.'

'Thank you; you are as insulting as the commander of the frigate. His ship was called the Tiger. He styled himself the fighting tiger, and his men the fighting cubs. He was going to make faggots of my ship, ready to roast me for his breakfast in the morning, but he has not yet come for his meal.'

'I wish he would; I'd feed him on forced (meat) balls for a short time, and try what sort of an indigestion he has got.'

'The devil seize him, I say, before he comes here again!'

'Your prayers will avail him nothing, so save them till you go to the church at Havre, and while he's away, let us make good use of our time in setting you on your legs again, for you are in a sorry plight to run through the channel fleet.'

'Sorry am I to be compelled to acknowledge it. But see yonder, there's the very rogue coming again."

'No matter, leave him to me; I'll settle him.'

'Confound your insolence,' muttered Henson, 'the very devil himself is in you;' then aloud he added—

'What do you intend doing?'

'Well, I shall send a score of hands to assist you in rigging again.'

'But about the frigate? This is madness, you know.'

'Leave him to me. I have a pill for him he will not easily swallow.'

'Confound the fellow! How tarnation close he is, and yet he is clever, and I dare not gainsay him,' muttered Henson, savagely, tugging at a few straggling hairs that served as an apology for a moustache.

'Are you going to fight him?' he yelled at length.

'Fight the devil! Get on with your work; here come my men."

The launch had been hoisted out, and a score of the best seamen on board the Golden Arrow leapt into her.

Gerald Stuart then turned his vessel's head in the direction of the frigate. His intention was to meet her and cause her delay, so as to allow Henson time to get his vessel a little in trim.

He then ordered the men to breakfast, and, having issued various orders to the officers, he went below.

When he returned on deck he beat to muster, and a smile passed over his features, as he looked along the lines of gallant fellows, radiant with health and full of good humour.

'Are all the men here?' asked Gerald of the mate.

'One only is absent, sir,' said the mate, touching his cap.

'And who is that?'

'Jack Happleton, sir.'

'Where is he?'

'Below, sir.' answered the mate, hesitatingly.

'Below,' iterated the captain, sternly. 'Why is he not here? Did he not hear the drummer beat to muster?'

'He did, sir, but'——

'But what?' shouted Gerald, seeing his reluctance in answering; 'but what, sir? Let us have no "buts" here; let me hear the truth.

'The boatswain can best explain to you,' said the mate, shrinking from Gerald's passionate gaze.

'Marline!'

'Ay, ay! sir.'

'What know you of John Happleton?'

Marline cast a vicious glance at the mate, then, mustering courage, he replied—

'Nothing, yer honour.'

'Do you hear that, sir?' asked Gerald, turning to the mate.

''Tis false.'

'It's truth, your honour; I was below when'—— He stopped short.

'What—what? Go on,' said Gerald, sternly.

'When the mate was on deck.'

A grin ran along the lines of faces, and even the

captain felt half inclined to smile, for the boatswain pulled such a serious face.

The captain had some difficulty in controlling the risible muscles of his face; and with a stern look and still sterner voice he said—

'I can plainly see that some mischief has been worked between you, something that neither of you have the spirit to own, but try to shift on each other's shoulders; whatever it is I shall punish accordingly.'

'You, Marline, go below and fetch Happleton. I am determined to sift this thing to the bott om.'

Old Squeaker, or Pipes, as the boatswain enigmatically called him, cast a rueful glance at the rows of grinning faces, and walked away scratching his head.'

'Bravo, Pipes! Bring him up with a luff tackle,' whispered Tom Tiller.

'Hallo, Spunyarn, your're bowled out this time,' said another.

Marline gave the speakers a significant look, just to assure them they would not be forgotten, and passed silently on.

Although silent, the old boatswain did not forget to heap a few blessings on his tormentors, and had not the captain been less angry, he would have given them a sharp retort.

The mate took the first opportunity that offered to slink away, and tried to conceal himself behind the helmsman; and the captain stood with eyes riveted on the forecastle hatch, down which the boatswain had taken a precipitate dive.

Some minutes of silence ensued, and then a suppressed giggle came from the lines of jolly tars.

Marline appeared at the hatchway, sweating under the weight of Happy Jack, who, with rueful countenance, was riding on his back.

The giggle would have burst into a laugh, but the stern aspect of the captain restrained it,

He looked rebukingly at the sailors, and then fixed his eye on Jack, whose right foot and ankle were swathed in bandages.

'How now—how came this about?' he demanded, imperatively. 'Is this amusement, crippling one another?'

'Please, your honour,' said Marline, resting his load on the companion hatch, 'it was—it was an accident.'

'Then why so much secrecy?—so much shuffling, eh? Speak out.'

'Please, your honour,' again stammered Marline, 'Jack knows *most* about it.'

'So it seems; and you deserve a good drilling to loosen your jawing tackle. I have a mind to punish you for the pains you have taken in eluding my questions, and your obstinacy in not divulging what you do know of this matter. What have you to say for yourself?' he asked of Jack.

Jack dropped his eyes on the deck, looked at his bandaged foot, twisted his hat round in his hands, something after the style of a tambourine-player, and then giving a perplexed look at the captain, answered—

'Nothing, cap'n.'

'Nothing, be hanged to you! You are all tarred with one brush. Confound it! have you all forgotten how to speak the truth?'

Captain Stuart was in a rage.

His men had never seen him so much put out before.

BLACK EYED SUSAN.

OR, PIRATES ASHORE.

THE FATAL PROOF.

The culprits trembled, and many of the others began to feel their shoes too tight for them.

Jack's feelings were of all the least pleasant.

Independent of the pain which at times made him wince, he could feel the burning gaze of the skipper fixed upon him, and the captain's rebuke stung him to the quick.

The few moments silence that followed the captain's speech seemed to him like so many hours, and it was a great relief to him when Gerald said—

'Well, since you know nothing, let me know what this nothing is.'

Jack lifted his eyes from the deck, and, not daring to look at the captain, turned them towards the galley and made answer.

'Please your honour, and Pat knows all about it.'

Gerald bit his lip.

His men would not betray one another, and at any other time this would have pleased Gerald Stuart, but in the present state of feeling he set it down as defying his power.

'Mutiny,' he muttered to himself; 'but I will let the rascals see that I am not to be toyed with. I would punish the ringleaders of this conspiracy could I discover them, even though we are in sight of an enemy's ship and the experiment might prove dangerous.'

The inward working of his passion was perceivable in his clouded brow and quivering lip, spite of the effort he made to conceal it.

Turning to Pat, who stood in awe before him, he said, in as calm a voice as he could command—

'Well, sir, have you fabricated your story?'

Pat stood lost in perplexity.

'Fab—fab!' he stammered out; 'sure is it confab your honour manes?'

The captain was obliged to turn his head to hide a smile.

Whether to laugh or to be angry with the Irishman he did not know

'Is it ignorance or his natural cunning,' he asked of himself; 'if the former he is to be pitied, if the latter he deserves keelhauling.'

Thus he was thinking, when a shot from the frigate's bow-gun warned him that time was too precious to waste in this manner; and, that if he were not quick in his decision, the object he had in mustering his men would be totally frustrated.

Turning fiercely upon Pat, he said—

'Now, sir, disclose the whole of this plot. Tell me how this man's foot got injured. It lays with you, I feel certain; but if you speak the truth, and at once, I will forgive you for breach of discipline in time of war; if not, I will have you flogged as long as you can'——

Bang! again went the frigate's gun.

'Confound the fellow! he grows impatient; but he must wait till I think fit to return the compliment. Now, sir, your story.'

Pat left off playing with the tormentor, a staff of office he invariably carried, which he had been balancing in his hands as though he fancied it a shillelah, and began his story.

'Shure and it was this morning, your honour, that the bos'un piped to breakfast before siven bells, and the boys thronged about the galley like Tim Mullgan's pigs round a shwill tub, and for the soul of me would they give me time to ladle out the cocoa at all—at all!'

'Well, well!'

'They shwore, and I cursed; for the divil himself had placed his body in the copper, and I baled and baled, and couldn't so much as get a dhrop!'

'What was the reason?' asked Gerald, impatiently.

'Shure, your honour, we didn't know. The ladle touched the bottom, and yet it didn't; and I cursed all hands, saving your honour's self, for they laughed at me, do you see? and I was ryled.'

Gerald stamped his foot.

'What was in the copper? Tell me at once, without this peramble.'

'Bless your honour! it was meself that soon found out. I seized the tormentor, and sez I to meself, "Divil or no divil, out you come!" and in I thrust it; but what was my surprise, yer honour, to find that instead of the divil, sparing yer honour's presence, it was a thirty-two pound shot! How I got it out, it's meself can't tell yer honour, for it bobbed and rolled and dodged round and round in such a manner, that would have puzzled the old one himself, sparing yer honour's presence, to catch a hoult on it.'

'But you caught it at last?'

'Caught, by the tarn! Had it been the dev—saving yer honour's presence—had it been twinty shots lashed in one I'd a caught it; but it gave me throuble enough, by St. Pater! and niver shall I forgit it.'

'But the foot—how did it get hurt?'

'I'm coming to it, yer honour, as the shot said as it shlipped out of the nit we'd made to catch it, and fell schalding hot as is was on Happy's foot and smashed his three toes, and peeled all the shkin off his foot as claen as you'd'——

'That will do,' said Gerald. 'I have heard sufficient.' Then turning to the men assembled, he addressed them thus—

'I hope this will be a warning for the future, and that all such skylarking, as you term it, but which in reality has turned out a serious misfortune to one of your shipmates, will for the future be abolished. Not only have you deprived yourselves of a meal you stand so much in need of, but you have aroused my anger to a pitch that might have proved grievous to all. You are aware that we are short handed, that every man's services is much needed, and that if fortune, who has proved generous to us, should desert us now, we would have to fight with an enemy more than three times our equal.'

'Look there,' he added, vehemently; "see you that ship? it is the Fighting Tiger. Many of you know her well, all have no doubt heard of her, and the renown of her fire-eating commander, Captain Bristle.'

'Ay, ay!' burst from the men with one accord.

'Well, then, it is to prepare you for this that I have mustered you, trusting that, in event of our having to fight, not one will be found wanting in courage or missed from his post; that you will fight as long as we have a plank to float, or a foot of bunting to show to the breeze."

'Ay, ay, we will,' was the general response, and Captain Gerald believed it sincere.

'Well done, my lads,' he continued; 'you will not be forgotten, from the cabin-boy upwards. Your reward shall be great, I need not say equal to your need; for I have faith enough to believe that every man will do his duty in the respective station he fills, and that the Golden Arrow will not lose one item of the honour and distinction she has already won.'

So saying, he descended to the cabin, but was

only a minute absent ere he returned to the deck attired in the disguise that had occasioned so much surprise on a former occasion, but now seemed quite familiar.

He had scarcely time to issue orders to the different officers, when the frigate ranged alongside.

'Ship ahoy!' was shouted through the speaking trumpet, though the vessels were within biscuit toss of each other.

'Well,' was the cool response of Gerald.

'What ship is that?—and why did you not answer my signal? It is a wonder you have escaped sinking.'

'It is the first I have heard of it.'

'Then it won't be the last,' thundered Bristle, 'so you will find. Why did you not heave-to, when I fired? and what were you doing alongside that vessel?'

'That is rather an impertinent question, I think,' said Gerald, provokingly. 'What is your opinion?'

'That you are a scoundrel!' vociferated Bristle, 'and '——

'You are what?'

'You shall know before we part.'

'Ah! I have a shrewd guess.'

'Indeed, sir! What do you mean?'

'That you are a fool to meddle with other people's business.'

Gerald had a reason for changing the theme, and the captain of the frigate was so infatuated as not to see through the dodge.

'Business,' repeated Bristle; 'what am I to suppose that word implies?'

'Boarding yonder ship, and taking'——

'Taking what?' thundered Bristle. "You boarded her, by heavens! after me crippling her last night, and standing by her till this morning to take her. Sir this is an insult I must resent. Heave-to, or I'll blow you out of the water.'

Gerald had veered his ship round, and brought her on the frigate's weather-quarter, so as to bring her between the Martinel and the Golden Arrow, so that, in case he should fail in deceiving Bristle, as he had done the others, both ships could engage the frigate.

Captain Henson had made good use of his armament, small as it was, for the frigate bore evidence of it both aloft and in her hull. Several shot plugs could be seen driven through her sides from the inside, and her sails were torn, and several of her stays and shrouds were stoppered in many places where they had been cut through.

This was the cause of the frigate hauling off, though Captain Bristle was too proud to acknowledge it; and Captain Stuart, on closer scrutiny, saw that her pumps had been worked during the night, which convinced him that she had received a shot below the water-line.

Aided by the Golden Arrow's men, Captain Henson soon got his vessel in trim.

Her topsails were mastheaded, fresh top-gallant sails, and royals bent, new running gear rove, fresh studding-sail booms lashed on the yards, and the gun tackling that had been shot away renewed.

Keeping on his way under easy sail, Captain Henson awaited either for a signal from Gerald, or the return of the Golden Arrow, which ever might come first.

Captain Stuart laughed at Bristle when he threatened to blow him out of the water, and this so exasperated the captain of the frigate, that, in spite of the British ensign floating at the Golden Arrow's peak, he felt inclined to fire into him without further parley.

The frigate's crew were at their quarters, the guns cast loose, and the upper half ports on the main deck triced up ready.

'Let down the lower half ports on the main deck, and run in the guns,' said Bristle to his lieutenant.

'Load the left-hand guns with grape, and the right-hand with round shot. That will warm them,' he added to himself, 'and teach them to show due respect to a king's ship.

The word was passed below, and the sailors obeyed the order with alacrity.

They were the fighting tigers, and smoke and battle was their watchword.

Incredulous and prodigious feats of valour were accredited to them by the various captains of vessels they had saved, when cruising on the coast of Barbary to protect the merchantmen from the depredations of the pirates, who captured and slaughtered the crews of any unfortunate vessel that chanced to be driven on the coast.

Sometimes they stood off to sea, and attacked them even in sight of the opposite shore, and on one occasion it was the fortune of Captain Bristle to rescue a nobleman and his family, who were returning to England, from the hands of these bloodthirsty wretches.

The captain had taken the precaution to hug the Italian and Spanish shores; but one morning when he considered all danger past, four large galleys, each containing about one hundred men, suddenly came in sight.

Captain Truman tried to avoid them, but they sailed so swift, and the long sweeps gave them so much advantage over him, that this was hopeless, and unless something unforeseen occurred, it was evident what would be their fate.

Two of the foremost galleys swept across his bows, and, wheeling round, lowered their sails and awaited their coming on the port side, the other two pulling swiftly up on the starboard.

Thus hemmed in, Captain Truman did not know what to do. Every precaution it was possible he had taken. His ship's sides had been greased from stem to stern with the cook's slush, and the carronades, of which there were four, were loaded and got into the best position.

The next difficulty was to work them with something like precision, for the second mate, who had been a gunner in the navy, and was the only one on board who understood practical firing, had lost his life in hauling in a shark; the line had got entangled in his legs in some way, and several of the hands, who were assisting him, having relaxed their hold, the mate was drawn over the taffrail, and, with the plunging fish, disappeared beneath the waves. Once he rose to the surface, and then, with one wild shriek, disappeared for ever.

The captain was a determined man, and strong of nerve, and he fired the four carronades as fast as they were loaded by the men, but with no effect; and two of the galleys stood towards them, their crews laughing derisively at their puny efforts.

The other two galleys had sighted fresh prey; it was a brig, and they made all speed towards her. She was coming on steadily, as though ignorant of her impending danger. When the galleys were within gun-shot, however, she turned, and made all sail in the opposite direction.

The pirates, fearful of losing their prey, redoubled their exertions at the sweeps, and fired their swivel guns and arquebuses at the sails and riggings. The sails, one after the other, came down by the run, and the brig's speed being thus diminished, the pirates came on either side of her.

It was fortunate they intended boarding her amidships instead of on the quarter (by this means they thought of pouring all hands on the deck at once), for they thus exposed themselves to the brig's broadside, which opened and poured into them such a deadly fire as sank both galleys at once.

This somewhat startled the others, who were alongside the barque endeavouring to board her.

The grease on the ship's side annoyed them much, especially as she was high out of the water, and they could get no hold of anything.

This grease affair had been practised so much of late, and baffled them so often, that the pirates had provided against it by carrying-ropes with grapnals attached, which they threw up into the rigging, and having thrown dry sand from a scoop on to the grease, tried to get a foot-hold.

But they were baffled again, for the cook, armed with a pan, kept pouring scalding fat on them, which caused them to retreat, and howl with pain.

Howling and cursing, the pirates leapt about like madmen, and then making a desperate effort under cover of a score of arquebusses, they almost effected a boarding.

One of the sailors was shot through the neck, he having lifted his head above the rail, and the cook shot a pirate on the port-side, just as he had gained a footing in the chains.

The captain and mate, armed with a musket, of which there were only two on board of any account, kept up a fire on both sides through the port.

In the meantime the brig settled accounts with the other two boats, and then bore down to the assistance of the barque.

A short and desperate struggle then ensued.

Captain Bristle (for it was he), being unable to fire his broadside guns for fear of riddling the barque, had to engage in the boats. and fight the pirates hand to hand.

Seeing their comrades likely to be beaten, the galley on the opposite side shoved off, and her crew pulled rapidly in the direction of the Barbary shore, but their companions' shouts caused them to return, and give them their assistance.

Bloody and fearful was the battle, the pirates numbering six to one of their plucky foes, who let them taste their steel with no niggard hand.

Captain Bristle drew up his few marines on the quarter, and as the second galley came round the barque's stern, he gave them a warm reception.

The pirates fought desperately, and the boat's crew, stimulated by the cries of their friends, cut down all before them.

From the ships little could be done, as the combatants were so mixed, and swayed about like a surging sea, but whenever a stray shot could find a victim, the opportunity was not lost.

Whilst the fight was at its height, the captain was startled by a scream in the cabin, and on rushing below, a sight presented itself that froze him with terror.

Two of the dusky wretches had found a way in at the cabin window, and the head of a third was just above the port sill. The foremost one held the youngest child in his arms, and with upraised scimetar, stood ready to sweep off its head. The other held the lady by the hair of her head, which was thrown back, so as to force her on her knees, and the point of a long knife, held daggerwise, was pressed to her fair bosom, down which the blood began to trickle.

The nobleman lay on the floor, half-stunned by a blow that left a deep gash on his forehead, unable to rise, or render them any assistance.

Sudden as was the sight presented to him, Captain Truman was not long in recovering his self-possession.

A bullet passed through the head of the wretch that held the lady, and a blow from the clubbed musket felled the other to the deck.

The third one seeing how matters stood, raised a pistol and fired at the captain, but fortunately it missed him, and the head disappeared with a groan.

Captain Truman had dealt him a blow similar to that he had given the villain who threatened the life of the child.

Having settled matters below, Captain Truman rushed on deck, where his men were engaged hand to hand with several of the crew who had boarded from the galley, and the captain having reloaded his musket, went forward.

A desperate and deadly struggle, that cost more than one sailor's life, and resulted in the defeat of the pirates, then ensued.

The marines' muskets did fearful execution on board the second galley, and the brig's stern-chaser, that had been brought to bear on her, poured in its grape and canister with terrible effect.

A panic then seized the pirates, and they leapt overboard in all directions to escape the murdering fire and the fatal blades of the men-of-war's-men.

Captain Bristle lost twelve men in that action; but he won a laurel for himself and the rest of his crew.

On board the galleys, neither of which were sunk for some time after, they found plenty of treasure, the plunder taken from many an unfortunate ship, and besides this, the captain and his noble passengers made him a handsome present, and made a good report of their actions when they arrived home.

With this recommendation Captain Bristle and his men were removed to the Tiger, where his glorious deeds and gallant bravery won him fresh laurels, and gained them the appellation of the fighting tigers.

Gerald Stuart heard the word passed, and watched the various preparations; but he only smiled, though he well knew what to expect should he receive the contents of the dark line of guns.

Taking the speaking trumpet in his hand for the first time, he shouted through it—

'Am I to consider you a pirate, and make prisoners of you in the king's name, that you would fire into a vessel sailing under his Majesty's orders?'

'The devil!' gasped Bristle, taken thoroughly aback; 'are you a '——

'Privateer,' interrupted Gerald; 'and here is my commission, as you would call it.'

'A letter of marque.'

'The same; and you can examine it of you like.'

At a signal from Gerald his gig was lowered, and in a few moments more he stood on the frigate's deck.

Captain Bristle opened the packet handed to him, and ran his eye over it.

Eyeing Gerald, he said—

'Then you are Captain Bullyton of the Lotus? You have changed much in appearance, though not in manners, since last I saw you. Your obstinacy will one day cost you dear.'

'How so?'

'Why the devil did you not show me this before? You might have caused me to waste my ammunition, and have parted from me with a ton of metal sticking in the Lotus's sides.'

'I have no fear of that,' said Gerald, laughing; 'but do you mean to say I have so changed that you did not recognise me?'

'You have.'

'For the better?'

'Slightly; though, I must say, that you exceed in rashness, and that will'——

'Carry me through the world.'

'Rather quicker than you will care for,' answered Bristle, slightly piqued; 'but I see your orders are limited. You cannot sail in the channel, so I will relieve you of your charge, and convey her to Portsmouth at once.'

'No, thank you, Captain Bristle,' said Gerald, smiling; 'the owners have fitted the Lotus out at some expense, and will, at least, expect something in return. I have captured yonder ship, and a prize crew is on board of her.'

'But you dare not carry her past the Eddystone. She will be captured again by the first king's ship you meet.'

'I dare any do anything with this,' said Gerald, coolly, handing as he spoke a piece of parchment to the astonished Bristle. 'That is signed, as you see,' he added, 'by Admiral Garthway, and dated but a day or two ago. I am to have assistance from any king's ship I may need it of, and also to pass up channel unmolested.'

'It is as you say,' said Bristle, rather dejectedly, 'and I cannot gainsay it, though it is strange he should give you so much power.'

'Will you affix your signature?'

'I will; come below.'

Gerald went below, and he could not help smiling to himself as he thought how nicely his ruse had succeeded.

Captain Bristle treated him cordially, and handed him wine and biscuits, and then sat down to write.

A vessel at that moment was reported from the masthead, and the middy entered the cabin to acquaint Bristle with that fact.

'What is she?' growled Bristle, vexed at being disturbed.

'A two-decker; but she shows no colours yet.'

'Is she coming this way?'

'Yes, sir, and is carrying every stitch she can aloft.'

Captain Bristle soon finished writing, and, handing the packet to Gregory, shook him warmly by the hand.

Gregory was in no humour to prolong his stay; he was uncertain what ship it might be that was coming down on them, so he took his leave, and just as he reached his own ship the stranger hoisted the English flag.

———

CHAPTER CXXV.

A NIGHT OF HORROR—THE 'THREE LUGGERS' HAS A STRANGE VISITOR.

SINCE the night of the tragical events recorded in a previous chapter, Silas Doggrass became an altered man.

Instead of the bold, threatening look that terrified all beneath him, and made those that by pecuniary circumstances were thrown in his power, quail before him. He now moved about as though some fearful doom hung over him.

He would start at times at the sound of his own footsteps, and stare fearfully about him when the noise of the tap-room roysterers became louder than usual.

The scene of that fearful night seemed to fix itself on his memory, and the sailor's pale visage, as the blood flowed from his wound, haunted his imagination.

Vain were his efforts to shake off the spell.

Fruitless were his attempts to drown his memory in the oft-repeated doses of ardent spirits.

It was of no use.

The trap, the stain upon the floor, reminded him of that which he would have given worlds to forget.

'Fool!' he muttered to himself, as one night he sat pouring tumbler after tumbler of the fiery fluid down his parched throat; 'fool that I am to be frightened at my own shadow. No one but myself knows the secret, so what need I fear? Aha!' he continued, 'I see my folly now. Silas Doggrass, you must shake off these babyish fears. Confound it! what makes my hand tremble so? that hand that would not have faltered in taking the life of my dearest friend! Yes,' he muttered, half aloud, as though debating some important question in his mind, 'I will remove the body to-night from beneath the hatch; it will at least be a comfort to know it is not beneath my feet.'

He rose to put his resolve into execution, but he trembled so, that his strength was only as a child's.

After great exertion he removed the table, and then raised the trap; but before descending, he fortified himself with another tumbler of spirits.

'Ah! that is the mainstay and renovator of nerves,' he said half aloud, as he replaced the empty glass on the table. 'I will now go boldly to my task.'

But his words were boastful.

His legs seemed to totter under him.

His whole frame shook with an inward fear.

As he took the candle it danced about in his palsied grasp, yet he did not relinquish his purpose, but slowly descended to the vault.

Straining his bleared eyes to pierce through the gloom, he looked about for the body, though half fearful of the sight that might meet his gaze.

'Strange! strange!' he muttered, as the object of his search did not reward his sight. 'He was here! By what means has the body been removed?'

He raised the light, and moved a few paces forward.

Still he could find no clue to the body.

Doggrass began to grow impatient.

His task was anything but a pleasant one, and he wanted to get through it.

'Curse his infernal carcase!' he burst out at

length. 'It laid here, I could swear. By what mysterious means it has been removed, I know not !'

He trembled at his own sacrilegious words, and timidly glanced around.

Still nothing could he see but the bare walls or mouldy casks, on which the cob-webs thickly hung.

Advancing two or three paces into the gloom, he was startled by a noise that sounded much like a footfall.

'Is it ? no ; it cannot be !' he muttered, banishing the thought as it rose to his mind. 'Nothing but rats infest this place, and perhaps it is to them the removal of the body is owing. If so, they have taken bones and all, for not a vestige remains.'

The sound that startled him so much was again heard, this time much plainer, and the old villain shook as though he had been seized with an attack of ague.

Suddenly, however, a sort of brute courage possessed him.

'I will search the vaults,' he muttered to himself; 'nothing more horrible than I have seen before can assail my vision. I will search. Ah ! confound it ! my legs seem too weak for my support.'

It was true his legs were too weak to hold him. They tottered in such a manner as to threaten him falling.

This altered his resolve, and he only thought how it was best for him to return, and clutching at the wall, he stood several minutes ere he dare essay to reach the steps.

After a time, he managed to do so with great difficulty, and as he turned to glance into the vault before ascending, a figure, clothed in white, assailed his eyes.

'God of heaven !' he gasped, for he could scarcely give utterance to that holy name; 'this is condemning me at once to perdition. Let me but live to repent of this, and my future life shall be one of penitence.'

'Wretched mortal !—thou hast too often promised that which thy avarice will not let thee perform,' said a voice, sepulchral and hollow, that froze the very marrow in his bones, and yet terrified him so that he scrambled up the ladder, and as soon as he reached the room, the trap he closed with a bang.

The secret spring held it secure, so that he had nothing to fear on that score, if the thing he saw was mortal; but he gazed in horror on the blood-stained floor, and fancied each moment to see some spectre rise up from it.

The horrors of that night were truly awful to him ; for he could not rise from the seat into which he had fallen, and, though, he gulped down all the brandy that lay within his reach, he was wide awake when daylight began to straggle into the apartment.

Susan rose as usual, and went about her accustomed duties with a seeming cheerfulness; yet there was that in her looks that told she had passed a sleepless night.

A something which the most casual observer would have detected, but which her uncle failed himself to notice.

'Susan, my child,' he said to her, as one by one the customers began to drop in, 'you must attend to the business. I leave all to you, as my bodily infirmities grow upon me daily, and deprive me of the power I once possessed.'

Mrs. Howard—or, Susan, as we must continue to call her—glanced in his face with a troubled look.

His husky voice and bloodshot eyes sent a thrill through her that she could not account for.

'You are ill,' she said, in a tone that betrayed her emotions; 'had you not better go to bed, and let Dame Howard attend you ?'

'No, no,' he replied, hastily casting an anxious glance at the table, which he had been unable to replace. 'I have not yet come to that. Go you into the tap, and serve those noisy vagrants, or they will grow bold, and help themselves.'

Having rid himself of his niece's presence, the old villain made a desperate effort, and got the table in its proper position.

He felt easier now, for he dreaded lest anyone should discover his horrible secret.

'She is a good girl,' he muttered to himself, 'and possesses not the curiosity of her sex, so that my secret rests safe from her; and, as to Dame Howard, the old woman has troubles enough to occupy her mind without interfering with the business of others.'

Silas Doggrass was wrong, however, in his calculation.

When Susan closed the door that separated the apartment from the bar, she stepped on to a stool, and looked through a small window, where she could observe him without his noticing her.

The noise of the customers silenced as she made her appearance.

The boisterous fishermen ceased their badinage, and began extolling her charms to one another in whispers.

The position offered them excellent opportunity for this, for Susan, in addition to her beautiful looks, had a faultless form and a delicate little foot, with well-turned ancle, which, owing to the shortness of her clothes and her elevated position, was exposed to the rude gaze of the critics.

Susan, owing to her husband's trial and the vicissitudes she had been subjected to, was a mark of admiration and wonderment to the people of Deal, and formed the chief topic of the conversation of visitors to the place, who seldom failed to drop into the Three Luggers to get a glimpse of her before leaving.

It so happened on this eventful morn that, when Susan had satisfied the wants of the fishermen, and they had taken their departure, two venerable old gentlemen, whom she had not before noticed, drew her attention to them.

'Tell me, pretty maid,' said one, in a joking tone, 'have you a room where we can sit undisturbed, and transact our business ?'

'Indeed, we have not. There is the common room ; but that is open to all comers,' Susan replied, with slight perturbation, for her mind was greatly troubled with unpleasant thoughts that had occurred to her. 'Stay,' she said, after a moment's reflection ; 'perhaps my uncle can accommodate you.'

Glancing into the room where she had left him, she found it empty, and she ushered them in.

'Thanks, my pretty one. It is not often we meet with such beauty in an outlandish port, especially at a tavern. Were you in London, those rosy lips and sparkling eyes would procure you a fortune.'

'I need none,' was Susan's modest reply, as she turned to leave. 'If you need anything, you will please to call, as my time is too precious to idle.'

'Stay,' said one, who had acted as spokesman,

divesting himself of his sword and hat, ' your hurry is not so great, I presume, but you can stay to receive our orders?'

'Believe me, it is,' said Susan, repenting her rashness in allowing them to enter without consulting her uncle, especially as they bore the appearance of holding a commission under government, and one of them had hung up his sword and hat as though he meant staying some time; 'my uncle will be angry if I neglect my work.'

'Your work! Sure your uncle is not such a scurvy knave as to let you work? Had I a niece half as beautiful, she should wait on none but me.'

'Indeed! Then it is a pity you have not one,' answered Susan, returning his amorous glance with a frown. 'As it is, I am thankful you are not my uncle.'

'Why?'

'Because your presence would not always suit me.'

'Ugh!' and he gave a sly glance at his companion as he spoke. 'Where is thy uncle that precedes me in this favour? Call him; let us see our worthy host.'

'You cannot; he is at present engaged. I can serve you with what you require; and, as I have given you the use of a private apartment to transact your business, I hope you will do so at once.'

Susan felt anything but easy in her mind.

She could not understand the character of her visitors, and dreading her uncle's displeasure, if she had done wrong in admitting them, she wished they were gone. But she had difficult customers to deal with, as she soon found.

'Ah, you are acting without permission,' said one. 'Well, we know what it is to disobey orders.'

'Practically, I suppose,' retorted Susan; 'unfortunately I am not; therefore'——

'Tut, tut. Use will soon accustom you to it; besides, one in your capacity must not be too exact. Your beauty would provide for your wants, if this tyrant of an uncle dismissed you.'

'Sir! I am surprised at you,' said Susan, indignantly, as the truth of his suggestions flashed to her mind. "You have mistaken me for some other'——

'No, no,' said he, interrupting her. 'Admiral Lanceville makes no mistake. You may hoist false lights and throw out false signals, but you cannot deceive me. I can read your character at a glance.'

Susan made no reply. With an indignant toss of her head, she hurriedly approached the door.

'Avast! my pretty one; don't make sail so fast. I see you are taken aback.'

As he spoke, the admiral caught her dress, and drew her from the door.

'Unhand me, sir!' she said, turning round fiercely. 'My Uncle Doggrass is not here to protect me from insult; but I would warn you to be careful how you tamper with the honour of a sailor's wife.'

'What! Are you married?' asked the admiral, in surprise.

'I am. And though circumstances have deprived me of the arm that should shield me, touch me not again at your peril.'

'Sorry am I that you should have mistaken my meaning,' said the admiral, soothingly. 'Did you not say your uncle's name was Doggrass?'

'I did. You must be a stranger here not to have known it.'

'Indeed I am. Important business has hurried me from town, and on leaving the coach, me and my friend dropped in here as the nearest tavern. Chance has thrown us in company with an angel, as you are, so I claim forgiveness for any offence I have given you. But, tell me,' said the admiral, 'is your name not Susan?'

As he spoke, he gradually dispelled the repugnance she at first felt towards him, and he clasped both her hands as he glanced good-humouredly in her face.

Susan remained some moments in silence with her eyes cast down, nor did she make any effort to free her hands, so great was the influence his speech held over her.

At length she replied—

'My name is Susan Howard; and, if you are truly Admiral Lanceville, you can remember my husband's name.'

'William Howard! In truth, do I. It was through my influence that Captain Crosstree obtained a discharge for him. I remember the disgraceful trial; but I am sorry to hear that he has made such bad use of it.'

Susan sighed.

'It was not of his own will. It was through the tyranny and designing craft of others that he became what he is,' said Susan. 'Truer man never served the king; but how were his services rewarded?'

'Poor fellow,' exclaimed the admiral, glancing meaningly at his friend; 'I heartily pity him, and did I know his whereabouts, I would do all in my power to raise him to a more exalted station. You are the only one, I presume, that he entrusts with his secret?'

Susan did not see the smile that played on his wily lips, as he put the question to her, and she answered, innocently—

'It is long since I have seen him, and many wish me to believe him dead. As to where he is, I know no more than you do.'

'Not so much, probably,' thought the admiral. 'I expect his arrival in the captured vessel, that was taken off Cherbourg; and I hope to-day to see him safe in irons, and lodged between four walls of stone.'

Such, indeed, was the wish of the crafty admiral.

For that purpose he had been posted to Deal, to fill the office of Admiral Garthway, who, as we have seen, had put to sea in the line-of-battle ship.

And now he had seen the lovely "Black-Eyed-Susan," that was causing much sensation in the metropolis, and, indeed, in every seaport town, he became enamoured of her charms, and longed to possess her.

This desire made him the more anxious for her husband's death.

As he did not wish to raise any suspicions by asking too many questions, he called for a bottle of wine, and held a long conference with his companion.

Doggrass, in the meantime, had taken Susan's advice, and retired to his room; but the sound of strange voices in the lower room aroused him, and he crept stealthily down, and listened.

Whatever was the subject of their conversation, it gave evident delight to the listener, for he grinned and chuckled to himself, and when they were about to depart, he peeped from his hiding-place, and, having gained a sufficient glance at their features, so as to know them again, he crept softly back to his room.

Susan was busily serving the crew of a man-of-war's launch, when the admiral called her, to settle for what they had had.

'Take this,' he said, 'for the trouble we have occasioned you,' and as he spoke, he slipped a guinea and a small note into her hand, in addition to the pay.

Scarce knowing what she was doing, Susan accepted it.

When she recovered from her surprise, the stranger had passed out, and, hearing footsteps descending the stairs, she returned to the bar.

The sailors, who had stolen away from the boat during the absence of their officer, to refresh themselves with a nip of spirits, were conversing earnestly about one of the parties just left.

'Did you sight his jib, Bill?' asked one.

'Ah, did I, and as piratical a figure-'ed as ever I saw, he carried under that three-cornered sky-sail of his.'

This allusion to the admiral's hat drew a grin from his mate.

The appearance of the coxswain, however, silenced their mirth.

'Now, lads, tumble down to the boats,' he said. 'Don't make a meal of a mouthful of grog. I 'spose you've clapped on the bilge pumps, and drained the grog monkey as dry as a purser's bread bag.'

'Avast! don't pay out your slack so cheery; Black-eyed Susan will give you a dipper of water if your throat's so parched, won't you, lass—eh?'

'That will I,' replied Susan with a smile.

'And a small wee drop of spirits in it just to kill the insects,' said the coxswain, grinning.

'But who was that fellow?' asked the coxswain, of Bill, rather seriously.

'What, he with the three-cornered scraper?'

'Ay, my hearty! I'll swear he's not one of the fleet.'

'You'll swear right; he's a reg'lar fresh-water gudgeon; I knows him. He was in the Inflexible, but somehow he got to join the board, and has a big house in London.'

'The swab-wringing rascal!' said the coxswain, as he swallowed up his grog; 'what's the Admiralty sent him sniffing down here for?'

'Well, I guess it's for this,' said a dry old tar sending a cloud of smoke from his lips, that threatened to choke all hands; 'he's come down here in search of a beef-eater to stick in the Tower.'

'And he'll get one, if he fall athwart you,' replied the coxswain; 'and I, for one of your messmates, will give you a good recommendation.'

'Swamp me! it will be taking the job out o' your hands; but come on, I see the recal hoisted.'

From the door of the Three Luggers they could see the frigate to which they belonged making a signal for the boat's return.

When they had gone Susan was alone, and she took the opportunity to examine the note which she had crushed, and thrust into her pocket.

It ran thus:—

"DEAR SUSAN,—

　"Come to the White Villa, at the hour of nine, or any time after dusk; I will see you, and you will likely hear something to your advantage.

　　"Your Sincere Friend,

　　　"ADMIRAL LANCEVILLE."

CHAPTER CXXVI.

THE PIRATES' DOOM—HORRIBLE SCENE ON BOARD THE SLAVE SHIP.

As the pale moon peeped from behind the fleeting clouds, and lit up the deck of the slaver, it revealed a horrible sight.

Here and there, weltering in gore, were the bodies of those slain in the affray.

Grouped about the deck was the remainder of the crew, stripped as they had leapt from their hammocks, and brandishing some formidable weapon in their hands.

Aft on the quarter-deck was the slaving captain and his mate.

A little apart stood Will Howard, stanching the blood that was flowing from a wound in the pirate captain's breast.

The rest of the pirates, who had escaped death, were battened down in the hold below.

'Now, villain!—murderer!' said the captain to Gregory Saunders; 'what is the meaning of this vile treachery? Have you been too well fed and cared for, that you turn upon us before the voyage has fairly commenced?'

The mate looked sullen, and made no reply.

'Speak!' added the captain, vexed at his silence.

'And if I do, what shall I gain by it?'

'That all depends on the defence you make. If you can give a just reason for your conduct, then I am ready to forgive you.'

'Very considerate of you, I must own.'

'Merciful, you should say.'

'Well, we won't quarrel about a difference of opinion.'

'Wretch! we shall quarrel soon, if you do not answer my question.'

'That will be no strange matter. We have been none of the best of friends since the night we left Havannah.'

'How was that?'

'You struck me; you must have soon forgotten it. I never shall.'

'It was excuseable. I was drunk.'

'If that excuses you, I have the same to plead.'

'Insolent rascal! this is too much!' vociferated the captain, savagely.

'As I surmised—our opinions differ. I had rathe kept silent.'

'You had better spoken the truth.'

'Aha! the truth!' laughed Gregory, in a bitter tone; 'the truth! 'Tis well for the captain of an *ebony* packet to talk of truthfulness, when his safety in every port depends upon the quantity of lies he can tell.'

'Fiend! if you taunt me, I will wring out your accursed heart!' cried the captain, fiercely. 'Monster! this badinage will avail you nothing.'

'Say on,' replied Gregory, affecting a tone of indifference quite foreign to his feeling. 'Say on, noble captain; chance has favoured you more than me.'

'And well it has so. You would have slain my man in cold blood, and the punishment for this shall be more terrible than you expect.'

'Is that villain dead?' he asked of Will.

'He is not. More than once I thought he had slipped his wind, but he hangs on to life as closely as ever ship did.'

BLACK EYED SUSAN.

OR, PIRATES ASHORE.

THE SPY ON DEAL BEACH.

M.U. SEARS. SC.

''Tis the way with such black-muzzled rascals,' said the captain, with a vicious grin.

'Ay, they have as many lives as a cat, and take as much killing as an elephant,' growled Will, as he poured some water down the pirate's throat, and threw some in the pirate's face to revive him, as he had fainted. 'Ah! you d—d swab!'

This exclamation burst from him as he sprang to his feet, and leapt towards Gregory.

He had taken advantage of the captain's attention being called for a moment to another part of the vessel, and seizing a knife, he was about to bury it in the captain's breast, when Will arrested his arm.

'Scoundrel!' Will hissed, as he wrenched it from his hand. 'I am half resolved to give you the length of its blade, but I would not stain my hands with the blood of so vile a cur! '

'Curse you! May thy slandering tongue wither!' yelled Gregory, as he closed with gallant Will; but the sailor frustrated his design to clutch him by the throat, and hurled him backward on the deck.

'Fiend! thou shalt curse the hour we met!' hissed Gregory through his clenched teeth, as he made an effort to rise.

A blow from the captain's pistol, however, floored him, and he laid on the deck senseless and bleeding from a wound in his forehead.

The captain strode forward.

'Now, lads, he said, to his men, 'it lays with you what shall be the fate of the mutineers.'

'We leave it to your better judgment,' replied one of the men.

'I would rather you would not,' replied the captain. You know our laws, and you know what crime the mate has committed. If not, I must tell you he has mutinied, and the punishment of mutiny is'——

'Death! death!' came from all quarters.

'Death, let it be, then, if you are so minded. I now give you half an hour to decide between yourselves what that death shall be.'

When the captain left, the men all grouped around Sancho.

'It appeared they looked upon him as their leader, and his tall herculean form looked noble as he stood in their midst.

'Well, comrades,' he asked as he raised his powerful voice, 'what do you propose—hanging, shooting, or a journey on the plank?'

'Let them be thrown overboard!' was the general cry. 'Let the sharks eat them alive.'

Sancho shuddered.

The slavers were indeed hard upon their enemies.

'Is that the opinion of all?' asked Sancho.

'Every one of us!' replied a voice.

'Then I will acquaint the captain with your wish. Shall I?'

'Yes, yes.'

'Before I go, mind,' said Sancho, 'I only repeat your wish. If there is any misunderstanding, or any of you are averse to this decision, I will not bear the blame.'

'You will not need to. We are agreed to a man.'

'It is enough,' said Sancho, as he walked aft.

'If such is their decree, I must abide by it,' said the captain, when Sancho had told him what passed.

'And a fit one, too,' said Will, who stood by; 'but see, the rascal is recovering from the blow you gave him.'

The pirate captain was coming round, and as his eyes opened, he glared around like a savage beast.

Wiping the clotted gore from his brow, he essayed to rise, but he seemed too weak for the effort, and failed.

'God!' he gasped hoarsely, 'aid me in my revenge; or if thou wilt not assist, I invoke the aid of all the foul fiends!'

'They will hear thy prayer, nay, listen to it,' said Will, who heard his words; 'the more so, as thou art one of the infernal legion.'

The pirate threw a glance of deadly hatred towards him, and muttered a bitter curse on his head.

The hatches were now opened, and the pirates brought on deck.

There was a hang-dog sort of look about them.

The men of the slaver treated them with little gentleness, for the fate of their comrades rankled in their breasts.

This feeling was rendered more bitter by the recollection of the fate they had so narrowly escaped.

The pirates looked around in sullen silence.

They could see that some terrible fate awaited them; but they could gain no clue as to what that fate would be.

Not a ray of pity could they see in the faces of their captors.

Their looks were stern and remorseless.

'Are these all that are left?' asked the captain of his men.

'Yes,' was the reply.

It was the second mate who spoke, and he stood ready, with sleeves rolled up, to act as executioner.

The pirates stood in a line, and the crew of the slaver stood over them, ready to cut any of them down that might offer resistance.

'Now, sir, do your duty,' said the captain; 'lead up the first. They need no time for praying. They have had sufficient time to atone for their sins during their stay in the hold.'

The pirate captain groaned and glanced at Will's pistol, as though he did not like its proximity.

"Make youself comfortable,' Will said; 'your turn is not yet come; as captain, it is your duty to see your men all safe on their journey and then to follow them.'

'H—l and furies!' raved the pirate captain; 'strike out, men; do not let these tyrants carry out their hellish work.'

Rendered desperate by their position, and goaded by the words of their captain, several of the pirates rushed upon the sailors who stood guard over them.

This rash act was a signal for their death.

Right and left the sailors cut and slashed, and the offenders soon lay bleeding and mangled on the deck.

The second mate was in the midst of the *melee*, and having sent his sword through one and pinned him to the mast, he seized another in his brawny arms, and hurled him overboard.

Sancho joined him in this.

He wanted to see the horrid work brought to a speedy end. As one or two of the other sailors joined together and aided in the task, the pirates were soon consigned to the deep.

The scene that followed was truly heartrending.

Some of the pirates were capital swimmers, and their struggles for life were great.

The ship was scarcely moving, and the shrieking wretches swam round about the sides, trying to fix their fingers between the planks, or hang to any projection.

They were quickly dislodged by Bill Clewline, who, armed with the lead and line, swung it about in such a manner as to clear the ship's side of the frantic wretches.

The second mate, having once commenced the work of death, seemed to glory in it.

Seizing hold of the dead, dying, or any that came in his way, he hurled them over the bulwarks, and if any of them chanced to clutch a rope or struggle with him, he resorted to the most brutal means to make them release their hold.

Gregory Saunders was one of those who fell into his ruthless hands.

His coward heart quailed, and he begged piteously for mercy; but none was shown to him, and he, with the rest, was hurled into the sea.

The whole of the pirate crew, with the exception of the captain, was now disposed of, and the second mate cast an inquiring glance at Will, as much as to say, 'Has his turn yet arrived?'

The captain of the slaver, who had stood with arms folded looking on, now spoke—

'Clap on sail, and see if we can get out of hearing of those shrieking wretches. It is quite enough to hear their oaths, without listening to their dying groans.'

'What do you intend doing with this fellow?' asked Will, when the captain had given this order.

'He shall walk the plank,' replied the captain, sternly. 'He came on board of his own accord, he shall leave it——Oh, curse you! God! he has stabbed me.'

The last words came from the captain's lips as Will grasped the pirate by the shoulder, and hurled him against the bulwark.

He had started suddenly to his feet, and plunged a knife to the hilt between the slaving captain's shoulders.

How he became possessed of the knife was a mystery.

The second mate rushed to the wounded man's assistance, and raised his head, but the pallid look and vacant gaze forewarned his approaching death.

'Fiend! hast thou added another murder to thy list of crimes?' cried Will Howard, scarce able to keep his hands from throttling him.

'Ay, and I will add more ere I leave this ship,' answered the pirate captain, his cheeks livid with rage, and his eyeballs glaring wildly.

'I will prevent you,' cried Will, seizing him round the waist, and calling to Sancho to approach. 'Bind his arms, Sancho. The serpent carries his sting to the very last.'

'It will be useless ever after this,' replied Sancho, as he bound the pirate so that he could not move, 'but the captain has no one to blame for this but his own folly.'

'Too late! I see it all,' gasped the captain of the slaver. 'He ought to have been first, so as to have led his men. I have prolonged his life, and he has shortened mine. Let him walk the plank. It is my dying wish.'

'And shall be fulfilled,' answered the second mate, who had been trying to stanch the blood. 'Ah! he is gone!'

Gazing mournfully into the captain's face, the second mate went so far as to shed a tear.

He had been his companion for many years, and his sudden loss affected him greatly.

Motioning Bill Clewline to assist him, he bore the body aft, and summoned the sail maker to sew him up in his cot.

The command of the vessel now fell to the share of the second mate, but he did not rejoice in it, for he was not sufficiently qualified to navigate the seas.

The additional sail increased the speed of the ship, but the shouts and cries of the wretched pirates, who still floated themselves by means of the handspikes, and various impliments they had used as weapons, and carried overboard with them, were still audible, and Will gave a shudder as he heard the shrieks that had told one of them had been seized by a shark.

The effect was not lost on the hardened pirate captain.

His eyeballs glanced hideously around, and his broad chest rose and fell like the swell of the ocean.

Horror was depicted in his every feature, for as the shrieks of his doomed men fell on his ears, it reminded him of the terrible fate that awaited himself.

'Fool! idiot! that I was, to listen to the words of the wily tempter,' he muttered, hoarsely. 'Had I waited patiently the ship would have been mine; but it is no use regretting it now. The die is cast, and I must yield.'

His resolution was shaken, however, when he saw the preparations being made for his execution.

His huge form trembled convulsively, and the veins of his forehead swelled nigh to bursting.

'I will not die!' he gasped, frantically, while his lurid eyeballs seemed ready to start out of his head.

'You will have no choice,' said Bill Clewline; 'so prepare for a launch into the next world, and pray to old Neptune to look you out as dry a berth as possible.'

The pirate gave a hideous smile as they unbound and led him to the plank.

The scond mate, as before, acted as executioner.

He ordered the pirate to walk the treacherous plank, which, as soon as he reached his foot beyond the bulwarks, would precipitate him into the sea.

As the pirate did not seem inclined to obey, he enforced his orders with a loaded pistol.

Thus urged, he seemed to comply, but it was only a feint. As he stepped upon the plank, he snatched the pistol from the hand of the second mate, and discharged it full at his head.

With an agonized cry, the second mate fell, and the pirate with an exultant laugh, hurled the pistol in the faces of the men, and then leaped overboard.

An unearthly shriek followed the dull splash, and the pirate was no more to be seen.

CHAPTER CXXVII.

RESCUED FROM THE WRECK—A PRISONER IN
THE SMUGGLERS' STRONGHOLD.

THE revenue cutter, disabled as she was, spite of
of the efforts of her crew, could make no headway
against the heavy sea that opposed her.

Fast upon the rocks she drove.

Nearer and nearer each wave hurled her to the
fatal spot.

When she struck, it was with a fearful shock
that shook her from truck to keel, and hurled
several of her crew overboard.

Lieutenant Pike, although smarting under his
wound, would not leave his post.

He was lashed to a part of the vessel, and continually gave his men orders.

Once fast on the rocks, his orders were of no
avail.

'Save yourselves as best you can, men,' he cried.
'I will stay and see the last of our gallant craft.'

There was a wide space of water between the
mainland and the rocks upon which the cutter
had fixed herself, and some of the men, grasping
pieces of the shattered spars that came down as
she struck, threw themselves in the sea hoping to
reach the shore.

Vain were the persuasions of the officers for the
lieutenant to make an effort to save his life.

He seemed fully resigned to his fate.

The approach of Bill Raker with the boat was
hailed joyfully by the gallant fellows; but it
seemed an impossibility that any could be saved
by her.

The sea ran very heavily, and the huge waves
rolled in mountainous masses over the doomed
ship, threatening her destruction, and also that of
the boat if it approached too near.

Bill Raker, well accustomed to such scenes,
handled his boat skilfully.

Turning her head to the sea, he allowed her to
drift down on the wreck, the men checking her
speed with the oars when she drifted too fast.

A line and buoy was floated to the wreck, and
one by one the brave fellows threw themselves
into the sea, and were hauled into the boat.

Lieutenant Pike resisted the solicitations of his
men until the very last, and it was only by main
force he was compelled to leave the cutter.

He was lashed to the line and thrown overboard
by the boatswain and gunner, who followed him
soon after.

The lightning still played with vividness, and
lit up the storm-lashed ocean with its momentary
flashes.

It was to this alone that the brave fellows owed
their guidance, for the night was one of great
darkness, and the rocks lay thickly studded
around.

A bright fire in the cavern cheered their return,
and everything was done for the comfort of the
sufferers.

A growl of disaffection came from some of the
men, however, when it was announced to the
smugglers that the shipwrecked mariners were
their sworn and inveterate enemies.

'Better have let them perish,' muttered one to
his companion. 'What say you, Rocket?'

'Well, it's hard to give an opinion. They say a
good act is never thrown away, so mayhap they
will do us a favour in return.'

'Ay,' muttered the smuggler, savagely, 'they'll
probably give us an introduction to the hangman.'

'And recommend us to his mercy,' suggested
another, with a meaning grin.

'You are right, Thowlpin; we have let the
sharks into our nest now for some purpose.'

The entrance of Hatchett put an end to their
grumbling.

'Well, lads,' he said, 'how does the stranger
get on?'

'All right,' replied Bill Raker; 'they have
plenty of grog, and what more does a sailor want?
and for that matter anyone else that has been out
on such a night as this.'

'Where is Pike?'

'In the inner cave.'

'Is he better?'

'Not much.'

'He gets on slowly, then.'

'The salt water has found his wound.'

'And how about your own?—did it not find
that?'

'Well, it did; but you see he has not taken the
same medicine as I. Had he a good bottle of our
strong brandy to pull at when he liked, the spirit
would have kept the water at bay.'

'That's your opinion.'

'And a very good one, inasmuch as I find the
benefit of it.'

'Ha! ha!' laughed Hatchett. 'I have always
told you that no life would suit you like a smuggler's; but let us hear what this Pike has to say
about it.'

The lieutenant was in great agony, and his coxswain was doing all in his power to allay the pain
when the smugglers entered.

'Well, lieutenant, how do you like our quarters?'
asked Hatchett.

'As much as ever,' was the reply. 'A den of
outlaws is no pleasant abode for a king's officer
at any time.'

'Ho, ho! that's how the wind blows, is it,
master Pike? Well, I hope you will soon be well
enough to leave us.'

'The sooner, the better I shall like it.'

'Not a very gentlemanly remark,' said Hatchett,
but'——

'The more honourable,' interposed the lieutenant. 'You have saved my life, and of course
I am indebted to you.'

'And will repay the debt, I hope, should I need
your aid. I hope that ever after this we shall be
friends.'

'Never!—it cannot be.'

'What?'

'It is impossible.

Tom Hatchett staggered back, and fixed his
dilating eyes on the lieutenant in astonishment.

'Do you know,' he said, 'that you are wholly in
our power—that a word from me would make you
the target for a hundred bullets? What I have
done for you is out of friendship, and it is but
right you return it when you have it in your
power.'

Lieutenant Pike raised himself on his elbow, and
looked firmly in the smuggler captain's face.

'Hatchett,' he said, 'you have spared my life,
and great praise is due to the brave fellows who
risked their own to save it; but it is not for me
to make conditions with such as you. We are

sworn enemies, and were it in my power, I would drag you to justice, where you would meet with the punishment thy crimes so justly merit.'

The face of the smuggler coloured with indignation.

'Were I the bloody rascal you take me for,' he said, 'I would order the tongue that can utter such words to be cut out; but I am more merciful; though it would be folly on my part to let one of you leave this cave, until you have sworn to keep our secret and molest us no further.'

'Then I tell you plainly you need not expect it.'

'Madman! you know not what you say.'

'I do perfectly well,' replied Pike, sternly.

'Then you must put up with what follows.'

'I am prepared to do so. I would fain save the lives of my men; but if it must not be, they must yield to fate.'

'You prefer death, then?'

'Anything to dishonour. I would rather you had hacked me to pieces, than to have made such dishonourble propositions.'

'Umph! You'll alter your opinions very soon.'

'Never! I will never betray my trust.'

'Then you will share the fate of all fools. With such impressions you can never expect to leave this place alive.'

'Then I will die if need be, and that nobly. The word dishonour shall never taint my name. I will die as I have lived, a loyal subject of the king.'

Hatchett turned away.

There was a melancholy in his looks, and a frown upon his brow.

He had been mistaken in his man.

He had hoped that by rescuing Lieutenant Pike, and getting him in his power, to have won him over in his favour. It was not to be, and Hatchett was mad at his failure.

CHAPTER CXXVIII.

THE CRUISE OF THE BOMBSHELL FRIGATE— MADELINE IN PERIL.

THE escape of the Black Pirate from the hands of Will Howard was the cause of a disaster they little anticipated.

The Bombshell man-of-war, carrying forty guns, and a crew of picked men, had been sent to cruise in the Mediterranean to cut up a fleet of privateers and small vessels of war that had sailed from the Gulf of Lyons.

Commodore Belcher, who had the command of the frigate, was a practical seamen, and a man of such stern determination as not to let a vessel pass him without thoroughly overhauling their papers, and making himself thoroughly acquainted with the object of their voyage.

One vessel he had captured, loaded with stores and ammunition for the French cruisers, and another one carrying dispatches of great import from the Sultan of Turkey to the French authorities.

These vessels he at once sent home, with a prize crew; and elated with his success, he scoured the sea in search of others.

The Black Pirate chanced to be the next to fall into his hands.

He was lashed alongside a brig of inferior size, and his crew were engaged with the sailors in deadly strife, when the Bombshell bore down with every stitch of sail set.

The pirate was taken by surprise.

He ordered the grapplings to be cast off, and the entangled rigging to be cut away, but it was no use; the brig swung off, and escaped in the smoke; but the pirate ship fell a victim to his superior foe.

Commodore Belcher, at the head of his men, leapt on board, and cut down all who opposed him; whilst the pirates, taken by surprise, could make but little resistance, though they were armed to the teeth.

'Hurrah, lads!—St. George for ever!' cried Bombshell, as he followed the retreating pirates to the fore part of the vessel. 'Spare them if they throw down their arms; if not, cut them up like junk.'

The sailors needed no such incentive.

They thoroughly hated the very name of a pirate and all connected with it.

They dealt about them with fierce and deadly blows, often forgetting the commodore's orders to grant mercy to those who sued for it.

The captain was the last to yield.

His body was covered with ghastly wounds, and one of his hands was severed from the wrist, when he sank to the deck with the commodore's sword in his breast.

'Water, water!' he gasped. 'Quick! I have not long to live.'

Water was soon procured, and when he had taken a good draught, the commodore, who saw that he had something to communicate before he died, raised his head.

It was some moments ere the wounded pirate could give utterance to another word.

His life-blood was fast ebbing from his wounds and his eyes were filming fast.

At length he spoke—

'The brig you saw us engaged with is Rock Elfin's, and he has several women on board that he has taken from various ships; amongst them is one he took a short time ago from my cabin, and she is the daughter of Lord Harry Garthway.'

'And where is she now?' asked the commodore.

'Far away, I fear; see is the brig still in sight.'

'She is not; if she is about here the haze precludes her from our vision.'

Although dying, the pirate could not restrain an oath.

'Curse him! May the devil catch him, if man cannot,' he said, with vehemence.

The commodore made no reply.

He was vexed.

He had long cherished an affection for Madeline; but as Gregory Saunders aspired to the favour of her hand, he kept his thoughts to himself.

'No matter; I will have her yet,' he thought, as he glanced in the direction the brig had taken; 'this Elfin shall deliver her up to me.'

The pirate ship was no mean prize.

Her coffers were well stored, and her ballast seemed mostly composed of valuables plundered from various ships.

The deck was soon cleared of the dead, and the living were placed in irons below.

Leaving just sufficient men on board to work her, Commodore Belcher made his way to the Bay of Gibraltar, where he intended leaving his prize until the manner of her disposal was decided, keeping a good look out as he went along, and a strict eye on every vessel he passed.

Commodore Belcher only waited long enough at Gibraltar to communicate with the admiral, when he put to sea again in the hopes of meeting with Rock Elfin.

Towards dusk one evening a vessel hove in sight that he thought must surely be the brig, but darkness coming on apace, she eluded him, although he gave chase vigorously.

Next morning another appeared, and soon after another.

They were both broad on the Bombshell's quarter, and the commodore no sooner saw them than he went about, and stood towards them.

One of the vessels began edging away, steering about two points defferent to the other, and when Belcher saw this his suspicions were aroused immediately.

'Enemies, by Jupiter!' he exclaimed; 'we'll overhaul 'em in a crack. Up studding sails and out booms; get the spritsail-yard across, and hoist the outer jib.'

All was bustle on board the frigate in an instant.

Ropes were thrown down, and busy feet hurried about the decks, creating such a noise as was anything but pleasant to those whose watch it was below.

Every inch—every stitch that could be carried, was spread to the breeze; and the frigate, like a lofty pyramid of canvas, bore away in the direction of her quarry.

Leaving them to the chase, we will follow the brig that escaped so miraculously from the hands of her would-be captors.

Rock Elfin glanced occasionally through the misty wreath of smoke occasioned by the firing of his guns, and at intervals an indistinct muttering left his lips.

His men were busy in clearing the deck of the dead and dying, and securing the guns that had been deserted at the first announcement of the frigate's propinquity, while some were aloft repairing the shattered rigging.

Deep sobs came from the cabin skylight that was raised to admit the fresh air, and the voice of a female could be heard pleading piteously to some one who appeared to pay but little heed to her solicitations.

'Curse you, hold your jaw!' were the words, uttered in a brutal tone; 'we've saved you from slavery, so make yourselves happy.'

'Happy! God! is it possible you can use that word so lightly? How can we be happy among such wretches?'

'Fool! I tell you, you will use that taunt too often. You are well treated here, and if you behave in any way becoming, you will find us true friends.'

'Merciful heavens! such mercy we might easily dispense with; but the time will come when you will have to answer for this insult. You forget I am the daughter of '——

'Silence, I tell you!' exclaimed the same brutal voice. 'What care we who you are, or where you come from? You are here now, and under our protection.'

'Too well I know it.'

'Then remain quiet.'

'I cannot.'

'Then I must use means of quieting you.'

Madeline Garthway, for it was she who had been

thus addressed, gave a shriek of terror as the sound of a blow followed the villain's threat.

Elfin looked down the skylight.

'What are you at, fool?' he inquired.

'Nothing, only clapping a stopper on this minx's jaws,' answered the man addressed.

It was the mate who spoke.

As callous, hard-hearted a wretch as ever stepped, was he.

He had managed, by his craft and villanous counsel, to make Elfin as bad as himself, and extinguished the small spark of feeling and humanity that Rock Elfin once possessed entirely out.

Black Dakin (the mate) was a man possessed of such power, that once his words were listened to, he could mould his hearers to his will, and thus it was he gained so much power over Rock Elfin.

The captain was about to descend to the cabin, when the carpenter announced that one of the bow planks had started, and it was necessary for them to put in somewhere, that the vessel might be heeled over.

Rock Elfin received the news with a ghastly grin.

'There is a bay down on our lee,' he said, 'where we may lay for a day or two secure. How long do you think it will take us to repair?'

'About three days.'

'Ah, and we can fit another topmast in the time during which you are busy about the hull.'

'Yes, sir.'

Rock Elfin gave another horrid grin.

It was the way he always expressed his displeasure to the officers.

'Square the yards,' he bawled to the men grouped on the forecastle. 'Ease tacks and sheets, and steady taut the braces.'

The order was obeyed, and the brig headed for the African shore.

The mate now came on deck.

'The place is infested with wild beasts and savages,' he replied, in answer to a question from Elfin; 'but we may hang it out in safety for the few days we shall require to put ourselves to rights.'

'At all events we'll try it,' said Elfin.

'It will be best to do so. Anything is better than ploughing the sea with those cursed pumps continually chattering in one's ear.'

'Well, how did you get on below there?' asked the captain.

'Badly, but it might have been worse. Women, you know, are naturally obstinate, but they gradually yield when they find themselves compelled to do so.'

'You are right, Dakin; all women are the same; and as to Madeline,' (he lowered his voice) 'I know she is a regular Tartar, but I must have revenge, be she what she may.'

'Nothing is to hinder you.'

'Certainly not; but'——

'There is no occasion for any buts about it,' said Black Dakin, interrupting him. 'Are not you and Gerald Stuart sworn enemies?'

'Indeed we are, and he would think no more of stringing me to the yard-arm, and blowing my ship into the air, than he would of sinking one of King George's gun-boats.'

'Then, why fear success?'

'Ah! you know not this Gerald, and it is well you do not.'

'D—n him! How can he harm us? what for have we to fear him so much?'

'Many things.'

'Name one.'

'A score, if it please you. You must first know, his vessel is more than double in superiority to ours.'

'Well.'

'His men are more than a match for treble our number, and his gunners are equally as good as any in the king's service.'

'But strategem, my man, will render us his equal.'

'His equal! I tell you you know him not, and your speech confirms my words. He is as crafty as the old one himself.'

'Where he that person in reality,' said Black Dakin, 'I would beat him.'

'Well, let us not quarrel about it. In less than an hour we shall double yonder headland; so see to our ground tackle, for the squalls that pour over these hills, and down the valleys, render the anchorage here not always safe.'

'In trouble again!' ejaculated Black Dakin. 'Why, you have not as much courage as a Turk, who heaves his ship to and goes below to pray, leaving his vessel to weather out, as best she may, the wildest storm.'

'Bah! cease thy prating, Dakin; it is not fit we should have preachers on board a vessel of our calling. Let us have a glass of the sparkling beverage we took from the Bordeaux trader.'

'With all my heart. I am confoundedly dry, and need a little refreshment.'

The pair descended to the cabin, and Rock Elfin gave a shudder as he beheld Madeline reclining on the after lockers.

For a moment the pale girl eyed him in silence. Presently she spoke.

'Rock Elfin,' she said, 'has pity totally deserted your breast? Are you so far depraved as to take advantage of a helpless girl?'

'Helpless!' replied Elfin, evasively. 'You are in better hands than you were a few hours ago.'

'Better! God help us! You should say, less merciful. The conduct of your partner has proved what company we are in!'

'Well, what have you to say against him?' growled Elfin.

'Judge for yourself. See you this?'

As she spoke she bared her eye, which was black and terribly swollen.

'This is a mark of his gentleness,' she added.

Rock Elfin glanced reprovingly at his mate, but the hardened villain met his gaze without flinching.

'That and much more she deserves,' he answered; 'the other two met their fate as becomes them.'

'Villain!' exclaimed Madeline, whilst her whole frame seemed to quiver with emotion; 'villain! you are fit to live only with the beasts of the jungle!'

'I know it,' replied Dakin; therefore, owe you nothing for the compliment.'

Rock Elfin had poured out the wine, and having drained the third tumbler, he desired his mate to follow his example.

Dakin required no urging.

He could have drained a dozen; he felt in the humour for it.

It was not long before the vessel reached the bay, which was well sheltered from observation seaward, and both anchors were dropped.

The female prisoners, an aged lady and her daughter, and Madeline, were taken on shore, and placed in hastily-erected tents.

The vessel was soon lightened of her heaviest articles, and other tents, made of sails, were formed for the accommodation of the men, whose services were required on shore.

Preparations were now made to guard against the savage beasts that were known to infest the forest that sheltered them behind, and good lookouts were placed in necessary positions.

These arrangements made, Rock Elfin and Black Dakin repaired to the principal tent.

It was a rude structure, but comparatively comfortable, couches and cushions having been brought from the ship, and other arrangements made by the carpenter.

Black Dakin and his chief remained in secret consultation for some time.

It was evident by their gestures that the women formed the subject of their talk.

Whatever were their opinions, and the subject each most dwelt on, it was evident the captain and his mate did not agree.

'You fool!' at length said Dakin, half-aloud; 'if you save the old hag we shall never know a moment's peace. Ease her wind, and all will be well.'

'I cannot.'

'You are a coward.'

'Liar!'

'Prove it.'

'How can I?'

'By settling her at once.'

'Mercy, Dakin! you are horrible.'

'These are horrible times. The old woman is but fit company for Old Davy. Let him have her.'

'I cannot. My heart revolts at further bloodshed.'

'Then you are a fool, and not fitted for the command of such a craft as you own. This once whispered amongst the men, and you are lost; besides, have we not one each? Three is one too many.'

'True. I see the force of your argument now; but how is it to be accomplished?'

'Have you not a knife?'

'I have; but can you not devise some other means?'

'None; unless you prefer'——

'Hush! Do not name it. Other ears may hear us.'

'True. Are you now resolved?'

'I am; and nothing shall divert me from my purpose.'

''Tis well. I am glad to see you have not become a woman; that you still have the spirit of a man.'

This discussion ended, Rock Elfin entered that part of the tent that was devoted to the females' use.

Everything that was possible had been done to render it comfortable.

Rolls of damask had been used to decorate the sides, and cushions of the softest had been spread to rest their delicate forms upon.

'Ladies,' said the captain, in a well-assumed tone, 'I fear you may think me neglectful that I have not ordered refreshment before; but important duties have called me elsewhere.'

'We need no excuse,' said Madeline, reproachfully; 'it is enough to bear with the horrors of our captivity, without being compelled to listen to the sound of thy lying lips.'

Rock Elfin scowled horribly as he retired.

'You shall repent this, madam,' he muttered, between his clenched teeth.

Supper was now served, and in one of the goblets of wine was mixed with a strong poison.

This was given to the old lady. She was an eyesore to the brace of villains who longed for her death, that they might have no witness to their wicked machinations.

The deadly draught was drank by the unsuspecting victim, and, after a few moments of horrible suffering, she was no more.

Her daughter, Jessie, was almost frantic, and Madeline was completely shocked.

All further concealment of their intentions was needless, and Black Dakin openly avowed his love for Jessie, announcing at the same time the fate of Madeline.

The deed done, Rock Elfin dismissed all scruples.

'You are mine now,' he said to Madeline.

She made no reply; she was too overpowered to speak.

The men who had to keep watch had lit a large fire around the encampment, and Rock Elfin summoned two of the men.

'Take the horrid carcase,' he said, pointing to the murdered woman, who was already turning black; 'take her beyond the pale of our encampment; she will add a morsel to the meal of some famished beast.'

Jessie came forward, and, in a paroxysm of grief, threw herself upon the body of her unfortunate parent.

'Pirate!' she cried, as the hot tears coursed each other down her cheeks; 'you shall not part us. Kill me, you may; but part us, you never shall.'

Black Dakin seized her roughly, and hurled her back upon the couch; and, in doing so, his arm came violently in contact with Madeline's face, bringing the sparks to her eyes and causing her to fall senseless.

This caused a quarrel between the two ruffians, and Rock Elfin, in his rage, drew his dirk, and plunged it into the heart of Black Dakin.

'Away with him! Clear the tent of this horrid scum,' cried Rock Elfin, trembling with rage. 'Let the wild beasts feed on his carrion carcase. And thus perish all who defy Rock Elfin.'

The men trembled as they listened to his fearful words, and quailed beneath his withering glance.

'You have heard my orders,' he said, with an impatient gesture; 'now obey them, and take this old withered hag with you,' he said to another of the band.

'Are you sure she's dead, cap'n?' inquired the man, who, in spite of the rude and boisterous life he was leading, could not help shuddering as he raised the inanimate form of the old woman.

A pang of remorse shot through his stony heart, for it reminded him that he once had a mother of his own.

'Dead!—of course she's dead; d—n you! have not I said so?' Take her away directly, and remember I am captain, and as such will be obeyed. Be careful how you play with me,' he added.

He glared furiously at the man as he spoke, and grasped the butt of a pistol.

This movement was observed by the man, who well knew his vindictive spirit.

Raising the woman in his arms, he bore her from the tent without deigning to offer a reply.

The watch fire burnt fiercely around their encampment, and the pirates, although fearing the threats of their captain, feared still more the fury of the raging elements.

It would be madness to attempt to pass the fiery barrier, and so intense was the heat that they could not with safety approach within two or three yards of the blazing circle within which they were enclosed.

'I arn't going to get roasted, Tom, if you are,' said the man who held the woman in his brawny arms. 'I can stand water, but I'm d——d if I can stand this blistering fire.'

'Same here, shipmate; I wouldn't go through that blaze for the best cap'n that trod a ship's plank. Let's lay 'em down here, mate.'

'Ay, ay, so say I, Tom,' replied the man, as he dropped the legs of the mate on a mound behind one of the tents.

The other man soon followed his example, laid the woman gently on the ground, and covered her over with a piece of sail cloth.

Having rid themselves of their unpleasant burdens, they entered the tent, where stood the captain feasting his gloating eyes on the fair and lovely form of the unfortunate girl as she lay almost in a state of nudity upon the rude couch, her fair breasts and marble limbs exposed to the intruding gaze of the rough men who surrounded her.

The poor girl, whose senses had been shattered by the fearful excitement, now gave signs of recovery.

A deep sigh escaped her breast, and a shudder pervaded her frame.

'She's coming round, cap'n,' said one of the men.

'So much the better,' rejoined Rock Elfin; 'the sooner she gets over this the sooner she'll have expended all her grief, and be able to listen to reason.'

'Reason!' muttered Tom, shrugging his shoulders.

'Or persuasion, or something else,' said the captain, turning fiercely towards Tom, who had spoken rather louder than he intended.

'What do you intend to do with her, cap'n?' inquired Tom, who appeared to possess the most feeling of any of the men assembled, for a look of pity stole over his features as he gazed upon the pale face of the poor young girl.

'Do with her?' iterated the captain, fiercely. 'Who gave you leave to question me? Am I not allowed to do as I think proper with her? She is my lawful prize.'

Tom fixed his steady eye upon the captain, and was about to reply, when, with another sigh, the suffering girl opened her eyes, and glanced upon the faces of those around in a bewildered manner.

Rock Elfin advanced, and placed his brawny arm under her head.

For some few moments the eyes of Jessie remained fixed on his own, then with a convulsive movement of the lips she shrieked—

'Murderer, murderer!'

At the sound of those fearful words as they echoed through the tent, the captain's face paled.

BLACK EYED SUSAN.

OR, PIRATES ASHORE.

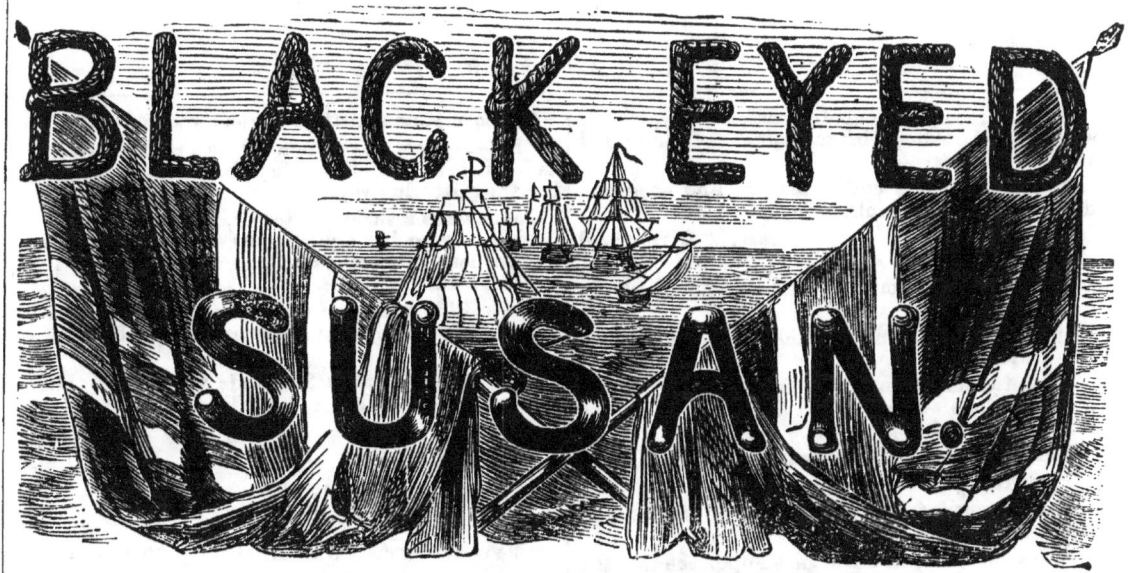

THE FALSE ACCUSATION.

But the momentary qualm passed away, and he was again the callous, brutal captain of a horde of villains.

A scornful smile curled his lip, and he gazed defiantly upon his helpless victim.

For a moment she met his gaze, and returned his scornful glance.

What a world of meaning did that single glance convey !

It was for an instant only that she lay powerless as a child.

With the fury of a tigress she tore herself from his loathsome embrace, and bounding up, stood before her cruel oppressor.

Her lustrous eyes flashed with an unearthly fire.

Her thin lips were compressed.

Her slender form was drawn up to its full height.

A few moments thus she gazed upon the swarthy visage of the captain, who had leaped to his feet.

Then her lips parted, and she hissed rather than spoke the word—

'Murderer !'

Beneath the glance that accompanied the expression the eye of Rock Elfin fell.

Before that proud and scornful attitude he cowered.

Raising her arm, and pointing her finger towards him, she exclaimed, in a calm but subdued tone—

'Murderer, where is my mother ?'

'Peace !' he yelled, starting forward, and grasping the wrist of her extended arm. 'Beware, or my dirk shall drink your heart's blood, and your fate shall be the same as that of him who defied me.'

'Assassin,' she replied; 'think of the work of your bloody hands. What have you done ? You have slain my only friend, my mother !'

'Bah !' said the captain, tauntingly; 'what harm have I done to you ? I love you too well to harm you.'

'Love me !' reiterated the girl, fiercely; 'love me ! A ruffian, the murderer of my aged mother, the destroyer of my happiness. Love me ! Does not the word love stick in your throat ? Does it not choke you ? '

He clenched his teeth firmly together, and seemed about to spring upon her.

But the glance of that suffering half-maddened girl held him rooted, as it were, to the spot.

'Fiend !'——

'Silence !' he exclaimed, as he bit his lips with passion, and grasped the handle of his long dirk ; 'another word, and '——

'Strike, assassin, if you have the courage !' exclaimed the young girl, interrupting him, and at the same time presenting her snowy breast to his upraised arm.

'Another word, and I bury it in your heart !' he hissed between his clenched teeth.

'Strike !' she answered in desperate coolness, 'and tarnish the bright blade with the blood of her whose mother you have murdered.'

Rock Elfin's hands fell powerless by his side.

'Coward ! you have not the courage to plunge your weapon into my breaking heart.'

'Beware how you taunt one who never forgets nor forgives,' exclaimed the captain, nervously clutching the handle of his dirk.

The woman's lips curled contemptuously.

'I scorn your threats, and defy your power.'

'By —— this is too much !' he cried hoarsely, as he rushed upon the defenceless girl, brandishing the glittering weapon.

Jessie gave a shriek of terror, and this aroused Madeline from her unconscious state, and springing to her feet, she caught the tyrant's arm in time to arrest the blow.

Rock Elfin gave a cry of mingled rage and disappointment, and, turning fiercely upon Madeline, he hissed—

'Thy life is doubly forfeited; now is the time for my long-cherished revenge !'

———

CHAPTER CXXIX.

THE FIGHT WITH THE FRIGATE—THE REPULSE OF THE BOARDERS.

IT needed no second glance from the experienced eye of Gerald Stuart to recognise the outlines of the Boomshell frigate as she bowled along before the wind; her lofty sail rivaling in whiteness the fleecy clouds that here and there studded the blue expanse of sky.

Captain Stuart made a signal to his consort to heave to.

The Martinet was some distance ahead of the Golden Arrow, and Henson felt rather annoyed at the signal, and felt inclined not to notice it.

Gerald, on the other hand, was determined he should, so kept the signal flying, and fired a gun to attract Henson's attention.

The list Admiral Garthway had given to Captain Stuart informed him of the name of the frigate's commander, and as Gerald was personally acquainted with him, he did not much care for his visit.

'Now, friend Henson,' cried Stuart, as his vessel ran up on the Martinet's quarter; 'there is a little fighting to be done, and you will have to assist.'

'What ! Do you mean to engage him ?' asked Henson, in surprise.

'I see no other way of ridding ourselves of him.'

'Can you not shake him off ?'

'I fear not.'

'Not by stratagem ?'

'Alas ! he is too old a cruiser to be gulled as were the others.'

Henson looked troubled.

His restless eye occasionally roved to the approaching frigate, and then turned to the head of his own ship, as though he were weighing the chances of escape.

'Had I not better sail in ?' he asked hoarsely.

Gerald Stuart eyed him askance.

After a moment's careful scrutiny, he said—

'First answer me. Are you prepared to run through the fleet ?'

'By hugging the land, I may chance to escape.'

'And if not, are you prepared to fight ?'

'I must be.'

'Why ?'

'There will be no other alternative.'

Gerald smiled.

He had a suspicion of the character of his man, and now he had proofs.

Fixing his keen glance on Henson, he said—

'Your answers to me are anything but satisfactory; in the first place, it would be much safer to keep in midchannel, as the light craft and look-out ships will of a certainty grope about in shore; and in the next place, if you are afraid of assisting me to give battle to a single ship, how would you fight your way through a squadron?'

Henson was completely trapped.

All escape seemed hopeless.

He must stay and join in the combat, though his inclination was greatly averse to it.

Captain Henson was a man who had distinguished himself for bravery, or he would not have been entrusted with the responsible mission that threw him in company with Gerald Stuart.

It was not absolute fear that made him as he was, it was over responsibility.

He had that on board his ship that might sway the destiny of a nation.

Its safe delivery might gain him an earldom.

Its failure might perhaps cost him his life, and not only his, but a score of other aspirants, who were looking forward to a life at court and the favour of a monarch.

With this knowledge, Gerald Stuart rather pitied than blamed him, though he could not help thinking in his own mind that he was a man unfit to be trusted with such a valuable freight.

Unlike Gerald Stuart, he was a man who could not face danger while there was the least chance of shunning it, and as we have seen, this would have resulted in serious results if it had been acted upon.

Both the Martinet and the Golden Arrow were now going under easy sail, with just sufficient distance between them to enable the captains to converse.

'Are your men at their quarters,' asked Gerald, as he eyed the rapidly nearing frigate.

'Yes,' was the reply; 'but do you think it advisable for me to stay.'

'Certainly, we must not part while a plank will float; we must drub this fellow and disable him, or we shall never see port again.'

The crew of the Golden Arrow were already at their guns, Happy Jack and his fellows were in glee at the prospect of another fight.

Silently they were crouched below the bulwarks, and their stern features and resolute mien told they were ready to fight to the death.

Pat was among them.

He could not stop in his galley, to be knocked down by a shot, without the chance of seeing where it came from.

'Arrah! ould Ireland for ever, you bog-throtting rogues!' he shouted, in high glee, as he placed the shot in the grommet; 'may we niver want for such praties as these whin an inimy's in sight; and whin they stand in need of iny, may we always dale 'em out with liberal hand, sure!'

'Bravo! Pat,' said Happy Jack, in a half-whisper. 'Bring us plenty of spuds, old boy, and I lay we'll keep the pot boiling.'

'Silence!'

The word went like magic along the deck.

'Port quarters, remain at your guns! Starboard quarters, attend the braces!'

By this time the frigate was within hail.

'What ship, and where bound?' shouted Belcher, through his trumpet.

'The Lotus; cruising,' was Gerald's reply.

'Then heave-to, you rascal, or I'll sink you!'

'The Lotus!' cried Gerald, affecting not to hear him.

'Heave-to!' thundered Belcher.

Captain Gerald knew that he was discovered; in fact, he did not dare to hope from the first that he could hoodwink the shrewd commander, who was as well acquainted with the build and rig of the Golden Arrow as he was himself.

Previous to this, he had given Henson orders how to act, and he had also arranged his own plans.

They were these.

Pretending to obey Belcher's order, he brought his ship's head round, at the same time delivering his broadside full into the frigate.

This movement left the Martinet's side clear, and she repeated the dose as well as her small armament would permit.

This daring and quite unexpected manoeuvre threw Belcher off his guard, and totally paralyzed his men, who were looking through the ports, never dreaming of such a reception from a vessel so totally inferior to their own in appearance.

The execution done by the double fire was terrific.

Shrieks and groans, mingled with the most fearful oaths, followed the loud boom of the cannon.

Belcher stamped and foamed like one mad.

'Give them a broadside!' he shouted to his lieutenant. 'Call down the men!' he yelled to the boatswain; and the sailors who were in the tops securing the stern-sails, and had ceased in their labours to gaze on the deck strewed with wounded, slid down on deck like so many spectres.

Whilst the idlers removed the dead or dying, the sailors got the guns into working order; but before they could do so, owing to the side tackles and breechings being out, the Golden Arrow wheeled under the frigate's stern, and raked her decks with her starboard guns.

This was disheartening to the bold British tars, especially as the Martinet hurled a shot or two from her midship-gun into the spars and sails that rent the canvas, and sent the splinters flying in continued showers.

With all this, the man-of-war's men did not shirk their duty.

They stuck to their posts through the blinding showers of wood and iron, with that stubborn persistence that none but British seamen can possess.

Belcher, in spite of the shattered state of his spars, handled his ship with admirable skill.

He hauled her to on the port tack, and fired his larboard broadside.

Had the ponderous missiles met with the resistance Belcher had anticipated against the side of the Golden Arrow, it must have sunk her; as it was, it passed over her long low hull, and did scarcely any damage to her rigging.

The fight now began in earnest.

Gerald Stuart glided about among his men, delivering his orders personally, and directing their fire to various parts of the enemy's ship.

By this means whole crews were swept from the frigate's guns, and, as their places were filled up with fresh men, the Golden Arrow's long gun vacated them again.

At first Gerald Stuart's men suffered severely, but as the action proceeded, and all his attention was directed towards the enemy's weak points, things began to turn in his favour.

At this juncture matters assumed a different form.

The Martinet, that had been playing at long-shot on the frigate's other side, suddenly ceased her firing.

What cause to attribute this to Gerald did not know, as the cloud of smoke that hung like a funeral pall over the engaged vessels was so dense as to obscure all objects that were not in the immediate vicinity.

A double-headed shot, too, cleared the six men from the after-gun, and a musket-bullet tore away one of the spokes of the wheel, and wounded the helmsman.

Still the fight raged furiously.

The words of command were drowned in shrieks, groans, and loud shouts of the sailors, as the partial clearing of the smoke revealed some damage done to the opposite vessel.

By this time the Golden Arrow had so crippled her opponent that all danger, except by boarding, seemed at an end.

The ponderous missiles, superior to many and equal to any carried by the men-of-war of that day, were more than the frigate could stand against.

Captain Belcher knew this.

And, as he had failed in bringing his ship round so as to expose his less battered side to the enemy, he was determined, if possible, to lay her alongside.

But he had a crafty and too skilful an opponent to do this.

Gerald had already weighed the chances and calculated the advantages of each.

Motioning Marline to his side, he whispered a few words in his ear.

The boatswain, though bleeding from a wound in his leg, hobbled away as best he could, and shouted to several men who were securing things aloft.

Rapidly they descended, and took their way to different parts of the ship, where they were soon lost in the smoke; and, at a signal from the boatswain's pipe, a thin, gauzy fabric rose up from the vessel's side.

Those on board the frigate could not see this, and Belcher, as a last resource, made up his mind to board.

Ordering the upper-deck guns to cease, and those that were not disabled on the main deck to keep on firing, he gave the word to prepare to board.

The brave fellows, armed with pikes, cutlasses, and pistols, flocked to the bow, where a pile of marines were already drawn up to clear a way for them with their muskets; and, as the vessels met with a crash, they sprang over the bulwark, and made a desperate leap.

Belcher had hoped to land his men on the deck of the Golden Arrow under cover of the smoke; but he found he had made a fearful mistake.

The slender fabric, which, owing to its fine texture, had not been observed by the boarders, stopped their impetuous course, and hurled them backwards with a rebound. Vainly some of them tried to stay their fall by clutching at the deceitful netting; but they could gain no hold, and those who did not immediately fall were pierced by the pikes of the repelling party, who thrust their weapons through the meshes of the network.

Horrible was the scene caused by this utterly fruitless sortie.

The frigate's men fell in all directions.

Some landed in fore channels, others fell overboard, and many were horribly crushed between the grinding ships.

This lasted but a moment when the vessels parted, for men had been stationed with hatchets in various parts of the Golden Arrow's netting, and cut away the grapplins before they could be secured.

This brought the battle to a close.

The firing was mutually suspended on both sides, though neither party felt satisfied.

Had Belcher succeeded in his scheme, he might have made a prize of the Golden Arrow; and had Henson thoroughly supported Captain Gerald, the frigate would have fallen an easy prey.

Gradually the smoke cleared, and both ships lay becalmed, two miserably shattered objects, their sails in ribbons, their spars ready to tumble on the heads of those below, and their respective flags drooping mournfully as though sorrowing for the lives of the brave fellows that lay weltering in their blood.

The heat and excitement at an end, the commanders seemed suddenly changed to beings of a different nature.

The sight of their mangled crews and dismantled vessels, as they lay like two gladiators resting from the fight, seemed to have softened their natures.

Marline was ready aloft with a party of his men, repairing the rigging; and as a light breeze sprang up, those of the Golden Arrow's sails that could be were set, and she gradually edged away from the frigate.

Gerald Stuart now began to look around him.

Since the commencement of the fight, he had not seen his consort, and he began to grow anxious about her.

He went aloft, and swept the horizon with his glass, but nothing with the exception of a small speck under the sun could he see.

Muttering a rather unfavourable blessing on Captain Henson for his obstinacy, and hoping he might withal reach his destined port in safety, he descended to the deck.

Having seen Gerald Stuart so far safe on his way, we must leave the fate of Captain Henson to form the subject of a future chapter.

CHAPTER CXXX.

A BRACE OF VILLAINS—BILL RAKER IN DANGER —TOM HATCHETT TO THE RESCUE.

ADMIRAL LANCEVILLE had scarcely left the Three Luggers when Doggrass's footstep was heard on the creaking stairs.

There was a paleness in his features, and a demoniacal smile played on his lip as he asked—

'Have you had company in my room, Susan?'

'In truth, uncle, I have, and I hope I have not done wrong.'

'That is the way with us all,' said Doggrass, bitterly. 'We all hope we have done no wrong, though at the same time we know we are doing that which is not right. Me thought I heard the rattle of a sword scabbard; was it so?'

Susan was rather confused; she knew not what to answer.

'Come, speak out!' cried Doggrass, eyeing her closely. 'I expect you to give me a lie, so out with it at once, and fire it point blank.'

'You are wrong,' replied Susan, bridling up. 'A stranger to the truth yourself, you think others must tell you a lie.'

'Then speak the truth! Who came here?' he said, sneeringly.

'Admiral Lanceville, if you must know, and '——

'His business?'

'You must ask him yourself. I hope you have done nothing wrong so as to have to fear him.'

Doggrass bit his lip.

'I hope I have done nothing wrong,' he said, sarcastically; 'but when one has to answer for others' actions, and when a man is surrounded by those who care not for his reputation, he never knows what he has to fear.'

'But you are not so situated?'

'I am, worse luck,' said Doggrass, emphatically; 'I am hedged around with sharks, who prey upon me, use me as a tool, care not what they do with me; in fact, serve me as you have done.'

'Me!' exclaimed Susan, in surprise, 'me! What have I done?'

'That which you ought not to—disobey my orders.'

'In what way?'

'Allowing strangers to enter that room. Not that I have anything to fear from them on that point. An honest man has no fear; but still I might have been dishonest for what you know, and they might have been excisemen, and what then?'

'That would have been your own look out; though I doubt whether a careful man like yourself would leave bait enough about to attract the nose of a shark; but you tremble.'

'It's weakness only.'

'Good heavens! it is weakness. Why, uncle, anyone that did not *know better* would think you had committed some great crime—a murder, for instance.'

'What!' gasped Doggrass, starting in horror. Do I look like a murderer—eh, lass?'

Susan, seeing her uncle change so suddenly, became alarmed, and she repented having let the words slip unconsciously from her lips.

'Uncle,' she said, 'far be it from my thoughts that you would do such a thing,' said Susan, though at the same time she could not banish the conviction that he would have done anything for gain. 'Sit down and compose yourself. I would not have anyone see you in this state. You look truly horrible.'

Silas staggered to a chair.

'Go! leave me, lass. Let me compose myself in quietude, and serve that noisy blusterer who is hammering at the bar as though trying to waken the dead.'

He glanced around on finding himself alone, for the last words he had uttered seemed to hang about the room, and echo in his ears.

'Wake the dead!' he groaned. 'Yes, well might they; but he sleeps too sound. 'Tis but a smuggler's motto I have acted upon. I put eternal silence on the clatter of his tongue, and he can never rise against me in evidence.'

Though Doggrass tried to console himself in this manner, he felt he was only deceiving himself. The sight of the trap leading to the secret vaults made him shudder.

'Ah!' he muttered to himself, 'how know I that I am not nestling a serpent under my roof? Susan, and even Dame Howard has just cause for revenge. Why did I have them here?—because I was a fool. Even now I believe she has some knowledge of my secret. Would I were certain,' he added, grinding his teeth; 'I would settle them with little compunction. I would prevent them doing me harm. It would be but a small sin added to the many, and only make the cup of guilt, which is now full, flow over.'

Thus he sat, musing and working himself to such a pitch that would have nerved him to commit the foulest deed, when a footstep disturbed him, and a man strode into the room.

Doggrass sprang from his seat.

'What means this intrusion?' he demanded, fiercely.

'Intrusion? Ha! ha!' laughed a voice, that he at once recognised as Bill Raker's; 'does a smuggling craft stay in the offing to make signals to the admiral before entering port? Aha! what a greenhorn you take me to be.'

'And what brings you here?' cried Doggrass, with difficulty smothering his rage.

'My legs; and pretty good ones they are, too; they'd carry me anywhere.'

'Ay! to destruction some day.'

'To the devil, for what I care,' growled Raker. 'I'm not a particular chap, as you know.'

'To my regret I do.'

'What regret? Silas Doggrass talk about regret, when it is the common talk of everyone in Deal and for miles around it that Silas Doggrass's breast is so full of guilt that there is not sufficient room for a pang of remorse to enter it.

'Cease thy ribaldry,' sneered Doggrass. 'What hellish design has brought you here?'

'Anxiety to learn your welfare.'

'Well?'

'And to let you see that though we are men of rough exterior and dangerous calling, we still have manliness enough in our hearts to remind us of our once having a friend.'

'And who is that friend?' demanded Doggrass, sarcastically.

'Need you ask?'

'Being ignorant, I must.'

'Can you not guess?'

'Probably.'

'Have a try. There will be no harm.'

'The devil!'

'Ha! ha!' laughed Raker, 'thou hast nearly guessed it. Now, will I tell you? It is yourself.'

'Villain!' gasped Doggrass, burning with rage. 'Have I not told Hatchett that I had done with you all? I wish to see you no more, for I am heartily tired of you.'

'So it seems; but we are not yet tired of you, friend Doggrass. You have escaped the swamping that threatened you; and now I have come to ask you if you'll be so kind as to set us on an even keel.'

'How? Have you again come to trouble me for money?'

'A little.'

'As I expected. You hang out like so many leeches sucking every drop of blood; but I tell you candidly it is no use, for money I have none.'

'Confound it !—how often have you told that tale, and yet you have found enough to do up the old house. Damme, I should like the overhauling of your memory. I lay you could soon remember where your little stow hole is located.'

'Indeed could I not, and it would be useless to say so; I hope you will stay no longer than is necessary, for I tell you honestly the place is watched, and if you are caught you will surely be hanged.'

'Fie! don't try to frighten me,' replied the smuggler, carelessly; 'our noses have been too well-trained to mistake the smell of rum for that of powder. Come, dub up the tin, and let me cause you no more uneasiness.'

Silas Doggrass rose from his chair. It was like parting with his blood to part with his money.

'Once for all,' he said, 'I cannot assist you. I have not therewith to do it, so depart at once peaceably, and while I am still your friend.'

'What! would you betray me?' asked Raker, fiercely.

'I cannot say what I may do if you remain here. A goaded man is not responsible for his actions.'

'Ah, I understand; you have given up smuggling?'

'Long since; I now wish to get my bread honestly.'

'Indeed!' cried Raker, with a sneer. 'Do you think you have honesty enough in your composition to do it? I would wager there is not one grain of honesty in your whole body.'

'You would lose,' said Doggrass collectedly; I am not the man you once knew me to be.'

'Then you have turned a peach I suppose? If so, and you are found out, I would not give a straw for your life.'

'Of one thing you may be sure,' replied Silas, I shall never ask you to purchase it. Look to your own life, man. It is worth five hundred pounds at this very moment.'

'Accept my thanks for the information, Silas Doggrass, though I take it to be a lie; or how is it you have allowed so great a sum to escape your avaricious grasp?'

'Have you not styled me your friend? How could I have the heart to do you an injury, think you?' asked Silas, with a cunning leer.

'You are right, Doggrass; give me your hand, said the crafty smuggler; 'you have indeed often befriended us, though, by-the-bye, you were never at a loss by it. Do us this favour, and I will ask no more?'

'First let me hear your wants? I will make no promise I cannot fulfil.'

'We want a few pounds just to fit out the Laughing Bird.'

'Do you meditate a cruise?'

'Yes.'

'Where to?'

'Holland.'

'What sum do you require?'

'Two hundred pounds.'

'Two hundred pounds' ejaculated Doggrass, starting.

'Even so; we can make up the rest.'

'Then it's true what has been reported?'

'What may that be?'

'That you have had an engagement with the revenue cutter, and sunk her and all hands.'

'Well, as to that,' replied the smuggler, carelessly, 'we did have a brush with them, but it was their own fault; and though we did not sink the cutter she will never float again.'

'What mean you? you speak in riddles.'

'It is as well I should do so, as I know not to whom I am speaking; the admission you made behoves me to be cautious.'

'Cautious? say rather distrustful,' said Doggrass, greatly annoyed at the smuggler's distrust. 'What have I given you to destroy the mutual confidence we have hitherto enjoyed?'

'Naught that I know of, saving your own words.'

'This is folly, and one day you may rue it, replied Doggrass, testily. 'I did but tell you that a price was on your head; I heard it from a private source, and know it to be true.'

'Who was your informant?'

'That is a secret; but I can tell you that six hundred pounds are offered for Tom Hatchett, and twenty pounds for any of the crew.'

'And did you say it was reported we sank the cutter?'

'A fisherman brought news of having seen you engaged muzzle to muzzle with your guns, and as the cutter did not return to her anchorage during the storm, and has not since been heard of, they concluded you sank her.'

'Well, it is nearly the same. We gave her a warning such as she asked for, and as the squall came on, we cut and run. She followed, and drifted on the devil's jaw, where she stuck until every plank was riven from the timbers and not a stick of her remained.'

'But what of her crew?'

'Those who escaped our fire and the water afterwards are safe.'

'And Lieutenant Pike?'

'He's right enough, too; though, like yourself, he's troubled with violent fits of temper.'

'D—n you!' burst out Doggrass, savagely; 'will you cease this badinage; you are enough to make a fellow swear.'

'Swear, and be hanged to you!' growled Raker, 'if you cannot bear to hear the truth. For my part, I care for no man.'

'So you have often boasted; but mark me, you will find yourself in error; the coast is well lined with spies.'

'And we can sit comfortable under their very feet and laugh at them,' said the smuggler; 'so that need occasion us but little trouble; besides, I have a passport wherever I go.'

Bill Raker produced a pistol from his pocket as he spoke, and Doggrass gave a sarcastic grin.

'That will fail you one of these times,' said he.

'It may, Doggrass. It may deceive me even as you have done.'

Bill Raker uttered the words, but it was thoughtlessly. He did not think at the time how soon they might be verified.

There was a deadly gleam in Doggrass's eye as he heard Bill's words, and his face seemed literally contorted with rage.

He was about to return some stinging retort, when the smuggler checked him by saying—

'Now, Silas, once for all, will you grant me this money?'

Doggrass eyed him demoniacally, and replied with bitter harshness—

'No; take this for an answer, and trouble me no more.'

Bill Raker bit his lip, but said nothing. He was trying to think of some plan for humbling the proud spirit of Doggrass.

He could find none at present, so he thought he would take a turn round the town, and then return.

His disguise was so effectual, that he had no fear of discovery; so he walked out boldly, merely nodding to a man dressed like a rustic as he passed out of the door.

He had not proceeded many paces, however, when a hand grasped him roughly by the shoulder, and a voice whispered harshly in his ear—

'Surrender; you are my prisoner!'

'By what authority?' asked Raker, turning round.

'The king's.'

'Then I dispute it?' cried Bill, savagely. drawing his cutlass from beneath his coat. 'Go back to your master, and deliver my message.'

'Smuggler! pirate! your time is come; you cannot escape.'

'I will try,' muttered the smuggler, hoarsely, and, as he spoke, he shook off the man's grasp.

As he freed himself, he followed up his would-be captor with his sword, and as the other was well armed, a desperate conflict ensued.

The clash of the weapons, and the shrieks of the women who stood near, soon brought a crowd to the spot, amongst which was a bevy of sailors belonging to a vessel in the roads.

'Help, in the king's name!' cried the officer, for such he appeared to be, by the superior finish of his weapons and haughty bearing. 'Seize the pirate, the murderer of Lieutenant Pike.'

'Liar!' thundered Raker, hurling his cutlass at the officer's head; 'I am no pirate, and I defy you to accuse me of murder.'

'Then yield, and submit yourself to a fair trial,' said the officer, as he still continued to beat off the blows threatened him by the smuggler.

'Fool! why should I yield to you?' demanded Rocket, hoarsely, as placing his back against a wall, he continued to battle fiercely with the officer, and kept the sailors, who were only partly armed, at bay with his pistol.

The officer eyed him with a look keen as his sword's point. There was a good reward within his grasp, and he was determined not to lose it without a struggle.

'Yield!' he cried again, fiercely, as he made a skilful thrust at Raker's breast. 'Yield, pirate, or I will pin you as you stand.'

'Never!' replied the smuggler, with fearful desperation; 'if you take me I must then submit.'

'Seize him, men!' thundered the officer to the sailors, who stood looking on without offering to assist; 'seize him, or I will report you to your commander.'

This had the effect of moving the men, who, to all appearance, would not have budged an inch without some incentive, and with fierce looks they began to close in on the smuggler.

It was now evident that unless something turned in his favour, Bill Raker would have to succumb, for one of the sailors, in the absence of any other weapon, seized a pitchfork from the hand of a gaping countryman, who stood amongst the crowd of lookers-on, and was about to rush to the charge, when a blow felled him to the earth.

The blow was a powerful one, and the man lay partly stunned by it; so that, before he could gain his feet, another was felled to keep him company.

This sudden turn of affairs caused quite a commotion amongst the sailors, and, seeing their comrades floored in this manner, they vented their rage in a volley of oaths.

'Keep close, men!' thundered the officer, as his quick eye caught sight of a party of smugglers hastening to the spot with bared cutlasses. 'Keep close; we are equal to them in courage, if not in numbers.'

'If you are not mistaken, as I fear you are,' cried Tom Hatchett, springing into their midst. 'Lay well about you, lads; we will show these sharks what mettle we are made of.'

The conflict now became general, for the sailors, who at first hesitated in joining in the fray, when only one man was opposed to them, fought with the courage of British seamen.

The officer continually cheered them with his words, and Hatchett, by the same means, kept the smugglers to their work, who, being better armed, had some slight advantage over the sailors, though the blue jackets were superior in numbers.

'Curse you, for a set of skulking swabs!' cried the officer, as he saw the sailors gradually being beaten. 'A round dozen or two under your jackets would liven you up a bit.'

'And that will assist to quicken you,' growled Raker, as he thrust his sword through the officer's right arm.

But the officer was a tough old sea-dog, and only winced at the first smart of pain, and, grasping his weapon in his left hand, he renewed the fight with a courage and desperation that were astonishing.

The sturdy veteran well-proved his skill in swordmanship, for Bill Raker had a very narrow escape of losing his life ere he could inflict another wound.

Even then he would not have been successful, had not the officer's foot slipped in the pool of blood that streamed from his wound, and, as he fell, Bill Raker's cutlass entered his shoulder.

Already several of the sailors strewed the ground or had been led away wounded, and the smugglers, driven to desperation by the thoughts of being captured, fought as only men can fight when similarly circumstanced.

'Hurrah, lads, and prepare for a retreat!' cried Hatchett, as a body of marines landed from a boat 'Stick together, the red-coats will be down on us in a crack.'

During the whole of the fight not a shot had been fired by either side.

Hatchett had reserved his pistols for a greater emergency.

'Crack on, my bullies!' he shouted at the pitch of his voice. 'Look out; keep a clear space in our rear.'

The marines were ascending the cliff at double time, their muskets at the trail and their bayonets unfixed; but as soon as they reached a spot convenient, they were halted and ordered to fix bayonets.

They were now so close, that the smugglers could distinctly hear the orders given, and Hatchett, seeing a favourable opportunity, gave the signal to retreat.

To gain the part they desired they had to cross an open space, and the officer of marines gave the word for his men to fire.

This they did, and it would have proved fatal to the smugglers, had they not been used to this mode of warfare, but they fell flat on the earth, allowing the shots to pass over them, and then springing hastily to their feet, made for a path down the cliff.

This latter movement was effected so rapidly, that when the marines arrived a moment or two after they were nowhere to be seen.

A shout directly after apprised them that they had gained the boat, and whilst they were standing between rage and astonishment, a boat pulled from beneath an overhanging rock, and they saw the smugglers waving their arms defiantly.

'Fire!' shouted the corporal, boiling with indignation. 'Put a bullet through their ugly carcases!'

But he might have saved his breath, for the shots passed over the smugglers' yawl, and as they bent vigorously to the oars, they soon pulled out of musket range.

Exasperated at their utter defeat, the marines faced about and returned to their boat, using not the most endearing terms in respect of those who had caused them their wild-goose chase.

The sailors conveyed their wounded comrades on board their ship, and the officer, who had suffered severely for his gallant attempt in capturing the band of desperate men, was conveyed to his own quarters.

———

CHAPTER CXXXI.

THE ACCUSATION—THE FATAL PROOF.

THE cause of the shriek that had so startled the pirates was soon known; a huge lion had dashed through the burning sands, seized one of the crew, and retreated with him to the forest to enjoy his meal in quietude.

This audacity on the part of the ferocious beast caused Rock Elfin to hurry his men on in the fitting of the ship, and to make his stay much shorter than he intended.

Once more afloat Rock Elfin began to look around him, for his crew was sadly reduced by one disaster and another, so that he resolved upon the daring project of running down on either the English or French coast, and picking up a few men.

With his knowledge of the state of the English channel his project seemed more the resolve of a madman than a rational being; but this did not deter Rock Elfin; he had faced dangers as great in his time, so he stood northward without the least hesitation.

In the cabin of the pirate ship, for it was no better than a pirate ship, the female prisoners were provided with every comfort that, in those days, was to be had at sea.

The cabin was elaborately furnished, the cushions were fresh covered with velvet or damask, and the ornaments that relieved the beams that supported the deck were made as charming to the eye as paint and gold could make them.

Jessie, though having become somewhat reconciled to the loss of her mother, had in some measure lost her reason, and at times she would rave and shout in such a manner as to cause Madeline to live in dread of some violence from her.

Sometimes she would pace the deck for hours together with her hair dishevelled and a cloak thrown loosely over her shoulders, muttering wild and incoherent sentences, from which Madeline could gather only sufficient to know that she was jealous of some one, hated them, and was only waiting an opportunity to wreak her vengeance on them.

Owing to his presence being required so much on deck, Rock Elfin could not much enjoy the society of his fair captives, but he was unremitting in his attentions to Madeline when he did come below.

Madeline was surprised at this; for she knew Gerald Stuart and he were at variance, and she thought he would rather have put an end to her than to have preserved her for his rival.

She was wrong; such vengeance as this Rock Elfin did not crave; he wanted to wean her affections—to gain a victory over her, and then return her, humbled and disgraced, to him who loved her dearer than life.

Madeline, in her innocence, did not dream of this; she attributed his kindness to some sudden change of mind—a turn for the better—as though he had been stricken with remorse.

Not so with Jessie; she was more acquainted with the world—she could read his intentions at a glance, and she became desperately jealous of Madeline, whom she considered her rival, although Rock Elfin was loathed and hated by her as though he had been a viper.

Under the belief that Rock Elfin had turned in the path of rectitude and was about to atone for his past sins by a charitable act, Madeline chatted and conversed with him more freely than she would otherwise have done, a circumstance which was noticed with flashing eyes by the half-witted Jessie.

Madeline was blind to all this, though she could not help noticing that Jessie sought on several occasions to quarrel with her on some trivial pretence not worth noticing.

This circumstance passed and Madeline thought no more of it, until Jessie, one day, openly accused her of allowing the captain a greater freedom with her than the rules of propriety allowed.

Madeline was too indignant at first to reply; but when her companion began to upbraid and accuse her of that which she was innocent, she stood up and defended herself in a manner becoming her.

'False woman!' she said, 'how dare you utter such vile insinuations? Do you know that every lie you utter you will have to answer for?'

'Of that I am perfectly aware,' replied Jessie, with provoking coolness; 'it is not from such lips as yours I need a remembrance.'

'You will need something more, I presume, if you follow up your vile assertions.'

'A proof! Ha! ha! I have it already.'

So saying, she removed a watch and chain from Madeline's neck, and holding it in her hand at arm's length, exclaimed—

'Now deny it if you can, while I hold the proof.

'But, but,' stammered Madeline, too flurried to explain.

'Ha! ha! your conscience accuses you I can see, the blush of shame mantles your brow, the hectic flush mounts to your cheek, a guilty knowledge fills you with remorse, and your tongue refuses to speak the lie you would utter.'

'Fiend! what mean you?' gasped Madeline, almost falling to the floor of the cabin.

'Need I explain? Tell me where you got this? Does it not belong to him—at least it did till he gave it to you.'

'Silence! let me hear no more!' cried Madeline, pressing her heated brow.

BLACK EYED
SUSAN.

OR, PIRATES ASHORE.

E.V. CAMPBELL Sc.

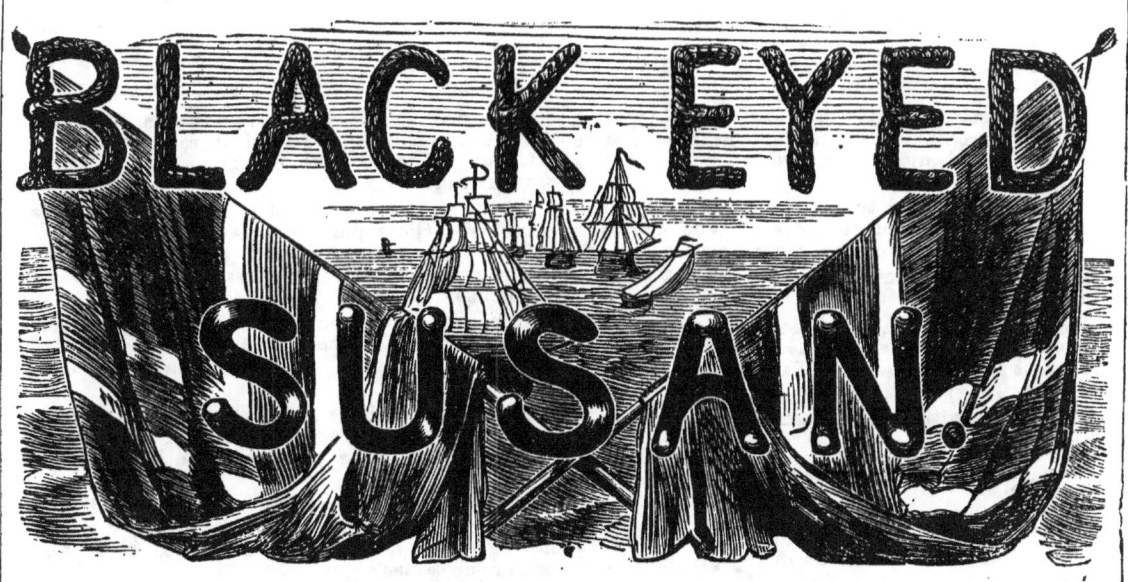

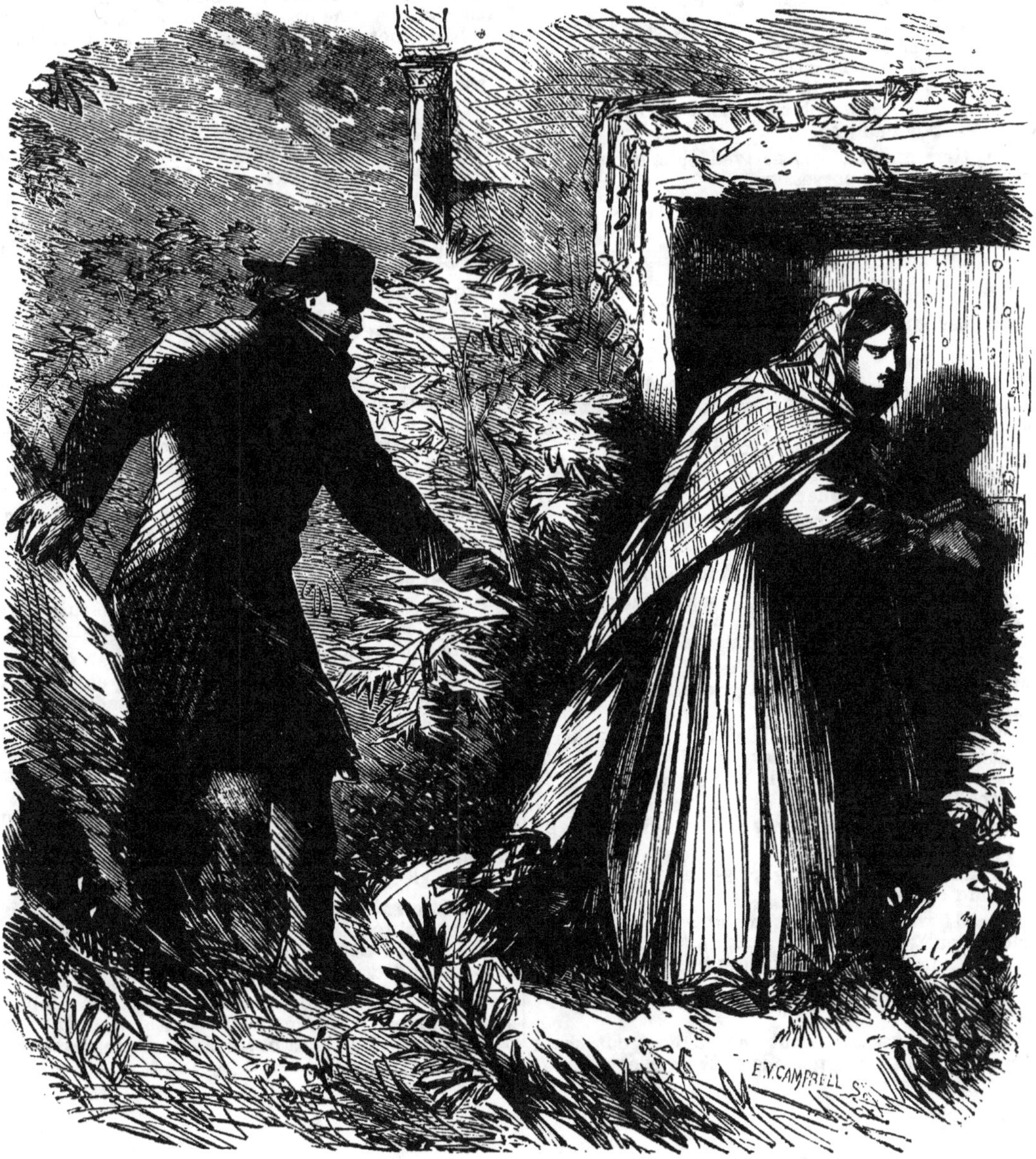

THE SECRET DISCOVERED.

'Well may you not wish to hear it!' cried Jessie, reproachfully. 'Had you granted him no favour, why should he make you such a present as this?'

Madeline listened to the woman's words until she could bear them no longer. Then she sank into a seat, and buried her face in her hands.

Jessie still continued to taunt her, but Madeline, made no reply.

Had the question have been put to her in a proper manner, she would have been able easily to account for her possession of the watch.

As it was her heart was too full to speak, so she put up with her companion's reproaches in silence.

A few words will explain how she became possessed of it.

Rock Elfin was hastily called on deck when enjoying his after dinner wine, and in his hurry he left the watch which he dearly prized on the table.

It was a beautiful specimen of workmanship and was of great value, and Madeline took it up to examine, and was very much taken with the portrait of a lady drawn on ivory that was set in the back, and ornamented with diamonds.

So deeply was her attention engrossed, that she tried it on her own neck to see how it would look, and being disturbed by the cabin boy entering, she hurried out of the cabin to her state room, intending to return the watch to a place of more safety when the boy had gone.

This time had not yet arrived, thus accounting for it being in her possession.

CHAPTER CXXXII.

DOGGRASS IN A FIX—THE RETURN OF LITTLE JACK.

THE affray with the smugglers caused some consternation in the town of Deal, and afforded much gossip for the idlers, who were glad to catch hold of any subject to pass away a dull hour.

'Did you hear of Bill Raker being killed?' asked one old dame of another.

'What, Raker, the noted smuggler!'

'Yes.'

'Lor' bless me, no! How did it happen?'

'There, that's the mystery,' replied the old hag, dwindling her voice down to a whisper; 'but I heard as much that old Doggrass had sold him.'

'Why, you don't say so! The old villain! He's rolling in riches now, without grabbing after blood money!'

'That's just what I say, Mrs. Clat. But, there, what bit of good is it having friends? You'd better be without them if they are not to be trusted!'

'Much better, Mrs. Jones; I would rather be dead than be like that!'

'And so would I, though, by-the-bye, I fancied you said Raker was dead.'

'Dead! woman; he was cut up awfully! I was told by one who helped to pick up the pieces, that there was not a piece two inches big left of him!'

'And did he have some of Tom Hatchett's men with him?'

'Oh! yes, a score; but the soldiers cut them down like grass, and not one of them escaped!'

This was the tale told two hours after the fray, and as at each recital it received a fresh addition, it must have become a tale of great wonderment before night.

As the public in general bore no ill-will to the smugglers, the report that Doggrass had turned informer brought on him the anger of the lovers of cheap spirits, and they threatened to pull down his house.

Doggrass, to escape their wrath, shut up what part of the shop he could, and then retired out of sight, leaving Susan to battle it out as best she could.

This was the wisest plan he could have done, inasmuch that his presence only served to excite the mob, and everything went on smoothly when he was gone.

It was when business was at its height, that a youth, care-worn and pale, entered the bar, and having called for refreshment, seated himself at one of the tables.

Susan was too busy when he entered to take much notice of him, but there was something in his voice and manner that led Susan to believe it was not the first time she had heard it.

As we have said, she was too busy to notice him further at the time he entered, but when the noisy mob had quieted down a little, he rose of his own accord, and approached her.

'Susan,' he said, pressing her hand in his thin, bony fingers; 'Susan, do you not remember me?'

'I do not; and yet methinks I have heard that voice before. What is your name?'

'Jack Murray, or Little Jack, as they used to call me,' he replied.

'Merciful heavens!' cried Susan looking at his pale and wasted face, 'is it possible? Long ere this I had given you up as dead.'

'I have had many narrow escapes, I can assure you, but I have weathered through them all. I will relate part of my adventures since last I saw you.'

'More dead than alive, I was taken off the raft by the mate of a ship, who having vainly tried to prevail on the captain to lower the boat, as the captain considered I was dead, jumped overboard, swam to the raft, and swam back with me to the ship.

'Once on board the vessel, and recovered, I soon learnt that she was a privateer, and that the captain, though a good man in many respects, had many failings.

'The grog-can he worshipped, and the ship was often neglected, and to this we owe the dreadful tragedy that followed my going on board.

'We had spent several days in giving chase to a small craft that we took for a pirate, and thus got in the mazes formed by the West India Islands, when we met with a sad mishap. I have mentioned it to no one since, as its memory gives me too much pain to delight in the recital.

'We had been enjoying a good breeze, when one evening the sea and the air were so calm that the vessel lay on the bosom of the water like a huge animal asleep, with her head towards the shore.

'Lieutenant Cook, the commander, who had been on the look-out for the pirate ship as long as twilight enabled him to do so, laid aside his glass and descended into the cabin.

'All above, and below, and around, was now lulled as in slumber; presently the mate, who was on deck, observed a small black cloud resting over the land.

'The cloud was gradually increasing, and although the mate saw no ground to apprehend danger, he thought it right to communicate the fact to his superior officer, believing that the land breeze was about to set in with unusual strength.

'Mr. Cook desired him to keep a sharp look-out and he would join him on the deck immediately.

'A moment after, a squall, as strong as it was sudden, burst from the cloud, and just as Cook had ascended to the deck, the schooner was born onward at a speed exceeding all belief, and though the men tried hard to take in the sail that was more than the ship would bear, it was impossible.

'Presently, as sudden as it had come on, the wind changed from N.N.E., where it had been blowing, to S.S.W., exactly the opposite point, and blew if anything ten times harder.

'The vessel thus suddenly taken aback, flew through the water, stern first, and from the commencement it was considered an hopeless task to try and save her.

'The captain (or Lieutenant Cook) shouted his orders hoarsely through his trumpet, and entreated the men to do their utmost, but like himself, when desired by the mate to lower the boat, they put it down as hopeless, and took no notice of his orders.

'When the vessel so sudden reversed her course, the wheel chains gave way before the sudden strain, so that the ship was totally unmanageable, and in less than a quarter of an hour she ploughed under an angry wave, that was coming to meet her, and went down stern first.

'Two of the crew were below, and they went down with her.

'The others, twenty-two in number, were left struggling in the deep, for the squall had passed, and sky and sea were again tranquil.

'It was now discovered that the boat had parted from the vessel, and floated.

'A rush was made towards her, and several of the men attempted to get into her on the same side.

'The consequence was, that she became half full of water, upset, rolled over and over, and at length lay with her keel upwards.

'Some got across her keel, others supported themselves by holding on to her with their hands, and thus all were for a time safe.

'Lieutenant Cook now reminded the crew that it was impossible for them to remain long in this predicament, and exhorted them to right the boat, and bale out the water from her.

'He was immediately attended to; the men on the keel relinquished their seats, the boat was turned over, and two men were ordered into her to bale out the water.

'This they commenced doing with their hats, and it seemed probable that by perseverance their task would be accomplished.

'At this moment a man called out that he saw the fin of a shark.

'Immediately all was confusion—everyone endeavoured to save himself, and in doing so rushed into needless danger.

'The mate begged them to persevere in attempting to clear the boat of water, and directed those not engaged in baling to keep splashing with their legs to frighten the sharks.

'Again he was attended to, four men were in the boat baling, and the water was rapidly decreasing, when a noise was heard, and more than a dozen sharks darted in among them.

'In the panic which ensued the boat was again upset, and the men were at the mercy of the marine monsters.

'At first the sharks played about amongst the men, occasionally rubbing against them, but presently a loud shriek arose from one of them—his leg was bitten from his body.

'The attack was now general.

'Shrieks arose from one and another; some were torn from the boat, and several sank into the abyss, either from being bitten, or through fear.

'In this trying moment we never lost courage, neither was Lieutenant Cook dismayed. He still gave orders to the crew firmly and coolly, and was still obeyed by them.

'The boat was again righted, and the baling again commenced, Cook clinging to the stern while he directed and encouraged his crew.

'For a moment he ceased to splash while he looked into the boat to see what progress his men were making.

'At this instant a shark bit off both his legs above the knees.

'With fortitude scarcely credible, he endeavoured to conceal the fact from his remaining crew, but, in spite of his effort to suppress it, a deep groan escaped him; he loosed his hold of the boat, and was about to sink, when two of his men caught hold of him, and placed him in the stern-sheets.

'Bleeding and in agony as he was, he still exerted himself for the benefit of his crew.

'At this instant some of the men endeavoured to get into the boat, which was thus drawn on one side, and Lieutenant Cook rolled overboard, and sunk to rise no more.

'The boat was now again upset.

'Some of the bleeding seamen placed themselves on the keel, but one by one dropped into the ocean.

'It was at eight o'clock when the Goldfinch sunk, and before nine all on board of her were eaten or drowned, with the exception of two, who succeeded in righting the boat and getting into her.

'They immediately began baling, and worked until they were nearly exhausted.

'The sharks swam round the boat and endeavoured to upset her, but failing, and perhaps gorged already, at length departed.

'The men worked at intervals, until the boat was nearly free from water, and then lay down and slept until after daylight.

'The morning was fine but sultry. The men were hungry, thirsty, and fatigued. They looked around them; an unbroken ocean, a cloudless sky, and a burning sun, were all that was within their view.

'They began to think of the only resource remaining—for either to kill his comrade and devour his flesh.

'They were men of equal strength, and both had knives.

'Each, however, seemed unwilling to resort to this horrible expedient, except in the last extremity.

'The man at the stern, for they were separated in mutual apprehension by nearly the whole length of the boat, knelt down and prayed, and his comrade followed the example.

'As the morning wore on they suffered intensely from thirst, and aggravated their suffering by attempting to allay it with salt water.

'The madness of despair was beginning to develop

itself in one of them, when a sail appeared in sight, which afterwards proved to be a brig steering towards them.

'One flung his jacket in the air, while the other hailed again and again, and sometimes they hailed both together, although the brig was at such a distance that it was not possible their cry should be heard.

'She approached nearer and nearer, and so riveted were their minds on the brig, that hunger and thirst were forgotten in the excitement of hope.

'The people on board the ship appeared to notice them, but just as they had reason to think this was the case, she changed her course and hoisted additional sail.

'Still they attempted to gain her attention, and endeavoured to propel the boat with their hands, but all was in vain, the ship was becoming every moment more distant, and their chance of release from their horrible condition of course fainter.

'At this moment one of the sailors conceived the bold project of swimming to the brig, which was by this time two miles and a half from them.

'His comrade remonstrated with him, so wild and hopeless did the undertaking appear to him, especially as the fins of sharks were again seen here and there above the water.

'After a little hesitation, caused by the appeal of his shipmate, and a short prayer, he jumped over.

'The splash occasioned by his doing so caused the sharks to disappear, and the man in the boat well knew they were in search of his comrade.

'Immediately after, three of them passed the boat towards him.

'With the greatest anxiety the sailor in the boat watched his messmate; he swam well, kicking and splashing as he went, to frighten the sharks.

'Once he beheld one of them close to him, but he only swam the faster, and kicked the more vigorously.

'The wind had freshened, the brig was sailing more swiftly, his cries were unheard by her crew, and he began to think he must yield himself up a prey to the sharks.

'While this melancholy thought was passing through his mind, he saw a man look over the side of the vessel; to attract his attention he held up both his hands, jumped up in the water, and used every means in his power to attain his end.

'He was successful; a boat was put out, the brave mariner was picked up, and was soon joined by his comrade on board the brig.

'I, for it was myself and the mate that had been so providentially saved, recognised at once in the features of the captain of the brig the face of one I well knew, and he asked me of his wife, and I told him all I knew, which, indeed, was not very much.'

'And who—who was it?' asked Susan, excitedly.

'Who do you think?'

'I do not know.'

'Your husband, William Howard.'

CHAPTER CXXXIII.

THE JOURNEY TO THE WHITE VILLA—THE CONSPIRATORS—SUSAN AGAIN IN DANGER.

THE sudden entrance of a party of coast-guardsmen put an end to the discourse between Susan and Jack Murray, and Susan having recovered sufficiently from her embarrassment, prepared to serve them.

Since the time when William's trial was pending, Deal had never been in such a commotion.

The daring of the smugglers occupied everybody's mind, and the parties of sailors, marines, and coastguardsmen that paraded the streets, led them to believe that some dreadful crisis was at hand.

To Susan it was a time of extreme torture, for now she fully believed from what she had heard from Murray, that her husband was in peril.

To add to this, Jack Murray had disappeared very suddenly when the coastguard entered.

It was a source of relief to her when the house was cleared for the night, and then she sat herself down, and burst into tears.

Having thus relieved herself, she drew the cramped note from her bosom, and received some consolation from its perusal.

'Something to my advantage!' she muttered. 'What can he mean? Will he really take an interest in my husband's welfare? At nine o'clock, too, he will be expecting me. I will go. My uncle will not miss me.'

So saying, she put on her hat and cloak, and took something from a drawer which she placed beneath her dress, and silently left the house.

The White Villa was a sharp walk of a few minutes from the Three Luggers, but as it was in a lonely quarter, Susan looked well about her as she proceeded.

Arrived at the house she knocked at the massive oak door with trembling hand, and an old withered hag answered her summons.

'Well, what do you want, miss?' she asked snappishly, as though she had been suddenly disturbed from a sound nap, and did not thank Susan for disturbing her.

'Admiral Lanceville, if you please.'

'Well, I don't please; I wish you'd come at a proper time of night. I wonder how a young woman like you dare venture out at such late hours!'

'That need not concern you,' replied Susan, annoyed. 'I wish to see Admiral Lanceville. Is he within?'

The old woman stood for a moment cogitating.

'What can she want with him or he with her,' she thought. 'Well, he told me he was not at home to anybody, so I'll tell her so plump. He's not a going to flirt with her and keep company with my daughter.'

Having settled this matter in her own mind, the old woman made answer—

'Admiral Lanceville is out—he's gone to dine with an officer on board the frigate laying in the downs.'

'He will not return to-night, then?'

'Certainly not. You must come to-morrow—and at a more seasonable hour than this, I hope.'

The old woman spoke as though she meant what she said, and closed the door in Susan's face without so much as saying good night.

This was a terrible disappointment to Susan; her heart seemed to sink like lead, and she stood for some seconds like one dumb-stricken, ere she ventured to move away.

A little to the right of where she stood was an old mansion which had long since yielded to the hand of time, and was now untenanted; in fact, no one could live in it, as in some parts the walls had crumbled and the roof fallen in.

The grounds of this house were extensive, and had been, therefore, used as a meeting-place for the disreputables of the town.

There smugglers had sought shelter from the law, and gallants had met to form their plans of villainy; for, as the place was reputed to be haunted, they had but little fear of being disturbed.

It was on this very night that a party were to meet for some purpose, and one, who had already arrived, seated himself on the stump of a fallen tree.

He was in deep meditation, and kept on muttering; but not sufficiently loud for a listener, if there had been any, to learn the subject of his thoughts.

'It is past the hour,' he muttered more loudly as the chime of some church clock broke the stillness of the air. 'This failure of promise at the onset forbodes a failure at the end.'

Then he continued his low mutterings again, and glanced uneasily around.

Each moment seemed to heighten his suspense, and every rustle of a leaf seemed to make him start. Then he would glance up at the blackened walls and sink again into deep reverie.

But his ears were still on the alert, and alive to the most trifling sound.

A low whistle, heard from some distance, apparently caused him to spring to his feet.

After a moment's pause, he bent low down, and placing something to his lips, blew three quick successive whistles.

In a moment the signal was answered as at first, and then the person within the grounds seemed to be satisfied, for he returned to his seat on the old stump, and again seated himself.

In a few moments a rustling and crackling in the bushes announced the approach of some one.

Then the branches on the side next the sea were pushed aside, and a young, handsomely-dressed cavalier stepped in the clear ground.

While he paused and re-adjusted his attire, which had been disarranged by the narrow passages, he spoke in a free and careless tone—

'This is a deuce of a place to have a fellow come to meet you, De Lorn; you might as well appoint purgatory at once. It has almost squeezed the breath out of me to get through among the trees.'

'Where are the others?' asked De Lorn; and his tone was bluff and stern.

'That's more than I know; I've had trouble enough to bring myself here, let alone keeping a look-out for them—but hark! there's a note from some of 'em!'

At the same instant another whistle was heard.

It was answered by De Lorn, and in a few moments two more persons stealthily entered the area.

'All but her—why does she play the laggard?' muttered De Lorn, as he glanced at the newcomers, one of whom was a man apparently as old as himself, and quite as odd in appearance, though differing much in style, for in his countenance could be read but one single passion—one single mark of character—and that was avarice.

His face was thin and sharp, his eyes were small, black, and glittered like the eyes of the adder when disturbed from its hole; his lips were thin, and like his face, pale and bloodless.

His brow was set off by two shaggy eyebrows of gray, which hung over his eyes, so sunken, like moss above a cavern's mouth.

He was armed with dagger, pistol, and cutlass; but he did not look as if his hand would be over ready to use them, or as if his thin, starved-looking figure had much strength in it to wield them.

The person who accompanied him was an officer to judge by his dress, and he looked more like a leader of banditti than anything else we can compare him to.

De Lorn arose as they entered the cleared space, and as he advanced, addressed the eldest by the name of Villiers, and the other as Clement.

'We want but one more here, and then we will proceed to business,' said De Lorn, after glancing again in the direction whence the others had appeared.

'Then you have no cause for delay,' said a clear, bird-like voice, which sounded so near him that De Lorn started back in surprise.

At the same moment a person stepped noiselessly from amid the branches, and, though clad in male apparel and armed like a cavalier, the beauty of her form and the lightness of her step, as well as her voice, betrayed that she was sailing under false colours.

She was tall, her eyes black as night's shade and bright as night's stars, over which drooped lashes, long, silky, and ebon, serving, with her cheek of olive hue and arched eyebrows, to denote her descent from the same race as De Lorn, and her very manner seemed to denote the woman of fiery passions—devoted in love, and bitter in hate—one whose hand would not hesitate to use the steel or poison, if love was thwarted or wrong committed, whether the steel or poison was for herself or others.

'Ah, Lady Catherine, is it you! I thought you would not fail at this meeting,' said De Lorn.

And a singular attempt at a smile contracted and worked his horrid features as if he had swallowed a young hedgehog.

'I never fail,' she said.

But how different her sweet, clear tones from the unwomanish look which her face wore as she spoke.

'Well, we are all here now, where we can talk, free from all observation, secure alike from lookers-on or listeners,' said De Lorn.

And then turning to the one who had first entered the area, the youngest of the men, he added—

'You, Lord Clive, are the only one here who does not already know of the business which led us here.'

'Then I presume I'm the next one to be informed upon the subject,' said the young man, carelessly.

'You are. I have been kind to you since you have been with us, have I not?'

'Yes, De Lorn, you have; but what in the world are you driving at? I don't want an hour's palaver about nothing, when five words will do as well as fifty. What do you want of me? You know my situation, and my wants. I am a ruined lord, one who owns a title without a crown to support it, save my paltry gains since I have joined you. I want money; money I will have; and if you have any plan to get money, speak out, and if the treasury were in purgatory, I'd go there to make a draw!'

'Don't talk so fast, my friend,' said De Lorn; 'you shall have money, never fear; and, if we meet with success, and our friends across the channel prove true to us, you shall have no just cause of complaint.'

'Had we not better explain the errand we are upon ?' asked Villiers.

'On reflection, I think not,' answered De Lorn.

'Why so ?'

'For this reason—that the less we speak on the subject while on these shores the better. We have heard of such a thing as walls having ears, and trees, when occupied by eavesdroppers, are not totally deaf.'

The hint given by De Lorn had its effect on all the party and met with their approval, and as to the gay young lord, he did not press them for further explanations.

'Well, what of the boat ?' asked Catherine.

'I have hired a lugger,' replied De Lorn, who seemed to be the leader of the party. 'She is a swift sailer, and her captain is a man we can depend on.'

'When do we start ?'

'Almost directly. It's fortunate for us there is no moon, and I am glad to find you all here. Hist ! I thought I heard a sound.'

All were silent, and strained their ears to catch the least sound.

A low whistle sounded near the road, and was answered from a different part of the grounds to that in which the party stood.

Presently the rattle of wheels was heard, and near an angle of the road the rumbling ceased.

Then followed another low whistle, the shriek of a female, and then the rumbling of the coach was continued till it was out of hearing.

As the party stood wondering what this could mean, a rustling of the branches disturbed them, and a man, in a thick pea-jacket buttoned close under his chin, made his appearance.

'Well, Philip, what news ?' asked De Lorn.

'Favourable as yet, your honour.'

'Is all clear ?'

'Ay—and the wind just in the quarter to send my lugger spinning across in a very few hours.'

'Glad to hear it. Have you made all preparations ?'

'Trust an old salt for that, your honour. The Curlew's cabin is as snug as any parlour for her ladyship to go into, and as for provisions, you won't find much better than I've provided.'

'As to that,' interposed Villiers, 'we don't want luxuries, a safe journey is all we need. We shall have to be cautious leaving the coast.'

'And we must land, if possible, without being seen,' suggested Lady Catherine.

'Of course; though I fear we shall have to do a bit of dodging, for, do you know, when I landed with the boat an hour since, the jetty was lined with soldiers and blue jackets.'

'Ah ! do you think they expect us ?'

'No; how could they know you were coming without either of us split ? I can swear they did not hear it from me, and there was none other, save your own selves to tell them.'

'But does not the matter seem strange to you ?'

'It certainly does; but from what I heard of their conversation they were on the look-out for William Howard, the pirate, as they called him; but, Lord love your hearts, he's as true a tar and as honest a one, I'll swear, as ever trod a plank.'

'Will Howard,' said Lady Catherine, with the uncertainty of one awaking from a dream. 'Was he not the friend of Gerald Stuart, the '——

'His lieutenant,' replied Philip, interrupting her ; 'but they have long been separated.'

'Indeed ! I have not heard of this.'

'It is true, nevertheless. Some little affair across the water parted them in some way, though I could never learn how ; and he took to smuggling, or something of that sort, and no one, not even his wife, as far as I could hear, knows of his whereabouts.'

'And what became of Gerald Stuart ?'

'I don't know, only that he's on some private expedition ; and I heard it said at the boat-house this morning that Admiral Garthway, when he sailed in the three-decker, swore he would not return until he had him dangling like a jewel-block from the yard-arm.'

'And yet he loved the admiral's daughter, did he not ?' asked Catherine, with an ill-suppressed sigh.

'Ay, did he, your ladyship! and a fine good-hearted lady, too, was Madeline Garthway. I shall never forget her kindness to me when my lugger was stove in, and I had two months on shore with a broken wing.'

'What—your arm broken ?'

'Yes, and my wife hove down with a fever. It was all through trying to save the crew of a schooner that struck on the shoals in a gale of wind.'

'Well, Philip, I think it is about time you cut your yarn, for we are losing time and wasting a favourable breeze,' said De Lorn, anxiously.

'I am ready to heave a-head at any moment,' replied the fisherman; 'say the word, and I drop my jawing tackle and take up the sweeps at once.'

'If there is danger lurking, as you say,' said De Lorn, 'we must proceed with caution. Have you any arms on board ?'

'Ay, and men to wield them. I can back my crew against any reasonable odds; they can handle a pike or a cutlass with as much ease as their nets, and throw a shot as true as they could throw a line.'

'That is well. Is the boat at the jetty ?'

'I should think not, rather.'

'How are we to reach her then ?'

'By a path down the cliff. Trust me for not being such a fool as to leave her under the nose of such a shark as Admiral Lanceville. He's prowling about here they say, and it's evident he has not left London for nothing.'

With this the fisherman turned the quid in his cheek, and led the way by an unfrequented route to the cliff, and in a very few minutes they were all seated in the boat.

Not a word was spoken as the sturdy crew bent to their oars, and propelled her swiftly towards a lugger that was lying with her sails half hoisted.

But they had not proceeded far, when a cutter, filled with men, pushed out from a shaded nook, and with muffled oars, proceeded in their wake.

Owing to the darkness and the shade of the cliff, Philip did not at first notice it, but as soon as it became apparent to his practised eye, he gave his men orders to 'give way.'

This they did with a spirit equal to the emergency, but owing to the heavy loading of the boat, the cutter gained upon them.

'Pull, lads, or we shall have to fight for it !

whispered the fisherman, hoarsely. 'Bend your backs, and stretch out handsomely.'

'Ay, ay,' growled the men, and they redoubled their exertions, but they did not reach the lugger till the cutter was within a fathom or so from the boat's stern.

Philip leapt on board and assisted his passengers to reach the deck, then securing the boat, set the sails, and the lugger out through the water, propelled by the gently rising breeze.

The cutter kept up the chase until all hopes of overtaking the lugger seemed fruitless; then the oars were abandoned, and a pistol volley discharged at her sails.

This did no material damage, however, and the sailors venting their rage in no very decorous manner, turned the cutter's head to the shore.

About ten miles from Deal, on the borders of a wood, stood a lone house, which had long been uninhabited, owing to a dispute between its claimants, who had placed it in chancery.

It was reached by a lone road, seldom frequented but by gipsies, or those who, for obvious reasons, sought its shelter not so much from choice as compulsion.

This lonely house, though sadly suffering from neglect, was still handsomely furnished, and one of its lower rooms was often used as a council chamber by a notorious band of highway robbers, who had a cavern in the wood where they stored their plunder.

It was in one of the rooms, in a part the most tenantable, that a female lay on a couch, and as the gray dawn struggled through the casement, she raised her head and looked around.

'Where am I?' she muttered, as she strove to shake off the drowsiness that, spite of her efforts, overcome her, and again she sinks into a state of slumber.

An hour passed, when she turns upon her side, her eyes slowly open, and she gazes vacantly around.

For several moments she gazes thus, her colourless lips gently part, and she mutters again—

'Where am I? Can it be a dream, or have I fallen a victim to some vile treachery?'

Silently her eyes wander around the apartment.

She is at a loss to conjecture into what place she has been thus suddenly transported.

In an agony of despair, she again dropped her head on her pillow.

Impulsively she starts.

A noise at the door had aroused her.

Then the door slowly opens and a man enters.

He is closely muffled; but, in spite of his disguise, she recognises him at once.

It is Admiral Lanceville, the visitor to the Three Luggers, and the female who has just aroused from a drugged stupor is Black-Eyed Susan.

With a fiendish smile the admiral gazes on the reclining female, and then, with jaunty step, nears her.

Scarcely recovered from the effects of the drug, Susan, more dead than alive, fixes her lustrous eyes on the intruder.

Struck with admiration at the lovely woman as she lay with hair and clothes dishevelled, the villain was about to clasp her to his breast.

But Susan, seeing his intention, sprang to her feet, and in a stern voice cried—

'Unhand me, villain, if you value your life, for by heavens I swear if you offer to violate me, I will lay you dead at my feet.'

'Come, come, my fair one,' responded Lanceville, coaxingly, 'you're too hasty by far.'

'Stand off!' she cried, 'or by heavens you shall pay for this rashness.'

Her hitherto pale face mantled with indignation as he embraced her, and her large dark eyes flashed fiercely.

Then with a scornful curl of the lip she cried imperatively—

'Admiral Lanceville! what means this outrage? Is this the conduct of a gentleman and an officer?'

'Pardon my presumption, Susan,' was his reply, as he drew her to his heart and strove to imprint a kiss upon her flushed cheek, 'when I tell you that love has prompted me thus to act.'

'Base wretch! how can you stand before me and utter such a falsehood? Are you not afraid the floor will sink beneath you?'

'Did I not have sufficient belief in its capabilities to bear me I might have cause for such fear,' replied the admiral, screwing up his face into what he supposed a smile. 'But,' he added, 'I place great confidence both in it and you.'

'Indeed,' cried Susan, indignantly, 'then I feel confident you are doing wrong. You will find me such as you little expect.'

The admiral quailed beneath her searching glance, yet still retaining one arm round her slender waist, said—

'Do you reject me? Is not my word to be taken before that of an outlaw? Is not my suit preferable to that of Will Howard?'

Susan's eye flashed fiercely at the mention of the brave sailor, and with a violent jerk she disengaged herself from his grasp.

'Fiend!' she cried, 'if he was here he would not suffer you thus to insult me. Your life would atone for this foul treachery.'

'Aha! my pretty minx, I have little to fear from him.'

'Do not be too confident. I know he will not rest until he has discovered the place of my captivity, and punished the perpetrators of this dark design.'

The admiral fixed his longing gaze on the fair girl as she uttered these words; then, in a malicious tone, said—

'You will never see Will Howard again—he is dead.'

'You cannot mean it?'

'I do.'

Susan could no longer repress her feelings, and she sank down on the couch burying her face in her hands.'

The admiral smiled demoniacly as he stood gazing upon her, and a gleam of evil shot from his fixed orbs.

For several moments he gazed thus.

Feasting on the agony of the heart-broken girl.

And as he did so his guilty thoughts were still at work, devising a plan for the furtherance of his scheme.

At length Susan, having relieved her bursting heart by a flood of tears, raised her head, and in a supplicating voice said—

'Tell me, is it true what you have spoken? Do not trifle with my feelings. Is my husband no more?'

'What I have said is the truth. The daring band of outlaws are routed—Will Howard with many of his followers are slain, whilst many are captured, and even now are awaiting their trial on board the flag ship.'

Susan again burst into tears.

In a voice scarcely audible with emotion, she said—

'I have nothing now on earth to live for—without him this world to me is a desert. Go, leave me to my solitude. Let me mourn for the loss of him who loved me dearer than his own life.'

'Foolish girl,' replied the admiral, reprovingly, 'you know not what you say. If he had lived he would have swung upon the gallows. Thank heaven you have escaped being dragged to prison.'

'Do not mock me,' answered Susan, sobbing; 'he was both brave and noble. Would to heaven that I had been there to close his dying eyes, and sooth his last moments with my prayers.'

'That was impossible, fair lady. He was shot dead by my own hand, when in the act of cutting down one of the coastguards who had arrested him. Soon after, as I came along the road, I saw a coach, and in it a female. I followed it, and I saw them enter here, and as the female was borne from the coach, I caught a slight glimpse of her face, and immediately recognised yourself.'

'Are you sure it was not by your own orders I was brought here.'

'Pardon me, madam; do you think I could be guilty of such villainy?'

'Then what brings you here,' asked Susan, eyeing him suspiciously.

'Suspecting some foul play on the part of those who brought you here, I waited till they had gone, and on searching the house I found you here in this room a prisoner.'

'For what purpose do you suppose they brought me here?' she asked.

'I cannot say: doubtless to starve you to death; and, if so, it is most fortunate that I have discovered your prison, and am thus enabled to frustrate their wicked designs.'

'Then why have you thus taken advantage of my weakness? Why did you not open my prison door, and lead me to liberty?'

Pardon my weakness, madam. In the fulness of my joy at discovering it was you, the thought quite slipped my memory, and I could not repress my desire at the moment to embrace you.'

Susan was now fully assured of his villainy, though she was undecided how to act.

She feared there was truth in the report of her husband's death, especially after what she had heard from Jack Murray.

'He might have been taken in trying to land,' she thought; 'perhaps betrayed by one of his crew,' for she had not heard of the wreck of the smuggling brig, and believed he had retained possession of that vessel up to the present.

The tale invented by the admiral seemed so feasible too, especially as she knew the inveterate enmity existing between her husband and the government, and the stringent measures they had adopted for his capture.

His acquaintance with Gerald Stuart too, who, as we have seen, had thrust his fingers into political affairs, strengthened the enmity of the government, who had not forgotten Captain Crosstree's defeat, nor the depredations to their shipping done by the Golden Arrow.

For some moments they regarded each other in silence, each wrapped in their own meditations, Susan at her wit's end to frame an answer suitable to the occasion, and Admiral Lanceville chafing inwardly at the prospect of his scheme being defeated.

Then the thought occurred to her that the admiral's story had been fabricated to deceive her, and she once more ventured to speak.

'Admiral Lanceville,' she said, slowly, 'do you think to deceive me? You must be a villain of the the blackest dye to invent such a tale. Go—leave me to myself.'

'I cannot, my fair one,' cried he, gazing affectionately in her face; 'too dearly do I love you.'

'What!' cried Susan, recoiling from him as though he were a serpent, 'this from you?—you love me? Have you not that already which claims your love?'

The admiral's cheek turned pale at these words, then suddenly turned purple with passion.

Fixing a look of unmitigated hatred on his intended victim, he hissed—

'Fool!—no longer will I bandy words with you. You shall yield to my will, if not willingly, by force.'

'Cowardly dastard!' cried Susan, as he moved towards her; 'approach me not, or, by heavens, I'll pierce your black polluted heart.'

'What! with those dark fiery eyes?' inquired the admiral, placing his arm around her waist.

'No, monster, with this!' she answered, drawing a poignard from beneath her robes.

The admiral drew back from the glittering blade, and, with a bitter oath, said—

'Curse you! you shall dearly repent this folly. I will wring your very heart-strings ere I have done with you.'

Susan drew her form erect, but spoke not.

Then pointing to the door, motioned him to leave.

With lowering brow and scornfully curling lip, the villain obeyed, muttering as he went—

'She shall yield to my wishes. I will starve her to submission. I will subdue her proud spirit, though I send my soul to perdition by so doing.'

At the threshold of the door he turned to cast one more threatening glance on his victim.

But the vindictive expression of his features was suddenly changed to one of fear when he heard footsteps on the stairs hastily descending.

CHAPTER CXXXIV.

THE CONVERSATION ON THE BEACH.

It was on the same evening, though some few hours later, on which Murray had paid his visit to the Three Luggers, that two men met on the beach some distance from Deal.

'Well, what news bring you?' asked one, stopping suddenly in his impatient walk as the other descended the narrow path down the cliff.

'None of the brightest, captain,' was the reply. 'It won't be safe to hang about here long.'

'Why?'

'The town's in a regular uproar.'

'From what cause?'

'Hatchett's run foul of the sharks again. I heard he'd sunk a cutter, and had a brush this afternoon with the king's men.'

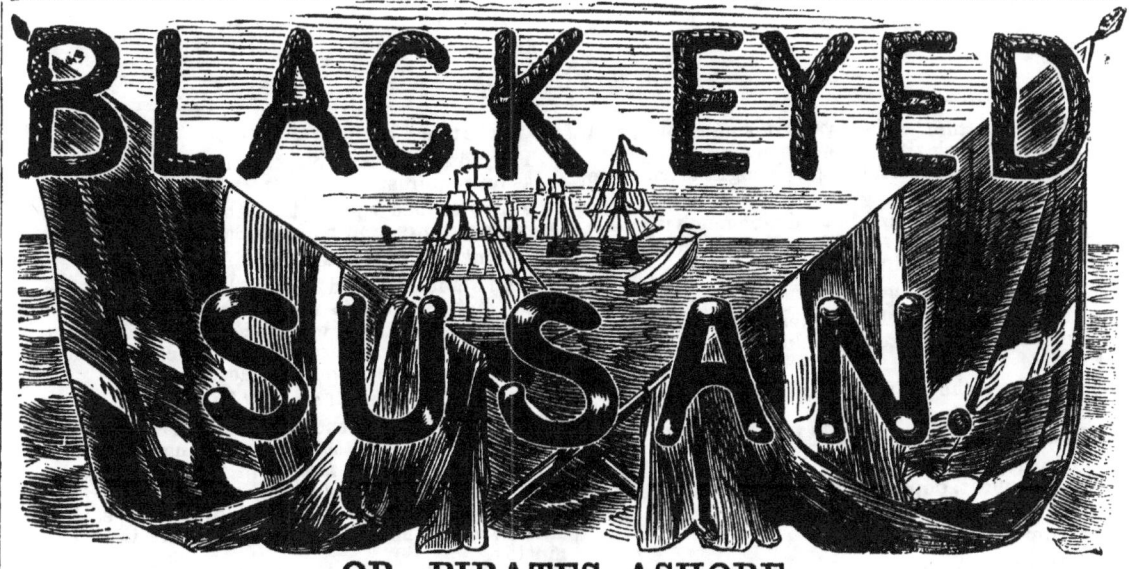

BLACK EYED SUSAN!

OR, PIRATES ASHORE.

THE COUNCIL.

'Confound him! he's always raising a dust, and especially at such time when we wish to be quiet. I should like to see him, though; I might learn some news from him.'

'You might, captain; but I doubt much whether he does not want advice himself, for the place is growing as hot for him as a cinder oven.'

'What has he been up to—running a cargo?'

'No—he seems to have given that work up for a time, but it's a mercy he didn't get clinched this time.'

'What was he doing on shore, then?' asked the captain.

'Paying old Doggrass a visit.'

'Visiting Doggrass, eh! Well, there is more mischief afloat, depend upon it; but did you see or hear anything of'——

'Your wife?'

'Yes.'

'Well, I did, captain, and I even spoke to her.'

'You did!' ejaculated the captain, hastily, his frame slightly quivering with emotion; 'and did you tell her I was safe?'

'Indeed, I did not—I had not time.'

'How was that?' asked the captain, his voice becoming hoarse.

'She was so taken aback by what I did tell her, that I was afraid we should attract attention, and that would not have been pleasant, as a party of coastguards entered at the time.

'And you '——

'Topped my boom and made all sail here; for I thought you would be anxious, and it was better than staying to be recognised.'

'True; but you might have whispered a few words to her, and told her I saw '——

'It was indeed possible—and yet, it would have been risking too much; you know those fellows have eyes and ears as sharp as a needle; besides, as matters are, they would have suspected me, perhaps have taken me to their quarters, and then what account could I give of myself?'

'True, Jack; but was she well, think you?'

'She looked as taut and trim as a jolly-boat, captain; one would think she had little to grieve her if we might judge from the roundness of her spars.'

'Well, well, that may be, though 'tis hard to judge a vessel's cargo by looking at her outer planks. It's a mystery to me what brings her in tow with her uncle—the old devil must have relented, and perhaps is trying to atone for his past sins. At all events, it does not seem he has given her over to the care of Hatchett.'

The captain's brow darkened as he mentioned the smuggler's name, and his teeth grated ominously as he tapped the hilt of his sword.

'Murray,' he said, sinking his voice to a hoarse whisper, 'that man has made himself my mortal foe; but this shall be my avenger, I will not spare him an inch.'

'At present it would not be well to treat him so. Let us first gain from him by stratagem that which we want to know.'

'Concerning Doggrass?'

'Yes; we shall do more by cunning than by force. I will visit the tavern again to-morrow, if you wish it.'

'No; I will go myself. I must see her, and then I will try and find out the smuggler's stronghold.'

'That will be no easy matter.'

'In what way?'

'They have several places, and shift about as occasion requires.'

'True,' replied the captain, thoughtfully; 'but Doggrass knows, and perhaps Susan.'

'I think not; Hatchett is artful.'

'And stands in need to be to keep his neck from harm; but he may do us a turn that no one else can. He knows every crack and crevice along the coast, and if we run across and get a cargo he will put us on to a good landing-place.'

'But why be in such a hurry?'

For this reason: those black bird-catchers on board do not like their time being idled; for though I shared the money in the ship equally, you heard they complained; and, if I do not do something to keep them employed and satisfy their wants, they will desert, or, what is worse, mutiny.'

'Of the latter you have little to fear, I should think.'

'I don't know, I would not trust nor tempt them too far; besides, they want a run ashore, and that's quite out of the question on this side the channel.'

'It would be madness to trust them here at least; if we were anchored in the Seine it would be different.'

'Yes, the Seine is the place,' muttered the captain, turning his face to seaward. 'But let us go on board, we can talk things over more comfortably there than here.'

They walked down towards a boat that lay a few yards from the beach with her men resting on their oars, and made a signal for them to pull her to.

The captain and Murray then stepped in, and the boat was soon heading towards a snug-looking craft that lay at anchor in the bay.

CHAPTER CXXXV.
DOGGRASS MEETS WITH AN OLD FRIEND.

LONG before the first visitors usually made their morning call at the Three Luggers, Doggrass was awake and moving.

He had passed a sleepless night, and wished he had not retired at all, for whenever he closed his eyes in the endeavour to sleep horrid visions seemed to rise before him.

It was a wonder, in fact, how such a wretch existed with the enormity of sins he had to carry; for there was scarcely a crime on record but what he had to answer for.

He had robbed the widow and the fatherless, taken the bed from beneath the dying man for the sake of a few shillings' rent; he had disgraced the daughter of one man whom he had ruined, and brought the son of another to the lowest dregs of misery and crime; he had steeped his hands in blood and committed successful forgery; he had robbed his fellow-man on every side; and last, if not the least, he had defrauded the revenue to such an extent that his coffers overflowed with wealth.

Haggard, careworn, and starting at even the sound of his own footsteps, the guilty wretch crawled about the house a miserable, despicable wretch, a prey to his own conscience, if he had any, and dragging out a weary existence.

'Strange, strange,' he muttered, as he listened at his door to hear if Susan was about. 'Strange it is indeed that she is not astir. I do not like to disturb her—I dare not, in fact; so I must open the door myself to those thirsty rascals who are already on their way to be served with their morning dram. The air feels chilly,' he added, as he shrugged his shoulders and gazed down at his ample attire; 'winter is fast approaching, and that reminds me that we soon shall close the events of another year. Yes,' he went on soliloquizing, 'I shall be sixty-five if I live another week, and how have I passed the last score of those years? In a manner too horrible to think upon, too horrible for inspection. Twenty years of crime; and yet,' he added, consolingly, 'there have been men more wicked than me—men who have wasted their wealth, which I have not, squandered their hard earnings and lived upon charity; of this crime at least my conscience is clear, for I never knew the sin of being poor.'

A loud knocking at the door, and a gruff voice pronouncing the name of Susan, aroused him from his reverie, and he listened to hear if it was answered from Susan's window, as it was her usual custom to do so.

All was silent but the throbbing of his own heart, which beat palpably against his ribs, and made him tremble. All was silent. Susan's merry voice did not salute his ear.

This filled him with superstitious fear, for he alike hated and feared the girl, and the conviction forced itself upon him that something wrong had happened.

Susan's room was opposite that of Dame Howard's, and he crept cautiously to the door and knocked.

'Who's there?' shouted the dame, alarmed at this unusual occurrence.

'Susa—an is ill, I fear,' he stammered in reply.

'Susan ill?' repeated the dame, in alarm; 'I will tend her at once, poor girl. I expected it would be so from what I saw of her yesterday.'

Doggrass tottered down to the door, his mind greatly harassed, although he might be said to have received some consolation in having conversed with a human being.

Amongst the customers who entered there was one whose features particularly struck Doggrass as being familiar.

They were of a man thick set and well-proportioned, muffled in a thick pea-jacket and fisherman's boots; a short pipe was stuck in his mouth, and a sou'-wester on his head, the flaps of which were drawn down closely over his face.

Doggrass tried to get a second look at him, but failed; he averted his face from him when he called for his liquor, and having been supplied, he walked away and seated himself with several men who, from their appearance, had evidently been out all night.

He was soon in conversation with them, and he could see he was putting several questions to them, which, by the bye, greatly annoyed Silas, inasmuch as he was too far from him to hear what was passing.

One thing he became cognisant of, and that only served to heighten his curiosity, and that was that the men answered his questions pretty freely, at least so it seemed, for they entered into a lively chat, and the man that caused Doggrass so much anxiety plied them liberally with grog.

Doggrass's attention was, however, soon turned in another channel.

Dame Howard informed him, with bewildered looks, that Susan was not to be found.

'Is she not in her room?' asked Doggrass, in alarm.

'She is not in the house that I can see,' answered the dame.

'Can you in any way account for her absence?'

'Not in the least.'

Doggrass bit his lip and trembled like a cat.

'Can she have betrayed me?' he thought, and his eye wandered to the stranger, through whose disguise he now fancied he saw the uniform of an officer.

Then he would console himself by muttering—

'Bah! what a fool I am! She knows nothing that would pay for her trouble in trying to sell me, thank God; I kept her too much in ignorance for that.'

Still, for all this he could not persuade himself that something was not wrong. He puzzled his brain to think of any incautious word that might have dropped from his lips, and which he knew her quick ear and sharp discernment would easily have picked up, and construed into a piece of wonderful information.

As he was thus cogitating, a man, with shaggy brows and wonderfully piercing eyes, entered the bar abruptly.

'Give us a nip of grog, old fellow,' were the first words he uttered gruffly.

'Good man, you appear in a hurry,' said Doggrass, nervously.

'It's hurrying times now, guv'ner; and though I feel to want a toothful of spirits most alarmingly, I don't want to lay myself open to the chance of taking my breakfast at the grating.'

'Why, what's the matter?' inquired Doggrass; 'have you captured a fleet of Frenchmen, or pounced on a cargo of contraband, that you'——

'No, but something as good. We've nabbed a prize.'

'Oh! a good one, I hope.'

'Well, I guess so, though I fear Jack's reward will be more in the form of glory than of prize money.'

'How is that?'

'Why, don't the officers always have the first cut, and leave us the bones?'

'I don't know but what you're right, my man; but what have you caught?—that infamous Hatchett and his crew?'

'Better than that. It's a craft we've had all the fleet looking after, and it's been their chance to miss them, and our good fortune to nab them; so, you see, it will recommend us to head-quarters; but I must be off, as I don't agree with the bo'sun's mate practising his art on my bare back.'

'But stay,' cried Doggrass, as the man turned to depart; 'what ship is it you have captured?'

'Why, the Martinet, if you have ever heard of her.'

'I have. How did you manage to catch her?'

'Catch her—my stars! we're just the boys that could do it. We sighted her in the morning, clapped on all sail, larboard and starboard, alow and aloft, got within range, gave her a few hundredweight of cold shot, boarded her, and found she was worth making a prize of; took her in tow, and now she is just off here, and I am going up to Admiral Lance—— something, whatever his name is, to tell him the news.'

This piece of news seemed to entirely take the attention of the listeners, and seemed to awaken a great deal of interest in the stranger.

Silas did not fail to notice this, and it only served to strengthen his opinions, that the stranger's visit boded him no good.

As the little party that had been so much engaged in chat had one by one left the house, the man with the slouched sou'-wester was soon left alone.

'How now, Mr. Landlord,' he said, rising from his seat; 'what have you done with that pretty niece of yours? Sent her out fishing—eh?'

Doggrass started, and trembled greatly. He was perplexed with the sudden question, and struck with the man's voice.

'My niece?' he said, endeavouring to collect himself; 'she's not very well.'

'Oh, indeed!' was the man's reply, and his eyes seemed to flash fire. 'No serious complaint, I hope.'

'No, nothing. Merely a—a'——

'Cold, I suppose? Well, can I see her?'

'You could not; she is confined to her room,' replied Doggrass, derisively.

The man bit his lip.

'There is no possibility of seeing her, then?' he said—

'None whatever. If you have any message for her you can leave it.'

'I have none for you,' thought Will, 'at least, at present; but there is some mystery in all this. She is purposely kept out of sight. Perhaps,' he muttered, as the thought occurred to him, 'perhaps he has sent her away. Hatchett may be taking especial care of her; if so,' he thought, 'I must act with caution, and punish those who are in fault. When, think you, it will be possible to see her?' he asked, breaking the silence.

'I do not know,' Silas replied, evasively; 'besides, I do not make it a practice to answer such questions.'

'Indeed! you may have to answer them a little oftener, much civiller, and a great deal more truthful before very long, mark you that, Silas Doggrass.'

'Scoundrel! what do you mean by such language?' asked Silas, white with passion. 'Know you not that what I have done for the girl is purely out of charity, and that I defy you or anyone else to take her from my keeping, unless she herself peremptorily refuses to stay with me.'

'You are a d—d rascal!' vociferated the man, 'and I will keep a sharp eye on you. I will set such a watch on your movements as you never had before.'

Doggrass burst into a rage, and began to swear vehemently; but the man appeared to take but little notice of his passion, and while Doggrass was in that state the man disappeared.

CHAPTER CXXXVI.

THE SMUGGLERS PROPOSE TO RID THEMSELVES OF AN ENEMY—TREACHERY.

LIEUTENANT PIKE was still in the stronghold of the smugglers, and though recovering rapidly from his wound, no decision as to his disposal had been arrived at.

Hatchett secretly wished him out of the way, though he did not wish to take his life in cold blood, and he hinted as much to Bill Raker.

'Why, as to that,' replied the smuggler, 'we must not be over-scrupulous. We must study our own interest in this affair; for, after what has happened, they will not hesitate in hanging us if they once get us in their clutches.'

'I know that; but still'——

'There is no buts in the case,' replied Raker, vehemently; 'it's our own safety we must study; besides, the men must have a voice in the matter.'

'They will be for killing him.'

'Quite right, too. We've brought him to our nest, and there are but two ways of keeping him in check, for he would betray us, as his words prove.'

'There are two alternatives you say? Name them, Bill.'

'One is hanging, the other confining him for life.'

'The first is an easy matter,' said Hatchett; 'but the second is out of all question. If we keep him here we must have him guarded, and then we have treachery to fear. We shall never feel safe, and besides he will learn all our plans, and see all we do.'

'That there is no denying; but if we put him out of the way he can trouble us no more.'

'But the men—what can we do with them?'

'Rocket seemed lost for an answer.

It would be wholesale murder to put an end to the lot.

'Can you not suggest anything?' asked Hatchett, impatient at his silence.

'Nothing; unless you blindfold them, and take them out to sea, put them adrift in a boat, and let them trust to chance.'

'That's a good plan, Bill, and one we will adopt. They shall go, and we will risk their escaping.'

With this the smuggler captain and his mate left the cave, and strolled out on the beach to prepare future arrangements.

While they were thus employed a party had secretly met in a hollow of the cliffs to talk over their grievances, and consult each other what should be done.

Foremost of these was Rocket, and he acted as spokesman.

He laid the law down to his mates in a manner best understood by them, and impressed fully upon their minds the necessity of doing something decisive, and with as little delay as possible.

'Look here, Ned,' he said to a bluff old sea-dog, 'it's sartin all things must have an end, and for my part I should like to see the end of that Pike and his ground sharks. It's the cap'n's fault for bringing him here; and I say, let's clear 'em out, whether he likes it or not.'

'Well, what you argufy is quite right,' replied Ned, giving his quid a vengeful nip. 'It's a no use in my eye a keeping 'em 'ere. 'They're a tarnal set o' cusses, and would not stand nice about giving us a leaden pill if they had the chance o' doing it; so I say clear the decks of 'em, for they're wus nor lumber.'

'But how are we to do it?' asked a grizzly bearded fellow who had the appearance of a very Judas in his face; 'how are we to do it? Answer me that.'

'Well, there's two or three ways,' replied Rocket.

'I can't see it; so perhaps you'll clear the fog from my dead lights, and oblige,' said the other.

'Well, in the first place, there's poison, and then there's the knife; but I votes for a douser from the cliff.'

'Ah! werry thoughtful,' replied Ned; 'we shan't have any bother about his burial; besides if he gets washed up, it'll look better to find him drowned than with his wizzen out.'

To this the others gave their consent, and they dispersed in several directions so as to reach the cave unobserved, previously agreeing to meet again, and talk it over.

When they had gone a man somewhat differently attired to the smugglers crept from a hole near where they had assembled.

'D——n em,' he muttered, as he glanced around to make sure he was not watched; 'let them look out; for as sure as I am here, and hope to get away in safety, they'll find their necks stretched as long as a hostrich's.'

'Ah!' he went on as he gave a quiet grin, 'they thought of having Tom Bolt, but they ain't cute enough; they never could find a French prison strong enough for me; and may I be flogged, which I may some day, if they can find moorings strong enough here to hold me.'

He took another survey around, and glanced upward at the towering cliff which seemed impossible to scale.

'Hang me for a swab! may I be fed on weavles and bilge water, if I suffer myself to be beaten. Oh! no, it won't do; I have got so far and it won't— Ah! what's that?'

The sound that disturbed his soliloquy was the sound of footsteps, and some one conversing in an undertone.

Scarcely had he ensconced himself in the hole he had just left, when Hatchett and Bill Raker rounded a point of the rock.

'To-night, it must be done to-night,' he could hear them say, and then they turned in their walk and disappeared again.

'Ha! ha! it shall be done to-night,' said Tom Bolt; 'to-night, ha! ha!' and he made an attempt to climb up the side of the cliff.

It was too steep, and having submitted to several nasty falls, he looked about for a road in another direction.

A narrow crevice had been formed by a huge rock having been rent asunder, evidently by the force of the last gale, for if it had been of longer duration, the smugglers would evidently have seen it, and would have filled up the gap, as, with the exception of this, the stronghold could only be reached from one particular point.

This entrance was a cavern in a dense wood about a mile inland, and was the entrance to a subterranean passage, which had been cut out by a band of notorious sea-robbers more than a hundred years ago.

With this, providing treachery was not employed, they were considered comparatively safe, and as they were completely sheltered from seaward, and the passage guarded by innumerable rocks, it was probable their secret might have remained intact for years.

That night, when the two parties that had been holding counsel in the morning were thinking of putting their plans into execution, each party ignorant of the other's arrangements, for Hatchett did not think it necessary to acquaint his men with that which he thought of doing till the last moment, and they, on the other hand, never intended to let him know their thoughts till after the deed was completed, a small boat might be seen making its way through the intricate passage between the rocks.

It was evident from the progress they made that the steersman had some knowledge of the place, though he proceeded with caution, and had a man in the boat's bow sounding with a boat-hook.

A small red flag was fastened in the stern—a precaution very necessary, as on the headland, occupied by the look-out, there was a gun fixed that would, at a given signal, have swept the boat and its occupants away for ever.

This could not from that distance have been seen by the naked eye; but those who did business with the smugglers were aware of its existence and locality.

Captain Hatchett was already apprised of the approach of the boat, and stood on the beach ready to receive the new-comer.

He had been previously recognised as the agent who had supplied Hatchett with his cargoes when captain of the Redbreast.

'Well, Doubledock, what brings you cruising in this quarter?' asked Tom Hatchett, eyeing him at first mistrustfully. 'Don't the discount satisfy you that you have to turn smuggler as well?"

'The discount satisfies me, Mr. Hatchett; but there is none to be got now, since you have all turned so honest. Why, it's an age almost since you last paid me a visit.'

'Well, it is a long time; but we can't be in two places at one time. But, had you waited a week or so, you would have seen me again. But to business. What brings you here now?'

Doubledock could not stand the smuggler's keen scrutiny. He kept his eyes averted, and there was something in his manner and tone that Hatchett did not like.

'I have got a cargo,' answered Doubledock, after some hesitation; 'but the devil of it is I have no place to land it.'

'So you dropped down here to ask my advice?'

'Exactly so; and if you can do anything with it, you know, why you may as well reap the benefit of it as a stranger.'

'Much better,' replied Hatchett, forcing a smile, 'and I must say it's very thoughtful of you. What sort of stuff is it?'

'Capital.'

'Yes, yes; but what do you call capital? I should like to see a sample, and I must also inform you that I have but little *capital*, and cannot pay for it at present.'

We shall not quarrel about that, for you see it would be better to pay you for warehousing it than to take it back and run the risk of its loss.'

'Calculating again; what a clever fellow you are,' said the smuggler captain, affecting an air of carelessness. 'But I'll leave you and Raker to arrange matters. I've other matters to look to.'

There was a meaning glance exchanged between the two smugglers, as Hatchett left the cave.

Doubledock, the name under which the agent transacted business with the smugglers, followed Hatchett's retreating form with his gaze, and muttered to himself, 'You will have other matters to look to of which you are not aware.'

Turning to Bill Raker, he said, 'He trusts all to you.'

'Ay, he leaves all to me, and I daresay we can come to terms.'

'Have you an inventory of the cargo?'

'I have,' was the ready reply; 'but it is on board; if you give me pen and paper, I can give you a copy.'

'I will,' responded Raker, and departed.

'My plans are prospering well,' muttered the agent, as he disappeared.

Then rubbing his hands in glee, he added—

'Little does he know what an invaluable cargo I have brought.'

'Here are both pen and paper,' said the smuggle on entering, and placing a small box on the table 'I must leave you for a short time, and when I return most likely you will have done.'

Bill Raker now took his way to the crow's nest.

It had been reported that the vessel in which Doubledock had arrived was being hotly chased by a revenue cutter.

But being a swift sailer, the cutter could not get within gunshot of her.

And she was now drawing the cutter off the land in order to baffle her in the fast approaching darkness of the coming night.

Long before he returned, the agent had finished writing, and was eyeing the inventory with evident signs of satisfaction.

'Thus far all prospers well,' he muttered. 'Tom Hatchett, you little know how dearly your friends cherish your remembrance. You forget the last business transaction we had, and how it terminated. But you shall rue it, or my name's not '——

He checked himself, and took a careful survey around, as though impressing all he saw well on his memory.

Thus he was amusing himself when Raker returned, saying—

'Your cargo has had a narrow squeak, my friend.'

'How? What mean you?' he asked, colouring slightly.

'She has been hotly pursued by one of the government sharks, and if she had not been a walker, and had good handling, she would have fallen into their jaws.'

'Is she safe?'

'Yes; he has made a board off the land, with the intention of stretching in under cover of night.'

'That is well,' said he, and handing the paper to Raker, he added, 'Read this.'

The smuggler ran his eye down the paper, on which were forty entries relating to things of the costliest kind, and a slight flush mantled his cheek, then again it turned whiter than marble.

The agent did not notice this, and Bill Raker, schooling his features so as not to betray his suspicions, said—

'Sit down awhile. Here is brandy and tobacco. I will go and prepare for the landing of the cargo. We shall have to be quick about it, or the land sharks may be down upon us, for I have no doubt the cutter threw out a signal.'

'Yes, yes. It will be as well to have all ready.'

The smuggler smiled faintly on leaving the Frenchman, and then entered another cave, when, drawing a note from his pocket, he compared the writing.

It was part of a note he had picked up on his way to the Three Luggers; and, though not looking at it at the time, he tore part of it off to light his pipe.

Had it been whole it would have disclosed a deep-laid plot and the name of its instigator, but, as it was, he could only make out part of the plans.

'They were written by the same hand, I swear,' said Raker, 'and Mr. Crapau has made up his mind to sell us, but he'll find himself bit. I must be cautious in my actions.'

As they had conjectured, the vessel again drew near the stronghold of the smugglers.

The smugglers were on the alert, and several large boats were quickly brought from their place of concealment, launched, and pulled off to the vessel.

The designing Frenchman eyed with pleasure each boat load as it was landed and stowed in the cave.

Approaching one of the cases, as though to examine if it had got wet in its passage from the ship to the shore, he gave it three gentle raps, and whispered—

'All goes well. Lay still until they have landed all, then I will release you, and we can achieve an easy victory. Thank God!' muttered he, as the last of the cargo was placed in the cave. 'Now I must watch my opportunity.'

But scarcely had these thoughts passed through his mind, when he was seized, and a pistol held close to his ear.

'Move,' cried Bill Raker, 'and I send a brace of bullets through your brain.'

He then led him prisoner to the cave.

Doubledock stared in astonishment at this act of the smuggler's, which he observing, said—

'Comrades all, this rascal is concerned in, if he is not the actual perpetrator of, a most foul crime. I accuse him of betraying me to the officer that caused us that little affray a day or two back, and I believe he is still acting with falseness towards us. However, I have proof sufficient to assure me he is no friend of ours, and his little game will have to be stopped.'

The smugglers eyed the prisoner threateningly, and would have made short work of him, had not Bill Rocket placed himself between them.

'Stay your hand!' he cried; 'be not too hasty.'

Then, drawing a brace of pistols from his belt, he held them towards the cringing wretch, and said in a calm but determined tone—

'Doubledock, you have fallen unconsciously into the lion's den—into the hands of those who have proved your friends—but who, through your treachery, have become your foes. I give you your choice, either to disclose your rascally plans, or '——

'Mercy! would you murder me innocently?' cried the agent.

'Murder you? no,' responded the smuggler, coolly; 'but I never break my promise.'

'Foiled—foiled!' he muttered to himself; 'foiled on the very eve of my success. Who could have betrayed me?'

Having allowed the Frenchman sufficient time to collect his scattered thoughts, he said—

'Have you decided how it is to be?'

'How can I? I swear I am ignorant of this you have charged me with, and therefore innocent.'

'Liar!' thundered Raker, darting a furious glance at him; 'I have proof of your guilt.'

'Show it to me.'

'Here you are,' cried the smuggler, producing a note; then, placing the paper Doubledock had so recently written beside it, he said—

'These you will allow were written by one hand.'

''Tis false as him who says so,' cried the agent, in terror.

'Abominable fiend and liar, confess at once ere I am tempted to pluck out your false tongue, and tear thy black heart from your guilty breast.'

'Mercy! mercy!' he cried. 'Oh! save me—spare my life, and I will tell you all.'

'That's what we want you to do; go on, but mind, adhere to the truth, or beware '——

'I will tell the truth; one of the merchants bribed me to write the letter, but I meant you no harm.'

'A merchant, do you say? what motive has prompted him to do this?'

'I have had no hand in it, I can assure you; he forced me to write that note, but he would not tell me his motives.'

'Am I to believe what you say?'

'You can rely on what I have spoken,' said the trembling agent.

'We shall see,' said Raker; then, turning to the smugglers, he said—

'Take the treacherous serpent away to the inner cave, and see that he is well ironed and guarded; on his safety depends your life; we will keep him prisoner till our captain returns.'

'Ay, ay,' cried two stalwart smugglers, who Bill Raker had pointed out.

CHAPTER CXXXVII.

WILL HOWARD A PRISONER—CAPTAIN ANDERSON IN A FIX.

WHAT Murray had told Will Howard about Deal being too hot for them was true, for scarcely had he walked half the way between the Three Luggers and the spot where he had left his boat, when he found himself suddenly surrounded by a score of stalwart men-of-war's men.

Will turned fiercely upon them; but he was so taken by surprise that he could not so much as possess himself of his pistol, and, borne down by numbers, he was compelled to yield.

In this way he was dragged down to the boat of a gun-brig that lay in the offing, and he soon found himself on board of her.

Captain Anderson commanded the brig, and as he had been junior lieutenant in the vessel to which Will Howard had belonged, it was no wonder he recognised him.

Anderson was not what might be termed a cruel man, nor exactly a tyrant; but duty to the service was his motto, and it was stamped on his every feature.

Will could not suppress a sigh on finding himself thus trapped.

Thoughts of his wife—his darling Black-Eyed Sue—flashed to his mind, and his feelings were anything but enviable.

'Now, what is your intention?' he asked.

'We shall take you to the flagship, where you will be tried,' answered the captain.

'And the result?'

'You will be hanged.'

It was not for information that Will asked these questions; he could see that his men had been made aware of his capture, for he could just see his vessel through one of the ports, and she was getting under weigh.

'If Sancho is at all lively, as I don't doubt he will be, there may yet be a chance of escape,' he thought. 'Jack Murray has seen my capture from the look-out.'

He was right in his conjectures; and, as he looked, the canvas was dropped from the yards, sheeted home, and the vessel headed towards the gun-brig.

The brigantine sailed gaily on, and Will was busy calculating how long it might be before they came up with them, when the voice of the captain disturbed him.

'Send the corporal of marines here,' he said to a middy standing by.

The middy obeyed, and the corporal forthwith made his appearance.

He touched his forelock to the captain, and awaited his further orders.

'Place this man in irons,' said Anderson, sternly; 'see that he is well guarded, and, at your peril, see that he does not escape.'

The corporal again touched his forelock, and motioned two of his men to seize the prisoner.

This enraged the gallant Will.

His face flushed, and his eyes lit fiercely.

With a well-directed blow, he sent the two marines, who were about to lay hands on him, reeling against the bulwarks, and with the speed of lightning snatched a cutlass from the sheath of a sailor standing by.

'Now take me!' he cried, in a voice rendered hoarse with desperation; 'but beware! the first that approaches dies!'

'William Howard,' cried the captain, drawing his sword, 'surrender; there is no chance of escape; you must now settle the great debt you owe to your country.'

'Surrender I never will,' said Will, as he brandished his cutlass above his head.

Captain Anderson was a brave man, and never flinched from shot or steel, but believing him so completely in his power, and galled at the daring of the smuggler, he sprang upon him with a fearful yell.

The clash of weapons now rang on the air, and the marines and blue jackets could not suppress a murmur of admiration, as they watched the rapid movements of the smuggler, who appeared but a stripling compared to the herculean form of the captain.

Captain Anderson fought with the fury of a tiger, as he tried to beat his opponent to the deck, whilst Will Howard, who had never for a moment lost his temper, guarded the furious blows of his assailant with that coolness for which he was so renowned; and at length by a dexterous movement dashed the cutlass from the hand of Captain Anderson, who was now at his mercy.

But Will, though pressed as he was by his assailants, and with death almost staring him in the face, could not take the life of the defenceless captain, and it was well for him he did not, or he would have fallen, pierced by a score of bullets from the muskets and pistols which were now pointed towards him.

At this moment, when Will's life was in jeopardy, a shot from the brigantine passed over the bows of the gun-brig.

This drew the attention of the brig's crew, and they seemed utterly confounded at the audacity of the brigantine's men in firing at a king's ship.

Captain Anderson, as soon as he had risen from the deck, and became aware of the circumstance, almost foamed with rage.

'Clear away the guns!' he shouted; 'we will blow them to atoms; but first,' he added, suddenly recollecting himself, 'secure the prisoners.'

But his order came too late.

Will Howard had disappeared, and though they searched for him high and low, he was not to be found.

CHAPTER CXXXVIII.

VILLAINY MEETS ITS REWARD.

'AH, so you are here, eh? You are sharp enough down on your prey; but you are not very ready in dubbing the coin.'

'What mean you? Did I not promise'——

'Ay, but we want you to perform; it is as well to settle accounts as we go on, then we need fear no bother.'

'Have you found any clue to the affair?' asked the admiral, biting his lip.

'None; neither care I to do so.'

'Why?'

'As the money is not forthcoming. You have failed to keep your promise, so I cry quits.'

'You are a mean scoundrel,' replied Lanceville, closing the door, that Susan might not hear them. 'Have you discovered aught of the pirate, Will Howard?'

'I have told you, and that is sufficient; money down, and then we go to work.'

'You ask too much; you certainly brought the girl here, and I have got to tame her, which is a task equal to all your trouble. Go, I shall not give you one farthing until you bring news of Will.'

'And this is your resolve? Mind, be careful what you say. One word, Admiral Lanceville; and he who has proved thy staunchest friend will be thy deadliest foe.'

'Fool! give your prating to the winds; I fear not your threats. Idiot, begone!'

'And leave you here,' said the man, sneeringly.

'Ay, leave me here; your presence is no longer needed.'

'What!' cried the man, his eyes flashing fire. Is this my reward? Beware, Lanceville, how you play with a desperate man.'

'Ha! ha! desperate enough, to be sure; at least you were when the murder was committed in the barn.'

There was a sneer on the admiral's lips and a sarcasm in his tone that seemed to wring the very heart of his listener; and before Lanceville had sufficiently delivered himself of the last word to pause, the man's hand was on his throat.

'Now taunt me!' he hissed, hoarsely; 'now goad me, Admiral Lanceville! the villain and seducer, the hirer of an assassin, the wretch that profited by my poverty, and urged me to commit a crime for paltry gold, a crime that stains my soul, and hangs about me like a pestilence.

'Night or day I sleep not; and in the balmy breeze of summer or the biting blast of winter I hear the cry for help ring in my ears. You, Admiral Lanceville, were the cause of this; and yet you dare to taunt me.'

'Help! mercy!' gasped the admiral, choking; 'mercy! spare me! Oh! for heaven's sake'——

'Heaven!' cried the man, 'can such a word find utterance from you? Heaven and justice have long forsaken you.'

A moan was all that came from the admiral's lips, and his face grew livid from the compression of his throat; then his eyes started wildly from their sockets, and he fell heavily on the floor.

'Thus perish the fiend that has made me the wretch that I am; this last act, had he paid me for it honestly, would have given me the means to lead an honest life, but fate ordained it otherwise, and my soul is stained with another crime.'

Dashing open the door with his foot, he said to Susan, who stood trembling—

'You are free to depart, lady; and if you can sit a horse, I will conduct you back to the spot you were taken from.'

Susan gladly complied, for she had heard most of what passed, and she shuddered as she gazed at the wretch who had lured her with false hopes, as he lay cold and stark, his heart for ever having ceased to beat.

'Now,' said the man, halting at a lonely spot near the White Villa, 'now must I make you promise one thing ere we part.'

'And that is'——

'Secrecy. Never must you divulge what you have seen.'

'I promise you.'

'Swear—you must swear.'

'I swear it, then, and you may believe me, for no man on earth did I hate more than him who now lies cold.'

'Enough,' cried the man, pressing her hand, and in an instant he was gone, much to the disappointment of Susan, who intended questioning him.

The look with which Doggrass regarded her when she entered the door of the Three Luggers was one of withering hate—a look such as never is to be forgotten when once seen—a look with which we might suppose a fiend would regard an angel.

Susan recoiled when she saw it, and then recovering herself, she walked boldly in.

'So you have come back,' said Silas, with a sneer. 'I was afraid the land sharks had made a meal of you.'

'They have not, you see; so your fears have been needless,' replied Susan, tartly.

'And where have you been to escape them?'

'It concerns you not, so trouble me with no questions; 'tis evident you did not seek me far.'

'Me, girl!' cried Silas, affecting surprise; 'me, girl! What had I to do with you? Once you told me you had a protector—a husband,' he added, with a sneer.

Susan's dark eyes flashed, and seemed to emit a light as her uncle spoke, then, with a frenzied cry, she raised a heavy chair, and dashed it at his head.

It missed, and the next moment Doggrass seized her, and, snatching a knife from the table, he was about to bury it in her bosom, when a strong grasp caught his wrist.

Doggrass muttered an oath, and turned half round to see who it was assailed him, and a cry of horror burst from his lips.

'It is his ghost. Away! away!' he cried, like a madman, holding up his hands, whilst his face was distorted with terror. 'Take him away; I did not murder him! Oh! take him from my sight, or I shall go mad!'

'Fiend! thy fate shall be worse!' whispered a harsh voice in his ear; 'the day of retribution is at hand—the day, Doggrass, when you shall atone for your many sins; the day when the guilty breast shall be laid open and disclose its secrets.'

Doggrass clasped his hands to his heated brow, and tried to shut out the sight that met his gaze, for the figure, features, and even the voice, that met his gaze and assailed his ears, were that of the sailor—the man he had killed!

'Can it be possible he comes to haunt me!' muttered Doggrass, hoarsely, as the big beads of agony poured down his furrowed cheeks. 'Has the dead risen to bear witness against me? Is it possible that my hour has come—that the cup, which my own deeds have rendered bitter, is so near my lips? No. I will not believe it; all men are liars; my own conscience even is false. Where is he? Gone! gone!' he muttered, clasping his brow in agony; 'and she, too; and yet I heard not the sound of feet; the doors, too, are closed. Where have they gone? Answer me, ye walls, or say that I am mad!'

BLACK EYED SUSAN.

OR, PIRATES ASHORE.

DEATH OF DOGGRASS.

CHAPTER CXXXIX.

THE FAILURE OF THE CONSPIRACY.

'THANK God, I have met you, Gerald, and that you are well,' said the gallant Will, as he grasped Captain Stuart's hand. 'It was a lucky chance I ran across old Phil; but there, in this world of riddles we must always be prepared for changes. Keep our signals at the masthead, our anchor ready at the bows, and our weather eye lifting for the shoals.'

'It is a strange coincidence that we should thus meet,' said Gerald Stuart; 'and especially at such a time, when the destiny of a nation hangs, as it were, upon a thread. To-night the grand council will be held, and the fate of a monarch will be decided.'

'You have still persevered in the cause, then?' asked Will.

'Ay, staunch as oak; and had you continued with me, I should have placed you in command of the vessel that now causes us so much concern.'

'What ship do you mean?'

'The Martinet. On board of her is that which can settle at once this great question. If she arrives safe all will be well; but if she is captured, as I fear, all is lost. But come, the bubble has burst; there is no need for further secrecy; you can pass in with me.'

In the large hall where the decisive council was to be held crowds had already assembled, and Gerald cast his eye uneasily around. 'Well, well,' he muttered unconsciously to Will, 'the game is up, with such a nest of hornets flocking to the hive. How can things prosper? I am heart sick, and '——

'Ah! is that you, Stuart? I am glad you have returned. You know me, I suppose; De Lorn is my name,' said a gaily dressed cavalier, grasping Gerald's hand.

'Know you, my staunchest, oldest friend? Good reason have I to do so. But I would hear from you what good is such an assembly as this to us?'

'What good? None whatever, my friend. And my words, though laughed at, will come true. But know you anything of '——

He whispered in Gerald's ear, and Gerald made answer—

'It was safe on board his ship, I swear; but I fear his obstinacy has thrown it into the hands of the king; and if so, our labour is all lost.'

'As I have thought myself, but I fear there are many traitors among us; know you that fellow with bleared eye glaring at us?'

'Indeed do I. If I mistake not, it is Gregory Saunders, and that fellow to his right is Rock Elfin, another of the villainous clan.'

'So I thought,' said De Lorn thoughtfully; 'and I must now tell you of an adventure I met with on my way here. A poor woman, whom I had known in former years when she was better circumstanced, stopped me, and inquired if I had heard of Captain Stuart lately?'

'And you told her '——

'I had not.'

'Her name.'

'Eurice, I think she said, though it was not by that name I knew her before.'

'By heavens! that is fortunate. Is she in the town, do you say?'

'She was destitute, and I provided apartments for her.'

'I must find her, then,' said Gerald, vehemently. 'She shall meet *him* to-night face to face. Justice shall be done at least in one quarter.'

'What is this? Hide not the secret from me, Gerald.'

'I must for the present, so press me no further. Said she aught about anyone else?'

'No, only there chanced to be lodging in the same hotel a fair creature named Madeline, the daughter of an admiral, and she knew her, or at least I fancied she did.'

Gerald started. 'What! Madeline Garthway?' he exclaimed.

'I think, if I remember rightly, that was the name.'

'Then I must away at once. You do not know what importance hangs upon my seeing her—in fact, seeing both; so I will leave you for the present, and my friend here, Will Howard, will accompany me.'

'It is best not to go alone, for the French spies are at every corner; the government has enlisted their services by bribery, and it is but right to guard against them.'

After holding a whispered conversation, De Lorn and Gerald Stuart parted; but they did not notice when they left the hall that they were followed.

Madeline and Eurice were seated in earnest conversation when Gerald disturbed them, and a cry, not only of surprise, but intensest joy burst from Madeline when she recognised him.

'Gerald—my dearest Gerald!' she cried passionately; 'oh! how glad I am to see you again. I despaired of ever doing so more—I thought you were dead.'

'Not yet; I have escaped danger so far, but I fear my dearest hopes will never be realized, so I will tempt danger no more and stay with you.'

'Thanks, thanks, dear Gerald, glad am I to hear you say so; but then,' she added, bitterly, 'I am poor, penniless, and without a friend but you.'

'Fear not for that, Madeline; though my rightful estates have been stolen from me, I have that wherewith we may live happy; but see, your companion has fainted, has she not?'

'Alas! yes; she is so weak, and trouble seems to have almost turned her brain, poor thing. Twice has she been taken thus since she came here.'

'And to what cause do you attribute it?'

'I know not, only that her heart is well nigh bursting with grief.'

'Well, tend to her, Madeline darling; I have a friend waiting at the corner; he will think it strange if I wait longer; I will fetch him here.'

Leaving Madeline to attend to the poor woman, Gerald made his way into the street; and, as he moved towards the corner where he had left Will, a figure, muffled in a cloak, crept from the shade of a portico and stealthily followed him.

''Tis he, and he shall die!' muttered the man, as he grasped the hilt of his poignard; and, stepping sharply up to Gerald, he was about to plunge it in his back, when his wrist was suddenly grasped, and a blow felled him to the earth.

'Good God! what has happened?' exclaimed Gerald, turning suddenly.

'An assassin,' replied Will, tearing the mask from the fellow's face. 'By Jupiter! 'tis your old enemy, Saunders.'

The villain started as though he had been shot when he recognised Will Howard's voice, and he winced with pain when the brave sailor took him in his iron grasp.

'It is well he has come here,' said Gerald, recovering his composure. 'He must accompany us, William.'

'Where to?' gasped the ruffian, glaring savagely at his intended victim. 'Where to, I say? By h——l! I will not leave this spot!'

'It will not lay to your choice!' said Gerald, sternly. 'Come quietly, or an inch of cold steel may induce you to alter your mind.'

'Would you murder me?' asked Saunders, with a savage leer; but his captors made no reply as they hurried him on.

A feather might have knocked the villain down as he entered the room where Madeline and Eurice were seated.

The latter had come-to after swallowing some strong brandy, and when Saunders was led in, she seemed suddenly possessed of supernatural strength.

'Gregory Saunders!' she exclaimed, starting from her seat, and passing her fingers through her silvery locks—'Gregory Saunders! the cause of all my woe! Has heaven spared thee to gaze upon this wreck, the shattered remains of her that was once thy wife. Would to heaven it had not been so! though 'twas its decree that made me so, and thy cruelty that made me as I am!'

'Ah! taunt me no more. My brain is on fire, a worm is gnawing at my vitals, the room seems in a whirl, and myriads of evil spirits and ghastly forms seem to rise about me. Release me! let me be gone, or I shall go mad!'

With a bound he sprang to the door, but Will's strong arm held him back, and the wretch sank exhausted to the floor.

'Wretch!' cried Eurice, springing upon him as he lay, 'you have made me a monster in human form, and I will have thy life, not as thou hast had mine, inch by inch, drop by drop, but thou shalt feel the fleshless talons thy cruelty hath made, and we will die together.'

She clenched her bony fingers in his throat, and dug them into his neck until the villain ceased to breath, then, with an hysterical laugh, she flung up her wasted arms and cried—

'Just heaven, that hath decreed we should be so long parted, I implore thee to let us sleep together in death Pardon our sins, and may we rest together in one grave until the last trump summons us hence. Farewell, farewell all! Now can I die in peace.'

For a few moments she knelt with her hands clasped, and her lips moving as though in prayer, and then she fell back into Madeline's arms, and when they looked she was dead.

When Will and Gerald returned to the hall the council had been broken up, a party of gensdarmes and secret police, headed by the emissaries of the English government, had entered suddenly, and after a brief but terrific conflict, those of the council that were not captured fled and sought safety where they could.

The main cause of this was attributed to the loss of the Martinet, which, owing to Captain Henson's obduracy, had fallen into the hands of the government, and exposed all their plot to them, so that they were able to counteract them at every point.

This was a sad blow to Gerald, and he fretted greatly about it, but the joy of meeting with Madeline soon banished it from his mind.

They buried the bodies of Gregory Saunders and Eurice, his ill-used wife, in one grave, in the little churchyard just out of the town, and then embarked as quietly as possible on board the Golden Arrow, Will having sold the slave ship to satisfy the claims and the grumblings of the men.

CHAPTER CXL.

THE SMUGGLER'S FRIEND TURNS OUT A FOE.

THE Frenchman's treachery was soon made known to the whole of the smugglers, and upon the casks and cases being opened, as Bill Raker had anticipated, instead of finding the costly articles described in the bill of lading, they were found to contain armed men.

Tom Hatchett, on his return, was so enraged at hearing of it, that he ordered the casks to be again headed up and rolled on to the beach, so as to be burnt.

Bill Raker would not hear of this. He argued that it would only be a landmark for their foes, a beacon to guide them to their stronghold, in which opinion the smugglers joined him.

It was then agreed that the casks should be placed one by one in the boat, and taken outside of the rocks and sunk, so that no one should know what became of them unless their remains washed up.

This seemed the most favourable, and the best suited to their views, so it was readily agreed upon.

Amongst those who had heard of this last decision was Lieutenant Pike, and as soon as he found out that there was such a strong force in the cave, he set his wits to work to turn it to his advantage.

He had managed by dint of bribes and promises to win the confidence of one of the men who watched over him, for all the sailors were not exempt from that unfortunate weakness, and Pike having learnt from him the exact number of men in the casks and cases, and the exact locality of the cave they were stowed in, he resolved upon a trial to liberate them.

He calculated that with his own men and the new reinforcement they would number two to one of the smugglers.

His ingenious mind was not long in forming a plan, and as soon as it was formed he put it into use.

'Mat, Mat,' he whispered to the smuggler who was keeping guard, 'I've got the cramp most fearfully; lift me up, old fellow, for I am unable to rise.'

The smuggler, whose mind was so busied on other matters, though at any other time he would have forgotten all to attend on the lieutenant, paid but little heed to him, but watched the torches flashing about near the entrance of the cave.

'Mat, Mat!' again cried the lieutenant, affecting much pain; 'come here, man, for God's sake—you unfeeling brute. I will give you anything if you only assist me.'

Mat was a dear lover of lucre, and he needed no second inviting; he sprang to the lieutenant's side like lightning at the prospect of being paid.

'Stoop down, man, and try to lift me,' said Pike, intermingling his speech with a groan. 'The pain is in my side.'

The smuggler obeyed, and bending his body over Pike, he placed his sinewy arms round his waist, at the same moment Pike caught him round the neck, and pressed his face on his breast till he was near stifled.

The smuggler relaxed his hold at once, and Pike, taking the advantage offered him, swung himself round, and worked himself on top of the smuggler, who soon went into a fit, and when he recovered sufficiently to look about he found himself minus of his own clothes and those of the lieutenant laying by his side, but Pike was gone.

It was too chilly for anyone not accustomed to it to go without clothes while there were any to get, so he at once donned the lieutenant's, and admired himself greatly, for they well fitted his figure.

'Well, well,' he thought to himself, 'how nice it must be to be a hofficer,' he thought, and scarcely had he entertained it when Lieutenant Pike rushed into the cave, sword in hand, followed by a score of stalwart men-of-war's men.

'Now, then, my hearties, rouse up, unless you desire a keel-hauling to wake you!' he shouted, a hint that was never lost for effect, and the men sprang to their feet, and were quickly divested of the ropes that bound their hands.

Such a fight as is seldom recorded then took place, and blood, smoke, and fire were on all sides.

'Down with them! give them no quarter if they will not yield!' cried Pike, heated with excitement. At that instant another party, headed by Bolt, rushed into the cave.

Bill Raker, seeing that his men were being rapidly overpowered, seized a torch, and rushed into the magazine.

A fearful explosion, that rent the rocks, followed this daring act, and Rocket, with a score of the smugglers, was buried in the debris.

The fight was now at an end.

Hatchett and the survivors of his crew were captured, and Pike and his party took charge of the ruins.

CHAPTER CXLI.

THE DENOUEMENT.

THE capture of the gang had a terrible effect on Doggrass, for he not only feared that after his treatment of Susan she would betray him, but there existed a probability of his being arrested as an accessory.

This so preyed on his mind, that he was unable to attend to the business, and being at length unable to leave his bed, he treated his niece with such kindness, that drove from her mind the memory of his former cruelty.

Dame Howard was now wholly occupied in attending upon him, and Susan found sufficient employment in managing the rapidly increasing business, which she performed with a light heart, having heard good news of her husband.

One morning Susan was surprised by the entrance of a man, whose sun-burnt features were too well concealed by a slouched hat for her to recognise, but his black, glossy ringlets, that flowed over his shoulders, reminded her of one whose memory she still cherished in her heart.

As she watched the man drink the grog she had served him with, she noticed that his form trembled, and a slight scream escaped her as she caught his eye when he turned.

One vault the man made, and cleared the counter that separated them, and clasping her to his arms, he cried fervently—

'Susan!—my bonny Black-Eyed Sue! have you forgotten your Will—your own sweet William, as you used to call him? Come, give us a kiss, lass, and dash the salt water from those bonny black eyes.'

Susan was so taken aback that she almost fainted, but the smack that emanated from the sailor's lips, as they met those of her own, soon brought her to again.

'Where's old Doggrass—that old shark of an uncle of yours?' cried Will, as with one arm still encircling her waist he gazed into her sparkling eyes. 'Come, spin out, old girl, and tell me where the old crocodile is to be found, that I may give the old devil a broadside such as he deserves.'

'Hush! calm yourself, dear Will,' said Susan; 'the old man is dying; and, besides, remember there are many spies about here that would not hesitate to betray you.'

'Betray me!' laughed Will, scornfully; 'it is beyond their power. In crossing the channel with the Golden Arrow we chanced to fall in with Admiral Garthway, who was opposed to a whole squadron of the French, and our timely aid prevented his capture. The service we did him, and the sight of his daughter, Madeline, made him relent, and he obtained our pardon of the king, and now Madeline is the bride of Gerald Stuart.'

Old Doggrass received the news of Will's return and his good fortune with sullen silence; but as the doctor had given him no hopes of his life, he began to relent, and as an atonement for his many sins, and the great wrong he had done the gallant sailor, he made over the whole of his property to his niece, Susan, who was his only relative then existing.

Silas Doggrass only survived long enough to hear of the terrible end of his companion in crime, who, with the rest of the smugglers that survived Raker's horrible deed, expiated his crimes on the scaffold; Rock Elfin shared the same fate at the yardarm of a frigate; and Doggrass died in a chair, falling into the arms of his niece.

Our hero gave him befitting interment in the little churchyard, and then took possession of his effects, which was such as to enable him to deal liberally with those who had suffered through Doggrass's villainy.

Andrew and Pauline, who by accident had fallen into each other's company, were united, and with Gerald Stuart and his doting bride went abroad to seek that peace of mind which was denied them in England; Jack Murray and the sailor, Bob Braddon, accompanied them; but the faithful Sancho, though hardly pressed, would not leave his true friend, Will, and he proved of much service to him.

We have only to add that Gnatbrain and Dolly Mayflower entered heart and soul into the marriage state, and Jacob Twig, who was fast advancing into years, took a partner to soothe his dismal life; whilst our hero, who had changed the name of the Three Luggers to that of the Sailor's Retreat, lived happily with Susan, his wife; and often when the boisterous weather drove the fishermen to seek shelter in the cozy tap-room, which was always provided with a good fire, he would amuse them with a stiff yarn, or Sancho would give them a stave of a favourite song.

THE END.